By Diana Gabaldon

(in chronological order)
OUTLANDER
DRAGONFLY IN AMBER
VOYAGER
DRUMS OF AUTUMN
THE FIERY CROSS
A BREATH OF SNOW AND ASHES
AN ECHO IN THE BONE
THE OUTLANDISH COMPANION *(nonfiction)*
THE EXILE *(graphic novel)*

(in chronological order)
LORD JOHN AND THE HELLFIRE CLUB *(novella)*
LORD JOHN AND THE PRIVATE MATTER
LORD JOHN AND THE SUCCUBUS *(novella)*
LORD JOHN AND THE BROTHERHOOD OF THE BLADE
LORD JOHN AND THE HAUNTED SOLDIER *(novella)*
CUSTOM OF THE ARMY *(novella)*
LORD JOHN AND THE HAND OF DEVILS *(collected novellas)*
THE SCOTTISH PRISONER
PLAGUE OF ZOMBIES *(novella)*

Other Outlander-related novellas
A LEAF ON THE WIND OF ALL HALLOWS
THE SPACE BETWEEN
VIRGINS

WRITTEN IN MY OWN HEART'S BLOOD

DIANA GABALDON

WRITTEN IN MY OWN HEART'S BLOOD

A NOVEL

DELACORTE PRESS
NEW YORK

A Delacorte Press International Edition

Copyright © 2014 by Diana Gabaldon

Title page art from an original photograph by Laura Shreck

Published by Delacorte Press, an imprint of Random House, a division of
Random House LLC, a Penguin Random House Company, New York.

DELACORTE PRESS and the HOUSE colophon are registered trademarks
of Random House LLC.

A hardcover edition has been published in the United States by Delacorte
Press, an imprint of Random House, a division of Random House LLC.

Gabaldon, Diana.
Written in my own heart's blood : a novel / Diana Gabaldon.
pages cm
ISBN 978-0-553-84113-8
eBook ISBN 978-0-440-24644-2
1. Philadelphia (Pa.)—History—Revolution, 1775–1783—Fiction.
2. United States—History—Revolution, 1775–1783—Fiction.   3. Scottish
Americans—Fiction.   4. Time travel—Fiction.
I. Title.
PS3557.A22W85 2014
813'.54—dc23   2013043591

Printed in the United States of America on acid-free paper

www.bantamdell.com

9 8 7 6 5 4 3 2

Book design by Virginia Norey

This book is dedicated to ALL of the people
(besides me) *who worked like fiends*
to produce it for you.
Especially to

Jennifer Hershey *(editor, U.S.)*
Bill Massey *(editor, U.K.)*
Kathleen Lord *(aka "Hercules"—copy editor)*
Barbara Schnell *(translator and trench-buddy, Germany)*
Catherine MacGregor, Catherine-Ann MacPhee,
and Adhamh Ò Broin *(Gaelic experts)*
Virginia Norey *(aka "Book Goddess"—designer)*
Kelly Chian, Maggie Hart, Benjamin Dreyer, Lisa Feuer,
and the rest of the Random House Production Team
and
Beatrice Lampe und Petra Zimmermann in München

CONTENTS

PART TWO
Meanwhile, Back at the Ranch . . .

PART THREE
A Blade Fresh-Made from the Ashes of the Forge

PART FOUR
Day of Battle

PART FIVE
Counting Noses

PART SIX
The Ties That Bind

PART SEVEN
Before I Go Hence

PART EIGHT
Search and Rescue

PART NINE

*"Thig crioch air an t-saoghal ach mairidh
ceol agus gaol."*

PROLOGUE

I N THE LIGHT OF eternity, time casts no shadow.

Your old men shall dream dreams, your young men shall see visions. But what is it that the old women see?

We see necessity, and we do the things that must be done.

Young women don't see—they *are,* and the spring of life runs through them.

Ours is the guarding of the spring, ours the shielding of the light we have lit, the flame that we are.

What have I seen? You are the vision of my youth, the constant dream of all my ages.

Here I stand on the brink of war again, a citizen of no place, no time, no country but my own . . . and that a land lapped by no sea but blood, bordered only by the outlines of a face long-loved.

PART ONE

Nexus

A HUNDREDWEIGHT OF STONES

June 16, 1778
The forest between Philadelphia and Valley Forge

IAN MURRAY STOOD with a stone in his hand, eyeing the ground he'd chosen. A small clearing, out of the way, up among a scatter of great lichened boulders, under the shadow of firs and at the foot of a big red cedar; a place where no casual passerby would go, but not inaccessible. He meant to bring them up here—the family.

Fergus, to begin with. Maybe just Fergus, by himself. Mam had raised Fergus from the time he was ten, and he'd had no mother before that. Fergus had known Mam longer than Ian had, and loved her as much. *Maybe more,* he thought, his grief aggravated by guilt. Fergus had stayed with her at Lallybroch, helped to take care of her and the place; he hadn't. He swallowed hard and, walking into the small clear space, set his stone in the middle, then stood back to look.

Even as he did so, he found himself shaking his head. No, it had to be two cairns. His mam and Uncle Jamie were brother and sister, and the family could mourn them here together—but there were others he might bring, maybe, to remember and pay their respects. And those were the folk who would have known Jamie Fraser and loved him well but wouldn't ken Jenny Murray from a hole in the—

The image of his mother *in* a hole in the ground stabbed him like a fork, retreated with the recollection that she wasn't after all in a grave, and stabbed again all the harder for that. He really couldn't bear the vision of them drowning, maybe clinging to each other, struggling to keep—

"*A Dhia!*" he said violently, and dropped the stone, turning back at once to find more. He'd seen people drown.

Tears ran down his face with the sweat of the summer day; he didn't mind it, only stopping now and then to wipe his nose on his sleeve. He'd tied a rolled kerchief round his head to keep the hair and the stinging sweat out of his eyes; it was sopping before he'd added more than twenty stones to each of the cairns.

He and his brothers had built a fine cairn for their father before he died, at the head of the carved stone that bore his name—all his names, in spite of the expense—in the burying ground at Lallybroch. And then later, at the funeral, members of the family, followed by the tenants and then the servants, had come one by one to add a stone each to the weight of remembrance.

Fergus, then. Or . . . no, what was he thinking? Auntie Claire must be the first he brought here. She wasn't Scots herself, but she kent fine what a cairn was and would maybe be comforted a bit to see Uncle Jamie's. Aye, right. Auntie Claire, then Fergus. Uncle Jamie was Fergus's foster father; he had a right. And then maybe Marsali and the children. But maybe Germain was old enough to come with Fergus? He was ten, near enough to being a man to understand, to be treated like a man. And Uncle Jamie was his grandsire; it was proper.

He stepped back again and wiped his face, breathing heavily. Bugs whined and buzzed past his ears and hovered over him, wanting his blood, but he'd stripped to a loincloth and rubbed himself with bear grease and mint in the Mohawk way; they didn't touch him.

"Look over them, O spirit of red cedar," he said softly in Mohawk, gazing up into the fragrant branches of the tree. "Guard their souls and keep their presence here, fresh as thy branches."

He crossed himself and bent to dig about in the soft leaf mold. A few more rocks, he thought. In case they might be scattered by some passing animal. Scattered like his thoughts, which roamed restless to and fro among the faces of his family, the folk of the Ridge—God, might he ever go back there? Brianna. Oh, Jesus, Brianna . . .

He bit his lip and tasted salt, licked it away and moved on, foraging. She was safe with Roger Mac and the weans. But, Jesus, he could have used her advice—even more, Roger Mac's.

Who was left for him to ask, if he needed help in taking care of them all?

Thought of Rachel came to him, and the tightness in his chest eased a little. Aye, if he had Rachel . . . She was younger than him, nay more than nineteen, and, being a Quaker, had very strange notions of how things should be, but if he had her, he'd have solid rock under his feet. He hoped he *would* have her, but there were still things he must say to her, and the thought of that conversation made the tightness in his chest come back.

The picture of his cousin Brianna came back, too, and lingered in his mind: tall, long-nosed and strong-boned as her father . . . and with it rose the image of his *other* cousin, Bree's half brother. Holy God, William. And what ought he to do about William? He doubted the man kent the truth, kent that he was Jamie Fraser's son—was it Ian's responsibility to tell him so? To bring him here and explain what he'd lost?

He must have groaned at the thought, for his dog, Rollo, lifted his massive head and looked at him in concern.

"No, I dinna ken that, either," Ian told him. "Let it bide, aye?" Rollo laid his head back on his paws, shivered his shaggy hide against the flies, and relaxed in boneless peace.

Ian worked awhile longer and let the thoughts drain away with his sweat and his tears. He finally stopped when the sinking sun touched the tops of his cairns, feeling tired but more at peace. The cairns rose knee-high, side by side, small but solid.

He stood still for a bit, not thinking anymore, just listening to the fussing of wee birds in the grass and the breathing of the wind among the trees. Then he sighed deeply, squatted, and touched one of the cairns.

"*Tha gaol agam oirbh, a Mhàthair,*" he said softly. *My love is upon you, Mother.* Closed his eyes and laid a scuffed hand on the other heap of stones. The dirt ground into his skin made his fingers feel strange, as though he could maybe reach straight through the earth and touch what he needed.

He stayed still, breathing, then opened his eyes.

"Help me wi' this, Uncle Jamie," he said. "I dinna think I can manage, alone."

2

DIRTY BASTARD

WILLIAM RANSOM, Ninth Earl of Ellesmere, Viscount Ashness, Baron Derwent, shoved his way through the crowds on Market Street, oblivious to the complaints of those rebounding from his impact.

He didn't know where he was going, or what he might do when he got there. All he knew was that he'd burst if he stood still.

His head throbbed like an inflamed boil. Everything throbbed. His hand— he'd probably broken something, but he didn't care. His heart, pounding and sore inside his chest. His foot, for God's sake—what, had he kicked something? He lashed out viciously at a loose cobblestone and sent it rocketing through a crowd of geese, who set up a huge cackle and lunged at him, hissing and beating at his shins with their wings.

Feathers and goose shit flew wide, and the crowd scattered in all directions.

"Bastard!" shrieked the goose-girl, and struck at him with her crook, catching him a shrewd thump on the ear. "Devil take you, *dreckiger Bastard!*"

This sentiment was echoed by a number of other angry voices, and he veered into an alley, pursued by shouts and honks of agitation.

He rubbed his throbbing ear, lurching into buildings as he passed, oblivious to everything but the one word throbbing ever louder in his head. *Bastard.*

"Bastard!" he said out loud, and shouted, "Bastard, bastard, *bastard!*" at the top of his lungs, hammering at the brick wall next to him with a clenched fist.

"Who's a bastard?" said a curious voice behind him. He swung round to see a young woman looking at him with some interest. Her eyes moved slowly down his frame, taking note of the heaving chest, the bloodstains on the facings of his uniform coat, and the green smears of goose shit on his breeches. Her gaze reached his silver-buckled shoes and returned to his face with more interest.

"I am," he said, hoarse and bitter.

"Oh, really?" She left the shelter of the doorway in which she'd been lingering and came across the alley to stand right in front of him. She was tall and slim and had a very fine pair of high young breasts—which were clearly visible under the thin muslin of her shift, because, while she had a silk petticoat, she wore no stays. No cap, either—her hair fell loose over her shoulders. A whore.

"I'm partial to bastards myself," she said, and touched him lightly on the arm. "What kind of bastard are you? A wicked one? An evil one?"

"A sorry one," he said, and scowled when she laughed. She saw the scowl but didn't pull back.

"Come in," she said, and took his hand. "You look as though you could do with a drink." He saw her glance at his knuckles, burst and bleeding, and she caught her lower lip behind small white teeth. She didn't seem afraid, though, and he found himself drawn, unprotesting, into the shadowed doorway after her.

What did it matter? he thought, with a sudden savage weariness. *What did anything matter?*

3

IN WHICH THE WOMEN,
AS USUAL, PICK UP THE PIECES

Number 17 Chestnut Street, Philadelphia
The residence of Lord and Lady John Grey

WILLIAM HAD LEFT the house like a thunderclap, and the place looked as though it had been struck by lightning. I certainly felt like the survivor of a massive electrical storm, hairs and nerve endings all standing up straight on end, waving in agitation.

Jenny Murray had entered the house on the heels of William's departure, and while the sight of her was a lesser shock than any of the others so far, it still left me speechless. I goggled at my erstwhile sister-in-law—though, come to think, she still *was* my sister-in-law . . . because Jamie was alive. *Alive.*

He'd been in my arms not ten minutes before, and the memory of his touch flickered through me like lightning in a bottle. I was dimly aware that I was smiling like a loon, despite massive destruction, horrific scenes, William's distress—if you could call an explosion like that "distress"—Jamie's danger, and a faint wonder as to what either Jenny or Mrs. Figg, Lord John's cook and housekeeper, might be about to say.

Mrs. Figg was smoothly spherical, gleamingly black, and inclined to glide silently up behind one like a menacing ball bearing.

"What's *this?*" she barked, manifesting herself suddenly behind Jenny.

"Holy Mother of God!" Jenny whirled, eyes round and hand pressed to her chest. "Who in God's name are you?"

"This is Mrs. Figg," I said, feeling a surreal urge to laugh, despite—or maybe because of—recent events. "Lord John Grey's cook. And, Mrs. Figg, this is Mrs. Murray. My, um . . . my . . ."

"Your good-sister," Jenny said firmly. She raised one black eyebrow. "If ye'll have me still?" Her look was straight and open, and the urge to laugh changed abruptly into an equally strong urge to burst into tears. Of all the unlikely sources of succor I could have imagined . . . I took a deep breath and put out my hand.

"I'll have you." We hadn't parted on good terms in Scotland, but I had loved her very much, once, and wasn't about to pass up any opportunity to mend things.

Her small firm fingers wove through mine, squeezed hard, and, as simply as that, it was done. No need for apologies or spoken forgiveness. She'd never had to wear the mask that Jamie did. What she thought and felt was there in her eyes, those slanted blue cat eyes she shared with her brother. She knew the truth now of what I was, and she knew I loved—and always had loved—her brother with all my heart and soul—despite the minor complications of my being presently married to someone else.

She heaved a sigh, eyes closing for an instant, then opened them and smiled at me, mouth trembling only a little.

"Well, fine and dandy," said Mrs. Figg shortly. She narrowed her eyes and rotated smoothly on her axis, taking in the panorama of destruction. The railing at the top of the stair had been ripped off, and cracked banisters, dented walls, and bloody smudges marked the path of William's descent. Shattered crystals from the chandelier littered the floor, glinting festively in the light that poured through the open front door, the door itself cracked through and hanging drunkenly from one hinge.

"*Merde* on toast," Mrs. Figg murmured. She turned abruptly to me, her small black-currant eyes still narrowed. "Where's his lordship?"

"Ah," I said. This was going to be rather sticky, I saw. While deeply disapproving of most people, Mrs. Figg was devoted to John. She wasn't going to be at all pleased to hear that he'd been abducted by—

"For that matter, where's my brother?" Jenny inquired, glancing round as though expecting Jamie to appear suddenly out from under the settee.

"Oh," I said. "Hmm. Well . . ." Possibly worse than sticky. Because . . .

"And where's my Sweet William?" Mrs. Figg demanded, sniffing the air. "He's been here; I smell that stinky cologne he puts on his linen." She nudged a dislodged chunk of plaster disapprovingly with the toe of her shoe.

I took another long, deep breath and a tight grip on what remained of my sanity.

"Mrs. Figg," I said, "perhaps you would be so kind as to make us all a cup of tea?"

WE SAT IN the parlor, while Mrs. Figg came and went to the cookhouse, keeping an eye on her terrapin stew.

"You don't want to scorch turtle, no, you don't," she said severely to us, setting down the teapot in its padded yellow cozy on her return. "Not with so much sherry as his lordship likes in it. Almost a full bottle—terrible waste of good liquor, that would be."

My insides turned over promptly. Turtle soup—with a lot of sherry—had certain strong and private associations for me, these being connected with Jamie, feverish delirium, and the way in which a heaving ship assists sexual intercourse. Contemplation of which would *not* assist the impending discussion in the slightest. I rubbed a finger between my brows, in hopes of dispelling the buzzing cloud of confusion gathering there. The air in the house still felt electric.

"Speaking of sherry," I said, "or any other sort of strong spirits you might have convenient, Mrs. Figg . . ."

She looked thoughtfully at me, nodded, and reached for the decanter on the sideboard.

"Brandy is stronger," she said, and set it in front of me.

Jenny looked at me with the same thoughtfulness and, reaching out, poured a good-sized slug of the brandy into my cup, then a similar one into her own.

"Just in case," she said, raising one brow, and we drank for a few moments. I thought it might take something stronger than brandy-laced tea to deal with the effect of recent events on my nerves—laudanum, say, or a large slug of straight Scotch whisky—but the tea undeniably helped, hot and aromatic, settling in a soft trickling warmth amidships.

"So, then. We're fettled, are we?" Jenny set down her own cup and looked expectant.

"It's a start." I took a deep breath and gave her a *précis* of the morning's events.

Jenny's eyes were disturbingly like Jamie's. She blinked at me once, then twice, and shook her head as though to clear it, accepting what I'd just told her.

"So Jamie's gone off wi' your Lord John, the British army is after them, the tall lad I met on the stoop wi' steam comin' out of his ears is Jamie's son—well, of course he is; a blind man could see that—and the town's aboil wi' British soldiers. Is that it, then?"

"He's not exactly *my* Lord John," I said. "But, yes, that's essentially the position. I take it Jamie told you about William, then?"

"Aye, he did." She grinned at me over the rim of her teacup. "I'm that happy for him. But what's troubling his lad, then? He looked like he wouldna give the road to a bear."

"What did you say?" Mrs. Figg's voice cut in abruptly. She set down the tray she had just brought in, the silver milk jug and sugar basin rattling like castanets. "William is *whose* son?"

I took a fortifying gulp of tea. Mrs. Figg did know that I'd been married to—and theoretically widowed from—one James Fraser. But that was all she knew.

"Well," I said, and paused to clear my throat. "The, um, tall gentleman with the red hair who was just here—you saw him?"

"I did." Mrs. Figg eyed me narrowly.

"Did you get a good look at him?"

"Didn't pay much heed to his face when he came to the door and asked where you were, but I saw his backside pretty plain when he pushed past me and ran up the stairs."

"Possibly the resemblance is less marked from that angle." I took another mouthful of tea. "Um . . . that gentleman is James Fraser, my . . . er . . . my—" "First husband" wasn't accurate, and neither was "last husband"—or even, unfortunately, "most recent husband." I settled for the simplest alternative. "My husband. And, er . . . William's father."

Mrs. Figg's mouth opened, soundless for an instant. She backed up slowly and sat down on a needlework ottoman with a soft *phumph.*

"William know that?" she asked, after a moment's contemplation.

"He does *now*," I said, with a brief gesture toward the devastation in the stairwell, clearly visible through the door of the parlor where we were sitting.

"*Merde* on— I mean, Holy Lamb of God preserve us." Mrs. Figg's second husband was a Methodist preacher, and she strove to be a credit to him, but her first had been a French gambler. Her eyes fixed on me like gun sights.

"You his mother?"

I choked on my tea.

"No," I said, wiping my chin with a linen napkin. "It isn't quite *that* complicated." In fact, it was more so, but I wasn't going to explain just how Willie had come about, either to Mrs. Figg or to Jenny. Jamie had to have told Jenny who William's mother was, but I doubted that he'd told his sister that William's mother, Geneva Dunsany, had forced him into her bed by threatening Jenny's family. No man of spirit likes to admit that he's been effectively blackmailed by an eighteen-year-old girl.

"Lord John became William's legal guardian when William's grandfather died, and at that point, Lord John also married Lady Isobel Dunsany, Willie's mother's sister. She'd looked after Willie since his mother's death in childbirth, and she and Lord John were essentially Willie's parents since he was quite young. Isobel died when he was eleven or so."

Mrs. Figg took this explanation in stride but wasn't about to be distracted from the main point at issue.

"James Fraser," she said, tapping a couple of broad fingers on her knee and looking accusingly at Jenny. "How comes he not to be dead? News was he drowned." She cut her eyes at me. "I thought his lordship was like to throw himself in the harbor, too, when he heard it."

I closed my own eyes with a sudden shudder, the salt-cold horror of that news washing over me in a wave of memory. Even with Jamie's touch still joyful on my skin and the knowledge of him glowing in my heart, I relived the crushing pain of hearing that he was dead.

"Well, I can enlighten ye on that point, at least."

I opened my eyes to see Jenny drop a lump of sugar into her fresh tea and nod at Mrs. Figg. "We were to take passage on a ship called *Euterpe*—my brother and myself—out o' Brest. But the blackhearted thief of a captain sailed without us. Much good it did him," she added, frowning.

Much good, indeed. The *Euterpe* had sunk in a storm in the Atlantic, lost with all hands. As I—and John Grey—had been told.

"Jamie found us another ship, but it landed us in Virginia, and we'd to make our way up the coast, partly by wagon, partly by packet boat, keepin' out of the way of the soldiers. Those wee needles ye gave Jamie against the seasickness work a marvel," she added, turning approvingly to me. "He showed me how to put them in for him. But when we came to Philadelphia yesterday," she went on, returning to her tale, "we stole into the city by night, like a pair o' thieves, and made our way to Fergus's printshop. Lord, I thought my heart would stop a dozen times!"

She smiled at the memory, and I was struck by the change in her. The shadow of sorrow still lay on her face, and she was thin and worn by travel, but the terrible strain of her husband Ian's long dying had lifted. There was color in her cheeks again and a brightness in her eyes that I had not seen since I had first known her thirty years before. She had found her peace, I thought, and felt a thankfulness that eased my own soul.

". . . so Jamie taps on the door at the back, and there's no answer, though we can see the light of a fire comin' through the shutters. He knocks again, makin' a wee tune of it—" She rapped her knuckles lightly on the table, *bump-ba-da-bump-ba-da-bump-bump-bump,* and my heart turned over, recognizing the theme from *The Lone Ranger,* which Brianna had taught him.

"And after a moment," Jenny went on, "a woman's voice calls out fierce, 'Who's there?' And Jamie says in the *Gàidhlig,* 'It is your father, my daughter, and a cold, wet, and hungry man he is, too.' For it was rainin' hammer handles and pitchforks, and we were both soaked to the skin."

She rocked back a little, enjoying the telling.

"The door opens then, just a crack, and there's Marsali wi' a horse pistol in her hand, and her two wee lasses behind her, fierce as archangels, each with a billet of wood, ready to crack a thief across his shins. They see the firelight shine on Jamie's face then, and all three of them let out skellochs like to wake the dead and fall upon him and drag him inside and all talkin' at once and greetin', askin' was he a ghost and why was he not drowned, and that was the first we learned that the *Euterpe* had sunk." She crossed herself. "God rest them, poor souls," she said, shaking her head.

I crossed myself, too, and saw Mrs. Figg look sideways at me; she hadn't realized I was a Papist.

"I've come in, too, of course," Jenny went on, "but everyone's talkin' at once and rushin' to and fro in search of dry clothes and hot drinks and I'm just lookin' about the place, for I've never been inside a printshop before, and the smell of the ink and the paper and lead is a wonder to me, and, sudden-like, there's a tug at my skirt and this sweet-faced wee mannie says to me, 'And who are you, madame? Would you like some cider?'"

"Henri-Christian," I murmured, smiling at thought of Marsali's youngest, and Jenny nodded.

"'Why, I'm your grannie Janet, son,' says I, and his eyes go round, and he lets out a shriek and grabs me round the legs and gives me such a hug as to make me lose my balance and fall down on the settle. I've a bruise on my bum the size of your hand," she added out of the corner of her mouth to me.

I felt a small knot of tension that I hadn't realized was there relax. Jenny did of course know that Henri-Christian had been born a dwarf—but knowing and seeing are sometimes different things. Clearly they hadn't been, for Jenny.

Mrs. Figg had been following this account with interest, but maintained her reserve. At mention of the printshop, though, this reserve hardened a bit.

"These folk—Marsali is your daughter, then, ma'am?" I could tell what she was thinking. The entire town of Philadelphia knew that Jamie was a Rebel—and, by extension, so was I. It was the threat of my imminent arrest that had caused John to insist upon my marrying him in the wake of the tumult following Jamie's presumed death. The mention of printing in British-occupied Philadelphia was bound to raise questions as to just *what* was being printed, and by whom.

"No, her husband is my brother's adopted son," Jenny explained. "But I raised Fergus from a wee lad myself, so he's my foster son, as well, by the Highland way of reckoning."

Mrs. Figg blinked. She had been gamely trying to keep the cast of characters in some sort of order to this point, but now gave it up with a shake of her head that made the pink ribbons on her cap wave like antennae.

"Well, where the devil—I mean, where on earth has your brother gone with his lordship?" she demanded. "To this printshop, you think?"

Jenny and I exchanged glances.

"I doubt it," I said. "More likely he's gone outside the city, using John—er, his lordship, I mean—as a hostage to get past the pickets, if necessary. Probably he'll let him go as soon as they're far enough away for safety."

Mrs. Figg made a deep humming noise of disapproval.

"And maybe he'll make for Valley Forge and turn him over to the Rebels instead."

"Oh, I shouldna think so," Jenny said soothingly. "What would they want with him, after all?"

Mrs. Figg blinked again, taken aback at the notion that anyone might not value his lordship to the same degree that she did, but after a moment's lip-pursing allowed as this might be so.

"He wasn't in his uniform, was he, ma'am?" she asked me, brow furrowed. I shook my head. John didn't hold an active commission. He was a diplomat, though technically still lieutenant colonel of his brother's regiment, and therefore wore his uniform for purposes of ceremony or intimidation, but he was officially retired from the army, not a combatant, and in plain clothes he would be taken as citizen rather than soldier—thus of no particular interest to General Washington's troops at Valley Forge.

I didn't think Jamie was headed for Valley Forge in any case. I knew, with absolute certainty, that he would come back. Here. For me.

The thought bloomed low in my belly and spread upward in a wave of warmth that made me bury my nose in my teacup to hide the resulting flush.

Alive. I caressed the word, cradling it in the center of my heart. Jamie was alive. Glad as I was to see Jenny—and gladder still to see her extend an olive branch in my direction—I really wanted to go up to my room, close the door, and lean against the wall with my eyes shut tight, reliving the seconds after he'd entered the room, when he'd taken me in his arms and pressed me to the wall, kissing me, the simple, solid, warm fact of his presence so overwhelming that I might have collapsed onto the floor without that wall's support.

Alive, I repeated silently to myself. *He's alive.*

Nothing else mattered. Though I did wonder briefly what he'd done with John.

DON'T ASK QUESTIONS YOU DON'T
WANT TO HEAR THE ANSWERS TO

In the woods,
an hour's ride outside Philadelphia

JOHN GREY HAD BEEN quite resigned to dying. Had expected it from the moment that he'd blurted out, *"I have had carnal knowledge of your wife."* The only question in his mind had been whether Fraser would shoot him, stab him, or eviscerate him with his bare hands.

To have the injured husband regard him calmly and say merely, *"Oh? Why?"* was not merely unexpected but . . . infamous. Absolutely infamous.

"Why?" John Grey repeated, incredulous. "Did you say *'Why?'* "

"I did. And I should appreciate an answer."

Now that Grey had both eyes open, he could see that Fraser's outward calm was not quite so impervious as he'd first supposed. There was a pulse beating in Fraser's temple, and he'd shifted his weight a little, like a man might do in the vicinity of a tavern brawl: not quite ready to commit violence but readying himself to meet it. Perversely, Grey found this sight steadying.

"What do you bloody *mean,* 'Why'?" he said, suddenly irritated. "And why aren't you fucking dead?"

"I often wonder that myself," Fraser replied politely. "I take it ye thought I was?"

"Yes, and so did your wife! Do you have the faintest idea what the knowledge of your death *did* to her?"

The dark-blue eyes narrowed just a trifle.

"Are ye implying that the news of my death deranged her to such an extent that she lost her reason and took ye to her bed by force? Because," he went on, neatly cutting off Grey's heated reply, "unless I've been seriously misled regarding your own nature, it would take substantial force to compel ye to any such action. Or am I wrong?"

The eyes stayed narrow. Grey stared back at them. Then he closed his own eyes briefly and rubbed both hands hard over his face, like a man waking from a nightmare. He dropped his hands and opened his eyes again.

"You are not misled," he said, through clenched teeth. "And you *are* wrong."

Fraser's ruddy eyebrows shot up—in genuine astonishment, Grey thought.

"Ye went to her because—from *desire?*" His voice rose, too. "And she let ye? I dinna believe it."

The color was creeping up Fraser's tanned neck, vivid as a climbing rose. Grey had seen that happen before and decided recklessly that the best—the only—defense was to lose his own temper first. It was a relief.

"We thought you were *dead,* you bloody arsehole!" he said, furious. "Both of us! Dead! And we—we—took too much to drink one night—very much too much . . . We spoke of you . . . and . . . Damn you, neither one of us was making love to the other—we were both fucking *you!*"

Fraser's face went abruptly blank and his jaw dropped. Grey enjoyed one split second of satisfaction at the sight, before a massive fist came up hard beneath his ribs and he hurtled backward, staggered a few steps farther, and fell. He lay in the leaves, completely winded, mouth opening and closing like an automaton's.

All right, then, he thought dimly. *Bare hands it is.*

The hands wrapped themselves in his shirt and jerked him to his feet. He managed to stand, and a wisp of air seeped into his lungs. Fraser's face was an inch from his. Fraser was in fact so close that Grey couldn't see the man's expression—only a close-up view of two bloodshot blue eyes, both of them berserk. That was enough. He felt quite calm now. It wouldn't take long.

"You tell me exactly what happened, ye filthy wee pervert," Fraser whispered, his breath hot on Grey's face and smelling of ale. He shook Grey slightly. "Every word. Every motion. *Everything.*"

Grey got just enough breath to answer.

"No," he said defiantly. "Go ahead and kill me."

FRASER SHOOK HIM violently, so that his teeth clacked painfully together and he bit his tongue. He made a strangled noise at this, and a blow he hadn't seen coming struck him in the left eye. He fell down again, his head exploding with fractured color and black dots, the smell of leaf mold pungent in his nose. Fraser yanked him up and set him on his feet once more, but then paused, presumably deciding how best to continue the process of vivisection.

What with the blood pounding in his ears and the rasp of Fraser's breath, Grey hadn't heard anything, but when he cautiously opened his good eye to see where the next blow was coming from, he saw the man. A rough-looking dirty thug, in a fringed hunting shirt, gawping stupidly from under a tree.

"Jethro!" the man bellowed, taking a tighter hold on the gun he carried.

A number of men came out of the bushes. One or two had the rudiments of a uniform, but most of them were dressed in homespun, though with the addition of the bizarre "liberty" caps, tight-knitted woolen affairs that fitted over the head and ears, which through John's watering eye gave the men the bluntly menacing aspect of animated bombshells.

The wives who had presumably made these garments had knitted such mottoes as LIBERTY or FREEDOM into the bands, though one bloodthirsty abigail had knitted the adjuration KILL! into her husband's hat. The husband in question was, Grey noted, a small and weedy specimen wearing spectacles with one shattered lens.

Fraser had stopped at the sound of the men's approach and now rounded on them like a bear brought to bay by hounds. The hounds stopped abruptly, at a safe distance.

Grey pressed a hand over his liver, which he thought had likely been ruptured, and panted. He was going to need what breath he could get.

"Who're you?" one of the men demanded, jabbing pugnaciously at Jamie with the end of a long stick.

"Colonel James Fraser, Morgan's Rifles," Fraser replied coldly, ignoring the stick. "And you?"

The man appeared somewhat disconcerted but covered it with bluster.

"Corporal Jethro Woodbine, Dunning's Rangers," he said, very gruff. He jerked his head at his companions, who at once spread out in a businesslike way, surrounding the clearing.

"Who's your prisoner, then?"

Grey felt his stomach tighten, which, given the condition of his liver, hurt. He replied through clenched teeth, not waiting for Jamie.

"I am Lord John Grey. If it's any business of yours." His mind was hopping like a flea, trying to calculate whether his chances of survival were better with Jamie Fraser or with this gang of yahoos. A few moments before, he had been resigned to the idea of death at Jamie's hands, but, like many ideas, that one was more appealing in concept than in execution.

The revelation of his identity seemed to confuse the men, who squinted and murmured, glancing at him dubiously.

"He ain't got a uniform on," one observed to another, *sotto voce.* "Be he a soldier at all? We got no business with him if he ain't, do we?"

"Yes, we do," Woodbine declared, regaining some of his self-confidence.

"And if Colonel Fraser's taken him prisoner, I reckon he has reason?" His voice went up, reluctantly questioning. Jamie made no reply, his eyes fixed on Grey.

"He's a soldier." Heads swung round to see who had spoken. It was the small man with the shattered spectacles, who had adjusted these with one hand, the better to peer at Grey through his remaining lens. A watery blue eye inspected Grey, then the man nodded, more certain.

"He's a soldier," the man repeated. "I saw him in Philadelphia, sittin' on the porch of a house on Chestnut Street in his uniform, large as life. He's an officer," he added unnecessarily.

"He is not a soldier," Fraser said, and turned his head to fix the spectacled man with a firm eye.

"Saw him," muttered the man. "Plain as day. Had gold braid," he murmured almost inaudibly, dropping his eyes.

"Huh." Jethro Woodbine approached Grey, examining him carefully. "Well, you got anything to say for yourself, Lord Grey?"

"Lord John," Grey said crossly, and brushed a fragment of crushed leaf off his tongue. "I am not a peer; my elder brother is. Grey is my family name. As for being a soldier, I have been. I still bear rank within my regiment, but my commission is not active. Is that sufficient, or do you want to know what I had for breakfast this morning?"

He was purposely antagonizing them, some part of him having decided that he would rather go with Woodbine and bear the inspection of the Continentals than remain here to face the further inspections of Jamie Fraser. Fraser was regarding him through narrowed eyes. He fought the urge to look away.

It's the truth, he thought defiantly. *What I told you is the truth. And now you know it.*

Yes, said Fraser's black gaze. *You think I will live quietly with it?*

"He is not a soldier," Fraser repeated, turning his back deliberately on Grey, switching his attention to Woodbine. "He is my prisoner because I wished to question him."

"About what?"

"That is not your concern, Mr. Woodbine," Jamie said, deep voice soft but edged with steel. Jethro Woodbine, though, was nobody's fool and meant to make that clear.

"I'll be judge of what's my business. Sir," he added, with a notable pause. "How do we know you're who you say you are, eh? You aren't in uniform. Any of you fellows know this man?"

The fellows, thus addressed, looked surprised. They looked uncertainly at one another; one or two heads shook in the negative.

"Well, then," said Woodbine, emboldened. "If you can't prove who you are, then I think we'll take this man back to camp for questioning." He smiled unpleasantly, another thought having evidently occurred to him. "Think we ought to take you, too?"

Fraser stood quite still for a moment, breathing slowly and regarding Woodbine as a tiger might regard a hedgehog: yes, he could eat it, but would the inconvenience of swallowing be worth it?

"Take him, then," he said abruptly, stepping back from Grey. "I have business elsewhere."

Woodbine had been expecting argument; he blinked, disconcerted, and half-raised his stick, but said nothing as Fraser stalked toward the far edge of the clearing. Just under the trees, Fraser turned and gave Grey a flat, dark look.

"We are not finished, sir," he said.

Grey pulled himself upright, disregarding both the pain in his liver and the tears leaking from his damaged eye.

"At your service, sir," he snapped. Fraser glared at him and moved into the flickering green shadows, completely ignoring Woodbine and his men. One or two of them glanced at the corporal, whose face showed his indecision. Grey didn't share it. Just before Fraser's tall silhouette vanished for good, he cupped his hands to his mouth.

"I'm not bloody sorry!" he bellowed.

5

THE PASSIONS OF YOUNG MEN

WHILE FASCINATED to hear about William and the dramatic circumstances under which he had just discovered his paternity, Jenny's true concern was for another young man.

"D'ye ken where Young Ian is?" she asked eagerly. "And did he find his young woman, the Quaker lassie he told his da about?"

I relaxed a little at this; Young Ian and Rachel Hunter were—thank God—*not* on the list of fraught situations. At least not for the moment.

"He did," I said, smiling. "As for where he is . . . I haven't seen him for several days, but he's often gone for longer. He scouts for the Continental army now and then, though since they've been in their winter quarters at Valley Forge for so long, there's been less need for scouting. He spends quite a bit of time there, though, because Rachel does."

Jenny blinked at that.

"She does? Why? Do Quakers not mislike wars and such?"

"Well, more or less. But her brother, Denzell, is an army surgeon—though he's a real physician, not the usual horse-leech or quack-salver the army usually gets—and he's been at Valley Forge since last November. Rachel comes and goes to Philadelphia—she can pass through the pickets, so she carries back food and supplies—but she works with Denny, so she's out there, help-ing with patients, much more often than she is here."

"Tell me about her," Jenny said, leaning forward intently. "Is she a good lass? And d'ye think she loves Young Ian? From what Ian told me, the lad's desperate in love with her but hadn't spoken to her yet, not knowing how she'd take it—he wasna sure she could deal with him being . . . what he is." Her quick gesture encompassed Young Ian's history and character, from Highland lad to Mohawk warrior. "God kens weel he'll never make a decent Quaker, and I expect Young Ian kens that, too."

I laughed at the thought, though in fact the issue might be serious; I didn't know what a Quaker meeting might think of such a match, but I rather thought they might view the prospect with alarm. I knew nothing about Quaker marriage, though.

"She's a very good girl," I assured Jenny. "Extremely sensible, very capable—and plainly in love with Ian, though I don't think she's told him so, either."

"Ah. D'ye ken her parents?"

"No, they both died when she was a child. She was mostly raised by a Quaker widow and then came to keep house for her brother when she was sixteen or so."

"That the little Quaker girl?" Mrs. Figg had come in with a vase of sum-mer roses, smelling of myrrh and sugar. Jenny inhaled strongly and sat up straight. "Mercy Woodcock thinks the world of her. She comes by Mercy's house every time she's in town, to visit that young man."

"Young man?" Jenny asked, dark brows drawing together.

"William's cousin Henry," I hastened to explain. "Denzell and I carried out a very serious operation on him during the winter. Rachel knows both William and Henry and is very kind about visiting to see how Henry is. Mrs. Woodcock is his landlady."

It occurred to me that I had meant to go check on Henry today myself. There were rumors of a British withdrawal from the city, and I needed to see whether he was fit enough yet to travel. He was doing well when I'd stopped by a week before but at that point had been able to walk only a few steps, leaning on Mercy Woodcock's arm.

And what about Mercy Woodcock? I wondered, with a small jolt at the pit of the stomach. It was clear to me, as it was to John, that there was a serious—and deepening—affection between the free black woman and her aristocratic young lodger. I had met Mercy's husband, very badly wounded, during the exodus from Fort Ticonderoga a year before—and, lacking any communica-tion from or about him, thought it very likely that he had died after being taken prisoner by the British.

Still, the possibility of Walter Woodcock returning miraculously from the dead—people *did,* after all, and a fresh bubble of joy rose under my heart at the thought—was the least of the matter. I couldn't imagine that John's brother, the very firm-minded Duke of Pardloe, would be delighted at hear-ing that his youngest son meant to marry the widow of a carpenter, whatever her color.

And then there was his daughter, Dottie, speaking of Quakers: she was betrothed to Denzell Hunter, and I did wonder what the duke would think of that. John, who liked a wager, had given me no better than even odds between Dottie and her father.

I shook my head, dismissing the dozen things I could do nothing about. During this minor reverie, Jenny and Mrs. Figg appeared to have been discussing William and his abrupt departure from the scene.

"Where would *he* go to, I wonder?" Mrs. Figg looked worriedly toward the wall of the stairwell, pocked with blood-smeared dents left by William's fist.

"Gone to find a bottle, a fight, or a woman," said Jenny, with the authority of a wife, a sister, and the mother of sons. "Maybe all three."

Elfreth's Alley

IT WAS PAST midday, and the only voices in the house were the distant chitterings of women. No one was visible in the parlor as they passed, and no one appeared as the girl led William up a foot-marked staircase to her room. It gave him an odd feeling, as though he might be invisible. He found the notion a comfort; he couldn't bear himself.

She went in before him and threw open the shutters. He wanted to tell her to close them; he felt wretchedly exposed in the flood of sunlight. But it was summer; the room was hot and airless, and he was already sweating heavily. Air swirled in, heavy with the odor of tree sap and recent rain, and the sun glowed briefly on the smooth top of her head, like the gloss on a fresh conker. She turned and smiled at him.

"First things first," she announced briskly. "Throw off your coat and waistcoat before you suffocate." Not waiting to see whether he would take this suggestion, she turned to reach for the basin and ewer. She filled the basin and stepped back, motioning him toward the washstand, where a towel and a much-used sliver of soap stood on worn wood.

"I'll fetch us a drink, shall I?" And with that, she was gone, bare feet pattering busily down the stairs.

Mechanically, he began to undress. He blinked stupidly at the basin but then recalled that, in the better sort of house, sometimes a man was required to wash his parts first. He'd encountered the custom once before, but on that occasion the whore had performed the ablution for him—plying the soap to such effect that the first encounter had ended right there in the washbasin.

The memory made the blood flame up in his face again, and he ripped at his flies, popping off a button. He was still throbbing all over, but the sensation was becoming more centralized.

His hands were unsteady, and he cursed under his breath, reminded by the broken skin on his knuckles of his unceremonious exit from his father's—no, *not* his bloody father's house. Lord John's.

"You bloody *bastard*!" he said under his breath. "You knew, you knew all along!" That infuriated him almost more than the horrifying revelation of his own paternity. His stepfather, whom he'd loved, whom he'd trusted more than anyone on earth—Lord John bloody Grey—had lied to him his whole life!

Everyone had lied to him.

Everyone.

He felt suddenly as though he'd broken through a crust of frozen snow and plunged straight down into an unsuspected river beneath. Swept away into black breathlessness beneath the ice, helpless, voiceless, a feral chill clawing at his heart.

There was a small sound behind him and he whirled by instinct, aware only when he saw the young whore's appalled face that he was weeping savagely, tears running down his own face, and his wet, half-hard cock flopping out of his breeches.

"Go away," he croaked, making a frantic effort to tuck himself in.

She didn't go away but came toward him, decanter in one hand and a pair of pewter cups in the other.

"Are you all right?" she asked, eyeing him sideways. "Here, let me pour you a drink. You can tell me all about it."

"No!"

She came on toward him, but more slowly. Through his swimming eyes, he saw the twitch of her mouth as she saw his cock.

"I meant the water for your poor hands," she said, clearly trying not to laugh. "I will say as you're a real gentleman, though."

"I'm not!"

She blinked.

"Is it an insult to call you a gentleman?"

Overcome with fury at the word, he lashed out blindly, knocking the decanter from her hand. It burst in a spray of glass and cheap wine, and she cried out as the red soaked through her petticoat.

"You *bastard*!" she shrieked, and, drawing back her arm, threw the cups at his head. She didn't hit him, and they clanged and rolled away across the floor. She was turning toward the door, crying out, "Ned! Ned!" when he lunged and caught her.

He only wanted to stop her shrieking, stop her bringing up whatever male enforcement the house employed. He got a hand on her mouth, yanking her back from the door, grappling one-handed to try to control her flailing arms.

"I'm sorry, I'm sorry!" he kept saying. "I didn't mean—I don't mean—oh, bloody *hell*!" She caught him abruptly in the nose with her elbow and he let go, backing away with a hand to his face, blood dripping through his fingers.

Her face was marked with red where he'd held her, and her eyes were wild. She backed away, scrubbing at her mouth with the back of her hand.

"Get . . . *out*!" she gasped.

He didn't need telling twice. He rushed past her, shouldered his way past a burly man charging up the stairs, and ran down the alley, realizing only when he reached the street that he was in his shirtsleeves, having left coat and waistcoat behind, and his breeches were undone.

"Ellesmere!" said an appalled voice nearby. He looked up in horror to find himself the cynosure of several English officers, including Alexander Lindsay.

"Good Christ, Ellesmere, what happened?" Sandy was by way of being a friend and was already pulling a voluminous snowy handkerchief from his sleeve. He clapped this to William's nose, pinching his nostrils and insisting that he put his head back.

"Have you been set upon and robbed?" one of the others demanded. "God! This filthy place!"

He felt at once comforted by their company—and hideously embarrassed by it. He was not one of them, not any longer.

"Was it? Was it robbery?" another said, glaring round eagerly. "We'll find the bastards who did it, 'pon my honor we will! We'll get your property back and teach whoever did it a lesson!"

Blood was running down the back of his throat, harsh and iron-tasting, and he coughed but did his best to nod and shrug simultaneously. He *had* been robbed. But no one was ever going to give him back what he'd lost today.

6

UNDER MY PROTECTION

THE BELL OF THE Presbyterian church two blocks away rang for half-two, and my stomach echoed it, reminding me that—what with one thing and another—I hadn't had any tea yet.

Jenny had had a bite with Marsali and the children but declared herself equal to dealing with an egg, if there might be one, so I sent Mrs. Figg to see whether there might, and within twenty minutes we were wallowing—in a genteel fashion—in soft-boiled eggs, fried sardines, and—for lack of cake—flapjacks with butter and honey, which Jenny had never seen before but took to with the greatest alacrity.

"Look how it soaks up the sweetness!" she exclaimed, pressing the spongy little cake with a fork, then releasing it. "Nay like a bannock at all!" She glanced over her shoulder, then leaned toward me, lowering her voice. "D'ye think her in the kitchen might show me the way of it, if I asked?"

A diffident rapping on the damaged front door interrupted her, and as I turned to look, it was shoved open and a long shadow fell across the painted canvas rug, narrowly preceding its owner. A young British subaltern peered into the parlor, looking disconcerted by the wreckage in the foyer.

"Lieutenant Colonel Grey?" he asked hopefully, glancing back and forth between Jenny and me.

"His lordship isn't in just now," I said, attempting to sound self-possessed.

I wondered just how many more times I might have to say that—and to whom.

"Oh." The young man looked further disconcerted. "Can you tell me where he is, mum? Colonel Graves sent a message earlier, asking Lieutenant Colonel Grey to attend General Clinton at once, and the general was, er . . . rather wondering why the lieutenant colonel hadn't arrived yet."

"Ah," I said, with a sidewise glance at Jenny. "Well. I'm afraid his lordship was rather urgently called away before he received the colonel's message." That must have been the paper John had received moments before Jamie's dramatic reappearance from a watery grave. He'd glanced at it but then shoved it unread into his breeches' pocket.

The soldier heaved a small sigh at this but was undaunted.

"Yes, mum. If you'll tell me where his lordship is, I'll go fetch him there. I really can't go back without him, you know." He gave me a woeful look, though with a touch of a charming smile. I smiled back, with a small touch of panic in my midsection.

"I'm so sorry, but I really don't *know* where he is right now," I said, standing up in hopes of driving him back toward the door.

"Well, mum, if you'll just tell me where he was heading, I shall go there and seek direction," he said, doggedly standing his ground.

"He didn't tell me." I took a step toward him, but he didn't retreat. This was escalating beyond absurdity into something more serious. I'd met General Clinton briefly at the Mischianza ball a few weeks ago—God, had it been only weeks? It seemed whole lifetimes—and while he'd been quite cordial to me, I didn't think he'd receive a *nolle prosequi* from me with any sort of complaisance. Generals tended to think highly of their own consequence.

"You know, his lordship doesn't hold an active commission," I said, in the faint hope of putting the young man off. He looked surprised.

"Yes, he does, mum. The colonel sent notice of it with the message this morning."

"What? He can't do that—er, can he?" I asked, a sudden dread creeping up my backbone.

"Do what, mum?"

"Just—just tell his lordship that his commission is active?"

"Oh, no, mum," he assured me. "The colonel of Lieutenant Colonel Grey's regiment re-called him. The Duke of Pardloe."

"Jesus H. Roosevelt Christ," I said, sitting down. Jenny snatched up her napkin to muffle what was plainly a laugh; it had been twenty-five years since she'd heard me say that. I gave her a look, but this was no time to be picking up the threads.

"All right," I said, turning to face the young man again and taking a deep breath. "I'd better go with you to see the general." I got to my feet again and only at this point realized that, having been surprised whilst changing, I was still wearing nothing but my shift and dressing gown.

"I'll help ye dress," Jenny said, standing up hurriedly. She gave the soldier a charming smile and gestured at the table, now strewn with toast, marmalade, and a steaming dish of kippers. "Have a bite while ye wait, lad. No point wasting good food."

JENNY POKED HER head out into the corridor and listened, but the faint sound of a fork on china and Mrs. Figg's voice from below indicated that the soldier had accepted her suggestion. She quietly closed the door.

"I'll go with ye," she said. "The town's full of soldiers; ye shouldna go out by yourself."

"I'll be—" I began, but then stopped, unsure. Most of the British officers in Philadelphia knew me as Lady John Grey, but that didn't mean that rank-and-file soldiers shared either that knowledge or the sense of respect that it normally engendered. I also felt like an imposter, but that was rather beside the point; it didn't show.

"Thank you," I said abruptly. "I'd be glad of your company." Unsure as I felt about everything save my conviction that Jamie was coming, I *was* glad of a little moral support—though I wondered whether I might need to warn Jenny of the need for circumspection when I talked to General Clinton.

"I shallna say a word myself," she assured me, grunting slightly as she pulled my laces tight. "D'ye think ye should tell him what's happened to Lord John?"

"No, I definitely don't," I said, exhaling forcefully. "That's . . . tight enough."

"Mmm." She was already deep in the armoire, picking through my gowns. "What about this one? It's got a deep décolletage, and your bosom's still verra good."

"I'm not meaning to seduce the man!"

"Oh, yes, ye are," she said matter-of-factly. "Or at least distract him. If ye're no going to tell him the truth, I mean." One sleek black eyebrow lifted. "If I were a British general and was told that my wee colonel had been abducted by a wicked great Hieland man, I think I might take it amiss."

I couldn't really contradict this piece of reasoning and, with a brief shrug, wriggled my way into the amber silk, which had cream-colored piping in the seams and ruched cream ribbons outlining the edge of the bodice.

"Oh, aye, that's good," Jenny said, tying my laces and stepping back to eye the effect with approval. "The ribbon's near the same color as your skin, so the neck looks even lower than it is."

"One would think you'd spent the last thirty years running a dressmaker's salon or a brothel, rather than a farm," I remarked, nervousness making me rather cross. She snorted.

"I've got three daughters, nine granddaughters, and there's sixteen nieces and great-nieces on Ian's sister's side. It's often much the same sort o' thing."

That made me laugh, and she grinned at me. Then I was blinking back tears, and so was she—the thought of Brianna and of Ian, our lost ones, coming suddenly—and then we were embracing, holding hard to each other to keep grief at bay.

"It's all right," she whispered, hugging me fiercely. "Ye've not lost your lass. She's still alive. And Ian's still wi' me. He'll never go from my side."

"I know," I said, choked. "I know." I let go and straightened up, smudging tears away with a finger, sniffing. "Have you got a handkerchief?"

She had one in her hand, in fact, but reached into the pocket at her waist and pulled out another, freshly washed and folded, which she handed me.

"I'm a grannie," she said, and blew her nose vigorously. "I've *always* got a spare hankie. Or three. Now, what about your hair? Ye canna be going out in the street like *that.*"

By the time we'd got my hair done up in something resembling order, corralled in a snood and pinned respectably under a broad-brimmed woven straw hat, I'd come up with at least a rough notion of what to tell General Clinton. *Stick to the truth as far as possible.* That was the first principle of successful lying, though it had been some time since I'd been last obliged to employ it.

Well, then. A messenger had come for Lord John—one had—bringing a note—he did. I had no idea what was in the note—totally true. Lord John had then left with the messenger but without telling me where they were going. Also technically true, the only variance being that it had been a different messenger. No, I hadn't seen in which direction they had gone; no, I didn't know whether they had walked or ridden—Lord John's saddle horse was kept at Davison's livery on Fifth Street, two blocks away.

That sounded good. If General Clinton chose to make inquiries, I was reasonably sure he'd discover the horse still in its stall and thus conclude that John was somewhere in the city. He would also presumably lose interest in me as a source of information and send soldiers round to whatever haunts a man such as Lord John Grey might be supposed to be visiting.

And with any luck at all, by the time the general had exhausted such possibilities as Philadelphia offered, John would be back and could answer his own damned questions.

"And what about Jamie?" Jenny asked, her face showing small signs of anxiety. "He'll not come back into the city, surely?"

"I hope not." I could scarcely draw breath, and not merely because of the tight lacing. I could feel the thudding of my heart against the placket of the stays.

Jenny gave me a long, considering look, eyes narrowed, and shook her head.

"No, ye don't," she said. "Ye think he'll come straight back here. For you. And ye're right. He will." She considered for a moment longer, her brow furrowed. "I'd best stay here," she said abruptly. "Should he come back whilst ye're wi' the general, he'll need to know what's the state o' things. And I dinna think I trust her in the kitchen not to stab him wi' a toasting fork, should he loom up in her doorway without notice."

I laughed, all too easily envisioning Mrs. Figg's response to a sudden Highlander in her midst.

"Besides," she added, "someone's got to clear up the mess, and I've had a good bit o' practice wi' *that,* too."

THE YOUNG SOLDIER greeted my belated reappearance with relief and, while not actually seizing my arm and hustling me down the pavement, offered me his own arm and then walked in such a fashion that I was urged into a near trot to keep up with him. It was not far to the mansion where Clinton had made his headquarters, but the day was warm and I arrived moist and gasping, with tendrils of hair escaping from under my straw hat and sticking to my neck and cheeks, and tendrils of sweat snaking their tickling slow way down inside my bodice.

My escort delivered me—with an audible sigh of relief—to another soldier in the spacious parquet-floored foyer, and I had a moment to shake the dust from my skirts, straighten and re-pin my hat, and blot my face and neck discreetly with a ladylike lace hankie. I was sufficiently taken up with this that it was a moment before I recognized the man sitting on one of the little gilded chairs on the other side of the foyer.

"Lady John," he said, standing up when he saw that I had noticed him. "Your servant, ma'am." He smiled slightly, though it lent no warmth at all to his eyes.

"Captain Richardson," I said flatly. "How nice." I didn't offer my hand and he didn't bow. There was no point in trying to pretend that we were anything but enemies—and not very cordial ones, either. He'd precipitated my marriage to Lord John by inquiring of John whether he, John, had any personal interest in me, as he, Richardson, was contemplating my immediate arrest on grounds of spying and of passing seditious materials. Both charges were quite true, and while John might not have known that, he took Richardson's word regarding his intentions, told Richardson politely that, no, there was no personal interest—also true as a statement, so far as it went—and two hours later I was standing in his parlor in a daze of shock and grief, mechanically saying, "I do," in response to questions that I neither heard nor comprehended.

I had barely heard Richardson's name at the time, let alone known him by sight. John had introduced me—with cold formality—when Richardson came up to us at the Mischianza, the huge ball thrown for the British officers by the Loyalist ladies of Philadelphia a month before. And only *then* had he told me about Richardson's threats, with a brief admonition to avoid the fellow.

"Are you waiting to see General Clinton?" I inquired politely. If he was, I had half a mind to execute a quiet sneak through the house and out of the back door whilst he was ensconced with the general.

"I am," he replied, adding graciously, "but you must certainly go before me, Lady John. My business will wait."

That had a mildly sinister ring to it, but I merely inclined my head politely, with a noncommittal "Hmm."

It was dawning upon me, like an incipient case of indigestion, that my position with regard to the British army in general, and Captain Richardson in particular, was on the verge of a marked reevaluation. Once it became common knowledge that Jamie wasn't dead—then I was no longer Lady John Grey. I was Mrs. James Fraser again, and while that was certainly cause for ecstatic rejoicing, it also removed any restraint on Captain Richardson's baser urges.

Before I could think of anything useful to say to the man, a lanky young lieutenant appeared to usher me into the general's presence. The drawing room, which had been converted to Clinton's main office, was now in a state of organized disarray, with packing crates lining one wall and bare flagstaffs tied together like a bundle of faggots, the military banners they usually sported being folded briskly into tidy packets by a corporal near the window. I'd heard—the whole city had probably heard—that the British army was withdrawing from Philadelphia. Evidently they were doing so with considerable dispatch.

There were several other soldiers carrying things in and out, but two men were seated, one on either side of the desk.

"Lady John," Clinton said, looking surprised but rising from his desk and coming to bow over my hand. "Your most obedient servant, ma'am."

"Good day to you, sir," I said. My heart had already been beating fast; it speeded up considerably at sight of the man who had risen from his chair and was standing just behind the general. He was in uniform and looked strikingly familiar, but I was sure I'd never seen him before. Who—?

"I am so sorry to have disturbed you, Lady John. I had hoped to surprise your husband," the general was saying. "But I understand that he is not at home?"

"Er . . . no. He's not." The stranger—an infantry colonel, though his uniform seemed to sport even more gold lace than the usual—raised a brow at this. The sudden familiarity of the gesture gave me a slight spinning sensation in the head.

"You're a relative of Lord John Grey's," I blurted, staring at him. He had to be. The man wore his own hair, as John did, though his was dark beneath its powder. The shape of his head—fine-boned and long-skulled—was John's, and so was the set of his shoulders. His features were much like John's, too, but his face was deeply weathered and gaunt, marked with harsh lines carved by long duty and the stress of command. I didn't need the uniform to tell me that he was a lifelong soldier.

He smiled, and his face was suddenly transformed. Apparently he had John's charm, too.

"You're most perceptive, madam," he said, and, stepping forward, smoothly took my limp hand away from the general and kissed it briefly in the continental manner before straightening and eyeing me with interest.

"General Clinton informs me that you are my brother's wife."

"Oh," I said, scrambling to recover my mental bearings. "Then you must be Hal! Er . . . I beg your pardon. I mean, you're the . . . I'm sorry, I know you're a duke, but I'm afraid I don't recall your title, Your Grace."

"Pardloe," he said, still holding my hand and smiling at me. "But my Christian name *is* Harold; do please use it if you like. Welcome to the family, my dear. I had no idea John had married. I understand the event was quite recent?" He spoke with great cordiality, but I was aware of the intense curiosity behind his good manners.

"Ah," I said noncommittally. "Yes, quite recent." It hadn't for an instant occurred to me to wonder whether John had written to tell his family about me, and if he had, they could barely have received the letter by now. I didn't even know who all the members of his family *were*—though I had heard about Hal, he being the father of John's nephew Henry, who—

"Oh, of course, you've come to see Henry!" I exclaimed. "He'll be so pleased to see you! He's doing very well," I assured him.

"I have already seen Henry," the duke assured me in turn. "He speaks with the greatest admiration of your skill in removing pieces of his intestine and reuniting the remnants. Though eager as I naturally was to see my son—and my daughter"—his lips compressed for a moment; apparently Dottie had informed her parents about her engagement—"and delighted as I shall be to meet my brother again, it is actually duty that called me to America. My regiment is newly landed in New York."

"Oh," I said. "Er . . . how nice." John plainly hadn't known that his brother, let alone his regiment, was coming. It occurred dimly to me that I ought to be asking questions and finding out what I could about the general's plans, but it didn't seem the time or place.

The general coughed politely.

"Lady John—do you happen to know the whereabouts of your husband at the moment?"

The shock of meeting Harold, Duke of Pardloe, had quite wiped the reason for my presence out of my mind, but this brought it back with a rush.

"No, I'm afraid I don't," I said, as calmly as possible. "I told your corporal. A messenger came a few hours ago, with a note, and Lord John went off with him. He didn't say where he was going, though."

The general's lips twitched.

"Actually," he said, still polite, "he didn't. Colonel Graves sent the messenger, with a note informing Lord John of his re-commission and directing him to come here at once. He didn't."

"Oh," I said, sounding as blank as I felt. Under the circumstances, it seemed all right to let that show, and I did. "Dear me. In that case . . . he did go off with *someone*."

"But you don't know with whom?"

"I didn't see him go," I said, neatly avoiding the question. "I'm afraid he didn't leave word as to where he was bound."

Clinton raised a strongly marked black brow and glanced at Pardloe.

"I suppose in that case he will return shortly," the duke said with a shrug. "The matter isn't urgent, after all."

General Clinton looked as though he differed somewhat with this opinion but, with a brief glance at me, said nothing. He clearly had little time to waste, though, and, bowing politely, bade me good day.

I took my leave with alacrity, barely pausing to assure the duke that I was pleased to have met him and to ask where might his brother send word . . . ?

"I have rooms at the King's Arms," Pardloe said. "Shall I—"

"No, no," I said hurriedly, to forestall his offer to see me home. "It's quite all right. Thank you, sir." I bowed to the general, then to Hal, and headed for the door in a whirl of skirts—and emotions.

Captain Richardson was no longer in the foyer, but I hadn't time to wonder where he had gone. I gave the soldier at the door a quick nod and smile and then was out in the open air, breathing as though I'd just escaped from a bathysphere.

Now what? I wondered, swerving to avoid two little boys with a hoop, who were caroming down the street, bouncing off the legs of the soldiers carrying parcels and furniture to a large wagon. The boys must belong to one of Clinton's officers, since the soldiers were tolerating them.

John had spoken fairly often of his brother and had remarked upon Hal's tendency toward ruthless high-handedness. All the current situation needed was a nosey parker with a taste for authority mixing in. I wondered briefly whether William was on good terms with his uncle; if so, perhaps Hal could be diverted and put to good use in talking sense to—no, no, of course not. Hal mustn't know—yet at least—about Jamie, and he couldn't exchange two words with Willie without finding out—if William *would* talk about it, but then—

"Lady John." A voice behind me stopped me in my tracks, only momentarily but long enough for the Duke of Pardloe to come up beside me. He took me by the arm, detaining me.

"You're a very bad liar," he remarked with interest. "What are you lying about, though, I wonder?"

"I do it better with a little warning," I snapped. "Though, as it happens, I'm *not* lying at the moment."

That made him laugh. He leaned closer, examining my face at close range. His eyes were pale blue, like John's, but the darkness of his brows and lashes gave them a particularly piercing quality.

"Perhaps not," he said, still looking amused. "But if you aren't lying, you aren't telling me everything you know, either."

"I'm not obliged to tell you *anything* I know," I said with dignity, trying to retrieve my arm. "Let go."

He did let go, reluctantly.

"I beg your pardon, Lady John."

"Certainly," I said shortly, and made to go round him. He moved smartly in front of me, blocking my way.

"I want to know where my brother is," he said.

"I should like to know that myself," I replied, trying to sidle past him.

"Where are you going, may I ask?"

"Home." It gave me an odd feeling, still, to call Lord John's house "home"—and yet I had no other. *Yes, you do,* a small, clear voice said in my heart. *You have Jamie.*

"Why are you smiling?" asked Pardloe, sounding startled.

"At the thought of getting home and taking off these shoes," I said, hastily erasing the smile. "They're killing me."

His mouth twitched a little.

"Allow me to offer you the use of my chair, Lady John."

"Oh, no, I really don't—" But he had taken a wooden whistle from his pocket and uttered a piercing blast on it that brought two squat, muscular men—who had to be brothers, such was their resemblance to each other—trotting round the corner, a sedan chair suspended on poles between them.

"No, no, this isn't necessary at all," I protested. "Besides, John says you suffer from the gout; you'll need the chair yourself."

He didn't like that; his eyes narrowed and his lips compressed.

"I'll manage, madam," he said shortly, and, seizing me by the arm again, dragged me to the chair and pushed me inside, knocking my hat over my eyes as he did so. "The lady is under my protection. Take her to the King's Arms," he instructed Tweedledum and Tweedledee, shutting the door. And before I could say, "Off with his head!" we were jolting down the High Street at a terrific pace.

I seized the door handle, intending to leap out, even at the cost of cuts and bruises, but the bastard had put the locking pin through the outside handle, and I couldn't reach it from the inside. I shouted at the chairmen to stop, but they ignored me completely, pounding along the cobbles as though bringing the news from Aix to Ghent.

I sat back, panting and furious, and jerked the hat off. What did Pardloe think he was doing? From what John had said, and from other remarks made by the duke's children about their father, it was clear to me that he was used to getting his own way.

"Well, we'll bloody see about *that*," I muttered, stabbing the long, pearl-headed hatpin through the hat brim. The snood that had contained my hair had come off with the hat; I crammed it inside and shook my loose hair out over my shoulders.

We turned in to Fourth Street, which was paved with brick rather than cobbles, and the jolting grew less. I was able to let go my grip on the seat and fumbled with the window. If I could get it open, I might be able to reach the locking pin, and even if the door flew open and decanted me into the street, it would put a stop to the duke's machinations.

The window worked on a sliding-panel arrangement but had no sort of latch by which to get a grip on it; the only way of opening it was by inserting the fingertips into a shallow groove at one side and pushing. I was grimly attempting to do this, in spite of the chair's renewed bucketing, when I heard the duke's voice choke and stop in the midst of some shouted direction to the chairmen.

"St . . . stop. I . . . can't . . ." His words trailed off, the chairmen faltered to a halt, and I pressed my face against the suddenly motionless window. The duke was standing in the middle of the street, a fist pressed into his waistcoat, struggling to breathe. His face was deeply flushed, but his lips were tinged with blue.

"Put me down and open this bloody door this instant!" I bellowed through the glass to one of the chairmen, who was glancing back over his shoulder, a look of concern on his face. They did, and I emerged from the chair in an explosion of skirts, stabbing the hatpin down into the placket of my stays as I did so. I might need it yet.

"Bloody sit down," I said, reaching Pardloe. He shook his head but let me lead him to the chair, where I forced him to sit, my feeling of satisfaction at this reversal of position somewhat tempered by the fear that he might just possibly be about to die.

My first thought—that he was having a heart attack—had vanished the moment I heard him breathe—or try to. The wheezing gasp of someone in the throes of an asthmatic attack was unmistakable, but I seized his wrist and checked his pulse just in case. Hammering but steady, and while he was sweating, it was the normal warm perspiration caused by hot weather rather than the sudden clammy exudation that often accompanied a myocardial infarction.

I touched his fist, still embedded in his midsection.

"Do you have pain here?"

He shook his head, coughed hard, and took his hand away.

"Need . . . pill . . . b . . ." he managed, and I saw that there was a small pocket in the waistcoat that he had been trying to reach into. I put in two fingers and pulled out a small enameled box, which proved to contain a tiny corked vial.

"What—never mind." I pulled the cork, sniffed, and wheezed myself as the sudden fumes of ammonia shot up my nose.

"No," I said definitely, putting the cork back in and shoving vial and box into my pocket. "That won't help. Purse your lips and blow out." His eyes bulged a bit, but he did it; I could feel the slight movement of air on my own perspiring face.

"Right. Now, relax, *don't* gasp for air, just let it come. Blow out, to the count of four. One . . . two . . . three . . . four. In for a count of two, same rhythm . . . yes. Blow out, count of four . . . let it come in, count of two . . . yes, good. Now, don't worry; you aren't going to suffocate, you can keep doing that all day." I smiled encouragingly at him, and he managed to nod. I straightened up and looked round; we were near Locust Street, and Peterman's ordinary was no more than a block away.

"You," I said to one of the chairmen, "run to the ordinary and fetch back a jug of strong coffee. He'll pay for it," I added, with a flip of the hand toward the duke.

We were beginning to draw a crowd. I kept a wary eye out; we were near enough to Dr. Hebdy's surgery that he might come out to see the trouble, and the very last thing I needed was that charlatan to materialize, fleam at the ready.

"You have asthma," I said, returning my attention to the duke. I knelt so that I could see into his face while I monitored his pulse. It was better, noticeably slower, but I thought I could feel the odd condition called "paradoxical pulse," a phenomenon you sometimes saw in asthmatics, wherein the heart rate speeded up during exhalation and dropped during inhalation. Not that I had been in any doubt. "Did you know that?"

He nodded, still pursing his lips and blowing.

"Yes," he managed briefly, before breathing in again.

"Do you see a doctor for it?" A nod. "And did he actually recommend *sal volatile* for it?" I gestured toward the vial in my pocket. He shook his head.

"For fain . . . ting," he managed. "All I . . . had."

"Right." I put a hand under his chin and tilted his head back, examining his pupils, which were quite normal. I could feel the spasm easing, and so could he; his shoulders were beginning to drop, and the blue tinge had faded from his lips. "You don't want to use it when you're having an asthma attack; the coughing and tearing will make matters worse by producing phlegm."

"Whatever are the idle lot of you doing, standing about? Go run and fetch the doctor, lad!" I heard a woman's sharp voice say in the crowd behind me. I grimaced, and the duke saw it; he raised his brows in question.

"You don't want *that* doctor, believe me." I stood up and faced the crowd, thinking.

"No, we don't need a doctor, thank you very much," I said, as charmingly as possible. "He's just been overtaken by the indigestion—something he ate. He's quite all right now."

"He don't look that good to me, ma'am," said another voice, doubtful. "I think we best fetch the doctor."

"Let him die!" came a shout from the back of the gathering crowd. "Fucking lobster!"

An odd sort of shimmer ran through the crowd at this, and I felt a knot of dread form in my stomach. They hadn't been thinking of him as a British soldier, merely as a spectacle. But now . . .

"I'll get the doctor, Lady John!" To my horror, Mr. Caulfield, a prominent Tory, had forced his way to the front, being tolerably free with his gold-headed walking stick. "Get away, you lice!"

He bent to peer into the sedan chair, lifting his hat to Hal.

"Your servant, sir. Help will be here presently, be assured of that!"

I seized him by the sleeve. The crowd was, thank God, divided. While there were catcalls and insults directed at Pardloe and at me, there were dissenting voices, too, those of Loyalists (or perhaps merely the saner sorts who didn't think attacking a sick man in the street part of their political philosophy) chiming in, with reason, protests—and not a few loud insults of their own.

"No, no!" I said. "Let someone else go for the doctor, please. We daren't leave His Grace here without protection!"

"His Grace?" Caulfield blinked, and carefully unfolding his gold-rimmed *pince-nez* from a little case, put them on his nose and bent to peer into the chair at Pardloe, who gave him a small, dignified nod, though he kept on assiduously with his breathing exercise.

"The Duke of Pardloe," I said hastily, still keeping a grip of Mr. Caulfield's sleeve. "Your Grace, may I present Mr. Phineas Graham Caulfield?" I waved a vague hand between them, then, spotting the chairman coming back at the gallop with a jug, I sprinted toward him, hoping to reach him before he got within earshot of the crowd.

"Thank you," I said, panting as I snatched the jug from him. "We've got to get him away before the crowd turns nasty—nastier," I amended, hearing a sharp *crack!* as a thrown pebble bounced off the roof of the sedan chair. Mr. Caulfield ducked.

"Oy!" shouted the chairman, infuriated at this attack upon his livelihood. "Back off, you lot!" He started for the crowd, fists clenched, and I seized him by the coattails with my free hand.

"Get him—*and* your chair—away!" I said, as forcefully as possible. "Take him to—to—" Not the King's Arms; it was a known Loyalist stronghold and would merely inflame anyone who followed us. Neither did I want to be at the duke's mercy, once inside the place.

"Take us to Number Seventeen Chestnut Street!" I said hurriedly, and, digging one-handed in my pocket, grabbed a coin and thrust it into his hand. "Now!" He didn't pause for thought but took the coin and headed for the chair at the run, fists still clenched, and I trotted after him as fast as my red morocco heels would take me, clutching the coffee. His number was stitched into a band round his sleeve: THIRTY-NINE.

A shower of pebbles was rattling off the sedan chair's sides, and the second chairman—Number Forty—was batting at them as though they were a swarm of bees, shouting, "Fuck OFF!" at the crowd, in a businesslike if repetitious fashion. Mr. Caulfield was backing him up in more genteel fashion, shouting, "Away with you!" and "Leave off at once!" punctuated with pokes of his cane at the more daring children, who were darting forward to see the fun.

"Here," I gasped, leaning into the chair. Hal was still alive, still breathing. He raised one brow at me and nodded toward the crowd outside. I shook my head and thrust the coffee into his hands.

"Drink . . . that," I managed, "and keep breathing." Slamming the door of the chair, I dropped the locking pin into its slot with an instant's satisfaction and straightened up to find Fergus's eldest son, Germain, standing by my side.

"Have ye got a bit of trouble started again, *Grand-mère?*" he asked, unperturbed by the stones—now augmented with clumps of fresh manure—whizzing past our heads.

"You might say so, yes," I said. "Don't—"

But before I could speak further, he turned round and bellowed at the crowd, in a surprisingly loud voice, "THIS'S MY GRANNIE. You touch ONE HAIR on her head and—" Several people in the crowd laughed at this, and I put up a hand to my head. I'd completely forgotten the loss of my hat, and my hair was standing out in a mushroom-like cloud round my head—what wasn't sticking to my sweating face and neck. "And I'll do you BROWN!" Germain yelled. "Aye, I mean YOU, Shecky Loew! And you, too, Joe Grume!"

Two half-grown boys hesitated, clumps of filth in hand. Evidently they knew Germain.

"And my grannie'll tell your da what you've been a-doing, too!" That decided the boys, who stepped back a pace, dropping their clods of dirt and trying to look as though they had no idea where they had come from.

"Come on, *Grand-mère*," Germain said, grabbing my hand. The chairmen, no slouches on the uptake, had already seized their poles and hoisted the chair. I'd never manage to keep up with them in the high-heeled shoes. As I was kicking them off, I saw plump Dr. Hebdy puffing down the street, in the wake of the hectoring woman who had suggested calling him and who was now sailing toward us on the breeze of her heroism, face set in triumph.

"Thank you, Mr. Caulfield," I said hurriedly, and, snatching up the shoes in one hand, followed the chair, unable to keep my skirts up off the grubby cobbles but not terribly concerned about that. Germain fell back a little, making threatening gestures to discourage pursuit, but I could tell from the sound of the crowd that their momentary hostility had turned to amusement, and though further catcalls followed us, no missiles came in their wake.

The chairmen slowed a little once we'd turned the corner, and I was able to make headway on the flat brick of Chestnut Street, coming up beside the chair. Hal was peering through the side window, looking considerably better. The coffee jug was on the seat beside him, evidently empty.

"Where are we . . . going, madam?" he shouted through the window when he saw me. So far as I could tell over the steady thump of the chairmen's shoes and through the glass of the window, he sounded much better, too.

"Don't worry, Your Grace," I shouted back, jogging along. "You're under my protection!"

7

THE UNINTENDED CONSEQUENCES
OF ILL-CONSIDERED ACTIONS

JAMIE SHOVED THROUGH the brush, heedless of ripping brambles and slapping branches. Anything that got in his way could get out of it or be trampled.

He hesitated for no more than an instant when he reached the two horses, hobbled and grazing. He untied them both and, slapping the mare, sent her snorting into the brush. Even if no one made off with the extra horse before the militia let John Grey go, Jamie didn't mean to make it easy for the man to get back to Philadelphia. Whatever must be dealt with there would be done much more easily without the complications of his lordship's presence.

And what *would* be done? he wondered, nudging his heels into his horse's sides and reining its head round toward the road. He noticed with some surprise that his hands were shaking, and squeezed hard on the leather to make it stop.

The knuckles of his right hand throbbed, and a white stab of pain where his missing finger had been ran through his hand, making him hiss through his teeth.

"What the devil did ye *tell* me for, ye wee idiot?" he said under his breath, urging his horse up into a gallop. "What did ye *think* I'd do?"

Just what ye damn well did was the answer. John hadn't resisted, hadn't fought back. *"Go ahead and kill me,"* the wee bugger had said. A fresh spurt of rage curled Jamie's hands as he imagined all too well doing just that. Would he have gone ahead and done it, if that pissant Woodbine and his militia hadn't turned up?

No. No, he wouldn't. Even as he longed momentarily to go back and choke the life out of Grey, he was beginning to answer his own question, reason fighting its way through the haze of fury. Why *had* Grey told him? There was the obvious—the reason he'd hit the man by sheer reflex, the reason he was shaking now. Because Grey had told him the truth.

"We were both fucking you." He breathed hard and deep, fast enough to make him giddy, but it stopped the shaking and he slowed a little; his horse's ears were laid back, twitching in agitation.

"It's all right, *a bhalaich*," he said, still breathing hard but slower now. "It's all right."

He thought for a moment that he might vomit, but managed not to, and settled back in the saddle, steadier.

He could still touch it, that raw place Jack Randall had left on his soul. He'd thought it so well scarred over that he was safe now, but, no, bloody John Grey had torn it open with five words. "We were both fucking you." And he couldn't blame him for it—oughtn't to, anyway, he thought, reason doggedly fighting back the fury, though he knew only too well how weak a weapon reason was against that specter. Grey couldn't have known what those words had done to him.

Reason had its uses, though. It was reason that reminded him of the second blow. The first had been blind reflex; the second wasn't. Thought of it brought anger, too, and pain, but of a different sort.

"I have had carnal knowledge of your wife."

"You bugger," he whispered, clutching the reins with a reflexive violence that made the horse jerk its head, startled. "Why? Why did ye tell me that, ye bugger!"

And the second answer came belatedly, but as clearly as the first: *Because she'd tell me, the minute she had a chance. And he kent that fine. He thought if I'd do violence when I heard, best I do it to him.*

Aye, she would have told him. He swallowed. *And she* will *tell me.* What might he say—or do—when she did?

He was trembling again and had slowed inadvertently, so the horse was nearly at a walk, head turning from side to side as it snuffed the air.

It's nay her fault. I know that. *It's nay her fault.* They'd thought him dead. He knew what that abyss looked like; he'd lived there for a long while. And he understood what desperation and strong drink could do. But the vision—or the lack of one . . . How did it happen? Where? Knowing it had happened was bad enough; not knowing the how and the why of it from her was almost unbearable.

The horse had stopped; the reins hung slack. Jamie was sitting in the middle of the road, eyes closed, just breathing, trying not to imagine, trying to pray.

Reason had limits; prayer didn't. It took a little while for his mind to relax its grip, its wicked curiosity, its lust to *know*. But, after a bit, he felt he could go on and gathered up the reins again.

All that could wait. But he needed to see Claire before he did anything else. Just now he had no idea what he would say—or do—when he saw her, but he needed to see her, with the same sort of need that a man might feel who'd been cast away at sea, marooned without food or water for weeks on end.

JOHN GREY'S BLOOD was thrumming in his ears so loudly that he barely heard the discussion among his captors, who—having taken the elementary precautions of searching him and tying his hands together in front of him—had gathered into a knot a few yards away and were heatedly hissing at one another like geese in a barnyard, casting occasional hostile glares in his direction.

He didn't care. He couldn't see out of his left eye and he was by now quite certain that his liver was ruptured, but he didn't care about that, either. He'd told Jamie Fraser the truth—the *whole* bloody truth—and felt the same fierce constellation of feelings that attends victory in battle: the bone-deep relief of being alive, the giddy surge of emotion that carries you on a wave much like drunkenness, then ebbs and leaves you staggering light-headed on the beach—and an absolute inability to count the cost 'til later.

His knees experienced much the same post-battle sensations and gave way. He sat down unceremoniously in the leaves and closed his good eye.

After a short interval in which he was aware of nothing much beyond the gradual slowing of his heart, the thrumming noise in his ears began to abate, and he noticed that someone was calling his name.

"Lord Grey!" the voice said again, louder, and close enough that he felt a warmly fetid gust of tobacco-laden breath on his face.

"My name is not Lord Grey," he said, rather crossly, opening his eye. "I told you."

"You said you were Lord John Grey," his interlocutor said, frowning through a mat of grizzled facial hair. It was the large man in the filthy hunting shirt who had first discovered him with Fraser.

"I am. If you bloody have to talk to me, call me 'my lord,' or just 'sir,' if you like. What do you want?"

The man reared back a little, looking indignant.

"Well, since you ask . . . *sir*, first off, we want to know if this elder brother of yours is Major General Charles Grey."

"No."

"No?" The man's unkempt eyebrows drew together. "Do you *know* Major General Charles Grey? Is he kin to you?"

"Yes, he is. He's . . ." Grey tried to calculate the precise degree, but gave it up and flapped a hand. "Cousin of some sort."

There was a satisfied rumble from the faces now peering down at him. The man called Woodbine squatted down next to him, a square of folded paper in his hand.

"Lord John," he said, more or less politely. "You said that you don't hold an active commission in His Majesty's army at present?"

"That's correct." Grey fought back a sudden unexpected urge to yawn. The excitement in his blood had died away now and he wanted to lie down.

"Then would you care to explain these documents, my lord? We found them in your breeches." He unfolded the papers carefully and held them under Grey's nose.

John peered at them with his working eye. The note on top was from General Clinton's adjutant: a brief request for Grey to attend upon the general at his earliest convenience. Yes, he'd seen that, though he'd barely glanced at it before the cataclysmic arrival of Jamie Fraser, risen from the dead, had driven it from his mind. Despite what had occurred in the meantime, he couldn't help smiling. *Alive.* The bloody man was *alive!*

Then Woodbine took the note away, revealing the paper beneath: the document that had come attached to Clinton's note. It was a small piece of paper, bearing a red wax seal and instantly identifiable; it was an officer's warrant, his proof of commission, to be carried on his person at all times. Grey blinked at it in simple disbelief, the spidery clerk's writing wavering before his eyes. But written at the bottom, below the King's signature, was another, this one executed in a bold, black, all-too-recognizable scrawl.

"Hal!" he exclaimed. "You *bastard!*"

"TOLD YOU HE was a soldier," the small man with the cracked spectacles said, eyeing Grey from under the edge of his knitted KILL! hat with an avidity that Grey found very objectionable. "Not just a soldier, neither; he's a spy! Why, we could hang him out o' hand, this very minute!"

There was an outburst of noticeable enthusiasm for this course of action, quelled with some difficulty by Corporal Woodbine, who stood up and shouted louder than the proponents of immediate execution, until those espousing it reluctantly fell back, muttering. Grey sat clutching the commission crumpled in his bound hands, heart hammering.

They bloody could hang him. Howe had done just that to a Continental captain named Hale, not two years before, when Hale was caught gathering intelligence while dressed as a civilian, and the Rebels would like nothing better than a chance to retaliate. William had been present, both at Hale's arrest and his execution, and had given Grey a brief account of the matter, shocking in its starkness.

William. Jesus, William! Caught up in the immediacy of the situation, Grey had had barely a thought to spare for his son. He and Fraser had absquatulated onto the roof and down a drainpipe, leaving William, clearly reeling with the shock of revelation, alone in the upstairs hallway.

No. No, not alone. Claire had been there, and the thought of her steadied him a bit. She would have been able to talk to Willie, calm him, explain . . . well, possibly not explain, and possibly not calm, either—but at least if Grey was hanged in the next few minutes, William wouldn't be left to face things entirely alone.

"We're taking him back to camp," Woodbine was saying doggedly, not for the first time. "What good would it do to hang him here?"

"One less redcoat? Seems like a good thing to *me*!" riposted the burly thug in the hunting shirt.

"Now, Gershon, I'm not saying as how we shouldn't hang him. I said, not here and now." Woodbine, musket held in both hands, looked slowly round the circle of men, fixing each one with his gaze. "Not here, not now," he repeated. Grey admired Woodbine's force of character and narrowly kept himself from nodding agreement.

"We're taking him back to camp. You all heard what he said; Major General Charles Grey's kin to him. Might be as Colonel Smith will want to hang him in camp—or might even be as he'll want to send this man to General Wayne. Remember Paoli!"

"Remember Paoli!" Ragged cries echoed the call, and Grey rubbed at his swollen eye with his sleeve—tears were leaking from it and irritating his face. Paoli? What the devil was Paoli? And what had it to do with whether, when, or how he should be hanged? He decided not to ask at just this moment and, when they hauled him to his feet, went along with them without complaint.

8

HOMO EST OBLIGAMUS AEROBE ("MAN IS AN OBLIGATE AEROBE")—HIPPOCRATES

THE DUKE'S FACE WAS dangerously flushed when Number Thirty-Nine ceremoniously opened the sedan chair's door, and not, I thought, from the heat.

"You wanted to see your brother, did you not?" I inquired, before he could gather enough breath to say any of the things on his mind. I gestured toward the house. "This is his house." The fact that John was not presently *in* the house could wait.

He gave me a marked look, but he was still short of breath and wisely saved it, irritably waving off Number Forty's helping hand as he struggled out of the sedan chair. He did pay the chairmen—rather fortunate, as I hadn't any more money with me—and, wheezing, bowed and offered me his arm. I took it, not wanting him to fall on his face in the front garden. Germain, who had kept up with the chair without noticeable effort, followed at a tactful distance.

Mrs. Figg was standing in the front doorway, watching our approach with interest. The broken door was now lying on a pair of trestles next to a camellia bush, having been removed from its hinges, and was presumably awaiting some sort of professional attention.

"May I present Mrs. Mortimer Figg, Your Grace?" I said politely, with a nod in her direction. "Mrs. Figg is his lordship's cook and housekeeper. Mrs. Figg, this is His Grace, the Duke of Pardloe. Lord John's brother."

I saw her lips form the words "*Merde* on toast," but fortunately without sound. She moved nimbly down the steps despite her bulk and took Hal by the other arm, shoring him up, as he was beginning to turn blue again.

"Purse your lips and blow," I said shortly. "Now!" He made an ugly choking noise but did start blowing, though making evil grimaces in my direction.

"What in the name of the everlasting Holy Ghost did you do to him?" Mrs. Figg asked me accusingly. "Sounds like he's about to die."

"Saved his life, to start with," I snapped. "Ups-a-daisy, Your Grace!" and between us we hoicked him up the steps. "Then I saved him from being stoned and beaten by a mob—with Germain's invaluable help," I added, glancing back at Germain, who grinned hugely. I was also in the act of abducting him, but I thought we needn't go into that.

"And I'm about to save his life again, I think," I said, pausing on the porch to pant for a moment myself. "Have we a bedroom we can put him in? William's, perhaps?"

"Will—" the duke began, but then started to cough spasmodically, going a nasty shade of puce. "Wh—wh—"

"Oh, I was forgetting," I said. "Of course, William's your nephew, isn't he? He's not here just now." I looked narrowly at Mrs. Figg, who snorted briefly but said nothing. "Blow, Your Grace."

Inside, I saw that some progress had been made toward restoring order. The debris had been swept into a neat pile by the open doorway, and Jenny Murray was sitting on an ottoman beside it, picking unbroken crystals from the fallen chandelier out of the rubbish and dropping them into a bowl. She lifted an eyebrow at me but rose unhurriedly to her feet, putting the bowl aside.

"What d'ye need, Claire?" she said.

"Boiling water," I said, grunting slightly as we maneuvered Pardloe—he was lean and fine-boned, like John, but a solid man, nonetheless—into a wing chair. "Mrs. Figg? Cups, several cups, and, Jenny, my medicine chest. Don't lose your rhythm, Your Grace—blow . . . two . . . three . . . four— *don't* gasp. Sip the air—you'll get enough, I promise." Hal's face was twitching, shining with sweat, and while he still had control over himself, I could see panic creasing the lines around his eyes as his airways closed.

I fought down a similar sense of panic; it wouldn't serve either of us. The fact was that he *could* die. He was having a severe asthmatic attack, and even with access to epinephrine injections and the facilities of a major hospital, people did die in such circumstances, whether of a heart attack brought on by stress and lack of oxygen or from simple suffocation.

His hands were clenched on his knees, the moleskin breeches crumpled and dark with sweat, and the cords of his neck stood out with strain. With some difficulty, I pried one of his hands loose and grasped it strongly in mine; I had to distract him from the panic darkening his mind, if he was to have any chance at all.

"Look at me," I said, leaning close and looking straight into his eyes. "It's going to be all right. Do you hear me? Nod if you can hear me."

He managed a short nod. He was blowing, but too fast; no more than a wisp of air touched my cheek. I squeezed his hand.

"Slower," I said, my voice as calm as I could make it. "Breathe with me, now. Purse your lips . . . blow . . ." I tapped out a regular count of four on his knee with my free hand, as slow as I dared. He ran out of air between two and three but kept his lips pursed, straining.

"Slow!" I said sharply as his mouth opened, gasping, starving for air. "Let it come by itself; one . . . two . . . blow!" I could hear Jenny hurrying down the stairs with my medicine chest. Mrs. Figg had departed like a great rushing wind in the direction of the cookhouse, where she kept a cauldron boiling—yes, here she came, three teacups looped over the fingers of one hand, a can of hot water wrapped in a towel clutched to her bosom with the other.

". . . three . . . four—joint fir, Jenny—one . . . two . . . blow *out*, two . . . three . . . four—a good handful in each cup—two, yes, that's it . . . blow . . ." Still holding his gaze, willing him to blow—it was all that was keeping his airways open. If he lost his rhythm, he'd lose what little air pressure he had, the airways would collapse, and then—I shoved the thought aside, squeezing his hand as hard as I could, and gave disjoint directions between chanting the rhythm. Joint fir . . . what the bloody hell else did I have?

Not much, was the answer. Bowman's root, jimsonweed—much too dangerously toxic, and not fast enough. "Spikenard, Jenny," I said abruptly. "The root—grind it." I pointed at the second cup, then the third. ". . . two . . . three . . . four . . ." A large handful of crumbled joint fir (aptly named; it looked like a pile of miniature sticks) had been placed in each cup and was already steeping. I'd give him the first as soon as it had cooled enough to drink, but it took a good half hour of steeping to get a truly effective concentration. "More cups, please, Mrs. Figg—in, one . . . two . . . that's good . . ."

The hand in mine was slick with sweat, but he was gripping me with all the strength he had; I could feel my bones grind, and twisted my hand a bit to ease them. He saw and released the pressure a little. I leaned in, cradling his hand in both of mine—not incidentally taking the opportunity to get my fingers on his pulse.

"You aren't going to die," I said to him, quietly but as forcefully as I could. "I won't let you." The flicker of something much too faint to be a smile passed behind those winter-sharp blue eyes, but he hadn't enough breath even to think of speaking. His lips were still blue and his face paper-white, in spite of the temperature.

The first cup of joint-fir tea helped briefly, the heat and moisture doing as much as the herb; joint fir did contain epinephrine and was the only really good treatment for asthma I had available—but there wasn't enough of the active principle in a cup of the stuff after only ten minutes' brewing. Even the momentary sense of relief steadied him, though. His hand turned, fingers linking with mine, and he squeezed back.

A fighter. I knew one when I saw one and smiled involuntarily.

"Start three more cups, please, Jenny?" If he drank them slowly—and he couldn't do more than sip briefly between gasps—and continuously, we should have got a decent amount of stimulant into him by the end of the sixth, most-concentrated cup. "And, Mrs. Figg, if you would boil three handfuls of the joint fir and half that of spikenard in a pint of coffee for a quarter hour, then let it steep?" If he wasn't going to die, I wanted a concentrated tincture of *Ephedra* easily on hand; this obviously wasn't his first attack, and—if it wasn't his last—there'd be another sometime. And quite possibly sometime soon.

The back of my mind had been ticking through diagnostic possibilities, and now that I was fairly sure he was going to survive the moment, I could spare time to think about them consciously.

Sweat was pouring down the fine-cut bones of his face; I'd got his coat, waistcoat, and leather stock off first thing, and his shirtfront was pasted to his chest, his breeches black-wet in the creases of his groin. No wonder, though, between the heat of the day, his exertions, and the hot tea. The blue tinge was fading from his lips, and there was no sign of edema in face or hands . . . no distention of the blood vessels in his neck, in spite of his effort.

I could hear the crackling rales in his lungs easily without a stethoscope, but he showed no thoracic enlargement; his torso was as trim as John's, a bit narrower through the chest. Probably not a chronic obstructive pulmonary condition, then . . . and I didn't *think* he had congestive heart failure. His color when I met him had been good, and his pulse was presently thumping against my fingers very steadily, fast, but no flutters, no arrhythmia . . .

I became aware of Germain hovering by my elbow, staring interestedly at the duke, who was now sufficiently himself as to lift an eyebrow in the boy's direction, though still unable to speak.

"Mmm?" I said, before resuming my now-automatic counting of breaths.

"I'm only thinking, *Grand-mère,* as how himself there"—Germain nodded at Pardloe—"might be missed. Had I maybe best carry a message to someone, so as they aren't sending out soldiers after him? The chairmen will talk, will they not?"

"Ah." That was a thought, all right. General Clinton, for one, certainly knew that Pardloe was in my company when last seen. I had no idea with whom Pardloe might be traveling or whether he was in command of his regiment. If he *was,* people would be looking for him right now; an officer couldn't be gone from his place for long without someone noticing.

And Germain—an observant lad, if ever there was one—was right about the chairmen. Their numbers meant they were registered with the central chairmen's agency in Philadelphia; it would be the work of a moment for the general's staff to locate numbers Thirty-Nine and Forty and find out where they'd delivered the Duke of Pardloe.

Jenny, who had been tending the array of teacups, stepped in now with the next and knelt by Pardloe, nodding to me that she would see to his breathing while I talked to Germain.

"He told the chairmen to bring me to the King's Arms," I said to Germain, taking him out onto the porch, where we could confer unheard. "And I met him at General Clinton's office in the—"

"I ken where it is, *Grand-mère.*"

"I daresay you do. Have you something in mind?"

"Well, I'm thinkin'—" He glanced into the house, then back at me, eyes narrowed in thought. "How long d'ye mean to keep him prisoner, *Grand-mère?*"

So my motives hadn't escaped Germain. I wasn't surprised; he undoubtedly had heard all about the day's excitements from Mrs. Figg—and, knowing as he did who Jamie was, had probably deduced even more. I wondered if he'd seen William. If so, he likely knew everything. If he didn't, though, there was no need to reveal *that* little complication until it was necessary.

"Until your grandfather comes back," I said. "Or possibly Lord John," I added as an afterthought. I hoped with all my being that Jamie would come back shortly. But it might be that he would find it necessary to stay outside the city and send John in to bring me news. "The minute I let the duke go, he'll be turning the city upside down in search of his brother. Always assuming for the sake of argument that he doesn't drop dead in the process." And the very last thing I wanted was to instigate a dragnet in which Jamie might be snared.

Germain rubbed his chin thoughtfully—a peculiar gesture in a child too young for whiskers, but his father to the life, and I smiled.

"That's maybe not too long," he said. "*Grand-père* will come back directly; he was wild to see ye last night." He grinned at me, then looked through the open doorway, pursing his lips.

"As to himself, ye canna hide where he is," he said. "But if ye were to send a note to the general, and maybe another to the King's Arms, saying as how His Grace was staying with Lord John, they wouldna start searching for him right away. And even if someone was to come here later and inquire, I suppose ye might give him a wee dram that would keep him quiet so ye could tell them he was gone. Or maybe lock him in a closet? Tied up wi' a gag if it should be he's got his voice back by then," he added. Germain was a very logical, thorough-minded sort of person; he got it from Marsali.

"Excellent thought," I said, forbearing to comment on the relative merits of the options for keeping Pardloe incommunicado. "Let me do that now."

Pausing for a quick look at Pardloe, who was doing better though still wheezing strongly, I whipped upstairs and flipped open John's writing desk. It was the work of a moment to mix the ink powder and write the notes. I hesitated briefly over the signature but then caught sight of John's signet on the dressing table; he hadn't had time to put it on.

The thought gave me a slight pang; in the overwhelming joy of seeing Jamie alive, and then the shock of William's advent, Jamie's taking John hostage, and the violence of William's exit—dear Lord, where was William now?—I had pushed John to the back of my mind.

Still, I told myself, he was quite safe. Jamie wouldn't let any harm come to him, and directly he came back into Philadelphia—the chiming of the carriage clock on the mantelpiece interrupted me, and I glanced at it: four o'clock.

"Time flies when you're having fun," I murmured to myself, and, scribbling a reasonable facsimile of John's signature, I lit the candle from the embers in the hearth, dripped wax on the folded notes, and stamped them with the smiling half-moon ring. Maybe John would be back before the notes were even delivered. And Jamie, surely, would be with me as soon as darkness made it safe.

9

A TIDE IN THE AFFAIRS OF MEN

JAMIE WASN'T ALONE on the road. He'd been dimly aware of horses passing by, heard the distant talk of men on foot, but now that he'd come out of his red haze, he was startled to see how many there were. He saw what was plainly a militia company—not marching, but on the move as a body, knots and clumps of men, solitary riders—and a few wagons coming from the city, piled with goods, women and children afoot beside them.

He'd seen a few folk leaving Philadelphia when he'd come in the day before—God, was it only *yesterday?*—and thought to ask Fergus about it, but in the excitement of arrival and the later complications had quite forgotten.

His sense of disturbance increased and he kicked up his horse to a faster pace. It was no more than ten miles to the city; he'd be there long before nightfall.

Maybe just as well if it's dark, he thought grimly. Easier to have things out with Claire alone and undisturbed—and whether the having-out led to beating or bed, he wanted no interference.

The thought was like the striking of one of Brianna's matches. Just the word "bed" and he was aflame with fresh rage.

"Ifrinn!" he said aloud, and slammed his fist against the pommel. All the trouble to calm himself, and all to waste in an instant! God *damn* it—damn him, damn her, John Grey—damn everything!

"Mr. Fraser!"

He jerked as though shot in the back, and the horse slowed at once, snorting.

"Mr. Fraser!" came the loud, wheezy voice again, and Daniel Morgan came trotting up alongside on a small, sturdy bay, grinning all over his big scarred face. "Knew that was you, knew it! Ain't no other rascal that size with that color hair, and if there is one, I don't want to meet him."

"Colonel Morgan," he said, noting auld Dan's unaccustomed uniform with the fresh insignia on the collar. "On your way to a wedding?" He did his best to smile, though the turmoil inside him was like the whirlpools off the rocks of Stroma.

"What? Oh, that," said Dan, trying to look sideways down his own neck. "Pshaw. Washington's a damned stickler for 'proper dress.' The Continental army got more generals than they got private soldiers, these days. An officer lives through more 'n two battles, they make him some kind of general on the spot. Now, gettin' any pay for it, that's a different kettle of fish."

He tipped back his hat and looked Jamie up and down.

"Just come back from Scotland? Heard you went with Brigadier Fraser's body—your kin, I suppose?" He shook his head regretfully. "Cryin' shame. Fine soldier, good man."

"Aye, he was that. We buried him near his home at Balnain."

They continued together, auld Dan asking questions and Jamie replying as briefly as good manners—and his real affection for Morgan—would allow. They hadn't met since Saratoga, where he'd served under Morgan as an officer of his Rifle Corps, and there was a good deal to say. Still, he was glad of the company, and even of the questions; they distracted him and kept his mind from catapulting him again into fruitless fury and confusion.

"I suppose we must part here," Jamie said, after a bit. They were approaching a crossroads, and Dan had slowed his pace a bit. "I'm bound into the city myself."

"What for?" Morgan asked, rather surprised.

"I—to see my wife." His voice wanted to tremble on the word "wife," and he bit it off sharp.

"Oh, yes? Could you maybe spare a quarter hour?" Dan was giving him a sort of calculating look that made Jamie instantly uneasy. But the sun was still high; he didn't want to enter Philadelphia before dark.

"Aye, maybe," he replied cautiously. "To do what?"

"I'm on my way to see a friend—want you to meet him. It's right close, won't take a moment. Come on!" Morgan veered right, waving at Jamie to follow, which, cursing himself for a fool, he did.

Number 17 Chestnut Street

I WAS SWEATING as freely as the duke was by the time the spasm eased enough for him to breathe without the positive-pressure exercise. I wasn't quite as tired as he was—he lay back in the chair, exhausted, eyes closed, drawing slow, shallow—but free!—breaths—but close. I felt light-headed, too; it's not possible to help someone breathe without doing a lot of it yourself, and I was hyperventilated.

"Here, *a piuthar-chèile.*" Jenny's voice spoke by my ear, and it was only when I opened my eyes in surprise that I realized they'd been closed. She put a small glass of brandy in my hand. "There's nay whisky in the house, but I expect this will help. Shall I give His Grace a dram, too?"

"Yes, you shall," the duke said, with great authority, though he didn't move a muscle or open his eyes. "Thank you, madam."

"It won't hurt him," I said, drawing myself up and stretching my back. "Or you, either. Sit down and have a drink. You, too, Mrs. Figg." Jenny and Mrs. Figg had worked nearly as hard as I had, fetching and grinding and brewing, bringing cool cloths to mop the sweat, spelling me now and then with the counting, and, by combining their not-inconsiderable force of will with mine, helping to keep him alive.

Mrs. Figg had very fixed notions of what was proper, and these didn't include sitting down to share a dram with her employer, let alone a visiting duke, but even she was obliged to admit that the circumstances were unusual. Glass in hand, she perched primly on an ottoman near the parlor door, where she could deal with any potential invasions or domestic emergencies.

No one spoke for some time, but there was a great sense of peace in the room. The hot, still air carried that sense of odd camaraderie that binds people who have passed through a trial together—if only temporarily. I gradually became aware that the air was carrying noises, too, from the street outside. Groups of people moving hurriedly, shouts from the next block, and a rumble of wagons. And a distant rattle of drums.

Mrs. Figg was aware of it, too; I saw her head rise, the ribbons of her cap atremble with inquisitiveness.

"Baby Jesus, have mercy," she said, setting down her empty glass with care. "Something's coming."

Jenny looked startled and glanced at me, apprehensive.

"Coming?" she said. "What's coming?"

"The Continental army, I expect," said Pardloe. He let his head fall back, sighing. "Dear God. What it is . . . to draw breath." His breath was still short, but not very much constrained. He raised his glass ceremoniously to me. "Thank you, my . . . dear. I was . . . already in your debt for your . . . kind services to my son, but—"

"What do you mean, 'the Continental army'?" I interrupted. I set down my own glass, now empty. My heart rate had calmed after the exertions of the last hour but now abruptly sped up again.

Pardloe closed one eye and regarded me with the other.

"The Americans," he said mildly. "The Rebels. What else . . . would I mean?"

"And when you say, 'coming . . .'" I said carefully.

"I didn't," he pointed out, then nodded at Mrs. Figg. "She did. She's right, though. General Clinton's . . . forces are with . . . drawing from Philadelphia. . . . I daresay Wa . . . Washington is . . . poised to rush in."

Jenny made a small sputtering noise, and Mrs. Figg said something really blasphemous in French, then clapped a broad pink-palmed hand to her mouth.

"Oh," I said, doubtless sounding as blank as I felt. I'd been so distracted during my meeting with Clinton earlier in the day that the logical consequences of a British withdrawal had not occurred to me at all.

Mrs. Figg stood up.

"I best go and be burying the silver, then," she said in a matter-of-fact sort of way. "It'll be under the laburnum bush by the cookhouse, Lady John."

"Wait," I said, raising a hand. "I don't think we need do that *just* yet, Mrs. Figg. The army hasn't yet left the city; the Americans aren't precisely snapping at our heels. And we'll need a few forks with which to eat our supper."

She made a low rumbling noise in her throat but seemed to see the sense in this; she nodded and began to collect the brandy glasses instead.

"What'll you be wanting for supper, then? I got a cold boiled ham, but I was thinking to make a chicken fricassee, William liking that so much."

She cast a bleak look at the hallway, where the bloody smudges on the wall-paper had now turned brown. "You think he's coming back for his supper?" William had an official billet somewhere in the town, but frequently spent the night at the house—particularly when Mrs. Figg was making chicken fricassee.

"God knows," I said. I hadn't had time to contemplate the William situation, what with everything else. *Might* he come back, when he'd cooled down, determined to have things out with John? I'd seen a Fraser on the boil, many times, and they didn't sulk, as a rule. They tended to take direct action, at once. I eyed Jenny speculatively; she returned the look and casually leaned her elbow on the table, chin in hand, and tapped her fingers thoughtfully against her lips. I smiled privately at her.

"Where *is* my nephew?" Hal asked, finally able to take note of something other than his next breath. "For that matter . . . where is my brother?"

"I don't know," I told him, putting my own glass on Mrs. Figg's tray and scooping his up to add to it. "I really wasn't lying about that. But I do expect he'll be back soon." I rubbed a hand over my face and smoothed my hair back as well as I could. First things first. I had a patient to tend.

"I'm sure John wants to see you as much as you want to see him. But—"

"Oh, I doubt it," the duke said. His eyes traveled slowly over me, from bare feet to disheveled hair, and the faint look of amusement on his face deepened. "You must tell me how John . . . happened to marry you . . . when there's time."

"A counsel of desperation," I said shortly. "But in the meantime we must get you to bed. Mrs. Figg, is the back bedroom—"

"Thank you, Mrs. Figg," the duke interrupted, "I shan't be . . . requiring . . ." He was trying to struggle up out of the chair and hadn't enough breath to talk. I walked up to him and gave him my best piercing head-matron look.

"Harold," I said in measured tones. "I am not merely your sister-in-law." The term gave me an odd *frisson,* but I ignored it. "I am your physician. If you don't—what?" I demanded. He was staring up at me with a most peculiar expression on his face, something between surprise and amusement. "You invited me to use your Christian name, didn't you?"

"I did," he admitted. "But I don't think anyone has . . . actually called me Harold since . . . I was three years old." He did smile then, a charming smile quite his own. "The family call me Hal."

"Hal, then," I said, smiling back but refusing to be distracted. "You're going to have a nice refreshing sponge bath, Hal, and then you're going to bed."

He laughed—though he cut it short, as he began to wheeze. He coughed a little, fist balled under his ribs, and looked uneasy, but it stopped, and he cleared his throat and glanced up at me.

"You'd think I *was* . . . three years old. Sister-in-law. Trying to send me . . . to bed without my tea?" He pressed himself gingerly upright, getting his feet under him. I put a hand on his chest and pushed. He hadn't any strength in his legs and fell back into the chair, astonished and affronted. And afraid: he hadn't realized—or at least had not admitted—his own weakness. A severe attack usually left the victim completely drained, and often with the lungs still dangerously twitchy.

"You see?" I said, tempering my tone with gentleness. "You've had attacks like this before, haven't you?"

"Well . . . yes," he said unwillingly, "but . . ."

"And how long were you in bed after the last one?"

His lips compressed.

"A week. But the fool doctor—"

I put a hand on his shoulder and he stopped—as much because he'd temporarily run short of air as because of the touch.

"You. Cannot. Breathe. Yet. On. Your. Own," I said, separating the words for emphasis. "Listen to me, Hal. Look what's happened this afternoon, will you? You had a fairly severe attack in the street; had that crowd on Fourth Street decided to set upon us, you would have been quite helpless—don't argue with me, Hal, I was there." I narrowed my eyes at him. He did the same back at me but didn't argue.

"Then the walk from the street to the door of the house—a distance of some twenty feet—threw you straight into a full-blown *status asthmaticus;* have you heard that term before?"

"No," he muttered.

"Well, now you have, and now you know what it is. And you were in bed for a week the last time? Was it as bad as this?"

His lips were a thin line and his eyes sparking. I imagined most people didn't speak to a duke—let alone the commander of his own regiment—like this. Be good for him, I thought.

"Bloody doctor . . . said it was my heart." His fist had uncurled and the fingers were slowly rubbing his chest. "Knew it wasn't that."

"I think you're probably right about that," I conceded. "Was this the same doctor who gave you smelling salts? Complete quack, if so."

He laughed, a brief, breathless sound.

"Yes, he is." He paused to breathe for a moment. "Though in . . . justice, he . . . he didn't give me . . . salts. Got them . . . myself. For fainting . . . told you."

"So you did." I sat down beside him and took hold of his wrist. He let me, watching curiously. His pulse was fine; it had slowed and was thumping along very steadily.

"How long have you been subject to fainting spells?" I asked, bending to look closely into his eyes. No sign of petechial hemorrhage, no jaundice, pupils the same size . . .

"A long time," he said, and pulled his wrist abruptly away. "I haven't time to chat about my health, madam. I—"

"Claire," I said, and put a restraining hand on his chest, smiling amiably at him. "You're Hal, I'm Claire—and you aren't going anywhere, Your Grace."

"Take your hand off me!"

"I'm seriously tempted to do just that and let you fall on your face," I told him, "but wait until Mrs. Figg finishes brewing the tincture. I don't want you thrashing about on the floor, gasping like a landed fish, and no way of getting the hook out of your mouth."

I did in fact take my hand off his chest, though, and, rising, I went out into the hall before he could find breath to say anything. Jenny had taken up a stand by the open doorway, looking up and down the street.

"What's going on out there?" I asked.

"I dinna ken," she said, not taking her eyes off a couple of rough-looking men who were lounging down the other side of the street. "But I dinna like the feel of it a bit. D'ye think he's right?"

"That the British army is leaving? Yes. They are. And very likely half the Loyalists in the city with them." I knew exactly what she meant by not liking the feel of things. The air was hot and thick, buzzing with cicadas, and the leaves of the chestnut trees along the street hung limp as dishrags. But *something* was moving in the atmosphere. Excitement? Panic? Fear? All three, I thought.

"Had I best go to the printshop, d'ye think?" she asked, turning to me with a slight frown. "Would Marsali and the weans be safer if I fetched them here, I mean? If there was to be a riot or the like?"

I shook my head.

"I don't think so. They're well-known Patriots. It's the Loyalists who will be in danger, if the British army is leaving. They won't have any protection, and the Rebels may well . . . do things to them. And"—a very unpleasant feeling snaked down my backbone, like a cold, slimy finger—"this is a Loyalist household." *"Without even a door to shut and bolt,"* I might have added, but didn't.

There was a loud thump from the parlor, as of a body hitting the floor, but Jenny didn't turn a hair, nor did I. We'd both had a lot of experience with stubborn men. I could hear him panting; if he started wheezing again, I'd go in.

"Will it put ye in danger, then, to have him here?" she asked, *sotto voce,* with a tilt of her head toward the parlor. "Maybe ye'd best come to the print-shop."

I grimaced, trying to evaluate the possibilities. The notes I'd sent with Germain would delay inquiries, and I could put off anyone who did come. But that also meant I could expect no immediate help from the army, if help was needed. And it might be; someone in that hostile crowd on Fourth Street might well have heard where I'd told the chairmen to come. That hostility now showed itself in a different light.

If the Rebels in the city were about to rise and turn upon the defenseless Loyalists—and the currents I sensed beginning to swirl through the streets were dark ones—

"Someone might just show up on your porch wi' a keg of tar and a bag o' feathers," Jenny observed, preempting my thought in a most unnerving way.

"Well, that wouldn't help His Grace's asthma a bit," I said, and she laughed.

"Had ye maybe better give him back to General Clinton?" she suggested. "I've had soldiers search my house, wi' a wanted man hidin' in the bottom o' my wardrobe and my newborn bairn in his arms. I dinna think it would be a great deal easier on the nerves to have the Sons o' Liberty come in here after His Grace, if half what Marsali told me about them is true."

"It probably is." A gunshot smacked through the heavy air, flat and dull, from somewhere near the river, and we both tensed. It wasn't repeated, though, and after a moment I drew breath again.

"The thing is, he's not stable. I can't risk taking him through streets filled with dust and tree pollen and then leaving him in the care of an army surgeon, or even that quack Hebdy. Were he to have another attack and no one able to get him through it . . ."

Jenny grimaced.

"Aye, ye're right," she said reluctantly. "And ye canna leave him here and go yourself, for the same reason."

"That's right." And Jamie would be coming here, to find me. I wouldn't leave.

"Ken, if Jamie came and didna find ye here, he'd go to the printshop next thing," Jenny observed, making the hair prickle on the back of my neck.

"Will you stop doing that!?"

"What?" she said, startled.

"Reading my mind!"

"Oh, that." She grinned at me, blue eyes creasing into triangles. "Everything ye think shows on your face, Claire. Surely Jamie's told ye that?"

A deep flush burned upward from my low-cut décolletage, and only then did I recall that I was still wearing the amber-colored silk, which was now soaked with sweat, rimed with dust, and altogether rather the worse for wear. And which had very tight stays. I rather hoped that *everything* I was thinking didn't show on my face, because there was quite a bit of information I didn't mean to share with Jenny just yet.

"Well, I canna tell *everything* ye think," she admitted—doing it *again,* dammit!—"but it's easy to tell when ye're thinking about Jamie."

I decided that I really didn't want to hear what I looked like when thinking about Jamie and was about to excuse myself to look in on the duke, who I could hear coughing and swearing breathlessly to himself in German, when my attention was distracted by a boy sprinting down the street as though the devil were after him, his coat on inside out and shirttails streaming.

"Colenso!" I exclaimed.

"What?" Jenny said, startled.

"Not what. Who. Him," I said, pointing at the grubby little creature panting up the walk. "Colenso Baragwanath. William's groom."

Colenso, who always looked as though he should be squatting atop a toadstool, came hurtling toward the door with such violence that Jenny and I both leapt out of the way. Colenso tripped on the doorsill and fell flat on his face.

"Ye look as though Auld Hornie himself was after ye, lad," Jenny said, bending down to hoick him to his feet. "And whatever's become of your breeks?"

Sure enough, the boy was barefoot and wearing only his shirt beneath his coat.

"They took 'em," he blurted, gasping for breath.

"Who?" I said, pulling his coat off and turning it right side out again.

"Them," he said, gesturing hopelessly toward Locust Street. "I put me head into the ordinary, to see was Lord Ellesmere there—he is, sometimes— and there was a knot o' men all buzzin' like a hive o' bees together. They was big lads with 'em, and one of 'em as knew me saw me and raises up a great cry, shoutin' as I'm a-spyin' on 'em and mean to take word back to the army, and then they grabbed me and they called me a turncoat and put me coat on backward and the one man said he'd beat me and teach me not to do such as that and pulled off me breeches and . . . and . . . anyway, I squirmed out of his hand and fell down on the floor and crawled out under the tables and took off a-runnin'." He wiped a sleeve under his runny nose. "His lordship here, ma'am?"

"No," I said. "Why do you want him?"

"Oh, I don't, ma'am," he assured me, with evident sincerity. "Major Findlay wants him. Now."

"Hmm. Well . . . wherever he is at the moment, he'll likely go back to his regular billet this evening. You know where that is, don't you?"

"Yes, ma'am, but I'm not a-goin' back in the street 'thout my breeches!" He looked both horrified and indignant, and Jenny laughed.

"Dinna blame ye a bit, lad," she said. "Tell ye what, though—my eldest grandson's likely got an old pair of breeches he could spare. I'll step round to the printshop," she said to me, "fetch the breeches, and tell Marsali what's ado."

"All right," I said, a little reluctant to see her go. "But hurry back. And tell her not to print *any* of this in the newspaper!"

10

THE DESCENT OF THE HOLY GHOST
UPON A RELUCTANT DISCIPLE

DAN MORGAN'S "IT" *WAS* nearby: a ramshackle cabin set in a little elm grove, down a short dirt lane off the main road. There was a big gray gelding hobbled and cropping grass nearby, his tack resting on the porch; he looked up briefly and whinnied at the newcomers.

Jamie ducked under the lintel after Dan and found himself in a dark, shabby room that smelled of cabbage water, grime, and the sharp reek of urine. There was one window, its shutters left open for air, and the sunlight coming in silhouetted the long-skulled head of a large man sitting at the table, who raised his head at the opening of the door.

"Colonel Morgan," he said, in a soft voice touched with the drawl of Virginia. "Have you brought me good news?"

"That's *just* what I brought you, General," auld Dan said, and shoved Jamie ahead of him toward the table. "I found this rascal on the road and bade him come along. This'll be Colonel Fraser, who I've told you of before. Just come back from Scotland, and the very man to take command of Taylor's troops."

The big man had risen from the table and put out a hand, smiling—though he smiled with his lips pressed tight together, as though afraid something might escape. The man was as tall as Jamie himself, and Jamie found himself looking straight into sharp gray-blue eyes that took his measure in the instant it took to shake hands.

"George Washington," the man said. "Your servant, sir."

"James Fraser," Jamie said, feeling mildly stunned. "Your . . . most obedient. Sir."

"Sit with me, Colonel Fraser." The big Virginian gestured toward one of the rough benches at the table. "My horse pulled up lame, and my slave's gone to find another. No notion how long it may take him, as I require a good sturdy beast to bear my weight, and those are thin on the ground these days." He looked Jamie up and down with frank appraisal; they were much of a size. "I don't suppose you have a decent horse with you, sir?"

"Aye, I do." It was clear what Washington expected, and Jamie yielded gracefully. "Will ye do me the honor to take him, General?"

Auld Dan made a disgruntled noise and shifted from foot to foot, clearly wanting to object, but Jamie gave him a brief shake of the head. It wasn't that far to Philadelphia; he could walk.

Washington looked pleased and thanked Jamie with grace in turn, saying that the horse should be returned to him as soon as another suitable mount might be procured.

"But it *is* somewhat necessary that I be nimble at present, Colonel," Washington remarked, with an air of apology. "You're aware, are you, that Clinton is withdrawing from Philadelphia?"

A shock went through Jamie like a hot penny dropped on butter.

"It—he—no, sir. I was not aware."

"I was just about to get to that," Dan said tetchily. "No one lets me get one word in edgewise, I tell you."

"Well, now you've got one," Washington said, amused. "You might get another, if you're quick enough to speak before Lee gets here. Sit down, gentlemen, if you will. I'm expecting—ah, there they are." Sounds from the dooryard indicated a number of horsemen arriving, and within a few moments the cabin was crowded with Continental officers.

They were a creased and weathered lot, for the most part, dressed in motley bits of uniform, these coupled uneasily with hunting shirts or homespun breeches. Even the complete suits of clothes were mud-spattered and worn, and the smell of men who'd been living rough quite overcame the gentler domestic reeks of the cabin.

Among the shuffling and excited greetings, Jamie spotted the source of the urinous smell, though: a thin-faced woman stood with her back pressed into a corner of the room, holding an infant wrapped in a ratty shawl against her bosom, her eyes darting to and fro among the intruders. A dark wet patch showed on the shawl, but it was plain the woman was afraid to move from her place to change the wean and instead shifted mechanically from foot to foot, patting the child to soothe it.

"Colonel Fraser! Well met! Well met!" The voice jerked his attention away, and, to his astonishment, he found his hand being pumped with enthusiasm by Anthony Wayne—known quite openly by now as "Mad Anthony"—whom he had last seen a few weeks before the fall of Ticonderoga.

"Is your wife well, sir, and your Indian nephew?" Wayne was asking, beaming up into Jamie's face. Anthony was short and stocky, with the full cheeks of a chipmunk, but also equipped with a sharp, poking sort of nose over which his eyes did now and then seem to glow with fire. At the moment, Jamie was relieved to see them merely alight with friendly interest.

"All well, sir, I thank ye. And—"

"Tell me, is your wife near at hand?" Wayne moved a little closer and lowered his voice a bit. "I've been having the most damnable time with my gouty foot, and she did wonders with the abscess at the base of my spine while we were at Ti—"

"Colonel Fraser, allow me to make you acquainted with Major General Charles Lee and with General Nathanael Greene." George Washington's voice drove a smooth Virginia wedge between himself and the base of Mad Anthony's spine, to Jamie's relief.

Besides Washington himself, Charles Lee was the best equipped of the lot, wearing complete uniform from gorget to polished boots. Jamie hadn't met him before but could have picked him out of a crowd as a professional soldier, no matter how he was dressed. An Englishman of the sort who seemed always to be smelling something dubious, but he shook hands cordially enough, with a clipped "Your servant, sir." Jamie knew exactly two things about Charles Lee, both told to him by Young Ian: to wit, that the man had a Mohawk wife—and that the Mohawk called him "Ounewaterika." Ian said it meant "Boiling Water."

Between Mad Anthony and Boiling Water, Jamie was beginning to feel that he should have spurred up and run for it when he met Dan Morgan on the road, but too late for regrets.

"Sit, gentlemen, we have no time to waste." Washington turned to the woman in the corner. "Have you anything to drink, Mrs. Hardman?"

Jamie saw her throat move as she swallowed, squeezing the child so hard that it squealed like a piglet and started to cry. He felt several of the men, doubtless fathers, wince at the sound.

"No, Friend," she said, and he realized she was a Quaker. "Naught but water from the well. Shall I fetch you a bucket?"

"Don't trouble thyself, Friend Hardman," Nathanael Greene said, soft-voiced. "I've two bottles in my saddlebag will do us." He moved slowly toward the woman, not to startle her, and took her gently by the arm. "Come outside. Thee needn't be disturbed by this business." He was a heavy, imposing man, who walked with a noticeable limp, but she seemed reassured by his plain speech and went with him, though looking back with an anxious face, as though fearing that the men might set fire to the place.

A quarter hour later, Jamie wasn't so sure that they might not ignite the cabin by the sheer force of their excitement. Washington and his troops had been bottled up at Valley Forge for the last six months, drilling and preparing, and the generals were on fire to be at the enemy.

Much talk, plans proposed, argued over, put aside, returned to. Jamie listened with half a mind; the other half was in Philadelphia. He'd heard enough from Fergus to know that the city was divided, with regular clashes between Patriots and Loyalists, these kept under control only by the presence of the British soldiers—but the Loyalists were a minority. The moment the army's protection was withdrawn, the Loyalists would be at the mercy of the Rebels—and Rebels who had been suppressed for months were not likely to be merciful.

And Claire . . . His mouth went dry. Claire was, so far as anyone in Philadelphia knew, the wife of Lord John Grey, a very visible Loyalist. And Jamie himself had just removed John Grey's protection from her, leaving her alone and helpless in a city about to explode.

How long did he have before the British left the city? No one at the table knew.

He took as little part as possible in the conversation, both because he was estimating how fast he could reach Philadelphia on foot—versus the possibility of going out to the privy and stealing back the horse he'd just given Washington—and because he hadn't forgotten what auld Dan had said to General Washington when he'd dragged Jamie in here. The very last thing he wanted was—

"And you, Colonel Fraser," Washington said. Jamie closed his eyes and commended his soul to God. "Will you do me the signal service of accepting command of Henry Taylor's battalion? General Taylor fell ill and died two days ago."

"I . . . am honored, sir," Jamie managed, thinking frantically. "But I have very urgent business . . . in Philadelphia. I should be happy to oblige ye, so soon as my business is accomplished—and I could, of course, bring back word of exactly how matters stand with General Clinton's forces." Washington had been looking severe during the first part of this speech, but the last sentence made Greene and Morgan hum with approval and Wayne nod his little chipmunk head.

"Can you manage your business within three days, Colonel?"

"Yes, sir!" It was no more than ten miles to the city; he could do that in two or three hours. And it wasn't going to take him more than thirty seconds to take Claire out of that house, once he reached it.

"Very well, then. You're appointed to a temporary field rank of General of the Army. That—"

"*Ifrinn!*"

"I beg your pardon, Colonel?" Washington looked puzzled. Dan Morgan, who'd heard Jamie say "Hell!" in *Gàidhlig* before, shook silently beside him.

"I—thank ye, sir." He swallowed, feeling a dizzy wave of heat pass over him.

"Though the Congress will have to approve your appointment," Washington went on, frowning a little, "and there's no guarantee as to what those contentious, shopkeeping sons of bitches will do."

"I understand, sir," Jamie assured him. He could only hope. Dan Morgan passed him a bottle, and he drank deep, hardly noticing what was in it. Sweating profusely, he sank back on the bench, hoping to avoid any further notice.

Jesus, now what? He'd meant to slip quietly into the city and out again with Claire, then head south to retrieve his printing press, perhaps establish a wee business in Charleston or Savannah until the war was over and they could go home to the Ridge. But he *had* known there was a risk; any man below the age of sixty could be compelled into militia service, and if it came down to it, he was likely a little safer being a general than a commander of militia. Maybe. And a general could resign; that was a heartening thought.

Despite all the talk and the worrying prospects of the immediate future, Jamie found himself paying more attention to Washington's face than to what he said, taking note of how the man talked and carried himself, so that he could tell Claire. He wished that he could tell Brianna; she and Roger Mac had sometimes speculated about what it might be like to meet someone like Washington—though having met a number of famous people himself, he'd told her that the experience was likely to prove a disappointment.

He would admit that Washington knew what he was about, though; he listened more than he talked, and when he said something, it was to the point. And he did give off an air of relaxed authority, though it was clear the present prospect excited him very much. His face was pockmarked, big-featured, and far from handsome, but had a good bit of dignity and presence.

His expression had become very animated, and he went so far as to laugh now and then, showing very bad, stained teeth. Jamie was fascinated; Brianna had told him they were false, made of wood or hippopotamus ivory, and he had a sudden dislocating recollection of his grandfather: the Old Fox had had a set of teeth made of beechwood. Jamie had thrown them on the fire during an argument at Beaufort Castle—and just for an instant he was there, smelling peat smoke and roasting venison, every hair on his body a-prickle with warning, surrounded by kinsmen who might just kill him.

And as suddenly he was back, pressed between Lee and auld Dan, smelling sweat and exhilaration and, despite himself, feeling the rising excitement among them begin to seep into his blood.

It gave him a queer feeling in his wame, to sit nay more than a foot away from a man whom he knew not at all but about whom he maybe kent more than the man himself.

True, he'd sat with Charles Stuart many evenings, knowing—and believing—what Claire had said would happen to him. But still . . . Christ had told doubting Thomas, *"Blessed are those who have not seen but have be-*

lieved." Jamie wondered what you called those who *had* seen and were obliged to live with the resultant knowledge. He thought "blessed" was maybe not the word.

IT WAS MORE than an hour before Washington and the others took their leave—an hour during which Jamie thought repeatedly that he might just stand up, flip the table over, and run out the door, leaving the Continental army to make shift without him.

He kent perfectly well that armies moved slowly, save when fighting. And clearly Washington expected that it would be a week or more before the British actually quit Philadelphia. But it was no use talking sense to his body, which as usual had its own measures of importance. He could ignore or suppress hunger, thirst, fatigue, and injury. He couldn't suppress the need to see Claire.

Likely it was what she and Brianna called testosterone poisoning, he thought idly—their term for the obvious things men did that women didn't understand. Someday he must ask her what testosterone was. He shifted uncomfortably on the narrow bench, forcing his mind back to what Washington was saying.

At long last, there came a rap on the door, and a black man put his head in and nodded to Washington.

"Ready, suh," he said, in the same soft Virginia accent as his master.

"Thank you, Caesar." Washington nodded back, then put his hands on the table and rose swiftly. "We are agreed, then, gentlemen? You're coming with me, General Lee. I'll see the rest of you in due course at Sutfin's farm, save you hear otherwise."

Jamie's heart leapt and he made to rise, too, but auld Dan put a hand on his sleeve.

"Set a bit, Jamie," he said. "You'll need to know something about your new command, won't you?"

"I—" he began, but there was no help for it. He sat and waited while Nathanael Greene thanked Mrs. Hardman for her hospitality and begged her to accept a small recompense from the army for her civil reception of them. Jamie would have wagered a good deal that the coins he plucked from his purse were his own and not the army's, but the woman took them, an acceptance too faint to be pleasure showing in her worn face. He saw her shoulders sag with relief as the door closed behind the generals and realized that their presence might have put her and her child in considerable peril, should the wrong people see uniformed Continental officers visiting her house.

She glanced consideringly at him and Dan, but they seemed to trouble her much less, in their rough civilian clothes. Dan had taken off his uniform coat and folded it inside out, laying it on the bench beside him.

"Feel any tongues of fire come down on your head just now, Jamie?" Dan asked, seeing his look.

"What?"

"Then the same day at evening, being the first day of the week, when the doors

were shut where the disciples were assembled for fear of the Jews, came Jesus and stood in the midst, and saith unto them, Peace be unto you," Dan quoted, and grinned wide at Jamie's look of astonishment.

"My Abigail's a reading woman, and she reads bits o' the Bible out to me regular, in hopes it'll do some good, though ain't much luck in that direction yet." He took up the rucksack he'd brought in and dredged about in it, coming out with a folded sheaf of dog-eared papers, an inkhorn, and a couple of tattered quills.

"Well, now that the Father, Son, and the Holy Ghost are gone off about their own business, let me write you down the names of your company commanders, what-all you got in the way of militia, and where they all are, 'cuz it ain't like they're all in barracks—or even in the same village. Missus Hardman, might I trouble you, ma'am, for a drop of water for my ink?"

Jamie bent his mind with difficulty to the business at hand, the better to dispatch it quickly, and within a quarter hour was gathering together the lists, made out in Dan's slow, crabbed hand. *Two hours to Philadelphia . . . maybe three . . .*

"Got any money on you to speak of?" Dan asked, pausing by the door.

"Not a penny," Jamie admitted, with a glance at the spot on his belt where his purse was normally fastened. He'd given it to Jenny to keep on the journey, as she delighted in making their small purchases. And this morning he'd been so much on fire to see Claire that he'd left the printshop with nothing but the clothes on his back and the packet of papers for Fergus. He spared an instant to wonder whether things would be different now, had he not been spotted giving the papers to Fergus and followed to Lord John's house by the soldiers—and William—but there was no point in regrets.

Dan pawed in his sack again, came out with a smaller bag and a clinking purse, both of which he tossed to Jamie.

"A bit of food for your journey, and an advance on your general's pay," he said, and chortled with amusement at his own wit. "You'll need to pay hard cash for a uniform these days; ain't a tailor in Philadelphia will take Continentals. And woe betide you if you show up before his worshipfulness George Washington without being dressed proper. He's a stickler for proper uniform, says you can't expect to command respect without lookin' like you deserve it. But I reckon you know all about that."

Dan, who had fought both battles of Saratoga in a hunting shirt, leaving his uniform coat hung over a tree branch in camp because of the heat, smiled broadly at Jamie, the scar on his upper lip where a bullet had torn through his face showing white against the weathered skin.

"Fare thee well, General Fraser!"

Jamie snorted but smiled nonetheless as he stood to shake Dan's hand. Then he turned back to the litter on the table, stowing the papers and purse— and a stray quill that Dan had abandoned, overlooked—into the bag. He was grateful for the food; the scent of jerked meat and journeycake floated out of the canvas depths, and he could feel the hard shape of apples at the bottom. He'd left the printshop without breakfast, too.

He straightened, and a pain like white lightning shot from the middle of his spine down the back of his leg to the sole of his foot. He gasped and collapsed onto a stool, his lower back and right buttock clenched with cramp.

"Jesus, Mary, and Bride—not *now*," he said between his teeth, and meant it somewhere between prayer and curse. He'd felt something small wrench or tear in his back when he'd hit John Grey, but in the heat of the moment it hadn't seemed important. It hadn't troubled him much walking—he'd barely noticed, with all there was on his mind—but now that he'd sat for a time and the muscles had chilled . . .

He tried rising, carefully, collapsed again. Bent sweating over the table with his fists clenched, he said a number of things in Gaelic that weren't at all prayerful.

"Is thee quite well, Friend?" The woman of the house leaned near, peering nearsightedly at him in concern.

"A . . . moment," he managed, trying to do as Claire told him and breathe through the spasm.

"Like labor pains," she'd told him, amused. He hadn't thought it was funny the first time and didn't now.

The pain eased. He extended his leg, then flexed it back under him, very gingerly. So far, so good. But when he once more tried to rise, his lower back was locked in a vise, and a pain that made him catch his breath stabbed down his buttock.

"Have ye . . . anything like . . . whisky? Rum?" If he could just get to his feet . . . But the woman was shaking her head.

"I'm sorry, Friend. I have not even small beer. Not even milk for the children any longer," she added with a certain bitterness. "The army took my goats away."

She didn't say which army, but he supposed it didn't matter to her. He made a sound of apology, just in case it had been the Continentals or the militia, and subsided, breathing heavily. This had happened three times before—just the same sudden flashing pain, the inability to move. Once, it had taken four days before he could hobble; the other two times, he had got to his feet within two days, and while it had twinged sporadically for weeks, he'd been able to walk, if slowly.

"Is thee ill? I could give thee rhubarb syrup," she offered. He managed to smile at that, shaking his head.

"I thank ye, ma'am. It's no but a clench in my back. When it eases, all will be well." The trouble was that *until* it eased, he was all but helpless, and the dawning realization of that gave him a sense of panic.

"Oh." The woman hesitated for a moment, hovering, but then the baby started to wail and she turned away to fetch it. A little girl—five or six, he thought, a stunted little creature—crawled out from under the bed and stared at him curiously.

"Is thee going to stay to supper?" she asked, in a high, precise voice. She gave him an appraising frown. "Thee looks like thee would eat a lot."

He revised his estimate of the girl's age to eight or nine and smiled at her. He was still sweating with the pain, but it was easing a bit.

"I'll not take your food, *a nighean*," he assured her. "In fact, there's a good loaf and some jerked meat in yon bag; it's yours." Her eyes went round as pennies, and he amended, "Your family's, I mean."

She glanced eagerly at the bag, swallowing painfully as her mouth watered; he could hear the tiny gulp and it wrung his heart.

"Pru!" she whispered, turning urgently toward the table. "Food!"

Another small girl crawled out and stood beside her sister. They were both plain as fence posts, though they otherwise didn't resemble each other much.

"I heard," the newcomer told her sister, and turned a solemn gaze on Jamie.

"Don't let Mam give thee rhubarb syrup," she advised him. "It makes thee shit like the blazes, and if thee can't get to the privy, it—"

"Prudence!"

Prudence obligingly shut her mouth, though she continued to look Jamie over with interest. Her sister knelt and rummaged under the bed, emerging with the family utensil, this a homely object of brown earthenware, which she presented gravely for his inspection.

"We'll turn our backs, sir, if thee should need to—"

"Patience!"

Red in the face, Mrs. Hardman took the piss pot from her daughter and shooed the little girls to the table, where—with a glance at Jamie to be sure he had meant it—she took the bread and meat and apples from his bag, dividing the food scrupulously into three parts: two large portions for the girls, and a smaller one for herself, put aside for later.

She had left the chamber pot on the floor beside the bed, and as she eased him gingerly onto the corn-shuck mattress, Jamie caught sight of lettering painted in white across the bottom. He squinted to make it out in the dim light, then smiled. It was a Latin motto, encircling a vividly executed bee with a jovial expression and a pronounced wink. *Iam apis potanda fineo ne.*

He'd seen the jest before—the brothel in Edinburgh where he'd once kept a room had been equipped throughout with utensils sporting a variety of Latin tags, most of them prurient, but some merely puns, like this one. It *was* a Latin sentence, if a foolish one—"Drink not the bee now"—but if read phonetically in English, ignoring the spacing, it read, "I am a piss pot and a fine one." He glanced up at Mrs. Hardman in speculation but thought it was likely not her work. The absent Mr. Hardman must be—*or have been,* he thought, given the obvious poverty of the household, and he crossed himself unobtrusively at the thought—an educated man.

The baby had waked and was fussing in her cradle, making small sharp yelps like a fox kit. Mrs. Hardman scooped the child out, pulling a worn nursing chair toward the fire with one foot. She laid the baby momentarily on the bed beside Jamie, opening her blouse with one hand, the other reaching automatically to save an apple that was rolling toward the edge of the table, nudged by a little girl's elbow.

The baby smacked her lips, hungry as her sisters. "And this will be wee Chastity, I make nay doubt?" he said.

Mrs. Hardman gaped at him. "How did thee know the child's name?"

He glanced at Prudence and Patience, who were silently stuffing bread and meat into their mouths as quickly as they could eat. "Well, I havena yet met a lassie named Sobriety or Fortitude," he said mildly. "The wean's sopping; have ye a clean clootie for her?"

There were two worn clouts hung to dry before the fire; she brought one, to find that Jamie had already unpinned the baby's soggy nappie—that's what Claire called them—and wiped the shit from her bottom, holding her tiny ankles in one hand.

"Thee has children, I see." Eyebrows raised, Mrs. Hardman took the soiled clout from him with a nod of thanks and dropped it into a bucket of vinegar and water that stood in the far corner.

"And grandchildren," he said, wiggling a finger in front of wee Chastity's nose. She gurgled and went cross-eyed, kicking her legs enthusiastically. "To say nothing of six nephews and nieces." *And where are Jem and wee Mandy, I wonder? Can she breathe easy now, poor lassie?* He gently tickled the baby's soft pink foot, remembering the strangely beautiful, heart-wrenching blue tinge to Mandy's perfect toes, long-jointed and graceful as a frog's.

"They're just like yours," Claire had told him, drawing a fingernail lightly down the sole of Mandy's foot, making the long big toe spring suddenly away from the others. What had she called that?

He tried it himself, gingerly, and smiled with delight to see it happen to Chastity's chubby toes.

"Babinski," he said to Mrs. Hardman, with a sense of deep satisfaction at recalling the name. "That's what it's called when a wean's great toe does that. A Babinski reflex."

Mrs. Hardman looked astonished—though much more so when he skillfully repinned the new clout and swaddled wee Chastity afresh in her blanket. She took the baby from him and, with an uncertain expression, sank down in the chair and pulled the ratty shawl over the baby's head. Unable to turn over easily, Jamie instead closed his eyes to afford her such privacy as he could.

11

REMEMBER PAOLI!

IT WAS HARD TO wipe away the sweat with his hands tied and impossible to keep the stinging salt out of his wounded eye, so puffed and slitted that he couldn't close it tightly. Water ran down his cheek in a steady flow, dripping off his chin. Blinking in a vain attempt to clear his vision, John Grey missed a fallen branch in his path and fell heavily.

Those behind him on the narrow trail halted abruptly, with sounds of mild collision, jangling weapons and canteens, confusion and impatience. Rough hands seized him and hauled him up again, but the tall, rawboned man deputed to be his escort said only, "Watch your step, me lord," in a mild tone of voice, and gave him a nudge down the path rather than a shove.

Encouraged by this evidence of consideration, he thanked the man and asked his name.

"Me?" The man sounded surprised. "Oh. Bumppo. Natty Bumppo." Adding, after a moment, "Folks mostly call me 'Hawkeye,' though."

"I don't wonder," Grey said, half under his breath. He bowed, as well as he could whilst walking, and nodded at the long rifle that bobbed in a sling at the man's back. "Your servant, sir. I deduce that you are a fine shot, then?"

"Reckon that would be a good deduction, your lordship." Bumppo's voice sounded amused. "Why? D'you want something shot? Or somebody?"

"I'm keeping a list," Grey told him. "I'll let you know when it's complete."

He felt, rather than heard, the other's laugh—the amusement was palpable, but it made little sound.

"Let me guess who's first on your list—the big Scotch fellow what put your light out?"

"He'd be fairly high on the list, yes." Actually, he couldn't decide who he'd rather see shot first: Jamie Fraser or his own bloody brother. Probably Hal, all things considered. Rather ironic, if Hal ended up getting *him* shot. Though his captors seemed quite convinced that hanging was the preferred method.

That reminded him of the uncomfortable bit of conversation that had preceded his being chivvied through the woods on a deer trail bountifully equipped with bramblish bushes, low-hanging branches, ticks, and biting flies the size of the ball of his thumb.

"Would you happen to know what—or possibly who—Paoli is, Mr. Bumppo?" he asked politely, kicking a fir cone out of his way.

"What's Paoli?" The man's voice was filled with astonishment. "Why, man, are you just come to this neck o' the woods?"

"Fairly recently," Grey replied guardedly.

"Oh." Bumppo considered, carefully matching his lengthy stride to Grey's shorter one. "Why, 'twas an infamous attack, to be sure. Your kinsman— Major General Grey, as they said—him and his troops snuck up by night to where General Wayne's men were camped. Grey didn't want to risk a stray flint sparking and giving them away, so he gives the order to take out all the flints from their guns and use the bayonets. Fell upon the Americans and bayoneted near a hundred men in their beds, in cold blood!"

"Really?" Grey tried to reconcile this account with any recent battle *he* knew of, and failed. "And . . . Paoli?"

"Oh. That's the name of the tavern nearby—Paoli's Tavern."

"Ah. Where is it? Geographically, I mean. And when, exactly, did this battle occur?"

Bumppo's prehensile lips pushed out in thought, then withdrew.

"Be up near Malvern, last September. The Paoli Massacre, they calls it," he added with a certain dubiousness.

"Massacre?" Grey echoed. The engagement had taken place before his own arrival, but he'd heard it talked about—briefly, and not in terms of massacre, to be sure. But, then, perceptions of the event were bound to be different, depending upon one's position in the matter. William Howe had spoken of it with approval—as a successful engagement in which a minimal number of British troops had routed an entire American division, with a loss of only seven men.

Bumppo seemed disposed to share Grey's opinion of the rhetorical nature of the name, albeit from yet a third perspective.

"Well, you know how folks will talk," he said, lifting one shoulder. "Ain't what *I'd* call a proper massacre, but, then, ain't many folk seen one, and I have."

"You have?" Glancing up at the tall, bearded ruffian, Grey thought it only too likely.

"Was raised as an Indian," Bumppo said, with visible pride. "By the Mohican, my own folks havin' died when I were just a tadpole. Aye, I've seen a massacre or two."

"Indeed?" Grey said, innate courtesy obliging him to invite the man to elaborate, should he wish to. Besides, it would pass the time; they seemed to have been walking for hours, and no end in sight—not that he was eagerly anticipating the end. . . .

As it was, Mr. Bumppo's reminiscences passed the time to such good effect that Grey was surprised when Corporal Woodbine, in the lead, called the company to a halt at the edge of a fairly sizable encampment. He was glad enough to stop, though; he was wearing city shoes, not suited for the terrain at all, and they had worn through his stockings and rubbed his feet to blood and blisters.

"Scout Bumppo," Woodbine said, with a short nod to Grey's companion. "You'll take the company on to Zeke Bowen's place. I'll deliver the prisoner to Colonel Smith."

This statement gave rise to vocal discontent, from which Grey gathered that the company wished very much to accompany Woodbine, in order not to miss Grey's execution, which they confidently expected to occur within moments of his delivery to the aforesaid Colonel Smith. Woodbine was firm about it, though, and with democratic mutterings and execrations, the militia moved reluctantly off under the guidance of Natty Bumppo.

Woodbine watched them out of sight, then drew himself up, brushing a stray caterpillar from the breast of his shabby coat and straightening his disreputable hat.

"Well, Lieutenant Colonel Grey. Shall we go?"

NATTY BUMPPO'S reminiscences of the proper way to conduct a massacre had left Grey with the feeling that perhaps, by contrast, hanging was not the worst way to die. But while he hadn't personally witnessed any first-rate massacres, he'd seen men hanged, very close to—and the memory of it dried his throat. The leakage from his eye hadn't stopped completely but had lessened; the skin felt raw and inflamed, though, and the swelling gave him the annoying sense that his head was grossly misshapen. Still, he drew himself upright and strode chin out into the ragged canvas tent ahead of Corporal Woodbine.

Colonel Smith looked up from his lap desk, startled at the intrusion—though not quite as startled as Grey.

He'd last seen Watson Smith in his own sister-in-law's drawing room in London two years ago, eating cucumber sandwiches. In the uniform of a captain of the Buffs.

"Mr. Smith," he said, recovering his wits first. He bowed very correctly. "Your servant, sir." He didn't bother trying to keep the edge out of his voice or his expression. He sat down upon a vacant stool without being invited and gave Smith as direct a stare as he could with one operant eye.

Smith's cheeks flushed, but he leaned back a little, gathering his own wits before replying, and returned Grey's stare, with interest. He was not a big man but had broad shoulders and considerable presence of manner—and Grey knew him to be a very competent soldier. Competent enough not to reply directly to Grey but to turn instead to Corporal Woodbine.

"Corporal. How comes this gentleman here?"

"This is Lieutenant Colonel Lord John Grey, sir," Woodbine said. He was near bursting with pride at his capture and placed Grey's King's warrant and Graves's accompanying note on the rickety table with the manner of a butler presenting a roast pheasant with diamond eyes to a reigning monarch. "We caught him in the woods near Philadelphia. Out of uniform. Er . . . as you see, sir." He cleared his throat in emphasis. "*And* he admits to being a cousin of Major General Charles Grey. You know—the Paoli Massacre."

"Really?" Smith picked up the papers but cocked an eyebrow at Grey. "What was he doing there?"

"Having the shit beaten out of him by Colonel Fraser, sir—he's one of Morgan's officers. He said," Woodbine added, with less certainty.

Smith looked blank.

"Fraser . . . don't believe I know him." Switching his attention to Grey, he addressed him for the first time. "Do *you* know Colonel Fraser . . . Colonel Grey?"

The elaborate hesitation spoke volumes. Well, he hadn't expected anything else. Grey wiped his nose as well as he could on a forearm and sat straight.

"I decline to answer your questions, sir. They are improperly put. You know my name, rank, and regiment. Beyond that, my business is my own."

Smith stared at him, eyes narrowed. Smith's eyes were rather attractive, a pale gray with black brows and lashes, very dramatic. Grey had noticed them when the man came to tea with Minnie.

Woodbine coughed.

"Er . . . Colonel Fraser said the man was his prisoner, sir. But he wouldn't say what for, and when I pressed the matter, he . . . er . . . left. That's when we searched Lord . . . er, the lord colonel here, and found his papers."

"He left," Smith repeated carefully. "And you allowed him to leave, Corporal?"

Woodbine was looking less confident in the virtue of his conduct but wasn't the sort to be easily cowed, Grey saw. He lowered his brow and gave Smith a look of his own.

"Couldn't have stopped him, short of shooting him. Sir," he added flatly. The flesh around Smith's nostrils whitened, and Grey had the distinct impression that the Englishman must find his new command not quite what he'd been used to.

The quarters certainly weren't. While Smith's Continental uniform was smart and well tended, and his wig in good order, his tent, while large, appeared to have been through several campaigns, being worn to the threads in places and patched in others. Not entirely a bad thing, Grey thought, briefly closing his eyes as a faint evening breeze came wafting through the walls of the tent, relieving the stifling heat. He had a noticeable headache, and even such minor relief was welcome.

"Very well, Corporal," Smith said after a moment, having evidently tried and failed to think of something new to ask. "Well done," he added, offering a belated note of congratulation.

"Thank you, sir." Woodbine hovered, obviously loath to surrender his share of the excitement. "If I may ask, sir—what do you mean to do with the prisoner?"

Grey opened his eye and a half, interested to hear what the answer might be, and found Smith eyeing him in what seemed a faintly carnivorous fashion. The turncoat smiled.

"Oh, I'll think of something, Corporal Woodbine," he said. "You are dismissed. Good night."

SMITH GOT UP and came over to Grey, leaning down to examine his face. Grey could smell his sweat, sharp and musky.

"Do you need a doctor?" he asked dispassionately, but without hostility.

"No," Grey said. Both his head and his side ached deeply, and he felt dizzy, but he doubted there was anything a doctor could do about either condition. And he found that after prolonged contact with Claire and her opinions, he had much less trust in physicians than heretofore—and he hadn't had much to begin with.

Smith nodded and, straightening up, went to a battered campaign chest and dug out two dented pewter cups and a stone bottle of what proved to be applejack. He poured two generous tots, and they sat in silence for a time, sipping.

So close to Midsummer Day, it was still bright light out, though Grey could hear the rattle and shuffle of a camp beginning the evening routine. A mule brayed loudly, and several more answered it in raucous chorus. Wagons, then . . . perhaps artillery? He breathed deeply, nostrils flaring; an artillery company had a distinct smell to it, a sort of distillation of sweat, black powder, and hot metal, much more pungent than the scent of an infantry company with their muskets—the scent of searing iron seeped into an artilleryman's clothes, as well as his soul.

What came to him was not the stink of guns but the smell of roasting meat. It drifted through the tent, and his stomach growled loudly; he'd eaten nothing since the beer that had been his preliminary to a preempted meal. He thought Smith's mouth twitched a little at the noise, but the colonel politely ignored it.

Smith finished his drink, refilled both cups, and cleared his throat.

"I will not plague you with questions, as you don't wish to answer them," he said carefully, "but in the interests of civil conversation, should you wish to make any inquiries of me, I should not take offense."

Grey smiled wryly.

"Very gracious of you, sir. Do you wish to justify your present allegiance to me? I assure you, it's unnecessary."

Small red patches sprang up immediately on Smith's cheekbones.

"That was not my intent, sir," he said stiffly.

"Then I apologize," Grey said, and took another mouthful. The sweet strong cider was assuaging his hunger pangs as well as the pain in his side, though it admittedly wasn't doing much for the dizziness. "What sort of question did you think I might ask? What is the current state of the Continental army? I could deduce that easily enough, I think, from the state of the gentlemen who captured me, and . . . other evidence." He let his eyes roam deliberately around the tent, taking in the chipped pottery utensil under the lopsided cot, the tail of dirty linen straggling out of a portmanteau in the corner; evidently Smith had either no orderly or an inept one. For an instant, Grey felt a pang of nostalgia for Tom Byrd, the best valet he had ever had.

Smith's flush had faded; he gave a small, ironic laugh. "I imagine you could. It's not much of a secret. No, I rather thought you might be curious as to what I propose to do with you."

"Oh, that." Grey put down his cup and rubbed gingerly at his forehead, trying not to touch the swollen area around his eye. "Frankly, I'd forgotten, in the surprise of seeing you. And the pleasure of your kind hospitality," he added, lifting the cup with no irony at all. "Corporal Woodbine and his men appeared to think I should be promptly hanged, both on the charge of spying and on the more serious one of being related to Major General Charles Grey, who I gather is believed to have committed some atrocity at a place called Paoli."

Smith's brow creased.

"Do you deny being a spy?"

"Don't be ridiculous, Smith. I'm a lieutenant colonel. What on earth would I be doing, spying in a deserted wood? Well, deserted until Woodbine and his merry men showed up," he added. His cup was empty; he stared into it, wondering how that had happened. With a small sigh, Smith refilled it.

"Besides, I was carrying no documents of information, no secret writings—no evidence whatever of spying."

"Doubtless you committed to memory whatever information you had gained," Smith said, sounding cynically amused. "I recall that you have a prodigious memory." He gave a small snort that could perhaps have been called a snigger. *"So sayeth Sally, nimble-fingered, as her grip upon his prick did linger . . ."*

In fact, Grey's memory was quite good. Good enough to remember a dinner at which a number of officers from different regiments had been guests. When the gentlemen were at their port, Grey had—upon invitation, and to thunderous applause—recited entirely from memory one of the longer, and very scabrous, odes from Harry Quarry's infamous *Certain Verses Upon the Subject of Eros,* copies of which were still eagerly sought and covertly passed around the circles of society, though the book had been published nearly twenty years before.

"What on earth is there to spy *on?*" he demanded, realizing the logical trap too late. Smith's mouth turned up at one corner.

"You expect me to tell you?" Because the answer, of course, was that Washington's entire force was likely on the move in his immediate vicinity, positioning for the move into Philadelphia—and, very possibly, for an attack on Clinton's withdrawing troops.

Grey dismissed Smith's question as rhetorical and took another tack—though a dangerous one.

"Woodbine gave you a correct assessment of the circumstances in which he discovered me," he said. "Plainly I was not discovered *in flagrante* by Colonel Fraser, as he would simply have done what Corporal Woodbine did and arrested me."

"Are you asserting that Colonel Fraser met you by arrangement, to pass on information?"

Jesus Christ. He'd known this tack was dangerous but hadn't foreseen *that* possibility—that Jamie Fraser could be suspected of being his confederate. But of course Smith would be particularly sensitive to such a possibility, given his own change of loyalties.

"Certainly not," Grey said, allowing a certain asperity to creep into his tone. "The encounter that Corporal Woodbine witnessed was of a purely personal nature."

Smith, who plainly knew a thing or two about interrogation, cocked a brow at him. Grey knew a thing or two about it, too, and sat back, sipping his applejack insouciantly, as though quite sure his statement had settled matters.

"They *will* probably hang you, you know," Smith said after a suitable pause. He spoke quite casually, eyes on the amber stream as he refilled both cups again. "After what Howe did to Captain Hale? Even more, after Paoli. Charles Grey is your cousin, is he not?"

"Second or third cousin, yes." Grey knew the man, though they didn't move in the same circles, either socially or militarily. Charles Grey was a pig-faced professional killer, rather than a soldier, and while he doubted that the Paoli Massacre had been entirely as described—what sort of idiots would lie on the ground waiting to be bayoneted in their beds? Because he didn't for an instant think a column of infantry was capable of sneaking up in the dark over rough country to within stabbing distance without giving some notice of their presence—he *did* know about Charles's merciless bayonet tactics at Culloden.

"Nonsense," Grey said, with as much confidence as he could summon. "Whatever one may think of the American high command, I doubt it is composed entirely of fools. My execution would yield nothing, whereas my exchange might be of value. My brother does have some small influence."

Smith smiled, not without sympathy.

"An excellent argument, Lord John, and one I'm sure would find favor with General Washington. Unfortunately, the Congress and the King remain at loggerheads over the matter of exchange; at present, there is no mechanism to allow the exchange of prisoners."

That one struck him in the pit of the stomach. He knew all too well that there were no official channels of exchange; he'd been trying to have William exchanged for months.

Smith upended the bottle, dribbling the last amber drops into Grey's cup. "Are you a Bible-reading man, Colonel Grey?"

Grey looked at him blankly.

"Not habitually. I have read it, though. Some of it. Well . . . bits. Why?"

"I wondered if you were familiar with the concept of a scapegoat." Smith rocked back a little on his stool, gazing at Grey with his lovely deep-set eyes, which seemed to hold a certain sympathy—though perhaps it was just the applejack. "Because I'm afraid that is where your chief value lies, Colonel. It is no secret that the Continental army is in poor condition, lacking money, disillusion and desertion rife. Nothing would hearten and unify the troops more—or send a more potent message to General Clinton—than the trial and very public execution of a high-ranking British officer, a convicted spy and close relation to the infamous 'No Flints' Grey."

He belched softly and blinked, eyes still fixed on Grey.

"You asked what I meant to do with you."

"No, I didn't."

Smith ignored this, leveling a long, knobby finger at him.

"I'm sending you to General Wayne, who, believe me, has 'Paoli' carved upon his heart."

"How very painful for him," Grey said politely, and drained his cup.

12

EINE KLEINE NACHTMUSIK

THE INTERMINABLE DAY was reluctantly ending, the heat at last beginning to fade from the forest along with the waning light. He didn't suppose that he would be taken directly to General Wayne, unless that worthy were close at hand, and he thought not. He could tell from the sounds and the feel of the camp that it was a small one, and plainly Colonel Smith was the senior officer present.

Smith had asked him, *pro forma,* to give his parole—and been substantially taken aback when Grey had courteously refused to do so.

"If I am in fact a duly commissioned British officer," Grey had pointed out, "then clearly it is my duty to escape."

Smith eyed him, the failing light shading his face with sufficient ambiguity that Grey was not sure whether he was fighting an impulse to smile or not. Probably not.

"You're not escaping," he said definitely, and went out. Grey could hear a brief, heated discussion, conducted in low voices outside the tent, as to just what to do with him. A militia camp on the move had no facilities for prisoners. Grey amused himself by composing a mental entertainment in which Smith was obliged to share his narrow cot with Grey, in the interests of keeping his prisoner secure.

In the end, though, a corporal came in, carrying a rusty set of fetters that looked as though they had last seen use during the Spanish Inquisition, and took Grey to the edge of camp, where a soldier who had been a blacksmith in private life banged them into place with a stout hammer, using a flattish rock as an anvil.

He felt the oddest sensations, kneeling on the ground in the twilight, an interested group of militiamen gathered round in a circle to watch. He was forced to lean forward in a crouching posture, hands laid before him, as though he were about to be beheaded, and the hammer blows echoed through the metal, into the bones of his wrists and arms.

He kept his eyes on the hammer, and not only from fear that the smith would miss his aim in the growing dusk and smash one of his hands. Under the influence of intoxication and a growing, deeper fear that he didn't want to acknowledge, he sensed the mingled curiosity and animus surrounding him and felt it as he would a nearby thunderstorm, electricity crawling over his skin, the threat of lightning annihilation so close he could smell its sharp odor, mixed with gunpowder and the heavy tang of the sweat of men.

Ozone. His mind seized on the word, a small escape into rationality. That's what Claire called the smell of lightning. He'd told her he thought it was from the Greek *ozon,* the neuter present participle of *ozein,* meaning "to smell."

He began to work his way methodically through the complete conjugation; by the time he'd finished, surely they would be done with it. *Ozein,* to smell. I smell . . .

He could smell his own sweat, sharp and sweet. In the old days, it was considered a better death, beheading. To be hanged was shameful, a commoner's death, a criminal's death. Slower. He knew that for a fact.

A final reverberating blow, and a visceral sound of satisfaction from the watching men. He was made prisoner.

THERE BEING NO shelter other than the brushy wigwams and scraps of canvas the militiamen rigged near their fires, he was escorted back to

Smith's big, threadbare tent, given supper—which he forced down, not much noticing what he ate—and then tethered to the tent pole with a long, thin rope run through the chain of his irons, with sufficient play as to allow him to lie down or use the utensil.

At Smith's insistence, he took the cot and did lie down with a slight groan of relief. His temples throbbed with each heartbeat, and so did the entire left side of his face, which was now radiating small jolts down into his upper teeth, very unpleasant. The pain in his side had dulled to a deep ache, almost negligible by comparison. Luckily, he was so tired that sleep swamped all discomfort, and he fell into it with a sense of profound gratitude.

He woke in the full dark sometime later, slicked with sweat, heart hammering from some desperate dream. He raised a hand to push the soaked hair off his face and felt the heavy, chafing weight of the fetters, which he'd forgotten about. They clanked, and the dark figure of a sentry silhouetted in the fire glow at the entrance of the tent turned sharply toward him, but then relaxed as he turned over on the cot, clanking further.

Bugger, he thought, still groggy with sleep. *Couldn't even masturbate if I wanted to.* The thought made him laugh, though fortunately it came out as a mere breath of sound.

Another body turned over, rustling, shifting heavily near him. Smith, he supposed, sleeping on a canvas bed sack stuffed with grass; Grey could smell the meadow scent of dry hay, faintly musty in the humid air. The bed sack was standard issue to the British army; Smith must have kept it, along with his tent and other equipment, changing only his uniform.

Why had he turned his coat? Grey wondered vaguely, peering at Smith's humped shape, just visible against the pale canvas. Advancement? Starved as they were for professional soldiers, the Continentals offered rank as inducement; a captain in any European army might become anything from a major to a general in the blink of an eye, whereas the only means of achieving higher rank in England was to find the money to purchase it.

What was rank without pay, though? Grey was no longer a spy, but he had been one, once—and still knew men who labored in those dark fields. From what he'd heard, the American Congress had no money at all and depended upon loans—these unpredictable in amount and erratic in occurrence. Some from French or Spanish sources, though the French wouldn't admit to it, of course. Some from Jewish moneylenders, said one of his correspondents. *Salomon, Solomon . . . some name like that.*

These random musings were interrupted by a sound that made him stiffen. A woman's laughter.

There were women in the camp, wives who had come along to war with their husbands. He'd seen a few when they took him across the campground, and one had brought his supper, glancing suspiciously up at him from under her cap. But he thought he *knew* that laugh—deep, gurgling, and totally unself-conscious.

"Jesus," he whispered under his breath. "Dottie?"

It wasn't impossible. He swallowed, trying to clear his left ear, to listen through the multitude of small sounds outside. Denzell Hunter was a Continental surgeon, and Dottie had—to her brother's, cousin's, and uncle's horror—joined the camp followers at Valley Forge in order to help her fiancé, though she rode into Philadelphia regularly to visit her brother Henry. If Washington's forces were moving—and very plainly they were—it was entirely possible that a surgeon might be anywhere among them.

A high, clear voice, raised in question. An English voice, and not common. He strained to hear but couldn't make out the words. He wished she'd laugh again.

If it *was* Dottie . . . he breathed deep, trying to think. He couldn't call out to her; he'd felt the avid hostility directed at him from every man in camp—letting the relationship be known would be dangerous for her and Denzell, both, and certainly wouldn't help Grey. And yet he had to risk it—they'd move him in the morning.

Out of sheer inability to think of anything better, he sat up on the cot and began to sing *"Die Sommernacht."* Quietly at first, but gathering strength and volume. As he hit *"In den Kulungen wehn"* at the top of his very resonant tenor voice, Smith sat up like a jack-in-the-box and said, *"What?"* in tones of utter amazement.

> *"So umschatten mich Gedanken an das Grab*
> *Meiner Geliebten, und ich seh' im Walde*
> *Nur es dämmern, und es weht mir*
> *Von der Blüte nicht her."*

Grey went on, reducing his volume somewhat. He didn't want Dottie—if it was Dottie—coming to look, only to let her know he was here. He'd taught her this *lied* when she was fourteen; she sang it often at musicales.

> *"Ich genoß einst, o ihr Toten, es mit euch!*
> *Wie umwehten uns der Duft und die Kühlung,*
> *Wie verschönt warst von dem Monde,*
> *Du, o schöne Natur!"*

He stopped, coughed a little, and spoke into the marked silence before him, slurring his words a bit, as though still drunk. In fact, he discovered, he was.

"Might I have some water, Colonel?"

"Will you sing anymore if I give it to you?" Smith asked, deeply suspicious.

"No, I think I'm finished now," Grey assured him. "Couldn' sleep, you know—too much to drink—but I find a song settles the mind rem-remarkably."

"Oh, does it?" Smith breathed heavily for a moment, but clambered to his feet and fetched the ewer from his basin. Grey could feel him repressing an urge to douse his prisoner with the contents, but Smith was a man of strong character and merely held the pitcher for him to drink, then put it back and resumed his own bed with no more than a few irritable snorts.

The *lied* had caused some comment in the camp, and a few musical souls took it as inspiration and began singing everything from "Greensleeves"—a very poignant and tender rendition—to "Chester." Grey quite enjoyed the singing, though it was only by exercise of his own strong character that he refrained from shaking his fetters at the end of:

> *"Let tyrants shake their iron rods. And slavery clank her galling chains."*

They were still singing when he fell asleep again, to dream in anxious fragments, the fumes of applejack drifting through the hollow spaces of his head.

Number 17 Chestnut Street

THE BELL OF the Presbyterian church struck midnight, but the city wasn't sleeping. The sounds were more furtive now, muffled by darkness, but the streets were still alive with hurrying feet and the sound of moving wagons—and, in the far distance, I heard a faint cry of "Fire!" being raised.

I stood by the open window, sniffing the air for smoke and watching out for any sign of flames that might spread in our direction. I wasn't aware of Philadelphia having ever burned to the ground like London or Chicago, but a fire that merely engulfed the neighborhood would be just as bad from my point of view.

There was no wind at all; that was something. The summer air hung heavy, damp as a sponge. I waited for a bit, but the cries stopped, and I saw no red glimmer of flames against the half-clouded sky. No trace of fire save the cool green sparks of fireflies, drifting among the shadowed leaves in the front garden.

I stood for a bit, letting my shoulders slump, letting go of my half-formed plans for emergency evacuation. I was exhausted but unable to sleep. Beyond the need to keep an eye on my unsettled patient, and the unsettled atmosphere beyond the quiet room, I was most unsettled in myself. I'd been listening all day, constantly on the alert for a familiar footstep, the sound of Jamie's voice. But he hadn't come.

What if he had learned from John that I had shared his bed on that one drunken evening? Would the shock of that, given without preparation or suitable explanation, be enough to have made him run away—for good?

I felt sudden tears come to my eyes and shut them, hard, to stem the flow, gripping the sill with both hands.

Don't be ridiculous. He'll come as soon as he can, no matter what. You know he will. I did know. But the shocked joy of seeing him alive had wakened nerves that had been numb for a long time, and while I might seem calm externally, on the inside my emotions were at a rolling boil. The steam was building up, and I had no way to release the pressure—save pointless tears, and I wouldn't give way to those.

For one thing, I might not be able to stop. I pressed the sleeve of my dressing gown briefly to my eyes, then turned back resolutely into the darkness of the room.

A small brazier burned near the bed under a tented wet cloth, casting a flickering red glow on Pardloe's sharp-cut features. He was breathing with an audible rasp and I could hear his lungs rattle with each exhalation, but it was a deep breathing, and regular. It occurred to me that I might not have been able to smell the smoke of a fire outside, had there been one: the atmosphere in the room was thick with oil of peppermint, eucalyptus . . . and cannabis. Despite the wet cloth, enough smoke had escaped the brazier to form a hanging cloud of purling wisps, moving pale as ghosts in the darkened air.

I sprinkled more water on the muslin tent and sat down in the small armchair beside the bed, breathing the saturated atmosphere in cautiously but with an agreeable small sense of illicit pleasure. Hal had told me that he was in the habit of smoking hemp to relax his lungs and that it seemed to be effective. He'd said "hemp," and that was undoubtedly what he'd been smoking; the psychoactive form of the plant didn't grow in England and wasn't commonly imported.

I hadn't any hemp leaves in my medical supply but did have a good bit of ganja, which John had acquired from a Philadelphia merchant who had two Indiamen. It was useful in the treatment of glaucoma, as I'd learned when treating Jamie's aunt Jocasta, it relieved nausea and anxiety—and it had occasional non-medicinal uses, as John had informed me, to my private amusement.

Thought of John gave me a small internal qualm, to add to my anxiety over Jamie, and I took a deep, deliberate breath of the sweet, spicy air. Where was *he*? What had Jamie done with him?

"Do you ever make bargains with God?" Hal's voice came quietly out of the half dark.

I must subconsciously have known he wasn't sleeping, for I wasn't startled.

"Everyone does," I said. "Even people who don't believe in God. Do you?"

There was the breath of a laugh, followed by coughing, but it stopped quickly. Perhaps the smoke *was* helping.

"Have you got such a bargain in mind?" I asked, as much from real curiosity as to make conversation. "You aren't going to die, you know. I won't let you."

"Yes, you said that," he replied dryly. After a moment's hesitation, he turned on his side to face me. "I do believe you," he said rather formally. "And . . . I thank you."

"You're quite welcome. I can't let you die in John's house, you know; he'd be upset."

He smiled at that, his face visible in the brazier's glow. We didn't speak for a bit but sat looking at each other, with no particular sense of self-consciousness, both of us calmed by the smoke and the sleepy chirping of crickets outside. The sound of wagon wheels had ceased, but there were still people passing by. Surely I would know Jamie's step, be able to distinguish his, even among so many. . . .

"You're worried about him, aren't you?" he asked. "John."

"No," I said quickly, but I saw one dark brow rise and remembered that he already knew me for a bad liar. "That is . . . I'm sure he's quite all right. But I *would* have expected him home by now. And with so much commotion in the city . . ." I waved a hand toward the window. "You don't know what might happen, do you?"

I heard him draw breath, his chest rattling faintly, and clear his throat.

"And you still decline to tell me where he is."

I lifted one shoulder and let it fall; it seemed pointless to repeat that I didn't know, even though that *was* the truth. Instead, I took up a comb from the table and began to deal slowly with my hair, untangling and smoothing the unruly mass, enjoying the cool feel of it in my hands. After we had bathed Hal and got him put to bed, I'd taken a quarter hour for a somewhat more leisurely wash of my own and had rinsed the sweat and dust from my hair, despite knowing it would take hours to dry in the humid air.

"The bargain I had in mind was not for my own life," he said after a bit. "As such."

"I'm sure John isn't going to die, either, if that's what you—"

"Not John. My son. My daughter. And my grandson. You have grandchildren, I collect? I believe I heard that rather stalwart young man call you 'Grannie' this afternoon, did I not?" His voice held a trace of amusement.

"You did, and I do. You mean Dorothea? Is something the matter with her?" A stab of alarm made me set down the comb. I'd seen Dottie only a few days before, at the house where her brother Henry was staying.

"Aside from the fact that she appears to be on the verge of marrying a Rebel and declares her intent to accompany the man onto battlefields and to live with him under the most insalubrious conditions imaginable?"

He sat up in bed and spoke with evident passion, but I couldn't help smiling at his mode of expression; evidently the Grey brothers shared the same habit of speech. I coughed to hide this, though, and replied as tactfully as possible.

"Um . . . you've seen Dottie, then?"

"Yes, I have," he said shortly. "She was with Henry when I arrived yesterday, and wearing the most extraordinary garment. Evidently the man to whom she considers herself affianced is a Quaker, and she declares that she has become one, as well!"

"So I understand," I murmured. "You . . . er . . . hadn't heard about it?"

"No, I had not! And I have a few things to say to John regarding both his cowardice in not telling me about it and his son's unpardonable machi . . . machinations . . ." The choler in this speech literally choked him, and he had to stop and cough, wrapping his arms round his knees to steady himself against the racking spasms.

I took up the fan I'd left on the table earlier and wafted a bit of smoke from the brazier into his face. He gasped, coughed harder for a moment, and then subsided, wheezing.

"I'd tell you not to excite yourself, if I thought there was the slightest chance of you listening," I remarked, handing him a cup of the boiled tincture of *Ephedra* in coffee. "Drink that. Slowly.

"As for John," I went on, watching him make faces over the bitter taste, "he considered writing to you when he found out what Dottie intended. He didn't, because at the time he thought it might be nothing more than a passing whim and that once she'd seen the reality of Denny's—er, that's her fiancé, Dr. Hunter—of his life, she might think better of it. And if she did, there was no need to alarm you and your wife. He never expected you to turn up here."

Hal coughed once, then drew breath in a tentative fashion.

"I didn't, either," he said, and, putting the cup aside, coughed again and lay back against the heaped pillows. "The War Office decided to send my regiment to support Clinton when the new strategy was decided upon; there wasn't time to write."

"Which new strategy is this?" I asked, only mildly interested.

"To sever the southern colonies from the north, suppress the rebellion there, and thus starve the north into submission. Keep the bloody French out of the West Indies, too," he added as an afterthought. "You think Dottie might change her mind?" He sounded dubious but hopeful.

"Actually, no," I said. I stretched and ran my fingers through my damp hair, which had settled softly on my neck and shoulders, curling light and tickling round my face. "I wondered whether it was you or your wife she took after in terms of willfulness, but the instant I met you, it was clear."

He gave me a narrow look but had the grace to smile.

"She does," he admitted. "So does Benjamin—my eldest son. Henry and Adam are both like my wife in terms of temperament. Which does not mean that they aren't capable of seeking their own way," he added thoughtfully. "Only that they're rather more diplomatic about it."

"I'd like to meet your wife," I said, smiling, too. "Her name is Minnie, John said?"

"Minerva," he said, his smile growing more genuine. "Minerva Cunnegunda, to be exact. Couldn't call her 'Cunny,' could I?"

"Probably not in public, no."

"Wouldn't try it in private, either," he assured me. "She's very demure—to look at."

I laughed, and darted a glance at the brazier. I hadn't thought the active principle in ganja would be very strong, burned as an atmospheric rather than smoked directly. Still, it was obviously having a beneficial effect on Hal's mood as well as his asthma, and I was conscious of a slight feeling of well-being beginning to creep into my own outlook. I was still worried about Jamie—and John—but the worry had lifted from my shoulders and seemed to be floating a little way above my head: still visible, and a dull purple-gray in color, but floating. *Like a lead balloon,* I thought, and gave a small, amused snort.

Hal was lying back, eyes half lidded, watching me with a sort of detached interest.

"You're a beautiful woman," he said, sounding faintly surprised. "Not demure, though," he added, and made a low chuckling noise. "What could John have been thinking?"

I knew what John had been thinking but didn't want to talk about it—for assorted reasons.

"What did you mean earlier," I asked curiously, "about making bargains with God?"

"Ah." His eyelids closed slowly. "When I arrived at General Clinton's office this morning—God, was that only this morning?—he had rather bad news for me—and a letter. Sent some weeks ago from New Jersey, forwarded eventually to him through the army post.

"My eldest son, Benjamin, was captured by the Rebels at the Brandywine," he said, almost dispassionately. Almost; there was enough light for me to see the bulge of his jaw muscle. "There is at present no agreement with the Americans involving the exchange of prisoners, so he remains in captivity."

"Where?" I asked, disturbed at the news.

"I don't know that," he said shortly. "Yet. But I shall discover his whereabouts as quickly as possible."

"Godspeed," I said sincerely. "Was the letter from Benjamin?"

"No." His jaw tightened a little further.

The letter had been from a young woman named Amaranthus Cowden, who informed His Grace the Duke of Pardloe that she was the wife of his son Benjamin—and the mother of Benjamin's son, Trevor Wattiswade Grey, aged three months. *Born after Benjamin was captured,* I thought, and wondered whether Benjamin knew about the baby.

The young Mrs. Grey found herself in difficult circumstances, she wrote, owing to her husband's sad absence, and therefore proposed to go to her relatives in Charleston. She felt some delicacy in approaching His Grace for assistance, but her state was such that she felt she had little choice in the matter and hoped that he would forgive her forwardness and look kindly upon her plea. She enclosed a lock of her son's hair, feeling that His Grace might like to have such a keepsake of his grandson.

"Dear me," I said. I hesitated for a moment, but the same thought must surely have occurred to him. "Do you think she's telling the truth?"

He sighed, a mixture of anxiety and aggravation.

"Almost certainly she is. My wife's maiden name was Wattiswade, but no one outside the family would know that." He nodded toward the wardrobe where Mrs. Figg had hung his uniform. "The letter is in my coat, should you wish to read it."

I waved a hand in polite dismissal.

"I see what you meant about making bargains with God. You want to live to see your grandchild—and your son, of course."

He sighed again, his lean body seeming to diminish slightly. Mrs. Figg had undone his queue—much against his will—brushed out his hair, and tied it in a loose tail that now fell over his shoulder, a soft dark brown shot with streaks of white that glinted red and gold in the fire glow.

"Not precisely. I do want that, of course, but—" He groped for words, quite unlike his earlier elegant loquacity. "You'd die for them, happily. Your family. But at the same time you think, *Christ, I can't die! What might happen to them if I weren't here?*" He gave me a wry and rueful smile. "And you know bloody well that you mostly can't help them anyway; they've got to do it—or not—themselves."

"Unfortunately, yes." A draft of air moved the muslin curtains and stirred the hanging pall of smoke. "Not the grandchildren, though. You can help them." And I suddenly missed Henri-Christian's soft weight, his solid head against my shoulder; I'd saved his life by removing his tonsils and adenoids, and I thanked God that I'd been in time to do it. And Mandy . . . *God, take care of her,* I prayed fiercely. I'd been able to tell Bree what was wrong and that it could be fixed—but *I* couldn't fix her heart defect, and I regretted that lack every day of my life. If I could have done the necessary surgery in this time, they'd all still be here. . . .

The curtains moved again, and the heavy atmosphere drew a clean, sudden breath. I inhaled deeply, catching the faint, sharp scent of ozone. "Rain," I said. "Rain's coming."

The duke didn't reply but turned, lifting his face toward the window. I got up and raised the sash higher, gratefully letting in a cool breeze. I looked out into the night again; clouds were drifting fast across the moon, so the light seemed to pulse rather than flicker, like the beat of a palpitating heart. The streets were dark, with no more than the occasional glow of a moving lantern to mark the muted agitation of the city.

Rain might damp the movement, both of fleeing Loyalists and the army readying itself to depart. Would the cover of the storm make it easier for Jamie to come into the city? A bad storm might hamper him, turning the roads to mud. How far away was he?

The lead balloon had come down on my head. My mood had taken a plunge, whether from fatigue, the oncoming storm, or merely as a natural effect of cannabinol, I didn't know. I shivered, though the air was still hot, unable to keep my brain from projecting vivid images of all the dire possibilities that could befall a man caught between two armies, alone in the night.

Maybe alone. What *had* he done with John? Surely he wouldn't have—

"I was twenty-one when my father died," Hal remarked out of the blue. "Grown. Had my own life, had a wife—" He broke off abruptly, his mouth twisting. "Didn't think I needed him at all, until he suddenly wasn't there."

"What could he have done for you?" I asked, sitting down again. I was curious—but also anxious to avoid my own racing thoughts.

Hal lifted one slender shoulder. The neck of the nightshirt was unbuttoned, both because of the heat and so I could more easily see the pulse in his neck. It fell open, the cloth limp with moisture, and his clavicle showed, high-arched and clean, shadowed sharp against his skin.

"Been there," he said simply. "Listened. Perhaps . . . approved of what I was doing." The last few words came low, barely audible. "Or maybe not. But . . . been there."

"I know what you mean," I said, more to myself than to him. I'd been lucky; I was very young when my parents died, and my uncle had stepped promptly into my life, to be there for me. And casual as his own life had been—he always *was* there. I'd felt his loss acutely when he died, but I'd been married then—a spasm of guilt seized me out of nowhere, thinking of Frank. And another, worse, thinking of Brianna. I'd left her, once—and then she had left me.

That unleashed a jumble of morbid thoughts: of Laoghaire, abandoned by both daughters, unlikely ever to see her grandchildren, now mine. Of Jem and Mandy . . . and Jamie.

Where *was* he? And why wasn't he here? Surely, whatever John might have told him . . .

"Oh, dear," I said hopelessly, under my breath. I could feel the tears prick and well, pressing up against the dam of my determination.

"Do you know, I'm most remarkably hungry," Hal said, sounding surprised. "Is there any food in the house?"

JAMIE'S STOMACH GROWLED, and he coughed to cover the sound, but there was no need. The little girls were curled up like a pair of capped hedgehogs under a tattered quilt by the hearth, back to back and snoring like drunken bumblebees. Mrs. Hardman was on the settle, singing to the baby under her breath. He couldn't make out the words, so he couldn't tell what song it was, but imagined it to be a lullaby. On the other hand, he'd heard Highland women sing their babes asleep often enough with things like *"Nighean Nan Geug,"* which dealt with severed heads and blood-soaked ground. But Mrs. Hardman was a Friend; presumably she'd have no truck with that sort of lullaby. Maybe "The Great Silkie of Sule Skerry," he thought, beginning to relax. Clearly Friends had no objection to carnal relations as such . . .

That reminded him of bloody John Grey, and he grimaced, then stifled a grunt as his back sent a warning shot down his leg, indicating that even that much movement wouldn't be tolerated.

The song was no more music to him than the snoring, but both were gentle sounds, and he eased himself cautiously, checked that knife and pistol were easily to hand, and shut his eyes. He was tired to the bone but doubted he'd sleep. He couldn't even shift himself in the bed without white stabs of pain jabbing him in the backside like the devil's pitchfork.

It had been years since his back had last done this to him. Ached frequently, now and then was stiff in the morning, but it hadn't done this in . . . ten years? He remembered it vividly. It was soon after they'd come to the Ridge, just after he and Ian built the cabin. He'd gone out a-hunting, sprung over a bank in pursuit of a fleeing elk, and found himself lying on his face at the foot of the bank, quite unable to move.

Claire, bless her, had come searching for him—he smiled wryly at thought of it; she'd been so proud of tracking him through the forest. If she hadn't found him . . . well, it would have been the luck of the draw as to whether a painter, bear, or wolf came upon him before his back released its clench and let him move. He supposed he wouldn't have died of cold, though he might well have lost a few toes to frostbite.

She—

A sound brought his head up, fast. His back stabbed viciously, but he set his teeth, ignoring it, and pulled the pistol out from underneath his pillow.

Mrs. Hardman's head jerked up at his movement. She stared at him, wide-eyed, then heard what he had heard and got up hastily. Feet on the path, more than one pair. She turned, looking for the cradle, but he shook his head.

"Keep the bairnie with ye," he said, low-voiced. "Answer when they knock, open if they ask."

He saw her swallow, but she did as he said. There were three or four, he thought, but not bent on mischief. There were feet on the porch, low murmurs, and a bit of laughing. A knock, and Mrs. Hardman called, "Who's there?"

"Friends, missus," said a man's voice, slurred with drink. "Let us in."

She cast a frightened glance at Jamie, but he nodded, and she lifted the latch, opening the door to the night. The first man started to come in but then saw Jamie on the bed and stopped, mouth open.

"Good evenin' to ye," Jamie said, polite, but holding the other man's eyes with his own. The pistol lay in plain sight, under his hand.

"Oh," said the other man, disconcerted. He was young and rather stout, dressed in hunting garb but with a militia badge; he glanced over his shoulder at his companions, who had stopped on the threshold. "I—er—good evening to you, sir. We didn't—er—we thought . . ." He cleared his throat.

Jamie smiled at him, well aware what he thought. Keeping the man in sight from the corner of his eye, he turned to Mrs. Hardman and gestured to her to sit down. She did and bent her head over the child, brushing her lips over Chastity's tiny cap.

"We've nothing to offer ye in the way of food, gentlemen," Jamie said. "But there's cold water from the well, and a bed in the shed, if ye need it."

The other two men stood outside, shuffling awkwardly. There was a strong smell of liquor coming off them, but they hadn't come in a mood to do damage.

"That's all right," the young man said, backing up to his friends. His round face was flushed, as much with embarrassment as with liquor. "We'll just . . . sorry to disturb you. Sir."

The other two bobbed their heads, and all three retreated, shuffling and bumping into one another in their haste to leave. The last one pulled the door to, but not all the way. Mrs. Hardman rose and pushed it to with a small bang, then leaned against it, her eyes closed, the child clasped against her bosom.

"Thank you," she whispered.

"It's all right," he said. "They'll not come back. Put the bairn down and bar the door, aye?"

She did, then turned and leaned against the door, her hands pressed flat against it. She looked at the floor between her feet, breathing audibly for a moment, then slowly straightened.

Her plain jacket was fastened with pins—he didn't know if this was to avoid the vanity of buttons, as the Moravians did, or whether she was simply too poor to have any. Her fingers fiddled nervously with the top pin, and then she suddenly pulled it out and laid it glinting on the shelf. She looked directly at him then, her fingers gripping the head of the next pin. Her long upper lip was pressed down, and a nervous sweat glistened on it.

"Dinna even think about it," he said bluntly. "In my present condition, I couldna swive a dead sheep. To say nothing of which, I'm old enough to be your father, lass—and I'm marrit, forbye."

Her mouth quivered slightly, though he couldn't tell whether with disappointment or relief. Her fingers relaxed, though, and her hand dropped to her side.

"Ye dinna need to pay me for the food, lass," he said. "It was a gift."

"I—yes, I know. I thank thee, Friend." She looked aside, swallowing a little. "I only—I hoped that perhaps—thee might stay. For a time."

"I'm marrit, lass," he repeated gently, then, after an uncomfortable pause, felt compelled to ask, "Do ye have such callers often?" It had been clear to him that the men were strangers to her—but she was not to them. They'd heard of the Quaker woman who lived alone with three young girls.

"I take them to the shed," she blurted, her face going redder than the flames made it. "After the girls are asleep."

"Mmphm," he said, after another pause that lasted much too long. His eyes went to the cradle but then shot away. He wondered how long Mr. Hardman had been gone from home, but it wasn't his business. Nor was it his business how she managed to feed her girls.

"Sleep, lass," he said. "I'll keep watch."

13

MORNING AIR AWASH WITH ANGELS

Next day

JAMIE AWOKE TO THE smell of frying meat and sat up straight in bed, forgetting his back.

"Lord have mercy," said Mrs. Hardman, looking over her shoulder. "I haven't heard a noise like that since the last time my husband, Gabriel, killed a pig." She shook her head and returned to her cookery, pouring batter into an oiled cast-iron spider that sat in the coals, smoking and spitting in a baleful sort of way.

"I beg your pardon, ma'am—"

"Silvia is my name, Friend. And thine?" she asked, raising one brow at him.

"Friend Silvia," he said through clenched teeth. "My name Is Jamie. Jamie Fraser." He'd raised his knees in the involuntary jerk that brought him upright, and now he wrapped his arms around them and laid his sweating face against the worn quilt that covered them, trying to stretch his recalcitrant back. The effort shot pain down his right leg and caused an instant sharp cramp in his left calf muscle, which made him grunt and pant until it let go.

"I'm pleased to see thee sit up, Friend Jamie," Silvia Hardman remarked, bringing him a plate filled with sausage, fried onions, and johnnycake. "Your back is some better, I collect?" She smiled at him.

"Somewhat," he managed, and smiled back as well as he could while trying not to groan. "You—have fresh food, I see."

"Yes, God be thanked," she said fervently. "I sent Pru and Patience out to the main road at dawn to watch for wagons coming in to the market in Philadelphia, and they came back with a pound of sausage, two of cornmeal, a sack of oats, and a dozen eggs. Eat up!" She placed the wooden plate on the bed beside him, with a wooden spoon.

Jamie could see Prudence and Patience behind their mother, industriously wiping sausage grease from their empty plates with chunks of johnnycake. Easing himself gingerly around in order to put his back against the wall, he stretched out his legs, picked up the plate, and followed their example.

The food filled him with a surprising sense of well-being, and he put down the empty plate determined upon enterprise.

"I propose to visit your privy, Friend Silvia. But I may need some assistance to rise."

Once on his feet, he found that he could make shift to stagger a few inches at a time, and Prudence and Patience at once rushed up to seize him by the elbows, in the manner of small flying buttresses.

"Don't worry," Prudence advised him, squaring her puny shoulders and looking confidently up at him. "We won't let thee fall."

"I'm sure ye won't," he said gravely. In fact, the little girls had a wiry strength that belied their fragile appearance, and he found their presence an actual help, as they provided something for him to hold on to for balance when it was necessary to stop—as it was every few feet.

"Tell me about the wagons that go into Philadelphia," he said at one such stop, as much to make conversation as because he required the information. "Do they come only in the early morning?"

"Mostly," Patience said. "They go back empty an hour or two before sunset." She set her feet wider, bracing herself. "It's all right," she assured him. "Lean on me. Thee seems summat shaky."

He squeezed her shoulder gently in thanks and let her take a very little of his weight. Shaky, indeed. It was more than half a mile to the main road; it would take over an hour to totter that far, even with the girls' assistance, and the likelihood of his back freezing again and stranding him midway was yet too high to risk it. To say nothing of the risk of arriving in Philadelphia completely unable to move. By tomorrow, though . . .

"And did ye see soldiers on the road?" he asked, essaying a ginger step that shot pain from hip to foot. "Ow!"

"We did," Patience said, taking a tighter grip on his elbow. "Courage, Friend. Thee will prevail. We saw two companies of militia, and one Continental officer on a mule."

"We saw some British solders, too, though," Prudence put in, eager not to be overlooked. "They were with a train of carts, going in the other direction."

"The other—away from Philadelphia?" Jamie asked, his heart jumping. Was the evacuation of the British army already begun? "Could you see what was in the carts?"

Prudence shrugged. "Furniture. Trunks and baskets. There were ladies riding atop some of the carts, though mostly they walked alongside. No room," she clarified. "Guard thy shirttail, Friend, or thy modesty will be at risk." The morning was cool and breezy, and an errant gust of wind had risen up, bellying his shirt—wonderful on his sweating body, but definitely a risk to maiden eyes.

"Shall I knot the tails between thy legs?" Patience inquired. "I can tie a granny knot, an overhand knot, or a square knot. My daddy taught me!"

"Don't be silly, Patience," her sister said crossly. "If thee knots his shirt, how will he lift it to shit? No one can untie her knots," she confided to Jamie. "She always makes them too tight."

"Oh, I do not, liar!"

"Fie upon thee, sister! I'll tell Mummy what thee said!"

"Where is your father?" Jamie interrupted, wanting to stop the acrimony before they began pulling each other's hair. They did stop and glanced at each other for a moment before replying.

"We don't know," Prudence said, her voice small and sad. "He went a-hunting one day a year ago and didn't come back."

"It might be that Indians took him," Patience said, trying to sound hopeful. "If so, may be that he'll escape one day and come home."

Prudence sighed.

"Maybe," she said flatly. "Mummy thinks the militia shot him."

"Why?" Jamie asked, looking down at her. "Why would they shoot him?"

"For being a Friend," Patience explained. "He wouldn't fight, and so they said he was a Loyalist."

"I see. Was—er, I mean—*is* he?"

Prudence looked at him, grateful for the "is."

"I don't think so. But Mummy says Philadelphia yearly meeting told everyone that all Friends should be for the King, as the King would keep peace and the Rebels seek to break it. So"—she shrugged—"people think all Friends are Loyalists."

"Daddy wasn't—*isn't*," Patience put in. "He used to say all kinds of things about the King, and Mummy would get worried and beg him to hold his tongue. Here's the privy," she announced unnecessarily, letting go of Jamie's elbow in order to open the door. "Don't wipe thyself with the towel; it's for hands. There are corncobs in the basket."

JOHN GREY WOKE feverish and heavy-limbed, with a pounding headache, and a stabbing pain in his left eye when he tried to open it. Both his eyes were crusted and gummy. He'd been dreaming in vivid, fractured swaths, a confusion of images, voices, emotions . . . Jamie Fraser had been shouting at him, face dark with passion, but then something changed, some sort of pursuit began, and he fell back into queasy nightmare. They were running together through a bog, a sucking quagmire that pulled at his steps, and Fraser was struggling just ahead of him, trapped, shouting at him to go back, but he couldn't, his feet were mired fast and he was sinking, flailing madly but unable to get a purchase on anything . . .

"Gaah!" A hand shook him by the shoulder, startling him out of the morass. He pried his good eye open and saw the wavering form of a neat young man in a dark coat and spectacles, peering down at him in an oddly familiar way.

"John Grey?" said the young man.

"I am," he said. He swallowed painfully. "Have I—the honor of your acquaintance, sir?"

The young man flushed a bit.

"Thee has, Friend Grey," he said, low-voiced. "I am—"

"Oh!" Grey said, sitting up in a rush. "Of course, you—oh. Oh, Jesus." His head, disturbed by the abrupt change of posture, had apparently decided to fly off his shoulders and thump into the nearest wall. The young man . . . *Hunter,* he thought, finding the name turn up with an odd neatness among the chaos inside his skull. *Dr.* Hunter. Dottie's Quaker.

"I think thee had best lie down, Friend."

"I think I had best vomit first."

Hunter snatched the pot out from under the cot just in time. By the time he had administered water—"Drink slowly, Friend, if thee wishes to keep it"—and eased Grey back down on the cot, Colonel Smith was looming up behind him.

"What do you say, Doctor?" Smith was frowning and seemed worried. "Is he in his right mind? He was singing last night, now he's been moaning and saying odd things, and the look of him . . ." Smith grimaced in a fashion that made Grey wonder what the devil he *did* look like.

"He's badly fevered," Hunter said, with a piercing look through his spectacles as he bent to take hold of Grey's wrist. "And thee sees the condition of his eye. It would be dangerous to move him. A further extravasation of blood into the brain . . ."

Smith made a discontented noise and compressed his lips. He nudged Hunter aside and bent over Grey.

"Can you hear me, Colonel?" he asked, speaking in the slow, distinct manner one used with idiots and foreigners.

"Ich bin ein Fisch . . ." Grey murmured beatifically, and closed his eyes.

"His pulse is much disordered," Hunter said warningly, his thumb pressing Grey's wrist. His hand was cool and firm; Grey found the touch comforting. "I really cannot answer for the consequences should he be moved abruptly."

"I see." Smith stood still for a moment; Grey could hear his heavy breathing but forbore opening his eyes. "Very well, then." He gave a short, humorless laugh. "If Mohammed cannot go to the mountain, then the mountain will jolly well have to come here. I'll send a note to General Wayne. Do what you can, please, to see that he's coherent, Doctor?"

HE COULD SEE Denzell Hunter out of his damaged eye; that was re-assuring: he wasn't blind. Yet. Hunter had removed his spectacles in order to peer more closely into the injured organ; he had very nice eyes himself, Grey thought—the iris just the light-brown color of the flesh of a ripe olive, with tiny streaks of deep green.

"Look up, please," Hunter murmured.

Grey tried to oblige.

"Ow!"

"No? Look down." This attempt was no more successful, nor could he move the eye to the right or left. It seemed to have solidified in its socket, like a hard-boiled egg. He put this theory to Hunter, who smiled, though in a rather worried way.

"There *is* a great deal of swelling, to be sure. Whatever struck thee did so with a good deal of force." Hunter's fingers moved gently over Grey's face, prodding here and there in a questioning manner. "Does this—"

"Yes, he did. Don't keep asking if it hurts; everything from my scalp to my chin hurts, including my left ear. What you said regarding extravasation of blood into the brain—did you mean it?"

"It's possible." Hunter did smile at that, though. "But since thee has shown no disposition to seizure or unconsciousness—save that due to alcohol—and thee apparently walked for several hours following the injury, I think perhaps the probability is lower. There *is* bleeding beneath the sclera, though." His cool fingertips brushed the puffy lid. "Thy eyeball is crimson, as is the lining of thy eyelid. It's rather . . . dramatic." There was a distinct tone of amusement in this, which Grey found reassuring.

"Oh, good," he said dryly. "How long will it take to go away?"

That made the Quaker grimace and shake his head.

"The blood will take a week to a month to clear; it's essentially the same as mere bruising—the bursting of small blood vessels under the skin. What worries me is thy inability to move the eye. I think thee has a fracture of the bony orbit, which is somehow trapping the orbicularis muscle. I do wish thy wife was here; she has a much greater—"

"My wife," Grey said blankly. "Oh!" Memory and realization collided, and he felt a sudden leap of spirit. "She isn't my wife! Not anymore," he added, and found himself grinning. He leaned forward to whisper into Hunter's astonished ear, "Jamie Fraser isn't dead!"

Hunter stared at him, blinked, put his spectacles back on, and resumed staring, obviously rethinking his appraisal of Grey's brain.

"He's the one who hit me," Grey said helpfully. "It's all right," he added at Hunter's frown. "I was asking for it."

"God be praised," Hunter whispered, breaking into a huge smile—apparently at the news of Fraser's survival rather than Grey's assurance of the morality of his actions. "Ian will be—" He broke off with a gesture indicating his inability to describe Ian Murray's probable emotions.

"And Friend Claire!" he exclaimed, eyes huge behind his spectacles. "Does she know?"

"Yes, but—" Approaching footsteps made Grey hurl himself back onto the cot, with a completely authentic exclamation of pain. He shut his eyes and rolled his head to one side, groaning.

"The mountain seems to be with General Washington," Smith said, plainly disedified. Grey felt him come to a stop by the cot, bumping it with his legs. "Do what you can to see that he's capable of travel by tomorrow, Doctor— we'll load him into one of the wagons, if necessary."

Number 17 Chestnut Street

HIS GRACE WOKE up in the morning red-eyed as a ferret and in roughly the same temper as a rabid badger. Had I a tranquilizing dart, I would have shot him with it without an instant's hesitation. As it was, I pre-scribed a large slug of brandy to be added to his breakfast coffee and—after a brief struggle with my Hippocratic conscience—added a very small amount of laudanum to it.

I couldn't give him much; it depressed the respiration, among other things. Still, I reasoned, counting the aromatic reddish-brown drops as they plinked into the brandy, it was a more humane way of dealing with him than crowning him with the chamber pot or calling Mrs. Figg to sit on him whilst I tied him to the bedstead and gagged him.

And I did require him to be both immobile and quiet for a short period. Mr. Figg, a preacher of the Methodist Society, was bringing round two young men of the society who were carpenters, to rehang the front door and nail boards over the shutters of the downstairs windows, in case of roving mobs. I'd told Mrs. Figg that of course she might confide our circumstances to her husband—I couldn't very well stop her—but that perhaps he might be per-suaded not to mention His Grace's presence, in the interests of protecting Lord John's safety and property—to say nothing of His Grace, who was, after all, Lord John's presumably beloved brother.

Mrs. Figg would cheerfully have handed the duke over to be tarred and feathered, but an appeal on Lord John's behalf would always carry weight with her, and she nodded in sober agreement. So long as His Grace didn't draw attention to himself by shouting out of the upstairs window or hurling things at the workmen, she thought his presence could be concealed.

"What you mean to do with him, though, Lady John?" she asked, glanc-ing warily toward the ceiling. We were standing in the back parlor, conferring in lowered voices while Jenny administered Hal's breakfast and made sure all the brandy-laced coffee was drunk. "And what if the army sends someone round to ask after him?"

I made a helpless gesture.

"I have no idea," I confessed. "I just need to keep him here until either Lord John or my—er, Mr. Fraser—comes. They'll know what to do with him. As for the army, if anyone comes asking after His Grace, I'll . . . um . . . speak to them."

She gave me a look indicating that she'd heard better plans, but nodded reluctantly and went off to fetch her marketing basket. The first thing that happens in a newly occupied city is a shortage of food, and with the Continental army poised to descend on Philadelphia like a plague of locusts, the wagons that normally brought in produce from the countryside would likely be sparse. If either army *was* on the road already, they'd be seizing anything that came along.

At the door, though, Mrs. Figg paused and turned around.

"What about William?" she demanded. "If he comes back . . ." She was obviously torn between hope that he *would* come back—she was worried for him—and consternation at what might happen if he encountered his uncle in captivity.

"I'll speak to him," I repeated firmly, and waved a hand toward the door.

Running upstairs, I found Hal yawning over a nearly empty breakfast tray and Jenny fastidiously wiping egg yolk off the corner of his mouth. She'd spent the night at the printshop but had come back to help, bringing with her a battered portmanteau filled with possibly useful items.

"His Grace made a good breakfast," she reported, stepping back to examine her work critically. "And he's moved his bowels. I made him do that afore he drank his coffee, just in case. Wasna sure how quick it might be."

Hal frowned at her, though whether in puzzlement or offense, I couldn't tell. His pupils were already noticeably constricted, which gave him a slightly staring look. He blinked at me and shook his head, as though trying to clear it.

"Let me have a quick check of your vital signs, Your Grace," I said, smiling and feeling like Judas. He was my patient—but Jamie was my husband, and I hardened my resolve.

His pulse was slow and quite regular, which reassured me. I took out my stethoscope, unbuttoned his nightshirt, and had a listen: a nice, steady heartbeat, no palpitations, but the lungs were gurgling like a leaky cistern, and his breathing was interrupted by small gasps.

"He'd best have some of the *Ephedra* tincture," I said, straightening up. It was a stimulant and would antagonize the opiate in his system, but I couldn't risk his stopping breathing while asleep. "I'll stay with him; will you go down and get a cup—don't bother heating it, cold will do." I wasn't sure he'd stay conscious long enough to have a cup heated.

"I really must go to see General Clinton this morning," Pardloe said, with surprising firmness, considering his foggy mental state. He cleared his throat and coughed. "There are arrangements to make. . . . My regiment . . ."

"Ah. Er . . . where *is* your regiment just now?" I asked cautiously. If they were in Philadelphia, Hal's adjutant would be starting to look for him in earnest at any minute. He might reasonably have spent the night with a son or daughter, but by now . . . and I didn't know precisely how much distraction value my forged notes might have had.

"New York," he replied. "Or at least I sincerely hope so." He closed his eyes, swayed slightly, then straightened his back with a jerk. "Landed there. I came down to Philadelphia . . . to see Henry . . . Dottie." His face twisted with pain. "Mean . . . to go back with Clinton."

"Of course," I said soothingly, trying to think. *When,* exactly, would Clinton and his troops leave? Assuming Pardloe to be sufficiently recovered that he wouldn't actually die without my attendance, I could give him back as soon as the exodus was under way. At that point, he'd have no way of starting a major search for John and endangering Jamie. But surely Jamie—with or without John—would come back at any moment?

Who did come back was Jenny, with the *Ephedra* tincture—and a hammer in the pocket of her apron and three stout laths under her arm. She handed me the cup without comment and proceeded to nail the laths over the window, in a surprisingly brisk and competent manner.

Hal sipped his *Ephedra* slowly, watching Jenny with bemusement.

"Why is she doing that?" he asked, though not as if he cared particularly what the answer was.

"Hurricanes, Your Grace," she said with a straight face, and zipped out to return the hammer to the carpenters, whose cheerful banging sounded like a battalion of woodpeckers attacking the house.

"Oh," Hal said. He was glancing vaguely round the room, possibly in search of his breeches, which Mrs. Figg had thoughtfully taken away and hidden in the cookhouse. His eye rested on the small pile of Willie's books I had moved to the top of the dressing table. Evidently he recognized one or more, because he said, "Oh. William. Where *is* William?"

"I'm sure Willie's very busy today," I said, and picked up his wrist again. "Perhaps we'll see him later." His heartbeat was slow but still strong. Just as his grip loosened, I caught the empty cup and set it on the table. His head drooped, and I eased him carefully back on the pillow, propped for easier breathing.

"If he comes back . . ." Mrs. Figg had said of Willie, with the obvious implication, *"what then?"*

What indeed?

Colenso had not returned, so presumably he had found William; that was reassuring. But what William was doing—or thinking . . .

14

INCIPIENT THUNDER

AN ASSIGNMENT BEFITTING your peculiar situation," Major Findlay had said. Findlay didn't know the half of it, William reflected bitterly. Not that his situation wasn't "peculiar," even without his recent discoveries.

He had surrendered at Saratoga, with the rest of Burgoyne's army, in October of '77. The British soldiers and their German allies had been obliged to yield their weapons but were not to be held prisoner; the Convention of Saratoga, signed by Burgoyne and by the Continental general, Gates, had stated that all troops would be allowed to return to Europe, once they had given their parole not to take up arms again in the American conflict.

But ships could not sail during the winter storms, and something had to be done with the captured soldiers. Referred to as the Convention army, they had been marched en masse to Cambridge, Massachusetts, there to await spring and repatriation. All but William and a few like him, who had either connections in America with influence, or connections with Sir Henry, who had succeeded Howe as commander in chief of the American campaign.

William, fortunate fellow, had both; he had served on Howe's personal staff, his uncle was the colonel of a regiment, and his father was an influential diplomat, presently in Philadelphia. He had been released under an exceptional personal parole, as a favor to General Lord Howe, and sent to Lord John. He was, however, still part of the British army, merely precluded from actual fighting. And the army had any number of obnoxious chores that did not involve fighting; General Clinton had been delighted to make use of him.

Deeply galled by his situation, William had begged his father to try to have him exchanged; that would remove the conditions of his parole and allow him to resume full military duties. Lord John had been quite willing to do this, but in January of 1778 there had been a falling-out between General Burgoyne and the Continental Congress over the former's refusal to provide a list of the surrendered *soldiers*. The Convention of Saratoga had been repudiated by the Congress, which then declared that it would detain the entire Convention army until the convention and the required list were ratified by King George—the Congress knowing damned well that the King would do no such thing, as such an act would be tantamount to acknowledging the independence of the colonies. The upshot of this was that there was at present no mechanism at all for the exchange of prisoners. Any prisoners.

Which left William in a deeply ambiguous position. Technically, he was an escaped prisoner, and in the highly unlikely event that he was recaptured by the Americans and discovered to be one of the Saratoga officers, he would promptly be marched off to Massachusetts to languish for the rest of the war. At the same time, no one was quite sure whether it was appropriate for him to take up arms again, since even though the convention had been repudiated, William had been given a personal parole.

Which had led to William's present invidious situation, in charge of troops assisting the evacuation of Philadelphia's richest Loyalists. The only thing he could think of that might be worse was driving a herd of swine through the eye of a needle.

While the poorer citizens who felt endangered by the proximity of General Washington's militias were obliged to brave the dangers of the road, making their exodus by wagon, handcart, and foot, the wealthier Loyalists were allowed a safer and theoretically more luxurious removal by ship. And not one of them could be brought to understand that there was but *one* ship presently available—General Howe's own ship—and very limited room aboard it.

"No, madam, I'm very sorry, but it's quite impossible to accommodate—"

"Nonsense, young man, my husband's grandfather purchased that tall clock in the Netherlands in 1670. It displays not only the time but also the phases of the moon and a complete table of tides for the Bay of Napoli! Surely you do not expect me to allow such an instrument to fall into the clutches of the Rebels?"

"Yes, madam, I'm afraid I do. No, sir, no servants; only the members of your immediate family and a very small amount of baggage. I'm sure that your bond servants will be perfectly safe following by—"

"But they'll starve!" exclaimed a cadaverous-looking gentleman who was loath to part with his talented cook and a plumply voluptuous housemaid, who, if not talented at sweeping, obviously had other desirable abilities, these clearly on display. "Or be abducted! They are my responsibility! Surely you cannot—"

"I can," said William firmly, with an appreciative sideways glance at the housemaid, "and I must. Corporal Higgins, please see Mr. Hennings's bond servants safely off the quay. No, madam. I agree that the matched armchairs are quite valuable, but so are the lives of the people who will drown if the ship sinks. You may take your carriage clock, yes." He raised his voice and bellowed, "Lieutenant Rendill!"

Rendill, face red and streaming, fought his way through the crowd of pushing, cursing, heaving, shrieking evacuees. Arriving in front of William, who was perched on a box in order to avoid being trampled or pushed into the water by the crowd, the lieutenant saluted but was rudely jostled by several people attempting to gain William's attention and ended with his wig pushed over his eyes.

"Yes, sir?" he said gamely, pushing it back and elbowing a gentleman out of the way as politely as possible.

"Here's a list of General Howe's particular acquaintances, Rendill. Go on board and see if they've all made it—if they haven't . . ." He cast an eloquent glance over the surging throng on the dock, surrounded by mountains of semi-abandoned possessions and trampled baggage, and thrust the list unceremoniously into the lieutenant's hand. "Find them."

"Oh, God," said Rendill. "I mean . . . yes, sir. At once, sir." And, with a hopeless air, he turned and began to swim through the crowd, doing a modified but vigorous form of breaststroke.

"Rendill!"

Rendill obediently turned and made his way resignedly back into earshot, a stout red porpoise surging his way through shoals of hysterical herring.

"Sir?"

William leaned down and lowered his voice to a level inaudible to the press of people around them, then nodded at the piles of furniture and baggage heaped unsteadily all over the dock—many of them dangerously close to the edge.

"As you pass, tell the fellows on the dock that they should take no great pains to preserve those heaps of things from falling into the river, would you?"

Rendill's perspiring face brightened amazingly.

"Yes, sir!" He saluted and swam off again, radiating renewed enthusiasm, and William, his soul slightly soothed, turned courteously to attend to the complaint of a harried German father with six daughters, all of them carrying what appeared to be their entire lavish wardrobes, anxious round faces peering out between the brims of their wide straw hats and the piles of silk and lace in their arms.

Paradoxically, the heat and incipient thunder in the air suited his mood, and the sheer impossibility of his task relaxed him. Once he'd realized the ultimate futility of satisfying all these people—or even one in ten of them—he stopped worrying about it, took what steps he could to preserve order, and let his mind go elsewhere while he bowed courteously and made noises of reassurance to the phalanx of faces pressing in upon him.

Had he been in a mood for irony, he reflected, there was plenty of it to go round. He was neither fish nor fowl nor good red beef, as the country folk said of an ambiguous cut of meat. Not a full soldier, not a free civilian. And, evidently, neither an Englishman nor an earl . . . and yet . . . how could he possibly not be an Englishman, for God's sake?

Once he had regained enough of his temper to think, he had realized that he was still *legally* the Ninth Earl of Ellesmere, regardless of his paternity. His parents—his real parents—his *theoretically* real parents—had undeniably been married at the time of his birth. At the moment, though, that seemed to make matters worse: how could he go about letting people think and act as though he were the heir of Ellesmere's ancient blood when he knew damned well that he was really the son of—

He choked that thought off, shoving it violently to the back of his mind. "Son of" had brought Lord John vividly to mind, though. He breathed deep of the hot, murky, fish-smelling air, trying to quell the sudden pang that came to him at thought of Papa.

He hadn't wanted to admit it to himself, but he'd been looking through the crowd all day, scanning the faces in search of his fa—yes, dammit, his father! John Grey was as much his father now as he ever had been. *Goddamned liar or not.* And William was growing worried about him. Colenso had reported that morning that Lord John had not returned to his house—and Lord John *should* have returned by now. And if he had, he would have come to find William, he was sure of that. Unless Fraser had killed him.

He swallowed bile at the thought. Why would he? The men had once been friends, good friends.

True, war severed such bonds. But even so—

On account of Mother Claire? He recoiled from that thought, too, but made himself come back to it. He could still see her face, glowing in spite of the uproar, fierce as flame with the joy of seeing Jamie Fraser, and felt a prick of jealousy on behalf of his father. If Fraser felt similarly impassioned, might he . . . but that was nonsense! Surely he must realize that Lord John had only taken her under his protection—and done that for the sake of his good friend!

But, then, they *were* married . . . and his father had always been quite open regarding matters of sex. . . . His face grew even hotter, with embarrassment at the vision of his father enthusiastically bedding the not-quite-ex-Mrs. Fraser. And if Fraser had discovered that—

"No, sir!" he said sharply to the importunate merchant who—he realized belatedly—had just tried to bribe him to admit the merchant's family to

Howe's ship. "How dare you? Begone, and think yourself fortunate that I have no time to deal with you as I ought!"

The man shuffled disconsolately away, and William felt a small pang of regret, but there was in fact little he could do. Even had he felt able to stretch a point in the merchant's favor, once a bribe was offered, he had no choice.

Even if it were true, how would Fraser have discovered it? Surely Lord John wouldn't have been foolish enough to tell him. No, it must be something else that was delaying Papa's return—doubtless the muddle of people leaving Philadelphia; the roads must be choked. . . .

"Yes, madam. I think we have room for you and your daughter," he said to a young mother, very frightened-looking, with a baby clutched against her shoulder. He reached out and touched the infant's cheek; she was awake, but not troubled by the crowd, and regarded him with soft brown long-lashed eyes. "Hallo, sweetheart. Want to go on a boat with your mummy?"

The mother gave a stifled sob of relief.

"Oh, thank you, Lord—it is Lord Ellesmere, is it not?"

"It is," he said automatically, and then felt as though someone had punched him in the belly. He swallowed and his face burned.

"My husband is Lieutenant Beaman Gardner," she said, offering the name in anxious justification of his mercy, and bobbed a short curtsy. "We've met. At the Mischianza?"

"Yes, of course!" he said, bowing, though he didn't recall Mrs. Lieutenant Gardner at all. "Honored to be of service to a brother officer's wife, ma'am. If you will be so good as to go on board directly, please? Corporal Anderson? Escort Mrs. Gardner and Miss Gardner on board."

He bowed again and turned away, feeling as though his insides had been scooped out. *Brother officer. My lord.* And what would Mrs. Lieutenant Gardner have thought if she'd known? What would the lieutenant himself think?

He sighed deeply, closing his eyes for an instant's escape. And when he opened them, found himself face-to-face with Captain Ezekiel Richardson.

"*Stercus!*" he exclaimed, startled into his uncle Hal's habit of Latin denunciation in moments of extreme stress.

"Indeed," Richardson remarked politely. "May I have a word with you? Yes, just so—Lieutenant!" He beckoned to the nearby Rendill, who was eyeball-to-eyeball with an elderly woman in black bombazine with no fewer than four small dogs yapping at her heels, these held by a long-suffering small black boy. Rendill made a quelling motion to her and turned to Richardson. "Sir?"

"Relieve Captain Lord Ellesmere, please. I require a moment of his time."

Before William could decide whether to object or not, Richardson had him by the elbow and was towing him out of the scrum and into the lee of a neat little sky-blue boathouse that stood on the riverbank.

William breathed deep with relief as the shade fell upon him but had by then gathered his wits. His first impulse had been to speak sharply to Richardson—followed perhaps by knocking him into the river—but wisdom spoke in his ear, advising otherwise.

It was at Richardson's instigation that William had become for a short time an intelligencer for the army, collecting information in the context of various journeys and delivering this to Richardson. On the last of these missions, though, a journey into the Great Dismal Swamp of Virginia, William had had the misfortune to become lost, be wounded, and suffer a fever that would certainly have killed him had Ian Murray not found and rescued him—in the course of the rescue informing William that he had almost certainly been gulled and sent not into the bosom of British allies but into a nest of Rebels, who would hang him should they discover who he was.

William was of two minds as to whether to believe Murray or not—particularly after the arrival of Jamie Fraser had made it patently clear that Murray was his own cousin but hadn't felt it necessary to apprise him of the fact. But a deep suspicion of Richardson and his motives remained, and it was no friendly face that he turned on the man.

"What do you want?" he said abruptly.

"Your father," Richardson replied, causing William's heart to give a great thump that he thought must be audible to the other. "Where is Lord John?"

"I haven't the slightest idea," William said shortly. "I haven't seen him since yesterday." *The day my bloody life ended.* "What do you want with him?" he asked, not bothering with any semblance of courtesy.

Richardson twitched an eyebrow but didn't otherwise respond to his tone. "His brother, the Duke of Pardloe, has disappeared."

"The—what?" William stared at him for a moment, uncomprehending. "His brother? Disappeared . . . from where? When?"

"Evidently from your father's house. As to when: Lady John said that he left the house just after tea yesterday afternoon, presumably in search of your father. Have you seen him since then?"

"I haven't seen him at all." William felt a distinct ringing in his ears—probably his brains trying to get out through them. "What—I mean, I had no idea he was in Philadelphia. In the colonies at all, for that matter. When did he arrive?" *Jesus, did he come to deal with Dottie and her Quaker? No, he can't have, he couldn't have had time . . . could he?*

Richardson was squinting at him, probably trying to determine whether he was telling the truth.

"I haven't seen either of them," William said flatly. "Now, if you'll excuse me, Captain . . ." There was a tremendous splash from the direction of the dock and a loud chorus of shock and dismay from the crowd. "Excuse me," William repeated, and turned away.

Richardson seized him by the arm and made an effort to fix William with his gaze. William looked deliberately in the direction of his neglected duty.

"*When* you see either one of them, Captain Ransom, be so good as to send word to me. It would be a great help—to many people."

William jerked his arm free and stalked off without reply. Richardson had used his family name instead of his title—did that mean anything beyond mere rudeness? At the moment, he didn't care. He couldn't fight, he couldn't help anyone, he couldn't tell the truth, and he wouldn't live a lie. God damn it, he was stuck like a hog, mired to the hocks.

He wiped the sweat from his face on his sleeve, squared his shoulders, and strode back into the fray. All there was to do was his duty.

15

AN ARMY ON THE MOVE

W E WERE JUST IN time. No sooner had I closed the bedroom door on Pardloe's gentle snore than a knock came on the
newly hung front door below. I hurried downstairs to find Jenny
face-to-face with a British soldier, this time a lieutenant. General Clinton was
escalating his inquiries.

"Why, no, lad," she was saying, in a tone of mild surprise, "the colonel
isn't here. He took tea with Lady John yesterday, but then he went off to
look for his brother. His lordship hasn't come back, and"—I saw her lean
closer, her voice lowered dramatically—"her ladyship's that worried. Ye'll not
have news of him, I suppose?"

This was my cue, and I came down from the landing, rather surprised to
find that I was indeed "that worried." Tending Hal had distracted me from
the situation temporarily, but by now there was no denying that something
had gone seriously wrong.

"Lady John. Lieutenant Roswell, your servant, ma'am." The lieutenant
bowed, with a professional smile that didn't hide the slight furrowing of his
brow. The army was getting worried, too, and that was bloody dangerous.
"Your servant, mum. Have you in fact had no word from Lord John or Lord
Melton—oh, I beg your pardon, my lady, I mean from His Grace?"

"D'ye think I'm a liar, lad?" Jenny said tartly.

"Oh! No, mum, not at all," he said, flushing. "But the general will want
to know that I spoke with her ladyship."

"Of course," I said soothingly, though my heart was pittering in my throat.
"Tell the general that I haven't heard from my husband"—*either of them*—
"at all. I'm most disturbed." I wasn't a good liar, but I wasn't lying now.

He grimaced.

"The thing is, mum, the army has begun withdrawing from Philadelphia,
and all Loyalists remaining in the city are being advised that they may wish
to . . . er . . . make preparations." His lips compressed for a moment as he
glanced at the stairwell, with its ruined banister and bloody fist marks. "I . . .
see that you have already experienced some . . . difficulty?"

"Och, no," Jenny said, and with a deprecating glance at me, stepped
nearer the lieutenant and put her hand on his arm, pushing him gently toward the door. He automatically moved away with her, and I heard her murmur, ". . . no but a wee family quarrel . . . his lordship . . ."

The lieutenant shot me a swift glance, in which surprise mingled with a certain sympathy. But the lines in his forehead eased. He had an explanation to take back to Clinton.

Blood flamed in my cheeks at his look—as though there truly had been a family row, during which Lord John had stamped out, leaving wreckage in his wake and a wife at the mercy of the Rebels. True, it *was* a family row, but the circumstances were more through-the-looking-glass than a matter of mere common scandal.

The White Rabbit shut our new door firmly on Lieutenant Roswell and turned to me, back pressed against it.

"Lord Melton?" she asked, one black eyebrow raised.

"It's one of the duke's titles, one he used before he became Duke of Pardloe. Lieutenant Roswell must have known him some years ago," I explained.

"Oh, aye. Well, lord or duke, how long can we keep him asleep?" she asked.

"The laudanum will keep him out for two or three hours," I replied, glancing at the gilt carriage clock on the mantel, which had somehow escaped the carnage. "But he had a very hard day yesterday and a rather disturbed night; he may well go straight off into a natural sleep as the drug wears off. If no one comes along to knock the house down round our ears," I added, wincing at sounds of a violent altercation somewhere nearby.

Jenny nodded. "Aye. I'd best go along to the printshop now, then, to see what the news in the city is. And perhaps Jamie will ha' gone there," she added hopefully. "Not thinking it safe to come here, I mean, wi' the streets full of soldiers."

A spark of hope at the suggestion flared up like a lit match. Though even as I envisioned the possibility, I knew that if Jamie was in the city at all, he'd be standing before me right now. Possibly enraged, possibly disturbed, but before me.

With the army already beginning its withdrawal, and the concomitant public disturbances, no one would have time or inclination to notice—let alone arrest—a tall Scotsman suspected of nothing more than passing suspicious documents. It wasn't as though there was an all points bulletin out on him—or at least I hoped not. William was the only soldier who knew that Jamie had taken Lord John hostage, and from his manner in leaving, I rather thought that the last thing William would have done was give a full report of the situation to his superiors.

I said as much to Jenny, though agreed that she ought to go back to the printshop, to check on the welfare of Fergus and Marsali's family, as well as to find out what was going on amongst the Rebels in the city.

"Will you be safe in the streets?" I asked, unfolding her cloak and holding it up for her to put on.

"Oh, I expect so," she said briskly. "No one much thinks to look at an auld woman. But I suppose I'd best put away my wee bawbee." The bawbee in question was a small silver chiming watch, with a delicately filigreed cover, which she wore pinned to the bosom of her dress.

"Jamie bought it for me in Brest," she explained, seeing me looking at it as she unpinned it. "I told him it was foolery; I didna need such a thing to ken the time, nay more than he did himself. But he said, no, I must have it, that knowing what o'clock it is gives ye the illusion that ye have some control over your circumstances. Ye ken how he is," she added, putting the watch carefully away in her pocket, "always explaining ye to yourself. Though I will say as he's no often wrong.

"Now, then," she added, turning to me as she opened the door. "I'll come back before him upstairs wakes up, unless I can't, and if I can't, I'll send Germain to say so."

"Why should you not be able to?" I asked, in some surprise.

"Young Ian," she said, equally surprised that I should not have thought of this. "Wi' the army leaving, he may have come back from Valley Forge by now—and ye ken, the poor lad thinks I'm dead."

16

ROOM FOR SECRETS

In the forest, five miles from Valley Forge

"D O QUAKERS BELIEVE in heaven?" Ian Murray asked. "Some do," Rachel Hunter replied, pausing to turn over a large toadstool with the toe of her shoe. "No, dog, don't touch that one. See the color of its gills?" Rollo, who had come to sniff at the fungus, dismissed it with a perfunctory sneeze and lifted his snout to the wind in hopes of more promising prey.

"Auntie Claire says dogs canna see colors," Ian remarked. "And what d'ye mean, 'Some do'? Is there a difference of opinion on the matter?" Quaker beliefs puzzled him beyond measure, but he found Rachel's explanations invariably entertaining.

"Perhaps they smell them instead. The dogs, I mean. But to return to thy question, we consider our life here on earth to be a sacrament, lived in the light of Christ. There may be an afterlife, but as no one has come back to say so, it's a matter of speculation, left to each person individually."

They had paused in the shade of a small walnut grove, and the soft green sun that fell flickering through the leaves gave Rachel herself an unearthly glow that any angel might have envied.

"Well, I havena been there, either, so I'll no just say that's wrong," he said, and bent to kiss her just above the ear. A faint rush of tiny gooseflesh stippled her temple for an instant, and the sight touched his heart.

"Why does thee think of heaven?" she asked curiously. "Does thee think there will be fighting in the city? I haven't known thee overly fearful for thy life before." Valley Forge had been hoaching like a grain sack full of weevils when they left it an hour before, the soldiers salvaging what they could from the camp, molding fresh musket balls and packing cartridges, preparing to march on Philadelphia when the word was given that Clinton's men had withdrawn.

"Och, no. There'll be nay fighting in the city. Washington will try to catch Clinton's men in retreat." He took her hand, small and brown and work-roughened but the fingers reassuringly strong as they turned and clasped his. "Nay, I was thinking of my mam—that I should ha' liked to show her places like this." He gestured toward the little clearing in which they stood, a tiny spring of an improbably deep blue welling up from the rock under their feet, overhung by a yellow wild-rose brier, humming with summer bees. "She had a big yellow rose brier growin' up the wall at Lallybroch; my grandmother planted it." He swallowed a small lump in his throat. "But then I thought, may be as she's happier in heaven with my da than she would be here without him."

Rachel's hand squeezed his, hard.

"She would be with him always, in life or in death," she whispered, and stood a-tiptoe to kiss him back. "And you will take me someday to see your grandmother's rose in Scotland."

They stood in silence for a bit, and Ian felt his heart, clenched with a sudden grief at the thought of his mother, ease in Rachel's sympathetic company. He hadn't said it, but what he most regretted was not his inability to show his mother the beauties of America but the fact that he couldn't show her Rachel.

"She'd have liked ye," he blurted. "My mam."

"I hope that she would," Rachel said, though with a tinge of dubiousness. "Did thee tell her about me, in Scotland? That I am a Friend, I mean. Some Catholics find us scandalous."

Ian tried to remember whether he *had* mentioned that to his mother, but couldn't. It made no difference, in any case, and he shrugged, dismissing it.

"I told her I loved ye. That seemed to be enough. Come to think, though—my da asked all kinds of questions about ye; he wanted to know everything he could. He kent ye were a Quaker, so that means she kent it, too." He took her elbow to help her down from the rock.

She nodded, thoughtful, but as she followed him out of the clearing, he heard her ask behind him, "Does thee think a married couple should be completely in each other's confidence—share not only their histories, I mean, but every thought?"

That sent a qualm skittering down his backbone like a mouse with cold feet, and he took a deep breath. He loved Rachel with every fiber of his being, but he found her apparent ability to read him like a book—if not to actually hear his thoughts, and sometimes he thought for sure she did that, too—unsettling.

He had in fact suggested that they walk together to Matson's Ford and meet Denzell with the wagon there, rather than ride with him from Valley

Forge, so that Ian might have sufficient time and solitude in which to share a few necessary things with her. He'd rather be tortured by Abenakis than tell her some of those things, but it was right she should know them, no matter what the result might be.

"Aye. I mean . . . well, so far as one can, I think they maybe should. Not every thought, I dinna mean, but important things. Ahh . . . history, like ye said. Here, come sit for a wee while." There was a big fallen log, half rotted and covered with moss and fuzzy gray lichens, and he led her to it, sitting down beside her in the fragrant shade of a big red cedar.

She didn't say anything, but lifted a brow in question.

"Well." He drew a deep breath, feeling that there wasn't enough air in the whole forest for this. "Did ye ken . . . I've been marrit before?"

Her face flickered, surprise overcome by determination so fast that he'd have missed it if he hadn't been watching so close.

"I did not," she said, and began to pleat the folds of her skirt, one-handed, clear hazel eyes fixed intently on his face. "Thee did say *been* married. Thee isn't now, I suppose?"

He shook his head, feeling a little easier—and very grateful to her. Not every young woman would have taken it so calmly.

"No. I wouldna have spoken to ye—asked ye to marry me, I mean—otherwise."

She pursed her lips a little and her eyes narrowed.

"In point of fact," she said thoughtfully, "thee never *has* asked me to marry thee."

"I didn't?" he said, staggered. "Are ye sure?"

"I would have noticed," she assured him gravely. "No, thee didn't. Though I recall a few very moving declarations, there was no suggestion of marriage among them."

"But—well." Heat had risen in his cheeks. "I—but you . . . ye said . . ." Maybe she was right. She *had* said . . . or had she? "Did ye not say ye loved me?"

Her mouth turned up just a little, but he could see her laughing at him at the back of her eyes.

"Not in so many words. But I did give thee to understand that, yes. Or at least I meant to."

"Oh. Well, then," he said, much happier. "Ye did." And he pulled her into his one sound arm and kissed her with great fervor. She kissed him back, panting a little, her fists curled in the fabric of his shirt, then broke away, looking mildly dazed. Her lips were swollen, the skin around them pink, scraped by his beard.

"Perhaps," she said, and swallowed, pushing him away with one hand flat on his chest, "perhaps thee should finish telling me about not being married, before we go further? Who was thy—thy wife—and what happened to her?"

He let go of her reluctantly but would not surrender her hand. It felt like a small live thing, warm in his.

"Her name is Wakyo'teyehsnonhsa," he said, and felt the accustomed inner shift at the speaking of it, as though the line between his Mohawk self and his white self had momentarily disappeared, leaving him awkwardly suspended somewhere in between. "It means 'Works With Her Hands.' " He cleared his throat. "I called her Emily. Most of the time."

Rachel's small, smooth hand jerked in his.

"Is?" she said, blinking. "Thee said *is*? Thy wife is *alive*?"

"She was a year ago," he said, and, with an effort, didn't cling to her hand but let her take it back. She folded her hands in her lap, fixed her eyes on him, and swallowed; he saw her throat move.

"All right," she said, with no more than a faint tremor in her voice. "Tell me about her."

He took another deep breath, trying to think how to do *that*, but then abandoned the effort and spoke simply.

"D'ye truly want to know that, Rachel? Or do ye only want to ken whether I loved her—or whether I love her now?"

"Start there," she said, lifting one brow. "*Does* thee love her?"

"I—yes," he said, helpless to speak other than the truth to her. Rollo, sensing some disturbance among his pack, got up from his resting place and padded over to Rachel. He sat down by her foot, making his allegiance in the matter clear, and gave Ian a yellow-eyed wolf look over Rachel's knee that bore an uncomfortable resemblance to the look in her own eye. "But . . ."

The brow lifted a fraction of an inch higher.

"She . . . was my refuge," he blurted. "When I left my own family and became a Mohawk, it was as much to be wi' her as because I had to."

"Had to . . . what?" She looked baffled, and he saw her eyes drop a little, tracing the tattooed lines across his cheekbones. "Thee had to become a Mohawk? Why?"

He nodded, feeling momentarily on firmer ground. He could tell her this story; it was only what had happened. Her eyes went round when he explained how he and Uncle Jamie had met Roger Wakefield, not realized who he was and thought him to be the man who had raped his cousin Brianna and got her with child, had come close to killing him, but had thought better of the notion—

"Oh, good," Rachel said, half under her breath. He glanced sidelong at her but couldn't tell if she meant this ironically or not, so he coughed and went on, telling how they had instead given the man to the Tuscarora, who in turn had sold him as a slave to the Mohawk farther north.

"We didna want to risk him ever comin' back to trouble Brianna, aye? Only then—" He swallowed, reliving in memory both the terror of his asking Brianna to marry him and the utter horror when cousin Bree had drawn a picture of the man she loved, the man she was waiting for—and the strong dark features of the man they had given to the Mohawk sprang into view.

"You asked thy cousin to marry thee? Did thee want to?" She looked wary; he supposed she must be thinking that he went about proposing to every third or fourth woman he met and hastened to correct this impression.

"Nay, I mean—well, Brianna's a . . . well, I didna *mind*, ken, we'd ha' got on fine, and she—well . . . I mean, no, not exactly," he added hurriedly, seeing Rachel's graceful brows draw together. The truth was that he'd been seventeen and Brianna several years older; she'd terrified him, but the thought of bedding her had— He choked that thought off as though it were a venomous snake.

"It was Uncle Jamie's idea," he said, with as much an air of casual dismissal as could be assumed on short notice. He lifted one shoulder. "To give the bairn a name, aye? I said I would, for the family honor."

"The family honor," she repeated, giving him a fishy look. "To be sure. But then—"

"But then we found it was Roger Mac—he'd taken back his own name of MacKenzie, is why we didna recognize him—that we'd given to the Indians by mistake, and so we went to retrieve him," he said quickly. By the time he'd finished explaining all the events that had culminated in his volunteering to take the place of a Mohawk killed during Roger's rescue, the washing of his body in the river, the Mohawk women scrubbing him with sand to remove the last trace of his white blood, the plucking of his hair and the tattoos, he thought his marriage to Emily might seem only one more picturesque detail.

But of course it didn't.

"I—" He stopped dead, realizing suddenly that the conversation was about to become even stickier than he'd thought. He glanced at her apprehensively, heart beating in his throat and ears. But she was still looking back; the pinkness round her mouth showing more vividly because she'd gone a little pale—but looking, clear and steady.

"I—wasna a virgin when I wed," he blurted.

The eyebrow went up again.

"Really, I am not quite sure what to ask," she said, examining him in the way he'd seen his auntie Claire appraise some horrible growth—fascinated rather than repelled, but with a firm air of deciding exactly how best to deal with the offending bit. He hoped fervently she didn't mean to cut him out of her life like a wart or amputate him like a gangrenous toe.

"I'll . . . tell ye anything ye want to know," he said bravely. "Anything."

"A generous offer," she said, "and one I shall accept—but I think I must offer thee the same accommodation. Thee does not wish to ask whether I am virgin?"

His mouth fell open, and her shoulders shook briefly.

"Ye're not?" he croaked.

"No, I am," she assured him, still quivering with the effort not to laugh. "But why should thee assume it?"

"Why?" He felt the blood rise in his face. "Because—anyone who looked at ye would know ye on the instant for a—a—a virtuous woman!" he concluded, with a sense of relief at having found a reasonable term.

"I might have been raped," she pointed out. "That would not mean I was not virtuous, would it?"

"I—well. No, I suppose not." He knew that a good many folk *would* think a raped woman was not virtuous—and Rachel knew that. He was on the verge of becoming completely confused, and she knew that, too; he could see her taking pains not to laugh. He squared his shoulders and gave a great sigh, then met her eyes directly.

"D'ye want to hear about every woman whose bed I've shared? Because

I'll tell ye, if so. I've never taken a woman unwilling—though they were mostly whores. I'm no poxed, though," he assured her. "Ye should ken that."

She considered that for a moment.

"I think I need not know the details," she said finally. "But should we ever meet a woman thee has bedded, I wish to know it. Thee does not mean to continue fornicating with prostitutes once we are wed, though, does thee?"

"No!"

"Good," she said, but rocked back a little on the log, hands linked around her knees, holding his gaze. "I do wish to hear more about thy wife. Emily."

He could feel the warmth of her leg, her body, close beside him. She hadn't moved away from him when he'd said about sleeping with whores. The silence grew around them, and a jay called somewhere in the wood beyond.

"We loved each other," he said at last, softly, eyes on the ground. "And I wanted her. I—could talk to her. Then, at least."

Rachel drew breath but didn't say anything. He took his courage in his hands and looked up. Her face was carefully expressionless, her eyes intent on his face.

"I dinna ken how to say it," he said. "It wasna the same way I want you—but I dinna mean to make it sound as though . . . as though Emily didna matter to me. She did," he added, very low-voiced, and glanced down again.

"And . . . she does?" Rachel asked quietly, after a long pause. After a longer one, he nodded, swallowing.

"But," he said, and stopped, searching for the way to go on, because now they were coming to the most perilous part of his confession, the thing that might make Rachel stand up and walk away, dragging his heart behind her through the rocks and brush.

"But?" she said, and her voice was gentle.

"The Mohawk," he began, and had to stop for a breath. "It's the woman's choice, about being married. If a woman should take against her husband for some reason—if he beats her, or he's a lazy sot, or smells too bad when he farts"—he stole a glance and saw the corner of her mouth twitch, which heartened him a little—"she puts his things out o' the longhouse, and he has to go back to live wi' the unmarried men—or find another woman who'll have him at her fire. Or leave altogether."

"And Emily put you out?" She sounded both startled and a bit indignant. He gave her a wee smile in return.

"Aye, she did. Not because I beat her, though. Because . . . of the bairns."

He felt the tears come to his eyes and clenched his hands in frustration on his knees. Damn, he'd sworn to himself that he wouldn't weep. Either she'd think he made a show of his grief to win her sympathy—or she'd see too deep; he wasn't ready . . . but he had to tell her, he'd started this on purpose to tell her, she had to know. . . .

"I couldna give her children," he blurted. "The first—we had a wee daughter, born too early, who died. I called her Iseabail." He wiped the back of his hand viciously under his nose, swallowing his pain. "After that, she—Emily—she got wi' child again. And again. And when she lost the third . . . her heart toward me died with it."

Rachel made a small sound, but he didn't look at her. Couldn't. Just sat hunched on the log like a toadstool, shoulders drawn up around his ears, and eyes blurred with the tears he couldn't shed.

A small warm hand settled on his.

"And your heart?" she asked. "Yours died, too?"

He closed his hand on hers and nodded. And then just breathed for a bit, holding on to her hand, until he could speak again without his voice breaking.

"The Mohawk think that the man's spirit fights wi' the woman's, when they . . . lie together. And she willna get with child unless his spirit can conquer hers."

"Oh, I see," Rachel said softly. "So she blamed you."

He shrugged.

"I canna say she was wrong." He turned a little on the log, to look at her directly. "And I canna say that it would be different—with us. But I did ask Auntie Claire, and she told me about things in the blood . . . well, perhaps ye should ask her to explain it; I wouldna make a decent job of it. But the end of it was that she thought it *might* be different wi' another woman. That I maybe could. Give ye bairns, I mean."

He only realized that Rachel had been holding her breath when she let it out, a sigh that brushed his cheek.

"Do ye—" he began, but she had risen a little, into him, and she kissed him gently on the mouth, then held his head against her breast and took the end of her kerchief and wiped his eyes and then her own.

"Oh, Ian," she whispered. "I do love thee."

17

FREEDOM!

GREY PASSED ANOTHER interminable—though less eventful—day, broken only by watching Colonel Smith write dispatches, which he did at a furious rate, quill scratching with the sound of a scuttling cockroach. This bit of imagery did nothing for Grey's digestion, which, in the aftermath of intoxication, hadn't dealt all that well with the cold grease-caked journeycake and burnt-acorn coffee he'd been given for breakfast.

In spite of physical infelicity and an uncertain future, though, he found himself surprisingly cheerful. Jamie Fraser *was* alive, and he, John, wasn't married. Given those two marvelous facts, the dubious prospects of escape and the much higher probability of being hanged seemed only mildly concerning. He settled himself to wait with what grace he could, sleeping as much as his head allowed, or singing softly to himself—a practice that caused Smith to hunch his shoulders up around his ears and scratch faster.

Messengers came and went with great frequency. If he hadn't already known that the Continentals were not only moving but preparing for a fight, it would have been clear to him within an hour. The hot air was burdened with the scent of molten lead and the whine of a sharpening wheel, and the camp had a sense of rising urgency that any soldier would have felt at once.

Smith made no attempt to keep him from hearing what was said by and to the messengers and subalterns; clearly he didn't expect the information gained to be of any use to Grey. Well . . . neither did Grey, to be honest.

Toward the evening, the tent's door was darkened by a slender female form, though, and Grey raised himself to a sitting position, careful of his tender head, because his heart had begun to beat strongly again and it made his eye throb.

His niece Dottie was in sober Quaker garb, but the soft blue of much-laundered indigo was surprisingly flattering to her English-rose coloring—and she was in amazing fine looks. She nodded to Colonel Smith and set down her tray upon his desk, before glancing over his shoulder at the prisoner. Her blue eyes widened in shock, and Grey grinned at her over the colonel's shoulder. Denzell must have warned her, but he supposed he must look a literal fright, with a grotesquely swollen face and a fixed and glaring crimson eye.

She blinked and swallowed, then said something low-voiced to Smith, with a brief questioning gesture in Grey's direction. He nodded impatiently, already taking up his own spoon, and she wrapped a thick rag around one of the steaming cans on the tray and came across to Grey's cot.

"Dear me, Friend," she said mildly. "Thee seems much injured. Dr. Hunter says thee may eat as much as is comfortable, and he will attend thee later to put a dressing on your eye."

"Thank you, young woman," he said gravely, and, glancing over her shoulder to be sure Smith's back was turned, nodded at her. "Is it squirrel stew?"

"Possum, Friend," she said. "Here, I brought thee a spoon. The stew is boiling; be careful." Putting herself carefully between him and Smith, she placed the rag-wrapped can between his knees and rapidly touched the rags, then the links of his fetters, her eyebrows raised. A horn spoon was produced from the pocket tied at her waist—and a knife with it, which was slipped under his pillow, quick as any conjurer could have managed it.

Her pulse was beating fast in her throat, and perspiration gleamed at her temples. He touched her hand once, softly, and picked up the spoon.

"Thank you," he said again. "Tell Dr. Hunter I look forward to seeing him again."

THE ROPE WAS horsehair and the knife dull, and it was very late and with innumerable small cuts stinging his hands and fingers that Grey rose cautiously from the cot. His heart was pounding; he could feel it thumping briskly behind his injured eye and hoped the eye itself was not going to explode under the impact.

He bent and picked up the tin chamber pot and used it; Smith was a very sound sleeper, thank God; if he roused at all, he would hear the familiar noise, be reassured, and—presumably—fall back asleep, subconsciously ignoring any further small noises as being Grey resettling himself.

Smith's breathing didn't change. He had a small, buzzing snore like a bee working in a flower, a tidy, busy sound that Grey found mildly comical. He lowered himself to his knees, slowly, between the cot and Smith's pallet, fighting a momentary insane impulse to kiss Smith on the ear—he had sweet, small ears, very pink. This vanished in an instant, and he crept on hands and knees to the edge of the tent. He'd threaded the rags and the gauze with which Denzell Hunter had packed his eye through the links of his fetters but still moved with the utmost caution. Being caught would be bad for him; it would be disastrous for Hunter and Dottie.

He'd been listening intently to the sentries for hours. There were two guarding the colonel's tent, but he was fairly sure that both were presently near the front flap, warming themselves at the fire; hot as the day had been, this late at night the forest's blood ran cold. So did his.

He lay down and squirmed as quickly as he could under the edge of the tent, clinging to the canvas to minimize any shaking of the tent itself—though he'd taken pains to jerk on his rope every so often through the evening, so that any shifting of the structure might be put down to his normal movements.

Out! He allowed himself one deep gulp of air—fresh, cold, and leafy—then rose, clutching the padded fetters close against his body, and walked as silently as possible away from the tent. He mustn't run.

He had had a short, sharp, whispered argument with Hunter during the latter's evening visit, seizing the brief moment when Smith had left the tent to visit the latrine. Hunter had insisted that Grey hide in his wagon; he was going into Philadelphia, everyone knew that, there would be no suspicion, and Grey would be safe from patrols. Grey appreciated Hunter's desire to rescue him, but he couldn't possibly put the doctor—let alone Dottie—at risk, and risk it would be. In Smith's place, the first thing he would do was prevent anyone from leaving, the second, search the camp and everything in it.

"There's no time," Hunter had said, briskly tucking in the end of the bandage he had wrapped around Grey's head, "and thee may be right." He glanced over his shoulder; Smith would be back any minute. "I'll leave a bundle of food and clothing in my wagon for thee. If thee chooses to make use of it, I'm glad. If not, God go with thee!"

"Wait!" Grey seized Hunter by the sleeve, making his fetters rattle. "How will I know which wagon is yours?"

"Oh." Hunter coughed, seeming embarrassed. "It . . . has a, um, sign painted on the tailboard. Dottie purchased it from— Now, you must take care, Friend," he said, abruptly raising his voice. "Eat generously but slowly, take no alcohol, and be careful in moving. Do not stand up too quickly."

Colonel Smith came in and, seeing the doctor present, came over to inspect the patient himself.

"Are you feeling better, Colonel?" he inquired politely. "Or are you still suffering from the need to burst into song? If so, might I suggest you do so now and get it out of your system, before I retire for the night?"

Hunter—who had of course heard *"Die Sommernacht"* the night before—made a small noise in his throat but managed to take his leave without losing control.

Grey grinned to himself, recalling Smith's glower—and imagining what the colonel might look like in a few hours, when he woke to discover that his songbird had flown. He made his way around the edge of the camp, avoiding the picket lines of mules and horses—easy to detect by the smell of manure. The wagons were parked nearby: no artillery, he noted.

The sky was overcast, a sickle moon glimmering uneasily between racing clouds, and the air held the scent of impending rain. Fine. There were worse things than being wet and cold, and rain would hamper pursuit, if anyone discovered his absence before daylight.

No abnormal sounds from the camp behind him; none he could hear above the noise of his own heart and breathing. Hunter's wagon was easy to find, even in the flickering dark. He'd thought by "sign" that the doctor meant a name, but it was one of the barn signs that some of the German immigrants painted on their houses and sheds. He smiled when the clouds parted, revealing this one clearly, and he saw why Dottie had chosen it: it was a large circle, in which two comical birds faced each other, beaks open in the manner of lovebirds. *Distlefink.* The word floated into his head; someone, somewhere, had told him the name of that sort of bird, saying it was a symbol of good luck.

"Good," he said under his breath, climbing up into the wagon. "I'll need it."

He found the bundle under the seat, where Hunter had told him, and took a moment to remove the silver buckles from his shoes, tying the flaps together instead with a length of leather lacing that had evidently been meant for his hair. He left the buckles tucked under the seat, put on the shabby coat, which smelled strongly of stale beer and what he thought was old blood, and peered at the knitted cap, which held two journeycakes, an apple, and a small canteen of water. Turning back the edge of the hat, he read by the fitful moonlight, LIBERTY OR DEATH, in bold white letters.

HE WASN'T HEADED in any particular direction; even had the sky been clear, he wasn't sufficiently familiar as to be able to chart his direction by the stars. His only goal was to get as far away from Smith as possible, without running into another militia company or a patrol of Continentals. Once the sun was up, he could orient himself; Hunter had told him that the main road lay south–southwest of the camp, about four miles away.

What the public might make of a man strolling down the main road in fetters was another question, but not one he needed to answer just now. After walking for an hour or so, he found a sheltered spot among the roots of an enormous pine tree and, taking out the knife, hacked off his hair as best he could. He stuffed the shorn locks well back under a root, rubbed his hands in the dirt, and then applied them vigorously to hair and face before donning his Phrygian cap.

Thus suitably concealed, he heaped a thick blanket of fallen dry needles over himself, curled up, and went to sleep to the sound of pattering rain in the trees above, once more a free man.

18

NAMELESS, HOMELESS, DESTITUTE,
AND VERY DRUNK INDEED

HOT, DISHEVELED, AND still thoroughly out of temper from his encounter with Richardson, William made his way back through the crowded streets. One more night in a decent bed, at least. Tomorrow he'd leave Philadelphia with the last few companies of the army, following Clinton north—and leaving the remaining Loyalists to fend for themselves. He was torn between relief and guilt at the thought but had little energy left to consider them.

He arrived at his billet to find that his orderly had deserted and had taken with him William's best coat, two pairs of silk stockings, a half bottle of brandy, and the seed-pearl-encrusted double miniature of William's mother, Geneva, and his other mother, her sister, Isobel.

This was so far over the bloody limit of what could be borne that he didn't even swear, merely sank down on the edge of the bed, closed his eyes, and breathed through clenched teeth until the pain in his stomach subsided. It left a raw-edged hollow. He'd had that miniature since he was born, was accustomed to bid it good night before he slept, though since he'd left home he did this silently.

He told himself it didn't matter; he was unlikely to forget what his mothers looked like—there were other paintings, at home at Helwater. He remembered Mama Isobel. And he could see the traces of his real mother in his own face. . . . Involuntarily, he glanced at the shaving mirror that hung on the wall—the orderly had somehow overlooked that in his flight—and felt the hollow inside him fill with hot tar. He no longer saw the curve of his mother's mouth, her dark wavy chestnut hair; he saw instead the too-long, knife-edged nose, the slanted eyes and broad cheekbones.

He stared at this blunt evidence of betrayal for an instant, then turned and stamped out.

"Fuck the resemblance!" he said, and slammed the door behind him.

He didn't care where he was going, but within a few streets he ran into Lindsay and another couple of fellows he knew, all intent on making the most of their last evening in a semi-civilized city.

"Come along, young Ellesmere," Sandy said, collaring him firmly and shoving him down the street. "Let's make a few memories to see us through the long winter nights up north, eh?"

Some hours later, viewing the world through the bottom of a beer glass, William wondered rather blearily whether memories counted if you didn't remember them. He'd lost count some time ago of what—and how many of what—he'd drunk. He thought he'd lost one or two or three of the companions with whom he'd started the evening, too, but couldn't swear to it.

Sandy was still there, swaying in front of him, saying something, urging him to his feet. William smiled vaguely at the barmaid, fumbled in his pocket, and laid his last coin on the table. That was all right, he had more in his trunk, rolled up in his spare pair of stockings.

He followed Sandy outside into a night that seized and clung, the hot air so thick that it was hard to breathe, clogged with the smell of horse droppings, human ordure, fish scales, wilted vegetables, and fresh-slaughtered meat. It was late, and dark; the moon had not yet risen, and he stumbled over the cobbles, lurching into Sandy, a blacker smudge on the night before him.

Then there was a door, a blur of light, and an enveloping hot scent of liquor and women—their flesh, their perfume, the smell more befuddling than the sudden light. A woman in a ribboned cap was smiling at him, greeting him, too old to be a whore. He nodded amiably at her and opened his mouth, only to be mildly surprised by the fact that he'd forgotten how to talk. He closed his mouth and went on nodding; the woman laughed in a practiced way and guided him to a shabby wing chair, where she deposited him as she might leave a parcel to be called for later.

He sat slumped in a daze for some time, the sweat running down his neck under his stock and dampening his shirt. There was a fire burning in a hearth near his legs, a small cauldron of rum punch steaming on the hob, and the scent of it made him queasy. He had the feeling that he was melting like a candle but couldn't move without being sick. He shut his eyes.

Some time later, he slowly became aware of voices near him. He listened for a little, unable to make sense of any words but feeling the flow vaguely soothing, like ocean waves. His stomach had settled now, and with his eyelids at half-mast, he gazed placidly at a shifting sand of light and shadow, pricked with bright colors, like darting tropical birds.

He blinked a few times, and the colors shimmered into coherence: the hair and ribbons and white shifts of women, the red coats of infantry, the blue of an artilleryman moving among them. Their voices had given him the impression of birds, high and trilling, squawking now and then, or scolding like the mockingbirds who lived in the big oak near the plantation house at Mount Josiah. But it wasn't the women's voices that caught his attention.

A pair of dragoons were lounging on the settee nearby, drinking rum punch and eyeing up the women. He thought they'd been talking for some time, but now he could make out the words.

"Ever buggered a girl?" one of the dragoons was saying to his friend. The friend giggled and flushed, shook his head, murmured something that sounded like, "Too dear for *my* purse."

"What you want's a girl that hates it." The dragoon hadn't moved his gaze from the women across the room. He raised his voice, just a little. "They clamp down, trying to get rid of you. But they can't."

William turned his head and looked at the man, repulsed, and making his disgust evident. The man ignored him. He seemed vaguely familiar, dark and heavy-featured, but no one William knew by name.

"Then you take her hand and make her reach back and feel you. God, the squirming—milk you like a dairymaid, she will!" The man laughed loudly, still staring across the room, and for the first time William looked to see the target of this brutish farrago. There were three women standing in a group, two in their shifts, the thin fabric molded damply to their bodies, one in an embroidered petticoat, but it was plain to see who the dragoon's insinuations were meant for: the tallish one in the petticoat, who stood there with her fists clenched, glaring back at the dragoon fit to burn a hole through his forehead.

The madam was standing a little apart, frowning at the dragoon. Sandy had disappeared. The other men present were drinking and talking with four girls at the far end of the room; they hadn't heard this vulgar impertinence. The dragoon's friend was scarlet as his coat, between liquor, amusement, and embarrassment.

The dark dragoon was flushed, too, a livid line across his heavy stubbled jowls where they pressed against the leather of his stock. One hand plucked absently at the sweat-stained crotch of his moleskin breeches. He was having too much fun with his prey to cut the chase short, though.

"Mind, you don't want one who's used to it. You want her tight." He leaned forward a little, elbows on his knees, eyes intent on the tall girl. "But you don't want one who's never had it before, either. Better if she knows what's coming, eh?"

His friend mumbled something indistinct, glanced at the girl and hastily away. William looked back at the girl, too, and as she made a small involuntary movement—not quite a flinch—the candlelight glowed for an instant on the smooth crown of her head: soft chestnut, with the gloss of a fresh conker. Jesus Christ.

Before he knew it, he was on his feet. He took two swaying paces to the madam's side, touched her shoulder politely, and when she turned a surprised face up to him—all her attention had been on the dragoon, a worried line between her brows—he said slowly, so as not to slur his words, "I'll take that one, please. The—the tall girl. In the petticoat. For the night."

The madam's plucked eyebrows all but vanished into her cap. She looked

quickly at the dragoon, who was still so fixed on his prey that he hadn't noticed William at all. His friend had, though; he nudged the dragoon and
muttered in his ear.

"Eh? What's that?" The man was already moving, scrambling to his feet.
William groped hastily in his pocket, remembering too late that he was penniless.

"What's this, Madge?" The dragoon was with them, dividing a glower
between the madam and William. William straightened instinctively—he had
six inches on the man—and squared up. The dragoon assessed his size and his
age and lifted the corner of his upper lip to show an eyetooth. "Arabella's
mine, sir. I'm sure Madge will find another young lady to accommodate
you."

"I am before you, sir," William said, and bowed, inclining his head a quarter inch, keeping a close eye on the cullion. Wouldn't put it past the filthy
bugger to try to kick him in the balls—the look on his face, he wouldn't stick
at it.

"He is, Captain Harkness," the madam said quickly, stepping between the
men. "He's already offered for the girl, and as you hadn't made up your
mind . . ." She wasn't looking at Harkness; she jerked her chin urgently at
one of the girls, who looked alarmed but swiftly vanished through a door at
the back. *Gone to fetch Ned,* William thought automatically, and wondered
dimly for an instant how he knew the doorkeeper's name.

"Haven't seen the color of his money yet, have you?" Harkness reached
into his bosom and pulled out a well-stuffed wallet, from which he withdrew
a careless sheaf of paper money. "I'll have her." He grinned unpleasantly at
William. "For the night."

William promptly whipped off his silver gorget, took the madam's hand,
and pressed the crescent into it.

"For the night," he repeated politely, and without further ado turned and
walked across the room, though the floor seemed to undulate slightly beneath his feet. He took Arabella—*Arabella?*—by the arm and steered her
toward the back door. She looked appalled—plainly she recognized him—
but a quick glance at Captain Harkness decided her that William was the
lesser of two weevils, as he'd heard a sailor friend of his father's put it.

He could hear Harkness's shout behind them, but just then the door
opened and a very large, tough-looking man walked in. He had but one eye,
but that one focused instantly on Harkness. The man advanced on the captain, walking lightly on the balls of his feet, fists half curled. *Ex-boxer,* William
thought, pleased. *Put that in your pipe and smoke it, Harkness!*

Then, a hand on the stairwell wall to stop from stumbling, he found himself following a round, agitated bum up the same worn, lye-soap-smelling
stairs he had trodden yesterday, wondering what the devil he'd say to her
when he reached the top.

HE'D BEEN VAGUELY hoping that it wouldn't be the same room,
but it was. It was night now, though, and the windows were open. The

warmth of the day lingered in the walls and floor, but there *was* a breeze, spicy with tree sap and the river's breath, that made the single candle flame flicker and bend. The girl waited for him to come in, then closed the door and stood with her back against it, her hand still on the knob.

"I won't hurt you," he blurted. "I didn't mean to, last time." Her hand relaxed a bit, though she continued to look narrowly at him. It was dark where she stood, and he could barely make out the gleam of her eyes. She didn't look friendly.

"You didn't hurt me," she said. "You spoilt my best petticoat, though, *and* a decanter of wine. Cost me a beating and a week's wages, that."

"I'm sorry," he said. "Truly. I'll—I'll pay for the wine and the petticoat." *Using what?* he wondered. It had belatedly occurred to him that the spare stockings in which he kept his cash had vanished with his orderly, and undoubtedly so had the cash. Well, he'd pawn something if he had to, or borrow a bit. "Can't do much about the beating. But I *am* sorry."

She made a small huffing noise through her nose but seemed to accept this. She took her hand off the doorknob and came a little way into the room, so he could see her face in the candlelight. She was very pretty, despite the look of suspicious wariness, and he felt a mild stirring.

"Well." She looked him up and down, much as she'd done when she met him in the alley. "William, you said your name is?"

"Yes." The silence lengthened a heartbeat past comfort, and he asked, almost at random, "Is your name really Arabella?"

That surprised her, and her mouth twitched, though she didn't laugh.

"No. I'm a fancy piece, though, and Madge thinks the fancies should have names like—like—ladies?" She raised a brow, and he wasn't sure whether she was questioning whether ladies had names like Arabella or what he thought of Madge's philosophy.

"I do *know* a couple of Arabellas," he offered. "One of them's six and the other's eighty-two."

"Are they ladies?" She waved a hand, dismissing the question as soon as it was asked. "Of course they are. You wouldn't know them, otherwise. Do you want me to send for wine? Or punch?" She gave him an assessing eye. "Only, if you want to do anything, I really think you'd best stay off the drink. Your choice, though." She put a hand to the tie of her petticoat in tepid invitation but didn't pull it loose. Clearly, she wasn't keen to induce him to "do anything."

He rubbed a hand over his sweating face, imagined he smelled the alcohol oozing from his pores, and wiped it on his breeches.

"I don't want wine, no. Nor do I want to . . . to do . . . well, that's not true," he admitted. "I do want to—very much," he added hurriedly, lest she think him insulting, "but I'm not going to."

She looked at him openmouthed.

"Why not?" she said at last. "You've paid well over the odds for anything you want to do. Including buggery, if that's your pleasure." Her lip curled a little.

He flushed to the scalp.

"You think I would save you from—that, and then do it *myself*?"

"Yes. Often men don't think of something until another mentions it, and then they're all eagerness to try it themselves."

He was outraged.

"You must have a most indifferent opinion of gentlemen, madam!"

Her mouth twitched again, and she gave him a look of such barely veiled amusement that the blood burned in his face and ears.

"Right," he said stiffly. "I take your point."

"Well, that's a novelty," she said, the twitch breaking into a malicious smile. "It's generally the other way round."

He breathed deeply through his nose.

"I . . . it is meant as an apology, if you like." It was a struggle to keep meeting her eye. "For what happened last time."

A faint breeze came in, ruffling the hair about her shoulders and filling the fabric of her shift so it billowed, which afforded him a glimpse of her nipple, like a dark rose in the candlelight. He swallowed and looked away.

"My . . . um . . . my stepfather . . . told me once that a madam of his acquaintance said to him that a night's sleep was the best gift you could give a whore."

"It runs in the family, does it? Frequenting brothels?" She didn't pause for a response to that. "He's right, though. Do you really mean that you intend for me to . . . sleep?" From her tone of incredulity, he might have asked her to engage in some perversion well past buggery.

He kept his temper with some difficulty.

"You can sing songs or stand on your head, if you prefer, madam," he said. "I don't propose to . . . er . . . molest you. Beyond that, your actions are quite up to you."

She stared at him, a small frown between her brows, and he could see that she didn't believe him.

"I . . . would go," he said, feeling awkward again, "but I have some concern that Captain Harkness might be still on the premises, and should he learn that you are alone . . ." And he somehow couldn't face his own dark, empty room. Not tonight.

"I imagine Ned's disposed of *him*," she said, then cleared her throat. "But don't go. If you do, Madge will send somebody else up." She took off her petticoat, with no display of coquetry or artifice in the motion. There was a screen in the corner; she went behind this, and he heard the splash of her using a chamber pot.

She came out, glanced at him, and with a brief wave at the screen said, "Just there. If you—"

"Uh . . . thank you." He did in fact need to piss fairly badly, but the thought of using her pot, so soon after her own use of it, caused him an unreasonable amount of embarrassment. "I'll be fine." He looked round, found a chair, and sat down in it, ostentatiously thrusting out his boots and leaning back in an attitude of relaxation. He closed his eyes—mostly.

Through slitted lids, he saw her observe him closely for a moment, then she leaned over and blew out the candle. Ghostlike in the darkness, she climbed into her bed—the ropes creaked with her weight—and drew up the quilt. A faint sigh came to him over the sounds of the brothel below.

"Er . . . Arabella?" He didn't expect thanks, exactly, but he did want *something* from her.

"What?" She sounded resigned, obviously expecting him to say that he'd changed his mind about buggery.

"What's your real name?"

There was silence for a minute, as she made up her mind. There was nothing tentative about the young woman, though, and when she did reply, it was without reluctance.

"Jane."

"Oh. Just—the one thing more. My coat—"

"I sold it."

"Oh. Er . . . good night, then."

There was a prolonged moment, filled with the unspoken thoughts of two people, then a deep, exasperated sigh.

"Come and get into bed, you idiot."

HE COULDN'T GET into bed in full uniform. He did keep his shirt on, with some idea of preserving her modesty and his original intent. He lay quite rigid beside her, trying to envision himself as the tomb figure of a Crusader: a marble monument to noble behavior, sworn to a chastity enforced by his stone embodiment.

Unfortunately, it was a rather small bed and William was rather large. And Arabella–Jane wasn't trying at all to avoid touching *him*. Granted, she wasn't trying to arouse him, either, but her mere presence did that without *half* trying.

He was intensely aware of every inch of his body and which of them were in contact with hers. He could smell her hair, a faint scent of soap mingled with the sweetness of tobacco smoke. Her breath was sweet, too, with the smell of burnt rum, and he wanted to taste it in her mouth, share the lingering stickiness. He closed his eyes and swallowed.

Only the fact that he needed desperately to pee made it possible to keep his hands off her. He was in that state of drunkenness where he could perceive a problem but could not analyze a solution to it, and sheer inability to think of two things at once prevented him either speaking to her or laying a hand on hers.

"What's the matter?" she whispered hoarsely. "You're wiggling like you've got tadpoles in your drawers—only you haven't any drawers on, have you?" She giggled, and her breath tickled his ear. He groaned softly.

"Here, now—" Her voice took on a tone of alarm, and she sat up in bed, twisting round to look at him. "You're not going to be sick in my bed! Get up! Get up right this minute!" She pushed at him with small, urgent hands, and he stumbled out of bed, swaying and clutching at furniture to keep from falling.

The window gaped before him, open to the night, a lovely sickle moon pale above. Taking this as the celestial invitation it surely was, he raised his shirt, gripped the window frame, and pissed into the night in a majestically arching rush of blinding bliss.

The sense of relief was so intense that he noticed nothing whatever in its wake, until Arabella–Jane seized him by the arm and pulled him away from the window.

"Get out of sight, for God's sake!" She risked a hasty glance downward, then dodged back, shaking her head. "Oh, well. It's not as though Captain Harkness was ever going to propose you for membership in his favorite club, is it?"

"Harkness?" William swayed toward the window, blinking. There was a remarkable amount of shouting and abuse coming from below, but he was having trouble in focusing his eyes and perceived nothing save the flicker of red uniforms, redder still in the light from the lantern over the establishment's door.

"Never mind. He'll likely think I did it," Arabella–Jane said, a dark note in her voice.

"You're a girl," William pointed out logically. "You couldn't piss out a window."

"Not without making a prime spectacle of myself, no," she agreed. "But 'tisn't unknown for a whore to throw the contents of her chamber pot out on someone, accidental on purpose. Well." She shrugged, went behind the screen, and emerged with the aforementioned receptacle, which she promptly upended out the open window. In response to renewed howls from below, she leaned out and shrieked several insults that a regimental sergeant would have been proud to author, before ducking back in and banging the shutters closed.

"May as well be hanged—or buggered—for a sheep as a lamb," she remarked, taking him by the arm again. "Come back to bed."

"It's only in Scotland that they bugger sheep," William said, obediently following her. "And maybe part of Yorkshire. Northumbria, too, maybe."

"Oh, really? Is Captain Harkness from one of those places, then?"

"Oh, him?" William sat down on the bed rather suddenly, as the room had begun to revolve in a stately manner round him. "No. I'd say maybe Devon, from his—his . . . speech," he concluded, pleased to have found the word.

"So they've got sheep in Devon, too, then, I suppose." Arabella–Jane was unbuttoning his shirt. He raised a hand to stop her, wondered why he should, and left the hand hanging in midair.

"Lot of sheep," he said. "Lot of sheep everywhere in England."

"God save the Queen, then," she murmured, intent on her work. The last button came free, and a faint draft of air stirred the hairs on William's chest.

He remembered then why he should have been stopping her, but she'd put her head inside the open front of his shirt and licked his nipple before he could make his arrested hand complete its motion, and when he did, it merely settled gently on her head, which was surprisingly warm. So was her breath. So was her hand, which had wrapped itself around his prick in a possessive sort of way.

"No," he said, after what seemed a very long time but could have been no more than seconds. His hand descended and closed—regretfully—over hers where it grasped him. "I . . . I meant it. I won't bother you."

She didn't let go but did sit up and regard him with an air of puzzled impatience, just visible in the lantern light that seeped through the shutters.

"If you bother me, I'll tell you to stop; how's that?" she offered.

"No," he repeated. He was concentrating fiercely now; it seemed exceedingly important that she understand. "Honor. It's my honor."

She made a small sound that might have been impatience or amusement.

"Maybe you should have considered your honor before you came to a whorehouse. Or did someone drag you inside against your will?"

"I came with a friend," he said with dignity. She still hadn't let go but couldn't move her hand, not with his clasped tightly around it. "That's . . . not what I mean. I mean . . ." The words that had come easily a moment before had slipped away again, leaving him blank.

"You could tell me later, once you've had a good think," she suggested, and he was startled to discover that she had *two* hands and knew what to do with the other one, too.

"Unhand my . . ." *Damn, what is the bloody word?* "Unhand my testicles if you please, madam."

"Just as you like," she replied crisply, and, doing so, put her head back inside his damp, smelly shirt, seized one nipple between her teeth, and sucked so hard that it pulled every last word out of his head.

Matters thereafter were unsettled but largely pleasant, though at one point he found himself rearing above her, sweat dripping from his face onto her breasts, muttering, "I'm a bastard, I'm a bastard, I'm a *bastard,* don't you understand?"

She didn't reply to this but stretched up a long white arm, cupped her hand round the back of his head, and pulled him down again.

"That's why." He came gradually to himself, aware that he was talking and evidently had been for some time, in spite of his head being cradled in the curve of her shoulder, his senses aswim in her musk (*like a sweating flower,* he thought dreamily), and her nipple a dark sweet thing an inch or two from his nose. "The only honor I have left is my word. Have to keep it." Then tears came suddenly to his eyes, with recollection of the moments just past. "Why did you make me break my word?"

She didn't answer for a while, and he would have thought she'd fallen asleep, save for the hand that roved over his bare back, gentle as a whisper.

"Ever think that maybe a whore has a sense of honor, too?" she said at last.

Frankly, he hadn't, and opened his mouth to say so, but once more his words had gone missing. He closed his eyes and fell asleep on her breast.

19

DESPERATE MEASURES

SILVIA HARDMAN STOOD regarding Jamie with a lowered brow, her lips pushed out in concentration. Finally she shook her head, sighed, and drew herself up.

"Thee means it, I suppose?"

"I do, Friend Silvia. I must be in Philadelphia as quickly as may be. And to do that, I must reach the road. I must be able to walk tomorrow morning, however haltingly."

"Well, then. Patience, fetch me thy father's special flask. And, Prudence, will thee grind a good measure of mustard seed . . ." She stepped a little closer to the bed, peering nearsightedly at Jamie's back as though to gauge the acreage. "A good handful—no, make it two; thy hands are small." She took a digging stick from the shelf near the door but hesitated before opening it. "Do not touch thy eyes or face, Pru—and by no means touch Chastity without washing thy hands first. Let Patience mind her if she cries."

Chastity was making fretful noises, though freshly fed and changed. Patience, though, had already run out the door, making Jamie wonder where her father's special flask might be. Hidden, apparently.

"Put the wean beside me," he suggested. "I can mind her for a bit."

Silvia did so without hesitation, which pleased him, and he lay face-to-face with wee Chastity, amusing them both by making faces at her. She giggled—and so did Prudence, as the pestle scraped and the hot smell of ground mustard thickened the air. He stuck out his tongue and waggled it; Chastity shook like a small jelly and put out a tiny pink tongue tip in turn, which made *him* laugh.

"What are you all laughing at?" Patience demanded, opening the door. She frowned censoriously from one sister to the other, making them all laugh harder. When Mrs. Hardman came in a few moments later with a large grubby root in her hand, they had reached the point of laughing at absolutely nothing, and she blinked in bewilderment, but then shook her head and smiled.

"Well, they do say laughter is good medicine," she remarked, when the hilarity had run its course, leaving the girls pink-faced and Jamie feeling slightly better—to his surprise. "May I borrow thy knife, Friend James? It is more suited to the purpose than mine."

This was patently true; her knife was a crude iron blade, badly sharpened, the haft bound with string. Jamie had a good ivory case knife, bought in Brest, of hardened steel, with an edge that would shave the hairs off his forearm. He saw her smile with involuntary pleasure at the feel of it in her hand

and had a momentary flash of memory—Brianna, delicately unfolding a blade of her Swiss Army knife, an air of pleased satisfaction on her face.

Claire appreciated good tools, too. But she touched tools with immediate thought of what she meant to do with them, rather than simple admiration for elegance and function. A blade in her hand was no longer a tool but an extension of her hand. His own hand closed, thumb rubbing gently against his fingertips, remembering the knife he had made for her, the handle carefully grooved and sanded smooth to fit her hand, to match her grip exactly. Then he closed his fist tight, not wanting to think of her so intimately. Not just now.

Bidding the girls stand well back out of the way, Silvia carefully peeled the root and grated it into a small wooden bowl, keeping her face averted as much as possible from the rising fumes of the fresh horseradish but still with tears streaming down her face. Then, wiping her eyes on her apron and taking up the "special flask"—this being a dark-brown stoneware bottle stained with earth (had the lass just dug it up?)—she cautiously poured a small amount of the very alcoholic contents. What was it? Jamie wondered, sniffing cautiously. Very old applejack? Twice-fermented plum brandy? It had probably started life as some sort of fruit, but it had been some time since that fruit hung on a tree.

Mrs. Hardman relaxed, putting the cork back into the bottle as though relieved that the contents had not in fact exploded upon being decanted.

"Well, then," she said, coming over to pick up Chastity, who squealed and fussed at being removed from Jamie, whom she plainly regarded as a large toy. "That must steep for a few hours. Thee needs heat. Thee should sleep, if thee can. I know thee passed a wakeful night, and tonight may not be much better."

JAMIE HAD STEELED himself to the prospect of drinking horseradish liquor with a mix of trepidation and curiosity. The first of these emotions was momentarily relieved when he discovered that Mrs. Hardman didn't mean him to drink it, but it returned in force when he found himself a moment later facedown on the bed with his shirt rucked up to his oxters and his hostess vigorously rubbing the stuff into his buttocks.

"Have a care, Friend Silvia," he managed, trying to turn his head enough to get his mouth clear of the pillow without either twisting his back or unclenching his bum. "If ye drip that down the crack of my arse, I may be cured wi' a somewhat sudden violence."

A small snort of amusement tickled the hairs in the small of his back, where the flesh was still smarting and tingling from her administrations.

"My grandmother did say this receipt would raise the dead," she said, her voice pitched low in order not to disturb the girls, who were rolled up on the hearth in their blankets like caterpillars. "Perhaps she was less careful in her applications."

"THEE NEEDS HEAT," she'd said. Between the horseradish liniment and the mustard plaster resting on his lower back, he thought he might suffer spontaneous combustion at any moment. He was sure his skin was blistering. *"I know thee passed a wakeful night, and tonight may not be much better."* She'd got that right.

He shifted, trying to turn stealthily onto his side without making noise or dislodging the plaster—she'd bound it to his lower back by means of strips of torn flannel tied round his body, but they had a tendency to slip. The pain when shifting was in fact much less, which encouraged him greatly. On the other hand, he felt as though someone was repeatedly passing a pine torch within inches of his body. And while she *had* been very careful while working the liniment into him from rib cage to knees, a bit of the ferocious liquid had touched his balls, giving him a not-unpleasant sense of remarkable heat between his legs but also an uncontrollable urge to squirm.

He hadn't, while she was working on him, and hadn't said a word. Not after seeing the state of her hands: red as a lobsterback's coat, and a milky blister rising on the side of her thumb. She hadn't said a word, either, just drawn down his shirt when she was done and patted him gently on the backside before going to wash and then smooth a little cooking grease gingerly into her hands.

She was asleep now, too, a hunched form curled up in the corner of the settle, little Chastity's cradle by her foot, safely away from the banked embers of the fire. Now and then one of the glowing chunks of wood split with a loud *crack!* and a small fountain of sparks.

He stretched gingerly, experimenting. Better. But whether he was cured in the morning or not, he was leaving—if he had to drag himself on his elbows to the road. The Hardmans must have their bed back—and he must have his. Claire's bed.

The thought made the heat in his flesh bloom up through his belly, and he did squirm. His thoughts squirmed, too, thinking of her, and he grabbed one, pinning it down like a disobedient dog.

It's nay her fault, he thought fiercely. *She's done me nay wrong.* They'd thought him dead—Marsali had told him so and told him that Lord John had wed Claire in haste following the news of Jamie's death, in order to protect not only her but Fergus and Marsali as well, from imminent arrest.

Aye, and then he took her to his bed! The knuckles of his left hand twinged as he curled his fist. *"Never hit them in the face, lad."* Dougal had told him that a lifetime ago, as they watched a knockdown fight between two of Colum's men in the courtyard at Leoch. *"Hit them in the soft parts."*

They'd hit *him* in the soft parts.

"Nay her fault," he muttered under his breath, turning restlessly into his pillow. What the bloody *hell* had happened, though? How had they done it—why?

He felt as though he was fevered, his mind dazed with the waves of heat that throbbed over his body. And like the half-glimpsed things in fever dreams, he saw her naked flesh, pale and shimmering with sweat in the humid night, slick under John Grey's hand . . .

We were both fucking you!

His back felt as though someone had laid a hot girdle on it. With a deep growl of exasperation, he turned onto his side again and fumbled at the bandages holding the scalding plaster to his skin, at last wriggling out of its torrid embrace. He dropped it on the floor and flung back the quilt that covered him, seeking the relief of cool air on body and mind.

But the cabin was filled to the rooftree with the fuggy warmth of fire and sleeping bodies, and the heat that flamed over him seemed to have rooted itself between his legs. He clenched his fists in the bedclothes, trying not to writhe, trying to calm his mind.

"Lord, let me stand aside from this," he whispered in *Gàidhlig.* "Grant me mercy and forgiveness. Grant me understanding!"

What his mind presented him with instead was a fleeting sense, a memory of cold, as startling as it was refreshing. It was gone in a flash but left his hand tingling with the touch of cold stone, cool earth, and he clung to the memory, closing his eyes, in imagination pressing his hot cheek to the wall of the cave.

Because it was his cave. The place where he'd hidden, where he'd lived, in the years after Culloden. He had throbbed there, too, pulsing with heat and hurt, rage and fever, desolation and the sweet brief consolation of dreams wherein he met his wife again. And he felt in mind the coldness, the dark chill that he'd thought would kill him, finding it now relief in the desert of his thoughts. He envisioned himself pressing his naked, scalded back to the rough damp of the cave wall, willing the coldness to pass into his flesh, to kill the fire.

His rigid body eased a little, and he breathed slower, stubbornly ignoring the ripe reeks of the cabin, the fumes of horseradish and plum brandy and mustard, of cooking and bodies washed infrequently. Trying to breathe the piercing cleanliness of the north wind, the scents of broom and heather.

And what he smelled was . . .

"Mary," he whispered, and his eyes flew open, shocked.

The scent of green onions and cherries, not quite ripe. A cold boiled fowl. And the warm smell of a woman's flesh, faintly acrid with the sweat in her clothes, overlaid by the mild, fatty smell of his sister's lye soap.

He took a deep breath, as though he might capture more of it, but the cool air of the Highlands had fled, and he inhaled a thick gulp of hot mustard, and coughed.

"Aye, all right," he muttered ungraciously to God. "Ye've made your point."

He hadn't sought out a woman, even in his most abject loneliness, living in the cave. But when Mary MacNab had come to him on the eve of his departure for an English prison, he'd found consolation for his grief in her arms. Not as replacement for Claire, never that—but only desperately needing, and gratefully accepting, the gift of touch, of not being alone for a little while. How could he possibly find it wrong that Claire had done the same?

He sighed, wriggling to find a more comfortable position. Little Chastity emitted a faint cry, and Silvia Hardman sat up at once in a rustle of clothes, bending down to the cradle with a sleepy murmur.

For the first time, the child's name struck him. The baby was perhaps three or four months old. How long had Gabriel Hardman been gone? More than a year, he thought, from what the little girls had said. Chastity, indeed. Was the name merely the natural companion to Prudence and Patience—or Mrs. Hardman's private, poignant bitterness, a reproach to her missing husband?

He closed his eyes and sought a sense of coolness in the dark. He thought he had burned long enough.

20

OF CABBAGES AND KINGS

HE WALKED TO THE road just before dawn, declining help from Prudence and Patience, though they insisted upon coming with him, in case he should fall flat on his face, be stricken with sudden paralysis, or step into a gopher's hole and twist an ankle. They had no great opinion of his powers but were well mannered enough to keep a distance of a foot or so on either side, their hands hovering like small white butterflies near his elbows, pale in the half dark.

"There's not so many wagons coming in, these last few days," Patience observed, in a tone somewhere between anxiety and hope. "Thee may not find a suitable conveyance."

"I should be satisfied wi' a dung cart or a wagon filled with cabbages," he assured her, already glancing down the road. "My business is somewhat urgent."

"We know," Prudence reminded him. "We were under the bed when Washington appointed you." She spoke with a certain reserve, as a Quaker opposed to the practice of war, and he smiled at her small, serious face, long-lipped and kind-eyed like her mother's.

"Washington is nay my greatest concern," he said. "I must see my wife, before . . . before anything else."

"Thee has not seen her in some time?" Prudence asked, surprised. "Why?"

"I was detained upon business in Scotland," he said, deciding not to observe that he'd seen her but two days ago. "Is that a wagon coming, d'ye think?"

It was a drover with a herd of swine, in fact, and they were obliged to scuttle back from the roadside with some haste, in order to avoid being either bitten or trampled. By the time the sun was fully up, though, regular traffic had begun to flow along the road.

Most of this was coming from Philadelphia, as the girls had told him: Loyalist families who could not afford to leave by ship, fleeing the city with what they could carry, some with wagons or handcarts, many with no more than what they could convey on their backs or in their arms. There were also British soldiers in groups and columns, presumably assisting the exodus and protecting the Loyalists from being attacked or looted, should Rebel militia suddenly come out of the wood.

That thought reminded him of John Grey—who had been mercifully absent from his mind for several hours. Jamie ruthlessly pushed him out again, muttering, "Aye, *stay* gone," under his breath. But a reluctant second thought occurred to him—what if Grey had been released by the militia at once and had already made his way back to Philadelphia? On the one hand, he would see to Claire's safety; he could trust the man for that. But on the other . . .

Aye, well. If he walked into the house and found Grey there with her, he'd just take her away with him and say nothing. Unless . . .

"Does thee still suffer from the horseradish, Friend Jamie?" Patience asked politely. "Thee snorts quite fearful. Perhaps thee had best take my hankie."

In the woods outside Philadelphia

GREY WOKE ABRUPTLY to full daylight and a musket barrel jabbed into his belly.

"Come out of there with your hands up," said a cold voice. He got his good eye sufficiently open as to see that his interlocutor wore a tattered Continental officer's coat over homespun breeches and an open-collared shirt, topped by a slouch hat turned up with a turkey feather through the brim. Rebel militia. Heart in his throat, he crawled stiffly out of his refuge and rose, hands in the air.

His captor blinked at Grey's battered face, then at the fetters, strips of muslin bandage hanging from the rusted links. He withdrew the musket slightly but didn't lower it. Now that Grey was on his feet, he could see several other men, as well, all peering at him with extreme interest.

"Ah . . . where did you escape from?" the officer with the musket asked carefully.

There were two possible answers, and he chose the riskier option. Saying "gaol" would have likely led to them leaving him alone or, at worst, taking him with them but leaving him in irons; either way, he'd still be wearing fetters.

"I was put in irons by a British officer who took me up as a spy," he said boldly. *Entirely true,* he reflected, *so far as it goes.*

A deep hum of interest ran among the men, who pressed closer to look at him, and the prodding musket barrel was withdrawn altogether.

"Indeed," said his captor, who had an educated English voice, with a slight Dorset accent. "And what might be your name, sir?"

"Bertram Armstrong," he replied promptly, using two of his middle names. "And may I have the pleasure of knowing your own name, sir?"

The man pursed his lips a little but answered readily enough.

"I am the Reverend Peleg Woodsworth, Captain of the Sixteenth Pennsylvania, sir. And your company?" Grey saw Woodsworth's eyes flick toward his liberty cap with its bold motto.

"I haven't yet joined a company, sir," he said, softening his own accent just a little. "I was on my way to do so, in fact, when I ran afoul of a British patrol and shortly thereafter found myself in the straits you see." He raised his wrists a little, clanking. The hum of interest came again, this time with a distinct note of approval.

"Well, then," Woodsworth said, and lifted his musket to his shoulder. "Come along with us, Mr. Armstrong, and I think we might be able to relieve your straits."

21

BLOODY MEN

ONCE THEY REACHED the trace, there were horses, mules, and wagons, as well as militia companies. Rachel was able to ride in a teamster's wagon filled with sacks of barley, Ian and Rollo trotting along beside, as far as Matson's Ford, where they were meant to meet Denzell and Dottie. They waited at the ford until midmorning, but there was no sign of Denzell's wagon, and none of the militia groups crossing there had seen him.

"He'll have had an emergency," Rachel said, lifting one shoulder in resignation. "We'd best go on by ourselves; perhaps we can find a wagon on the main road that will carry us into the city." She wasn't troubled; any doctor's family was used to fending for themselves unexpectedly. And she loved being alone with Ian, talking, looking at his face.

Ian agreed that this was good sense, and they splashed across, shoes in hand, the cold water a relief. Even in the forest, the air was close and hot, restless with prowling thunder that never came close enough to do much good.

"Here," he said to Rachel, and handed her his moccasins, his rifle, and his belt, with powder horn, shot bag, and dirk. "Stand back a bit, aye?" He could see a scour in the streambed, where a persistent eddy had carved a deep hole, a dark, inviting shadow in the ripples of the creek. He leapt from stone to stone and jumped from the last one, going into the hole with a *PLUNK!* like a dropped boulder. Rollo, belly-deep in the ford and soaked to the shoulders, barked and showered Rachel with water from a huge wagging tail.

Ian's head lunged back into view, streaming water, and he reached a long, skinny arm toward her leg, beckoning her to join him. She didn't retreat but held his rifle out at arm's length and raised one brow, and he dropped his invitation, scrambling out of the hole on hands and knees. He stood up in the ford and shook himself like Rollo, spattering her with icy drops.

"Want to go in?" he asked, grinning as he took back his weapons. He wiped water from his brows and chin with the back of his hand. "It'll cool ye right down."

"I would," she said, smearing the cold droplets over her sweating face with one hand, "if my clothes were as impervious to the elements as thine are." He had on his worn buckskin leggings and breechclout, with a calico shirt so faded that the red flowers on it were nearly the same color as the brown background. Neither water nor sun would make any difference, and he would look just the same wet or dry—while she would look like a drowned rat all day, and an immodest drowned rat at that, shift and dress half transparent with water and sticking to her.

The casual thought coincided with Ian's buckling of his belt, and the movement drew her eye to the flap of his linen breechclout—or, rather, to where it had been before he raised it to pull it over his belt.

She drew in her breath audibly and he looked up at her, surprised.

"Eh?"

"Never mind," she said, her face going hot despite the cool water. But he looked down, following the direction of her gaze, and then looked back, right into her eyes, and she had a strong impulse to jump straight into the water, damage to her wardrobe notwithstanding.

"Are ye bothered?" he said, eyebrows raised, as he plucked at the wet cloth of his breechclout, then dropped the flap.

"No," she said with dignity. "I've seen one before, thee knows. *Many* of them. Just not . . ." *Not one with which I am soon to be intimately acquainted.* "Just not . . . yours."

"I dinna think it's anything out o' the ordinary," he assured her gravely. "But ye can look, if ye like. Just in case. I wouldna want ye to be startled, I mean."

"Startled," she repeated, giving him a look. "If thee thinks I am under any illusions about either the object or the process, after living for months in a military camp . . . I doubt I shall be shocked, when the occasion a—" She broke off, a moment too late.

"Rises," he finished for her, grinning. "I think I'll be verra disappointed if ye're not, ken?"

IN SPITE OF the hot blush, which seemed to run from her scalp straight down into her nether regions, she didn't begrudge him fun at her expense. Anything that made him smile like that was balm to her own spirit.

He'd been deeply oppressed, ever since the dreadful news of the ship's sinking had come, and while he'd borne up with a stoicism she thought natural to both Highlanders and Indians, saying little about it, he hadn't tried to hide his desolation from her, either. She was glad of that, despite her own sadness for Mr. Fraser, for whom she had a deep respect and affection.

She did wonder about Ian's mother and how she might have got on with that lady. At the best, she might have had a mother again herself—and that would have been a great blessing. She hadn't been expecting the best, though; she doubted that Jenny Murray would have been any more pleased at the notion of her son marrying a Friend than a Quaker meeting might be to hear of Rachel's intention of marrying a man of blood—and a Catholic, to boot. She wasn't sure which of those would be more cause for consternation but *was* sure that Ian's tattoos would pale in contrast to his affiliation with the Pope.

"How shall we be wed, d'ye think?" Ian, who had been walking in front of her to push branches out of her way, paused and turned to let her come alongside, the path here being wide enough to walk abreast for a little.

"I don't know," she told him frankly. "I think I cannot in good conscience be baptized Catholic, no more than you in good conscience could live as a Friend."

"Do Friends marry only other Friends, then?" One side of his mouth curled. "I'd think the choice might be a bit sparse. Or d'ye all end up marrying your cousins?"

"They marry other Friends or they get put out of meeting," she told him, ignoring the gibe about cousins. "With rare exceptions. A marriage between a Friend and a non-Friend might be allowed in case of dire circumstance—after a committee on clearness had conferred with both bride and groom—but it's rare. I fear that even Dorothea may have difficulty, in spite of her very evident sincerity of conversion."

Ian laughed at thought of Denny's fiancée. Lady Dorothea Jacqueline Benedicta Grey was no one's notion of a demure Quaker—though, for that matter, Rachel thought that anyone who supposed female Friends to be demure had never met one.

"Have ye asked Denny what they mean to do?"

"I haven't," she admitted. "To tell the truth, I am somewhat afraid to ask."

Ian's feathery brows shot up.

"Afraid? Why?"

"Both on his account and ours. You know we were put out of our meeting in Virginia—or, rather, he was, and I went with him. It affected him very much, and I know he wishes above all things to marry Dottie properly, before the witness of a meeting to which they both belong."

Ian shot her a quick glance, and she knew he was about to ask if she felt likewise. She hurried on, to forestall him.

"There are other Friends in his same case, though: men who cannot abide the thought of capitulation to the King and who feel obliged to assist the Continental army. 'Fighting Quakers,' they call themselves." She couldn't help smiling at the name; it conjured such incongruous images.

"Some such held meeting now and then at Valley Forge, but they aren't accepted by Philadelphia yearly meeting. Denny has to do with them but hasn't joined them as yet."

"Aye?" The trail had narrowed again and Ian moved ahead, turning his head to speak over his shoulder so she would know he attended. She was somewhat distracted herself; the buckskin was drying slowly, molding itself damply to Ian's long, sinewy shanks, and reminding her of his breechclout.

"Yes," she said, recovering her train of thought. "The thing is—is thee familiar with religious disputation, Ian?"

That made him laugh again.

"I thought not," she said dryly. "I am. And the thing is, when a group of . . . of . . . persons who disagree with a central teaching of—"

"Heretics?" he offered helpfully. "Quakers wouldna burn folk, would they?"

"Those who are led of the spirit to follow a different path, let us say," she said, a little tersely. "And, no, they wouldn't. But the point I am making is that when such a group breaks away over some point of doctrine, they are inclined to cling even more rigorously to the rest of their beliefs and be more fierce even than the original group."

Ian's head lifted; so did Rollo's. Both hunters turned to and fro, nostrils flaring, but then shook themselves slightly and resumed walking. "Aye, so?" Ian said, reminding her of her point.

"So even if Denny should become convinced that he should belong to a meeting of Fighting Quakers, they might be that much more reluctant to accept a member such as Dottie. Though, on the other hand, should they be willing to do so, that *might* mean that they would at least consider our marriage. . . ." She tried to sound hopeful about that prospect but in truth thought pigs might fly before any meeting of Friends accepted Ian Murray—or vice versa.

"Is thee attending, Ian?" she asked a little sharply, for man and dog were still moving but with a new wariness. Rollo's ears cocked alertly and Ian shifted his rifle from shoulder to hand. Within a few steps, she heard what they had heard—the distant sounds of wagon wheels and marching feet. An army on the move, and the thought made the fine hairs prickle on her arms, in spite of the heat.

"What?" Ian turned a blank face toward her, then came to himself and smiled. "Well, no. I was wondering what a dire circumstance might be. To Friends."

Rachel had wondered that herself, if only briefly. "Well . . ." she began dubiously. In truth, she had no idea what sort of dire circumstance would make such a marriage thinkable, let alone acceptable.

"I was only thinking," he went on, before she could think of anything. "Uncle Jamie told me how it was when his parents wed. His father stole his mother away from her brothers, and they were obliged to hide where they could, for the MacKenzies of Leoch werena anything ye'd want to face, when roused."

His face was animated, telling the story.

"They couldna be marrit in kirk, for the banns couldna be called, and they'd be discovered the moment they came out of hiding to speak to a priest. So they stayed hidden until Ellen—that would be my grannie, aye?—was big wi' child, and then came out. Her brothers couldna object to the marriage at that point, and so they were wed." He shrugged. "So I was only wondering: would Friends think a coming child a dire circumstance?"

Rachel stared at him.

"If thee thinks that I will lie with thee without marriage, Ian Murray," she said, in measured tones, "thee has no notion just how dire thy own circumstances might become."

BY THE TIME they reached the main road that led to Philadelphia, the sound had grown amazingly—and so had the traffic making it. Normally a busy road, carrying travelers and wagons full of produce to and from the nearby countryside, it was all but choked now, mules braying, children shrieking, harried parents calling out for their offspring, pushing handcarts and barrows full of possessions along the road, often with a resentful pig towed alongside by a rope round its neck or a basket of chickens wobbling atop the pile.

And in, around, and through the struggling knots of civilians fleeing at footpace was the army. Marching columns, two by two, leather straps and gaiters creaking as they sweated through their coats, faces more crimson in the heat than their fading uniforms. Small platoons of cavalry, still fine on their horses, knots of green-clad Hessians, and, here and there, companies of infantry stationed at the side of the road, providing support for officers who were stopping wagons, sometimes commandeering them, sometimes waving them on.

Ian paused in the shadow of the trees, judging the situation. The sun was nearly overhead—plenty of time. And they had nothing that the army would want; no one would stop them.

He was aware of the militia companies, too. They had met several, passing through the woods. These for the most part stayed off the road, making their way carefully through the verges in ones and twos and threes, not hiding, but not drawing attention to themselves, either.

"Look!" Rachel exclaimed, her hand tightening on his arm. "It's William!" She pointed at a tall officer on the far side of the road and looked up at Ian, her face bright as sun on water. "We must speak to him!"

Ian's hand had tightened on her shoulder in response, and he felt the urgency of her flesh—but also the terrible fragility of the bones under it.

"Not you," he said, and lifted his chin toward the plodding ranks of disgruntled troops, sweating and dust-stained. "I dinna want ye anywhere in sight o' them."

Her eyes narrowed just a trifle—but Ian had been married once and took his hand off her shoulder promptly.

"I mean," he said hastily, "I'll go and talk to William. I'll bring him here to ye."

Rachel opened her mouth to reply, but he snooved his way hastily through the screening bushes before she could speak.

"Stay," he said sternly to Rollo, turning back for an instant. The dog, who had not stirred from his comfortable spot at Rachel's feet, twitched one ear.

William was standing by the roadside, looking hot, tired, disheveled, and thoroughly unhappy. As well he might, Ian thought with some sympathy. He kent William had surrendered at Saratoga; he was likely bound for England—if he was lucky—or for a long parole in some rough lodging somewhere far to the north. In either case, his active role as a soldier was over for some time.

His face changed abruptly at sight of Ian. Surprise, the beginnings of indignation, then a quick glance round, decision clamping down upon his features. Ian was surprised for a moment that he could read William's face so easily but then remembered why. Uncle Jamie guarded his own expression in company—but not with Ian. Ian's own face didn't show his knowledge, though, any more than William's now showed more than an irritable acknowledgment.

"Scout," William said, with the briefest of nods. The corporal to whom he had been talking gave Ian a brief, incurious look, then saluted William and plunged back into the trudging stream.

"What the bloody hell do *you* want?" William drew a grubby sleeve across his sweating face. Ian was mildly surprised at this evident hostility; they'd parted on good terms the last time they had seen each other—though there had been little conversation at the time, William having just put a pistol ball through the brain of a madman trying to kill Rachel, Ian, or both, with an ax. Ian's left arm had healed enough to dispense with a sling, but it was still stiff.

"There's a lady who'd like to speak with ye," he said, ignoring William's narrowed eyes. The eyes relaxed a little.

"Miss Hunter?" A small gleam of pleasure lit William's eyes, and Ian's own narrowed slightly. *Aye, well,* he thought, *let her tell him, then.*

William waved to another corporal down the line, who waved back, then he stepped off the road after Ian. A few soldiers glanced at Ian, but he was unremarkable, the double line of dotted tattooing on his cheeks, his buckskin breeches, and his sun-browned skin marking him as an Indian scout—a good many of these had deserted the British army, but there were still a good many left, mostly Loyalists like Joseph Brant, who held land in Pennsylvania and New York; there were also still some ranging parties from the Iroquois nations who had come down to fight at Saratoga.

"William!" Rachel flew across the little clearing and clasped the tall captain's hands, beaming up at him with such joy that he smiled back at her, all irritability vanished. Ian hung back a bit, to give her time. There hadn't been any, really, what with Rollo roaring and tearing at Arch Bug's miserable auld carcass, Rachel sprawled on the floor, frozen with horror, himself lying on the floor pouring blood, and half the street outside screaming bloody murder.

William had pulled Rachel to her feet and thrust her into the arms of the first woman available, who, as it happened, was Marsali.

"Get her out of here!" William had snapped. But Rachel, Ian's nut-brown maiden—her brownness much splattered with blood—had pulled herself together in an instant and, gritting her teeth—Ian had seen her do it, bemused by shock as he lay on the floor, watching things happen as though in a dream—had stepped over auld Arch's body, fallen to her knees in the mess of brains and blood, wrapped her apron tight about Ian's wounded arm and tied it with her kerchief, and then, with Marsali, had dragged him bodily out of the printshop and into the street, where he'd promptly passed out, waking only when Auntie Claire began stitching his arm.

Ian hadn't had time to thank William, even had he been able to speak, and he meant to convey his own thanks as soon as he might. But clearly Rachel wanted to talk to him first, and he waited, thinking how beautiful she looked, her eyes the clouded hazel of thicket and greenbrier, face clever and quick as flame.

"But thee is tired, William, and thin," she was saying, drawing a finger disapprovingly down the side of his face. "Do they not feed thee? I'd thought it was only the Continentals who went short of rations."

"Oh. I—I haven't had time of late." The happiness that had lit William's face while he talked with Rachel faded noticeably. "We—well, you see." He waved an arm toward the invisible road, where the hoarse chants of the sergeants rang like the calling of disgruntled crows above the shuffle of feet.

"I do see. Where is thee going?"

William rubbed the back of his hand across his mouth and glanced at Ian.

"I suppose he oughtn't to say," Ian said, coming across and touching Rachel's arm, smiling at William in apology. "We're the enemy, *mo nighean donn.*"

William looked sharply at Ian, catching the tone of his voice, then back at Rachel, whose hand he was still holding.

"We are betrothed, William—Ian and I," she said, gently pulling her hand out of his and putting it on Ian's.

William's face changed abruptly, losing its look of happiness altogether. He eyed Ian with something remarkably close to dislike.

"Are you," he said flatly. "I suppose I must wish you every happiness, then. Good day." He turned on his heel, and Ian, surprised, reached out to pull him back.

"Wait—" he said, and then William turned and hit him in the mouth.

He was lying on his back in the leaves, blinking in disbelief, as Rollo hurtled over him and sank his teeth into some soft part of William, judging by the yelp and the brief cry of startlement from Rachel.

"Rollo! *Bad* dog—and thee is a bad dog, too, William Ransom! What the devil does thee mean by this?"

Ian sat up, tenderly fingering his lip, which was bleeding. Rollo had retreated a little under Rachel's scolding but kept a yellow eye fixed on William and a curled lip raised over bared teeth, the faintest rumble of a growl coming from his huge chest.

"*Fuirich,*" Ian said to him briefly, and got to his feet. William had sat down and was examining the calf of his leg, which was bleeding through his torn silk hose, though not badly. When he saw Ian, he scrambled to his feet. His face was bright red and he looked as though he meant to either do murder or burst into tears. *Maybe both,* Ian thought in surprise.

He was careful not to touch William again but stood back a bit—in front of Rachel, just in case the man meant to go off again. He *was* armed, after all; there was a pistol and knife at his belt.

"Are ye all right, man?" Ian asked, in the same tone of mild concern he'd heard his da use now and then on his mam or Uncle Jamie. Evidently it was in fact the right tone to take with a Fraser about to go berserk, for William breathed like a grampus for a moment or two, then got himself under control.

"I ask your pardon, sir," he said, back stiff as a stick of rock maple. "That was unforgivable. I shall . . . leave you. I—Miss Hunter . . . I—" He turned, stumbling a little, and that gave Rachel time to dart round in front of Ian.

"William!" Her face was full of distress. "What is it? Have I—"

He looked down at her, his face contorted, but shook his head.

"You haven't done anything," he said, with an obvious effort. "You . . . you could never do anything that—" He swung round toward Ian, fist clenched on his sword. "But *you,* you fucking bas—you son of a bitch! *Cousin!*"

"Oh," said Ian stupidly. "Ye know, then."

"Yes, I bloody know! You could have fucking told me!"

"Know what?" Rachel looked from him to William and back again.

"Don't you bloody tell her!" William snapped.

"Don't be silly," Rachel said reasonably. "Of course he'll tell me, the minute we're alone. Does thee not wish to tell me thyself? I think perhaps thee might not trust Ian to say it aright." Her eye rested on Ian's lip, and her own mouth twitched. Ian might have taken offense at this, save that William's distress was so apparent.

"It isna really a disgrace—" he began, but then stepped hastily back as William's clenched fist drew back.

"You think not?" William was so furious, his voice was nearly inaudible. "To discover that I am—am—the . . . the get of a Scottish criminal? That I am a fucking *bastard*?"

Despite his resolve to be patient, Ian felt his own dander start to rise.

"Criminal, forbye!" he snapped. "Any man might be proud to be the son of Jamie Fraser!"

"Oh," said Rachel, forestalling William's next heated remark. "That."

"What?" He glared down at her. "What the devil do you mean, '*that*'?"

"We thought it must be the case, Denny and I." She lifted one shoulder, though keeping a close watch on William, who looked as if he were about to go off like a twelve-pound mortar. "But we supposed that thee didn't wish the matter talked about. I didn't know that thee—how could thee not have known?" she asked curiously. "The resemblance—"

"Fuck the resemblance!"

Ian forgot Rachel and hit William on the head with a double-fisted thump that knocked him to his knees, then kicked him in the stomach. Had the kick landed where he'd meant it to, it would have finished the matter right there, but William was a good deal faster than Ian expected him to be. He twisted sideways, caught Ian's foot, and yanked. Ian hit the ground on one elbow, rolled up, and got hold of William's ear. He was dimly aware of Rachel screaming and was momentarily sorry for it, but the relief of fighting was too great to think of anything else, and she disappeared as his fury surged.

There was blood in his mouth and his ears were ringing, but he had one hand on William's throat and the other stabbing forked for his eyes, when hands seized him by the shoulders and jerked him off his cousin's squirming body.

He shook his head to clear it, panting and pulling at whoever was holding him—there were two of the villains. That earned him a thump in the ribs that knocked out what little breath he had.

William wasn't doing much better. He got to his feet, wiping the back of his hand under his nose, which was bleeding profusely. He glanced at the result and grimaced in disgust, wiping the hand on his coat.

"Take him," he said, half breathless but in control of himself. One of his eyes was swelling shut, but the other gave Ian a look of straightforward bloodlust—and, despite the circumstances, Ian was once more startled at seeing one of Uncle Jamie's expressions on another face.

There was a thunderous growl from Rollo. Rachel had the big dog's scruff twisted tight, but Ian kent well enough that she couldn't hold him if he decided to savage William. *"Fuirich, a cu!"* he said, with all the authority he could summon. The soldiers would kill Rollo without a second thought if he lunged for William's throat. The dog eased back down on his haunches but stayed tensed, his lips drawn back from saliva-dripping fangs and a deep, constant growl echoing through his body.

William glanced at Rollo, then turned his back on the dog. He sniffed, hawked, and spat blood to one side, then continued, still breathing heavily. "Take him to the head of the column, to Colonel Prescott. He's under arrest for assaulting an officer; he'll be dealt with at camp this evening."

"What does thee mean, 'dealt with'?" Rachel demanded, pushing her way past the two soldiers holding Ian. "And how dare thee, William Ransom? How—how . . . how *dare* thee?!" She was white-faced with fury, small fists clenched and shaking at her sides, and Ian grinned at her, licking fresh blood from his split lip. She was paying no attention to him, though, all her ire focused on William, who drew himself up to his full height and glared down the steep bridge of his nose at her.

"This is no longer your concern, madam," he said, as coldly as a man who was red as a piece of flannel and shooting sparks out of his ears could manage.

Ian thought Rachel might actually kick William in the shins, and would have paid good money to see that, but her Quaker principles got the better of the situation and she drew herself up to her own not insignificant height— she was as tall as Auntie Claire—and thrust her chin pugnaciously up at William.

"Thee is a coward and a brute," she declared at the top of her voice. Swinging round toward the men holding Ian, she added, "And so are you brutes and cowards, to be following an order so lacking in justice!"

One of the soldiers sniggered, then coughed as he caught William's bloodshot eye upon him.

"Take him," William repeated. "Now." And, turning on his heel, stalked off. There was a broad stripe of pale road dust down the back of his coat and a good deal of it in his hair.

"Best bugger off, miss," one of the soldiers advised Rachel, not unkindly. "You don't want to be down amongst the troops, like, not on your own."

"I will not bugger off," Rachel said, narrowing her eyes at the man in a way that reminded Ian of a panther about to spring. "What does thee intend to do to this man?" She gestured at Ian, who was getting his own breath back by now.

"Rachel," he began, but was interrupted by the other soldier.

"Assaulting an officer? Probably five hundred lashes. Wouldn't hang him, I don't s'pose," the man added dispassionately. "Seeing as young Galahad's not maimed, I mean."

Rachel went even whiter at this, and Ian jerked hard at his arms, getting his feet solidly under him.

"It'll be all right, *a nighean*," he said, hoping he sounded reassuring. "Rollo! *Sheas!* But he's right—the camp's nay place for ye, and ye canna do me any good by coming. Go back to the city, aye? Tell Auntie Claire what's happened—she can speak to L—*ungk!*" A third soldier, coming out of nowhere, had hit him in the pit of the stomach with a musket butt.

"What are you lot hangin' about for? Get on! And you—" The soldier turned on Rachel and the dog, glowering. "Shoo." He jerked his head at Ian's captors, who obligingly hauled Ian around.

Ian tried to turn his head to give Rachel a final word, but they jerked him back and firmly down the road.

He stumbled along, in preference to being dragged, thinking furiously. Auntie Claire was his best chance—likely his only one. If she could make Lord John take a hand, either speaking to Willie or directly to this Colonel Prescott . . . He glanced up at the sun. Noon, more or less. And the British on the march carried out routine flogging and other punishment after the evening meal; he'd seen it now and then, and he'd seen his uncle's back now and then, too. A cold worm crawled through his sore belly.

Six hours. Maybe.

He risked another quick glance back. Rachel was running, Rollo loping alongside.

WILLIAM SWABBED HIS face with what was left of his handkerchief. His features felt foreign to him, lumped and swollen, and he explored the inside of his mouth gingerly with his tongue: no teeth missing, a couple maybe loose, and a stinging cut inside his cheek. Not bad. He thought he'd done worse to Murray and was glad of it.

He was still trembling—not with shock but with the urge to rip someone limb from limb. At the same time, he was beginning to *feel* shock, though conscious thought still came in fleeting snatches. What the devil had he done?

A short column of soldiers marched past, a few of them openly staring at him. He gave them a vicious look, and their heads snapped forward so fast he could hear the leather of their stocks creak.

He hadn't done it. Murray had attacked *him*. Where did Rachel Hunter get off, calling *him* a coward and a brute? He felt the tickle of blood crawling down from one nostril and stanched it, snorting into the filthy rag. He saw someone approaching, coming up the road, accompanied by a large dog. He straightened, stuffing the handkerchief into his pocket.

"Speak of the bloody she-devil," he muttered, and coughed, his throat raw with the iron taste of blood.

Rachel Hunter was pale with rage. Apparently she hadn't turned round to apologize for her insults. She had snatched off her cap and held it clutched in one hand—did she mean to throw it at him? he wondered in fogged amazement.

"Miss Hunter—" he began in a rasping voice, and would have bowed, save he was afraid the motion would make his nose bleed again.

"Thee cannot mean it, William!"

"Mean what?" he said, and she gave him a look that might have singed the small hairs off his body, had he not still been hot himself.

"Do not be obtuse!" she snapped. "What possessed thee, to—"

"What possessed your—your *fiancé*?" he snapped back. "Did I attack him? No!"

"Yes, you did! You struck him in the mouth, without the slightest provocation—"

"And he hit me on the head, without the least warning! If anyone is a coward—"

"Don't you dare call Ian Murray coward, you—you—"

"I'll call him what I bloody like—what he bloody *is*. Just like his goddamned uncle, goddamned Scottish bastard fu— I mean . . ."

"His uncle? Thy *father*?"

"Shut up!" he bellowed, and felt the blood surge into his face, stinging all the raw places. "Don't call him my father!"

She breathed stertorously through her nose for a moment, glaring up at him.

"If thee allow this to be done, William Ransom, I will—I will—"

William could feel the blood pool in his belly and thought he might faint, but not because of her threats.

"You'll what?" he asked, half breathless. "You're a Quaker. You don't believe in violence. Ergo, you can't—or at least won't"—he corrected himself, seeing the dangerous look in her eye—"stab me. You probably won't even strike me. So what did you have in mind?"

She did strike him. Her hand whipped out like a snake and slapped him across the face hard enough to make him stagger.

"So now thee has doomed thy kinsman, repudiated thy father, and caused me to betray my principles. What next?!"

"Oh, bloody hell," he said, and grabbed her arms, pulled her roughly to him, and kissed her. He let go and stepped back quickly, leaving her bug-eyed and gasping.

The dog growled at him. She glared at him, spat on the ground at his feet, then wiped her lips on her sleeve and, turning away, marched off, the dog at her heels casting a red-eyed look at William.

"Is spitting on people a part of your bloody *principles?*" he shouted after her.

She swung round, fists clenched at her sides.

"Is assaulting women part of thine?" she bellowed back, to the amusement of the infantrymen who had been standing still by the road, leaning on their weapons and gaping at the show provided.

Flinging her cap on the ground at his feet, she whirled on her heel and stamped away, before he could say more.

JAMIE CAUGHT SIGHT of a small group of redcoats coming down the road and slumped on the wagon's seat, hat pulled down over his eyes. No one would be looking for him, with the British army on the move, and even were he recognized, probably no one would bother trying to detain or question him in the midst of such an exodus—but the sight of British soldiers would likely put a knot in his tailbone for the rest of his life, and today was no exception.

He turned his head casually away toward the far side of the road as the soldiers passed, but then heard a loud *"Ifrinn!"* in a very familiar voice, and jerked round in reflex to find himself staring straight into his nephew Ian's startled, horrified face.

He was equally startled—and nearly as horrified—to see Ian, hands tied behind his back, smeared with dirt and blood and obviously the worse for wear, being shoved along by two cross-looking British privates, red-faced and sweating in their heavy uniforms.

He stifled his immediate urge to leap off the wagon and stared hard at Ian, willing the lad not to speak. He didn't, just goggled back with his eyes bulging out of his head and his face pale, as though he'd seen a ghost, and walked past, speechless.

"Jesus," Jamie murmured under his breath, realizing. "He thinks he *has* seen my fetch."

"Who thinks what?" asked the driver, though without much interest.

"I think I must get down here, sir, if ye'd be so civil as to stop? Aye, thanks." Without thought of his back, he swung down off the wagon; it twinged, but there was no warning stab of pain down his leg—and if there had been, he would still have gone up the road as fast as he could, because he saw a small figure a little way ahead, running like a rabbit with its tail on fire. The figure was plainly female, it was accompanied by a large dog, and he had the sudden thought that it might be Rachel Hunter.

It was, and he just managed to catch her up, seizing her by the arm as she ran, petticoats kirtled up in her arms and feet hammering the dust.

"Come with me, lass," he said urgently, grabbed her round the waist, and pulled her off the road. She uttered a stifled shriek—and then a much louder one, when she looked up and saw his face.

"No, I'm not dead," he said hurriedly. "Later, aye? Step back on the road wi' me now, or someone's going to come see am I raping ye in the bushes.

Ciamar a tha thu, a choin?" he added to Rollo, who was sniffing him industriously.

She made an odd gargling noise in her throat and continued to stare, but
after an instant blinked and nodded and they were back on the road. Jamie
smiled and acknowledged a man who had stopped in the middle of the road,
dropping the handles of a barrow he was trundling. The man looked suspiciously at them, but Rachel, after a moment's stunned bewilderment, waved
at him with a ghastly smile, and he shrugged and picked up his barrow.

"Wh-what—" she croaked. She looked as though she might collapse or
vomit, chest heaving and her face going scarlet and white and scarlet again.
She'd lost her cap, and her dark hair was matted with sweat and sticking to
her face.

"Later," he said again, but gently. "What's happened to Ian? Where are
they taking him?"

Between wrenching gasps, she told him what had happened.

"A mh'ic an diabhail," he said softly, and wondered for a split second
what—or who—he meant by that. The thought vanished, though, as he
looked up the road. Perhaps a quarter mile back, he could see the large, slow-
moving knot of evacuees, a sprawling mass of slow wagons and trudging
people, with the neat scarlet columns of soldiers splitting to flow round them,
coming on now four abreast.

"Aye, then," he said grimly, and touched Rachel's shoulder. "Dinna fash,
lassie. Get your breath and go back after Ian, but dinna get close enough that
the soldiers take notice of ye. When he's free, tell him the two of ye must
come back to the city straightaway. Go to the printshop. Oh—and best leash
the hound wi' your sash. Ye dinna want him to eat anyone."

"Free? But what—what are you going to do?" She'd got the hair out of
her eyes and was calmer, though the whites of her eyes still showed all round.
She reminded him of a young badger at bay, baring its teeth in panic, and the
thought made him smile a little.

"I mean to have a word with my son," he said, and, leaving her, strode
purposefully up the road.

HE MADE OUT William at a considerable distance. The young man
was standing at the side of the road, bare-headed, disheveled, and slightly
battered, but evidently attempting to look collected; his hands were folded
behind his back, and he appeared to be counting the wagons that passed him.
He was alone, and Jamie hastened his step to reach the lad before anyone
came along to talk to him; he needed privacy for his own conversation.

He was reasonably sure Rachel hadn't told him everything about the recent stramash and wondered whether she herself had been partly the cause of
it. She *had* said the trouble began just after she'd told William about her
betrothal to Ian. Her account had been slightly confused overall, but he'd
got the gist of it well enough, and his jaw tightened as he came up to William
and saw the look on his face.

Christ, do I look like that in a temper? he wondered briefly. It was off-putting to speak to a man who looked as though he asked nothing more of the world than the chance to rend someone limb from limb and dance on the pieces.

"Well, rend away, lad," he said under his breath. "And we'll see who dances." He stepped up beside William and took off his hat.

"You," he said baldly, not wishing to call the lad by either title or name, "come aside wi' me. Now."

The look on William's face changed from incipient murder to the same look of startled horror Jamie had just surprised on Ian's. Had matters been otherwise, he'd have laughed. As it was, he gripped William hard by the upper arm, pushed him off-balance, and had him into the shelter of a scrim of saplings before he could set his feet hard.

"You!" William blurted, wrenching loose. "What the devil are you doing here? And where is my—what have you—" He made a convulsive gesture of dismissal. "What are you *doing* here?"

"Talking to you, if ye'll close your mouth for a moment," Jamie said coldly. "Listen to me, lad, because I'm telling ye what you're going to do."

"You're not telling me *anything*," William began furiously, and cocked a fist. Jamie grabbed him by the upper arm again, and this time dug his fingers hard into the spot Claire had shown him, on the underside of the bone. William let out a strangled "Agh!" and started to pant, his eyes bulging.

"You're going to catch up the men ye sent Ian with and tell them to set him free," Jamie said evenly. "If ye don't, I go down under a flag of truce to the camp where they're taking him, introduce myself, tell the commander who *you* are, and explain the reason for the fight. Ye'll be right there beside me. Do I make myself clear?" he asked, increasing the pressure of his fingers.

"Yes!" The word came out in a hiss, and Jamie let go suddenly, folding his fingers into a fist to hide the fact that they were trembling and twitching from the effort.

"God damn you, sir," William whispered, and his eyes were black with violence. "God damn you to hell." His arm hung limp and must have hurt, but he wouldn't rub it, not with Jamie watching.

Jamie nodded. "Nay doubt," he said quietly, and went into the forest. Once out of sight of the road, he leaned against a tree, feeling sweat stream down his face. His back felt cast in cement. His whole body was trembling, but he hoped that William had been too distrait to notice.

God, should it have come to blows, I couldna take him.

He closed his eyes and listened to his heart, which was thumping like a bodhran. After a little, he heard the sound of hooves on the road, a horse galloping, and, turning to peer through the trees, caught a glimpse of William thundering past, heading in the direction Ian had been taken.

22

THE GATHERING STORM

B Y BREAKFAST ON Thursday, I'd come to the firm conclusion that it was the Duke of Pardloe or me. If I stayed in the house, only one of us would remain alive by sundown. Denzell Hunter must have come into the city by now, I reasoned; he'd call in daily at Mrs. Woodcock's house, where Henry Grey was convalescing. A very kind and capable doctor, he could easily manage Hal's recovery—and perhaps his future father-in-law would be grateful for his professional attention.

The thought made me laugh out loud, despite my increasing anxiety.

To Dr. Denzell Hunter
From Dr. C. B. R. Fraser

I am called away to Kingsessing for the day. I surrender His Grace the Duke of Pardloe to your most competent care, in the happy confidence that your religious scruples will prevent your striking him in the head with an ax.

Yours most sincerely,
C.

Postscriptum: I'll bring you back some asafoetida and ginseng root as recompense.

Post-postscriptum: Strongly suggest you don't bring Dottie, unless you possess a pair of manacles. Preferably two.

I sanded this missive, gave it to Colenso for delivery to Mrs. Woodcock's house, and executed a quiet sneak out the front door before Jenny or Mrs. Figg should pop up and demand to know where I was going.

It was barely seven o'clock, but the air was already warming, gradually heating up the city. By noon, the pungent mix of animals, humans, sewage, rotting vegetable matter, resinous trees, river mud, and hot brick would be stifling, but for the moment, the faint scent lent a piquant touch to the gentle air. I was tempted to walk, but even my most utilitarian shoes weren't up to an hour's walk on country roads—and if I waited for sundown and the cooling evening to make my way back, I'd be remarkably late.

Neither was it a good idea for a woman to be alone on the roads, on foot. Day *or* night.

I thought I could manage the three blocks to the livery stable without incident, but at the corner of Walnut I was hailed by a familiar voice from a carriage window.

"Mrs. Fraser? I say, Mrs. Fraser!"

I looked up, startled, to see the hawk-nosed face of Benedict Arnold smiling down at me. His normally fleshy features were gaunt and lined, and his usually ruddy complexion had faded to an indoor pallor, but there was no mistaking him.

"Oh!" I said, and made a quick bob. "How nice to see you, General!"

My heart had sped up. I'd heard from Denny Hunter that Arnold had been appointed military governor of Philadelphia but hadn't expected to see him so soon—if at all.

I should have left it there but couldn't help asking, "How's the leg?" I knew he'd been badly injured at Saratoga—shot in the same leg that had been wounded a short time before, and then crushed by his horse falling with him in the storming of Breymann Redoubt—but I hadn't seen him then. The regular army surgeons had attended him, and from what I knew of their work, I was rather surprised that he was not only alive but still *had* two legs.

His face clouded a bit at that, but he continued to smile.

"Still present, Mrs. Fraser. If two inches shorter than the other. Where are you going this morning?" He glanced automatically behind me, registering my lack of a maid or companion, but didn't seem disturbed by it. He'd met me on the battlefield and knew me—and appreciated me—for what I was.

I knew what he was, too—and what he would become.

The hell of it was that I *liked* the man.

"Ah . . . I'm on my way out to Kingsessing."

"On foot?" His mouth twitched.

"Actually, I had it in mind to hire a gig from the livery stable." I nodded in the general direction of Davison's stable. "Just round the corner there. Lovely to see you, General!"

"Wait a moment, Mrs. Fraser, if you would . . ." He turned his head toward his aide, who was leaning over his shoulder, nodding toward me, and saying something inaudible. Next thing I knew, the carriage door popped open and the aide jumped down, offering me an arm.

"Do come up, ma'am."

"But—"

"Captain Evans here says the livery is closed, Mrs. Fraser. Allow me to put my carriage at your service."

"But—" Before I could think of anything to complete this protest, I was handed up opposite the general and the door firmly shut, Captain Evans hopping nimbly up beside the driver.

"I gather that Mr. Davison was a Loyalist," General Arnold said, eyeing me.

"*Was?*" I said, rather alarmed. "What's happened to him?"

"Captain Evans says that Davison and his family have left the city."

They had. The carriage had turned in to Fifth Street, and I could see the livery stable, its doors hanging open—one of them pulled entirely off and lying in the street. The stable was empty, as was the stable yard—the wagon, the gig, and the small coach gone with the horses. Sold, or stolen. From the Davisons' house, next to the stable, the tatters of Mrs. Davison's lace curtains fluttered limp in a broken window.

"Oh," I said, and swallowed. I darted a quick look at General Arnold. He'd called me "Mrs. Fraser." Obviously, he didn't know what my current situation was—and I couldn't make up my mind whether to tell him. On impulse, I decided not to. The less official inquiry there was into events at Number 17 Chestnut Street, the better, whether the inquiry was British or American.

"I'm told the British kept quite a clamp on Whigs in the city," he went on, looking me over with interest. "I hope you weren't much troubled, you and the colonel?"

"Oh, no," I said. "Not really." I took a deep breath, groping for some means of diverting the conversation. "But I have been rather short of news—er, American news, I mean. Have there been any . . . remarkable developments of late?"

He laughed at that, but wryly.

"Where shall I start, madam?"

Despite my unease at meeting Benedict Arnold again, I was glad for his courtesy in offering me a ride; the air was thick with moisture and the sky white as a muslin sheet. My shift was moist with perspiration after only a brief walk; I would have been wringing wet—and likely on the verge of heatstroke—by the time I had walked as far as Kingsessing.

The general was excited, both by his new appointment and by the impending military developments. He was not at liberty to tell me what those were, he said—but Washington was on the move. Still, I could see that his excitement was much tempered by regret; he was a natural warrior, and sitting behind a desk, no matter how important and ornate, was no substitute for the bone-deep thrill of leading men into a desperate fight.

Watching him shift in his seat, hands clenching and unclenching on his thighs as he talked, I felt my uneasiness deepen. Not just about him, but about Jamie. They were quite different kinds of men—but Jamie's blood roused at the scent of battle, too. I could only hope he wasn't going to be anywhere in the vicinity of whatever battle might be impending.

The general set me down at the ferry; Kingsessing was on the other side of the Schuylkill. He got out himself to hand me down from the carriage, in spite of his bad leg, and pressed my hand in parting.

"Shall I send the carriage to retrieve you, Mrs. Fraser?" he asked, glancing up at the hazy white sky. "The sky looks untrustworthy."

"Oh, no," I assured him. "I shouldn't be much longer than an hour or two about my business; it won't rain before four o'clock—it never does at this time of year. Or so my son assures me."

"Your son? Do I know your son?" His brow wrinkled; he prided himself on his memory, Jamie had said.

"I don't think you would. Fergus Fraser, he's called; he's my husband's adopted son, really. He and his wife own the printshop on Market Street."

"Indeed?" His face lighted with interest, and he smiled. "A newspaper called . . . *The Onion?* I heard it mentioned in the ordinary where I breakfasted this morning. A Patriot periodical, I gather, and somewhat given to satire?"

"L'Oignon," I agreed, laughing. "Fergus is a Frenchman, and his wife has a sense of humor. They do print other things, though. And they sell books, of course."

"I shall call upon them," Arnold declared. "I'm quite without books, having left such belongings as I possess to follow after me. But really, my dear, how will you get back to Philadelphia?"

"I'm sure I can borrow some form of transportation from the Bartrams," I assured him. "I've been to their gardens several times; they know me." In fact, I intended to walk—I was in no hurry to return to the Chestnut Street house and my cantankerous prisoner (what the devil was I going to do with *him?* Particularly now that the British had left . . .), and it was no more than an hour on foot—but knew better than to tell him that, and we parted with mutual expressions of esteem.

It was only a quarter hour's walk from the ferry to Bartram's Garden, but I took my time about it, as much because my mind was still on General Arnold as because of the heat.

When? I wondered uneasily. When would it begin to happen? Not yet; I was almost sure of that. What was it, what would it be, that turned this gallant, honorable man from patriot to traitor? Who would he talk to, what would plant the deadly seed?

Lord, I thought in a moment of sudden, horrified prayer, *please! Don't let it be something I said to him!*

The very idea made me shudder, in spite of the oppressive heat. The more I saw of how things worked, the less I knew. Roger worried a lot about it, I knew: the *why* of it. Why were a few people able to do this? What effect— conscious or unconscious—did travelers have? And what ought they to do about it if they—we—did?

Knowing what would happen to Charles Stuart and the Rising hadn't stopped him, and it hadn't stopped our being dragged into the tragedy, either. But it had—maybe—saved the lives of a number of men whom Jamie had led from Culloden before the battle. It *had* saved Frank's life, or so I thought. Would I have told Jamie, though, if I'd known what the cost would be to him and me? And if I *hadn't* told him, would we have been dragged into it anyway?

Well, there weren't any bloody answers, no more than there had been the hundreds of other times I'd asked those bloody questions, and I heaved a sigh of relief as the gate to Bartram's Garden came in sight. An hour in the midst of acres of cool greenery was just what I needed.

23

IN WHICH MRS. FIGG
TAKES A HAND

JAMIE'S BREATH CAME SHORT, and he found that he was clenching and unclenching his fists as he turned in to Chestnut Street. Not as a means of controlling his temper—he had it well leashed and it would stay that way—but only to let out more of the energy inside him.

He was trembling with it, with the need to see her, touch her, have her tight against him. Nothing else mattered. There'd be words, there needed to be words—but those could wait. Everything could wait.

He'd left Rachel and Ian at the corner of Market and Second, to go on to the printshop to find Jenny, and he spared an instant's quick prayer that his sister and the wee Quaker might get on well together, but this vanished like smoke.

There was a burning just under his ribs that spread through his chest and throbbed in his restless fingers. The city smelled like burning, too; smoke hung under a lowering sky. He noted automatically the signs of looting and violence—a half-burnt wall, the smudge of soot like a giant thumbprint on the plaster, broken windows, a woman's cap snagged on a bush and left to hang limp in the heavy air—and the streets around him were full of people, but not those going about their business. Mostly men, many of them armed, half of them walking warily, glancing about, the rest standing in loose knots of excited conversation.

He didn't care what was happening, providing only that it wasn't happening to Claire.

There it was, Number 17; the neat brick three-story house that he'd rushed into—and out of—three days ago. The sight of it hit him in the pit of the stomach. He'd been in there perhaps five minutes and recalled every second. Claire's hair, half brushed and clouding up around his face as he bent to her, smelling of bergamot, vanilla, and her own green scent. Her warmth and solidness in his arms, his hands; he'd grabbed her by the arse, her lovely round arse so warm and firm under the thin shift, and his palms tingled with the memory of instant lust. And no more than an instant later . . .

He pushed the vision of William out of his mind. William could wait, too.

His knock at the door was answered by the rotund black woman he'd seen on his first arrival, and he greeted her in much the same way, though with not quite the same words.

"Good day to ye, madam. I've come for my wife." He stepped inside, past her open mouth and raised brows, and paused, blinking at the damage.

"What happened?" he demanded, rounding on the housekeeper. "Is she all right?"

"I expect she is, if you're meaning Lady John," the woman said, with a heavy emphasis on the name. "As to all this"—she rotated smoothly on her axis, gesturing toward the gouged, blood-smeared wall, the broken banister, and the iron skeleton of a chandelier, lying drunkenly in a corner of the foyer—"that would be Captain Lord Ellesmere. Lord John's *son*." She narrowed her eyes and glared at Jamie in a way that made it apparent to him that she knew damned well what had happened in the hallway above when he'd come face-to-face with William—and she was not at all pleased.

He hadn't time to worry about her feelings and pushed past her as politely as possible, heading up the stairs as quickly as his twitching back muscles would allow.

As he reached the top of the stair, he heard a woman's voice—but not Claire's. To his astonishment, it was his sister's voice, and he approached the farthest bedroom to see her back blocking the doorway. And over her shoulder . . .

He'd felt unreal ever since his conversation with William at the roadside. Now he was convinced that he was hallucinating, because what he *thought* he saw was the Duke of Pardloe, face contorted in annoyance, rising from a chair, clad in nothing but a nightshirt.

"Sit down." The words were spoken quietly, but their effect on Pardloe was instantaneous. He froze, and everything in his face save his eyes went blank.

Leaning forward, Jamie peered over Jenny's shoulder to see a large Highland dag in her hand, its eighteen-inch barrel trained steady on the duke's chest. What he could see of her face was white and set like marble. "Ye heard me," she said, her voice little more than a whisper.

Very slowly, Pardloe—yes, it really was him, Jamie's eyes informed his dazed mind—took two steps backward and lowered himself into the chair. Jamie could smell the gunpowder in the priming pan and thought the duke very likely could, too.

"Lord Melton," Jenny said, moving slightly so as to have him silhouetted against the dim light that filtered through the shutters. "My good-sister said that you're Lord Melton—or were. Is that so?"

"Yes," Pardloe said. He wasn't moving, but Jamie saw that he had sat down with his legs flexed under him; he could be out of the chair in one lunge, if he chose. Very quietly, Jamie edged to the side. He was close enough that Jenny should have sensed him behind her, but he could see why she didn't; her shoulder blades were pressed together in concentration, sharp-edged under the cloth as a pair of hawk's wings.

"It was your men who came to my house," she said, her voice low. "Came more than once, to loot and destroy, to take the food from our mouths. Who took my husband away"—for an instant, the barrel trembled, but then steadied again—"away to the prison where he took the ill that killed him. Move one inch, my lord, and I'll shoot ye in the guts. Ye'll die quicker than he did, but I daresay ye willna think it fast enough."

Pardloe didn't say a word but moved his head a fraction of an inch to indicate that he'd understood her. His hands, which had been clutching the arms of the chair, relaxed. His eyes left the pistol—and saw Jamie. His mouth fell open, his eyes sprang wide, and Jenny's finger whitened on the trigger.

Jamie got a hand under the gun just as it went off in a puff of black smoke, the crack of the firing simultaneous with the explosion of a china figure on the mantelpiece.

Pardloe sat frozen for an instant, then—very carefully—reached up and removed a large shard of porcelain from his hair.

"Mr. Fraser," he said, in a voice that was almost steady. "Your servant, sir."

"Your most obedient, Your Grace," Jamie replied, suffering an insane urge to laugh, and kept from it only by the sure knowledge that his sister would immediately reload and shoot him at point-blank range if he did. "I see ye're acquainted with my sister, Mrs. Murray."

"Your—dear lord, she is." Pardloe's eyes had flicked back and forth between their faces, and he now drew a long, slow breath. "Is your entire family given to irascibility?"

"We are, Your Grace, and I thank ye for the compliment," Jamie said, and laid a hand on Jenny's back. He could feel her heart going like a trip-hammer, and her breath was coming in shallow pants. Putting the pistol aside, he took her hand in both of his. It was cold as ice in spite of the temperature in the room, which was slightly hotter than Hades, with the window shuttered and boarded over.

"Would ye be so amiable as to pour out a dram of whatever's in that decanter, Your Grace?"

Pardloe did and approached warily, holding out the glass—it was brandy; Jamie could smell the hot fumes.

"Don't let him out," Jenny said, getting hold of herself. She glared at Pardloe and took the brandy, then glared at Jamie. "And where in the name of St. Mary Magdalene have *you* been these three days past?"

Before he could answer, heavy footsteps came hastily down the hallway and the black housekeeper appeared in the doorway, breathing audibly and holding a silver-inlaid fowling piece in a manner suggesting that she knew what to do with it.

"The two of you can just sit yourselves down this minute," she said, moving the barrel of the gun back and forth between Pardloe and Jamie in a businesslike fashion. "If you think you're going to take that man out of here, you—"

"I told you—I beg your pardon, madam, but would ye honor me with your name?"

"You—what?" The housekeeper blinked, disconcerted. "I—Mrs. Mortimer Figg, if it's any of your business, and I doubt *that*."

"So do I," Jamie assured her, not sitting down. The duke, he saw, had. "Mrs. Figg, as I said to ye downstairs, I've come for my wife and nothing more. If ye'll tell me where she is, I'll leave ye to your business. Whatever that may be," he added, with a glance at Pardloe.

"*Your* wife," Mrs. Figg repeated, and the barrel swiveled toward him.

"Well, now. I'm thinking that perhaps you ought just to sit down and wait until his lordship comes and we see what he has to say about all this."

"Dinna be daft, Jerusha," said Jenny, rather impatiently. "Ye ken Claire's my brother's wife; she told ye that herself."

"Claire?" exclaimed Pardloe, standing up again. He had been drinking from the decanter and still held it carelessly in one hand. "*My* brother's wife?"

"She's no such thing," Jamie said crossly. "She's mine, and I'll thank someone to tell me where the devil she is."

"She's gone to a place called Kingsessing," Jenny said promptly. "To pick herbs and the like. We've been doctoring this *mac na galladh*—" She scowled at Pardloe. "Had I kent who ye were, *a mh'ic an diabhail*, I'd ha' put ground glass in your food."

"I daresay," Pardloe murmured, and took another gulp from the decanter. He turned his attention to Jamie. "I don't suppose that *you* know where my brother is at the moment?"

Jamie stared at him, a sudden feeling of unease tickling the back of his neck. "Is he not here?"

Pardloe made a wide gesture round the room, wordlessly inviting Jamie to look. Jamie ignored him and turned to the housekeeper. "When did ye see him last, madam?"

"Just before he and you skedaddled out the attic window," she replied shortly, and prodded him in the ribs with the barrel of the fowling piece. "What have you done with him, *fils de salope*?"

Jamie edged the barrel gingerly aside with one finger. The fowling piece was primed but not yet cocked.

"I left him in the woods outside the city, two days ago," he said, a sudden feeling of disquiet tightening the muscles at the base of his spine. He backed against the wall, discreetly pressing his arse into it to ease his back. "I expected to find him here—with my wife. Might I inquire how you come to be here, Your Grace?"

"Claire kidnapped him," Jenny said, before Pardloe could speak. The duke's eyes bulged slightly, though whether at the remark or at the fact that Jenny was reloading her pistol, Jamie couldn't tell.

"Oh, aye? What did she want him for, did she say?"

His sister gave him a look.

"She was afraid he'd turn the city upside down looking for his brother and you'd be taken up in the kerfuffle."

"Aye, well, I think I'm safe enough now," he assured Jenny. "Ought ye to turn him loose, d'ye think?"

"No," she said promptly, pounding home her ball and patch. She reached into her apron and came out with a tiny powder horn. "We canna do that; he might die."

"Oh." He considered this for a moment, watching the duke, whose face had assumed a slight purple tinge. "Why is that?"

"He canna breathe properly, and she was afraid if she let him loose before he was quite over it, he'd die in the street, and her conscience wouldna let her do that."

"I see." The urge to laugh was back, but he controlled it manfully. "So ye were about to shoot him in the house, in order to keep him from dyin' in the street."

Her dark-blue eyes narrowed, though she kept her gaze fixed on the powder she was pouring into the priming pan.

"I wouldna really have shot him in the guts," she said, though from the press of her lips it was apparent that she'd have liked nothing more. "I'd just have winged him in the leg. Or maybe shot off a couple o' toes."

Pardloe made a sound that might have been outrage, but, knowing the man as he did, Jamie recognized it as smothered laughter. He hoped his sister wouldn't. He opened his mouth to ask just how long Pardloe had been held captive, but before he could speak, there was a knock at the door below. He glanced at Mrs. Figg, but the housekeeper was still regarding him with narrowed eyes and made no move either to lower the fowling piece or to go downstairs and answer the door.

"Come in!" Jamie shouted, sticking his head out into the hall, then jerking back into the room before Mrs. Figg should take it into her head that he was attempting to escape and discharge a load of buckshot into his backside.

The door opened, closed, and there was a pause as the caller apparently looked around the devastated entry, then light, quick steps came up the stairs.

"Lord John!" breathed Mrs. Figg, her stern face lightening.

"In here!" called the duke, as the steps reached the landing. An instant later, the slight, bespectacled form of Denzell Hunter appeared in the doorway.

"*Merde!*" said Mrs. Figg, bringing her shotgun to bear on the newcomer. "I mean, Shepherd of Judea! Who in the name of the Holy Trinity are *you?*"

HUNTER WAS NEARLY as pale as Jenny, Jamie thought. Nonetheless, he didn't blink or pause but walked up to Pardloe and said, "I am Denzell Hunter, Friend Grey. I am a physician, come at the request of Claire Fraser to attend thee."

The duke dropped the decanter, which fell over and disgorged the few drops it still contained onto the braided hearth rug.

"You!" he said, drawing himself abruptly to his full height. He was in fact no taller than Hunter, but it was obvious that he had the habit of command. "You are the skulking fellow who has had the temerity to seduce my daughter, and you dare come here and offer to physic me? Get out of my sight, before I—" At this point, it dawned on Pardloe that he was in his nightshirt and unarmed. Nothing daunted, he seized the decanter from the floor and swung it at Denzell's head.

Denzell ducked, and Jamie got hold of Pardloe's wrist before he could try again. Denny straightened up, fire glinting behind his spectacles.

"I take issue both with thy description of my behavior and thy slur upon thy daughter's reputation," he said sharply. "I can only conceive that the order of thy mind is deranged by illness or drugs, for surely the man who sired and reared such a person as Dorothea could not speak so meanly of her or have so little faith in her strength of character and her virtue as to think that anyone might seduce her."

"I'm sure His Grace didna mean physical seduction," Jamie said hastily, twisting Pardloe's wrist to make him let go of the decanter.

"Is it the act of a gentleman, sir, to induce a young woman to run away with him? Ow! Let go, damn you!" he said, dropping the decanter as Jamie jerked his arm up behind his back. It fell to the hearth and burst in a shower of glass, but the duke disregarded this entirely.

"A gentleman would have sought the approval of the young lady's father, sir, before ever venturing to speak to her!"

"I did," Denzell said more mildly. "Or, rather, I did write to thee at once, apologizing for having been unable to speak with thee in person beforehand, and explaining that Dorothea and I wished to become betrothed and sought thy blessing upon our desire. I doubt thee received my letter before embarking for America, though."

"Oh, thee did, did thee? Your *desire*?" Pardloe snorted, tossing a hank of loosened hair out of his face. "Will you let go of me, you bloody Scotchman! What do you think I'm going to do, strangle him with his own neckcloth?"

"Ye might," Jamie said, easing his grip but keeping hold of Pardloe's wrist. "Jenny, would ye put that pistol somewhere out of His Grace's reach?"

Jenny promptly handed the freshly loaded pistol to Denzell, who took it by reflex, then regarded the thing in his hand in astonishment. "You need it more than I do," she said, and looked grimly at the duke. "If ye shoot him, we'll all swear it was self-defense."

"We will *not*," said Mrs. Figg indignantly. "If you think I'm going to tell his lordship I let his brother be murdered in cold blood—"

"Friend Jamie," Denny interrupted, holding out the pistol. "I should feel much happier was thee to release Dorothea's father and take charge of this. I think that might increase the civility of our conversation."

"It might," Jamie said dubiously, but let go of Pardloe and took the pistol.

Denny approached the duke, edging glass shards out of the way, and looked carefully into his face.

"I will be pleased to speak and counsel with thee, Friend, and offer any reassurances that lie within my power regarding thy daughter. But thy breathing alarms me, and I would examine thee first."

The duke was in fact making a faint wheezing noise, and Jamie noted that the purple tinge to his face had become more pronounced. At Denzell's remark, this was augmented by a wash of dull red.

"You don't touch me, you qu . . . quack-salver!"

Denzell glanced round and seized upon Jenny as the most likely source of information.

"What did Friend Claire say regarding him, in terms of ailment and treatment?"

"Asthma, and joint fir brewed in coffee. She calls it *Ephedra*." Jenny replied promptly, turning to add to Pardloe, "Ye ken, I didna have to tell him that. I might ha' let ye strangle, but I suppose that's no a Christian way to carry on. Are Quakers Christians, by the by?" she asked Denny curiously.

"Yes," he replied, advancing cautiously on Pardloe, whom Jamie had forced to sit down by pressing on his shoulder. "We believe the light of Christ is present in all men—though in some cases, perceiving it is somewhat difficult," he added, under his breath but loud enough for Jamie—and the duke—to hear.

Pardloe appeared to be trying to whistle, blowing with pursed lips, meanwhile glaring at Denzell. He gasped in air and managed a few more words.

"I will . . . not be doctored . . . by you, sir." Another pause for blowing and gasping. Jamie noticed Mrs. Figg stir uneasily and take a step toward the door. "I will not . . . leave my . . . daughter in your . . . clutches—" Blow. Gasp. "If you kill me." Blow. Gasp. "Nor risk . . . you sav . . . ing my life . . . and putting . . . me in . . . your . . . debt." The effort involved in getting that one out turned him a ghastly gray, and Jamie was seriously alarmed.

"Has he medicine, Jenny?" he asked urgently. His sister compressed her lips but nodded, and, with a final glare at the duke, scurried out of the room.

With the ginger air of one embracing a crocodile, Denzell Hunter crouched, took hold of the duke's wrist, and peered closely into his eyes, these organs repaying his inspection by narrowing in the most threatening fashion manageable by a man dying of suffocation. Not for the first time, Jamie suffered a reluctant admiration for Pardloe's strength of character—though he was likewise obliged to admit that Hunter's nearly matched it.

His concentration on the tableau before him was broken by the sound of an excited fist hammering the front door below. The door opened, and he heard his nephew Ian exclaim, "Mam!" in a hoarse voice, concurrent with his sister's astonished "Ian!" Jamie stepped out of the room and, reaching the shattered banister in a few steps, saw his sister engulfed and all but obliterated by her tall son's embrace.

Ian's eyes were closed and his cheeks wet, arms wrapped tight round his small mother, and Jamie felt a sudden lump in his own throat. What would he not give to embrace his daughter that way once more?

A slight motion drew his eye, and he saw Rachel Hunter standing shyly back, smiling at mother and son, her own eyes filled with tears. She dabbed at her nose with a handkerchief, then, happening to glance up, saw Jamie above and blinked.

"Miss Rachel," he said, smiling down at her. He pointed at a jug standing on the occasional table by the door, which he assumed was Pardloe's medicine. "Might ye bring that wee jug up here? Quickly?" He could hear Pardloe's heavy breathing from the room behind him; it didn't seem to be getting worse but was still worrying.

The gasping was momentarily drowned out by the footsteps of Mrs. Figg, appearing behind him with her fowling piece. She peered over the banister at the touching scene below, then at Rachel Hunter, trotting up the stairs, jug in hand.

"And who is *this?*" she demanded of Jamie, not quite brandishing her weapon under his nose.

"Dr. Hunter's sister," he told her, interposing his body between Rachel, who looked taken aback, and the agitated housekeeper. "Your brother wants the stuff in the jug, Miss Rachel."

Mrs. Figg made a low rumbling noise but stepped back and allowed Rachel to pass. With a bleak look down at Jenny and Ian, who had now separated enough to speak and were waving their hands and interrupting each other in excited *Gàidhlig*, she vanished back into the bedroom on Rachel's heels. Jamie hesitated, wanting to rush out the front door and head for King-sessing, but a sense of morbid responsibility obliged him to follow her.

Denny had pulled up the stool from the dressing table and was still holding Pardloe's wrist, addressing him in calm tones.

"Thee is in no immediate danger, as thee likely knows. Thy pulse is strong and regular, and while thy breathing is clearly compromised, I think—ah, is this the tincture the Scotswoman mentioned? I thank thee, Rachel; will thee pour—" But Rachel, long accustomed to medical situations, was already decanting into the brandy glass some blackish-brown stuff that looked like the contents of a spittoon.

"Shall I—" Denzell's attempt to hold the glass for the duke was preempted by Pardloe's seizing the glass for himself and taking a gulp that all but choked him on the spot. Hunter calmly observed the coughing and spluttering, then handed him a handkerchief.

"I have heard it theorized that such cataclysms of breath as thee is experiencing may be precipitated by violent exercise, a rapid change of temperature, exposure to smoke or dust, or, in some cases, by a surge of violent emotion. In the present instance, I believe I may possibly have caused thy crisis by my appearance, and if so, I ask thy pardon." Denny took the handkerchief and handed Pardloe back the glass, wise enough not to tell him to sip the stuff.

"Perhaps I may make some recompense for this injury, though," he said. "I gather thy brother is not at home, since I can't suppose that he would remain absent from this gathering unless he were dead in the cellar, and I should hope that's not the case. Has thee seen him recently?"

"I have—not." Pardloe's breathing was in fact growing smoother and his face a more normal color, though the expression on it was still feral. "Have you?"

Hunter took off his spectacles and smiled, and Jamie was struck by the kindness of his eyes. He glanced at Rachel; her eyes were hazel, rather than her brother's soft olive brown and, while good-natured, were much warier. Jamie thought wariness a good thing in a woman.

"I have, Friend. Thy daughter and I discovered him in a militia camp some distance from the city. He had been taken prisoner, and—" Pardloe's exclamation collided with Jamie's, and Hunter patted the air with his hand, begging attention. "We were able to assist his escape, and, since he'd been injured during his capture, I treated him; his injuries were not intrinsically serious."

"When?" Jamie asked. "When did ye see him?" His heart had given a small, disquietingly happy lurch at the news that John Grey was not dead.

"Last night," Denny told him. "We heard of his escape this morning and heard nothing of his recapture as we made our way back to Philadelphia, though I asked each group of regulars or militia we encountered. He will have needed to go with care, both woods and roads being alive with men, but I imagine he'll be with you soon."

Pardloe drew a long, deep breath.

"Oh, God," he said, and closed his eyes.

24

WELCOME COOLNESS IN THE HEAT,
COMFORT IN THE MIDST OF WOE

THERE WAS PLENTY OF cool greenery available; the gardens covered the best part of a hundred acres, with trees, bushes, shrubs, vines, and flowers of all descriptions—and the odd exotic fungus thrown in here and there for variety. John Bartram had spent the greater part of a long life combing the Americas for botanical specimens, most of which he had hauled home and induced to grow. I regretted not having met the old gentleman; he had died a year before, leaving his famous garden in the capable hands of his children.

I found Young Mr. Bartram—he was about forty, but so called to distinguish him from his elder brother—in the center of the gardens, sitting under the shade of an immense creeper that covered half the porch of his house, a sketchbook open on the table before him, making careful drawings of a handful of pale, leggy roots that lay on a napkin.

"Ginseng?" I asked, bending to peer at them.

"Yes," he said, not taking his eyes off the delicate line of his pen. "Good morning, Lady John. You're familiar with the root, I see."

"It's fairly common in the mountains of North Carolina, where I . . . used to live." The casual sentence caught in my throat with a sudden unexpectedness. Out of nowhere, I smelled the woods on Fraser's Ridge, pungent with balsam fir and poplar sap, heavy with the musty scent of wood ears and the tang of wild muscats.

"Yes, indeed." Reaching the end of his line, he set down his pen, removed his spectacles, and looked up at me with the bright face of a man who lives for plants and fully expects the world to share his obsession. "These are Chinese ginseng; I want to see whether I might be able to persuade it to grow here—" He waved a hand toward the encompassing acres of lush garden. "The Carolina variety languishes, and the Canadian ginseng stubbornly refuses even to try!"

"How very perverse of it. Though I expect it's too hot," I observed, taking the stool he gestured me to and setting down my basket on the floor. My shift was sticking to me, and I could feel a large splotch of spreading wetness between my shoulder blades, where my hair dripped sweat down my back. "They like cold weather."

The vivid memory of the woods had blossomed into a visceral longing for the Ridge, so immediate that I felt the ghost of my vanished house rise around me, a cold mountain wind thrumming past its walls, and thought that, if I reached down, I could feel Adso's soft gray fur under my fingers. I swallowed, hard.

"It *is* hot," he said, though he himself looked as dry as one of the roots on the table, dappled with shade from his vine. "May I offer you some refreshment, Lady John? I have some iced negus in the house."

"I'd love it," I said, meaning it. "But—iced?"

"Oh, we have quite a large icehouse by the river, Sissy and I," he said proudly. "Let me just tell her . . ."

I *had* had sufficient forethought as to bring a fan with me and now pulled this out of my basket. The sense of longing had turned suddenly into a new— and wonderful—realization. *We could go home.* Jamie had been released from service with the Continental army in order to see his cousin's body back to Scotland. He'd meant, when we returned, to go back to North Carolina, reclaim his printing press, and take up arms on behalf of the revolution via the pen rather than the sword.

That plan had vanished, along with the rest of my life, when he'd been reported drowned. But now . . . A thrill of excitement ran through me and must have shown on my face, for Mr. and Miss Bartram both blinked at me as they came out onto the porch. They were twins, and while their faces bore only a faint similarity of feature, they often shared the same expression and were doing so presently, both looking slightly bewildered but pleased.

I could barely keep myself from sharing my wonderful thought with them, but that wouldn't do, and I managed to sip the negus—port mixed with hot water, sugar, and spices, then chilled to a cold—*truly* cold!—water-beaded delight—and engage in civil admiration of the ongoing improvements to Bartram's Garden, these being already famous for their beauty and variety. Old Mr. Bartram had been planning and planting and extending them for fifty years, and his children had evidently inherited the family mania, as well as the gardens.

". . . and we've improved the river path, and we've just put up a *much* bigger potting shed," Sissy Bartram was saying eagerly. "So many customers wanting potted vines and flowers for their drawing rooms and conservatories! Though I don't know . . ." Her eagerness faded a little, and she made a moue of doubt. "With all this kerfuffle—war is *so* bad for business!"

Mr. Bartram coughed a little. "It does depend on the sort of business," he said mildly. "And I'm afraid we shall have a much increased demand for the medicinals."

"But if the army is leaving . . ." Miss Bartram began hopefully, but her brother shook his head, his face growing sober.

"Does thee not feel it in the air, Sissy?" he said softly. "Something is coming." He lifted his face, as though scenting something on the heavy air, and she reached to put a hand on his arm, silent, listening with him for the sound of distant violence.

"I hadn't realized that you were Friends, Mr. Bartram," I said, to break the ominous quiet. Both of them blinked and smiled at me.

"Oh," said Miss Bartram. "Father was read out of meeting some years ago. But sometimes the habits of childhood come back when you least expect them." She lifted one plump shoulder, smiling, but with something regretful behind it. "I see you have a list, Lady John?"

That recalled me abruptly to my business, and the next hour was spent in busy exploration, discussion of the merits and drawbacks of various medicinals, the selection of dried herbs from the vast drying sheds, and cutting of fresh ones from the beds. With my sudden realization that we might return to the Ridge quite soon, and Mr. Bartram's very acute observation about the impending demand for medicinals, I bought much more than I had originally intended, replenishing not only my usual stocks (including a pound of dried Chinese joint fir, just in case. What *was* I going to do with the bloody man?), but also a good quantity of Jesuit bark, elecampane, and even lobelia, plus the asafoetida and ginseng I'd promised Denny.

In the end, there was too much for my basket, and Miss Bartram said she would put it up into a package and have one of the assistant gardeners who lived in Philadelphia bring it into the city when he went home in the evening.

"Would you like to see the river path, before you go?" she asked me, with a quick glance skyward. "It's not finished yet, of course, but we have some amazing things put in, and it is wonderfully cool at this time of day."

"Oh, thank you. I really—wait. You wouldn't have fresh arrowhead down there, would you?" I hadn't thought to put that on my list, but if it was available . . .

"Oh, yes!" she cried, beaming. "Masses of it!" We were standing in the largest of the drying sheds, and the late-afternoon light falling through the boards striped the walls with bars of swimming gold, illuminating the constant rain of tiny pollen grains from the drying flowers. There was a scatter of tools on the table, and she plucked a wooden trowel and a stubby knife from the litter without hesitation. "Would you like to dig your own?"

I laughed with pleasure. The opportunity to grub around in the wet mud wasn't an offer that most women would have made—especially to another woman dressed in pale-blue muslin. But Miss Bartram spoke my language. I hadn't had my hands in the earth in months, and the mere suggestion made my fingers tingle.

THE RIVER PATH was lovely, edged with willow and silver birch that cast a flickering shade over banks of nasturtium and azalea and the floating masses of dark-green cress. I felt my blood pressure drop as we strolled, chatting of this and that.

"Do you mind if I ask you something about the Friends?" I asked. "I have a colleague who was read out of meeting—he and his sister—because he volunteered as a surgeon with the Continental army. Since you mentioned your father . . . I wondered, how important a thing is that? Belonging to a meeting, I mean?"

"Oh!" She laughed, rather to my surprise. "I imagine it depends upon the individual—everything does, really, as a Friend. My father, for instance: he *was* read out of meeting, for refusing to acknowledge the divinity of Jesus

Christ, but he went right on going to meeting; it made no particular difference to him."

"Oh." That was rather reassuring. "What if—what is a Quaker marriage like? Would one have to belong to a meeting in order to get married?"

She thought that interesting and made low humming noises for a bit.

"Well, a marriage between Friends is . . . between the Friends marrying. No clergyman, I mean, and no specific prayer or service. The two Friends marry *each other,* rather than it being considered a sacrament administered by a priest or the like. But it does need to be done before witnesses—other Friends, you know," she added, a small crease forming between her brows. "And I think that there might be considerable objection if the Friends involved—or one of them—had been formally expelled."

"How interesting—thank you." I wondered how this might affect Denzell and Dorothea; even more, how it might affect Rachel and Ian. "Can a Friend marry a, er, non-Friend?"

"Oh, yes, of course. Though I think they would be put out of meeting as a result," she added dubiously. "But there might be special consideration for dire circumstances. The meeting would appoint a committee of clearness to look into the situation, I suppose."

I hadn't got so far as worrying about dire circumstances, but thanked her, and the conversation went back to plants.

She'd been right about the arrowhead: there *were* masses of it. She smiled happily at my amazement but then left me to my digging, assuring me that I might take some of the lotus and some Sweet Flag rhizomes, as well, if I liked. "And fresh cress, of course!" she added over her shoulder, waving a blithe hand at the water. "All you like!"

She'd thoughtfully brought along a burlap sack for me to kneel on; I spread it carefully, not to crush anything, and kirtled up my skirts out of the way as best I could. There was a faint breeze; there always is, over moving water, and I sighed in relief, both at the coolness and the sudden sense of solitude. The company of plants is always soothing, and after the incessant—well, you couldn't call it sociability, exactly, but at least the incessant *presence* of people requiring to be conversed with, directed, hectored, scolded, conferred with, persuaded, lied to—that I had experienced over the last few days, I found the rooted silence, rushing stream, and rustling leaves balm to the spirit.

Frankly, I thought, my spirit could use a bit of balm. Between—or rather, among—Jamie, John, Hal, William, Ian, Denny Hunter, and Benedict Arnold (to say nothing of Captain Richardson, General Clinton, Colenso, and the whole bloody Continental army), the male of the species had been rather wearing on my nerves of late.

I dug slowly and peaceably, lifting the dripping roots into my basket and packing each layer between mats of watercress. Sweat was running down my face and between my breasts, but I didn't notice it; I was melting quietly into the landscape, breath and muscle turning to wind and earth and water.

Cicadas buzzed heavily in the trees nearby, and gnats and mosquitoes were beginning to collect in uneasy clouds overhead. These were luckily only a nuisance when they flew up my nose or hovered too close to my face; apparently my twentieth-century blood wasn't attractive to eighteenth-century insects, and I was almost never bitten—a great blessing to a gardener. Lulled into mindlessness, I had quite lost track of time and place, and when a pair of large, battered shoes appeared in my field of view, I merely blinked at them for a moment, as I might at the sudden appearance of a frog.

Then I looked up.

"OH," I SAID, a little blankly. Then, "There you are!" I said, dropping my knife and scrambling to my feet in a surge of joyous relief. "Where the bloody hell have you *been?*"

A smile flickered briefly across Jamie's face, and he took my hands, wet and muddy as they were. His were large and warm and solid.

"In a wagon full of cabbages, most recently," he said, and the smile took hold as he looked me over. "Ye look well, Sassenach. Verra bonny."

"You don't," I said frankly. He was grubby, very thin, and he plainly hadn't been sleeping well; he had shaved, but his face was gaunt and shadowed. "What's happened?"

He opened his mouth to reply but then seemed to think better of it. He let go my hands, cleared his throat with a low Scottish noise, and fixed his eyes on mine. The smile had gone.

"Ye went to bed with John Grey, aye?"

I blinked, startled, then frowned at him. "Well, no, I wouldn't say that."

His eyebrows rose.

"He told me ye did."

"Is that what he said?" I asked, surprised.

"Mmphm." Now it was his turn to frown. "He told me he'd had carnal knowledge of ye. Why would he lie about such a thing as that?"

"Oh," I said. "No, that's right. Carnal knowledge is a very reasonable description of what happened."

"But—"

"'Going to bed,' though . . . For one thing, we didn't. It started on a dressing table and ended—so far as I recall—on the floor." Jamie's eyes widened noticeably, and I hastened to correct the impression he was obviously forming. "For another, that phraseology implies that we decided to make love to each other and toddled off hand in hand to do so, and that wasn't what happened at all. Umm . . . perhaps we should sit down?" I gestured toward a rustic bench, standing knee-deep in creamy drifts of ranunculus.

I hadn't had a single thought of that night since learning Jamie was alive, but it was beginning to dawn on me that it might quite possibly seem important to Jamie—and that explaining what *had* happened might be somewhat tricky.

He nodded, rather stiffly, and turned toward the bench. I followed, noting with some concern the set of his shoulders.

"Have you hurt your back?" I asked, frowning as I saw the care with which he sat down.

"What *did* happen?" he asked, ignoring the question. Politely, but with a distinct edge.

I took a deep breath, then blew out my cheeks in a helpless gesture.

He growled. I glanced at him, startled, having never heard such a noise from him before—at least, not aimed at me. Apparently it was somewhat more than important.

"Er . . ." I said cautiously, sitting down beside him. "What did John say, *exactly?* After telling you about the carnal knowledge, I mean?"

"He desired me to kill him. And if ye tell me ye want me to kill *you* rather than tell me what happened, I warn ye, I willna be responsible for what happens *next.*"

I looked at him narrowly. He seemed self-possessed, but there was an undeniable tension in his posture.

"Well . . . I remember how it began, at least. . . ."

"Start there," he suggested, the edge more pronounced.

"I was sitting in my room, drinking plum brandy and trying to justify killing myself, if you must know," I said, with an edge of my own. I stared at him, daring him to say something, but he merely cocked his head at me in a "Go on, then" gesture.

"I ran out of brandy and was trying to decide whether I might walk downstairs to look for more without breaking my neck, or whether I'd had enough not to feel guilty about drinking the whole bottle of laudanum instead. And then John came in." I swallowed, my mouth suddenly dry and sticky, as it had been that night.

"He did say there was drink taken," Jamie observed.

"Lots. He seemed nearly as drunk as I was, save that he was still on his feet." I could see John's face in memory, white as bone save for his eyes, which were so red and swollen that they might have been sandpapered. And the expression in those eyes. "He looked the way a man looks just before he throws himself off a cliff," I said quietly, eyes on my folded hands. I took another breath.

"He had a fresh decanter in his hand. He put it down on the dressing table beside me, glared at me, and said, '*I will not mourn him alone tonight.*'" A deep quiver ran through me at the memory of those words.

"And . . . ?"

"And he didn't," I said, a little sharply. "I told him to sit down and he did, and he poured out more brandy and we drank it, and I have not one single notion what we said, but we were talking about you. And then he stood up, and I stood up. And . . . I couldn't bear to be alone and I couldn't bear for *him* to be alone and I more or less flung myself at him because I very much needed someone to touch me just then."

"And he obliged ye, I take it."

The tone of this was distinctly cynical, and I felt a flush rise in my cheeks, not of embarrassment but of anger.

"Did he bugger you?"

I looked at him for a good long minute. He meant it.

"You absolute bastard," I said, as much in astonishment as anger. Then a thought occurred to me. "You said he desired you to kill him," I said slowly. "You . . . didn't, did you?"

He held my eyes, his own steady as a rifle barrel.

"Would ye mind if I did?" he asked softly.

"Yes, I bloody well would," I said, with what spirit I could summon up amongst the growing confusion of my feelings. "But you didn't—I *know* you didn't."

"No," he said, even more softly. "Ye don't know that."

Despite my conviction that he was bluffing, a small chill prickled the hairs on my forearms.

"I should have been within my rights," he said.

"You would not," I said, chill fading into crossness. "You didn't have any rights. You were bloody dead." Despite the crossness, my voice broke a bit on the word "dead," and his face changed at once.

"What?" I said, turning my own face away. "Did you think it didn't *matter?*"

"No," he said, and took my mud-stained hand in his. "But I didna ken it mattered quite that much." His own voice was husky now, and when I turned back to him, I saw that tears stood in his eyes. With an incoherent noise, I flung myself into his arms and clung to him, making foolish hiccuping sobs.

He held me tight, his breath warm on the top of my head, and when I stopped at last, he put me away a little and cupped my face in his hands.

"I have loved ye since I saw you, Sassenach," he said very quietly, holding my eyes with his own, bloodshot and lined with tiredness but very blue. "I will love ye forever. It doesna matter if ye sleep with the whole English army—well, no," he corrected himself, "it would matter, but it wouldna stop me loving you."

"I didn't think it would." I sniffed and he pulled a handkerchief from his sleeve and handed it to me. It was worn white cambric and had the initial "P" embroidered awkwardly in one corner in blue thread. I couldn't imagine where he'd got such a thing but didn't bother asking, under the circumstances.

The bench was not very large, and his knee was within an inch or two of mine. He didn't touch me again, though, and my heart rate was beginning to speed up noticeably. He meant it, about loving me, but that didn't mean the next while was going to be pleasant.

"It was my impression that he told me because he was sure that *you* would tell me," he said carefully.

"So I would have," I said promptly, wiping my nose. "Though I might possibly have waited 'til you'd got home, had a bath, and been fed supper. If there's one thing I know about men, it's that you don't break things like this to them on an empty stomach. When did you last eat?"

"This morning. Sausages. Dinna be changing the subject." His voice was level, but there was a good deal of feeling bubbling under it; he might as well have been a pan of simmering milk. One extra degree of heat and there'd be an eruption and scorched milk all over the stove. "I understand, but I want—I need—to know what happened."

"You understand?" I echoed, sounding surprised even to my own ears. I hoped he *did* understand, but his manner was more than a little at odds with his words. My hands were no longer cold; they were starting to sweat, and I gripped the skirt over my knees, heedless of mud stains.

"Well, I dinna *like* it," he said, not quite between clenched teeth. "But I understand it."

"You do?"

"I do," he said, eyeing me. "Ye both thought I was dead. And I ken what ye're like when you're drunk, Sassenach."

I slapped him, so fast and so hard that he hadn't time to duck and lurched back from the impact.

"You—you—" I said, unable to articulate anything bad enough to suit the violence of my feelings. "How bloody *dare* you!"

He touched his cheek gingerly. His mouth was twitching.

"I . . . uh . . . didna quite mean that the way it sounded, Sassenach," he said. "Besides, am I no the aggrieved party here?"

"No, you bloody *aren't*!" I snapped. "You go off and get—get drowned, and leave me all alone in the m-midst of spies and s-soldiers and with children—you and Fergus both, you bastards! Leave me and Marsali to-to—" I was so choked with emotion that I couldn't go on. I was damned if I'd cry, though, *damned* if I'd cry any more in front of him.

He reached out carefully and took my hand again. I let him, and let him draw me closer, close enough to see the faint dusting of his beard stubble, to smell the road dust and dried sweat in his clothes, to feel the radiant heat from his body.

I sat quivering, making small huffing sounds in lieu of speech. He ignored this, spreading my fingers out between his own, gently stroking the palm of my hand with a large, callused thumb.

"I didna mean to imply that I think ye a drunkard, Sassenach," he said, making an obvious effort to be conciliatory. "It's only that ye think wi' your body, Claire; ye always have."

With a tremendous effort of my own, I found words.

"So I'm a—a—what are you calling me now? A loose woman? A trollop? A strumpet? And you think that's better than calling me a drunkard?!?"

He gave a small snort of what might have been amusement. I yanked at my hand, but he wouldn't let go.

"I said what I meant, Sassenach," he said, tightening his grip on my hand, and augmenting it with another hand on my forearm, preventing me from rising. "Ye think wi' your body. It's what makes ye a surgeon, no?"

"I—oh." Overcoming my dudgeon momentarily, I was obliged to admit that there was something in this observation.

"Possibly," I said stiffly, looking away from him. "But I don't think that's what you meant."

"Not entirely, no." There was a very slight edge to his voice again, but I wouldn't meet his eyes. "Listen to me."

I sat stubbornly silent for a moment, but he simply held on, and I knew that he was more stubborn by nature than I could be if I worked at it for a hundred years. I was going to hear what he had to say—and I was going to tell him what he wanted to hear—whether I liked it or not.

"I'm listening," I said. He drew breath and relaxed a little but didn't lessen his grip.

"I've taken ye to bed a thousand times at least, Sassenach," he said mildly. "Did ye think I wasna paying attention?"

"Two or three thousand at least," I said, in the interests of strict accuracy, staring at the digging knife I'd dropped on the ground. "And no."

"Well, then. I ken what ye're like in bed. And I see—all too well," he added, his mouth compressing momentarily, "—how this likely was."

"No, you bloody don't," I said warmly.

He made another Scottish noise, this one indicating hesitation.

"I do," he said, but carefully. "When I lost ye, after Culloden—I kent ye weren't dead, but that made it all the worse, if ye ask me . . . eh?"

I had made a noise of my own but gestured briefly at him to go on.

"I told ye about Mary MacNab, aye? How she came to me, in the cave?"

"Several years after the fact," I said rather coldly. "But, yes, you did get round to it eventually." I gave him a look. "I certainly didn't blame you for that—and I didn't ask you for the gory details, either."

"No, ye didn't," he admitted. He rubbed the bridge of his nose with a knuckle. "Maybe ye weren't jealous. I am." He hesitated. "I'd tell ye, though—how it was—if ye wanted to know."

I looked at him, biting my lip dubiously. *Did* I want to know? If I didn't— and I wasn't at all sure whether I did or not—would he take that as evidence that I didn't care? And I was quite conscious of that brief *"I am."*

I took a deep breath, accepting the implied bargain.

"Tell me," I said. "How it was."

Now he did look away, and I saw his throat move as he swallowed.

"It . . . was tender," he said quietly, after a moment. "Sad."

"Sad," I echoed. "How?"

He didn't look up but kept his eyes fixed on the flowers, following the movements of a big black bumblebee among the furled blooms.

"Both of us mourning things that were lost," he said slowly, brows drawn down in thought. "She said she meant to keep ye alive for me, to let me . . . to let me imagine it was you, I suppose she meant."

"Didn't work quite that way?"

"No." He looked up then, straight on, and his eyes went through me like a rapier through a scarecrow. "There couldna be anyone like you."

It wasn't said with an air of compliment, more one of flat finality—or, even, of resentment.

I lifted a shoulder briefly. There wasn't much response I could make. "And?"

He sighed and looked back at his knotted hands. He was squeezing the fingers of his narrowed right hand with his left, as though to remind himself of the missing finger.

"It was quiet," he said to his thumb. "We didna talk, really, not once we'd . . . begun." He closed his eyes, and I wondered, with a small twinge of curiosity, just what he saw. I was surprised to realize that curiosity was all I felt—with, perhaps, pity for them. I'd seen the cave in which they'd made love, a cold granite tomb, and I knew how desperate the state of things had been in the Highlands then. Just the promise of a little human warmth . . . *"Both of us mourning things that were lost,"* he'd said.

"It was just the once. It didna last very long; I—it had been a long time," he said, and a faint flush showed across his cheekbones. "But . . . I needed it, verra much. She held me after, and . . . I needed that more. I fell asleep in her arms; she was gone when I woke. But I carried the warmth of her with me. For a long time," he said very softly.

That gave me a quite unexpected stab of jealousy, and I straightened a little, fighting it back with clenched hands. He sensed it and turned his head toward me. He'd felt that flame ignite—and had one to match it.

"And you?" he said, giving me a hard, direct look.

"It wasn't tender," I said with an edge. "And it wasn't sad. It should have been. When he came into my room and said he wouldn't mourn you alone, and we talked, then I got up and went to him, expecting—if I had so much as an expectation; I don't think I had any conscious thoughts. . . ."

"No?" He matched my edge with his own. "Blind drunk, were ye?"

"Yes, I bloody was, and so was he." I knew what he was thinking; he wasn't making any effort to hide it, and I had a sudden, vivid recollection of sitting with him in the corner of a tavern in Cross Creek, his taking my face suddenly between his hands and kissing me, and the warm sweetness of wine passing from his mouth to mine. I sprang to my feet and slapped my hand on the bench.

"Yes, I bloody was!" I said again, furious. "I was drunk every damned day since I heard you were dead."

He drew a deep, deep breath, and I saw his eyes fix on his hands, clenched on his knees. He let it out very slowly.

"And what did he give ye, then?"

"Something to hit," I said. "At least to begin with."

He looked up at me, startled.

"Ye hit him?"

"No, I hit *you*," I snapped. My fist had curled, without my realization, clenched against my thigh. I remembered that first blow, a blind, frenzied punch into unwary flesh, all the force of my grief behind it. The flex of recoil that took away the sensation of warmth for an instant, brought it back with a smash that flung me onto the dressing table, borne down by a man's weight, his grip tight on my wrists, and me screaming in fury. I didn't remember the specifics of what came next—or, rather, I recalled certain things very vividly but had no idea of the order in which they happened.

"It was a blur," people say. What they really mean is the impossibility of anyone truly entering such an experience from outside, the futility of explanation.

"Mary MacNab," I said abruptly. "She gave you . . . tenderness, you said. There should be a word for what this was, what John gave me, but I haven't thought of it yet." I needed a word that might convey, encapsulate.

"Violence," I said. "That was part of it." Jamie stiffened and gave me a narrow look. I knew what he was thinking and shook my head. "Not that. I was numb—deliberately numb, because I couldn't bear to feel. He could; he had more courage than I did. And he made me feel it, too. That's why I hit him."

I'd been numb, and John had ripped off the dressing of denial, the wrappings of the small daily necessities that kept me upright and functioning; his physical presence had torn away the bandages of grief and showed what lay below: myself, bloody and unhealed.

I felt the air thick in my throat, damp and hot and itching on my skin. And finally I found the word.

"Triage," I said abruptly. "Under the numbness, I was . . . raw. Bloody. *Skinned*. You do triage, you . . . stop the bleeding first. You stop it. You stop it, or the patient dies. He stopped it."

He'd stopped it by slapping his own grief, his own fury, over the welling blood of mine. Two wounds, pressed together, blood still flowing freely—but no longer lost and draining, flowing instead into another body, and the other's blood into mine, hot, searing, not welcome—but life.

Jamie said something under his breath in Gaelic. I didn't catch most of the words. He sat with his head bent, elbows on his knees and head in his hands, and breathed audibly.

After a moment, I sat back down beside him and breathed, too. The cicadas grew louder, an urgent buzz that drowned out the rush of water and the rustling of leaves, humming in my bones.

"Damn him," Jamie muttered at last, and sat up. He looked disturbed, angry—but not angry at me.

"John, um, *is* all right, isn't he?" I asked hesitantly. To my surprise—and my slight unease—Jamie's lips twisted a little.

"Aye. Well. I'm sure he is," he said, in a tone admitting of a certain doubt, which I found alarming.

"What the bloody hell did you do to him?" I said, sitting up straight.

His lips compressed for an instant.

"I hit him," he said. "Twice," he added, glancing away.

"Twice?" I echoed, in some shock. "Did he fight you?"

"No," he said shortly.

"Really." I rocked back a bit, looking him over. Now that I had calmed down enough to take notice, I thought he was displaying . . . what? Concern? Guilt?

"Why did you hit him?" I asked, striving for a tone of mild curiosity, rather than one of accusation. Evidently I was less than successful with this, as he turned on me like a bear stung in the rump by a bee.

"*Why?* Ye dare to ask me *why?*"

"Certainly I do," I said, discarding the mild tone. "What did he do to make you hit him? And *twice?*" Jamie had no problem with mayhem, but he normally did require a reason.

He made a deeply disgruntled Scottish noise, but he'd promised me honesty a long time ago and hadn't seen fit to break that promise yet. He squared his shoulders and looked at me straight.

"The first was between him and me; it was a blow I've owed him for a good while."

"And you just seized the opportunity to punch him, because it was convenient?" I asked, a bit wary of asking directly what the devil he meant by "between him and me."

"I couldna help it," he said testily. "He said something and I hit him."

I didn't say anything but inhaled through my nose, meaning him to hear it. There was a long moment of silence, weighted with expectation and broken only by the shush of the river.

"He said the two of ye hadna been making love to each other," he finally muttered, looking down.

"No, we weren't," I said, somewhat surprised. "I told you. We were both—oh!"

He did look up at me then, glaring.

"Oh," he said, the word dripping with sarcasm. "Ye were both fucking me, he said."

"Oh, I see," I murmured. "Well. Um. Yes, that's quite true." I rubbed the bridge of my nose. "I see," I said again, and thought I probably did. There was a deep friendship of long standing between Jamie and John, but I was aware that one of the pillars it rested on was a strict avoidance of any reference to John's sexual attraction toward Jamie. If John had lost his composure sufficiently as to kick that pillar out from under the two of them . . .

"And the second time?" I asked, choosing not to ask him to elaborate any further on the first.

"Aye, well, that one was on your account," he said, both voice and face relaxing a little.

"I'm flattered," I said, as dryly as possible. "But you really shouldn't have."

"Well, I ken that now," he admitted, flushing. "But I'd lost my temper already and hadna got it back again. *Ifrinn*," he muttered, and, stooping, picked up the discarded digging knife and jammed it hard into the bench beside him.

He closed his eyes then, pressed his lips tight, and sat tapping the fingers of his right hand against his leg. He hadn't done that since I'd amputated the remains of his frozen fourth finger, and I was taken aback to see him do it now. For the first time, I began to appreciate the true complexities of the situation.

"Tell me," I said, in a voice not much louder than the cicadas. "Tell me what you're thinking."

"About John Grey. About Helwater." He drew a deep, exasperated breath and opened his eyes, though he didn't look at me. "I managed there. Staying numb, as ye said. I suppose I might have stayed drunk, too, had I been able to afford it." His mouth twisted, and he folded his right hand into a fist, then looked down at it in surprise; he hadn't been able to do that for thirty years. He opened it and put his hand flat on his knee.

"I managed," he repeated. "But then there was Geneva—and I told ye how that was, too, did I not?"

"You did."

He sighed. "And then there was William. When Geneva died and it was my fault, it was a knife in my heart—and then William . . ." His mouth softened. "The bairn cut me wide open, Sassenach. He spilled my guts out into my hands."

I put my hand on his, and he turned it, his fingers curling over mine.

"And that bloody English sodomite bandaged me," he said, so low I could scarcely hear him above the sound of the river. "With his friendship."

He drew breath again and let it out explosively. "No, I didna kill him. I dinna ken if I'm glad of it or not—but I didn't."

I let out my own breath in a deep sigh and leaned against him.

"I knew that. I'm glad."

The haze had thickened into steel-gray clouds, coming purposefully up the river, muttering with thunder. I took a deep, lung-filling whiff of ozone and then another, of his skin. I detected the basic male animal, very appetizing in itself, but he seemed to have acquired a rather unusual—though savory—bouquet in addition: a faint whiff of sausage, the strong bitter scent of cabbage, and . . . yes, mustard, underlaid with something oddly spicy. I sniffed again, repressing the urge to lick him.

"You smell like—"

"I smell like a large plate of *choucroute garnie,*" he interrupted, with a slight grimace. "Give me a moment; I'll have a wash." He made as though to get up and go toward the river, and I reached out and seized him by the arm.

He looked at me for a moment, then drew a deep breath and, reaching slowly out in turn, pulled me against him. I didn't resist. In fact, my own arms went round him in reflex, and we both sighed in unison, in the sheer relief of embrace.

I would have been quite content to sit there forever, breathing the musky, dusty, cabbage-laced smell of him and listening to the thump of his heart under my ear. All the things we'd said—all the things that had happened—hovered in the air around us like the cloud of troubles from Pandora's box,—but for this one moment, there was nothing but each other.

After a bit, his hand moved, smoothing the loose, damp curls behind my ear. He cleared his throat and shifted a little, drawing himself up, and I reluctantly let go of him, though I left my hand on his thigh.

"I wish to say something," he said, in the tone of one making a formal statement before a court. My heart had quieted while he held me; now it fluttered in renewed agitation.

"What?" I sounded so apprehensive that he laughed. Only a breath, but he did laugh, and I was able to breathe again. He took my hand firmly and held it, looking into my eyes.

"I don't say that I dinna mind this, because I do. And I don't say that I'll no make a fuss about it later, because I likely will. But what I do say is that there is nothing in this world or the next that can take ye from me—or me from you." He raised one brow. "D'ye disagree?"

"Oh, no," I said fervently.

He breathed again, and his shoulders came down a fraction of an inch.

"Well, that's good, because it wouldna do ye any good if ye did. Just the one question," he said. "Are ye my wife?"

"Of course I am," I said, in utter astonishment. "How could I not be?"

His face changed then; he drew a huge breath and took me into his arms. I embraced him, hard, and together we let out a great sigh, settling with it, his head bending over mine, kissing my hair, my face turned into his shoulder, openmouthed at the neck of his open shirt, our knees slowly giving way in mutual relief, so that we knelt in the fresh-turned earth, clinging together, rooted like a tree, leaf-tossed and multi-limbed but sharing one single solid trunk.

The first drops of rain began to fall.

HIS FACE WAS open now and his eyes clear blue and free of trouble— for the moment, at least. "Where is there a bed? I need to be naked with ye."

I was entirely in sympathy with this proposition, but the question took me momentarily aback. Of course we couldn't go to John's house—or at least not in order to go to bed together. Even if John himself was in no position to object, the thought of what Mrs. Figg would say if I walked into the house with a large Scotsman and immediately ascended the stairs to my bedroom with him . . . and then there was Jenny . . . On the other hand, eager as I was, I really didn't want to be naked with him among the ranunculus, where we might be interrupted at any moment by Bartrams, bumblebees, or rain.

"An inn?" I suggested.

"Is there one where folk wouldna ken ye? A decent one, I mean?"

I knit my brows, trying to think of one. Not the King's Arms, definitely not that. Otherwise . . . I was familiar only with the two or three ordinaries where Marsali bought ale or bread—and people most assuredly knew me there—as Lady John Grey.

It wasn't that Jamie by himself needed to avoid notice anymore—but his supposed death and my marriage to John had been the subject of a tremendous amount of public interest, by reason of its tragedy. For it to become widely known that the presumably deceased Colonel Fraser had suddenly reappeared from the dead to reclaim his wife would be a subject of conversation that would dwarf the withdrawal of the British army from the city. I had a quick flash of memory—our wedding night, witnessed at close quarters by a crowd of raucously drunk Highland clansmen—and imagined a reprise of this experience, with interested commentary by the ordinary's patrons.

I glanced at the river, wondering whether, after all, a nice, sheltering bush—but it was late in the afternoon, cloudy, and the gnats and mosquitoes were hanging in small carnivorous clouds of their own beneath the trees. Jamie stooped suddenly and swept me up in his arms.

"I'll find a place."

THERE WAS A wooden thump as he kicked open the door of the new potting shed, and suddenly we were in a light-streaked darkness smelling of sun-warmed boards, earth, water, damp clay, and plants.

"What, *here?*"

It was abundantly clear that he wasn't seeking privacy for the purpose of further inquiry, discussion, or reproach. For that matter, my own question was largely rhetorical.

He stood me on my feet, turned me about, and began undoing my laces. I could feel his breath on the bare skin of my neck, and the tiny hairs there shivered.

"Are you—" I began, only to be interrupted by a terse "Hush." I hushed. I could hear then what he'd heard: the Bartrams, in conversation with each other. They were some distance away, though—on the back porch of the house, I thought, screened from the river path by a thick hedge of English yew.

"I don't think they can hear us," I said, though I lowered my voice.

"I've done wi' talking," he whispered, and, leaning forward, closed his teeth gently on the nape of my exposed neck.

"Hush," he said again, though mildly. I hadn't actually said anything, and the sound I'd made was too high-pitched to draw the attention of anything save a passing bat. I exhaled strongly through my nose and heard him chuckle deep in his throat.

My stays came loose, and cool air flooded through the damp muslin of my shift. He paused, one hand on the tapes of my petticoats, to reach round with the other and gently lift one breast, heavy and free, thumb rubbing the nipple, hard and round as a cherry stone. I made another sound, this one lower-pitched.

I thought vaguely how fortunate it was that he was left-handed, as that was the hand nimbly engaged in undoing the tapes of my skirts. These fell in a swishing heap round my feet, and I had a sudden vision—as his hand left my breast and the shift whiffed up round my ears—of Young Mr. Bartram suddenly realizing a dire need to pot up a batch of rosemary seedlings. The shock probably wouldn't kill him, but . . .

"May as well be hung for sheep as lambs," Jamie said, having evidently divined my thought from the fact that I'd turned round and was shielding my more private bits in the manner of Botticelli's Venus. "And I'll have ye naked."

He grinned at me, whipped off his own dirt-streaked shirt—he'd thrown off his coat when he set me down—and yanked down his breeks without pausing to undo the flies. He was thin enough to make this possible; the breeches hung on his hipbones, barely staying up by themselves, and I saw the shadow of his ribs beneath his skin as he bent to shed his stockings.

He straightened and I put a hand on his chest. It was damp and warm, and the ruddy hairs prickled into gooseflesh at my touch. I could smell the hot, eager scent of him, even over the agricultural fug of the shed and the lingering smell of cabbage.

"Not so fast," I whispered.

He made a Scottish sound of interrogation, reaching for me, and I dug my fingers into the muscle of his breast.

"I want a kiss first."

He put his mouth against my ear and both hands firmly on my bottom.

"Are ye in a position to make demands, d'ye think?" he whispered, tightening his grasp. I caught the faint barb in *that*.

"Yes, I bloody am," I said, and adjusted my own grip somewhat lower. *He* wouldn't be attracting any bats, I thought.

We were eyeball-to-eyeball, clasped and breathing each other's breath, close enough to see the smallest nuance of expression, even in the dimness. I saw the seriousness that underlay the laughter—and the doubt beneath the bravado.

"I *am* your wife," I whispered, my lips brushing his.

"I ken that," he said, very softly, and kissed me. Softly. Then closed his eyes and brushed his lips across my face, not so much kissing as feeling the contours of cheekbone and brow, of jaw and the tender skin below the ear, seeking to know me again past skin and breath, to know me to the blood and bone, to the heart that beat beneath.

I made a small sound and tried to find his mouth with my own, pressing against him, bare bodies cool and damp, hair rasping sweetly, and the lovely firmness of him rolling between us. He wouldn't let me kiss him, though. His hand gripped the tail of my hair at the base of my neck, cupping my head, the other hand pursuing the same game of blind man's buff.

There was a rattling thump; I had backed into a potting bench, setting a tray of tiny seedling pots to vibrating, the spicy leaves of sweet basil trembling in agitation. Jamie pushed the tray aside with one hand, then grasped me by the elbows and lifted me onto the bench.

"Now," he said, half breathless. "I must have ye now."

He did, and I ceased caring whether there were splinters in the bench or not.

I wrapped my legs round him and he laid me flat and leaned over me, hands braced on the bench, with a sound halfway between bliss and pain. He moved slowly in me and I gasped.

The rain had grown from a patter to a ringing din on the tin roof of the shed, covering any sounds I might make, and a good thing, too, I thought dimly. The air had cooled but was full of moisture; our skins were slick, and heat sprang up where flesh touched flesh. He was slow, deliberate, and I arched my back, urging him. In response, he took me by the shoulders, bent lower, and kissed me lightly, barely moving.

"I willna do it," he whispered, and held tight when I struggled against him, trying vainly to goad him into the violent response I wished—I needed.

"Won't do what?" I was gasping.

"I willna punish ye for it," he said, so softly I could barely hear him, close as he was. "I'll not do that, d'ye hear?"

"I don't frigging *want* you to punish me, you bastard." I grunted with effort, my shoulder joints creaking as I tried to break free of his grasp. "I want you to . . . God, you know what I want!"

"Aye, I do." His hand left my shoulder and cupped beneath my buttock, touching the flesh of our joining, stretched and slippery. I made a small sound of surrender, and my knees loosened.

He pulled back, then came back into me, strongly enough that I gave a small, high-pitched cry of relief.

"Ask me to your bed," he said, breathless, hands on my arms. "I shall come to ye. For that matter—I shall come, whether ye ask it or no. But remember, Sassenach—I am your man; I serve ye as I will."

"Do," I said. "*Please* do. Jamie, I want you so!"

He seized my arse in both hands, hard enough to leave bruises, and I arched up into him, grasping, hands sliding on his sweat-slick skin.

"God, Claire, I need ye!"

Rain was roaring on the tin roof now, and lightning struck close by, blue-white and sharp with ozone. We rode it together, forked and light-blind, breathless, and the thunder rolled through our bones.

25

GIVE ME LIBERTY . . .

AND AS THE SUN set on the third day since he had left his home, Lord John William Bertram Amstrong Grey found himself once more a free man, with a full belly, a swimming head, a badly mended musket, and severely chafed wrists, standing before the Reverend Peleg Woodsworth, right hand uplifted, reciting as prompted:

"I, Bertram Armstrong, swear to be true to the United States of America, and to serve them honestly and faithfully against all their enemies and opposers whatsoever, and to observe and obey the orders of the Continental Congress and the orders of the generals and officers set over me by them."

Bloody hell, he thought. *What next?*

PART TWO

Meanwhile, Back at the Ranch . . .

26

A STEP INTO THE DARK

Craigh na Dun

October 30, 1980
Craigh na Dun

A BLOTCH OF SWEAT darkened the shirt between William Buccleigh's shoulder blades; the day was cool, but it was a steep climb to the top of Craigh na Dun—and the thought of what awaited them at the top was enough to make anybody sweat.

"Ye haven't got to come," Roger said to Buccleigh's back.

"Get stuffed," his great-great-great-great-great-grandfather replied briefly. Buck spoke absentmindedly, though, all his attention, like Roger's, focused on the distant crest of the hill.

Roger could hear the stones from here. A low, sullen buzz, like a hive of hostile bees. He felt the sound move, crawling under his skin, and scratched viciously at his elbow, as though he could root it out.

"Ye've got the stones, aye?" Buck stopped, clinging one-handed to a birch sapling as he looked back over his shoulder.

"I have," Roger said shortly. "D'ye want yours now?"

Buck shook his head and wiped shaggy fair hair off his brow with the back of his free hand.

"Time enough," he said, and began to climb again.

Roger knew the diamonds were there—he knew Buck knew, too—but put a hand into his jacket pocket anyway. Two rough pieces of metal clinked together, the halves of an old brooch Brianna had cut apart with the poultry shears, each half with a scatter of tiny diamonds, barely more than chips. He hoped to God they'd be enough. If not—

The day was only cool, but a bone-deep shudder ran through him. He'd done it twice—three times, if he counted the first attempt, the one that had almost killed him. It got worse each time. He'd thought he wouldn't make it the last time, coming back on Ocracoke, mind and body shredding in that place that was neither place nor passage. It had only been the feel of Jem in his arms that made him hold on, come through. And it was only the need to find Jem now that would make him do it again.

A hydroelectric tunnel
under the Loch Errochty dam

HE MUST BE getting near the end of the tunnel. Jem could tell by the way the air pushed back against his face. All he could see was the red light on the service train's dashboard—did you call it a dashboard on a train? he wondered. He didn't want to stop, because that meant he'd have to get out of the train, into the dark. But the train was running out of track, so there wasn't much else he could do.

He pulled back a bit on the lever that made the train go, and it slowed down. More. Just a little more, and the lever clicked into a kind of slot and the train stopped with a small jerk that made him stumble and grab the edge of the cab.

An electric train didn't make any engine noise, but the wheels rattled on the track and the train made squeaks and clunks as it moved. When it stopped, the noise stopped, too. It was really quiet.

"Hey!" he said out loud, because he didn't want to listen to his heart beating. The sound echoed, and he looked up, startled. Mam had said the tunnel was really high, more than thirty feet, but he'd forgotten that. The idea that there was a lot of empty space hanging over him that he couldn't see bothered him a lot. He swallowed and stepped out of the tiny engine, holding on to the frame with one hand.

"Hey!" he shouted at the invisible ceiling. "Are there any bats up there?"

Silence. He'd kind of been hoping there *were* bats. He wasn't afraid of them—there were bats in the old broch, and he liked to sit and watch them come out to hunt in the summer evenings. But he was alone. Except for the dark.

His hands were sweating. He let go of the metal cab and scrubbed both hands on his jeans. Now he could hear himself breathing, too.

"Crap," he whispered under his breath. That made him feel better, so he said it again. Maybe he ought to be praying, instead, but he didn't feel like that, not yet.

There was a door, Mam said. At the end of the tunnel. It led into the service chamber, where the big turbines could be lifted up from the dam if they needed fixing. Would the door be locked?

Suddenly he realized that he'd stepped away from the train and he didn't know whether he was facing the end of the tunnel or back the way he'd come. In a panic, he blundered to and fro, hands out, looking for the train. He tripped over part of the track and fell, sprawling. He lay there for a second, saying, "Crap-*crap-crap-crap-crap!*" because he'd skinned both knees and the palm of his hand, but he was okay, really, and now he knew where the track was, so he could follow it and not get lost.

He got up, wiped his nose, and shuffled slowly along, kicking the track every few steps to be sure he stayed with it. He thought he was in front of where the train had stopped, so it didn't really matter which way he was going—either he'd find the train or he'd find the end of the tunnel. And then the door. If it *was* locked, maybe—

Something like an electric shock ran right through him. He gasped and fell over backward. The only thing in his mind was the idea that somebody had hit him with a lightsaber like Luke Skywalker's, and for a minute he thought maybe whoever it was had cut off his head.

He couldn't feel his body, but he could see in his mind his body lying bleeding in the dark and his head sitting right there on the train tracks in the dark, and his head couldn't see his body or even know it wasn't attached anymore. He made a breathless kind of a noise that was trying to be a scream, but it made his stomach move and he felt that, he *felt* it, and suddenly he felt a lot more like praying.

"Deo . . . gratias!" he managed to gasp. It was what Grandda said when he talked about a fight or killing something, and this wasn't quite that sort of thing, but it seemed like a good thing to say anyway.

Now he could feel all of himself again, but he sat up and grabbed his neck, just to be sure his head was still on. His skin was jumping in the weirdest way. Like a horse's does when a horsefly bites it, but all over. He swallowed and tasted sugared silver and he gasped again, because now he knew what had hit him. Sort of.

This wasn't quite like it had been when they'd all walked into the rocks on Ocracoke. One minute he'd been in his father's arms, and the next minute it was as if he'd been scattered everywhere in little wiggly pieces like the spilled quicksilver in Grannie's surgery. Then he was back together again, and Da was still holding him tight enough to squeeze his breath out, and he could hear Da sobbing and that scared him, and he had a funny taste in his mouth and little pieces of him were still wiggling around trying to get away but they were trapped inside his skin . . .

Yeah. That was what was making his skin jump now, and he breathed easier, knowing what it was. That was okay, then; he was okay; it would stop.

It was stopping already, the twitchy feeling going away. He still felt kind of shaky, but he stood up. Careful, because he didn't know where it was.

Wait—he *did* know. He knew exactly.

"That's weird," he said, out loud without really noticing, because he wasn't scared by the dark anymore; it wasn't important.

He couldn't *see* it, not with his eyes, not exactly. He squinted, trying to think how he *was* seeing it, but there wasn't a word for what he was doing. Kind of like hearing or smelling or touching, but not really any of those.

But he knew where it was. It was right *there,* a kind of . . . shiver . . . in the air, and when he stared at it, he had a feeling in the back of his mind like pretty sparkly things, like sun on the sea and the way a candle flame looked when it shone through a ruby, but he knew he wasn't really *seeing* anything like that.

It went all the way across the tunnel, and up to the high roof, too, he could tell. But it wasn't thick at all; it was thin as air.

He guessed that was why it hadn't swallowed him like the thing in the rocks on Ocracoke had. At least . . . he thought it hadn't and, for an instant, worried that maybe he'd gone sometime else. But he didn't think so. The tunnel felt just the same, and so did he, now that his skin had stopped jumping. When they'd done it, on Ocracoke, he'd known right away it was different.

He stood there for a minute, just looking and thinking, and then shook his head and turned around, feeling with his foot for the track. He wasn't going back through *that*, no matter what. He'd just have to hope the door wasn't locked.

The laird's study,
Lallybroch estate

BRIANNA'S HAND closed on the letter opener, but even as she calculated the distance involved, the obstacle of the desk between Rob Cameron and herself, and the flimsiness of the wooden blade, she was reluctantly concluding that she couldn't kill the bastard. Not yet.

"Where's my son?"

"He's okay."

She stood up suddenly, and he jerked a little in reflex. His face flushed and he hardened his expression.

"He'd bloody well *better* be okay," she snapped. "I said, where is he?"

"Oh, no, hen," he said, rocking back on his heels, affecting nonchalance. "That's no how we're playing it. Not tonight."

God, why didn't Roger keep a hammer or a chisel or something *useful* in his desk drawer? Did he expect her to *staple* this jerk? She braced herself, both hands flat on the desk, to keep from leaping over it and going for his throat.

"I'm not playing," she said through her teeth. "And neither are you. *Where's Jemmy?*"

He leveled a long finger at her.

"You're no longer the boss lady, *Ms.* MacKenzie. I call the shots now."

"Oh, you think so, do you?" she asked, as mildly as she could. Her thoughts were slipping past like grains of sand in an hourglass, a slithering cascade of *what if, how, shall I, no, yes . . .*

"I do, aye." His color, already high, rose higher, and he licked his lips. "Ye're gonna find out what it's like to be on the bottom, hen."

Cameron's eyes were very bright, and his hair was clipped so short that she could see beads of sweat glittering above his ears. Was he high on something? She thought not. He was wearing track pants, and his fingers flicked unconsciously across the front, where a substantial bulge was beginning to show. Her lips tightened at the sight.

Not on your life, buddy.

She widened her gaze as much as possible, to take him in without letting his eyes move from hers. She didn't *think* he was armed, though the pockets of his jacket had stuff in them. He really thought he could make her have sex with him, without a set of manacles and a sledgehammer?

He twirled his finger, pointing to the floor in front of him.

"Come round here, hen," he said softly. "And take your jeans down. Might do ye good to learn what it's like to take it up the arse regularly. Ye've done it to me for months—fair's fair, isn't it?"

Very slowly, she came around the desk but stopped well short of him, keeping out of reach. She fumbled cold-fingered at the button of her fly, unwilling to look down, unwilling to take her eyes off him. Her heart was beating so hard in her ears that she could barely hear his heavy breathing.

The tip of his tongue showed briefly, involuntarily, as she pushed the jeans down over her hips, and he swallowed.

"The knickers, too," he said, half breathless. "Take them off."

"You don't rape people very often, do you?" she said rudely, stepping out of the puddled jeans. "What's your rush?" She bent and picked the heavy denim pants up, shook out the legs, and turned as though to lay them on the desk. Then whipped back, clutching the jeans at the ankle, and lashed them as hard as she could at his head.

The heavy cloth with its zipper and brass fly button struck him full in the face, and he staggered back with a grunt of surprise, clutching at the jeans. She let go of them instantly, leapt onto the desk, and launched herself at him, shoulder-first.

They fell together with a crash that shook the hardwood floor, but she landed on top, kneed him hard in the belly, and then grabbed him by both ears and thumped his head on the floor as hard as she could. He let out a cry of pain, reached for her wrists, and she promptly let go of his ears, leaned backward, and grabbed for his crotch.

Had she been able to get a decent grip on his balls through the soft fabric, she would have crushed them. As it was, she managed a glancing squeeze but one hard enough to make him yelp and convulse, nearly dislodging her from her perch.

She couldn't win a fistfight. Couldn't let him hit her. She scrambled to her feet, looking wildly round the office for something heavy to hit him with, seized the wooden letter box, and smashed it over his head as he started to rise. He didn't fall down but bobbed his head, dazed amongst the cascade of letters, and she kicked him in the jaw as hard as she could, her own teeth clenched. It was a sliding, sweaty impact, but she'd hurt him.

She'd hurt herself, too, had kicked him with her heel, as much as she could, but she felt a burst of pain in the middle of her foot; she'd torn or broken something, but it didn't matter.

Cameron shook his head violently, trying to clear it. He was on his hands and knees now, crawling toward her, reaching for her leg, and she backed up against the desk. With a banshee shriek, she kneed him in the face, squirmed out of his grasp, and ran for the hall, limping heavily.

There were weapons on the walls of the foyer, a few targes and broadswords kept for ornament, but all hung high, to be out of the children's reach. There was a better one easily to hand, though. She reached behind the coat rack and grabbed Jem's cricket bat.

You can't kill him, she kept thinking, dimly surprised at the fact that her mind was still working. *Don't kill him. Not yet. Not 'til he says where Jemmy is.*

"Fucking . . . *bitch*!" He was nearly on her, panting, half blinded by blood running down his forehead, half sobbing through the blood pouring from his nose. "Fuck you, split you open, fuck you up the—"

"*Caisteal DOOON!*" she bellowed, and, stepping out from behind the coat rack, swung the bat in a scything arc that caught him in the ribs. He made a gurgling noise and folded, arms across his middle. She took a deep breath, swung the bat as high as she could, and brought it down with all her strength on the crown of his head.

The shock of it vibrated up her arms to her shoulders and she dropped the bat with a *clunk* and stood there gasping, trembling and drenched with sweat.

"Mummy?" said a tiny, quavering voice from the foot of the stair. "Why is you not got pants on, Mummy?"

THANK GOD FOR instinct was her first coherent thought. She'd crossed the length of the foyer, snatched Mandy up in her arms, and was patting her comfortingly before any sort of conscious decision to move had been made.

"Pants?" she said, eyeing the limp form of Rob Cameron. He hadn't twitched since he'd fallen, but she didn't think she'd killed him. She'd have to take more-certain steps to neutralize him, and fast. "Oh, pants. I was just getting ready for bed when this naughty man showed up."

"Oh." Mandy leaned out of her arms, peering at Cameron. "Iss Mr. Rob! Iss a burglar? Iss a bad man?"

"Yes, both," Brianna said, deliberately casual. Mandy's speech showed the sibilance it had when she got excited or upset, but the little girl seemed to be recovering pretty fast from the shock of seeing her mother crown a burglar in the front hall while wearing only a T-shirt and underpants. The thought made her want to stomp on Cameron's balls, but she choked it back. No time for that.

Mandy clung to her neck, but Brianna set her firmly on the stairs.

"Mummy wants you to stay here, *a ghraidh*. I have to put Mr. Rob someplace safe, where he can't do anything bad."

"No!" Mandy cried, seeing her mother head toward the crumpled Cameron, but Brianna waved in what she hoped was a reassuring manner, picked up the cricket bat as insurance, and nudged her prisoner in the ribs with a cautious toe. He wobbled but didn't stir. Just in case, she moved round behind him and prodded him rudely between the buttocks with the cricket bat, which made Mandy giggle. He didn't move, and she drew a deep breath for the first time in what seemed like hours.

Going back to the stairs, she gave Mandy the bat to hold and smiled at her. She pushed a strand of sweaty hair behind her ear.

"Okay. We're going to put Mr. Rob in the priest's hole. You go and open the door for Mummy, all right?"

"I hit him?" Mandy asked hopefully, clutching the bat.

"No, I don't think you need to do that, darling. Just open the door."

Her work tote was hanging from the coat rack, the big roll of duct tape easily to hand. She trussed Cameron's ankles and wrists, a dozen turns each, then bent and, clutching him by the ankles, dragged him toward the swinging baize door at the far end of the hall, which separated the kitchen from the rest of the house.

He began to stir as they negotiated the big table in the kitchen, and she dropped his feet.

"Mandy," she said, keeping her voice as calm as possible. "I need to have a grown-up talk with Mr. Rob. Give me the bat. Then you go right on out to the mudroom and wait for me there, okay?"

"Mummy . . ." Mandy was shrinking back against the sink cabinet, eyes huge and fixed on the moaning Cameron.

"*Go*, Mandy. Right now. Mummy will be there before you can count to a hundred. Start counting *now*. One . . . two . . . three . . ." She moved between Cameron and Mandy, motioning firmly with her free hand.

Reluctantly, Mandy moved, murmuring, "Four . . . five . . . six . . . seven . . ." and disappeared through the back kitchen door. The kitchen was warm from the Aga, and despite her lack of clothes, Bree was still streaming with sweat. She could smell herself, feral and acrid, and found that it made her feel stronger. She wasn't sure she'd ever truly understood the term "bloodthirsty" before, but she did now.

"Where's my son?" she said to Cameron, keeping a wary distance in case he tried to roll at her. "Answer me, you piece of crap, or I'll beat the shit out of you and then call the police."

"Yeah?" He rolled slowly onto his side, groaning. "And tell them what, exactly? That I took your boy? What proof of that d'ye have?" His words were slurred; his lip was puffed out on one side, where she'd kicked him.

"Fine," she snapped. "I'll just beat the shit out of you."

"What, beat a helpless man? Fine example for your wee lassie." He rolled onto his back with a muffled grunt.

"As for the police, I can tell them you broke into my house and assaulted me." She pointed one foot at him, so he could see the livid scratches on her leg. "You'll have my skin cells under your fingernails. And while I'd rather not have Mandy go through it all again, she'd certainly tell them what you were saying in the hallway." *She would, too*, Bree thought. Mandy was a very faithful tape recorder, especially where bad language was concerned.

"Nng." Cameron had closed his eyes, grimacing against the light over the sink, but now opened them again. He was less dazed; she could see the light of calculation back in his eyes. Like most men, she thought, he was probably smarter when he wasn't sexually aroused—and she'd taken care of *that*.

"Aye. And I tell them it was just a wee sex game that got out of hand, and you say it wasn't, and they say, 'Aye, fine, missus, and where's your husband, then?'" The undamaged side of his mouth twisted up. "You're not that swift tonight, hen. But, then, ye're not usually."

His mention of Roger made the blood surge in her ears. She didn't reply but grabbed him by the feet and pulled him roughly through the kitchen and into the back passageway. The grating that covered the priest's hole was hidden by a bench and several boxes of milk bottles, bits of farm equipment awaiting repair, and other items that didn't go anywhere else. She dropped Rob's feet, shoved the bench and boxes aside, and pulled up the grating. There was a ladder leading down into the shadowy space; she pulled this up and slid it behind the bench. *That* little amenity wouldn't be needed.

"Hey!" Rob's eyes widened. Either he hadn't known there really was a priest's hole in the house or he hadn't thought she'd do it. Without a word, she seized him under the arms, dragged him to the hole, and shoved him in. Feetfirst, because if he broke his neck, he couldn't tell her where Jem was.

He fell with a shriek, which was cut short by a heavy thump. Before she could worry that he'd managed to land on his head after all, she heard him moaning and a rustle as he started to stir. A muttering of very bad language further reassured her that he was in good enough shape to answer questions. She fetched the big flashlight from the kitchen drawer and shone it down into the hole. Cameron's face, congested and streaked with blood, glared up at her. He curled up and with some difficulty managed to wriggle into a sitting position.

"You've broken my leg, you fucking bitch!"

"Good," she said coldly, though she doubted it. "Once I get Jem back, I'll take you to a doctor."

He breathed heavily through his nose, making a nasty snuffling noise, and swiped at his face with his bound hands, smearing the blood across one cheek.

"You want him back? You get me out of here, and fast!"

She'd been considering—and discarding—different plans of action, shuffling through them like a mental pack of cards, ever since she'd duct-taped him. And letting him out wasn't one she'd considered. She *had* thought of fetching the .22 rifle the family used to hunt rats and winging him in a few nonessential places—but there was some risk of either disabling him too badly to be of help or killing him accidentally by hitting something vital if he squirmed.

"Think fast," he shouted up at her. "Your wee lass will hit a hundred and be back any second!"

Despite the situation, Brianna smiled. Mandy had very recently been introduced to the idea that numbers were infinite and had been enchanted by the concept. She wouldn't stop counting until she ran out of breath or someone stopped her. Still, she wasn't going to engage in pointless conversation with her prisoner.

"Okay," she said, and reached for the grate. "We'll see how talkative you are after twenty-four hours without food or water, shall we?"

"You bloody bitch!" He tried to surge to his feet but fell over onto his side, writhing impotently. "You—you just think about this, aye? If I'm without food and water, so's your wee lad!"

She froze, the metal edge of the grate digging into her fingers.

"Rob, you're not bright," she said. She was amazed that her voice sounded conversational; waves of horror and relief and renewed horror were rippling across her shoulders, and something primitive in the back of her mind was screaming.

A sullen silence from below, as he tried to work out what he'd just given away.

"Now I know you didn't send Jem back through the stones," she clarified for him. She carefully didn't shriek, *But you sent Roger back to look for him! And he'll never find him. You . . . you . . .* "He's still here, in this time."

Another silence.

"Yeah," he said slowly. "Okay, you know that. But you don't know where he is. And you're not going to, until you turn me loose. I meant it, hen—he'll be thirsty by now. *And* hungry. It'll be a lot worse for him by morning."

Her hand tightened on the grate. "You had better be lying," she said evenly. "For your sake." She shoved the grate back into place and stepped on it, clicking it down into its frame. The priest's hole was literally a hole: a space about six feet by eight, and twelve feet deep. Even if Rob Cameron hadn't been bound hand and foot, he couldn't jump high enough to get hold of the grate, let alone reach the latch that held it down.

Ignoring the furious shouts from below, Brianna went to retrieve her daughter and her jeans.

THE MUDROOM WAS empty, and for an instant she panicked—but then she saw the tiny bare foot sticking out from under the bench, long toes relaxed as a frog's, and her heart rate dropped. A little.

Mandy was curled up under Roger's old mac, thumb half in her mouth, sound asleep. The impulse was to carry her to her bed, let her sleep 'til daylight. Brianna laid a soft hand on her daughter's black curly hair—black as Roger's—and her heart squeezed like a lemon. There was another child to consider.

"Wake up, sweetheart," she said, gently shaking the little girl. "Wake up, honey. We need to go and look for Jem."

It took no little cajoling and the administration of a glass of Coca-Cola—a rare treat, and absolutely unheard of so late at night, how exciting!—to get Mandy into a state of alertness, but once there she was all eagerness to go and hunt for her brother.

"Mandy," Bree said as casually as she could, buttoning her daughter's pink quilted coat, "can you feel Jem? Right now?"

"Uh-huh," Mandy replied offhandedly, and Brianna's heart leapt. Two nights before, the child had waked screaming from a sound sleep, weeping hysterically and insisting that Jem was gone. She had been inconsolable, wailing that her brother had been eaten by "big wocks!"—an assertion that had terrified her parents, who knew the horrors of those particular rocks all too well.

But then, a few minutes later, Mandy had suddenly calmed. Jem was there, she said. He was there in her head. And she had gone back to sleep as though nothing had happened.

In the consternation that had followed this episode—the discovery that Jem had been taken by Rob Cameron, one of Brianna's fellow employees at the hydroelectric plant, and presumably taken through the stones into the past—there had been no time to recall Mandy's remark about Jem being back in her head, let alone to make further inquiries. But now Brianna's mind was moving at the speed of light, bounding from one horrifying realization to the next, making connections that might have taken hours to make in cooler blood.

Horrifying Realization Number 1: Jem hadn't gone into the past, after all. While by itself this was undeniably a *good* thing, it made Horrifying Realization Number 2 that much worse: Roger and William Buccleigh *had* undoubtedly gone through the stones, searching for Jemmy. She hoped they were in fact in the past and not dead—traveling through whatever sort of thing the stones were was a bloody dangerous proposition—but, if so, that brought her back to Horrifying Realization Number 1: Jem *wasn't* in the past. And if he wasn't there, Roger wasn't going to find him. And since Roger would never give up looking . . .

She pushed Horrifying Realization Number 3 aside with great force, and Mandy blinked, startled.

"Why you making faces, Mummy?"

"Practicing for Halloween." She rose, smiling as best she could, and reached for her own duffel coat.

Mandy's brow creased in thought.

"When's Halloween?"

Cold rippled over Brianna, and not just from the draft through the crack under the back door. *Did they make it?* They thought the portal was most active on the sun feasts and fire feasts—and Samhain was an important fire feast—but they couldn't wait the extra day, for fear that Jem would be taken too far from Craigh na Dun after passing through the stones.

"Tomorrow," she said. Her fingers slipped and fumbled on the fastenings, shaky with adrenaline.

"Goody, goody, goody!" Mandy said, hopping to and fro like a cricket. "Can I wear my mask to look for Jemmy?"

27

NOTHING'S SO HARD BUT
SEARCH WILL FIND IT OUT

HE'D FELT THE DIAMONDS explode. For some time, that was the only thought in his mind. *Felt it.* One instant, briefer than a heartbeat, and a pulse of light and heat in his hand and then the throb of something going through him, surrounding him, and then . . .

Not "then," he thought muzzily. *Wasn't any then. Wasn't any now. Now there is, though . . .*

He opened his eyes to find that there was a now. He was lying on stones and heather and there was a cow breathing—no, not a cow. He made to rise and managed to turn his head half an inch. It was a man, sitting huddled on the ground. Taking huge, irregular, gasping sobs of breath. *Who . . . ?*

"Oh," he said aloud, or almost. "'S you." The words came out in a mangle that hurt his throat, and he coughed. That hurt, too. "You . . . okay?" he asked hoarsely.

"No." It came out in a grunt, filled with pain, and alarm got Roger up onto hands and knees, head spinning. He did a bit of gasping himself but crawled as fast as he could toward Buck.

William Buccleigh was curled over, arms crossed, gripping his left upper arm with his right hand. His face was pale and slicked with sweat, lips pressed so tight together that a ring of white showed round his mouth.

"Hurt?" Roger lifted a hand, not sure where or whether to prod. He couldn't see any blood.

"My . . . chest," Buck wheezed. "Arm."

"Oh, Jesus," Roger said, the last remnants of muzziness stripped away by a blast of adrenaline. "Are you having a bloody heart attack?"

"What . . ." Buck grimaced, then something seemed to ease a little. He gulped air. "How would *I* know?"

"It's—never mind. Lie down, will you?" Roger looked wildly round, though even as he did, he realized the sheer pointlessness of doing so. The area near Craigh na Dun was wild and unpopulated in his own time, let alone this one. And even should someone appear out of the stones and heather, the chances of whoever it was being a doctor were remote.

He took Buck by the shoulders and eased him gently down, then bent and put his ear to the man's chest, feeling like an idiot.

"D'ye hear anything?" Buck asked anxiously.

"Not with you talking, no. Shut up." He thought he could make out a heartbeat of some sort but had no idea whether there was anything wrong with it. He stayed bent a moment longer, if only to compose himself.

Always act as if you know what you're doing, even if you don't. He'd been given that bit of advice by a number of people, from performers he'd shared a stage with to academic advisers . . . and, much more recently, by both of his in-laws.

He put a hand on Buck's chest and looked into the man's face. He was still sweating and plainly scared, but there was a little more color in his cheeks. His lips weren't blue; that seemed a good sign.

"Just keep breathing," he advised his ancestor. "Slow, aye?"

He tried to follow that bit of advice himself; his own heart was hammering and sweat was running down his back, in spite of a cold wind that whined past his ears.

"We did it, aye?" Buck's chest was moving more slowly under his hand. He turned his head to look round. "It's . . . different. Isn't it?"

"Yes." In spite of the current situation and the overwhelming worry for Jem, Roger felt a surge of jubilation and relief. It *was* different: from here, he could see the road below—now no more than an overgrown drovers' trace rather than a gray asphalt ribbon. The trees and bushes, they were different, too—there were pines, the big Caledonian pines that looked like giant stalks of broccoli. They *had* made it.

He grinned at Buck. "We made it. Don't die on me now, you bugger."

"Do my best." Buck was gruff but maybe starting to look better. "What happens if ye die out of your time? D'ye just disappear, like ye never were?"

"Maybe ye explode into bits. I don't know, and I don't want to find out. Not while I'm standing next to you, at least." Roger got his feet under him and fought down a wave of dizziness. His own heart was still beating hard enough that he felt it in the back of his head. He breathed as deep as he could and stood up.

"I'll . . . get ye some water. Stay there, aye?"

ROGER HAD BROUGHT a small empty canteen, though he'd worried about what might happen to the metal in transit. Evidently whatever it was that vaporized gemstones wasn't bothered about tin, though; the canteen was intact, and so was the small knife and the silver pocket flask of brandy.

Buck was sitting up by the time Roger came back from the nearest burn with water, and after mopping his face with the water and drinking half the brandy, he declared himself recovered.

Roger wasn't all that sure; the look of the man was a little off-color still—but he was much too anxious about Jem to suggest waiting any longer. They'd talked about it a bit on the drive to Craigh na Dun, agreeing on a basic strategy, at least to start.

If Cameron and Jem had made it through without mishap—and Roger's heart misgave him at that thought, recalling Geillis Duncan's careful collection of news reports involving people found near stone circles, most of them dead—they had to be on foot. And while Jem was a sturdy little boy and capable of walking a good distance, he doubted they could make much more than ten miles in a day over rough country.

The only road was the drovers' track that led near the base of the hill. So one of them would take the direction that would intersect with one of General Wade's good roads that led to Inverness; the other would follow the track west toward the pass that led to Lallybroch and, beyond it, Cranesmuir.

"I think Inverness is the most likely," Roger repeated, probably for the sixth time. "It's the gold he wants, and he knows that's in America. He can't be meaning to walk from the Highlands to Edinburgh to find a ship, not with winter breathing down his neck."

"He won't find a ship anywhere in the winter," Buck objected. "No captain would cross the Atlantic in November!"

"D'ye think he knows that?" Roger asked. "He's an amateur archaeologist, not a historian. And most folk in the twentieth century have trouble thinking anything was ever different in the past, save the funny clothes and no indoor plumbing. The notion that the weather could stop them going anywhere they'd a mind to—he may well think ships run all the time, on a regular timetable."

"Mmphm. Well, maybe he means to hole up in Inverness with the lad, maybe find work, and wait 'til the spring. D'ye want to take Inverness, then?" Buck lifted his chin in the direction of the invisible town.

"No." Roger shook his head and began patting his pockets, checking his supplies. "Jem knows this place." He nodded toward the stones above them. "I brought him here, more than once, to make sure he never came upon it unawares. That means he knows—approximately, at least—how to get home—to Lallybroch, I mean—from here. If he got away from Cameron—and, God, I hope he did!—he'd run for home."

He didn't trouble saying that even if Jem wasn't there, Brianna's relatives were, her cousins and her aunt. He'd not met them, but they knew from Jamie's letters who he was; if Jem wasn't there—and, Lord, how he hoped he was—they'd help him search. As to how much he might try to tell them . . . that could wait.

"Right, then." Buck buttoned his coat and settled the knitted comforter round his neck against the wind. "Three days, maybe, to Inverness and time to search the town, two or three back. I'll meet ye here in six days' time. If ye're not here, I follow on to Lallybroch."

Roger nodded. "And if I've not found them but I've heard some word of them, I'll leave a message at Lallybroch. If . . ." He hesitated, but it had to be said. "If ye find your wife, and things fall out—"

Buck's lips tightened.

"They've already fallen," he said. "But, aye. If. I'll still come back."

"Aye, right." Roger hunched his shoulders, anxious to go, and awkward with it. Buck was already turning away but suddenly about-faced and gripped Roger's hand, hard.

"We'll find him," Buck said, and looked into Roger's eyes, with those bright-moss eyes that were the same as his. "Good luck." He gave Roger's hand one sharp, hard shake and then was off, arms outstretched for balance as he picked his way down through the rocks and gorse. He didn't look back.

28

WARMER, COLDER

"CAN YOU TELL, when Jem's at school?"

"Yes. He goes on da bus." Mandy bounced a little on her booster seat, leaning to peer out the window. She was wearing the Halloween mask Bree had helped her make, this being a mouse princess: a mouse face drawn with crayons on a paper plate, with holes pierced for eyes and at either side for pink yarn ties, pink pipe cleaners glued on for whiskers, and a precarious small crown made with cardboard, more glue, and most of a bottle of gold glitter.

Scots celebrated Samhain with hollowed-out turnips with candles in them, but Brianna had wanted a slightly more festive tradition for her half-American children. The whole seat sparkled as though the car had been sprinkled with pixie dust.

She smiled, despite her worry.

"I meant, if you played warmer, colder with Jem, could you do it if he wasn't answering you out loud? Would you know if he was closer or farther away?"

Mandy kicked the back of the seat in meditative fashion.

"Maybe."

"Can you try?" They were headed toward Inverness. That was where Jem was supposed to be, spending the night with Rob Cameron's nephew.

"Okay," Mandy said agreeably. She hadn't asked where Rob Cameron was. Brianna spared a thought as to the fate of her prisoner. She really *would* shoot him through the ankles, elbows, knees, or anything else necessary to find out where Jem was—but if there were quieter ways of interrogation, it would be better all round. It wouldn't be good for Jem and Mandy to have their mother sent to prison for life, particularly if Roger— She choked that thought off and stepped harder on the gas.

"Colder," Mandy announced, so suddenly that Brianna nearly stalled the car.

"What? Do you mean we're getting farther away from where Jemmy is?"

"Uh-huh."

Brianna took a deep breath and made a U-turn, narrowly avoiding an on-coming panel truck, which hooted at them in annoyance.

"Right," she said, gripping the wheel with sweaty hands. "We'll go the other way."

THE DOOR WASN'T locked. Jem opened it, heart pounding in relief, and then it pounded harder, as he realized the lights weren't on in the tur-bine chamber, either.

There was *some* light. The little windows up at the top of the huge space, up where the engineers' room was: there was light coming from there. Just enough so he could see the monsters in the huge room.

"They're just machines," he muttered, pressing his back hard against the wall beside the open door. "Justmachinesjustmachinesjustmachines!" He knew the names of them, the giant pulley hoists that ran overhead with the big hooks dangling, and the turbines, Mam had told him. But he'd been up *there* then, where the light was, and it had been daylight.

The floor under his feet vibrated, and he could feel the knobs on his back-bone knocking against the wall as it shook from the weight of the water rushing through the dam under him. Tons of water, Mummy said. Tons and tons and tons of black dark water, all around him, under him . . . If the wall or the floor broke, it—

"Shut up, baby!" he said fiercely to himself, and rubbed his hand hard over his face and wiped it on his jeans. "You got to move. *Go!*"

There were stairs; there had to be stairs. And they were somewhere in here, among the big black humps of the turbines that poked up. They stood higher than the big stones on the hill where Mr. Cameron had taken him. That thought calmed him down some; he was lots more scared of the stones. Even with the deep roaring noise the turbines made—that was making his bones twitch, but it didn't really get *inside* his bones.

The only thing that kept him from going right back into the tunnel and hoping for someone to find him in the morning was the . . . thing in there. He didn't want to be anywhere near that.

He couldn't hear his heart anymore. It was too noisy in the turbine chamber to hear anything. He sure couldn't hear himself think, but the stairs had to be near the windows, and he wobbled that way, keeping as far as he could from the huge black double humps sticking up through the floor.

It was only when he finally found the door, yanked it open, and fell into the lighted staircase that it occurred to him to wonder whether Mr. Cameron was maybe up there, waiting for him.

29

RETURN TO LALLYBROCH

ROGER HAULED HIS WAY laboriously toward the summit of the mountain pass, muttering under his breath (as he had been doing for the last several miles):

> *"If you had seen this road before it was made,*
> *You would lift up your hands and bless General Wade."*

The Irish General Wade had spent twelve years building barracks, bridges, and roads all over Scotland, and if that bit of admiring verse was not in fact carved into a stone on one of the general's roads, it ought to have been, Roger thought. He had picked up one of the general's roads near Craigh na Dun, and it had carried him as swiftly as he could walk to within a few miles of Lallybroch.

These last few miles, though, had not had the benefit of Wade's attention. A rocky trail, pitted with small mud bogs and thickly overgrown with heather and gorse, led up through the steep pass that overlooked—and protected— Lallybroch. The lower slopes were forested with beeches, alders, and stout Caledonian pines, but up this high there was neither shade nor shelter, and a strong, cold wind battered him as he climbed.

Could Jem have come this far by himself, if he'd escaped? Roger and Buck had cast round in the vicinity of Craigh na Dun, hoping that perhaps Cameron had stopped to rest after the strain of the passage, but there had been no sign—not so much as the print of a size-4 trainer in a muddy patch of ground. Roger had come on then by himself, as fast as he could, pausing to knock at the door of any croft he came to—and there weren't many along this way—but he'd made good time.

His heart was pounding, and not only from the exertion of the climb. Cameron had maybe a two-day lead, at the most. If Jem hadn't got away and run for home, though . . . Cameron wouldn't come to Lallybroch, surely. But where *would* he go? Follow the good road, left now ten miles behind, and head west, maybe, into the MacKenzies' territory—but why?

"Jem!" He shouted now and then as he went, though the moors and mountains were empty save for the rustling of rabbits and stoats and silent but for the calling of ravens and the occasional shriek of a seagull winging high overhead, evidence of the distant sea.

"Jem!" he called, as though he could compel an answer by sheer need, and in that need imagined sometimes that he heard a faint cry in response. But when he stopped to listen, it was the wind. Only the wind, whining in his ears, numbing him. He could walk within ten feet of Jem and never see him, and he knew that.

His heart rose, in spite of his anxiety, when he came to the top of the pass and saw Lallybroch below him, its white-harled buildings glowing in the fading light. Everything lay peaceful before him: late cabbages and turnips in orderly rows within the kailyard walls, safe from grazing sheep—there was a small flock in the far meadow, already bedding for the night, like so many woolly eggs in a nest of green grass, like a kid's Easter basket.

The thought caught at his throat, with memories of the horrible cellophane grass that got everywhere, Mandy with her face—and everything else within six feet of her—smeared with chocolate, Jem carefully writing *Dad* on a hard-boiled egg with a white crayon, then frowning over the array of dye cups, trying to decide whether blue or purple was more Dad-like.

"Lord, let him be here!" he muttered under his breath, and hurried down the rutted trail, half sliding on loose rocks.

The dooryard was tidy, the big yellow rose brier trimmed back for the winter, and the step swept clean. He had the sudden notion that if he were simply to open the door and walk in, he would find himself in his own lobby, Mandy's tiny red galoshes flung helter-skelter under the hall tree where Brianna's disreputable duffel coat hung, crusty with dried mud and smelling of its wearer, soap and musk and the faint smell of her motherhood: sour milk, fresh bread, and peanut butter.

"Bloody hell," he muttered, "be weeping on the step, next thing." He hammered at the door, and a huge dog came galloping round the corner of the house, baying like the bloody hound of the Baskervilles. It slid to a stop in front of him but went on barking, weaving its huge head to and fro like a snake, ears cocked in case he might make a false move that would let it devour him with a clear conscience.

He wasn't risking any moves; he'd plastered himself against the door when the dog appeared and now shouted, "Help! Come call your beast!"

He heard footsteps within, and an instant later the door opened, nearly decanting him into the hall.

"Hauld your wheesht, dog," a tall, dark man said in a tolerant tone. "Come ben, sir, and dinna be minding him. He wouldna eat you; he's had his dinner."

"I'm pleased to hear it, sir, and thank ye kindly." Roger pulled off his hat and followed the man into the shadows of the hall. It was his own familiar hall, the slates of the floor just the same, though not nearly as worn, the dark-wood paneling shining with beeswax and polishing. There *was* a hall tree in the corner, though of course different to his; this one was a sturdy affair of wrought iron, and a good thing, too, as it was supporting a massive burden of jackets, shawls, cloaks, and hats, which would have crumpled a flimsier piece of furniture.

He smiled at it, nonetheless, and then stopped dead, feeling as though he'd been punched in the chest.

The wood paneling behind the hall tree shone serene, unblemished. No sign of the saber slashes left by frustrated redcoat soldiers searching for the outlawed laird of Lallybroch after Culloden. Those slashes had been carefully preserved for centuries, were still there, darkened by age but still distinct, when he had owned—would own, he corrected mechanically—this place.

"We keep it so for the children," Bree had quoted her uncle Ian as saying. *"We tell them, 'This is what the English are.'"*

He had no time to deal with the shock; the dark man had shut the door with a firm Gaelic adjuration to the dog and now turned to him, smiling.

"Welcome, sir. Ye'll sup wi' us? The lass has it nearly ready."

"Aye, I will, and thanks to ye," Roger bowed slightly, groping for his eighteenth-century manners. "I—my name is Roger MacKenzie. Of Kyle of Lochalsh," he added, for no respectable man would omit to note his origins, and Lochalsh was far enough away that the chances of this man—who was he? He hadn't the bearing of a servant—knowing its inhabitants in any detail was remote.

He'd hoped that the immediate response would be, *"MacKenzie? Why, you must be the father of wee Jem!"* It wasn't, though; the man returned his bow and offered his hand.

"Brian Fraser of Lallybroch, your servant, sir."

ROGER FELT ABSOLUTELY nothing for a moment. There was a faint clicking that reminded him of the noise a car's starter makes when the battery is dead, and for a disoriented moment he assumed it was being made by his brain. Then his eyes focused on the dog, which, prevented from eating him, had come into the house and was walking down the passage, its toenails clicking on the parquet floor.

Oh. So that's what left those scratches on the kitchen door, he thought, dazed, as the beast reared up and heaved its weight at the swinging door at the end of the passage, then shot through as it opened.

"Are ye quite well, sir?" Brian Fraser was looking at him, thick black brows drawn down in concern. He reached out a hand. "Come into my study and sit. I'll maybe fetch ye a dram?"

"I—thank you," Roger said abruptly. He thought his knees might give way at any second, but he managed to follow the master of Lallybroch into the speak-a-word room, the laird's office and study. His own study.

The shelves were the same, and behind his host's head was the same row of farm ledgers that he'd often thumbed through, conjuring up from their faded entries the phantom life of an earlier Lallybroch. Now the ledgers were new, and Roger felt himself the phantom. He didn't like the feeling at all.

Brian Fraser handed him a small, thick, flat-bottomed glass half full of spirit. Whisky, and very decent whisky, too. The smell of it began to bring him out of his shock, and the warm burn of it down his gullet loosened the tightness in his throat.

How was he to ask what he so desperately needed to know? *When?!* He glanced over the desk, but there was no half-finished letter, conveniently dated, no planting almanac that he might glance casually through. None of the books on the shelf were of help; the only one he recognized was Defoe's *THE LIFE AND STRANGE SURPRIZING ADVENTURES OF ROBINSON CRUSOE, OF YORK, MARINER,* and that had been published in 1719. He knew he must be later than that; the house itself hadn't yet been built in 1719.

He forced down the rising tide of panic. It didn't matter; it didn't matter if it wasn't the time he'd expected—not if Jem was here. And he must be. He *must* be.

"I'm sorry to disturb your family, sir," he said, clearing his throat as he set down the glass. "But the fact is that I've lost my son and am in search of him."

"Lost your son!" exclaimed Fraser, eyes widening in surprise. "Bride be with ye, sir. How did that come about?"

Just as well to tell the truth where he could, he thought, and, after all, what else could he say?

"He was kidnapped two days ago and carried away—he's no but nine years old. I have some reason to think the man who took him comes from this area. Have ye by chance seen a tall man, lean and dark, traveling with a young red-haired lad, about so tall?" He put the edge of his hand against his own arm, about three inches above the elbow; Jem was tall for his age and even taller for this age—but, then, Brian Fraser was a tall man himself, and *his* son . . .

A fresh shock went through Roger with the thought: Was Jamie here? In the house? And if he was, how old might he be? How old had he been when Brian Fraser die—

Fraser was shaking his head, his face troubled.

"I have not, sir. What's the name of the man who's taken your lad?"

"Rob—Robert Cameron, he's called. I dinna ken his people," he added, falling naturally into Fraser's stronger accent.

"Cameron . . ." Fraser murmured, tapping his fingers on the desk as he searched his memory. The motion flicked something in Roger's memory; it was the ghost of one of Jamie's characteristic gestures when thinking—but Jamie, with his frozen finger, did it with the fingers flat, where his father's came down in a smooth ripple.

He picked up the glass again and took another sip, glancing as casually as he might at Fraser's face, searching for resemblance. It was there but subtle, mostly in the cock of the head, the set of the shoulders—and the eyes. The face was quite different, square in the jaw, broader of brow, and Brian Fraser's eyes were a dark hazel, not blue, but the slanted shape of them, the wide mouth—that was Jamie.

"There're nay many Camerons nearer than Lochaber." Fraser was shaking his head. "And I've heard nothing of a wanderer in the district." He gave Roger a direct look, not accusing but definitely questioning. "Why is it ye think the man came this way?"

"I—he was seen," Roger blurted. "Near Craigh na Dun."

That startled Fraser.

"Craigh na Dun," he repeated, leaning back a little, his eyes gone wary. "Ah . . . and where might ye have come from yourself, sir?"

"From Inverness," Roger replied promptly. "I followed him from there." *Close enough.* He was trying hard not to recall that he'd left on his quest to find Cameron and Jem from the very spot in which he was now sitting. "I—a friend—a kinsman—came with me. I sent him toward Cranesmuir to search."

The news that he apparently wasn't a solitary nutter seemed to reassure Fraser, who pushed back from the desk and stood up, glancing at the window, where a big rose brier curved up gaunt and black against the fading sky.

"Mmphm. Well, bide for a bit, sir, and ye will. It's late in the day, and ye'll make no great distance before dark falls. Sup with us, and we'll gie ye a bed for the night. Mayhap your friend will catch ye up with good news, or one of my tenants may ha' seen something. I'll send round in the morning, to ask."

Roger's legs were quivering with the urge to leap up, rush out, *do* something. But Fraser was right: it would be pointless—and dangerous—to blunder round the Highland mountains in the dark, losing his way, perhaps be caught in a killing storm this time of year. He could hear the wind picking up; the rose brier beat at the glass of the window. It was going to rain soon. *And is Jem out in it?*

"I—yes. I thank you, sir," he said. "It's most kind of ye."

Fraser patted him on the shoulder, went out into the hallway, and called, "Janet! Janet, we've a guest for supper!"

Janet?

He'd risen to his feet without thinking and came out of the office as the kitchen door swung open—and a small, slender shape was momentarily silhouetted against the glow of the kitchen, rubbing her hands on her apron.

"My daughter, Janet, sir," Fraser said, drawing his daughter into the fading light. He smiled fondly at her. "This is Mr. Roger MacKenzie, Jenny. He's lost his wee lad somewhere."

"He has?" The girl paused, halfway through a curtsy, and her eyes went wide. "What's happened, sir?"

Roger explained again briefly about Rob Cameron and Craigh na Dun, but all the time was consumed by the desire to ask the young woman how old she was. Fifteen? Seventeen? Twenty-one? She was remarkably beautiful, with clear white skin that bloomed from the heat of cooking, soft curly black hair tied back from her face, and a trim figure that he tried hard not to stare at— but what was most disturbing was that, despite her obvious femininity, she bore a startling resemblance to Jamie Fraser. *She might be his daughter,* he thought, and then brought himself up short, realizing afresh—and remembering, with a stab of the heart that nearly dropped him to his knees—who Jamie Fraser's daughter really was.

Oh, God. Bree. Oh, Jesus, help me. Will I ever see her again?

He realized that he'd fallen silent and was staring at Janet Fraser with his mouth open. Apparently she was used to this sort of response from men, though; she gave him a demure, slant-eyed smile, said that supper would be on the table in a few moments and maybe Da should show Mr. MacKenzie the way to the necessary? Then she was walking back down the hallway, the big door swung to behind her, and he found he could breathe again.

THE SUPPER WAS plain but plentiful and well cooked, and Roger found that food restored him amazingly. No wonder—he couldn't remember when he'd last eaten.

They ate in the kitchen, with a pair of housemaids called Annie and Senga and a man-of-all-work named Tom McTaggart sharing the table with the family. All of them were interested in Roger and, while giving him great sympathy in the matter of his missing son, were even more interested in where he might come from and what news he might bear.

Here he was at something of a loss, as he had no firm notion what year it was *(Brian died—God, will die—when Jamie was nineteen, and if Jamie was born in May of 1721—or was it 1722?—and he was two years younger than Jenny . . .)* and thus no idea what might have been happening in the world of late, but he delayed a bit, explaining his antecedents in some detail—that was good manners, for one thing, and for another, his birthplace in Kyle of Lochalsh was far enough away from Lallybroch that the Frasers were unlikely to have met any of his people.

Then at last he had a bit of luck, when McTaggart told about taking off his shoe to shake out a stone, then seeing one of the pigs wriggle under the fence and head for the kailyard at a trot. He rushed after the pig, of course, and succeeded in catching it—but had dragged it back to the pen only to find that the other pig had likewise wriggled out and was peacefully eating his shoe.

"This was all she left!" he said, pulling half a shredded leather sole out of his pocket and waving it at them reproachfully. "And a rare struggle I had to pull it from her jaws!"

"Why did ye bother?" Jenny asked, wrinkling her nose at the dank object. "Dinna trouble yourself, Taggie. We'll slaughter the pigs next week, and ye can have a bit o' the hide to make yourself a new pair of shoon."

"And I suppose I'm to go barefoot 'til then, am I?" McTaggart asked, disgruntled. "There's frost on the ground in the morn, aye? I could take a chill and be dead of the pleurisy before yon pig's eaten its last bucket o' slops, let alone been tanned."

Brian laughed and lifted his chin toward Jenny. "Did your brother no leave a pair of his outgrown shoon behind when he left for Paris? I mind me he did, and if ye havena given them to the poor, might be as Taggie could manage wi' them for a bit."

Paris. Roger's mind worked furiously, calculating. Jamie had spent not quite two years in Paris at the *université* and had come back . . . when? When he was eighteen, he thought. Jamie would have been—will be—eighteen in May of 1739. So it was now 1737, 1738, or 1739.

The narrowing of uncertainty calmed him a little, and he managed to put his mind to thinking of historical events that had occurred in that gap that he might offer as current news in conversation: absurdly, the first thing that came to mind was that the bottle opener had been invented in 1738. The second was that there had been an enormous earthquake in Bombay in 1737.

His audience was initially more interested by the bottle opener, which he was obliged to describe in detail—inventing wildly, as he had no notion what the thing actually looked like, though there were sympathetic murmurs regarding the residents of Bombay and a brief prayer for the souls of those crushed under falling houses and the like.

"But where *is* Bombay?" asked the younger of the housemaids, wrinkling her brow and looking from one face to another.

"India," said Jenny promptly, and pushed back her chair. "Senga, fetch the cranachan, aye? I'll show ye where India is."

She vanished through the swinging door, and the bustle of removing dishes left Roger with a few moments' breathing space. He was beginning to feel a little easier, getting his bearings, though still agonized with worry for Jem. He did spare a moment's thought for William Buccleigh and how Buck might take the news of the date of their arrival.

Seventeen thirty-something . . . Jesus, Buck himself hadn't even been born yet! But, after all, what difference did that make? he asked himself. *He* hadn't been born yet, either, and had lived quite happily in a time prior to his birth before. . . . Could their proximity to the beginning of Buck's life have something to do with it, though?

He did know—or thought he knew—that you couldn't go back to a time during your own lifetime. Trying to exist physically at the same time as yourself just wasn't on. It had just about killed him once; maybe they'd got too close to Buck's original lifeline, and Buck had somehow recoiled, taking Roger with him?

Before he could explore the implications of *that* unsettling thought, Jenny returned, carrying a large, thin book. This proved to be a hand-colored atlas, with maps—surprisingly accurate maps, in many cases—and descriptions of "The Nations of the World."

"My brother sent it to me from Paris," Jenny told him proudly, opening the book to a double-page spread of the Continent of India, where the starred circle indicating Bombay was surrounded by small drawings of palm trees, elephants, and something that upon close scrutiny turned out to be a tea plant. "He's at the *université* there."

"Really?" Roger smiled, being sure to look impressed. He was, the more so at realization of the effort and expense involved in going from this remote mountain wilderness to Paris. "How long has he been there?"

"Oh, almost two years now," Brian answered. He put out a hand and touched the page gently. "We do miss the lad cruelly, but he writes often. And he sends us books."

"He'll be back soon," Jenny said, though with an air of conviction that seemed somewhat forced. "He said he'd come back."

Brian smiled, though this too was a little forced.

"Aye. I'm sure I hope so, *a nighean*. But ye ken he may have found opportunities that keep him abroad for a time."

"Opportunities? Ye mean that de Marillac woman?" Jenny asked, a distinct edge in her voice. "I dinna like the way he writes about her. Not one bit."

"He could do worse for a wife, lass." Brian lifted one shoulder. "She's from a good family."

Jenny made a very complicated sound in her throat, indicating sufficient respect for her father as to prevent her expressing a fuller opinion of "that woman" while still making that opinion plain. Her father laughed.

"Your brother's no a *complete* fool," he assured her. "I doubt he'd marry a simpleton or a—a—" He'd obviously thought better of saying "whore"— his lips had begun to shape the word—but couldn't think of a substitute in time.

"He would," Jenny snapped. "He'd walk straight into a cob's web wi' his eyes wide open, if the cob had a pretty face and a round arse."

"Janet!" Her father tried to look shocked but failed utterly. McTaggart guffawed openly, and Annie and Senga giggled behind their hands. Jenny glowered at them but then drew herself up with dignity and addressed herself to their guest.

"So, then, Mr. MacKenzie. Is your own wife living, I hope? And is she your wean's mother?"

"Is she—" He felt the question like a blow in the chest but then remembered when he was. The odds of a woman surviving childbirth were no more than even in many places. "Yes. Yes, she's—in Inverness, with our daughter."

Mandy. Oh, my sweet baby. Mandy. Bree. Jem. All at once, the enormity of it struck him. He'd managed so far to ignore it by concentrating on the need to find Jem, but now a cold wind whistled through the holes in his heart left by hurtling odds. The odds were that he would never see any of them again. And they would never know what had happened to him.

"Oh, sir." Jenny whispered it, leaning forward to lay a hand on his arm, her eyes wide with horror at what she'd provoked. "Oh, sir, I'm sorry! I didna mean to—"

"It's all right," he managed, forcing the words through his mangled larynx in a croak. "I'm—" He waved a hand in blind apology and stumbled out. He went straight out through the mudroom at the back of the house and found himself in the night outside.

There was a narrow crack of sullen light just at the tops of the mountains, where the cloud had not quite settled, but the yard about him was deep in shadow, and the wind touched his face with the scent of cold rain. He was shaking, but not from chill, and sat down abruptly on the big stone by the path where they pulled the children's wellies off when it was muddy.

He put his elbows on his knees and his face in his hands, overcome for a moment. Not only for his own situation—but for those in the house. Jamie Fraser was coming home soon. And soon after there would come the afternoon when red-coated soldiers marched into the yard at Lallybroch, finding Janet and the servants alone. And the events would be set in train that would end with the death of Brian Fraser, struck down by an apoplexy while watching his only son flogged—he thought—to death.

Jamie . . . Roger shivered, seeing in mind not his indomitable father-in-law but the lighthearted young man who, among the distractions of Paris, still thought to send books to his sister. Who—

It had begun to rain, with a quiet thoroughness that slicked his face in seconds. At least no one would know if he wept in despair. *I can't stop it,* he thought. *I can't tell them what's coming.*

A huge shape loomed out of the darkness, startling him, and the dog leaned heavily against him, nearly pushing him off the stone he sat on. A large, hairy nose was thrust sympathetically into his ear, whoofling and wetter than the rain.

"Jesus, dog," he said, half-laughing in spite of everything. "God." He put his arms round the big, smelly creature and rested his forehead against its massive neck, feeling inchoate comfort.

He thought of nothing for a little and was inexpressibly relieved. Little by little, though, coherent thought came back. It maybe wasn't true that things—the past—couldn't be changed. Not the big things, maybe, not kings and battles. But maybe—just maybe—the small ones could. If he couldn't come right out and tell the Frasers of Lallybroch what doom was to come upon them, perhaps there was *something* he could say, some warning that might forestall—

And if he did? If they listened? Would that good man in the house die of his apoplexy anyway, some weakness in his brain giving way as he came in from the barn one day? But that would leave his son and his daughter safe—and then what?

Would Jamie stay in Paris and marry the flirtatious Frenchwoman? Would he come home peaceably to live at Lallybroch and mind his estate and his sister?

Either way, he wouldn't be riding near Craigh na Dun in five or six years, pursued by English soldiers, wounded and needing the assistance of a random time traveler who had just stepped out of the stones. And if he didn't meet Claire Randall. . . . *Bree,* he thought. *Oh, Christ. Bree.*

There was a sound behind him—the door of the house opening—and the beam of a lantern fell onto the path nearby.

"Mr. MacKenzie?" Brian Fraser called into the night. "Are ye all right, man?"

"God," he whispered, clutching the dog. "Show me what to do."

30

LIGHTS, ACTION, SIRENS

T HE DOOR AT THE top of the staircase *was* locked. Jem pounded on it with his fists, kicked it with his feet, and shouted. He could feel *it* back down there behind him, in the dark, and the feel of it crawled up his back, as if it were coming to get him, and the thought of that scared him so bad that he shrieked like a *ban-sìdhe* and threw himself hard against the door, over and over, and—

The door flew open and he fell flat on a dirty lino floor, all footmarks and cigarette butts.

"What the devil—who are you, laddie, and what in God's name were ye doing in there?"

A big hand grabbed him by the arm and pulled him up. He was out of breath from yelling and almost blubbering from relief, and it took a minute to remember who he was.

"Jem." He swallowed, blinking in the light, and wiped his face on his sleeve. "Jem MacKenzie. My mam's . . ." He went blank, suddenly unable to remember what Mam's first name was. "She works here sometimes."

"I know your mam. No mistaking *that* hair, laddie." The man who'd pulled him up was a security guard; the patch on his shirtsleeve said so. He tilted his head to one side and the other, looking Jem over, light flashing off his bald head, off his glasses. The light was coming from those long tube lights in the ceiling Da said were fluorescent; they buzzed and reminded him of the thing in the tunnel, and he turned round fast and shoved the door shut with a bang.

"Is someone chasin' ye, lad?" The guard reached a hand toward the doorknob, and Jem put his back hard against the door.

"No!" He could feel it back there, behind the door. Waiting. The guard was frowning at him. "I—I just—it's really dark down there."

"Ye were down in the dark? However did ye come to be there? And where's your mother?"

"I don't know." Jem started being scared again. *Really* scared. Because Mr. Cameron had shut him up in the tunnel so he could go somewhere. And he might have gone to Lallybroch.

"Mr. Cameron put me in there," he blurted. "He was supposed to take me to spend the night with Bobby, but instead he took me to Craigh na Dun, and then he took me to his house and locked me in a room overnight, and then the next morning he brought me here and shut me up in the tunnel."

"Cameron—what, Rob Cameron?" The guard crouched down so he could frown right into Jem's face. "Why?"

"I—I don't know." *Don't ever tell anyone,* Da had said. Jem swallowed hard. Even if he wanted to tell, he didn't know how to start. He could say Mr. Cameron took him up the hill at Craigh na Dun, to the stones, and pushed him into one. But he couldn't tell what had happened then, not any more than he could tell Mr. MacLeod—that's what it said on his badge, JOCK MACLEOD—what the shiny thing in the tunnel was.

Mr. MacLeod made a thinking noise in his throat, shook his head, and stood up.

"Well, I'd best be calling your parents to come and fetch ye home, aye? They can say if they maybe want to speak to the polis."

"Please," Jem whispered, feeling his knees turn to water at the thought of Mam and Da coming to get him. "Yes, please."

Mr. MacLeod took him along to a little office where the phone was, gave him a warm can of Coke, and told him to sit down just there and say his parents' telephone number. He sipped the drink and felt lots better right away, watching Mr. MacLeod's thick finger whirl the telephone dial. A pause, and then he could hear ringing on the other end. *Breep-breep . . . breep-breep . . . breep-breep . . .*

It was warm in the office, but he was starting to feel cold around his face and hands. Nobody was answering the phone.

"Maybe they're asleep," he said, stifling a Coke burp. Mr. MacLeod gave him a sideways look and shook his head, pushed down the receiver, and dialed the number again, making Jem say the numbers one at a time. *Breep-breep. . . . breep-breep . . .*

He was concentrating so hard on willing somebody to pick up the phone that he didn't notice anything until Mr. MacLeod suddenly turned his head toward the door, looking surprised.

"What—" the guard said, and then there was a blur and a thunking noise like when cousin Ian shot a deer with an arrow, and Mr. MacLeod made an awful noise and fell right out of his chair onto the floor, and the chair shot away and fell over with a crash.

Jem didn't remember standing up, but he was pressed against the filing cabinet, squeezing the can so hard that the bubbly Coke blurped out and foamed over his fingers.

"You come with me, boy," said the man who'd hit Mr. MacLeod. He was holding what Jem thought must be a cosh, though he'd never seen one. He couldn't move, even if he'd wanted to.

The man made an impatient noise, stepped over Mr. MacLeod like he was a bag of rubbish, and grabbed Jem by the hand. Out of sheer terror, Jem bit him, hard. The man yelped and let go, and Jem threw the can of Coke right at his face, and when the man ducked, he tore past him and out of the office and down the long hallway, running for his life.

IT WAS GETTING late; they passed fewer and fewer cars on the road, and Mandy's head began to nod. The mouse-princess mask had ridden up on top of her head, its pipe-cleaner whiskers poking up like antennae. Seeing this in the rearview mirror, Brianna had a sudden vision of Mandy as a tiny radar station, scanning the bleak countryside for Jem's small, pulsing signal.

Could she? She shook her head, not to dispel the notion but to keep her mind from slipping all the way out of reality. The adrenaline of her earlier rage and terror had all drained away; her hands shook a little on the steering wheel, and the darkness around them seemed vast, a yawning void that would swallow them in an instant if she stopped driving, if the feeble beam of the headlights ceased . . .

"Warm," Mandy murmured sleepily.

"What, baby?" She'd heard but was too hypnotized by the effort of keeping her eyes on the road to take it in consciously.

"Warm . . . *er.*" Mandy struggled upright, cross. The yarn ties of her mask were stuck in her hair, and she made a high-pitched cranky noise as she yanked at them.

Brianna pulled carefully onto the verge, set the hand brake, and, reaching back, began to disentangle the mask.

"You mean we're going toward Jem?" she asked, careful to keep her voice from trembling.

"Uh-huh." Free of the nuisance, Mandy yawned hugely and flung out a hand toward the window. "Mmp." She put her head down on her arms and whined sleepily.

Bree swallowed, closed her eyes, then opened them, looking carefully in the direction Mandy had pointed. There was no road . . . but there was, and with a trickle of ice water down her spine, she saw the small brown sign that said: SERVICE ROAD. NO PUBLIC ACCESS. NORTH OF SCOTLAND HYDRO ELECTRIC BOARD. Loch Errochty dam. The tunnel.

"Damn!" said Brianna, and stomped the gas, forgetting the hand brake. The car jumped and stalled, and Mandy sat bolt upright, eyes glazed and wide as a sun-stunned owl's.

"Iss we home yet?"

JEM PELTED DOWN the hallway and threw himself at the swinging door at the end, so hard that he skidded all the way across the landing on the other side and fell down the stairs beyond, bumping and banging and ending up in a dazed heap at the bottom.

He heard the footsteps coming fast toward the door above and, with a small, terrified squeak, scrambled on all fours round the second landing and launched himself headfirst down the next flight, tobogganing on his stomach for a few stairs, then tipping arse over teakettle and somersaulting down the rest.

He was crying with terror, gulping air and trying not to make a noise, stumbling to his feet, and everything hurt, everything—but the door: he had to get outside. He staggered through the half-dark lobby, the only lights shining through the glass window where the receptionist usually sat. The man was coming; he could hear him cursing at the bottom of the stairs.

The main door had a chain looped through the bars. Swiping tears on his sleeve, he ran back in to the reception, looking wildly round. EMERGENCY EXIT—there it was, the red sign over the door at the far end of another small corridor. The man burst into the lobby and saw him.

"Come back here, you little bugger!"

He looked round wildly, grabbed the first thing he saw, which was a rolling chair, and pushed it as hard as he could into the lobby. The man cursed and jumped aside, and Jem ran for the door and flung himself against it, bursting into the night with a scream of sirens and the flash of blinding lights.

"WHASSAT, MUMMY? Mummy, I scared, I SCARED!"

"And you think I'm not?" Bree said under her breath, heart in her mouth. "It's okay, baby," she said aloud, and pressed her foot to the floor. "We're just going to get Jem."

The car slewed to a stop on the gravel, and she leapt out but dithered for a moment, needing urgently to rush toward the building, where sirens and lights were going off over an open door at the side, but unable to leave Mandy alone in the car. She could hear the rush of water down the spillway.

"Come with me, sweetheart," she said, hastily undoing the seat belt. "That's right, here, let me carry you . . ." Even as she spoke, she was looking here, there, from the lights into the darkness, every nerve she had screaming that her son was here, he was *here,* he had to be . . . rushing water . . . her mind filled with horror, thinking of Jem falling into the spillway, or Jem in the service tunnel—God, why hadn't she gone there first? Of course Rob Cameron would have put him there, he had the keys, he . . . but the lights, the sirens . . .

She'd almost made it—at a dead run, impeded only slightly by thirty pounds of toddler—when she saw a big man at the edge of the drive, thrashing through the bushes with a stick or something, cursing a blue streak.

"What do you think you're *doing?*" she bellowed. Mandy, alarmed anew, let out a screech like a scalded baboon, and the man jumped, whirling to face them, stick raised.

"What the bleedin' hell are you doing here?" he said, so taken aback that he spoke almost normally. "You're supposed to be—"

Bree had peeled Mandy off. Setting her daughter down behind her, she prepared to take the man apart with her bare hands, if necessary. Evidently this intent showed, because the man dropped the stick and abruptly vanished into the darkness.

Then flashing lights washed over the drive and she realized that it wasn't her own aspect that had frightened him. Mandy was clinging to her leg, too frightened even to wail anymore. Bree picked her up, patting her gently, and turned to face the two police officers who were advancing cautiously toward her, hands on their batons. She felt wobbly-legged and dreamlike, things fading in and out of focus with the strobing lights. The rush of tons of falling water filled her ears.

"Mandy," she said into her daughter's warm curly hair, her own voice almost drowned out by the sirens. "Can you feel Jem? Please tell me you can feel him."

"Here I am, Mummy," said a small voice behind her. Convinced she was hallucinating, she lifted a restraining hand toward the police officers and pivoted slowly round. Jem was standing on the drive six feet away, dripping wet, plastered with dead leaves, and swaying like a drunk.

Then she was sitting splay-legged on the gravel, a child clutched in each arm, trying hard not to shake, so they wouldn't notice. She didn't start to sob, though, until Jemmy lifted a tearstained face from her shoulder and said, "Where's Daddy?"

31

THE SHINE OF A
ROCKING HORSE'S EYES

F RASER DIDN'T ASK BUT poured them each a dram of whisky, warm-smelling and smoke-tinged. There was something comfortable in drinking whisky in company, no matter how bad the whisky. Or the company, for that matter. This particular bottle was something special, and Roger was grateful, both to the bottle and its giver, for the sense of comfort that rose from the glass, beckoning him, a genie from the bottle.

"*Slàinte,*" he said, lifting the glass, and saw Fraser glance at him in sudden interest. Lord, what had he said? "*Slàinte*" was one of the words that had a distinct pronunciation, depending on where you came from—men from Harris and Lewis said "*Slàn-ya,*" while far north it was more like "*Slànj.*" He'd used the form he'd grown up with in Inverness; was it strikingly wrong for where he'd said he came from? He didn't want Fraser to think him a liar.

"What is it ye do for yourself, *a chompanaich*?" Fraser asked, having taken a sip, closing his eyes in momentary respect to the drink, then opening them to regard Roger with a kind curiosity—tinged perhaps with a little wariness, lest his visitor be unhinged. "I'm accustomed to know a man's work at once by his dress and manner—not that ye find many folk truly unusual up here." He smiled a bit at that. "And drovers, tinkers, and gypsies dinna take much effort to descry. Clearly you're none of those."

"I have a bit of land," Roger replied. It was an expected question; he was ready with an answer—but found himself longing to say more. To tell the truth—so far as he himself understood it.

"I've left my wife wi' the running of things whilst I came to search for our lad. Beyond that—" He lifted one shoulder briefly. "I was trained as a minister."

"Oh, aye?" Fraser leaned back, surveying him with interest. "I could see ye're an educated man. I was thinkin' maybe a schoolmaster or a clerk—perhaps a lawyer."

"I've been both schoolmaster and clerk," Roger said, smiling. "Havena quite risen—or fallen, maybe—to the practice of law yet."

"And a good thing, too." Fraser sipped, half-smiling.

Roger shrugged. "Law's a corrupt power but one acceptable to men by reason of having arisen from men—it's a way of getting on wi' things, is the best ye can say for it."

"And not a mean thing to say for it, either," Fraser agreed. "The law's a necessary evil—we canna be doing without it—but do ye not think it a poor substitute for conscience? Speakin' as a minister, I mean?"

"Well . . . aye. I do," Roger said, somewhat surprised. "It would be best for men to deal decently with one another in accordance with—well, with God's principles, if ye'll pardon my putting it that way. But what are ye to do, first, if ye have men to whom God is of no account, and, second, if ye have men—and you do, always—who own no power greater than their own?"

Fraser nodded, interested.

"Aye, well, it's true that the best conscience willna avail a man who willna mind it. But what d'ye do when conscience speaks differently to men of goodwill?"

"As in political disputes, you mean? Supporters of the Stuarts versus those of the . . . the House of Hanover?" It was a reckless thing to say, but it might help him to figure out when he was, and he meant to say nothing that might make it look as though he had a personal stake on either side.

Fraser's face underwent a surprising flow of expression, from being taken aback to mild distate, this then ending in a look of half-amused ruefulness.

"Like that," he agreed. "I fought for the House of Stuart in my youth, and while I'd not say that conscience didna come into it, it didna come very far onto the field wi' me." His mouth quirked at the corner, and Roger felt again the tiny *plop!* of a stone tossed into his depths, the ripples of recognition spreading through him. Jamie did that. Brianna didn't. Jem did.

He couldn't stop to think about it, though; the conversation was teetering delicately on the precipice of an invitation to political disclosure, and that, he couldn't do.

"Was it Sheriffmuir?" he asked, making no effort to disguise his interest.

"It was," Fraser said, openly surprised. He eyed Roger dubiously. "Ye canna have gone yourself, surely . . . did your faither maybe tell ye?"

"No," said Roger, with the momentary twinge that thought of his father always brought. In fact, Fraser was only a few years older than himself, but he knew the other man doubtless took him for a decade younger than he was.

"I . . . heard a song about it. 'Twas two shepherds met on a hillside, talking about the great fight—and arguing who'd won it."

That made Fraser laugh.

"Well they might! We were arguing that before we finished pickin' up the wounded." He took a sip of whisky and washed it meditatively round his mouth, clearly reminiscing. "So, then, how does the song go?"

Roger breathed deep, ready to sing, and then remembered. Fraser had seen his rope scar and been tactful enough not to remark on it, but no need to make the damage obvious. Instead, he chanted the first few lines, tapping his fingers on the desk, echoing the rhythm of the big bodhran that was the song's only accompaniment.

> *"O cam ye here the fight to shun,*
> *Or herd the sheep wi' me, man?*
> *Or were ye at the Sherra-moor,*
> *Or did the battle see, man?"*
> *I saw the battle, sair and teugh,*
> *And reekin-red ran mony a sheugh;*
> *My heart, for fear, gaed sough for sough,*
> *To hear the thuds, and see the cluds*
> *O' clans frae woods, in tartan duds,*
> *Wha glaum'd at kingdoms three, man.*

It went better than he'd thought; the song really *was* more chanted than sung, and he managed the whole of it with no more than the odd choke or cough. Fraser was rapt, glass forgotten in his hand.

"Oh, that's braw, man!" Fraser exclaimed. "Though yon poet's got the devil of an accent. Where's he come from, d'ye ken?"

"Er . . . Ayrshire, I think."

Fraser shook his head in admiration and sat back.

"Could ye maybe write it down for me?" he asked, almost shyly. "I wouldna put ye to the trouble of singin' it again, but I'd dearly love to learn the whole of it."

"I—sure," Roger said, taken aback. Well, what harm could it do to let Robert Burns's poem loose in the world some years in advance of Burns himself? "Ken anyone who can play a bodhran? It's best wi' the drum rattlin' in the background." He tapped his fingers in illustration.

"Oh, aye." Fraser was rustling about in the drawer of his desk; he came out with several sheets of foolscap, most with writing on them. Frowning, he flicked through the papers, picked one, and pulled it from the sheaf, placing it facedown in front of Roger, offering him the blank back side.

There were goose quills, rather tattered from use but well trimmed, in a jar on the desk, and a brass inkstand, which Fraser offered him with a generous sweep of one broad hand.

"My son's friend plays well—he's gone for a soldier, though, more's the pity." A shadow crossed Fraser's face.

"Ach." Roger clicked his tongue in sympathy; he was trying to make out the writing that showed faintly through the sheet. "Joined a Highland regiment, did he?"

"No," Fraser said, sounding a little startled. *Christ, were there Highland regiments yet?* "He's gone to France as a mercenary soldier. Better pay, fewer floggings than the army, he tells his da."

Roger's heart lifted; yes! It was a letter or maybe a journal entry—whatever it was, there was a date on it: 17 . . . was that a 3? Had to be, couldn't be an 8. 173 . . . it might be a 9 or a 0, couldn't tell for sure through the paper—no, it had to be a 9, so 1739. He breathed a sigh of relief. Something October, 1739.

"Probably safer," he said, only half attending to the conversation as he began to scratch out the lines. It was some time since he'd written with a quill, and he was awkward.

"Safer?"

"Aye," he said, "from the point of view of disease, mostly. Most men that die in the army die of some sickness, ken. Comes from the crowding, having to live in barracks, eat army rations. I'd think mercenaries might have a bit more freedom."

Fraser muttered something about "freedom to starve," but it was half under his breath. He was tapping his own fingers on the desk, trying to catch the rhythm as Roger wrote. He was surprisingly rather good; by the time the song was finished, he was singing it softly in a pleasant low tenor and had the drumming down pretty well.

Roger's mind was divided between the task in front of him and the feel of the letter under his hand. The feel of the paper and the look of the ink reminded him vividly of the wooden box, filled with Jamie's and Claire's letters. He had to stop himself from glancing at the shelf where it would be kept when this room was his.

They'd been rationing the letters, reading them slowly—but when Jem was taken, all bets were off. They'd rushed through the whole of the box, looking for any mention of Jem, any indication that he might have escaped from Cameron and found his way to the safety of his grandparents. Not a word about Jem. Not one.

They'd been so distraught that they'd scarcely noticed anything else the letters said, but occasional phrases and images floated up in his mind, quite randomly—some of them distinctly disturbing—Brianna's uncle Ian had died—but scarcely noticeable at the time.

They weren't anything he wanted to think about now, either.

"Will your son be studying the law, then, in Paris?" Roger asked abruptly. He picked up the fresh dram Brian had poured for him and took a sip.

"Aye, well, he'd maybe make a decent lawyer," Fraser admitted. "He could argue ye into the ground, I'll say that for him. But I think he hasna got the patience for law or politics." He smiled suddenly. "Jamie sees at once what he thinks should be done and canna understand why anyone else should think otherwise. And he'd rather pound someone than persuade them, if it comes to that."

Roger laughed ruefully.

"I understand the urge," he said.

"Oh, indeed." Fraser nodded, leaning back a little in his chair. "And I'll no say as that's not a necessary thing to do on occasion. Especially in the Highlands." He grimaced but not without humor.

"So, then. Why do ye think this Cameron has stolen your lad?" Fraser asked bluntly.

Roger wasn't surprised. As well as they'd been getting on together, he'd known Fraser had to be wondering just how much Roger was telling and how truthful he was. Well, he'd been ready for that question—and the answer was at least a version of the truth.

"We lived for a time in America," he said, and felt a pang with the saying of it. For an instant, their snug cabin on the Ridge was around him, Brianna asleep with her hair loose on the pillow beside him and the children's breath a sweet fog above them.

"America!" Fraser exclaimed in astonishment. "Where, then?"

"The colony of North Carolina. A good place," Roger hastened to add, "but not without its dangers."

"Name me one that is," Fraser said, but waved that aside. "And these dangers made ye come back?"

Roger shook his head, a tightness in his throat at the memory.

"No, it was our wee lass—Mandy, Amanda, she's called. She was born with a thing wrong with her heart, and there was no physician there who could treat it. So we came . . . back, and while we were in Scotland, my wife inherited some land, and so we stayed. But . . ." He hesitated, thinking how to put the rest, but knowing what he did of Fraser's antecedents and his history with the MacKenzies of Leoch, the man probably wouldn't be overly disturbed at his story.

"My wife's father," he said carefully, "is a good man—a very good man—but the sort who . . . draws attention. A leader of men, and one that other men . . . Well, he told me once that his own father had said to him that, since he was a large man, other men would try him—and they do."

He watched Brian Fraser's face carefully at this, but, beyond the twitch of an eyebrow, there was no apparent response.

"I'll not go into all the history of it"—*since it hasn't happened yet*—"but the long and the short of it is that my father-in-law was left in possession of a large sum in gold. He doesna regard it as his own property but as something held in trust. Still, there it is. And while it's been kept secret so far as possible . . ."

Fraser made a sympathetic sound, acknowledging the difficulties of secrecy in such conditions.

"So this Cameron learned of the treasure, did he? And thought to extort it from your father-in-law by taking the bairn captive?" Fraser's dark brow lowered at the thought.

"That may be in his mind. But beyond that—my son kens where the gold is hidden. He was with his grandfather when it was put away safe. Only the two of them ken the whereabouts—but Cameron learned that my son knew the place."

"Ah." Brian sat for a moment staring into his whisky, thinking. Finally he cleared his throat and looked up, meeting Roger's eyes. "I maybe shouldna say such a thing, but it may be in your own mind already. If he's taken the boy only because the lad kens where yon treasure is . . . well, was I a wicked man with no scruples, I think I might force the information out of the lad, so soon as I had him alone."

Roger felt the cold slide of the suggestion down into the pit of his belly. It *was* something that had been at the back of his own mind, though he hadn't admitted it to himself.

"Make him tell—and then kill him, you mean."

Fraser grimaced unhappily.

"I dinna want to think it," he said. "But without the lad, what is there to mark him out? A man alone—he could travel as he liked, without much notice."

"Yes," Roger said, and stopped to breathe. "Yes. Well . . . he didn't. I—I know the man, a little. I don't think he'd do that, mur—" His throat closed suddenly, and he coughed violently. "Murder a child," he finished hoarsely. "He wouldn't."

THEY GAVE HIM a room at the end of the hallway on the second floor. When his family would live here, this would be the children's playroom. He undressed to his shirt, put out the candle, and got into bed, resolutely ignoring the shadows in the corners that held the ghosts of giant cardboard building blocks, of dollhouses, six-guns, and chalkboards. The fringed skirt of Mandy's Annie Oakley costume fluttered at the corner of his eye.

He ached from follicles to toenails, inside and out, but the panic engendered by his arrival had passed. How he felt didn't matter, though; the question was—what now? They hadn't gone where they thought, he and Buck, but he had to assume that they *had* ended up in the right place. The place where Jem was.

How else could they have come here? Perhaps Rob Cameron knew more now about how the traveling worked, could control it, and had deliberately brought Jem to this time, in order to frustrate pursuit?

He was too exhausted to keep hold of his thoughts, let alone string them into coherence. He pushed everything out of his mind, so far as he could, and lay still, staring into the dark, seeing the shine of a rocking horse's eyes.

Then he got out of bed, knelt on the cold boards, and prayed.

32

"FOR MANY MEN WHO STUMBLE AT THE THRESHOLD ARE WELL FORETOLD THAT DANGER LURKS WITHIN"

Lallybroch
October 31, 1980

BRIANNA COULDN'T open her own front door. She kept trying, rattling the big iron key all over the escutcheon plate, until the WPC took it from her shaking hand and got it into the keyhole. She hadn't started to shake until the police car turned up the lane to Lallybroch.

"Rather an old lock," the police constable observed, giving it a dubious look. "Original to the house, is it?" She lifted her head, peering up the white-harled front of the house, pursing her lips at sight of the lintel, with its carved date.

"I don't know. We don't usually lock the door. We've never had burglars." Brianna's lips felt numb, but she thought she'd managed a weak smile. Luckily, Mandy was unable to contradict this bald-faced lie, as she'd seen a toad in the grass by the path and was following it, poking at it with the toe of her shoe to make it hop. Jemmy, glued protectively to Brianna's side, made a low noise in his throat that reminded her startlingly of her father, and she looked down at him, narrowing her eyes.

He made the noise again and looked away.

There was a rattle and click as the lock opened, and the constable straightened up with a pleased sound.

"Aye, that's done it. Now, you're quite sure as you'll be all right, will you, Mrs. MacKenzie?" the woman said, giving her a dubious look. "Out here by yourself, and your man away?"

"He'll be home soon," Brianna assured her, though her stomach went hollow at the words.

The woman eyed her consideringly, then gave a reluctant nod and pushed open the door.

"Well, then, you know best, I expect. I'll just check to see that your phone's in order and all the doors and windows locked, shall I, while you have a look round to be sure everything's as it should be?"

The lump of ice that had formed in her middle during the long hours of questioning shot straight up into her chest.

"I—I—I'm sure everything's fine." But the constable had already gone inside and was waiting impatiently for her. "Jem! Bring Mandy inside and take her up to the playroom, will you?" She couldn't bear to leave the kids outside by themselves, exposed. She could scarcely bear to have them out of her sight. But the *very* last thing she needed was to have Mandy tagging helpfully along, chatting to Constable Laughlin about Mr. Rob in the priest's hole. Leaving the door open, she hurried after the WPC.

"The phone's in there," she said, catching up with Constable Laughlin in the hall and gesturing toward Roger's study. "There's an extension in the kitchen. I'll go and check that and see to the back door." Not waiting for an answer, she strode down the hall and nearly threw herself through the swinging door that led to the kitchen.

She didn't pause to check anything but jerked open the junk drawer and snatched up a big rubber-covered flashlight. Meant to assist farmers lambing at night or searching for lost stock, the thing was a foot long and weighed nearly two pounds.

The .22 rifle was in the mudroom, and for an instant, as she walked through the house, she debated killing him, in a dispassionate way that would probably scare her if she had time to think about it. She had Jem back, after all—but no. Constable Laughlin would certainly recognize the sound of a shot, in spite of the muffling green baize on the kitchen door. And there was apparently more she needed to learn from Rob Cameron. She'd knock him unconscious and tape his mouth.

She stepped into the mudroom and quietly closed the kitchen door behind her. There was a deadbolt, but she couldn't lock it from this side without the key, and her keys were on the table in the foyer, where Constable Laughlin had left them. Instead, she dragged the heavy bench over and jammed it catty-corner between the door and the wall, concentrating on the logistics. Where was the best place to hit someone on the head so as to render them unconscious without fracturing their skull? She had a vague memory of her mother mentioning that once . . . the occiput?

She'd expected an outcry from Cameron at the sound of her entry, but he didn't peep. She could hear footsteps above, the confident stride of an adult going down the hall. Constable Laughlin on her tour of inspection, no doubt checking the first-floor windows, ladder-bearing burglars in mind. She closed her eyes for an instant, envisioning the constable sticking her head into the playroom just as Mandy was regaling her brother with the details of her own adventures the night before.

Nothing to be done about that. She took a deep breath, lifted the grate over the priest's hole, and shone the light down into the shadows. The empty shadows.

For a few moments she went on looking, swinging the torch beam from one side of the priest's hole to the other, then back, then back again . . . her mind simply refusing to believe her eyes.

The light caught the dull gleam of duct tape—two or three discarded wads, flung into a corner. There was a cold feeling at the back of her neck, and she jerked round, flashlight raised—but it was no more than apprehension; no one was there. The outer door was locked, the mudroom windows secure.

The door was locked. She made a small, frightened sound and clapped her hand hard over her mouth. Like the door between mudroom and kitchen, the mudroom's outer door locked with a deadbolt—from the inside. If someone had gone out that way and left the door locked behind him—he had a key to the house. And her rifle was gone.

⁂

THEY'RE TOO LITTLE, she kept thinking. *They shouldn't know about things like this; they shouldn't know it's possible.* Her hands were shaking; it took three tries to open the sticky drawer in Mandy's dresser, and after the third failure, she pounded it in fury with the side of her fist, whispering through gritted teeth, "You goddamned fucking bloody buggering *thing*! Don't you *dare* get in my way!" She crashed her fist on top of the dresser, raised her foot, and smashed the sole of her sneaker into the thing so hard that it rocked back and thumped into the wall with a bang.

She grabbed the drawer pulls and yanked. The terrorized drawer shot out, and she snatched the whole thing free and flung it into the opposite wall, where it struck and exploded in a rainbow spray of underpants and tiny striped T-shirts.

She walked over and looked down at the battered drawer, lying upside down on the floor.

"So there," she said calmly. "Teach *you* to get in my way when I have things to think about."

"Like what, Mam?" said a cautious voice from the doorway. She looked up to see Jemmy hovering there, eyes flicking from her to the mistreated drawer and back.

"Oh." She thought of trying to explain the drawer but instead cleared her throat and sat down on the bed, holding out a hand to him. "Come here, *a bhalaich.*"

His ginger brows flicked up at the Gaelic endearment, but he came willingly, cuddling into her arm. He hugged her hard, burying his head in her shoulder, and she held him as tightly as she could, rocking back and forth and making the sorts of soft noises she'd made to him when he was tiny.

"It'll be all right, baby," she whispered to him. "It will."

She heard him swallow and felt his small, square back move under her hand.

"Yeah." His voice quivered a little and he sniffed hard, then tried again. "Yeah. But *what's* going to be all right, Mam? What's going on?" He drew away a little then, looking up at her with eyes that held more questions and more knowledge than any nine-year-old should reasonably have.

"Mandy says you put Mr. Cameron in the priest's hole. But he's not there now—I looked."

A cold hand stroked her nape as she remembered the shock of the empty hole.

"No, he's not."

"But you didn't let him out, did you?"

"No. I didn't let him out. He—"

"So somebody else did," he said positively. "Who, do you think?"

"You have a very logical mind," she said, smiling a little, despite herself. "You get it from your Grandda Jamie."

"He said I got it from Grannie Claire," Jem replied, but automatically; he wasn't to be distracted. "I thought maybe it was the man who chased me at the dam—but he couldn't have been here letting Mr. Cameron out at the same time he was chasing me. Could he?" A sudden fear showed in his eyes, and she choked back the overwhelming urge to hunt the man down and kill him like a rabid skunk.

The man had got away at the dam, running off into the dark when the police showed up, but, God help her, she was going to find him one day, and then—but this was not the day. The problem now was to stop him—or Rob Cameron—from getting anywhere near her kids again.

Then she got what Jemmy was saying and felt the chill she'd carried in her heart spread like hoarfrost through her body.

"You mean there has to be another man," she said, surprised at how calm she sounded. "Mr. Cameron, the man at the dam—and whoever let Mr. Cameron out of the priest's hole."

"It could be a lady," Jemmy pointed out. He seemed less scared, talking about it. That was a good thing, because her own skin was rippling with fear.

"Do you know what Grannie called—calls—goose bumps?" She held out her arm, the fine reddish hairs all standing on end. "Horripilation."

"Horripilation," Jemmy repeated, and gave a small, nervous giggle. "I like that word."

"Me, too." She took a deep breath and stood up. "Go pick out a change of clothes and your PJs, would you, sweetheart? I have to make a couple of phone calls, and then I think we're going to go visit Auntie Fiona."

33

IT'S BEST TO SLEEP IN A HALE SKIN

ROGER WOKE SUDDENLY, but without shock. No sense of abandoned dreams, no half-heard noise, but his eyes were open and he was fully aware. It was perhaps an hour before sunrise. He'd left the shutters open; the room was cold and the clouded sky the color of a black pearl.

He lay motionless, listening to his heart beat, and realized that for the first time in several days it wasn't pounding. He wasn't afraid. The fear and turmoil of the night, the terror of the last few days, had vanished. His body was completely relaxed; so was his mind.

There *was* something floating in his mind. Absurdly, it was a line from "Johnny Cope": *"It's best to sleep in a hale skin; for 'twill be a bluidy morning."* Weirder still, he could hear—could almost feel—himself singing it, in his old voice, full of power and enthusiasm.

"Not that I'm ungrateful," he said to the whitewashed ceiling beams, his morning voice cracked and rough. "But what the hell?"

He wasn't sure whether he was talking to God or to his own unconscious, but the likelihood of getting a straight answer was probably the same in either case. He heard the soft thud of a closing door somewhere below and someone outside whistling through his or her teeth—Annie or Senga, maybe, on the way to the morning milking.

A knock came on his own door: Jenny Murray, tidy in a white pinny, dark curly hair tied back but not yet capped for the day, with a jug of hot water, a pot of soft soap, and a razor for shaving.

"Da says can ye ride a horse?" she said without preamble, looking him up and down in an assessing sort of way.

"I can," he replied gruffly, taking the towel-wrapped jug from her. He needed badly to clear the phlegm from his throat and spit but couldn't bring himself to do that in front of her. Consequently, he just nodded and muttered, *"Taing,"* as he took the razor, instead of asking why.

"Breakfast'll be in the kitchen when you are," she said matter-of-factly. "Bring the jug down, aye?"

AN HOUR LATER, filled to bursting with hot tea, parritch, bannocks with honey, and black pudding, he found himself on an autumn-shaggy horse, following Brian Fraser through the rising mist of early morning.

"We'll go round to the crofts nearby," Fraser had told him over breakfast, spooning strawberry preserves onto a bannock. "Even if no one's seen your lad—and to be honest," his wide mouth twisted in apology, "I think I should ha' heard already if anyone had seen a stranger in the district—they'll pass on the word."

"Aye, thanks very much," he'd said, meaning it. Even in his own time, gossip was the fastest way of spreading news in the Highlands. No matter how fast Rob Cameron might travel, Roger doubted he could outpace the speed of talk, and the thought made him smile. Jenny caught it and smiled back sympathetically, and he thought again what a very pretty lass she was.

The sky was still low and threatening, but impending rain had never yet deterred anyone in Scotland from doing anything and wasn't likely to start now. His throat felt much better for the hot tea, and the odd sense of calm with which he'd waked was still with him.

Something had changed in the night. Maybe it was sleeping in Lallybroch, among the ghosts of his own future. Perhaps that had settled his mind while he slept.

Maybe it was answered prayer and a moment of grace. Maybe it was no more than Samuel Beckett's bloody existential *I can't go on; I'll go on.* If he had a choice—and he did, Beckett be damned—he'd go with grace.

Whatever had caused it, he wasn't disoriented any longer, thrown off-balance by what he knew about the futures of the people around him. There was still a deep concern about them—and the need to find Jem still filled him. But now it was a quiet, hard thing in his core. A focus, a weapon. Something to brace his back against.

He straightened his shoulders as he thought this and, at the same time, saw Brian's straight, flat back and the broad, firm shoulders under the dark sett of his tartan coat. They were the echo of Jamie's—and the promise of Jem's.

Life goes on. It was his job above all to rescue Jem, as much for Brian Fraser's sake as for his own.

And now he knew what had changed in him and gave thanks to God for what was indeed grace. He'd slept—and waked—in a whole skin. And however bloody the mornings to come, he had direction now, calmness and hope, because the good man who rode before him was on his side.

THEY VISITED MORE than a dozen crofts in the course of the day and stopped a tinker they met along the way, as well. No one had seen a stranger recently, with or without a red-haired lad, but all promised to spread the word and all without exception offered their prayers for Roger and his quest.

They stopped for supper and the night with a family named Murray that had a substantial farmhouse, though nothing to rival Lallybroch. The owner, John Murray, turned out in the course of conversation to be Brian Fraser's factor—the overseer of much of the physical business of Lallybroch's estate—and he lent his grave attention to Roger's story.

An elderly, long-faced man with rawboned, muscular arms, he sucked his teeth consideringly, nodding his head.

"Aye, I'll send one of my lads down in the morn," he said. "But if ye've found nay trace o' this fellow up along the Hieland passes . . . might be as ye should go down to the garrison and tell your tale, Mr. MacKenzie."

Brian Fraser cocked a dark brow, half-frowning at this, but then nodded.

"Aye, that's no a bad thought, John." He turned to Roger. "It's some distance, ken—the garrison's in Fort William, down by Duncansburgh. But we can ask along our way, and the soldiers send messengers regularly betwixt the garrison, Inverness, and Edinburgh. Should they hear a thing about your man, they could get word to us swiftly."

"And they could maybe arrest the fellow on the spot," Murray added, his rather melancholy countenance brightening a bit at the idea.

"Moran taing," Roger said, bowing a little to them both in acknowledg-

ment, then turning to Fraser. "I'll do that, and thanks. But, sir—ye needna go with me. You've business of your own to tend to, and I wouldna—"

"I'll come, and glad to," Fraser interrupted him firmly. "The hay's long since in and naught to do that John canna take care of for me."

He smiled at Murray, who made a small noise, halfway between a sigh and a cough, but nodded.

"Fort William's in the midst of the Camerons' land, forbye," Murray observed absently, gazing off toward the dark fields. They had dined with his family but then come out to the dooryard, ostensibly to share a pipe; it smoldered in Murray's hand, disregarded for the moment.

Brian made a noncommittal sound in his throat, and Roger wondered just what Murray meant. Was it a warning that Rob Cameron might have relatives or allies to whom he was heading? Or was there some tension or difficulty between some of the Camerons and the Frasers of Lovat—or between the Camerons and the MacKenzies?

That presented some difficulty. If there *was* a feud of any importance going on, Roger ought already to know about it. He gave a small, grave "hmp" himself and resolved to approach any Camerons with caution. At the same time . . . *was* Rob Cameron intending to seek refuge or help with the Camerons of this time? Had he maybe come to the past before and had a hiding place prepared among his own clan? That was an evil thought, and Roger felt his stomach tighten as though to resist a punch.

But no; there hadn't been time. If Cameron had only learned about time travel from the guide Roger had written for his children's eventual use, he wouldn't have had time to go to the past, find ancient Camerons, and . . . no, ridiculous.

Roger shook off the tangle of half-formed thoughts as though they were a fishing net thrown over his head. There was nothing more to be done until they reached the garrison tomorrow.

Murray and Fraser were leaning on the fence now, sharing the pipe and chatting casually in Gaelic.

"My daughter bids me ask after your son," Brian Fraser said, with an air of casualness. "Any word?"

Murray snorted, smoke purling from his nostrils, and said something very idiomatic about his son. Fraser grimaced in sympathy and shook his head.

"At least ye ken he's alive," he said, dropping back into English. "Like enough, he'll come home when he's had his fill of fighting. We did, aye?" He nudged Murray gently in the ribs, and the taller man snorted again, but with less ferocity.

"It wasna boredom that led us here, *a dhuine dhubh*. Not you, anyway." He raised one shaggy graying brow, and Fraser laughed, though Roger thought there was a regretful edge in it.

He remembered the story very well: Brian Fraser, a bastard of old Lord Lovat's, had stolen Ellen MacKenzie from her brothers Colum and Dougal, the MacKenzies of Castle Leoch, and had ended up at last with her at Lallybroch, the pair of them more or less disowned by both clans but at least left alone by them. He'd seen the portrait of Ellen, too—tall, red-haired, and undeniably a woman worth the effort.

She'd looked very much like her granddaughter Brianna. By reflex, he closed his eyes, breathed deep of the cold Highland evening, and thought he felt her there at his side. If he opened them again, might he see her standing in the smoke?

I'll come back, he thought to her. *No matter what,* a nighean ruaidh—*I'm coming back. With Jem.*

34

SANCTUARY

I T WAS NEARLY AN hour's drive over the narrow, twisting Highland roads from Lallybroch to Fiona Buchan's new house in Inverness. Plenty of time for Brianna to wonder if she was doing the right thing, if she had any right to involve Fiona and her family in a matter that looked more dangerous by the moment. Plenty of time to get a stiff neck from looking over her shoulder—though if she was being followed, how would she know?

She'd had to tell the kids where Roger was, as gently and briefly as possible. Mandy had put a thumb in her mouth and stared gravely at her, round-eyed. Jem . . . Jem hadn't said anything but had gone white under his freckles and looked as though he was about to throw up. She glanced in the rearview mirror. He was hunched in a corner of the backseat now, face turned to the window.

"He'll come back, honey," she'd said, trying to hug him in reassurance. He'd let her but stood stiff in her arms, stricken.

"It's my fault," he'd said, his voice small and wooden as a puppet's. "I should have got away sooner. Then Dad wouldn't—"

"It's *not* your fault," she'd said firmly. "It's Mr. Cameron's fault and no one else's. You were *very* brave. And Daddy will come back really soon."

Jem had swallowed hard but said nothing in reply. When she'd let him go, he swayed for a moment, and Mandy had come up and hugged his legs.

"Daddy'll come back," she said encouragingly. "For supper!"

"It might take a little bit longer than that," Bree said, smiling in spite of the panic packed like a snowball under her ribs.

She drew a deep breath of relief as the highway opened out near the airport and she could go faster than 30 mph. Another wary glance in the mirror, but the road was empty behind her. She stepped on the gas.

Fiona was one of the only two people who knew. The other one was in

Boston: her mother's oldest friend, Joe Abernathy. But she needed sanctuary for Jem and Mandy, right now. She couldn't stay with them at Lallybroch; the walls were two feet thick in places, yes, but it was a farm manor, not a fortified tower house, and hadn't been built with any notion that the inhabitants might need to repel invaders or stand off a siege.

Being in the city gave her a sense of relief. Having people around. Witnesses. Camouflage. Help. She pulled up in the street outside the Craigh na Dun Bed-and-Breakfast (three AA stars) with the sense of an exhausted swimmer crawling up onto shore.

The timing was good. It was early afternoon; Fiona would have finished the cleaning and it wouldn't yet be time to check in new guests or start the supper.

A little painted bell in the shape of a bluebell tinkled when they opened the door, and one of Fiona's daughters instantly popped an inquiring head out of the lounge.

"Auntie Bree!" she shouted, and at once the lobby was filled with children, as Fiona's three girls pushed one another out of the way to hug Bree, pick up Mandy, and tickle Jem, who promptly dropped to all fours and crawled under the bench where folk left their wraps.

"What—oh, it's you, hen!" Fiona, coming out of the kitchen in a workmanlike canvas apron that said PIE QUEEN on the front, smiled with delight at sight of Bree and enveloped her in a floury hug.

"What's wrong?" Fiona murmured in her ear, under cover of the embrace. She drew back a bit, still holding Bree, and looked up at her, squinting in half-playful worry. "Rog playing away from home, is he?"

"You . . . could say that." Bree managed a smile but evidently not a very good one, because Fiona at once clapped her hands, bringing order out of the chaos in the lobby, and dispatched all the children to the upstairs lounge to watch telly. Jem, looking hunted, was coaxed out from under the bench and reluctantly followed the girls, looking back over his shoulder at his mother. She smiled and made shooing motions at him, then followed Fiona into the kitchen, glancing by reflex over her own shoulder.

THE TEAKETTLE SCREAMED, interrupting Brianna, but not before she'd got to the most salient point of her story. Fiona warmed and filled the pot, purse-lipped with concentration.

"Ye say he took the rifle. Ye've still got your shotgun?"

"Yes. It's under the front seat of my car at the moment."

Fiona nearly dropped the pot. Brianna shot out an arm and grabbed the handle, steadying it. Her hands were freezing, and the warm china felt wonderful.

"Well, I wasn't going to leave it in a house the bastards have a key to, now, was I?"

Fiona set down the pot and crossed herself. *"Dia eadarainn 's an t-olc."* *God between us and evil.* She sat, giving Brianna a sharp look. "And ye're quite sure as it's bastards, plural?"

"Yes, I bloody am," Bree said tersely. "Even if Rob Cameron managed to grow wings and fly out of my priest's hole—let me tell you what happened to Jem at the dam."

She did, in a few brief sentences, by the end of which Fiona was glancing over her own shoulder at the closed kitchen door. She looked back at Bree, settling herself. In her early thirties, she was a pleasantly rounded young woman with a lovely face and the calm expression of a mother who normally has the Indian sign on her offspring, but at the moment she had a look that Brianna's own mother would have described as "blood in her eye." She said something very bad in English regarding the man who'd chased Jem.

"So, then," she said, picking up a paring knife from the nearby drainboard and examining the edge critically, "what shall we do?"

Bree drew a breath and sipped cautiously at the hot, milky tea. It was sweet, silky, and very comforting—but not nearly as comforting as that "we."

"Well, first—would you let Jem and Mandy stay here while I go do a few things? It might be overnight; I brought their pajamas, just in case." She nodded at the paper sack that she'd set down on one of the chairs.

"Aye, of course." A small frown formed between Fiona's dark brows. "What . . . *sorts* of things?"

"It's—" Brianna began, intending to say, *"better if you don't know,"* but in fact someone *had* better know where she was going and what she was doing. Just in case she didn't come back. A little bubble of what might be either fear or anger rose up through the sense of warmth in her middle.

"I'm going to visit Jock MacLeod in hospital. He's the night watchman who found Jem at the dam. He might know the man who hit him and tried to take Jem. And he *does* know Rob Cameron. He can maybe tell me who Cameron's mates are outside of work or in lodge."

She rubbed a hand down over her face, thinking.

"After that . . . I'll talk to Rob's sister and his nephew. If she's not involved in whatever he's up to, she'll be worried. And if she *is* involved—then I need to know that."

"D'ye think ye'll be able to tell?" Fiona's frown had eased a bit, but she still looked worried.

"Oh, yes," Brianna said, with grim determination. "I'll be able to tell. For one thing, if someone I talk to *is* involved, they're probably likely to try to stop me asking questions."

Fiona made a small noise that could best be spelled as *"eeengh,"* indicating deep concern.

Brianna drank the last of her tea and set down the cup with an explosive sigh.

"And then," she said, "I'm going back to Lallybroch to meet a locksmith and have him change all the locks and install burglar alarms on the lower windows." She looked questioningly at Fiona. "I don't know how long it might take. . . ."

"Aye, that's why ye brought the kids' nighties. Nay problem, hen." She chewed her lower lip, eyeing Brianna.

Bree knew what she was thinking, debating whether to ask or not, and saved her the trouble.

"I don't know what I'm going to do about Roger," she said steadily.

"He'll come back, surely," Fiona began, but Bree shook her head. Horrifying Realization Number 3 couldn't be denied any longer.

"I don't think so," she said, though she bit her lip as if to keep the words from escaping. "He—he can't know that Jem isn't there. And he'd never ab-abandon him."

Fiona was clasping Brianna's hand in both of her own.

"No, no, of course he wouldna do that. But if he and the other fellow go on searching and find no trace . . . eventually, surely he'd think . . ." Her voice died away as she tried to imagine *what* Roger might think under those circumstances.

"Oh, he'll be thinking, all right," Bree said, and managed a small, shaky laugh. The thought of Roger's determination, the growing sense of fear and desperation that must inevitably eat away at it, his fight to keep going—because he would; he'd never give up and come back to tell her Jem was lost for good. For if he didn't find any trace of Jem, what could he think? That Cameron had maybe killed Jem, hidden his body, and gone to America in search of the gold? Or that they had both been lost in that horrifying space between one time and another, never to be found?

"Well, and he'll be praying, too," Fiona said with a brisk squeeze of Bree's hand. "I can help wi' that."

That made tears well, and she blinked hard, scrubbing at her eyes with a paper napkin.

"I can't cry now," she said, in a choked voice. "I *can't*. I haven't got time." She stood up suddenly, pulling her hand free. She sniffed, blew her nose hard on the napkin, and sniffed again.

"Fiona . . . I—I know you haven't told anybody about . . . us," she began, and even she could hear the doubt in her own voice.

Fiona snorted.

"I have not," she said. "I'd be taken off to the booby hatch, and what would Ernie do wi' the girls and all? Why?" she added, giving Brianna a hard look. "What are ye thinking?"

"Well . . . the women who—who dance at Craigh na Dun. Do you think any of them know what it is?"

Fiona sucked in one cheek, thinking.

"One or two o' the older ones might have an idea," she said slowly. "We've been callin' down the sun on Beltane there for as far back as anyone knows. And some things do get passed down, ken. Be strange if nobody ever wondered. But even if someone kent for sure what happens there, they'd not speak—no more than I would."

"Right. I just wondered—could you maybe find out, quietly, if any of the women have ties to Rob Cameron? Or maybe . . . to the Orkneys?"

"To what?" Fiona's eyes went round. "Why the Orkneys?"

"Because Rob Cameron went on archaeological digs there. And I think that's what made him interested in stone circles to start with. I know one man named Callahan, a friend of Roger's—who worked up there with him, and I'll talk to him, too—maybe tomorrow; I don't think I'll have time today. But if there's anyone else who might be connected with things like that . . ."

It was more than a long shot, but at the moment she was inclined to look under any stone she could lift.

"I'll call round," Fiona said thoughtfully. "And speak of calling—telephone me if ye're not coming back tonight, aye? Just so as I know ye're safe."

Bree nodded, her throat tight, and hugged Fiona, taking one more moment's strength from her friend.

Fiona saw her down the hall to the front door, pausing at the foot of the stair, and glanced toward the chatter coming from above. Did Bree want to say goodbye to Jem and Mandy? Wordless, Brianna shook her head. Her feelings were too raw; she couldn't hide them sufficiently and didn't want to scare the kids. Instead, she pressed her fingers to her lips and blew a kiss up the stairs, then turned to the door.

"That shotgun—" Fiona began behind her, and stopped. Brianna turned and raised an eyebrow.

"They canna get ballistics off buckshot, can they?"

35

AN GEARASDAN

THEY REACHED Fort William in early afternoon of the second day's travel.

"How large is the garrison?" Roger asked, eyeing the stone walls of the fort. It was modest, as forts went, with only a few buildings and a drill yard within the surrounding walls.

"Maybe forty men, I'd say," Brian replied, turning sideways to allow a pair of red-coated guards carrying muskets to pass him in the narrow entry passage. "Fort Augustus is the only garrison north of it, and that's got maybe a hundred."

That was surprising—or maybe not. If Roger was right about the date, it would be another three years before there was much talk of Jacobites in the Highlands—let alone enough of it to alarm the English crown into sending troops en masse to keep a lid on the situation.

The fort was open, and any number of civilians appeared to have business with the army, judging from the small crowd near one building. Fraser steered him toward another, smaller one with a tilt of his head, though.

"We'll see the commander, I think."

"You know him?" A worm of curiosity tickled his spine. Surely it was too early for—

"I've met him the once. Buncombe, he's called. Seems a decent fellow, for a Sassenach." Fraser gave his name to a clerk in the outer room, and within a moment they were ushered into the commander's office.

"Oh . . ." A small, middle-aged man in uniform with tired eyes behind a pair of half spectacles half-rose, half-bowed, and dropped back into his seat as though the effort of recognition had exhausted him. "Broch Tuarach. Your servant, sir."

Perhaps it had, Roger thought. The man's face was gaunt and lined, and his breath whistled audibly in his lungs. Claire might have known specifically what was up with Captain Buncombe, but it didn't take a doctor to know that something was physically amiss.

Still, Buncombe listened civilly to his story, called in the clerk to make a careful note of Cameron's description and Jem's, and promised that these would be circulated to the garrison and that any patrols or messengers would be advised to ask after the fugitives.

Brian had thoughtfully brought along a couple of bottles in his saddlebags and now produced one, which he set on the desk with a gurgling thump of enticement.

"We thank ye, sir, for your help. If ye'd allow us to present a small token of appreciation for your kindness . . ."

A small but genuine smile appeared on Captain Buncombe's worn face.

"I would, sir. But only if you gentlemen will join me . . . ? Ah, yes." Two worn pewter cups and—after a brief search—a crystal goblet with a chip out of the rim were produced, and the blessed silence of the dram fell upon the tiny office.

After a few moments' reverence, Buncombe opened his eyes and sighed.

"Amazing, sir. Your own manufacture, is it?"

Brian inclined his head with a modest shake.

"Nay but a few bottles at Hogmanay, just for the family."

Roger had himself seen the root cellar from which Brian had chosen the bottle, lined from floor to ceiling with small casks and with an atmosphere to it that would have knocked a moose flat had he stayed to breathe it long. But an instant's thought told him that it was probably wiser not to let a garrison full of soldiers know that you kept any sort of liquor in large quantities on your premises, no matter what terms you were on with their commander. He caught Brian's eye, and Fraser looked aside with a small "mmphm" and a tranquil smile.

"Amazing," Buncombe repeated, and tipped another inch into his glass, offering the bottle round. Roger followed Brian's lead and refused, nursing his own drink while the other two men fell into a sort of conversation he recognized very well. Not friendly but courteous, a trade of information that might be of advantage to one or both—and a careful avoidance of anything that might give the other too *much* advantage.

He'd seen Jamie do it any number of times, in America. It was headman's talk, and there were rules to it. Of course . . . Jamie must have seen his da do it any number of times himself; it was bred in his bones.

He thought Jem maybe had it. He had *something* that made people look at him twice—something beyond the hair, he amended, and smiled to himself.

While Buncombe occasionally directed a question to him, Roger was for the most part able to leave them to it, and he gradually relaxed. The rain had passed, and a beam of sun from the window rested on his shoulders, warming him from without as the whisky warmed him within. He felt for the first time that he might be accomplishing something in his search, rather than merely flailing desperately round the Highlands.

"And they could maybe arrest the fellow," John Murray had remarked, anent the soldiers and Rob Cameron. A comforting thought, that.

The clan angle, though . . . he didn't *think* Cameron could have accomplices here, but—he straightened in his chair. *He* had an accomplice from this time, didn't he? Buck had the gene, and while it was clearly less frequent to travel forward from one's original lifeline—well, Roger *thought* it was less frequent (his own lack of knowledge was an unnerving realization in itself)—Buck had done it. If Cameron was a traveler, he'd got the gene from an ancestor who could also have done it.

Chill was running through his veins like iced wine, killing the whisky's warmth, and a sinister tangle of cold worms came writhing into his mind. Could it be a conspiracy, maybe, between Buck and Rob Cameron? Or Buck and some ancient Cameron from his own time?

He'd never thought Buck was telling the whole truth about himself or his own journey through the stones. Could all this have been a plot to lure Roger away from Lallybroch—away from Bree?

Now the worms were bloody *eating* his brain. He picked up his cup and threw back the rest of the whisky at a gulp to kill them. Buncombe and Fraser both glanced at him in surprise but then courteously resumed their conversation.

In the cold light of his present state of mind, something else now cast new shadows. Brian Fraser. While Roger had taken Fraser's bringing him to the garrison as purely a helpful gesture toward finding Jem, it had another function, didn't it? It displayed Roger to Captain Buncombe, in a context that made it clear that he had no claim of clan obligation or personal friendship on Fraser, just in case Roger turned out not to be what he said he was. And it allowed Fraser to see whether Buncombe recognized Roger or not. Just in case he wasn't what he said he was.

He took a deep breath and pressed his hands on the desktop, concentrating on the feel of the wood grain under his fingers. All right. Perfectly reasonable. How many times had he seen Jamie do the same sort of thing? For these men, the welfare of their own people always came first; they'd protect Lallybroch, or Fraser's Ridge, above all, but that didn't mean they were unwilling to help when help was in their power to give.

And he did believe that Fraser meant to help him. He clung to the thought and found that it floated.

Fraser glanced at him again, and something in the man's face eased at whatever it saw in his own. Brian picked up the bottle and poured another inch into Roger's glass.

"We'll find him, man," he said softly, in Gaelic, before turning to serve Captain Buncombe in turn.

He drank and put everything out of his mind, concentrating on the trivia of the conversation. It was all right. Everything was going to be all right.

He was still repeating this mantra to himself when he heard shouts and whistles from outside. He glanced toward the window, but it showed nothing save a view of the fort's wall. Captain Buncombe looked startled—but Brian Fraser was on his feet, and moving fast.

Roger followed, emerging into the fort's drill yard to see a fine-looking young woman mounted on a large, fine-looking horse and glaring down at a small cluster of soldiers who had gathered round her stirrup, pushing one another, snatching at the reins, and shouting remarks up at her. The horse plainly didn't like it, but she was managing to keep it under control. She was also holding a switch in one hand and, from the look on her face, was plainly choosing a target amongst those presenting themselves.

"Jenny!" Brian roared, and she looked up, startled. The soldiers were startled, too; they turned and, seeing Captain Buncombe come out behind the Scot, instantly melted away, heads down as they hurried off about their business.

Roger was at Brian's shoulder when he grabbed the horse's bridle.

"What in the name of the Blessed Mother are you—" Brian began, furious, but she interrupted him, looking straight at Roger.

"Your kinsman," she said. "William Buccleigh. He sent word to Lallybroch that he's taken bad and will ye come at once. They said he may not live."

IT TOOK A good day and a half to make the journey, even in good weather. Given that it was raining, that the journey back was uphill, and that the latter portion of it involved stumbling around in the dark, hunting for a nearly invisible trail, they covered the distance in a surprisingly short time.

"I'll come in with ye," Brian had said, swinging off his horse in the dooryard. "They're no my tenants, but they know me."

The household—it was a modest crofter's cottage, dull white as a pebble in the light of a gibbous moon—was closed up tight for the night, shutters drawn and the door bolted. Fraser thumped on the door and shouted in Gaelic, though, identifying himself and saying that he'd brought the sick man's kinsman to him, and presently the door swung open, framing a squat, bearded gentleman in shirt and nightcap, who peered at them for a long moment before stepping back with a gruff "Come ben."

Roger's first impression was that the house was crammed to the rafters with odorous humanity. These lay in small snuggled heaps on the floor near the hearth or on pallets by the far wall, and here and there tousled heads poked up like prairie dogs, blinking in the glow of the smoored fire to see what was to do.

Their host—introduced by Fraser as Angus MacLaren—nodded curtly to Roger and gestured toward a bedstead drawn into the center of the room.

Two or three small children were sleeping on it, but Roger could just make out the blur of Buck's face on the pillow. Christ, he hoped Buck didn't have anything contagious.

He leaned in close, whispering, "Buck?" so as not to wake anyone who hadn't waked already. He couldn't make out much of Buck's face in the gloom—and it was covered with beard stubble, as well—but his eyes were closed, and he didn't open them in response to Roger's saying his name. Nor in response to Roger's laying a hand on his arm. The arm did feel warm, but given the suffocating atmosphere in the cottage, he thought it likely Buck would feel warm even if he'd been dead for hours.

He squeezed the arm, lightly at first, then harder—and at last Buck gave a strangled cough and opened his eyes. He blinked slowly, not seeming to recognize Roger, then closed them again. His chest heaved visibly, though, and he breathed now with a slow, clearly audible gasping note.

"He says as there's something the matter wi' his heart," MacLaren told Roger, low-voiced. He was leaning over Roger's shoulder, watching Buck intently. "It flutters, like, and when it does, he goes blue and canna breathe or stand up. My second-eldest lad found him out in the heather yesterday afternoon, flat as a squashed toad. We fetched him down and gave him a bit to drink, and he asked would we send someone to Lallybroch to ask after his kinsman."

"Moran taing," said Roger. "I'm that obliged to ye, sir." He turned to Brian, who was lurking behind MacLaren, looking at Buck with a small frown.

"And thank ye, too, sir," Roger said to him. "For all your help. I can't thank ye enough."

Fraser shrugged, dismissing this.

"I imagine ye'll stay with him? Aye. If he's able to travel in the morn, bring him along to Lallybroch. Or send, if there's aught we can do." Fraser nodded to MacLaren in farewell but then paused, squinting through the murk at Buck's face. He glanced at Roger, as though comparing their features.

"Is your kinsman from Lochalsh, as well?" he asked, curious, and looked back at Buck. "He's the look of my late wife's people about him. The MacKenzies of Leoch." Then he noticed the small squat shape of what must be Mrs. MacLaren—glowering under her cap—and he coughed, bowed, and took his leave without waiting for an answer.

Mr. MacLaren went to bolt the door, and the lady of the house turned to Roger, yawned cavernously, then motioned toward the bed, scratching her bottom unself-consciously.

"Ye can sleep wi' him," she said. "Push him oot the bed if he dies, aye? I dinna want ma quilts all spoilt."

HAVING TAKEN OFF his boots, Roger lay down gingerly on the quilt beside Buck—readjusting the position of the small children, who were limp and flexible as cats in sunshine—and spent the remainder of the night listening to his ancestor's irregular snoring, poking him whenever it seemed to stop. Toward dawn, though, he dozed off, to be waked sometime later by the thick warm smell of porridge.

Alarmed by the fact that he'd fallen asleep, he raised up on one elbow to find Buck pale-faced and breathing stertorously through his mouth. He seized his ancestor by the shoulder and shook him, causing Buck to start up in bed, glaring wildly round. Spotting Roger, he punched him solidly in the stomach.

"Bugger off wi' that!"

"I just wanted to be sure you were alive, you bastard!"

"What are ye doing here in the first place?" Buck rubbed a hand through his disheveled hair, looking cross and confused.

"Ye sent for me, fool." Roger was cross, too. His mouth felt as though he'd been chewing straw all night. "How are you, anyway?"

"I—not that well." Buck's face changed abruptly from crossness to a pale apprehension, and he put a hand flat on his chest, pressing hard. "I—it—it doesna feel right."

"Lie down, for God's sake!" Roger squirmed off the bed, narrowly avoiding stepping on a little girl who was sitting on the floor, playing with the buckles of his boots. "I'll get ye some water."

A row of children was watching this byplay with interest, ignored by Mrs. MacLaren and two of the older girls, who were respectively stirring a huge cauldron of parritch and rapidly laying the large table for breakfast, slapping down wooden plates and spoons like cards in a game of old maid.

"If ye need the privy," one of the girls advised him, pausing in her rounds, "ye'd best go now. Robbie and Sandy've gone to tend the kine, and Stuart's no got his shoon on yet." She lifted her chin toward a stripling of twelve or so, who was crawling slowly about on hands and knees, with one worn shoe in one hand, peering under the sparse furniture in search of its mate. "Oh— and since your kinsman's lived the night, Da's gone for the healer."

36

THE SCENT OF A STRANGER

S HE'D BROUGHT Jock MacLeod the traditional hospital present of grapes. And a bottle of eighteen-year-old Bunnahabhain, which had brightened his face—or what could be seen of it behind the bandage that wrapped his head and the bruising that narrowed both eyes to bloodshot slits.

"Oh, I'm a bit peely-wally," he'd told her, wrapping the bottle in his dressing gown and handing it to her to stash in his bedside cabinet, "but no bad, no bad. A wee dunt on the head, is all. I'm only glad the lad got away. D'ye ken how he came to be in the tunnel, lass?"

She'd given him the official version, listened patiently to his speculations, and then asked if he'd maybe recognized the man who hit him?

"Well, I did, then," Jock had said, surprising her. He leaned back on his pillows. "Which is not to say as I know his name. But I've seen him, aye, often. He skippers a boat on the canal."

"What? A charter boat, or one of the Jacobite cruise boats?" Her heart beat faster. The Caledonian Canal, he meant. It ran from Inverness to Fort William and carried a huge amount of water traffic, much of it visible from the road.

"Nice wee motor sailer—must be a charter. I only noticed because my wife's cousin has one like it; we went out wi' him the once. Ten-meter, I think it is."

"You told the police, of course."

"I did, so." He tapped blunt fingers on the coverlet, glancing sideways at her. "I described the man so well as I could—but, ken, he didna really look unusual. I'd know him again—and maybe your wee lad would—but I don't know as the polis would pick him out easy."

She'd brought her Swiss Army knife out of her pocket as she talked, playing with it meditatively, flicking the blades open and shut. She opened the corkscrew, testing the sharp end of it with the ball of her thumb.

"Do you think you could maybe describe him to me? I draw a bit; I could make a stab at a picture."

He grinned at her, eyes disappearing into the bruised flesh.

"Pour me a dram, lass, and we'll have a go."

BRIANNA REACHED Lallybroch again in the late afternoon, just in time for her four o'clock appointment with the locksmith. A scrap of white tacked to the door fluttered in the autumn wind; she yanked it off and fumbled it open with chilled fingers.

> *Had an emergency call in Elgin; won't be back 'til late. Will call by in the morning. Apologies, Will Tranter*

She crumpled the note and stuffed it into her jacket pocket, muttering under her breath. Bloody kidnapping rapist bastards walking in and out of her house like it was the public highway and this *wasn't* an emergency?

She hesitated, fingers wrapped around the big antique key in her pocket, looking up at the white-harled front of the house. The sinking sun flashed in the upper windows, glazing them with red, hiding whatever might be behind them. *They had a key.* Did she really want to go in there alone?

She glanced round, self-conscious, but saw nothing out of the ordinary. The home fields lay tranquil, the small flock of sheep already bedding down in the setting sun. She breathed deeply, turning from side to side as she would when hunting with Da in the North Carolina forest, as though she might catch the tang of deer on the breeze.

What was she looking for now? *Exhaust fumes. Rubber, hot metal, unlaid dust in the air, the ghost of a car.* Or maybe something else, she thought, remembering the stink of Rob Cameron's sweat. The scent of a stranger.

But the cold air brought her only the smell of dead leaves, sheep shit, and a hint of turpentine from the Forestry Commission's pine plantation to the west.

Still. She'd heard her father mention a feeling at the back of his neck when something was wrong, and she felt the hairs on her nape prickle now. She turned away, got back into her car, and drove off, glancing automatically behind her every few minutes. There was a petrol station a few miles up the road; she stopped there to call Fiona and say she'd pick the kids up in the morning, then bought a few snacks and drove back, taking the farm track that circled the far edge of Lallybroch's land and led up into the pine plantation.

At this time of year, it got dark by 4:30 P.M. Up the hillside, the track was no more than a pair of muddy ruts, but she bumped carefully along until she came to one of the clearings where the foresters piled slash for burning. The air was rough with the smell of wood fire, and a big blackened patch of earth and ember still sent up wisps of smoke, but all the fires were out. She drove the car behind a heap of fresh-cut branches, piled ready for the next day, and cut the ignition.

As she came down out of the plantation, carrying the shotgun in one hand, something large shot past her head in total silence, and she stumbled, gasping. An owl; it disappeared, a pale blur in the dark. In spite of her pounding heart, she was glad to see it. White animals were harbingers of good luck in Celtic folklore; she could use any luck going.

"Owls are keepers of the dead, but not just the dead. They're messengers between worlds." For an instant Roger was next to her, solid, warm in the cold night, and she put out a hand by impulse, as though to touch him.

Then he was gone and she was standing alone in the shadow of the pines, looking toward Lallybroch, the shotgun cold in her hand. "I'll get you back, Roger," she whispered under her breath, and curled her left hand into a fist, clenching the copper ring with which he'd married her. "I *will*." But first she had to make sure the kids were safe.

Night rose up around the house and Lallybroch faded slowly out of sight, a paler blotch against the dark. She checked the safety on the gun and moved silently toward home.

SHE CAME UP the hill behind the broch, as quietly as she could. The wind had come up, and she doubted anyone would hear her steps over the rustling of the gorse and dry broom that grew thick back here.

If they were waiting for her, wanting to do harm, surely they'd be in the house. But if they just wanted to know where she was . . . they might be watching the house instead, and this was the place to do it from. She paused by the wall of the broch and put a hand on the stones, listening. Faint rustling, punctuated by an occasional dovish coo. The bats would have gone out long since, hunting, but the doves were abed.

Pressing her back against the stones, she sidled around the broch, pausing near the door, and reached out a hand, groping for the latch. The padlock was cold in her hand; intact and locked. Letting out her breath, she fumbled the bunch of keys out of her pocket and found the right one by touch.

The sleeping doves erupted in a mad flutter when the wind from the open door whooshed up to the rafters where they roosted, and she stepped hastily back against the wall, out of the way of a pattering rain of panicked incontinence. The doves calmed in a moment, though, and settled down again in a murmurous rustle of indignation at the disturbance.

The upper floors had long since fallen in and the timbers cleared away; the broch was a shell, but a sturdy shell, its outer stones repaired over the years. The stair was built into the wall itself, the stone steps leading up between the inner and outer walls, and she broke the gun over her shoulder and went up slowly, feeling her way one-handed. There was a torch in her pocket but no need to risk using it.

A third of the way up, she took up station by a window slit that commanded a view of the house below. It was cold sitting on the stones, but her jacket was down-filled and she wouldn't freeze. She pulled a bar of Violet Crumble from her pocket and settled down to wait.

She'd called the Hydro Board and asked for a week's leave in order to deal with a family emergency. News of what had happened at the Loch Errochty dam last night had spread, so there'd been no difficulty, save in deflecting the flood of sympathetic exclamations and curious questions—all of which she'd claimed not to be able to answer, owing to the ongoing police inquiry.

The police . . . they *might* be of help. Jock had told them about the man at the dam; they'd be following that up. She'd had to tell them about Rob Cameron. And, with some reluctance, she'd told them about his coming into the house and threatening her, since Mandy would likely blow the gaff about that. She told them about his open disgruntlement over having a woman supervisor and his harassing her at work—though that seemed like a paltry motive for kidnapping a child. She hadn't mentioned most of the physical stuff, the priest's hole, or Cameron's assisted escape, though. Just said she'd hit him—first with the letter box, and then with the cricket bat—and he'd run away. She'd gone with Mandy to find Jem, that being obviously more urgent than calling the police. The police didn't agree with that assessment, but they were British and thus polite about their disapproval.

She'd said Cameron had told her where Jem was. If the police found him, he wasn't going to be in any position to contradict her. She *did* hope they picked him up. It might cause complications, but she'd feel safer if he wasn't wandering around loose. With her rifle. Possibly lurking in her house.

Her hand curled up in the deep pocket of her jacket, fingering the comforting shapes of a dozen shotgun shells.

37

COGNOSCO TE

THE HEALER ARRIVED in midafternoon. He was a short man but not slight; he looked like an amateur wrestler, with shoulders nearly as broad as Roger's own. He didn't introduce himself but nodded politely to Mrs. MacLaren, his eyes flicking round the room in a brief, all-encompassing glance, then focused on Buck, who had fallen into an uneasy sleep and did not wake even to the disturbance caused by the healer's entrance.

"He says his heart—" Roger began awkwardly. The man glanced sharply sideways at him, then flicked a hand in dismissal and, walking over, peered closely at Buck for a moment. All the MacLarens waited in breathless silence, clearly expecting something spectacular.

The man nodded to himself, removed his coat, and turned back his shirt-sleeves, displaying sun-browned forearms corded with muscle.

"Well, then," he said, sitting down by the bed and laying a hand on Buck's chest. "Let me—" His face went quite blank and he stiffened, his hand jerking back as though he'd received an electric shock. He gave a quick, hard shake of the head and pulled Buck's shirt open, plunging both hands into the opening and laying them flat on Buck's laboring chest.

"Jesu," he whispered. *"Cognosco te!"*

Quite suddenly the hairs on Roger's body lifted, prickling as though a thunderstorm was coming. The man had spoken in Latin, and what he had said was, *"I know you!"*

THE MACLARENS ALL watched the healer work, with great respect and not a little awe. Roger, who had learned a good bit about the psychology of healing from Claire, was just as impressed. And, to be frank, scared shitless.

The healer had stood motionless for a long moment, hands on Buck's chest, his head thrown back and eyes closed, his face contorted in an expression of the deepest concentration, as though listening to something far, far off. He had murmured what Roger recognized as the Pater Noster—from the looks on the faces of the MacLarens, it might as well have been the Abracadabra. Then, keeping his hands in place, he had raised one thick forefinger and begun to tap, delicately, in a slow, regular rhythm, his finger rebounding each time as though he were striking a piano key.

Thup . . . thup . . . thup. It went on for a long time, so long that everyone in the room began to draw breath again—even Buck, whose labored gasping began to ease, his lungs filling naturally again. Then it was two fingers, *Thup-tup . . . thup-tup . . . thup-tup.* Slow. Regular as a metronome. On and on and on and on . . . Soothing. Hypnotic. And Roger realized that the rhythm was that of a beating heart—his *own* heart. Looking round the room at the wide eyes and slightly open mouths of the adenoidal MacLaren clan, he had the most peculiar sense that *all* their hearts were beating to precisely the same rhythm.

He knew they were breathing as one; he could hear the susurrus of indrawn breath and the sea-foam rush of exhalation. He *knew* it—and was helpless to change his own rhythm, to resist the sense of unity that had formed insensibly among all the people in the cabin, from Angus MacLaren down to little Josephine, round-eyed as the rest in her mother's arms.

All of them were breathing, hearts beating as one—and somehow they were supporting the stricken man, holding him as part of a larger entity, embracing him, bracing him. Buck's injured heart lay in the palm of Roger's hand: he realized it quite suddenly and, just as suddenly, realized that it had been there for some time, resting as naturally in the curve of his palm as rounded river rock, smooth and heavy. And . . . beating, in time with the heart in Roger's chest. What was much stranger was that none of this felt in any way out of the ordinary.

Odd—and impressive—as it was, Roger could have explained this. Mass suggestion, hypnosis, will and willingness. He'd done much the same thing himself any number of times, singing—when the music caught the audience up with him, when he knew they were with him, would follow him anywhere. He'd done it once or twice, preaching; felt the people warm to him and lift him up as he lifted them. It was impressive to see it done so quickly and thoroughly without any sort of warm-up, though—and much more disquieting to feel the effects in his own flesh. What was scaring him, though, was that the healer's hands were blue.

No doubt about it. It wasn't a trick of the light—there wasn't any to speak of, bar the dull glow of the smoored fire. It wasn't a huge thing; no fiery coruscations or neon. But a soft blue tinge had come up between the healer's fingers, crept over the backs of his hands—and now spread in a faint haze *around* his hands, seeming to penetrate Buck's chest.

Roger glanced to one side, then the other, without moving his head. The MacLarens were paying rapt attention but showed no sign of seeing anything startling. *They don't see it.* The hairs on his forearms lifted silently. *Why do I see it?*

Thup-tup . . . thup-tup . . . thup-tup . . . Tireless, regular—and yet Roger became aware of some subtle change. Not in the healer's rhythm—that didn't vary at all. But something had shifted. He glanced down involuntarily into his palm, where he still imagined that Buck's heart lay, and was now scarcely surprised to see it there, a ghostly round object, transparent but pulsing gently, regularly. On its own.

Thup-tup . . . . . . thup-tup . . . . . . thup-tup. The healer now was following, not leading. Not slowing the beats but pausing for a longer period between them, letting Buck's heart beat alone between them.

At last, the faint sound stopped, and there was silence in the room for the length of three heartbeats. And then the silence popped like a soap bubble, leaving the onlookers blinking and shaking their heads, as those awakened from dreaming. Roger closed his empty hand.

"He'll be all right," the healer said to Mrs. MacLaren, in a matter-of-fact manner. "Let him sleep as long as he can, give him something to eat when he wakes up."

"Much obliged, sir," Mrs. MacLaren murmured. She patted Josephine, who had fallen asleep with her mouth open, a glimmering trail of saliva falling from the corner of her mouth to her mother's shoulder. "Will I make up a pallet for ye by the fire?"

"Ah, no," the healer said, smiling. He shrugged back into his coat, put on his cloak, and reached for his hat. "I'm staying no great distance away."

He went out, and Roger waited for a moment, just long enough for people to turn back to their own conversations, and then followed, shutting the door quietly behind him.

THE HEALER WAS a little way down the road; Roger saw the man's dark figure kneeling in prayer before a tiny shrine, the ends of his cloak fluttering in the wind. Roger came up to him slowly, hanging back so as not to disturb his devotions—and, on impulse, bowed his own head toward the small statue, so weathered as to be faceless. *Take care of them, please,* he prayed. *Help me get back to them—to Bree.* That was all he had time for, before the healer rose to his feet—but that was all he had to say, in any case.

The healer hadn't heard him; he rose and turned, surprised at seeing Roger but recognizing him at once. He smiled, a little wearily, clearly expecting some medical question of a private nature.

Heart thumping, Roger reached out and grasped the healer's hand. The man's eyes widened with shock.

"*Cognosco te,*" Roger said, very softly. *I know you.*

"WHO ARE YE, then?" Dr. Hector McEwan stood squinting against the wind, his face wary but excited. "The two of ye—who are ye?"

"I think ye maybe ken that better than I do," Roger told him. "That—the light in your hands . . ."

"You could see it." It wasn't a question, and the wary excitement in McEwan's eyes blazed into life, visible even in the dimming light.

"Aye, I could. Where did ye . . ." Roger groped for the best way to ask, but, after all, how many ways were there? "*When* did ye come from?"

McEwan glanced involuntarily over his shoulder toward the croft, but the door was shut, smoke pouring from the hole in the roof. It was beginning to rain, a premonitory pattering among the mounded heather near the path. He moved abruptly, taking Roger's arm.

"Come," he said. "We canna be standing out here, dreich as it is; we'll catch our deaths."

"Dreich" was the word; the rain set to in good earnest and Roger was half soaked in minutes, having come out without hat or cloak. McEwan led the way quickly up a winding path through thickets of dark gorse, emerging onto a stretch of moorland where the remains of a tumbledown croft offered some shelter. The rooftree had been burned, and recently; the smell still lingered. A corner of thatch remained, though, and they huddled inside, close beneath its scanty protection.

"Anno Domini eighteen hundred and forty-one," McEwan said matter-of-factly, shaking rain from his cloak. He looked up at Roger, one thick brow raised.

"Nineteen hundred and eighty," Roger replied, heart hammering. He cleared his throat and repeated the date; the cold had affected his throat, and the words emerged in a strangled croak. McEwan leaned close at the sound, peering at him.

"What's that?" the man asked sharply. "Your voice—it's broken."

"It's noth—" Roger began, but the healer's fingers were already groping behind his head, undoing his neckcloth in nothing flat. He closed his eyes, not resisting.

McEwan's broad fingers were cold on his neck; he felt the icy touch delicate on his skin as it traced the line of the rope scar, then firmer as the healer prodded gently round his damaged larynx—it gave him an involuntary choking sensation, and he coughed. McEwan looked surprised.

"Do that again," he said.

"What, cough?" Roger said, hoarse as a crow.

"Aye, that." McEwan fitted his hand snugly round Roger's neck, just under the chin, and nodded. "Once, then wait, then do it again." Roger hacked obligingly, feeling a slight pain with each expulsion of breath where the healer's hand pressed. The man's face brightened with interest, and he removed his hand.

"Do you know what a hyoid bone is?"

"If I had to guess, it's something in the throat." Roger cleared his throat hard and rubbed at it, feeling the roughness of the scar under his palm. "Why?" He wasn't sure whether to be offended at the personal intrusion or—something else. His skin tingled slightly where McEwan had touched it.

"It's just *there*," the healer said, pressing with his thumb, high up under Roger's chin. "And if it had been *here*"—he moved the thumb down an inch—"you'd have been dead, sir. It's a fragile wee bone. Easy to strangle someone by breaking it—with your thumbs *or* a rope." He drew back a little, eyes intent on Roger's; the curiosity was still plain on his face, but the wariness had returned. "Are you and your friend fleeing from . . . something? Someone?"

"No." Roger felt at once very tired, the strain of everything catching up to him, and looked round for something to sit on. There was nothing but a few dark chunks of rock that had fallen from the cottage's wall when the burning thatch had been pulled down. He pushed two blocks together and sat on one, knees up round his ears. "I—this—" He touched his throat briefly. "It was a long time ago, nothing to do with what we—we—we're looking for my son. He's only nine."

"Oh, dearie me." McEwan's broad face creased in sympathy. "How—"

Roger lifted a hand. "You first," he said, and cleared his throat again. "I'll tell ye everything I know, but . . . you first. Please."

McEwan pursed his lips and glanced aside, thinking, but then shrugged and lowered himself, grunting, to his own rude seat.

"I was a doctor," he said abruptly. "In Edinburgh. I came up to the Highlands to shoot grouse with a friend. Do folk still do that, a hundred years hence?"

"Aye. Grouse are still tasty," Roger said dryly. "It was at Craigh na Dun that ye came through, then?"

"Yes, I—" McEwan halted abruptly, realizing what that question implied. "Dear Lord in heaven, do ye mean to be telling me there are other places? Where . . . *it* happens?"

"Yes." The hairs rippled on Roger's arms. "Four that I know of; likely there are others. How many stone circles are there in the British Isles?"

"I've no idea." McEwan was clearly shaken. He got up and went to the doorway, the jamb of it scorched and the lintel burned almost away. Roger hoped none of the stones above it would fall on the man's head—at least not until he found out more.

Dr. McEwan stayed for a long time, staring out into the rain, which had gone the silvery gray of cat's fur. Finally he shook himself and came back, mouth set in firm decision.

"Aye, nothing to be gained from secrecy. And I hope nothing to be lost by honesty." This last was not quite a question, but Roger nodded and tried to look earnest.

"Well, then. Grouse, as I say. We were on the moor, just below that hill where the standing stones are. All of a sudden a fox shot out of the bracken, right by my foot, and one of the dogs lost his head and chased it. Brewer— that was my friend, Joseph Brewer—started after it, but he has—he *had*," McEwan corrected, with an expression of mild irritation that made Roger want to smile, because he was so familiar with the feeling that dealing with the phenomenon caused, "a clubfoot. He managed all right with a special boot, but climbing and chasing . . ." He shrugged.

"So you went after the dog, and . . ." Roger shuddered involuntarily at the memory, and so did McEwan.

"Exactly."

"Did the dog . . . go?" Roger asked suddenly. McEwan looked surprised and vaguely affronted.

"How should I know? It didn't turn up where I did, I can tell ye that much."

Roger made a brief gesture of apology.

"Just curious. We—my wife and I—we've been trying to puzzle out as much as we can, for the sake of the children." "Children" caught in his throat, coming out in no more than a whisper, and McEwan's expression softened.

"Aye, of course. Your son, you said?"

Roger nodded and managed to explain what he could, about Cameron, the letters . . . and, after a moment's hesitation, about the Spaniard's gold, for, after all, he'd have to give a reason for Cameron's taking Jem in the first place, and his sense of Dr. McEwan was one of solid kindness.

"Dearie me," the doctor murmured, shaking his head in dismay. "I'll ask among my patients. Perhaps someone . . ." He trailed off, his face still troubled. Roger had the distinct impression that the sense of trouble wasn't all down to Jem, or even to the staggering discovery that there were other—

He stopped, seeing plainly in his mind's eye the soft blue glow surrounding McEwan's fingers—and the look of surprised delight on his face. *Cognosco te. I know you.* Delight, not just shock. He and Buck weren't the first time travelers this man had known. But the doctor hadn't said as much. Why not?

"How long have you been here?" Roger asked, curious.

McEwan sighed and rubbed a hand over his face.

"Maybe too long," he said, but then pushed that away, straightening up. "Two years, about. Speaking of too long, though . . ." He straightened, pulling the cloak over his shoulders. "It'll be dark in less than an hour. I'll need to go, if I'm to reach Cranesmuir by nightfall. I'll come again tomorrow to tend your friend. We can talk a bit more then."

He turned abruptly, but just as suddenly turned back and, reaching out, took Roger's throat in his hand.

"Maybe," he said, as though to himself. "Just maybe." Then he nodded once, let go, and was gone, his cloak fluttering like bat wings behind him.

38

THE NUMBER OF THE BEAST

AFTER *FRAGGLE ROCK*, the telly went to the evening news, and Ginger reached to turn it off but stopped abruptly as Jem's last year's school picture flashed on the screen. She stared at the television, mouth half open, then looked incredulously at Jem.

"That's you!" she said.

"Ken that fine," he said crossly. "Turn it off, aye?"

"No, I want to see." She blocked him as he lunged for the screen; Ginger was eleven and bigger than him.

"Turn it off!" he said, then, with cunning inspiration, "It'll scare Mandy and she'll howl."

Ginger shot Mandy a quick glance—she had good lungs, did Mandy—then reluctantly turned the TV off.

"Mmphm," she said, and lowered her voice. "Mam told us what happened, but she said we weren't to trouble ye about it."

"Good," Jem said. "Don't." His heart was hammering and he felt sweaty, but his hands were going cold and hot and cold again.

He'd got away by the skin of his teeth, diving under the bushes planted at the top of the spillway and crawling down the concrete edging 'til he found a ladderway that went down into the water. He'd shoggled down it as far as he could and clung on so hard his hands went numb, with the black water rumbling inches under his feet and surging down the spillway past him, drenching him with cold spray. He could still feel his bones shake with it.

He believed he might throw up if he thought about it anymore, so he turned away and went to look into the wee girls' toy chest. It was full of girlie toys, of course, but maybe if they had a ball . . . They did. It was pink but one of the good high-bouncy kind.

"We could go out to the garden, maybe, and have a bit o' catch?" he suggested, bouncing the ball on the floor and catching it.

"It's dark and rainin' like the clappers," Tisha said. "Dinna want to get wet."

"Ach, it's no but a saft drizzle! What are ye, made of sugar?"

"Yes," said Sheena, with a simper. "Sugar and spice 'n everything nice, that's what little girls are made of. Snips and snails and puppy-dog tails—"

"Come play dollies," suggested Tisha, waggling a naked doll invitingly at him. "Ye can have GI Joe if ye want. Or would ye rather Ken?"

"Nay, I'm no playin' dollies," Jem said firmly. "Canna be doing wi' the clothes and all."

"I play dollies!" Mandy muscled her way between Tisha and Sheena, eager hands stretched out for a Barbie in a pink frilly ball gown. Sheena grabbed it away just in time.

"Aye, aye," she soothed Mandy's impending screech, "you can play, sure. Ye have to play nice, though; ye dinna want to spoil her dress. Here, sit down, pet, I'll give ye this one. See her wee comb and brush? Ye can fix her hair."

Jem took the ball and left. The upstairs hall had carpet, but the landing was bare wood. He popped the ball off it and it shot up and hit the ceiling with a smack, just missing the hanging light fixture. It bounced off the floor and he caught it before it could get away, clutching it to his chest.

He listened for a second, to be sure Mrs. Buchan hadn't heard. She was back in the kitchen, though; he could hear the sound of her singing along to the radio.

He was halfway down the stairs when the bell over the front door went, and he looked over the banister to see who it was coming in. Who it was was Rob Cameron, and Jem nearly swallowed his tongue.

JEM PRESSED himself back against the wall of the landing, his heart pounding so loud he could barely hear Mrs. Buchan come out of the kitchen.

Should he go get Mandy? There wasn't any way out of the house but by the stairs; he couldn't drop Mandy out the lounge window, there wasn't a tree or anything . . .

Mrs. Buchan was saying hello and she was sorry if the gentleman was wanting a room, because she was booked full every day this week. Mr. Cameron was being polite, saying, no, thank ye kindly, he was only wondering might he have a wee word . . .

"If ye're selling anything—" she started, and he interrupted her.

"No, missus, nothing like that. It's a few questions I have about the stones at Craigh na Dun."

Jem was gasping for air. His lungs were heaving, but he'd pressed a hand over his mouth so Mr. Cameron wouldn't hear. Mrs. Buchan didn't gasp, but he could hear her take breath, then stop, deciding what to say.

"Stones?" she said, and even he could tell she was faking puzzlement. "I dinna ken anything about stones."

Rob made a polite laugh.

"I apologize, missus. I should have introduced myself, first. My name's Rob Cameron—and—is something wrong, missus?" She'd not only gasped really loud, Jem thought she must have stepped back without looking and hit the wee table in the hall, because there was a thump and an "Ach!" and the splat of picture frames falling over.

"No," Mrs. Buchan said, getting ahold of herself. "No. Had a wee turn, that's all—I've the high blood pressure, ken. Get that wee bit dizzy. Your name's Cameron, is it?"

"Aye. Rob Cameron. I'm cousin by marriage to Becky Wemyss. She told me a bit about the dancing up at the stones."

"Oh." That "oh" meant trouble for Becky Wemyss, thought Jem, who knew a lot about mothers' voices.

"I'm a bit of a scholar of the auld ways, see. I'm writing a wee book . . . Anyway, I wondered if I could maybe talk to you for a few minutes. Becky said ye'd know more about the stones and the dancing than anybody else."

Jem's breathing slowed down, once he realized that Mr. Cameron hadn't come because Mr. Cameron knew Mandy and he were here. Or maybe he did and was trying it on with Mrs. Buchan 'til he could make an excuse to use the loo and come poke round in search of them? He looked apprehensively up the half flight of stairs that led from the landing, but the lounge door above was closed, and while he could hear Mandy's giggling fine through it, probably Mr. Cameron couldn't.

Mrs. Buchan was taking Mr. Cameron back to the kitchen. Her voice when she'd said, "Come ben. I'll tell ye what I can," hadn't sounded at all friendly. Jem wondered whether she might be going to put rat poison in Mr. Cameron's tea.

Maybe Mrs. Buchan didn't have any rat poison, though. He took a step one way, then the other, then back. He really, really wanted to run down the stairs and out the door and keep going. But he couldn't leave Mandy.

His havering stopped at once when the kitchen door opened, but he could hear it was Mrs. Buchan's step, and just hers, coming fast and light.

She turned up the stairs but started back when she saw him on the landing, a hand to her chest. Then she ran up to him and hugged him tight, whispering in his ear.

"Bloody heck, lad. What're you—well, never mind, I was coming to find you. Ye saw him?"

Jem nodded, wordless, and Mrs. Buchan's mouth pressed flat.

"Aye. I'm going to take ye out the door. Go left out the gate. Two houses down is Mrs. Kelleher. Knock and tell her I sent ye to use the phone. Ye call the polis and tell them the man that kidnapped you is here—ye ken the address here?"

He nodded. He'd seen the number when he visited before with Mam and Dad and remembered it because it was 669; Dad had said it should by rights be 666, but that was the number of the beast. Jem had asked whether it was Mr. or Mrs. Buchan that was the beast, and Mam and Dad both laughed like loons.

"Good," said Mrs. Buchan, letting go of him. "Come on, then."

"Mandy—" he started, but she shushed him.

"I'll mind her. Come!"

He ran down the stairs after her, trying not to make any noise, and, at the door, she stood on her toes and held the little bell so it wouldn't ring.

"Run!" she whispered.

He ran.

MRS. KELLEHER WAS an old lady and kind of deaf. Jem was out of breath and so scared that he couldn't put his words together right, so it was a long time before she took him to the telephone, and then the lady at the police station put the phone down on him twice, because she thought he was some bampot wean who'd got hold of the phone and was playing tricks.

"I'm Jeremiah MacKenzie!" he bellowed, next time she answered. "I was kidnapped!"

"Ye were?" said Mrs. Kelleher, very startled. She grabbed the phone away from him. "Who's this?" she demanded of it. Faint squawking—at least the police lady hadn't hung up again. Mrs. Kelleher turned and squinted through her spectacles at him.

"Who was it ye were wanting to call, lad? Ye've got the polis by mistake."

He really wanted to hit something, but he couldn't hit Mrs. Kelleher. He said something very bad in Gaelic, and her mouth fell open. She'd let the phone fall away from her ear, though, and he grabbed it.

"The man that kidnapped me is *here*," he said, as slow as he could. "I need somebody to come! Before—" Inspiration struck. "Before he hurts my little sister! It's 669 Glenurquhart Road. Come right away!" Then *he* put the phone down, before the lady could ask him questions.

Mrs. Kelleher had plenty of those, and he didn't want to be rude, so he asked could he use the loo and locked the door against her, then hung out the upstairs window, watching for the police.

Nothing happened for what seemed forever. The raindrops started to drip off his hair and eyelashes, but he was afraid of missing anything. He was rubbing the water out of his eyes when all of a sudden the door of 669 flew open and Rob Cameron came running out, jumped in a car, and drove off with the tires squealing.

Jem almost fell out the window but then rushed back and barreled out of the bathroom, nearly knocking Mrs. Kelleher over.

"Thank you, Mrs. Kelleher!" he yelled over his shoulder, taking the stairs three at a time, and shot out the front door.

There was a lot of screaming and crying going on inside the Buchans' house, and he felt his chest go so tight he couldn't breathe.

"Mandy!" He tried to call, but her name came out in a whisper. The front door was hanging open. Inside, there were girls everywhere, but he picked Mandy out of the muddle in the lounge instantly and ran to grab her. She wasn't crying, but she latched on to him like a leech, burying her black curly head in his stomach.

"It's okay," he told her, squeezing the stuffing out of her in relief. "It's okay, Man. I gotcha. I gotcha."

His heart started to slow down a little, and he saw that Mrs. Buchan was sitting on the sofa, holding a towel full of ice cubes to her face. Some of the ice had fallen out and was lying on the rug at her feet. Tisha and Sheena were holding on to their mother and crying, and Ginger was trying to pat her mam's hair and comfort her sisters at the same time, but her face was dead white and tears were running silently down it.

"Mrs. Buchan . . . are ye all right?" Jem asked timidly. He had an awful feeling in the bottom of his stomach. Somehow, he was sure this was his fault.

Mrs. Buchan looked up at him. One side of her face was puffy and the eye on that side was swollen half shut, but the other one had fire in it, and that made him feel a little better.

"Aye, fine, Jem," she said. "Dinna fash, girls! It's well enough; no but a black eye. Quit your caterwauling, will ye? I canna hear myself think." She gave a small, good-natured shake to detach the clinging girls, pushing and patting at them with her free hand. Then there was a knock on the doorjamb, and a man's voice from the front hall.

"Police, here! Anyone to home?"

Jem could have told Mrs. Buchan what happened once you called the police. Questions, and questions, and more questions. And if there were things you couldn't *tell* the police . . . At least Mrs. Buchan wouldn't let them take Jem or her to the police station to answer questions, insisting that she couldn't leave the girls on their own. By the time the police gave up, Mandy and Sheena were both asleep on the couch, curled up together like a pair of kittens, and Ginger and Tisha had made everyone tea, then sat yawning in the corner together, blinking now and then to keep awake.

A few minutes after the police left, *Mr.* Buchan came home for his supper, and all the explaining was to do all over again. There really wasn't much to it: Mrs. Buchan had sat Mr. Cameron down in the kitchen and told him a bit about the dancing—it wasn't secret, most folk who'd lived in Inverness for a long time knew about it—but she'd left the radio playing while they were talking, and all of a sudden the newscaster was saying the name "Robert Cameron" and how Robert Cameron was wanted for questioning in the kidnapping of a local boy, and—

"And then the wee bastard jumps up, and so do I, and he must have thought I meant to stop him—I was betwixt him and the door, anyroad— and he belts me one in the eye, pushes me into the wall, and he's away off!"

Mr. Buchan was giving Jem a hard look now and then and seemed like *he* wanted to start asking questions, but instead he said they'd all go into the town and have a fish supper as it was so late, and everyone started feeling better at once. Jem could see the looks going back and forth between the Buchans, though, and he kind of wondered whether Mr. Buchan maybe meant to drop him and Mandy off at the police station on the way back. Or maybe just leave them by the side of the road.

39

THE GHOST OF A HANGIT MAN

THE HEAVENS OPENED, and Roger was soaked to the skin by the time he got back to the MacLarens' cottage. Amid cries of dismay from Mrs. MacLaren and her ancient mother, he was hastily stripped, wrapped up snug in a ragged quilt, and stood to steam before the fire, where his presence greatly impeded the preparations for supper. Buck, propped up on pillows with the two smallest MacLarens curled up in sleep on the bed beside him, lifted a brow at Roger in inquiry.

Roger moved his hand slightly, in a tell-you-later gesture. He thought Buck looked better; there was color in his face, and he was sitting upright, not slumped into the bedding. For a brief instant, Roger wondered what would happen if he were to lay his own hand on Buck. Would it glow blue?

The thought sent a shiver through him, and Allie, one of the MacLaren daughters, pushed the trailing edge of his quilt away from the fire with a squeak of alarm.

"Take care, sir, do!"

"Aye, do," said Grannie Wallace, pulling the blackened iron spider—this spitting hot grease—well away from his bare legs and making shooing motions. "Take a spark, and ye'll go up like tinder." She was blind in one eye, but the other was sharp as a needle and gave him a piercing look. "Tall as ye are, ye'd likely set the rooftree afire, and then where should we all be, I'd like tae know!"

There was a general titter at that, but he thought the laughter had an uneasy note to it and wondered why.

"Moran taing," Roger said in polite thanks for the advice. He moved a foot or so farther from the hearth, fetching up against the settle on which Mr. Angus MacLaren was sitting, mending his pipe stem. "Since ye speak of rooftrees—there's a wee croft just over the hill that's been burnt out. Cooking accident, was it?"

The room went silent, and people froze for an instant, all looking at him.

"Evidently not," he said, with an apologetic cough. "I'm sorry to make light—were folk killed, then?"

Mr. MacLaren gave him a brooding sort of look, quite at odds with his earlier geniality, and set the pipe on his knee.

"No by the fire," he said. "What led ye up there, man?"

Roger met MacLaren's eye directly.

"Searching for my lad," he said simply. "I dinna ken where to look—so I look everywhere. Thinkin' what if he's got away, what if he's wandering about by himself . . . maybe taking shelter where he can find it . . ."

MacLaren took a deep breath and sat back, nodding a little.

"Aye, well. Ye'll want to keep well away from that croft."

"Haunted, is it?" Buck asked, and all heads swung round to look at him—then swung back to Mr. MacLaren, waiting for him to give the answer.

"It might be," he said, after a reluctant pause.

"It's cursed," Allie whispered to Roger under her breath.

"Ye didna go in, sir, did ye?" said Mrs. MacLaren, the permanent worry crease deepening between her brows.

"Och, no," he assured her. "What was it happened there?" McEwan hadn't had any hesitation about going into the croft; did he not know whatever they were concerned about?

Mrs. MacLaren made a small "Mmp!" noise and, with a shake of her head, swung the cauldron out on its bracket and began to scoop out boiled neeps with a wooden spoon. Not her place to speak of such goings-on, said her primly sealed mouth.

Mr. MacLaren made a somewhat louder noise and, leaning forward, got ponderously to his feet.

"I'll just be going to check the beasts before supper, ken," he said, and gave Roger an eye. "Perhaps ye'd like to come along and be oot the way o' the lasses and their doings."

"Oh, aye," Roger said, and, with a small bow to Mrs. MacLaren, hitched the quilt up higher over his shoulders and followed his host into the byre. He caught Buck's eye in passing and gave him a brief shrug.

In the usual way, the cattle's quarters were separated from the people's by no more than a stone wall with a large space at the top, allowing the considerable heat—along with floating bits of straw and a strong scent of piss and manure—generated by several large cows to percolate into the ben. The MacLarens' was a snug byre, well kept and piled with clean straw at one end, with three fat, shaggy red cows and a diminutive black bull who snorted fiercely at Roger, nostrils red-black in the dim light and the brass ring in his nose agleam.

The ben of the croft was far from cold—what with nine people crammed into it and a good peat fire on the hearth—but the byre was filled with an encompassing warmth and a sense of peace that made Roger sigh and drop his shoulders, only then realizing that they'd been up round his ears for what seemed hours.

MacLaren made no more than a cursory check of his beasts, scratching the bull between the ears and administering a comforting slap to a cow's flank. Then he led Roger to the far end of the byre with a jerk of his head.

Ever since his conversation with Hector McEwan, Roger had had an uneasy feeling, caused by something he felt he had heard and not understood. And now, as MacLaren turned to speak to him, it was there suddenly, clear in his head. *Cranesmuir.*

"Twa strangers built the croft up there," MacLaren said. "They came from nowhere seemingly; just one day they were there. A man and a woman, but we couldna tell were they man and wife, or maybe a man and his daughter, for he seemed a good bit older than she did. They said they came from the isles—and I think he maybe did, but her speech wasna like any islander I've heard."

"Was she Scots?"

MacLaren looked surprised.

"Oh, aye, she was. She had the *Gàidhlig.* I'd have said she came from somewhere up northwest of Inverness—maybe Thurso—but there again . . . it wasna quite . . . *right.*"

Not quite right. Like someone out of their proper place, pretending.

"What did she look like?" Roger said. His voice was thick; he had to clear his throat and repeat himself.

MacLaren's lips pursed but not in condemnation; it was the sort of soundless whistle of appreciation one gives at sight of something remarkable.

"Bonny," he said. "Verra bonny, indeed. Tall and straight, but . . . er . . . not so straight in places, if ye take my meaning." He ducked his head, half embarrassed, and Roger realized that his reluctance to talk in front of the womenfolk perhaps wasn't due entirely to the scandalous nature of his story.

"I do," Roger said, lowering his own voice to MacLaren's confidential level. "Did they keep to themselves, then?" If they hadn't, surely the whole district would have known about them and quickly discovered whether they were man and wife.

MacLaren frowned.

"Aye, they did . . . though he was friendly enough; I met him now and again, out on the moor, and we'd have a word, and I'd always come away thinkin' as how he was a good wee fellow, and yet when I came to tell my Maggie about it, I couldna just charge my memory wi' anything he'd *said.*"

MacLaren said somehow word got round that the woman was something that wee bit odd—a root doctor, but maybe would give you a bit more than a grass cure, if you found her alone in the house. . . .

There was no light in the byre save the dull glow from the hearth fire next door, but, even so, Roger could see that MacLaren had grown flushed and discomfited. Roger was beginning to feel uncomfortable himself, but not for the same reason.

Cranesmuir. He knew the name, had known it when McEwan said it. The MacLarens had said the healer came from Draighhearnach. Cranesmuir was in the opposite direction—and two miles farther on. Why was he going there tonight?

"There were stories. Always are, about a woman like that." MacLaren cleared his own throat. "But she was good wi' the grass cures—and wi' charms, as well. Or so folk said."

But then the man had gone, MacLaren said. No one knew where; they just didn't see him anymore, and the woman went on as before, but now more of her visitors were men. And the women stopped taking their bairns up there, though they'd go sometimes themselves, quietly, in secret.

And then on the day before Samhain, as the sun was sinking and the great fires being built up for the evening, a woman from nearby had gone up to the lonely croft and run down again, screaming.

"She'd found the door o' the croft standing wide, the woman and her things all gone—and a man hanging from the rooftree, stone dead wi' a rope around his neck."

The shock tightened Roger's own throat. He couldn't speak.

MacLaren sighed, head bent. A cow had come up behind him, nudging gently, and he laid one hand on her back as though seeking support from the animal, who went on placidly chewing her cud.

"It was the priest who said we should cleanse the place with fire, for it had the smell of evil about it, and no one kent the man. We couldna tell was it just a poor fellow as took his life by despair—or was it murder."

"I . . . see." Roger forced the words through the burn in his throat, and MacLaren looked up suddenly at him. He saw the man's mouth drop open, his eyes bulging, and realized that in the warmth he'd let the quilt slide back on his shoulders. MacLaren was looking straight at his throat, where the livid and unmistakable scar of hanging must show plain in the dim red light.

MacLaren backed away, or tried to, but there was nowhere to go. He plastered himself against one beast's shaggy flank, making a low gobbling noise. The cow seemed annoyed by this and brought her hoof down solidly on MacLaren's foot. The consequent anguish and fury at least brought MacLaren out of his fright, and when he had extricated himself—by means of thumps and curses—he turned bravely on Roger, jaw thrust out.

"Why come ye here, *a thaibse*?" he said, fists clenched but his voice low. "Whatever sin I might have done, I did naught to you. I'd nay part in your death—and I said they must bury your body beneath the hearthstone before they fired the place. The priest wouldna have ye in the kirkyard, aye?" he added, evidently fearing that the ghost of the hangit man had come to complain about the unsancitifed disposal of his mortal remains.

Roger sighed and rubbed a hand over his face, the stubble rasping against his palm. He could see several curious faces, attracted by MacLaren's cries, peering into the shadows of the byre from the glow of the room beyond.

"Have ye got a rosary in the house, sir?" he said.

IT WAS A long and restless night. Grannie Wallace had snatched the children off Buck's bed, as though fearing he might devour them the moment her back was turned, and put them to bed with her in the trundle, while the older children slept either with their parents or rolled up in quilts by the hearth. Roger shared the pariah's bed with Buck, for while his ability to hold the rosary in his hand, kiss the crucifix, and then lead the family in saying the rosary had—barely—kept Angus MacLaren from throwing him out into the night and pissing on the gateposts to keep him from coming back in, it hadn't made him much more popular.

He doubted Buck had slept much better than himself, for his ancestor had rolled out of bed at first light, declaring an urgent necessity to visit the privy. Roger had as hastily arisen, saying, "I'll help ye," and pulled on a still-damp shirt and breeks.

He was pleased to see that Buck didn't actually appear to need help. He walked stiffly and limped a little, but his shoulders were square and he wasn't gasping or turning blue.

"If they think ye're a vengeful ghost, what the devil do they think *I* am?" Buck inquired, the instant they were clear of the cottage. "And surely to goodness ye could ha' just said the Lord's Prayer once and not dragged everyone through five decades o' the rosary and ruined the supper!"

"Mmphm." Buck had a point there, but Roger had been too much upset at the time to think of that. Besides, he'd wanted to give them time to recover from the shock. "It wasn't ruined," he said crossly. "Only the neeps a bit scorched."

"Only!" Buck echoed. "The place still reeks. And the women hate ye. They'll put too much salt in your porridge, see if they don't. Where d'ye think we're going? It's that way."

He pointed at a path on the left that did indeed lead to the privy, this sitting in plain sight.

Roger made another testy sound but followed. He was off-kilter this morning, distracted. No wonder about why, either.

Now? He wondered, watching the door of the privy close behind Buck. It was a two-seater, but he wasn't minded to broach what he had to say under conditions of *that* much intimacy, no matter how private the subject matter was.

"The healer," he said instead through the door, choosing the simplest place to start. "McEwan. He said he'd come back today to see to ye."

"I don't need seeing to," Buck snapped. "I'm fine!" Roger had known the man long enough to recognize bravado covering fear, and replied accordingly.

"Aye, right. What did it feel like?" he asked curiously. "When he put his hand on you?"

Silence from the privy.

"Did ye feel *anything*?" he asked, after the silence had lengthened well past any time required for natural functions.

"Maybe," said Buck's voice, gruff and reluctant. "Maybe no. I fell asleep whilst he was tapping on my chest like a yaffle after tree grubs. Why?"

"Did you understand what it was he said to ye? When he touched you?" Buck had been a lawyer in his own time; he must have studied Latin.

"Did you?" A slight creak of wood and a rustling of cloth.

"I did. And I said it back to him, just before he left."

"I was asleep," Buck repeated doggedly. Clearly he didn't want to talk about the healer, but he wasn't going to have a choice about that, Roger thought grimly.

"Come out of there, will ye? The MacLarens are all out in the dooryard, crossing their legs." He glanced over his shoulder and was surprised to see that in fact the MacLarens *were* out in the dooryard.

Not all of them—it was only Angus and a tall boy, plainly a MacLaren, too, from the shape of him. He seemed familiar—had he been at the house the evening before? They were bent close together, talking in evident excitement, and the boy was pointing off toward the distant road.

"Come out," Roger repeated, sudden urgency in his voice. "Someone's coming. I hear horses."

The privy door flew open and Buck sprang out like a jack-in-the-box, stuffing his shirt into his breeks. His hair was matted and dirty, but his eyes were alert, and he looked entirely capable; that was reassuring.

The horses had come up over the brow of the hill now—six of them: four of the shaggy Highland ponies called garrons, one indifferent rangy bay, and a startlingly fine chestnut with a black mane. Buck seized Roger's arm with a grip like a horse's bite.

"*A Dhia,*" Buck said, half under his breath. "Who's that?"

40

ANGELS UNAWARE

ROGER HAD NO IDEA who the tall man with the good horse was, but it was crystal clear *what* he was, both from the deferential manner of the MacLarens and from the way in which his companions fell naturally into place a step behind him. The man in charge.

A tacksman of the MacKenzies? he wondered. Most of the men wore a hunting tartan with a sett in green, brown, and white, but Roger wasn't yet familiar enough with the local patterns as to tell whether they came from somewhere close by or not.

The tall man glanced over his shoulder at MacLaren's nod, and his eyes rested on Roger and Buck with an air of casual interest. There was nothing threatening in his manner, but Roger felt himself draw up to his own full height and wished for an instant that he wasn't barefoot and unshaven, breeks flapping unbuckled at his knees.

At least he did have someone at his own back: Buck had fallen a step behind him. He hadn't time to be surprised at that before he came within the stranger's ken.

The man was an inch or two shorter than himself and close to his own age, dark and good-looking in a faintly familiar sort of . . .

"Good morn to ye, sir," the dark man said, with a courteous inclination of the head. "My name is Dougal MacKenzie, of Castle Leoch. And . . . who might you be?"

Dear Jesus bloody hell, he thought. The shock rippled through him, and he hoped it didn't show on his face. He shook hands firmly.

"I am Roger Jeremiah MacKenzie, of Kyle of Lochalsh," he said, keeping his voice mild and—he hoped—assured, as some compensation for his shabby appearance. His voice sounded nearly normal this morning; if he didn't force it, with luck it wouldn't crack or gurgle.

"Your servant, sir," MacKenzie said with a slight bow, surprising Roger with his elegant manners. He had deep-set hazel eyes, which looked Roger over with frank interest—and a faint touch of what appeared to be amusement—before shifting to Buck.

"My kinsman," Roger said hastily. "William Bu—William MacKenzie." *When?* he thought in agitation. *Was Buck born yet? Would Dougal recognize the name William Buccleigh MacKenzie? But, no, he can't be born yet; you can't exist twice in the same time—can you?!?*

A question from Dougal MacKenzie interrupted this stream of confusion, though Roger missed hearing it. Buck answered, though.

"My kinsman's son was taken," he said, looking Dougal over with exactly —*oh, Jesus, exactly*—the same attitude of insouciant confidence that the other MacKenzie carried. "About a week past, abducted by a man named Cameron. Robert Cameron. Will ye maybe ken such a man?"

Dougal of course did not—not surprising, as Cameron hadn't existed here until a week ago. But he conferred with his men, asked intelligent questions, and expressed an open sympathy and concern that at once comforted Roger and made him feel as though he was about to vomit.

To this point, Dougal MacKenzie had been no more than a name on the historical page, momentarily, if vividly, illustrated by Claire's disjunct memories. Now he sat solid in the early-morning sun beside Roger on the bench outside the MacLarens' cottage, his plaid rough and smelling faintly of piss and heather, two days' stubble rasping as he scratched his jaw in thought.

I like him, God help me. And, God help me, I know what's going to happen to him. . . .

His eyes fixed in helpless fascination on the hollow of Dougal's throat, sun-brown and strong, framed in the open collar of his crumpled shirt. Roger jerked his eyes away, glancing instead at the russet hairs on Dougal's wrist, these catching the sunlight as he motioned toward the east, talking of his brother, chieftain of the clan MacKenzie.

"Colum doesna travel, himself, but he'd be glad to welcome the two of ye, should you find yourselves near Leoch in your search." He smiled at Roger, who smiled back, warmed by it. "Where d'ye mean to go now?"

Roger took a deep breath. Where, indeed?

"South, I think. William found no trace of Cameron in Inverness, so I'm thinking that he might be headed toward Edinburgh, meaning to take ship there."

Dougal pursed his lips, nodding in thought.

"Well, then." He turned to his men, who had sat down on the rocks that lined the path, and called to them. "Geordie, Thomas—we'll lend your beasts to these men; get your bags. Ye'd have little chance of catching up to the villain on foot," he said, turning back to Roger. "He must be mounted himself, and moving fast, or ye'd have found some trace of him."

"I—thank you," Roger managed. He felt a deep chill, in spite of the sun on his face. "You must—I mean—that's very kind. We'll bring them back as soon as we can—or send them, if—if we should be detained anywhere."

"*Moran taing,*" Buck murmured, nodding to Geordie and Thomas, who nodded back, looking dour but philosophical at the prospect of walking back to wherever they'd come from.

Where have *they come from?* Apparently, Angus MacLaren had sent his son off last night before supper, to summon Dougal to come and have a look at his alarming guests. But Dougal and his men had to have been somewhere close at hand . . .

The chink of metal as Jock dumped an obviously heavy bag on the ground beside Dougal gave him a clue. *Quarter Day.* Dougal was collecting the rents for his brother—and likely on his way back to Leoch. A lot of the rents would have been paid in kind—hams, chickens, wool, salt fish—probably Dougal's party was accompanied by one or more wagons, which they'd left behind wherever they'd stayed last night.

Angus MacLaren and his oldest son stood a little to the side, eyes fixed suspiciously on Roger as though he might sprout wings and fly away. Dougal turned to Angus with a smile and said in *Gàidhlig,* "Don't trouble, friend; they're nay more ghosts than the lads and I are."

"*Do not forget to entertain strangers,*" Buck said in the same language, "*for thereby some have entertained angels unawares.*"

There was a startled pause at that, everyone staring at him. Then Dougal laughed, and his men followed him. Angus merely made a polite noise in his throat but shifted his weight and visibly relaxed. As though this had been a signal—and perhaps it was—the door opened, and Mrs. MacLaren and Allie came out, with a stack of wooden bowls and a steaming pot of parritch. One of the smaller MacLarens came after, carefully bearing a saltcellar in both hands.

In the general hubbub of serving and eating—the women *had* oversalted his porridge, though not badly—Roger said quietly to Dougal, "Did MacLaren actually send to have you come and see whether I was a ghost?"

Dougal looked surprised but then smiled, one side of his mouth turning up. It was the way Brianna smiled when she wanted to acknowledge a joke she didn't think was funny—or when she saw something funny that she didn't mean to share with the company. A searing pang followed the jolt of recognition, and Roger was obliged to look down for a moment and clear his throat in order to get control of his voice.

"No, man," Dougal said casually, also looking down as he wiped his bowl with a bit of hard journeycake taken from his saddlebag. "He thought I might be of help to ye in your search." He looked up then, straight at Roger's neck, and raised one dark, heavy brow. "Not that the presence of a half-hangit man at your door doesna raise questions, ken?"

"At least a half-hangit man can answer the questions," Buck put in. "Not like him from the croft above, aye?"

That startled Dougal, who put down his spoon and stared at Buck. Who stared back, one fair brow raised.

Holy Lord . . . do they see it? Either of them? It wasn't warm, despite the sun, but Roger felt sweat begin to trickle down his spine. It was more a matter of posture and expression than of feature—and yet the echo of similarity between the two faces was plain as the . . . well, as the long, straight nose on both faces.

Roger could see the thoughts flickering across Dougal's face: surprise, curiosity, suspicion.

"And what have ye to do with him above?" he asked, with a slight lift of his chin in the direction of the burnt-out croft.

"Not a thing, so far as I ken," Buck answered, with a brief shrug. "Only meaning as how if ye want to know what happened to my kinsman, ye can ask him. We've nothing to hide."

Thanks a lot, Roger thought, with a sideways look at his ancestor, who smiled blandly back at him and resumed gingerly eating his salty parritch. *Why the bloody hell did you say* that, *of all things?*

"I was hanged in mistake for another man," he said, as casually as possible, but he heard the voice grate in his throat, tightening, and had to stop to clear it. "In America."

"America," Dougal repeated, in open astonishment. All of them were staring at him now, men-at-arms and MacLarens both. "What took ye to America—and what brought ye back, come to that?"

"My wife has kin there," Roger replied, wondering what the devil Buck was up to. "In North Carolina, on the Cape Fear River." He very nearly named Hector and Jocasta Cameron, before remembering that Jocasta was Dougal's sister. Also that it was Culloden that had sent them to America—and Culloden hadn't happened yet.

And he won't live to see it, he thought, watching Dougal's face as he spoke, feeling a state of bemused horror. Dougal would die, hours before the battle, in the attics of Culloden House near Inverness, with Jamie Fraser's dirk sunk in the hollow of his throat.

He told the story of his hanging and rescue briefly, leaving out the context of the War of the Regulation—and leaving out Buck's role in getting him hanged, too. He could feel Buck there beside him, leaning forward, intent, but didn't look at him. Couldn't look at him without wanting to strangle him. Wanted to strangle him anyway.

He could barely speak by the time he finished, and his heart was thumping in his ears with suppressed rage. Everyone was looking at him, with a range of emotions from awe to sympathy. Allie MacLaren was openly sniffing, her apron hem at her nose, and even her mother looked as though she somewhat regretted the salt. Angus coughed and handed him a stone bottle of what turned out to be beer, and a very grateful beverage it was, too. He muttered thanks and gulped it, avoiding all eyes.

Dougal nodded soberly, then turned to Angus.

"Tell me about the man above," he said. "When did that happen—and what d'ye ken about it?"

MacLaren's face lost a little of its natural high color, and he looked as though he wanted his beer back.

"Six days past, *a ghoistidh.*" He gave a brief, and much less atmospheric, account than he had the night before—but it was the same story.

Dougal looked thoughtful, tapping his fingers gently on his knee.

"The woman," he said. "D'ye ken where she's gone?"

"I . . . uh . . . heard as how she'd gone to Cranesmuir, sir." MacLaren's color had all come back, with interest, and he carefully avoided his wife's hard eye.

"Cranesmuir," Dougal repeated. "Aye, well. Perhaps I'll seek her out, then, and just have a word. What's her name?"

"Isbister," MacLaren blurted. "Geillis Isbister."

Roger didn't actually feel the earth shake under his feet but was surprised that it hadn't.

"Isbister?" Dougal's brows went up. "From the northern isles, is she?"

MacLaren shrugged in elaborate pantomime of ignorance—and unconcern. He looked as though someone had made a serious attempt to boil his head, and Roger saw Dougal's mouth twitch again.

"Aye," he said dryly. "Well, an Orkneywoman maybe won't be hard to find, then, in a place the size of Cranesmuir." He lifted his chin in the direction of his men, and they all rose as one when he stood. So did Roger and Buck.

"Godspeed to ye, gentlemen," he said, bowing to them. "I'll have word put about regarding your wee lad. If I hear anything, where shall I send?"

Roger exchanged glances with Buck, nonplussed. He couldn't ask for word to be sent to Lallybroch, knowing what he knew of the relations between Brian Fraser and his brothers-in-law.

"Do ye ken a place called Sheriffmuir?" he asked, groping for some other place he knew that existed at the present time. "There's a fine coaching inn there—though not much else."

Dougal looked surprised but nodded.

"I do, sir. I fought at Sheriffmuir with the Earl of Mar, and we supped there with him one night, my father and brother and I. Aye, I'll send word there, if there is any."

"Thank you." The words came half choked but clear enough. Dougal gave him a sympathetic nod, then turned to take leave of the MacLarens. Stopped by a sudden thought, though, he turned back.

"I dinna suppose ye really are an angel, are ye?" he asked, quite seriously.

"No," Roger said, smiling as best he could, despite the coldness in his belly. *And it isn't you that's talking to a ghost.*

He stood with Buck, watching the MacKenzies depart, Geordie and

Thomas keeping up with little effort, as the horses went slowly on the steep, rocky path.

The phrase *"Blessed are those who have not seen but have believed"* floated through his head. It was maybe not the believing that was the blessing; it was the not having to look. Seeing, sometimes, was bloody awful.

ROGER DELAYED their own departure as long as he decently could, hoping for the return of Dr. McEwan, but as the sun rose high in the sky, it was plain that the MacLarens wanted them gone—and Buck wanted to go.

"I'm fine," he said crossly, and thumped his chest with a fist. "Sound as a drum."

Roger made a skeptical noise in his throat—and was surprised. It hadn't hurt. He stopped himself putting a hand to his own throat; no need to draw attention to it, even if they were leaving.

"Aye, all right." He turned to Angus MacLaren and Stuart, who'd helpfully filled Roger's canteen in the hope of hurrying them on their way and was standing with it dripping in his hands. "I thank ye for your hospitality, sir, and your kindness to my kinsman."

"Och," said MacLaren, a distinct look of relief coming over his face at what was plainly farewell. "That's fine. Nay bother."

"If—if the healer should come along, would ye thank him for us? And say I'll try to come and see him on our way back."

"On your way back," MacLaren repeated, with less enthusiasm.

"Aye. We're bound into Lochaber, to the Cameron lands. If we find nay trace of my son there, though, we'll likely come back this way—perhaps we'll call at Castle Leoch for news."

MacLaren's face cleared at that.

"Och, aye," he said heartily. "Good thought. Godspeed!"

41

IN WHICH THINGS CONVERGE

"NOW, IT'S NOT that I dinna want to be helping your mam," Mr. Buchan said, for the third time. "But I canna be having ructions going on in my house, and criminals coming and goin,' not with my girls there, now, can I?"

Jem shook his head obediently, though Mr. Buchan wasn't looking at him; he was peering into his rearview mirror and looking over his shoulder now and then, like he thought somebody might be following them. It made Jem want to look, too, but he couldn't see behind without getting up on his knees and turning round, and Mandy was passed out asleep, half on his lap.

It was late, and he yawned, forgetting to cover his mouth. He thought of saying, "Excuse me," but he didn't think Mr. Buchan had noticed. He felt a burp coming and did cover his mouth this time, tasting vinegar from the fish and chips. Mr. Buchan had bought an extra fish supper for Mam; it was in a brown-paper bag on the floor by Jem's feet, so as not to get grease on the seat.

"Ken when your da's expected back?" Mr. Buchan asked abruptly, glancing down at him. Jem shook his head, feeling the fish and chips rise up in a queasy ball.

Mr. Buchan's mouth pressed tight, like he wanted to say something he thought he shouldn't.

"Daddy . . ." Mandy murmured, then pushed her head into his ribs, snorted, and went back to sleep. He felt terrible. Mandy didn't even know where Da was; she probably thought he was just at lodge or something.

Mam said Da would come back, as soon as he figured out that Jem wasn't there with Grandda. *But how?* he thought, and had to bite his lip hard not to cry. *How would he know?* It was dark, but there was a glow from the dashboard. If he cried, Mr. Buchan would maybe see.

Headlights flashed in the rearview mirror and he looked up, brushing his sleeve furtively under his nose. He could see a white panel truck coming up behind them. Mr. Buchan said something under his breath and stepped on the gas pedal harder.

BRIANNA HAD SETTLED into the hunter's wait: a state of physical detachment and mental abeyance, mind and body each minding its own business but able to spring into unified action the moment something worth eating showed up. Her mind was on the Ridge, reliving a possum hunt with her cousin Ian. The pungent stickiness and eye-watering smoke of pine-knot torches, a glimpse of glowing eyes in a tree, and a sudden bristling possum like a nightmare in the branches, needle-toothed and gaping threats, hissing and growling like a flatulent motorboat . . .

And then the phone rang. In an instant she was standing, gun in hand, every sense trained on the house. It came again, the short double *brr!* muffled by distance but unmistakable. It was the phone in Roger's study, and even as she thought this, she saw the brief glow of a light inside as the study door was opened, and the ringing phone abruptly stopped.

Her scalp contracted, and she felt a brief kinship with the treed possum. But the possum hadn't had a shotgun.

Her immediate impulse was to go and flush out whoever was in her house and demand to know the meaning of this. Her money was on Rob Cameron, and the thought of flushing him like a grouse and marching him out at the point of a gun made her hand tighten on said gun with anticipation. She had Jem back; Cameron would know she didn't need to keep him alive.

But. She hesitated in the door of the broch, looking down.

But whoever was in the house had answered the phone. *If I was a burglar, I wouldn't be answering the phone in the house I was burgling. Not unless I thought it would wake up the people inside.*

Whoever was in her house already knew no one was home.

"Quod erat demonstrandum," her father's voice said in her mind, with a grim satisfaction. Someone in the house was expecting a call.

She stepped outside, with a deep breath of the fresh cold scent of gorse replacing the dank musk of the broch, her heart beating fast and her mind working faster. *Who would be calling him—them? To say what?*

Maybe someone had been watching earlier, seen her coming down the forestry road. Maybe they were calling to tell Rob she was outside, in the broch. No, that didn't make sense. Whoever was in the house, they'd *been* in there when she arrived. If someone had seen her come, they'd have called the house then.

"Ita sequitur . . ." she murmured. *Thus it follows:* if the call wasn't about her, it must be either a warning that someone—the police, and why?—was coming toward Lallybroch—or news that whoever was on the outside had found the kids.

The metal of the barrel was slick under her sweating palm, and it took a noticeable effort to keep a firm grip on the gun. Even more of an effort not to run toward the house.

Aggravating as it was, she had to wait. If someone had found the kids, she couldn't reach Fiona's house in time to protect them; she'd have to depend on Fiona and Ernie and the City of Inverness police. But if that was the case, whoever was in the house would surely be coming out right away. *Unless that bastard Rob means to hang around in hopes of catching me unawares, and . . .* Despite the gun in her hand, that thought gave her an unpleasant squirm deep inside—one she recognized as the ghostly touch of Stephen Bonnet's penis.

"I killed you, Stephen," she said under her breath. "And I'm glad you're dead. You may have company in hell pretty soon. Make sure the fire's lit for him, okay?"

That restored her nerve, and dropping to her haunches, she duckwalked through the gorse, coming down the hillside at an angle that would bring her out near the kailyard, not by the path, which was visible from the house. Even in the dark, she was taking no chances; there was a rising half-moon, though it showed erratically through scudding cloud.

The sound of a car coming made her lift her head, peering over a tuft of dry broom. She put a hand in her pocket, thumbing through the loose shot-gun shells. Fourteen. That should be enough.

Fiona's remark about ballistics flitted through her mind, along with a faint reminder of the possibility of going to prison for wholesale manslaughter. She might risk it, for the satisfaction of killing Rob Cameron—but the unwel-come thought occurred to her that while she didn't need him to locate Jem anymore, she *did* need to find out what the hell was going on. And while the police might track down the man from the dam, if there was some sort of gang involved, Rob was likely the only way of finding out who the others were—and what they wanted.

The headlights jounced down the lane and into the dooryard, and she stood up abruptly. The motion-detecting light had come on, showing her Ernie's white panel truck, unmistakable, with BUCHAN ELECTRICS/FOR ALL YOUR CURRENT NEEDS, CALL 01463 775 4432 on the side, with a drawing of a severed cable, spitting sparks.

"Bloody hell," she said. "Bloody, *bloody* hell!"

The truck's door opened and Jem tumbled out, then turned round to help Mandy, who was no more than a short dark blot in the recesses of the truck.

"GET BACK IN THE TRUCK!" Brianna bellowed, leaping down the slope, skittering on rolling stones and bending her ankles in spongy patches of heather. "JEMMY! GET BACK!"

She saw Jem turn, his face white in the glare of the light, but it was too late. The front door flew open and two dark figures rushed out, running for the truck.

She wasted no more breath but ran for all she was worth. A shotgun was useless at any distance—or maybe not. She skidded to a halt, shouldered the gun, and fired. Buckshot flew into the gorse with a whizzing sound like tiny arrows, but the bang had halted the intruders in their tracks.

"BACK IN THE TRUCK!" she roared, and fired again. The intruders galloped toward the house, and Jem, bless his heart, leapt into the truck like a startled frog and slammed the door. Ernie, who had just got out, stood for a moment gawking up the slope, but then, realizing what had happened, came suddenly to life and dived for his own door.

She reloaded in the glow of the spotlight. How long would the light stay on with no one moving in its range? She racked a fresh shell and ran for Ernie's truck. More headlights jerked her attention toward the lane. Holy Mary, Mother of God, who was this? *Please, God, let it be the police . . .*

The light winked out, then on again almost at once, as the second vehicle roared into the dooryard, moving fast. The people inside the house were hanging out of the drawing room casement, yelling something at the new truck—yes, it was another panel truck, much like Ernie's, save that it said POULTNEY'S, PURVEYOR OF FINE GAME and had a picture of a wild boar.

"Holy Mary, Mother of God, pray for us sinners now and at the hour of our death . . ." She had to get to Ernie's truck before—too late. The FINE GAME truck revved up and rammed Ernie's truck in the side, shunting it several yards. She could hear Mandy's scream above everything, sharp as an augur through her heart.

"Bloody Mother of . . . Jesus H. Roosevelt Christ!" She couldn't take time to circle the dooryard. She ran straight across it, took close aim, and shredded the front tire of the FINE GAME truck with a blast of buckshot.

"STAY IN THE TRUCK!" she shouted, chambering the second shell and pointing the gun at the windshield in the same motion. A blur of white as at least two people ducked down out of sight below the dash.

The men—yes, both men—inside the house were yelling at each other, and at the people in the truck, and at her. Useless adjurations and insults, mostly, but one of them was now pointing out to the others that her weapon *was* a shotgun. Useless except at short range, and only two shots.

"You can't cover us all, hen!"

That was Rob Cameron, shouting from the Poultney's truck. She didn't bother replying but ran to get in range of the house, and the drawing room window dissolved in a shower of glass.

Sweat was running down her sides, tickling. She broke the gun and thumbed two more shells into place. She felt as though she were moving in slow motion—but the rest of the world was moving slower. With no sense of hurry, she walked to Ernie's truck and put her back against the door behind which Jem and Mandy were sheltering. A strong waft of fish and malt vinegar floated out as the window cranked down a few inches.

"Mam—"

"Mummy! Mummy!"

"Bloody hell, Brianna! What's going on?"

"A bunch of nutters are trying to kill me and take my kids, Ernie," she said, raising her voice over Mandy's wailing. "What does it look like? How about you start the engine, hmm?"

The other truck was out of effective shotgun range from here, and she could see only one side of it. She heard its door open on the other side and saw a flicker of movement inside the shattered window of the house.

"*Now* would be a good time, Ernie." She wasn't forgetting that one of the bastards had her rifle. She could only hope they didn't know how to use it.

Ernie was frantically turning the key and stomping the gas. She could hear him praying under his breath, but he'd flooded the engine; the starter whirred uselessly. Lower lip tucked under her teeth, she strode round the front of the truck in time to catch one of the people from the FINE GAME truck—to her surprise, this one was a woman, a short, dumpy shape in a balaclava and an old Barbour. She raised the shotgun to her shoulder, and the woman tried to run backward, tripped, and fell on her backside with an audible "Oof!"

She wanted to laugh but then saw Cameron climbing out of the truck, her rifle in hand, and the urge left her.

"Drop it!" She strode toward him, gun at her shoulder. He *didn't* know how to use the rifle; he glanced wildly from her to the gun, as though hoping it would aim itself, then changed his mind and dropped it.

The front door of the house slammed open, and she heard running feet coming fast. She whirled on her heel and ran, too, reaching Ernie's truck barely in time to hold off the two men from the house. One immediately began to sidle round, clearly meaning to circle the other truck and collect his idiot comrades. Rob Cameron was now advancing on her slowly, hands held up to show his non-offensive—*ha*—intent.

"Look, Brianna, we don't mean ye any harm," he said.

She racked a fresh shell in answer to that, and he took a step back.

"I mean it," he said, an edge in his voice. "We want to talk to you, is all."

"Aye, pull the other one," she said, "it's got bells on. *Ernie?*"

"Mam—"

"Don't you dare open that door until I say so, Jemmy!"

"Mam!"

"Get down on the floor, Jem, right now! Take Mandy!" One of the men from the house and the dumpy woman were moving again; she could hear them. And the second man from the house had disappeared into the dark outside the circle of light. "ERNIE!"

"But, Mam, somebody's coming!"

Everyone froze for an instant, and the sound of an engine advancing down the farm track came clearly through the night. She turned and grabbed the door handle, jerking it open just as Ernie's engine finally coughed into full-throated life. She hurled herself into the seat, her feet narrowly missing Jem's head as he peered up from the footwell, eyes huge in the dim light.

"Let's go, Ernie," she said, very calmly under the circumstance. "Kids, you stay down there."

A rifle butt struck the window near Ernie's head, starring the glass, and he yelped but didn't, God bless him, flood the engine again. Another blow and the glass broke in a cascade of glittering fragments. Brianna dropped her own gun and lunged across Ernie, reaching for the rifle. She got a hand on it, but the man holding it wrenched it free. Grabbing wildly, she scrabbled at the balaclava'd shape, and the woolly helmet came off in her hand, leaving the man beneath openmouthed with shock.

The spotlight went off, plunging the yard into darkness, and bright spots danced in front of her eyes. It popped back on again as the new vehicle roared into the yard, horn blaring. Brianna lifted herself out of Ernie's lap, trying to see out through the windshield, then flung herself toward the other side of the truck.

It was an ordinary car, a dark-blue Fiat, looking like a toy as it circled the yard, horn blatting like a sow in heat.

"Friend, d'ye think?" Ernie asked, his voice strained but not panicked. "Or foe?"

"Friend," she said, breathless, as the Fiat charged three of the intruders who were standing together: the unmasked rifle-wielder, the woman in the Barbour jacket, and whoever the guy who wasn't Rob Cameron was. They scattered like cockroaches into the grass, and Ernie slammed a fist on the dash in exultation.

"That'll show the buggers!"

Bree would have liked to stay and watch the rest of the show, but wherever Cameron was, he was undoubtedly too close.

"*Go*, Ernie!"

He went, with a terrible crunching and screeching of metal. The van lurched badly; the back axle must be damaged. She could only hope a wheel didn't come off.

The blue Fiat was prowling the dooryard; it honked and flashed its lights at Ernie's truck, and a hand waved from the driver's window. Brianna stuck her head out cautiously and returned the wave, then dropped back into her seat, panting. Black spots were swimming in her field of vision and her hair stuck to her face, lank with sweat.

They limped down the lane in first gear, with a horrible grinding noise; from the sound of it, the back wheel well had caved in.

"Mam." Jemmy stuck his head up over the edge of the seat like a prairie dog. "Can I come up now?"

"Sure." She took a deep breath and helped Mandy scramble up after him. The little girl plastered herself at once to Brianna's chest, whimpering.

"It's okay, baby," she whispered into Mandy's hair, clinging to the solid small body as much as Mandy clung to her. "Everything will be fine." She glanced down at Jem, riding between Ernie and herself. He was hunched into himself and shivering visibly in his checked wool jacket, even though it was warm in the cab. She reached out a hand and took him by the back of the neck, shaking him gently. "Okay there, pal?"

He nodded, but without saying anything. She folded her hand over his, clenched into a small fist on his knee, and held it tight—both in reassurance and to stop her own hand shaking.

Ernie cleared his throat.

"I'm sorry, Brianna," he said gruffly. "I didna ken that—I mean, I thought it would be okay to bring the bairns back, and after yon Cameron came to the house and hit Fiona, I—" A trickle of sweat gleamed as it ran down behind his ear.

"He what?" After the events of the last hour, this news registered only as a blip on her personal seismograph, obscured by the bigger shock waves that were only now dying down. But she asked questions, and Jem began to come out of his own shell shock, telling about his part, gradually becoming indignant about Mrs. Kelleher and the police dispatcher. She felt a quiver in the pit of her stomach that wasn't quite laughter but close enough.

"Don't worry about it, Ernie." She brushed off his renewed attempts at apology. Her voice rasped, her throat sore from shouting. "I'd have done the same, I expect. And we'd never have got away without you." They'd never have *been* there without him in the first place, but he knew that as well as she did; no point in rubbing it in.

"Aye, mmphm." He drove in silence for a moment, then remarked conversationally, looking in the rearview mirror, "Yon wee blue motor's following us, ken." His throat moved as he swallowed.

Brianna rubbed a hand over her face, then looked. Sure enough, the Fiat was trundling after them at a discreet distance.

Ernie coughed. "Ehm . . . where d'ye want to go, Bree? Only, I'm none sae sure we'll make it all the way into the town. But there's a petrol station with a garridge bay on the main road—if I was to stop there, they'd have a phone. Ye could call the polis while I deal wi' the van."

"Don't call the polis, Mam," Jemmy said, his nostrils flaring with disgust. "*They're* no help."

"Mmphm," she said noncommittally, and raised an eyebrow at Ernie, who nodded and set his jaw.

She was inclined against calling the police herself—but out of concern lest they be *too* inquisitively helpful. She'd managed to deflect them from the touchy question of just where her husband was last night, telling them he was in London to visit the British Museum Reading Room and that she'd call him as soon as they got home. If the police found out about the shoot-out at the O.K. Corral, there was going to be a lot more scrutiny of her private affairs.

And it took no stretch of imagination at all to conclude that the police might really suspect her of having something to do with Roger's disappearance, since she couldn't produce him and couldn't tell them where he was. *Might never be able to.* She swallowed, hard.

The only recourse would be to claim that they'd had a fight and he'd walked out on her—but that would sound pretty flimsy, in light of recent events. And she wouldn't say something like that in front of the kids, regardless.

But stopping at the petrol station was the only thing she could see to do at the moment. If the blue Fiat followed them there, at least she might discover an ally. And if it was the police, incognito . . . well, she'd cross that bridge when she came to it. Adrenaline and shock had both left her now; she felt detached, dreamy, and very, very tired. Jemmy's hand had relaxed in hers, but his fingers were still curled around her thumb.

She leaned back, closing her eyes, and slowly traced the curve of Mandy's spine with her free hand. Her little girl had relaxed into sleep against her chest, her son with his head on her shoulder, the weight of her children's trust heavy on her heart.

THE PETROL STATION was next to a Little Chef café. She left Ernie to talk to the garageman while she extracted the kids. She didn't bother looking over her shoulder; the blue Fiat had fallen back to a respectful distance, not crowding them as they crawled clanking and grinding down the motorway at 20 mph. If the driver didn't mean to talk to her, he'd have driven off and disappeared. Maybe she'd manage a cup of tea before she had to deal with him.

"Can't wait," she muttered. "Get the door, please, Jem?"

Mandy was inert as a bag of cement in her arms but began to stir at the smell of food. Bree gagged at the reek of stale frying oil, burnt chips, and synthetic pancake syrup, but ordered ice cream for Jem and Mandy, with a cup of tea for herself. Surely even this place couldn't ruin tea?

A cup of barely warm water and a PG Tips tea bag convinced her otherwise. It didn't matter; her throat was so tight that she doubted she could swallow even water.

The blessed numbness of shock was lifting, much as she would have preferred to keep it wrapped blanket-like around her. The café seemed too bright, with acres of foot-marked white lino; she felt exposed, like a bug on a grimy kitchen floor. Prickles of apprehension sparked unpleasantly over her scalp, and she kept her eyes fixed on the door, wishing she'd been able to bring the shotgun inside.

She didn't realize that Jem had also been watching the door until he stiffened to attention beside her in the booth.

"Mam! It's Mr. Menzies!"

For a moment, neither the words nor the sight of the man who had just entered the café made any sense. She blinked several times, but he was still there, striding toward them with an anxious face. Jem's school principal.

"Mrs. MacKenzie," he said, and, reaching across the table, shook her hand fervently. "Thank God you're all right!"

"Er . . . thanks," she said feebly. "You—was that *you*? In the blue Fiat?" It was like being keyed up to confront Darth Vader and coming face-to-face with Mickey Mouse.

He actually blushed behind his glasses.

"Ehm . . . well, aye. I—er . . ." He caught Jem's eye and smiled awkwardly. "You're taking good care of your mother, then, Jem?"

"Aye, sir." Jem was quite obviously about to burst with questions. Bree forestalled him with a quelling look and gestured to Lionel Menzies to sit down. He did and took a deep breath, about to say something, but was interrupted by the waitress, a solid, middle-aged woman with thick stockings and a cardigan and an air that indicated that she didn't care whether they were space aliens or cockroaches, so long as they didn't complicate her life.

"Don't order the tea," Bree said, with a nod toward her cup.

"Aye, thanks. I'll have . . . a bacon butty and an Irn-Bru?" he asked tentatively, looking up at the waitress. "With tomato sauce?" She scorned to reply but flipped her pad shut and trundled off.

"Right," Menzies said, squaring his shoulders like one about to face a firing squad. "Tell me the one thing, would you? Was it Rob Cameron there at your house?"

"It was." Bree spoke tersely, recalling belatedly that Cameron was related to Menzies in some way—a cousin or something? "Why?"

He looked unhappy. A pale-faced man with slightly receding curly brown hair and glasses, he wasn't remarkable in any way and yet usually had a presence, a friendliness and quiet air of authority about him that drew the eye and made one feel reassured in his company. This was notably lacking tonight.

"I was afraid that it might be. I heard—on the evening news. That Rob was being looked for by the police"—he lowered his voice, though there was no one within earshot—"in connection with . . . well, with"—he nodded discreetly toward Jem—"taking Jeremiah, here."

"He did!" Jem said, dropping his spoon and sitting up straight. "He did, Mr. Menzies! He said he was going to take me to spend the night with Bobby, only he didn't, he took me up to the rocks and—"

"Jem." Brianna spoke quietly, but it was her Shut Up Right Now voice, and he did, though with an audible snort and a glare at her.

"Yes, he did," she said levelly. "What do you know about it?"

He blinked in surprise.

"I—why, nothing. I can't imagine why he—" He broke off, coughed, and taking his glasses off, pulled a pocket handkerchief out and polished them. By the time he put them back on, he'd pulled himself together.

"You may remember, Rob Cameron's my cousin. And he's in lodge, of course. I was knocked off my perch to hear this about him. So I thought I'd maybe come out to Lallybroch, have a word with you and your husband"—he lifted an eyebrow, but she didn't respond to this obvious hint about Roger, and he went on—"see that Jem was all right—are ye all right, Jem?" he broke off to ask seriously, glancing at the boy.

"Oh, aye, fine," Jem replied airily, though he seemed tense. "Sir," he added belatedly, and licked a smear of chocolate ice cream off his upper lip.

"That's good." Menzies smiled at Jem, and Brianna saw a little of his usual warmth light up behind the glasses. The warmth was still in his eyes, though he was serious when he looked at her. "I wanted to ask if there'd maybe been a mistake, but I'm thinking that there likely wasn't? In light of . . . all that." He tilted his head in the direction of Lallybroch and swallowed.

"Yes, there was," she said grimly, shifting Mandy's weight on her lap, "and Rob Cameron made it."

He grimaced, drew a deep breath, but nodded.

"I'd like to help," he said simply.

"You definitely did," she assured him, wondering what on earth to do with him now. "Ick! Mandy, you're dribbling all over everywhere! Use a napkin, for heaven's sake." She swabbed Mandy's face briskly, ignoring her daughter's cranky whine. *Could* he help? She wanted badly to believe him; she was still shaking internally and all too ready to grab at any offer of assistance.

But he *was* Rob Cameron's relative. And maybe he'd come out to the house to talk, and maybe he'd come for some other reason. He might, after all, have intervened to keep her from blasting Rob into bloody shreds, rather than to save her and the kids from Rob and his masked sidekicks.

"I spoke to Ernie Buchan," Menzies said, nodding toward the plate-glass window. "He, um, seemed to think that you might not want the police involved?"

"No." Bree's mouth was dry; she sipped the lukewarm tea, trying to think. It was getting harder by the moment; her thoughts scattered like drops of quicksilver, wobbling away in a dozen directions. "Not—not just yet. We were at the police station half of last night. I really can't deal with any more questions tonight." She took a deep breath and stared at him directly.

"I don't know what's going on," she said. "I don't know why Rob Cameron should have kidnapped Jemmy—"

"Yes, you d—" Jem started, and she whipped her head round and glared at him. He glared back, red-eyed and clench-fisted, and with a jolt of alarm she recognized the Fraser temper, about to go off with a bang.

"You do so know!" he said, loudly enough that a couple of truckers at the counter turned round to look at him. "I *told* you! He wanted me to—" Mandy, who had started to drop off again, jerked awake and started to wail.

"I want Daddeeeee!"

Jem's face was bright red with fury. At this, it went white.

"Shut up, shut up, shut up!" he shrieked at Mandy, who yelped in terror and screamed louder, trying to scramble up Brianna's body.

"DADDEEE!"

"Jem!" Lionel Menzies was on his feet, reaching for the boy, but Jem was absolutely beside himself, literally hopping up and down with rage. The entire restaurant was gaping at them.

"Go AWAY!" Jem roared at Menzies. "DAMMIT! Don't you touch me! Don't touch my mam!" And, in an excess of passion, he kicked Menzies hard on the shin.

"Jesus!"

"Jem!" Bree had a grip on the struggling, bawling Mandy but couldn't reach Jem before he picked up his dish of ice cream, flung it at the wall, and then ran out of the café, crashing the door open so hard that a man and woman on the verge of entering were forced to leap aside to avoid being knocked over as he rocketed past.

Brianna sat down quite suddenly, as all the blood left her head. *Holy Mary, Mother of God, pray for us . . .*

The room was silent, save for Mandy's sobbing, though this was dying down as her panic subsided. She burrowed into Brianna's chest, burying her face in the padded coat.

"Hush, sweetie," Bree whispered, bending her head so that Mandy's curls brushed her lips. "Hush, now. It's all right. Everything will be all right."

A muffled mumble ended with a tearful ". . . Daddy?"

"Yes," Bree said firmly. "We'll see Daddy soon."

Lionel Menzies cleared his throat. He'd sat down to massage his shin but left off doing this to gesture toward the door.

"Had I . . . better go after Jem?"

"No. He's all right . . . I mean . . . he's with Ernie. I can see him." They were in the parking lot, just visible in the glow of light from the neon sign. Jem had cannoned into Ernie, who was coming toward the restaurant, and was clinging to him like a limpet. As Brianna watched, Ernie, an experienced father, knelt down and hugged Jem to him, patting his back and smoothing his hair, talking earnestly to him.

"Mmphm." It was the waitress with Menzie's butty, her stolid face melted into sympathy. "The wee lassie's tired, nay doubt."

"I'm sorry," Bree said feebly, and nodded at the shattered dish and splotch of chocolate ice cream on the wall. "I'll, um, pay for it."

"Och, dinna fash, lass," the waitress said, shaking her head. "I've had weans. I can see ye've got enough trouble to be goin' on with. Let me fetch ye oot a nice cup o' tea."

She trundled off. Without speaking, Lionel Menzies popped the tab on his can of Irn-Bru and shoved it in her direction. She picked it up and gulped it. The advertising implied that the stuff was made from rusty iron girders salvaged from Glasgow shipyards. Only in Scotland would this have been considered a good selling point, she reflected. But it was about half sugar, and the glucose hit her bloodstream like the elixir of life.

Menzies nodded, seeing her straighten up like a wilting flower revived.

"Where *is* Roger?" he asked softly.

"I don't know," she said, just as softly; Mandy had given a final hiccuping sigh and fallen heavily asleep, face still buried in Brianna's coat. She twitched the quilted fabric aside so Mandy wouldn't suffocate. "And I don't know when he's coming back."

He grimaced, looking unhappy and strangely embarrassed; he was having trouble meeting her eyes.

"I see. Mmphm. Was it—I mean, did he . . . leave because of what Rob . . . er . . . did to Jem?" His voice dropped even lower and she blinked at him. Rising blood sugar had brought her thoughts back into focus, though, and suddenly the penny dropped, and the blood rushed into her face.

He thought Rob had abducted Jemmy in order to—and Jemmy had said, *"You know what he did,"* and she'd shut him up sharp . . . and she'd said she didn't want the police involved . . . oh, dear Lord. She took a deep breath and rubbed a hand over her face, wondering whether it was better to let him think Rob had molested Jemmy—and was now trying to murder her in order to cover that up—or to tell him some halfway believable version of some part of the truth.

"Rob came to my house last night and tried to rape me," she said, leaning over Mandy's head in order to keep her voice low enough to escape the flapping ears of the truckers sitting at the counter, who were glancing covertly over their shoulders at her. "He'd already taken Jem, and Roger had left to try to find him. We thought he'd taken Jem away to . . . to Orkney." *That seems far enough.* "I . . . left messages; I expect Roger'll be back any time now—as soon as he hears that Jemmy's been found." She crossed her fingers under the table.

Menzies's face went blank, all his previous assumptions colliding with new ones.

"He—he—oh." He paused for a moment, mechanically took a swallow of her cold tea, and made a face. "You mean," he said carefully, "that you think Rob took Jem in order to lure your husband away, so that he . . . ehm . . . could—"

"Yes, I do." She seized on this suggestion gratefully.

"But . . . those other people. With the—" He passed a hand vaguely over his head, indicating the balaclavas. "What on earth . . . ?"

"I have *no* idea," she said firmly. She wasn't going to mention the Spanish gold unless or until she had to. The fewer people who knew about that, the better. And as for the other thing . . .

But the mention of "those other people" reminded her of something, and she groped in her capacious pocket, drawing out the balaclava that she'd snatched off the man who'd broken the window with the rifle. She'd caught the barest glimpse of his face amidst the shifting light and shadow and had had no time to think about it. But now she did, and a fresh qualm went through her.

"Do you know a man named Michael Callahan?" she asked, trying to keep her voice casual. Menzies glanced at the balaclava, then at her, eyes widening.

"Of course I do. He's an archaeologist, something to do with ORCA—Orkney Research Centre, I mean. Orkney . . . You're no telling me he was with the people who—"

"Pretty sure. I saw his face for just a second when I pulled this off him. And"—she grimaced in distaste, plucking a tuft of sandy hair from the inside of the balaclava—"apparently that's not all I pulled off him. Rob knows him. He came out to Lallybroch to give us an opinion on some ruins up behind the house, and stayed to supper."

"Oh, dearie me," Menzies murmured, seeming to sink back into his seat. He took off his glasses and massaged his forehead for a bit. She watched him think, feeling increasingly remote.

The waitress hove to and put down a fresh cup of hot, milky tea, already sugared and stirred. Brianna thanked her and sat sipping it, watching the night outside. Ernie had taken Jem off in the direction of the garage, doubtless to check on his van.

"I can see why you don't want trouble," Menzies said carefully at last. He'd eaten half his butty; the rest of it lay on the plate, oozing ketchup in a queasy sort of way. "But really, Mrs.—may I call you Brianna?"

"Bree," she said. "Sure."

"Bree," he said, nodding, and one corner of his mouth twitched.

"Yes, I know what it means in Scots," she said dryly, seeing the thought cross his face. A bree was a storm or a great disturbance.

Lionel's face broke into a half smile.

"Yes. Well . . . what I'm thinking, Bree—I hate to suggest it, but what if Rob's done some harm to Roger? Would it not be worth the questions to get the police to look for him?"

"He hasn't." She felt unutterably tired and wanted only to go home. "Believe me, he hasn't. Roger went with his—his cousin, Buck. And if Rob had managed to hurt them somehow, he'd certainly have gloated about that when he . . . well." She took a breath that went all the way down to her aching feet and shifted her weight, getting a solid hold on Mandy.

"Lionel. Tell you what. Drive us home, will you? If that lot's still lurking around, then we'll go to the police right away. If not—it can wait 'til the morning."

He didn't like it, but he was suffering from the aftereffects of shock and fatigue, too, and after more argument finally agreed, done in by her implacable stubbornness.

Ernie had telephoned for a ride, after being assured that Lionel would see them home. Lionel was tense on the way back to Lallybroch, hands whiteknuckled on the steering wheel, but the Fiat's headlights showed the dooryard empty, save for a discarded tire lying in the gravel, shredded rubber spraying out like the wings of some gigantic vulture shot out of the sky.

Both the kids were sound asleep; Lionel carried Jem in, then insisted on searching the house with Bree, nailing up laths across the shattered window in the parlor while she combed the rooms—again—suffering déjà vu.

"Had I not better spend the night?" Lionel asked, hesitating at the door. "I'd be happy to sit up and keep watch, you know."

She smiled, though it took a lot of effort.

"Your wife will already be wondering where you are. No, you've done enough—more than enough for us. Don't worry; I'll . . . take steps in the morning. I just want the kids to be able to have a good night's sleep in their own beds."

He nodded, lips drawn in in worry, and glanced round the foyer, its gleaming walnut paneling serene in the lamplight, even the English saber slashes somehow grown homely and peaceful with age.

"Do you maybe have family—friends—in America?" he asked abruptly. "I mean, it might not be a bad idea to get right away for a bit, aye?"

"Yes," she said. "I was thinking that myself. Thanks, Lionel. Good night."

42

ALL MY LOVE

SHE WAS SHAKING. Had been shaking ever since Lionel Menzies left. With a faint sense of abstraction, she held out her hand, fingers spread, and watched it vibrate like a tuning fork. Then, irritated, made a fist and smacked it hard into the palm of her other hand. Smacked it again and again, clenching her teeth in fury, until she had to stop, gasping for breath, her palm tingling.

"Okay," she said under her breath, teeth still clenched. *"Okay."* The red haze had lifted like a cloud, leaving a pile of cold, icy little thoughts under it.

We have to go.

Where?

And when?

And the coldest of all:

What about Roger?

She was sitting in the study, the wood paneling glowing softly in the candlelight. There was a perfectly good reading lamp, as well as the ceiling fixture, but she'd lit the big candle instead. Roger liked to use that when he wrote late at night, writing down the songs and poems he'd memorized, sometimes with a goose quill. He said it helped him recall the words, bringing back an echo of the time where he'd learned them.

The candle's smell of hot wax brought back an echo of *him.* If she closed her eyes, she could hear him, humming low in his throat as he worked, stopping now and then to cough or clear his damaged throat. Her fingers rubbed softly over the wooden desk, summoning the touch of the rope scar on his throat, passing round to cup the back of his head, bury her fingers in the thick black warmth of his hair, bury her face in his chest . . .

She was shaking again, this time with silent sobs. She curled her fist again, but this time just breathed until it stopped.

"This will *not* do," she said out loud, sniffed deeply, and, clicking on the light, she blew out the candle and reached for a sheet of paper and a ballpoint pen.

WIPING THE TEARS off her face with the back of her hand, she folded the letter carefully. Envelope? No. If anybody found this, an envelope wouldn't stop them. She turned the letter over and, sniffing, wrote *Roger,* in her best parochial-school penmanship.

She groped in her pocket for a Kleenex and blew her nose, feeling obscurely that she should do something more . . . ceremonial? . . . with the letter, but other than putting it in the fireplace and touching a match to it so the north wind would carry it, as her parents had done with her childhood letters to Santa, nothing occurred to her.

In her present state of mind, she found it comforting that Santa had always come through.

She opened the big drawer and was groping at the back for the catch that released the secret hiding place when something else did occur to her. She slammed the big drawer shut and yanked open the wide shallow one in the center, which held pens and paper clips and rubber bands—and a lipstick left in the downstairs powder room by some random dinner guest.

It was pink but a dark pink, and it didn't matter that it clashed with her hair. She applied it hastily by feel, then pressed her lips carefully over the word *Roger*.

"I love you," she whispered, and, touching the pink kiss with one fingertip, opened the big drawer again and pushed the spot that unlocked the hiding place. It wasn't a secret drawer but a space built into the underside of the desk. A sliding panel let you reach up into a shallow hole about six inches by eight.

When Roger discovered it, it had three stamps printed with the head of Queen Victoria in it—unfortunately, all run-of-the-mill late-Victorian postage rather than a helpfully valuable One-Penny Black—and a wispy curl of a child's fine blond hair, faded with age, tied with white thread and a tiny scrap of heather. They'd left the stamps there—who knew, maybe they *would* be valuable by the time another few generations inherited the desk—but she'd put the lock of hair between the pages of her Bible and said a small prayer for the child and his—her?—parents, whenever she came across it.

The letter fit easily into the heart of the old desk. A moment of panic: should she have included locks of the kids' hair? *No*, she thought fiercely. *Don't be morbid. Sentimental, yes. Morbid, no.*

"Lord, let us all be together again," she whispered, pushing down the fear, and, closing her eyes, shut the panel with a little *click*.

If she hadn't opened her eyes right as she withdrew her hand, she'd never have seen it. Just the edge of something hanging down at the back of the big drawer, barely visible. She reached up and found an envelope, far back, attached to the underside of the desk with Scotch tape. This had dried with age; her earlier slamming of the drawer had probably loosened it.

She turned the envelope over with a sense of something happening in a dream and was, dreamlike, not surprised to see the initials *B.E.R.* written on the yellowed envelope. Very slowly, she opened it.

Dearest Deadeye, she read, and felt each tiny hair on her body rise slow and silent, one at a time.

Dearest Deadeye,

You've just left me, after our wonderful afternoon among the clay pigeons. My ears are still ringing. Whenever we shoot, I'm torn between

*immense pride in your ability, envy of it—and fear that you may some-
day need it.*

*What a queer feeling it is, writing this. I know that you'll eventually
learn who—and perhaps, what—you are. But I have no idea how you'll
come to that knowledge. Am I about to reveal you to yourself, or will this
be old news when you find it? If we're both lucky, I may be able to tell you
in person, when you're a little older. And if we're very lucky, it will come
to nothing. But I daren't risk your life in that hope, and you're not yet
old enough that I could tell you.*

*I'm sorry, sweetheart, that's terribly melodramatic. And the last
thing I want to do is alarm you. I have all the confidence in the world in
you. But I am your father and thus prey to the fears that afflict all
parents—that something dreadful and unpreventable will happen to
one's child, and you powerless to protect her.*

"What the hell, Daddy?" She rubbed hard at the back of her neck to ease
the prickling there.

*Men who've lived through war usually don't talk about it, save to
other soldiers. Men from my part of the Service don't talk to anyone, and
not only because of the Official Secrets Act. But silence eats at the soul. I
had to talk to someone, and my old friend Reggie Wakefield became my
confessor.*

*(That's the Reverend Reginald Wakefield, a Church of Scotland min-
ister who lives in Inverness. If you're reading this letter, I'll very likely be
dead. If Reggie is still alive and you are of age, go to see him; he has my
permission to tell you anything he knows at that point.)*

"Of age?" Hastily, she tried to calculate when this had been written. Clay
pigeons. Sherman's—the shooting range where he'd taught her to use a
shotgun. The shotgun had been a present for her fifteenth birthday. And her
father had died soon after her seventeenth birthday.

*The Service has nothing directly to do with this; don't go looking in
that direction for information. I mention it only because that's where I
learned what a conspiracy looks like. I also met a great many people in
the war, many of them in high places, and many of them strange; the two
overlap more often than one might wish.*

*Why is this so hard to say? If I'm dead, your mother may have told you
already the story of your birth. She promised me that she would never
speak of it, so long as I lived, and I'm sure she hasn't. If I'm dead,
though, she might—*

*Forgive me, darling. It's hard to say, because I love your mother and I
love you. And you are my daughter forever, but you were sired by another
man.*

*All right, that's out. Seeing it in black and white, my impulse is to rip
this paper to bits and burn them, but I won't. You have to know.*

Shortly after the war ended, your mother and I came to Scotland.

Something of a second honeymoon. She went out one afternoon to pick flowers—and never came back. I searched—everyone searched—for months, but there was no sign, and eventually the police stopped—well, in fact they didn't stop suspecting me of murdering her, damn them, but they grew tired of harassing me. I had begun to put my life back together, made up my mind to move on, perhaps leave Britain—and then Claire came back. Three years after her disappearance, she showed up in the Highlands, filthy, starved, battered—and pregnant.

Pregnant, she said, by a Jacobite Highlander from 1743 named James Fraser. I won't go into all that was said between us; it was a long time ago and it doesn't matter—save for the fact that IF your mother was telling the truth, and did indeed travel back in time, then you may have the ability to do it, too. I hope you don't. But if you should—Lord, I can't believe I'm writing this in all seriousness. But I look at you, darling, with the sun on your ruddy hair, and I see him. I can't deny that.

Well. It took a long time. A very long time. But your mother never changed her story, and though we didn't speak about it after a while, it became obvious that she wasn't mentally deranged (which I had rather naturally assumed to be the case, initially). And I began . . . to look for him.

Now I must digress for a moment; forgive me. I think you won't have heard of the Brahan Seer. Colorful as he was—if, in fact, he existed—he's not really known much beyond those circles with a taste for the more outlandish aspects of Scottish history. Reggie, though, is a man of immense curiosity, as well as immense learning, and was fascinated by the Seer— one Kenneth MacKenzie, who lived in the seventeenth century (maybe), and who made a great number of prophecies about this and that, sometimes at the behest of the Earl of Seaforth.

Naturally, the only prophecies mentioned in connection with this man are the ones that appeared to come true: he predicted, for instance, that when there were five bridges over the River Ness, the world would fall into chaos. In August 1939 the fifth bridge over the Ness was opened, and in September, Hitler invaded Poland. Quite enough chaos for anyone.

The Seer came to a sticky end, as prophets often do (do please remember that, darling, will you?), burnt to death in a spiked barrel of tar at the instigation of Lady Seaforth—to whom he had unwisely prophesied that her husband was having affairs with various ladies while away in Paris. (That one was likely true, in my opinion.)

Amongst his lesser-known prophecies, though, was one called the Fraser Prophecy. There isn't a great deal known about this, and what there is is rambling and vague, as prophecies usually are, the Old Testament notwithstanding. The only relevant bit, I think, is this: "The last of Lovat's line will rule Scotland."

Pause if you will, now, dear, and look at the paper I am enclosing with this letter.

Fumbling and clumsy with shock, she dropped the sheets altogether and had to retrieve them from the floor. It was easy to tell which paper he meant;

the paper was flimsier, a photocopy of a handwritten chart—some sort of family tree—the writing not her father's.

Yes. Well. This bit of disturbing information came into my hands from Reggie, who'd had it from the wife of a fellow named Stuart Lachlan. Lachlan had died suddenly, and as his widow was clearing out his desk, she found this and decided to pass it on to Reggie, knowing that he and Lachlan had shared an interest in history and in the Lovat family, they being local to Inverness; the clan seat is in Beauly. Reggie, of course, recognized the names.

You likely know nothing about the Scottish aristocracy, but I knew Simon Lovat, Lord Lovat that is, in the war—he was Commandos, then Special Forces. We weren't close friends but knew each other casually, in the way of business, you might say.

"Whose business?" she said aloud, suspicious. "His, or yours?" She could just see her father's face, with the hidden smile in the corner of his mouth, keeping something back but letting you know it was there.

The Frasers of Lovat have a fairly straightforward line of descent, until we come to Old Simon—well, they're all called Simon—the one they call the Old Fox, who was executed for treason after the Jacobite Rebellion—the '45, they call it. (There's quite a bit about him in my book on the Jacobites; don't know if you'll ever read that, but it's there, should you feel curious.)

"Should I feel curious," she muttered. "Ha." Brianna sensed a definite, if muted, note of accusation there and pressed her lips together, as much annoyed at herself for not having read her father's books yet as at him for mentioning it.

Simon was one of the more colorful Frasers, in assorted ways. He had three wives but was not famous for fidelity. He did have a few legitimate children, and God knows how many illegitimate ones (though two illegitimate sons were acknowledged), but his heir was Young Simon, known as the Young Fox. Young Simon survived the Rising, though attainted and stripped of his property. He eventually got most of it back through the courts, but the struggle took him most of a long life, and while he married, he did so at a very advanced age and had no children. His younger brother, Archibald, inherited, but then died childless, as well.

So Archibald was the "last of Lovat's line"—there's a direct line of descent between him and the Fraser of Lovat who would have been concurrent with the Brahan Seer—but clearly he wasn't the Scottish ruler foreseen.

You see the chart, though. Whoever made it has listed the two illegitimate sons, as well as Young Simon and his brother. Alexander and Brian, born to different mothers. Alexander entered the priesthood and became the abbot of a monastery in France. No known children. But Brian—

She tasted bile and thought she might throw up. *But Brian*—She closed her eyes in reflex, but it didn't matter. The chart was burned on the inside of her eyelids.

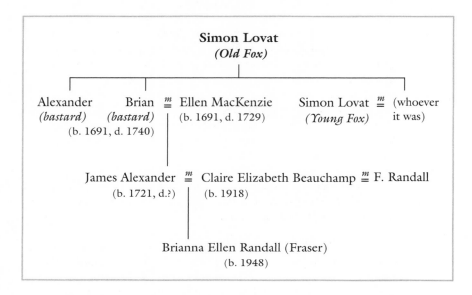

She stood up, pushing back the chair with a screak, and lurched out into the hallway, heart thundering in her ears. Swallowing repeatedly, she went to the lobby and got the shotgun from its place behind the coat rack. She felt a little better with it in hand.

"It isn't right." She hadn't realized that she'd spoken aloud; her own voice startled her. "It's not right," she repeated, in a low, fierce voice. "They left people out. What about Aunt Jenny? She had *six* kids! What about them?"

She was stomping down the hallway, gun in hand, swinging the barrel from side to side as though she expected Rob Cameron—or *somebody,* and the thought made her shudder—to jump out of the parlor or the kitchen or come sliding down the banister. That thought made her look up the stairs— she'd left all the lights on when she came down from tucking in the kids—but the landing was empty and no noise came from above.

A little calmer, she searched the ground floor carefully, testing every door and window. And the priest's hole, whose empty blackness gaped mockingly up at her.

Jem and Mandy were all right. She knew they were. But she still went upstairs, soft-footed, and stood by their beds for a long time, watching the pale glow of the Snow White night-light on their faces.

The longcase clock in the hall below struck the hour, and then a single *bong!* She drew a deep breath and went down to finish reading her father's letter.

The current line of Fraser of Lovat is descended from a collateral branch; presumably the Fraser Prophecy isn't referring to one of them— though there are plenty of heirs in that line.

I don't know who drew this chart, but I do intend to find out. This letter is in case I don't. In case of a number of things.

One of those things being the possibility that your mother's story is true—I still have difficulty believing it, when I wake in the morning beside her and everything is so normal. But late at night, when I'm alone with the documents . . . Well, why not admit it? I found the record of their marriage. James Alexander Malcolm MacKenzie Fraser and Claire Elizabeth Beauchamp. I'm not sure whether to be grateful or outraged that she didn't marry him using my name.

Forgive me, I'm rambling. It's hard to keep emotion out of it, but I'll try. The essence of what I'm saying is this: if you can indeed go back in time (and possibly return), you are a person of very great interest to a number of people, for assorted reasons. Should anyone in the more shadowed realm of government be halfway convinced that you are what you may be, you would be watched. Possibly approached. (In earlier centuries, the British government pressed men into service. They still do, if less obviously.)

That's a very remote contingency, but it is a real one; I must mention it.

There are private parties who would also have a deep interest in you for this reason—and evidently there is someone who has spotted you and is watching. The chart showing your line of descent, with dates, indicates that much. It also suggests that this person's or persons' interest may be a concern with the Fraser Prophecy. What could be more intriguing to that sort of person than the prospect of someone who is "the last of Lovat's line" and is also a time traveler? These sorts of people—I know them well—invariably believe in mystic powers of all sorts—nothing would draw them more powerfully than the conviction that you hold such power.

Such people are usually harmless. But they can be very dangerous indeed.

If I find whoever drew this chart, I will question them and do my best to neutralize any possible threat to you. But as I say—I know the look of a conspiracy. Nutters of this sort thrive in company. I might miss one.

"Neutralize them," she murmured, the chill in her hands spreading through her arms and chest, crystallizing around her heart. She had no doubt at all what he'd meant by that, the bland matter-of-factness of the term notwithstanding. And had he found him—them?

Don't—I repeat, don't—go anywhere near the Service or anyone connected with it. At best, they'd think you insane. But if you are indeed what you may be, the last people who should ever know it are the funny buggers, as we used to be known during the war.

And if worse should come to worst—and you can do it—then the past may be your best avenue of escape. I have no idea how it works; neither does your mother, or at least she says so. I hope I may have given you a few tools to help, if that should be necessary.

And . . . there's him. Your mother said that Fraser sent her back to me, knowing that I would protect her—and you. She thought that he died immediately afterward. He did not. I looked for him, and I found him. And, like him, perhaps I send you back, knowing—as he knew of me—that he will protect you with his life.

I will love you forever, Brianna. And I know whose child you truly are.

With all my love,
Dad

43

APPARITION

THE LOCHABER DISTRICT, according to the North of Scotland Hydro Electric Board (as interpreted by Brianna), is a "high glaciated landscape."

"That means it goes up and down a lot," Roger explained to Buck, as they fought their way through what he thought was part of the Locheil Forest, looking for the edge of Loch Lochy.

"Ye don't say?" Buck glanced bleakly over his shoulder at the distant hump of Ben Nevis, then back at Roger. "I'd not noticed."

"Cheer up, it's all downhill for a bit now. And the midgies are all dead wi' the cold. Count your blessings." Roger felt unaccountably cheerful this morning—perhaps only because the walking *was* downhill, after a strenuous week of combing the Cameron clan lands, a bewildering network of corries, tarns, moraines, and Munros, those deceptive summits with their gently rounded tops and their unspeakable slopes. Thank God no one lived on top of them.

Perhaps also because, while they hadn't found Jem or any trace of him, it was progress, of a sort. The Camerons on the whole had been hospitable, after the initial surprise, and they'd had the luck to find a tacksman of Lochiel, the clan chieftain, who'd sent a man to Tor Castle for them. Word had come back a day later: no word of a stranger matching Rob Cameron's description—though, in fact, Rob looked like half the people Roger had met in the last few days—or Jem's, he being a lot more noticeable.

They'd worked their way back along the shores of Loch Arkaig—the fastest way for someone to travel from the Great Glen, if heading for the ocean. But no word of a boat stolen or hired, and Roger began to feel that Cameron had not, after all, sought refuge or help among his ancient clan—a relief, on the whole.

"Blessings, is it?" Buck rubbed a hand over his face. Neither of them had shaved in a week, and he looked as red-eyed and grubby as Roger felt. He scratched his jaw consideringly. "Aye, well. A fox took a shit next to me last night, but I didna step in it this morning. I suppose that'll do, for a start."

The next day and night dampened Roger's mood of optimism somewhat: it rained incessantly, and they spent the night under heaps of half-dry bracken on the edge of a black tarn, emerging at dawn chilled and frowsty, to the shrieks of plovers and killdeer.

He hesitated momentarily as they rode past the place where they might turn toward Cranesmuir; he wanted badly to talk again with Dr. McEwan. His hand found his throat, thumb stroking the scar. *"Maybe,"* the healer had said. *"Just maybe."* But McEwan couldn't aid them in looking for Jem; that visit would have to wait.

Still, he felt his heart rise as they came over the pass and saw Lallybroch below. It was bittersweet, coming home to a home that was not his and might never be again. But it promised refuge and succor, if only temporarily—and it promised hope, at least in these last few minutes before they reached the door.

"Och, it's you!" It was Jenny Fraser who opened the door, her look of wariness changing to one of pleased welcome. Roger heard Buck behind him making a small humming noise of approval at sight of her, and, despite his determination not to hope too much, Roger felt his own spirits rise.

"And this will be your kinsman?" She curtsied to Buck. "Welcome to ye, sir. Come ben; I'll call Taggie to mind the horses." She turned in a flicker of white apron and petticoats, beckoning them to follow. "Da's in the speak-a-word," she called over her shoulder as she headed for the kitchen. "He's something for you!"

"Mr. MacKenzie and . . . this would be also Mr. MacKenzie, aye?" Brian Fraser came out of the study, smiling, and offered Buck his hand. Roger could see him looking Buck over with close attention, a slight frown between his dark brows. Not disapproval—puzzlement, as though he knew Buck from somewhere and was trying to think where.

Roger knew exactly where and felt again that peculiar quiver he'd felt on meeting Dougal MacKenzie. The resemblance between father and son was by no means instantly striking—their coloring was very different, and Roger thought most of Buck's features came from his mother—but there was a fugitive similarity, nonetheless, something in their manner. Men cocksure of their charm—and no less charming for knowing it.

Buck was smiling, making commonplace courtesies, complimenting the house and its estate. . . . The puzzlement faded from Brian's eyes, and he invited them to sit, calling down the hall to the kitchen for someone to bring them a bite and a dram.

"Well, then," Brian said, pulling out the chair from behind his desk in order to sit with them. "As ye havena got the lad with ye, I see he's not found yet. Have ye heard any news of him, though?" He looked from Buck to Roger, worried but hopeful.

"No," Roger said, and cleared his throat. "Not a word. But—your daughter said that you . . . might have heard something?"

Fraser's face changed at once, lighting a little.

"Well, it's nay so much *heard* anything, but . . ." He rose and went to rummage in the desk, still talking.

"A captain from the garrison came by here twa, three days ago, wi' a small party of soldiers. The new man in charge—what was his name, Jenny?" For Jenny had come in with a tray, this holding a teapot, cups, a small bottle of whisky, and a plate of cake. The smell made Roger's stomach rumble.

"Who? Oh, the new redcoat captain? Randall, he said. Jonathan Randall." Her color rose a little, and her father smiled to see it. Roger felt the smile freeze on his own face.

· "Aye, he took to you, lass. Wouldna be surprised if he came back one of these days."

"Precious little good it will do him if he does," Jenny snapped. "Have ye lost that thing, *an athair?*"

"No, no, I'm sure I put . . ." Brian's voice trailed off as he scrabbled in the drawer. "Oh. Erm, aye." He coughed, hand in the drawer, and, through his shock, Roger realized what the trouble was. The desk had a secret compartment. Evidently Brian had put the "thing," whatever it was, in the hiding place and was now wondering how to get it out again without revealing the secret to his visitors.

Roger rose to his feet.

"Will ye pardon me, mistress?" he asked, bowing to Jenny. "I'd forgot something in my saddlebag. Come with me, aye?" he added to Buck. "It's maybe in with your things."

Jenny looked surprised but nodded, and Roger blundered out, Buck making little grunts of annoyance at his heels.

"What the devil's wrong wi' you?" Buck said, the minute they were out the door. "Ye went white as a sheet in there, and ye still look like a fish that's been dead a week."

"I feel like one," Roger said tersely. "I know Captain Randall—or, rather, I know a lot of things about him. Leave it that he's the last person I'd want to have any knowledge of Jem."

"Oh." Buck's face went blank, then firmed. "Aye, well. We'll see what it is he brought, and then we'll go and have it out with him if we think he might have the lad."

What it is he brought. Roger fought back all the horrible things that phrase conjured—Jem's ear, a finger, a lock of his hair—because if it had been anything like that, surely the Frasers wouldn't be calm about it. But if Randall had brought some hideous token in a box?

"Why, though?" Buck was frowning, plainly trying to read Roger's expression, which, judging from Buck's own, must be appalling. "Why would this man mean you and the lad ill? He's never met ye, has he?"

"That," Roger said, choking down his feelings, "is an excellent question. But the man is a—do you know what a sadist is?"

"No, but it's plainly something ye dinna want close to your wean. Here, sir! We'll be taking those in, thank ye kindly." They'd come right round the house by now, and McTaggart the hired man was coming down the path from the stable, their saddlebags in either hand.

McTaggart looked surprised but surrendered the heavy bags gladly and went back to his work.

"I ken ye just wanted to get us out of there so to give your man a bit of privacy to work the secret drawer," Buck remarked. "And he kens that fine. Do we need to take in something, though?"

"How do you know about—" Buck grinned at him, and Roger dismissed the question with an irritable gesture. "Yes. We'll give Miss Fraser the cheese I bought yesterday."

"Ah, Mrs. Jenny." Buck made the humming noise again. "I wouldna blame Captain Randall. That skin! And those bubs, come to that—"

"Shut up right this minute!"

Buck did, shocked out of his jocularity.

"What?" he said, in quite a different tone. "What is it?"

Roger unclenched his fist, with an effort.

"It's a bloody long story; I haven't time to tell it to ye now. But it's—something I know from the other end. From my time. In a year or so, Randall's coming back here. And he's going to do something terrible. And, God help me, I don't think I can stop it."

"Something terrible," Buck repeated slowly. His eyes were boring into Roger's own, dark as serpentine. "To that bonnie wee lass? And ye think ye can't *stop* it? Why, man, how can ye—"

"Just shut up," Roger repeated doggedly. "We'll talk about it later, aye?"

Buck puffed out his cheeks, still staring at Roger, then blew out his breath with a sound of disgust and shook his head, but he picked up his saddlebag and followed without further argument.

The cheese—a thing the size of Roger's outstretched hand, wrapped in fading leaves—was received with pleasure and taken off to the kitchen, leaving Roger and Buck alone once more with Brian Fraser. Fraser had regained his own composure and, picking up a tiny cloth-wrapped parcel from his desk, put it gently in Roger's hand.

Too light to be a finger . . .

"Captain Randall said that Captain Buncombe sent word out wi' all the patrols, and one of them came across this wee bawbee and sent it back to Fort William. None of them ever saw such a thing before, but because of the name, they were thinking it might have to do wi' your lad."

"The name?" Roger untied the cord and the cloth fell open. For an instant, he didn't know what the hell he was seeing. He picked it up; it was light as a feather, dangling from his fingers.

Two disks, made of something like pressed cardboard, threaded onto a bit of light woven cord. One round, colored red—the other was green and octagonal.

"Oh, Jesus," he said. "Oh, Christ Jesus."

J. W. MacKenzie was printed on both disks, along with a number and two letters. He turned the red disk gently over with a shaking fingertip and read what he already knew was stamped there.

RAF

He was holding the dog tags of a Royal Air Force flier. Circa World War II.

44

AMPHISBAENA

"YE CANNA BE SURE those things name your father." Buck nodded at the dog tags, their cord still wrapped round Roger's hand, the tiny disks themselves folded tight in his palm. "How many MacKenzies are there, for God's sake?"

"Lots." Roger sat down on a big lichen-covered boulder. They were at the top of the hill that rose behind Lallybroch; the broch itself stood on the slope just below them, its conical roof a broad black whorl of slates. "But not so bloody many who flew for the Royal Air Force in World War Two. And even fewer who disappeared without a trace. As for those who might be time travelers . . ."

Roger couldn't remember what he'd said when he saw the dog tags or what Brian Fraser had said to him. When he'd started to notice things again, he was sitting in Brian's big wheel-backed chair with a stoneware mug of hot tea cupped between his hands and the entire household crammed into the doorway, regarding him with looks ranging from compassion to curiosity. Buck was squatting in front of him, frowning in what might have been concern or simply curiosity.

"Sorry," Roger had said, cleared his throat, and set the tea undrunk on the desk. His hands throbbed from the heat of the cup. "Rather a shock. I—thank you."

"Is it something to do wi' your wee boy, then?" Jenny Fraser had asked, deep-blue eyes dark with concern.

"I think so, yes." He'd got his wits back now and rose stiffly, nodding to Brian. "Thank ye, sir. I canna thank ye enough for all ye've done for me—for us. I . . . need to think a bit what's to do now. If ye'll excuse me, Mistress Fraser?"

Jenny nodded, not taking her eyes from his face but shooing the maids and the cook away from the door so he could pass through it. Buck had followed him, murmuring reassuring things to the multitude, and come along with him, not speaking until they reached the solitude of the craggy hilltop. Where Roger had explained just what the dog tags were and to whom they had belonged.

"Why two?" Buck asked, reaching out a tentative finger to touch the tags. "And why are they different colors?"

"Two in case one was destroyed by whatever killed you," Roger said, taking a deep breath. "The colors—they're made of pressed cardboard treated with different chemicals—substances, I mean. One resists water and the other resists fire, but I couldn't tell ye which is which."

Speaking of technicalities made it just barely possible to speak. Buck, with unaccustomed delicacy, was waiting for Roger to bring up the unspeakable.

How did the tags turn up here? *And when—and under what circumstances— had they become detached from J(eremiah) W(alter)MacKenzie, Roman Catholic, serial number 448397651, RAF?*

"Claire—my mother-in-law—I told ye about her, did I not?"

"A bit, aye. A seer, was she?"

Roger laughed shortly. "Aye, like I am. Like you are. Easy to be a seer if what you see has already happened."

What's already happened . . .

"Oh, God," he said out loud, and curled over, pressing the fist that held the dog tags hard against his forehead.

"All right, there?" Buck asked after a moment. Roger straightened up with a deep breath.

"Know the expression 'damned if ye do, damned if ye don't'?"

"No, though I wouldna think it was one a minister would use." Buck's mouth twitched into a half smile. "Are ye not dedicated to the notion that there's always one sure way out o' damnation?"

"A minister. Aye." Roger breathed deep again. There was a lot of oxygen on a Scottish hilltop, but somehow there didn't seem quite enough just this minute. "I'm not sure that religion was constructed with time travelers in mind."

Buck's brows rose at that.

"Constructed?" he echoed, surprised. "Who builds God?"

That actually made Roger laugh, which made him feel a little better, if only momentarily.

"We all do," he said dryly. "If God makes man in His image, we all return the favor."

"Mmphm." Buck thought that one over, then nodded slowly. "Wouldna just say ye're wrong about that. But God's *there,* nonetheless, whether we ken quite what He is or not. Isn't He?"

"Yeah." Roger wiped his knuckles under his nose, which had begun to run with the cold wind. "Ever hear of Saint Teresa of Avila?"

"No." Buck gave him a look. "Nor have I heard of a Protestant minister who has to do wi' saints."

"I take advice where I can get it. But St. Teresa once remarked to God, 'If this is how you treat your friends, no wonder you have so few of them.' God's got his own ways."

Buck smiled; it was one of his rare, unwary smiles, and it heartened Roger enough to try to come to grips with the situation.

"Well, Claire—my mother-in-law—she told Brianna and me a good bit. About the things that happened when she went through the stones in 1743, and about things that had happened before that. Things about Captain Randall." And in sentences as brief and unemotional as he could make them, he told the story: Randall's raid on Lallybroch while Brian Fraser was away, his attack on Jenny Murray, and how Jamie Fraser—newly returned from Paris and wondering what to do with his life—had fought for his home and his sister's honor, been arrested and taken to Fort William, where he had been flogged nearly to death.

"Twice," Roger said, pausing for air. He swallowed. "The second time . . . Brian was there. He thought Jamie *was* dead, and he had a stroke—an apoplexy—on the spot. He . . . died." He swallowed again. "Will die."

"Jesus, Mary, and Bride." Buck crossed himself. His face had gone pale. "Your man in the house? He'll be dead in a year or two?"

"Yes." Roger looked down at Lallybroch, pale and peaceful as the sheep that browsed its pastures. "And . . . there's more. What happened later, just before the Rising."

Buck raised a hand.

"I say that's more than enough. I say we go down to Fort William and do for the wicked bugger now. Preemptive action, ye might say. That's a legal term," he explained, with an air of kindly condescension.

"An appealing notion," Roger said dryly. "But if we did—what *would* happen four years from now?"

Buck frowned, not comprehending.

"When Claire came through the stones in 1743, she met—will meet— Jamie Fraser, an outlaw with a price on his head, coming home from France. But if what happened with Captain Randall *doesn't* happen—Jamie won't be there. And if he isn't . . . ?"

"Oh." The frown grew deeper, comprehension dawning. "Oh, aye. I see. No Jamie, no Brianna . . ."

"No Jem or Mandy," Roger finished. "Exactly."

"Oh, God." Buck bent his head and massaged the flesh between his brows with two fingers. "Damned if ye do, damned if ye don't, did ye say? Enough to make your head spin like a top."

"Yes, it is. But I have to do something, nonetheless." He rubbed a thumb gently over the dog tags' surfaces. "I'm going down to Fort William to talk to Captain Randall. I have to know where these came from."

BUCK LOOKED squiggle-eyed at the tags, lips pressed together, then switched the look to Roger.

"D'ye think your lad's with your father, somehow?"

"No." That particular thought hadn't occurred to Roger, and it shook him for a moment. He shrugged it away, though.

"No," he repeated more firmly. "I'm beginning to think that maybe . . . maybe Jem's not here at all." The statement hung there in the air, revolving slowly. He glanced at Buck, who seemed to be glowering at it.

"Why not?" his kinsman asked abruptly.

"A, because we've found no hint of him. And B, because now there's *these*." He raised the tags, the light cardboard disks lifting in the breeze.

"Ye sound like your wife," Buck said, half amused. "She does that, aye? Layin' things out, A, B, C, and all."

"That's how Brianna's mind works," Roger said, feeling a brief surge of affection for her. "She's very logical."

And if I'm right, and Jem's not here—where is he? Has he gone to another time—or did he not travel at all? As though the word "logical" had triggered it, a whole array of horrifying possibilities opened out before him.

"What I'm thinking—we were both concentrating on the name 'Jeremiah' when we came through, aye?"

"Aye, we were."

"Well . . ." He twirled the cord between his fingers, making the disks spin slowly. "What if we got the wrong Jeremiah? That was my father's name, too. And—and if Rob Cameron *didn't* take Jem through the stones—"

"Why would he not?" Buck interrupted sharply. He transferred the glower to Roger. "His truck was there at Craigh na Dun. He wasn't."

"Plainly he wanted us to *think* he'd gone through. As to why—" He choked on the thought. Before he could clear his throat, Buck finished it for him.

"To get us away, so he'd have your missus to himself." His face darkened with anger—part of it aimed at Roger. "I told her yon man had a hot eye for her."

"Maybe he does," he said shortly. "But think, aye? Beyond whatever he may have had in mind with regard to Brianna—" The mere words conjured up pictures that made the blood shoot up into his head. "Whatever he had in mind," he repeated, as calmly as he could, "he likely also wanted to see whether it was true. About the stones. About whether we—or anyone—really could go through. Seeing's believing, after all."

Buck blew out his cheeks, considering.

"Ye think he was there, maybe? Watching to see if we disappeared?"

Roger shrugged, momentarily unable to speak for the thoughts clotting his brain.

Buck's fists were clenched on his knees. He looked down at the house, then behind him at the rising mountains, and Roger knew exactly what he was thinking. He cleared his throat with a hacking growl.

"We've been gone for two weeks," Roger said. "If he meant Brianna harm . . . he'll have tried." *Jesus. If he—no.* "She'll not have let him harm her or the kids," he went on, as steadily as he could. "If he tried anything, he'll either be in jail or buried under the broch." He lifted his chin toward the tower below, and Buck snorted in reluctant amusement.

"So, then. Aye, I want to rush straight back to Craigh na Dun, too. But think, man. We ken Cameron *went* to the stones after he took Jem. Would he not make Jem touch them, to see? And if he did . . . what if Cameron can't travel but Jem did—to get away from him?"

"Mmphm." Buck thought that one over and gave a reluctant nod. "So ye're maybe thinkin' that if the lad was scairt of Cameron and popped through accidental, he maybe wouldn't try to come straight back?"

"He maybe couldn't." Roger was dry-mouthed and swallowed hard to generate enough saliva to speak. "He didn't have a gemstone. And even with one . . ." He nodded at Buck. "Ken what happened to you, even with one. It *does* get worse each time. Jemmy might have been too scared to try." *And he might have tried, not made it, and now he's lost for good . . . NO!*

Buck nodded.

"So. Ye think he's maybe with your da, after all?" He sounded dubious in the extreme.

Roger couldn't bear sitting any longer. He stood up abruptly, thrusting the dog tags into the breast pocket of his coat.

"I don't know. But this is the only solid bit of evidence we have. I have to go and see."

45

THE CURE OF SOULS

"**Y**E'RE OUT OF YOUR wee pink mind, ye ken that, aye?" Roger looked at Buck in amazement.

"Where the devil did you get *that* expression?"

"From your wife," Buck replied. "Who's a verra bonnie lass and a well-spoken one, forbye. And if ye mean to get back to her bed one of these days, ye'll think better of what ye mean to do."

"I've thought," Roger said briefly. "And I'm doing it." The entrance to Fort William looked much as it had when he'd come here with Brian Fraser nearly two weeks earlier, but this time with only a few people hastening in, shawls over their heads, and hats pulled down against the rain. The fort itself now seemed to have a sinister aspect, the gray stones bleak and streaked black with wet.

Buck reined up, grimacing as the horse shook its head and sprayed him with drops from its soaking mane.

"Aye, fine. I'm no going in there. If we have to kill him, it's best if he doesna ken me, so I can get behind him. I'll wait at yonder tavern." He lifted his chin, indicating an establishment called the Peartree, a few hundred feet down the road from the fort, then kicked his horse into motion. Ten feet on, he turned and called over his shoulder, "One hour! If ye're not with me by then, I'm comin' in after ye!"

Roger smiled, despite his apprehension. He waved briefly to Buck and swung off his horse.

Bless me, Lord, he prayed. *Help me to do the right thing—for everyone. Including Buck. And* him.

He hadn't actually stopped praying at any time since Jem had disappeared, though most of it was just the frantic, reflexive *Dear Lord, let it be all right* of everyone facing crisis. Over time, either the crisis or the petitioner wears down, and prayer either ceases or . . . the person praying starts to listen.

He knew that. And he was listening. But he was still taken aback to get an answer.

He had enough experience in the business of prayer to recognize an answer when it showed up, though, however unwelcome. And the pointed reminder, arriving as a random thought in the middle of their mud-spattered, rain-sodden journey—that Jack Randall's soul was in as much danger as Brian Fraser's life—was damned unwelcome.

"Well, then," Buck had said, brightening under the soggy brim of his hat when Roger had shared his disturbance at this insight. "All the more reason to kill him now. Save yon Frasers, and keep the wicked wee sod from going to hell—if he hasn't done something already as would send him there," he'd added as an afterthought. "Two birds wi' one stone, aye?"

Roger had squelched along for a moment before replying.

"Out of sheer curiosity—were you a solicitor or a barrister, when ye did law?"

"Solicitor. Why?"

"No wonder you failed at it. All your talents lie in the other direction. Can ye not have a conversation without arguing?"

"Not wi' *you*," Buck had said pointedly, and kicked his horse into a trot, sending up thumping clods of mud in his wake.

Roger gave his name and asked the army clerk if he might have a word with Captain Randall, then stood by the peat fire, shaking off as much water as he could before the man came back to lead him to Randall's office.

To his surprise, it was the same office where he and Brian Fraser had had their audience with Captain Buncombe almost two weeks before. Randall was seated behind the desk, quill in hand, but looked up with a courteous expression at Roger's entrance and half rose, with a small bow.

"Your servant, sir. Mr. MacKenzie, is that right? You've come from Lallybroch, I collect."

"Your most obedient, sir," Roger replied, adjusting his accent back to his normal Scots-tinged Oxbridge. "Mr. Brian Fraser was good enough to give me the object that you brought. I wanted both to thank you for your kind assistance—and to ask whether you might be able to tell me where the object was discovered."

He knew about the banality of evil; human monsters came in human shapes. Even so, he was surprised. Randall was a handsome man, rather elegant in bearing, with a lively, interested expression, a humorous curve to his mouth, and warm dark eyes.

Well, he is human. And perhaps he's not a monster yet.

"One of my messengers brought it in," Randall replied, wiping his quill and dropping it into a stoneware jar full of such objects. "My predecessor, Captain Buncombe, had sent dispatches to Fort George and Fort Augustus about your son—I am very sorry for your situation," he added rather formally. "A patrol from Ruthven Barracks had brought the ornament in. I'm afraid I don't know where they discovered it, but perhaps the messenger who brought it from Ruthven does. I'll send for him."

Randall went to the door and spoke to the sentry outside. Coming back, he paused to open a cupboard, which revealed a wig stand, a powdering shaker, a pair of hairbrushes, a looking glass, and a small tray with a cut-glass decanter and glasses.

"Allow me to offer you refreshment, sir." Randall poured a cautious inch into each glass and offered one to Roger. He picked up his own, his nostrils flaring slightly at the scent of the whisky. "The nectar of the country, I'm given to understand," he said with a wry smile. "I am told I must develop a taste for it." He took a wary sip, looking as though he expected imminent death to result.

"If I might suggest . . . a bit of water mixed with it is customary," Roger said, carefully keeping all trace of amusement out of his voice. "Some say it opens the flavor, makes it smoother."

"Oh, really?" Randall put down his glass, looking relieved. "That seems sensible. The stuff tastes as though it's flammable. Sanders!" he shouted toward the door. "Bring some water!"

There was a slight pause, neither man knowing quite what to say next.

"The, um, *thing*," Randall said. "Might I see it again? It's quite remarkable. Is it a jewel of some kind? An ornament?"

"No. It's a . . . sort of charm," Roger said, fishing the dog tags out of his pocket. He felt an ache in his chest at thought of the small personal rituals that the fliers did—a lucky stone in the pocket, a special scarf, the name of a woman painted on the nose of a plane. Charms. Tiny bits of hopeful magic, protection against a vast sky filled with fire and death. "To preserve the soul." *In memory, at least.*

Randall frowned a little, glancing from the dog tags to Roger's face, then back. He was clearly thinking the same thing Roger was: *And if the charm is detached from the person it was meant to protect . . .* But he didn't say anything, merely touched the green tag gently.

"J. W. Your son's name is Jeremiah, I understand?"

"Yes. Jeremiah's an old family name. It was my father's name. I—" He was interrupted by the entrance of Private MacDonald, a very young soldier, dripping wet and slightly blue with cold, who saluted Captain Randall smartly, then gave way to a rattling cough that shook his spindly frame.

Once recovered, he complied at once with Randall's order to tell Roger all he knew about the dog tags—but he didn't know much. One of the soldiers stationed at Ruthven Barracks had won them in a dice game at a local pub. He did recall the name of the pub—the Fatted Grouse; he'd drunk there himself—and he thought the soldier had said he'd won the bawbee from a farmer come back from the market in Perth.

"Do you recall the name of the soldier who won them?" Roger asked.

"Oh, aye, sir. 'Twas Sergeant McLehose. And now I think—" A broad grin at the recollection showed crooked teeth. "I mind me of the farmer's name, too! 'Twas Mr. Anthony Cumberpatch. It did tickle Sergeant McLehose, bein' foreign and soundin' like 'cucumber patch.'" He sniggered, and Roger smiled himself. Captain Randall cleared his throat, and the sniggering stopped abruptly, Private MacDonald snapping to a sober attention.

"Thank you, Mr. MacDonald," Randall said dryly. "That will be all."

Private MacDonald, abashed, saluted and left. There was a moment's silence, during which Roger became aware of the rain, grown harder now, clattering like gravel on the large casement window. A chilly draft leaked around its frame and touched his face. Glancing at the window, he saw the drill yard below, and the whipping post, a grim crucifix stark and solitary, black in the rain.

Oh, God.

Carefully, he folded up the dog tags again and put them away in his pocket. Then met Captain Randall's dark eyes directly.

"Did Captain Buncombe tell you, sir, that I am a minister?"

Randall's brows rose in brief surprise.

"No, he didn't." Randall was plainly wondering why Roger should mention this, but he was courteous. "My younger brother is a clergyman. Ah . . . Church of England, of course." There was the faintest implied question there, and Roger answered it with a smile.

"I am a minister of the Church of Scotland myself, sir. But if I might . . . will ye allow me to offer a blessing? For the success of my kinsman and myself—and in thanks for your kind help to us."

"I—" Randall blinked, clearly discomfited. "I—suppose so. Er . . . all right." He leaned back a little, looking wary, hands on his blotter. He was completely taken aback when Roger leaned forward and grasped both his hands firmly. Randall gave a start, but Roger held tight, eyes on the captain's.

"Oh, Lord," he said, "we ask thy blessing on our works. Guide me and my kinsman in our quest, and guide this man in his new office. May your light and presence be with us and with him, and your judgment and compassion ever on us. I commend him to your care. Amen."

His voice cracked on the last word, and he let go Randall's hands and coughed, looking away as he cleared his throat.

Randall cleared his throat, too, in embarrassment, but kept his poise.

"I thank you for your . . . er . . . good wishes, Mr. MacKenzie. And I wish you good luck. And good day."

"The same to you, Captain," Roger said, rising. "God be with you."

46

BABY JESUS, TELL ME . . .

Boston, November 15, 1980

D R. JOSEPH ABERNATHY pulled into his driveway, looking forward to a cold beer and a hot supper. The mailbox was full; he pulled out a handful of circulars and envelopes and went inside, tidily sorting them as he went.

"Bill, bill, occupant, junk, junk, more junk, charity appeal, bill, idiot, bill, invitation . . . hi, sweetie—" He paused for a fragrant kiss from his wife, followed by a second sniff of her hair. "Oh, man, are we having brats and sauerkraut for dinner?"

"You are," his wife told him, neatly snagging her jacket from the hall tree with one hand and squeezing his buttock with the other. "I'm going to a meeting with Marilyn. Be back by nine, if the rain doesn't make the traffic too bad. Anything good in the mail?"

"Nah. Have fun!"

She rolled her eyes at him and left before he could ask if she'd bought Bud. He tossed the half-sorted mail on the kitchen counter and opened the refrigerator to check. A gleaming red-and-white six-pack beckoned cheerily, and the warm air was so tangy with the smells of fried sausage and vinegar that he could taste it without even taking the lid off the pan sitting on the stove.

"A good woman is prized above rubies," he said, inhaling blissfully and pulling a can loose from its plastic ring.

He was halfway through the first plate of food and two-thirds of the way into his second beer when he put down the sports section of the *Globe* and saw the letter on top of the spilled pile of mail. He recognized Bree's handwriting at once; it was big and round, with a determined rightward slant—but there was something wrong with the letter.

He picked it up, frowning a little, wondering why it looked strange . . . and then realized that the stamp was wrong. She wrote at least once a month, sending photos of the kids, telling him about her job, the farm—and the letters all had British stamps, purple and blue heads of Queen Elizabeth. This one had an American stamp.

He slowly set down the letter as though it might explode and swallowed the rest of the beer in one gulp. Fortified, he set his jaw and picked it up.

"Tell me you and Rog took the kids to Disneyland, Bree," he murmured, licking mustard off his knife before using it to slit the envelope. She'd talked about doing that someday. "Baby Jesus, tell me this is a photo of Jem shaking hands with Mickey Mouse."

Much to his relief, it *was* a photo of both children at Disneyland, beaming at the camera from Mickey Mouse's embrace, and he laughed out loud. Then he saw the tiny key that had fallen out of the envelope—the key to a bank's safe-deposit box. He set down the photo, went and got another beer, and sat down deliberately to read the brief note enclosed with the photo.

> *Dear Uncle Joe,*
>
> *I'm taking the kids to see Grandma and Grandpa. I don't know when we'll be back; could you please see to things while we're gone? (Instructions in the box.)*
> *Thank you for everything, always. I'll miss you. I love you.*
>
> *Bree*

He sat for a long time next to the cold grease congealing on his plate, looking at the bright, happy photo.

"Jesus, girl," he said softly. "What's happened? And what do you mean *you're* taking the kids? Where the hell's Roger?"

PART THREE

A Blade New-Made from

the Ashes of the Forge

47

SOMETHING SUITABLE IN
WHICH TO GO TO WAR

June 19, 1778
Philadelphia

I WOKE COMPLETELY disoriented, to the splat of water dripping into a wooden bucket, the sharp smells of wood pulp and printer's ink, the softer musk of Jamie's body and frying bacon, the clank of pewter plates, and the loud braying of a mule. The latter noise brought back memory at once, and I sat up, sheet clutched to my bosom.

I was naked, and I was in the loft of Fergus's printshop. When we had left Kingsessing the day before, during a brief pause in the rain, we had found Fergus patiently sheltering in a toolshed near the gates, Clarence the mule and two horses tethered under its eaves.

"You haven't been out here all this time!" I'd blurted upon seeing him.

"Did it take that long?" he inquired, cocking a dark brow at Jamie and giving him the sort of knowing look that Frenchmen appear to be born with.

"Mmphm," Jamie replied ambiguously, and took my arm. "I rode Clarence out, Sassenach, but I asked Fergus to come on a wee bit later wi' a horse for you. The mule canna carry us both, and my back willna stand walking that far."

"What's the matter with your back?" I asked, suspicious.

"Nothing that a night's sleep in a good bed willna cure," he replied, and, stooping so I could put a foot in his hands, tossed me up into the saddle.

It had been past dark when we made it back to the printshop. I'd sent Germain at once to Jenny at Number 17 with word where I was but had gone to bed with Jamie before he came back. I wondered vaguely who else was at the house on Chestnut Street and what they were doing: was Hal still a captive, or had Young Ian decided to release him? If not, had Hal assassinated Denny Hunter, or had Mrs. Figg shot him?

Jamie had told me he'd left Ian in charge of the situation—or situations; there seemed to have been a great deal going on the day before. All of it seemed unreal and dreamlike, both the events I'd participated in and the ones Jamie had told me about on the ride back. The only vividly real recollection I had was of our conversation in the garden—and what followed it, in the potting shed. My flesh still felt the echoes.

Breakfast was plainly preparing below; besides the delectable scent of frying bacon, I could smell toasted yeast bread and fresh honey. My stomach gave a loud gurgle at this, and as though the sound had caused it, the ladder leading up into the loft began to shake. Someone was coming up, moving slowly, and in case it wasn't Jamie, I seized my shift and pulled it hastily over my head.

It wasn't. A pewter tray rose slowly into sight, laid with a plate piled with food, a bowl of porridge, and a pottery mug of something steaming; it couldn't be tea and didn't smell like coffee. As the tray levitated, Henri-Christian's beaming face appeared below it; he was balancing the thing on his head.

I held my breath until he'd stepped off the ladder, and then, as he removed the tray from his head and presented it to me with a ceremonious little bow, applauded.

"Merveilleux!" I told him, and he grinned from ear to ear.

"Félicité wanted to try," he told me proudly, "but she can't do it with a full tray yet. She spills."

"Well, we can't have that. Thank you, sweetheart." I leaned forward to kiss him—his dark wavy hair smelled of woodsmoke and ink—and took the mug. "What's this?"

He looked at it dubiously and shrugged. "It's hot."

"So it is." I cradled the mug in my hands. The loft had been warm the night before, the day's heat trapped under the roof, but it had rained most of the night, and the chilly damp had come through the holes in the roof—four or five vessels placed under the leaks made a symphony of plinking sounds. "Where's *Grand-père*?"

Henri-Christian's face at once went bright red, his lips pressed tight together, and he shook his head vigorously.

"What?" I said, surprised. "Is it a secret?"

"Don't you tell her!" Joanie's shrill voice floated up from the shop below. *"Grand-père* said not to!"

"Oh, a surprise, is it?" I asked, smiling. "Well, perhaps you'd best go down and help your mama, then, so you don't give it away by mistake."

He giggled, hands pressed over his mouth, then reached up over his head, gave a convulsive leap, and flipped over backward, landing adroitly on his hands. He walked on them to the ladder, stocky little legs splayed to keep his balance, and for an instant my heart was in my mouth as he reached the edge and I thought he might try to go down the ladder upside down. He flipped over again, though, landing neatly on the top rung, and scampered out of sight like a squirrel, giggling all the way down.

Smiling, I plumped up the sparse bedding—we had slept on a flattened pallet of worn straw from the stable, which smelled rather strongly of Clarence, and on our half-dried cloaks, covered with a spare sheet and a ragged blanket, though Joanie and Félicité had given us one of their feather pillows, they sharing the other—and sat back against the wall, the tray perched on a keg of ink powder. I was surrounded by stacks of paper, these shielded by oilcloth from the leaks. Some of it was blank reams awaiting the press, some of it pamphlets, circulars, posters, or the guts of unbound books, awaiting delivery to customers or to the bookbinder.

I could hear Marsali's voice below, back in the living quarters behind the shop, raised in maternal command. No male voices but Henri-Christian's, though; Fergus and Germain must have gone out with Clarence the mule to make the morning deliveries of *L'Oignon,* the satirical newspaper started by Fergus and Marsali in North Carolina.

Normally, *L'Oignon* was a weekly paper, but there was a copy on my tray of the special edition for today, with a large cartoon on the first page, showing the British army as a horde of cockroaches, fleeing Philadelphia with tattered flags dragging behind them and trailing ribbon banners filled with speeches of futile threat. A large buckled shoe labeled *General Washington* was squashing some of the more laggard roaches.

There was a large glob of opaque yellow-white honey melting slowly in the middle of the porridge; I stirred it in, poured a bit of cream over it, and settled down to enjoy breakfast in bed, along with an article noting the imminent entrance into Philadelphia of General Arnold, who was taking office as the military governor of the city, welcoming him and praising his military record and gallant exploits at Saratoga.

How long? I thought then, setting down the paper with a small shiver. *When?* I had the feeling that it had been—would be—much later in the war, when circumstance turned Benedict Arnold from patriot to traitor. But I didn't know.

It didn't matter, I told myself firmly. I couldn't change it. And long before that happened, we would be safely back on the Ridge, rebuilding our house and our lives. Jamie was alive. Everything would be all right.

The bell over the shop door below rang, and there was an excited gabble as the children stampeded out of the kitchen. The soft rumble of Jamie's voice floated up over the confusion of shrill greetings, and I caught Marsali's voice among them, stunned.

"Da! What have ye *done?*"

Alarmed, I scrambled out of my nest and went on hands and knees to the edge of the loft to look down. Jamie stood in the middle of the shop, surrounded by admiring children, his loose hair spangled with raindrops, cloak folded over his arm—dressed in the dark blue and buff of a Continental officer.

"Jesus H. Roosevelt *Christ!*" I exclaimed. He looked up and his eyes met mine like those of a guilty puppy.

"I'm sorry, Sassenach," he said apologetically. "I had to."

HE'D COME UP to the loft and pulled the ladder up behind him, to prevent the children coming up. I was dressing quickly—or trying to—as he told me about Dan Morgan, about Washington and the other Continental generals. About the coming battle.

"Sassenach, I *had* to," he said again, softly. "I'm that sorry."

"I know," I said. "I know you did." My lips were stiff. "I—you—I'm sorry, too."

I was trying to fasten the dozen tiny buttons that closed the bodice of my gown, but my hands shook so badly that I couldn't even grasp them. I stopped trying and dug my hairbrush out of the bag he'd brought me from the Chestnut Street house.

He made a small sound in his throat and took it out of my hand. He threw it onto our makeshift couch and put his arms around me, holding me tight with my face buried in his chest. The cloth of his new uniform smelled of fresh indigo, walnut hulls, and fuller's earth; it felt strange and stiff against my face. I couldn't stop shaking.

"Talk to me, *a nighean,*" he whispered into my tangled hair. "I'm afraid, and I dinna want to feel so verra much alone just now. Speak to me."

"Why has it always got to be *you?*" I blurted into his chest.

That made him laugh, a little shakily, and I realized that all the trembling wasn't coming from me.

"It's no just me," he said, and stroked my hair. "There are a thousand other men readying themselves today—more—who dinna want to do it, either."

"I know," I said again. My breathing was a little steadier. "I know." I turned my face to the side in order to breathe, and all of a sudden began to cry, quite without warning.

"I'm sorry," I gasped. "I don't mean—I don't want t-to make it h-harder for you. I—I—oh, Jamie, when I knew you were alive—I wanted so much to go home. To go home with you."

His arms tightened hard round me. He didn't speak, and I knew it was because he couldn't.

"So did I," he whispered at last. "And we will, *a nighean.* I promise ye."

The sounds from below floated up around us: the sounds of children running back and forth between the shop and the kitchen, Marsali singing to herself in Gaelic as she made fresh ink for the press from varnish and lampblack. The door opened, and cool, rainy air blew in with Fergus and Germain, adding their voices to the cheerful confusion.

We stood wrapped in each other's arms, taking comfort from our family below, yearning for the others we might never see again, at once at home and homeless, balanced on a knife edge of danger and uncertainty. But together.

"You're not going off to war without me," I said firmly, straightening up and sniffing. "Don't even *think* about it."

"I wouldna dream of it," he assured me gravely, went to wipe his nose on his uniform sleeve, thought better of it, and stopped, looking at me helplessly. I laughed—tremulous, but it was a laugh nonetheless—and gave him the handkerchief I'd tucked automatically into my bosom when I fastened my stays. Like Jenny, I *always* had one.

"Sit down," I said, swallowing as I picked up the hairbrush. "I'll plait your hair for you."

He'd washed it this morning; it was clean and damp, the soft red strands cool in my hands and smelling—oddly—of French soap, scented with bergamot. I rather missed the scent of sweat and cabbage that had surrounded me all night.

"Where did you bathe?" I asked curiously.

"At the house on Chestnut Street," he answered, a little tersely. "My sister made me. She said I couldna turn up to be a general smelling like a stale dinner, and there was a tub and hot water to spare."

"Did she?" I murmured. "Um . . . speaking of Chestnut Street . . . how is His Grace, the Duke of Pardloe?"

"Gone before dawn, Jenny said," he said, bending his head to aid in the plaiting. His neck was warm under my fingers. "According to Ian, Denny Hunter said he was well enough to go, provided that he took along a flask of your magic potion. So Mrs. Figg gave him back his breeches—wi' some reluctance, I understand—and he went."

"Went *where?*" I asked. His hair was more heavily traced with silver than it had been. I didn't mind that; I minded that I hadn't been there to see it slowly change, day by day.

"Ian didna ask him. But he said Mrs. Figg told the duke the names of some friends of Lord John's—Loyalists that might be still in the city. And his son's staying in a house here, no? Dinna be worrit on his account, Sassenach." He turned his head to smile sideways at me. "His Grace is a man who's hard to kill."

"I suppose it takes one to know one," I said tartly. I didn't ask why Jamie had gone to Chestnut Street; Hal, Jenny, and all other concerns notwithstanding, I knew he wanted to know whether John had reappeared. Apparently not, and a small chill frosted my heart.

I was groping in my pocket for a ribbon with which to club his queue, when a fresh draft swept through the loft, lifting the oilcloth and fluttering the papers beneath. I turned to see the source of the breeze and beheld Germain, swinging off the pulley rope to come in by the shuttered doors through which bales and kegs could be lowered from the loft to wagons below.

"*Bonjour, Grand-père,*" he said, wiping a cobweb off his face as he landed and bowing to Jamie with great formality. He turned and bowed to me, as well. "*Comment ça va, Grand-mère?*"

"Fi—" I began automatically, but was interrupted by Jamie.

"No," he said definitely. "Ye're not coming."

"Please, Grandda!" Germain's formality disappeared in an instant, replaced by pleading. "I could be a help to ye!"

"I know," Jamie said dryly. "And your parents would never forgive me if ye were. I dinna even want to know what your notion of help involves, but—"

"I could carry messages! I can ride, ye ken that, ye taught me yourself! And I'm nearly twelve!"

"Ye ken how dangerous that is? If a British sharpshooter didna take ye out of the saddle, someone from the militia would club ye over the head to steal the horse. And I can count, ken? Ye're no even eleven yet, so dinna be tryin' it on with me."

Obviously, danger held no fears whatever for Germain. He shrugged, impatient.

"Well, I could be an orderly, then. I can find food anywhere," he added, cunning. He was in fact a very accomplished scrounger, and I looked at him thoughtfully. Jamie intercepted my glance and glowered at me.

"Dinna even think about it, Sassenach. He'd be taken up for theft and hanged or flogged within an inch of his life, and I couldna do a thing to stop it."

"Nobody's ever caught me!" Germain said, his professional pride outraged. "Not once!"

"And they're not going to," his grandfather assured him, fixing him with a steely eye. "When ye're sixteen, maybe—"

"Oh, aye? Grannie Janet says ye were *eight* when ye first went raiding with your da!"

"Lifting cattle's no the same as war, and I wasna anywhere near the fighting," Jamie said. "And your Grannie Janet should keep her mouth shut."

"Aye, I'll tell her ye said so," Germain retorted, disgruntled. "She says ye got bashed on the head with a sword."

"I did. And with luck ye'll live to be an auld man with your brains unscrambled, unlike your grandsire. Leave us, lad, your grannie needs to put her stockings on." He stood up and, lifting the ladder, slid it down from the loft and pushed Germain firmly onto it.

He stood looking sternly down until Germain had reached the floor below, marking his displeasure by skipping the last few rungs and landing with a loud thud.

Jamie sighed, straightened up, and stretched himself gingerly, groaning a little.

"God knows where we'll sleep tonight, Sassenach," he remarked, glancing at our rude couch as he sat down for me to finish clubbing his hair. "For the sake of my back, I hope it's a bit softer than this." He grinned at me suddenly. "Did ye sleep well?"

"Never better," I assured him, smoothing out the ribbon. In fact, I ached in almost every place it was possible to ache, save perhaps the top of my head. For that matter, I'd barely slept, and neither had he; we'd passed the hours of darkness in slow and wordless exploration, finding again each other's body . . . and, toward dawn, had touched each other's soul again. I touched the back of his neck now, gently, and his hand rose to mine. I felt simultaneously wonderful and wretched, and didn't know from moment to moment which feeling was uppermost.

"When will we leave?"

"As soon as ye put your stockings on, Sassenach. And tidy your hair. And do up your buttons," he added, turning and catching sight of my excessive décolletage. "Here, I'll do that."

"I'll need my medicine box," I said, going cross-eyed as I watched his nimble fingers flicking down my chest.

"I brought it," he assured me, and frowned a bit, eyes intent on a recalcitrant button. "It's a bonny bit of furniture. I expect his lordship bought it for ye?"

"He did." I hesitated a moment, rather wishing he had said "John" rather than "his lordship." I also wished I knew where John was—and that he was all right. But this didn't seem the moment to say any of those things.

Jamie leaned forward and kissed the top of my breast, his breath warm on my skin.

"I dinna ken whether I'll have a bed at all tonight," he said, straightening up. "But whether it's feathers or straw, promise ye'll share it with me?"

"Always," I said, and, picking up my cloak, shook it out, swirled it round my shoulders, and smiled bravely at him. "Let's go, then."

JENNY HAD SENT my medicine chest from Chestnut Street and with it the large parcel of herbs from Kingsessing, which had been delivered there the night before. With the forethought of a Scottish housewife, she'd also included a pound of oatmeal, a twist of salt, a package of bacon, four apples, and six clean handkerchiefs. Also a neat roll of fabric with a brief note, which read:

> *Dear Sister Claire,*
>
> *You appear to own nothing suitable in which to go to war. I suggest you borrow Marsali's printing apron for the time being, and here are two of my flannel petticoats and the simplest things Mrs. Figg could find amongst your wardrobe.*
> *Take care of my brother, and tell him his stockings need darning, because he won't notice until he's worn holes in the heel and given himself blisters.*
>
> *Your Good-sister,*
> *Janet Murray*

"And just how is it that *you* own something suitable in which to go to war?" I asked, eyeing Jamie in his indigo splendor. His uniform appeared to be complete, from coat with epaulets and a brigadier general's insignia to buff waistcoat and cream silk stockings. Tall and straight, with auburn hair neatly clubbed and ribboned in black, he distinctly drew the eye.

He drew his chin back and looked down his nose at himself.

"Well, the sark and smallclothes were mine already; I had them when I came from Scotland. But when I came back to Philadelphia to find ye yesterday, I found Jenny first, and I told her about General Washington and asked her would she see to it. So she took my measurements and found a tailor and his son who do uniforms and browbeat them into working all night to make the coat and waistcoat—poor wretches," he added, gingerly pulling a loose thread from the edge of his cuff. "How is it that ye don't, Sassenach? Did his lordship think it unseemly for ye to doctor folk and make ye burn your working clothes?"

This was said with the sort of jesting tone that's meant to suggest perfect innocence on the part of the speaker while making it perfectly apparent that malice is intended. *"I don't say that I'll no make a fuss about it later."* I looked pointedly at the medical chest John had given me, then back at him, narrowing my eyes ever so slightly.

"No," I said, with great casualness. "I spilled vitriol on them, making—

making ether." The memory made my hands shake slightly, and I had to set down the cup of nettle tea I was drinking.

"Jesus, Sassenach." Jamie spoke under his breath—Félicité and Joan were kneeling at his feet, arguing with each other as they busily burnished his brass shoe buckles—but he met my eyes over their heads, appalled. "Tell me ye werena doing that drunk."

I took a deep breath, at once reliving the experience and trying not to. Standing in the hot, semi-dark shed behind the house, the rounded glass slick in my sweating hands . . . then the flying liquid—it had barely missed my face—and the sickly smell and magically widening, smoking holes that burned straight through my heavy canvas apron and the skirt beneath. I hadn't really cared at the time whether I lived or died—until it looked as though I was going to die in the next few seconds. That made rather a difference. It hadn't convinced me not to commit suicide—but the shock of the near accident did make me think more carefully about how. Slitting one's wrists was one thing; dying in slow, disfiguring agony was another.

"No, I wasn't," I said, and, taking up the cup, managed a deliberate mouthful. "I—it was a hot day. My hands were sweating, and the flask slipped."

He closed his eyes briefly, all too clearly envisioning the scene himself, then reached across Félicité's sleek dark head to cup my cheek.

"Dinna be doing that again, aye?" he said softly. "Don't make it any-more."

To be honest, the thought of making ether again made my palms sweat. It wasn't chemically difficult, but it *was* terribly dangerous. One wrong move, a little too much vitriol, a few degrees of heat too much . . . And Jamie knew as well as I did just how explosive the stuff was. I could see the memory of flames in his eyes, the Big House going up around us. I swallowed.

"I don't want to," I said honestly. "But—without it, Jamie, I can't do things that I can do with it. If I hadn't had it, Aidan would be dead—so would John's nephew Henry."

He compressed his lips and looked as though he considered that Henry Grey might be disposable—but he was fond of little Aidan McCallum Hig-gins, whose appendix I'd removed on the Ridge with the assistance of my first batch of ether.

"Grannie *has* to help people feel better, *Grand-père,*" Joanie said reproach-fully, rising from her spot at Jamie's feet and frowning up at him. "It's her callin', Mam says. She can't just *not.*"

"I ken that fine," he assured her. "But she needna blow herself to king-dom come doing it. After all, who's going to look after all the sick folk, if your grannie's lying about in pieces?"

Félicité and Joanie both thought that image hilarious; I was less amused, but didn't say anything further until they'd taken their rags and vinegar back to the kitchen. We were left in the sleeping part of the living quarters, assem-bling our bags and bundles for departure, and momentarily alone.

"You said you were afraid," I said quietly, eyes on the spools of coarse thread and twists of silk floss I was stowing in a wooden box with several suture needles. "But that won't stop you doing what you think you have to do, will it? *I'm* afraid *for* you—and that certainly won't stop you, either." I was careful to speak without bitterness, but he was as sensitive to tones of voice this morning as I was.

He paused for a moment, regarding his shining shoe buckles, then lifted his head and looked at me straight.

"Do ye think that because ye've told me the Rebels will win, I am free to walk away?"

"I—no." I slid the box lid shut with a snick, not looking at it. I couldn't look away from him. His face was still, but his eyes held mine, intent. "I know you have to. I know it's part of what you are. You can't stand aside and still be what you are. That was more or less my point, about—"

He interrupted me, stepping forward and seizing me by the wrist.

"And what is it that ye think I am, Sassenach?"

"A bloody *man*, that's what!" I pulled loose and turned away, but he put a hand on my shoulder and turned me back to face him.

"Aye, I *am* a bloody man," he said, and the faintest trace of rue touched his mouth, but his eyes were blue and steady.

"Ye've made your peace with what I am, ye think—but I think ye dinna ken what that means. To be what I am doesna mean only that I'll spill my own blood when I must. It means I must sacrifice other men to the ends of my own cause—not only those I kill as enemies, but those I hold as friends . . . or as kin."

His hand dropped away, and the tension left his shoulders. He turned toward the door, saying, "Come when ye're ready, Sassenach."

⸻

I STOOD THERE for an instant, blinking, then ran after him, leaving my half-packed bag behind.

"Jamie!" He was standing in the printshop, Henri-Christian in his arms, bidding goodbye to the girls and Marsali. Germain was nowhere in sight, doubtless sulking. Jamie looked up, startled, then smiled at me.

"I wasna going to leave ye behind, Sassenach. And I didna mean to hurry ye, either. Do ye—"

"I know. I just—I have to tell you something."

All the little heads turned toward me like a nestful of baby birds, soft pink mouths open in curiosity. It occurred to me that I might better have waited until we were on the road, but it had seemed urgent that I tell him now—not only to relieve his anxieties, but to make him know I *did* understand.

"It's William," I blurted, and Jamie's face clouded for an instant, like a breathed-on mirror. Yes, I had understood.

"Come to me, *a bhalaich*," Marsali said, taking Henri-Christian from Jamie and setting him on the floor. "Oof! Ye weigh more than I do, wee man! Come away now, lassies, Grandda isn't going just yet. Help me fetch out Grannie's things."

The children obediently scampered off behind her, though still looking back at us in frustrated curiosity. Children hate secrets, unless they're the ones keeping them. I glanced after them, then turned back to Jamie.

"I didn't know if they knew about William. I suppose Marsali and Fergus do, since—"

"Since Jenny told them. Aye, they do." He rolled his eyes in brief resignation, then fixed them on my face. "What is it, Sassenach?"

"He can't fight," I said, letting out a half-held breath. "It doesn't matter what the British army is about to do. William was paroled after Saratoga—he's a conventioner. You know about the Convention army?"

"I do." He took my hand and squeezed it. "Ye mean he's not allowed to take up arms unless he's been exchanged—and he hasn't been, is that it?"

"That's it. Nobody *can* be exchanged, until the King and the Congress come to some agreement about it."

His face was suddenly vivid with relief, and I was relieved to see it.

"John's been trying to have him exchanged for months, but there isn't any way of doing it." I dismissed Congress and the King with a wave of my free hand and smiled up at him. "You won't have to face him on a battlefield."

"Taing do Dhia," he said, closing his eyes for an instant. "I've been thinking for days—when I wasna fretting about *you,* Sassenach—" he added, opening his eyes and looking down his nose at me, "—the third time's the charm. And that would be an evil charm indeed."

"Third time?" I said. "What do you—would you let go my fingers? They've gone numb."

"Oh," he said. He kissed them gently and let go. "Aye, sorry, Sassenach. I meant—I've shot at the lad twice in his life so far and missed him by no more than an inch each time. If it should happen again—ye canna always tell, in battle, and accidents do happen. I was dreaming, during the night, and . . . och, nay matter." He waved off the dreams and turned away, but I put a hand on his arm to stop him. I knew his dreams—and I'd heard him moan the night before, fighting them.

"Culloden?" I said softly. "Has it come back again?" I actually hoped it *was* Culloden—and not Wentworth. He woke from the Wentworth dreams sweating and rigid and couldn't bear to be touched. Last night, he hadn't waked, but had jerked and moaned until I'd got my arms around him and he quieted, trembling in his sleep, head butted hard into my chest.

He shrugged a little and touched my face.

"It's never left, Sassenach," he said, just as softly. "It never will. But I sleep easier by your side."

48

JUST FOR THE FUN OF IT

I T WAS A PERFECTLY ordinary red-brick building. Modest—no pediments, no carved stone lintels—but solid. Ian looked at it warily. The home of Philadelphia Yearly Meeting, the weightiest meeting of the Society of Friends in the Americas. Aye, very solid.

"Will this be like the Vatican?" he asked Rachel. "Or more like an archbishop's palace?"

She snorted.

"Does it look like any sort of palace to thee?" She spoke normally, but he could see the pulse beat quick in the soft spot just beneath her ear.

"It looks like a bank," he said, and that made her laugh. She cut it short, though, glancing over her shoulder as though afraid someone might come out and scold her for it.

"What do they do in there?" he asked, curious. "Is it a great meetinghouse?"

"It is," she said. "But there is also business to be done, thee knows. The yearly meetings deal with matters of . . . I suppose thee would call it principle. We call it Faith and Practice; there are books, rewritten every so often, to reflect the present sense of the meeting. And queries." She smiled suddenly, and his heart gave a small extra thump. "I think thee would recognize the queries—they're much like thee has described the examination of conscience before thy confession."

"Och, aye," he said agreeably, but declined to pursue the subject. He hadn't been to confession in some years and didn't feel sufficiently wicked at present to trouble about it. "This Faith and Practice—is that where they say ye mustn't join the Continental army, even if ye dinna take up arms?"

He was immediately sorry he'd asked; the question dimmed the light in her eyes, but only momentarily. She drew a deep breath through her nose and looked up at him.

"No, that would be an opinion—a formal opinion. Friends talk over every possible point of consideration before they give an opinion—whether it's a positive one or not." There was the barest hesitation before "not," but he heard it and, reaching out, pulled out her hatpin, gently straightened her straw hat, which had slid a little askew, and pushed the pin back in.

"And if in the end it's not, and we canna find a meeting that will have us, lass—what will we do?"

Her lips pressed together, but she met his eyes straight on.

"Friends are not married *by* their meeting. Or by priest or preacher. They marry each *other*. And we will marry each other." She swallowed. "Somehow."

The small bubbles of misgiving that had been rising through his wame all morning began to pop, and he put a hand over his mouth to stifle a belch. Being nervous took him in the innards; he'd not been able to eat breakfast. He turned a little away, from politeness, and spied two figures coming round the far corner. "Och! There's your brother now, and lookin' gey fine for a Quaker, too."

Denzell was dressed in the uniform of a Continental soldier and looked self-conscious as a hunting dog with a bow tied round its neck. Ian suppressed his amusement, though, merely nodding as his future brother-in-law drew to a stop before them. Denny's betrothed had no such compunctions.

"Is he not *beautiful?*" Dottie crowed, standing back a little to admire him. Denzell coughed and pushed his spectacles up his nose. He was a tidy man, not over-tall, but broad in the shoulder and strong in the forearm. He did look fine in the uniform, Ian thought, and said so.

"I will try not to let my appearance engorge my vanity," Denzell said dryly. "Is thee not also to be a soldier, Ian?"

Ian shook his head, smiling.

"Nay, Denny. I shouldna be any kind of soldier—but I'm a decent scout." He saw Denzell's eyes fix on his face, tracing the double line of tattooed dots that looped across both cheekbones.

"I expect thee would be." A certain tenseness in Denny's shoulders relaxed. "Scouts are not required to kill the enemy, are they?"

"No, we've our choice about it," Ian assured him, straight-faced. "We can kill them if we like—but just for the fun of it, ken. It doesna really count."

Denzell blinked for an instant at that, but Rachel and Dottie both laughed, and he reluctantly smiled.

"Thee is late, Denny," Rachel said, as the public clock struck ten. "Was Henry in difficulty?" For Denzell and Dottie had gone to take farewell of Dottie's brother, Henry, still convalescent from the surgery Denny and Ian's auntie Claire had done.

"Thee might say so," Dottie said, "but not from any physical ill." The look of amusement faded from her face, though a faint gleam still lingered in her eyes. "He is in love with Mercy Woodcock."

"His landlady? Love's no usually a fatal condition, is it?" Ian asked, raising one brow.

"Not if thy name is neither Montague nor Capulet," Denny said. "The difficulty is that while Mercy loves him in return, she may or may not still have a husband living."

"And until she finds out he's dead . . ." Dottie added, lifting one slim shoulder.

"Or alive," Denny said, giving her a look. "There is always the possibility."

"Not much of one," Dottie replied bluntly. "Auntie—I mean Friend—Claire doctored a man called Walter Woodcock who'd been badly wounded at Ticonderoga, and she said he was near death then and taken p-prisoner." She stumbled slightly on the last word, and Ian was reminded suddenly that her eldest brother, Benjamin, was a prisoner of war.

Denzell saw the cloud cross her face and gently took her hand in his.

"Both thy brothers will survive their trials," he said, and warmth touched his eyes behind the glass. "So will we, Dorothea. Men have died from time to time and worms have eaten them—but not for love."

"Hmph!" said Dottie, but gave him a small, grudging smile. "All right, then—go ahead. There's *such* a lot to do before we go."

To Ian's surprise, Denzell nodded, took a folded sheaf of papers from his bosom, and, turning, went up the step to the door of the meetinghouse.

Ian had supposed the place was only a convenient spot to meet—he would be catching up his uncle and Auntie Claire on the road to Coryell's Ferry but had lingered to help with the loading, for Denny, Dottie, and Rachel were driving a wagon filled with medical supplies—but evidently Denny had business with Philadelphia Yearly Meeting.

Was he seeking advice in how to be married as a Quaker even while flouting their . . . what would you call it, edict—no, Rachel had said it was an opinion, but a "weighty" opinion—regarding support of the rebellion?

"He's giving them his witness—his testimony," Dottie said matter-of-factly, seeing the puzzlement in Ian's face. "He wrote it all out. Why he thinks it's right to do what he's doing. He's going to give it to the clerk of the yearly meeting and request that his views be mentioned and discussed."

"D'ye think they will?"

"Oh, yes," Rachel said. "They may disagree with him, but they won't stifle him. And good luck to them if they thought to try," she added, half under her breath. She pulled a handkerchief out of her bosom, very white against the soft brown of her skin, and patted tiny droplets of sweat away from her temples.

Ian felt a sudden and profound longing for her and glanced involuntarily toward the clock tower. He'd need to be on the road soon and hoped there'd be time for a precious hour alone with Rachel first.

Dorothea's eyes were still fixed on the door through which Denny had passed.

"He *is* so lovely," she said softly, as though to herself. Then glanced self-consciously at Rachel. "He felt badly for wearing his uniform to see Henry," she said, a tone of apology in her voice. "But the time was so short . . ."

"Was thy brother upset?" Rachel asked sympathetically. Dottie's brows drew down.

"Well, he didn't *like* it," she said frankly. "But it's not as though he didn't know that we're Rebels; I told him some time ago." Her expression relaxed a little. "And he *is* my brother. He won't disown me."

Ian wondered whether the same was true of her father, but didn't ask. She hadn't mentioned the duke. He wasn't really attending to Dottie's family concerns, though—his mind was busy with thought of the coming battle and all that needed to be done immediately. Ian caught Rachel's eye and smiled, and she smiled back, all worry melting from her face as she met his gaze.

He had concerns himself, certainly, annoyances and worries. At the bottom of his soul, though, was the solid weight of Rachel's love and what she had said, the words gleaming like a gold coin at the bottom of a murky well. *"We will marry each other."*

49

UNCERTAINTY PRINCIPLE

AS JAMIE EXPLAINED to me on the way out of Philadel-
phia, the problem lay not in finding the British but in catching up to
them with enough men and matériel to do some good.

"They left with several hundred wagons and a verra large number of Loyalists who didna feel quite safe in Philadelphia. Clinton canna be protecting
them and fighting at the same time. He must make all the speed he can—
which means he must travel by the most direct road."

"I suppose he can't very well be legging it cross-country," I agreed. "Have
you—meaning General Washington—got any idea how big a force he has?"

He lifted one shoulder and waved off a large horsefly with his hat.

"Maybe ten thousand men. Maybe more. Fergus and Germain watched
them assemble to march out, but ye ken it's not easy to judge numbers when
they're crawlin' out of the side streets and all."

"Mmm. And . . . um . . . how many men do we have?" Saying *"we"* gave
me an odd sensation that rippled through my lower body. Something between tail-curling apprehension and an excitement that was startlingly close
to sexual.

It wasn't that I'd never felt the strange euphoria of war before. But it had
been a very long time; I'd forgotten.

"Fewer than the British," Jamie said, matter-of-fact. "But we willna ken
how many until the militia have gathered—and pray it's not too late when we
do."

He glanced aside at me, and I could see him wondering whether to say
something further. He didn't speak, though, just gave a little shrug and settled himself in the saddle, putting on his hat again.

"What?" I said, tilting my head to peer up at him from under the brim of
my own broad straw. "You were about to ask me something."

"Mmphm. Aye, well . . . I was, but then I realized that if ye did know
anything about . . . what might happen in the next few days, ye'd surely have
told me."

"I would." In fact, I didn't know whether to regret my lack of knowledge
or not. Looking back at those instances where I'd thought I knew the future,
I hadn't known nearly enough. Out of nowhere, I thought of Frank . . . and
Black Jack Randall, and my hands gripped the reins so strongly that my mare
jerked her head with a startled snort.

Jamie looked round, startled, too, but I waved a hand and leaned forward
to pat the horse's neck in apology.

"Horsefly," I said, in explanation. My heart was thumping noticeably against the placket of my stays, but I took several deep breaths to quiet it. I wasn't about to mention my sudden thought to Jamie, but it hadn't left me.

I'd thought I knew that Jack Randall was Frank's five-times-great-grandfather. His name was right there, on the genealogical chart that Frank had shown me many times. And, in fact, he *was* Frank's ancestor—on paper. It was Jack's younger brother, though, who had sired Frank's bloodline but then had died before being able to marry his pregnant lover. Jack had married Mary Hawkins at his brother's request and thus given his name and legitimacy to her child.

So many gory details didn't show up on those tidy genealogical charts, I thought. Brianna was Frank's daughter, on paper—and by love. But the long, knife-blade nose and glowing hair of the man beside me showed whose blood ran through her veins.

But I'd thought I *knew*. And because of that false knowledge, I'd prevented Jamie killing Jack Randall in Paris, fearing that if he did, Frank might never be born. What if he *had* killed Randall then? I wondered, looking at Jamie sidelong. He sat tall, straight in the saddle, deep in thought, but with an air now of anticipation; the dread of the morning that had gripped us both had gone.

Anything might have happened; a number of things might not. Randall wouldn't have abused Fergus; Jamie wouldn't have fought a duel with him in the Bois de Boulogne . . . perhaps I would not have miscarried our first child, our daughter Faith. Likely I would have—miscarriage was usually physiological in basis, not emotional, however romantic novels painted it. But the memory of loss was forever linked to that duel in the Bois de Boulogne.

I shoved the memories firmly aside, turning my mind away from the half-known past to the complete mystery of the waiting future. But just before the images blinked out, I caught the edge of a flying thought.

What about the child? The child born to Mary Hawkins and Alexander Randall—Frank's true ancestor. He was, in all probability, alive now. Right now.

The ripple I'd experienced before came back, this time running from my tailbone up my spine. *Denys.* The name floated up from the parchment of a genealogical chart, calligraphic letters that purported to capture a fact, while hiding nearly everything.

I knew his name was Denys—and he was, so far as I knew, actually Frank's four-times great-grandfather. And that was all I knew—likely all I ever would know. I fervently hoped so. I wished Denys Randall silently well and turned my mind to other things.

50

THE GOOD SHEPHERD

TWELVE. BLOODY. *MILES!* The train of baggage wagons stretched as far as the eye could see in either direction and raised a cloud of dust that nearly obscured the mules negotiating a bend in the road a half mile away. The people trudging beside the wagons on either side were coated with the fine brown stuff—and so was William, though he kept as much distance as he could from the slow-moving cavalcade.

It was mid-afternoon of a hot day, and they'd been on the march since before dawn.

He paused to slap dust from the skirts of his coat and take a mouthful of tin-tasting water from his canteen. Hundreds of refugees, thousands of camp followers, all with packs and bundles and handcarts, with here and there a laden horse or mule that had somehow escaped the army teamsters' rapacity, were strung over the twelve miles between the two main bodies of the army. They spread out in a straggling mass that reminded him of the plague of locusts from the Bible. Was that the book of Exodus? Couldn't recall, but it seemed apposite.

Some of them looked over their shoulders now and then. He wondered if it was fear of pursuit or thoughts of what they'd left behind—the city itself was long out of sight.

Well, if there was any danger of turning to a pillar of salt, it would be owing to sweat, not yearning, he thought, wiping his sleeve across his face for the dozenth time. He was himself eager to shake the dust of Philadelphia from his boots and never think of it again.

If it weren't for Arabella–Jane, he'd likely have forgotten it already. He certainly *wanted* to forget everything else that had happened in the last few days. He twitched his reins and nudged his horse back toward the trudging horde.

It could be worse; nearly *had* been much worse. He'd come close to being dispatched back to England or sent north to join the other conventioners in Massachusetts. Thank Christ that Papa—that is, *Lord John,* he corrected himself firmly—had made him learn German, along with French, Italian, Latin, and Greek. Besides the divisions commanded by Sir Henry and Lord Cornwallis, the army included a huge body of mercenary troops under General von Knyphausen—nearly all of them from Hesse-Kassel, whose dialect William could manage with no trouble.

It had still taken a good deal of persuasion, but in the end he'd landed up as one of Clinton's dozen aides-de-camp, charged with the tedious chore of riding up and down the ponderously moving column, collecting reports, delivering dispatches, and dealing with any small difficulties that developed en route—a more or less hourly occurrence. He kept a running mental note of where the various surgeons and hospital orderlies were; he lived in horror of having to attend the delivery of one of the camp followers' babies—there were at least fifty very pregnant women with the column.

Maybe it was the proximity of these ladies, gravid and pale, their swollen bellies borne like burdens, balanced with the ones on their backs, that made him think of . . .

Surely whores knew how to avoid pregnancy? He didn't recall Arabella–Jane doing anything . . . but he wouldn't have noticed, drunk as he was.

William thought of her whenever he touched the spot on his breast where his gorget should be. If asked, he would have said he put the thing on with his uniform and forgot about it—but from the number of times he found Arabella–Jane in his mind, he was apparently in the habit of fiddling with it constantly.

The loss of the gorget had cost him an unpleasant five-minute analysis of his character, dress, hygiene, and personal failings from Clinton's chief aide, Captain Duncan Drummond, and a ten-shilling fine for being out of proper uniform. He didn't grudge her the cost.

He did find himself keeping an eye out for Captain Harkness. He couldn't recall enough of their encounter to have any idea of Harkness's regiment, but there weren't that many dragoon companies with the present army. He was working his way back along the column now, doing his daily round on Visigoth, a big bay gelding with good wind. The horse wasn't pleased with the slow pace and kept twitching under him, wanting to break into a gallop, but William held him to a steady trot, nodding as he passed each company, looking to the corporals and sergeants to see if any were in difficulty or needed assistance.

"Water's coming!" he called to a particularly wilted-looking group of Loyalist refugees who had stopped on the verge of the road, taking pause in the scant shade provided by a scatter of oak saplings and a handcart precariously piled with their belongings.

This reassurance made the women look up hopefully from under their bonnets, and the gentleman rose to his feet, waving William down.

He reined in and recognized Mr. Endicott, a well-to-do Philadelphia merchant, and his family. He'd been to dinner at their house and had danced with the two older Misses Endicott at several parties.

"Your servant, sir," he said, sweeping off his hat with a bow and nodding in turn to the ladies. "And yours, Mrs. Endicott. Miss Endicott, Miss Sally . . . and your most humble and obedient, Miss Peggy." Miss Peggy Endicott, aged nine, went pink as a young strawberry at being singled out, and her elder sisters exchanged raised brows over her head.

"Is it true, Lord Ellesmere," Endicott said, "that we are closely pursued by the Rebels?" He was holding a large red-flannel handkerchief, with which he wiped a perspiring round face. "The . . . er . . . the ladies find themselves summat worried by the prospect."

"The ladies have no cause for concern, sir," William assured him. "You are under the protection of His Majesty's army, you know."

"Well, yes, we do know that," Mr. Endicott said, rather testily. "Or so we hope, at least; certainly wouldn't be here else, I can tell you. But have you any news of Washington's whereabouts, is what I'd like to know?"

Visigoth shifted his weight and danced a little, eager to be off, but William pulled his head round, clicking his tongue in rebuke.

"Why, yes, sir," he said respectfully. "We have had several deserters from the Rebel camp, come in last night. They say that Washington is gathering his troops, no doubt in hopes of catching up to us—but he has no more than two thousand regulars, with a few scrubby militia companies."

Mr. Endicott looked somewhat reassured at this, but the girls and their mother didn't. Mrs. Endicott plucked at her husband's sleeve and murmured something. He flushed more deeply.

"I said I'll deal with it, madam!" he snapped. He had taken off his wig because of the heat and wore a spotted silk handkerchief tied over his head against the sun; his grizzled hair was cropped short, and tiny bristles stuck out from the edge of the kerchief like the feelers of angry insects.

Mrs. Endicott's lips pressed tight, but she stepped back, jerking her head in a small nod. Miss Peggy, though, emboldened by Captain Ellesmere's particularity, scampered forward and seized hold of his stirrup. Visigoth, startled by the flying scrap of calico at the corner of his vision, shied violently; Peggy shrieked, stumbled back, and went flying. All of the Endicott ladies were shrieking, but William could do nothing about that; he fought the horse's head round and held on grimly while Goth crow-hopped and whirled, then settled down gradually, snorting and jerking at the bit. He could hear passing infantrymen being profanely amused as their column swerved to go round him.

"Is Miss Peggy quite all right?" he inquired, breathing heavily as he finally brought the horse back to the verge. Miss Anne Endicott was standing near the edge of the road, waiting for him; the rest of her family had retreated, and he heard a loud howling coming from behind the handcart.

"Aside from being spanked by Papa for nearly being killed, yes," Miss Endicott replied, looking amused. She drew a little closer, keeping a wary eye on Goth, but the horse was calm enough now, stretching his neck to grab a mouthful of grass.

"I'm sorry to have been the cause of her distress," William said politely, and groped in his pocket, coming out with nothing but a crumpled handkerchief and a stray sixpence. He handed the coin down to Anne, smiling. "Give her that, will you, with my apologies?"

"She will be fine," Anne said, but took the coin. She glanced over her shoulder, then drew a step closer and spoke rapidly, lowering her voice. "I . . . hesitate to ask, Lord Ellesmere . . . but, you see, the cart has broken a wheel, my father cannot fix it, he *won't* abandon our belongings—and my mother is terrified that we will be overtaken and captured by Washington's men." Her dark eyes—very fine dark eyes—fixed on his with a brilliant intensity. "Can you help? Please? That was what my little sister meant to ask you."

"Oh. What exactly is the trouble with—never mind. Let me have a look." It would do Goth no harm to settle for a few minutes. He swung down and tied the horse to one of the saplings, then followed Miss Endicott to the handcart.

It was overflowing with the same higgledy-piggledy assortment of goods he'd seen on the docks two days ago—a tall clock stuck out of heaped clothing and linens, and a homely earthenware chamber pot was stuffed with handkerchiefs, stockings, and what was probably Mrs. Endicott's jewel case. The sight of this particular mess gave him a sudden pang, though.

These were remnants of a real home, one he'd been a guest in—the rubbish and treasures of people he knew . . . and liked. He'd heard that very clock, with its pierced-work crown, strike midnight just before he'd stolen a kiss from Anne Endicott in the shadows of her father's hallway. He felt the mellow *bong, bong* now, deep in his vitals.

"Where will you go?" he asked quietly, a hand on her arm. She turned to him, flushed and harried, her dark hair coming out of her cap—but still with dignity.

"I don't know," she said, just as quietly. "My aunt Platt lives in a small village near New York, but I don't know that we can travel so far, as we are . . ." She nodded at the unwieldy cart, surrounded by bags and half-wrapped bundles. "Perhaps we can find a safe place closer and wait there while my father goes to make . . . arrangements." Her lips pressed suddenly tight, and he realized that she was holding on to her composure by dint of great effort. And that it was unshed tears that made her eyes so bright. He took her hand and kissed it, gently.

"I'll help," he said.

Easier said than done. While the axle of the cart was intact, one wheel had struck a jagged rock and not merely popped off but had in the process lost the flat-iron tire that encircled the felloes—which in consequence had come apart, being badly glued. The wheel lay in pieces in the grass, and a gaudy orange-and-black butterfly perched on the disjunct hub, lazily fanning its wings.

Mrs. Endicott's fears weren't unfounded. Neither was Mr. Endicott's anxiety—which he was attempting with little success to disguise as irritability. If they were stranded for too long, and left behind . . . even if Washington's regular troops were moving too fast for looting, there were always scavengers on the outskirts of an army—any army.

A respectful period of inspection allowed Mr. Endicott, still red-faced but more settled, to emerge from his domestic imbroglio, followed by Peggy, also red-faced and downcast. William nodded to the merchant and gestured, summoning him to join in contemplation of the wreckage, out of hearing of the women.

"Are you armed, sir?" William asked quietly. Endicott's face paled noticeably, and his Adam's apple bobbed above his dirt-grimed stock.

"I have a fowling piece that belonged to my father," he said, in a voice so low as to be scarcely audible. "I—it's—not been fired in twenty years." *God,* William thought, appalled. William felt himself naked and edgy without weapons. Endicott had to be fifty, at least, and alone here with four women to protect?

"I'll find you help, sir," William said firmly. Mr. Endicott drew a deep, deep breath. William thought the man might sob if obliged to speak, and turned without haste toward the women, talking as he went.

"There will be a cooper or wainwright somewhere along the column. Ah, and here's the water carrier coming!" He extended a hand to Peggy. "Will you come with me to catch him, Miss Margaret? I'm sure he'll stop for a pretty face." She didn't smile, but she sniffed, wiped her nose on her sleeve, drew herself up, and took his hand. The Endicott ladies were nothing if not courageous.

A bored-looking mule pulled a cart with several barrels of water, passing slowly down the column, the driver pausing when hailed. William waded determinedly into the fray, lifting Peggy in his arms for safety—to her evident delight—and deflected the carrier to the Endicotts' service. Then, with a sweep of his hat to the ladies, he mounted again and made his way down the road in search of a cooper.

The army traveled with the equivalent of several villages' worth of artisans and those men called "supportives": coopers, carpenters, cooks, smiths, farriers, wainwrights, drovers, hauliers, orderlies. To say nothing of the vast swarm of laundresses and sempstresses among the camp followers. It wouldn't take long to find a cooper or a wainwright and persuade him to deal with the Endicotts' trouble. William glanced at the sun; nearly three.

The army was proceeding briskly, but that didn't mean it was moving at any great rate of speed. Clinton had given orders to march an additional two hours per day, though, a strain in the increasing heat. Another two hours before they made camp; with luck, the Endicotts might be whole again by then and able to keep up tomorrow.

A rumble of hooves and catcalls from the infantry caught his attention and made him glance over his shoulder, heart speeding up. Dragoons, plumes fluttering. He reined up and rode Goth straight at them, glancing from face to face as he passed down their double line. Several of them stared at him, and an officer made irritated motions at him, but he ignored that. A small voice in the back of his mind inquired what he meant to do if he *found* Harkness among them, but he ignored that, too.

He passed the end of the company, circled to the rear, and rode up the other side of the column, looking back over his shoulder at the rank of puzzled faces staring at him, some affronted, some amused. No . . . no . . . no . . . maybe? Would he even recognize the fellow? he wondered. He'd been very drunk. Still, he thought Harkness would recognize *him*. . . .

They were all staring at him by this time, but none with an aspect either of alarm or violence. Their colonel reined up a little and called to him.

"Ho, Ellesmere! Lost something, have you?"

He squinted against the sun and made out the vivid face of Ban Tarleton, red-cheeked and grinning under his flamboyant plumed helmet. He jerked his chin up in invitation, and William wheeled his horse and fell in beside him.

"Not lost, exactly," he said. "Just looking for a dragoon I met in Philadelphia—named Harkness; you know him?"

Ban pulled a face.

"Yes. He's with the Twenty-sixth. Randy bugger, always after women."

"And you aren't?" Ban wasn't a close friend, but William had been out on the randan with him once or twice in London. He didn't drink much, but he didn't need to; he was the sort of man who always seemed a little intoxicated.

Tarleton laughed, face flushed with the heat and red-lipped as a girl.

"Yes. But Harkness doesn't care about anything *but* women. Known him to have three at once, in a brothel."

William considered that one for a moment.

"All right. I can see a use for two, maybe . . . but what's the third one for?"

Ban, who was maybe four years older than William, gave him the sort of pitying look reserved for virgins and confirmed bachelors, then ducked back, laughing, when William punched him in the arm.

"Right," William said. "That aside, I'm looking for a wainwright or a cooper. Any close by?"

Tarleton straightened his helmet and shook his head.

"No, but there's bound to be one or two in that mess." He gestured negligently at the train of baggage wagons. "Which regiment are you with, these days?" He frowned at William, seeming to realize that something was amiss with his dress. "Where's your sword? And your gorget?"

William gritted his teeth—and they really did grit, there being so much coarse dust in the air—and apprised Tarleton of his situation in the minimum number of words. He didn't mention where or under what circumstances he had lost his gorget, and with a brief salute of farewell to the colonel, reined round and went down the column again. He was breathing as though he'd run the length of London Bridge, and pulses of electricity were running down his arms and legs, jolting at the base of his spine.

His anger over his situation had been rekindled by his conversation with Tarleton and—unable to do any bloody thing about any of it—turned his mind to what he wanted to do to Harkness, should he meet the 26th Light Dragoons. He touched his chest by reflex, and his sudden urge to do violence changed at once to an equally sudden rush of desire that made him light-headed.

Then he recalled his original errand, and hot blood washed through his face. He rode more slowly, calming his mind. Harkness could wait. The Endicotts couldn't.

Thought of the family pained him—and not only because he was ashamed of letting himself be distracted from their difficulty. But in recollecting them now, he realized that for those few moments with the Endicotts, concerned with their troubles, he'd forgotten. Forgotten the burden he'd been carrying like a pound of lead in his chest. Forgotten who he really was.

What would Anne Endicott have done, if she knew? Her parents? Even . . . well, no. He smiled, despite his disquiet. He didn't think Peggy Endicott would mind if he told her he was secretly a cutpurse or a cannibal, let alone a—

Everyone *else* he knew, though . . . The Endicotts were only one Loyalist family who'd welcomed him into their home, and he'd not taken proper leave of any of those who chose to stay in Philadelphia, too ashamed to see them, knowing the truth.

He looked back over his shoulder; the Endicotts were barely visible, now sitting in the grass in a companionable circle, sharing food of some kind. He felt a keen pang at the sight of their companionability. He'd never be part of a decent family, couldn't ever marry a woman even of such modest origins as Anne Endicott.

Her father might well be ruined, might have lost his wealth and business, the family might descend into poverty—but they would remain who they were, firm in their courage and the pride of their name. Not him. His name didn't belong to him.

Well . . . he *could* marry, he grudgingly admitted to himself, making his way gingerly through a group of camp followers. But only a woman who wanted nothing but his title and money would have him, and to wed under such circumstances, knowing that your wife despised you . . . and to know that you passed the taint of your blood to your sons . . .

This morbid train of thought stopped abruptly with the appearance of a small group of artisans, trudging beside a large wagon that undoubtedly held their tools.

He came down on them like a wolf on a flock of startled sheep and ruthlessly cut out a fine, fat wainwright, whom he persuaded by threats and bribery to mount behind him and thus carried his prey back to the Endicotts.

With his spirit soothed by their gratitude, he turned northward again, toward the head of the army, camp, and his supper. Absorbed in thoughts of roast chicken and gravy—he ate with Clinton's staff, and thus ate very well—he didn't notice at once that another horseman had come up alongside him, matching his pace.

"Penny for your thoughts?" said a pleasant, half-familiar voice, and he turned to find himself looking into the smiling face of Denys Randall-Isaacs.

WILLIAM REGARDED Randall-Isaacs with something between annoyance and curiosity. The man had to all effects abandoned him in Quebec City a year and a half before and vanished, leaving him to spend the winter snowbound with nuns and *voyageurs*. The experience had improved both his French and his hunting abilities, but not his temper.

"Captain Randall-Isaacs," he said in acknowledgment, rather coldly. The captain smiled sunnily at him, not at all put off by his tone.

"Oh, just Randall these days," he said. "My father's name, you know. The other bit was a courtesy to my stepfather, but as the old man's passed on now . . ." He lifted one shoulder, leaving William to draw the obvious conclusion: that a Jewish-sounding surname couldn't be an asset to an ambitious officer.

"Surprised to see you here," Randall went on, chummy, as though they'd seen each other at a ball last month. "You were at Saratoga with Burgoyne, weren't you?"

William's hand tightened on the reins, but he patiently explained his peculiar status. For possibly the twentieth time.

Randall nodded, respectful.

"Certainly better than cutting hay in Massachusetts," he said, with a glance at the marching columns they were passing. "Thought of going back to England, though?"

"No," William said, somewhat startled. "Why? For one thing, I doubt I can, by the terms of parole. For another—why should I?" *Why, indeed?* he thought, with a fresh stab. He'd not even begun to think about what awaited him in England, at Helwater, at Ellesmere. In London, for that matter . . . oh, Jesus . . .

"Why, indeed?" Randall said, unconsciously echoing him. The man sounded thoughtful. "Well . . . not much opportunity for distinguishing yourself here, is there?" He glanced very briefly at William's belt, bare of weapons, and away again directly, as though the sight was somehow shameful—which it was.

"And what is it you think I could do there?" William demanded, keeping his temper with some difficulty.

"Well, you *are* an earl," Randall pointed out. William felt the blood rise up his neck, but couldn't say anything. "You have a seat in the House of Lords. Why not use it to accomplish something? Take up politics. Doubt your parole says anything about that—and as long as you weren't going back to rejoin the army, I shouldn't think the travel itself would be a problem."

"I'd never thought of it," William said, striving for politeness. He couldn't think of anything he'd less rather do than be political—unless it was be political while acting a sham.

Randall tilted his head amiably to and fro, still smiling. He was much as he'd been when William had seen him last: dark hair tied back without powder, good-looking rather than handsome, slender without being slight, graceful in movement, with a constant expression of sympathetic geniality. He hadn't changed much—but William had. He was two years older now, much more experienced, and was both surprised and a little gratified to discover that he realized that Randall was playing him like a hand of bezique. Or trying to.

"I suppose there are other possibilities," he said, guiding his horse around an enormous puddle of muddy urine that had collected in a dip in the road.

Randall's horse had paused to add to it. Randall sat as composedly as one can in such a situation, but didn't try to raise his voice over the noise. He picked his way out of the mud and caught William up before continuing the conversation.

"Possibilities?" He sounded genuinely interested, and probably was, William thought—but why? "What were you thinking of doing?"

"You recall Captain Richardson, of course?" William asked casually, but with an eye on Randall's face. One dark brow rose a bit, but otherwise he showed no particular emotion at hearing the name.

"Oh, yes," Randall replied, as casual as William. "Have you seen the good captain recently?"

"Yes, a couple of days ago." William's temper had abated, and he waited with interest to see what Randall might have to say to this.

The captain didn't look taken aback, exactly, but his air of pleasant inconsequence had definitely sharpened into something else. William could actually *see* him wondering whether to ask bluntly what Richardson had wanted or to take another tack, and the perception gave him a small thrill.

"Is Lord John with Sir Henry?" Randall asked. That was enough of a non sequitur to make William blink, but there was no reason not to answer.

"No. Why should he be?"

The brow lifted again.

"You didn't know? The Duke of Pardloe's regiment is in New York."

"It is?" William was more than startled by that, but hastened to collect himself. "How do you know?"

Randall waved a well-manicured hand, as though the answer to this was irrelevant—as perhaps it was.

"Pardloe left Philadelphia this morning with Sir Henry," he explained. "As the duke has recalled Lord John to duty, I thought—"

"He *what?*" William's horse jerked his head and snorted at the exclamation, and William stroked the big neck, using the gesture to avert his face for a moment. His father was *here?*

"I stopped at his lordship's house in Philadelphia yesterday," Randall explained, "and a rather odd Scotchwoman—she must be his lordship's housekeeper, I collect?—told me that his lordship had been gone for several days. But if you haven't seen him . . ."

Randall raised his head, looking ahead. A haze of woodsmoke was already showing above the trees, cook fires, wash fires, and watch fires all marking the growing camp, their tang a pleasant spice in the nostrils. It made William's stomach growl.

"Hup! Hup! At the double, quick . . . march!" A sergeant's bellow came from behind them, and they pulled aside for a double column of infantry, who hadn't needed the exhortation; they were eager for their dinner and the chance to lay down their arms for the night.

The pause gave William room for a moment's thought: ought he to ask Randall to sup with him later, try to draw him out? Or get the hell away from the man as quickly as possible, using his need to wait on Sir Henry as excuse? But what if Lord John really *was* with Sir Henry right this moment? *And* bloody Uncle Hal—all he needed in the present circumstance!

Randall had evidently used the pause for thought, as well, and come to his own decision. He came up close beside William, and after a quick glance to be sure no one was near them, leaned close and spoke in a low voice.

"I say this as a friend, Ellesmere—though I grant you've no reason to trust me, I hope you'll listen. Don't, for God's sake, engage in any enterprise that Richardson suggests. Don't go with him anywhere, no matter what the circumstances. If you can avoid it, don't even talk to him again."

And with that, he reined his horse's head around, spurred up abruptly, and was off down the road at a gallop, heading away from the camp.

51

SCROUNGING

GREY WOULDN'T MIND, if it weren't for the headaches. The ache in his side had faded to something tolerable; he thought a rib might be cracked, but as long as he didn't have to run, that wouldn't be a problem. The eye, though . . .

The injured eye stubbornly refused to move but jerked in its socket, pulling against whatever obstruction held it—an orbicularis muscle? Was that what Dr. Hunter had called it?—in an attempt to focus with its fellow. This was painful and exhausting in itself but also led to double vision and crushing headaches, and he found himself often unable to eat when they halted, wanting only to lie down in darkness and wait for the throbbing to cease.

By the time they stopped to make camp on the evening of the second day of march, he could barely see out of his good eye, and his stomach was heaving with nausea.

"Here," he said, thrusting his hot journeycake at one of his fellows, a tailor from Morristown named Phillipson. "You take it. I can't, not just . . ." He couldn't go on, but pressed the heel of his hand hard against his closed eye. Green and yellow pinwheels and brilliant flashes of light erupted behind his eyelid, but the pressure eased the pain for a moment.

"You save it for later, Bert," Phillipson said, tucking the journeycake into Grey's rucksack. He bent close and peered at Grey's face in the firelight. "You need a patch for that eye," he declared. "Keep you from rubbing at it, at least; it's red as a whore's stocking. Here."

And with that, he took off his own battered felt hat and, whipping a small pair of scissors from his bosom, cut a neat round patch from the brim, rubbed a bit of spruce gum round the edge to make it stick, and then bound it carefully in place over the injured orb with a spotted handkerchief contributed by one of the other militiamen. All of them clustered round to watch, with the kindest expressions of concern, offers of food and drink, suggestions as to which company had a surgeon that might come to let his blood, and so on. Grey, in the weakness of pain and exhaustion, thought he might weep.

He managed to thank them all for their concern, but at last they left off, and after a swig of something unidentifiable but strongly alcoholic from Jacobs's canteen, he sat on the ground, shut his good eye, leaned his head back against a log, and waited for the throbbing in his temples to lessen.

Despite his bodily discomfort, he felt comforted in spirit. The men with him weren't soldiers, and God knew they weren't an army—but they were men, engaged in common purpose and mindful of one another, and that was a thing he knew and loved.

". . . and we bring our needs and desires before thee, O great Lord, and implore thy blessing upon our deeds . . ."

The Reverend Woodsworth was conducting a brief service of prayers. He did this every evening; those who wished might join him; those who didn't occupied themselves in quiet conversation or small tasks of mending or whittling.

Grey had no real idea where they were, save somewhere to the northeast of Philadelphia. Messengers on horseback met them now and then, and confused bits of news and speculation spread like fleas through the group. He gathered that the British army was heading north—clearly to New York—and that Washington had left Valley Forge with his troops and was intending to attack Clinton somewhere en route, but no one knew where. The troops were to muster at a place called Coryell's Ferry, at which point they might, possibly, be told where they were going.

He didn't waste energy on thinking about his own position. He could escape easily enough in the darkness, but there was no point in doing so. Wandering around the countryside in the midst of converging militia companies and regular troops, he ran more risk of ending up back in the custody of Colonel Smith, who would probably hang him out of hand, than he did in remaining with Woodsworth's militia.

The danger might increase when they *did* join Washington's troops—but large armies really couldn't hide from each other, nor did they try to avoid notice. If Washington got anywhere near Clinton, Grey could at that point easily desert—if one considered it desertion—and cross the lines into British hands, risking only being shot by an overenthusiastic sentry before he could surrender and make himself known.

Gratitude, he thought, hearing Mr. Woodsworth's prayer through a haze of growing drowsiness and fading pain. Well, yes, there were a few more things he could count on his list of blessings.

William was still on parole and thus a noncombatant. Jamie Fraser had been released from the Continental army to escort Brigadier Fraser's body back to Scotland. Though he'd returned, he was no longer in the army; he wouldn't be in this fight, either. His nephew Henry was healing, but in no way fit for combat. There was no one likely to be involved in the coming battle—if there was one—over whom he need worry. Though come to think. . . . His hand found the empty pocket of his breeches. *Hal.* Where the bloody hell *was* Hal?

He sighed, but then relaxed, breathing in the scents of woodsmoke, pine needles, and roasted corn. Wherever Hal was, he'd be safe enough. His brother could take care of himself.

The prayers over, one of his companions had started to sing. It was a song he knew, but the words were quite different. His version, picked up from an army surgeon who'd fought with the Colonials during the French and Indian war, went:

> *Brother Ephraim sold his Cow*
> *And bought him a Commission;*
> *And then he went to Canada*
> *To fight for the Nation;*
>
> *But when Ephraim he came home*
> *He proved an arrant Coward,*
> *He wouldn't fight the Frenchmen there*
> *For fear of being devour'd.*

Dr. Shuckburgh hadn't had much opinion of the colonials, and neither had the composer of the newer version, used as a marching song. He'd heard that one in Philadelphia and hummed along under his breath.

> *Yankee Doodle came to town,*
> *For to buy a firelock,*
> *We will tar and feather him,*
> *And so we will John Hancock!*

His present companions were now singing—with gusto—the latest evolution:

> *Yankee Doodle went to town*
> *A-riding on a pony,*
> *Stuck a feather in his cap*
> *And called it Macaroni!*

He wondered, yawning, whether any of them knew that the word *dudel* meant "simpleton" in German. He doubted Morristown, New Jersey, had ever seen a macaroni, those affected young men who went in for pink wigs and a dozen face patches.

As his headache eased, he began to appreciate the simple pleasure of reclining. The shoes with their makeshift laces fit him badly and, as well as rubbing his heels raw, gave him shooting pains in the shins from the effort of constantly clenching his toes in order to keep the bloody things on. He stretched his legs gingerly, almost enjoying the tenderness in his muscles, so near bliss by contrast with walking.

He was distracted from his catalog of meager blessings by a small, hungry gulp near his ear, followed by a young, low voice.

"Mister . . . if ye're not meanin' to eat that journeycake yourself . . ."

"What? Oh . . . yes. Of course."

He struggled to sit up, one hand pressed protectively over his bad eye, and turned his head to see a boy of eleven or twelve sitting on the log just beside him. He had his hand inside his sack, rummaging for the food, when the boy let out a gasp, and he looked up, vision wavering in the firelight, to discover himself face-to-face with Claire's grandson, fair hair in a tousled halo round his head and a look of horror on his face.

"Hush!" he said in a whisper, and grabbed the child's knee in such a sudden grip that the boy gave a small yelp.

"Why, what's that you've got there, Bert? Caught you a thief?" Abe Shaffstall, distracted from a desultory game of knucklebones, looked over his shoulder, peering shortsightedly at the boy—Christ, what was his name? His father was French; was it Claude? Henri? No, that was the younger boy, the dwarf. . . .

"Tais-toi!" he said under his breath to the boy, and turned to his companions. "No, no—this is a neighbor's son from Philadelphia—er . . . Bobby. Bobby Higgins," he added, grabbing at the first name that offered itself. "What's brought you out here, son?" he asked, hoping that the boy was as quick-witted as his grandmother.

"Lookin' for my grandda," the boy replied promptly, though his eyes shifted uneasily round the circle of faces, now all aimed in his direction as the singing died away.

"My mam sent me with some clothes and food for him, but some wicked fellows in the wood pulled me off my mule and . . . and t-took everything." The boy's voice trembled realistically, and Grey noticed that, in fact, his dirty cheeks showed the tracks of tears.

This provoked a rumble of concern round the circle and the immediate production from pokes and pockets of hard bread, apples, dried meat, and dirty handkerchiefs.

"What's your grandpa's name, son?" Joe Buckman inquired. "What company is he with?"

The boy looked nonplussed at this and shot a quick glance at Grey, who answered for him.

"James Fraser," he said, with a reassuring nod that made his head throb. "He'd be with one of the Pennsylvania companies, wouldn't he, Bobby?"

"Aye, sir." The boy wiped his nose on the proffered handkerchief and gratefully accepted an apple. *"Mer—"* He interrupted himself with an artful coughing fit and amended this to "Thank ye kindly, sir. And you, sir." He handed back the handkerchief and set himself to ravenous consumption, this limiting his replies to nods and shakes of the head. Indistinct mumbles indicated that he had forgotten the number of his grandfather's company.

"No matter, boy," Reverend Woodsworth said comfortingly. "We're all a-going to the same place to muster. You'll find your grandpa with the troops there, surely. You think you can keep up with us, though, a-foot?"

"Oh, aye, sir," Germain—*that was it! Germain!*—said, nodding fast. "I can walk."

"I'll take care of him," Grey said hastily, and that seemed to settle it.

He waited impatiently until everyone had forgotten the boy's presence and begun to ready themselves for sleep, then rose, muscles protesting, and jerked his head at Germain to follow him, muffling an exclamation of pain at the movement.

"Right," he said in a low voice, as soon as they were out of earshot. "What the devil are you doing out here? And where *is* your bloody grandfather?"

"I *was* lookin' for him," Germain replied, unbuttoning his flies to piss. "He's gone to—" He paused, obviously unsure what his relationship with

Grey now was. "Beg pardon, my lord, but I dinna ken should I tell ye that or not. I mean . . ." The boy was no more than a silhouette against the darker black of the undergrowth, but even the outline of his body expressed an eloquent wariness. *"Comment se fait-il que vous soyez ici?"*

"How did I come to be here," Grey repeated under his breath. *"Comment,* indeed. Never mind. I'll tell *you* where we're going, shall I? I gather we're bound for a place called Coryell's Ferry to join General Washington. Does that ring a bell?"

Germain's slender shoulders relaxed, and a soft pattering on the earth indicated that apparently it did. Grey joined him, and, finished, they turned back toward the glow of the campfire.

Still in the shelter of the woods, Grey put his hand on Germain's shoulder and squeezed. The boy stopped dead.

"Attendez, monsieur," Grey said, low-voiced. "If the militia learn who I am, they'll hang me. Instantly. My life is in your hands from this moment. *Comprenez-vous?"*

There was silence for an unnerving moment.

"Are you a spy, my lord?" Germain asked softly, not turning round.

Grey paused before answering, wavering between expediency and honesty. He could hardly forget what he'd seen and heard, and when he made it back to his own lines, duty would compel him to pass on such information as he had.

"Not by choice," he said at last, just as softly.

A cool breeze had risen with the setting of the sun, and the forest murmured all around them.

"Bien," Germain said at last. "And thank ye for the food." He turned then, and Grey could see the glint of firelight on one fair brow, arched in inquisitiveness.

"So I am Bobby Higgins. Who are you, then?"

"Bert Armstrong," Grey replied shortly. "Call me Bert."

He led the way then toward the fire and the blanket-humped rolls of sleeping men. He couldn't quite tell, above the rustling of the trees and the snoring of his fellows, but he *thought* the little bugger was laughing.

52

MORPHIA DREAMS

WE SLEPT THAT NIGHT in the public room of an ordinary in Langhorne. Bodies were sprawled on tables and
benches, curled *under* the tables, and laid in haphazard arrangements on pallets, folded cloaks, and saddlebags, as far away from the hearth
as they could get. The fire was banked, but it still radiated considerable heat.
The room was filled with the bitter scents of burning wood and boiling bodies. I estimated the temperature in the room at something like ninety-five
degrees Fahrenheit, and the slumbering bodies on display were largely un-
clad, pale haunches, shoulders, and bosoms glimmering in the sullen glow of
the embers.

Jamie had been traveling in shirt and breeches, his new uniform and its
dazzling smallclothes carefully folded into a portmanteau until we got within
range of the army, so his disrobing was a simple matter of unbuttoning his
flies and pulling off his stockings. Mine was complicated by the fact that my
traveling stays had leather laces, and over the course of a sweat-drenched day,
the knot had tightened into a stubborn nodule that resisted all attempts.

"Are ye no coming to bed, Sassenach?" Jamie was already lying down,
having found a remote corner behind the bar counter and spread out our
cloaks.

"I've broken a fingernail trying to get this bloody thing loose, and I can't
bloody reach it with my teeth!" I said, on the verge of breaking into tears of
frustration. I was swaying with weariness, but couldn't bring myself to sleep
in the clammy confines of my stays.

Jamie reached up an arm out of the darkness, beckoning.

"Come lie down wi' me, Sassenach," he whispered. "I'll do it."

The simple relief of lying down, after twelve hours in the saddle, was so
exquisite that I nearly changed my mind about sleeping in my stays, but he'd
meant it. He squirmed down and bent his head to nuzzle at my laces, an arm
round my back to steady me.

"Dinna fash," he murmured into my midsection, voice somewhat muffled.
"If I canna nibble it loose, I'll prise it wi' my dirk."

He looked up with an inquiring noise, as I'd uttered a strangled laugh at
the prospect.

"Just trying to decide whether being accidentally disemboweled would be
worse than sleeping in my stays," I whispered, cupping his head. It was warm,
the soft hair at his nape damp to the touch.

"My aim's no that bad, Sassenach," he said, pausing in his labors for an instant. "I'd only risk stabbin' ye in the heart."

As it was, he accomplished his goal without recourse to weapons, gently jerking the knot loose with his teeth until he could finish the job with his fingers, opening the heavy seamed canvas stays like a clamshell to expose the whiteness of my shift. I sighed like a grateful mollusk opening at high tide, plucking the fabric out of the creases the stays had made in my flesh. Jamie pushed away the discarded stays but remained where he was, his face near my breasts, rubbing his hands gently over my sides.

I sighed again at his touch; he'd done it by habit, but it was a habit I'd missed for the last four months, and a touch I'd thought never to feel again.

"Ye're too thin, Sassenach," he whispered. "I can feel every rib. I'll find ye food tomorrow."

I had been too much preoccupied in the last few days to think about food, and was much too tired at the moment to be hungry, but made an agreeable sound in response and stroked his hair, tracing the curve of his skull.

"I love you, *a nighean*," he said, very softly, his breath warm on my skin.

"I love you," I answered just as softly, taking the ribbon from his hair and loosening his plait between my fingers. I pressed his head closer to me, not in invitation, but out of the sudden urgent need to *keep* him close to me, to protect him.

He kissed my breast and turned his head, laying it in the hollow of my shoulder. He took one deep breath, one more, and then was asleep, the relaxing weight of his body against me both protection and trust.

"I love you," I said, almost soundless, my arms wrapped tight about him. "Oh, dear God, I love you."

IT MIGHT HAVE been the sense of overwhelming fatigue, or the smell, the mingling of alcohol and unwashed bodies, that made me dream of the hospital.

I was walking down the little hall beyond the men's ward at the hospital where I'd done my nurse's training, the tiny bottle of morphia grains in my hand. The walls were dingy gray; so was the air. At the end of the hall was the alcohol bath where the syringes were kept.

I lifted one out, cold and slippery, careful not to drop it. But I did drop it; it slid from my hand and shattered on the floor, spraying glass shards that cut my legs.

I couldn't worry about that; I had to get back with the morphine injection—men were calling out behind me, desperate, and somehow it was the sound of the operating tent in France back there, men moaning, screams and hopeless sobbing, and my fingers shook with urgency, groping in the cold steel bath among glass syringes that rattled like bones.

I pulled one out, gripping it so tightly that it, too, broke in my hand, and blood ran down my wrist, but I wasn't conscious of pain. Another, I must have another; they were in dreadful pain and I could stop it, if *only* . . .

Somehow I had a clean syringe and had got the top off the tiny bottle of morphia grains, but my hand was shaking, the grains spilling like salt; Sister Amos would be furious. I needed tweezers, forceps; I couldn't grasp the tiny pellets with my fingers and, in a panic, shook several of them into the syringe, a whole grain, not the quarter grain called for, but I *had* to get to the men, had to stop their pain.

Then I was running back down the endless gray hall toward the cries, shards of glass glinting among the red blood drops on the floor, both as bright as dragonfly wings. But my hand was growing numb, and the last syringe fell from my fingers before I reached the door.

And I woke up with a jolt that seemed to stop my heart. I gulped smoke and the fug of beer and bodies, not knowing where I was.

"Jesus, Sassenach, are ye all right?" Jamie, startled out of sleep, rolled up onto his elbow above me, and I came back into the present with as much of a jolt as my awakening had been. My left arm was numb from the shoulder down, and there were tears on my cheeks; I felt the coolness on my skin.

"I . . . yes. Just a . . . a bad dream." I felt ashamed to confess it, as though it were his privilege alone to suffer nightmares.

"Ah." He lowered himself beside me with a sigh and gathered me to him with one arm. He ran a thumb over my face and, finding wetness, blotted it matter-of-factly with his shirt. "All right now?" he whispered, and I nodded, thankful that I needn't talk about it.

"Good." He stroked the hair off my face and rubbed my back gently, the circles of his hand growing gradually slower until he fell asleep again.

It was deep night, and a deep sleep lay upon the room. The whole of it seemed to breathe in unison, snores and gasps and grunts all fading into something like the waves of a receding tide, rising and falling and bearing me with them, safely back into the depths of sleep.

Only the pins and needles of feeling returning to my dead arm kept me from it, and that only momentarily.

I could still see the blood and the shards of glass and heard against the susurrus of snores the crash of falling crystal, saw the bloody smudges on the wallpaper at Number 17.

Dear Lord, I prayed, listening to Jamie's heart under my ear, slow and steady. *Whatever happens, let him have a chance to talk to William.*

53

TAKEN AT A DISADVANTAGE

WILLIAM LED HIS HORSE down among the rocks to a level place where both of them could drink. It was midafternoon, and after a day spent riding to and fro along the column in the blazing sun, he was parched as a piece of last year's venison jerky.

His present horse was Madras, a cob with a deep chest and a steady, stolid disposition. The horse waded purposefully into the stream, hock-deep, and sank his nose into the water with a blissful snort, shivering his coat against the cloud of flies that appeared instantly out of nowhere whenever they stopped.

William waved a couple of insects away from his own face and took off his coat for a moment's relief from the heat. He was tempted to wade in, too—up to his neck, if the creek was deep enough—but . . . well . . . He looked cautiously over his shoulder, but he was well out of sight, though he could hear the sounds of the baggage train on the distant road. Why not? Just for a moment. It wasn't as though the dispatch he was carrying was urgent; he'd seen it written, and it contained nothing more than an invitation for General von Knyphausen to join General Clinton for supper at an inn with a reputation for good pork. Everyone was wringing with sweat; dampness would be no telltale.

He hastily shucked shoes, shirt, stockings, breeches, and smalls, and walked naked into the purling water, which barely reached his waist but was wet and cool. He closed his eyes in blissful relief—and opened them abruptly a half second later.

"William!"

Madras flung up his head with a startled snort, showering William with droplets, but he barely noticed in the shock of seeing two young women standing on the opposite bank.

"What the devil are *you* doing here?" He tried to squat a little lower in the water without being conspicuous about it. Though a dim voice in the back of his mind wondered aloud why he bothered: Arabella–Jane had already seen anything he had. "And who's that?" he demanded, jerking his chin at the other girl. Both of them were flushed as summer roses, but he thought—he hoped—it was the result of the heat.

"This is my sister, Frances," Jane said, with the elegance of a Philadelphia matron, and gestured to the younger girl. "Curtsy to his lordship, now, Fanny."

Fanny, a very lovely young girl with dark curls peeping out under her cap—what was she, eleven, twelve?—bobbed him a sweet curtsy, blue-and-red-calico petticoats outspread, and dropped long lashes modestly over the big, soft eyes of a young doe.

"Your most humble servant, mademoiselle," he said, bowing with as much grace as possible, which, judging from the expressions on the girls' faces, was probably a mistake. Fanny clapped a hand over her mouth and went much redder from the effort not to laugh.

"I am charmed to meet your sister," he said to Jane, rather coldly. "But I fear you take me at something of a disadvantage, madam."

"Yes, that's a piece of luck," Jane agreed. "I couldn't think how we were to find you in that moil, and when we saw you ride past like the fiend was after you—we'd got a ride on a baggage wagon—I didn't think we'd ever catch you. But we took the chance, and . . . *voilà! Fortuna favet audax,* you know." She wasn't even trying to *pretend* she wasn't laughing at him!

He scrabbled for some cutting rejoinder in Greek, but the only thing that came to his inflamed mind was a humiliating echo from his past, something his father had said to him on the occasion when he'd accidentally fallen into a privy: *"What news from the underworld, Persephone?"*

"Turn your backs," he said curtly. "I'm getting out."

They didn't. Gritting his teeth, he turned his own back on them and deliberately climbed the bank, feeling the itch of four interested eyes focused on his dripping backside. He grabbed his shirt and wrestled his way into it, feeling that even that much shelter would enable him to carry on the conversation in a more dignified manner. Or maybe he'd just tuck his breeches and boots under his arm and leave without further chat.

The sound of heavy splashing whilst he was still enveloped in the folds of his shirt made him whirl round, head popping free just in time to see Madras lunge up out of the creek on the girls' side, lips already reaching for the apple Jane was holding out to him.

"Come back here, sir!" he shouted. But the girls had more apples, and the horse paid no attention whatever—nor did he object when Arabella–Jane took his reins and looped them casually round the trunk of a young willow.

"I noticed that you didn't ask how we came to be here," she said. "Doubtless surprise has deprived you of your usual exquisite manners." She dimpled at him and he eyed her severely.

"I did," he said. "I distinctly recall saying, 'What. The. Devil. Are. You. Doing. Here.'"

"Oh, so you did," she said, without a blush. "Well, not to put too fine a point on the matter, Captain Harkness came back."

"Oh," he said, in a slightly different tone. "I see. You, um, ran away, then?"

Frances nodded solemnly.

William cleared his throat. "Why? Captain Harkness is doubtless *with* the army. Why would you come here, of all places, instead of staying safe in Philadelphia?"

"No, he isn't," Jane said. "He was detained on business in Philadelphia. So we came away. Besides," she added carelessly, "there are *thousands* of women with the army. He'd never find us, even if he was looking—and why should he be?"

That was reasonable. Still . . . he knew what the life of an army whore was like. He also had a strong suspicion that the girls had run out on their contract with the brothel; very few saved enough from their wages to buy their way out, and both of these girls were much too young to have made much money. To abandon the reasonable comfort of clean beds and regular meals in Philadelphia in order to accommodate filthy, sweating soldiers amidst mud and flies, paid in blows as often as in coin . . . Yet he was obliged to admit that he'd never been buggered by a vicious sod like Harkness and thus had no true basis for comparison.

"I expect you want money, to assist in your escape?" he said, an edge in his voice.

"Well, perhaps," said Jane. Reaching into her pocket, she held up something shiny. "Mostly, I wanted to give this back to you."

His gorget! He took an involuntary step toward her, toes squelching in the mud.

"I—thank you," he said abruptly. He'd felt its lack every time he dressed, and felt even more the weight of his fellow officers' eyes on the empty spot where it should rest. He'd been obliged to explain to Colonel Desplains what had happened—more or less—saying that he'd been robbed in a bawdy house. Desplains had chewed him bloody, but then had given him reluctant leave to appear without a gorget until he might get another in New York.

"What I—we, I mean—*really* want is your protection," Jane said, doing her best to look winsomely earnest, and doing it damned well.

"You *what*?"

"I don't think I should have any difficulty in making a living with the army," she said frankly, "but 'tisn't really what I want for my dear sister, that sort of life."

"Er . . . no. I imagine not," William said warily. "What else did you have in mind?" *"Lady's maid?"* he wanted to suggest sarcastically, but in light of the return of his gorget, he refrained.

"I haven't quite made up my mind," she said, fastening her gaze on the ripples where the creek ran over rocks. "But if you could help us to get safely to New York—and maybe find us a place there . . ."

William ran a hand down his face, wiping away a layer of fresh sweat.

"Don't want much, do you?" he said. On the one hand, if he didn't give her some assurance of help, he wouldn't put it past her to fling his gorget into the water in a fit of pique. And on the other . . . Frances was a lovely child, delicate and pale as a morning-glory blossom. And on the third hand, he hadn't any more time to spare in argument.

"Get on the horse and come across," he said abruptly. "I'll find you a new place with the baggage train. I have to ride a dispatch to von Knyphausen just now, but I'll meet you in General Clinton's camp this evening—no, not this evening, I won't be back until tomorrow. . . ." He fumbled for a moment, wondering where to tell her to find him; he could *not* have two young whores asking for him at General Clinton's headquarters. "Go to the surgeons' tent at sundown tomorrow. I'll—think of something."

54

IN WHICH I MEET A TURNIP

DURING THE NEXT DAY'S ride, we encountered a messenger, sent back from Washington's command with a note for Jamie. He read this leaning against a tree, while I made an unobtrusive visit to a nearby clump of brush.

"What does he say?" I asked, straightening my clothes as I emerged. I was still rather awed that Jamie had actually spoken with George Washington, and the fact that he was frowning at a letter presumably *written* by the future Father of the Country . . .

"Two or three things," he replied with a shrug, and, refolding the note, stuffed it into his pocket. "The only important bit o' news is that my brigade is to be under the command of Charles Lee."

"Do you know Charles Lee?" I got my foot into the stirrup and heaved myself into the saddle.

"I know *of* him." What he knew appeared to be rather problematic, judging from the line between his brows. I raised my own; he glanced at me and smiled.

"I met him, ken, when I first met General Washington. I made it my business to learn a bit more about him since."

"Oh, so you didn't like him," I observed, and he gave me a small snort.

"No, I didn't," he said, nudging his horse into a walk. "He's loud and unmannerly and a sloven—I could see that much for myself—but from what I've heard since, he's also jealous to the bone and doesna trouble to hide it verra well."

"Jealous? Of whom?" Not Jamie, I hoped.

"Of Washington," he answered matter-of-factly, surprising me. "He thought he should have command o' the Continental army and doesna like playin' second fiddle."

"Really?" I'd never once heard of General Charles Lee, which seemed odd, if he had such prominence as to have made that a reasonable expectation. "Why does he think that, do you know?"

"I do. He feels he has a good deal more in the way of military experience than Washington—and that's maybe true: he was in the British army for some time and fought a number of successful campaigns. Still—" He lifted one shoulder and dropped it, dismissing General Lee for the moment. "I wouldna have agreed to do this, had it been Lee who asked me."

"I thought you didn't want to do it, regardless."

"Mmphm." He considered for a moment. "It's true I didna want to do this—I don't now." He looked at me, apologetic. "And I truly dinna want you to be here."

"I'm going to be where you are for the rest of our lives," I said firmly. "If that's a week or another forty years."

"Longer," he said, and smiled.

We rode for a time in silence, but deeply aware of each other. We had been, since that conversation in the gardens at Kingsessing.

"I will love ye forever. It doesna matter if ye sleep with the whole English army—well, no, it would matter, but it wouldna stop me loving you."

"I've taken ye to bed a thousand times at least, Sassenach. Did ye think I wasna paying attention?"

"There couldna be anyone like you."

I hadn't forgotten a word we'd said—and neither had he, though neither one of us had spoken of it again. We weren't walking on tiptoe with each other, but we were feeling our way . . . finding our way into each other, as we'd done twice before. Once, when I'd returned to find him in Edinburgh—and at the beginning, when we'd found ourselves wed by force and joined by circumstance. Only later, by choice.

"What would you have wanted to be?" I asked, on impulse. "If you hadn't been born the laird of Lallybroch?"

"I wasn't. If my elder brother hadna died, ye mean," he said. A small shadow of regret crossed his face, but didn't linger. He still mourned the boy who had died at eleven, leaving a small brother to pick up the burden of leadership and struggle to grow into it—but he had been accustomed to that burden for a very long time.

"Maybe that," I said. "But what if you'd been born elsewhere, maybe to a different family?"

"Well, I wouldna be who I am, then, would I?" he said logically, and smiled at me. "I may quibble wi' what the Lord's called me to do now and then, Sassenach—but I've nay argument wi' how he made me."

I looked at what he was—the strong, straight body and capable hands, the face so full of everything he was—and had no argument, either.

"Besides," he said, and tilted his head consideringly, "if it had been different, I wouldna have you, would I? Or have had Brianna and her weans?"

If it had been different . . . I didn't ask whether he thought his life as it was had been worth the cost.

He leaned over and touched my cheek.

"It's worth it, Sassenach," he said. "For me."

I cleared my throat.

"For me, too."

⁂

IAN AND ROLLO caught us up a few miles from Coryell's Ferry. Darkness had fallen, but the glow of the camp was faintly visible against the sky, and we made our way cautiously in, being stopped every quarter mile or so by sentries who popped unnervingly out of the dark, muskets at the ready.

"Friend or foe?" the sixth of these demanded dramatically, peering at us in the beam of a dark lantern held high.

"General Fraser and his lady," Jamie said, shielding his eyes with his hand and glaring down at the sentry. "Is that friendly enough for ye?"

I muffled a smile in my shawl; he'd refused to stop to find food along the way, and I'd refused to let him consume uncooked bacon, no matter how well smoked. Jenny's four apples hadn't gone far, we'd found no food since the night before, and he was starving. An empty stomach generally woke the fiend that slept within, and this was clearly in evidence at the moment.

"Er . . . yes, sir, General, I only—" The lantern's beam of light shifted to rest on Rollo, catching him full in the face and turning his eyes to an eerie green flash. The sentry made a strangled noise, and Ian leaned down from his horse, his own face—Mohawk tattoos and all—appearing suddenly in the beam.

"Dinna mind us," he said genially to the sentry. "We're friendly, too."

TO MY SURPRISE, there was actually a good-sized settlement at the Ferry, with several inns and substantial houses perched on the bank of the Delaware.

"I suppose that's why Washington chose this as the rendezvous point?" I asked Jamie. "Good staging, I mean, and some supply."

"Aye, there's that," he said, though he spoke abstractedly. He'd risen a little in his stirrups, looking over the scene. Every window in every house was lit, but a large American flag, with its circle of stars, flapped above the door of the largest inn. Washington's headquarters, then.

My chief concern was to get some food into Jamie before he met with General Lee, if the aforementioned indeed had a reputation for arrogance and short temper. I didn't know what it was about red hair, but many years' experience with Jamie, Brianna, and Jemmy had taught me that while most people became irritable when hungry, a redheaded person with an empty stomach was a walking time bomb.

I sent Ian and Rollo with Jamie to find the quartermaster, discover what we might have in the way of accommodation, and unload the pack mule, then followed my nose toward the nearest scent of food.

The dug-in camp kitchens would long since have banked their fires, but I'd been in many army camps and knew how they worked; small kettles would be simmering all night, filled with stew and porridge for the morning—the more so as the army was in hot pursuit of General Clinton. Amazing to think that I had met him socially only a few days before—

I'd been so focused on my quest that I hadn't seen a man come out of the half dark and nearly ran into him. He seized me by the arms and we waltzed a dizzy half-turn before coming to rest.

"*Pardon, madame!* I am afraid I have stepped upon your foot!" said a young French voice, very concerned, and I looked straight into the very concerned face of a very young man. He was in shirtsleeves and breeches, but I could see that his shirtsleeves sported deep, lace-trimmed cuffs. An officer, then, in spite of his youth.

"Well, yes, you have," I said mildly, "but don't worry about it. I'm not damaged."

"*Je suis tellement désolé, je suis un navet!*" he exclaimed, striking himself in the forehead. He wore no wig, and I saw that despite his age, his hair was receding at a rapid pace. What was left of it was red and inclined to stand on end—possibly owing to his apparent habit of thrusting his fingers through it, which he was now doing.

"Nonsense," I said in French, laughing. "You aren't a turnip at all."

"Oh, yes," he said, switching to English. He smiled charmingly at me. "I once stepped on the foot of the Queen of France. She was much less gracious, *sa Majesté*," he added ruefully. "*She* called me a turnip. Still, if it hadn't happened—I was obliged to leave the court, you know—perhaps I would never have come to America, so we cannot bemoan my clumsiness altogether, *n'est-ce pas?*"

He was exceedingly cheerful and smelled of wine—not that that was in any way unusual. But given his exceeding Frenchness, his evident wealth, and his tender age, I was beginning to think—

"Have I the, um, honor of addressing—" Bloody hell, what was his actual title? Assuming that he really was—

"*Pardon, madame!*" he exclaimed, and, seizing my hand, bowed low over it and kissed it. "*Marie Joseph Paul Yves Roch Gilbert du Motier, Marquis de La Fayette, a votre service!*"

I managed to pick "La Fayette" out of this torrent of Gallic syllables and felt the odd little thump of excitement that happened whenever I met someone I knew of from historical accounts—though cold sober realism told me that these people were usually no more remarkable than the people who were cautious or lucky enough *not* to end up decorating historical accounts with their blood and entrails.

I gathered sufficient composure to inform him that I was Madame General Fraser and that I was sure my husband would shortly be along to pay his respects, directly I had located some supper.

"But you must come and dine with me, madame!" he said, and, having not let go of my hand, was in a position to tuck it cozily into his elbow and tow me off toward a large building that looked like an inn of some sort. An inn was precisely what it was, but an inn that had been commandeered by the Rebel forces and was now General Washington's headquarters—as I discovered when *le marquis* led me under a fluttering banner, through the taproom, and into a large back room where a number of officers were sitting at table, presided over by a large man who did not look precisely like the image on a dollar bill, but close enough.

"*Mon Général,*" the marquis said, bowing to Washington and then gesturing to me. "I have the honor to present to you Madame General Fraser, the personification of grace and loveliness!"

The table rose as one, with a screeching of wooden benches, and the men—in fact, there were only six of them—rose and bowed to me in turn, murmuring, "Your servant," and "Your most obedient, ma'am." Washington himself stood up at the head of the table—*My God, he's as tall as Jamie*, I thought—and gave me a very graceful bow, hand on his bosom.

"I am honored by your presence, Mrs. Fraser," he said, in a soft Virginia drawl. "Dare I hope that your husband accompanies you?"

I had a moment's insane impulse to reply, *"No, he sent me to fight instead,"* but managed not to say it.

"He does," I replied instead. "He's . . . er . . ." I gestured helplessly toward the doorway, where—with remarkably good timing—Jamie himself now appeared, brushing pine needles off his sleeve and saying something to Young Ian, behind him.

"There ye are!" he exclaimed, spotting me. "Someone told me ye'd gone off with a strange Frenchman. What—" He stopped abruptly, having suddenly realized that I wasn't merely in the company of a strange Frenchman.

The table fell about laughing, and La Fayette rushed up to Jamie and seized his hand, beaming.

"Mon frère d'armes!" He clicked his heels together, doubtless by reflex, and bowed. "I must apologize for having stolen your lovely wife, sir. Allow me, please, to make recompense by inviting you to dinner!"

I'd met Anthony Wayne before, at Ticonderoga, and was pleased to see him again. I was also delighted to see Dan Morgan, who gave me a hearty buss on both cheeks, and I admitted to a certain thrill at having my hand kissed by George Washington, though noticing the halitosis that accompanied his notorious dental problems. I wondered how I might make an opportunity to inspect his teeth, but gave such speculations up immediately with the arrival of a procession of servants with trays of fried fish, roast chicken, buttermilk biscuits with honey, and an amazing selection of ripe cheeses, these having been—he told me—brought by the marquis himself from France.

"Try this one," he urged me, cutting a slab of an extremely fragrant Roquefort, green-veined and crumbly. Nathanael Greene, who sat on the other side of the marquis, pinched his nose unobtrusively and gave me a small private smile. I smiled back—but in fact I quite liked strong cheese.

I wasn't the only one. Rollo, who had come in—naturally—with Young Ian and was sitting behind him, across the table from me, lifted his head and poked a long, hairy snout between Ian and General Lee, sniffing interestedly at the cheese.

"Good Christ!" Lee apparently hadn't noticed the dog before this and flung himself to one side, nearly ending in Jamie's lap. This action distracted Rollo, who turned to Lee, sniffing him with close attention.

I didn't blame the dog. Charles Lee was a tall, thin man with a long, thin nose and the most revolting eating habits I'd seen since Jemmy had learned to feed himself with a spoon. He not only talked while he ate and chewed with his mouth open, but was given to wild gestures while holding things in his hand, with the result that the front of his uniform was streaked with egg, soup, jelly, and a number of less identifiable substances.

Despite this, he was an amusing, witty man—and the others seemed to give him a certain deference. I wondered why; unlike some of the gentlemen at the table, Charles Lee never attained renown as a Revolutionary figure. He treated *them* with a certain . . . well, it wasn't scorn, certainly—condescension, perhaps?

I was taken up in conversation—mostly with the marquis, who was putting himself out to be charming to me, telling me how much he missed his wife (Good Lord, how old was he? I wondered. He didn't look more than twenty, if that), who had been responsible for the cheese. No, no, not making it herself, but it came from their estate at Chavaniac, which his wife ran most ably in his absence—but now and then caught a glimpse of Jamie. He took part in the conversation, but I could see his eyes flick round the table, appraising, judging. And they rested most often on General Lee, beside him.

Of course, he knew Wayne and Morgan quite well—and he knew what I'd been able to tell him about Washington and La Fayette. God, I hoped what I thought I knew about them was halfway accurate—but we'd find out soon enough if it wasn't.

Port wine was brought—evidently the meal was being hosted by the marquis; I had the distinct feeling that the high command of the Continental army didn't always eat this well. The men had largely avoided talking about the impending battle during the meal, but I could feel the subject looming like an approaching thunderstorm, bright-rimmed black clouds, excitingly shot with flickers of lightning. I began to rearrange my skirts and make gestures of incipient leave-taking, and saw Jamie, seated next to Lee across the table, notice and smile at me.

Lee noticed, too—he'd been gazing in an absent way at my décolletage—and broke off the anecdote he'd been telling Ian, seated on his other side.

"Such a pleasure to make your acquaintance, ma'am," he said cordially. "Your husband obliges us extremely by allowing us the delight of your company. I—"

Lee stopped abruptly in mid-sentence—and mid-bite, staring at Rollo, who had unobtrusively moved closer and was now standing no more than a couple of feet from the general. Given the low bench on which Lee was sitting and Rollo's size, this proximity placed them roughly eye-to-eye.

"Why is that dog looking at me like that?" Lee demanded, swinging round to glare at Ian.

"He's waitin' to see what ye drop next, I expect," Ian said, chewing placidly.

"If I were you, sir," Jamie put in politely, "I'd drop something quickly."

IAN, ROLLO, AND I took our leave of the generals and went out into the dark to find our beds, escorted by an orderly with a lantern. Fires burned high all up and down the bank of the Delaware, and many of the boats on the river had lanterns or open fires as well, the lights reflecting in the water like shoals of glimmering fish.

"Do you know anything about the man who ate beside you?" I asked Ian, in my hesitant Gaelic. He laughed—he and Jamie *always* laughed when I spoke Gaelic—but lifted one shoulder in a negative shrug.

"I do not, but I will find out," he said. "He is an Englishman, I can tell you that much."

He used the word "Sassenach," which gave me a mild shock. It had been a long time since I'd heard a Scot use that word in the way it was meant.

"Yes, he is. Do you think it makes a difference?" Technically, they were *all* still Englishmen—well, bar La Fayette, von Steuben, Kosciuszko, and similar oddities—but it was true that most of the Continental officers had been born and spent their lives in America. Lee hadn't. Ian made a derisory Scottish noise, indicating that it did.

"But I hear that he was adopted into the Kahnyen'kehaka, too," I objected.

Ian was silent for a moment, then took my arm, leaning close to speak in my ear.

"Auntie," he said softly. "D'ye think I ever stopped bein' a Scot?"

55

VESTAL VIRGINS

JAMIE AND I WERE billeted at the home of the Chenowyths, a pleasant—if understandably somewhat anxious—family whose home stood at the end of the single road that ran through Coryell's Ferry. Mrs. Chenowyth was in her wrapper, but greeted me kindly with a candlestick and took me to a small bedroom at the back of the house—this showing the evidence of hasty evacuation by a number of young Chenowyths, these presumably now sharing their parents' room, judging from the sounds of mixed heavy breathing.

The single bed was fairly large, though Jamie's feet would still stick out by a good six inches. There was a washbasin and ewer full of fresh water; I picked this up carefully and drank from it; my throat was dry from too much French wine. I replaced the ewer and sat down on the bed, feeling rather strange.

Possibly it was the wine. Possibly it was the fact that the room had no windows, and Mrs. Chenowyth had thoughtfully closed the door behind her. It was a small room, perhaps ten feet by eight. The air was still and the candle's flame burned high and steady, pure against the bricks of the wall. Perhaps it was the candle that brought to mind Uncle Lamb and the day he'd told me about vestal virgins, showing me a blue chalcedony carving from the temple of Vesta.

"Should a virgin betray her vows," he'd said, waggling his eyebrows at me,

"she'd be whipped, then sealed up alive in a small underground tomb, equipped with a table and chair, some water, and a single candle. And there she would die, when the air ran out."

I'd considered that with a sort of morbid relish—I might have been ten— and then asked with interest just *how* a vestal might betray her vows. Which is how I learned what used to be called "the facts of life," Uncle Lamb not being one to shirk any fact that wandered across his path, or mine. And while Uncle Lamb had assured me that the cult of Vesta had long since ceased operations, I had at that point resolved not to be a virgin, just in case. On the whole, a good resolution, though sleeping with men did have the most peculiar side effects.

Ian had brought along my saddlebags, which he'd dumped in the corner of the room before going off with Rollo to find his own sleeping place. I got up and fumbled for my toothbrush and tooth powder, though it seemed quite surreal to be brushing my teeth on what might be the eve of battle. Not *quite* rearranging the deck chairs on the Titanic . . . or at least I hoped not.

I knew that Washington and the marquis were going to survive whatever happened—and spared a thought for the strangeness of now thinking of them as men and not names. The large pores on George Washington's nose as he'd bent over my hand, and the shadowed pits of old smallpox scars across his lower cheeks; the smell of him, starch and sweat, wine and wig powder— for he wore his wig, hot as it was—the sweetly nasty smell of dental decay . . . I picked up my toothbrush, reminded, and set to work with some vigor. He'd smelled of blood, too; I wondered why—bleeding gums, perhaps?

I wriggled my way out of gown, jacket, and stays and stood for a bit flapping my shift, in hopes of admitting a little air. It made the candle flicker but didn't have much effect beyond that, so I blew the candle out and lay down.

I didn't expect to sleep. Adrenaline had been jolting through me like the current in a faulty circuit ever since we'd left Philadelphia, but now it was settling down to a steady humming in my blood. The conversation over dinner had been fairly general, but the atmosphere had been electric with anticipation. Clearly, once Ian and I had left and the plates had been removed . . . It was as close as I had ever been to a council of war, and the vibrations of it were still tingling through me.

There was anxiety tingling, too, to be sure—there had been amongst the men, as well. But given a suitable outlet, anxiety can be transformed into very effective action, and that's plainly what Washington and his generals were now doing, hammering out plans, assigning troops, drawing up strategies . . . I wished I was amongst them. It would be much easier than lying in the pitch dark, staring up into a boring infinity—nasty way to die, that.

I sat up, gulping air, and went hastily to the door. No sounds, no light seeping under the door. I patted round on the floor 'til I located my shoes and the puddle of my cloak and, swinging this over my shoulders, slipped out and made my way silently through the half-dark house, past the smoldering hearth and out.

The door was unbolted and on the latch; perhaps Mr. Chenowyth was out and expected back. I supposed there was some danger of my being locked out, but at this point spending the night in the midst of a military camp in my shift seemed preferable to sleeping—or, rather, not sleeping—in a tomb. Besides, I was sure that one of the small Chenowyths had wee'd in the bed fairly recently.

No one took any notice of me as I walked back along the road. The taverns and ordinaries were crammed full and spilling customers all over the road. Continental regulars in their blue and buff, swaggering about, the envy—they hoped—of the militiamen. Any number of women, too, and not all whores, by any means. But above all . . . air.

The heat of the day had largely gone, and while the air wasn't cold by any means, it wasn't stifling, either. Having escaped entombment, I reveled in the feeling of freedom—and what amounted to invisibility, for tall as I was, with my cloak on and my hair tied back in a plait for bed, I looked much like many of the militiamen in the dark; no one glanced twice at me.

The street and the camp beyond were electric; I recognized the feeling, and it gave me the oddest sense of dislocation—for I recognized it in its various forms from half of the battlefields I'd served near, from France in 1944 to Prestonpans and Saratoga. It wasn't always this way; often the sense of the occasion was one of dread—or worse. I remembered the night before Culloden and felt a wave of cold wash through me so strongly that I staggered and nearly fell against the wall of a building.

"Friend Claire?" said a voice, in amazement.

"Denzell?" Half-blinded by a number of torches being borne past, I blinked at the shape that had manifested before me.

"What is thee doing out here?" he said, alarmed. "Is anything wrong? Is it Jamie?"

"Well, you could say it's Jamie," I said, getting back my composure. "But there's nothing wrong, no. I was just getting a bit of air. What are *you* doing here?"

"I was fetching a pitcher of beer," he said, and took me firmly by the arm, steering me down the street. "Come with me. Thee ought not be in the street with the fighting men. Those that aren't drunk now will be shortly."

I didn't argue. His hand on my arm felt good, steadying me against the strange currents of the night that seemed to carry me willy-nilly into the past—and the future—and back again without warning.

"Where are Rachel and Dottie?" I asked, as we turned right at the end of the street and began to thread our way through the campfires and rows of tents.

"Rachel's gone somewhere with Ian; I didn't inquire. Dottie's in our medical tent, dealing with a case of acute indigestion."

"Oh, dear. What did she eat?"

He laughed softly. "The indigestion isn't hers. A woman named Peabody, who came in complaining of colic pains. Dorothea said she would administer something appropriate, if I would go and fetch her some beer—it being not safe for her to venture to the ordinary alone."

I thought I detected a small note of reproach in his voice, but I made an indeterminate "hmm" in response and he said no more about my wandering the streets *en déshabillé*. Possibly because he hadn't noticed that I was *en déshabillé,* until we entered the Hunters' big medical tent and I took my cloak off.

Denny gave me one brief, shocked look, coughed, and, picking up a canvas apron, managed to hand it to me without looking directly at me. Dottie, who was massaging the massive back of a very large woman seated hunched over on a stool in front of her, grinned at me over the woman's capped head.

"How are you, Auntie. Restless tonight?"

"Very," I replied frankly, putting on the apron. "This is Mrs. Peabody?"

"Yes." Dottie smothered a yawn with her shoulder. "The indigestion seems to be better—I gave her gripe water and peppermint," she added, to Denny. "But she's complaining of pains in her back, as well."

"Hmm." I came over and squatted down in front of the woman, who appeared to be half asleep—until I caught a whiff of her breath, which was eighty proof, at least. I put my hand on her belly to see if I could feel the location of the trouble, when she coughed thickly in a way I'd heard all too often before, choked—and I leapt back just in time.

"Thank you for the apron, Denny," I said mildly, brushing off some of the higher flecks of mud and vomit that had spattered on me. "I don't suppose you brought a birthing stool with you?"

"A birthing stool. To a battle?" he said faintly, his eyes bulging slightly behind his spectacles as he looked at the woman, now swaying ponderously to and fro, like a large bell making up its mind whether to ring or not.

"I rather think it may be one," I said, glancing round. "*If* she's in labor. Can you find a blanket, Dottie? I think we'll have to lay her on the ground; she'll collapse the cot."

It took all three of us to wrestle Mrs. Peabody—who relapsed comfortably into unconsciousness the moment we touched her—onto a blanket spread on the ground under the lantern. There was an almost instant insurgence of moths, as they came fluttering in, attracted not only by the light but by the assorted smells thickening the air.

Mrs. Peabody had lapsed not merely into unconsciousness but into what appeared to be an alcoholic coma. After a certain amount of discussion, we'd turned her onto one side, in case she should vomit again, and the position had allowed her belly to flow away from the rest of her corpulent body, so that it lay on the ground in front of her, gravid and sac-like. She looked like the queen of some order of social insect, ready to deliver in the thousands, but I refrained from mentioning this, as Dottie was still pale.

Denzell had recovered from the shock and was keeping an eye—or rather a hand—on her wrist, keeping track of her pulse. "Amazingly strong," he said at last, letting go, and looked up at me. "Does thee think she is near her time?"

"I really hope *not,*" I said, looking down. "But there's no telling without . . . er . . . closer examination." I took a deep breath and a grip on my more generous instincts. "Would you like me to . . . er . . . ."

"I'll go and find clean water," he said, springing to his feet and seizing a bucket.

Given that Dottie was engaged to Denny, I refrained from calling him a coward in her presence and merely waved him off in a reserved manner. Mrs. Peabody made me uneasy on a number of scores. I had no idea whether she might be about to go into labor, or, if she did, how her comatose state might affect it. The level of alcohol in her blood was certainly affecting the child's; would a drunken newborn be able to breathe? It wouldn't vomit, as there wasn't anything in its stomach *to* vomit, but might it void its bowels in utero and aspirate the material? That was a remarkably dangerous thing to happen even in a modern hospital with a full delivery-suite staff attending—most of the babies who did that died of suffocation, lung injury, or infection.

I was very much ashamed to admit to myself that my chief fear, though, was that something would happen during delivery that would require me to remain with mother and/or child for a prolonged period. I could not, by my oath as a physician—and what I conceived my responsibilities to be—abandon a patient in dire need of me.

But I *would* not abandon Jamie. I knew beyond all doubt that he was going into battle, and soon. He wasn't going without me.

A slight noise jerked me out of my hypothetical moral quandary. Dottie had started unpacking and had dropped an amputation saw. She stooped to pick it up and said something under her breath in German that I thought was probably a bad word—John always swore in German; perhaps it was a family habit.

Thought of John added another layer of guilt to my complicated feelings—though the logical part of my brain firmly rejected this as undeserved. Still, the worry for him couldn't be rejected so easily, though I did my best to tuck it away for the present.

"You needn't stay up, Dottie," I said. "I can take care of matters here. Nothing's going to happen immediately, regardless—I can make up the surgical kits."

"No, that's all right," she said, and then yawned involuntarily, gaping so widely that she startled herself and clapped a hand belatedly over her mouth. "Oh, dear. I do beg your pardon, Mrs. Fraser." That made me smile; she had John's elegant manners—perhaps Hal did, too, when he wasn't engaging in undiluted bastardliness.

"Actually," she said, fixing me directly with her striking gaze, "I'm pleased to have a chance to talk with you in privacy."

"Oh?" I said, squatting to put a hand on Mrs. Peabody's belly. I wasn't feeling any movement from the baby, but they usually did go quiet if labor was impending. I could have used my stethoscope to listen for a fetal heartbeat, but it was in one of the boxes or bags that Ian and the orderly had carried off somewhere. Besides, whatever I heard or didn't would make no difference to the immediate protocol.

"Yes." Dottie sat down on a packing case as though it were a throne—like all the Greys I'd met, she had excellent posture. "I want to know the correct way of performing sexual intercourse."

"Oh. Erm . . ."

She glanced down at Mrs. Peabody.

"And whether there is any way of preventing . . . er . . ."

"Pregnancy. To be sure." I cleared my throat. I rather thought the sight of Mrs. Peabody would have put most young women off the idea of childbearing—if not sex—altogether. Dorothea Grey, though, was plainly a young woman of blood and iron.

"Don't mistake me, Auntie," she said earnestly. "Or do I mean Friend Claire? I *do* want children—want them terribly. But if there is any choice about giving birth on a battlefield or a moving ship, say—"

I seized on this last, in part to give myself time to compose something coherent in the way of advice. I'd rather thought Rachel might want to talk about such things at some point, having no mother, but . . .

"A ship? Are you thinking of going home to England, then?"

She grimaced in a way that brought her father vividly before me, and I nearly laughed but fortunately didn't.

"I don't know. I dearly want to see Mama again, of course, and Adam . . . and my . . . well, actually, I doubt I should see any of my friends again." She waved a hand, dismissing the friends. "Not that there aren't any Quakers in society, but they're all very rich, and we won't be."

She bit her lip, but in a way indicating calculation rather than chagrin.

"If I can contrive to make Denny marry me here, so that we arrived in England as husband and wife already, it would be a simple matter to find a London meeting that would welcome us. Whereas here—" She flung out a hand toward the hum of the camp around us. "His involvement in the war would always stand in his way, you see?"

"Even after the war is over?"

She gave me a patient look, too old for her face.

"Papa says that wars take three generations to fade from the ground where they're fought. And from what I've seen, Friends have quite long memories, as well."

"He might just have a point." Mrs. Peabody had begun to snore wetly, but I felt no sense of contraction. I rubbed a hand through my hair and braced my back more comfortably against one of the packing crates set against the wall. "All right. Perhaps . . . a little basic anatomy, to begin with."

I really had no idea how much—if anything—a nobly born young woman might have been told, or found out by other means, so began with female reproductive anatomy, starting with the womb—for surely she knew what that was—and leading outward, part by part.

"You mean it has a *name?*" she exclaimed, charmed, when I got to the clitoris. "I'd always thought of it as just, you know . . . *that* bit." Her tone of voice made it abundantly clear that I needn't explain what *that* bit did, and I laughed.

"To the best of my knowledge, it's the only structure of the human body that appears to have no function whatever save the pleasure of the owner."

"But men . . . don't they . . . ?"

"Well, yes, they do," I said. "And very pleasurable they find theirs, too. But a penis is extremely functional, as well. You, er . . . do know how it . . . works? In terms of intercourse?"

"Denzell won't let me touch his naked member, and I'm *longing* to see it at my leisure—not just the odd glimpse when he, well, you know." Her eyes sparkled at the thought. "But I know what it feels like through his breeches.

I was amazed, the first time it went stiff under my hand! However does it do that?"

I explained the concept of hydrostatic pressure as simply as possible, already seeing what was coming next. I cleared my throat and rose to my knees.

"I need to examine Mrs. Peabody for any sign of labor. And while we must be respectful of her privacy—so far as such a thing exists under these conditions"—for Dottie had snorted loudly—"since you're assisting me here, there's no reason why you shouldn't observe what I'm doing, and I'll explain it to you as we go. How things . . . work."

She hummed with interest as I gingerly unveiled Mrs. Peabody's nether regions, which were thickly forested but still identifiably—very identifiably—feminine.

"When the cervix—that's the opening to the womb—when it begins to open in order for the baby to come out, there's often some blood and mucus released, but it's quite harmless. I don't see any sign of it yet, though." That heartened me.

"Oh," said Dottie, rather faintly. But she leaned intently over my shoulder as I carefully inserted my freshly washed hand. "Oh!" Dottie said, in tones of extreme revelation. "*That's* where it goes!"

"Well, yes, it is," I said, trying not to laugh—and failing. "Denzell would have told you, I expect. Did you ask him?"

"No," she said, sitting back a little on her heels but still watching closely as I put a hand on Mrs. Peabody's abdomen and felt the cervix. Softened, but still firm. I began to breathe again.

"No?" I said, only half-attending.

"No." She drew herself up. "I didn't want to seem ignorant. Denny's so—I mean, he's *educated*. I can read, of course, and write, but only letters, and play music, but that's useless. I bustle round after him and help where I can, of course, and he's always so good about explaining things . . . but . . . well, I kept having this vision of our wedding night and him explaining it to me in just the same way he'd tell me how to suck the snot out of a child's nose with a tube or hold the skin together so he could stitch a wound. And . . ." She made a graceful little moue, which had to be her mother's legacy. "And I made up my mind it wasn't going to be that way."

"Very . . . um . . . commendable." I withdrew my hand and wiped it, recovered Mrs. Peabody, and checked her pulse again—slow, but strong as a tympani; the woman must have the heart of an ox. "How—er—how *do* you want it to be? Bearing in mind," I hastened to add, "that this sort of thing is rather variable." Another thought occurred to me. "Has Denzell ever . . . ? Though I don't suppose you'd know."

Her soft white brow wrinkled in thought.

"I don't know; I never thought of asking him. I just assumed—well, I have brothers. I know *they* have, because they talk about it—whores, I mean—with their friends. I suppose I thought all men . . . but, come to think, perhaps Denny wouldn't go to a prostitute. Do you think he might have?" Her brow furrowed a little, but she didn't seem upset at the thought. Of course, it was probably commonly accepted in the Greys' social circle that men, or soldiers at least, naturally would.

With very vivid memories of my own wedding night—and my stupefaction upon being informed that my bridegroom was a virgin—I temporized a bit.

"Possibly not. Now, being a medical man, plainly he must know the essential mechanics. But there *is* more to it than that."

Her eyes grew brighter and she leaned forward, hands on her knees. "Tell me."

"RATHER LIKE EGG white mixed with a drop or two of civet. Theoretically good for the skin, though frankly—" I was saying, when I heard the sound of voices just outside the tent.

Rachel and Ian had returned, looking cheerful, flushed, and quite like young people who had just passed the last hour or two doing the sorts of things in which I'd been instructing Dottie. I saw her glance sideways at Rachel, then—very briefly—at Ian's breeches. Her color went up a notch.

Rachel didn't notice, her attention having fixed at once on Mrs. Peabody—well, everyone's attention was fixed on Mrs. Peabody; it was really impossible to look at anything else. She frowned at the supine woman on the ground and then looked at me.

"Where's Denzell?"

"An excellent question. He left a quarter of an hour ago to find water. There's beer, though, if you're thirsty." I nodded at the neglected pitcher.

Ian poured a cup for Rachel, waited while she drank it, then refilled it for himself, eyes still fixed on Mrs. Peabody, who was emitting a remarkable variety of noises, though still out cold.

"Does Uncle Jamie ken where ye are, Auntie?" he asked. "He was lookin' for ye just now. He said he'd put ye somewhere safe to sleep, but ye'd escaped. Again," he added with a broad grin.

"Oh," I said. "He's finished with the generals for the night, then?"

"Aye, he went to make the acquaintance o' some of the militia captains under him, but most had gone to sleep by then, so he went to join ye at the Chenowyths. Mrs. Chenowyth was a bit taken aback to find ye gone," he added delicately.

"I just came out for a little air," I said, defensive. "And then—" I gestured at the patient on the floor, who had now settled down to a rhythmic snore. Her color was looking better; that was heartening. "Er . . . is Jamie put out, do you think?"

Ian and Rachel both laughed at that.

"No, Auntie," Ian said. "But he's dead tired, and he wants ye bad."

"Did he tell you to say that?"

"Not in precisely those words," Rachel said, "but his meaning was plain." She turned to Ian, with a quick squeeze of his arm. "Would thee go and find Denny, Ian? Claire can't leave this woman alone—I think?" she asked, arching a brow at me.

"Not yet," I said. "She doesn't seem to be going into labor immediately"—I crossed my fingers against the possibility—"but she oughtn't to be left alone in this state."

"Aye, of course." Ian yawned suddenly, widely, but then shook himself back into alertness. "If I come across Uncle Jamie, I'll tell him where ye are, Auntie."

He left, and Rachel poured another cup of beer, which she offered me. It was room temperature—and a warm room, at that—but refreshingly sour and strong. I hadn't really thought I was tired, but the beer revivified me astonishingly.

Dottie, having checked Mrs. Peabody's pulse and breathing, laid a ginger hand on the distended bulge of pregnancy. "Has thee attended a birth before, good-sister?" Dottie asked Rachel, being careful of her plain speech.

"Several," Rachel replied, squatting down by Mrs. Peabody. "This looks somewhat different, though. Has she suffered some injur—oh!" The brewery reek hit her, and she reared back and coughed. "I see."

Mrs. Peabody uttered a loud moan and everyone stiffened. I wiped my hands on my apron, just in case. She relaxed again, though, and after a few moments' contemplative silence to see if Mrs. Peabody would do it again, Dottie took a deep breath.

"Mrs.—I mean, Friend Claire was just telling me some very interesting things. Regarding . . . er . . . what to expect on one's wedding night."

Rachel looked up with interest.

"I should welcome any such instruction myself. I know where the . . . um . . . parts go, because I've seen them go there fairly frequently, but—"

"You *have*?!?" Dottie gawked at her, and Rachel laughed.

"I have. But Ian assures me that he has more skill than the average bull or billy goat, and my observations are limited to the animal world, I'm afraid." A small line showed between her brows. "The woman who cared for me after the death of my parents was . . . very dutiful in informing me of my womanly obligations, but her instructions consisted largely of 'Spread thy legs, grit thy teeth, girl, and let him.'"

I sat down on the packing case and stretched to ease my back, suppressing a groan. God knew how long it might take Ian to find Jamie among the teeming hordes. And I did hope that Denny hadn't been knocked on the head or trampled by a mule.

"Pour me another cup of beer, will you? And have some more yourselves. I suspect we may need it."

". . . and if he says, 'Oh, God, oh, God,' at some point," I advised, "take note of what you were just doing, so you can do it again next time."

Rachel laughed, but Dottie frowned a little, looking slightly cross-eyed.

"Do you—does thee—think Denny would take the Lord's name in vain, even under those circumstances?"

"I've heard him do it on much less provocation than that," Rachel assured her, stifling a burp with the back of her hand. "He tries to be perfect in thy company, thee knows, for fear thee will change thy mind."

"He does?" Dottie looked surprised but rather pleased. "Oh. I wouldn't, thee knows. Ought I to tell him?"

"Not until he says, 'Oh, God, oh, God,' for thee," Rachel said, succumbing to a giggle.

"I wouldn't worry," I said. "If a man says, 'Oh, God,' in that situation, he nearly always means it as a prayer."

Dottie's fair brows drew together in concentration.

"A prayer of desperation? Or gratitude?"

"Well . . . that's up to you," I said, and stifled a small belch of my own.

Approaching male voices outside the tent made us all glance self-consciously at the empty beer pitcher and sit up straight, poking at our slightly disheveled hair, but none of the gentlemen who came in were in any condition to cast stones.

Ian had found Denzell *and* Jamie, and somewhere along the way they had acquired a small, stout companion in a cocked hat, with his hair in a stumpy pigtail. All of them were flushed and, while certainly not staggering, were surrounded by a distinct haze of fermented barleycorn.

"There ye are, Sassenach!" Jamie brightened still further at seeing me, and I felt a small rush of delight at it. "Are ye—who's this?" He had been advancing toward me, hand outstretched, but stopped abruptly at sight of Mrs. Peabody, who was lying with her arms flung out, mouth wide open.

"That's the lady I told ye about, Uncle Jamie." Ian wasn't staggering, either, but was distinctly swaying and took hold of the tent pole to steady himself. "The one that's . . . ehm . . ." He gestured with his free hand to the gentleman in the cocked hat. "She's his wife."

"Oh? Aye, I see." He edged gingerly around Mrs. Peabody's recumbent form. "She's no dead, is she?"

"No," I said. "I think I would have noticed." He might have been somewhat inebriated, but still caught the faint dubious emphasis I'd placed on "think." He knelt down carefully and put a hand in front of her open mouth.

"Nay, only drunk," he said cheerfully. "Shall we lend ye a hand to take her home, Mr. Peabody?"

"Better lend him a wheelbarrow," Dottie whispered to Rachel, beside me, but luckily no one noticed.

"That would be kindly of you, sir." Surprisingly, Mr. Peabody appeared to be the only sober one of the lot. He knelt and smoothed the damp hair tenderly off his wife's brow. "Lulu? Wake up, darling. Time to be going now."

To my surprise, she opened her eyes and, after blinking several times in confusion, appeared to fix her gaze on her husband.

"There you are, Simon!" she said, and, with a rapturous smile, fell soundly back asleep.

Jamie rose slowly, and I could hear the small bones in his back pop as he eased himself. He was still flushed and smiling, but Ian had been right—he *was* dead tired. I could see the deep lines of weariness in his face and the hollows under his bones.

Ian saw them, too.

"Auntie Claire's in need of her bed, Uncle Jamie," he said, squeezing Jamie's shoulder and giving me a meaning look. "It's been a long night for her. Take her along, aye? Denny and I can help Mr. Peabody."

Jamie gave his nephew a sharp look and then turned the same look on me, but I obligingly yawned widely enough to make my jaw crack—no great effort—and with a final quick look at Mrs. Peabody to be *sure* she was neither dying nor going into labor, I took his arm and towed him determinedly outside, waving briefly in farewell.

Outside, we both drew deep breaths of fresh air, sighed in unison, and laughed.

"It *has* been rather a long night, hasn't it?" I put my forehead against his chest and my arms around him, slowly rubbing the knobs of his vertebrae through his coat. "What happened?"

He sighed again and kissed the top of my head.

"I've command of ten companies of mixed militia from Pennyslvania and New Jersey; the marquis has command of a thousand men—including mine—and is in charge of a plan to go and bite the British army in the arse."

"Sounds like fun." The racket of the camp had died down considerably, but the thick air still held the vibrations of many men, awake or uneasily asleep. I thought I could feel that same expectant vibration pass through Jamie, in spite of his obvious tiredness. "You need sleep, then."

His arm tightened round me and his free hand traveled slowly down my back. I'd left Denny's apron in the tent, and my cloak was over my arm; the thin muslin of my shift might as well have not existed.

"Oh, God," he said, and his big, warm hand cupped my buttock with a sudden urgency. "I need *you*, Sassenach. I need ye bad."

The shift was just as thin in front as in back; I could feel his waistcoat buttons—and a few other things—through it. He did want me bad.

"Do you mind doing it in a crypt that smells of wee?" I asked, thinking of the Chenowyths' back bedroom.

"I've taken ye in worse places, Sassenach."

Before I could say, "Name three," the tent flap opened to disgorge a small procession, this consisting of Denzell, Dottie, Rachel, and Ian, each couple carrying one end of a canvas sheet on which lay the protuberant form of Mrs. Peabody. Mr. Peabody led the way, lantern held high.

We were standing in shadow, and they passed without noticing us, the girls giggling at the occasional stumble, the young men grunting with effort, and Mr. Peabody calling out encouragement as they made their laborious way through the darkness, presumably heading for the Peabody abode.

The tent stood before us, dark and invitingly empty.

"Aye?"

"Oh, yes."

The stretcher bearers had taken the lantern, and the setting moon was the barest sliver above the horizon; the inside of the tent was filled with a soft, dusty black that rose up around us in a fragrantly alcoholic cloud—with a faint tang of vomit—when we stepped inside.

I recalled exactly where things were, though, and we managed to push together four of the packing crates. I spread my cloak on these, he took off his coat and waistcoat, and we lay down precariously in the beery dark together.

"How long do you think we have?" I asked, undoing his flies. His flesh was warm and hard under my hand, and his skin there soft as polished silk.

"Long enough," he said, and brushed my nipple with his thumb, slowly, in spite of his own apparent urgency. "Dinna hurry yourself, Sassenach. There's no telling when we'll have the chance again."

He kissed me lingeringly, his mouth tasting of Roquefort and port. I could feel the vibration of the camp here, too—it ran through both of us like a fiddle string pegged tight.

"I dinna think I've got time to make ye scream, Sassenach," he whispered in my ear. "But I've maybe time to make ye moan?"

"Well, possibly. It's some time 'til dawn, isn't it?"

Whether it was the beer and premarital explanations, the late hour and lure of secrecy—or only Jamie himself and our increasing need to shut out the world and know only each other—he had time, and to spare.

"Oh, God," he said at last, and came down slowly on me, his heart beating heavy against my ribs. "Oh . . . God."

I felt my own pulse throb in hands and bones and center, but couldn't manage any response more eloquent than a faint "Ooh." After a bit, though, I recovered enough to stroke his hair.

"We'll go home again soon," I whispered to him. "And have all the time in the world."

That got me a softly affirmative Scottish noise, and we lay there for a bit longer, not wanting to come apart and get dressed, though the packing cases were hard and the possibility of discovery increasing with each passing minute.

At last he stirred, but not to rise.

"Oh, God," he said softly, in another tone altogether. "Three hundred men." And held me tighter.

56

STINKING PAPIST

THE SUN WASN'T YET above the horizon, but the horse park was busy as an anthill, full of grooms, foragers, teamsters, and farriers, all scurrying about their business in an incongruous soft pink light filled with the sound of hundreds of pairs of steadily champing jaws. William picked up the bay gelding's hoof and held out his hand for the hoof pick his new, small groom was clutching nervously to his chest.

"Now, come here, Zeb," he said coaxingly. "I'll show you how it's done; there's nothing to it."

"Yes, sir." Zebedee Jeffers edged an inch closer, eyes flicking back and forth from the hoof to the towering mass of horseflesh. Jeffers did not like horses. He particularly didn't like Visigoth. William thought it was just as well that Zeb likely didn't know what a Visigoth was.

"All right. See there?" He tapped the pick against the shadow: the edge of a small rock that had trapped itself under the curve of the iron shoe during the night. "It's only a little one, but it feels just like a pebble in your own shoe would feel, and he'll go lame if we don't take care of it. Here, it's not stuck fast; do you want to try?"

"No, sir," Zeb said honestly. Zebedee came from the shore of Maryland and knew about oysters, boats, and fish. Not horses.

"He won't hurt you," William said, with a touch of impatience. He'd be riding back and forth along the columns a dozen times a day, carrying dispatches and gathering reports; both his horses needed to be kept ready, his regular groom, Colenso Baragwanath, was down with a fever, and he hadn't time to find another servant.

"Yes, he will. Sir," Zeb added as an afterthought. "See?" He held out a scrawny arm, displaying what was undoubtedly a festering bite mark.

William suppressed the urge to ask what the devil the boy had been doing to the horse. Visigoth wasn't a bad-tempered horse on the whole, but he could be irritable, and Zeb's nervous fidgeting was enough to try anyone, let alone a tired and hungry horse.

"All right," he said with a sigh, and pried the rock loose with one sharp dig. "Better, then?" he said to the horse, running a hand down the leg and then patting Goth's flank. He felt in his pocket and drew out a bunch of limp carrots, bought the night before from a farmwoman who'd come through camp with baskets of produce on a yoke across her broad shoulders.

"Here. Give him that; make friends with him," he suggested, handing a carrot to Zeb. "Hold it flat on your hand." Before the boy could extend this putative olive branch, though, the horse reached down and snatched it from his fingers with an audible crunch of big yellow teeth. The boy uttered a small shriek and took several steps back, collided with a bucket, and fell over it, arse over teakettle.

Torn between annoyance and an unseemly urge to laugh, William smothered both and went to pick his groom out of a manure pile.

"Tell you what," he said, dusting the boy off with a firm hand, "you see that *all* my dunnage is aboard the baggage wagon, see if Colenso needs anything, and make sure there's something for me to eat tonight. I'll ask Sutherland's groom to tend the horses."

Zeb sagged with relief.

"Thank you, sir!"

"And go see one of the surgeons and have that arm tended to!" William shouted after him, above the rising sound of braying and whickering. The boy's shoulders rose up around his ears and he walked faster, pretending he hadn't heard.

William saddled Goth himself—he always did, not trusting anyone else to check tack that his life might depend on—then left him with his other horse, Madras, and went to find Lord Sutherland's groom. Despite the bustle, he had no trouble finding the string; Sutherland had ten horses, all prime creatures of sixteen hands or so, and at least a dozen grooms to tend them. William was just concluding negotiations with one of these when he caught sight of a familiar face among the throng.

"Shit," he said, under his breath, but Captain Richardson had seen him and was coming toward him, smiling genially.

"Captain Lord Ellesmere. Your servant, sir."

"Yours, sir," William said, as pleasantly as he could. *What did the scoundrel want now?* he wondered. Not that Richardson *was* a scoundrel—or not necessarily one, despite Randall's warning. It might, after all, be Randall who was the scoundrel. But he did hold rather a grudge against Richardson, on Mother Claire's account, as well as his own. The thought of Mother Claire stabbed him unexpectedly, and he forced it back. None of it was *her* fault.

"I'm surprised to see you here, your lordship," Richardson said, glancing round at the roiling camp. The sun was up, and bands of gold lit the fog of dust rising from the mules' rough coats. "You are a conventioneer, are you not?"

"I am," William said coldly. Richardson certainly knew he was. William felt obliged to defend himself, though against what, he wasn't sure. "I cannot fight." He spread his arms slightly. "As you see, I carry no weapons." He made polite motions indicating his immediate need to be elsewhere, but Richardson went on standing there, smiling with that very ordinary face, so unremarkable that his own mother probably couldn't pick him out of a crowd, save for a large brown mole on the side of his chin.

"Ah, to be sure." Richardson drew a little closer, lowering his voice. "That being the case . . . I wonder whether—"

"No," William said definitely. "I am one of General Clinton's aides, and I cannot leave my duty. You will excuse me, sir; I am expected."

He turned on his heel and made off, his heart hammering—and realized rather belatedly that he had left his horse behind. Richardson was still standing at the far side of the horse park, talking to a groom who was taking down the pickets, coiling the rope around one shoulder as he did so. The crowd of horses and mules was swiftly diminishing, but there were enough still near Visigoth to enable William to duck in and pretend to be fiddling with his saddlebags, head bent to hide his face until Richardson should go away.

The conversation had left him with an unsettling image of his erstwhile stepmother as he had last seen her, disheveled and *en déshabillé* but glowing with a radiant life he had never seen. He didn't suppose she was his stepmother anymore, but he'd liked her. Belatedly, it occurred to him that Claire now-Fraser still *was* his stepmother—by a different father. . . . Bloody hell.

He set his teeth, rummaging in the saddlebag for his canteen. Now that that Scotch bugger had returned from his watery grave, throwing everything and everyone into confusion . . . why couldn't he have drowned and never come back?

Never come back.

"You are a stinking Papist, and your baptismal name is James." He froze as though shot in the back. He bloody remembered it. The stables at Helwater, the warm smell of horses and mash, and the prickle of straw that worked its

way through his stockings. Cold stone floors. He'd been crying . . . Why? All he recalled was a huge wash of desolation, total helplessness. The end of the world. Mac leaving.

He took a long, slow breath and pressed his lips together. Mac. The word didn't bring back a face; he couldn't remember what Mac had looked like. He'd been big, that was all. Bigger than Grandfather or any of the footmen or the other grooms. *Safety. A sense of constant happiness like a soft, worn blanket.*

"Shit," he whispered, closing his eyes. And had that happiness been a lie, too? He'd been too little to know the difference between a groom's deference to the young master and real kindness. But . . .

"'You are a stinking Papist,'" he whispered, and caught his breath on something that might have been a sob. "'And your baptismal name is James.'"

"It was the only name I had a right to give ye."

He realized that his knuckles were pressed against his chest, against his gorget—but it wasn't the gorget's reassurance that he sought. It was that of the little bumps of the plain wooden rosary that he'd worn around his neck for years, hidden under his shirt where no one would see it. The rosary Mac had given him . . . along with his name.

With a suddenness that shocked him, he felt his eyes swim. *You went away. You left me!*

"Shit!" he said, and punched his fist so hard into the saddlebag that the horse snorted and shied, and a bolt of white-hot pain shot up his arm, obliterating everything.

57

DO NOT GO GENTLE INTO THAT GOOD NIGHT

IAN WOKE JUST BEFORE dawn to find his uncle squatting beside him.

"I'm away to break bread wi' the captains of my companies," Jamie said without preamble. "Ye'll report to Colonel Wilbur as a scout. And will ye see about horses, Ian? I'll need a spare mount, gun-broke, and so will you." He dropped a purse on Ian's chest, smiled, and vanished into the morning mist.

Ian rolled slowly out of his blanket, stretching. He'd chosen his resting spot well away from the main camp, on a small rise of ground near the river. He didn't bother wondering how Uncle Jamie had found him, or waste time in marveling at his uncle's recuperative powers.

He took his time about his preparations, dressed carefully, and found some food, thinking over the things that must be done. He'd dreamed during the night, and the dream was still on him, though he couldn't recall the details. He'd been in thick woods, and something was there with him, hiding among the leaves. He wasn't sure what it was, or even if he'd seen it, but the sense of danger lingered uneasily between his shoulder blades. He'd heard a raven calling in his dream, and that was certainly a warning of some kind—but then the raven had flown past him, and it wasn't a raven at all but a white bird of some kind. Its wing had touched his cheek in flight, and he could still feel the brush of its feathers.

White animals were messengers. Both the Mohawk and the Highlanders said so.

He was an Indian and a Highlander; dreams were not to be dismissed. Sometimes the meaning of a dream floated to the surface of your mind like a drowned leaf rising. He let it go, hoping the dream would return to explain itself, and went about his work, seeing Colonel Wilbur, finding and haggling for two reasonable horses, big enough to bear a large man through battle . . . but the white bird stayed by him all day long, hovering just above his right shoulder, a glimpse now and then in the corner of his eye.

IN THE LATE afternoon, his business done for the moment, he returned to the main camp and found Rachel standing in line with a number of other women at the well in the yard of the Goose and Grapes, two buckets resting at her feet.

"I could take those down to the river for ye," he offered. She was flushed with the heat of the day but looked beautiful, her bare arms brown and the curving muscle of them so neat and delicate that it lifted his heart to look at them.

"I thank thee, Ian, but no." She smiled up at him and reached to tweak one of the two eagle feathers he'd knotted into his hair. "Thy auntie says the boats throw their waste into the river, and half the army is pissing in it, as well, and she's right. I should need to walk a mile upstream to find a clean place from which to draw water. Is thee about thy business, then?"

She spoke with interest but with no sense of concern or disapproval, and he appreciated that.

"I willna kill anyone unless I have to, Rachel," he said softly, and touched her cheek. "I'm signed on as a scout. I shouldna have to."

"But things happen," she said, and looked away, to keep him seeing the sudden shadow in her eyes. "I know."

With an unexpected spurt of impatience, he wanted to ask her: would she rather he kill or *be* killed for the sake of his soul's grace? But he smothered the impulse, and the tinge of anger with it. She loved him, he didn't doubt that. It was maybe a fair question to put to a Quaker, but not to his betrothed.

Her eyes were on his face, interested and thoughtful, and he felt a slight flush rise in his cheeks, wondering just how much of his thoughts showed.

"Thy life's journey lies along its own path, Ian," she said, "and I cannot share thy journey—but I can walk beside thee. And I will."

The woman standing behind them in the line heaved a deep, contented sigh.

"Now, that's a very pretty and right thing to say, sweetheart," she said to Rachel, in approving tones. And, switching her gaze to Ian, looked him skeptically up and down. He was dressed in buckskins, clout, and calico shirt, and, bar the feathers in his hair and the tattoos, didn't look too outlandish, he thought.

"You probably don't deserve her," the woman said, shaking her head doubtfully. "But try, there's a good lad."

HE CARRIED THE water for Rachel, making their way through the sprawl of the camp toward the place where Denzell had set up his medical practice. The tent was still standing, but Denzell's wagon with its painted goldfinches on the tailboard was drawn up beside it, Dottie standing in it, and Denzell handing up parcels and boxes to her.

Rachel stood on tiptoe to kiss his cheek, then vanished into the tent to help with the packing.

"Wilt thee join us later, Ian?" Denny looked up from the pack he was strapping together.

"Anywhere, *a bhràthair*," Ian said, smiling. "Where are ye bound, then?"

"Oh. Nowhere." Denny took off his spectacles, polishing them absently on the tail of his shirt. "It's not yet First Day, but we may well be engaged in battle then; we thought to hold meeting before supper tonight. We would be pleased if thee feels it good to sit with us, but if not . . ."

"No, I'll come," Ian said quickly. "To be sure. Ah . . . where . . . ?" He waved a hand vaguely, indicating the half-ordered chaos of the camp surrounding them. New companies of militia were still coming in from New Jersey and Pennsylvania to join the Continental soldiers, and while officers had been assigned to receive and organize these and help them find campgrounds, they were swiftly overwhelmed. Men were making camp anywhere they could find open ground, and there was great to-ing and fro-ing in search of water and food, arguments and raised voices, and the sound of industrious shoveling and muttered curses nearby indicated the creation of yet another set of sanitary trenches. A constant small procession of persons who couldn't wait visited a nearby copse in hopes of a private moment. Ian made a mental note to step wary if he walked that way.

"Ye dinna mean to do it here, surely?" People came in and out all day, in need of the doctor's attention, and wouldn't be likely to stop, only because meeting was being held.

"Friend Jamie says he will provide us a refuge," Denny assured him. "We'll go as soon as—who has thee there, Dorothea?"

Dottie was stowing supplies but had paused to talk with a young girl who had climbed up to kneel on the wagon's seat and was addressing Dorothea earnestly.

"It's a woman in childbed, Denny," she called. "Three campfires over!"

"Urgent?" Denny at once began unstrapping the pack he had just done up.

"This child says so." Dottie straightened up and tucked her straggling fair hair back under her cap. "It's her mother's fourth; no trouble with the first three, but given the conditions . . ." She sidled past the baggage to the lowered tailboard, and Ian gave her a hand to hop down.

"She really wanted Mrs. Fraser," Dottie said to Denny, *sotto voce*. "But she'll settle for you." She dimpled. "Is thee flattered?"

"I see my reputation spreads like pomade on a silken pillow," he replied tranquilly. "And thy use of plain speech inflames me. Thee had best come with me. Will thee watch the wagon, Ian?"

The two of them made off through the maze of wagons, horses, and stray pigs—some enterprising farmer had driven a dozen lean hogs into camp, seeking to sell them to the quartermaster, but the pigs had taken fright at the inadvertent explosion of a musket nearby and run off among the crowd, causing mass confusion. Rollo had run one down and broken its neck; Ian had bled and eviscerated the carcass and—after giving Rollo the heart and lights—stashed it under damp canvas, hidden beneath Denzell's wagon. Should he meet the distraught swineherd, he'd pay him for the beast, but he wasn't letting it out of his sight. He stole a quick glance under the skirting board, but the canvas-covered lump was still there.

Rollo moved a little and made an odd sound, not quite a whine, that shifted Ian's attention at once to the dog.

"How is it, *a choin?*" he asked. Rollo at once licked his hand and panted in a genial fashion, but Ian slid off the wagon tongue and knelt in the leaves, feeling his way over the big, shaggy body, just in case. Palpating, Auntie Claire called it, a word that always made Ian smile.

He found a little tenderness where the dog had been shot the autumn before, in the meat of the shoulder just above the foreleg, but that was always there. And a spot on his spine, a few inches forward of the beast's tail, that made him splay his legs and groan when it was pressed. Maybe Rollo had strained himself taking down the hog.

"None sae young as ye used to be, are ye, *a choin?*" he asked, scratching Rollo's whitened jaw.

"None of us are, *a mac mo pheathar,*" said his uncle Jamie, coming out of the gloaming and sitting down on the stump Dottie had been using to mount the wagon. He was wearing full uniform and looked hot. Ian passed over his canteen and Jamie took it with a nod of thanks, wiping his sleeve across his face.

"Aye, day after tomorrow," he said, in answer to Ian's raised brow. "First light, if not before. Wee Gilbert's got command of a thousand men and permission to go after the rear guard."

"You—I mean us"—Ian corrected himself—"with him?"

Jamie nodded and drank deep. Ian thought he looked a bit tense, but, after all, he was in command of three hundred men—if all of them were going with La Fayette . . .

"I think they're sending me with him in hopes that my ancient wisdom will balance the Seigneur de La Fayette's youthful enthusiasm," Jamie said, lowering the canteen with a sigh. "And it's maybe better than staying back wi' Lee." He grimaced. "Boiling Water thinks it beneath his dignity to marshal no but a thousand men and declined the command."

Ian made a noise indicating amusement at this and faith in his uncle's sagacity. It might be fun, harrying the British rear. He felt a tingle of anticipation at thought of putting on his war paint.

"Where's Denzell gone?" Jamie asked, glancing at the wagon.

"Attending a childbirth over yon," Ian said, lifting his chin in the direction Denzell and Dottie had taken. "He says ye're hosting a Quaker meeting tonight."

Jamie lifted a thick brow glistening with droplets of sweat.

"Well, I wasna planning to join in, but I said they might use my tent and welcome. Why, are ye going yourself?"

"Thought I might," Ian said. "I was invited, after all."

"Were ye?" Jamie looked interested. "D'ye think they mean to convert ye?"

"I dinna think that's how Quakers work," Ian said, a little ruefully. "And good luck to them if they do. I think the power o' prayer must have limits."

That made his uncle snort with amusement, but Jamie shook his head. "Never think it, laddie," he advised. "If wee Rachel sets her mind to it, she'll have your sword beaten into a plowshare before ye can say Peter Piper picked a peck o' pickled peppers. Well, twice," he added. "Or maybe three times."

Ian made a dissentient noise through his nose. "Aye, and if I were to try bein' a Friend, who would there be to protect the lot of 'em? Rachel and her brother and Dottie, I mean. Ye ken that, don't ye? That they can only be what they are because you and I are what we are?"

Jamie leaned back a little, purse-lipped, then gave him the ghost of a wry smile.

"I ken that fine. And so does Denzell Hunter; it's why he's here, though it's cost him his home and his meeting. But, mind, they're worth protecting— beyond you bein' in love wi' Rachel, I mean."

"Mmphm." Ian wasn't in the mood to discuss philosophy, and he doubted his uncle was, either. The light was in that long hour before darkfall, when the things of the forest pause and draw breath, slowing for the night. It was a good time to hunt, because the trees slowed first, so you saw the animals still moving among them.

Uncle Jamie kent that. He sat, relaxed, nothing moving save his eyes. Ian saw his gaze flick up and turned his own head to see. Sure enough, a squirrel clung to the trunk of a sycamore, ten feet away. He'd not have seen it, had he not caught the last flick of its tail as it stilled there. He met Jamie's eyes, and they both smiled and sat silent for a while, listening to the racket of the camp, even this beginning to mute itself.

Denzell and Dottie hadn't come back; perhaps the birth was more complicated than Denny had thought. Rachel would be going to Jamie's tent soon, for the meeting.

He wondered about that. You needed a meeting, to counsel the two of you, then to approve and witness the marriage. Might Denny have it in his mind to establish a new Friends meeting, within which he could marry Dottie—and Rachel might wed Ian?

Jamie sighed and stirred, getting ready to rise.

"Ahh . . . Uncle," Ian said, in a casual tone that made his uncle instantly focus attention on him.

"What?" said his uncle warily. "Ye havena got your lass wi' child, have ye?"

"I have not," Ian said, offended—and wondering vaguely how his uncle had known he was thinking of Rachel. "And why would ye think a thing like that, ye evil-minded auld mumper?"

"Because I ken well enough what 'Ahh . . . Uncle' usually means," Jamie informed him cynically. "It means ye've got yourself into some confusion involving a lass and want advice. And I canna think what ye could be confused about wi' regard to wee Rachel. A more straightforward lass I've never met—bar your auntie Claire, that is," he added, with a brief grin.

"Mmphm," Ian said, not best pleased by his uncle's acuity, but obliged to admit the truth of it. "Well, then. It's only . . ." Despite the completely benign intent—the *innocence,* even—of the question that had come into his mind, he felt his face go hot.

Jamie raised his brows.

"Well, if ye must know, then—I've never lain wi' a virgin." Once he'd got it out, he relaxed a little, though his uncle's brows nearly met his hairline. "And, aye, I'm sure Rachel is one," he added defensively.

"I'm sure, too," his uncle assured him. "Most men wouldna consider it a problem."

Ian gave him a look. "Ye ken what I mean. I want her to like it."

"Verra commendable. Have ye had complaints from women before?"

"Ye're in a rare mood, Uncle," Ian said coldly. "Ye ken verra well what I mean."

"Aye, ye mean if ye're paying a woman to bed ye, ye're no likely to hear anything ye dinna like regarding your own performance." Jamie rocked back a little, eyeing him. "Did ye tell Rachel ye're in the habit of consorting wi' whores?"

Ian felt the blood rush to his ears and was obliged to breathe evenly for a moment before replying.

"I told her everything," he said between clenched teeth. "And I wouldna call it a 'habit.'" He did know better than to go on with, *"It's no more than other men do,"* because he kent fine what sort of answer he'd get to *that.*

Fortunately, Jamie seemed to have reined in his jocularity for the moment and was considering the question.

"Your Mohawk wife," he said delicately. "She, er . . ."

"No," Ian said. "The Indians see bedding a bit differently." And, seizing the opportunity to get a bit of his own back, added, "D'ye not recall the time we went to visit the Snowbird Cherokee and Bird sent a couple of maidens to warm your bed?"

Jamie gave him an old-fashioned sort of look that made him laugh.

"Tell me, Ian," he said, after a pause, "would ye be having this conversation with your da?"

"God, no."

"I'm flattered," Jamie said dryly.

"Well, see . . ." Ian had answered by reflex and found himself fumbling for an explanation. "It—I mean . . . it's no that I wouldna talk to Da about things, but if he'd told me anything about . . . it would ha' been to do with him and Mam, wouldn't it? And I couldna . . . well, I couldn't, that's all."

"Mmphm."

Ian narrowed his eyes at his uncle.

"Ye're no going to try and tell me that my mother—"

"Who's my sister, aye? No, I wouldna tell ye anything like that. I see your point. I'm only thinkin' . . ." He trailed off and Ian gave him a pointed look. The light was fading, but there was still plenty. Jamie shrugged.

"Aye, well. It's only—your auntie Claire was widowed when I wed her, aye?"

"Aye. So?"

"So it was me that was virgin on our wedding night."

Ian hadn't thought he'd moved, but Rollo jerked his head up and looked at him, startled. Ian cleared his throat.

"Oh. Aye?"

"Aye," said his uncle, wry as a lemon. "And I was given any amount of advice beforehand, too, by my uncle Dougal and his men."

Dougal MacKenzie had died before Ian was born, but he'd heard a good bit about the man, one way and another. His mouth twitched.

"Would ye care to pass on any of it?"

"God, no." Jamie stood up and brushed bits of bark from the tails of his coat. "I think ye already ken ye should be gentle about it, aye?"

"Aye, I'd thought of that," Ian assured him. "Nothing else?"

"Aye, well." Jamie stood still, considering. "The only useful thing was what my wife told me on the night. 'Go slowly and pay attention.' I think ye canna go far wrong wi' that." He settled his coat on his shoulders. "*Oidhche mhath*, Ian. I'll see ye at first light—if not somewhat before."

"*Oidhche mhath*, Uncle Jamie."

As Jamie reached the edge of the clearing, Ian called after him.

"Uncle Jamie!"

Jamie turned to look over his shoulder.

"Aye?"

"And was she gentle with ye?"

"God, no," Jamie said, and grinned broadly.

58

CASTRAMETATION

T HE SUN WAS LOW in the sky by the time William reached
Clinton's camp, and lower still before he'd turned Goth over to
Sutherland's grooms. Zeb was nowhere in sight. Perhaps he was with
Colenso.

He delivered his cartouche of dispatches to Captain von Munchausen, saw
the company clerk, and found the tent he shared with two other young captains, both of the 27th Foot. Randolph Merbling was sitting outside, reading
by the last of the sun, but there was no sign of Thomas Evans—nor of Colenso Baragwanath. Nor of Zebedee Jeffers. Nor of William's baggage.

He breathed for a moment, then shook himself like a dog shedding water.
He was so tired of being angry that he just couldn't be arsed anymore. He
shrugged, borrowed a towel from Merbling, washed his face, and went to
find a bite to eat.

He'd made up his mind not to think about anything whatever until he'd
had some food and largely succeeded, letting roast chicken, bread, cheese,
and beer fill at least some of his empty spaces. As he finished, though, a sudden sharp image punctured his pleasant digestive reverie. A flushed, pretty
face, with wary eyes the exact color of the cider he was drinking.

Jane. Bloody hell! What with one thing and another, he'd quite forgotten
the whore and her sister. He'd told them to meet him at the surgeon's tent
at sundown. . . . Well, the sun wasn't down yet. He was on his feet and on his
way, but then had a second thought and, going back to the cook, wangled a
couple of loaves and some cheese, just in case.

Castrametation was the science of laying out a proper military camp.
Drainage, sanitary trenches, where to put the powder depot to avoid flooding if it rained . . . He'd had a brief course in it once. He'd likely never need
to do it himself, but it did help in locating things, if you knew where they
were supposed to be. And when in camp, the hospital was meant to be on the
opposite side from command headquarters, close to water but on a height, if
one was available.

One was, and he found the large green-canvas tent without difficulty.
Could have found it with his eyes closed. Surgeons carried the smell of their
work around with them, and the whiff of dried blood and the uneasy tang of
sickness and recent death were perceptible at a hundred yards. It was worse—
much worse—after a battle, but there was always illness and accident, and the
stink lingered even on peaceful days, aggravated now by the muggy heat that
lay like a wet blanket over the camp.

There were men, and not a few women, clustered round the tent, waiting for attention. He gave them a quick glance, but didn't see Jane. His heart had sped up a little at thought of seeing her, and he felt unaccountably disappointed. No reason why, he told himself. She and her sister would be nothing but trouble to him. They must have grown tired waiting, and—

"You're very late, my lord," said an accusatory voice at his elbow, and he whirled round to see her looking down her nose at him—as well as someone who was shorter than he could do, which wasn't very well. He found himself smiling down at her, absurdly.

"I said sundown," he replied mildly, nodding toward the west, where a thin slice of brilliance still glowed through the trees. "Not down yet, is it?"

"The sun takes a bloody long time to go down out here." She switched her disapproval to the orb in question. "It's much faster in the city."

Before he could argue with this ridiculous assertion, she'd glanced back at him, frowning.

"Why aren't you wearing your gorget?" she demanded, hands on her hips. "I went to a deal of trouble to get it back for you!"

"I'm exceedingly grateful to you, ma'am," he said, striving for gravity. "I thought it might provoke inquiries, though, should I turn up suddenly in the midst of camp wearing it, and I thought you and your sister might just possibly wish to avoid . . . tedious explanations?"

She sniffed, but not without amusement.

"How thoughtful. Not quite so thoughtful of your servants, though, are you?"

"What do you mean?"

"Come with me." She linked her arm with his and towed him off toward the wood before he could protest. She led him to a small lean-to shelter in the undergrowth, which seemed to have been constructed of an unstuffed army bed sack and two petticoats. Bending down at her invitation, he discovered her sister, Fanny, within, sitting next to a bed sack that had been stuffed with fresh grass, upon which crouched both Colenso and Zeb, both looking bewildered. On sight of him, they crouched further.

"What the devil are you doing here?" he demanded. "And where is my dunnage, Zeb?"

"Back there, sir," Zeb quavered, jerking a thumb toward the growth behind the lean-to. "I couldn't find your tent and I didn't want to leave it, see."

"But I told you—and what about you, Baragwanath? Are you still ill?" William demanded, kneeling down suddenly and thrusting his head into the shelter. Colenso looked bad, pale as a cup of soured milk, and plainly in pain, curled up into himself.

"Oh . . . 'tisn't nothin', sir," he said, swallowing heavily. "Just must have . . . ate . . . something."

"Did you see the surgeon?"

Colenso turned his face into the bed sack, shoulders hunched. Zeb was edging away, apparently thinking of making a run for it.

William grabbed him by the arm; the little groom yelped and he let go. "What's wrong? Did you not have that arm seen to?"

"They're afraid of the surgeons," Jane said sharply.

William drew himself up to his full height and glared down at her.

"Oh? Who told them they should be afraid of the surgeons? And how do they come to be in *your* care, may I ask?"

Her lips pressed tight together, and she glanced involuntarily into the shelter. Fanny was looking out at them, doe eyes huge in the fading light. She swallowed and put a protective hand on Colenso's shoulder. Jane sighed deeply and took William's arm again.

"Come with me."

She led him away a short distance, still within sight of the little shelter but out of earshot.

"Fanny and I were waiting for you when those boys came along together. The bigger one—*what* did you say his name is?"

"Colenso Baragwanath. He's Cornish," William added shortly, seeing a look of amusement flit across her face.

"Really. I hope it isn't catching. Well, he was so ill he couldn't stand, and sank down on the ground near us, making the most horrid noises. The little one—yes, I know he's Zebedee, thank you—was beside himself, half-weeping with confusion. My sister is a most tenderhearted creature," she said, rather apologetically. "She went to help, and I followed." She shrugged.

"We got Colenso into the wood far enough to get his britches down in time, and I gave him a little water." She touched a small wooden canteen that hung from her shoulder, and he wondered briefly where she'd got it. She hadn't had it when he'd met the girls by the creek yesterday.

"I am much obliged to you, ma'am," he said formally. "Now—why is it, exactly, that you did not then take the boys in to see the surgeons?"

For the first time, her composure showed signs of cracking. She turned a little away from him, and he noticed the last rays of the sun polishing the smooth crown of her head with a faint, familiar gleam of chestnut. The sight of it brought back memory of his first meeting with her with the force of a thunderclap—and, with it, the memory of his mingled shame and arousal. Especially the latter.

"Answer me," he said, more roughly than he'd intended, and she turned on him, eyes narrowed at his tone.

"There was a finger lying on the ground by the surgeon's tent," she snapped. "It frightened my sister, and the boys took fright from her."

William rubbed a knuckle down the bridge of his nose, eyeing her.

"A finger." He had himself seen piles of amputated limbs outside the surgeons' tents at Saratoga, and aside from a quick prayer of gratitude that none of the disconnected arms and legs was his, had experienced no particular qualms. "Whose was it?"

"How should I know? I was too much occupied in keeping your orderly from shitting himself to ask."

"Ah. Yes. Thank you," he said, rather formally. He glanced toward the shelter again and was surprised to see that Fanny had come out and was hovering a little way from her sister, a wary look on her lovely face. Did he look threatening? he wondered. Just in case, he relaxed his posture a bit and smiled at Fanny. She didn't change expression, but continued to stare at him suspiciously.

He cleared his throat and took the sack off his shoulder, holding it out to Jane. "I thought you might have missed your supper. Have the boys—well, Zeb, at least—eaten anything?"

Jane nodded and took the bag with a celerity suggesting that it had been some time since the girls had had a meal. "He ate with the other grooms, he said."

"All right, then. I'll take him in to have his arm seen to and perhaps get a dose for Colenso, while you and your sister refresh yourselves. Then, madam, we can discuss your own situation."

He'd been intensely aware of her physical presence for some moments, but when he said that, she turned the full effect of her eyes on him—*cider*, he thought vaguely, *or sherry wine?*—and seemed somehow to *flow*, shifting in some indefinable way. He hadn't seen her move, but suddenly she was standing near enough to touch, and he smelled the odor of her hair and imagined he felt the warmth of her skin through her clothes. She took his hand briefly, and her thumb moved across the palm, slowly. The palm tingled and the hairs on his arm rippled.

"I'm sure we can come to a reasonable accommodation, my lord," she said, very grave, and let him go.

He dragged Zeb into the surgeon's tent like a recalcitrant colt and stood by, only half-attending, as a young Scottish surgeon with freckles swabbed the boy's wound clean of dirt. Arabella–Jane didn't smell of the whorish scent she'd worn at the brothel, but, by Christ, she smelled good.

"We should cauterize the wound, sir," the young doctor's voice was saying. "It will stop an abscess forming, aye?"

"No!" Zeb jerked away from the doctor and made a dash for the door, knocking into people and sending one woman flying with a shriek. Jolted out of his random thoughts, William made a reflexive dive and knocked the boy flat.

"Come on, Zeb," he said, hauling Zeb to his feet and propelling him firmly back to Dr. MacFreckles. "It won't be that bad. Just a moment or two, and then it's all over."

Zeb appearing patently unconvinced by this, William deposited him firmly on a stool and pulled up his own right cuff.

"Look," he said, displaying the long, comet-shaped scar on his forearm. "*That's* what happens when you get an abscess."

Both Zeb and the doctor peered at the scar, impressed. It had been a splinter wound, he told them, caused by a lightning-struck tree.

"Wandered round the Great Dismal Swamp for three days in a fever," he said. "Some . . . Indians found me and got me to a doctor. I nearly died, and"—he lowered his brows and gave Zeb a piercing look—"the doctor was just about to *cut off my arm*, when the abscess burst and he cauterized it. You might not be so lucky, hey?"

Zeb still looked unhappy, but reluctantly agreed. William gripped him by the shoulders and said encouraging things while the iron was heating, but his own heart was beating as fast as it might have had he been awaiting cautery himself.

Indians. One, in particular. He'd thought he'd exhausted his anger, but there it bloody was again, bursting into bright fresh flame like an ember smashed open with a poker.

Bloody fucking Ian Murray. Fucking Scot and sometime Mohawk. His bloody fucking *cousin,* which made it all that much worse.

And then there was Rachel. . . . Murray had taken him to Dr. Hunter and Rachel. He drew a deep, ragged breath, remembering her worn indigo gown, hanging on its peg in the Hunters' house. Grabbing a handful of the cloth and pressing it to his face, breathing in her scent as though starved of air.

That was where Murray had met Rachel himself. And now she was *betrothed* to that—

"Ow!" Zeb writhed, and William realized belatedly that he was digging his fingers into the boy's shoulder, just like—he let go as though Zeb were a hot potato, feeling the memory of James Fraser's iron grip on his arm and the agonizing pain that had numbed him from shoulder to fingertip.

"Sorry," he said, voice shaking a little with the effort to hide his fury. "Sorry, Zeb." The surgeon was ready with the glowing iron; William took Zeb's arm, as gently as he could, and held it still while the thing was done. Rachel had held his own.

He'd been right; it was quick. The surgeon pressed the hot iron to the wound and counted five, slowly, then took it away. Zeb went stiff as a tent pole and sucked in enough breath to supply three people, but didn't scream.

"It's done," the doctor said, taking the iron away and smiling at Zeb. "Here, I'll put a bit of sweet oil on and bandage it. Ye did well, laddie."

Zeb's eyes were watering, but he wasn't crying. He sniffed deeply and wiped the back of his hand across his face, looking up at William.

"Well done, Zeb," William said, squeezing his shoulder gently, and Zeb managed a tiny smile in return.

By the time they'd returned to the girls and Colenso, William had managed to tamp down the rage—again. Was he never going to be able to get rid of it? *Not 'til you make up your mind what to do about things,* he thought grimly. But there wasn't anything that could be done right now, so he squashed all the sparks in his head firmly into one dense red ball and rolled it to the back of his mind.

"Here, let Fanny do it. He trusts her." Jane took the vial containing the dose Dr. MacFreckles had made up for Colenso and gave it to her sister. Fanny promptly sat down beside Colenso, who was pretending as hard as he could to be asleep, and began stroking his head, murmuring something to him.

William nodded and, gesturing to Jane to accompany him, withdrew far enough to be out of earshot. Rather to his surprise, part of his brain had apparently been analyzing the problem and coming to conclusions while the rest was occupied, for he had a rough plan.

"What I suggest is this," he said, without preamble. "I will make provision for you and your sister to receive regular army rations, as camp followers, and to travel under my protection. Once in New York, I will give you five pounds, and you're on your own. In return . . ."

She didn't quite smile, but a dimple showed in one cheek.

"In return," he repeated more firmly, "you will mind my orderly and my groom, tend their ills, and make sure they're reasonably cared for. You will also be my laundress."

"Your laundress?!" The dimple had disappeared abruptly, replaced by an expression of sheer astonishment.

"Laundress," he repeated doggedly. He knew what she'd been expecting him to propose and was rather surprised himself that he hadn't, but there it was. He couldn't, not with his thoughts of Rachel and of Anne Endicott so fresh in his mind. Not with the deep, smothered rage fueled by the thought that he deserved no woman but a whore.

"But I don't know how to do laundry!"

"How hard can it be?" he asked, as patiently as he could. "You wash my clothes. Don't put starch in my drawers. That's about it, isn't it?"

"But—but—" She looked aghast. "One needs a . . . a kettle! A fork, a paddle, something to stir with . . . Soap! *I* haven't any soap!"

"Oh." That hadn't occurred to him. "Well . . ." He dug in his pocket, found it empty, and tried the other, which held a guinea, tuppence, and a florin. He handed her the guinea. "Buy what you need, then."

She looked at the golden coin in her palm, her face utterly blank. She opened her mouth, then closed it again.

"What's the matter?" he asked impatiently. She didn't answer, but a soft voice behind him did.

"The duffent know how."

He whirled to find Fanny looking up at him from under her cap, her delicate cheeks flushed red by the sunset.

"What did you say?"

Fanny's soft mouth pressed tight and her cheeks grew redder, but she repeated it, dogged. "The . . . duffent . . . know *how*."

Jane reached Fanny in two steps, putting an arm around her sister's shoulders and glaring at William.

"My sister's tongue-tied," she said, daring him to say anything. "That's why she's afraid of the surgeons. She thinks they will amputate her tongue if they find out."

He drew a deep, slow breath.

"I see. And what she said to me . . . 'She doesn't know how'? She means you, I collect? What is it, pray, that you don't know how?"

"Muddy," whispered Fanny, now staring at the ground.

"Mud—money?" He stared at Jane. "You don't know how to—"

"I've never *had* any money!" she snapped, and threw the guinea on the ground at his feet. "I know the names of the coins, but I don't know what you can buy with them, except—except—what you can buy in a brothel! My cunt is worth six shillings, all right? My mouth is three. And my arse is a pound. But if someone gave *me* three shillings, I wouldn't know if I could buy a loaf of bread or a horse with them! I've never bought *anything*!"

"You—you mean—" He was so flabbergasted, he couldn't string words into a sentence. "But you have wages. You said—"

"I've been a brothel whore since I was ten years old!" Her fists clenched, knuckles sharp under the skin. "I never *see* my wages! Mrs. Abbott spends them—she says—for my—our—food and clothes. I've never had a penny to my name, let alone spent one. And now you hand me . . . *that*"—she stamped her foot on the guinea, driving it into the ground—"and tell me to buy a kettle?!? Where? How? From whom?!"

Her voice shook and her face was a deal redder than the setting sun could make it. She was furious, but also very near to tears. He wanted to take her in his arms and soothe her, but thought that might be a good way to lose a finger.

"How old is Fanny?" he asked instead. She jerked her head up, panting.

"Fanny?" she said blankly.

"I'm e-lev-en," Fanny's voice said behind him. "You weve her *awone!*"

He turned to see the girl glaring up at him, a stick clutched in her hand. He might have laughed, if not for the expression on her face—and if not for what he'd just realized. He took a step back, so as to see both girls at once, and like magnet and iron, they came together and clung, both staring distrustfully at him.

"How much is her maidenhead worth?" he asked Jane baldly, with a nod at Fanny.

"Ten pounth," Fanny answered automatically, just as Jane shouted, "She's not for sale! To you or any other bugger!" She pressed Fanny fiercely closer, daring him to make a move toward the girl.

"I don't *want* her," he said through his teeth. "I don't fornicate with children, for God's sake!"

Jane's hard expression didn't alter, and she didn't loosen her grip on her sister.

"Then why did you ask?"

"To verify my suppositions regarding your presence here."

Jane snorted. "Those being?"

"That you ran away. Presumably because your sister has now reached an age where . . . ?" He raised an eyebrow, nodding at Fanny. Jane's lips compressed, but she gave him a tiny, grudging nod.

"Captain Harkness?" he asked. It was a shot in the dark, but well aimed. Harkness hadn't been pleased at being deprived of his prey and, unable to come at William, might well have decided to take his revenge elsewhere.

The light bathed everything in tones of gold and lavender, but he could see Jane's face go pale, nonetheless, and felt a tightening in his loins. If he found Harkness . . . He resolved to go looking tomorrow. The man might be in Philadelphia, as she'd said—but he might not. It would be a welcome focus for his rage.

"Right, then," he said, as matter-of-factly as he could. He stooped and pried the guinea out of the soft earth, realizing as he did so that he'd been a fool to offer it to her. Not because of what she'd told him but because someone like her—or Colenso—would never have such a sum. They'd be suspected of stealing it and very likely would be relieved of it by the first person to see it.

"Just look after the boys, will you?" he said to Jane. "And the both of you keep clear of the soldiers until I can find you simple clothes. Dressed like that"—he gestured at their dust-smudged, sweat-stained finery—"you'll be taken for whores, and soldiers don't take no for an answer."

"I am a whore," Jane said, in a strange, dry voice.

"No," he said, and felt his own voice as oddly separate from himself but very firm. "You're not. You travel under my protection. I'm not a pimp—so you're not a whore. Not until we reach New York."

59

A DISCOVERY IN THE RANKS

THE 16TH PENNSYLVANIA militia company, Captain the Reverend Peleg Woodsworth in command, marched into camp in good order, having paused just outside to tidy themselves, clean their weapons, and wash their faces. Lord John knew no one would take notice but approved of the preparations on grounds of good military discipline, as he explained to Germain.

"Slovenly troops make bad fighters," he said, critically examining a large rent in the sleeve of his filthy black coat. "And soldiers must be in the habit of obeying orders, no matter what those orders are."

Germain nodded. "Aye, that's what my mam says. Doesn't matter whether ye see the point or not, ye do as ye're told, or else."

"Your mother would make an admirable sergeant," Grey assured his orderly. He'd encountered Marsali Fraser once or twice, at her printshop. "Splendid grasp of the essence of command. Speaking of 'or else,' though—what, exactly, do you expect to happen when you go home?"

It was evident that Germain hadn't given much thought to the prospect, but after a moment he uncreased his brow.

"Likely it'll depend how long I've been gone," he said, with a shrug. "If I went back tomorrow, I'd get my ears blistered and my arse, too. But I think if I was to be gone longer than a week, she'd be pleased I wasna deid."

"Ah. Have you heard the story of the Prodigal Son, by chance?"

"No, me lo—er . . . Bert." Germain coughed. "How does it go?"

"It's—" he began automatically, but then stopped dead, feeling as though a stake had been driven through his chest. The company had already begun to fray and straggle; the few men behind him merely skirted him and went past. Germain twisted round to see what he was looking at.

"It's that man who pretends to be a Frenchman. My father doesn't like him."

Grey stared at the gentleman in the suit of very fashionable blue and gray-striped silk, who was likewise staring at Grey, mouth slightly open, ignoring the small knot of Continental officers accompanying him.

"I know a lot of Frenchmen," Grey said, recovering his breath. "But you're right; that's not one of them." He turned his back on the man, mind awhirl, and gripped Germain by the arm.

"Your grandfather has to be in this moil somewhere," he said, forcing resolution into his voice. "Do you see the building over there, with the flag?" He nodded at the limp banner, on the far side of the sprawling camp, but clearly visible. "Go there. That will be the commander in chief's headquarters. Tell one of the officers who you're looking for; they'll find him for you among the militia."

"Oh, they won't have to," Germain assured him. "*Grand-père* will be there."

"Where?"

"With General Washington," Germain said, with the exaggerated patience of those forced to consort with dunces. "He's a general, too; did ye not know that?" Before Grey could respond to this piece of flabbergasting intelligence, Germain had scampered away in the direction of the distant banner.

Grey risked a glance over his shoulder, but Perseverance Wainwright had disappeared, as had the Continental officers, leaving only a couple of lieutenants in conversation.

He thought several blasphemous things in a row, alternating between Jamie Fraser and Percy Wainwright as the recipients of assorted violent assaults of a personal nature. What the fucking *hell* was either of them doing here? His fingers twitched, wanting to strangle someone, but he fought back this useless impulse in favor of deciding what the devil to do now.

He began to walk hastily, with no clear notion where he was going. Percy had seen him, he knew that much. Jamie hadn't, but might at any moment. *A general? What the—no time to worry about that just now.* What might either one of them do about it?

He hadn't seen Percy—ex-lover, ex-brother, French spy, and all-around shit—since their last conversation in Philadelphia, some months before. When Percy had first reappeared in Grey's life, it had been with a last attempt at seduction—political rather than physical, though Grey had an idea that he wouldn't have balked at the physical, either. . . . It was an offer for the British government: the return to France of the valuable Northwest Territory, in return for the promise of Percy's "interests" to keep the French government from making an alliance with the American colonies.

He had—as a matter of duty—conveyed the offer discreetly to Lord North and then expunged it—and Percy—from his mind. He had no idea what, if anything, the First Minister had made of it.

Too late now in any case, he thought. France had signed a treaty with the rebellious colonies in April. It remained to be seen, though, whether that treaty would result in anything tangible in the way of support. The French were notoriously unreliable.

So now what? His instinct toward self-preservation urged him to fade quietly through the camp and disappear as quickly as possible. Germain wouldn't tell Jamie he was here; they'd agreed that much in advance. Two considerations held him back, though: first, the minor matter that he didn't yet know where the British army was or how far away. And second . . . a sense of curiosity about Percy that he himself recognized as dangerously reckless.

He'd kept moving, since to stand still was to be knocked over and trampled, and now found himself walking beside the Reverend Woodsworth. The tall minister's face was suffused with an excitement that kept breaking through the man's normal mien of calm dignity, and Grey couldn't help smiling at it.

"God has brought us safe thus far, Bert," Woodsworth said, looking about him with shining eyes. "And He will grant us victory, I know it!"

"Ah." Grey groped for some reply, and finding—to his surprise—that he was incapable of agreeing with this statement, settled for, "I suppose we cannot presume to divine the Almighty's intent, but I do trust He will preserve us, in His mercy."

"Very well said, Bert, very well said." And Woodsworth clapped him resoundingly on the back.

60

QUAKERS AND QUARTERMASTERS

JAMIE FOUND NATHANAEL Greene in his tent and still in shirtsleeves, the remains of breakfast on a table before him, frowning at a letter in his hand. He put this down at once upon seeing Jamie and rose to his feet.

"Come in, sir, do! Have you et anything yet today? I've a spare egg going to waste." He smiled, but briefly; whatever had troubled him about the letter still lurked in the creases of his brow. Jamie glanced at it from the corner of his eye; from the blots and ragged edge, it looked a piece of domestic correspondence, rather than an official note.

"I have, I thank ye, sir," Jamie said, with a slight bow of acknowledgment toward the egg, which sat neglected in a little wooden cup with a flowered heart painted on it. "I only wondered, if ye meant to ride out today, might I come with ye?"

"Of course!" Greene looked surprised but pleased. "I should welcome your advice, General."

"Perhaps we might trade wisdom, then," Jamie suggested. "For I should value your own advice, though perhaps on a different matter."

Greene paused, coat half-pulled on.

"Really? Advice on what sort of matter?"

"Marriage."

Greene's face struggled between astonishment, a courteous attempt to suppress the astonishment, and something else. He glanced behind him at the letter lying on the table and settled his coat on his shoulders.

"I could use sound advice on *that* matter myself, General Fraser," he said, with a wry twist of the lips. "Let's be off, then."

They rode out of camp north by northwest—Greene was equipped with a battered compass, and Jamie wished for a moment that he still possessed the gold-plated astrolabe that William had sent from London at the behest of Lord John. That had perished when the Big House burned, though the spurt of dark feeling that went through him now had more to do with the thought of John Grey than with the fire and its aftermath.

Conversation at first dealt only with the business at hand: the location of supply dumps along the probable line of march—and, if necessary, retreat, though no one spoke of that possibility. There was no particular doubt as to where the British army was headed; a body that large, with an enormous baggage train and outlying flocks of camp followers, was limited in its choice of roads.

"Aye, that would do," Jamie said, nodding in agreement at Greene's suggestion of an abandoned farmstead. "D'ye think the well's good?"

"I'm minded to find out," Greene said, turning his horse's head toward the farm. "It's hot as Hades already. Scorch our ears off by noon, I reckon."

It was hot; they'd left off their stocks and waistcoats and were riding in shirtsleeves, coats across their saddlebows, but Jamie felt the linen of his shirt sticking to his back and sweat trickling over his ribs and down his face. Fortunately, the well *was* still good; water glimmered visibly below, and a stone dropped in gave back a satisfactory *plunk!*

"I confess I'm surprised to find you in want of advice regarding marriage, General," Greene said, having first drunk his fill and then upended a bucketful of water luxuriously over his head. He blinked water off his lashes, shook himself like a dog, and handed the bucket to Jamie, who nodded thanks. "I should have thought your own union most harmonious."

"Aye, well, it's not my own marriage I'm worrit for," Jamie said, grunting a little as he pulled up a fresh full bucket—hand over hand, for the windlass had rotted away and he'd been obliged to fetch a rope from his saddlebag. "Will ye ken a young scout named Ian Murray? He's my nephew."

"Murray. Murray . . ." Greene looked blank for a moment, but then comprehension dawned. "Oh, him! Yes, drat him. Your nephew, you say? Thought he was an Indian. Cost me a guinea on that race. My wife won't be happy about that at all. Not that she's happy at the moment, regardless," he added with a sigh. Evidently the letter *had* been domestic.

"Well, I might persuade him to give it ye back," Jamie said, suppressing a smile, "if ye might be able to help him to wed."

He raised the bucket overhead and gave himself over to a moment of joy as the drench of water quenched the heat. He drew one deep, grateful breath of coolness, tasting of the dank stones at the bottom of the well, and likewise shook himself.

"He means to marry a Quaker lass," he said, opening his eyes. "I kent that ye were a Friend yourself, havin' heard ye speak to Mrs. Hardman when we met. So I wondered, maybe, if ye could tell me just what's needed in the way of requirement for such a marriage?"

If Greene had been surprised to find that Ian was Jamie's nephew, this news seemed to knock him speechless. He stood for a moment, pushing his lips in and out, as though they might suck up a word he could spit back out, and at last found one.

"Well," he said. He paused for a bit, considering, and Jamie waited patiently. Greene was a man of fairly strong opinions, but he didn't give them hastily. Jamie did wonder what there was to consider in his question, though— were Quakers even stranger in their customs than he thought?

"Well," Greene said again, and exhaled, settling his shoulders. "I must tell you, General, that I no longer consider myself a Friend, though I was indeed raised in that sect." He shot Jamie a sharp look. "And I must also tell you that the cause of my departure was a mislike of their narrow-minded, superstitious ways. If your nephew means to turn Quaker, sir, I'd recommend you do your best to dissuade him."

"Och. Well, that's part of the difficulty, I gather," Jamie replied equably. "He doesna mean to turn Quaker himself. And I think that a wise decision; he isna suited for it at all."

Greene relaxed a little at that and went so far as to smile, if wryly.

"I'm glad to hear it. But he has no objection to his wife remaining a Friend?"

"I think he's better sense than to suggest otherwise."

That made Greene laugh. "Perhaps he'll manage marriage well enough, then."

"Oh, he'll make a bonny husband for the lass, I've nay doubt. It's the getting them wed that seems a difficulty."

"Ah. Yes." Greene glanced round the homestead, wiping his wet face with a wadded handkerchief. "That might in fact be *very* difficult, if the young woman . . . well. Let me think for a moment. In the meantime . . . the well's good, but we can't store powder here; there's not much roof left, and I'm told this weather often presages thunderstorms."

"There's likely a root cellar at the back," Jamie suggested.

There was. The door had gone and a tangle of spindly, pallid vines had sprouted from a rotted sack of potatoes abandoned in the corner, tendrils crawling in slow desperation toward the light.

"It'll do," Greene decided, and made a penciled note in the small book he carried everywhere. "Let's move on, then."

They let the horses drink, poured more water over themselves, and rode on, gently steaming. Greene was not a chatterer, and there had been no conversation for a mile or two, when he finally reached a conclusion of his mental processes.

"The principal thing to bear in mind regarding Friends," he said, without preliminary, "is that they depend very much upon one another's company and opinion—often to the exclusion of the world outside their meetings." He shot Jamie a glance. "The young woman—is your nephew known to her meeting?"

"Mmphm," Jamie said. "As I understand from her brother, they were both put out of their meeting—in a small place in Virginia when he decided to become a surgeon in the Continental army. Or perhaps he was put out, and she merely went with him; I dinna ken whether it makes a difference."

"Oh, I see." Greene plucked the wet shirt away from his body in hopes of admitting a little air to his skin, but it was a vain hope. The air lay thick as a woolen blanket on the simmering countryside. "A 'fighting Quaker,' as they call it?"

"No, he willna take up arms," Jamie assured Greene, "but apparently his merely being connected with the army offended his meeting." Greene snorted in what appeared to be a personal way, and Jamie cleared his throat. "In fact, Denzell Hunter—Dr. Hunter—also is engaged to be married. Though his path may be somewhat smoother, in that his bride has become a Friend herself."

"Has she a home meeting?" Greene asked sharply. Jamie shook his head.

"No, it appeared to be a . . . private event. The conversion, I mean. I am told that Quakers dinna have either clergy or ritual . . . ?" He left that hanging delicately, and Greene snorted again.

"Nor do they. But I assure you, General, there is nothing truly private in a Friend's life—certainly no spiritual matter. My own father opposed reading, as being a practice likely to separate one from God, and when as a young man I not only read but began to collect works on military strategy, in which I had an interest, I was brought before an examination committee from our meeting and subjected to such questions as to—well, as I say, I am no longer a member of that sect."

He blew out his lips and made small rumbling noises for a bit, frowning at the road ahead—though Jamie saw that, even in his preoccupation, Greene was taking note of their surroundings, with an eye to logistics.

He himself had become aware of a certain vibration in the air and wondered if Greene sensed it. Not quite noise, it was a disturbance that he knew well: a large body of men and horses, too far away to see their dust—but there. They'd found the British army. He slowed a little, looking carefully at the trees ahead in case of British scouts—for the British must surely know by now that they were pursued.

Greene's hearing was less acute, though, or perhaps he was only preoccupied, for he glanced at Jamie in surprise, though he slowed, as well. Jamie raised a hand to stop him speaking and lifted his chin—there was a rider coming toward them, following the road. The sound of hooves was audible, and Jamie's own mount flung up his head and whickered with interest, nostrils flaring.

Both men had come armed; Greene set a hand on the musket balanced across his saddle. Jamie left his rifle in its sling but checked the priming of the pistols in his saddle holsters. Awkward to fire a long gun from horseback.

The rider was coming slowly, though; Jamie's hand on the pistol's grip relaxed, and he shook his head at Greene. They reined up, waiting, and a moment later the rider came in view.

"Ian!"

"Uncle Jamie!" Ian's face blossomed with relief at sight of him, and no wonder. He was dressed like a Mohawk, in buckskin leggings and calico shirt, with feathers in his hair, and a long, hairy gray carcass lay across his saddle-bow, blood dripping slowly from it down the horse's leg.

The beast wasn't dead, though; Rollo twitched and raised his head, giving the newcomers a yellow wolf glare, but recognized Jamie's scent and barked once, then let his tongue loll out, panting.

"What's happened to the hound, then?" Jamie rode up alongside and leaned forward to look.

"The numpty fell into a deadfall trap," Ian said, frowning rebuke at the dog. Then he gently scratched the big dog's ruff. "Mind, I'd ha' fallen in it myself, if he hadna gone before me."

"Bad hurt?" Jamie asked. He didn't think so; Rollo was giving General Greene his usual look of appraisal—a look that made most people take a few steps back. Ian shook his head, his hand curled into Rollo's fur to keep him steady.

"Nay, but he's torn his leg and he's lame. I was looking for a safe place to leave him; I've got to report in to Captain Mercer. Though seein' as you're here—oh, good day to ye, sir," he said to Greene, whose horse *had* backed up in response to Rollo and was presently indicating a strong desire to keep going, in spite of his rider's inclination. Ian sketched a salute and turned back to Jamie. "Seein' as you're here, Uncle Jamie, could ye maybe fetch Rollo back to the lines with ye and get Auntie Claire to tend his leg?"

"Oh, aye," Jamie said, resigned, and swung down from the saddle, grop-ing for his soggy handkerchief. "Let me bind his leg first. I dinna want blood all over my breeks, and the horse willna like it, either."

Greene cleared his throat.

"As you mention reporting, Mr. . . . . Murray?" he asked, with a sideways glance at Jamie, who nodded. "Perhaps you'd be so good as to give me, as well as Captain Mercer, the benefit of your report?"

"Aye, sir," Ian said agreeably. "The army's divided into three bodies now, wi' a great long line o' baggage wagons in between. Sae far as I could tell—I exchanged words wi' another scout who'd gone all the way up the column—they're headed toward a place called Freehold. The ground's no verra good for attack—folded up like a used napkin, all cut up wi' ravines and bitty creeks—though the other scout told me there's meadows beyond that might do for a fight, and ye could lure them or drive them out there."

Greene asked sharp questions, some of which Ian could answer and some he couldn't, while Jamie tended to the ginger business of binding up the dog's leg—there was a nasty stake wound, though not too deep; he hoped the stake hadn't been poisoned. Indians would do that sometimes, in case a wounded deer or wolverine might spring out of the trap.

Jamie's horse was not enthused at the prospect of carrying a wolf on his back but eventually was persuaded, and with no more than a nervous eye roll backward now and then, they were mounted.

"Fuirich, a choin," Ian said, leaning over and scratching Rollo behind the ears. "I'll be back, aye? *Taing,* Uncle!" And with a brief nod to Greene, he was away, his own horse clearly wanting to put as much distance between himself and Rollo as possible.

"Dear Lord," Greene said, wrinkling his nose at the dog's reek.

"Aye, well," Jamie said, resigned. "My wife says ye get used to any sort of smell after a bit of smelling it. And I suppose she'd know."

"Why, is she a cook?"

"Och, no. A physician. Gangrene, ken, festering bowels and the like."

Greene blinked.

"I see. You have a most interesting family, Mr. Fraser." He coughed and looked after Ian, rapidly vanishing in the distance. "You might be wrong about him never becoming a Quaker. At least he doesn't bow his head to a title."

61

A VISCOUS THREE-WAY

JAMIE CAME BACK from his ride with General Greene looking damp, wrinkled, and completely disheveled but otherwise refreshed—and with Rollo, bloody and disgruntled but not badly hurt.

"He'll be fine," I said, scratching Rollo gently behind the ears. The gash had bled a lot, but wasn't deep. "I don't think I'll stitch it."

"Dinna blame ye a bit, Sassenach," Jamie said, glancing at the dog, who had suffered my cleaning, salving, and bandaging his leg but didn't look at all inclined to stand for more fiddling. "Where are my good stockings?"

"In the portmanteau with your other linen," I replied patiently. "Where they are every morning. Surely you know that?"

"I do," he admitted. "I just like ye to tend to me."

"All right," I said, obligingly pulling them out. "D'you want me to put them on for you?"

"Nay, I can manage that," he said, taking them. "Could ye find my shirt, though?"

"I think I can do that, yes," I replied, taking the shirt out of the same portmanteau and shaking it out. "How was General Greene this morning?"

"Good. I asked him about the Quaker way of marriage," he said, pulling a fresh white shirt—his *only* fresh white shirt, as I pointed out—over his head. "Evidently the difficulty is with Denzell and Rachel not havin' a home meeting, as it's called. It's no that they canna marry, but to do it in the proper way, it would involve the whole meeting. There's a thing called a Clearness Committee, which meets wi' the bride and groom to counsel them and make sure they're suited and that they've some notion what they're in for." He shrugged into the sleeves and grinned at me. "I couldna help thinking, while he was tellin' me, what a committee like that would have had to say about us when we wed."

"Well, they wouldn't have had any more notion what we were in for than we did," I said, amused. "Do you think they would have thought us well suited?"

"If they'd seen the way I looked at ye, Sassenach, when ye didna see me lookin'—then, aye, they would." He kissed me briefly and looked round for the hairbrush. "Can ye club up my hair for me? I canna be reviewing my troops like this." His hair was tied back carelessly with a leather thong, damp stray wisps sticking to his face.

"Of course. How many of them are you reviewing? And when?" I sat him down on the stool and set to work with the brush. "Have you been burrowing through the countryside headfirst? You have foxtails and leaves in your hair, and those winged seeds that elder trees make. Ooh! To say nothing of *this*." I carefully removed a tiny green caterpillar that had become entangled in his tresses and showed it to him, perched inquisitively on my forefinger.

"Thalla le Dia," he said to the caterpillar. *Go with God.* And taking it carefully onto his own finger, brought it to the tent flap and loosed it into the grass.

"All of them, Sassenach," he said, returning and sitting down again. "My last two companies came in this morning; they'll have been fed now and rested a bit. I meant to ask," he added, twisting round to look up at me, "would ye come with me, Sassenach, and have a look at them? To see if any should be left back from the fighting or to tend any that might need the odd bit o' repair."

"Yes, of course. When?"

"Come to the parade ground in an hour, if ye would." He passed a hand over the neatly gleaming auburn queue, doubled on itself and ribboned in a club at his nape. "Aye, that's grand. Am I decent otherwise?"

He stood up and brushed bits of discarded leaf from his sleeve. The crown of his head brushed the tent, and he was glowing—with sun, energy, and the suppressed excitement of impending action.

"You look like bloody Mars, god of war," I said dryly, handing him his waistcoat. "Try not to scare your men."

His mouth quirked as he shrugged into the waistcoat, but he spoke seriously, eyes on mine.

"Och, I want them frightened of me, Sassenach. It's the only way I'll have a chance of bringing them out of it alive."

WITH AN HOUR to spare, I took my kit of everyday medical supplies and went out to the big tree where the sick among the camp followers tended to gather. The army surgeons would tend camp followers as well as soldiers, if they had time—but they wouldn't be having time today.

There was the usual assortment of minor ailments and injuries: a deeply embedded splinter (infected, requiring the application of drawing salve, followed by excavation, disinfection, and bandage); a dislocated toe (caused by the patient having kicked a fellow in play, but the work of a moment to reduce); a split lip (requiring one stitch and a little gentian ointment); a badly gashed foot (the result of inattention whilst chopping wood, requiring twenty-eight stitches and a large dressing); one child with an ear infection (an onion poultice and willow-bark tea prescribed); another with the bellyache (peppermint tea and a strong admonition against eating eggs of unknown age out of birds' nests of unknown provenance) . . .

The few patients requiring medicines I put aside until I'd dealt with the injuries. Then—with a wary eye on the sun—I led them off to my tent to dispense packets of willow bark, peppermint, and hemp leaves.

The tent flap was open; surely I had left it closed? I ducked my head into the gloom of the tent and stopped abruptly. A tall figure stood before me, apparently in the act of rifling my medicine chest.

"What the devil are you doing with that?" I asked sharply, and the figure jerked, startled.

My eyes had now become accustomed to the diffuse light, and I saw that the thief—if that's what he was—was a Continental officer, a captain.

"I beg your pardon, madam," he said, giving me a perfunctory bow. "I had heard that there was a supply of medicaments here. I—"

"There is, and they're mine." This seemed a trifle ungracious—though I certainly thought his own attitude rather brusque—and I softened the remark a little. "What is it that you need? I imagine I can spare a little—"

"Yours?" He glanced from the chest—very clearly an expensive professional bit of furniture—to me, and his brows rose. "What are *you* doing with a thing like that?"

Several possible replies flitted through my head, but I'd recovered from the surprise of seeing him sufficiently as not to make any of them. I settled for a neutral "May I ask who you are, sir?"

"Oh." Mildly flustered, he bowed to me. "I beg pardon. Captain Jared Leckie, your servant, ma'am. I am a surgeon with the Second New Jersey."

He eyed me consideringly, clearly wondering who the devil *I* was. I was wearing a canvas apron with capacious pockets over my gown, these pockets presently stuffed with all manner of small instruments, dressings, bottles and jars of ointments and liquids. I'd also taken off my broad-brimmed hat when I came into the tent and, as usual, was not wearing a cap. I *had* bound up my hair, but it had come loose and was coiling damply round my ears. He obviously suspected me of being a laundress, come to collect soiled linen—or possibly something worse.

"I am Mrs. Fraser," I said, drawing myself up with what I hoped was a gracious nod. "Er . . . Mrs. *General* Fraser, that is," I added, seeing that he appeared unimpressed.

His eyebrows shot up, and he looked me openly up and down, his eyes lingering on the top pockets of my apron, these featuring an unwieldy rolled dressing in the act of coming unrolled and trailing down my front and a jar of asafoetida, whose cork was loose, thus allowing the reek of it to waft gently above the other notable smells of the camp. It was known commonly as "dev-il's dung," and for good reason. I pulled the jar out and pushed the cork in more securely. This gesture seemed somehow to reassure him.

"Oh! The general is a physician, I perceive," he said.

"No," I said, beginning to see that I should have uphill work with Captain Leckie, who appeared young and not overbright. "My husband is a soldier. *I* am a physician."

He stared at me as though I'd told him I was a prostitute. Then he made the mistake of assuming that I was joking and laughed heartily.

At this point, one of my patients, a young mother whose one-year-old son had an ear infection, poked her neatly capped head hesitantly into the tent. Her little boy was in her arms, howling and red-faced.

"Oh, dear," I said. "I'm so sorry to keep you waiting, Mrs. Wilkins. Do bring him in; I'll get the bark for him directly."

Captain Leckie frowned at Mrs. Wilkins and beckoned her closer. She looked nervously at me, but allowed him to lean down and look at little Peter.

"He has a difficult tooth," Leckie said, rather accusingly, after running a large, unwashed thumb through Peter's drooling mouth. "He ought to have the gum slit, to let the tooth come through." He began to fumble in his pocket, where he doubtless had a highly insanitary scalpel or lancet.

"He is teething," I agreed, shaking out a quantity of crumbled willow bark into my mortar. "But he also has an ear infection, and the tooth will come through of its own accord within the next twenty-four hours."

He rounded on me, indignant and astonished.

"Are you contradicting me?"

"Well, yes," I said, rather mildly. "You're wrong. You want to have a good look in his left ear. It's—"

"I, madam, am a diplomate of the Medical College of Philadelphia!"

"I congratulate you," I said, beginning to be provoked. "You're still wrong." Having thus rendered him momentarily speechless, I finished grind-ing the bark into powder and poured it into a square of gauze, which I folded into a neat packet and handed to Mrs. Wilkins, with instructions as to the brewing of the infusion and how to administer it, as well as how to apply an onion poultice.

She took the packet as though it might explode and, with a hasty glance at Captain Leckie, fled, little Peter's howls receding like a siren in the distance.

I drew a deep breath.

"Now," I said, as pleasantly as possible. "If you're in need of simples, Dr. Leckie, I have a good supply. I can—"

He had drawn himself up like a crane eyeing a frog, beady-eyed and hos-tile.

"Your servant, ma'am," he said curtly, and stalked past me.

I rolled my eyes up toward the canvas overhead. There was a small gecko-like creature clinging to the cloth, who viewed me with no particular emo-tion.

"How to win friends and influence people," I remarked to it. "Take note."

Then I pushed the tent flap back and beckoned for the next patient to come in.

I HAD TO hurry in order to make my rendezvous with Jamie, who was just about to begin his review when I dashed up, twisting my hair into a mass and pinning it hastily under my broad-brimmed hat. It was a terribly hot day; being in the open sun for only a few minutes had made my nose and cheeks tingle warningly.

Jamie bowed gravely to me and began his advance along the line of men drawn up for review, greeting men, saluting officers, asking questions, giving his aide-de-camp notes of things to be done.

He had Lieutenant Schnell with him as aide-de-camp—a nice German boy from Philadelphia, perhaps nineteen—and a stout gentleman I didn't know but assumed from his uniform to be the captain in charge of whatever companies we were inspecting. I followed them, smiling at the men as I passed, while looking them over sharpish for any overt signs of illness, injury, or disability—I was sure that Jamie could spot excessive drunkenness without my expert opinion.

There were three hundred men, he'd told me, and most of them were quite all right. I kept walking and nodding, but wasn't above beginning to fantasize some dangerous circumstance in which I found Captain Leckie writhing in pain, which I would graciously allay, causing him to grovel and apologize for his objectionable attitude. I was trying to choose between the prospect of a musket ball embedded in his buttock, testicular torsion, and something temporarily but mortifyingly disfiguring, like Bell's palsy, when my eye caught a glimpse of something odd in the lineup.

The man in front of me was standing bolt upright, musket at port arms, eyes fixed straight ahead. This was perfectly correct—but no other man in the line was doing it. Militiamen were more than capable, but they generally saw no point in military punctilio. I glanced at the rigid soldier, passed by—then glanced back.

"Jesus H. Roosevelt Christ!" I exclaimed, and only sheer chance kept Jamie from hearing me, he being distracted by the sudden arrival of a messenger.

I took two hasty steps back, bent, and peered under the brim of the dusty slouch hat. The face beneath was set in fierce lines, with a darkly ominous glower—and was completely familiar to me.

"Bloody effing hell," I whispered, seizing him by the sleeve. "What are you *doing* here?"

"You wouldn't believe me if I told you," he whispered back, not moving a muscle of face or body. "Do walk on, my dear."

Such was my astonishment, I might actually have done it, had my attention not been drawn by a small figure skulking about behind the line, trying to avoid notice by crouching behind a wagon wheel.

"Germain!" I said, and Jamie whirled about, eyes wide.

Germain stiffened for an instant and then turned to flee, but too late; Lieutenant Schnell, living up to his name, sprang through the line and grabbed Germain by the arm.

"Is he yours, sir?" he asked, glancing curiously from Jamie to Germain and back.

"He is," Jamie said, with a tone that had turned many a man's blood to water. "What the devil—"

"I'm an orderly!" Germain said proudly, trying to detach himself from Lieutenant Schnell's grip. "I'm supposed to be here!"

"No, you're not," his grandfather assured him. "And what do ye mean, an orderly? Whose orderly?"

Germain at once glanced in John's direction, then, realizing his mistake, jerked his eyes back, but it was too late. Jamie reached John in a single stride and ripped the hat off his head.

The face was identifiable as that of Lord John Grey, but only by someone who knew him well. He wore a black felt patch over one eye, and the other was all but obscured by dirt and bruises. He'd cut his luxuriant blond hair to roughly an inch in length and appeared to have rubbed dirt into it.

With considerable aplomb, he scratched his head and handed Jamie his musket.

"I surrender to you, sir," he said, in a clear voice. "To you, personally. So does my orderly," he added, putting a hand on Germain's shoulder. Lieutenant Schnell, quite flabbergasted, let go of Germain as though he were red-hot.

"I surrender, sir," Germain said solemnly, and saluted.

I'd never seen Jamie at a complete loss for words, and didn't now, but it was a near thing. He inhaled strongly through his nose, then turned to Lieutenant Schnell.

"Escort the prisoners to Captain McCorkle, Lieutenant."

"Er . . ." I said apologetically. A hard blue eye swiveled in my direction, brow raised.

"He's injured," I said, as mildly as I could, with a brief gesture in John's direction. Jamie's lips compressed for an instant, but he nodded.

"Take the prisoners—and Mrs. Fraser"—I daresay it was merely sensitivity on my part that perceived a certain emphasis on "Mrs. Fraser"—"to my tent, Lieutenant."

With scarcely a breath, he turned on John.

"I accept your surrender, Colonel," he said, with icy politeness. "And your parole. I will attend you later."

And, with that, he turned his back on the three of us, in what could only be described as a marked manner.

"WHAT ON EARTH happened to your eye?" I demanded, peering at it. I had John on the cot in my small medical tent, the flap open to admit as much light as possible. The eye was swollen half shut and surrounded by a sticky black ring where the felt patch had been peeled away, the underlying flesh a lurid palette of green, purple, and ghastly yellow. The eye itself was red as a flannel petticoat and, from the irritated state of the eyelids, had been watering more or less constantly for some time.

"Your husband punched me when I told him I'd bedded you," he replied, with complete composure. "I do hope he didn't take any similarly violent actions upon being reunited with you?"

Had I been capable of a convincing Scottish noise, I might have resorted to one. As it was, I merely glared at him.

"I decline absolutely to discuss my husband with you," I said. "Lie down, blast you."

He eased himself back on the cot, wincing.

"He said he hit you twice," I remarked, watching this. "Where was the second one?"

"In the liver." He gingerly touched his lower abdomen. I pulled up his shirt and inspected the damage, which amounted to further spectacular bruising around the lower ribs, with blue streaks draining down toward the ilial crest, but little more.

"That's not where your liver is," I informed him. "It's on the other side."

"Oh." He looked blank. "Really? Are you sure?"

"Yes, I am," I assured him. "I'm a doctor. Let me look at your eye."

I didn't wait for permission, but he didn't resist, lying back and staring up at the canvas roof while I spread the eyelids as far as possible. The sclera and conjunctiva were badly inflamed, and even the dim light made the eye water profusely. I held up two fingers.

"Two," he said, before I could ask. "And before you start ordering me to look to and fro and up and down . . . I can't. I can see out of it—though it's a bit blurry, and I see everything doubled, which is very disagreeable—but I can't move it at all. Dr. Hunter opined that some muscle or other was trapped by some sort of bone. He didn't feel competent to deal with it."

"I'm flattered that you think I might be."

"I have the fullest confidence in your abilities, Dr. Fraser," he said politely. "Besides, have I any choice?"

"No. Keep quite still, there . . . Germain!" I had caught sight of a telltale flutter of pink calico from the corner of my eye, and the runaway came sidling in, looking vaguely guilty.

"Don't tell me what you have in your shirt," I said, noting a suspicious bulge or two. "I don't want to be an accessory to crime. No, wait—is it alive?"

Germain prodded the bulge, as though not quite sure, but it didn't move, and he shook his head. "No, *Grand-mère.*"

"Good. Come here and hold this, will you?"

I handed him my pocket looking glass and, adjusting the tent flap so that a ray of light shone in, then adjusted Germain's hand so that the reflected light shone directly from the mirror into the affected eye. John yelped slightly when the light struck his eye, but obediently clutched the sides of the cot and didn't move, though his eye watered terribly. All the better; it would wash out bacteria and perhaps make it easier to move the eyeball.

Denny was most likely right, I thought, selecting my smallest cautery iron and slipping it gently under the lower lid. It was the best thing I could find for the job, being flat, smooth, and spade-shaped. I couldn't move the globe of the eyeball upward at all; even slight pressure made him go white. I could move it slightly from side to side, and given the sensitivity of John's face just below the eye, I began to form a mental picture of the damage. It was almost certainly what was called a "blowout" fracture, which had cracked the delicate bone of the orbital floor and forced a displaced bit of it—along with part of the inferior rectus muscle—down into the maxillary sinus. The edge of the muscle was caught in the crack, thus immobilizing the eyeball.

"Bloody, bloody-minded, effing *Scot,*" I said, straightening up.

"Not his fault," said John. "I provoked him." He sounded excessively cheerful, and I turned a cold look on him.

"I'm not any more pleased with you," I informed him. "You aren't going to like this, and it will serve you right. How in heaven's name did you—no, don't tell me now. I'm busy."

He folded his hands across his stomach, looking meek. Germain sniggered, but desisted when I gave him a glare of his own.

Tight-lipped, I filled a syringe—Dr. Fentiman's penis syringe, as it happened; how appropriate—with saline solution for irrigation and found my small pair of needle-nosed forceps. I had another peek at the site with my makeshift spatula and prepared a tiny, curved needle with a wet catgut suture, cut very fine. I *might* manage without needing to stitch the inferior rectus—it depended whether the edge of the muscle had frayed very badly, by reason of its long entrapment, and how it survived being dislodged—but best to have the suture handy, in case of need. I hoped the need wouldn't occur; there was so much swelling . . . but I couldn't wait several days for it to subside.

What was troubling me was not so much the immediate reduction of the fracture and freeing of the muscle but the longer-term possibility of adhesion. The eye should be kept fairly immobile, to aid healing, but doing that might cause the muscle to adhere to the orbit, literally freezing the eye permanently. I needed something slippery with which to dress the site, something biologically inert and non-irritating—in my own time, sterile glycerin drops would have been instantly available, but here . . .

Egg white, perhaps? Probably not, I thought; body heat might coddle it, and then what?

"John!"

A shocked voice behind me made me turn, needle in hand. A very dapper-looking gentleman in a stylish wig and a gray-blue velvet suit was standing just inside the tent flap, staring aghast at my patient.

"What's happened to him?" Percy Beauchamp demanded, spotting me in the background.

"Nothing serious," I said. "Are you—"

"Leave," said John, in a voice I'd never heard him use before. He sat up, fixing the newcomer with as steely a look as could be managed with one badly watering crimson eye. "Now."

"What in God's name are you doing here?" Beauchamp demanded. His accent was English, but English faintly tinged with French. He took a step nearer and lowered his voice. "Surely you have not become a Rebel?"

"No, I bloody haven't! Leave, I said."

"Dear God, you mean you—what the devil *happened* to you?" He'd come close enough now to behold the complete picture: filthy cropped hair, filthy disheveled clothes, filthy stockinged feet with holes in toe and heel, and a distorted visage now directing a glare of bloodshot venom at him.

"Now, look here—" I began, turning on Percy with determined firmness, but Germain stopped me.

"He's the man who was looking for Papa in New Bern last year," Germain said. He'd put down the looking glass and was watching the evolving scene with interest. "*Grand-père* thinks he's a villain."

Percy cast Germain a startled look, but recovered his composure with remarkable speed.

"Ah. The proprietor of distinguished frogs," he said, with a smile. "I recall. Peter and Simon were their names? One yellow and one green."

Germain bowed respectfully.

"Monsieur has an excellent memory," he said, with exquisite politeness. "What do you want with my papa?"

"An excellent question," said John, putting one hand over his injured eye, the better to glare at Monsieur Beauchamp.

"Yes, that *is* a good question," I said mildly. "Do sit down, Mr. Beauchamp—and bloody explain yourself. And, *you*," I added, taking John firmly by both shoulders, "lie down."

"That can wait," John said shortly, resisting my attempt to flatten him. He swung his legs over the side of the cot. "What are you doing here, Percy?"

"Oh, you know him, do you?" I said, beginning to be provoked.

"Certainly. He's my brother—or was."

"What?" Germain and I exclaimed as one. He looked at me and giggled.

"I thought Hal was your only brother," I said, recovering. I glanced back and forth between John and Percy. There was no resemblance at all between them, whereas John's resemblance to Hal was as marked as if they'd been stamped from the same mold.

"Stepbrother," John said, still more shortly. He got his feet under him, preparing to rise. "Come with me, Percy."

"You're not going anywhere," I said, raising my voice slightly.

"How do you propose to stop me?" John was on his feet, staggering a little as he tried to focus his eyes. Before I could answer, Mr. Beauchamp had lunged forward and grabbed his arm, to keep him from falling. John jerked violently away from him, nearly falling again as he stumbled backward into the cot. He caught his balance and stood glowering at Beauchamp, his fists half clenched.

Beauchamp's gaze was locked with his, and the air between them was . . . electric. *Oh,* I thought, glancing from one to the other, suddenly enlightened. *Oh.*

I must have made some small movement, because Beauchamp's gaze flicked suddenly toward my face. He looked startled at whatever he saw there, then, recovering himself, smiled wryly and bowed.

"*Madame,*" he said. Then, in perfect, accentless English, "He is really my stepbrother, though we haven't spoken in . . . some time. I am here as the guest of the Marquis de La Fayette—amongst other things. Do allow me to take his lordship to meet the marquis. I promise to bring him back in one piece." He smiled at me, warm-eyed and sure of his charm, which was considerable.

"His lordship is a prisoner of war," said a very dry Scottish voice from behind Beauchamp. "And my responsibility. I regret that he must remain here, sir."

Percy Beauchamp whirled round, gaping at Jamie, who was filling the tent flap in a most implacable fashion.

"I *still* want to know what he wants with Papa," Germain said, small blond brows drawn down in a suspicious glower.

"I should like to know that, too, monsieur," Jamie said. He came into the tent, ducking, and nodded toward the stool I had been using. "Pray be seated, sir."

Percy Beauchamp glanced from Jamie to Lord John and back again. His face had gone smooth and blank, though the lively dark eyes were full of calculation.

"Alas," he said, the slight French accent back. "I am engaged to *le marquis*—and General Washington—just now. You will excuse me, I am sure. *Bonjour, Mon Général.*" He marched to the tent flap, head held high, turning at the last moment to smile at John. *"Au revoir, mon frère."*

"Not if I bloody see you first."

⁂

NOBODY MOVED FOR the space of nine heartbeats—I counted them—following Percy Beauchamp's dignified exit. Finally, John sat down abruptly on the cot, exhaling audibly. Jamie caught my eye and, with a slight nod, sat down on the stool. Nobody spoke.

"You mustn't hit him again, *Grand-père*," Germain said earnestly, breaking the silence. "He's a very good man, and I'm sure he won't take Grannie to bed anymore, now that you're home to do it."

Jamie gave Germain a quelling look, but his mouth twitched. From my position behind the cot, I could see the back of John's neck flush a deep pink.

"I'm much obliged to his lordship for his care of your grannie," Jamie told Germain. "But if ye think makin' impertinent remarks regarding your elders is going to save your arse—think again."

Germain shifted uneasily, but rolled his eyes at Lord John in a "worth a try" sort of way.

"I'm obliged to you for your good opinion, sir," John told him. "And I reciprocate the compliment—but I trust you are aware that good intent alone does not absolve one from the consequences of rash conduct."

Jamie was beginning to flush as deeply as John.

"Germain," I said. "Do go away. Oh—see if you can find me some honey, would you?"

All three of them looked at me, startled at this apparent non sequitur.

"It's viscous," I said, with a slight shrug. "And antibacterial."

"Of course it is," John said under his breath in a hopeless sort of way.

"What does 'viscous' mean?" Germain asked, interested.

"Germain," said his grandfather, in a menacing tone, and he hastily disappeared without waiting for enlightenment.

Everyone took a deep breath.

"Lie down *now*," I said to John, before anything regrettable might be said. "Have you got a moment, Jamie? I need someone to hold the mirror while I fix his eye."

With no more than an instant's hesitation, they both obeyed, not looking at each other. I was nearly ready; when I'd got Jamie positioned and the ray of light focused on the eye, I once more irrigated the eye and socket gently with saline solution, then rinsed my fingers thoroughly with the same stuff.

"I need you both to hold completely still," I said. "I'm sorry, John, but there's no other way to do this, and if we're lucky, it will be quick."

"Aye, I've heard that one before," Jamie muttered, but desisted when I shot a sideways look at him.

I was afraid to use the forceps, for fear of puncturing his eyeball. So I spread the lids of John's affected eye with the fingers of my left hand, wedged the fingertips of my right as deeply into the eye socket as I could, and squeezed.

He made a shocked, strangled sort of noise, and Jamie gasped but didn't drop the mirror.

There are not many things in the world slipperier than a wet eyeball. I tried to squeeze as lightly as I could, but there was no help for it; a light pressure merely allowed the eyeball to pop out of my fingers like an oiled grape. I clenched my teeth and tried again, gripping harder.

On the fourth try, I managed to get a sufficient grip as to allow me to try to rotate the eyeball in its socket. I didn't quite manage it, but at least got a better idea of how it might go.

Five minutes later, John was trembling like a blancmange, hands clenched tight on the rails of the cot, Jamie was praying under his breath in Gaelic, and all three of us were drenched with sweat.

"Once more," I said, drawing breath and wiping sweat from my chin with the back of my hand. I rinsed my fingers again. "If I can't get it this time, we'll have a rest and try again later."

"Oh, God," said John. He closed both eyes briefly, swallowed hard, and opened them as wide as he could. Both eyes were watering badly, and tears washed down his temples.

I felt Jamie move slightly next to me. He refocused the mirror—but I saw that he had also moved nearer to the cot, so that his leg pressed against the rail, just next to John's gripping fingers. I wiggled my wet fingers in preparation, said a brief prayer to St. Claire, patron of sore eyes, and thrust my fingers as deeply into the socket as I could manage.

By this time, I had a very clear mental image of the fracture, a dark line beneath the torn conjunctiva, and the line of the inferior rectus muscle wedged into it. I twisted, a short, sharp jerk, before my fingers slipped—and felt the muscle pop free. John shuddered the full length of his body and gave a little moan.

"Glory be," I said, and laughed from sheer relief. There was a little blood—not much—on my fingers, and I wiped them on my apron. Jamie flinched and looked away.

"Now what?" he asked, carefully not looking at John.

"Now what—Oh." I considered that one for a moment, then shook my head.

"He has to lie down for several hours with the eye covered—a day or two, ideally. If Germain finds me some honey, I'll lubricate the eye socket with a bit of it, to prevent adhesion."

"I mean," Jamie said patiently, "does he require to be kept under a doctor's care?"

"Not all the time," I said, surveying John critically. "Someone—me, I mean—needs to check the eye every so often, but there's really nothing else to be done for it; the swelling and bruises will take care of themselves. Why? What were you planning to do with him?"

Jamie made a small gesture of frustration.

"I *would* hand him over to Washington's staff for interrogation," he said. "But—"

"But I surrendered to you personally," John said helpfully. He glanced at me out of his working eye. "That means I'm his responsibility."

"Aye, thank ye for that," Jamie muttered, giving him an irritable look.

"Well, you aren't going to tell him anything useful, either, are you?" I asked, putting a hand on John's forehead. Slightly warm, but no gross fever. "Such as the nature of the relations between yourself and the recent Mr. Beauchamp?"

Jamie gave a brief snort.

"I ken fine what his relations are wi' that wee sodomite," he said bluntly. He gave John a piercing stare. "Ye dinna mean to tell me what he's doing here, do ye?"

"No," John said cheerfully. "Though it almost certainly wouldn't help you if I did."

Jamie nodded, having evidently expected nothing better, and rose with an air of decision.

"Well, then. I've work to do, and so have you, Sassenach. Wait here for Germain, if ye will, and when ye've finished with the honey, tell Germain he's to be in charge of his lordship. He's no to leave his lordship under any circumstances, save you or I tell him he may—and should Monsieur Beauchamp pay another call, Germain is to be present at any conversation. He speaks French verra fluently," he advised John. "And should ye think of attempting to subvert my grandson's loyalty—"

"Sir!" John said, looking shocked at the mere idea.

"Mmphm," Jamie said darkly, and left.

62

THE MULE DISLIKES YOU

I DIDN'T KNOW QUITE what to say to John, in the wake of recent events. He seemed similarly at a loss, but coped with the social awkwardness by closing his eyes and pretending to be asleep. I couldn't leave him until Germain got back with the honey—assuming he found any, but I had a fair amount of faith in his abilities.

Well, no point in sitting about with my hands folded. I took out my mortar and pestle and set to work grinding gentian root and garlic for antibiotic ointment. This occupied my hands, but unfortunately not my mind, which was scampering in circles like a hamster on a wheel.

I had two main anxieties at the moment, one of which I could do nothing about: that being the escalating sense of oncoming battle. I knew it very well; I couldn't be mistaken. Jamie hadn't told me explicitly, perhaps because he hadn't had written orders yet—but I knew as clearly as if it had been shouted by a town crier. The army would move soon.

I stole a glance at John, who lay like a tomb effigy, hands neatly crossed at his waist. All it wanted was a small dog curled up at his feet. Rollo, snoring under the cot, would have to do, I supposed.

John, of course, was the other anxiety. I had no idea how he'd come to be where he was, but enough people had seen him surrender that his presence would be common knowledge by nightfall. And once it *was* . . .

"I don't suppose you'd consider escaping, if I left for a moment?" I asked abruptly.

"No," he said, not opening his eyes. "I gave my parole. Besides, I wouldn't make it outside the camp," he added.

The silence resumed, broken by the *brumm* of a large bumblebee, which had blundered into the tent, and the more distant shouts and drumbeats of soldiers drilling and the low thrashing noises of daily camp life.

The only good thing—if one chose to regard it that way, and I might as well—was that the rising sense of battle urgency was likely to preclude official curiosity about John. What the devil would Jamie do with him when the army decamped in the morning? I wondered.

"Grand-mère, Grand-mère!" Germain burst into the tent, and Rollo—who had slept through Percy Beauchamp's visit without stirring a whisker—shot out from under the cot with an explosive *WOOF!* that nearly overturned the cot and John with it.

"Hush, dog," I said, seeing him glaring wildly round, and took a restraining grip on his scruff. "And what the he—I mean the dev—I mean what's the matter, Germain?"

"I saw him, Grannie! I saw him! The man who took Clarence! Come quick!" And without waiting for response, he turned and raced out of the tent.

John began to sit up, and Rollo tensed under my hand.

"Sit!" I said to both of them. "And bloody stay!"

THE HAIRS ON my forearms were prickling, even as sweat streamed down my neck. I'd left my hat behind and the sun blazed on my cheeks; I was panting by the time I caught up with Germain, as much from emotion as from heat.

"Where—"

"Just there, Grannie! The big bugger wi' the kerchief round his arm. Clarence must ha' bitten him!" Germain added, with glee.

The bugger in question *was* big: roughly twice my size, with a head like a pumpkin. He was sitting on the ground under the shade of what I thought of as the hospital tree, nursing his kerchief-wrapped arm and glowering at nothing in particular. A small group of people seeking medical treatment—you could tell as much from their hunched and drooping attitudes—was keeping a distance from him, looking warily at him from time to time.

"You'd best keep out of sight," I murmured to Germain, but, hearing no answer, glanced round to discover that he'd already faded artfully from view, canny child that he was.

I walked up, smiling, to the little group of waiting people—mostly women with children. I didn't know any of them by name, but they clearly knew who and what I was; they bobbed their heads and murmured greetings, but cut their eyes sideways at the man under the tree. *"Take him first before he does something messy"* was the clear message. Just as clear as the sense of badly contained violence that the man was radiating in all directions.

I cleared my throat and walked over to the man, wondering what on earth I was to say to him. *"What have you done with Clarence the mule?"* or *"How dare you rob my grandson and leave him in the wilderness alone, you bloody bastard?"*

I settled for "Good morning. I'm Mrs. Fraser. What happened to your arm, sir?"

"Bleedin' mule bit me to the bone, gaddamn his stinkin' hide," the man replied promptly, and glowered at me under eyebrows ridged with scar tissue. So were his knuckles.

"Let me see it, will you?" Not waiting for permission, I took hold of his wrist—it was hairy and very warm—and unwrapped the kerchief. This was stiff with dried blood, and no wonder.

Clarence—if it was Clarence—actually *had* bitten him to the bone. Horse and mule bites could be serious but usually resulted only in deep bruising; equines had powerful jaws, but their front teeth were designed for tearing grass, and as most bites were through clothing, they didn't often break skin. It could be done, though, and Clarence had done it.

A flap of skin—and a good chunk of flesh—about three inches wide had been partially detached, and I could see past the thin fatty layer to the gleam of tendon and the red membranous covering of the radius. The wound was recent but had stopped bleeding, save for a little oozing at the edges.

"Hmm," I said noncommittally, and turned his hand over. "Can you close your fingers into a fist?" He could, though the ring finger and little finger wouldn't fold in completely. They did move, though; the tendon wasn't severed. "Hmm," I said again, and reached into my bag for the bottle of saline solution and a probe. Saline was a little less painful for disinfection than dilute alcohol or vinegar—and it was somewhat easier to get hold of salt, at least when living in a city—but I kept a tight grip on the enormous wrist as I poured the liquid into the wound.

He made a noise like a wounded bear, and the waiting onlookers took several steps back, as a body.

"Rather a vicious mule," I observed mildly, as the patient subsided, panting. His face darkened.

"Gonna beat the gaddamn bastarding fucker to death, soon as I get back," he said, and bared his yellow teeth at me. "Skin him, I will, and sell his meat."

"Oh, I wouldn't advise that," I said, keeping a grip on my temper. "You don't want to be using that arm violently; it could bring on gangrene."

"It could?" He didn't go pale—it wasn't possible, given the temperature—but I'd definitely got his attention.

"Yes," I said pleasantly. "You've seen gangrene, I daresay? The flesh goes green and putrid—beastly smell—limb rots, dead in days . . . that sort of thing?"

"I seen it," he muttered, eyes now fixed on his arm.

"Well, well," I said soothingly, "we'll do our best here, won't we?" I would normally have offered a patient in such a case a fortifying draft of whatever liquor was available—and, thanks to the marquis, I had quite a good supply of French brandy—but in the present instance, I wasn't feeling charitable.

In fact, my general feeling was that Hippocrates could turn a blind eye for the next few minutes. Do no harm, forsooth. Still, there wasn't a great deal I could do to him, armed with a two-inch suture needle and a pair of embroidery scissors.

I stitched the wound as slowly as I could, taking care to slosh more saline over it periodically and glancing covertly round for assistance. Jamie was with Washington and the high command as they strategized the imminent engagement; I couldn't summon him out to deal with a mule thief.

Ian had vanished on his pony, scouting the British rear guard. Rollo was with Lord John. Rachel had gone off with Denny and Dottie in the Quakers' wagon, to look for supplies in the nearest village. And good luck to them, I thought; General Greene's foragers had spread out like locusts over the face of the earth the moment the army halted, stripping farmsteads and storage barns in their path.

The patient was cursing in a rather monotonous and uninspired fashion, but showed no signs of keeling over in a convenient faint. What I was doing to his arm was unlikely to improve his temper; what if he actually *did* intend to go straight off and beat Clarence to death?

If Clarence was loose, I'd put good odds on the mule to win any such encounter, but he was very likely tied or hobbled. But then . . . a horrid thought struck me. I *knew* where Germain was, and what he was doing—or trying to do.

"Jesus H. Roosevelt Christ," I muttered, bending my head over the teamster's arm to hide an undoubtedly appalled expression. Germain was an extremely talented pickpocket, but stealing a mule out of the middle of a gang of teamsters . . .

What had Jamie said? *"He'd be taken up for theft and hanged or flogged within an inch of his life, and I couldna do a thing to stop it."* Teamsters being what they were, they'd likely just break his neck and be done with it, rather than waiting for any sort of military justice.

I swallowed hard and glanced quickly over my shoulder, to see if I could spot the teamsters' encampment. If I could see Germain . . .

I didn't see Germain. What I saw was Percy Beauchamp, regarding me thoughtfully from the shadow of a nearby tent. Our eyes met, and he instantly came toward me, straightening his coat. Well, I was in no position to look a gift horse—or mule—in the mouth, was I?

"Madame Fraser," he said, and bowed. "Are you in need of some assistance?"

Yes, I bloody did need assistance; I couldn't drag my surgical repairs out much longer. I darted a look at my massive patient, wondering whether he had any French.

Apparently my face was just as transparent as Jamie had always told me it was; Percy smiled at me and said conversationally in French, "I don't think this clot of decaying menstrual blood is capable of understanding more English than it takes to hire the sort of poxed and imbecile whore who would let him touch her, let alone understand the tongue of angels."

The teamster went on muttering, "Shit-fire, shit-fire, fucking shit-ass fucking-ass mule, that gaddamn *hurts* . . ."

I relaxed a little and replied in French. "Yes, I need help—with the utmost urgency. My grandson is trying to steal the mule this oaf stole from him. Can you retrieve him from the teamsters' camp before someone notices?"

"À votre service, madame," he replied promptly, and, clicking his heels smartly together, bowed and went off.

I TOOK AS long as I could over the final dressing of the wound, worried that should my foul-mouthed patient find Germain among the teamsters, Percy's French manners might be unequal to the occasion. And I couldn't really expect Hippocrates to continue turning a blind eye, were I compelled to do something drastic if the man tried to break Germain's neck.

I heard a familiar loud braying behind me, though, and turned sharply to see Percy, flushed and a trifle disheveled, leading Clarence toward me. Germain sat atop the mule, his face set in lines of vindictive triumph as he glared at my patient.

I stood up hastily, groping for my knife. The teamster, who had been gingerly prodding the fresh bandage round his arm, looked up, startled, then surged to his feet with a roar.

"Shit-*FIRE!*" he said, and started purposefully toward them, fists clenched.

Percy, to his credit, stood his ground, though he paled a little. He handed the reins up to Germain, though, and stepped firmly forward.

"Monsieur . . ." he began. I would have liked to know just what he had in mind to say but didn't find out, as the teamster didn't bother with colloquy, instead driving a hamlike fist into Percy's belly. Percy sat down hard and folded up like a fan.

"Bloody *hell—Germain!*" For Germain, nothing daunted by the sudden loss of support, had gathered up Clarence's reins and tried to lash the teamster across the face with them.

This might possibly have been effective, had he not telegraphed his intention quite so clearly. As it was, the teamster ducked and reached out, clearly intending to grab either the reins or Germain. The crowd around me had realized what was happening by now, and women started screaming. At this point, Clarence decided to become involved and, laying back his ears, curled his lips and snapped at the teamster's face, coming within a toucher of taking off the man's nose.

"SHIT-ASS FUCKING MULE!!" Deeply inflamed, the teamster leapt at Clarence and fixed his teeth in the mule's upper lip, clinging like grim death to his neck. Clarence screamed. The women screamed. Germain screamed.

I didn't scream, because I couldn't breathe. I was elbowing my way through the crowd, fumbling for the slit in my skirt so I could reach my knife. Just as I laid my hand on the hilt, though, a hand came down on my shoulder, halting me in my tracks.

"Pardon me, milady," said Fergus, and, stepping purposefully past me, walked up beside the lunging mass of mule, teamster, and shrieking child, and fired the pistol in his hand.

Everything stopped, for a split second, and then the shouting and screaming started again, everyone surging toward Clarence and his companions to see what had happened. For a long moment, it wasn't apparent what *had* happened. The teamster had let go his grip in astonishment and turned toward Fergus, eyes bulging and blood-tinged saliva running down his chin. Germain, with more presence of mind than I would have had in such a situation, got hold of the reins and was hauling on them with all his strength, trying to turn Clarence's head. Clarence, whose blood was plainly up, was having none of it.

Fergus calmly put the fired pistol back into his belt—I realized at this point that he must have fired into the dirt near the teamster's feet—and spoke to the man.

"If I were you, sir, I would remove myself promptly from this animal's presence. It is apparent that he dislikes you."

The shouting and screaming had stopped, and this made several people laugh.

"Got you there, Belden!" a man near me called. "The mule dislikes you. What you think of that?"

The teamster looked mildly dazed but still homicidal. He stood with his fists clenched, legs braced wide apart and shoulders hunched, glowering at the crowd.

"What I think . . . ?" he began. "*I* think—"

But Percy had managed to get to his feet and, while still somewhat hunched, was mobile. Without hesitation, he walked up and kicked the teamster smartly in the balls.

This went over well. Even the man who appeared to be a friend of Belden's whooped with laughter. The teamster didn't go down but curled up like a dried leaf, clutching himself. Percy wisely didn't wait for him to recover, but turned and bowed to Fergus.

"*À votre service, monsieur.* I suggest that you and your son—and the mule, of course—might withdraw?"

"*Merci beaucoup,* and I suggest you do the same, *tout de suite,*" Fergus replied.

"Hey!" shouted the teamster's friend, not laughing now. "You can't steal that mule!"

Fergus rounded on him, imperious as the French aristocrat Percy had implied he might be.

"I cannot, sir," he said, inclining his head a quarter of an inch in acknowledgment. "Because a man cannot steal that which already belongs to him, is this not so?"

"Is that not . . . is *what* not so?" demanded the man, confused.

Fergus scorned to answer this. Lifting one dark brow, he strode off several paces, turned, and shouted, "Clarence! *Écoutez-moi!*"

With the teamster's collapse, Germain had succeeded in getting Clarence somewhat under control, though the mule's ears were still laid out flat in displeasure. At the sound of Fergus's voice, though, the ears rose slowly upright and swiveled in his direction.

Fergus smiled, and I heard a woman behind me sigh involuntarily. Fergus's smile was remarkably charming. He reached into his pocket and withdrew an apple, which he skewered neatly on his hook.

"Come," he said to the mule, extending his right hand and twiddling the fingers in a head-scratching motion. Clarence came, disregarding Mr. Belden, who had now sat down and was clutching his knees, the better to contemplate his state of inner being. The mule ducked his head to take the apple, nudging Fergus's elbow, and allowed his forehead to be scratched. There was a murmur of interest and approbation from the crowd, and I noticed a few censorious glances being shot at the groaning Mr. Belden.

The sense of being about to faint had left me, and now my insides began to unclench. With some effort, I slid the knife back into its sheath without stabbing myself in the thigh and wiped my hand on my skirt.

"As for *you, sans crevelle,*" Fergus was saying to Germain, with a low-voiced menace that he'd plainly learned from Jamie, "we have a few things to discuss presently."

Germain turned a rather sickly shade of yellow. "Yes, *Papa,*" he murmured, hanging his head in order to avoid his father's minatory eye.

"Get down," Fergus said to him, and, turning to me, raised his voice.

"Madame General, permit me to present this animal personally to General Fraser, in the service of liberty!"

This was delivered in such a tone of ringing sincerity that a few souls applauded. I accepted, as graciously as possible, on behalf of General Fraser. By the conclusion of these proceedings, Mr. Belden had got awkwardly to his feet and stumbled off toward the teamsters' camp, tacitly ceding Clarence to the cause.

I took Clarence's reins, relieved and glad to see him again. Apparently it was mutual, for he nosed me familiarly in the shoulder and made chummy huffing noises.

Fergus, meanwhile, stood for a moment looking down at Germain, then squared his shoulders and turned to Percy, who still looked a little pale but had straightened his wig and regained his self-possession. Percy bowed very formally to Fergus, who sighed deeply, then bowed back.

"And I suppose that we, too, have matters to discuss, monsieur," he said, resigned. "Perhaps a little later?"

Percy's handsome face lighted.

"*À votre service . . . seigneur,*" he said, and bowed again.

63

AN ALTERNATE USE FOR
A PENIS SYRINGE

GERMAIN HAD, IN FACT, found some honey, and now that the excitement of recovering Clarence was over, he produced a large chunk of sticky honeycomb, wrapped in a dirty black kerchief, from the recesses of his shirt.

"What are you going to do wi' that, Grannie?" he asked, curious. I'd set the oozing chunk of comb in a clean pottery dish and was again employing the useful penis syringe—carefully sterilized with alcohol—to suck up honey, being careful to avoid bits of wax and noticeable pollen grains. Having been designed for irrigation rather than puncture, the syringe had a blunt, smoothly tapered tip: just the thing for dribbling honey into someone's eye.

"I'm going to lubricate his lordship's bad eye," I said. "Fergus, will you come and steady his lordship's head, please? Put your hand on his forehead. And, Germain, you'll hold his eyelids open."

"I can keep still," John said irritably.

"Be quiet," I said briefly, and sat down on the stool beside him. "No one can keep still while having things poked into their eye."

"You were poking your bloody *fingers* into my eye not an hour since! And I didn't move!"

"You squirmed," I said. "It's not your fault, you couldn't help it. Now, be quiet; I don't want to accidentally stab you in the eyeball with this."

Breathing audibly through his nose, he clamped his mouth shut and suffered Fergus and Germain to immobilize him. I'd debated whether to dilute the honey with boiled water, but the heat of the day had made it sufficiently thin that I thought it better to use it at full strength.

"It's antibacterial," I explained to the three of them, using my cautery iron again to lift the eyeball and squirting a slow dribble of honey under it. "That means it kills germs."

Fergus and Germain, to whom I had explained germs more than once, nodded intelligently and tried to look as though they believed in the existence of such things, which they didn't. John opened his mouth as though to speak, but then shut it again and exhaled strongly through his nose.

"But the chief virtue of honey in the present instance," I went on, anointing the eyeball generously, "is that it's viscous. Let go now, Germain. Blink, John. Oh, *very* good!" The handling had of course made the eye water, but even dilute honey retains its viscosity; I could see the altered gleam of the light across the sclera, indicating the presence of a thin, soothing—I hoped—layer of honey. Some had overflowed, of course, and amber beads were sliding down his temple toward his ear; I stanched the flow with a handkerchief.

"How does it feel?"

John opened and closed his eye a couple of times, very slowly.

"Everything looks blurry."

"Doesn't matter; you aren't going to be looking out of that eye for a day or two anyway. Does it feel any better?"

"Yes," he said, in a distinctly grudging manner, and the other three of us made approving noises that made him look embarrassed.

"Right, then. Sit up—carefully! Yes, that's it. Close your eye and hold this to catch the drips." And, handing him a clean handkerchief, I unrolled a length of gauze bandage, thumbed a pad of lint carefully into the eye socket, and rolled the bandage round his head a few times, tucking in the ends. He strongly resembled a figure in an old painting titled *The Spirit of '76*, but I didn't mention it.

"All right," I said, exhaling and feeling rather pleased with myself. "Fergus, why don't you and Germain go and find some food? Something for his lordship, and something for the road tomorrow. I rather think it will be a long day."

"This one's been quite long enough already," John said. He was swaying a little, and I pushed him gently back down with little resistance. He stretched his neck to ease it, then settled on the pillow with a sigh. "Thank you."

"It was my pleasure," I assured him. I hesitated, but, with Fergus's departure, I didn't think I'd have a better chance to ask what was in my mind. "I don't suppose *you* know what Percival Beauchamp wants with Fergus, do you?"

The good eye opened and looked at me.

"You mean you don't think he believes Fergus to be the lost heir to a great fortune? No, I don't, either. But if Mr. Fraser will take a bit of unsolicited advice, I'd strongly suggest having as little as possible to do with Monsieur Beauchamp." The eye closed again.

Percy Beauchamp had taken his leave—very gracefully—after Clarence's rescue, explaining that he must attend *le marquis* but adding that he would seek out Fergus on the morrow.

"When things are quieter," he'd added, with a genteel bow.

I regarded John thoughtfully.

"What did he do to you?" I asked. He didn't open his eye, but his lips tightened.

"To me? Nothing. Nothing at all," he repeated, and turned over on his side with his back to me.

64

THREE HUNDRED AND ONE

THREE HUNDRED MEN. Jamie stepped into the darkness beyond the 16th New Jersey's campfire and paused for a moment to let his eyes adjust. Three *hundred* bloody men. He'd never led a band of more than fifty. And never had much in the way of subalterns, no more than one or two men under him.

Now he had ten militia companies, each with its own captain and a few informally appointed lieutenants, and Lee had given him a staff of his own: two aides-de-camp, a secretary—now, *that* he could get used to, he thought, flexing the fingers of his maimed right hand—three captains, one of whom was striding along at his shoulder, trying not to look worrit, ten of his own lieutenants, who would serve as liaison between him and the companies under his command, a cook, an assistant cook—and, of course, he had a surgeon already.

Despite the preoccupations of the moment, the memory of Lee's face when Jamie'd told him exactly why he didn't need an army surgeon assigned to him made him smile.

"Indeed," Lee had said, his long-nosed face going blank. Then he'd gathered his wits and gone red in the face, thinking himself practiced upon. But Jamie had pushed back his cuff and shown Lee his right hand, the old white scars on his fingers like tiny starbursts where the bones had come through, and the broad one, still red but neat, straight, and beautifully knit, running down between the middle finger and the little one, showing where the missing finger had been amputated with such skill that one had to look twice to see why the hand seemed strange.

"Well, General, your wife seems a most accomplished needlewoman," Lee said, now amused.

"Aye, sir, she is," he'd said politely. "And a verra bonny hand with a blade, too."

Lee gave him a sardonic look and spread out the fingers of his own right hand; the outer two were missing.

"So was the gentleman who took these off me. A duel," he added off-handedly, seeing Jamie's raised brows, and curled up his hand again. "In Italy."

He didn't know about Lee. The man had a reputation, but he was a boaster, and the two didn't often go together. On the other hand, he was proud as one of Louis's camels, and arrogance sometimes did mark a man who kent his worth.

The plan to attack the British rear guard, at first intended as a quick strike by La Fayette and a thousand men—Lee scorning such a minor command—had grown more elaborate, as such things always did if you gave commanders time to think about them. Once Washington had decided that the expeditionary force should be five thousand men, Lee had graciously condescended to this more appropriate command—leaving La Fayette in charge of his own smaller force, for the sake of the marquis's *amour-propre,* but with Lee in command overall. Jamie had his doubts, but it wasn't his place to voice them.

He glanced to his left, where Ian and his dog were ambling along, the former whistling to himself and the latter a huge, shaggy shape in the dark, panting from the heat.

"Iain," he said casually in *Gàidhlig,* "did your friends with the feathers have aught to say about Ounewaterika?"

"They had, Uncle," Ian replied in the same language. "Not much, though, for they know him only by repute. He's a most ferocious fighter, or so it's said."

"Mmphm." The Mohawk were certainly ferocious and did set great store by personal courage—but he thought they had a negligible grasp of strategy, tactics, and judgment. He was about to ask about Joseph Brant, who was likely the closest thing to a general—in the formal sense—among the Mohawk, but was interrupted by a tall, gangling form stepping out in front of him.

"I beg your pardon, sir. Might I have a word?" the man said, and, looking right and left at Jamie's companions, added, "A private word."

"Certainly, Captain . . . Woodsworth," he replied, hoping his hesitation in finding the man's name was small enough to pass unnoticed. He'd memorized all the militia captains as he met them—and as many men as he could—but their names wouldn't come easy to him for a bit yet.

After a moment's further hesitation, he nodded to Ian to go on with Captain Whewell to the next fire.

"Tell them what's afoot, Captain," he said, for the next fire was one of Whewell's assigned companies, "but wait for me there, aye?"

"What's afoot?" Woodsworth repeated, sounding alarmed. "What's happening? Are we to go now?"

"Not yet, Captain. Come aside, aye? Else we'll be trampled." For they were standing in the path that led from the fires to a set of hastily dug latrine trenches; he could smell the acrid tang of ordure and quicklime from here.

Leading Woodsworth aside, he acquainted him with the change of commander for the morning, but assured him that this would make no real difference to the militia companies under Jamie's command; they would receive their orders in the normal way.

He thought privately that it wouldn't make a difference in how the companies operated—it might well make a difference as to whether they met battle on the morrow or not, and whether they survived if they did—but there was no telling whether the better odds lay with La Fayette or Lee. Chances were that sheer accident, Fate, or, just possibly, God, would decide.

"Now, sir," he said. "Ye wished to speak wi' me?"

"Oh." Woodsworth inhaled through his nose and straightened himself, hastily retrieving the words of whatever speech he'd composed. "Yes, sir. I wished to inquire after the—er—the disposition made of Bertram Armstrong."

"Bertram . . . what?"

"The man you took from my—er, from the lines earlier today, with the little boy."

Jamie didn't know whether to laugh or be annoyed. *Bertram?*

"The man is well enough disposed for the present, sir. My wife's seen to his eye, and he's been fed."

"Oh." Woodsworth shuffled his feet, but stood his ground. "I'm glad of that, sir. But what I meant—I am concerned for him. There is talk about him."

"I'm sure there is," Jamie said, not bothering to hide the edge in his voice. "And what is your concern, sir?"

"They are saying—the men from Dunning's company—that Armstrong is a government spy, that he is a British officer who concealed himself among us. That they found a commission upon him, and correspondence. I—" He paused and gulped breath, the next words coming out in a rush. "I cannot believe it of him, sir, nor can any of us. We feel that some mistake must have been made, and we—we wish to say that we hope nothing . . . hasty will be done."

"No one has suggested anything of the sort, Captain," Jamie assured him, alarm running down his spine like quicksilver. *Only because they haven't had time.* He'd been able to ignore the thorny problem Grey presented as a prisoner, in the fierce rush of preparation and the fiercer rush of his own feelings, but he couldn't ignore it much longer. He should have notified La Fayette, Lee, *and* Washington of Grey's presence immediately, but had gambled on the confusion of imminent battle to disguise his delay.

His eyes had grown used to the scattered light of stars and fire; he could see Woodsworth's long face, apologetic but determined.

"Yes. I hesitate to speak so frankly, sir, but the sorry fact is that when men's passions run high, regrettable actions—irretrievable actions—may be taken." Woodsworth swallowed audibly. "I should not like to see that."

"Ye think someone might see fit to take such action? Now?" He glanced round at the encircling fires. He could see bodies moving, restless as the flames, dark shadows in the woods—but he caught no sense of riot, no pulse of anger. A murmur of talk, to be sure, voices raised in excitement, bursts of laughter and even singing, but it was the nervous spirit of anticipation, expectation, not the sullen rumble of a mob.

"I am a clergyman, sir." Woodsworth's voice was stronger now, urgent. "I know how men may turn to evil conversation and how quickly such conversation may turn to action. One drink too many, a careless word . . ."

"Aye, ye're right about that," Jamie said. He cursed himself for not having thought of this possibility; he'd let his own feelings cloud his mind. Of course, he'd had no idea when he left Grey that he'd been carrying a commission—but that was no excuse. "I've sent word to General Lee about . . . Mr. Armstrong. Should ye hear any more talk about the man, ye might let it be known that the matter is in official hands. That might prevent anything . . . regrettably informal happening."

Woodsworth's sigh of relief was palpable.

"Yes, sir," he said, with gratitude. "I shall certainly let that be known." He stepped aside, bobbing his head, but then stopped, struck by a thought. "Oh."

"Aye?" Jamie spoke impatiently; he felt assailed from all sides by swarms of tiny, stinging troubles, and was inclined to swat this one.

"I trust you will forgive my persistence, General. But I just thought—the boy who was with Armstrong. Bobby Higgins, he's called."

All Jamie's senses were instantly alert.

"What about him?"

"He—I mean Armstrong—the boy said he was in search of his grandfather, and Armstrong said he knew the man—and that his name was James Fraser. . . ."

Jamie shut his eyes. If no one lynched John Grey before dawn, he might throttle the man himself.

"The boy is indeed my grandson, Captain," he said, as evenly as he could, opening his eyes. *Which means, aye, I ken bloody Bert Armstrong.* And if that small bit of information became generally known, there were going to be a lot of very awkward questions asked, by people in a position to demand answers. "My wife is caring for him."

"Oh. Good. I just wished to—"

"To make known your concern. Aye, Captain. I thank ye. Good night."

Woodsworth bowed and stepped back, murmuring, "Good night," in his turn, and disappeared into a night that was far from good and getting worse by the moment.

Jamie jerked his coat straight and strode on. Three hundred men to inform and command, to rouse, lead, and control. Three hundred lives in his hands.

Three hundred and bloody *one*.

65

MOSQUITOES

JAMIE WALKED INTO the light of the fire quite late, smiled at me, and sat down suddenly.

"Is there food?" he asked.

"There is, sir," said the woman who was stirring it. "And you'll have some, too, ma'am," she added firmly, giving me a look that strongly suggested that I was not looking my very best. I wasn't disposed to care, but accepted with thanks a wooden bowl of something hot and a chunk of bread to eat it with.

I barely noticed what I ate, though I was ravenous. The day had been so filled with activity that I hadn't had time to eat—would not have eaten at all, in fact, had I not brought food for John, at which point he insisted that I sit down for ten minutes and eat with him. Percy Beauchamp had not come back; that was something on the plus side of the ledger, I supposed.

There had been a couple of dozen men from Jamie's companies that I rejected by reason of disfirmity—crippled, asthmatic, collapsed with age—and perhaps three dozen more who were essentially sound but sporting some injury requiring attention, these mostly the result of fistfights or falling down while under the influence of drink. Several of them were *still* under the influence of drink and had been sent off under guard to sleep it off.

I did wonder for a moment how many men normally went into battle drunk. In all honesty, I'd be strongly tempted to do it myself, were I required to do what these men were about to do.

There was still a tremendous bustle, but the earlier sense of exhilaration had transmuted into something more concentrated, more focused and sober. Preparations were being made in earnest.

I'd finished my own, or hoped I had. A small tent for shelter from the blazing sun, packs of medical supplies, surgical kits, each equipped with a jar of wet sutures, a wad of lint for mopping up blood, and a bottle of dilute alcohol—I'd run out of salt and couldn't summon the will to badger or beg more from the commissary officer; I'd try to do it in the morning. And the emergency kit that I carried over my shoulder, no matter what.

I sat close to the fire, but despite that and in spite of the warmth of the night itself, I began to feel chilled and heavy, as though I were slowly ossifying, and only then realized how tired I was. The camp hadn't gone to sleep entirely—there was still talk around the fires, and the occasional rasp of a scythe or a sword being sharpened, but the volume had dropped. The atmosphere had settled with the sinking of the moon, even those souls most excited at the prospect of imminent battle succumbing to sleep.

"Come and lie down," I said softly to Jamie, and rose from my seat with a muffled groan. "It won't be for long, but you need *some* rest—and so do I."

"Aye, all right, but I canna be under canvas," he said, low-voiced, following me. "I feel half smothered; couldna breathe in a tent."

"Well, plenty of room outside," I said, nobly suppressing a twinge at the thought of sleeping on the ground. Fetching a couple of blankets, I followed him, yawning, a little way along the riverbank, until we found a private spot behind the scrim of willows that dragged their leaves in the water.

In fact, it was surprisingly comfortable; there was a thick growth of springy grass on which to spread the blankets, and, so close to the water, the air was at least moving, cool on my skin. I shucked out of my petticoats and took my stays completely off, with a blissful shiver of relief as the coolness stirred gently through my damp shift.

Jamie had stripped to his shirt and was rubbing his face and legs with mosquito ointment, the presence of hordes of these insects accounting for the lack of company near the water. I sat down beside him and helped myself to a small scoop of the mint-smelling grease. Mosquitoes seldom bit me, but that didn't stop them whining past my ears and poking inquisitively into my mouth and nostrils, which I found disconcerting in the extreme.

I lay back, watching as he finished his more thorough anointing. I could feel the distant approach of morning, but longed all the more for whatever brief oblivion I could get before the sun rose and all hell broke loose.

Jamie closed the tin and stretched out beside me with a low groan, black leaf shadows trembling over the paleness of his shirt. I rolled toward him just as he rolled toward me, and we met with a blind and groping kiss, smiling against each other's mouth, wriggling and squirming to find a good way of lying together. Warm as it was, I wanted to be touching him.

He wanted to be touching me, too.

"Really?" I said, astonished. "How can you possibly—you've been up for hours!"

"No, only the last minute or two," he assured me. "I'm sorry, Sassenach. I ken ye're tired and I wouldna ask—but I'm desperate." He let go of my bottom long enough to pull up his shirt, and I rather resignedly started disentangling my shift from my legs.

"I dinna mind if ye fall asleep while I'm about my business," he said in my ear, feeling his way one-handed. "I willna take long about it. I just—"

"The mosquitoes will bite your arse," I said, wiggling my own arse into a better position and opening my legs. "Hadn't I best put some—oh!"

"Oh?" he said, sounding pleased. "Well, it's all right if ye want to stay awake, of course . . ."

I pinched his buttock, hard, and he gave a small yelp, laughed, and licked my ear. The fit was a bit dry, and he fumbled for the tin of mosquito ointment.

"Are you sure—" I began dubiously. "Oh!" He was already applying the half-liquid ointment, with more enthusiasm than dexterity, but the fact of his enthusiasm was more arousing than skill might have been. Having a small amount of oil of peppermint vigorously applied to one's private parts was a rather novel sensation, too.

"Make that noise again," he said, breathing heavily in my ear. "I like it."

He was right; it didn't take long. He lay half on and half off me, panting, his heart beating slow and hard against my breast. I had my legs wrapped round him—I could feel the flutter of tiny insects on my ankles and bare feet as they swarmed, avid for his unprotected bare flesh—and didn't mean to let him go. I squeezed him close, rocking gently, slippery and tingling and . . . I didn't take long, either. My quivering legs relaxed, releasing him.

"Shall I tell you something?" I said, after a bit of mint-scented heavy breathing. "The mosquitoes won't bite your cock."

"I dinna mind if they carry me off to their lair to feed to their bairns," he murmured. "Come here, Sassenach."

I pushed damp hair out of my face and settled contentedly in the hollow of his shoulder, his arm around me. By now, I had reached that sense of accommodation with the humid atmosphere in which I stopped trying to keep track of my own body's boundaries and simply melted into sleep.

I slept without dreaming and without moving, until a touch of cramp in my left foot roused me enough to shift a little. Jamie raised his arm a bit, then replaced it as I settled again, and I became aware that he wasn't asleep.

"You . . . all right?" I murmured, thick-tongued with drowsiness.

"Aye, fine," he whispered, and his hand smoothed the hair from my cheek. "Go back to sleep, Sassenach. I'll wake ye when it's time."

My mouth was sticky, and it took a moment to locate any words.

"You need to sleep, too."

"No," he said, soft but definite. "No, I dinna mean to sleep. So close to the battle . . . I have dreams. I've had them the last three nights, and they get worse."

My own arm was lying across his midsection; at this, I reached up involuntarily, putting my hand over his heart. I knew he'd dreamed—and I had a very good idea what he'd dreamed about, from the things he'd said in his sleep. And the way he'd wakened, trembling. *"They get worse."*

"Shh," he said, and bent his head to kiss my hair. "Dinna fash, *a nighean*. I want only to lie here wi' you in my arms, to keep ye safe and watch ye sleep. I can rise then with a clear mind . . . and go to do what must be done."

66

WAR PAINT

"**N**ESSUN DORMA." *None shall sleep.* It was a song—an aria, Brianna had called it—from an opera she knew; she'd played a part in it at her university, dressed up in Chinese robes. Ian smiled at thought of his cousin, taller than most men, striding up and down on a stage, swishing her silk robes about her; he wished he'd seen that.

He'd thought of her from the moment he'd opened the little deerskin bag that held his paints. She was a painter, Bree, and a good one. She ground her own pigments, and she'd made his red ochre for him, and the black and white from charcoal and dried clay—and made for him, too, a deep green from ground malachite, and a brilliant yellow from the gall of the buffalo she and her mother had killed; no other man had such deep colors to his paint, and he wished for a moment that Eats Turtles and some of his other Mohawk clan brothers could be with him to admire them.

The noise of the distant camp was like the singing of cicadas in the trees near a river: a buzz too loud to think through, but one that went away as you got used to it. *None shall sleep* . . . The women and children, they might sleep—but the whores surely didn't. Not tonight.

He felt a twitch at the thought, but dismissed it. Thought of Rachel, and dismissed her, too, but reluctantly.

He opened the willow-bark box of deer fat and anointed his face and chest and shoulders with it, slowly, focusing his mind. Normally he'd speak to the spirits of the earth as he did this, and then to his own particular saints, Michael and Bride. But he wasn't seeing Michael or Bride; Brianna was still faintly with him, but what he was feeling was a strong sense of his da, which was disconcerting.

It didn't seem respectful to be dismissing his own father. He stopped what he was doing and closed his eyes instead, waiting to see if maybe Da had a thing to tell him.

"I hope ye're no bringing me word of my death, aye?" he said aloud. "Because I dinna mean to die until I've lain wi' Rachel, at least."

"Well, there's a noble goal, to be sure." The dry voice was Uncle Jamie's, and Ian's eyes popped open. His uncle was standing among the trailing fronds of a river willow, dressed in nothing but his shirt.

"Out of uniform, are ye not, Uncle?" he said, though his heart had leapt in his chest like a startled deer mouse. "General Washington willna be pleased." Washington was a great stickler for proper uniform. Officers *must* be dressed suitably at all times; he said the Continentals couldn't be taken seriously as an army, did they come to the field looking and acting like a rabble in arms.

"I'm sorry to interrupt ye, Ian," Uncle Jamie said, stepping out from the willow. The moon was nearly down; he was nay more than a ghost, bare-legged in his floating sark. "Who were ye speaking to, though?"

"Oh. My da. He was just . . . there in my mind, ken? I mean, I think of him often, but it's not sae often I feel him *with* me. So I wondered had he come to tell me I'd die this day."

Jamie nodded, not seeming bothered at the thought.

"I doubt it," he said. "Ye're putting on your paint, aye? Getting ready, I mean."

"Aye, I was about to. Ye want some, too?" It was only half said in jest, and Jamie took it that way.

"I would, Ian. But I think General Washington might have me strung up by the thumbs and flogged, should I come before him wi' my troops all marshaled and me wi' war paint on."

Ian made a small sound of amusement and scooped two fingers into the dish of red ochre, which he began to rub on his chest.

"And what are ye doin' out here in your sark, then?"

"Washing," Jamie said, but in a tone indicating that that wasn't all of it. "And . . . talkin' to my ain dead."

"Mmphm. Anyone in particular?"

"My uncle Dougal, and Murtagh, him who was my godfather. They're the two I'd most want with me, in battle." Jamie made a small restless movement. "If I can, I make a wee moment to be alone before a fight. To wash, ken, and pray a bit, and then . . . to just ask if they'll bide with me as I go."

Ian thought this interesting; he hadn't known either man himself—they'd both died at Culloden—but he'd heard stories.

"Bonnie fighters," he said. "Did ye ask my da, too? To go with ye, I mean. Perhaps that's why he's about."

Jamie turned his head sharply toward Ian, surprised. Then relaxed, shaking his head.

"I never had to ask Ian Mòr," he said softly. "He was always . . . just with me." He gestured briefly to the darkness on his right.

Ian's eyes stung and his throat closed. But it was dark; it didn't matter.

He cleared his throat and held out one of the tiny dishes. "Will ye help me, Uncle Jamie?"

"Oh? Aye, surely. How d'ye want it?"

"Red across my forehead—I can do that bit. But black from the wee dots to the chin." He drew a finger across the line of tattooed dots that curved under his cheekbones. "Black's for strength, aye? It declares ye're a warrior. And yellow means ye're no afraid to die."

"Och, aye. Are ye wantin' the yellow today?"

"No." He let the smile show in his voice, and Jamie laughed.

"Mmphm." Jamie dabbed with the rabbit-foot brush, then spread the color evenly with his thumb. Ian closed his eyes, feeling strength come into him with the touch.

"Do ye usually do this alone, Ian? Seems hard, save ye've a looking glass."

"Mostly. Or sometimes we'd do it together, and a clan brother would paint ye. If it's an important thing—a big raid, say, or going to make war on someone—then the medicine man would paint us, and sing."

"Tell me ye dinna want me to sing, Ian," his uncle murmured. "I mean, I'd *try*, but . . ."

"I'll do without, thanks."

Black for the lower face, red on the forehead, and a band of the malachite green following the line of his tattoos, from ear to ear, across the bridge of his nose.

Ian peered at the small dishes of pigment; it was easy to spot the white, and he pointed to it.

"Can ye maybe draw a wee arrow, Uncle? Across my forehead." He drew a finger from left to right, showing where.

"I can, aye." Jamie's head was bent over the paint dishes, hand hovering. "Did ye not tell me once the white is for peace, though?"

"Aye, should ye be going to parley or trade, ye use a good deal of white. But it's for the mourning, too—so if ye go to avenge someone, ye'd maybe wear white."

Jamie's head came up at that, staring at him.

"This one's no for vengeance," Ian said. "It's for Flying Arrow. The dead man whose place I took, when I was adopted." He spoke as casually as he could, but he felt his uncle tighten and look down. Neither one of them was ever going to forget that day of parting, when he'd gone to the Kahnyen'ke-haka, and both of them had thought it was forever. He leaned over and put a hand on Jamie's arm.

"That day, ye said to me, '*Cuimhnich,*' Uncle Jamie. And I did." *Remember.*

"So did I, Ian," Jamie said softly, and drew the arrow on his forehead, his touch like a priest's on Ash Wednesday, marking Ian with the sign of the cross. "So did we all. Is that it?"

Ian touched the green stripe gingerly, to be sure it was dry enough.

"Aye, I think so. Ken Brianna made me the paints? I was thinking of her, but then I thought I maybe shouldna take her with me that way."

He felt Jamie's breath on his skin as his uncle gave a small snort and then sat back.

"Ye always carry your women wi' ye into battle, Ian Òg. They're the root of your strength, man."

"Oh, aye?" That made sense—and was a relief to him. Still . . . "I was thinkin' it maybe wasna right to think of Rachel in such a place, though. Her being Quaker and all."

Jamie dipped his middle finger into the deer fat, then delicately into the white clay powder, and drew a wide, swooping "V" near the crest of Ian's right shoulder. Even in the dark, it showed vividly.

"White dove," he said with a nod. He sounded pleased. "There's Rachel for ye."

He wiped his fingers on the rock, then rose and stretched. Ian saw him turn to look toward the east. It was still night, but the air had changed, just in the few minutes they'd sat. His uncle's tall figure was distinct against the sky, where a little before he'd seemed part of the night.

"An hour, nay more," Jamie said. "Eat first, aye?" And, with that, turned and walked away to the stream and his own interrupted prayers.

67

REACHING FOR THINGS
THAT AREN'T THERE

WILLIAM WISHED he could stop reaching for things that weren't there. A dozen times today—oftener!—he'd reached for the dagger that should have been on his belt. Once or twice, for one of his pistols. Slapped an impotent hand against his hip, missing his sword, missing the small, solid weight of his shot pouch, the swing of his cartridge box.

And now he lay sweating naked on his cot, hand slapped flat on his chest where he'd reached without thinking for the wooden rosary. The rosary that, if he'd had it, would no longer be the comfort it had been for so many years. The rosary that, if he'd had it, no longer said *"Mac"* to him. If he *did* still have it, he'd have snatched it off and thrown it into the nearest fire. That's likely what James Fraser had done with it after William had thrown the rosary in the bastard's face. But, then, Fraser wasn't the bastard here, was he?

He muttered *"Scheisse!"* and flung himself irritably over. Three feet away, Evans stirred and farted in his sleep, a sudden, muffled sound like distant cannon. On his other side, Merbling went on snoring.

Tomorrow. He'd gone to bed late after an exhausting day and would be up in an hour, maybe, but he lay wide awake, eyes so adapted to the dark that he could see the pale blur of the tent canvas overhead. No chance of sleep, he knew. Even if he'd see no action himself—and he wouldn't—the proximity of battle had him so keyed up that he could have leapt from bed and gone straight for the enemy right now, sword in hand.

There'd be a battle. Maybe not a big one, but the Rebels were yapping at their heels, and tomorrow—today—there would be a meeting. It might put paid to Washington's ambitions, though Sir Henry was firm that this was not his goal. He meant to get his army and the people under its protection to New York; that was all that mattered—though if his officers should choose to demonstrate their military superiority while doing so, he had no great objection.

William had stood at attention behind Sir Henry's chair at dinner, his back against the tent wall, listening attentively while the plans were drawn up. Had in fact had the honor of carrying the formal written orders to von Knyphausen, whose troops were to march to Middletown, while Clinton's brigade would form up at the rear, to engage the Rebels while my lord Cornwallis's escorted the baggage train on to safety. That's why he'd been so late getting to bed.

He yawned suddenly, surprising himself, and settled back, blinking. Maybe he *could* sleep a bit, after all. Thinking of dinner and orders and such mundanities as the color of von Knyphausen's nightshirt—it was pink silk, with purple pansies embroidered round the neck—rather than the oncoming battle had calmed his mind amazingly. Distraction. That's what he needed.

Worth a try, he supposed. . . . He squirmed into the most comfortable attitude he could manage, closed his eyes, and began mentally extracting the square roots of numbers greater than one hundred.

He'd got to the square root of 117 and was muzzily groping for the product of 12 and 6 when he felt the sudden stir of air on his damp skin. He sighed and opened his eyes, thinking that Merbling had got up for a piss, but it wasn't Merbling. A dark figure stood just inside the tent flap. The flap wasn't closed, and the figure was clearly visible against the faint glow from the banked campfires outside. A girl.

He sat up fast, groping one-handed for the shirt he'd tossed to the foot of his cot.

"What the devil are you doing here?" he whispered, as softly as he could.

She'd been hovering, uncertain. But hearing him speak, she came straight for him, and next thing he knew, her hands were on his shoulders, her hair brushing his face. He put up his own hands in reflex and found that she was in her shift, her breasts free and warm under it, a few inches from his face.

She pulled back, and in what seemed like the same motion, skimmed the shift off over her head, shook out her hair, and straddled him, her moist round thighs pressing his.

"Get off!" He grabbed her by the arms, pushing her away. Merbling stopped snoring. Evans's bedclothes rustled.

William stood up, snatched up her shift and his shirt, and, taking her by the arm, marched her out of the tent, as quietly as he could.

"What the devil do you think you're doing? Here, put that on!" He thrust the shift unceremoniously into her arms and hastily pulled his shirt on. They were not in full view of anyone, but might be at any moment.

Her head emerged from the shift like a flower popping out of a snowbank. A rather angry flower.

"Well, what do you *think* I was doing?" she said. She pulled her hair free of the shift and fluffed it violently. "I was trying to do you a kindness!"

"A—what?"

"You're going to fight tomorrow, aren't you?" There was enough light to see the shine of her eyes as she glared at him. "Soldiers always want to fuck before a fight! They need it."

He rubbed a hand hard over his face, palm rasping on his sprouting whiskers, then took a deep breath.

"I see. Yes. Very kind of you." He suddenly wanted to laugh. He also—very suddenly—wanted to take advantage of her offer. But not enough to do it with Merbling on one side and Evans on the other, ears flapping.

"I'm not going to fight tomorrow," he said, and the pang it caused him to say that out loud startled him.

"You're not? Why not?" She sounded startled, too, and more than a little disapproving.

"It's a long story," he said, struggling for patience. "And it's not your business. Now, look. I appreciate the thought, but I told you: you're not a whore, at least not for the time being. And you're not *my* whore." Though his imagination was busy with images of what might have happened had she stolen into his cot and taken hold of him before he was fully awake . . . He put the thought firmly aside and, taking her by the shoulders, turned her round.

"Go back to your own bed now," he said, but couldn't stop himself from patting her very nice arse in farewell. She turned her head and glared at him over her shoulder.

"Coward!" she said. "A man that won't fuck won't fight."

"What?" For an instant, he didn't think she'd really said it, but she had.

"You heard me. Good—fucking—night!"

He reached her in two strides, seized her shoulder, and whirled her round to face him.

"And who gave you that bit of wisdom, may I ask? Your good friend Captain Harkness?" He wasn't truly angry, but the shock of her unexpected arrival was still reverberating in his blood and he *was* annoyed. "Did I save you from buggery so you could throw my circumstances in my face?"

Her chin drew back, and she breathed hard, but not in apparent distress.

"What circumstances?" she demanded.

"I told you—bloody hell. Do you know what the Convention army is?"

"No."

"Well, that's the long story, and I'm not telling you it standing in my shirt in the middle of camp. Now, bugger off and take care of your sister and the lads. That's your job; I'll take care of myself."

She exhaled sharply, with a *puh!* sound.

"Doubtless you *will*," she said, with the maximum of sarcasm and a pointed glance at his cock, which was poking absurdly at his shirt, making its own urgent preferences known.

"Scheisse," he said again, briefly, then grabbed her in a bear hug that pressed her body against his all the way down and kissed her. She struggled, but after the first moment he realized that the struggle was not meant to procure her release but to provoke him further. He tightened his grip until she stopped, but didn't quit kissing her for some time thereafter.

He finally let go, panting and bedewed with perspiration; the air was like breathing hot tar. She was panting, too. He could take her. Wanted to. Push her down on her knees in the grass beside the tent, pull up her shift, and have her from behind—it wouldn't take more than seconds.

"No," he said, and wiped his mouth on the back of his hand. "No," he said again, more positively. Every nerve in his body wanted her, and had he been sixteen, it would have been long over by this time. But he wasn't, and he had just enough self-control to turn her round again. He gripped her by scruff and buttock to keep her from turning back and held her immobile.

"When we get to New York," he whispered, bending to speak in her ear, "I'll think again."

She stiffened, her buttock rounding hard in his hand, but didn't pull away or try to bite him, which he'd half-expected.

"Why?" she said, in a calm voice.

"That's a long story, too," he said. "Good night, Jane." And, releasing her, stalked away into the dark. Nearby, the drums of reveille began.

PART FOUR

Day of Battle

68

GO OUT IN DARKNESS

I AN HAD BEEN OVER the land briefly the day before, scouting. "And a good thing, too," he said, under his breath. It was the dark of the moon, and he must go canny and keep the road. He wasn't risking his horse's legs over the rough land before he had to, and Bride grant him the sky would be fully light by then.

Still, he was glad of the dark, and the solitude. Not that the land was still; the woods lived at night, and many things came out in the strange dawn hour when the light began to swell. But neither the rustle of hares and voles nor the sleepy call of waking birds demanded his notice or took any notice of him. He had finished his own prayers after Uncle Jamie left him, then departed alone in silence, and the peace of his preparations was still on him.

When he had lived with the Mohawk—particularly when things had gone wrong with Emily—he would leave the longhouse for days, hunting alone with Rollo, until the wilderness had eased his spirit enough to go back, strengthened. He glanced down by reflex, but Rollo had been left behind with Rachel. The wound from the deadfall trap was clean; Auntie Claire had put something on it that helped—but he wouldn't have let Rollo come to a battle like this one offered to be, even had he been whole and a good deal younger than he was.

There was no doubt of the coming battle. He could smell it. His body was rising toward the fight; he could feel the tingling of it—but he treasured this momentary stillness the more for that.

"Won't last long, mind," he said softly to the horse, who ignored him. He touched the white dove on his shoulder and rode on, still quiet but not alone.

THE MEN HAD lain on their arms all night, by Sir Henry's orders. While one didn't actually lie *on* a musket and cartridge box, there was something about sleeping with a gun touching your body that kept you alert, ready to rouse from sleep in nothing flat.

William had no arms to lie on, and hadn't needed rousing, as he hadn't slept, but was no less alert for the lack. He wouldn't be fighting, and deeply regretted that—but he would be out in it, by God.

The camp was a-bustle, drums rattling up and down the aisles of tents, summoning the soldiers, and the air was full of the smells of baking bread, pork, and hot pease porridge.

There was no visible sign of dawn yet, but he could feel the sun there, just below the horizon, rising with the slow inevitability of its daily dominion. The thought reminded him, vividly, of the whale he had seen on the voyage to America: a dark shadow below the ship's side, easily dismissed as the change of light on the waves—and then, slowly, the growing bulk, the realization and the breathless wonder of seeing it rise, so close, so huge—and suddenly *there*.

He fastened his garters and tugged them tight before buckling his knee bands and pulling on his Hessian boots. At least he had his gorget back, to lend a touch of ceremony to the mundane task of getting dressed. The gorget, of course, reminded him of Jane—was he ever going to be able to wear it *without* thinking of the damned girl?—and of recent events.

He'd regretted not accepting her offer, and still did. He could still smell her scent, musky and soft, like putting his face in thick fur. Her remark still rankled, too, and he snorted, settling his coat on his shoulders. Perhaps he'd think again *before* they reached New York.

These idle thoughts were interrupted by the appearance of another of Sir Henry's aides, Captain Crosbie, who popped his head through the tent flap, clearly in a great flurry.

"Oh, there you are, Ellesmere. Hoped I'd catch you—here." He tossed a folded note in William's general direction and vanished.

William snorted again and picked it up off the ground. Evans and Merbling had both left, they having actual troops to inspect and command; he envied them bitterly.

It was from General Sir Henry Clinton, and hit him in the stomach like a blow: . . . *in view of your peculiar status, I think it best that you remain with the clerical staff today* . . .

"*Stercus!*" he said, finding German insufficient to his feelings. "*Excrementum obscaenum! Filius mulieris prostabilis!*"

His chest was tight, blood was pounding in his ears, and he wanted to hit something. It would be useless to appeal to Sir Henry, he knew that much. But to spend the day essentially kicking his heels in the clerks' tent—for what was there for him to *do*, if he wasn't allowed to carry dispatches or even do the lowly but necessary work of shepherding the camp followers and Loyalists? What—was he to fetch the clerks' dinner in, or hold a torch in each hand when it got dark, like a fucking candelabra?

He was about to crumple the note into a wad, when yet another unwelcome head intruded itself, followed by an elegant body: Captain André, dressed for battle, sword at his side and pistols in his belt. William eyed him with dislike, though in fact he was an amiable fellow.

"Oh, there you are, Ellesmere," André said, pleased. "Hoped you hadn't gone off yet. I need you to run me a dispatch, quickly. To Colonel Tarleton—with the British Legion, the new Provincials, green chaps—you know him?"

"I do, yes." William accepted the sealed dispatch, feeling odd. "Certainly, Captain."

"Good man." André smiled and squeezed his shoulder, then strode out, ebullient with the promise of imminent action.

William drew a deep breath, carefully folded Sir Henry's note back into its original shape, and placed it on his cot. Who was to say that he hadn't met André first and, owing to the urgency of his request, left immediately, without reading Sir Henry's note?

He doubted he'd be missed, in any case.

69

SPARROW-FART

IT WAS PERHAPS four o'clock ack emma. Or before sparrow-fart, as the British armed forces of my own time used to put it. That sense of temporal dislocation was back again, memories of another war coming like a sudden fog between me and my work, then disappearing in an instant, leaving the present sharp and vivid as Kodachrome. The army was moving.

No fog obscured Jamie. He was big and solid, his outlines clearly visible against the shredding night. I was awake and alert, dressed and ready, but the chill of sleep still lay upon me, making my fingers clumsy. I could feel his warmth and drew close to him, as I might to a campfire. He was leading Clarence, who was even warmer, though much less alert, ears sagging in sleepy annoyance.

"You'll have Clarence," Jamie told me, putting the mule's reins in my hand. "And these, to make sure ye keep him, if ye should find yourself on your own." "These" were a heavy pair of horse pistols, holstered and strung on a thick leather belt that also held a shot bag and powder horn.

"Thank you," I said, swallowing as I wrapped the reins around a sapling in order to belt the pistols on. The guns were amazingly heavy—but I wouldn't deny that the weight of them on my hips was amazingly comforting, too.

"All right," I said, glancing toward the tent where John was. "What about—"

"I've seen to that," he said, cutting me off. "Gather the rest of your things, Sassenach; I've nay more than a quarter hour, at most, and I need ye with me when we go."

I watched him stride off into the mêlée, tall and resolute, and wondered—as I had so often before—*Will it be today? Will this be the last sight I remember of him?* I stood very still, watching as hard as I could.

When I'd lost him the first time, before Culloden, I'd remembered. Every moment of our last night together. Tiny things would come back to me through the years: the taste of salt on his temple and the curve of his skull as I cupped his head; the soft fine hair at the base of his neck, thick and damp in my fingers . . . the sudden, magical well of his blood in dawning light when I'd cut his hand and marked him forever as my own. Those things had kept him by me.

And when I'd lost him this time, to the sea, I'd remembered the sense of him beside me, warm and solid in my bed, and the rhythm of his breathing. The light across the bones of his face in moonlight and the flush of his skin in the rising sun. I could hear him breathe when I lay in bed alone in my room at Chestnut Street—slow, regular, never stopping—even though I knew it *had* stopped. The sound would comfort me, then drive me mad with the knowledge of loss, so I pulled the pillow hard over my head in a futile attempt to shut it out—only to emerge into the night of the room, thick with woodsmoke and candle wax and vanished light, and be comforted to hear it once more.

If this time—but he had turned, quite suddenly, as though I'd called his name. He came swiftly up to me, grasped me by the arms, and said in a low, strong voice, "It willna be today, either."

Then he put his arms around me and drew me up on tiptoe into a deep, soft kiss. I heard brief cheers from a few of the men nearby, but it didn't matter. Even if it should be today, I would remember.

JAMIE STRODE toward his waiting companies, loosely assembled near the river. The breath of the water and the mist rising from it comforted him, keeping him wrapped for a little while longer in the peace of the night and the deep sense of his kin, there at his shoulder. He'd told Ian Mòr to stay with Ian Òg, as was right, but had the odd sense that there were three men with him, still.

He'd need the strength of his dead. Three hundred men, and he'd known them for only days. Always before, when he'd taken men into battle, they were men of his blood, of his clan, men who knew him, trusted him—as he knew and trusted them. These men were strangers to him, and yet their lives were in his hands.

He wasn't worried by their lack of training; they were rough and undisciplined, a mere rabble by contrast with the Continental regulars who'd drilled all winter under von Steuben—the thought of the little barrel-shaped Prussian made him smile—but his troops had always been this kind of men: farmers and hunters, pulled from their daily occupations, armed with scythes and hoes as often as with muskets or swords. They'd fight like fiends for him—with him—if they trusted him.

"How is it, then, Reverend?" he said softly to the minister, who had just blessed his flock of volunteers and was hunched among them in his black coat, arms still half spread like a scarecrow protecting his misty field at dawn. The man's face, always rather stern in aspect, lightened upon seeing him, and he realized that the sky itself had begun to glow.

"All well, sir," Woodsworth said gruffly. "We are ready." He didn't, thank God, mention Bertram Armstrong.

"Good," said Jamie, smiling from face to face, and seeing them all lighten in turn as the dawn touched them. "Mr. Whelan, Mr. Maddox, Mr. Hebden—ye're all well in yourselves this morning, I hope?"

"We are," they murmured, looking shyly gratified that he knew their names. He wished he knew them all, but had had to do the best he could, learning the names and faces of a handful of men in each company. It might give them the illusion that he did know every man by name—he hoped so; they needed to know he cared for them.

"Ready, sir." It was Captain Craddock, one of his three captains, stiff and self-conscious with the importance of the occasion, and Judah Bixby and Lewis Orden, two of Jamie's lieutenants, behind him. Bixby was no more than twenty, Orden maybe a year older; they could barely repress their excitement, and he smiled at them, feeling their joy in their young manhood echo in his own blood.

There were some *very* young men among the militia, he noticed. A couple of half-grown boys, tall and spindly as cornstalks—who were they? Oh, yes, Craddock's sons. He remembered now; their mother had died only a month ago, and so they had come with their father into the militia.

God, let me bring them back safe! he prayed.

And felt—actually felt—a hand rest briefly on his shoulder, and knew who the third man was who walked with him.

Taing, Da, he thought, and blinked, raising his face so the tears in his eyes might be thought due to the brightness of the growing light.

I TIED CLARENCE to a picquet and made my way back into the tent, less troubled, though still keyed up. Whatever was going to happen was going to happen fast, and likely with little warning. Fergus and Germain had gone to find breakfast; I hoped they would show up before I had to leave—because when the time came, I would have to leave, no matter my reservations about abandoning a patient. Any patient.

This particular patient was lying on his back, under the lantern, his working eye half closed, singing to himself in German. He desisted when I came in, and turned his head to see who it was, blinking at sight of my armament.

"Are we expecting imminent invasion and capture?" he asked, sitting up.

"Lie back down. No, this is Jamie being provident." I touched one of the pistols gingerly. "I don't know if they're loaded yet."

"Certainly they are. The man is nothing if not thorough." He eased himself back down, groaning slightly.

"You think you know him awfully well, don't you?" I asked, with an edge that rather surprised me.

"Yes, I do," he answered promptly. He smiled slightly at my expression. "Not nearly as well as you do in some matters, I'm sure—but perhaps better in others. We are both soldiers." He tilted his head, indicating the military racket going on outside.

"If you know him that well," I said, nettled, "you should have known better than to say whatever you did say to him."

"Ah." The smile disappeared and he looked up at the canvas overhead in contemplation. "I did. Know better. I just said it anyway."

"Ah," I replied, and sat down next to the pile of bags and supplies that had made it thus far. Much of this would have to be abandoned. I could take a good deal in Clarence's packs and saddlebags, but not everything. The army had been instructed to abandon almost everything they carried, save weapons and canteens, in the interests of speed.

"Did he tell you what it was?" John asked after a moment, his voice elaborately casual.

"What you said? No, but I could very likely guess." I compressed my lips and didn't look at him, instead lining up bottles on top of a chest. I'd got salt from the innkeeper—not without trouble—and had made up a couple of bottles of crude saline solution, and there was the alcohol . . . I picked up the candle and began to dribble wax carefully over the corks, lest they loosen and the bottles discharge their contents along the way.

I didn't want to pursue the history of John's eye any further. Other considerations aside, any discussion might lead a little too close to Wentworth Prison for comfort. However close a friend Jamie might have considered John during the last few years, I was positive that he'd never told John about Black Jack Randall and what had happened at Wentworth. He'd told his brother-in-law Ian, many years ago—and therefore Jenny must know, too, though I doubted she'd ever spoken of it to Jamie—but no one else.

John would likely assume that Jamie had hit him purely from revulsion at something overtly sexual from John—or from jealousy over me. It was perhaps not quite fair to let him think that—but fairness didn't come into it.

Still, I regretted the trouble between them. Beyond whatever personal awkwardness I found in the present situation, I knew how much John's friendship had meant to Jamie—and vice versa. And while I was more than relieved not to be married to John anymore, I did care for him.

And—while the noise and movement all around urged me to forget everything else but the urgency of departure—I couldn't forget that this might be the last time I ever saw John, too.

I sighed and began to wrap the waxed bottles in towels. I should add whatever I could find room for from my Kingsessing haul, but . . .

"Don't be troubled, my dear," John said gently. "You know it will all come right—provided that we all live long enough."

I gave him a marked look and nodded toward the tent flap, where the clatter and clash of a military camp on the verge of movement was escalating.

"Well, *you'll* likely survive," I said. "Unless you say the wrong thing to Jamie before we leave and he really does break your neck this time."

He glanced—as briefly as possible—toward the pale shaft of dust-filled light, and grimaced.

"You've never had to do it, have you?" I said, seeing his face. "Sit and wait through a battle, wondering if someone you care for will come back."

"Not with regard to anyone other than myself, no," he replied, but I could see that the remark had gone home. He *hadn't* thought of that, and he didn't like the thought one bit. *Welcome to the club,* I thought sardonically.

"Do you think they'll catch Clinton?" I asked, after a moment's silence. He shrugged, almost irritably.

"How should I know? I haven't the slightest idea where Clinton's troops are—I have no idea where Washington is, or where we are, for that matter."

"General Washington would be about thirty yards that way," I said, picking up a basket of bandages and lint, and nodding toward where I'd last seen the commander. "And I would be surprised if General Clinton is very much farther off."

"Oh? And why is that, madam?" he asked, now half amused.

"Because the order came down an hour ago to jettison all unnecessary supplies—though I don't know if he actually said 'jettison,' come to think; that may not be a word in common use now. That's why we were inspecting the men, when we found you—to leave back any who aren't capable of a long forced march on short rations, should that be necessary. Apparently it is.

"But you know what's happening," I added, watching him. "*I* can hear it. You surely can." Anyone with ears or eyes could sense the nervous excitement in camp, see the hasty preparations being made, the small fights and outbreaks of cursing as men got in each other's way, the bawling of officers, only a hair short of eye-rolling, horn-tossing violence, the braying of mules—I hoped no one would steal Clarence before I got back to him.

John nodded, silent. I could see him turning the situation over in his mind, along with the obvious implications.

"Yes, 'jettison' is certainly a word in common use," he said absently. "Though you hear it more in terms of sea cargo. But—" He jerked a little, realizing the further implications of what I'd said, and stared hard at me with his uncovered eye.

"Don't do that," I said mildly. "You'll hurt the other one. And what I am or am not isn't important just now, is it?"

"No," he muttered, and shut the eye for a moment, then opened it, staring upward at the canvas overhead. Dawn was coming; the yellowed canvas was beginning to glow, and the air around us was thick with dust and the odor of dried sweat.

"I know very little that would be of interest to General Washington," he said, "and I would be surprised if he didn't know that little already. I am not a serving officer—or . . . well, I wasn't, until my bloody brother decided to reenter me on the rolls of his bloody regiment. Do you know, he nearly got me *hanged*?"

"No, but it sounds extremely like him," I said, laughing despite my disquiet.

"What do you—oh, God. You've *met* Hal?" He'd reared up on one elbow, blinking at me.

"I have," I assured him. "Lie down, and I'll tell you." Neither of us was going anywhere for a few minutes at least, and I was able to give him the entire story of my adventures with Hal in Philadelphia, while I wound up bandages, put my medical box in good order, and extracted what I thought the most important items from the supplies I'd brought. In an emergency, I might be reduced to what I could carry on my back at a dead run, and I made up a small rucksack with that contingency in mind, whilst regaling John with my opinions of his brother.

"Jesus, if he thinks he's a chance in hell of preventing Dorothea from marrying Dr. Hunter . . . I believe I'd pay good money to overhear the conversation when he meets Denzell," he remarked. "Who would you bet on—given that Hal hasn't got a regiment at his back to enforce his opinions?"

"He likely *has* met him by now. As to odds—Denzell, three to two," I said, after a moment's consideration. "He's got not only God but love—and Dorothea—on his side, and I do think that will outweigh even Hal's brand of . . . of . . . autocratic conviction?"

"I'd call it undiluted bastardliness, myself, but, then, I'm his brother. I'm allowed liberties."

The sound of voices speaking French announced the arrival of Fergus and Germain, and I stood up abruptly.

"I may not—" I began, but he raised a hand, stopping me.

"If not, then goodbye, my dear," he said softly. "And good luck."

70

A SINGLE LOUSE

IT WAS BARELY AN hour past dawn and it would doubtless be another beastly hot day, but for the moment the air was still fresh and both William and Goth were happy. He threaded his way through the boiling mass of men, horses, limbers, and the other impedimenta of war, quietly whistling "The King Enjoys His Own Again."

The baggage wagons were already being readied; a great dust cloud rose, roiling and shot through with gold from the rising sun, from the teamsters' park near von Knyphausen's division, encamped a quarter mile away, on the other side of Middletown. They'd be off directly, heading for Sandy Hook—and Jane, Fanny, Zeb, and Colenso with them, he sincerely hoped. A brief sensory recollection of the skin inside Jane's thighs sparked through his mind and he stopped whistling for an instant, but then shook it out of his head. Work to be done!

No one quite knew where the new British Legion was, though it was assumed to be somewhere in the vicinity of Clinton's division, it being one of his personal regiments, raised only a month ago in New York. That might be chancy, but William was quite willing to wager that he could evade Sir Henry's notice, under the conditions.

"Like picking one louse out of a Frenchie's wig," he murmured, and patted Goth's neck. The horse was fresh and frisky, couldn't wait to reach the open road and break into a gallop. Clinton's division was holding the rear guard at Middletown—enough distance to take the edge off Goth's bounciness. First, though, they'd have to get through the spreading mass of camp followers, struggling out of sleep into a desperate haste. He kept Goth on a short rein, lest he trample a child—there were dozens of the little buggers, swarming over the ground like locusts.

Glancing up from the ground, he caught sight of a familiar form, standing in line for bread, and his heart gave a small leap of pleasure. Anne Endicott, dressed for day but without her cap, dark hair in a thick plait down her back. The sight of it gave him a *frisson* of intimacy, and he barely stopped himself calling out to her. Time enough, after the fight.

71

FOLIE À TROIS

FERGUS HAD BROUGHT me a sausage roll and a cannikin of coffee—real coffee, for a wonder.

"Milord will send for you shortly," he said, handing these over.

"Is he nearly ready?" The food was warm and fresh—and I knew it might be the last I got for some time—but I barely tasted it. "Have I time to dress Lord John's eye again?" The pervading air of haste was clearly perceptible to me, and my skin had started twitching as though I were being attacked by ants.

"I will go and see, milady. Germain?" Fergus tilted his head toward the tent flap, beckoning Germain to go with him.

But Germain, out of what might have been either loyalty to John or fear of finding himself alone with Jamie—who had rather plainly meant what he said regarding the future of Germain's arse—wanted to stay in the tent.

"I'll be fine," John assured him. "Go with your father." He was still pale and sweating, but his jaw and hands had relaxed; he wasn't in severe pain.

"Yes, he will be fine," I said to Germain, but nodded to Fergus, who went out without further comment. "Fetch me some fresh lint, will you? Then you can come and help me while his lordship rests. As for you—" I turned to John. "You lie flat, keep your eye closed, and bloody stay out of trouble, if such a thing is possible."

He swiveled his good eye in my direction, wincing slightly as the movement pulled on the bad one.

"Are you accusing *me* of causing the imbroglio that resulted in my injury, madam? Because I distinctly recall your playing some minor role in its origins." He sounded rather cross.

"I had nothing whatever to do with your ending up *here*," I said firmly, though I could feel my cheeks flush. "Germain, have you found the lint?"

"Will the honey not draw flies, Grannie?" Germain handed me the requested lint but stood by the cot, frowning down at its occupant. "Ken what they say, aye? Ye catch more flies wi' honey than ye do wi' vinegar. Ye couldna pour vinegar on him, I suppose?"

"Hmmm." He had a point. We were no great distance from the teamsters; I could hear mules snorting and braying, and newly wakened flies, still heavy with sleep, had been buzzing round my ears even as I unwrapped the old bandage. "Right. Not vinegar, but mint might help. Find the tin with the fleur-de-lis, then, and rub ointment on his lordship's face and hands—*don't* get it in his eyes. Then bring the small box—"

"I am certainly capable of rubbing ointment on myself," John interrupted, and extended a hand to Germain. "Here, give it to me."

"Lie still," I said, rather cross myself. "As for what you're capable of, I shudder to think." I had set a small dish of honey to warm near the lantern; I filled my syringe and injected the honey around his bad eye, made a small pad of lint, thumbed it gently into his eye socket, and bound a clean length of gauze round his head to hold it in place, thinking as I did so.

"Germain . . . go and fill the canteen, will you?" It was half full already, but he obligingly took it and went, leaving me alone with John.

"Shall I leave Germain with you?" I asked, stuffing the last few items into my first-aid kit. "And Fergus?" I added hesitantly.

"No," he said, slightly startled. "What for?"

"Well . . . protection. In case Monsieur Beauchamp should come back, I mean." I didn't trust Percy in the slightest. I was also dubious about putting Fergus in close proximity to him, but it had occurred to me that perhaps John might be some protection to *him*.

"Ah." He closed his good eye for a moment, then opened it again. "Now, *that* imbroglio is indeed of my own making," he said ruefully. "But while Germain is admittedly a formidable presence, I shan't need a bodyguard. I rather doubt that Percy intends either to assault or to kidnap me."

"Do you . . . care for him?" I asked curiously.

"Is it your business if I do?" he replied evenly.

I flushed more deeply, but took a few breaths before answering.

"Yes," I said at last. "Yes, I rather think it is. Whatever my role in the origins of this . . . this . . . er . . ."

"*Folie à trois?*" he suggested, and I laughed. I'd told him what a *folie à deux* was, with reference to Mrs. Figg's and the laundress's shared obsession with starched drawers.

"That will do. But, yes, it is my business—on Jamie's behalf, if not yours." But it was on his behalf, as well. The shock and rush of recent events had prevented my thinking through the situation, but I was quite sure that Jamie had. And now that I was thoroughly awake and undistracted by my own affairs, my thoughts were catching up with uncomfortable rapidity.

"Do you recall a Captain André?" I asked abruptly. "John André. He was at the Mischianza."

"I may have lost a few things over the course of the last few days," he said, with some acerbity, "but neither my memory nor my wits. Yet," he added, in a marked manner. "Of course I know him. A very sociable and artistic young man; he was invited everywhere in Philadelphia. He's on General Clinton's staff."

"Did you know that he's also a spy?" My heart was thumping in my ears, and my stays felt suddenly too tight. Was I about to do something hideously irrevocable?

He blinked, obviously startled.

"No. Why on earth should you think that?" And, a half second later, "And why the devil would you tell me about it, if you do think so?"

"Because," I said, as evenly as I could, "he'll be caught doing it, in another year or two. He'll be found behind the American lines, in civilian clothes, with incriminating documents on his person. And the Americans will hang him."

The words hung in the air between us, visible as though they were written in black smoke. John opened his mouth, then shut it again, clearly nonplussed.

I could hear all the sounds of the camp around us: talk, occasional shouting, and the sounds of horses and mules, the beat of a drum in the distance, summoning men to . . . what? Someone at close range practicing a fife, the shrill note breaking in the same place each time. The constant rumble and shriek of the grinding wheel, frenziedly sharpening metal for the last time. And the increasing buzz of flies.

They were drifting into the tent in small clouds of carnivory; two of them landed on John's forehead, to be irritably brushed away. The tin of bug repellent lay on the cot where Germain had put it down; I reached for it.

"No," he said, rather sharply, and took it from my hand. "I can—I—don't touch me, if you please." His hand trembled, and he had a moment's difficulty in getting the lid off, but I didn't help him. I'd gone cold to the fingertips, in spite of the stifling atmosphere in the tent.

He'd surrendered to Jamie personally, given his parole. It would be Jamie who would eventually have to hand him over to General Washington. Would *have* to; too many people had seen the incident, knew where John was—and, by this time, what he was.

John didn't sit up, but managed to thumb a glob of the mentholated grease from the tin and rub it on his face and neck.

"You didn't have anything in your clothes," I ventured, with a faint hope. "No incriminating documents, I mean."

"I had my warrant of commission in my pocket when the Rebel militia took me, outside Philadelphia," he said, but spoke in an abstract tone, as though it didn't really matter. He rubbed ointment briskly over his hands and wrists. "Not proof of spying in itself—but certainly proof that I was a British officer, out of uniform and arguably behind the American lines at the time. Don't talk anymore, my dear; it's very dangerous."

He snapped the lid onto the tin and held it out to me.

"You'd better go," he said, looking me in the eye and speaking in a low voice. "You must not be found alone with me."

"Grannie?" Germain pushed back the tent flap, red as a beet under his shaggy bangs. "Grannie! Come quick! *Papa* says *Grand-père* wants you!"

He disappeared and I hastily snatched up my equipment, bedizening myself with bags and boxes. I made for the tent flap, but paused for an instant, turning to John.

"I should have asked—does he care for *you*?" I said.

He shut his good eye and his lips compressed for a moment.

"I hope not," he said.

I HURRIED AFTER Germain with my medical satchel full of gurgling bottles slung over my shoulder, a small box of extra instruments and sutures under my arm, Clarence's reins in hand, and a mind so agitated I could hardly see where I was going.

I realized now that I hadn't been telling John anything he didn't know. Well . . . bar the account of Captain André's future fate, and while that was chilling enough, it wasn't of direct importance at the moment.

He'd stopped me speaking, because he'd already known how much danger he stood in—and what the effects were likely to be on Jamie, and on me. *"You must not be found alone with me."*

Because I'd been at one point his wife, he meant. That's what he'd been thinking but hadn't wanted to tell me, until I forced the issue.

If anything happened—well, be blunt about it: if he broke his parole and escaped—I'd very likely be suspected of having a hand in it, but the suspicion would be a great deal more pronounced if anyone could testify to having seen us in private conversation. And Jamie would be suspected of complicity at worst, or, at best, of having a wife who was disloyal both to him and to the cause of independence. . . . I could easily end up in a military prison. So might Jamie.

But if John *didn't* escape . . . or escaped and was recaptured . . .

But the road lay before me, and Jamie was there on his horse, holding the reins of my mare. And it was Jamie with whom I'd cross the Rubicon today—not John.

THE MARQUIS de La Fayette was waiting for them at the rendezvous, face flushed and eyes bright with anticipation. Jamie couldn't help smiling at sight of the young Frenchman, got up regardless in a glorious uniform with red silk facings. He wasn't inexperienced, though, despite his youth and his very obvious Frenchness. He'd told Jamie about the battle at Brandywine Creek a year before, where he'd been wounded in the leg, and how Washington had insisted that he lie beside him and wrapped him in his own cloak. Gilbert idolized Washington, who had no sons of his own, and who clearly felt a deep affection for the wee marquis.

Jamie glanced at Claire, to see if she was appreciating La Fayette's stylish toilette, but her gaze was fixed—with a small frown—on a group of men in the far distance, beyond the Continental regulars drawn up in orderly formations. She wasn't wearing her spectacles; he could see easily at a distance and half-stood in his stirrups to look.

"General Washington and Charles Lee," he told her, sitting back in the saddle. La Fayette, spotting them, as well, swung himself into his own saddle and rode toward the senior officers. "I suppose I'd best go join them. D'ye see Denzell Hunter yet?" He had it in mind to confide Claire to Hunter's care; he didn't mean her to be wandering the battlefield—if there was one—on her own, no matter how helpful she might be there, and was wary of leaving her alone.

Hunter was driving his wagon, though, and that couldn't keep up with the marching men. Clouds of dust rose in the air, stirred by thousands of eager feet; it tickled in his chest, and he coughed.

"No," she said. "Don't worry." And she smiled at him, brave, though her face was pale despite the heat, and he could feel the flutter of her fear in his own wame. "Are you all right?" She always looked at him in that searching way when he set out to a fight, as though committing his face to memory in case he was killed. He kent why she did it, but it made him feel strange—and he was already unsettled this morning.

"Aye, fine," he said, and taking her hand, kissed it. He should have spurred up and gone, but lingered for a moment, loath to let go.

"Did you—" she began, and then stopped abruptly.

"Put on clean drawers? Aye, though it's like to be wasted effort, ken, when the guns start firin'." It was a feeble enough jest, but she laughed, and he felt better.

"Did I what?" he prompted, but she shook her head.

"Never mind. You don't need anything else to think of now. Just—be careful, will you?" She swallowed visibly, and his heart turned over.

"I will," he said, and took up the reins but looked back over his shoulder, in case Young Ian should be coming. She was safe enough, in the midst of the forming companies, but he'd still be happier with someone to look after her. And if he told her that, she'd likely—

"There's Ian!" she exclaimed, squinting to see. "What's the matter with his horse, I wonder?"

He looked where she was looking and saw the cause at once. His nephew was afoot, leading the halting horse, and both of them were looking crankit.

"Lame," he said. "And badly lamed, too. What's amiss, Ian?" he called.

"Stepped on summat sharp, coming up the bank, and cracked his hoof, right down into the quick." Ian ran a hand down the horse's leg and the animal all but leaned on him, picking up its unshod hoof at once. Sure enough, the crack was visible, and deep enough to make Jamie wince in sympathy. Like having a toenail torn off, he supposed, and having to walk a distance with it.

"Take my horse, Ian," Claire said, and slid off in a flurry of petticoats. "I can ride Clarence. No need for me to be fast, after all."

"Aye, all right," Jamie said, though a bit reluctant. Her mare was a good one, and Ian had to have a mount. "Shift the saddles, then, and, Ian, watch out for Dr. Hunter. Dinna leave your auntie 'til he comes, aye? Goodbye, Sassenach; I'll see ye later in the day." He could wait no longer, and nudged his horse away into the crowd.

Other officers had gathered around Washington; he'd barely be in time. But it wasn't the risk of being conspicuously late that cramped his bowels. It was guilt.

He ought to have reported John Grey's arrest at once. He kent that fine, but had delayed, hoping . . . hoping what? That the ridiculous situation would somehow evaporate? If he *had* reported it, Washington would have had Grey taken into custody and locked up somewhere—or hanged him out of hand, as an example. He didn't think that likely, but the possibility had been enough to keep him from saying anything, counting on the chaos of the impending exodus to keep anyone from noticing.

But what was eating at his insides now was not guilt over duty deferred, or even over exposing Claire to danger by keeping the wee sodomite in his own tent instead of turning him over. It was the fact that he had not thought to revoke Grey's parole this morning when he left. If he had, Grey might easily have escaped in the confusion of leaving, and even if there had been trouble later over it . . . John Grey would be safe.

But it was too late, and with a brief prayer for the soul of Lord John Grey, he reined up beside the Marquis de La Fayette and bowed to General Washington.

72

MORASSES AND IMBROGLIOS

THERE WERE THREE CREEKS running through the land, cutting it up. Where the earth was soft, the water had cut deep and the creek ran at the bottom of a steep ravine, the banks of it thick with saplings and underbrush. A farmer he'd spoken to while scouting the day before had told him the names of them—Dividing Brook, Spotswood Middle Brook, and Spotswood North Brook—but Ian wasn't at all sure he kent for sure which this one was.

The ground here was wide and low; the creek ran out into a sunken, marshy sort of place, and he turned away; bad footing for either man or horse. One of the farmers had called the ravines "morasses," and he thought that a good word. He looked up the creek, searching for good watering places, but the ravine fell too steeply. A man could make shift to scramble down to the water, maybe, but not horses or mules.

Ian felt them before he saw them. The sense of a hunting animal, lying concealed in the wood, waiting for prey to come down to drink. He turned his horse sharply and rode along the creek bank, watching the trees on the other side.

Movement, a horse's head tossing against flies. A glimpse of a face—faces—painted, like his own.

A thrill of alarm shot up his spine and instinct flattened him against the horse's neck, as the arrow whizzed over his head. It stuck, quivering, in a nearby sycamore.

He straightened, his own bow in hand, nocked an arrow in the same movement, and sent it back, aiming blind for the spot where he'd seen them. The arrow shredded leaves as it went but struck nothing—he hadn't expected it to.

"Mohawk!" came a derisory shout from the other side, and a few words in a language he didn't understand but whose intended meaning was clear enough. He made a very Scottish gesture, whose meaning was also clear, and left them laughing.

He paused to yank the arrow out of the sycamore. Fletched with a yaffle's tail feathers, but not a pattern he knew. Whatever they'd been speaking wasn't an Algonquian tongue. Might be something northern like Assiniboine—he'd know, if he got a clear look at them—but might equally be something from nearer to hand.

Very likely working for the British army, though. He kent most of the Indian scouts presently with the Rebels. And while they hadn't been trying to kill him—they could have done so, easily, if they'd really wanted to—this was rougher teasing than might be expected. Perhaps only because they'd recognized him for what he was.

Mohawk! To an English speaker, it was just easier to say than "Kahnyen'ke-haka." To any of the tribes who lived within knowledge of the Kahnyen'ke-haka, it was either a word to scare children with or a calculated insult. "Man-eater," it meant, for the Kahnyen'kehaka were known to roast their enemies alive and devour the flesh.

Ian had never seen such a thing, but he knew men—old men—who had and would tell you about it with pleasure. He didn't care to think about it. It brought back much too vividly the night the priest had died in Snaketown, mutilated and burned alive—the night that had inadvertently taken Ian from his family and made him a Mohawk.

The bridge lay upstream, perhaps sixty yards from where he was. He paused, but the woods on the other side were silent, and he ventured across, his horse's hooves a careful clopping on the boards. If there were British scouts here, the army was not too far beyond.

There were broad meadows past the woods on the far side, and beyond these the fields of a good-sized farm; he could see a snatch of the buildings through the trees—and the movement of men. He turned hastily, circling a copse and coming out into ground open enough to see.

There were green-coated soldiers on the ridgeline beyond the farm buildings, and he could smell the sulfur of their slow match on the heavy air. Grenadiers.

He wheeled his horse and headed back, to find someone to tell.

WILLIAM FINALLY discovered the cavalry detachment of the British Legion, filling their canteens from a well in the yard of a farmhouse. They had a picket out, though, who gave a warning shout at sight of a lone horseman, and half the company swung round, on the alert. A well-trained company; Banastre Tarleton was a good, energetic officer.

Tarleton himself was standing relaxed in the shade of a big tree, his ornately plumed helmet cradled in one arm, mopping his face with a green silk kerchief. William rolled his eyes briefly at this bit of affectation, but not so Tarleton could see. He came to a walk and rode up beside Tarleton, leaning down to give him the dispatch.

"From Captain André," he said. "Been busy?" The men had been fighting; he could smell the smoke on them, and a couple of men with what looked like minor wounds were sitting against the barn, uniforms streaked with blood. The barn doors hung open on emptiness, and the yard was trampled and spotted with dung; he wondered for a moment whether the farmer had driven his own stock away, or whether one or another of the armies had taken the animals.

"Not nearly busy enough," Tarleton replied, reading the note. "This may help, though. We're to go reinforce my lord Cornwallis." His face was flushed with the heat, and his leather stock was clearly cutting into his thick, muscular neck, but he looked exceedingly cheerful at the prospect.

"Good," said William, reining up to turn and go, but Tarleton stopped him with a raised hand. He tucked the dispatch away in his pocket, along with the green kerchief.

"Since I see you, Ellesmere—saw a tasty piece last night in camp, in the bread line," he said. Tarleton sucked his lower lip for an instant and released it, red and wet. "*Very* tasty, and a sweet little sister with her, too, though that one's not quite ripe enough for me." William raised his brows, but felt himself tense in thighs and shoulders.

"Made her an offer," Tarleton said, overtly careless but with a swift glance at William's hands. William relaxed them with an effort. "She declined, though—said she was yours?" This last was not quite a question, but not quite not.

"If her name is Jane," William said shortly, "she and her sister are traveling under my protection."

Tarleton's quizzical look flowered into open amusement.

"Your protection," he repeated. His full lips twitched. "I believe she told me that her name was Arabella, though—perhaps we're thinking of different girls."

"No, we're not." William did *not* want to be having this conversation, and gathered up his reins. "Don't fucking touch her."

That was a mistake; Tarleton never passed up a challenge. His eyes sparkled and William saw him set himself, legs spread.

"Fight you for her," he said.

"What, here? Are you insane?" There were bugles in the distance, and not a very far distance, either. To say nothing of Tarleton's troops, many of them clearly listening to this exchange.

"Wouldn't take long," Tarleton said softly, rocking back on his heels. His left fist was loosely curled and he rubbed his right hand flat on the side of his breeches, coat pushed back. He glanced over his shoulder, to the empty barn. "My men wouldn't interfere, but we could go in there, if you're shy." *"Shy"* said with that particular intonation that made it clear that cowardice was meant.

It had been on the tip of William's tongue to say, *"I don't* own *the girl"*— but to make that admission was to give Tarleton license to go after her. He'd seen Ban with girls often enough; he wasn't violent with them, but he was insistent. Never left without getting what he wanted, one way or another.

And after Harkness . . . His thoughts hadn't caught up with his body; he was on the ground, shucking his coat, before he'd made a conscious decision.

Ban laid his helmet on the ground, grinning, and took off his own coat in a leisurely fashion. The motion attracted all his men at once, and in seconds they were surrounded by a circle of dragoons, whistling and hooting encouragement. The only dissenter was Ban's lieutenant, who had gone a sickly shade of gray.

"Colonel!" he said, and William realized that the man's fear had all to do with taking issue with Ban and not the consequences of what might happen if he didn't. He meant to do his duty, though, and reached out a hand to grip Tarleton's arm. "Sir. You—"

"Let go," Ban said, not taking his eyes off William. "And shut up." The lieutenant's hand dropped away as though someone had punched him in the shoulder.

William felt at once detached, as though he were watching this from somewhere outside himself, above it all—and that part of him wanted to laugh at the ridiculousness of the situation. And some very tiny remnant of conscience was appalled. But the fleshly part of him was grimly exultant, and very much in charge.

He'd seen Ban fight before, and didn't make the mistake of waiting for any sort of signal. The moment the green coat hit the ground, William launched himself and—ignoring a ferocious hook that slammed into his ribs—grabbed Tarleton by both shoulders, jerked him forward, and butted him in the face with a horrid sound of cracking bone.

He let go, pushed Ban hard in the chest, and sent him staggering backward, blood flying from his broken nose and a surprised look on his face that turned immediately to berserk fury. Tarleton dug in his heels and leapt at William like a rabid dog.

William had six inches and forty pounds on Ban, and three older cousins who had taught him to fight. Banastre Tarleton had an unshakable conviction that he was going to win any fight he started.

They were struggling on the ground, so locked that neither was actually able to hit the other effectively, when William dimly heard the lieutenant's voice, full of panic, and a rush all round them. Hands seized him and dragged him away from Tarleton; more hands pushed him frantically toward his horse. There were drums coming down the lane and the sound of marching feet.

He mounted in a daze, a taste of blood in his mouth, and spat by reflex. His coat was thrown across his lap, and someone slapped his horse with a sharp "T'cha!" that nearly unseated William, whose feet were nowhere near the stirrups.

He pressed knees and calves into the horse's sides, urging Goth into a gallop, and burst from the lane directly in front of an infantry column, whose sergeant recoiled with a shout of alarm. Scots. He saw the checkered trews and caps, and heard a few uncouth shouts in what might be Scots or Gaelic, but didn't care. They belonged to a regiment he didn't know—and so their officers wouldn't know him.

Tarleton could give what explanations he liked. William's left ear was ringing, and he shook his head and pressed the flat of his hand against the ear to quiet it.

When he took the hand away, the ringing had eased, and a number of people were singing "Yankee Doodle" instead. He glanced over his shoulder, incredulous, and saw a number of blue-coated Continentals, dragging a number of cannon, making for the distant ridgeline.

Go back and tell the Scots infantry and Tarleton's men? Head south to Cornwallis?

"Hey, redcoat!" A shout from his left made him look in that direction, and just in time. A group of ten or fifteen men in hunting shirts was bearing down on him, most of them armed with scythes and hoes. One man was aiming a musket at him; apparently he was the one who had shouted, for he did so again: "Drop your reins and get off!"

"The devil I will," William replied, and booted Goth, who took off as though his tail were on fire. William heard the boom of the musket, but crouched low over the horse's neck and kept going.

73

PECULIAR BEHAVIOR OF A TENT

WHILE NOT EAGER to be removed to a prison of some sort, John Grey was beginning to wish at least for solitude. Fergus Fraser and his son had insisted on remaining with him until someone came for him. Presumably so they could tell Jamie how he had been disposed of.

He was peculiarly disinterested in the method and means of that disposal, content to await developments. What he wanted solitude for was a contemplation of Percy Wainwright's presence, motives, and possible action. With La Fayette, he'd said. Adviser. John shuddered to think what sort of advice might be given by that . . . and what about his interests in Fergus Fraser?

He glanced at said printer, presently engaged in argument with his precocious offspring.

"You did it!" Germain glowered up at his father, face flushed red with righteous indignation. "Ye told me so yourself, a dozen times or more! How you went to war with *Grand-père,* and stabbed a man in the leg, and rode on a cannon when the soldiers dragged it back from Prestonpans—and ye weren't even as old as I am now when ye did all that!"

Fergus paused for an instant, regarding his offspring through narrowed eyes, obviously regretting his previous prolixity. He breathed steadily through his nose for a moment, then nodded.

"That was different," he said evenly. "I was milord's employee at the time, not his son. I had a duty to attend him; he had no responsibility to prevent me doing so."

Germain blinked, frowning uncertainly.

"You weren't his son?"

"Of course not," Fergus said, exasperated. "If I told you about Prestonpans, surely I have told you that I was an orphan in Paris when I met your *grand-père.* He hired me to pick pockets for him."

"He did?" John hadn't meant to interrupt, but couldn't help it. Fergus glanced at him, startled; evidently he hadn't really noticed John's presence, focused as he was on Germain. He bowed.

"He did, my lord. We were Jacobites, you understand. He required information. Letters."

"Oh, indeed," John murmured, and took a sip from his flask. Then, recalling his manners, offered it to Fergus, who blinked in surprise, but then accepted it with another bow and took a healthy gulp. Well, it must be thirsty work, pursuing an errant child through an army. He thought briefly of Willie, and thanked God his son was safe—or was he?

He'd known that William would of course have left Philadelphia when Clinton withdrew the army—perhaps as a non-fighting aide-de-camp to a senior officer. But he hadn't thought about that supposition in conjunction with the apparent present fact that General Washington was now in hot pursuit of Clinton and might just possibly catch up with him. In which case, William . . .

These thoughts had distracted him from the ongoing tête-à-tête, and he was jerked out of them by a question directed to him by Germain.

"Me? Oh . . . sixteen. I might have gone to the army earlier," John added apologetically, "had my brother's regiment been formed, but he only raised it during the Jacobite Rising." He looked at Fergus with new interest. "You were at Prestonpans, were you?" That should have been his own first battle, too—and would have been, save for his happening to meet one Red Jamie Fraser, notorious Jacobite, in a mountain pass two nights before.

"Did you kill anybody?" Germain demanded.

"Not at Prestonpans. Later, at Culloden. I wish I hadn't." He stretched out a hand for the flask. It was nearly empty, and he drained it.

A moment later, he was glad of his celerity; had he not drained the flask already, he might have choked. The tent flap folded back, and Percy Wainwright/Beauchamp stuck his head in, then froze in surprise, dark eyes darting from one to another of the tent's inhabitants. John had an impulse to throw the empty flask at him, but thought better of it, instead saying coldly, "I beg your pardon, sir; I am engaged."

"So I see." Percy didn't look at John "Mr. Fergus Fraser," he said softly, coming into the tent, hand outstretched. "Your servant, sir. *Comment ça va?*"

Fergus, unable to avoid him, shook his hand with reserve and bowed slightly but said nothing. Germain made a small growling noise in his throat, but desisted when his father gave him a sharp glance.

"I am so pleased finally to have encountered you in private, Monsieur Fraser," Percy said, still speaking French. He smiled as charmingly as possible. "Monsieur—do you know who you are?"

Fergus regarded him thoughtfully.

"Few men know themselves, monsieur," he said. "For my part, I am entirely content to leave such knowledge to God. He can deal with it far better than I could. And having come to this conclusion, I believe that is all I have to say to you. *Pardonnez-moi.*" With that, he shouldered past Percy, taking him off-guard and knocking him off-balance. Germain turned at the tent flap and stuck out his tongue.

"Damned frog!" he said, then disappeared with a small yelp as his father jerked him through the flap.

Percy had lost one of his silver-buckled shoes in trying to stay upright. He brushed dirt and vegetable matter from the bottom of his stocking and screwed his foot back into the shoe, lips compressed and a rather attractive flush showing across his cheekbones.

"Oughtn't you to be with the army?" John inquired. "Surely you want to be there, if Washington does meet Clinton. I imagine your 'interests' would want a full report by an eyewitness, wouldn't they?"

"Shut up, John," Percy said briefly, "and listen. I haven't got much time." He sat down on the stool with a thump, folded his hands on his knee, and looked intently at John, as though evaluating his intelligence. "Do you know a man—a British officer—called Richardson?"

FERGUS MADE HIS way through the shambles left by the exodus of the army, holding Germain firmly by the hand. The camp followers and such men as had been left behind as unfit were setting to the work of salvage, and no one gave the Frasers more than a glance. He could only hope that the horse was where he had left it. He touched the pistol tucked under his shirt, just in case.

"Frog?" he said to Germain, not bothering to keep amusement out of his voice. "Damned *frog*, you said?"

"Well, he *is*, Papa." Germain stopped walking suddenly, pulling his hand free. "Papa, I need to go back."

"Why? Have you forgotten something?" Fergus glanced over his shoulder at the tent, feeling an uneasiness between his shoulder blades. Beauchamp couldn't force him to listen, let alone to do anything he didn't wish to, and yet he had a strong aversion to the man. Well, call it fear; he seldom bothered lying to himself. Though why he should fear a man such as that . . .

"No, but . . ." Germain struggled to choose among several thoughts that were plainly all trying to emerge into speech at once. "*Grand-père* told me I must stay with his lordship and if Monsieur Beauchamp should come, I must listen to anything they said."

"Really? Did he say why?"

"No. But he said it. And, also, I was—I *am*—his lordship's servant, his orderly. I have a duty to attend him." Germain's face was touchingly earnest, and Fergus felt his heart squeeze a little. Still . . .

Fergus had never mastered the Scottish way of making crude but eloquent noises in the throat—he rather envied them—but was not bad with similar communications made via the nose.

"According to what the soldiers said, he is a prisoner of war. Do you mean to accompany him to whatever dungeon or hulk they put him in? Because I think *Maman* would come and hoick you out of it by the scruff of your neck. Come along, she's very worried and waiting to hear that you're safe."

Mention of Marsali had the hoped-for effect; Germain cast down his eyes and bit his lip.

"No, I don't—I mean, I'm not . . . well, but, Papa! I *have* to just go and be sure that Monsieur Beauchamp isn't doing anything bad to him. And maybe see that he has some food before we leave," he added. "You wouldna have him starve, would you?"

"Milord looked reasonably well nourished," Fergus said, but the urgency on Germain's face drew him a reluctant step back toward the tent. Germain at once glowed with relief and excitement, seizing his father's hand again.

"Why do you think Monsieur Beauchamp means his lordship harm?" Fergus asked, holding Germain back for a moment.

"Because his lordship doesna like him, and neither does *Grand-père*," the boy said briefly. "Come on, Papa! His lordship is unarmed, and who knows what that sodomite has in his pocket?"

"Sodomite?" Fergus stopped dead in his tracks.

"*Oui, Grand-père* says he's a sodomite. Come *on*!" Germain was nearly frantic now and drew his father on by sheer willpower.

Sodomite? Well, that was interesting. Fergus, observant and very much experienced in the ways of the world and of sex, had some time ago drawn his own conclusions regarding milord Grey's preferences but had naturally not mentioned these to Jamie, as the English lord was his father's good friend. Did he know? Regardless, that might make his lordship's relationship with this Beauchamp a good deal more complex, and he approached the tent with a heightened sense of both curiosity and wariness.

He was prepared to clap his hand over Germain's eyes and drag him away, should anything untoward be going on in that tent, but before they came close enough to see through the flap, he saw the canvas quiver in a very odd way, and pulled Germain to a halt.

"*Arrête,*" he said softly. He couldn't conceive of even the most depraved sexual practices causing a tent to behave in that way and, gesturing to Germain to stay put, moved soft-footed to one side, keeping a little distance among the camp debris.

Sure enough, Lord John was wriggling out under the back edge of the tent, cursing quietly in German. Eyes on this peculiar exhibition, Fergus didn't notice that Beauchamp had emerged from the front of the tent until he heard Germain's exclamation and turned to find the boy behind him. He was impressed at Germain's ability to move quietly, but this was not the time for praise. He motioned to his son and withdrew a little farther, taking cover behind a pile of spiled barrels.

Beauchamp, with a high color in his face, walked off briskly, dusting chaff from the elegant skirts of his coat. Lord John, scrambling to his feet, made off in the other direction, toward the woods, not bothering about his own costume, and no wonder. What on earth had the man been doing, dressed in such a way?

"What shall we do, Papa?" Germain whispered.

Fergus hesitated only a moment, glancing after Beauchamp. The man was heading toward a large inn, likely General Washington's erstwhile center of command. If Beauchamp were remaining with the Continental army, he could be found again—if that proved necessary.

"Shall we follow Lord John, Papa?" Germain was vibrating with anxiety, and Fergus put his hand on the boy's shoulder to calm him.

"No," he said, firmly but with some regret—he himself was more than curious. "Clearly his business is urgent, and our presence would be more likely to cause him danger than to help." He didn't add that Lord John was almost certainly headed for the battlefield—if there should be one. Such an observation would only make Germain more eager.

"But—" Germain had his mother's sense of Scottish stubbornness, and Fergus suppressed a smile at seeing his small blond brows draw down in Marsali's exact expression.

"He will be looking either for your *grand-père* or for his compatriots," Fergus pointed out. "Either will take care of him, and in neither case would our presence be useful to him. And your mother will assassinate both of us if we don't return to Philadelphia within the week."

He also didn't mention that the thought of Marsali and the other children alone in the printshop caused him a great uneasiness. The exodus of the British army and a horde of Loyalists hadn't rendered Philadelphia safe, by any means. There were a good many looters and lawless men who had moved in to pick over the leavings of those who had fled—and there were plenty still left with Loyalist sympathies who didn't admit them openly but might easily act upon them under cover of darkness.

"Come," he said more gently, and took Germain by the hand. "We'll need to find some food to eat along the way."

JOHN GREY MADE his way through the wood, stumbling now and then by reason of having only one working eye; the ground wasn't always where he thought it was.

Once away from the campsite, he made no effort to keep out of sight; Claire had packed his eye with cotton lint and wrapped his head in a most professional manner with a gauze bandage to keep the lint in place. It would protect the bad eye while allowing air to dry the skin around it, she said. He supposed it was working—his eyelids weren't as raw and sore as they had been, only rather sticky—but at the moment was only grateful that he looked like a wounded man who'd been left behind by the rushing American army. No one would stop or question him.

Well, no one save his erstwhile comrades of the 16th Pennsylvania, should he have the misfortune to encounter them. God only knew what they'd thought when he surrendered to Jamie. He felt badly about them—they'd been very kind to him and must feel their kindness betrayed by the revelation of his identity, but there hadn't been much bloody choice about it.

There wasn't much choice about this, either.

"They mean to take your son." It was probably the one thing Percy could have said that would have made him attend.

"They who?" he'd said sharply, sitting up. "Take him where? And what for?"

"The Americans. As to what for—you and your brother." Percy had looked him over, shaking his head. "Do you have the slightest notion of your value, John?"

"Value to whom?" He'd stood up then, swaying perilously, and Percy had grabbed his hand to steady him. The touch was warm and firm and startlingly familiar. He withdrew his hand.

"I'm told I have considerable value as a scapegoat, should the Americans decide to hang me." Where was that bloody note from Hal . . . who had it now? Watson Smith? General Wayne?

"Well, that won't do at all, will it?" Percy appeared undisturbed at thought of Grey's imminent demise. "Don't worry. I'll have a word."

"With whom?" he asked, curious.

"General La Fayette," Percy said, adding with a slight bow, "to whom I have the honor of being an adviser."

"Thank you," Grey said dryly. "I am not concerned with the possibility of being hanged—at least not right this minute—but I want to know what the devil you mean about my son, William."

"This would be much easier over a bottle of port," Percy said, with a sigh, "but time doesn't permit, alas. Sit down, at least. You look as though you're going to fall on your face."

Grey sat, with as much dignity as he could muster, and glared up at Percy.

"To put it as simply as possible—and it's not simple, I assure you—there is a British officer named Richardson—"

"I know him," Grey interrupted. "He—"

"I know you do. Be quiet." Percy flapped a hand at him. "He's an American spy."

"He—what?" For an instant, he thought he might really fall on his face, despite the fact of sitting down, and grasped the cot's frame with both hands to prevent this. "He told me that he proposed to arrest Mrs. Fraser for distributing seditious materials. That was what caused me to marry her. I—"

"You?" Percy goggled at him. "*You* married?"

"Certainly," Grey said crossly. "So did you, or so you told me. Go on about bloody Richardson. How long has he been spying for the Americans?"

Percy snorted but obliged.

"I don't know. I became aware of him in the spring of last year, but he may well have been at it before that. Active fellow, I'll give him that. And not content with merely gathering information and passing it on, either. He's what one might call a *provocateur*."

"He's not the only one who's provoking," Grey muttered, resisting the urge to rub his bad eye. "What's he got to do with William?" He was beginning to have an unpleasant feeling in his abdomen. *He* had given William permission to undertake small intelligence-gathering missions for Captain Richardson, who—

"Put as bluntly as possible, he's tried more than once to lure your son into a position where he might appear to have sympathies with the Rebels. I gather that last year he sent him into the Great Dismal in Virginia, with the intention that he should be captured by a nest of Rebels who have a bastion there—presumably they would let it be known that he had deserted and joined their forces, while actually holding him prisoner."

"What for?" Grey demanded. "Will you bloody sit down? Looking up at you is giving me a headache."

Percy snorted again and sat—not on the conveniently placed stool, but beside Grey on the camp bed, hands on his knees.

"Presumably to discredit your family—Pardloe was making rather inflammatory speeches in the House of Lords at the time, about the conduct of the war." He made a small, impatient gesture that John recognized, a quick flutter of the fingers. "I don't know everything—yet—but what I *do* know is that he's arranged to have your son taken, during the journey to New York. He's not bothering with indirection or politics; things have changed, now that France has come into the war. This is simple abduction, with the intent of demanding your—and Pardloe's—cooperation in the matter of the Northwest Territory—and possibly something else—as the price of the boy's life."

Grey closed his good eye, in an effort to stop his head spinning. Two years before, Percy had abruptly reentered his life, bearing a proposal from certain French "interests"—to wit, that these interests wanted the return of the valuable Northwest Territory, presently held by England, and in return for assistance in achieving that goal would offer their influence to keep France from entering the war on the side of the Americans.

"Things have changed," he repeated, with an edge.

Percy inhaled strongly through his nose.

"Admiral d'Estaing sailed from Toulon with a fleet, in April. If he's not already off New York, he will be shortly. General Clinton may or may not know that."

"Jesus!" He clenched his fists on the bedframe, hard enough to leave marks from the nailheads. So the bloody French *had* now officially entered the war. They'd signed a Treaty of Alliance with America in February, and declared war on England in March, but talk was cheap. Ships and cannon and men cost money.

Suddenly he grasped Percy's arm, squeezing hard.

"And where do you come into this?" he said, voice level and cold. "Why are you telling me all this?"

Percy drew breath, but didn't jerk away. He returned Grey's stare, brown eyes clear and direct.

"Where I come into it doesn't matter," he said. "And there isn't time. You need to find your son quickly. As to why I tell you . . ."

John saw it coming and didn't pull away. Percy smelled of bergamot and petitgrain and the red wine on his breath. John's grip on Percy's arm loosened.

"Pour vos beaux yeux," Percy had whispered against his lips—and laughed, damn him.

74

THE SORT OF THING THAT WILL
MAKE A MAN SWEAT AND TREMBLE

WE FOLLOWED IN the wake of the army. Because of the speed of march, the soldiers had been instructed to jettison their nonessential equipment, and I had had to abandon many of my supplies, as well. Still, I was mounted and thus would be able to keep up, even loaded with what I managed to keep. After all, I reasoned, it would do me no good to catch up with the army if I had nothing with which to treat wounds when I did.

I had Clarence packed with as much as he could reasonably be expected to carry. As he was a large mule, this was a substantial amount, including my small tent, a folding camp bed for surgery, and all I could cram in, in terms of bandages, lint, and disinfectant—I had both a small cask of purified saline solution and a couple of bottles of straight ethyl alcohol (these disguised as poison, with large skull-and-crossbones labels painted on). Also a jug of sweet oil for burns, my medicine chest, and bundles of raw herbs, large jars of prepared ointment, and dozens of small bottles and vials of tinctures and infusions. My surgical instruments, stitching needles, and sutures were in their own small box, this in a haversack with extra bandage rolls, to be carried on my person.

I left Clarence tied and went to find out where the hospital tents were to be set up. The camp was milling with non-combatants and support personnel, but I was finally able to locate Denny Hunter, who told me that on the basis of General Greene's reports, the surgeons were to be dispatched to the village of Freehold, where there was a large church that could be used as a hospital.

"The last thing I've heard is that Lee has taken command of the force attacking the British rear and means to encircle the British," he said, polishing his spectacles on the tail of his shirt.

"Lee? But I thought he didn't think it an important command and wouldn't take it." I wouldn't care one way or the other—save that Jamie and his companies would be engaged in that mission, and I had my own doubts about General Lee.

Denzell shrugged, putting his spectacles back on and tucking in his shirt-tail.

"Apparently Washington decided that a thousand men were insufficient to his purpose and raised the number to five thousand, which Lee considered more appropriate to his . . . sense of his own importance." Denny's mouth twisted a little at this. He looked at my face, though, and touched my arm gently.

"We can but put our trust in God—and hope that the Lord has his eye upon Charles Lee. Will thee come with the girls and me, Claire? Thy mule will bide with us willingly."

I hesitated for no more than a moment. If I rode Clarence, I could take only a fraction of the equipment and supplies he could otherwise carry. And while Jamie had said he wanted me with him, I knew quite well that what he really meant was that he wanted to be assured of where I was, and that I was near at hand if he needed me.

"Thy husband does trust me with thy welfare," Denny said, smiling, having plainly divined what I was thinking.

"*Et tu, Brute?*" I said rather curtly, and, when he blinked, added more civilly, "I mean—does *everyone* know what I'm thinking, all of the time?"

"Oh, I doubt it," he said, and grinned at me. "If they did, I expect a number of them would take a deal more care in what they said to thee."

I rode in Denny's wagon with Dottie and Rachel, Clarence pacing stolidly along behind, tied to the tailboard. Dottie was flushed with heat and excitement; she had never been near a battle before. Neither had Rachel, but she had helped her brother during a very bad winter at Valley Forge and had much more idea of what the day might hold.

"Does thee think perhaps thee should write to thy mother?" I heard Rachel ask seriously. The girls were behind Denny and me, sitting in the bed of the wagon and keeping things from bouncing out when we hit ruts and mud bogs.

"No. Why?" Dottie's tone was wary—not quite hostile, but very reserved. I knew she had written to tell her mother that she intended to wed Denzell

Hunter, but she hadn't received a reply. Given the difficulties of correspondence with England, though, there was no assurance that Minerva Grey had ever read the letter.

It occurred to me, with a sudden qualm, that I hadn't written a letter to Brianna in several months. I hadn't been able to bear to write about Jamie's death, and there hadn't been time since his return even to think about it.

"It *is* a war, Dottie," Rachel said. "Unexpected things may happen. And thee would not wish thy mother to . . . well . . . to discover that thee had perished without some assurance that she was in thy heart."

"Hmm!" said Dottie, clearly taken aback. Beside me, I felt Denzell shift his weight, bending a little forward as he took a fresh grip on the reins. He glanced aside at me, and his mouth turned up in an expression that was as much grimace as smile, acknowledging that he'd been listening to the girls' talk, too.

"She worries for me," he said very quietly. "Never for herself." He let go the reins with one hand to rub a knuckle under his nose. "She has as much courage as her father and brothers."

"As much pigheadedness, you mean," I said under my breath, and he grinned, despite himself.

"Yes," he said. He glanced over his shoulder and so did I, but the girls had moved to the tailboard and were talking over it to Clarence, brushing flies off his face with the needles of a long pine twig. "Does thee think it a familial lack of imagination? For in the case of the men of her family, it cannot be ignorance of the possibilities."

"No, it certainly can't," I agreed, with a note of ruefulness. I sighed and stretched my legs a little. "Jamie is the same way, and *he* certainly doesn't lack for imagination. I think it's . . ." I made a small helpless gesture. "Perhaps 'acceptance' is the word."

"Acceptance of the fact of mortality?" He was interested and pushed his spectacles back into place. "We have discussed that—Dorothea and I." He nodded back toward the girls. "Friends live in the certain knowledge that this world is temporary and there is nothing to fear in death."

"Some of that, perhaps." In fact, almost everyone in this time had a very matter-of-fact acceptance of mortality; death was a constant presence at everyone's elbow, though they regarded that presence in a variety of ways. "But they—those men—what they do is something different, I think. It's more an acceptance of what they think God made them."

"Really?" He seemed slightly startled by that, and his brows drew together in consideration. "What does thee mean by that? That they believe God has created them deliberately to—"

"To be responsible for other people, I think," I said. "I couldn't say whether it's the notion of *noblesse oblige*—Jamie was a laird, you know, in Scotland—or just the idea that . . . that's what a man does," I ended, rather lamely. Because "that" was plainly not what Denzell Hunter thought a man should do. Though I did wonder a bit. Plainly the question troubled him a little.

As well it might, given his position. I could see that the prospect of battle excited him and that the fact that it did troubled him a great deal.

"You're a very brave man," I said quietly, and touched his sleeve. "I saw that. When you played Jamie's deserter game, after Ticonderoga."

"It wasn't courage, I assure thee," he said, with a short, humorless laugh. "I didn't seek to be brave; I only wanted to prove that I was."

I made a rather disrespectful noise—I wasn't in either Jamie's or Ian's class, but I *had* picked up a few pointers—and he glanced at me in surprise.

"I do appreciate the distinction," I told him. "But I've known a lot of brave men in my time."

"But how can thee know what lies—"

"Be quiet." I waved my fingers at him. " 'Brave' covers everything from complete insanity and bloody disregard of other people's lives—generals tend to go in for that sort—to drunkenness, foolhardiness, and outright idiocy—to the sort of thing that will make a man sweat and tremble and throw up . . . and go and do what he thinks he has to do *anyway.*

"Which," I said, pausing for breath and folding my hands neatly in my lap, "is exactly the sort of bravery you share with Jamie."

"Thy husband does not sweat and tremble," he said dryly. "I've seen him. Or, rather, I have *not* seen him do such things."

"He does the sweating and trembling on the inside, mostly," I replied. "Though he really does often vomit before—or during—a battle."

Denzell blinked, once, and didn't speak for a bit, absorbed—apparently—in steering his way past a large hay wagon whose oxen had suddenly decided they didn't want to go any farther and stopped dead in the middle of the road.

At last he took a breath and let it out explosively.

"I am not afraid to die," he said. "That isn't my difficulty."

"What is?" I asked, curious. "Are you afraid of being maimed and left helpless? I certainly would be."

"No." His throat moved as he swallowed. "It's Dorothea and Rachel. I'm afraid I would lack the courage to see them die without trying to save them, even if that meant killing someone."

I couldn't think of anything to say to this, and we jolted on in silence.

LEE'S TROOPS LEFT Englishtown at about 6 A.M., heading east toward Monmouth Courthouse. Lee arrived at the courthouse at about nine-thirty, to find that the bulk of the British army had left—presumably moving toward Middletown, as that was where the road went.

Lee was prevented from following, though, by the presence of a small but very belligerent rear guard under the command of General Clinton himself. Or so Ian told Jamie, having got close enough to see Clinton's regimental banners. Jamie had communicated this information to Lee, but saw no evidence that it affected either that gentleman's plan of action (always assuming that he had one) or his disinclination to send out more scouts to reconnoiter.

"Go round this lot and see can ye find out where Cornwallis is," Jamie told Ian. "The grenadiers ye saw are likely Hessians, so they'll be close to von Knyphausen."

Ian nodded and took the full canteen Jamie offered him.

"Shall I tell General Lee, if I do? He didna seem much interested in what I had to say."

"Aye, tell him if ye see him before ye see me—tell the marquis, too, should ye come within reach of him—but find me, regardless, aye?"

Ian grinned at him and slung the canteen over his pommel.

"Good hunting, *a Bhràthair-mathàr*!"

Jamie had had two companies blooded by midmorning, skirmishing near Monmouth Courthouse, but no one killed yet and only three wounded badly enough to retire. Colonel Owen had requested cover for his artillery—only two cannon, but any artillery was welcome—and Jamie had sent Thomas Meleager's Pennsylvanians to deal with that.

He'd sent one of Captain Kirby's companies to reconnoiter toward what he thought was the creek and kept back the rest, waiting for orders from La Fayette or Lee. La Fayette was somewhere ahead of him, Lee well behind and to the east with the main body of his troops.

The sun stood just short of ten o'clock when a messenger appeared, crouched dramatically in his saddle as though dashing through a hail of bullets, though in fact there was not a British soldier in sight. He pulled his lathered horse to a stop and gasped out his message.

"There's dust clouds in the east—might be more redcoats comin'! And the marky says there's redcoat cannon in the cider orchard, sir, and will you do summat about it, please."

The sweating messenger gulped air, loosening his rein in obvious preparation for dashing off again. Jamie leaned over and seized the horse's bridle to prevent it.

"Where *is* the cider orchard?" he asked calmly. The messenger was young, maybe sixteen, and wild-eyed as his rawboned horse.

"Dunno, sir," he said, and began glancing to and fro, as though expecting the orchard to materialize suddenly out of the meadow they were standing in. A sudden distant boom reverberated in Jamie's bones, and his horse's ears pricked up.

"Never mind, lad," he said. "I hear them. Breathe your horse, or he's like to die under ye before the sun's high."

Letting go the bridle, he waved to Captain Craddock and turned his own horse's head toward the sound of cannon.

THE AMERICAN ARMY had several hours' lead on him, and the British army very much more—but a man alone could move a great deal faster than even a company of light infantry. Neither was John burdened with weapons. Or food. Or water.

You know perfectly well that he's lying to you.

"Oh, be quiet, Hal," Grey muttered to his brother's shade. "I know Percy a great deal better than you do."

I said, you know perfectly well . . .

"I do. What am I risking if he is lying—and what am I risking if he's *not*?"

Hal was high-handed, but logical. He was also a father; that shut him up.

What he was risking if Percy *was* lying was being shot or hanged out of hand if anyone recognized him. Anyone. If the Americans found him out before he reached the British lines, they'd arrest him for breaking his parole and promptly execute him as a spy. If the British *didn't* recognize him in time, they'd shoot him on sight as Rebel militia. He put a hand in the pocket where he'd wadded the LIBERTY OR DEATH cap and debated the wisdom of throwing it away, but, in the event, kept it.

What he was risking if Percy wasn't lying was Willie's life. No great effort required to call the odds.

It was midmorning, and the air was like treacle, thick and sweet with flowers, sticky with tree sap, and completely unbreathable. His good eye was beginning to itch from the floating pollen grains, and flies were buzzing interestedly round his head, drawn by the scent of honey.

At least the headache had gone away, dispelled by the burst of alarm—and a brief flare of lust, might as well admit it—occasioned by Percy's revelation. He wouldn't begin to speculate as to Percy's motives, but . . .

" 'For your beautiful eyes,' indeed!" he muttered, but couldn't help smiling at the impudence. A wise man would not touch Percy Wainwright with a ten-foot pole. Something shorter, though . . .

"Oh, do be quiet, will you?" he murmured to himself, and made his way down a clay bank to the edge of a tiny creek, where he could throw cold water on his heated face.

IT WAS PERHAPS eight o'clock in the morning when we reached Freehold, where Tennent Church was to be established as the main hospital. It was a large building, set in the midst of a huge, sprawling churchyard, an acre or more of ground whose headstones were as individual as doubtless their owners had been in life. No neat aisles of uniform white crosses here.

I spared a thought for the graves of Normandy and wondered whether those rows upon rows of faceless dead were meant to impose a sort of postmortem tidiness on the costs of war—or whether it was meant rather to underline them, a solemn accounting carried out in endless rows of naughts and crosses.

But I didn't think long. Battle had been joined already—somewhere—and there were already wounded coming in, a number of men sitting in the shade of a large tree next to the church, more coming down the road, some staggering with the help of friends, some being carried on litters—or in someone's arms. My heart lurched at the sight, but I tried not to look for Jamie or Ian; should they be among the early wounded, I'd know it soon enough.

There was a bustle near the church's porch, where the double doors had been flung wide to accommodate passage, and orderlies and surgeons were coming and going in haste—but organized haste, so far.

"Go and see what's happening, why don't you?" I suggested to Denzell. "The girls and I will unload things."

He paused long enough to unhitch his own two mules and hobble them, then hastened into the church.

I found the buckets and dispatched Rachel and Dottie to find a well. The day was already uncomfortably hot; we were going to need a good deal of water, one way or another.

Clarence was showing a strong urge to go join Denny's mules in cropping grass among the headstones, jerking his head against the pull of his tether and uttering loud cries of annoyance.

"All right, all right, all *right*," I said, hurrying to undo the packing straps and lift his burdens off. "Hold your—oh, dear."

A man was staggering toward me, giving at the knees with every step and lurching dizzily. The side of his face was black, and there was blood down the facing of his uniform. I dropped the bundle of tenting and poles and rushed to catch him by the arm before he should trip over a headstone and fall face-first into the dirt.

"Sit down," I said. He looked dazed and appeared not to hear me, but as I was pulling on his arm, he did go down, letting his knees relax abruptly and nearly taking me with him as he landed on a substantial stone commemorating one Gilbert Tennent.

My patient was swaying as though about to fall over, and yet a hasty check showed me no significant wounds; the blood on his coat was from his face, where the blackened skin had blistered and split. It wasn't just the soot of black powder—the skin had actually been burned to a crisp, the underlying flesh seared, and my patient smelled appallingly like a pork roast. I took a firm grip on my lurching stomach and stopped breathing through my nose.

He didn't respond to my questions but stared hard at my mouth, and he seemed lucid, despite his continued swaying. The penny finally dropped.

"Ex . . . plo . . . sion?" I mouthed with exaggerated care, and he nodded vigorously, then stopped abruptly, swaying so far that I had to grasp him by the sleeve and pull him upright.

Artilleryman, from his uniform. So something big had exploded near him—a mortar, a cannon?—and not only burned his face nearly to the bone but also likely burst both his eardrums and disturbed the balance of his inner ear. I nodded and set his hands to grip the stone he sat on, to keep him in place while I hastily finished unloading Clarence—who was making the welkin ring with frustration; I should have realized at once that the artilleryman was deaf, as he was taking no notice of the racket—hobbled him, and set him loose to join Denny's mules in the shade. I dug what I needed out of the packs and set about to do what little I could for the injured man, this consisting mostly of soaking a towel in saline and applying it to his face like a poultice, to remove as much soot as I could without scrubbing.

I thanked God that I'd had the forethought to bring a jug of sweet oil for burns—and cursed my lack of it for not having asked for aloe at Bartram's Garden.

The girls hadn't yet returned with water; I hoped there was a well somewhere close at hand. Creek water so close to an army couldn't be used without boiling it. That thought led me to look round for a spot where a fire could be lighted and to make a mental note to send the girls to look for wood next.

My mind was jerked from my rapidly expanding mental checklist, though, by Denny's sudden emergence from the church. He wasn't alone; he appeared to be having a passionate argument with another Continental officer. With a brief exclamation of exasperation, I dug in my pocket and found my silk-wrapped spectacles. With these on my nose, the face of Denny's interlocutor sprang into clear focus—Captain Leckie, diplomate of the Medical College of Philadelphia.

My patient tugged at my skirt and, when I turned to him, apologetically opened his mouth and mimed drinking. I held up a finger, adjuring him to wait one moment, and went to see whether Denzell required reinforcement.

My appearance was greeted by an austere look from Captain Leckie, who viewed me rather as he might have looked at something questionable on the bottom of his shoe.

"Mrs. Fraser," he said coldly. "I have just been telling your Quaker friend that there is no room inside the church for cunning-women or—"

"Claire Fraser is the most skillful surgeon I have seen operate!" Denzell said. He was flushed and fairly bristling with anger. "You will do your patients great harm, sir, by not allowing her to—"

"And where did you obtain your training, *Dr.* Hunter, that you are so confident of your own opinion?"

"In Edinburgh," Denny said through his teeth. "Where I was trained by my cousin, John Hunter." Seeing that this made no impact on Leckie, he added, "And his brother, William Hunter—*accoucheur* to the queen."

That took Leckie aback, but unfortunately also got up his nose.

"I see," he said, dividing a faint sneer evenly between us. "I congratulate you, sir. But as I doubt the army requires a man midwife, perhaps you should assist your . . . colleague"—and here he actually flared his nostrils at me, the pompous little swine—"with her seeds and potions, rather than—"

"We haven't time for this," I interrupted firmly. "Dr. Hunter is both a trained physician and a duly appointed surgeon in the Continental army; you can't bloody keep him out. And if my experience of battle—which I venture to suggest may be somewhat more extensive than your own, *sir*—is anything to go on, you'll need every hand you can get." I turned to Denzell and gave him a long, level look.

"Your duty is with those who need you. So is mine. I told you about triage, did I not? I have a tent and my own surgical instruments and supplies. I'll do triage out here, deal with the minor cases, and send in anyone requiring major surgery."

I had a quick look over my shoulder, then turned back to the two fuming men.

"You'd best go inside and be quick about it. They're starting to pile up."

This was not a metaphorical expression. There was a crowd of walking wounded under the trees, a few men lying on makeshift stretchers and sheets of canvas . . . and a small, sinister heap of bodies, these presumably men who had died of their wounds en route to the hospital.

Fortunately, Rachel and Dottie appeared at this moment, each lugging a heavy bucket of water in each hand. I turned my back on the men and went to meet them.

"Dottie, come and put up the tent poles, will you?" I said, taking her buckets. "And, Rachel—you know what arterial bleeding looks like, I imagine. Go and look through those men and bring me anyone who's doing it."

I gave my burnt artilleryman water, then helped him to his feet. As he stood up, I saw behind his legs the epitaph carved into Gilbert Tennent's headstone:

O READER HAD YOU HEARD HIS LAST TESTIMONY YOU WOULD HAVE BEEN CONVINCED OF THE EXTREME MADNESS OF DELAYING REPENTANCE.

"I suppose there are worse places to be doing this," I remarked to the artilleryman, but, unable to hear me, he simply raised my hand and kissed it before swaying off to sit down on the grass, the wet towel pressed to his face.

75

THE CIDER ORCHARD

THE FIRST SHOT took them by surprise, a muffled boom from the cider orchard and a slow roll of white smoke. They didn't run, but they stiffened, looking to him for direction. Jamie said to those near him, "Good lads," then raised his voice. "To my left, now! Mr. Craddock, Reverend Woodsworth—circle them; come into the orchard from behind. The rest—scatter to the right and fire as ye can—" The second crash drowned his words, and Craddock jerked like a puppet with his strings cut and dropped to the ground, blood spraying from the blackened hole in his chest. Jamie's horse shied violently, nearly unseating him.

"Go with the reverend!" he shouted at Craddock's men, who stood there drop-jawed, staring at their captain's body. "Go *now!*" One of the men shook himself, grabbed the sleeve of another, pulled him away, and then they all began to move as a body. Woodsworth, bless him, raised his musket overhead and roared, "To me! Follow me!" and broke into the stork-legged shamble that passed with him for running—but they followed him.

The gelding had settled but was moving uneasily. He was—supposedly— used to the sound of guns, but he didn't like the strong smell of blood. Jamie didn't like it, either.

"Shouldn't we . . . bury Mr. Craddock?" a timid voice suggested behind him.

"He's not *dead,* lackbrain!"

Jamie glanced down. He wasn't—but it wouldn't be more than a few seconds longer.

"Go with God, man," he said quietly. Craddock didn't blink; his eyes were fixed on the sky, not yet dull but sightless.

"Go wi' your fellows," he said to the two lingerers, then saw that they were Craddock's two sons, maybe thirteen and fourteen, white-faced and staring as sheep. "Say farewell to him," he said abruptly. "He'll still hear ye. Then . . . go." He thought for a moment to send them to La Fayette, but they'd be no safer there. "Run!"

They ran—they were a deal safer running—and with a gesture to Lieutenants Orden and Bixby, he wheeled his horse to the right, following Guthrie's company. The cannon were firing more regularly from the orchard. He saw a ball bounce past, ten feet away, and the air was thickening with smoke. He could still smell Craddock's blood.

He found Captain Moxley and sent him with a full company to look at the farmhouse on the far side of the orchard.

"At a distance, mind. I want to know if the redcoats are in it or if the family's still there. If the family's there, surround the house; go inside if they'll let ye, but don't force your way. If there are soldiers inside and they come out after you, engage them and take the house if ye think ye can. If they stay inside, don't stir them up; send someone back to tell me. I'll be at the back o' the orchard; the north side."

Guthrie was waiting for him, the men lying flat in the long grass behind the orchard. He left the two lieutenants with his horse, which he tied to a fence rail well out of range of the orchard, and scrambled along to the company, keeping low. He dropped to his belly by Bob Guthrie.

"I need to know where the cannon are—exactly where they are, and how many. Send three or four men in from different directions, goin' canny—ye know what I mean? Aye. They're not to do anything; see what they can and come out again, fast."

Guthrie was panting like a dog, stubbled face awash with sweat, but he grinned and nodded and wormed his way off through the grass.

The meadow was dry, brown and brittle in the summer heat; Jamie's stockings prickled with foxtails, and the warm sharp scent of ripe hay was stronger than that of black powder.

He gulped water from his canteen; it was nearly empty. It wasn't yet noon, but the sun was coming down on them like a flatiron. He turned to tell one of the lieutenants who'd been following him to go and find the nearest water, but nothing moved in the grass behind him save hundreds of grasshoppers, whirring up like sparks. Gritting his teeth against the stiffness in his knees, he scrambled up onto hands and feet and scuttled back toward his horse.

Orden was lying ten feet away, shot through one eye. Jamie froze for an instant, and something whirred close past his cheek. It might be a grasshopper and it might not. He was flat to the earth beside the dead lieutenant, heart pounding in his ears before the thought had fully formed.

Guthrie. He daren't raise his head to call out—but had to. He got his feet under him as best he could, shot out of the grass, and ran like a rabbit, to and fro, zigging away from the orchard as best he could while still going in the direction he'd sent Guthrie.

He could hear the shots now: more than one sniper in the orchard, protecting the cannon, and the sound was the flat *crack!* of a rifle. Jaegers? He flung himself down and crawled madly, now shouting for Guthrie.

"Here, sir!" The man popped up suddenly beside him like a groundhog, and Jamie seized Guthrie's sleeve, pulling him back down.

"Get . . . your men back." He gulped air, chest heaving. "Shooting—from the orchard. This side. They'll be picked off."

Guthrie was staring at him, mouth half open.

"Get them!"

Shaken out of his shock, Guthrie nodded like a puppet and started to rise. Jamie grabbed him by the ankle and jerked him flat, pressed him down with a hand on his back.

"Don't . . . stand up." His breathing was slowing and he managed to speak calmly. "We're still in range here. Get your men and retire with your company—back to the ridgeline. Join Captain Moxley; tell him to come round and join me . . ." His mind went blank for a moment, trying to think of some reasonable place for a rendezvous. "South of the farmhouse. With Woodbine's company." He took his hand off Guthrie.

"Aye, sir." The man scuffed up onto hands and knees, reaching for the hat that had fallen off. He glanced back at Jamie, eyes full of earnest concern.

"Are you hit bad, sir?"

"Hit?"

"There's blood all down your face, sir."

"It's nothing. Go!"

Guthrie swallowed, nodded, wiped his face on his sleeve, and made off through the grass, as fast as he could go. Jamie put a hand to his own face, belatedly aware of a slight sting across his cheekbone. Sure enough, his fingers came away bloody. Not a grasshopper, then.

He wiped his fingers on the skirt of his coat and noticed mechanically that the seam of the sleeve had burst at the shoulder, showing the white shirt beneath. He rose a little, cautious, looking round for Bixby, but there was no sign of him. Maybe dead in the long grass, too; maybe not. With luck, he'd seen what was happening and run back to warn the companies coming up. The horse was still where he'd left it, thank God, tethered to a fence, fifty yards away.

He hesitated for a moment, but there wasn't time to lose in looking for Bixby. Woodsworth and his two companies would be coming round the orchard in a few minutes, and right into range of the German rifles. He popped up and ran.

Something tugged at his coat, but he didn't stop, and reached his horse, gasping for air.

"*Tiugainn!*" he said, swinging up into the saddle. He turned away from the orchard and galloped through a potato field, though it bruised his farmer's heart to see what the armies' passing had done to it already.

I DON'T KNOW when physicians began calling it "the Golden Hour," but surely every battlefield medic from the time of the *Iliad* onward knows about it. From the time of an accident or injury that isn't immediately fatal, the victim's chances of living are best if he receives treatment within an hour of sustaining the injury. After that, shock, continued loss of blood, debility due to pain . . . the chance of saving a patient goes sharply downhill.

Add in blazing temperatures, lack of water, and the stress of running full out through fields and woods, wearing wool homespun and carrying heavy weapons, inhaling powder smoke, and trying either to kill someone or avoid being killed, just prior to being injured, and I rather thought we were looking at a Golden fifteen minutes or so.

Given also the fact that the wounded were having to be carried or to *walk*—probably more than a mile—to a place where they could find assistance . . . I supposed we were doing well to save as many as we were. *If only temporarily,* I added grimly to myself, hearing the screaming from inside the church.

"What's your name, dear?" I said to the young man in front of me. He couldn't be more than seventeen and was precious near to bleeding to death. A bullet had gone through the meat of his upper arm, which would normally be a fortuitous location for a wound. Unfortunately, in this instance the ball had passed through the underside of the arm and nicked the brachial artery, which had been spurting blood in a slow but earnest manner until I'd taken a death grip on his arm.

"Private Adams, ma'am," he replied, though his lips were white and he was shaking. "Billy, they call me," he added politely.

"Pleased to meet you, Billy," I said. "And you, sir . . . ?" For he'd been brought in staggering, leaning on another boy of about his own age—and nearly as white-faced, though I thought he wasn't hurt.

"Horatio Wilkinson, ma'am," he said, dipping his head in an awkward bow—the best he could manage while holding his friend upright.

"Lovely, Horatio," I said. "I've got him now. Would you pour him out a little water, with a splash of brandy in it? Just there." I nodded at the packing case I was using for a table, on which one of my brown bottles marked POISON stood, along with a canteen full of water and wooden cups. "And as soon as he's drunk it, give him that leather strip to bite down on."

I'd have told Horatio to have a tot, too, save that there were only two cups, and the second one was mine. I was sipping water steadily—my bodice was soaked and clung to me like the membrane inside an eggshell, and sweat ran steadily down my legs—and I didn't want to be sharing the germs of assorted soldiers who didn't brush their teeth regularly. Still, I might have to tell him to take a quick gulp direct from the brandy bottle; someone was going to have to apply pressure to Billy Adams's arm while I stitched his brachial artery, and Horatio Wilkinson didn't presently look equal to the task.

"Would you—" I began, but I was holding a scalpel and a suture needle with a dangling ligature in my free hand, and the sight of these overcame young Mr. Wilkinson. His eyes rolled up in his head and he dropped, boneless, into the gravel.

"Wounded?" said a familiar voice behind me, and I turned my head to see Denzell Hunter looking down at Mr. Wilkinson. He was nearly as pale as Horatio and, with strands of hair come loose and clinging to his cheeks, very much the antithesis of his usual collected self.

"Fainted," I said. "Can you—"

"They are idiots," he said, so pale—with rage, I now realized—that he could barely speak. "Regimental surgeons, they call themselves! A good quarter of them have never seen a man wounded in battle before. And those who have are barely capable of anything in the way of treatment save the crudest amputation. A company of barbers would do better!"

"Can they stop bleeding?" I asked, taking his hand and wrapping it round my patient's upper arm. He automatically pressed his thumb to the brachial artery near the armpit, and the spurting that had started when I took my own hand away stopped again. "Thank you," I said.

"Not at all. Yes, most of them can do that," he admitted, calming down just a little. "But they are so jealous of privilege—and so much affiliated with their own regiments—that some are letting a wounded man die because he is not one of theirs and his own regimental surgeon is otherwise occupied!"

"Scandalous," I murmured, and, "Bite hard now, Private," as I thrust the leather between his teeth and made a quick incision to enlarge the wound enough to find the end of the severed artery. He did bite, and made no more than a low grunting noise as the scalpel sliced into his flesh; perhaps he was sufficiently in shock that he didn't feel it much—I hoped not.

"We haven't a lot of choice," I observed, glancing toward the big shade trees that edged the graveyard. Dottie was minding the victims of heatstroke, giving them water and—as time and buckets permitted—dousing them with it. Rachel was in charge of depressed head fractures, abdominal wounds, and other serious wounds that couldn't be treated by amputation or binding and splinting. In most cases, this amounted to nothing more than comforting them as they died, but she was a good, steady girl, who had seen a great many men die during the winter at Valley Forge; she didn't shrink from the job.

"We have to let them"—I jerked my chin toward the church, my hands being occupied in holding Private Adams's arm and ligating the severed vessel—"do what they're able to do. Not that we could bloody *stop* them."

"No." Denny breathed out, let go of the arm as he saw I had the vessel tied off, and wiped his face on his coat. "No, we can't. I just needed to express my anger where it wouldn't cause more trouble. And to ask if I may have some of thy gentian ointment; I saw thee had two good-sized tubs made up."

I gave him a small, wry laugh.

"Be my guest. That ass Leckie sent an orderly out a little while ago to try to appropriate my stock of lint and bandages. Do you need some, by the way?"

"If thee has them to spare." He cast a bleak eye over the dwindling pile of supplies. "Dr. McGillis has sent an orderly to scavenge the neighborhood for items of use and another to carry word back to camp and bring more."

"Take half," I said, with a nod, and finished wrapping Billy Adams's arm with as miserly a bandage as would still do the job. Horatio Wilkinson had recovered himself a little and was sitting up, though still rather pale. Denny hoisted him to his feet and dispatched him with Billy to sit in the shade for a bit.

I was digging through one of my packs for the gentian ointment when I noticed the approach of another party and straightened up to see what their state of need might be.

None of them appeared to be wounded, though all were staggering. They weren't in uniform and bore no weapons save clubs; no telling whether they were militia, or . . .

"We hear you've some brandy, missus," one of them said, reaching out in a quasi-friendly manner and seizing me by the wrist. "Come and share it with us, eh?"

"Let go of her," Denzell said, in a tone of deep menace that made the man holding my wrist actually let go in surprise. He blinked at Denzell, whom he evidently hadn't noticed before.

"Who the hell're *you?*" he asked, though more in tones of befuddled astonishment than confrontation.

"I'm a surgeon with the Continental army," Denzell said firmly, and moved to stand beside me, thrusting a shoulder between me and the men, all of whom were clearly very drunk. One of them laughed at this, a high *heeheehee* sound, and his fellow giggled and poked him, repeating, "surgeon with the Continental *ar-my.*"

"Gentlemen, you must go," Denzell said, edging farther in front of me. "We have wounded men who need attention." He stood with his fists loosely curled, in the attitude of a man ready to do battle—though I was fairly sure he wouldn't. I hoped intimidation would do the trick, but glanced at my bottle; it was three-quarters empty—perhaps it would be better to give it to them and hope they went away. . . .

I could see a small party of wounded Continentals coming down the road, two on stretchers, and a few more stumbling, stripped to their bloodied shirts, coats in their hands being dragged in the dust. I reached for the bottle, intending to thrust it at the intruders, but a movement at the corner of my eye made me look toward the shade where the girls were tending prisoners. Both Rachel and Dottie were standing upright, watching the proceedings, and at this point, Dottie, with a strong look of determination on her face, began to walk toward us.

Denny saw her, too; I could see the sudden shift in his posture, a touch of indecision. Dorothea Grey might be a professed Quaker, but her family blood clearly had its own ideas. And I could—rather to my surprise—tell exactly what Denzell was thinking. One of the men had already noticed Dottie and had turned—swaying—in her direction. If she confronted them and one or more of them attacked her . . .

"Gentlemen." I interrupted the hum of interest among our visitors, and three pairs of bloodshot eyes turned slowly toward me. I withdrew one of the pistols Jamie had given me, pointed it into the air, and pulled the trigger.

It went off with a violent jerk and a *blam* that momentarily deafened me, along with a puff of acrid smoke that made me cough. I wiped streaming eyes on my sleeve in time to see the visitors departing hastily, with anxious looks back over their shoulders. I located a spare handkerchief tucked into my stays and wiped a smear of soot from my face, emerging from the damp linen folds to find the doors of the church occupied by several surgeons and orderlies, all goggling at me.

Feeling rather like Annie Oakley, and repressing the urge to try to twirl my pistol—mostly for fear I would drop it; it was nearly a foot long—I re-holstered my weapon and took a deep breath. I felt a trifle light-headed.

Denzell was regarding me with concern. He swallowed visibly and opened his mouth to speak.

"Not now," I said, my own voice sounding muffled, and nodded toward the men coming toward us. "There isn't time."

76

THE DANGERS OF SURRENDER

FOUR BLOODY HOURS. Hours spent slogging through an undulant countryside filled with mobs of Continental soldiers, clots of militia, and more bloody rocks than anyplace required for proper functioning, if you asked Grey. Unable to stand the blisters and shreds of raw skin any longer, he'd taken off his shoes and stockings and thrust them into the pockets of his disreputable coat, choosing to hobble barefoot for as long as he could bear it.

Should he meet anyone whose feet looked his size, he thought grimly, he'd pick up one of the omnipresent rocks and avail himself.

He *knew* he was close to the British lines. He could feel the tremble in the air. The movement of large bodies of men, their rising excitement. And somewhere, no great distance away, the point where excitement was turning to action.

He'd felt the presence of fighting since just past daylight. Sometimes heard shouting and the hollow boom of muskets. *What would I do if I were Clinton?* he'd wondered.

Clinton couldn't outstrip the pursuing Rebels; that was clear. But he would have had time enough to choose decent ground on which to stand and to make some preparation.

Chances were, some part of the army—Cornwallis's brigade, maybe; Clinton wouldn't leave von Knyphausen's Hessians to stand alone—would have taken up some defensible position, hoping to hold off the Rebels long enough for the baggage train to get away. Then the main body would wheel and take up its own position—perhaps occupying a village. He'd walked through two or three such, each with its own church. Churches were good; he'd sent many a scout up a steeple in his day.

Where's William most likely to be? Unarmed and unable to fight, chances were that he was with Clinton. That's where he *should* be. But he knew his son.

"Unfortunately," he muttered. He would, without hesitation, lay down both life and honor for William. That didn't mean he was pleased at the prospect of having to do so.

Granted, the current circumstance was not William's fault. He had to admit—reluctantly—that it was at least in part his own. He'd allowed William to undertake intelligence work for Ezekiel Richardson. He should have looked much more closely into Richardson . . .

The thought of having been gulled by the man was almost as upsetting as what Percy had told him.

He could only hope to run across Richardson in circumstances that would allow him to kill the man unobtrusively. But if it had to be at high noon in full view of General Clinton and his staff—so bloody be it.

He was inflamed in every particular of his being, knew it, and didn't care.

There were men coming, rumbling up the road behind him. Americans, disorderly, with wagons or caissons. He stepped off the road and stood still in the shade of a tree, waiting for them to pass.

It was a group of Continentals, pulling cannon. Fairly small: ten guns, and only four-pounders. Pulled by men, not mules. It was the only artillery he'd seen in the course of the morning, though; was it all Washington possessed?

They didn't notice him. He waited a few minutes, until they were out of sight, and followed in their wake.

HE HEARD MORE cannon, some way to his left, and paused to listen. British, by God! He'd had somewhat to do with artillery, early in his military career, and the rhythm of a working gun crew was embedded in his bones.

Sponge piece!
Load piece!
Ram!
Fire!

A single artillery unit. Ten-pounders, six of them. They had something in range but weren't being attacked; the firing was sporadic, not that of hot combat.

Though, to be fair, any physical effort whatever had to be described as "hot" today. He lunged into a patch of trees, exhaling in relief at the shade. He was ready to expire in his black coat and took it off for a moment's respite. Dare he abandon the bloody thing altogether?

He'd seen a band of militia earlier, shirtsleeved, some with kerchiefs tied over their heads against the sun. Coated, though, he might bluff his way as a militia surgeon—the beastly garment smelled badly enough.

He worked his tongue, bringing a little saliva to his dry mouth. Why the devil had he not thought to bring a canteen when he'd fled? Thirst decided him to make his move now.

Dressed as he was, he might well be shot by any infantryman or dragoon who saw him, before he could speak a word. But while cannon were very effective indeed against a massed enemy, they were almost useless against a single man, as the aim couldn't be adjusted quickly enough to bear, unless the man was fool enough to advance in a straight line—and Grey was not *that* foolish.

Granted, the officer in charge of each gun's crew would be armed with sword and pistol, but a single man approaching an artillery unit on foot could be no conceivable danger; sheer amazement would likely let him get within earshot. And pistols were so inaccurate at anything over ten paces, he wasn't risking much anyway, he reasoned.

He hastened his step as much as he could, a wary eye out. There were a lot of Continental troops in his vicinity now, marching furiously. The regulars would take him for walking wounded, but he daren't try to surrender to the British lines while combat was joined, or he'd be the walking dead in short order.

The artillery in the orchard might be his best chance, hair-raising as it was to walk into the mouths of the guns. With a muffled oath, he put his shoes back on and began to run.

HE RAN HEAD-ON into a militia company, but they were headed somewhere at the trot and gave him no more than a cursory glance. He swerved aside into a hedgerow, where he floundered for a moment before breaking through. He was in a narrow field, much trampled, and on the other side of it was an apple orchard, only the crowns of the trees showing above a heavy cloud of white powder smoke.

He caught a glimpse of movement beyond the orchard and risked a few steps to the side to look—then ducked back hastily out of sight. American militia, men in hunting shirts or homespun, a few shirtless and glistening with sweat. They were massing there, likely planning a rush into the orchard from behind, in hopes of capturing or disabling the guns.

They were making a good deal of noise, and the guns had stopped firing. Plainly the artillerymen knew the Americans were there and would be making preparations to resist. Not the best time to come calling, then . . .

But then he heard the drums. Well in the distance, to the east of the orchard, but the sound carried clearly. British infantry on the march. A better prospect than the artillery in the orchard. Moving, infantry wouldn't be disposed or prepared to shoot a single, unarmed man, no matter how he was dressed. And if he could get close enough to attract the attention of an officer . . . but he'd still have to cross the open ground below the orchard in order to reach the infantry before they'd marched off out of reach.

Biting his lip with exasperation, he shoved through the hedgerow and ran through the clouds of drifting smoke. A shot cracked the air much too near him. He flung himself into the grass by instinct, but then leapt up and ran again, gasping for breath. Christ, there were riflemen in the orchard, defending the cannon! *Jaegers.*

But most of the riflemen must be facing the other way, ready to meet the gathering militia, for no more shots came on this side of the orchard. He slowed down, pressing a hand to the stitch in his side. He was past the orchard now. He could still hear the drums, though they were drawing away . . . keep going, keep going . . .

"Hoy! You there!" He *should* have kept going but, short of breath and unsure who was calling, paused for an instant, half-turning. Only half, because a solid body hurtled through the air and knocked him down.

He hit the ground on one elbow and was already grappling the man's head with his other hand, wet greasy hair sliding through his fingers. He jabbed at the man's face, squirmed eel-like out from under his weight, kneeing the fellow in the stomach as he moved, and made it lurching to his feet.

"Stop right there!" The voice cracked absurdly, shooting up into a falsetto, and startled him so that he *did* stop, gasping for breath.

"You . . . no-account . . . filthy . . ." The man—no, by God, it was a boy!—who'd knocked him down was getting to his feet. He had a large stone in his hand; his brother—it had to be his brother; they looked like two peas in a pod, both half grown and gawky as turkey poults—had a good-sized club.

Grey's hand had gone to his waist as he'd risen, ready to draw the dagger Percy had given him. He'd seen these boys before, he thought—the sons of the commander of one of the New Jersey militia companies?—and, rather clearly, they'd seen him before, too.

"Traitor!" One of them yelled at him. "Bloody fucking *spy!*" They were between him and the distant infantry company; the orchard was at his back, and the three of them were well within range of any Hessian rifleman who happened to look in their direction.

"Look—" he began, but could see that it was pointless. Something had happened; they were crazed with something—terror, anger, grief?—that made their features shift like water and their limbs tremble with the need to do something immediate and violent. They were boys, but both taller than he was and quite capable of doing him the damage they clearly intended.

"General Fraser," he said loudly, hoping to jar them into uncertainty. "Where is General Fraser?"

77

THE PRICE OF BURNT SIENNA

"COMPANIES ALL, present, sir!" Robert MacCammon rushed up, panting. He was a heavyset man, and even the gently rolling fields and meadows were hard on him; the dark stains in his oxters were the size of dinner plates.

"Aye, good." Jamie glanced beyond Major MacCammon and saw Lieutenant Herbert's company emerging from a small wood, glancing cautiously round, their weapons in their hands. They were doing well, untrained as they were, and he was pleased with them.

Lord, let me bring them through it as best I can.

This prayer barely formed in his mind, he turned to look toward the west, and froze. On the slope below him, no more than a hundred yards away, he saw the two Craddock boys, armed with a rock and a stick, respectively, menacing a man whose back was turned to him but whose bare, cropped blond head was instantly recognizable, even without the stained bandage tied round it.

Then he saw Grey put a hand to his waist and knew beyond the shadow of doubt that it was a knife he reached for.

"*Craddock!!*" he bellowed, and the boys both started. One dropped his rock and stooped to pick it up again, exposing his scrawny neck to Grey. Grey looked at the vulnerable expanse of flesh, glanced bleakly at the older boy, gripping his stick like a cricket bat, then up the slope at Jamie, and let both hands and shoulders drop.

"*Ifrinn!*" Jamie muttered under his breath. "Stay here," he said briefly to Bixby, and ran down the slope, stumbling and pushing his way through a thick growth of alders that left sticky sap all over his hands.

"Where the devil is your company?" he demanded without preamble, breathing hard as he came up with the boys and Grey.

"Oh. Er . . ." The younger Craddock looked to his brother to answer.

"We couldn't find 'em, sir," the older boy said, and swallowed. "We were looking, when we run into a party of redcoats and had to scamper pretty quick to get away."

"Then we saw *him*," the younger Craddock said, thrusting out his chin at Grey. "Everybody in camp had said as how he was a redcoat spy, and, sure enough, there he was, makin' for them, waving and callin' out."

"So we thought as how it was our duty to stop him, sir," the older boy put in, anxious not to be eclipsed by his brother.

"Aye, I see." Jamie rubbed the spot between his eyebrows, which felt as though a small, painful knot had formed there. He glanced over his shoulder. Men were still running up from the south, but the rest of Craddock's company was nearly all there, milling anxiously and looking in his direction. No wonder: he could hear British drums, near at hand. Doubtless that was the company the boys had run into—the one Grey had been making for.

"Wenn ich etwas sagen dürfte," Grey said in German, with a glance at the Craddocks. *If I might speak . . .*

"You may not, sir," Jamie replied, with some grimness. There wasn't time—and if these two wee blockheids survived to get back to camp, they'd recount every word that had passed between Grey and him to anyone who would listen. The last thing he could afford was for them to report him involved in foreign confabulation with an English spy.

"I am in search of my son!" Grey switched to English, with another glance at the Craddocks. "I have reason to believe he's in danger."

"So is everyone else out here," Jamie replied with an edge, though his heart jerked in his chest. So that was why Grey had broken his parole. "In danger from whom?"

"Sir! *Sir!*" Bixby's voice was shouting from the other side of the alders, high and urgent. He had to go, and quickly.

"Coming, Mr. Bixby!" he shouted. "Why didn't you kill them?" he asked Grey abruptly, and jerked his head toward the Craddocks. "If you got past them, you could have made it."

One fair brow arched above the handkerchief binding Grey's bad eye.

"You'd forgive me for Claire—but not for killing your . . . men." He glanced at the two Craddocks, spotty as a pair of raisin puddings and—Grey's look implied—likely no brighter.

For a split second, the urge to punch him again surged up from Jamie's bowels, and for the same split second, the knowledge of it showed on John Grey's face. He didn't flinch, and his good eye widened in a pale-blue stare. This time, he'd fight back.

Jamie closed his eyes for an instant, forcibly setting anger aside.

"Go with this man," he said to the Craddocks. "He is your prisoner." He pulled one of the pistols from his belt and presented it to the elder Craddock, who received it with wide-eyed respect. Jamie didn't bother telling the lad it was neither loaded nor primed.

"And you," he said evenly to Grey. "Go with them behind the lines. If the Rebels still hold Englishtown, guide them there."

Grey nodded curtly, lips compressed, and turned to go.

He reached out and caught Grey by the shoulder. The man whipped round, blood in his eye.

"Listen to me," Jamie said, speaking loudly enough to be sure the Craddock boys could hear him. "I revoke your parole." He fixed Grey's single-eyed glare with one of his own. "D'ye understand me? When you reach Englishtown, ye'll surrender yourself to Captain McCorkle."

Grey's mouth twitched, but he said nothing and gave the merest nod of acknowledgment before turning away.

Jamie turned, too, running for his waiting companies, but risked a single glance over his shoulder.

Shooing the Craddocks before him, awkward and flapping as a pair of geese bound for market, Grey was headed smartly to the south, toward the American lines—if the concept of "lines" held any meaning in this god-damned battle.

Grey had certainly understood, and despite the present emergency, a weight lifted from Jamie's heart. With his parole revoked, John Grey was once more a prisoner of war, in the custody of his jailors, officially without freedom of movement. But also without the obligation of honor that would hold him prisoner on his own recognizance. Without parole, his primary duty now was that of any soldier in the hands of his enemy—escape.

"*Sir!*" Bixby arrived at his shoulder, panting. "There are redcoats—"

"Aye, Mr. Bixby. I hear them. Let's be having them, then."

IF IT WEREN'T for the coloring book, I might not have noticed imme-diately. In third or fourth grade, Brianna had had a coloring book featuring scenes from the American Revolution. Sanitized, suitably romantic scenes: Paul Revere flying through the night on a galloping horse, Washington cross-ing the Delaware while exhibiting (as Frank pointed out) a lamentable lack of seamanship . . . and a double-paged spread featuring Molly Pitcher, that gal-lant woman who had carried water to the heat-stricken troops (left-hand page) and then taken her wounded husband's place to serve his cannon (right-hand page)—at the Battle of Monmouth.

Which, it had dawned on me, was very likely what the battle we were en-gaged in was going to be called, once anyone got round to naming it. Mon-mouth Courthouse was only two or three miles from my present location.

I wiped my face once more—this gesture did nothing for the perspiration, which was instantly renewed, but, judging from the state of my three soggy handkerchiefs, was removing a fair amount of dirt from my countenance—and glanced toward the east, where I had been hearing distant cannon fire most of the day. Was she there?

"Well, George Washington certainly is," I murmured to myself, pouring out a fresh cup of water and returning to my work rinsing out bloody cloths in a bucket of salt water. "Why not Molly Pitcher?"

It had been a complicated picture to color, and as Bree had just got to the phase where she insisted that things be colored "real," the cannon could *not* be pink or orange, and Frank had obligingly drawn several crude cannon on a sheet of paper and tried out everything from gray (with shadings of black, blue, blue-violet, and even cornflower) to brown, with tints of burnt sienna and gold, before they finally settled—Frank's opinion as to actual historicity of cannon being diffidently advanced—on black with dark green shadings.

Lacking credentials, I had been relegated to coloring in the grass, though I also got to help with the dramatic shading of Mrs. Pitcher's raggedly stream-ing clothes, once Brianna got tired of it. I looked up, the smell of crayons strong in my memory, and saw a small group coming down the road.

There were two Continental regulars—and a man in what I recognized as the light-green uniform of Skinner's Greens, a Provincial Loyalist regiment.

He was stumbling badly, though supported on both sides by the Continentals. The shorter of these also seemed to be wounded; he had a bloodstained scarf wrapped around one arm. The other was looking from side to side as though on guard, but didn't seem to be wounded.

At first I'd looked at the Provincial, who must be a prisoner. But then I looked more closely at the wounded Continental supporting him. And with Molly Pitcher so clearly and recently in mind, I realized with a small shock that the Continental was a woman. The Continental's coat covered her hips, but I could plainly see the way in which her legs slanted in toward the knee; a man's thighbones run straight up and down, but a woman's width of pelvic basin compels a slightly knock-kneed stance.

It also became clear, by the time they reached me, that the wounded soldiers were related: both were short and thin, with squared-off chins and sloping shoulders. The Provincial was definitely male, though—his face was thickly stubbled—while his . . . sister? They seemed close in age . . . was clear-skinned as an egg and nearly as white.

The Provincial was not. He was red as a blast furnace and nearly as hot to the touch. His eyes were white slits, and his head wobbled on his spindly neck.

"Is he wounded?" I asked sharply, putting a hand under his shoulder to ease him down onto a stool. He went limp the moment his buttocks touched it and would have fallen to the ground had I not tightened my grip. The girl gave a frightened gasp and put out a hand toward him, but she also staggered and would have fallen, had the other man not seized her by the shoulders.

"He took a blow to the head," the male Continental said. "I—hit him with the hilt of my sword." This admission was made with some embarrassment.

"Help me lay him down." I ran my hand over the Provincial's head, detecting an ugly, contused wound under his hair, but found no crepitation, no sense of a skull fracture. Concussion, likely, but maybe no worse. He began to twitch under my hand, though, and the tip of his tongue protruded from his mouth.

"Oh, dear," I said, under my breath, but not far enough under, for the girl gave a small, despairing cry.

"It's heatstroke," I told her at once, hoping this might sound reassuring. The reality was far from it; once they collapsed and fell into seizures, they usually died. Their core temperature was far above what the systems of the body could tolerate, and seizing like that was often an indication that brain damage had started to occur. Still—

"Dottie!" I bellowed, and made urgent gestures at her, then turned to the sound—but very frightened-looking—Continental soldier. "See that young woman in gray? Drag him over into the shade where she is; she'll know what to do." It was simple. Pour water over him and—if possible—into him. That was the sum total of what *could* be done. Meanwhile . . .

I got hold of the girl by the non-wounded arm and sat her down on the stool, hastily pouring most of what remained in my brandy bottle into a cup. She didn't look as though she had much blood left.

She didn't. When I got the scarf off, I discovered that her hand was missing, and the forearm badly mangled. She hadn't bled to death only because someone had twined a belt round her upper arm and fastened the tourniquet tight with a stick thrust through it. It had been a long time since I'd fainted at sight of anything, and I didn't now, but did have one brief moment when the world shifted under my feet.

"How did you do that, sweetheart?" I asked, as calmly as possible. "Here, drink this."

"I—grenado," she whispered. Her head was turned away, not to see the arm, but I guided the cup to her lips and she drank, gulping the mix of brandy and water.

"She—he picked it up," said a low, choked voice at my elbow. The other Continental was back. "It rolled by my foot and he—she picked it up."

The girl turned her head at his voice, and I saw his anguished look.

"She came into the army because of you, I suppose?" Clearly the arm would have to be amputated; there was nothing below the elbow that could be saved, and to leave it in this state was to doom her to death by infection or gangrene.

"No, I didn't!" the girl said, huffing for breath. "Phil—" She gulped air and twisted her head to look toward the trees. "He tried to make me go with him. Loyalist c-camp . . . follower. Wouldn't." With so little blood remaining in her body, she was having trouble getting enough oxygen. I refilled the cup and made her drink again; she emerged from it spluttering and swaying, but more alert. "I'm a patriot!"

"I—I tried to make her go home, ma'am," the young man blurted. "But wasn't anyone left to look out for her." His hand hovered an inch from her back, wanting to touch her, waiting to catch her if she fell over.

"I see. Him—" I nodded toward Dottie's station under the trees, where the man with heatstroke lay in the shade. "Your brother?"

She hadn't the strength to nod, but closed her eyes briefly in acquiescence.

"Her father died just after Saratoga." The young man looked completely wretched. Christ, he couldn't be more than seventeen, and she looked about fourteen, though she must be older. "Phillip was already gone; he'd broke with his father when he joined the Provincials. I—" His voice broke, and he shut his mouth hard and touched her hair.

"What's your name, dear?" I said. I'd loosened the tourniquet to check that there was still blood flow to the elbow; there was. Possibly the joint could be saved.

"Sally," she whispered. Her lips were white, but her eyes were open. "Sarah." All my amputation saws were in the church with Denzell—I couldn't send her in there. I'd stuck my head in once and nearly been knocked over by the thick smell of blood and excrement—even more by the atmosphere of pain and terror and the sounds of butchery.

There were more wounded coming along the road; someone would have to tend them. I hesitated for no more than a minute.

Both Rachel and Dottie had the necessary resolve to deal with things and the physical presence to command distraught people. Rachel's manner came from months of experience at Valley Forge, Dottie's more from a habit of autocratic expectation that people would of course do what she wanted them to. Both of them inspired confidence, and I was proud of them. Between them, they were managing as well as could be expected, and—I thought— much better than the surgeons and their assistants in the church, though these were commendably quick about their bloody business.

"Dottie!" I called again, and beckoned. She rose and came at the trot, wiping her face on her apron. I saw her look at the girl—at Sarah—then turn with a brief look at the bodies on the grass, and turn back with a look in which curiosity, horror, and a desperate compassion were blended. So the brother was dead already, or dying.

"Go and get Denzell, Dottie," I said, moving just a little so that she could see the mangled arm. She turned white and swallowed. "Tell him to bring my bow-frame saw and a small tenaculum."

Sarah and the young man made small gasps of horror at the word "saw," and then he moved swiftly, touching her at last, gripping her by her sound shoulder.

"You'll be all right, Sally," he said fiercely. "I'll marry you! Won't make a blind bit of difference to me. I mean—your—your arm." He swallowed, hard, and I realized that he needed water, too, and passed over the canteen.

"Like . . . hell," Sally said. Her eyes were dark and bright as unfired coal in her white face. "I won't—be married for pity. Damn . . . you. Nor guilt. Don't . . . need you!"

The young man's face was blank with surprise—and, I thought, affront.

"Well, what are you going to live on?" he demanded, indignant. "You don't own a thing in this world but that damned uniform! You—you—" He pounded a fist on his leg in frustration. "You can't even whore, with one arm!"

She glared at him, breathing slow and hard. After a moment, a thought crossed her face and she nodded a little and turned to me.

"You reckon the army might . . . pay me . . . a pension?" she asked.

I could see Denzell now, blood-splattered but collected, hurrying across the gravel with the box of surgical instruments. I would have sold my soul for ether or laudanum, but had neither. I took a deep breath of my own.

"I expect they will. They'll give Molly Pitcher one; why not you?"

78

IN THE WRONG PLACE
AT THE WRONG TIME

WILLIAM TOUCHED his jaw gingerly, congratulating himself that Tarleton had only managed to hit him in the face once, and it hadn't been in the nose. His ribs, arms, and abdomen were another matter, and his clothes were muddy and his shirt rent, but it wouldn't be apparent to a casual observer that he'd been in a fight. He *might* just get away with it—so long as Captain André didn't happen to mention the dispatch to the British Legion. After all, Sir Henry had had his hands full during the morning, if half what William had heard along his way was true.

A wounded infantry captain on his way back to camp had told of seeing Sir Henry, in command of the rear guard, lead a charge against the Americans, getting so far out to the front that he was nearly captured before the men behind came up to him. William had burned, hearing this—he would have loved to be part of that. But at least he hadn't stayed mewed up in the clerks' tent. . . .

He was no more than a quarter mile along his way back to Cornwallis's brigade when Goth threw a shoe. William said something very bad, pulled up, and swung down to have a look. He found the shoe, but two nails had gone and a quick search didn't turn them up; no chance of hammering it back on with the heel of his boot, which had been his first thought.

He shoved the shoe in his pocket and looked round. Soldiers swarmed in every direction, but there was a company of Hessian grenadiers on the opposite side of the ravine, forming up at the bridgehead. He led Goth across, stepping gingerly.

"Hallo!" he called to the nearest fellow. *"Wo ist der nächste Hufschmied?"*

The man glanced indifferently at him and shrugged. A young fellow, though, pointed across the bridge and called out, *"Zwei Kompanien hinter uns kommen Husaren!"* Hussars are coming, two companies behind!

"Danke!" William called back, and led Goth into the sparse shade of a stand of spindly pines. Well, that was luck. He wouldn't have to walk the horse a long way; he could wait for the farrier and his wagon to come to him. Still, he fretted at the delay.

Every nerve was keyed tight as a harpsichord string; he kept touching his belt, where his weapons would normally be. He could hear the sounds of musket fire in the far distance, but couldn't see a thing. The countryside was folded up like a leporello, rolling meadow diving suddenly into wooded ravines, then springing back out, only to disappear again.

He dug out his handkerchief, so soggy by now that it served only to sluice the sweat from his face. He caught a faint breath of coolness wafting up from the creek, forty feet below, and walked nearer the edge in hopes of more. He drank warm water from his canteen, wishing he could scramble down and drink from the stream, but he daren't; he might get down the steep slope without trouble, but coming back up would be an awkward climb, and he couldn't risk missing the farrier.

"Er spricht Deutsch. Er gehört!" Heard what? He hadn't been paying attention to the grenadiers' sporadic conversation, but these hissed words came to him clearly, and he glanced round to see who it was they were saying spoke German, only to see two of the grenadiers quite close behind him. One of them grinned nervously at him, and he stiffened.

Suddenly two more were there, between him and the bridge. *"Was ist hier los?"* he demanded sharply. *"Was machst Ihr da?"* What is this? What are you doing?

A burly fellow pulled an apologetic face.

"Verzeihung. Ihr seid hier falsch."

I'm in the wrong place? Before William could say anything more, they closed on him. He elbowed, punched, kicked, and butted wildly, but it didn't last more than a few seconds. Hands pulled his arms behind him, and the burly fellow said once more, *"Verzeihung,"* and, still looking apologetic, bashed him in the head with a rock.

He didn't lose consciousness altogether until he hit the bottom of the ravine.

THERE WAS THE devil of a lot of fighting, Ian thought—but that was about all you could say about it. There was a good deal of movement—particularly among the Americans—and whenever they met with a group of redcoats, there was fighting, often ferocious fighting. But the countryside was so irregular, the armies seldom came together anywhere in large numbers.

He had found his way around several companies of British infantry more or less lying in wait, though, and beyond this vanguard were a goodly number of British, regimental banners in the midst of them. Would it help to know who was in command here? He wasn't sure he could tell, even if he was close enough to make out the details of the banners.

His left arm ached, and he rubbed it absently. The ax wound had healed well, though the scar was still raised and tender—but the arm hadn't yet recovered anything like its full strength, and loosing an arrow at the Indian scouts earlier had left the muscles quivering and jumping, with a burning deep in the bone.

"Best not try that again," he murmured to Rollo—then remembered that the dog wasn't with him.

He looked up and discovered that one of the Indian scouts *was* with him, though. Or at least he thought so. Twenty yards away, an Abenaki warrior sat on a rawboned pony, eyeing Ian thoughtfully. Yes, Abenaki, he was sure of it, seeing the scalp shaved clean from brows to crown and the band of black paint across the eyes, the long shell earrings that brushed the man's shoulders, their nacre glittering in the sun.

Even as he made these observations, he was turning his own mount, seeking shelter. The main body of men was a good two hundred yards distant, standing in open meadow, but there were stands of chestnut and poplar, and perhaps a half mile back the way he'd come, the rolling land dipped into one of the big ravines. Wouldn't do to be trapped in the low ground, but if he had enough lead, it was a good way to disappear. He kicked his horse sharply and they shot off, turning abruptly left as they passed a patch of thick growth— and a good thing, too, because he heard something heavy whiz past his head and go crashing into the growth. Throwing stick? Tomahawk?

It didn't matter; the only important thing was that the man who'd thrown it was no longer holding it. He did look back, though—and saw the second Abenaki come round the grove from the other side, ready to cut him off. The second one shouted something and the other answered—hunting cries. *Beast in view.*

"*Cuidich mi, a Dhia!*" he said, and jammed his heels hard into his horse's sides. The new mare was a good horse, and they made it out of the open ground, crashed through a small copse of trees and out the other side to find a rail fence before them. It was too close to stop, and they didn't; the horse dropped her hindquarters, bunched, and soared over, back hooves clipping the top rail with a solid *whank!* that made Ian bite his tongue.

He didn't look back but bent low over his horse's neck, and they ran flat out for the curving land he could see before him, dropping down. He turned and ran at an angle, not wanting to hit the edge of the ravine straight on, in case it should be steep just there. . . . No sound from behind save the rumble and clash of the army massing. No yelps, no hunting calls from the Abenaki.

There it was, the thick growth that marked the edge of the ravine. He slowed and now risked a look over his shoulder. Nothing, and he breathed and let the horse slow to a walk, picking their way along the edge, looking for a good way down. The bridge was just visible above him, maybe fifty yards distant, but no one was on it—yet.

He could hear men fighting *in* the ravine—perhaps three hundred yards from where he was—but there was sufficient growth that he was hidden from them. Only a scuffle, from the sounds—he'd heard or seen that a dozen times already today; men on both sides, driven by thirst down to the creeks that had carved the ravines, occasionally meeting and going for one another in a bloody splash among the shallows.

The thought of it reminded him of his own thirst—and the horse's, for the creature was stretching out her neck, nostrils greedily flaring at the scent of water.

He slid off and led the way down to the creek's edge, careful of loose stones and boggy earth—the creek bank here was mostly soft mud, edged with mats of duckweed and small reedbeds. A glimpse of red caught his eye and he tensed, but it was a British soldier, facedown in the mud and clearly dead, his legs swaying in the current.

He shucked his moccasins and edged out into the water himself; the creek was fairly wide here and only a couple of feet deep, with a silty bottom; he sank in ankle-deep. He edged out again and led the horse farther up the ravine, looking for better footing, though the mare was desperate for the water, pushing Ian with her head; she wouldn't wait long.

The sounds of the skirmish had faded; he could hear men up above and some way off, but nothing in the ravine itself anymore.

There, that would do. He let the horse's reins fall, and she lunged for the creek, stood with her forefeet sunk in mud but her hind feet solid on a patch of gravel, blissfully gulping water. Ian felt the pull of the water nearly as much and sank to his knees, feeling the blissful chill as it soaked his clout and leggings, that sensation fading instantly to nothingness as he cupped his hands and drank, and cupped and drank again and again, choking now and then in the effort to drink faster than he could swallow.

At last he stopped—reluctantly—and dashed water over his face and chest; it was cooling, though the bear grease in his paint made the water bead and run off his skin.

"Come on," he said to the horse. "Ye'll burst and ye keep on like that, *amaidan*." It took some struggle, but he got the horse's nose out of the creek, water and bits of green weed sloshing out of the loose-lipped mouth as the horse snorted and shook her head. It was while hauling the horse's head round in order to lead her up the bank that he saw the other British soldier.

This one was lying near the bottom of the ravine, too, but not in the mud. He was lying facedown, but with his head turned to one side, and . . .

"Och, Jesus, *no!*" Ian flung his horse's reins hastily round a tree trunk and bounded up the slope. It was, of course. He'd known it from the first glimpse of the long legs, the shape of the head, but the face made it certain, even masked with blood as it was.

William was still alive; his face twitched under the feet of a half-dozen black flies feeding on his drying blood. Ian put a hand under his jaw, the way Auntie Claire did, but, with no idea how to find a pulse or what a good one should feel like, took it away again. William was lying in the shadow of a big sycamore, but his skin was still warm—it couldn't help but be, Ian thought, even if he was dead, on a day like this.

He'd risen to his feet, thinking rapidly. He'd need to get the bugger onto the horse, but maybe best undress him? Take off the telltale coat, at least? But what if he were to take him back toward the British lines, find someone there to take charge of him, get him to a surgeon? That was closer.

Still need to take the coat off, or the man might die of the heat before he got anywhere. So resolved, he knelt again, and thus saved his own life. The tomahawk chunked into the sycamore's trunk just where his head had been a moment before.

And, a moment later, one of the Abenaki raced down the slope and leapt on him with a shriek that blasted bad breath into his face. That split second of warning, though, was enough that he'd got his feet under him and pushed to the side, heaving the Abenaki's body over his hip in a clumsy wrestling throw that landed the man in the mud four feet away.

The second one was behind him; Ian heard the man's feet in the gravel and weeds and whirled to meet the downward strike, catching the blow on his forearm, grabbing for the knife with his other hand.

He caught it—by the blade, and hissed through his teeth as it cut into his palm—and chopped down on the man's wrist with his half-numbed arm. The knife jarred loose. Hand and knife were slippery with blood; he couldn't get hold of the hilt but had got it away—he turned and threw it as far as he could upstream, and it plunked into the water.

Then they were both on him, punching, kicking, and tearing at him. He staggered backward, lost his balance but not his grip on one of his attackers, and succeeded in falling into the creek with the man atop him. After that, he lost track.

He had one of the Abenaki on his back in the water, was trying earnestly to drown him, while the other rode his own back and tried to get an arm around his neck—and then there was a racket on the other side of the ravine and everything stopped for a moment. A lot of men, moving in a disorganized sort of way—he could hear drums, but there was a noise like the distant sea, incoherent voices.

The Abenaki stopped, too, just for an instant, but that was long enough: Ian twisted, flinging the man off his back, and bounded awkwardly through the water, slipping and sinking in the muddy bottom, but made it to shore and ran for the first thing that met his eye—a tall white oak. He flung himself at the trunk and shinned up, grabbing at branches as they came in reach to pull himself higher, faster, reckless of his wounded hand, the rough bark scraping his skin.

The Indians were after him, but too late; one leapt and slapped at his bare foot but failed to get a grip, and he got a knee over a large branch and clung, panting, to the trunk, ten feet up. Safe? He thought so, but after a moment peered down cautiously.

The Abenaki were casting to and fro like wolves, glancing up at the noise above the rim of the ravine, then up at Ian—then across the creek toward William, and that made Ian's wame curl up. God, what could he do if they should decide to go cut the man's throat? He hadn't even got a stone to throw at them.

The one good thing was that neither of them seemed to have either a gun or a bow; must have left those with their horses, up above. They couldn't do anything but throw stones at *him,* and they seemed disinclined.

More noise from above—a *lot* of men up there; what were they shouting?— and the Abenaki abruptly abandoned Ian. They splashed back across the stream, their leggings clinging with water and streaked with black mud, paused briefly to turn William over and rummage his clothes—evidently he'd already been robbed, for they found nothing—and then untied Ian's horse and with a last mocking call of "Mohawk!" disappeared with the mare into a growth of pussy willows downstream.

IAN HAD DRAGGED himself one-handed up the slope, crawled some distance, and then lay for a while under a fallen log on the edge of a clearing, spots coming and going before his eyes like a swarm of midgies. There was a lot going on nearby, but none of it near enough to cause him immediate concern. He closed his eyes, hoping that would make the spots go away. They didn't, instead turning from black to a horrid constellation of swimming pink and yellow blobs that made him want to vomit.

He hastily opened his eyes again, in time to see several powder-blackened Continental soldiers, stripped to their shirts, some bare to the waist, dragging a cannon down the road. They were followed in short order by more men and another cannon, all staggering with the heat and white-eyed with exhaustion. He recognized Colonel Owen, stumping along between the limbers, sooty face set in unhappy desperation.

Some sense of stirring drew Ian's wandering eye away toward a group of men, and he realized with a faint sense of interest that it was a very large group of men, with a standard hanging limp as an unstuffed haggis against its pole.

That in turn stirred recognition. Sure enough, there was General Lee, long-nosed and frowning but looking very keen, riding out of the mass toward Owen.

Ian was too far away and there was too much noise to hear a word, but the trouble was obvious from Owen's gestures and pointings. One of his cannon was broken, burst, probably from the heat of firing, and another had broken free of its limber and was being dragged with ropes, its metal scraping on the rocks as it juddered along.

A dim sense of urgency was reasserting itself. *William.* He needed to tell someone about William. Plainly it wasn't going to be the British.

Lee's brows drew in and his lips thinned, but he kept his composure. He had bent down from his saddle to listen to Owen; now he nodded, spoke a few words, and straightened up. Owen wiped a sleeve across his face and waved to his men. They picked up their ropes and leaned into the weight, disconsolate, and Ian saw that three or four were wounded, cloths wrapped round heads or hands, one half-hopping with a bloody leg, a hand on one of the cannon for support.

Ian's wame had begun to settle now, and he was desperately thirsty, despite having drunk his fill at the creek only a short time before. He'd taken no notice where he was going but, seeing Owen's cannon come down the road, knew he must be near the bridge, though it was out of sight. He crawled out of his hiding place and managed to stand up, holding on to the log for a moment while his vision went black and white and black again.

William. He had to find someone to help . . . but first he had to find water. He couldn't manage without it. Everything he'd drunk at the creek had run off him as sweat, and he was parched to the bone.

It took several tries, but he got water at last from an infantryman who had two canteens hanging round his neck.

"What happened to you, chum?" the infantryman asked, eyeing him with interest.

"Had a fight with a British scout," Ian replied, and reluctantly handed back the canteen.

"Hope you won it, then," the man said, and waved without waiting for an answer, moving off with his company.

Ian's left eye was stinging badly and his vision was cloudy; a cut in his eyebrow was bleeding. He groped in the small bag at his waist and found the handkerchief wrapped round the smoked ear he carried. The cloth was a small one, but big enough to tie round his brow.

He wiped his knuckles over his mouth, already longing for more water. What ought he to do? He could see the standard now being vigorously waved, flapping heavily in the thick air, summoning the troops to follow. Plainly Lee was headed over the bridge; he knew where he was going, and his troops with him. No one would—or could—stop to climb down a ravine to aid a wounded British soldier.

Ian shook his head experimentally and, finding that his brains didn't seem to rattle, set off toward the southwest. With luck, he'd meet La Fayette or Uncle Jamie coming up, and maybe get another mount. With a horse, he could get William out of the ravine alone. And whatever else might happen today, he'd settle the hash of those Abenaki bastards.

79

HIGH NOON

ONE OF LA FAYETTE'S men came up at this point with orders to fall back, to rejoin La Fayette's main body near one of the farms between Spotswood South Brook and Spotswood Middle-brook. Jamie was pleased to hear it; there was no reasonable way for half-armed militia companies to lay siege to the artillery entrenched in the orchard, not with rifles guarding the cannon.

"Gather your companies, Mr. Guthrie, and join me on the road up there," Jamie said, pointing. "Mr. Bixby, can ye find Captain Kirby? Tell him the same thing; I'll fetch along Craddock's troops."

Captain Craddock's companies had been badly demoralized by his death, and Jamie had brought them under his own direct command to prevent them scattering like bumblebees.

They made their way across the fields, picking up Corporal Filmer and his men at the farmhouse—it was deserted; no need to leave anyone there—and across the bridge over one of the creeks. He slowed a little as his horse's hooves thudded on the planks, feeling the blessed cool dampness coming up from the water thirty feet below. They should stop, he thought, for water—

they hadn't, since early morning, and the canteens would be running dry—but it would take too long for so many men to work their way along the ravine, down to the creek, and back up. He thought they could make it to La Fayette's position; there were wells there.

He could see the road ahead and peeled an eye for lurking British. He wondered, with a moment's irritation, where Ian was; he would have liked to know where the British *were.*

He found out an instant later. A gunshot cracked nearby, and his horse slipped and fell. Jamie yanked his foot free and rolled out of the saddle as the horse hit the bridge with a thud that shook the whole structure, struggled for an instant, neighing loudly, and slid over the edge into the ravine.

Jamie scrambled to his feet; his hand was burning, all the skin taken off his palm when he'd skidded on the splintered boards.

"Run!" he shouted, with what breath he had left, and waved an arm wildly, gathering the men, pointing them down the road toward a growth of trees that would cover them. *"Go!"*

He found himself among them, the surge of men carrying him with them, and they stumbled into cover, gasping and wheezing with the effort of running. Kirby and Guthrie were sorting out their companies, the late Captain Craddock's men were clustering near Jamie, and he nodded, breathless, to Bixby and Corporal Greenhow to count noses.

He could still hear the sound the horse had made, hitting the ground below the bridge.

He was going to vomit; he felt it rising and knew better than to try to hold it back. He made a quick staying motion toward Lieutenant Schnell, who wanted to speak to him, stepped behind a large pine, and let his stomach turn itself out like an emptied sporran. He stayed bent for a moment, mouth open and forehead pressed against the rough bark for support, letting the gush of saliva wash the taste of it from his mouth.

Cuidich mi, a Dhia . . . But his mind had lost all notion of words for the moment, and he straightened up, wiping his mouth on his sleeve. As he came out from behind the tree, though, all thought of what might be going on and what he might have to do about it vanished. Ian had come out of the trees nearby and was making his way across the open space. The lad was afoot and moving slowly, but doggedly. Jamie could see the bruises, even from a distance of forty feet.

"That one of ourn or one of theirn?" a militiaman asked doubtfully, raising his musket to bear on Ian, just in case.

"He's mine," Jamie said. "Don't shoot him, aye? Ian! *Ian!*" He didn't run—his left knee hurt too much to run—but made his way toward his nephew as fast as possible and was relieved to see the glassy look in Ian's eyes shatter and brighten into recognition at sight of him.

"Uncle Jamie!" Ian shook his head as though to clear it and stopped abruptly with a gasp.

"Are ye bad hurt, *a bhalaich?*" Jamie asked, stepping back and looking for blood. There was some, but nothing dreadful. The lad wasn't clutching himself as though wounded in the vitals. . . .

"No. No, it's—" Ian worked his mouth, trying to get up the spit to make words, and Jamie thrust his canteen into Ian's hand. There was pitifully little water left in it, but some, enough, and Ian gulped it.

"William," Ian gasped, lowering the empty canteen. "Your—"

"What about him?" Jamie interrupted. There were more men coming down the road, some of them half-running, looking back. "*What?*" he repeated, grasping Ian's arm.

"He's alive," Ian said at once, correctly gauging both intent and intensity of the question. "Someone hit him on the head and left him in the bottom of yon ravine." He gestured vaguely toward the scouts. "Maybe three hundred yards west o' the bridge, aye? He's no dead, but I dinna ken how bad hurt he may be."

Jamie nodded, making instant calculations.

"Aye, and what happened to *you?*" He could only hope that William and Ian hadn't happened to each other. But if William was unconscious, it couldn't be he who'd taken Ian's horse, and plainly someone had, for—

"Two Abenaki scouts," Ian replied with a grimace. "The buggers have been following me for—"

Jamie was still holding Ian by the left arm and felt the impact of the arrow and the shock of its reverberation through the lad's body. Ian glanced unbelievingly at his right shoulder, where the shaft protruded, and gave at the knees, his weight pulling him from Jamie's grasp as he keeled over.

Jamie launched himself over Ian's body and hit the ground rolling, avoiding the second arrow; he heard it rip the air near his ear. Heard the militiaman's gun speak just above him and then a confusion of screaming and shouting, a group of his men breaking, running toward the source of the arrows, bellowing.

"Ian!" He rolled his nephew onto his back. The lad was conscious, but as much of his face as showed under the paint was white and ghastly, his throat working helplessly. Jamie grasped the arrow; it was lodged in what Claire called the deltoid, the fleshy part of the upper arm, but it didn't budge when he shook it gently.

"I think it's struck the bone," he said to Ian. "No bad, but the tip's stuck fast."

"I think so, too," Ian said faintly. He was struggling to sit up, but couldn't. "Break it off, aye? I canna be going about wi' it sticking out like that."

Jamie nodded, got his nephew sitting unsteadily upright, and broke the shaft between his hands, leaving a ragged stub a few inches long with which to pull the arrow out. There wasn't much blood, only a trickle running down Ian's arm. Claire could see to getting the arrowhead out later.

The shouting and confusion were becoming widespread. A glance showed him more men coming down the road, and he heard a fife signaling in the distance, thin and desperate.

"D'ye ken what's happened up there?" he said to Ian, nodding toward the noise. Ian shook his head.

"I saw Colonel Owen comin' down wi' his cannon all in shambles. He stopped to say a word to Lee and then came on, but he wasna running."

A few men *were* running, though in a heavy, clumsy way—not as though pursuit was close. But he could feel alarm beginning to spread through the men around him and turned to them at once.

"Stay by me," he said calmly to Guthrie. "Keep your men together, and by me. Mr. Bixby—say that to Captain Kirby, as well. Stay by me; dinna move save on my word."

The men from Craddock's company who had run after the Abenaki—he supposed that to be the source of the arrows—had vanished into the woods. He hesitated for an instant, but then sent a small party after them. No Indian he'd ever met would fight from a fixed position, so he doubted he was sending his men into ambush. Perhaps into the face of the oncoming British, but if that was the case, best he knew about it as soon as possible, and at least one or two would likely make it back to tell him.

Ian was getting his feet under him; Jamie bent and gave the lad an arm under his good shoulder and got him standing. His legs shook in their buckskins and sweat ran in sheets down his bare torso, but he stood.

"Was it you who called my name, Uncle Jamie?" he asked.

"Aye, I did when I saw ye come out of the trees." Jamie nodded toward the wood, keeping one eye out for anyone coming back that way. "Why?"

"Not then. Just before this—" He touched the ragged end of the arrow shaft gingerly. "Someone called out behind me; that's what made me move, and a good thing, too. I'd ha' taken this square in the chest otherwise."

Jamie shook his head and felt that faint sense of bemusement that always attended brushes with ghosts—if that's what this was. The only strangeness of it was that it never seemed strange at all.

But there was no time to think of such things; there were calls now of "Retreat! Retreat!" and the men behind him stirred and rippled like wheat in a rising wind.

"Stay by me!" he said, in a loud, firm voice, and the ones nearest him took a grip of their weapons and stood.

William. Thought of his son sparked a flare of alarm in his bones. The arrow that had struck Ian had jolted the vision of William, sprawled and bloody in the mud, out of his head, but now . . . Christ, he couldn't send men after the lad, not with half the army pouring back in this direction, and the British maybe on their heels. . . . A sudden ray of hope: if the British *were* headed this way, they'd maybe come across the lad and care for him.

He wanted badly to go himself. If William was dying . . . but he could in no circumstances leave his men, and particularly not in these circumstances. A terrible urgency seized him.

Christ, if I never speak to him—never tell him—

Now he saw Lee and his aides coming down the road. They were moving slowly, no air of haste about it, but deliberate—and looking back now and then, almost surreptitiously, glancing quickly again to the front, sitting straight in their saddles.

"Retreat!" The cry was springing up now all around them, growing stronger, and men were streaming out of the woods. "Retreat!"

"Stay by me," Jamie said, softly enough that only Bixby and Guthrie heard him—but it was enough. They stiffened, stood by him. Their resolve would help to hold the rest. If Lee came even with him, ordered him . . . then they would have to go. But not 'til then.

"Shit!" said one of the men behind him, surprised. Jamie glanced back, saw a staring face, then whipped round to look where the man was looking. Some of Craddock's men were coming out of the wood, looking pleased with themselves. They had Claire's mare with them, and over her saddle was the limp body of an Indian, his long, greased scalp locks nearly dragging the ground.

"Got him, sir!" One of the men—Mortlake—saluted, grinning white-toothed from the shade of a hat that he didn't think to remove. His face gleamed like oiled leather, and he nodded to Ian in a friendly fashion, jerking his thumb at the mare. "Horse—you?"

"It is," Ian said, and his Scots accent made Mortlake blink. "I thank ye, sir. I think my uncle had best take the horse, though. Ye'll need her, aye?" he added to Jamie, lifting an eyebrow toward the ranks of men behind them.

Jamie wanted to refuse; Ian looked as if he could barely walk. But the lad was right. Jamie would have to lead these men, whether forward or back—and he'd need them to be able to see him. He nodded reluctantly, and the body of the Abenaki was dragged from the saddle and tossed carelessly into the brush. He saw Ian's eyes follow it, dark with dislike, and thought for a split second of the smoked ear his nephew carried in his sporran, and hoped that Ian wouldn't—but, no, a Mohawk took no trophies from another's kill.

"There were two of them, ye said, Ian?"

Ian turned from contemplation of the dead Abenaki and nodded.

"Saw t'other one," Mortlake answered the implied question. "Ran when we shot this villain." He coughed, glancing at the increasing streams of men coming down the road. "Beg pardon, sir, but oughtn't we be moving, too?"

The men were fidgeting, craning their necks to see, murmuring when they spotted Lee, whose aides were spreading out, trying to marshal the swarming men into some kind of orderly retreat but being roundly ignored. Then something, some change of atmosphere, made Jamie turn, and half the men with him.

And here came Washington up the road on Jamie's erstwhile white stallion, galloping, and a look on his big, rough face that would have melted brass.

The incipient panic in the men dissolved at once as they pressed forward, urgent to learn what was afoot. There was chaos in the road. Some companies scattered, stopping abruptly to look round for their fellows, some noticing Washington's sudden appearance, others still coming down the road, colliding with those standing still—and, in the midst of it, Washington pulled his horse up beside Charles Lee's and leaned toward him, flushed like an apple with heat and anger.

"What do you mean by this, sir?!" was all that Jamie heard clearly, the words carried to him by some freak of the heavy air, before noise and dust and smothering heat settled so thickly on the scene that it was impossible to hear anything over the clishmaclaver, save the disquieting echo of musket volleys and the occasional faint popping of grenadoes in the distance.

He didn't try to shout above the noise; it wasn't necessary. His men were going nowhere, as riveted to the spectacle before them as he was.

Lee's long-nosed face was pinched with fury, and Jamie saw him for a brief instant as Punch, the furious puppet in a Punch-and-Judy show. An unhinged urge to laugh bubbled up, as the necessary corollary irresistibly presented itself: George Washington as Judy, the mobcapped shrew who belabored her husband with a stick. For an instant, Jamie feared he had succumbed to the heat and lost his mind.

Once envisioned, though, he couldn't escape the thought, and for an instant he was standing in Hyde Park, watching Punch feed his baby to the sausage machine.

For that was what Washington was very clearly doing. It lasted no more than three or four minutes, and then Washington made a furious gesture of disgust and dismissal and, wheeling his horse, set off at a trot, circling back to pass the troops who had clotted along the roadside, watching in fascination.

Emerging from his own fascination with a jolt, Jamie put a foot in the mare's stirrup and swung up.

"Ian—" he said, and his nephew nodded, putting a hand on his knee—as much to steady himself, he thought, as to reassure his uncle.

"Give me a few men, Uncle Jamie," he said. "I'll see to . . . his lordship."

There was barely time to summon Corporal Greenhow and detail him to take five men and accompany Ian, before Washington came close enough to spot Jamie and his companies. The general's hat was in his hand and his face was afire, anger and desperation subsumed in eagerness, and the whole of his being radiating something Jamie had seldom seen, but recognized. Had felt himself, once. It was the look of a man risking everything, because there was no choice.

"Mr. Fraser!" Washington shouted to him, and his wide mouth stretched wider in a blazing grin. "Follow me!"

80

PATER NOSTER

WILLIAM CAME AWAKE slowly, feeling terrible. His head hurt and he wanted to vomit. He was horribly thirsty, but the thought of drinking anything made his gorge rise and he retched feebly. He was lying in grass and bugs; there were bugs crawling on him. . . . He saw, for one vivid moment, a line of tiny ants climbing busily through the dark hairs on his wrist and tried to dash his hand against the ground to dislodge them. His hand didn't move, though, and his conscious-ness faded.

It came back with a throbbing rush and jounce. The world was jigging dizzily up and down, and he couldn't breathe. Then he made out the dark things that went in and out of his field of view as being a horse's legs and realized that he was belly-down over a saddle, being carried somewhere. *Where . . . ?*

There was a lot of shouting going on nearby, and the noise hurt his head very much.

"Stop!" shouted an English voice. "What are you doing with him? Stand! Stand or I'll kill you!"

"Leave him! Push him off! Run!" A vaguely familiar voice, Scottish.

Then a confusion of noise and somewhere in it the Scottish voice again, shouting, "Tell my—" But then he hit the ground with a thud that knocked out both wit and wind, and slid back into darkness, headfirst.

IN THE END, it was simplicity itself. John Grey walked down a cattle track, following the hoofprints toward what must be water, and walked straight into a startled group of British soldiers filling their canteens at a muddy ford. Light-headed from thirst and heat, he didn't bother trying to identify or explain himself, just put his hands in the air and gave himself up with an intense feeling of relief.

The soldiers gave him water, at least, and then he was marched off under the guard of a nervous boy with a musket and into the yard of a farmhouse that appeared to be deserted. No doubt the owners had fled upon realizing that they were in the middle of twenty thousand or so armed troops bent on mayhem.

Grey was hustled over to a large wagon half filled with cut grass, made to sit down on the ground with several other captured prisoners—in the shade, thank God—and left there under the guard of two middle-aged privates, armed with muskets, and a nervous child of fourteen or so in a lieutenant's uniform, who twitched every time the sound of a volley echoed off the trees.

This might be his best chance. If he could shock or intimidate the boy into sending him to Cornwallis or Clinton . . .

"Sir!" he barked at the boy, who blinked at him, startled. So did the cap-tured Americans.

"What is your name, sir?" he demanded, in his command voice. That rat-tled the young lieutenant badly; he took two involuntary steps backward before stopping himself. He flushed, though, and rallied.

"You be quiet!" he said, and, stepping forward, aimed a cuff at Grey's ear.

Grey caught him by the wrist by reflex, but before he could release the boy, one of the privates had taken a stride toward him and brought down the butt of his musket on Grey's left forearm.

" 'E said be quiet," the private said mildly. "I'd do it, was I you."

Grey *was* quiet, but only because he couldn't speak. That arm had been broken twice before—once by Jamie Fraser, once by a cannon explosion—

and the third time was definitely not the charm. His vision went black for a moment, and everything inside him contracted into a ball of hot lead. Then it started to hurt, and he could breathe again.

"What's that you just said?" the man sitting next him said under his breath, eyebrows raised. "'Tain't English, is it?"

"No," said Grey, and paused for another breath, clutching the arm against his belly. "It's German for 'Oh, shit.'"

"Ah." The man nodded understandingly and—with a wary glance at the guards—brought a small flask out from under his coat and pulled the cork before handing it to Grey. "Try that, friend," he whispered.

The scent of overripe apples surged directly into his brain and very nearly made him vomit. He managed to swallow, though, and handed back the flask with a nod of thanks. Sweat ran down his face in streams, stinging his good eye.

No one spoke. The man who'd given him the applejack was a Continental regular, middle-aged, with a haggard face and only half his teeth remaining. He sat hunched, elbows on his knees, eyes fixed on the distance, where the sound of fighting was. The others were doing the same thing, he realized—all craning toward the battle.

Colonel Watson Smith popped into his mind, doubtless summoned up by the fumes of applejack, but appearing so suddenly that Grey jerked a little, and one of the guards stiffened, giving him a hard look. Grey looked away, though, and the man relaxed.

Shocked with pain, exhausted and thirsty, he lay down, nursing his throbbing arm against his chest. The buzzing of insects filled his ears, and the volley of muskets retreated into the meaningless rumble of distant thunder. He let himself lapse into a not unpleasant catatonia visualizing Smith shirtless, lying on the narrow cot under a lantern, cradling Grey in his arms, stroking his back with a comforting hand. At some point, he drifted into an uneasy sleep, punctuated by the sounds of guns and shouting.

He woke suddenly, with a mouth like cotton, to find that several more prisoners had been delivered and that there was an Indian sitting beside him. Grey's working eye was gummy and bleared, and it took a moment before he recognized the face under the remnants of black and green war paint.

Ian Murray gave him a long, level look that said plainly, *"Don't talk,"* and he didn't. Murray raised an eyebrow at his wounded arm. Grey lifted his good shoulder in a brief shrug and focused his attention on the water cart that had come to a halt on the nearby road.

"You and you, come with me." One of the privates jerked a thumb at two of the prisoners and led them off toward the cart, from which they returned shortly, carrying buckets of water.

The water was blood-warm and tasted of sodden, half-rotted wood, but they drank greedily, spilling it down their clothes in their haste. Grey wiped a wet hand across his face, feeling somewhat more settled in his mind. He flexed his left wrist experimentally; perhaps it was only a brui—no, it wasn't.

He'd drawn in his breath with a hiss, and Murray, as though in response, closed his eyes, steepled his hands together, and began to intone the Pater Noster.

"What in b-buggery is *that*?" the lieutenant demanded, stamping over to him. "Are you talking Indian, sir?"

Ian opened his eyes, regarding the child with a mild stare.

"It's Latin. I'm sayin' my prayers, aye?" he said. "D'ye mind?"

"Do I—" The lieutenant stopped, baffled as much by being addressed in a Scottish accent as by the circumstance. He stole a glance at the privates, who looked off into the distance. He cleared his throat.

"No," he said shortly, and turned away, pretending absorption in the distant cloud of white powder smoke that hung low over the trees.

Murray cut his eyes at Grey and, with a slight nod, began the Pater Noster again. Grey, somewhat puzzled, joined him, stumbling a bit. The lieutenant stiffened, but didn't turn round.

"Do they not know who you are?" Murray asked in Latin at the end of the prayer, not varying his intonation.

"I told them; they don't believe me," Grey replied, adding a random *"Ave Maria"* at the end for verisimilitude.

"Gratia plena, Dominus tecum. Shall *I* tell them?"

"I have no idea what comes next. I suppose it couldn't hurt."

"Benedicta tu in mulieribus, et benedictus fructus ventris tui, Jesu," Murray replied, and rose to his feet.

The guards swung round immediately, raising their muskets to their shoulders. Murray ignored this, addressing the lieutenant.

"It's maybe no my business, sir," he said mildly. "But I shouldna like to see ye ruin your career over a wee mistake."

"Be qui—what mistake?" the lieutenant demanded. He had taken off his wig because of the heat but now crammed it back on his head, evidently thinking it might lend him authority. He was mistaken in this impression, as the wig was a good deal too large and immediately slipped sideways over one ear.

"This gentleman," Murray said, gesturing to Grey, who sat up straight and stared impassively at the lieutenant. "I canna imagine what's brought him here or why he should be dressed as he is—but I ken him well. This is Lord John Grey. The, ehm, brother of Colonel Grey, the Duke of Pardloe?" he added delicately.

The hue of the young lieutenant's face changed noticeably. He glanced quickly back and forth between Murray and Grey, frowning, and absently shoved his wig back into place. Grey rose slowly, keeping an eye on the guards.

"That's ridiculous," the lieutenant said, but without force. "Why should Lord John Grey be here, looking like—like *that*?"

"The exigencies of war, Lieutenant," said Grey, keeping his voice level. "I see you belong to the Forty-ninth, which means that your colonel is Sir Henry Calder. I know him. If you will be so kind as to lend me paper and pencil, I will write him a short note, asking him to send an escort to fetch me. You can send the note via the water carrier," he added, seeing a wild look come into the boy's eyes, and hoping to calm him before he panicked and decided that the simplest way out of this imbroglio was to shoot Grey.

One of the privates—the one who had broken Grey's arm—coughed gently.

"We'm goin' to need more men, sir, in any case. Three of us with a dozen prisoners . . . and doubtless more comin'?" The lieutenant looked blank, and the private had another go. "I meantersay . . . might be you'd mean to send for reinforcements anyroad." The man caught Grey's eye and coughed again.

"Accidents happen," Grey said, though with no great charity, and the guards relaxed.

"All right," the lieutenant said. His voice broke on it and he repeated, "All right!" in a gruff baritone, looking belligerently around. No one was foolish enough to laugh.

Grey's knees were wanting to tremble, and he sat down rather abruptly to prevent it. Murray's face—well, the faces of all the prisoners—were carefully blank.

"*Tibi debeo,*" Grey said quietly. *I acknowledge the debt.*

"*Deo gratias,*" Murray murmured, and only then did Grey see the trail of blood that streaked Murray's arm and side, staining his breechclout—and the stub of a broken arrow protruding from the flesh of his right shoulder.

WILLIAM CAME round again lying on something that didn't move, thank God. There was a canteen being pressed to his lips, and he drank, gulping, lips reaching for more water even as it was drawn away.

"Not that fast, you'll be sick," said a familiar voice. "Breathe once, and you can have more." He breathed and forced his eyes open against a glare of light. A familiar face appeared over him, and he reached up a wavering hand toward it.

"Papa . . ." he whispered.

"No, but the next best thing," said his uncle Hal, taking a firm hold on the groping hand and sitting down beside him. "How's the head?"

William closed his eyes and tried to focus on something other than the pain.

"Not . . . that bad."

"Pull the other one, it's got bells on," his uncle murmured, cupping William's cheek and turning his head to the side. "Let's have a look."

"Let's have more water," William managed, and his uncle gave a small snort and put the canteen back to William's lips.

When William stopped to breathe again, his uncle set the canteen down and inquired, in a perfectly normal tone of voice, "Can you sing, do you think?"

His vision was going in and out; there were momentarily two of his uncle, then one, then two again. He closed one eye, and Uncle Hal steadied.

"You want me to . . . *sing*?" he managed.

"Well, perhaps not right this minute," the duke said. He sat back on his stool and began to whistle a tune. "Recognize that, do you?" he asked, breaking off.

"'Lillibulero,'" William said, beginning to feel rather cross. "Why, for God's sake?"

"Knew a chap once who was hit on the head with an ax and lost his ability to make out music. Couldn't tell one note from another." Hal leaned forward, holding up two fingers. "How many fingers am I holding up?"

"Two. Stick them up your nose," William advised him. "Go away, will you? I'm going to be sick."

"Told you not to drink too fast." But his uncle had a basin under his face and a strong hand on his head, bracing him while he heaved and coughed and shot water out of his nose.

By the time he had subsided back onto his pillow—it *was* a pillow, he was lying on a camp cot—he'd recovered enough of his senses to be able to look around and determine that he was in an army tent—probably his uncle's, judging from the battered campaign chest and the sword that lay across it—and the glare of light was coming from the low afternoon sun flooding in through the open tent flap.

"What happened?" he asked, wiping his mouth on the back of his hand.

"What's the last thing you recall?" Uncle Hal countered, handing him the canteen.

"The—er—" His mind was full of confused bits and pieces. The last thing he truly remembered was Jane and her sister, laughing at him as he stood bare-arsed in the creek. He sipped water and put cautious fingers to his head, which seemed to be wrapped in a bandage. It felt sore to the touch. "Taking my horse down to drink at a creek."

Uncle Hal raised one eyebrow. "You were found in a ditch, near a place called Spottiswood or some such thing. Von Knyphausen's troops were holding a bridge there."

William started to shake his head, but thought better of it and closed his eyes against the light.

"Don't remember."

"It will likely come back to you." His uncle paused. "Do you happen to remember where you last saw your father?"

William felt an unnatural calm come over him. He just bloody didn't care anymore, he told himself. The whole world was going to know, one way or another.

"Which one?" he said flatly, and opened his eyes. His uncle was regarding him with interest, but no particular surprise.

"You've met Colonel Fraser, then?" Hal asked.

"I have," William said shortly. "How long have *you* known about it?"

"Roughly three seconds, in the sense of certainty," his uncle replied. He reached up and unfastened the leather stock around his neck, sighing with relief as it came off. "Good Lord, it's hot." The stock had left a broad red mark; he massaged this gently, half-closing his eyes. "In the sense of thinking there was something rather remarkable in your resemblance to the aforesaid Colonel Fraser . . . since I met him again in Philadelphia recently. Prior to that, I hadn't seen him for a long time—not since you were very small, and I never saw him in close conjunction with you then, in any case."

"Oh."

They sat in silence for a bit, gnats and black flies caroming off the canvas and falling onto William's bed like snowflakes. He became aware of the noises of a large camp surrounding them, and it occurred to him that they must be with General Clinton.

"I didn't know you were with Sir Henry," he said at last, breaking the silence. Hal nodded, pulling his worn silver flask out of his coat pocket before tossing the coat itself over the campaign chest.

"I wasn't; I've been with Cornwallis. We—the regiment, that is—arrived in New York about two weeks ago. I came down to Philadelphia to see Henry and John and make inquiries about Benjamin. I arrived just in time to leave the city with the army."

"Ben? What's he done that you're inquiring about?"

"Got married, had a son, and been mug enough to be captured by the Rebels, evidently," his uncle replied lightly. "Thought he might do with a bit of help. If I give you a sip of this, can you keep it down?"

William didn't reply, but reached for the flask. It was filled with good brandy; he breathed it in cautiously, but it seemed not to trouble his wobbly stomach, and he risked a sip.

Uncle Hal watched him for a bit, not speaking. The resemblance between him and Lord John was considerable, and it gave William an odd feeling to see him—something between comfort and resentment.

"Your father," Hal said after a few moments. "Or my brother, if you prefer. Do you recall when you saw him last?"

Resentment sparked abruptly into anger.

"Yes, I bloody do. On the morning of the sixteenth. In his house. With my *other* father."

Hal made a low humming noise, indicating interest.

"That when you found out, was it?"

"It was."

"Did John tell you?"

"No, he bloody didn't!" Blood surged to William's face, making his head throb with a fierce suddenness that made him dizzy. "If I hadn't come face-to-face with the—the fellow, I don't suppose he'd ever have told me!"

He swayed and put out a hand to keep from falling over. Hal grabbed him by the shoulders and eased him back down onto the pillow, where he lay still, teeth clenched, waiting for the pain to ebb. His uncle took the flask from his unresisting hand, sat down again, and took a meditative sip.

"You might have done worse," his uncle observed after a moment. "In the way of sires, I mean."

"Oh, really?" William said coldly.

"Granted, he is a Scot," the duke said judiciously.

"And a traitor."

"And a traitor," Hal agreed. "Damned fine swordsman, though. Knows his horses."

"He was a fucking *groom*, for God's sake! Of course he knows horses!" Fresh outrage made William jerk upright again, despite the thunder in his temples. "What am I bloody going to do?!"

His uncle sighed deeply and put the cork back in the flask.

"Advice? You're too old to be given it and too young to take it." He glanced aside at William, his face very like Papa's. Thinner, older, dark brows beginning to beetle, but with that same rueful humor in the corners of his eyes. "Thought of blowing your brains out?"

William blinked, startled.

"No."

"That's good. Anything else is bound to be an improvement, isn't it?" He rose, stretching, and groaned with the movement. "God, I'm old. Lie down, William, and go to sleep. You're in no condition to think." He opened the lantern and blew it out, plunging the tent into warm gloom.

A rustling as he raised the tent flap, and the searing light of the sinking sun outlined the duke's slender figure as he turned.

"You *are* still my nephew," he said in a conversational tone. "Doubt that's much comfort to you, but there it is."

81

AMONG THE TOMBSTONES

THE SUN WAS LOW and shining directly into my eyes, but the casualties had come so fast that I couldn't take time to move my equipment round. They'd fought all day; it was still going on— I could hear it, close by, but saw nothing when I glanced up, blinking against the sun. Still, the shouts and banging of muskets and what I thought must be grenades—I'd never heard a grenade explode, but something was making a sort of irregular hollow *poong!* that was quite different from the boom of cannon or the slow percussion of musket fire—were loud enough to drown the sounds of groaning and crying from the shade trees and the relentless buzzing of the flies.

I was swaying with weariness and heat and, for my own part, was nearly indifferent to the battle. Until, that is, a young man in militia brown staggered in, blood streaming down his face from a deep cut in his forehead. I had stanched the bleeding and half-wiped his face before I recognized him.

"Corporal . . . Greenhow?" I asked dubiously, and a small spurt of fear penetrated the fog of fatigue. Joshua Greenhow was in one of Jamie's companies; I'd met him.

"Yes, ma'am." He tried to bob his head, but I stopped him, pressing firmly on the wad of lint I'd slapped on his forehead.

"Don't move. General Fraser—have you . . ." My mouth dried, sticky, and I reached automatically for my cup, only to find it empty.

"He's all right, ma'am," the corporal assured me, and reached out a long arm to the table, where my canteen lay. "Or at least he was last time I saw him, and that was no more 'n ten minutes gone." He poured water into my cup, tossed it into his own mouth, breathed heavily for an instant in relief, then poured more, which he handed to me.

"Thank you." I gulped it; it was so warm that it was barely discernible as wet, but it eased my tongue. "His nephew—Ian Murray?"

Corporal Greenhow started to shake his head, but stopped.

"Haven't seen him since about noon, but I haven't seen him dead, either, ma'am. Oh—sorry, ma'am. I meant—"

"I know what you meant. Here, put your hand there and keep the pressure on." I placed his hand on the lint and fished a fresh suture needle threaded with silk out of its jar of alcohol. My hands, steady all day, trembled a little, and I had to stop and breathe for a moment. Close. Jamie was so close. And somewhere in the midst of the fighting I could hear.

Corporal Greenhow was telling me something about the fighting, but I was having trouble attending. Something about General Lee being relieved of his command and—

"Relieved of command?" I blurted. "What the devil for?"

He looked startled by my vehemence, but replied obligingly.

"Why, I don't quite know, ma'am. Was something to do with a retreat and how he oughtn't to have told them to do it, but then General Washington come up on his horse and cursed and swore like the dickens—saving your presence, ma'am," he added politely. "Anyway, I *saw* him! General Washington. Oh, ma'am, it was so . . ." Words failed him, and I handed him the canteen with my momentarily free hand.

"Jesus H. Roosevelt Christ," I murmured under my breath. Were the Americans winning? Holding their own? Had bloody Charles Lee cocked things up after all—or not?

Corporal Greenhow luckily hadn't noticed my language, but was coming to life like a flower in the rain, enthused by his account.

"And so we rushed straight after him, and he was all along the road and the ridgeline, shouting and waving his hat, and all the troops trudging back down . . . why, they all looked up with their eyes staring out of their heads and then they turned round and fell in with us, and the whole army, we just—we just *threw* ourselves on the damned redcoats. . . . Oh, ma'am, it was just *wonderful!*"

"Wonderful!" I echoed dutifully, catching a trickle of blood that threatened to run into his eye. The shadows of the tombstones in the graveyard stretched out long and violet, and the sound of the flies buzzed in my ears, louder than the ringing of the shots that still came—were coming closer—to the frail barrier of the dead. And Jamie with them.

Lord, keep him safe! I prayed in the silence of my heart.

"Did you say something, ma'am?"

JAMIE RUBBED a blood-wet sleeve across his face, the wool rasping his skin, sweat burning in his eyes. It was a church they'd chased the British into—or a churchyard. Men were dodging through the tombstones, vaulting them in hot pursuit.

The British had turned at bay, though, an officer shouting them into a ragged line, and the drill began, the muskets grounded, ramrods drawn . . .

"Fire!" Jamie bellowed, with all the power left in his cracked voice. "Fire on them! Now!"

Only a few men had loaded weapons, but sometimes it took only one. A shot rang out from behind him, and the British officer who was shouting stopped shouting and staggered. He clutched himself, curling up and falling to his knees, and someone shot him again. He jerked backward, then fell over sideways.

There was a roar from the British line, which dissolved at once into a rush, some men pausing long enough to fix their bayonets, others wielding their guns like clubs. The Americans met them, mindless and shrieking, with guns and fists. One militiaman reached the fallen officer, seized him by the legs, and began to drag him away toward the church, perhaps with the notion to take him prisoner, perhaps to get him help. . . .

A British soldier threw himself upon the American, who stumbled backward and fell, loosing his hold on the officer. Jamie was running, shouting, trying to gather the men, but it was no use; they'd lost their wits altogether in the madness of fighting, and whatever their original intent in seizing the British officer, they'd lost that, too.

Leaderless, so had the British soldiers, some of whom were now engaged in a grotesque tug-of-war with two Americans, each grasping the limbs of the dead—for surely he must be now, if he hadn't been killed outright—British officer.

Appalled, Jamie ran in among them, shouting, but his voice failed altogether under strain and breathlessness, and he realized he was making no more than faint cawing noises. He reached the fight, grasped one soldier by the shoulder, meaning to pull him back, but the man rounded on him and punched him in the face.

It was a glancing blow off the side of his jaw but made him lose his grip, and he was knocked off-balance by someone shoving past him to grab some part of the hapless officer's body.

Drums. A drum. Someone in the distance was beating something urgent, a summons.

"Retreat!" someone shouted in a hoarse voice. "Retreat!"

Something happened; a momentary pause—and suddenly it was all different and the Americans were coming past him, hasty but no longer frantic, a few of them carrying the dead British officer. Yes, definitely dead; the man's head lolled like a rag doll's.

Thank God they're not dragging him through the dirt was all he had time to think. Lieutenant Bixby was at his shoulder, blood pouring down his face from an open flap of scalp.

"There you are, sir!" he said, relieved. "Thought you was taken, we did." He took Jamie respectfully by the arm, tugging him along. "Come away, sir, will you? I don't trust those wicked buggers not to come back."

Jamie glanced in the direction Bixby was pointing. Sure enough, the British were retiring, under the direction of a couple of officers who had come forward out of a mass of redcoats forming up in the middle distance. They showed no disposition to come closer, but Bixby was right: there were still random shots being fired, from both sides. He nodded, fumbling in his pocket for his extra kerchief to give the man to stanch his wound.

The thought of wounds made him think of Claire, and he recalled suddenly what Denzell Hunter had said: *"Tennent Church, the hospital's set up there."* Was this Tennent Church?

He was already following Bixby toward the road but glanced back. Yes, the men who had the dead British officer were taking him into the church, and there were wounded men sitting near the door, more of them near a small white—God, that was Claire's tent, was she—

He saw her at once, as though his thought had conjured her, right there in the open. She was standing up, staring openmouthed, and no wonder—there was a Continental regular on a stool beside her, holding a bloodstained cloth, and more such cloths in a basin at her feet. But why was she out here? She—

And then he saw her jerk upright, clap a hand to her side, and fall.

A SLEDGEHAMMER hit me in the side, making me jerk, the needle dropping from my hands. I didn't feel myself fall but was lying on the ground, black and white spots flashing round me, a sense of intense numbness radiating from my right side. I smelled damp earth and warm grass and sycamore leaves, pungent and comforting.

Shock, I thought dimly, and opened my mouth, but nothing but a dry click came out of my throat. *What* . . . The numbness of the impact began to lessen, and I realized that I had curled into a ball, my forearm pressed by reflex over my abdomen. I smelled burning, and fresh blood, very fresh. *I've been shot, then.*

"Sassenach!" I heard Jamie's bellow over the roaring in my ears. He sounded far off, but I heard the terror in his voice clearly. I wasn't disturbed by it. I felt very calm.

"*Sassenach!*" The spots had coalesced. I was looking down a narrow tunnel of light and spinning shadow. At the end of it was the shocked face of Corporal Greenhow, the needle dangling by its thread from the half-sewn gash in his forehead.

PART FIVE

Counting Noses

82

EVEN PEOPLE WHO WANT TO GO TO HEAVEN DON'T WANT TO DIE TO GET THERE

I SWAM DIZZILY TO the surface of consciousness, thinking, *What was it Ernest Hemingway had said, about how one is supposed to pass out from the pain but you don't?* I just had, but he was more or less right; the unconsciousness hadn't lasted more than a few seconds. I was curled into a tight ball, both hands pressed against my right side, and I could feel the blood welling between my fingers, hot and cold and sticky, and it was beginning to hurt . . . very much . . .

"Sassenach! Claire!" I swam out of the fog again and managed to open one eye. Jamie was kneeling by me. He was touching me, had his hands on me, but I couldn't feel it. . . .

Sweat or blood or something ran burning into my eyes. I could hear someone gasping—short, shallow, panting breaths. *Me, or Jamie?* I was cold. *I shouldn't be cold, it was hot as blazes today.* . . . I felt jellied, quivering. And it hurt. A lot.

"Sassenach!"

Hands turned me. I screamed. Tried to. I felt it wrench my throat but couldn't hear it; there was a roaring in my ears. *Shock,* I thought. I couldn't feel my limbs, my feet. I felt the blood leaving my body.

It hurt.

The shock's wearing off, I thought. *Or is it getting worse?* I could see the pain now, going off in bursts like black lightning, jagged and searing.

"Sassenach!"

"What?" I said through clenched teeth. "Auh!"

"Are ye dying?"

"Probably."

Gutshot. The word formed unpleasantly in my mind, and I hoped vaguely that I hadn't spoken it out loud. Even if I had, though . . . surely Jamie could see the wound . . .

Someone was trying to pull my hands away, and I struggled to keep them in place, keep pressing, but my arms had no strength and I saw one hand hanging limp as they lifted it, the nails outlined black with blood, fingers coated scarlet, dripping. Someone rolled me onto my back and I thought I screamed again.

It hurt unspeakably. *Jellied. Impact shock. Cells blasted to shreds and goo. No function . . . organ failure.*

Tightness. Couldn't breathe. Jerking, and someone cursing above me. My eyes were open, I saw color, but the air was thick with pulsing spots.

Shouting. Talk.

I couldn't draw breath. Something tight around my middle. *What's gone? How much?*

God, it hurt. *Oh, God.*

JAMIE COULDN'T take his eyes off Claire's face, lest she die in the second when he looked away. He fumbled for a kerchief, but he'd given it to Bixby, and in desperation seized a fold of her skirt and pressed it hard to her side. She made a horrible sound and he nearly let go, but the ground under her was already darkening with blood and he pressed harder, shouting, "Help! Help me, Rachel! Dottie!"

But no one came, and when he risked a split second's glance around, he saw nothing but clumps of wounded and dead under the trees some distance away and the flickering forms of soldiers, some running, some wandering dazed through the tombstones. If the girls had been nearby, they must have been forced to run when the skirmish rolled through the graveyard.

He felt the slow tickle of Claire's blood running over the back of his hand and shouted again, his dry throat tearing with the effort. *Someone* must hear.

Someone did. He heard running footsteps on the gravel and saw a doctor named Leckie whom he knew racing toward him, white-faced, hurdling a tombstone as he came.

"Shot?" Leckie asked, breathless, collapsing onto his knees beside Jamie. Jamie couldn't speak, but nodded. Sweat was running down his face and the crease of his spine, but his hands seemed frozen to her body; he couldn't pull them away, couldn't let go until Leckie, pawing in one of Claire's baskets, seized a wad of lint and jerked Jamie's hand out of the way in order to clap it in place.

The surgeon elbowed him ruthlessly aside and he scuttled crabwise a foot or two away, then rose to his feet, swaying helplessly. Jamie couldn't look away but became slowly aware that a knot of soldiers had gathered, appalled, shuffling among themselves, not knowing what to do. Jamie gulped air, seized the nearest of these, and sent him running to the church in search of Dr. Hunter. She'd want Denny. If she survived long enough for him to come—

"Sir! General Fraser!" Not even the shouting of his own name made him look away from the spectacle on the ground: the blood, so much of it, soaking her clothes, making a hideous dark red puddle that stained the knees of Leckie's breeches as he knelt over her; her hair, untied and spilling wild, full of grass and bits of leaf from the ground she lay on, her face—oh, Christ, her face.

"Sir!" Someone grabbed his arm to compel his attention. He drove his elbow hard into whoever it was, and the man grunted in surprise and let go.

A gabble of whispers, agitation, people telling the newcomer that it was the general's wife, hurt, shot, dead or dying . . .

"She's not dying!" he turned and bellowed at them. He thought dimly that he must look demented; their blackened faces were aghast. Bixby stepped out and touched his shoulder gingerly, as though he were a lighted grenade that might go off in the next second. He thought he might.

"Can I help, sir?" Bixby said quietly.

"No," he managed to say. "I—he—" He gestured to Leckie, busy on the ground.

"General," said the newcomer, at his other elbow. He turned to find a blue-clad regular, a very young man in a baggy lieutenant's uniform, face set in dogged earnestness. "I dislike to intrude, sir, but as your wife's not dying—"

"Go away!"

The lieutenant flinched, but stood his ground.

"Sir," he said stubbornly. "General Lee has sent me urgently to find you. He requires that you attend him at once."

"Bugger Lee," said Bixby, very rudely, saving Jamie the trouble, and advanced on the newcomer, fists clenched.

The lieutenant was already flushed with heat, but at this grew redder. He ignored Bixby, though, attention focused on Jamie.

"You *must* come, sir."

VOICES . . . I heard words, disjointed, coming out of the fog like bullets, striking randomly.

". . . find Denzell Hunter!"

"General—"

"No!"

"—but you're needed at—"

"No!"

"—orders—"

"NO!"

And another voice, this one stiff with fear.

". . . could be shot for treason and desertion, sir!"

That focused my wandering attention and I heard the reply, clearly.

"Then they'll shoot me where I stand, sir, for I will not leave her side!"

Good, I thought, and, comforted, lapsed into the spinning void again.

"TAKE OFF YOUR coat and waistcoat, lad," Jamie said abruptly. The boy looked completely bewildered, but—stimulated by a menacing movement from Bixby—did as he was told. Jamie took him by the shoulder, turned him round, and said, "Stand still, aye?"

Stooping swiftly, he scooped a handful from the horrifying puddle of bloody mud and, standing, wrote carefully on the messenger's white back with a finger:

I resign my commission. J. Fraser.

He made to fling the remnants of mud away but, after a moment's hesitation, added a smeared and reluctant *Sir* at the top of the message, then clapped the boy on the shoulder.

"Go and show that to General Lee," he said. The lieutenant went pale.

"The general's in a horrid passion, sir," he said. "I dassen't!"

Jamie looked at him. The boy swallowed, said, "Yes, sir," shrugged on his garments, and went at a run, unbuttoned and flapping.

Rubbing his hands heedlessly on his breeches, Jamie knelt again beside Dr. Leckie, who spared him a quick nod. The doctor was pressing a wad of lint and a handful of skirt hard against Claire's side with both hands. The surgeon's hands were red to the elbow, and sweat was running down his face, dripping from his chin.

"Sassenach," Jamie said softly, afraid to touch her. His own clothes were sodden with sweat, but he was cold to the core. "Can ye hear me, lass?"

She'd regained consciousness, and his heart rose into his throat. Her eyes were closed, shut tight in a furious grimace of pain and concentration. She did hear him; the golden eyes opened and fixed on him. She didn't speak; her breath hissed through clenched teeth. She did see him, though, he was sure of that—and her eyes weren't clouded with shock, nor dim with imminent death. Not yet.

Dr. Leckie was looking at her face, too, intent. He let out his own breath, and the tension in his shoulders eased a little, though he didn't relax the pressure of his hands.

"Can you get me more lint, a wad of bandage, anything?" he asked. "I *think* the bleeding is slowing."

Claire's bag lay open a little way behind Leckie. Jamie lunged for it, upended it on the ground, and snatched up a double handful of rolled bandages from the litter. Leckie's hand made a sucking sound as he pulled it away from the sopping wad of cloth and grabbed the fresh bandages.

"You might cut her laces," the doctor said calmly. "I need her stays off. And it will help her to breathe more easily."

Jamie fumbled his dirk free, hands shaking in his haste.

"Un . . . *tie* . . . them!" Claire grunted, scowling ferociously.

Jamie grinned absurdly at hearing her voice, and his hands steadied. So she thought she'd live to need her laces. He gulped air and set himself to undo the knot. Her stay laces were leather and as usual soaked with sweat—but she used a very simple granny knot, and he got it loose with the tip of his dirk.

The knot fell free and he jerked the laces loose, wrenching the stays wide apart. Her bosom rose white as she gasped, and he felt an instant's embarrassment as he saw her nipples stiffen through the sweat-soaked fabric of her shift. He wanted to cover her.

There were flies everywhere, black and buzzing, drawn by the blood. Leckie shook his head to dislodge one that lighted on his eyebrow. They were swarming round Jamie's own ears, but he didn't bother about them, instead brushing them away as they crawled on Claire's body, over her twitching, pallid face, her hands half curled and helpless.

"Here," Leckie said, and, seizing one of Jamie's hands, pushed it down on the fresh compress. "Press hard on that." He sat back on his heels, grabbed another bandage roll, and unfurled it. With some lifting and grunting and a terrible moan from Claire, together they contrived to pass the cingulum round her body, securing the dressing in place.

"Right." Leckie swayed for a moment, then got laboriously to his feet. "The bleeding's mostly stopped—for now," he said to Jamie. "I'll come back when I can." He swallowed and looked directly at Claire's face, wiping his chin on his sleeve. "Good luck to you, ma'am."

And with that, he simply strode off toward the open doors of the church, not looking back. Jamie felt such a rush of fury that he would have gone after the man and dragged him back, could he have left Claire's side. He'd left— just left her, the bastard! Alone, helpless!

"May the devil eat your soul and salt it well first, you whore!" he shouted in *Gàidhlig* after the vanished surgeon. Overcome by fright and the sheer rage of helplessness, he dropped to his knees beside his wife and pounded a fist blindly on the ground.

"Did you just . . . call him a . . . whore?" The whispered words made him open his eyes.

"Sassenach!" He was scrambling for his discarded canteen, lost in the rubble of stuff from her bag. "Here, let me get ye water."

"No. Not . . . yet." She managed to raise one hand halfway, and he stopped dead, canteen in hand.

"Why not?" She was the gray of rotted oats and slick with sweat, trembling like a leaf. He could *see* her lips beginning to crack in the heat, for God's sake.

"I don't . . . know." She worked her mouth a moment before finding the next words. "Don't . . . know where it is." The trembling hand touched the dressing—already showing a stain of blood seeping through. "If it's perf . . . perf'rated the . . . bowel. Drink would . . . kill me. Fast. Intestin'l . . . sh-sh-shock."

He sat down by her slowly and, closing his eyes, breathed deliberately for a few seconds. For the moment, everything had disappeared: the church, the battle, the screams and shouts and the rumble of limber wheels along the rutted road through Freehold. There wasn't anything but her and him, and he opened his eyes to look on her face, to fix it in his mind forever.

"Aye," he said, keeping his voice as steady as he could. "And if that's the case . . . and if it didna kill ye quick . . . I've seen men die gutshot. Balnain died that way. It's long and it's foul, and I willna have ye die like that, Claire. I won't!"

He meant it, truly he did. But his hand squeezed the canteen hard enough to dent the tin. How could he give her the water that might kill her right before his eyes, right . . . *now?*

Not now, he prayed. *Please, don't let it be now!*

"I'm not . . . keen . . . either way," she whispered, after a long pause. She blinked away a green-bellied fly, shining like emerald, that had come to drink her tears. "I need . . . Denny." A soft gasp. "Quick."

"He's coming." He could barely breathe, and his hands hovered over her, afraid to touch anything. "Denny's coming. Hold on!"

The answer to this was a tiny grunt—her eyes were squinched shut and her jaw set hard—but she'd heard him, at least. With the vague recollection that she always said you must cover folk suffering from shock and lift their feet, he took off his coat and put it over her, then took off his waistcoat, rolled it up, and shoved it under her feet. At least the coat covered the blood that had now soaked the whole side of her dress. It terrified him to see that.

Her fists were clenched, both driven hard into her wounded side; he couldn't hold her hand. He put a hand on her shoulder, so she'd know he was there, shut his eyes, and prayed with his whole being.

83

SUNDOWN

T HE SUN WAS NEARLY down, and Denzell Hunter was laying out his knives. The air was thick with the sweetness of corn liquor; he'd dipped his instruments in it, and they lay gleaming wetly on the clean napkin Mrs. Macken had put down on the sideboard.

Young Mrs. Macken herself was hovering in the doorway, a hand pressed over her mouth and her eyes big as a cow's. Jamie tried to give her a reassuring smile, but whatever his expression was, it wasn't a smile and appeared to alarm her further, for she retreated into the darkness of her pantry.

She'd likely been alarmed all day, like everyone else in the village of Freehold; she was heavily pregnant and her husband was fighting with the Continentals. And still more alarmed for the last hour, ever since Jamie had pounded on her door. He'd battered six doors before hers. She was the first to answer, and, in poor return for her hospitality, now found a badly injured woman lying on her kitchen table, oozing blood like a fresh-killed deer.

That image unnerved him still further—Mrs. Macken was not the only one in the house who was shaken by events—and he came close and took Claire's hand, as much to reassure himself as her.

"How is it, Sassenach?" he said, low-voiced.

"Bloody awful," she replied hoarsely, and bit her lip to keep from saying more.

"Had ye best have a wee nip?" He moved to pick up the bottle of rough corn liquor from the sideboard, but she shook her head.

"Not quite yet. I don't *think* it struck the bowel—but I'd rather die of blood loss than sepsis or shock, if I'm wrong."

He squeezed her hand. It was cold, and he hoped she would keep talking, though at the same time he knew he ought not to make her talk. She'd need all her strength. He tried as hard as he could to will some of his own strength into her without hurting her.

Mrs. Macken edged into the room, carrying a candlestick with a fresh wax candle; he could smell the sweetness of the beeswax, and the scent of honey reminded him of John Grey. He wondered for an instant whether Grey had made it back to the British lines, but he had no real attention for anything but Claire.

Right this moment, he was busy regretting that he'd ever disapproved of her making ether. He would have given anything he possessed to spare her awareness of the next half hour.

The setting sun washed the room in gold, and the blood seeping through her bandages showed dark.

"ALWAYS CONCENTRATE when you're using a sharp knife," I said weakly. "You might lose a finger, else. My granny used to say that, and my mother, too."

My mother had died when I was five, my granny a few years later—but I hadn't seen her often, as Uncle Lamb spent at least half his time on archaeological expeditions round the world, with me as part of his baggage.

"Did you frequently play with sharp knives as a child?" Denny asked. He smiled, though his eyes stayed fixed on the scalpel he was carefully sharpening on a small oilstone. I could smell the oil, a soft murky scent under the tang of blood and the resinous smell of the unfinished rafters baking overhead.

"Constantly," I breathed, and shifted my position as slowly as I could. I bit my lip hard and managed to ease my back without groaning aloud. It made Jamie's knuckles go white when I did.

He was standing by the window at the moment, clutching the sill as he looked out.

Seeing him there, broad shoulders outlined by the sinking sun, brought back a sudden memory, surprising in its sharpness. Or rather, memories, for the layers of experience came back altogether, in a wodge, and I was seeing Jamie rigid with his fear and grief, the slight black figure of Malva Christie leaning toward him—and remembered feeling both a vague affront and a tremendous sense of peace as I began to leave my body, carried on the wings of fever.

I shook the memory off at once, frightened even to think of that beckoning peace. The fear was reassuring; I wasn't yet so close to death as to find it appealing.

"I'm sure it went through the liver," I said to Denny, gritting my teeth. "That much blood . . ."

"I'm sure thee is right," he said, pressing gently on my side. "The liver is a great mass of densely vascularized tissue," he added, turning to Jamie, who didn't turn from the window but hunched his shoulders against the possibility of being told anything else of a horrifying nature.

"But the excellent thing about a wound to the liver," Denny added cheerfully, "is that the liver, unlike the other organs of the body, will regenerate itself—or so thy wife tells me."

Jamie cast me a brief, haunted look, and went back to staring out the window. I breathed as shallowly as I could, trying to ignore the pain, and trying even harder not to think about what Denny was about to do.

That little exercise in self-discipline lasted about three seconds. If we were all lucky, it would be simple, and quick. He had to widen the bullet's entrance wound enough to see the direction of its track and to insert a probe along it, in hopes of finding the bullet before he had to dig for it. Then a quick— I could only hope—insertion of whichever one of his jawed forceps looked most appropriate. He had three, of different lengths, plus a davier: good for grasping a rounded object, but the jaws were much bigger than the tips of a forceps and would cause more bleeding.

If it wasn't simple or quick, I'd very likely be dead within the next half hour. Denny was entirely correct in what he'd told Jamie: the liver is hugely vascularized, an enormous sponge of tiny blood vessels crossed by very large ones like the hepatic portal vein. That's why the wound, superficially tiny, had bled so alarmingly. None of the major vessels had been damaged—yet— because I would have bled to death in minutes if they had been.

I was trying to breathe shallowly, because of the pain, but had an overwhelming need to draw deep, gasping breaths; I needed oxygen, because of the blood loss.

Sally flitted through my mind, and I seized on thought of her as distraction. She'd survived the amputation, screaming through a leather gag, Gabriel—yes, Gabriel, that was the name of the young man with her—white-eyed as a panicked horse, fighting to hold her steady and not to faint himself. She *had* fainted, luckily, toward the end—*So sucks to you, Ernest*, I thought blearily—and I'd left them both in Rachel's care.

"Where's Rachel, Denny?" I asked, suddenly thinking to wonder. I thought I'd glimpsed her briefly in the churchyard after I'd been shot, but couldn't be sure of anything that had happened in that blur of black and white.

Denny's hand stopped for an instant, the cautery iron he was holding suspended over a tiny brazier he'd set fuming at the end of the sideboard.

"She is searching for Ian, I believe," he said quietly, and laid the iron very gently in the fire. "Is thee ready, Claire?"

Ian, I thought. *Oh, God. He hasn't come back.*

"As I'll ever be," I managed, already imagining the stench of burning flesh. Mine.

If the bullet was resting near one of the large vessels, Denny's probing and grasping could rupture it and I'd hemorrhage internally. The cauterization might cause shock suddenly to set in and assassinate me without warning. Most likely, I'd survive the surgery but die of lingering infection. Consoling thought . . . At least in that case I'd have time to write a brief note to Brianna—and perhaps warn Jamie to be more careful about who he married next time. . . .

"Wait," Jamie said. He didn't raise his voice, but there was enough urgency in it to freeze Denny.

I closed my eyes, rested a hand gingerly on the dressing, and tried to envision just where the damned bullet might be. Was it only *in* the liver, or had it gone all the way through? There was so much trauma and swelling, though, that the pain was generalized over the whole right side of my abdomen; I couldn't pick out a single, vivid line of bright pain leading to the ball.

"What is it, Jamie?" Denny asked, impatient to be about his business.

"Your betrothed," Jamie said, sounding bemused. "Coming up the road with a gang of soldiers."

"Does thee think she is under arrest?" Denny asked, with a fair assumption of calm. I saw his hand tremble slightly as he picked up a linen napkin, though.

"I dinna think so," Jamie said doubtfully. "She's laughing wi' a couple of them."

Denny took his spectacles off and wiped them carefully.

"Dorothea is a Grey," he pointed out. "Any member of her family would pause on the gallows to exchange witty banter with the hangman before graciously putting the noose about his neck with his own hands."

That was so true that it made me laugh, though my humor was cut off at once by a jolt of pain that took my breath away. Jamie looked at me sharply, but I flapped a hand weakly at him, and he went to open the door.

Dorothea popped in, turning to wave over her shoulder and call good-bye to her escort, and I heard Denny sigh in relief as he put his spectacles back on.

"Oh, good," she said, going to kiss him. "I hoped you hadn't started yet. I've brought a few things. Mrs. Fraser—Claire—how are you? I mean, how is thee?" She put down the large basket she was carrying and came at once to the table I was lying on, to take my hand and gaze sympathetically at me with her big blue eyes.

"I've been slightly better," I said, making an effort not to grit my teeth. I felt clammy and nauseated.

"General La Fayette was most concerned to hear that you'd been hurt," she said. "He has all of his aides telling their rosary beads for you."

"How kind," I said, meaning it, but rather hoping the marquis hadn't sent a complicated greeting that I might need to compose a reply to. Having got this far, I wanted to get the bloody business over with, no matter *what* happened.

"And he sent this," she said, a rather smug look on her face as she held up a squat green-glass bottle. "Thee will want this first, I think, Denny."

"What—" Denny began, reaching for the bottle, but Dorothea had pulled the cork, and the sweet cough-syrup smell of sherry rolled out—with the ghost of a very distinctive herbal scent beneath it, something between camphor and sage.

"Laudanum," said Jamie, and his face took on such a startling look of relief that only then did I realize how frightened he had been for me. "God bless ye, Dottie!"

"It occurred to me that Friend Gilbert might just possibly have a few things that might be useful," she said modestly. "All the Frenchmen I know are dreadful cranks about their health and have enormous collections of tonics and pastilles and clysters. So I went and asked."

Jamie had me half sitting, with his arm braced behind my back and the bottle at my lips, before I could add my own thanks.

"Wait, will you?" I said crossly, putting my hand over the bottle's open mouth. "I haven't any idea how strong this stuff is. You won't do me any good by killing me with opium."

It cost me something to say so; my instinct was to drain the bottle forthwith, if it would stop the beastly pain. That nitwit Spartan who allowed the fox to gnaw his vitals had *nothing* on me. But, come right down to it, I didn't want to die, either of gunshot, fever, or medical misadventure. And so Dottie borrowed a spoon from Mrs. Macken, who watched in grisly fascination from the door while I took two spoonfuls, lay down, and waited an interminable quarter of an hour to judge the effects.

"The marquis sent all sorts of delicacies and things to aid your recovery," Dottie said encouragingly, turning to the basket and starting to lift things out by way of distraction. "Partridge in jelly, mushroom *pâté*, some *terrible*-smelling cheese, and—"

My sudden desire to vomit ceased just as suddenly, and I half-sat up, causing Jamie to emit a cry of alarm and grab me by the shoulders. Just as well that he did; I would have fallen onto the floor. I wasn't attending, though, my attention fixed on Dottie's basket.

"Roquefort," I said urgently. "Is it Roquefort cheese? Sort of gray, with green and blue veins?"

"Why, I don't know," she said, startled by my vehemence. She gingerly plucked a cloth-wrapped parcel out of the basket and held it delicately in front of me. The odor wafting from it was enough, and I relaxed—very slowly—back down.

"Good," I breathed. "Denzell—when you've finished . . . pack the wound with cheese."

Used to me as he was, this still made Denny's jaw drop. He glanced from me to the cheese, plainly thinking that fever must have set in with unusual speed and severity.

"Penicillin," I said, swallowing and waving a hand at the cheese. My mouth felt sticky from the laudanum. "The mold that makes that sort of cheese is a species of *Penicillium*. Use the stuff from the veins."

Denny shut his mouth and nodded, determined.

"I will. But we must begin soon, Claire. The light is going."

The light *was* going, and the sense of urgency in the room was palpable. But Mrs. Macken brought more candles, and Denny assured me that it was a simple operation; he would do quite as well by candlelight.

More laudanum. I was beginning to feel it—a not unpleasant dizzy sensation—and I made Jamie lay me down again. The pain was definitely less.

"Give me a bit more," I said, and my voice didn't seem to belong to me.

I took as deep a breath as I could and eased myself into a good position, looking with distaste at the leather gag that lay beside me. Someone—perhaps Dr. Leckie—had slit my shift up the side earlier in the proceedings. I spread the edges of the opening wide and stretched out my hand to Jamie.

The shadows grew between the smoke-stained rafters. The kitchen fire was banked, but still live, and the glow of it began to show red on the hearth. Looking up at the flickering rafters in my drugged state reminded me too much of the time I had nearly died of bacterial poisoning, and I shut my eyes.

Jamie was holding my left hand, curled on my breast, his other hand gently stroking my hair, smoothing damp wisps of it off my face.

"Better now, *a nighean*?" he whispered, and I nodded—or thought I did. Mrs. Macken murmured some question to Dottie, received an answer, and went out. The pain was still there but distant now, a small, flickering fire that I could shut out by closing my eyes. The thud of my heartbeat was more immediate, and I was beginning to experience . . . not hallucinations, quite. Disconnected images, though—the faces of strangers that faded in and out behind my eyes. Some were looking at me, others seemed oblivious; they smiled and sneered and grimaced but had nothing, really, to do with me.

"Again, Sassenach," Jamie whispered, lifting my head and putting the spoon to my lips, sticky with sherry and the bitter taste of opium. "One more." I swallowed and lay back. If I died, would I see my mother again? I wondered, and experienced an urgent longing for her, shocking in its intensity.

I was trying to summon her face before me, bring her out of the floating horde of strangers, when I suddenly lost my grip on my own thoughts and began to float off into a sphere of dark, dark blue.

"Don't leave me, Claire," Jamie whispered, very close to my ear. "This time, I'll beg. Dinna go from me. Please." I could feel the warmth of his face, see the glow of his breath on my cheek, though my eyes were closed.

"I won't," I said—or thought I said—and went. My last clear thought was that I'd forgotten to tell him not to marry a fool.

THE SKY OUTSIDE was lavender, and Claire's skin was washed with gold. Six candles burned around the room, the flames tall and still in the heavy air.

Jamie stood by her head, a hand on her shoulder as though he could comfort her. In fact, it was the sense of her, still alive under his hand, that was keeping him on his feet.

Denny made a small sound of satisfaction behind his highwayman's mask, and Jamie saw the muscle of his bared forearm tense as he slowly drew the instrument out of Claire's body. Blood gushed from the wound, and Jamie tensed like a cat, ready to spring forward with a pledget, but no spurt followed and the blood died to a trickle, with a final small blurt of blood as the jaws of the instrument emerged, something dark clamped between them.

Denny dropped the ball into the palm of his hand and peered at it, then made an irritable noise; his glasses were fogged with the sweat of his efforts. Jamie snatched them off the Quaker's nose and rubbed them hastily on his shirttail, replacing them before Hunter could blink twice.

"I thank thee," Denny said mildly, returning his attention to the musket ball. He turned it delicately and let out an audible breath.

"Whole," he said. "Thank God."

"*Deo gratias,*" Jamie echoed fervently, and reached out a hand. "Let me see it, will ye?"

Hunter's brows rose, but he dropped the thing in Jamie's hand. It was startlingly warm, warm from her body. Warmer even than the air or Jamie's own sweating flesh, and the feel of it made him fold his fist over it. He stole a look at Claire's chest: rising, falling, though with alarming slowness. Almost as slowly, he opened his hand.

"What is thee looking for, Jamie?" Denny asked, pausing to re-sterilize his beaked probe.

"Marks. A slit, a cross—any mark of tampering." He rolled the ball carefully between his fingers, then relaxed, a small spurt of gratitude making him murmur, *"Deo gratias,"* again.

"Tampering?" There were vertical lines between Denny's brows, deepening as he looked up. "To make the ball fragment, thee means?"

"That—or worse. Sometimes a man will rub something into the marks—poison, say, or . . . or shit. Just in case the wound itself isna fatal, aye?"

Hunter looked shocked, his appalled expression clear even behind the shielding handkerchief.

"If ye mean to kill a man, ye mean him harm," Jamie said dryly.

"Yes, but . . ." Hunter looked down, laying his tool carefully on the towel as though it were made of porcelain, not metal. His breath fluttered the handkerchief tied over his mouth. "But it is one thing, surely, to kill in battle, to shoot at an enemy when it is a matter of one's own life . . . and to form the cold-blooded intent that your enemy should die a horrible and lingering death . . ."

Claire made a ghastly moaning noise and twitched under his hands as Denny gently squeezed the flesh on either side of the wound. Jamie gripped her by the elbows, to keep her from turning. Denny picked up the jawed thing again.

"You wouldn't do it yourself," Hunter said with certainty. His eyes were intent on his delicate probing, a pledget held to catch the blood that dribbled slowly from the wound. Jamie felt the loss of each drop as though it left his own veins, and felt cold; how much could she lose and still live?

"No. It would be a cowardly thing." But he spoke automatically, scarcely attending. She had gone limp; he saw her fingers uncurl, droop, and looked at her face, her throat, searching for a visible pulse. He felt one, in his thumb where it pressed the bone of her arm, but couldn't tell whether it was her heart that beat there or his own.

He was acutely conscious of Denny's breath, audible behind his mask. It stopped for an instant, and Jamie glanced up from his scrutiny of Claire's face to see the Quaker's look of intentness as he drew the thing free once more—this time clutching a tiny clump of something unrecognizable. Denny opened the jaws of his forceps and dropped the clump on the towel, then used the tool to poke at it, trying to spread it, and Jamie saw the prickle of tiny dark threads as the blood soaked away into a bright red stain on the towel. Cloth.

"What does thee think?" Denny asked him, frowning at the thing. "Is it a bit of her shift, or the—the bodice—or material from her stays? For from the hole in her stays, I should think . . ."

Jamie rootled hastily in his sporran, pulled out the little silk bag in which he kept the spectacles he used for reading, and clapped these on his nose.

"Ye've at least two separate bits there," he announced, after an anxious perusal. "Canvas from the stays, and a lighter bit of cloth. See?" He took up a probe and delicately teased the fragments apart. "I think that one bit's her shift."

Denny glanced at the disconsolate pile of bloodstained garments on the floor, and Jamie, at once divining his intent, reached in, stirred about, and pulled out the remnants of her dress.

"It's a clean hole," Denny said, looking at the fabric Jamie spread out on the table. "Maybe . . ." He picked up the forceps and turned back, not finishing.

More probing, deeper, and Jamie gritted his teeth not to cry out in protest. *"The liver is so vascular,"* she'd said, talking Denny through what he must do. *"The risk of hemorrhage . . ."*

"I know," Denny murmured, not looking up. The sweat had plastered the handkerchief to his face, molding itself to nose and lips, so his speech was visible. "I'm being . . . careful."

"Ken that," Jamie said, but so softly he didn't know whether Hunter heard him. *Please. Please let her live. Blessed Mother, save her . . . saveher, saveher, saveher . . .* The words all ran together in an instant and he lost the sense of them, but not the sense of desperate entreaty.

The red stain on the toweling under her had grown to alarming proportions by the time Hunter set down his tool again and sighed, shoulders slumping.

"I think—I hope—I have it all."

"Good. I—what will ye do next?"

He saw Denny smile a little behind the sodden cloth, olive-brown eyes soft and steady over it.

"Cauterize it, bind the wound, and pray, Jamie."

84

NIGHTFALL

IT WAS PAST DARK when Lord John Grey, accompanied by a respectful escort and a slightly damaged Indian, limped into Clinton's camp.

Things were much as might be expected after a battle: strong currents of mingled agitation and exhaustion, the latter prevailing. No carousing amid the tents, no music. Men around the fires and camp kitchens, though, eating, getting themselves sorted, talking it over in low tones. No sense of celebration—more a sense of irritation, of disgruntled surprise. The scent of roast mutton came strongly through the smells of dust, mules, and sweating humanity, and Grey's mouth watered so much that he had to swallow before replying to Captain André's solicitous inquiry as to his immediate desires.

"I need to see my brother," he replied. "I'll attend upon General Clinton and my lord Cornwallis later. When I've washed and changed," he added, shucking the horrible black coat for what he sincerely hoped was the last time.

André nodded understandingly, taking the vile garment from him.

"Of course, Lord John. And . . . um . . . ?" He nodded delicately in the direction of Ian Murray, who was attracting glances, if not stares, from passersby.

"Ah. He'd best come, too."

He followed André through the orderly aisles of tents, hearing the clinking of mess kits and feeling the comfort of the army's stolid routine settle into place around him. Murray paced at his heel, silent. He'd no idea what the man was thinking and was too weary to care.

He did feel Murray's step falter, though, and automatically looked over his shoulder. Murray had turned, all his attention focused on a nearby fire, this an open wood fire, around which sat several Indians. Grey wondered dimly whether these might be friends of Murray's . . . and corrected this impression in the next second, as Murray took three giant strides, grabbed one of the Indians with a forearm round his throat, and punched him in the side with such force as to drive the other's wind out in an audible whoop.

Murray then threw the Indian on the ground, dropped on him with both knees—Grey winced at the impact—and gripped the man by the throat. The other Indians lurched out of the way, laughing and making high-pitched yips of encouragement or derision, Grey couldn't tell which.

He stood there blinking, swaying slightly, and unable either to intervene or to look away. Murray had declined to let one of the field surgeons remove the arrowhead from his shoulder, and fresh blood spattered from the wound as he punched his opponent viciously—and repeatedly—in the face.

The Indian—he had a shaved scalp and dangling earrings of shell; Grey noticed these when Murray ripped one out of the ear and stuffed it into his opponent's mouth—was making a stout attempt at resistance and retaliation, in spite of his being taken at such a disadvantage.

"Do you suppose they are acquainted?" Captain André asked Grey. He had turned back, hearing the outcries, and was now standing beside Grey, watching the affray with interest.

"I think they must be," Grey replied absently. He glanced briefly at the other Indians, none of whom seemed to have any interest in assisting their fellow, though a few of them appeared to be making wagers on the result. They'd plainly been drinking, but seemed no more intoxicated than the average soldier at this time of day.

The combatants were now squirming on the ground, evidently striving for possession of a large knife worn by the man Murray had attacked. The fight was attracting attention from other quarters; a number of men had hurried over from nearby fires and were clustered behind Grey and André, making speculations and hasty bets, offering shouted advice.

Grey was conscious, through his fatigue, of a certain concern for Murray—and not only on Murray's own account. On the off chance that he might at some point in future actually speak with Jamie Fraser again, he didn't want the first subject raised to be the demise of Fraser's nephew while more or less in Grey's custody. He couldn't think what the hell to do about it, though, and thus continued to stand there, watching.

Like most fights, it didn't last very long. Murray gained possession of the knife, by the brutal but effective expedient of bending one of his opponent's fingers backward 'til it broke and grabbing the hilt as the man let go.

As Murray pressed the blade against the other man's throat, it belatedly occurred to Grey that he might really intend to kill him. The men around him certainly thought so; there was a universal gasp as Murray drew the blade across his enemy's throat.

The momentary silence engendered by this was enough for most of the assembled to hear Murray say, with a noticeable effort, "I give you back your life!" He rose off the Indian's body, swaying and staring as though blind drunk himself, and hurled the knife into the darkness—causing considerable consternation and not a little cursing among those in whose direction he'd hurled it.

In the excitement, most of the crowd likely didn't hear the Indian's reply, but Grey and André did. He sat up, very slowly, hands shaking as they pressed a fold of his shirt to the shallow cut across his throat, and said, in an almost conversational tone, "You will regret that, Mohawk."

Murray was breathing like a winded horse, his ribs visible with each gasp. Most of the paint had gone from his face; there were long smears of red and black down his glistening chest, and only a horizontal streak of some dark color remained across his cheekbones—that and a smudge of white on the point of his shoulder, above the arrow wound. He nodded to himself, once, then twice. And, without haste, stepped back into the circle of firelight, picked up a tomahawk that was lying on the ground, and, swinging it high with both hands, brought it down on the Indian's skull.

The sound froze Grey to the marrow and silenced every man present. Murray stood still for a moment, breathing heavily, then walked away. As he passed Grey, he turned his head and said, in a perfectly conversational tone of voice, "He's right. I would have," before disappearing into the night.

There was a sudden, belated stir among the spectators, and André glanced at Grey, but he shook his head. The army took no official notice of what went on among the Indian scouts, save there was an incident involving regulars. And they didn't get more irregular than the gentleman who had just left them.

André cleared his throat.

"Was he your . . . er . . . prisoner, my lord?"

"Ah . . . no. A, erm . . . relation by marriage."

"Oh, I see."

IT WAS FULL dark before the battle ended. William gathered as much from the orderly who'd brought him supper, and he could hear the sounds of a camp slowly reassembling itself as companies of soldiers came in, were dismissed, and scattered to drop their equipment and find food. Nothing like the usual sense of relaxation that lay on a camp after sunset. Everything was agitated and restless—and so was William.

His head ached horribly and someone had stitched his scalp; the stitches were tender and itching. Uncle Hal hadn't come back, and he'd had no news whatever beyond the orderly's sketchy report, which indicated only that there had been no clear victory over the Americans but that all three parts of Clinton's army had withdrawn in good order, though with considerable casualties.

He wasn't sure he *wanted* any further news, to be honest. There was going to be a moment of reckoning with Sir Henry about that ignored order—though he supposed Sir Henry might just possibly be too preoccupied to realize . . .

Then he heard the sound of footsteps and sat up. His fretting disappeared on the instant when the tent flap lifted and he saw his father—*Lord John,* he corrected himself, but as an absent afterthought. His father seemed surprisingly small, almost fragile, and as Lord John limped slowly into the lantern light, William saw the stained bandage round his head, the makeshift sling, and when William cast his eyes down, he saw, too, the state of his father's bare feet.

"Are you—" he began, shocked, but Lord John interrupted him.

"I'm fine," he said, and tried for a smile, though his face was white and creased with fatigue. "Everything's all right, Willie. As long as you're alive, everything's all right."

He saw his father sway, put out a hand as though to steady himself, and, finding nothing to take hold of, withdraw it and force his body upright. Lord John's voice was hoarse, and his exposed eye bloodshot and exhausted but . . . tender. William swallowed.

"If you and I have things to say to each other, Willie—and of course we do—let it wait until tomorrow. Please. I'm not . . ." He made a vague, wavering gesture that ended nowhere.

The lump in William's throat was sudden and painful. He nodded, hands clenched tight on the bedding. His father nodded, too, drew a deep breath, and turned toward the tent flap—where, William saw, Uncle Hal was hovering, eyes fixed on his brother and brows drawn with worry.

William's heart seized, in a lump more painful than the one in his throat.

"Papa!" His father stopped abruptly, turning to look over his shoulder.

"I'm glad you're not dead," William blurted.

A smile blossomed slowly on his father's battered face.

"Me, too," he said.

IAN MADE HIS way out of the British camp, looking neither to right nor to left. The night was throbbing slowly round him. It was like being trapped inside a huge heart, he thought, feeling the thick walls squeeze him breathless, then draw away to leave him floating and weightless.

Lord John had offered to have an army surgeon tend his wound, but he couldn't bear to stay. He needed to go, to find Rachel, find Uncle Jamie. Had refused the offer of a horse, as well, unsure that he could stay on it. He'd do better walking, he'd told his lordship.

And he was walking all right, though obliged to admit that he didn't feel just that well in himself. His arms were still trembling from the shock of the killing blow. It had come up from his bowels and was still echoing through his bones, couldn't seem to find a way out of his body. Well, it would settle soon enough—this wasn't the first time, though he hadn't killed anyone in a long while, and a longer while since he'd done it with that much violence.

He tried to think who the last one had been, but couldn't. He could hear and see and feel things, but while his senses *worked*, they weren't joined up aright with the things he sensed. Troops were still marching past him into the camp. The battle must have ceased now with the darkness; the soldiers were coming home. He could hear the din they made, marching, their tin cups and canteens jangling against their cartridge boxes—but he heard it clanging long after they'd passed, and he couldn't always tell the light of distant campfires from the glow of fireflies near his feet.

The Scottish overseer. At Saratoga. The man's face was suddenly there in his memory, and just as suddenly his body remembered the feel of the blow. The violent punch of his knife, hard up under the man's back ribs, straight into the kidney. The huge, strange flexing he'd felt in his own body as the man's life surged up and then rushed out.

He wondered for a dazed moment whether butchers felt it—that echo—when they slaughtered a beast. You did, sometimes, when you cut a deer's throat, but usually not if it was just wringing a chicken's neck or crushing a weasel's skull.

"Or maybe ye just get used to it," he said.

"Maybe ye'd best try not to get used to it. Canna be good for your soul, *a bhalaich,* bein' used to that sort of thing."

"No," he agreed. "But ye mean when it's with your hands, aye? It's no the same wi' a gun or an arrow, now, is it?"

"Och, no. I did wonder sometimes, does it make a difference to the man ye kill, as well as yourself?"

Ian's feet blundered into a knee-high growth of thick weed and he realized that he'd stumbled off the road. It was just past the dark of the moon, and the stars still faint overhead.

"Different," he murmured, steering back into the roadway. "How d'ye mean, different? He'd be dead, either way."

"Aye, that's so. I'm thinkin' it's maybe worse to feel it's personal, though. Bein' shot in battle's more like bein' struck by lightning, ken? But ye canna help it bein' personal when ye do a man to death wi' your hands."

"Mmphm." Ian walked a bit farther in silence, the thoughts in his head circling like leeches swimming in a glass, going this way and that.

"Aye, well," he said at last—and realized suddenly that he'd spoken aloud for the first time. "It *was* personal."

The trembling in his bones had eased with the walking. The huge throbbing of the night had shrunk and come to rest in the arrow wound, the ache of it pulsing to the beat of his own heart.

It made him think of Rachel's white dove, though, flying serene above the hurt, and his mind steadied. He could see Rachel's face now, and he could hear crickets chirping. The cannon fire in his ears had stopped and the night grew slowly peaceful. And if his da had more to say on the subject of killing, he chose to keep his silence as they walked toward home together.

JOHN GREY EASED his battered feet into the pan, teeth gritted against the expected sensation, but to his surprise found that it caused him little pain, in spite of the torn skin and ruptured blisters.

"What—that's not hot water, is it?" he asked, leaning forward to look.

"Sweet oil," his brother said, his worn face relaxing a little. "And it had better be warm, not hot, or my orderly will be crucified at dawn."

"I'm sure the man trembles in his boots. Thank you, by the way," he added, gingerly dabbling. He was sitting on Hal's cot, his brother perched on the campaign chest, pouring something out of a canteen into one of the scarred pewter cups that had accompanied him for decades.

"You're welcome," Hal said, handing him the cup. "What the devil happened to your eye? And is your arm broken? I've called for a surgeon, but it may be some time." He waved a hand, encompassing the camp, the recent battle, and the stream of the returning wounded and sun-stricken.

"I don't need one. At first I thought my arm was broken, but I'm fairly sure it's just badly bruised. As for the eye . . . Jamie Fraser."

"Really?" Hal looked surprised and bent forward to peer at Grey's eye, now unwrapped from the bandages and—so far as Grey himself could tell—much improved. The constant watering had stopped, the swelling had gone down quite a bit, and he could, with caution, move it. From the look on Hal's face, though, the redness and bruising had perhaps not quite disappeared.

"Well, first Jamie, and then his wife." He touched the eye lightly. "He punched me, and then she did something excruciating to fix it and put honey in it."

"Having been subject to the lady's notions of medical treatment, I am not even faintly surprised to hear that." Hal lifted his cup in brief salute; Grey did the same and they drank. It was cider, and a dim recollection of applejack and Colonel Watson Smith floated through Grey's mind. Both seemed remote, as though they'd happened years ago rather than days.

"Mrs. Fraser doctored you?" Grey grinned at his brother. "What did she do to *you*?"

"Well . . . saved my life, to be perfectly frank." It was hard to tell in the lantern light, but Grey thought his brother was blushing slightly.

"Oh. In that case, I'm doubly obliged to her." He raised the cup again ceremoniously, then drained it. The cider went down gratefully after a hot day with no food. "How the hell did you fall into her clutches?" he asked curiously, extending the cup for more.

"I was looking for *you*," Hal said pointedly. "If you'd been where you were *supposed* to be . . ."

"You think I'm supposed to be sitting somewhere waiting for you to turn up without warning and involve me in—do you know you nearly got me *hanged*? Besides, I was busy being kidnapped by James Fraser at the time."

Hal raised one eyebrow and poured more cider. "Yes, you did say he'd punched you. What for?"

Grey rubbed two fingers between his brows. He hadn't really noticed the headache before, only because he'd had it all day. Hal was definitely making it worse, though.

"I couldn't begin to explain it, Hal," he said tiredly. "Can you find me a bed? I think I'm going to die, and if by some unfortunate chance I don't, I'll have to speak to Willie tomorrow about . . . well, never mind." He drank the last of the cider and set down the cup, preparing reluctantly to lift his feet from the soothing oil.

"I know about William," Hal said.

Grey stopped abruptly, looking dubiously at his brother, who shrugged.

"I saw Fraser," he said simply. "In Philadelphia. And when I said something to William this afternoon, he confirmed it."

"Did he?" Grey murmured. He was surprised but somewhat heartened by that. If Willie had calmed down sufficiently as to talk to Hal about the matter, Grey's own conversation with his son might be a trifle less fraught than he'd feared.

"How long have you known?" Hal asked curiously.

"For certain? Since Willie was two or three." He suddenly gave an enormous yawn, then sat blinking stupidly. "Oh—meant to ask. How did the battle go?"

Hal looked at him with something between affront and amusement. "You were bloody *in* it, weren't you?"

"My part of it didn't go that well. But my perspective was somewhat limited by circumstance. That, and having only one working eye," he added, gently prodding the bad one. A good night's sleep . . . Longing for bed made him sway, narrowly catching himself before simply falling into Hal's cot.

"Hard to tell." Hal fished a crumpled towel out of a basket of laundry lurking disreputably in a corner and, kneeling down, lifted Grey's feet out of the oil and blotted them gently. "Hell of a mess. Terrible ground, chopped up by creeks, either farmland or half covered in trees . . . Sir Henry got away with the baggage train and refugees all safe. But as for Washington . . ." He shrugged. "So far as I can tell from what I saw and heard, his troops acquitted themselves well. Remarkably well," he added thoughtfully. He rose to his feet. "Lie down, John. I'll find a bed somewhere else."

Grey was much too tired to argue. He simply fell over and rolled onto his back, not bothering to undress. The bad eye felt gritty, and he wondered dimly whether to ask Hal to find some honey but decided that could wait 'til morning.

Hal took the lantern from its hook and turned toward the tent flap, but paused for an instant, turning back.

"Do you think Mrs. Fraser—by the way, tomorrow I want to know how on earth she came to marry you—do you think she knows about William and James Fraser?"

"Anyone with eyes who'd seen the two of them would know," Grey murmured, eyes half closed. "She never mentioned it, though."

Hal grunted. "Apparently everyone knew—save William. Little wonder he's . . ."

"That's one word for it."

"I hadn't found one yet."

"Does it matter?" Grey's eyes closed all the way. Through the drifting mists of sleep, he heard Hal's quiet voice, by the tent flap.

"I've had word of Ben. They say he's dead."

85

LONG ROAD HOME

JAMIE SAT BY THE tiny window in his shirt and breeches, watching his wife's hair dry.

It was hot as a forge in the tiny spare room Mrs. Macken had given them, and his sweat lay on him in a heavy dew that broke under its own weight and ran down his sides with any movement, but he was careful not to block any faint breath of air that might seep into the room; the air reeked of Roquefort cheese and blood.

He'd soaked her hair with water from the ewer Mrs. Macken had brought and wetted her shift; it clung to her body, the round of her buttock showing pink through the fabric as it dried. It showed the thick wad of the dressing, too, and the bloody stain that spread slow upon the cloth.

Slow. His lips formed the word and he thought it passionately but didn't speak aloud. *Slow!* Stopping altogether would be much better, but he'd settle for slow just now.

Eight pints. That's how much blood she said a human body had. It must vary some, though; clearly a man his size had more than a woman of hers. Single hairs were beginning to rise from the soaking mass, curling as they dried, delicate as an ant's feelers.

He wished he might give her some of his blood; he had plenty. She'd said it was possible, but not in this time. Something to do with things in the blood that mightn't match.

Her hair was a dozen colors, brown, molasses, cream and butter, sugar, sable . . . gleams of gold and silver where the dying light touched it. A broad streak of pure white at her temple, nearly the shade of her skin. She lay on her side facing him, one hand curled against her bosom, the other loose, up-turned, so the inside of her wrist showed pure white, too, the blue veins heartbreaking.

She'd said she thought of cutting her wrists when she believed him dead. He didn't think he'd do it that way, if she died. He'd seen it: Toby Quinn with his wrist cut to the bone and all his blood run out across the floor, the room stinking of butchery and the word *"teind"* written on the wall above him in blood, his confession. A tithe to hell, it meant, and he shuddered in spite of the heat and crossed himself.

She'd said it was maybe the blood that had made Young Ian's bairns all die—the blood not matching betwixt him and his Mohawk wife—and that maybe it would be different with Rachel. He said a quick Ave, that it might be so, and crossed himself again.

The hair that lay upon her shoulders was coiling now, sinuous, slow as rising bread. Ought he rouse her to drink again? She needed the water, to help make more blood, to cool her with sweat. But while she slept, the pain was less. A few moments longer, then.

Not now. Please, not now.

She shifted, moaning, and he saw that she was different; restless now. The stain on her bandage had changed color, darkened from scarlet to rust as it dried. He laid a hand softly on her arm and felt the heat.

The bleeding had stopped. The fever had begun.

NOW THE TREES were talking to him. He wished they'd stop. The only thing Ian Murray wanted just now was silence. He was alone for the moment, but his ears buzzed and his head still throbbed with noise.

That always happened for a bit after a fight. You were listening so hard, to start with, for the sounds of the enemy, the direction of the wind, the voice of a saint behind you . . . you began to hear the voices of the forest, like you did hunting. And then you heard the shots and shouting, and when there were moments when that stopped, you heard the blood pounding round your body and beating in your ears, and, all in all, it took some time for the racket to die down afterward.

He had brief flashes of things that had happened during the day—milling soldiers; the thud of the arrow that struck him; the face of the Abenaki he'd killed by the fire; the look of George Washington on his big white horse, racing up the road, waving his hat—but these came and went in a fog of con-fusion, appearing as though revealed to him by a stroke of lightning, then disappearing into a buzzing mist.

A wind went whispering through the branches over him, and he felt it on his skin as though he'd been brushed with sandpaper. What might Rachel say, when he told her what he'd done?

He could still hear the sound when the tomahawk caved in the Abenaki's skull. He could still feel it, too, in the bones of his arms, in the bursting pain of his wound.

Dimly, he realized that his feet were no longer keeping to the road; he was stumbling over clumps of grass, stubbing his moccasin-clad toes on rocks. He looked back to find his path—he saw it, plain, a wavering line of black . . . Why was it wavering?

He didn't want silence, after all. He wanted Rachel's voice, no matter what she might say to him.

It came to him dimly that he couldn't go any farther. He was aware of a faint sense of surprise but was not afraid.

He didn't remember falling but found himself on the ground, his hot cheek pressed against the cool prickle of pine needles. Laboriously, he got to his knees and scraped away the thick layer of fallen needles. Then he was lying with his body on damp earth, the blanket of needles half pulled over him; he could do no more and said a brief prayer to the tree, that it might protect him through the night.

And as he fell headlong into darkness, he did hear Rachel's voice, in memory.

"Thy life's journey lies along its own path, Ian," she said, *"and I cannot share thy journey—but I can walk beside thee. And I will."*

His last thought was that he hoped she'd still mean it when he told her what he'd done.

86

IN WHICH ROSY-FINGERED DAWN

SHOWS UP MOB-HANDED

GREY WOKE TO THE drums of reveille, not startled by the accustomed rattle but with no clear idea where he was. *In camp.* Well, that much was obvious. He swung his legs out of the cot and sat up slowly, taking stock. His left arm hurt a lot, one of his eyes was stuck shut, and his mouth was so dry he could barely swallow. He'd slept in his clothes, smelled rank, and needed badly to piss.

He groped under the cot, found a utensil, and used it, noting in a rather dreamy way that his urine smelled of apples. That brought back the taste of cider and, with it, full recollection of the day and night before. Honey and flies. Artillery. Jamie, blood down his face. Rifle butt and the crack of bone. William . . . Hal . . .

Almost full recollection. He sat down and remained quite still for a moment, trying to decide whether Hal had really told him that his eldest son, Benjamin, was dead. Surely not. It must have been a shred of nightmare, lingering in his mind. And yet he had the dreadful feeling of doomed certainty that comes down like a curtain on the mind, smothering disbelief.

He stood up, staggering a little, determined to go and find his brother. He hadn't yet found his shoes, though, when the flap was thrown back and Hal came in, followed by an orderly with a basin, a steaming pitcher, and shaving implements.

"Sit down," Hal said, in a completely ordinary voice. "You'll have to wear one of my uniforms, and you're not doing it smelling like that. What the devil happened to your hair?"

Grey had forgotten his hair and flattened a palm on top of his head, surprised at the bristly stubble there.

"Oh. A *ruse de guerre.*" He sat down slowly, eyes on his brother. The bad eye had come open, though it was unpleasantly crusty, and so far as Grey could see, Hal looked much as he usually did. Tired, of course, worn, and a little haunted, but everyone looked like that the day after a battle. Surely if it were true, he'd look different. Worse, somehow.

He would have asked, but Hal didn't linger, going off and leaving John in the hands of the orderly. Before the ablutions were complete, a young Scottish surgeon with freckles appeared, yawning as though he hadn't slept all night, and blinked blearily at Grey's arm. He prodded this in a professional manner, pronounced the bone cracked but not broken, and put it in a sling.

The sling had to be removed almost at once, in order for him to dress—another orderly arrived with a uniform and a tray of breakfast—and by the time he was made tidy and had been forcibly fed, he was wild with impatience.

He would have to wait for Hal to reappear, though; no point going out to scour the camp for him. And he really must talk to his brother before seeking out William. A small dish of honey had been provided with his toast, and he was dipping a dubious finger into it, wondering whether he ought to try dabbing it into his eye, when at last the flap opened again and his brother was with him.

"Did you actually tell me that Ben is dead?" he blurted at once. Hal's face contracted a bit, but his jaw was set.

"No," Hal said evenly. "I told you that I'd had news of Ben, and they *said* he was dead. I don't believe it." He gave John a stare defying him to contradict this belief.

"Oh. Good," Grey said mildly. "Then I don't believe it, either. Who told you, though?"

"That's why I don't believe it," Hal replied, turning to lift the tent flap and peer out—evidently to be sure of not being overheard, and the thought made Grey's belly flutter a little. "It was Ezekiel Richardson who brought me the news, and I wouldn't trust that fellow if he told me I had a hole in the seat of my breeches, let alone something like that."

The flutter in Grey's belly became a full-blown beating of wings.

"Your instincts haven't led you amiss there," he said. "Sit down and have a piece of toast. I have a few things to tell you."

WILLIAM WOKE with a shattering headache and the conviction that he had forgotten something important. Clutching his head, he discovered a bandage wound round it, chafing his ear. He pulled it off impatiently; there was blood on it, but not much and all dried. He recalled vague bits of things from the night before—pain, nausea, his head swimming, Uncle Hal . . . and then an image of his father, white-faced and fragile . . . "*If you and I have things to say to each other . . .*" Christ, had he dreamed that?

He said something bad in German, and a young voice repeated it, rather doubtfully.

"What's that mean, sir?" asked Zeb, who had popped up beside his cot with a covered tray.

"You don't need to know, and don't repeat it," William said, sitting up. "What happened to my head?"

Zeb's brow creased.

"You don't remember, sir?"

"If I did, would I be asking you?"

Zeb's brow creased in concentration, but the logic of this question escaped him, and he merely shrugged, set down the tray, and answered the first one.

"Colonel Grey said you was hit on the head by deserters."

"Desert—oh." He stopped to consider that. British deserters? No . . . there was a reason why German profanity had sprung to his mind. He had a fleeting memory of Hessians, and . . . and what?

"Colenso's got over the shits," Zeb offered helpfully.

"Good to know the day's starting out well for somebody. Oh, Jesus." Pain crackled inside his skull, and he pressed a hand to his head. "Have you got anything to drink on that tray, Zeb?"

"Yes, sir!" Zeb uncovered the tray, triumphantly revealing a dish of coddled eggs with toast, a slice of ham, and a beaker of something that looked suspiciously murky but smelled strongly of alcohol.

"What's in this?"

"Dunno, sir, but Colonel Grey says it's a hair-of-the-dog-what-bit-you sort of thing."

"Oh." So it hadn't been a dream. He shoved that thought aside for the moment and regarded the beaker with a cautious interest. He'd had the first of his father's restoratives when he was fourteen and had mistaken the punch being prepared for Lord John's dinner party as the same sort that ladies had at garden parties. He'd had a few more in the years since and found them invariably effective, if rather startling to drink.

"Right, then," he said, and, taking a deep breath, picked up the beaker and drained it, swallowing heroically without pausing for breath.

"Cor!" said Zeb, admiring. "The cook said he could send some sausages, was you up to eating 'em."

William merely shook his head—being momentarily incapable of speech—and picked up a piece of toast, which he held for a moment, not quite ready to consider actually inserting it into his mouth. His head still hurt, but the restorative had jarred loose a few more bits from the detritus in his brain.

"*. . . Advice? You're too old to be given it and too young to take it. . . .*"

"*. . . Er spricht Deutsch. Er gehört! . . .*" He speaks German. He heard.

"I heard," he said slowly. "What did I hear?"

Zeb appeared to think this another rhetorical question and, instead of trying to answer it, asked one of his own.

"What happened to Goth, sir?" His thin face was solemn, as though he expected to receive bad news.

"Goth," William repeated blankly. "Has something happened to Goth?"

"Well, he's gone, sir," Zeb said, apparently trying to be tactful. "That is—when the regulars took you and the Indian away from the Rebels, you wasn't on him."

"When the . . . what Indian?—what the devil *happened* yesterday, Zeb?"

"How would I know?" Zeb said, affronted. "Wasn't there, was I?"

"No, of course—bloody hell. Is my uncle—the Duke of Pardloe—in camp? I need to talk to him."

Zeb looked dubious.

"Well, I can go and look for him, I s'pose."

"Do, please. Now." William waved him off, then sat still for a moment, trying to stick the jagged fragments of his memory back together. Rebels? Goth . . . He did recall *something* about Goth, but what was it? Had he run into Rebels, who took the horse? But what was this about Indians and deserters, and why did he keep hearing echoes of German speech in the back of his brain?

And who, come to think of it, was the Colonel Grey that Zeb had referred to? He'd assumed it was Uncle Hal—but his father's rank was lieutenant colonel, and he'd also be addressed as "Colonel" in common use. He glanced at the tray and the empty beaker. Uncle Hal certainly knew about the hair of the dog, but . . .

"*As long as you're alive, everything's all right.*"

He put the untouched toast down, a sudden lump in his throat. Again. He'd had the lump last night, when he saw Papa. When he'd said to his father—yes, God damn it, his father!—"*I'm glad you're not dead.*"

He maybe wasn't quite ready to talk to Papa—or Papa to him—and he didn't quite agree that everything was all right, but . . .

A shaft of brilliant sunlight lanced into his face as the tent flap was shoved aside, and he sat bolt upright, swinging his legs out of bed to be ready to meet—

But it wasn't either his uncle or his father who appeared out of the eye-watering blur of sunlight. It was Banastre Tarleton, in uniform but wigless and unbuttoned, looking indecently cheerful for someone whose face seemed to have been beaten badly not too long ago.

"Alive, are you, Ellesmere?" Ban spotted the dish and, scooping up a coddled egg in his fingers, gulped it. He licked his buttery fingers, making pleased noises.

"Christ, I'm hungry. Been up since dawn. Killing on an empty stomach leaves you rare sharp-set, I'll say that. Can I have the rest?"

"Be my guest. Who've you been killing for breakfast? Rebels?"

Tarleton looked surprised, arrested with a mouthful of toast. He chewed this imperfectly and bolted the bite before answering with a shower of crumbs.

"No, Washington's troops withdrew to the south, so far as I know. Hessian deserters. The same lot that crowned you and left you for dead, or so I assume. They had your horse; recognized him." He reached for another egg, and William thrust a spoon into his hand.

"For God's sake, eat like a Christian. Do you *have* my horse?"

"I do. He's lame in the right fore, but I don't think it's bad. Mmm . . . have you got your own cook?"

"No, he's my uncle's. Tell me about the deserters. They knocked me on the head, and my memory's a bit spotty." More than a bit, but chunks of it were beginning to come back pretty fast now.

Between bites, Tarleton gave him the story. A company of mercenaries under von Knyphausen had made up their minds to desert during the battle, but not all the men were of the same mind. Those in favor of desertion had drawn away a bit and were quietly discussing whether it was necessary to kill the dissenters, when William had shown up unexpectedly in their midst.

"That knocked them a bit skew-ways, as you might surmise." Tarleton, having finished the eggs and most of the toast, picked up the beaker and looked disappointed at finding it empty.

"There's probably water in that canteen," William said, motioning toward the battered tin-and-leather object hanging from the tent pole. "So that's it. . . . They looked a bit nervous, but when I asked one of them in German whether there was a farrier nearby—that was it! Goth threw a shoe, that's why he—but then I heard someone whispering, sounding frantic, and he was saying, 'He heard! He knows!' Must've meant he thought I'd overheard them plotting and knew what they were up to."

He breathed out in relief at having this much of the previous day restored to him.

Tarleton nodded. "Imagine so. They *did* kill some of the dissenters—gather a barney broke out after they bashed you on the head and threw you into the ravine—but not all of them."

A few of the mercenaries had escaped and headed for von Knyphausen, who, upon hearing the news, had sent a dispatch to Clinton asking for assistance in dealing with the miscreants.

William nodded at this. It was always better to have matters like desertion or treason dealt with by troops outside the affected companies. And knowing Ban Tarleton, he would have leapt at the chance to track down the deserters and—

"Were you told to kill them?" he asked, striving for casualness.

Tarleton gave him an eggy grin and wiped a few lingering crumbs off his chin.

"Not specifically. Got the impression that as long as I brought a few back to tell the tale, no one much cared how many. And there *was* a hint of *pour encourager les autres* in my orders."

Politely suppressing his shock at the revelation that Tarleton could read, let alone read Voltaire, William nodded.

"I see. My orderly said something rather curious: mentioned that I'd been found by Rebels—with an Indian. D'you know anything about that?"

Tarleton looked surprised, but shook his head.

"Not a thing. Oh—" He'd sat down on the stool and now rocked back a little, hands clasped about one knee, looking pleased with himself. "I *do* know something, though. Recall you asked me about Harkness?"

"Harkness . . . oh, yes!" William's exclamation had less to do with mention of Captain Harkness and more to do with the important thing he'd forgotten, which had just come back to him: Jane and her sister.

He had an immediate impulse to get up and go find her, make sure they were all right. The fugitive Loyalists and camp followers would have been well clear of the actual battle, of course—but the violence and agitation that attended fighting didn't simply stop when the fighting did. And it wasn't only deserters and scavengers who looted, raped, and hunted among the hapless sheep.

He spared a flickering thought for Anne Endicott and her family—but they did at least have a man to protect them, however ill-equipped. Jane and Fanny . . . but surely Zeb would have known, if anything—

"What?" He looked blankly at Tarleton. "What did you say?"

"That knock on the head affected your hearing, too, did it?" Ban took a swig from the canteen. "I said I made inquiries. Harkness never joined his regiment. For all anyone knows, he's still in Philadelphia."

William's mouth felt dry. He reached for the canteen and took a swallow; the water was warm and tin-tasting, but wet.

"Absent without leave, do you mean?"

"Very much without leave," Tarleton assured him. "Last anyone recalls seeing him, he was promising to go back to some brothel and give some whore a proper seeing-to. Maybe she saw to him, instead!" He laughed heartily at the thought.

William stood up abruptly, then—for something to do—reached to replace the canteen on its nail. The tent flap was down, but a stray beam of dust-filled sunlight still fell through the gap, catching the glitter of metal. His officer's gorget hung from the nail, its silver gleaming in the sun.

"PERCIVAL WAINWRIGHT?" John hadn't seen Hal so disconcerted since the events concerning their father's death—which had also involved Percy, come to think of it.

"In the—very fashionable—flesh. He's apparently an adviser to the Marquis de La Fayette."

"Who's that?"

"A flash young frog with a lot of money," Grey said with a one-shouldered shrug. "Rebel general. Said to be very close to Washington."

"Close," Hal repeated, with a sharp look at Grey. "Close to Wainwright, too, you think?"

"Probably not that way," he replied calmly, though his heart beat a little faster. "I gather you're not altogether surprised that he isn't dead. Percy, I mean." He was vaguely affronted; he'd gone to a lot of trouble to make it appear that Percy had died in prison while awaiting trial for sodomy.

Hal merely snorted. "Men like that never die so conveniently. Why the bloody hell is he telling you this, do you think?"

Grey suppressed the vivid memory of bergamot, red wine, and petitgrain.

"I don't know. But I *do* know he's deeply involved with French interests, and—"

"Wainwright's never been involved with any interests other than his own," Hal interrupted brusquely. He gave John a sharp look. "You'd do well to remember that."

"I doubt I shall ever see the fellow again," John replied, overlooking the implication that his brother considered him gullible—or worse. He was entirely aware that while Hal was treating Richardson's news of Ben with scorn, and was very likely right to do so, neither of them could completely ignore the possibility that the man had been telling the truth.

Hal verified this assumption by smacking his fist down on the campaign chest, making the pewter cups jump and fall over. He stood abruptly.

"Bloody hell," he muttered. "Stay here!"

"Where are you going?"

Hal paused at the tent flap for an instant. His face was still haggard, but John recognized the battle light in his eyes.

"To arrest Richardson."

"You can't arrest him yourself, for God's sake!" Grey was on his feet, too, reaching for Hal's sleeve.

"Which regiment does he belong to?"

"The Fifth, but he's detached. I told you he was an intelligencer, did I not?" The word "intelligencer" dripped with contempt.

"All right—I'll speak to Sir Henry first."

John had got a grip on Hal's arm and tightened his hold at this. "I should have thought you'd had enough of scandal by now," he said, trying for calmness. "Take a breath and imagine what will likely happen if you do that. Assuming that Sir Henry would take the time to consider your request. Today, for God's sake?" He could hear the army moving outside; there was no danger of pursuit from Washington's troops, but Clinton was not going to hang about. His division, with its baggage and refugees under its wing, would be on the road within the hour.

Hal's arm was hard as marble under John's hand and stayed that way. But he *did* stop, breathing with a slow, deep regularity. At last he turned his head and looked into his brother's eyes. A beam of sunlight threw every line in his face into stark relief.

"Name one thing you think I wouldn't do," he said quietly, "in order not to have to tell Minnie that Ben is dead."

Grey drew one long, deep breath of his own and nodded, letting go.

"Point taken. Whatever you mean to do, I'll help. But first I have to find William. What Percy said—"

"Ah." Hal blinked and his face relaxed a fraction. "Yes, of course. Meet you here in half an hour."

WILLIAM HAD BARELY finished dressing before the message he'd been halfway expecting arrived from Sir Henry, delivered by Lieutenant Foster, whom he knew slightly. Foster grimaced sympathetically when handing it over.

William observed Sir Henry Clinton's personal seal: not a good sign. On the other hand, if he was to be arrested for being absent without leave the previous day, Harry Foster would have brought an armed escort and taken him off without a by-your-leave. That was mildly heartening, and he broke the seal without hesitation.

In the event, it was a terse note advising him that he was relieved of duty until further notice—but that was all. He exhaled, only then realizing that he'd been holding his breath.

But of course Sir Henry wouldn't imprison him—how and where, with the army on the move? Short of putting him in irons and transporting him by wagon . . . Realistically, Clinton couldn't even confine him to quarters; the quarters in question were beginning to shake overhead as his uncle's orderly set to dismantling the tent.

All right, then. He stuffed the note into his pocket, stuffed his feet into his boots, seized up his hat, and went out, feeling not that bad, all things considered. He had a headache, but it was bearable, and he'd managed to eat what breakfast Tarleton had left.

When things settled down and Sir Henry got round to taking official notice of his disobedience of orders, William could fish up Captain André and have him explain about going to find Tarleton, and all would be well. Meanwhile, he'd go down to the camp followers' area and find Jane.

There was a strong bitter smell of fresh cabbage floating over the sprawl of makeshift shelters and human detritus, and a scatter of farm wagons drawn up along the road, with women crowding round them. The army cooks fed the refugees, but rations were sparse—and had doubtless been disrupted by the battle.

He walked along the road, keeping an eye out for Jane or Fanny, but didn't spot either one. His eye attuned for a young girl, though, he did see Peggy Endicott, trudging down the road with a bucket in either hand.

"Miss Peggy! May I offer my assistance, ma'am?" He smiled down at her and was warmed to see her own face—somewhat anxious before—bloom into delight under her cap.

"Captain!" she cried, nearly dropping her buckets in her excitement. "Oh,

I'm *so* happy to see you! We were all so worried for you, you know, in the battle, and we all said a prayer for your safety, but Papa told us you would surely prevail over the wicked Rebels and God would see you safe."

"Your lovely prayers were to great effect," he assured her gravely, taking the buckets. One was full of water and the other of turnips, their green tops wilting over the rim. "Are your mama and papa well, then, and your sisters?"

They walked along together, Peggy dancing on her toes and chattering like an affable small parrot. William kept an eye peeled for Jane or Fanny among the laundresses; it was safer near those redoubtable ladies than in some other parts of the camp. There were no kettles boiling this morning, of course, but the scent of lye soap floated on the humid air like scum on a cauldron full of dirty clothes.

There was no sign of Jane and Fanny by the time he'd reached the Endicotts' wagon—still on all four wheels, he was glad to see. He was greeted warmly by all the Endicotts, though the girls and Mrs. Endicott made a great fuss of the lump on his head when he took his hat off to help with the loading of their wagon.

"Nothing, ma'am, the merest bruise," he assured Mrs. Endicott for the ninth time, when she urged him to sit down in the shade and drink some water with the tiniest bit of brandy in it, for they still had some, thank goodness. . . .

Anne, who had maneuvered herself close to him, passing him items to be loaded, leaned in with a tea chest and let her hand brush his—deliberately, he was sure.

"Will you stay in New York, do you think?" she asked, stooping to pick up a portmanteau. "Or perhaps—you must excuse my prying, but people *will* talk—go back to England? Miss Jernigan said that you might."

"Miss . . . oh, of course." He recalled Mary Jernigan, a very flirtatious blond piece with whom he'd danced at a ball in Philadelphia. He glanced over the throng of Loyalist refugees. "Is she here?"

"Yes," Anne replied, a little tersely. "Dr. Jernigan has a brother in New York; they will stay with him for a time." She collected herself—he could see that she was regretting having recalled his attention to Mary Jernigan—and smiled at him, deeply enough as to invoke the dimple in her left cheek. "You needn't take refuge with reluctant relatives, though, need you? Miss Jernigan said that you have a great vast estate awaiting you in England."

"Mmm," he said noncommittally. His father had warned him early on about marriage-minded young women with an eye to his fortune, and he'd met quite a few of them. Still, he *liked* Anne Endicott and her family and was inclined to think they had a real regard for him, as well, despite his position and the pragmatical considerations that must now afflict Anne and her sisters, with their father's affairs so precarious.

"I don't know," he said, taking the portmanteau from her. "I truly have no idea what's to become of me. Who does, in wartime?" He smiled, a little ruefully, and she seemed to feel his sense of uncertainty, for she impulsively laid a hand on his sleeve.

"Well, be assured that you have friends, at least, who care what becomes of you," she said softly.

"Thank you," he said, and turned his face toward the cart, lest she see how much that touched him.

In turning, though, his eye caught a purposeful movement, someone threading toward him through the crowd, and Anne Endicott's soft dark eyes disappeared abruptly from his mind.

"Sir!" It was his groom Colenso Baragwanath, gasping from the effort of running. "Sir, have you—"

"There you are, Baragwanath! What the devil are you doing here, and where have you left Madras? Good news, though: Goth's come back. Colonel Tarleton has him and—what, for God's sake?" For Colenso was squirming as though he had a snake in his breeches, his square Cornish face contorted with information.

"Jane and Fanny're gone, sir!"

"Gone? Gone where?"

"Dunno, sir. But they've gone. I came back to get my jacket and the shelter was still up, but their things were gone and I couldn't find 'em and when I asked the folk who camps near us, they said as the girls had rolled up their bundles and sneaked off!"

William didn't waste time inquiring how one could possibly sneak out of an open camp of several thousand people, let alone why that should be necessary.

"Which way did they go?"

"That way, sir!" Colenso pointed down the road.

William rubbed a hand over his face and stopped abruptly when he inadvertently touched the bruised swelling on his left temple.

"Ouch. Well, bloody hell—oh, I beg your pardon, Miss Endicott." For at this point he became aware of Anne Endicott at his elbow, eyes round with curiosity.

"Who are Jane and Fanny?" she asked.

"Ahh . . . two young ladies who are traveling under my protection," he said, knowing exactly what effect *that* information was likely to have, but there wasn't much help for it. "*Very* young ladies," he added, in the vain hope of improving things. "Daughters of a . . . um, distant cousin."

"Oh," she said, looking distinctly unconvinced. "But they've run off? Whyever should they do such a thing?"

"Damned if I—er, beg pardon, ma'am. I don't know, but I must go and find out. Will you make my excuses to your parents and sisters?"

"I—of course." She made a small, abortive gesture toward him, putting out her hand and then withdrawing it. She looked both startled and slightly affronted. He regretted it, but there wasn't time to do anything about it.

"Your servant, ma'am," he said, and, bowing, left her.

IN THE END, it was half a day, rather than half an hour, before John saw Hal again. He found his brother, quite by chance, standing by the road that led northward, watching the marching columns go past. Most of the camp had already left; only the cook wagons and laundry kettles were trundling past now, the disorderly sprawl of camp followers spreading out behind them like the plague of lice over the land of Egypt.

"William's gone," he said to Hal without preamble.

Hal nodded, face somber. "So is Richardson."

"Bloody hell."

Hal's groom was standing by, holding two horses. Hal jerked his head at a dark-bay mare and took the reins of his own horse, a light-bay gelding with a blaze and one white stocking.

"Where do you think we're going?" John inquired, seeing his brother turn the gelding's head south.

"Philadelphia," Hal replied, tight-lipped. "Where else?"

Grey could himself think of any number of alternatives, but recognized a rhetorical question when he heard one and contented himself with asking, "Have you got a clean handkerchief?"

Hal gave him a blank look, then rummaged in his sleeve, pulling out a crumpled but unused linen square.

"Apparently. Why?"

"I expect we're going to need a flag of truce at some point. The Continental army lying presently between us and Philadelphia, I mean."

"Oh, that." Hal stuffed the handkerchief back up his sleeve and said no more until they had negotiated their way past the last trailing remnants of the horde of refugees and found themselves more or less alone on the road leading south.

"No one could be sure, in the confusion," he said, as though he'd last spoken ten seconds before. "But it looks very much as though Captain Richardson has deserted."

"What?!"

"Not a bad moment to choose, really," Hal said reflectively. "No one would have noticed he was gone for days, had I not come looking for him. He was in camp last night, though, and unless he's disguised himself as a teamster or a laundress, he's not here any longer."

"The contingency seems remote," Grey said. "William *was* here this morning—both your orderly and his young grooms saw him, and so did a Colonel Tarleton of the British Legion, who breakfasted with him."

"Who? Oh, him." Hal waved off Tarleton as a distraction. "Clinton values him, but I never trust a man with lips like a girl's."

"Regardless, he seems to have had nothing to do with William's disappearance. The groom Baragwanath thinks that William went off to see about a couple of . . . young women among the camp followers."

Hal glanced at him, one brow raised.

"What sort of young women?"

"Probably the sort you're thinking," John replied, a little tersely.

"At that hour of the morning, after being bashed on the head the night before? And young women, plural? The boy's got stamina, I'll say that for him."

Grey could have said a number of other things about William at this point, but didn't. "So you think Richardson's deserted." That would explain Hal's focus on Philadelphia; if Percy was right and Richardson was in fact an American agent, where else might he go at this point?

"It seems the most likely possibility. Also . . ." Hal hesitated for a moment, but then his mouth firmed. "If I believed that Benjamin was dead, what might I be expected to do?"

"Go and make inquiries into his death," Grey replied, suppressing the queasy feeling the notion induced. "Claim his body, at the least."

Hal nodded. "Ben was—or is—being held at a place in New Jersey called Middletown Encampment. I've not been there, but it's in the middle of Washington's strongest territory, in the Watchung Mountains. Nest of Rebels."

"And you'd be unlikely to undertake that sort of journey with a large armed guard," John observed. "You'd go alone, or perhaps with an orderly, an ensign or two. Or me."

Hal nodded. They rode for a bit, each alone with his thoughts.

"So you're not going to the Watchung Mountains," Grey said at last. His brother sighed deeply and set his jaw.

"Not immediately. If I can catch up with Richardson, I may find out what's really happened—or not happened—to Ben. After that . . ."

"Do you have a plan for proceeding once we reach Philadelphia?" Grey inquired. "Given that it's in the hands of the Rebels?"

Hal's lips compressed. "I will have, by the time we get there."

"I daresay. I have one now, though."

Hal looked at him, thumbing a hank of damp hair behind his ear. His hair was carelessly tied back; he'd not bothered to have it plaited or clubbed this morning, a sure sign of his agitation. "Does it involve anything patently insane? Your better plans always do."

"Not at all. We're certain to encounter the Continentals, as I said. Assuming we aren't shot on sight, we produce your flag of truce"—he nodded at his brother's sleeve, from which the edge of the handkerchief was drooping—"and demand to be taken to General Fraser."

Hal gave him a startled look.

"*James* Fraser?"

"The same." Grey's knotted stomach clenched a little tighter at the thought. At both the thought of speaking to Jamie again—and the thought of telling him that William was missing. "He fought with Benedict Arnold at Saratoga, and his wife is friendly with the man."

"God help General Arnold, in that case," Hal murmured.

"And who else has a better reason for helping us in this matter than does Jamie Fraser?"

"Who indeed?" They rode for some time in silence, Hal apparently lost in thought. It wasn't until they paused to find a creek and water the horses that he spoke again, water streaming down his face where he'd splashed it.

"So you've not only somehow married Fraser's wife, but you've accidentally been raising his illegitimate son for the last fifteen years?"

"Apparently so," Grey said, in a tone that he hoped indicated complete unwillingness to talk about it. For once, Hal took the hint.

"I see," he said, and, with no further questions, wiped his face with the flag of truce and mounted up.

87

MOONRISE

I T HADN'T BEEN a peaceful day. Apparently Jamie had somehow retained sufficient presence of mind last night to write a brief note—though he didn't recall doing so—to La Fayette, explaining what had happened and confiding care of his troops to the marquis. This he had sent with Lieutenant Bixby, with instructions to notify the captains and militia commanders of his companies. After which, he'd forgotten everything but Claire.

Everything had not forgotten him, though. The sun was barely up before a stream of officers appeared at Mrs. Macken's door, in search of General Fraser. Mrs. Macken took every arrival as being the possible bearer of bad news concerning her still-missing husband, and the reek of burnt porridge rose through the house, seeping into the walls like the smell of fear.

Some came with questions, some with news or gossip—General Lee was relieved of duty, was under arrest, had gone to Philadelphia, had turned his coat and joined Clinton, had hanged himself, had challenged Washington to a duel. A messenger arrived from General Washington with a personal note of sympathy and good wishes; another came from La Fayette with an enormous hamper of food and a half-dozen bottles of claret.

Jamie couldn't eat, but gave the food to Mrs. Macken. He retained a couple of bottles of the wine, though, which he'd opened and kept by him through the day, taking occasional gulps to sustain him as he sponged and watched and prayed.

Judah Bixby came and went like a helpful ghost, appearing and disappearing, but always seeming to be there if something was needed.

"The militia companies . . ." Jamie began, but then couldn't think what he'd meant to ask concerning them. "Are they . . . ?"

"Most of them have gone home," Bixby told him, unloading a basket full of beer bottles. "Their enlistment ends on the thirtieth—that's tomorrow, sir," he added gently, "but they mostly set off first thing this morning."

Jamie let out a breath he hadn't known he was holding and felt a small measure of peace.

"I reckon it'll be months before anyone knows was it a victory or not," Bixby remarked. He drew the cork from one bottle, then another, and handed one to Jamie. "But it surely wasn't defeat. Shall we drink to it, sir?"

Jamie was worn out with worry and praying, but managed a smile for Judah and a quick word of thanks to God for the boy.

Once Judah had left, a somewhat longer prayer on behalf of his nephew.

Ian hadn't returned, and none of Jamie's visitors had had any word of him. Rachel had come back late the night before, white-faced and silent, and had gone out again at daybreak. Dottie had offered to go with her, but Rachel had refused; the two of them were needed to deal with the wounded still being brought in and those sheltering in the houses and barns of Freehold.

Ian, Jamie thought in anguish, addressing his brother-in-law. *For God's sake, have an eye to our lad, because I canna do it. I'm sorry.*

Claire's fever had risen fast during the night, then seemed to fall a little with the coming of the light; she was conscious now and then and capable of a few words, but for the most part she lay in a uneasy doze, her breath coming in shallow pants punctuated by sudden deep, tearing gasps that woke her—she dreamed that she was being suffocated, she said. He would give her as much water as she would take and douse her hair again, and she would drop back into fever dreams, muttering and moaning.

He began to feel as though he were living in a fever dream himself: trapped in endless repetitions of prayer and water, these broken by visitations from some vanished, alien world.

Perhaps this was purgatory, he thought, and gave a wan smile at memory of himself, waking on Culloden Moor so many years ago, his eyelids sealed with blood, thinking himself dead and grateful for it, even if his immediate prospect was a spell in purgatory—that being a vague, unknown circumstance, probably unpleasant but not one he feared.

He feared the one that might be imminent.

He *had* come to the conclusion that he couldn't kill himself, even if she died. Even could he bring himself to commit a sin of that magnitude, there were people who needed him, and to abandon them would be a greater sin even than the willful destruction of God's gift of life. But to live without her—he watched her breathe, obsessively, counting ten breaths before he would believe she hadn't stopped—that would certainly be his purgatory.

He didn't think he'd taken his eyes off her, and maybe he hadn't, but he came out of his reverie to see that her own eyes were open, a soft smudged black in the white of her face. The light had faded to the final cusp of twilight and all color had washed from the room, leaving them in a luminous dusty haze that wasn't daylight any longer but not yet night. He saw that her hair was nearly dry, curling in masses over the pillow.

"I've . . . decided . . . not to die," she said, in a voice little more than a whisper.

"Oh. Good." He was afraid to touch her, for fear of hurting her, but couldn't bear not to. He laid a hand as lightly as he could over hers, finding it cool in spite of the heat trapped in the small attic.

"I *could,* you know." She closed one eye and looked accusingly at him with the other. "I *want* to; this is . . . bloody horrible."

"I know," he whispered, and brought her hand to his lips. Her bones were frail, and she hadn't the strength to squeeze his hand; her fingers lay limp in his.

She closed her eyes and breathed audibly for a little.

"Do you know why?" she said suddenly, opening her eyes.

"No." He'd thought of making some jesting remark about her needing to write down her receipt for making ether, but her tone was dead serious, and he didn't.

"Because," she said, and stopped with a small grimace that squeezed his heart. "Because," she said through clenched teeth, "I know what it felt . . . like when I . . . thought you were dead, and—" A small gasp for breath, and her eyes locked on his. "And I wouldn't do that to *you*." Her bosom fell and her eyes closed.

It was a long moment before he could speak.

"Thank ye, Sassenach," he whispered, and held her small, cold hand between his own and watched her breathe until the moon rose.

I COULD SEE the moon through the tiny window; we were in the attic of the house. It was the first breath of the new moon, but the whole of it was visible, a perfect ball of violet and indigo cupped in a sickle of light, luminous among the stars. "The new moon with the old," country folk called it in England. On the Ridge, people called it "holding water."

The fever had left me. It had also left me drained, light-headed, and weak as a newborn mouse. My side was swollen from hip to oxter, hot and tender to the touch, but I was sure this was only surgical trauma. There wasn't any significant infection, only a little inflammation near the surface of the incision.

I felt rather like the new moon: the shadow of pain and death was still clearly visible to me—but only because the light was there to throw it into perspective. On the other hand, there were still small practicalities and indignities to be dealt with. I had to pee, and I couldn't sit up by myself, let alone squat over a chamber pot.

I had no idea what time it was, though with the moon like that, it couldn't be the middle of the night. The house was still, though—Lieutenant Macken had returned safely in late afternoon, bringing with him several other men, but they had been too exhausted for celebration; I could hear faint snoring from the floor below. I couldn't disturb everyone by calling out for Loretta Macken's assistance. With a sigh, I leaned gingerly over the side of the bed and cleared my throat.

"Sassenach? Are ye all right?" A segment of the darkness on the floor moved suddenly and resolved itself into a Jamie-shaped shadow.

"Yes. Are you?"

That got me the breath of a laugh.

"I'll do, Sassenach," he said softly, and I heard the rustle of his movement as he got his feet under him. "I'm glad ye feel well enough to ask. D'ye need water?"

"Er . . . rather the opposite, really," I said.

"Oh? Oh." He stooped, a pale blur in his shirt, to reach under the bed. "D'ye need help?"

"If I didn't, I wouldn't have waked you up," I said, a little testily. "I didn't think I could wait for Mrs. Macken or Dottie, though." He snorted a little and got me under the arms, lifting me into a sitting position.

"Now, then," he murmured. "It's no like ye've not done this—and a good many worse things—for me."

While this was true, it didn't make matters easier.

"You can let go now," I said. "Perhaps leave the room?"

"Perhaps not," he said, still mildly, but with a tone indicating that his mind was made up on the subject. "If I let go, ye'll fall on your face, and ye ken that perfectly well, so stop talkin' and be about your business now, aye?"

It took some time—anything that put pressure on my abdomen, including the act of urinating, hurt remarkably—but the business was accomplished and I was eased back down onto the pillow, gasping. Jamie bent and picked up the chamber pot, clearly intending to hurl the contents out the window in customary Edinburgh fashion.

"No, wait!" I said. "Keep that 'til morning."

He paused.

"What for?" he asked cautiously. Clearly he suspected I might still be unhinged from fever and be contemplating some grossly irrational use of the pot's contents, but he didn't like to say so, in case I had something logical, if bizarre, in mind. I would have laughed, but it hurt too much.

"I need to check, once there's light, to be sure there's no blood," I said. "My right kidney's very sore; I want to be sure there's no damage."

"Ah." He set the utensil down carefully and, to my surprise, opened the door and glided out, moving soft-footed as a hunting fox. I heard one squeak as he stepped on a stair tread, but nothing more until a glow betokened his return with a candlestick.

"Have a look, then," he said, picking up the pot again and bringing it to me. "I kent ye'd just fret about it did ye have to wait for daybreak."

He sounded resigned, but this small thoughtfulness brought me close to tears. He heard the catch in my breathing and leaned close, alarmed, bringing the light up to my face.

"Are ye all right, Sassenach? Is it bad, then?"

"No," I said, and wiped my eyes hastily on a corner of the sheet. "No—it—it's fine. I just—oh, Jamie, I love you!" I did give way to tears, then, snuffling and blubbering like an idiot. "I'm sorry," I said, trying to get hold of myself. "I'm all right, there's nothing wrong, it's just—"

"Aye, I ken fine what it's just," he said, and, setting the candle and pot on the floor, lay down on the bed beside me, balancing precariously on the edge.

"Ye're hurt, *a nighean*," he said softly, smoothing my hair off my wet cheeks. "And fevered and starved and worn to a shadow. There's no much of ye left, is there, poor wee thing?"

I shook my head and clung to him. "There's not much of you left, either," I managed to say, mumbling wetly into the front of his shirt.

He made a small amused noise and rubbed my back, very gently. "Enough, Sassenach," he said. "I'm enough. For now."

I sighed and fumbled under the pillow for a hankie to blow my nose.

"Better?" he asked, sitting up.

"Yes. Don't go, though." I put a hand on his leg, hard and warm under my hand. "Can you lie with me a minute? I'm awfully cold." I was, though I realized from the damp and salt on his skin that the room was quite hot. But loss of so much blood had left me chilled and gasping; I couldn't get through a sentence without stopping to breathe, and my arms were permanently goose-pimpled.

"Aye. Dinna move; I'll go round." He came round the bed and edged carefully in behind me. It was a narrow bed, barely wide enough to hold us closely pressed together.

I exhaled gingerly and relaxed against him in slow motion, reveling in the feel of his warmth and the solid comfort of his body.

"Elephants," I said, drawing the shallowest possible breath compatible with speaking. "When a female elephant is dying, sometimes a male will try to mate with her."

There was a marked silence behind me, and then a big hand came round and rested assessingly on my forehead.

"Either ye're fevered again, Sassenach," he said in my ear, "or ye have verra perverse fancies. Ye dinna really want me to—"

"No," I said hastily. "Not right this minute, no. And I'm not dying, either. The thought just came to me."

He made an amused Scottish noise and, lifting the hair off my neck, kissed my nape.

"Since ye're no dying," he said, "maybe that will do for the moment?"

I took his hand and placed it on my breast. Slowly I grew warmer, and my chilly feet, pressed against his shins, relaxed. The window now was filled with stars, hazy with the moistness of the summer night, and I suddenly missed the cool, clear, black-velvet nights of the mountains, the stars blazing huge, close enough to touch from the highest ridge.

"Jamie?" I whispered. "Can we go home? Please?"

"Aye," he said softly. He held my hand and the silence filled the room like moonlight, both of us wondering where home might be.

88

A WHIFF OF ROQUEFORT

I HADN'T SEEN ANY of the previous day's flock of visitors, though Jamie had told me about them. This day, though, brought one for me. Mrs. Macken brought him up the stairs, in spite of her advanced state of pregnancy, and showed him into my tiny room with great respect.

He wasn't in uniform and was—for him—quite subfusc, in a coat and breeches of the dull gray that was referred to (with accuracy) as "sad-colored," though he *had* taken the trouble to wear a dove-gray waistcoat with it that flattered his coloring.

"How are you, my dear?" he asked, taking off his hat. Not waiting for an answer, he came down on one knee by the bed, took my hand, and kissed it lightly. His blond hair had been washed, I saw—I smelled his bergamot soap—and trimmed to a uniform length. As that length was roughly an inch, the overall effect reminded me irresistibly of a fuzzy duckling. I laughed, then gasped and pressed a hand to my side.

"Dinna make her laugh!" Jamie said, glowering at John. His tone was cold, but I saw him take in John's aspect, and the corner of his own mouth twitched.

"I know," John said ruefully to me, passing a hand over his head and ignoring Jamie completely. "Isn't it dreadful? I ought really to wear a wig for the sake of public decency, but I couldn't bear it in the heat."

"Don't know that I blame you," I told him, and ran a hand through the damp mass of my own hair, drying on my shoulders. "Though I haven't yet got to the point of wanting to shave my head," I added pointedly, not quite turning my head toward Jamie.

"Don't. It wouldn't suit you at all," John assured me.

"How is your eye?" I asked, gingerly trying to raise myself on the pillow. "Let me have a look at it."

"Stay there," he said, and, leaning over me, opened both eyes wide. "I think it's quite good. It's still a bit tender to the touch and gets the odd twinge when I move it too far up or to the right, but—do you smell French cheese?" He sounded slightly startled.

"Mmm." I was gently prodding the flesh around the orbit, which showed only a slight residual swelling. The sclera was still quite bloodshot, but the bruising was much better. I thumbed down the lower lid to inspect the conjunctiva: a nice slippery pink, no sign of infection. "Does it water?"

"Only in strong sunlight, and not very much," he assured me, straightening up. He smiled at me. "Thank you, my dear."

Jamie didn't say anything, but the way he breathed had a distinctly edgy feel about it. I ignored him. If he chose to make a fuss, I couldn't bloody stop him.

"What are ye doing here?" he asked abruptly. John looked up at him, one brow raised, as though surprised to see him looming on the other side of my bed. John rose slowly to his feet, holding Jamie's eyes with his own.

"What do you think I'm doing?" he asked quietly. There was no hint of challenge in the question, and I could see Jamie suddenly check his own hostility, frowning slightly as he looked John over, considering.

One side of John's mouth turned up a little.

"Do you think I've come to fight you for the favors of this lady? Or to seduce her from your side?"

Jamie didn't laugh, but the line between his brows smoothed out.

"I don't," he said dryly. "And as ye dinna seem to be much damaged, I doubt ye've come to be doctored."

John gave an amiable bob of the head, indicating that this line of reasoning was correct.

"And I doubt, as well," Jamie continued, an edge creeping into his voice, "that ye've come to continue our previous discussion."

John inhaled slowly, and exhaled even slower, regarding Jamie with a level gaze. "Is it your opinion that anything remains to be said, regarding any part of that discussion?"

There was a marked silence. I glanced from one to the other, Jamie's eyes narrowed and John's eyes wide, both with fixed blue stares. All it lacked was growling and the slow lashing of tails.

"Are you armed, John?" I inquired pleasantly.

He glanced at me, startled. "No."

"Good," I said, grunting slightly as I struggled to sit up. "Then you obviously aren't going to kill *him*"—I nodded at Jamie, standing over me with fists half curled—"and if he didn't break your neck the first time, he isn't going to do it now. Are you?" I inquired, arching a brow at Jamie.

He looked down his nose at me, but I saw the slight relaxation of his mouth. And his hands. "Probably not."

"Well, then." I brushed the hair back from my face. "No point in hitting each other. And harsh language would detract from the pleasant nature of this visit, wouldn't it?"

Neither of them chose to answer this.

"That was not actually a rhetorical question," I said. "But let that go." I turned to John, folding my hands in my lap. "Flattered as I am by the attention, I don't think you came *solely* to inquire after my well-being. So if you'll pardon my vulgar curiosity . . . why *are* you here?"

He finally relaxed and, at my nod, took the stool, linking his fingers round his knee.

"I've come to ask your help," he said directly to Jamie. "But also"—it was slight, but I noticed the hesitation—"to make you an offer. Not as quid pro quo," he added. "The offer is not contingent on your assistance."

Jamie made a Scottish noise indicating deep skepticism but willingness to listen.

John nodded and took a breath before continuing. "You once mentioned to me, my dear, that—"

"Dinna be calling her that."

"Mrs. Fraser," John amended, and, with a polite bow to me, turned his attention to Jamie, "once mentioned that she—and you, I would imagine— had some acquaintance with General Arnold."

Jamie and I exchanged puzzled looks. He shrugged and folded his arms. "Aye, we do."

"Good. What I—and my brother"—I felt, rather than saw, Jamie's start at mention of Hal—"would ask of you is a note of introduction to Arnold, with your personal request that the general allow us official entrance into the city—and whatever aid he might find it convenient to give us—for the purpose of making a search for my son."

John let out the rest of his breath and sat, head down, not moving. Nobody moved.

At last, Jamie let out a long sigh and sat down on the room's other stool.

"Tell me," he said, resigned. "What's the wee bastard done now?"

THE STORY FINISHED, John inhaled, made to rub his bad eye, and luckily stopped in time.

"I'll put a bit more honey in that before you leave," I told him. "It will ease the grittiness." This non sequitur helped to bridge the awkward gap in the conversation left by Jamie's being struck momentarily speechless.

"Jesus," he said, and rubbed a hand hard over his face. He was still wearing the bloodstained shirt and breeches in which he'd fought; he hadn't shaved in three days, had barely slept or eaten, and looked like something you wouldn't want to meet in broad daylight, let alone a dark alley. He took a deep breath and shook his head like a dog shedding water.

"So ye think the two of them have gone to Philadelphia—William and this Richardson?"

"Probably not together—or at least not to begin with," John said. "William's groom said he left to find a couple of . . . er . . . girls who had gone from the camp. But we strongly suspect that this was a ploy by Richardson, to decoy William out of camp and intercept him on the road."

Jamie made an irascible noise.

"I should *like* to think the lad's no such a fat-heided gomerel as to go off wi' this Richardson. Not after the man sent him into the Great Dismal last year and nearly killed him."

"He told you that?"

"Oh. He didna tell ye that?" Jamie's voice might possibly have held a shade of scorn, had one been listening closely.

"I'm damned sure he didn't tell *you* anything," John replied, with an edge. "He hadn't seen you for years before he met you at Chestnut Street, I'd bet money he hasn't seen you since, and I'm reasonably sure I would have noticed had he mentioned Richardson in the hallway there."

"No," Jamie said briefly. "He told my nephew, Ian Murray. Or at least," he amended, "Ian got it from what he said, raving wi' fever when Ian got him out of the swamp. Richardson sent him wi' a message for some men in Dismal Town—men he said were Loyalists. But half the men in Dismal Town are named Washington."

John's appearance of pugnacity had vanished. He looked pale, and the fading bruises stood out like leprosy against his skin. He took a deep breath, glanced round the room, and, seeing a half-empty bottle of claret on the table, picked it up and drank a quarter of it without stopping.

He set it down, stifled a belch, rose with a brief nod and a "wait a moment," and went out, leaving Jamie and me staring at each other in bafflement.

This was not significantly assuaged by the reappearance of John, followed by the Duke of Pardloe. Jamie said something remarkably creative in *Gàidhlig*, and I gave him a look of startled appreciation.

"And a good day to you, too, General Fraser," Hal said, with a correct bow. Like John, he was dressed in civvies, though with a rather loud mulberry striped waistcoat, and I did wonder where he'd got it from.

"I have resigned my commission," Jamie said coldly. " 'Mr. Fraser' will do. May I ask to what we owe the honor of your presence, Your Grace?"

Hal's lips pressed tight together, but, with a glance at his brother, he obliged with a brief précis of his personal concern with Captain Richardson.

"And I do, of course, wish to retrieve my nephew, William—should he in fact be with Richardson. My brother informs me that you have doubts as to the probability of this being the case?"

"I do," Jamie said shortly. "My son is not a fool, nor a weakling." I caught the faint emphasis on *"my son,"* and so did both Greys, who stiffened slightly. "He wouldna go off on some feeble pretext, nor would he allow someone of whom he was suspicious to take him captive."

"You have a bloody lot of faith in a boy you haven't seen since he was six," Hal observed conversationally.

Jamie smiled, with considerable rue.

"I had the making of him until he was six," he said, and turned his gaze on John. "I ken what he's made of. And I ken who shaped him after that. Tell me I'm wrong, my lord."

There was a marked silence, broken only by Lieutenant Macken's voice below, calling plaintively to his wife about the location of his clean stockings.

"Well, then," Hal said with a sigh. "Where do *you* think William's gone, if he's not with Richardson?"

"He's gone after the girls he spoke of," Jamie said, lifting one shoulder in a shrug. "He told his groom so, did he not? D'ye ken who these lassies are?"

The Greys exchanged looks of muted chagrin, and I coughed, very carefully, holding a pillow to my stomach.

"If that's the case," I said, "then presumably he'll come back, once he's either found them or given up looking for them. Wouldn't he? Would he go AWOL over them—er . . . absent without leave, I mean?"

"He wouldn't have to risk that," Hal said. "He's been relieved of duty."

"What?" John exclaimed, rounding on his brother. "What the devil for?"

Hal sighed, exasperated. "Leaving camp when he was ordered to stay there in the middle of a battle, what else? Getting into a fight with another officer, ending up at the bottom of a ravine with a dent in his skull through being in the wrong place at the wrong time, and in general being a bloody nuisance."

"You're right, he *is* your son," I said to Jamie, amused. He snorted, but didn't look altogether displeased.

"Speaking of nephews," Jamie said to Hal, "ye seem remarkably well informed, Your Grace. Might ye know anything of an Indian scout named Ian Murray?"

Hal looked blank, but John's head turned quickly in Jamie's direction.

"Yes," he said. "I do. He was taken prisoner late on the day of battle and walked with me into camp, whereupon he killed another scout with a tomahawk and walked out again."

"Blood will tell," I murmured, though privately both shocked and worried. "Er . . . was he injured?"

"Aye, he was," Jamie answered brusquely. "He'd been shot wi' an arrow, in the shoulder. I couldna pull it, but I broke the shaft for him."

"And . . . no one's seen him since the night of the battle?" I asked, striving to keep my voice steady. The men exchanged glances, but none of them would meet my eyes.

"I, um, did give him a canteen of water mixed with brandy," John said, a little diffidently. "He wouldn't take a horse."

"Rachel will find him," Jamie said, as firmly as he could. "And I've asked Ian Mòr to watch out for the lad. He'll be all right."

"I trust your faith in your blood will be justified, sir," Hal said with a sigh, evidently meaning it. "But as we can do nothing about Murray, and the question of William's whereabouts is apparently moot for the moment . . . I hesitate to intrude my concerns regarding *my* blood, but I have stringent reasons for finding Captain Richardson, quite apart from anything he may have done or not done with William. And to that end . . ."

"Aye," Jamie said, and the tension in his shoulders relaxed. "Aye, of course, Your Grace. Sassenach, will ye have the goodness not to die whilst I go and ask Mrs. Macken for paper and ink?"

"We have some," John said, reaching into the leather pouch he'd been carrying under his arm. "Allow me." And proceeded to lay out paper, an inkhorn, a small bundle of quills, and a stub of red sealing wax.

Everyone watched as Jamie mixed the ink, trimmed a quill, and began. Knowing how laborious writing was for him and how much he'd hate being watched, I pushed myself up a little more, stifling a groan, and turned to Hal.

"John mentioned that you wanted to make us an offer," I said. "Of course we're happy to help, regardless. But out of curiosity—"

"Oh." Hal blinked but changed gears rapidly, fixing his gaze on me. "Yes. The offer I had in mind has nothing to do with Mr. Fraser's kind accommodation," he said. "John suggested it, as a matter of convenience for all concerned." He turned to his brother, who smiled at me.

"My house on Chestnut Street," John said. "Plainly I shan't be living there for the foreseeable future. And I understand that you had taken refuge with the printer's family in Philadelphia. Given your present fragile state of health"—he nodded delicately at the small heap of bloody dressings in the corner—"clearly it would be more comfortable for you to resume residence at my house. You—"

A deep Scottish noise interrupted him, and he looked up at Jamie, startled.

"The last time I was compelled to accept assistance from your brother, my lord," Jamie said precisely, staring at John, "I was your prisoner and incapable of caring for my own family. Now I am no man's prisoner, nor ever will be again. I shall make provision for my wife."

In dead silence, with all eyes fixed on him, he bent his head to the paper and slowly signed his name.

89

ONE DAY, COCK OF THE WALK—

NEXT DAY, A FEATHER DUSTER

H E'D GONE BY INSTINCT to fetch Madras, but paused to think on the way. If he found the girls, he couldn't bring them both back with him on the horse. He changed direction and plunged into the teamsters' park, emerging a brief time later with an ammunition cart, now sans ammunition, pulled by a large, rugged gray mule with half of one ear missing.

The mule was disinclined to move fast, but still made better time than two girls on foot might. How long a head start did they have? Maybe an hour, from what Zebedee had said, maybe longer.

"Heya!" he shouted, and snapped the whip over the mule's rump. The animal was surly, but not a fool, and lurched into a faster pace—though William suspected that this effort might be as much to outrun the swarming flies as in response to his own urging.

Once solidly in motion, though, the mule seemed able to keep it up without noticeable effort, and they trotted down the road at a tooth-rattling pace, easily passing farm carts, foragers, and a couple of scouting parties. Surely he would catch the girls up in no time.

He didn't. He drove nearly ten miles, by his estimation, before concluding that there was no way the girls could possibly have outrun him, and he turned back, searching carefully along the few farm roads that led off into fields. To and fro he went, inquiring of everyone he saw, growing hotter and more irritated by the moment.

Midway through the afternoon, the army caught up with him, marching columns overtaking the mule, which had slowed to a walk by now. Reluctantly, he turned about and continued with the army to camp. Perhaps Colenso had been wrong; maybe the girls hadn't left at all. In which case, he'd find them once the camp settled for the night.

He did not. He did find Zeb, though, and Colenso with him. Both were adamant that the girls were indeed gone—and William found no trace of them, though he made stubborn inquiries among the laundresses and cooks.

At last, he trudged through the camp in search of either Papa or Uncle Hal. Not that he expected either man to have any notion regarding the girls—but he somehow felt that he could not abandon his search without at least soliciting their help in putting out word of the girls. Two half-grown girls couldn't possibly outstrip an army, and—

He stopped dead in the middle of camp, letting men on their way to supper flow around him.

"Bloody hell," he said, too hot and tired even to make it an exclamation. "Colenso, you left-handed little bugger." And barely containing his exasperation—with himself as much as with his groom—he set off grimly to find Colenso Baragwanath.

Because Colenso *was* a left-handed little bugger. William had noticed that immediately, as he suffered from the same affliction himself. Unlike Colenso, though, William could tell the difference between his right hand and his left—and had a sense of direction. Colenso . . . didn't, and William wanted to kick himself for not remembering that.

"You bloody *idiot*," he muttered, wiping a sleeve across his sweating, dusty face. "Why didn't you think of that?"

Because it made little sense—once he paused to think about it—for the girls to have run off *ahead* of the army. Even if they were afraid of someone in the army, and even if they meant to reach New York, they would have been better served to have gone the other way, at least temporarily. Let the army march on well ahead, and then make their way wherever they meant to go.

He glanced at the sun, just barely still above the horizon, and heaved a deep, exasperated breath. Whatever else she might be, Jane wasn't a fool. First he'd find some supper, and then Colenso—but he'd give good odds that the morrow would find him on the road back toward Middletown.

HE FOUND THEM, just before noon. They saw him coming, but he'd seen them first: the two of them walking down the side of the road, each with a bundle in either hand. They glanced over their shoulders at the sound of his wheels, saw nothing alarming, turned back—and then Jane whirled round again, her face aghast as she realized who she'd just seen.

She dropped one of her bundles, clutched her younger sister by the wrist, and jerked her off the road. The road led through farmland here, with open fields on either side—but there was a sizable chestnut grove a few hundred yards ahead, and, despite William's shout, the girls ran for this as though the devil himself were after them.

Muttering under his breath, he pulled up, dropped the reins, and leapt out. Long-legged as he was, he failed to catch them before they reached the edge of the wood.

"Stop, for God's sake!" he bellowed. "I'm not going to hurt you!"

Fanny, hearing this, seemed disposed to stop, but Jane yanked her urgently on and they vanished among the rustling leaves.

William snorted and slowed down. Jane could make up her own mind—if she had one, which he was strongly inclined to doubt at the moment—but she hadn't any business to be dragging her little sister off through land that had been a battlefield only two days ago.

Broken trails and big crushed patches marred the fields, from soldiers running or artillery being dragged through it. He could smell death when he drew a deep breath; it made him uneasy. The stink of uncollected corpses swelling in the sun, bursting open, weltering with flies and maggots . . . On the one hand, he hoped the girls wouldn't stumble over such a sight. On the other, if they did, they'd likely come haring back out into his arms, screaming.

And corpses might not be the only things hiding in the folds and furrows of the countryside. His hand went automatically to his waist, groping for the hilt of his knife—which, of course, wasn't there.

"Fucking buggering shit-fucking *hell*!"

As though this had been a signal, a sudden racket broke out in the trees. Not a corpse; he could hear male voices, cursing, cajoling, and high-pitched shrieks. He snatched up a fallen branch and charged into the grove, shouting at the top of his lungs. He could hear them; they could certainly hear him, and the tone of the shouting changed. The girls were still shrieking, but less frantically, and the men—yes, more than one . . . two, three? Not more— were arguing, agitated, fearful. *Not English . . . not speaking English . . .*

"*Mistkerle!*" he bellowed at the top of his lungs. *Bloody stinking Hessians!* "*Feiglinge!*" *Shit-eating cowards!*

A great thrashing of leaves and snapping branches, and, peering through the trees, he saw that the lot of them—judging by the noise, the girls were still with them—were heading for the road.

He stopped yelling and instantly altered his own course, charging back toward the road, crashing heedless through brush and low-hanging branches, half-ripe chestnuts thumping off his head and shoulders. There! He saw a man push out of the trees, stumbling onto the road, and lunge back, grabbing. A louder shriek and Fanny came stumbling out in turn, the man gripping her by the neck.

William veered toward them and burst out running, shouting incoherent curses, brandishing his makeshift club. He must nonetheless have looked frightening in his uniform, for the man holding Fanny let go of her at once, turned, and ran like a rabbit, dust spurting from his feet. Fanny staggered and fell to her knees, but there was no blood, she was all right. . . .

"Jane!" He shouted. "Jane! Where are you?"

"Here! He—" Her voice was cut off suddenly, but he could see where she was, no more than ten feet from him, and dived for the wildly waving branches.

There were two men with her, one with a hand over her mouth, the other struggling to detach the bayonet from a brown Bess musket. William kicked the gun out of his hands, then lunged at the man, and in moments was on the ground, grappling with a burly man who might not know what to do with a bayonet but certainly was acquainted with battle of a more primitive sort.

They rolled to and fro, panting and gouging, twigs breaking with a sound like gunshots, cracking beneath their bodies. He heard dimly a screech from the other man—perhaps Jane had bitten him; good girl!—but had no attention to spare for anything but the man who was trying earnestly to throttle him. He had a grip on the man's wrists, and, with a faint memory of Ban Tarleton, jerked the man closer and butted him in the face.

It worked again; there was a horrible crunch, hot blood spattered his face, and the man's grip relaxed. William squirmed away, his head swimming, only to find himself facing the other man, who had evidently succeeded in freeing the bayonet, for he had a foot of sharpened steel in his hand.

"Here! Here!" Jane popped out of a bush right beside William, startling him, and shoved something into his hand. It was, thank God, a knife. Nothing to rival the bayonet, but a weapon.

Jane was still by him; he grasped her arm and began to walk backward, knife held low and threatening in his other hand. The Hessian—Christ, was it one of the sons of bitches who'd hit him in the head? He couldn't tell; there were spots floating in front of his eyes, and the men had thrown away their telltale green coats. Did all sons of bitches wear green coats? he wondered muzzily.

Then they were on the road, and things became confused. He thought he'd stuck one of the men, and the girls were screaming again, and once he found himself in the roadway, choking on dust, but came up again before one of the bastards could kick him in the face . . . and then there was a shout and the pounding of hooves, and he let go of the man whose arm he was gripping and whirled round to see Rachel Hunter on a mule, coming fast down the road, swinging her bonnet from its strings and shouting, "Uncle Hiram! Cousin Seth! Hurry! Come on! Come on! Help me!"

His mule jerked its head up from the grass and, seeing Rachel's mount, brayed in greeting. This seemed to be the last straw for the deserters, who stood gaping for one stunned moment, then turned and galloped down the road after their vanished fellow.

William stood swaying for a moment, gasping for breath, then dropped his knife and sat down abruptly.

"What," he said, in a voice that sounded petulant even to his own ears, "are *you* doing here?"

Rachel ignored him. She swung down from her mule, landing with a small thump, and led it to William's mule, tethering it to the cart. Only then did she walk over to where William sat, slowly brushing dirt from his knees and counting his limbs.

"You wouldn't happen to have seen a couple of girls, would you?" he asked, tilting his head back to look up at Rachel.

"Yes. They ran into the trees," she said, nodding toward the chestnut grove. "As for what I am doing here, I have been up and down this road three times, looking for thy cousin, Ian Murray." She gave him a hard look as she said this, as though daring him to contradict her assertion regarding his kinship with Murray. Under other circumstances, he might have taken offense, but at the moment he hadn't the energy. "I assume that if thee had seen him, dead or alive, thee would tell me?"

"Yes," he said. There was a swollen knot between his eyes, where he had butted the deserter, and he rubbed this gingerly.

She drew a deep breath, sighed loudly, and wiped her sweating face on her apron, before replacing her bonnet. She looked him over, shaking her head.

"Thee is a rooster, William," Rachel said mournfully. "I saw this in thee before, but now I know it for certain."

"A rooster," he repeated coldly, brushing dirt from his sleeve. "Indeed. A vain, crowing, gaudy sort of fellow—that's what you think me?"

Her brows went up. They were not the level brows of classic beauty; they quirked up at the ends, even when her face was at rest, giving her a look of interested intelligence. When she was *not* at rest, they slanted with a sharp, wicked sort of look. They did this for an instant now, but then relaxed. A little.

"No," she said. "Has thee ever kept chickens, William?"

"Not for some years," he said, examining the hole torn in the elbow of his coat, the hole ripped in the shirt beneath, and the bloody scrape upon his bare elbow. Bloody hell, one of the buggers had come close to taking his arm off with that bayonet. "What with one thing and another, my recent acquaintance with chickens has been limited largely to breakfast. Why?"

"Why, a rooster is a creature of amazing courage," Rachel said, rather reproachful. "He will throw himself into the face of an enemy, even knowing he will die in the attack, and thus buy his hens time to escape."

William's head jerked up.

"My *hens?*" he said, outrage bringing the blood to his face. "*My* hens?" He glanced in the direction Jane and Fanny had taken, then glared back at Rachel. "Do you not realize that they are whores?"

She rolled her eyes at him in exasperation. She bloody rolled her eyes at him!

"I expect I have been living with an army for somewhat longer than thee has thyself," she said, making a decided effort to look down her nose at him. "I am familiar with women who lack both property and protection and are thus reduced to the dreadful expedient of selling their bodies, yes."

" 'Dreadful expedient'?" he repeated. "You realize that I—"

She stamped a foot and glared at him.

"Will thee stop repeating everything I say?" she demanded. "I was attempting to pay thee a compliment—while, as thy friend, lamenting the end thy roosterishness will surely bring thee to. Whether thy companions are whores or not—and whether thee pays for their company—is irrelevant to the matter."

"Irre—" William began in indignation, but choked the word off before he could be further accused of repetition. "I don't bloody pay them!"

"Irrelevant," she repeated, doing it herself, by God! "Thee has behaved in exactly the same way on my own behalf, after all."

"You—" He stopped abruptly. "I have?"

She exhaled strongly, eyeing him in a manner suggesting that she would have kicked him in the shins or stamped on his toes if not reminded of her Quaker principles.

"Twice," she said, elaborately polite. "The occasions were so negligible, I suppose—or I was—that thee has forgotten?"

"Remind me," he said dryly, and, ripping a chunk from the torn lining of his coat, used it to wipe the mud—and blood, he saw—from his face.

She snorted briefly, but obliged. "Does thee not recall the odious creature who attacked us in that dreadful place on the road in New York?"

"Oh, that." His belly clenched in recollection. "I didn't exactly do it on your account. Nor did I have much choice in the matter. He bloody tried to cave my head in with an ax."

"Hmph. I think thee has some fatal attraction for ax-wielding maniacs," she said, frowning at him. "That Mr. Bug actually *did* hit thee in the head with an ax. But when thee killed him later, it was to protect Ian and me from a similar fate, was it not?"

"Oh, indeed," he said, a little crossly. "How do you know it wasn't just revenge for his attacking *me*?"

"Thee may be a rooster, but thee is not a vengeful rooster," she said reprovingly. She pulled a kerchief from her pocket and blotted her face, which was growing shiny with perspiration again. "Should we not look for thy . . . companions?"

"We should," he said, with a degree of resignation, and turned toward the grove. "I think they'll run if I go in after them, though."

Rachel made an impatient noise and, pushing past him, stomped into the woods, rustling through the brush like a hungry bear. The thought made him grin, but a sudden yelp wiped the smile off his face. He started after her, but she was already backing out, yanking Jane by one arm, meanwhile trying to avoid the wild swipes Jane was making with her free hand, fingers clawed and slashing toward Rachel's face.

"Stop that!" William said sharply, and, stepping forward, grabbed Jane by the shoulder and jerked her out of Rachel's grasp. She turned blindly on *him*, but he had longer arms than Rachel and could easily hold her at bay.

"Will you quit that?" he said crossly. "No one's going to hurt you. Not now."

She did stop, though she looked back and forth between him and Rachel like a cornered animal, panting and the whites of her eyes showing.

"He's right," Rachel said, edging cautiously toward her. "Thee is quite safe now. What is thy name, Friend?"

"She's called Jane," William said, gradually loosing his hold, ready to grab her again if she bolted. "I don't know her surname."

She didn't bolt, but didn't speak, either. Her dress was torn at the neck, and she put a hand to the torn edge automatically, trying to fit it back in place.

"Have you seen my bundle?" she said, in an almost ordinary voice. "I have a housewife in it. I need a needle."

"I'll look for it," Rachel said soothingly. "Did thee drop it in the wood?"

"Thir!" Fanny spoke quite sharply behind William, and he became aware that she'd been there for a few moments; she'd said it once or twice before.

"What?" he said impatiently, half-turning toward her while trying to keep both Jane and Rachel in view.

"There'th an Indian in there," she said, and pointed toward the woods. "Ian!"

Rachel ran across the road, fleet as a snipe, and vanished into the trees. William followed hastily, hand on his knife. There was likely more than one Indian in these woods, and if it *wasn't* Murray . . .

But he could tell from Rachel's exclamation of mingled horror and relief from the depths of the wood that it was.

Murray was crumpled into a heap in the deep shadow at the base of a big pine tree, needles half-scuffled over him; evidently he'd tried to disguise himself but had passed out before managing the job.

"He's breathing," Rachel said, and he heard the catch in her voice.

"Good," William said briefly, and, squatting beside her, put a hand on Murray's shoulder to turn him over. The apparently insensible body gave a shriek, contorted violently, and ended on his knees, swaying and glaring wildly round, clutching the shoulder William had seized. Only then did William see the dried blood streaked down the arm and the fresh dribbles running down from the broken shaft of an arrow embedded in the swollen flesh.

"Ian," Rachel said. "Ian, it's me. It's all right now. I have thee." Her voice was steady, but her hand trembled as she touched him.

Murray gulped air, and his bleared gaze seemed to clear, traveling from Fanny and Jane, who had come into the grove after William, pausing briefly with a frown at William's face, then settling and easing as he saw Rachel. He closed his eyes and let out a long breath.

"Taing do Dhia," he said, and sank back on his haunches.

"Water," Rachel said urgently, shaking the empty canteen that lay on the ground beside Ian. "Has thee got any water, William?"

"I have," said Jane, stirring out of her trance and groping for the canteen round her neck. "Will he be all right, do you think?"

Rachel didn't answer but helped Murray to drink, her face pale with anxiety. Murray's own face bore the remnants of war paint, William saw with interest, and a brief ripple raised the hairs on his scalp, wondering whether Murray had killed any of the British soldiers. At least the bugger wasn't sporting any scalps on his belt, British or otherwise.

Rachel was conversing now in low tones with Murray, glancing now and then at William, a certain speculation in her gaze.

William was mildly surprised to find that he knew exactly what she was thinking. Though perhaps it wasn't so surprising; he'd been wondering much the same thing: could Murray ride the mule? Plainly he couldn't walk far. And if he couldn't . . . could Rachel persuade William to take Murray and her into the city in the wagon?

He felt his stomach clench at the thought of going back to Philadelphia.

His own gaze flicked toward Jane—only to discover that she wasn't there. Neither was Fanny.

He was halfway to his feet when he heard Rachel's mule bray in protest, and he made it to the road in seconds, to find Jane engaged in a futile struggle to push Fanny up into the saddle. The younger girl was trying valiantly, clutching at the mule's bristly mane and attempting to get a leg up, but the mule was objecting strenuously to this sort of interference, tossing his head and backing away from Jane, leaving Fanny's legs kicking desperately in the air.

William reached her in three paces and clasped her about the waist.

"Let go, sweetheart," he said calmly. "I've got you." Fanny was surprisingly solid, given her fragile appearance. She smelled sweet, too, though her neck was grubby and her clothes grimed with mud and road dust.

He put her down and turned a firm eye on Jane, who was looking defiant. He'd been acquainted with her long enough now, though, to see that the uplifted chin and tight jaw were covering fear, and, in consequence, spoke more gently than he might have.

"Where were you planning to go?" he asked, in a tone of mild interest.

"I—well, New York," she answered, but uncertainly, and her eyes were darting to and fro, as though expecting some threat to manifest itself from the peaceful countryside.

"Without me? I'm hurt, madam, that you should have conceived a sudden dislike of my company. What have I done to offend you, pray?"

She pressed her lips tight together, but he could see that his jesting tone had settled her a little; she was still red in the face from exertion, but not breathing in that jerky way.

"I think we must part, Lord Ellesmere," she said, with a touchingly absurd attempt at formality. "I—we—shall make our own way now."

He folded his arms, leaned back against the wagon, and looked down his nose at her.

"How?" he inquired. "You haven't any money, you don't have a mount, and you wouldn't get five miles on foot without running into someone else like those German fellows."

"I—have a little money." She smoothed a hand over her skirt, and he saw that there was indeed a bulge where her pocket lay. Despite his intent to remain calm, there was still a spring of anger in him, and it burst forth at this.

"Where did you get it?" he demanded, straightening up and grabbing her by the wrist. "Did I not forbid you to whore?"

She yanked her hand smartly free and took two quick steps back.

"You haven't any right to forbid me to do any damned thing I want!" she snapped, color burning high in her cheeks. "And it's none of your business, but I didn't make this money on my back!"

"What, then? Pimping your sister?"

She slapped him, hard. He shouldn't have said it and knew it, but the knowledge—and his stinging cheek—only made him angrier.

"I *should* bloody leave you here, you—"

"Good! That's just what I want you to do! You—you—"

Before either of them could decide upon an epithet, Rachel and Ian emerged from the wood, the tall Scot leaning heavily on her. William gave Jane a final glare and went to help, taking Murray's weight on one side. The man stiffened, resisting for a moment, but then yielded; he had to.

"What happened?" William asked, nodding at the broken arrow shaft. "A private quarrel or just bad aim?"

That made Murray's mouth twitch, reluctantly.

"Fortunes of war," he said hoarsely, and sat down at the open tailboard of the wagon. He was breathing like a winded ox, but had possession of himself. He gave William a brief glance.

"What are ye doing here, *a fang Sassunaich?*"

"None of your business, but a good job I was," William replied, just as briefly. He turned to Rachel, having made up his mind on the moment.

"Take the wagon and see the girls somewhere safe."

"That—" Rachel began, but then looked round, startled, as Jane and Fanny ran past her, crossed the road, and dived into the wood. "Where are they going?"

"Oh, bloody hell," William said, already striding across the road. "Wait here."

THEY COULDN'T outrun him, and they had nothing in the way of woodcraft that would enable them to lie hidden. He caught Fanny—again the slower of the two—by the back of her pinafore as she was scrambling over a log. To his astonishment, she squirmed round in his grasp and launched herself at him, scratching at his face and screaming, "Wun, Janie, *wun!*"

"Will you bloody stop that?" he said crossly, holding her at arm's length. "Ow!" For she had sunk her teeth into his wrist, and he dropped her.

She eeled over the log and bounded away like a rabbit, still screaming her head off. He started to follow her, and then thought better. On the one hand, he had a strong impulse to abandon them, but on the other . . . He remembered Mac telling him about plovers one day as they sat near Watendlath Tarn, eating bread and cheese, watching the birds.

"Bugger off, Mac," he said under his breath, and shoved thought of both Helwater and the groom ruthlessly away. But remembered, whether he wanted to or not.

"They run about and call out as though wounded, see?" Mac's arm had been round him, keeping him from going too close to the fluttering bird. *"But it's to draw ye away from their nest, lest ye crush the eggs or damage the young. Look canny, though, and ye'll see them."*

William stood quite still, calming his own breath and looking round, slow and careful, barely moving his head. And there indeed was the plover's nest: alas for Jane, she had worn her pink calico today, and her rosy buttocks rounded smoothly up out of the grass ten feet away, quite like a pair of eggs in a nest, at that.

He walked quietly, without haste. Nobly resisting the strong urge to smack her beguilingly curved behind, he instead laid a hand flat on her back.

"Tag," he said. "You're it."

She wriggled out from under his hand and shot up onto her feet.

"What?" she said. "What the bloody hell do you mean?" She was wild-eyed and nervy, but cross, as well.

"You've never played tag?" he asked, feeling foolish even as he said it.

"Oh," she said, and let out her breath a little. "It's a game. I see. Yes, but not for a long time."

He supposed one *didn't* play tag in a brothel.

"Look," she said tersely, "we want to go. I—I appreciate what you've done for me—for us. But—"

"Sit down," he said, and compelled her to do so, leading her to the log over which her sister had escaped and pressing on her shoulder until she reluctantly sat. He then sat down beside her and took her hand in his. It was very small, cold and damp from the grass where she'd hidden.

"Look," he said, firmly but not—he hoped—unkindly, "I'm not letting you run off. That's flat. If you want to go to New York with the army, I'll take you; I've already said so. If you want to return to Philadelphia—"

"No!" Her terror at the thought was clear now. She pulled desperately at her hand, but he wouldn't let go.

"Is it because of Captain Harkness? Because—"

She gave a cry that might have come from the throat of a wild bird caught in a trap, and he tightened his grip on her wrist. It was fine-boned and slender, but she was surprisingly strong.

"I know you stole the gorget back" he said. "It's all right. No one's going to find out. And Harkness won't touch you again; I promise you that."

She made a small bubbling noise that might have been a laugh or a sob.

"Colonel Tarleton—you know, the green dragoon that made advances to you?—he told me that Harkness was absent without leave, hasn't come back to his regiment. Do you know anything about that?"

"No," she said. "Let me go. Please!"

Before he could answer this, a small, clear voice piped up from the trees a few yards away.

"You'd best tew him, Janie."

"Fanny!" Jane swung round toward her sister, momentarily forgetting that she was pinioned. "Don't!"

Fanny stepped out of the shadows, wary but curiously composed.

"If you don't, I wiw," she said, her big brown eyes fixed on William's face. "He won't thtop." She came a little closer, cautious but not afraid. "If I tew you," she said, "do you pwomise not to take us back?"

"Back where?"

"To Phiwadelphia," she said. "*Or* the army."

He sighed, exasperated, but short of torturing the answer out of one of the girls, clearly no progress would be made unless he agreed. And he was beginning to have a cold feeling under the ribs about just what the answer might be.

"I promise," he said, but Fanny hung back, distrustful.

"Sweaw," she said, folding her arms.

"Sw—oh. Bloody hell. All right, then—I swear on my honor."

Jane made a small, dreary noise that was still a laugh. That stung.

"Do you think I haven't got any?" he demanded, turning on her.

"How would I know?" she countered, sticking out her chin. It wobbled, but she stuck it out. "What does honor look like?"

"For your sake, you'd better hope it looks a lot like me," he told her, but then turned to Fanny. "What do you want me to swear on?"

"Your mudder's head," she said promptly.

"My mother's dead."

"Your favver, den."

He drew a long, deep breath. *Which one?*

"I swear on my father's head," he said evenly.

And so they told him.

⁓

"I KNEW HE'D come back," Jane said. She was sitting on the log, hands clasped between her thighs and eyes on her feet. "They always do. The bad ones." She spoke with a sort of dull resignation, but her lips tightened at the memory. "They can't stand to think you've got away without . . . without. I thought it would be me, though."

Fanny was sitting beside her sister, as close as she could get, and now she put her arms around Jane and hugged her, her face in Jane's calico shoulder.

"I'm sowwy," she whispered.

"I know, lovie," Jane said, and patted Fanny's leg. A fierce look came into her face, though. "It's not your fault, and don't ever—*ever*—think so."

William's throat felt thick with disgust at the thought. That beautiful, flower-faced little girl, taken by—

"Her maidenhead's worth ten pound," Jane reminded him. "Mrs. Abbott was saving her, waiting for a rich man with a taste for new-hatched chicks. Captain Harkness offered her twenty." She looked directly at William for the first time. "I wasn't having that," she said simply. "So I asked Mrs. Abbott to send us up together; I said I could help keep Fanny from making a fuss. I knew what he was like, see," she said, and pressed her lips involuntarily together for an instant. "He wasn't the sort to plow you like a bull and have it done. He'd play with you, making you undress a bit at a time and—and do things—while he told you all about what *he* meant to do."

And so it had been easy to come behind him while he was watching Fanny, with the knife she'd taken from the kitchen hidden in the folds of her petticoats.

"I meant to stab him in the back," she said, looking down again. "I saw a man stabbed that way once. But he saw on Fanny's face what I—it wasn't her fault, she couldn't help it showing," she added quickly. "But he turned round quick and there wasn't any choice."

She'd plunged the knife into Harkness's throat and wrenched it free, intending to stab again. But that hadn't been necessary. "There was blood everywhere." She'd gone pale in the telling, her hands wrapped in her apron.

"I frew up," Fanny added matter-of-factly. "It was a mess."

"I expect it was," William said dryly. He was trying not to envision the scene—the candlelight, the spraying blood, the panicked girls—with remarkably little success. "How did you get away?"

Jane shrugged. "It was my room, and he'd bolted the door. And nobody was surprised when Fanny started screaming," she added, with a trace of bitterness.

There was a basin and pitcher of water, the usual rags for mess; they'd washed themselves hastily, changed clothes, and climbed out the window.

"We found a ride on a farmer's wagon, and . . . you know the rest." She closed her eyes for a moment, as though reliving "the rest," and then opened them and looked up at him, her gaze dark as shadowed water.

"Now what?" she asked.

WILLIAM HAD BEEN asking himself that question for the last several moments of Jane's story. Having met Harkness himself, he had considerable sympathy for Jane's action, but—

"You planned it," he said, giving her a sharp look. Her head was bent, her unbound hair hiding her face. "You took the knife, you had clothes to change into, you knew how to get down from the window and get away."

"Tho?" said Fanny, in a remarkably cold voice for a girl of her age.

"So why kill him?" he asked, transferring his attention to Fanny, but keeping a wary eye on Jane. "You were going to leave anyway. Why not just escape before he came?"

Jane raised her head and turned it, looking him directly in the eye.

"I wanted to kill him," she said, in a perfectly reasonable voice that chilled him despite the warmth of the day.

"I . . . see."

He saw more than the vision of Jane, with her delicate white wrists, plunging a knife into Captain Harkness's thick red throat while her little sister screamed. He saw Rachel's face, pale among the leaves, six feet away. From her expression, it was apparent that she had heard everything.

He cleared his throat.

"Is, um, Mr. Murray all right?" he asked politely. Jane and Fanny whirled, wide-eyed.

"He fainted," Rachel replied. She was eyeing the younger girls in much the same way that they were looking at her, with a gaze of fascinated horror. "His shoulder is badly inflamed. I came to see if thee had any brandy."

He fumbled in his pocket and withdrew a small silver flask with the Grey family arms engraved upon it.

"Whisky do for you?" he asked, handing it over. Rachel looked surprised; whisky wasn't a popular drink, but Lord John had always had a taste for it and William had taken to it himself—though now, knowing the truth about his disgraceful taint of Scottish blood, he wasn't sure he'd ever be able to drink the stuff again.

"It will, I thank thee." She stood holding it for a moment, clearly wanting to go to Murray but also hesitant to leave. He felt rather grateful to her for that hesitancy; he would as soon not be alone with Jane and Fanny—or, rather, he didn't want to be alone with the decision as to what the devil to do about them.

Rachel appeared to correctly interpret this feeling, for with a brief "I'll bring it right back," she disappeared in the direction of the road.

No one spoke. After that one direct look, Jane had bent her head again and sat quietly, though one hand restlessly smoothed the fabric of her skirt across one round thigh, over and over.

Fanny ran a hand over the crown of Jane's head in a protective gesture, while staring at William with a complete lack of expression. He found it unnerving.

What *was* he to do with them? Of course they couldn't go back to Philadelphia. And he dismissed as unworthy the impulse simply to abandon them to their own devices. But—

"Why not go to New York with the army?" he asked, his voice seeming unnaturally loud, harsh to his own ears. "What made you run yesterday?"

"Oh." Jane looked up slowly, her eyes a little unfocused, as though she had been dreaming. "I saw *him* again. The green dragoon. He'd wanted me to go with him the night before, and I wouldn't. But I saw him again yesterday morning and thought he was looking for me." She swallowed. "I told you—I know the ones who don't give up."

"Very perceptive of you," he said, eyeing her with some respect. "He doesn't. You misliked him on sight, then?" Because he didn't think for an instant that his having forbidden her to ply her trade would have stopped her, had she wanted to.

"It wasn't that," she said, and flicked Banastre Tarleton away with the sort of abrupt gesture one uses to shoo insects. "But he'd come to the brothel before, last year. He didn't go with me then, he chose another girl—but I knew if he spent much time with me, he'd likely remember why I seemed familiar to him. He said I did," she added, "when he came up to me in the bread line."

"I see." He paused. "So you did want to go to New York—but not with the army. Is that right?"

Jane shrugged, angry. "Does it matter?"

"Why the devil shouldn't it matter?"

"When has it *ever* mattered what a whore wants?" She sprang up and stamped across the clearing, leaving him staring after her in astonishment.

"What's wrong with her?" he demanded, turning to Fanny. The younger girl eyed him dubiously, lips pressed together, but then gave a little shrug.

"She thinks you might give her to a conthable or a magith-trate," she said, struggling a bit with "magistrate." "Or maybe to the army. It was a tholdier she killed."

William rubbed a hand over his face. In fact, the thought of delivering Jane to justice *had* flitted through his mind, in the wake of the shock of learning of her crime. The thought hadn't outlasted its birth, though.

"I wouldn't do that," he said to Fanny, striving to sound reasonable. She looked at him skeptically, under level dark brows.

"Why wouldn' you?"

"Excellent question," he said dryly. "And I haven't got an answer. But I suppose I don't need one."

He lifted a brow at her, and she gave a small snort of a laugh. Jane was edging along the far side of the clearing, glancing back toward Fanny every few seconds; her intent was clear—but she wouldn't go without her sister. He was sure of that much.

"Since you're here with me," he observed, "and *not* over there with your sister . . . you don't want to run, and you know she won't go without you. Ergo, I conclude that you don't think I'd give her up to justice."

She shook her head, slow and solemn as an owl.

"Jane says I don' know anyting about men yed, but I *do*."

He sighed.

"God help me, Frances, you do."

THERE WAS NO further conversation until Rachel returned a few minutes later.

"I can't lift him," she said directly to William, ignoring the girls for the moment. "Will thee help me?"

He rose at once, relieved by the prospect of physical action, but glanced over his shoulder at Jane, still hovering by the far side of the clearing like a hummingbird.

"We'll be heah," Fanny said quietly. He gave her a nod, and went.

He found Murray lying by the side of the road, near the wagon. The man wasn't unconscious, but the influence of the fever upon him was clear; his gaze was bleared and his speech slurring.

"I c'n walk."

"Like hell you can," William said briefly. "Hold on to my arm."

He got the man sitting upright and had a look for himself at the wounded shoulder. The wound itself wasn't that bad; it was apparent no bones were broken and it hadn't bled a lot. On the other hand, the flesh was red and swollen and starting to suppurate. He leaned close and took an unobtrusive sniff—not unobtrusive enough: Rachel noticed.

"There's no gangrene," she said. "I think there will not—I think things will be well, so long as we can get him to a doctor soon. What does thee mean to do about thy girls?" she added abruptly.

He didn't bother telling her again that they weren't *his*. Evidently they were, at least in terms of immediate responsibilities.

"I don't know," he admitted, rising to his feet. He glanced into the woods, but the clearing was far enough in that there was no flicker of garment or movement visible.

"They can't go to Philadelphia, and I can't take them back to the army. The best I can think of just now is to find them some place of refuge in one of the little villages hereabouts and cache them there until I can make some provision to get them to . . . to someplace safer." *Wherever the hell that might be. Canada?* he wondered wildly.

Rachel shook her head decidedly.

"Thee has no notion how people talk in small places—or how quickly news and rumor spread." She glanced down at Murray, who was still sitting upright but swaying, his eyes half closed.

"They have no other profession," she said. "And it would be quickly apparent to anyone what that profession is. They require not only refuge but refuge with people who will not cast them out once that becomes known."

She was brown with the sun—her blue calico bonnet had fallen off in the struggle with Jane and hung back over her shoulders—but her face paled when she looked at Murray. She clenched her fists, closed her eyes for an instant, then opened them, straightening to her full height, and looked William in the eye.

"There is a small settlement of Friends, perhaps two hours' travel from here. No more than three or four farms. I know of it from one of the women who came to Valley Forge with her husband. The girls could be kept safe there, for a while, at least."

"No!" Murray said. "Ye canna be . . ." He paused, eyes going out of focus, and braced himself on his sound arm, still swaying. He swallowed thickly. "No," he repeated. "Not . . . safe."

"It isn't," William agreed. "Three young women on the road, alone? And without even a pistol to defend yourselves?"

"If I had a pistol I would not use it," Rachel pointed out with some asperity. "Nor a cannon, come to that."

Murray laughed—or at least made a noise that might pass for amusement.

"Aye," he managed, and stopped to breathe before getting the next words out. "You take them," he said to William. "I'll . . . do here, fine."

"Thee bloody *won't*," Rachel said fiercely. She grabbed William's arm and pulled him closer to Murray. "Look at him! Tell him, since he professes not to believe me."

William looked, reluctantly, glancing at Murray's face, pale as suet and slick with an unhealthy sweat. Flies clustered thick on Murray's shoulder; he lacked the strength to brush them away.

"Merde," William muttered under his breath. Then louder, though still with reluctance, "She's right. You need a doctor, if you're to have a chance of keeping your arm."

That thought evidently hadn't struck Murray; death, yes—amputation, no. He turned his head and frowned at the wound.

"Bloody hell," William said, and turned to Rachel.

"All right," he said. "Tell me where this settlement is. I'll take them."

She grimaced, fists balling up at her sides. "Even Friends may not take well to the sudden appearance of a stranger who asks them to give indefinite sanctuary to a murderess. I am not a stranger and can plead the girl's case better than thee can." She drew a breath that swelled her bosom noticeably and looked at Murray, then turned her head to give William a piercing look.

"If I do this, thee must see him safe."

"*I* must?"

"Rachel!" Murray said hoarsely, but she ignored him.

"Yes. We'll have to take the wagon, the girls and I."

William drew a breath of his own, but he could see that she was right. He could also see just what the decision to save Jane was costing her.

"All right," he said tersely. He reached up and took the gorget from his neck and handed it to her. "Give Jane this. She may need it, if they find themselves on their own." Oddly, the removal of the gorget seemed a weight off his mind, as well. Even the possibility of being arrested if anyone in Philadelphia recognized him didn't trouble him overmuch.

He was about to remove his incriminating coat and waistcoat—he'd have to hide those somewhere—when Rachel stepped close to him and laid a hand on his arm.

"This man is my heart and my soul," she said simply, looking up into his face. "And he is thy own blood, whatever thee may presently feel about the fact. I trust thee to see him safe, for all our sakes."

William gave her a long look, thought of several possible replies, and made none of them, but gave a curt nod.

"Where should I take him?" he asked. "To my—to Lady J—I mean, to Mrs. F—I *mean*, God damn it," he amended, feeling the blood rise in his cheeks, "to his aunt?"

Rachel looked at him, startled.

"Thee doesn't know? Of course thee doesn't, how could thee?" She waved off her own denseness, impatient. "His aunt was shot in the course of the battle, outside Tennent Church, where she was tending the wounded."

William's annoyance was doused at once, as though ice water had been poured on his head, flooding his veins.

"Is she dead?"

"By the grace of our Lord, no," she said, and he felt the tightness in his chest relax a little. "Or at least she wasn't yesterday," she amended with a frown. "Though very badly hurt." The tightness returned.

"She is in the Macken house in the village of Freehold—about six miles in that direction." She nodded down the road. "My brother is likely there, as well, or nearby; there are still wounded from the battle there. He can deal with I-Ian's wound." For the first time, her voice lost its steadiness as her eyes went to her betrothed.

Murray's eyes were sunken and glazed with fever, but he had sufficient command of himself to reach out his good hand to her. The movement put weight on the bad arm and he grimaced, but Rachel was kneeling beside him in an instant, arms around him.

William coughed and turned discreetly away to leave them a moment's privacy in which to make their farewells. Whatever his own feelings, they deserved that. He'd seen many wounds go bad, and reckoned Murray's chances as no better than even. On the other hand, the man was apparently both a bloody Scot *and* a Mohawk, and both races were notoriously hard to kill.

He had walked away from the road, and his eye now caught the flutter of pink fabric behind a bush.

"Jane!" he called. "Is that you?"

"Yes," she said. She stepped out into the open, folded her arms, and pointed her chin at him. "What do you mean to do? With me, I mean."

"Miss Hunter is going to take you and Fanny to a safe place," he said, as gently as he could. In spite of her brave façade, she reminded him of a fawn, dappled light coming through the trees mottling her face and gown, making her seem shy and insubstantial, as though she might fade into the forest in the next breath. "I'll send word to you there when I've made some . . . suitable arrangement."

"Her?" Jane shot a surprised glance toward the road. "Why? Why can't you take us? Doesn't she want to stay with her—the Indian?"

"Miss Hunter will have time to explain everything to you on the way." He hesitated, unsure what else to say to her. From the road, he heard the distant murmur of voices, Rachel and Ian Murray. He couldn't make out the words, but it didn't matter; what they were saying to each other was plain. He felt a small, sharp pain under his third waistcoat button and coughed, trying to dislodge it.

"Thank you, thir," said a soft voice behind him, and he turned to find Fanny at his elbow. She took his hand, turned it palm upward, and planted a small, warm kiss in the center.

"I—you're most welcome, Miss Fanny," he said, smiling at her in spite of everything. She nodded to him, very dignified, and walked out to the road, leaving him with Jane.

For a moment, they stood staring at each other.

"I offered you a lot more than a kiss," she said quietly. "You didn't want it. I haven't got anything else to give you in thanks."

"Jane," he said. "It's not—I didn't—" And then stopped, desperately sorry but helpless to think of anything he could possibly say in reply. "Safe travels, Jane," he said at last, his throat tight. "Goodbye."

90

IT'S A WISE CHILD
WHO KNOWS HIS FATHER

IT WAS APPARENT that, while sound, Rachel's mule wasn't up to the weight of two men the size of William and Ian Murray. No matter; they couldn't go any faster than a walk in any case; Murray could ride, and William would walk alongside to make sure the bastard didn't fall off.

Murray managed to get up into the saddle, in spite of having only one functional hand; Rachel had roughly bandaged his wounded arm and put it into a sling torn from her underpetticoat. William didn't offer him assistance, feeling reasonably sure that such an offer would be neither welcomed nor accepted.

Watching the laborious process, though, William was interested to note that while the fabric of the sling was much-laundered and faded, it had been embroidered with small blue and yellow sunbursts along one edge. Did Quaker women commonly wear attractive undergarments beneath their sober gowns?

As they set off at a cautious walk, the sound of the wagon was still audible, though fading into the rush of trees.

"Are ye armed?" Murray asked suddenly.

"Slightly." He still had the knife Jane had pushed into his hand, now wrapped in a handkerchief and tucked in his pocket, as he had no sheath for it. He fingered the wooden handle, wondering whether it was the same knife that she . . . Well, of course it was.

"I'm not. Will ye find me a club?"

"You don't trust me to see you safe?" William asked sarcastically.

Murray's shoulders were slumped and his head thrust forward, nodding a little with the mule's gait, but he turned and gave William a look that was heavy-eyed with fever, but still surprisingly alert.

"Oh, I trust ye fine. It's men like the ones ye just fought I dinna trust."

This was a fair point; the roads were far from safe, and the knowledge gave William a severe pang of conscience on behalf of the women he'd just dispatched, unarmed and unprotected, to drive miles over those very roads with a valuable mule and cart. *I should have gone with them, insisted we all go together . . .*

"My mam always says there's no one more stubborn than my uncle Jamie," Murray observed mildly, "but a Quaker lass wi' her mind made up could give Uncle Jamie a run for his money, I'll tell ye. I couldna have stopped her—and neither could you."

William wasn't in a mood to discuss any of the persons mentioned, nor yet engage in philosophical discussions of relative stubbornness. He put a hand on the bridle and pulled the mule to a halt.

"Stay here. I see something that might do." He'd already seen that there was little in the way of fallen branches near the road; there never was, when an army's foragers had recently passed through. But he saw an orchard of some kind, a little way from the road, with a farmhouse beyond.

As he made his way toward the orchard, he could see that artillery had been hauled through it; there were deep furrows in the ground, and many of the trees had broken limbs, hanging like jackstraws.

There was a dead man in the orchard. American militia, by his hunting shirt and homespun breeches, lying curled among the gnarled roots of a big apple tree.

"Should have culled that one," William said aloud, keeping his voice steady. Old apple trees never yielded much; you took them out after fifteen, twenty years and replanted. He turned away from the body, but not fast enough to avoid seeing the greedy flies rise up in a buzzing cloud from what was left of the face. He walked three paces away and threw up.

No doubt it was the cloying smell of rotting apples that rose above the ghost of black powder; the whole orchard hummed with the noise of wasps gorging themselves on the juices. He unwrapped the handkerchief from Jane's knife and thrust the knife through his belt without looking to see if there were bloodstains on it. He wiped his mouth, then, after a moment's hesitation, went and laid the handkerchief over the Rebel's face. Someone had stripped the body; he had neither weapons nor shoes.

"THIS DO YOU?" He laid a three-foot length of applewood across the saddlebow. He'd broken it at both ends, so it made a serviceable club, about the thickness of his own forearm.

Murray seemed to wake from a doze; he drew himself slowly upright, took hold of the club, and nodded.

"Aye, that'll do," he said softly. His voice sounded thick, and William looked at him sharply.

"You'd best drink some more," he said, handing up the canteen again. It was getting low; probably no more than a quarter full. Murray took it, though moving sluggishly, drank, and gave it back with a sigh.

They walked without conversation for a half hour or so, leaving William time at last to sort through the events of the morning. It was well past noon now; the sun was pressing on his shoulders like a heated flatiron. How far did Rachel say it was it to Freehold? Six miles?

"D'ye want me to tell ye, or no?" Murray said suddenly.

"Tell me what?"

There was a brief sound that might have been either amusement or pain.

"Whether ye're much like him."

Possible responses to this came so fast that they collapsed upon themselves like a house of cards. He took the one on top.

"Why do you suppose I should wonder?" William managed, with a coldness that would have frozen most men. Of course, Murray was blazing with such a fever, it would take a Quebec blizzard to freeze him.

"I would, if it was me," Murray said mildly.

That defused William's incipient explosion momentarily.

"Perhaps you think so," he said, not trying to hide his annoyance. "You may know him, but you know nothing whatever about me."

This time, the sound was undeniably amusement: laughter, of a hoarse, creaking sort.

"I helped fish ye out of a privy ten years ago," Murray said. "That was when I first kent it, aye?"

Shock struck William almost dumb, but not quite.

"What—that . . . that place in the mountains—Fraser's Ridge . . . ?!" He'd succeeded, for the most part, in forgetting the incident of the snake in the privy, and with it, most of a miserable journey through the mountains of North Carolina.

Murray took William's choler for confusion, though, and chose to elucidate.

"The way ye came out o' the muck, your eyes bleezin' blue and your face set for murder—that was Uncle Jamie to the life, when he's roused." Murray's head bobbed forward alarmingly. He caught himself and straightened up with a muffled groan.

"If you're going to fall off," William said, with elaborate courtesy, "do it on the other side, will you?"

"Mmphm."

They paced another hundred yards before Murray came to life again, resuming the conversation—if it could be called that—as though there had been no pause.

"So when I found ye in the swamp, I kent who ye were. I dinna recall ye thankin' me for saving your life that time, by the way."

"You can thank *me* for not strapping you into a travois with a dead panther and dragging you for miles through the dirt now," William snapped.

Murray laughed, gasping a little.

"Ye'd likely do it, if ye had a dead panther." The effort of laughing seemed to deprive him of balance, and he swayed alarmingly.

"Fall off and I'll do it anyway," William said, grabbing him by the thigh to steady him. "Dead panther or not." Christ, the man's skin was so hot he could feel it through the buckskin leggings.

Despite his fog, Murray noticed his reaction.

"You lived through the fever," he said, and took a deep breath. "I will, too; dinna fash."

"If by that expression you mean that I ought not to be concerned that you'll die," William said coldly, "I'm not."

"I'm no worrit, either," Murray assured him. The man wobbled slightly, reins held loose in one hand, and William wondered if he could be sunstruck. "Ye promised Rachel, aye?"

"Yes," William said, adding almost involuntarily, "I owe her and her brother my life, as much as I do you."

"Mmphm," Murray said agreeably, and fell silent. He seemed to be going a nasty grayish color under the sun-browned skin. This time he stayed silent for a good five minutes before coming suddenly to life again.

"And ye dinna think I ken much about ye, after listening to ye rave wi' fever for days?"

"I do not," William said. "No more than I think I'll know a great deal about you by the time I get you to Freehold."

"Maybe more than ye think. Stop, aye? I'm going to puke."

"Whoa!" The mule obligingly halted, though it clearly didn't like either the sound or the smell of what was going on behind its head, and kept sidling round in circles, trying to escape it.

William waited 'til it was over, then handed up his canteen without comment. Murray drained it and handed it back. His hand was shaking, and William began to be worried.

"We'll stop as soon as I find water," he said. "Get you into the shade." Neither of them had a hat; he'd left his in the copse, rolled up with his uniform coat under a bush.

Murray didn't reply to this; he was not precisely raving, but seemed to be pursuing a separate conversation in his head.

"I maybe dinna ken ye that well, but Rachel does."

That was undeniably true and gave William an oddly mixed sense of shame, pride, and anger. Rachel and her brother *did* know him well; they'd saved his life and nursed him back to health, had traveled with him for weeks and shared both food and danger.

"She says ye're a good man."

William's heart squeezed a little.

"I'm obliged for her good opinion," he said. The water hadn't helped that much; Murray was definitely swaying in the saddle, his eyes half closed.

"If you die," William said loudly, "I'll marry her."

That worked; Murray's eyelids lifted at once. He smiled, very slightly.

"Ken that," he said. "Ken I'm no going to die? And, besides, ye owe me a life, Englishman."

"I don't. I saved your bloody life, too; I saved the both of you from that maniac—Bug, was he?—with the ax in Philadelphia. We're quits."

Some interminable time later, Murray roused himself again.

"I doubt it," he said.

91

KEEPING SCORE

JAMIE SAW THE GREYS out of the house and came back with an air of grim satisfaction. I would have laughed if it hadn't hurt to do it, but settled for smiling at him.

"*Your* son, *your* nephew, *your* wife," I said. "Fraser, three; Grey, nil."

He gave me a startled look, but then his face truly relaxed for the first time in days. "You're feeling better, then," he said, and, coming across the room, bent and kissed me. "Talk daft to me some more, aye?" He sat down heavily on the stool and sighed, but with relief.

"Mind," he said, "I havena the slightest idea how I'm going to keep ye, with no money, no commission, and no profession. But keep ye I will."

"No profession, forsooth," I said comfortably. "Name one thing you can't do."

"Sing."

"Oh. Well, besides that."

He spread his hands on his knees, looking critically at the scars on his maimed right hand.

"I doubt I could make a living as a juggler or a pickpocket, either. Let alone a scribe."

"You haven't got to write," I said. "You have a printing press—Bonnie, by name."

"Well, aye," he admitted, a certain light coming into his eyes. "I do. But she's in Wilmington at the moment." His press had been shipped from Edinburgh in the care of Richard Bell, who was—presumably—keeping her in trust until her real owner should come to repossess her.

"We'll go and get her. And then—" But I stopped, afraid to jinx the future by planning too far. It was an uncertain time for everyone, and no telling what the morrow might bring.

"But first," I amended, reaching out to squeeze his hand, "you should rest. You look as though you're about to die."

"Dinna talk that sort of daft," he said, and laughed and yawned simultaneously, nearly breaking his jaw.

"Lie down," I said firmly. "Sleep—at least until Lieutenant Bixby shows up again with more cheese." The American army had withdrawn to Englishtown, some seven miles away, only an hour's ride. The British army had decamped entirely, but as many of the militia units' enlistments had expired soon afterward, the roads were still very busy with men going home, mostly afoot.

He did lie down on his pallet, with surprisingly little protest—a good in-dication of just how exhausted he really was—and was asleep in seconds.

I was very tired myself, still very weak and easily exhausted, even by some-thing like the Greys' visit, and I lay back and dozed, stirring to wakefulness every so often when some sound roused me, but Jamie slept deeply, and it eased my heart to hear his soft, regular snore.

I woke some time later, hearing a distant knocking below. As I raised my head blearily off the pillow, I heard a voice shouting, "Hallo, the house!" and snapped into instant alertness. I knew that voice.

I glanced quickly down, but Jamie was dead asleep, curled up like a hedge-hog. With excruciating slowness, I managed to swing my legs off the bed and—moving like a geriatric tortoise and clinging to the bed frame—took the two steps that brought me to the window, where I clung to the sill.

There was a handsome bay mule in the dooryard, with a half-naked body laid over the saddle. I gasped—and immediately doubled in pain, but didn't let go the sill. I bit my lip hard, not to call out. The body was wearing buck-skins, and his long brown hair sported a couple of bedraggled turkey feathers.

"Jesus H. Roosevelt Christ," I breathed, through gritted teeth. "Please, God, don't let him be—" But the prayer was answered before I'd finished speaking it; the door below opened, and in the next moment William and Lieutenant Macken walked out and lifted Ian off the mule, put his arms about their shoulders, and carried him into the house.

I turned, instinctively reaching for my medical bag—and nearly fell. I saved myself by a grab at the bed frame but let out an involuntary groan that brought Jamie up into a crouch, staring wildly about.

"It's . . . all right," I said, willing my belly muscles into immobility. "I'm fine. It's—Ian. He's come back."

Jamie sprang to his feet, shook his head to clear it, and at once went to the window. I saw him stiffen and, clutching my side, followed him. William had come out of the house and was preparing to mount the mule. He was dressed in shirt and breeches, very grubby, and the sun licked his dark chestnut hair with streaks of red. Mrs. Macken said something from the door, and he turned to answer her. I don't think I made a noise, but something made him look up suddenly and he froze. I felt Jamie freeze, too, as their eyes met.

William's face didn't change, and after a long moment he turned to the mule again, mounted, and rode away. After another long moment, Jamie let out his breath.

"Let me put ye back to bed, Sassenach," he said calmly. "I'll have to go and find Denny to put Ian right."

92

I WILL NOT HAVE THEE BE ALONE

SOMEONE HAD GIVEN HIM laudanum before setting to work on his shoulder. Strange stuff, that. He'd had it before, he thought, a long time ago, though he hadn't known the name at the time. Now Ian lay on his back, blinking slowly as the drug ebbed from his mind, trying to decide where he was and what was real. He was pretty sure most of what he was looking at right now wasn't.

Pain. That was real and something to use as an anchor. It hadn't entirely gone away—he'd been aware of it, but remotely, as a disagreeable muddy green strand like a stream of dirty water meandering through his dreams. Now that he was awake, though, it was becoming more disagreeable by the minute. His eyes didn't want to focus yet, but he forced them to roll about in search of something familiar.

He found it at once.

Girl. Lass. Ifrinn, *what was her*—"Rachel," he croaked, and she rose instantly from what she was doing and came to him, her face worried but alight.

"Rachel?" he said again, uncertain, and she took hold of his good hand, pressing it to her bosom.

"Thee is awake, I see," she said softly, her eyes searching his face. "But still much fevered, from the heat of thy skin. How does thee feel?"

"Better for seein' ye, lass." He tried to lick his dry lips. "Is there maybe water?"

She made a small sound of distress that he'd had to ask, and hurried to bring a cup to his lips. It was perhaps the best thing he'd ever tasted, made better by her holding his head in her hand as he drank—he was very dizzy. He didn't want to stop, but she took the cup away.

"More presently," she promised. "Thee must not drink too much, too fast, or thee will vomit. And between the dirt and the blood, thee has made enough mess already," she said, smiling.

"Mmphm," he said, lying back. He was mostly clean, he discovered. Someone had washed away the last of the deer fat and paint, and a good deal of sweat and blood with it. His shoulder was bound up with a poultice of some kind; it smelled tangy and familiar, but his hazy mind was a long way yet from allowing him to think of the name of the herb.

"Did Auntie Claire bind my arm?" he asked. Rachel glanced at him, her brows furrowing.

"Thy aunt is ill," she said carefully. "Thee remembers I told thee that she was wounded—shot—in the battle?"

"No," he said, feeling blank and confused. He had no recollection of the last couple of days or of battle. "No. What—is she all right, then?"

"Denny removed the ball, and thy uncle Jamie is with her. Both of them say very firmly that she will be well." Her mouth twitched a bit, halfway between a smile and worry. He did his best to smile back.

"Then she'll be fine," he said. "Uncle Jamie's a verra stubborn man. Can I have more water?"

This time he drank more slowly and got more down before she took it away. There was a regular clanging noise somewhere; for a time he had taken it for some phantom of hearing left over from the dreams, but now it ceased for a moment, punctuated by a loud curse.

"What—where are we?" he asked, beginning to be able to look at things again. His wavering sight convinced him that he was indeed in a tiny cow byre; it was new hay he'd been smelling, and the warm scent of fresh cow dung. He was lying on a blanket spread over a mound of hay, but the cow was absent for the moment.

"A place called Freehold. The battle was fought nearby; Washington and the army have withdrawn to Englishtown, but a good many wounded soldiers have been given refuge by the inhabitants here. We currently enjoy the hospitality of the local smith, a gentleman named Heughan."

"Oh." The forge. That was the source of the clanging and cursing. He closed his eyes; that helped with the dizziness, but he could see shadows of his dreams on the inside of his eyelids and opened them again. Rachel was still there; that was good.

"Who won the battle?" he asked.

She shrugged, impatient. "So far as anyone has said anything sensible about it, no one. The Americans are cock-a-hoop at not having been defeated, to be sure—but the British army surely wasn't, either. All I care about is thee. And thee will be fine," she said, and laid her hand gently on his forehead. "*I* say so. And I am as stubborn as any Scot thee cares to name—including thyself."

"I need to tell ye something, lass." He hadn't meant to say that, but the words felt familiar in his mouth, as though he'd said them before.

"Something different?" She had been turning away but paused now, looking wary.

"Different? Did I tell ye things while I was . . ." He tried to wave a hand in illustration, but even his good arm was heavy as lead.

Rachel caught her upper lip between her teeth, regarding him.

"Who is Geillis?" she asked abruptly. "And what in the name of—of goodness did she *do* to thee?"

He blinked, startled and yet relieved to hear the name. Yes, that was what he'd been dreaming—oh, Jesus. The relief departed at once.

"What did I say?" he asked warily.

"If thee doesn't recall it, I don't wish to bring it back to thee." She knelt down by him, skirts rustling.

"I remember what happened—I just want to ken what I said about it."

"What happened," she repeated slowly, watching his face. "In thy dreams, thee means? Or—" She broke off, and he saw her throat move as she swallowed.

"Likely both, lass," he said softly, and managed to reach for her hand. "I spoke of Geillis Abernathy, though?"

"Thee only said 'Geillis,'" she said, and covered his hand with both of hers, holding fast. "Thee was afraid. And thee called out in pain—but of course thee *was* in pain, so . . . but then . . . it—whatever thee saw, it—"

Color rose slowly up her neck and washed her face, and with a slight relapse into the dream, he saw her for an instant as an orchid with a dusky throat into which he could plunge his— He cut that vision off and found that he was breathing fast.

"It seemed that thee experienced something other than pain," she said, frowning.

"Aye, I did," he said, and swallowed. "Can I have a bit more water?"

She gave it to him, but with a fixed look indicating that she didn't mean to be distracted from his story by his physical needs.

He sighed and lay back again. "It was a long time agone, *a nighean,* and nothing to fash about now. I was taken—kidnapped—for a brief time, when I was maybe fourteen or so. I stayed wi' a woman named Geillis Abernathy, on Jamaica, until my uncle found me. It wasna very pleasant, but I wasna damaged, either."

Rachel raised an elegant brow. He loved to watch her do that, but sometimes more than others.

"There were other lads there," he said, "and they were not so lucky." For a long time afterward, he'd been afraid to close his eyes at night, because he saw their faces. But they'd faded away, little by little—and now he felt a spasm of guilt because he'd let them go into darkness.

"Ian," Rachel said softly, and her hand stroked his cheek. He felt the rasp of his beard stubble as she touched him, and a pleasant gooseflesh ran down his jaw and shoulder. "Thee needn't speak of it. I would not bring it back to thee."

"It's all right," he said, and swallowed a little easier. "I'll tell ye—but later. It's an old story, and one ye dinna need to hear just now. But—" He stopped short and she raised the other brow.

"But what I *do* have to tell ye, lass . . ." And he told her. Much of the previous two days' events was still a blur, but he recalled vividly the two Abenaki who had hunted him. And what he'd finally done, in the British camp.

She was silent for so long that he began to wonder whether he'd really waked and had this conversation or was still dreaming.

"Rachel?" he said, shifting uneasily on his bed of prickly hay. The door of the byre was open and there was light enough, but he couldn't read her face at all. Her gaze rested on his own face, though, hazel-eyed and distant, as though she were looking *through* him. He was afraid she was.

He could hear Heughan the smith outside, walking to and fro and making clanking sounds, pausing to apostrophize some uncooperative implement in coarse terms. He could hear his own heart beating, too, an uncomfortable, jerky thump.

Finally a shiver went over Rachel, as though she shook herself awake, and she put a hand on his forehead, smoothing back his hair as she looked into his eyes, her own now soft and fathomless. Her thumb came down and traced the tattooed line across his cheekbones, very slowly.

"I think we can't wait any longer to be married, Ian," she said softly. "I will not have thee face such things alone. These are bad times, and we must be together."

He closed his eyes and all the air went out of him. When he drew breath again, it tasted of peace.

"When?" he whispered.

"As soon as thee can walk without help," she said, and kissed him, lightly as a falling leaf.

93

THE HOUSE ON
CHESTNUT STREET

THE HOUSE WAS occupied; there was smoke drifting from the west chimney. The door was locked, though, and bolted to boot. "I wonder what happened to the old door?" John said to Hal, trying the knob again, just in case. "It used to be green."

"If you knock on this one, you might conceivably get someone to come out and tell you," Hal suggested. They weren't in uniform, but Hal was noticeably on edge, and had been since their call on General Arnold.

The general had been understandably reserved, but civil, and after reading Fraser's letter over three or four times, had agreed to give them passes to remain in the city and to make such inquiries as they saw fit.

"With the understanding," Arnold had said, a flash of his reputed arrogance showing through the façade of governorship, "that if I hear of anything untoward, I'll have you both arrested and ridden out of the city on a rail."

"On a what?" Hal had said incredulously, he having not encountered this peculiarly American method of making guests feel unwelcome.

"A rail," Arnold had repeated, smiling genially. "Long piece of wood? Used for fences, I believe?"

Hal had turned to John, one eyebrow raised, as though inviting him to translate the speech of some Hottentot randomly encountered. John sighed internally, but did so.

"An undesirable person is mounted on the object in question," he said, "straddling it. Whereupon a party of men lift either end and set off through the streets with it, decanting the rider outside the city. I believe tar and feathers are sometimes applied as a preliminary gesture, though the physical effects of the rail are generally presumed to be sufficient."

"Flatten your ball sac like a horse stepped on it," Arnold said, still smiling. "Won't do your arse any good, either."

"I should imagine not," Hal said politely. His color was somewhat higher than usual, but he gave no other indication of offense, which Grey thought a reasonable indication—not that he needed one—of the importance of their mission to Hal.

The sound of the bolt grating free interrupted his recollection. The door swung open, revealing his housekeeper and cook, Mrs. Figg, fowling piece in hand.

"Lord John!" she exclaimed, dropping the gun with a clatter.

"Well, yes," he said, stepping in and picking it up. He smiled, feeling affection well up in his bosom at sight of her—substantial, tidy, and beribboned as always. "It's very good to see you again, Mrs. Figg. Allow me to make you acquainted with my brother, the—"

"We've met," Hal said, a wry edge to his voice. "How do you do, madam?"

"Better than Your Grace, by the looks of you," Mrs. Figg replied, narrowing her eyes at him. "Still breathing, though, I see." She sounded as though this was not entirely a desirable state of affairs, but Hal smiled broadly at her.

"Did you manage to bury the silver in time?" he asked.

"Certainly," she replied with dignity, and, turning to John, asked, "You come to get it, my lord? I can have it dug up right smart."

"Perhaps not just yet," John said. He looked round, noting the missing banister railing on the upper landing, the smudged and pockmarked wall by the staircase, and— "What's happened to the chandelier?"

Mrs. Figg sighed and shook her head darkly.

"That'd be Master William," she said. "How is he, my lord?"

"I'm afraid I don't know, Mrs. Figg. I was in some hopes that he might have been here—but I gather not?"

She looked disturbed at this.

"No, sir. We've not seen him since—well, since the day you went away yourself." She looked hard at him, taking in everything from the cropped hair to the fading bruises and the undistinguished suit, shook her head and sighed, but then straightened her broad shoulders, determined to be cheerful. "And glad we are to see you, sir! And Your Grace," she added as a definite afterthought. "Go sit yourselves down and I'll have you up a nice cup of tea in two minutes."

"You have tea?" Hal said, brightening.

"We buried the tea chest first thing," she informed him. "But I just brought in a brick for Miss Dottie, so—"

"Dottie's here?"

"To be sure," said Mrs. Figg, pleased to be the bearer of good news. "I'll just step out to the kitchen and fetch her."

This proved to be unnecessary, as the sound of the back door opening betokened Dottie's entrance, carrying an apronful of lumpy objects. These proved to be vegetable marrows from the kitchen garden, which cascaded over the floor in a bouncing flood of green and yellow as she let go the apron in order to leap at her father and embrace him.

"Papa!"

For an instant, Hal's face changed entirely, soft with love, and Grey was surprised and disconcerted to feel tears come to his own eyes. He turned away, blinking, and wandered over to the sideboard, meaning to give them a private moment.

The silver tea service was gone, of course, but his Meissen porcelain plates were in their accustomed spots on the plate rail. He touched the cool gilt-ribboned border of one, feeling oddly disembodied. *And his place shall know him no more.*

But Dottie was talking now to both of them; Grey turned round to her, smiling.

"I'm so glad you're both safe and both *here*!" Her cheeks were flushed, her eyes sparkling—and Grey's heart misgave him at the knowledge that this state of happiness would be quenched within the next minute, as soon as Hal told her the reason for their presence. Before any such doom could fall, though, Dottie had seized the reins of the conversation and driven it off in another direction entirely.

"Since you *are* here—Uncle John, could we possibly use your house? For the wedding, I mean. Please, please?"

"The wedding?" Hal disengaged himself gently and cleared his throat. "*Your* wedding?"

"Of course I mean my wedding, Papa. Don't be silly." She beamed at her uncle, placing a coquettish hand on his sleeve. "May we, Uncle John? We cannot be married in a meetinghouse, but we must have witnesses for a proper marriage of Friends, and, really, I'm sure Papa wouldn't want to see me married in the public room of a tavern. Would you?" she appealed, turning to Hal, whose expression had reverted to its earlier guardedness.

"Well, certainly you may, my dear," John said, glancing round his parlor. "Assuming that I retain possession of this place long enough for the marriage to take place. When is the ceremony to be, and how many witnesses will we need to accommodate?"

She hesitated, tapping a fingernail against her teeth.

"I'm not really sure. There will be some of the conscientious Friends who, like Denny, have been put out of meeting for joining the Continental army. And some friends—friends in the lowercase, meaning no disrespect—if any are left in Philadelphia. And . . . family?" She hesitated again, looking at her father sideways, from under her lashes. John suppressed a smile.

Hal closed his eyes and sighed deeply.

"Yes, I'll come to your wedding," he said, opening them with resignation.

"And so will Henry, if I have to drag him by the scruff of the neck. I suppose Mrs. Woodcock must be invited, too," he added, with a marked lack of enthusiasm. "But of course Adam . . . and—and Ben—"

John thought for a moment that he must tell her now, but his brother's lips closed, firmed with determination. He didn't look at John, but John caught the *"Not now, for God's sake. Let her be happy for a bit longer,"* as clearly as if it had been spoken aloud.

"No, that's too bad," Dottie said with regret, and met her father's eyes directly. "I'm sorry about Mama. I did write to her, though."

"Did you, sweetheart?" Hal said, sounding almost normal. "That was thoughtful." He tilted his head at her, though, eyes narrowing a bit. "What else?"

"Oh." Her color, which had returned to normal, rose again, and she began absently pleating her apron with one hand. "Well. Did you know that Rachel—Denzell's sister—is affianced to Ian Murray? That's Mr. James—no, no, we don't use 'Mister,' sorry—he's the nephew of James Fraser. You know—"

"I do know," Hal said, in a tone cutting off further amendation. "Who he is, I mean. What are you saying, Dottie? Without embroidery, if you please."

She sniffed at him but didn't appear to be discomposed in the least.

"Well, then. Rachel and Ian wish to be married as soon as they can, and so do Denny and I. As all the witnesses will be present, why not have both marriages at the same time?"

This time, Hal did look at John. Who returned the look, somewhat taken aback.

"Ah . . . well. I suppose that would mean additional guests? Including the aforementioned Mr. Fraser? I'm sure you will excuse my using his title, my dear; I'm accustomed to such social excesses."

"Well, yes. Rachel says that Mrs. Fraser is enough recovered that they will return to Philadelphia tomorrow or next day. And then of course there's Fergus and his wife, Marsali, and perhaps the children, and I don't know if there are other friends who—I don't *think* Ian has any Mohawk relations nearby, but—"

"One, two, three, four, five . . ." John turned and began counting the small gilt chairs that stood rigidly to attention beneath the wainscoting. "I think we shall be somewhat cramped, Dottie, but if—"

Mrs. Figg cleared her throat. The sound was sufficiently impressive that everyone else stopped talking and looked at her.

"Beg pardon, gentlemen," she said, and a faint flush was visible on her round face. "I don't mean to be forward or presuming . . . but so happens that I mentioned to the Reverend Figg about Miss Dottie and Friend Denzell needing a place to be married in."

She cleared her throat, the blush growing deeper beneath her dark skin, so that she bore a surprising resemblance to a just-fired cannonball, Grey thought, charmed by the notion.

"And . . . well, the long and the short of it, ma'am and gentlemen, is that the reverend and his congregation would be pleased was you to consider being married in the new church building, you having been so kind as to contribute to it. 'Tain't anyways fancy, mind, but—"

"Mrs. Figg, you are a marvel." Grey clasped her hands in his, an attention that flustered her to the point of speechlessness. Seeing this, he let go, though this allowed Dottie to swoop in and kiss the housekeeper, exclaiming in gratitude. That was all right, but when Hal took Mrs. Figg by the hand and kissed it, the poor lady was reduced nearly to the point of suffocation and, snatching back her hand, retreated in haste, muttering disjointedly about tea and narrowly avoiding tripping on a marrow.

"Is it all right to be married in a church?" Hal asked Dottie, once Mrs. Figg had retired to a safe distance. "It's not like Jews, is it? We needn't be circumcised in order to attend? Because if so, I think your guest list may be substantially reduced."

"Oh, I'm sure it's not . . ." Dottie began rather vaguely, but her attention was distracted by something seen through the front window. "Goodness, is that . . . ?"

Not bothering to complete her thought, she flew to the unbolted door and yanked it open, revealing a startled William on the stoop.

"Dottie!" he said. "What—" And then caught sight of John and Hal. William's face underwent a lightning shift that made a *frisson* run straight down John's back to his tailbone. He'd seen that exact expression on Jamie Fraser's face a hundred times, at least—but had never before seen it on William's.

It was the look of a man who doesn't like his immediate prospects one bit—but who feels himself entirely capable of dealing with them. William stepped inside, repelling by force of will Dottie's abortive attempt to embrace him. He removed his hat and bowed to Dottie, then, punctiliously, to John and Hal.

"Your servant, ma'am. Sirs."

Hal snorted, looking his nephew over from head to toe. William was dressed much as John and Hal were, in ordinary clothes—though clothes of good cut and quality, John observed; clearly his own.

"And where the devil have *you* been for the last three days, may I ask?"

"No, you mayn't," William replied briefly. "Why are *you* here?"

"Looking for you, for one thing," John replied equably, before Hal could stick his oar in again. He'd put the fowling piece on the mantel, easily within Hal's reach, but was reasonably sure it wasn't loaded. "And for Captain Richardson, for another. Have you seen him recently?"

William's expression of surprise made John heave an internal sigh of relief. "No, I haven't." William glanced shrewdly from one man to the other. "Is that what you were doing at Arnold's headquarters? Looking for Richardson?"

"Yes," John answered, surprised. "How did you—oh. You were watching the place." He smiled. "I did wonder how you happened to appear here so fortuitously. You followed us from General Arnold's."

William nodded and, stretching out a long arm, drew out one of the chairs from the wall. "I did. Sit down. Things need to be said."

"*That* sounds rather ominous," Dottie murmured. "Perhaps I'd best fetch the brandy."

"Please do, Dottie," John said. "Tell Mrs. Figg we want the '57, if you would. If it isn't buried, I mean."

"I think everything of an alcoholic nature is in the well, actually. I'll fetch it."

Mrs. Figg herself arrived at this point with a rattling tea tray, apologizing for the lowly earthenware pot in which the beverage was brewing, and within a few moments, everyone was provided with a steaming cup and a small glass of the '57.

"Thank you, sweetheart," Hal said, accepting a glass from Dottie, then adding pointedly, "You needn't stay."

"I'd rather you did, Dottie," William said quietly, but with an overt stare at Hal. "There are things you ought to know, I think."

With no more than a brief glance at her father, Dottie, who had been picking up the scattered squash, sat down on the ottoman, opposite her cousin.

"Tell me, then," she said simply.

"Nothing out of the way," he assured her, with an assumption of casualness. "I've recently discovered that I am the natural son of one James Fraser, who—"

"Oh," she said, and looked at him with renewed interest. "I *did* think General Fraser reminded me of someone! Of course, that's it! Goodness, Willie, you *do* look like him!"

William looked flabbergasted, but quickly pulled himself together.

"He's a general?" he asked Hal.

"He was," Hal said. "He's resigned his commission."

William made a small, humorless noise. "Has he? Well, so have I."

After a long silent moment, John placed his cup carefully on its saucer with a small clink.

"Why?" he asked mildly, at the same moment that Hal, frowning, said, "Can you do such a thing while technically a prisoner of war?"

"I don't know," William said tersely, and evidently in answer to both questions. "But I've done it. Now, as to Captain Richardson . . ." and he recounted his astonishing encounter with Denys Randall-Isaacs on the road.

"Or, rather, Denys Randall, as he now calls himself. Evidently his stepfather's a Jew, and he wishes to avoid the association."

"Sensible," Hal said briefly. "I don't know him. What else do you know about him, William? What's his connection with Richardson?"

"I haven't the faintest idea," William said, and, draining his cup, reached for the pot and poured another. "There *is* one, obviously, and prior to this, I would have assumed that Randall perhaps worked with, or for, Richardson."

"Perhaps he still does," John suggested, a slight edge in his voice. He'd been a spy himself for some years and was disinclined to take things said by known intelligencers at face value.

That seemed to take William aback for a moment, but he nodded reluctantly.

"All right," he conceded. "But tell me—why the devil are *you* two interested in Richardson?"

They told him.

At the conclusion, Hal was perched anxiously on the ottoman beside Dottie, an arm round her shaking shoulders. She was weeping silently, and he was dabbing at her face with his handkerchief, this now a grubby rag following its service as a flag of truce.

"I don't believe it," he was repeating doggedly, for the sixth or seventh time. "Do you hear me, darling, I do *not* believe it, and I won't have you believe it, either."

"N-no," she said obediently. "No . . . I won't. Oh, *Ben!*"

In some hopes of distracting her, John turned back to William.

"And what business brought you to Philadelphia, may I ask? You can't have come in search of Captain Richardson, because when you left camp, you didn't know he'd disappeared."

"I came on a personal matter," William said, in a tone suggesting that the matter was still personal and was going to remain that way. "But also . . ." He pressed his lips together for a moment, and again John had that odd sense of dislocation, seeing Jamie Fraser. "I was going to leave this here for you, in case you came back to the city. Or ask Mrs. Figg to send it to New York, if . . ." His voice trailed away, as he pulled a letter from the breast of his dark-blue coat.

"But I needn't now," he concluded firmly, and put it away again. "It's only saying what I've already told you." A slight flush touched his cheek-bones, though, and he avoided John's eye, turning instead to Hal.

"I'll go and find out about Ben," he said simply. "I'm not a soldier any longer; there's no danger of my being taken up as a spy. And I can travel much more easily than you can."

"Oh, William!" Dottie took the handkerchief from her father and blew her nose with a small, ladylike honk. She looked at him with brimming eyes. "Will you, really? Oh, *thank* you!"

That was not, of course, the end of it. But it was no revelation to Grey that William possessed a stubbornness so obviously derived from his natural father that no one but Hal would even have thought of arguing with him. And even Hal didn't argue long.

In due course, William rose to go.

"Give Mrs. Figg my love, please," he said to John, and, with a small bow to Dottie, "Goodbye, cousin."

John followed him to the door to let him out, but at the threshold put a hand on his sleeve.

"Willie," he said softly. "Give me the letter."

For the first time, William looked a little less than certain. He put his hand to his breast, but left it there, hesitant.

"I won't read it—unless you don't come back. But if you don't . . . I want it. To keep."

William drew breath, nodded, and, reaching into his coat, removed a sealed cover and handed it over. Grey saw that it had been sealed with a thick daub of candle wax and that William hadn't used his signet, preferring instead to stamp it with his thumbprint, firm in the hot wax.

"Thank you," he said through the lump in his throat. "Godspeed. Son."

94

THE SENSE OF THE MEETING

THE METHODIST CHURCH was a modest wooden
building with plain glass windows, and, while it did have an altar,
might otherwise easily have passed as a Quaker meetinghouse, bar
three framed cross-stitched samplers bearing Bible verses that hung on one
wall. I heard Rachel let out her breath as she stopped just inside, looking
around.

"No flowers?" Mrs. Figg had said the day before, scandalized. "I understand plain, but *God* made flowers!"

"A Friends' meetinghouse would not have flowers," Rachel had said, smiling. "We think them somewhat pagan, and a distraction to worship. But we
are thy guests, and surely a guest must not tell his host how to keep his own
house."

Mrs. Figg blinked at the word "pagan," but then made a low humming
noise and settled back into benignity.

"Well and good, then," she said. "His lordship has three good rosebushes,
and there's sunflowers in every yard in town. Lot of honeysuckle, too," she
added thoughtfully. There was; everyone planted honeysuckle by the privy.

As a nod to the Quakers' sensibilities, though, there was only one vase of
flowers—a very plain glass vase—between the two wooden benches that had
been set at the front of the room, and the faint perfume of honeysuckle and
pink cabbage roses mingled with the turpentine smell of hot pine boards and
the pungent scents of fairly clean but very hot people.

Rachel and I stepped outside again, joining the rest of what I supposed
might be called the wedding party, in the shade under a big lime tree. People
were still arriving in ones and twos, and I caught a good many curious looks
directed at us—though these were not aimed at the two brides.

"You are being married in . . . *that?*" Hal said, eyeing Dottie's Sunday-
best gown of soft gray muslin with a white fichu and a bow at the back of the
waist. Dottie raised one smooth blond brow at him.

"Ha," she said. "Mummy told me what *she* wore when you married her in
a tavern in Amsterdam. *And* what your first wedding was like. Diamonds and
white lace and St. James's Church didn't help all that much, did they?"

"Dorothea," Denzell said mildly. "Don't savage thy father. He has enough
to bear."

Hal, who had flushed at Dottie's remarks, went somewhat redder at Denny's and breathed in a menacing rasp, but didn't say anything further. Hal
and John were both wearing full dress uniform and far outshone the two

brides in splendor. I thought it rather a pity that Hal wouldn't get to walk Dottie down the aisle, but he had merely inhaled deeply when the form of the marriage was outlined to him and said—after being elbowed sharply in the ribs by his brother—that he was honored to witness the event.

Jamie, by contrast, did not wear uniform, but his appearance in full Highland dress made Mrs. Figg's eyes bulge—and not only hers.

"Sweet Shepherd of Judea," she muttered to me. "Is that man wearing a woolen *petticoat*? And what sort of pattern is that cloth? Enough to burn the eyes out your head."

"They call it a *Fèileadh beag*," I told her. "In the native language. In English, it's usually called a kilt. And the pattern is his family tartan."

She eyed him for a long moment, the color rising slowly in her cheeks. She turned to me with her mouth open to ask a question, then thought better and shut it firmly.

"No," I said, laughing. "He isn't."

She snorted. "Either way, he's like to die of the heat," she predicted, "and so are those two gamecocks." She nodded at John and Hal, glorious and sweating in crimson and gold lace. Henry had also come in uniform, wearing his more modest lieutenant's apparel. He squired Mercy Woodcock on his arm and gave his father a stare daring him to say anything.

"Poor Hal," I murmured to Jamie. "His children are rather a trial to him."

"Aye, whose aren't?" he replied. "All right, Sassenach? Ye look pale. Had ye not best go in and sit down?"

"No, I'm quite all right," I assured him. "I just *am* pale, after a month indoors. It's good to be in the fresh air." I had a stick, as well as Jamie, to lean on but was feeling quite well, bar a slight stitch in my side, and was enjoying the sensations of mobility, if not the sensation of wearing stays and petticoats in hot weather again. It was going to be even hotter, sitting packed together once the meeting began; the Reverend Mr. Figg's congregation was there, of course, it being their church, and the benches were filled with bodies.

The church had no bell, but a few blocks away the bell of St. Peter's began to toll the hour. It was time, and Jamie, I, and the Grey brothers made our way inside and found our places. The air hummed with murmured conversation and curiosity—the more so at the British uniforms and Jamie's plaid, though both he and the Greys had left their swords at home, in deference to the Friends' meeting.

Both curiosity and conversation rose to a much higher pitch when Ian walked in. He wore a new shirt, white calico printed with blue and purple tulips, his buckskins and breechclout, moccasins—and an armlet made of blue and white wampum shells, which I was reasonably sure that his Mohawk wife, Works With Her Hands, had made for him.

"And here, of course, is the best man," I heard John whisper to Hal. Rollo stalked in at Ian's heel, disregarding the further stir *he* caused. Ian sat down quietly on one of the two benches that had been set at the front of the church, facing the congregation, and Rollo sat at his feet, scratched himself idly, then collapsed and lay panting gently, surveying the crowd with a yellow stare of lazy estimation, as though judging them for eventual edibility.

Denzell came in, looking a little pale, but walked up and sat down on the bench beside Ian. He smiled at the congregation, most of whom murmured and smiled back. Denny wore his best suit—he owned two—a decent navy broadcloth with pewter buttons, and while he was both shorter and less ornamental than Ian, did not by any means disappear beside his outlandish brother-in-law-to-be.

"You're no going to be sick, lass?" Jamie said to Rachel. She and Dottie had come in, but hovered near the wall. Rachel's hands were clenched in the fabric of her skirt. She was white as a sheet, but her eyes glowed. They were fastened on Ian, who was looking at no one but her, his own heart in his eyes.

"No," she whispered. "Come with me, Dottie." She held out a hand, and the two girls walked together to the other bench and sat down. Dottie's color was high, and so was her head. Rachel folded her hands in her lap and resumed looking at Ian. I felt Jamie sigh a little and relax. On Jamie's far side, Jenny craned to see round him, then smiled with gratification.

She'd made Rachel's dress herself, for after the exigencies of recent months, Rachel owned nothing that wasn't near rags. And while Jenny was generally in favor of modesty in dress, she knew her way around a bustline. The dress was a pale-green chintz with a small pattern of dark-green curling vines, and fitted like a glove. With her dark-brown hair shining loose on her shoulders and hazel eyes huge in her face, Rachel looked like some denizen of the forest—perhaps a tree nymph.

I was about to share this fancy with Jamie when the Reverend Mr. Figg walked up to the front of the church, turned, and smiled at the congregation.

"Blessings to you all this day, brothers and sisters!" he said, and was answered by a genial rumble of "Blessings to you, brother!" and discreet "Amens."

"Well, now." He glanced from Ian and Denny to the girls, then back to the congregation. "We're gathered here for a wedding today. But the ladies and gentlemen being married belong to the Society of Friends, so it will be a Quaker wedding—and that's maybe a little different from ones you've seen before, so I take the liberty of telling you how it goes."

A little hum of interest and speculation, which he quieted with one hand. Mr. Figg was small and dapper in black suit and high white stock, but had immense presence, and every ear was tuned attentively to his explanations.

"We have the honor to host this meeting—for that's what the Friends call their worship. And for them, a wedding is just a normal part of meeting. There's no priest or minister involved; the lady and the gentleman just . . . marry each other, when they feel like it's the right time."

That caused a ripple of surprise, perhaps a little disapproval, and I could see the color rise in Dottie's cheeks. Mr. Figg turned to smile at the girls, then back to his congregation.

"I think perhaps one of our Quaker friends might tell us a little bit about their notion of meeting, as I'm sure they know more about it than I do." He turned expectantly toward Denzell Hunter—but it was Rachel who rose to her feet. Mr. Figg didn't see her and started with surprise when she spoke behind him, making everyone laugh.

"Good morning," she said, soft-spoken but clear, when the laughter had died down. "I thank you all for your presence here. For Christ said, 'Wherever two or more of you are gathered in my name, there am I.' And that is all the essence of a meeting of Friends: that Christ may make His presence known among us—and within us." She spread her hands a little. "So we gather, and we listen—both to one another and to the light within us. When a person is moved of the spirit to speak, he or she does speak."

"Or sing, if thee likes," Dottie put in, dimpling at John.

"Or sing," Rachel agreed, smiling. "But we do not fear silence, for often God speaks loudest in the quiet of our hearts." And with that, she sat down again, composed.

A moment of shuffling and blinking among the crowd was succeeded in fact by an expectant silence—this broken by Denny, who rose deliberately and said, "I am moved to tell you how grateful I am for your gracious use of us. For I was put out of meeting, and my sister with me, for my stated intent to join the Continental army. And for the same reason, we are not welcome as members of Philadelphia meeting." He glanced at Rachel, light glinting from his spectacles.

"This is a grievous thing to a Friend," he said quietly. "For our meeting is where our lives and souls abide, and when Friends marry, the whole of their meeting must approve and witness the marriage, for the community itself will support the marriage. I have deprived my sister of this approval and support, and I beg she will forgive me."

Rachel gave an unladylike snort. "Thee followed thy conscience, and if I hadn't thought thee right, I would have said so."

"It was my responsibility to take care of thee!"

"Thee has taken care of me!" Rachel said. "Do I look malnourished? Am I naked?"

A ripple of amusement ran through the congregation, but neither of the Hunters was noticing.

"I took thee from thy home and from the meeting that cared for thee and obliged thee to follow me into violence, into an army full of violent men."

"That would be me, I expect," Ian interrupted, clearing his throat. He looked at Mr. Figg, who seemed somewhat stunned, then at the rapt assemblage on the benches. "I'm no a Friend myself, ye ken. I'm a Highlander and a Mohawk, and they dinna come much more violent than that. By rights, I shouldna wed Rachel, and her brother shouldna let me."

"I should like to see him stop me!" said Rachel, sitting bolt upright with her fists curled on her knees. "Or thee, either, Ian Murray!"

Dottie appeared to be finding the conversation amusing; I could see her struggling not to laugh—and, glancing sideways along the bench in front of me, I could see precisely the same expression on her father's face.

"Well, it's on my account that ye couldna be wed in a proper Quaker meeting," Ian protested.

"No more than on mine," Denny said, grimacing.

"*Mea culpa, mea culpa, mea maxima culpa,*" Jamie murmured in my ear. "D'ye think I should say it's all my fault, for leaving Ian wi' the Indians and bein' a bad example to him?"

"Only if the spirit moves you," I said, not taking my eyes off the show. "Personally, I'd advise you and the spirit to stay out of it."

Mrs. Figg was not disposed to stay out of it. She cleared her throat loudly.

"Now, pardon me for interrupting, but from what I understand, you Friends think a woman's equal to a man, is that right?"

"It is," Rachel and Dottie said firmly together, and everyone laughed.

Mrs. Figg flushed like a ripe black plum, but kept her composure. "Well, then," she said. "If these ladies want to marry with you gentlemen, why do you think you got any business trying to talk them out of it? Have you maybe got your own reservations about the matter?"

A distinctly feminine murmur of approval came from the congregation, and Denny, who was still standing, seemed to be struggling for his own composure.

"Does he have a cock?" came a French-accented whisper from behind me and an unhinged giggle from Marsali in response. "You can't get married without a cock."

This reminiscence of Fergus and Marsali's unorthodox wedding on a Caribbean beach made me stuff my lace handkerchief into my mouth. Jamie shook with suppressed laughter.

"I do have reservations," Denzell said, taking a deep breath. "Though not," he added hastily, with a glance at Dottie, "regarding my desire to wed Dorothea or the honor of my intentions toward her. My reservations—and perhaps Friend Ian's, though I must not speak for him—lie entirely the other way. That is, I—we, perhaps—feel that we must lay bare our failings and limitations as . . . as husbands—" And for the first time, he, too, blushed. "That Dorothea and Rachel may . . . may come to a proper—er . . ."

"That they know what they may be getting into?" Mrs. Figg finished for him. "Well, that's a fine sentiment, Dr. Hunter—"

"Friend," he murmured.

"*Friend* Hunter," she said, with a minimal roll of the eyes. "But I tell you two things. One, your young lady probably knows more about you than you do." More laughter. "And two—speaking as a woman with some experience—I can tell you that nobody knows what being married's going to be like until you find yourself in the midst of it." She sat down with an air of finality, to a hum of approbation.

There was a certain amount of glancing to and fro and a sense of movement on the left side of the church, where several men sat together. I had seen them come in, with women who were plainly their wives; the women had separated, though, and gone to sit on the right side of the church, which made me think that they might be Quakers, though there was nothing in their dress that differentiated them from the other workmen and merchants in the congregation. I could see them come to some sort of silent consensus now, and one of them rose.

"I am William Sprockett," he said formally, and cleared his throat. "We have come to speak in support of Friend Hunter. For we also are Friends who have followed the dictates of our conscience to involvement with rebellion and other matters that a Friend would normally seek to avoid. And in consequence . . . have been read out of meeting."

He paused, brow furrowed, evidently not sure how to go on. A small woman in yellow rose on the other side and spoke clearly.

"What my husband seeks to say, friends, is that a man who would not do as his inner light tells him to is no man. And that while a man of conscience can be mighty inconvenient at times, it don't make him a bad husband." She smiled at Mr. Sprockett and sat down.

"Yes," said Mr. Sprockett gratefully. "As my wife is kind enough to say, going to fight don't unfit us for marriage. So we've all come"—he swept a broad hand around him, indicating his companions and the wives across the aisle—"to approve and witness thy marriage, Friend Hunter."

"And we will support thy marriage, Dorothea," Mrs. Sprockett put in, with a bob of her head. "And thine, Rachel."

Denny Hunter had remained standing while all this colloquy was going on.

"I . . . thank you, Friends," he said, and sat down abruptly, followed more slowly by the Sprocketts.

A hush fell upon the room, and for a little while there was no sound but the remote noise of the streets outside. Here and there a cough, the clearing of a throat, but, overall, silence. Jamie laid a hand on mine, and my fingers turned to intertwine with his. I could feel his pulse in my own fingertips, the solid bones of knuckle and phalanges. His right hand, battered and marked with the scars of sacrifice and labor. Marked also with the signs of my love, the crude repairs done in pain and desperation.

Blood of my blood, bone of my bone . . .

I wondered whether people who are unhappily married think of their own nuptials when they witness a wedding; I thought that those who are happy always do. Jenny's head was bowed, her face calm and inward but peaceful; did she think now of Ian and her wedding day? She did; her head turned a little to one side, she laid a hand lightly on the bench and smiled at the ghost who sat by her side.

Hal and John sat on the bench in front of us, a little to the side, so I could catch glimpses of their faces, so much alike and yet so different. Both of them had been married twice.

It was a slight shock, in fact, to recall that John's second marriage had been to me, for he felt entirely separate from me now, our brief partnership seeming so removed in time as almost to be unreal. And then . . . there was Frank.

Frank. John. Jamie. Sincerity of intention wasn't always enough, I thought, looking at the young people on the benches at the front of the church, none of them now looking at one another but staring at their folded hands, the floor, or sitting with closed eyes. Perhaps realizing that, as Mrs. Figg had said, a marriage is made not in ritual or in words but in the living of it.

A movement pulled me out of my thoughts; Denny had risen to his feet and held out a hand to Dottie, who rose as though mesmerized and, reaching out, clasped both his hands in hers, hanging on for dear life.

"Does thee feel the sense of the meeting clear, Dorothea?" he asked softly, and at her nod, spoke:

"In the presence of the Lord, and before these our Friends, I take thee, Dorothea, to be my wife, promising, with divine assistance, to be unto thee a loving and faithful husband so long as we both shall live."

Her voice was low but clearly audible as, face shining, she replied:

"In the presence of the Lord, and before these our Friends, I take thee, Denzell, to be my husband, promising, with divine assistance, to be unto thee a loving and faithful wife so long as we both shall live."

I heard Hal catch his breath, in what sounded like a sob, and then the church burst into applause. Denny looked startled at this but then broke into a brilliant smile and led Dottie, beaming on his arm, out through the congregation to the back of the church, where they sat close together on the last bench.

People murmured and sighed, smiling, and the church gradually quieted— but not to its former sense of contemplation. There was now a vibrant sense of expectation, tinged perhaps with a little anxiety, as attention focused on Ian and Rachel—no longer looking at each other but down at the floor.

Ian took a breath audible to the back benches, raised his head, and, taking the knife from his belt, laid it on the bench beside him.

"Aye, well . . . Rachel kens I was once married, to a woman of the Wolf clan of the Kahnyen'kehaka. And the Mohawk way of marriage is maybe none so different from the way Friends do it. We sat beside each other before the people, and our parents—they'd adopted me, ken—spoke for us, sayin' what they kent of us and that we were of good character. So far as *they* knew," he added apologetically, and there was a breath of laughter.

"The lass I was to wed had a basket on her lap, filled wi' fruit and vegetables and other bits o' food, and she said to me that she promised to feed me from her fields and care for me. And I—" He swallowed and, reaching out, laid a hand on his knife. "I had a knife, and a bow, and the skins of some otters I'd taken. And I promised to hunt for her and keep her warm wi' my furs. And the people all agreed that we should be married, and so . . . we were."

He stopped, biting his lip, then cleared his throat and went on.

"But the Mohawk dinna take each other for as long as they live—but only for as long as the woman wishes. My wife chose to part wi' me—not because I hurt or mistreated her, but for . . . for other reasons." He cleared his throat again, and his hand went to the wampum armlet round his biceps.

"My wife was called Wakyo'teyehsnonhsa, which means 'Works With Her Hands,' and she made this for me, as a love token." Long brown fingers fumbled with the strings, and the strip of woven shells came loose, slithering into his hand. "Now I lay it down, as witness that I come here a free man, that my life and my heart are once more mine to give. And I hope I may be allowed now to give them forever."

The blue and white shells made a soft clicking noise as he laid them on the bench. He let his fingers rest on them for a moment, then took his hand away.

I could hear Hal's breathing, steady now but with a faint rasp. And Jamie's, thick in his throat.

I could feel all sorts of things moving like wraiths in the thick, still air of the church. Sentiment, sympathy, doubt, apprehension . . . Rollo growled very softly in his throat and fell silent, yellow-eyed and watchful at his master's feet.

We waited. Jamie's hand twitched in mine, and I looked up at him. He was looking at Ian, intent, his lips pressed tight, and I knew he was wondering whether to stand up and speak on Ian's behalf, to assure the congregation— and Rachel—of Ian's character and virtue. He caught my glance, though, shook his head very slightly, and nodded toward the front. It was Rachel's part to speak, if she would.

Rachel sat still as stone, face bleached as bone and her eyes on Ian, burning. But she said nothing.

Neither did she move, but something moved in her; I could see the knowledge of it cross her face, and somehow her body changed, straightening and settling. She was listening.

We all listened with her. And the silence kindled slowly into light.

There was a faint throb in the air then, not quite a sound, and people began to look up, called from the silence. A blur appeared between the benches at the front, and a hummingbird materialized, drawn through the open window, a tiny blur of green and scarlet hovering beside the coral trumpets of the native honeysuckle.

A sigh came from the heart of the church, and the sense of the meeting was made clear.

Ian rose, and Rachel came to meet him.

A CODA IN THREE-TWO TIME

DENZELL AND DOROTHEA

IT WAS THE BEST party that Dorothea Jacqueline Benedicta Grey had ever attended. She had danced with earls and viscounts in the most beautiful ballrooms in London, eaten everything from gilded peacock to trout stuffed with shrimp and riding on an artful sea of aspic with a Triton carved of ice brandishing his spear over all. And she'd done these things in gowns so splendid that men blinked when she hove into view.

Her new husband didn't blink. He stared at her so intently through his steel-rimmed spectacles that she thought she could feel his gaze on her skin, from across the room and right through her dove-gray dress, and she thought she might burst with happiness, exploding in bits all over the taproom of the White Camel tavern. Not that anyone would notice if she did; there were so many people crammed into the room, drinking, talking, drinking, singing, and drinking, that a spare gallbladder or kidney underfoot would pass without notice.

Just possibly, she thought, one or two whole people might pass without notice, too—right out of this lovely party.

She reached Denzell with some difficulty, there being a great many well-wishers between them, but as she approached him, he stretched out a hand and seized hers, and an instant later they were outside in the night air, laughing like loons and kissing each other in the shadows of the Anabaptist Meeting House that stood next door to the tavern.

"Will thee come home now, Dorothea?" Denny said, pausing for a momentary breath. "Is thee . . . ready?"

She didn't let go of him but moved closer, dislodging his glasses and enjoying the scent of his shaving soap and the starch in his linen—and the scent of him underneath.

"Are we truly married now?" she whispered. "I am thy wife?"

"We are. Thee is," he said, his voice slightly husky. "And I am thy husband."

She thought he'd meant to speak solemnly, but such an uncontainable smile of joy spread across his face at the speaking that she laughed out loud.

"We didn't say 'one flesh' in our vows," she said, stepping back but keeping hold of his hand. "But does thee think that principle obtains? Generally speaking?"

He settled his glasses more firmly on his nose and looked at her with intense concentration and shining eyes. And, with one finger of his free hand, touched her breast.

"I'm counting on it, Dorothea."

SHE'D BEEN IN his rooms before. But first as a guest, and then as an assistant, coming up to pack a basket with bandages and ointments before accompanying him to some professional call. It was quite different now.

He'd opened all the windows earlier and left them so, careless of flying insects and the butcher's shop down the street. The second floor of the building would have been suffocating after the day's heat—but with the gentle night breeze coming through, the air was like warm milk, soft and liquid on the skin, and the meaty smells of the butcher's shop were now overborne by the night perfume of the gardens at Bingham House, two streets over.

All trace of his profession had been cleared away, and the light of the candle he lit shone serenely on a plainly furnished but comfortable room. Two small wing chairs sat beside the hearth, a single book on the table between them. And, through the open door, a bed fresh-made with a smooth counterpane and plump white pillows beckoned enticingly.

The blood still thrummed through her body like wine, though she'd had very little to drink. Still, she felt unaccountably shy and stood for a moment just inside the door, as though waiting to be invited in. Denny lit two more candles and, turning, saw her standing there.

"Come," he said softly, stretching out a hand to her, and she did. They kissed lingeringly, hands roaming slowly, clothes beginning to loosen. Her hand drifted casually down and touched him through his breeches. He drew breath and would have said something, but wasn't quick enough.

"One flesh," she reminded him, smiling, and cupped her hand. "I want to see thy half of it."

"THEE *HAS* SEEN such things before," Denny said. "I know thee has. Thee has brothers, for one thing. And—and in the course of . . . of treating wounded men . . ." He was lying naked on the bed, and so was she, fondling the object in question, which seemed to be enjoying the attention immensely. His fingers were sliding through her hair, playing with her earlobes.

"I hope thee doesn't think I ever did this to any of my brothers," she said, sniffing him with pleasure. "And those of wounded men aren't generally in a condition to be appreciated at all."

Denny cleared his throat and stretched himself a little, not quite squirming.

"I think thee should allow me to appreciate thy own flesh for a bit," he said. "If thee expects me to be able to make thee a wife tonight."

"Oh." She looked down at his cock and then at herself, surprised. "What do—does thee—mean? Why wouldn't thee be able to?"

"Ah." He looked pleased and eager—he was so young without his glasses—and bounced off the bed, going into the outer room, his bottom pale and tidy in the candlelight. To Dottie's astonishment, he came back with the book she'd noticed on the table and handed it to her. It was bristling with bookmarks, and as she took it, it fell open in her hands, displaying several drawings of a naked man in cross section, his private parts in various stages of operation.

She looked up at Denny in disbelief.

"I thought—I know thee is a virgin; I didn't want thee to be frightened, or unprepared." He was blushing like a rose, and instead of collapsing in howls of laughter, which she badly wanted to do, she shut the book gently and took his face between her hands.

"Is thee a virgin, too, Denny?" she said softly. His blush grew fierce, but he kept her gaze.

"Yes. But—I do know *how.* I'm a physician."

That was too much, and she did laugh, but in small, half-stifled blurts of giggling, which infected him, and in seconds they were in each other's arms on the bed, shaking silently, with occasional snorts and repetitions of "I'm a physician," which sent them into fresh paroxysms.

At last she found herself on her back, breathing heavily, Denny lying on top of her, and a slick of perspiration oiling them. She lifted a hand and touched his chest, and gooseflesh rippled over him, the dark hairs of his body curly and bristling. She was trembling, but not with either fear or laughter.

"Is thee ready?" he whispered.

"One flesh," she whispered back. And they were.

THE CANDLES had burned down nearly to their sockets, and the naked shadows on the wall moved slowly.

"Dorothea!"

"Thee should probably be quiet," she advised him, briefly removing her mouth in order to talk. "I've never done this before. Thee wouldn't want to distract me, now, would thee?" Before he could summon a single word, she had resumed her alarming actions. He groaned—he couldn't help it—and laid his hands gently, helplessly, on her head.

"It's called fellatio, did thee know that?" she inquired, pausing momentarily for breath.

"I did. How . . . I mean . . . Oh. Oh, God."

"What did you say?" Her face was beautiful, so flushed that the color showed even by candlelight, her lips deep rose and wet . . .

"I said—oh, God."

A smile lit her shadowed face with happiness, and her already firm grip on him tightened. His shadow jerked.

"Oh, *good,*" she said, and with a small, triumphant crow of laughter, bent to slay him with her sharp white teeth.

IAN AND RACHEL

IAN LIFTED THE GREEN gown off in a whuff of fabric, and Rachel shook her head hard, shedding hairpins in all directions with little pinging sounds. She smiled at him, her dark hair coming damply down in chunks, and he laughed and plucked out a few more of the little wire hoops.

"I thought I should die," she said, running her fingers through her loosened hair, which Jenny had put up before the party at the White Camel tavern. "Between the pins sticking into my head and the tightness of my stays. Unlace me, will thee—husband?" She turned her back to him but looked over her shoulder, eyes dancing.

He hadn't thought it possible to be more moved in his feelings or more excited in body—but that one word did both. He wrapped one arm around her middle, making her squeak, pulled the knot of her laces loose, and gently bit the back of her neck, making her squeak much louder. She struggled, and he laughed, holding her tighter as he loosened the laces. She was slim as a willow sapling and twice as springy; she squirmed against him, and the small struggle heated his blood still further. If he had had no self-control, he would have had her pinned to the bed in seconds, stays and shift and stockings be damned.

But he did and let her go, easing the stay straps off her shoulders and the stays themselves over her head. She shook herself again, smoothing down the damp shift over her body, then stood tall, preening for him. Her nipples stood out hard against the limp fabric.

"I won thy wager for thee," she said, passing a hand over the delicate blue satin ribbon threaded through the neck of her shift and fluttering the hem, adorned with embroidered flowers in blue and yellow and rose.

"How did ye hear about that?" He reached for her, pulled her close, and clasped both hands on her arse, bare under the shift. "Christ, ye've got a sweet round wee bum."

"Blasphemy, on our wedding night?" But she was pleased, he could tell.

"It's not blasphemy, it's a prayer of thanksgiving. And who told ye about the wager?" Fergus had bet him a bottle of stout that a Quaker bride would have plain linen undergarments. He hadn't known, himself, but had had hopes that Rachel wouldn't feel that pleasing her husband was the same thing as making a vain show for the world.

"Germain, of course." She put her own arms around him and clasped him in similar manner, smiling up. "Thine is neither wee nor round, but no less sweet, I think. Does thee need help with thy fastenings?"

He could tell she wanted to, so he let her kneel and unbutton the flies of his breeches. The sight of the top of her dark, disheveled head, bowed earnestly to the task, made him put his hand gently on it, feeling her warmth, wanting the touch of her skin.

His breeches fell and she stood up to kiss him, her hand caressing his standing cock as though by afterthought.

"Thy skin is so soft there," she said against his mouth. "Like velvet!"

Her touch wasn't tentative but very light, and he reached down and wrapped his fingers round hers, showing her the way of it, how to grasp it firmly and work it a bit.

"I like it when thee moans, Ian," she whispered, pressing closer and working it more than a bit.

"I'm not moaning."

"Yes, thee is."

"I'm only breathin' a bit. Here . . . I like that . . . but . . . here." Swallowing, he picked her up—she made a little whoop—and carried her the two steps to the bed. He dropped her onto the mattress—she made a louder whoop—and landed beside her, scooping her into his arms. There was a certain amount of writhing, giggling, and inarticulate noises, and she got him out of his calico shirt, while he had her shift pulled up at the bottom and down at the top but still puddled round her waist.

"I win," she said, wiggling the wadded shift down over her hips and kicking it off.

"Ye think that, do ye?" He bent his head and took her nipple in his mouth. She made a very gratifying noise and clutched his head. He butted her gently under the chin, then lowered his head and sucked harder, flicking his tongue like an adder's.

"I like it when ye moan, Rachel," he said, pausing for breath and grinning down at her. "D'ye want me to make ye scream?"

"Yes," she said, breathless, one hand on her wet nipple. "Please."

"In a bit." He'd paused to breathe, lifting himself above her to let a bit of air in between them—it was a small room, and hot—and she reached up to feel his chest. She rubbed a thumb lightly over his nipple, and the sensation shot straight down to his cock.

"Let me," she said softly, and lifted herself, a hand round his neck, and suckled him, very gently.

"More," he said hoarsely, bracing himself against her weight. "Harder. Teeth."

"Teeth?" she blurted, letting go.

"Teeth," he said breathlessly, rolling onto his back and pulling her on top. She drew breath and lowered her head, hair spilling across his chest.

"Ow!"

"Thee *said* teeth." She sat up anxiously. "Oh, Ian, I'm sorry. I didn't mean to hurt thee."

"I—ye didn't . . . well, ye did, but . . . I mean—do it again, aye?"

She looked at him, dubious, and it occurred to him that when Uncle Jamie told him to go slow and gentle with his virgin, it might not have been all to do with sparing the virgin.

"Here, *mo nighean donn*," he said, drawing her down beside him. His heart was hammering and he was sweating. He brushed the hair back from her temple and nuzzled her ear. "Slow for a bit, aye? Then I'll show ye what I mean by teeth."

IAN SMELLED OF wine and whisky and musky male skin—he burned astonishingly under her hands and smelled now something like a distant skunk, but in a much better way. She pressed her face into the curve of his shoulder, breathing him in with pleasure. She had his cock in her hand, gripping firmly . . . but curiosity made her loose her hold and grope lower, fingers probing through the thickness of his pubic hair. He breathed out very suddenly when she cupped his scrotum, and she smiled against his shoulder.

"Does thee mind, Ian?" she whispered, rolling the lovely egg-like shapes of his balls in her palm. She'd seen male scrota many times, baggy and wrinkled, and while she wasn't disgusted, had never thought them more than mildly interesting. This was wonderful, drawn up tight, the skin so soft and so hot. Daring, she scooted down a little and felt farther back between his legs.

He had an arm about her shoulders and it tightened, but he didn't tell her to stop, instead spreading his legs a little, allowing her to explore him. She'd wiped men's arses hundreds of time, and the fleeting thought occurred to her that not all of them took great care . . . but his hair was curly and very clean, and her hips moved against him involuntarily as her fingertip slid tentatively between his buttocks. He twitched, tensing involuntarily, and she stopped, feeling him shiver. Then she realized that he was laughing, shaking silently.

"Am I tickling thee?" she asked, raising up on one elbow. The light of the single candle flickered over his face, hollowing his cheeks and making his eyes shine as he smiled up at her.

"Aye, that's one word for it." He ran a hand half roughly up her back and gripped her by the nape. He shook his head slowly, looking at her. His hair had come loose from its binding and spread out dark behind his head. "Here I am, tryin' to go slow, tryin' to be gentle . . . and next thing I ken, ye're squeezin' my balls and stickin' your fingers up my arse!"

"Is that wrong?" she asked, feeling a slight qualm. "I didn't mean to be . . . er, too . . . bold?"

He pulled her down and hugged her close.

"Ye canna be too bold wi' me, lass," he whispered in her ear, and ran his own hand down her back—and down farther. She gasped.

"Shh," he whispered, and went on—slowly. "I thought—ye'd maybe be scairt at first. But ye're no scairt a bit, are ye?"

"I am. I'm t-terrified." She felt the laughter bubble up through her chest, but there was some truth in it, too—and he heard that. His hand stopped moving and he drew back enough to look at her, squinting a little.

"Aye?"

"Well . . . not terrified, exactly. But—" She swallowed, suddenly embarrassed. "I just—this is so nice. But I know when you—when we—well, it does hurt, the first time. I—I'm somewhat afraid that . . . well, I don't want to stop what we're doing, but I . . . I'd like to get that part over with, so I needn't worry about it."

"Over with," he repeated. His mouth twitched a bit, but his hand was gentle on the small of her back. "Well, then." He eased his other hand down and cupped her, very delicately, between the legs.

She was swollen there, and slippery—had been growing more so ever since he'd lifted her gown off over her head. His fingers moved, one and then two, playing, stroking . . . and . . . and . . .

It took her entirely by surprise, a feeling she knew but bigger, bigger, and then she gave way to it entirely, washed through with ecstasy.

She settled slowly into limpness, throbbing. Everywhere. Ian kissed her lightly.

"Well, that didna take verra long, did it?" he murmured. "Put your hands on my arms, *mo chridhe,* and hold on." He moved over her, agile as a big cat, and eased his cock between her legs, sliding slow but firm. Very firm. She flinched, clenching involuntarily, but the way was slick and her flesh swollen in welcome and no amount of resistance would keep him out.

She realized that her fingers were digging into his arms, but didn't let go.

"Am I hurting ye?" he said softly. He'd stopped moving, his full length inside her, stretching her in a most unnerving way. Something had torn, she thought; it burned a little.

"Yes," she said, breathless. "I don't . . . mind."

He lowered himself very slowly and kissed her face, her nose, her eyelids, lightly. And all the time the awareness of it—*him*—inside her. He pulled back a little and moved. She made a small, breathless noise, not quite protest, a little pain, not *quite* encouragement . . .

But he took it as that and moved more strongly.

"Dinna be worrit, lass," he said, a little breathless, too. "I won't take long, either. Not this time."

ROLLO WAS snoring in the corner, lying on his back for coolness, legs folded like a bug's.

She tasted faintly sweet, of her own musk and a trace of blandness with an animal tang that he recognized as his own seed.

He buried his face in her, breathing deep, and the slight salt taste of blood made him think of trout, fresh-caught and barely cooked, the flesh hot and tender, pink and slick in his mouth. She jerked in surprise and arched up into him, and he tightened his hold on her, making a low *hmmm* of reassurance.

It *was* like fishing, he thought dreamily, hands under her hips. Feeling with your mind for the sleek dark shape just under the surface, letting the fly come down just so . . . She drew her breath in, hard. And then engagement, the sudden sense of startlement, and then a fierce awareness as the line sprang taut, you and the fish so focused on each other that there was nothing else in the world . . .

"Oh, God," he whispered, and ceased to think, only feeling the small movements of her body, her hands on his head, the smell and taste of her, and her feelings washed through him with her murmured words.

"I love thee, Ian. . . ."

And there was nothing else in the world but her.

JAMIE AND CLAIRE

THE LIGHT OF a low yellow half-moon shone through gaps in the trees, glimmering on the dark rushing waters of the Delaware. So late at night, the air was cool by the river, very welcome to faces and bodies heated by dancing, feasting, drinking, and generally being in close proximity to a hundred or so other hot bodies for the last six or seven hours.

The bridal couples had escaped fairly early: Denzell and Dottie very inconspicuously, Ian and Rachel to the raucous shouts and indelicate suggestions of a roomful of festive wedding guests. Once they'd left, the party had settled down to serious merrymaking, the drinking now unhampered by the interruption of wedding toasts.

We'd taken our leave of the Grey brothers—Hal, as father of one of the brides, was hosting the party—sometime after midnight. Hal had been sitting in a chair near a window, very drunk and wheezing slightly from the smoke, but sufficiently composed as to stand and bow over my hand.

"You want to go home," I advised him, hearing the faint squeak of his breathing over the winding-down noises of the party. "Ask John if he's got any more ganja, and if he does, smoke it. It will do you good." And not only in a physical way, I thought.

"I thank you for your kind advice, madam," he said dryly, and, too late, I recalled our conversation the last time he had been exposed to ganja: his worry over his son Benjamin. If he thought of it, too, though, he said nothing, and merely kissed my hand and nodded to Jamie in farewell.

John had stood by his brother's side most of the evening and stood behind him now as we took our leave. His eyes met mine briefly, and he smiled but didn't step forward to take my hand—not with Jamie at my shoulder. I wondered now briefly if I should ever see either of the Greys again.

We hadn't gone back to the printshop but had wandered down by the river, enjoying the coolness of the night air and chatting about the young couples and the excitements of the day.

"I imagine their nights are bein' a bit more exciting still," Jamie remarked. "Reckon the lassies will be sore come morning, poor wee things."

"Oh, it may not be just the girls," I said, and he sniffed with amusement.

"Aye, well, ye may be right about that. I seem to recall wakin' the next morning after our wedding and wondering for a moment whether I'd been in a fight. Then I saw you in the bed wi' me and *knew* I had."

"Didn't slow you down any," I remarked, dodging a pale stone in my path. "I seem to recall being rather rudely awakened next morning."

"Rude? I was verra gentle with ye. More than ye were with me," he added, a distinct grin in his voice. "I told Ian so."

"You told Ian *what*?"

"Well, he wanted advice, and so I—"

"Advice? *Ian*?" To my certain knowledge, the boy had begun his sexual career at the age of fourteen, with a prostitute of similar age in an Edinburgh brothel, and hadn't looked back. Besides his Mohawk wife, there were at least half a dozen other liaisons that I knew of, and I was sure I didn't know them all.

"Aye. He wanted to know how to deal kindly wi' Rachel, her bein' virgin. Something new to him," he added wryly.

I laughed.

"Well, they'll be having an interesting night of it, then—all of them." I told him about Dottie's request in camp, Rachel's advent, and our ad hoc session of premarital counseling.

"Ye told them *what*?" He snorted with amusement. "Ye make *me* say, 'Oh, God,' all the time, Sassenach, and it's mostly not to do wi' bed at all."

"I can't help it if you're naturally disposed to that expression," I said. "You *do* say it in bed with no little frequency. You even said it on our wedding night. Repeatedly. I remember."

"Well, little wonder, Sassenach, wi' all the things ye did to me on our wedding night."

"What I did to *you*?" I said, indignant. "What on earth did I do to you?"

"Ye bit me," he said instantly.

"Oh, I did not! Where?"

"Here and there," he said evasively, and I elbowed him. "Oh, all right—ye bit me on the lip when I kissed ye."

"I don't recall doing that at all," I said, eyeing him. His features were invisible, but the moonglow off the water as he walked cast his bold, straight-nosed profile in silhouette. "I remember you kissing me for quite a long time while you were trying to unbutton my gown, but I'm sure I didn't bite you then."

"No," he said thoughtfully, and ran a hand lightly down my back. "It was later. After I went out to fetch ye some food, and Rupert and Murtagh and the rest all chaffed me. I know, because it was when I drank some o' the wine I'd fetched back, I noticed it burned the cut in my lip. And I bedded ye again before I got round to the wine, so it must ha' been that time."

"Ha," I said. "By that time, you wouldn't have noticed if I'd bitten your head off like a praying mantis. You'd got it properly up your nose and thought you knew everything."

He put an arm round my shoulders, pulled me close, and whispered in my ear, "I'd got it properly up *you, a nighean.* And ye weren't noticing all that much yourself, besides what was goin' on between your legs."

"Rather hard to ignore that sort of carry-on," I said primly.

He gave the breath of a laugh and, stopping under a tree, gathered me in and kissed me. He had a lovely soft mouth.

"Well, I willna deny ye taught me my business, Sassenach," he murmured. "And ye made a good job of it."

"You caught on reasonably quickly," I said. "Natural talent, I suppose."

"If it was a matter of special training, Sassenach, the human race would ha' died out long since." He kissed me again, taking more time over it.

"D'ye think Denny kens what he's about?" he asked, letting go. "He's a virtuous wee man, aye?"

"Oh, I'm sure he knows everything he needs to," I protested. "He's a physician, after all."

Jamie gave a cynical laugh.

"Aye. While he may see the odd whore now and then, it's likely in the way of his profession, not hers. Besides . . ." He moved close and, putting his hands through the pocket slits in my skirt, took a firm and interesting grip on my bottom. "Do they teach ye in medical college how to spread your wife's wee hams and lick her from tailbone to navel?"

"*I* didn't teach you that one!"

"Indeed ye didn't. And you're a physician, no?"

"That—I'm sure that doesn't make any sense. Are you drunk, Jamie?"

"Dinna ken," he said, laughing. "But I'm sure *you* are, Sassenach. Let's go home," he whispered, leaning close and drawing his tongue up the side of my neck. "I want ye to make me say, 'Oh, God,' for ye."

"That . . . could be arranged." I'd cooled down during our walk, but the last five minutes had lit me like a candle, and if I'd wanted to go home and take off my stays before, I was now wondering whether I could wait that long.

"Good," he said, pulling his hands out of my skirt. "And then I'll see what I can make *you* say, *mo nighean donn.*"

"See if you can make me say, 'Don't stop.' "

PART SIX

The Ties That Bind

95

THE BODY ELECTRIC

Redondo Beach, CA
December 5, 1980

I F SHE HADN'T NEEDED stamps, she wouldn't have stopped in at the post office. She'd have clipped this batch of letters to the mailbox for the postman to collect, or posted them in the corner mailbox when she took the kids down to the beach to look for pelicans.

But she did need stamps; there were at least a dozen more niggling things to deal with: things needing notarization or photocopies or tax returns or . . .

"S-word," she muttered, sliding out of the car. "Bloody F-wording S-word!" This was small relief to her feelings of anxiety and oppression. It really wasn't fair. Who needed the relief of occasional bad language more than a mother of small children?

Maybe she should start using her mother's "Jesus H. Roosevelt Christ!" instead. Jem had incorporated that one into his own collection of expletives before he turned four and had long since taught it to Mandy; they wouldn't be warped by hearing it.

It hadn't been this hard, last time. Well, no, she corrected herself. It had been a lot harder, in the most important respect. But this . . . this . . . this quagmire of pettifogging details—property, bank accounts, leases, notifications . . . She flicked the sheaf of sealed envelopes in her hand against her thigh with irritation. Some days, she would have taken Jem and Mandy by their hands and run, not walked, straight into the stones with no feeling save relief at abandoning all this bloody Stuff.

She hadn't really had much Stuff when she did it the first time. And, of course, she'd had someone to leave it with. Her heart squeezed a little, remembering the day she'd nailed down the lid on the wooden shipping crate that held her family's modest history: the silver passed down through her father's family, cabinet photographs of her mother's parents, the collection of her father's first editions, her mother's World War II Queen Alexandra uniform cap, still with a faint but detectible odor of iodine about it. And taken such pains in writing the note to Roger to go with it: *You told me once that . . . everyone needs a history. This is mine. . . .*

Almost sure then that she'd never see Roger again, let alone the silverware.

She blinked hard and shoved the door of the post office open with so much force that it crashed into the wall, and everyone in the lobby turned to stare at her. Hot-faced, she grabbed the doorframe and closed it with exaggerated care, then crossed the lobby soft-footed, avoiding all eyes.

She shoved the envelopes through the collection-box slot one by one, with a certain feeling of grim satisfaction at each tedious thing disposed of. Preparing to disappear into the past, leaving all Stuff behind, was one thing; preparing to disappear while thinking that you might eventually come *back* and need that Stuff again—or that your children might come back twenty years later, without you . . . She swallowed. That was something else again, as her father was inclined to say. She couldn't just dump it all on Uncle Joe; he didn't—

She turned, glancing across the lobby automatically at her PO box, and stopped, seeing the letter. She felt the hairs rising on her forearm as she strode across the grubby linoleum and reached for the knob, even before her mind had consciously registered the fact that it didn't look like a utility bill, a credit-card application, or any other sort of official mail.

G-H-I-D-E-I . . . the tumblers of the combination lock fell and the heavy little door swung open. And right there in the post office, she smelled heather and peat smoke and the breath of the mountains, so strongly that her eyes blurred and her own breath caught in her throat.

It was a regular white envelope, addressed to her in Joe Abernathy's round, capable hand. She could feel something inside it, another envelope, this one with a lump on it—a seal of some kind? She made it to her rented car before ripping it open.

It wasn't an envelope but a sheet of paper, folded and sealed with wax, blurs of black ink bleeding through the paper where a quill had scratched too deep. An eighteenth-century letter. She pressed it to her face, inhaling, but the scent of smoke and heather was gone—if it had ever been there. It smelled now only of age and brittle paper; not even the tang of the iron-gall ink was left.

There was a brief note from Uncle Joe, a slip of paper folded next to the letter.

> *Bree, darlin'—*
>
> *Hope this catches you in time. It came from the estate agent in Scotland. He said when the new tenant at Lallybroch went to put the furniture in storage, they couldn't get that big old desk through the door of the study. So they called an antiques guy to take the thing apart—very carefully, he assured me. And when they did, they found three Queen Victoria stamps and this.*
>
> *I didn't read it. If you haven't left yet, let me know if you want the stamps; Lenny Jr. collects them and will give them a good home, if not.*
>
> *All my love,*
> *Uncle Joe*

She folded the note carefully, pressing the creases, tucking it into her handbag. She felt as though she ought to go somewhere else to read the letter, somewhere private and quiet, so she could go to pieces without anyone noticing. The seal was sooty gray candle wax, not sealing wax, and Roger had sealed it with his thumbprint. It wasn't necessary—she'd recognized the writing immediately—but there was no doubt of the tiny hook-shaped scar left when a scaling knife had slipped while he was cleaning a salmon he and Jem had caught in Loch Ness. She'd kissed it while the cut was healing, and a dozen times since.

But she couldn't wait and, hands trembling, opened her pocketknife and carefully pried off the seal, trying not to break it. It was old and brittle; the candle grease had seeped into the paper over the years, making a shadow around the glob of wax, and it shattered in her hand. She clutched the fragments convulsively and turned the folded paper over.

Brianna Randall Fraser MacKenzie, he'd written on the front. *To be kept until called for.*

That made her laugh, but the sound came out as a sob, and she dashed the back of her hand across her eyes, desperate to read.

The very first words made her drop the letter as though it were on fire.

November 15, 1739

She snatched it back up. Lest she somehow miss it, he'd underlined *1739*.

"How in bloody *hell* did you—" she said aloud, and clapped a hand over her mouth, where she kept it as she read the rest.

> *My Dearest Heart,*
>
> *I know what you're thinking, and I don't know. My best idea is that I've come in search of Jeremiah and found him—or may have found him—but not the person I thought I was looking for.*
>
> *I sought help at Lallybroch, where I met Brian Fraser (you would like him, and he, you), and through him—with the assistance of one Captain Jack Randall, of all people—came into possession of a set of RAF identification disks. I recognized the information on them.*
>
> *We (Buck is still with me) have been searching for Jem since our arrival and have found no sign at all. I won't give up—of course you know that—but as our inquiries have borne no fruit in the northern clan lands, I feel I must follow the one clue I have and see if I can locate the owner of those tags.*
>
> *I don't know what might happen, and I had to leave you some word, however faint the chance that you'll ever see it.*
>
> *God bless you and Jem—wherever he is, poor little guy, and I can only hope and pray he's safe—and my sweet Mandy.*
>
> *I love you. I'll love you forever.*
>
> *R.*

She didn't realize that she was crying, until the tears running down her face tickled her hand.

"Oh, Roger," she said. "Oh, dear *God.*"

IN THE LATE evening, with the kids safely asleep and the sound of the Pacific Ocean washing through the open balcony doors, Brianna took out a bound notebook, brand-new, and a Fisher Space Pen (guaranteed to write upside down, underwater, and in conditions of zero gravity), which she thought entirely appropriate to this particular piece of composition.

She sat down under a good light, paused for a moment, then got up and poured a glass of cold white wine, which she set on the table beside her notebook. She'd been composing bits of this in her mind all day and so began with no difficulty.

There was no telling how old the kids might be when—or if—they read it, so she made no effort to simplify things. It wasn't a simple matter.

A PRACTICAL GUIDE FOR TIME TRAVELERS—PART II

Right. Dad's written down what we think we know about this, in terms of observation of occurrence, physical effects, and morality. This next part could best be described as preliminary hypotheses of cause: how time travel might work. I'd call it the scientific part, but you can't actually apply the scientific method very far with the scanty data we have available.

Any scientific approach starts with observations, though, and we have enough of those to maybe construct a rough series of hypotheses. Testing those . . .

The idea of testing those made Brianna's hand shake so badly that she was obliged to set down her pen and breathe slowly for two or three minutes, until the black spots stopped swarming in front of her eyes. Gritting her teeth, she wrote:

Hypothesis 1: That the time passages/vortices/whatever the bloody hell they are/ are caused by or occur at the crossing of ley lines. (Defined here as lines of geomagnetic force, rather the folkloric definition of straight map lines drawn between ancient structures like hill forts, henges, or places of ancient worship, like saints' pools. Supposition is that folkloric lines may be identical or parallel with geomagnetic lines, but no hard evidence to this effect.)

Evidence in Support of Hypothesis: Some. But to start with, we don't know whether the standing stones are part of the vortex thingy or just markers set up when ancient people saw other ancient people step on the grass right . . . there . . . and poof!

"Poof," she muttered to herself, and reached for the glass of wine. She'd planned to drink it as a reward when she'd finished, but at the moment felt more in need of first aid than reward. "I *wish* it was just poof." One sip, two, then she set it down, the citric edge of the wine lingering pleasantly on her tongue.

"Where were we? Oh, poof . . ."

Dad was able to connect a lot of the folkloric leys to standing stone circles. It would theoretically be possible to check the geomagnetic polarity of the rock around standing stone circles; that should actually go some way toward supporting Hypothesis 1, but might be a little difficult to execute. That is, you can measure the earth's magnetic field—Carl Friedrich Gauss figured out how to do it back in 1835 or so—but it isn't the sort of thing individuals do much.

   Governments that do geological surveys have the equipment for it; I know the British Geological Survey's Eskdalemuir Observatory does, because I saw a write-up on them. And I quote: "Such observatories can measure and forecast magnetic conditions such as magnetic storms that sometimes affect communications, electric power, and other human activities."

"Other human activities," she muttered. "Riiight . . ."

The army does this sort of thing, too, she wrote as an afterthought. "Yes, I'll get the army right on that. . . ."

The pen hovered over the page as she thought, but she couldn't add anything else useful there, and so went on:

Hypothesis 2: That entering a time vortex with a gemstone (preferably faceted, vide *remarks made by Geillis Duncan to this effect) offers some protection to the traveler in terms of physical effect.*

   Query: why facets? We used mostly unfaceted ones coming back through Ocracoke, and we know of other travelers using plain unfaceted ones.

   Speculation: Joe Abernathy told me about one of his patients, an archaeologist who told him about some study done on standing stones up in Orkney, where they discovered that the stones have interesting tonal qualities; if you strike them with wooden sticks or other stones, you get a kind of musical note. Any kind of crystal—and all gems have a crystalline interior structure—has a characteristic vibration when struck; that's how quartz watches work.

   So what if the crystal you carry has vibrations that respond to—or stimulate, for that matter—vibrations in the standing stones nearby? And if they did . . . what might be the physical effect? D.B.K. *

She made a swift note at the bottom of the page: **D.B.K.—*Don't Bloody Know,* and returned to her writing.

Evidence: There really isn't any, other than the aforesaid remarks from Geillis Duncan (though she may have noted some anecdotal material in her journals, which you'll find in the large safe-deposit box at the Royal Bank of Scotland in Edinburgh. Uncle Joe will have the key or will have made provisions for you to get it).

   NB: Grannie Claire traveled the first two times without any stones (though note that she was wearing a gold wedding ring the first time, and a gold and a silver ring on the second journey).

Grannie said that going with a stone seemed slightly easier—but given the subjectivity of the experience, I don't know how much weight to put on that. Doing it with a stone is the most horrible thing I . . .

Maybe better not to say that. She hesitated for some time, but, after all, her own experiences were data, and given how little there was of it . . . She finished the sentence, then went on.

Hypothesis 3: That traveling with a gemstone allows one better control in choosing where/when to emerge.

She stopped, frowning, and crossed out *where*. There wasn't any indication of people traveling *between* sites. Be bloody handy if they could, though. . . . She sighed and went on.

Evidence: Pretty sketchy, owing to lack of data. We know of a few travelers other than ourselves, and of these, five Native Americans (part of a political group called the Montauk Five) traveled with the use of stones. One of these is known to have died in the attempt, one survived and traveled back about 200 years, and another, a man named Robert Springer (aka "Otter-Tooth"), traveled back more than the usual distance, arriving (approximately) 250–260 years prior to his year of departure. We don't know what happened to the two other members of this group; they may have traveled to a different time and we haven't found any mention of them (difficult to track down a time traveler, if you don't know when they may have gone, what their real names are, or what they look like), may have been blown out of the time vortex for unknown reasons, or may have died inside it.

That little possibility unnerved her so much that she set down the pen and took several large swallows of wine before resuming.

By the evidence of Otter-Tooth's journal, these men all did travel with gemstones, and he procured a large opal with which he intended to make the return trip. (This is the stone Jemmy made explode, in North Carolina, presumably because fire opals have a high water content.)

It hadn't—and, thinking back, she couldn't imagine how it hadn't—occurred to her at the time to see whether Jemmy could make water boil by touching it. Well, she could see why it hadn't occurred to her, in retrospect; the last thing she'd wanted was any more dangerous peculiarity near her children, much less dangerous peculiarities being inherent in them.

"I wonder how often it happens that two time travelers marry each other?" she said aloud. No telling what the frequency of the gene—if it was a gene, but that looked to be a decent bet—in the general population was, but it couldn't be *very* common, or people would be walking into Stonehenge and

Callanish and going *poof!* on a daily basis. . . . "Somebody would have noticed," she concluded, and sat twiddling the pen for a bit in meditation.

Might she have met and married Roger if it weren't for the time-traveling thing? No, because it was her mother's need to find out what had happened to the men of Lallybroch that had led them to Scotland.

"Well, I'm not sorry," she said aloud to Roger. "In spite of . . . everything."

She flexed her fingers and picked up the pen, but didn't write at once. She hadn't thought further with her hypotheses and wanted them to be clear in her mind, at least. She had vague notions about how a time vortex might be explained in the context of a unified field theory, but if Einstein couldn't do it, she didn't think she was up to it right this minute.

"It has to be in there *somewhere,* though," she said aloud, and reached for the wine. Einstein had been trying to form a theory that dealt both with relativity and electromagnetism, and plainly they were dealing with relativity here—but a sort in which it maybe wasn't the speed of light that was limiting. What, then? The speed of time? The *shape* of time? Did electromagnetic fields crisscrossing in some places warp that shape?

What about the dates? Everything they thought they knew—precious little as it was—indicated that travel was easier, safer, on the sun feasts and fire feasts; the solstices and equinoxes. . . . A little ripple ran up her back. A few things were known about standing stone circles, and one of the common things was that many had been built with astronomical prediction in mind. Was the light striking a specific stone the signal that the earth had reached some planetary alignment that affected the geomagnetism of that area?

"Huh," she said, and sipped, flipping back over the pages she'd written. "What a hodgepodge." This wouldn't do anyone much good: nothing but disconnected thoughts and things that didn't even qualify as decent speculation.

Still, her mind wouldn't let go of the matter. *Electromagnetism* . . . Bodies had electric fields of their own, she knew that much. Was that maybe why you didn't just disintegrate when you traveled? Did your own field keep you together, just long enough to pop out again? She supposed that might explain the gemstone thing: you *could* travel on the strength of your own field, if you were lucky, but the energy released from the molecular bonds in a crystal might well add to that field, so perhaps . . . ?

"Bugger," she said, her overworked mental processes creaking to a halt. She glanced guiltily at the hallway that led to the kids' room. They both knew that word, but they oughtn't to think their mother did.

She sank back to finish the wine and let her mind roam free, soothed by the sound of the distant surf. Her mind wasn't interested in water, though; it seemed still concerned with electricity.

"*I sing the Body Electric,*" she said softly. "*The armies of those I love engirth me.*"

Now, there was a thought. Maybe Walt Whitman had been onto something . . . because if the electric attraction of *the armies of those I love* had an effect on time-traveling, it would explain the apparent effect of fixing your attention on a specific person, wouldn't it?

She thought of standing in the stones of Craigh na Dun, thinking of Roger. Or of standing on Ocracoke, mind fixed fiercely on her parents—she'd read all the letters now; she knew exactly where they were. . . . Would that make a difference? An instant's panic, as she tried to visualize her father's face, more as she groped for Roger's . . .

The expression of the face balks account. The next line echoed soothingly in her head. *But the expression of a well-made man appears not only in his face;*

> *It is in his limbs and joints also, it is curiously in the joints of his hips and wrists;*
> *It is in his walk, the carriage of his neck, the flex of his waist and knees—dress does not hide him;*
> *The strong, sweet supple quality he has, strikes through the cotton and flannel;*
> *To see him pass conveys as much as the best poem, perhaps more;*
> *You linger to see his back, and the back of his neck and shoulder-side.*

She didn't remember any more, but didn't need to; her mind had calmed. "I'd know you anywhere," she said softly to her husband, and lifted the remains of her glass. *"Slàinte."*

96

NAY GREAT SHORTAGE
OF HAIR IN SCOTLAND

MR. CUMBERPATCH proved to be a tall, ascetic person with an incongruous crop of red curls that sat on his head like a small, inquisitive animal. He had, he said, taken the disks in trade for a sucking pig, along with a tin pan whose bottom had been burnt through but could easy be patched, six horseshoes, a looking glass, and half a dresser.

"Not really a tinker by trade, see?" he said. "Don't travel much. But things come and find me, they do."

Evidently they did. Mr. Cumberpatch's tiny cottage was crammed to its rafters with items that had once been useful and might be so again, once Mr. Cumberpatch got round to fixing them.

"Sell much?" Buck asked, raising an eyebrow at a disassembled carriage clock that sat on the hearth, its internal organs neatly piled into a worn silver comfit dish.

"Happen," Mr. Cumberpatch said laconically. "See anything ye like?"

In the interests of cooperation, Roger haggled politely for a dented canteen and a canvas bed sack with only a few small charred holes at one end, these the result of some soldier taking his rest too close to a campfire. And received in turn the name and general direction of the person from whom Mr. Cumberpatch had got the disks.

"Flimsy sort of jewel," his host said, with a shrug. "And t'old woman said she wouldn't have it in t'house, all those numbers might be to do with magic, aye? Her not holdin' with sorcery and t'like."

The old woman in question was possibly twenty-five, Roger thought, a tiny, dark-eyed creature like a vole, who—summoned to provide tea—sized them up with a shrewd glance and proceeded to sell them a small, flabby-looking cheese, four turnips, and a large raisin tart, at an extortionate price. But the price included her own observations on her husband's transaction—well worth it, so far as Roger was concerned.

"That ornament—strange thing, no?" she said, narrowing her eyes at the pocket where Roger had replaced it. "Man what sold it to Anthony said he'd had it from a hairy man, one of them as lives on the wall."

"Which wall would this be, missus?" Buck asked, draining his cup and holding it out for more. She gave him a look from her bead-bright eyes, obviously thinking him a simpleton, but they *were* paying customers, after all. . . .

"Why, the Roman one, to be sure," she said. "They say the old king o' the Romes put it up, so as to keep the Scots from coming into England." The thought made her grin, small teeth gleaming. "As though anybody'd want to be a-going *there* in t'first place!"

Further questions elicited nothing more; Mrs. Cumberpatch had no idea what was meant by "a hairy man"; that was what the man said, and she hadn't wondered about it. Declining an offer from Mr. Cumberpatch for his knife, Roger and Buck took their leave, the food wrapped in the bed sack. But as they did so, Roger saw a pottery dish containing a tangle of chains and tarnished bracelets, and a stray gleam of rainy light struck a tiny red glow.

It must have been Cumberpatch's description of the disks as a jewel—a common way to refer to a pendant ornament—that had made his mind sensitive. He stopped and, stirring the dish with a forefinger, drew out a small pendant, blackened, cracked, and with a broken chain—it looked as though it had been in a fire—but set with a fairly large garnet, caked with grime but faceted.

"How much for this?" he said.

IT WAS DARK by four o'clock, and long cold nights to be sleeping out of doors, but Roger's sense of urgency drove them on, and they found themselves benighted on a lonely road, with nothing but a wind-gnarled Caledonian pine for shelter. Starting a fire with tinder and damp pine needles was no joke, but after all, Roger reflected, grimly bashing steel and flint for the hundredth time—and his finger for the twentieth—they had nothing but time.

Buck had, with a forethought born of painful experience, brought a sack of peats, and after a quarter hour of frantic blowing on sparks and thrusting grass-stems and pine needles into the infant flame, they succeeded in getting two of these miserable objects to burn with sufficient heat as to roast—or at least sear—the turnips and warm their fingers, if not the rest of them.

There hadn't been any conversation since they'd left the Cumberpatch establishment: impossible to talk with the cold wind whistling past their ears as they rode, and no breath with which to do it during the struggle with fire and food.

"What'll you do if we find him?" Buck asked suddenly, mid-turnip. "If J. W. MacKenzie really is your father, I mean."

"I've speg"—Roger's throat was clogged from the cold and he coughed and spat, resuming hoarsely—"spent the last three days wondering that, and the answer is, I don't know."

Buck grunted and unwrapped the raisin tart from the bed sack, divided it carefully, and handed Roger half.

It wasn't bad, though Mrs. Cumberpatch couldn't be said to have a light hand with pastry.

"Filling," Roger remarked, thriftily dabbing crumbs off his coat and eating them. "D'ye not want to go, then?"

Buck shook his head. "Nay, I canna think of anything better to do. As ye say—it's the only clue there is, even if it doesna seem to have aught to do with the wee lad."

"Mmphm. And there's the one good thing—we can head straight south to the wall; we needn't waste time looking for the man Cumberpatch got the disks from."

"Aye," Buck said dubiously. "And then what? Walk the length of it, askin' after a hairy man? How many o' those do ye think there might be? Nay great shortage of hair in Scotland, I mean."

"If we have to," Roger said shortly. "But if J. W. MacKenzie—and not just his identity disks—was anywhere in the neighborhood, I'm thinking he would have caused a good bit of talk."

"Mmphm. And how long's this wall, d'ye know?"

"I do, yes. Or, rather," Roger corrected, "I know how long it was when it was built: eighty Roman miles. A Roman mile being just slightly shorter than an English one. No idea how much of it's still there now, though. Most of it, likely."

Buck grimaced. "Well, say we can walk fifteen, twenty miles in a day—the walkin' will be easy, if it's along a bloody wall—that's only four days to cover the lot. Though . . ." A thought struck him and he frowned, pushing his damp forelock back. "That's if we could walk from end to end. If we hit it midway, though, what then? We might cover half and find nothing, and then have to go all the way back to where we started." He looked accusingly at Roger.

Roger rubbed a hand over his face. It was coming on to rain, and the mizzle was misting on his skin.

"I'll think about it tomorrow, aye?" he said. "We'll have plenty of time to make plans on our way." He reached for the canvas bed sack, shook out a limp turnip frond and ate it, then pulled the sack over his head and shoulders. "Want to join me under this, or are ye for bed?"

"Nay, I'm all right." Buck pulled his slouch hat lower and sat hunched, toes as close to the remnants of the fire as he could get.

Roger drew his knees up and tucked in the ends of the bed sack. The rain made a gentle pittering on the canvas, and in the fatigue of exhaustion and cold, but with the comfort of a full stomach, he allowed himself the further comfort of imagining Bree. He did this only at night but looked forward to it with a greater anticipation than he did supper.

He envisioned her in his arms, sitting between his knees, her head lying back on his shoulder, snug under the canvas with him and her soft hair spangled with raindrops that caught the faint light of the fire. Warm, solid, breathing against his chest, his heart slowing to beat with hers . . .

"I wonder what I'd say to my own father," Buck said suddenly. "Had I ever kent him, I mean." He blinked at Roger from under the shadowed brim of his hat. "Did yours—does he, I mean—know about you?"

Roger suppressed his annoyance at being disturbed in his fantasy, but answered shortly. "Yes. I was born before he disappeared."

"Oh." Buck rocked back a little, looking meditative, but said no more. Roger found, though, that the interruption had made his wife vanish. He concentrated, trying to bring her back, imagining her in the kitchen at Lallybroch, the steam of cooking rising up around her, making wisps of red hair curl round her face and moisture gleam on the long straight bridge of her nose . . .

What he was hearing, though, was her arguing with him about whether he should tell Buck the truth of his begetting.

"Don't you think he has a right to know?" she'd said. *"Wouldn't you want to know something like that?"*

"Actually, I don't think I would," he'd said at the time. But now . . .

"Do you know who your father was?" Roger asked suddenly. The question had been in his mind for months, he unsure whether he had any right to ask it.

Buck gave him a baffled, faintly hostile glance.

"What the devil d'ye mean by that? Of course I do—or did. He's dead now." His face twisted suddenly, realizing. "Or—"

"Or maybe he's not, since ye're not born yet. Aye, it gets to ye after a bit, doesn't it?"

Apparently, it had just gotten to Buck. He stood up abruptly and stalked off. He stayed gone for a good ten minutes, giving Roger time to regret saying anything. But at last Buck came out of the dark and sat down again by the smoldering peat. He sat with his knees pulled up, arms locked round them.

"What did ye mean by that?" he asked abruptly. "Did I ken my father, and that."

Roger took in a deep breath of damp grass, pine needles, and peat smoke. "I mean ye werena born to the house ye grew up in. Did ye ken that?"

Buck looked wary and slightly bewildered. "Aye," he said slowly. "Or—

not kent it straight out, I mean. My parents didna have any bairns besides me, so I thought there was maybe—well, I thought I was likely a bastard born to my father's sister. She died, they said, about the time I was born, and she wasna marrit, so . . ." He shrugged, one-shouldered. "So, no." He turned his head and looked at Roger, expressionless. "How d'ye come to know, yourself?"

"Brianna's mother." He felt a sharp, sudden longing for Claire and was surprised at it. "She was a traveler. But she was at Leoch, about that time. And she told us what happened." He had the hollow-bellied feel of one about to jump off a precipice into water of unknown depth, but there was no way to stop now.

"Your father was Dougal MacKenzie of Castle Leoch—war chieftain of the clan MacKenzie. And your mother was a witch named Geillis."

Buck's face was absolutely blank, the faint firelight shimmering on the broad cheekbones that were his father's legacy. Roger wanted suddenly to go and take the man in his arms, smooth the hair back from his face, comfort him like a child—like the child he could so plainly see in those wide, stunned green eyes. Instead, he got up and went off into the night, giving his four-times great-grandfather what privacy he could in which to deal with the news.

IT HADN'T HURT. Roger woke coughing, and drops of moisture rolled tickling down his temples, dislodged by the motion. He was sleeping under the empty canvas bed sack rather than on it, valuing its water-resilience more than its potential comfort when stuffed with grass, but he hadn't been able to bear having it over his head.

He put a hand cautiously to his throat, feeling the thickened line of the rope scar cutting across the lower swell of his larynx. He rolled over, lifted himself on one elbow, and cleared his throat experimentally. It didn't hurt this time, either.

"Do you know what a hyoid bone is?" He did; as a result of a number of medical consultations about his damaged voice, he understood the anatomy of his throat quite well. And thus had known what Dr. McEwan meant; his own hyoid was placed slightly higher and farther back than the usual, a fortunate circumstance that had saved his life when he was hanged, as the crushing of that wee bone would have suffocated him.

Had he been dreaming of McEwan? Or of being hanged? Yes, that. He'd had dreams like that often in the months afterward, though they'd grown less frequent in later years. But he remembered looking up through the lacy branches of the tree, seeing—in the dream—the rope tied to the branch above him, and the desperate struggle to scream a protest through the gag in his mouth. Then the ineluctable sliding under him as the horse he sat on was led away . . . but this time it hadn't hurt. His feet had struck the ground and he waked—but waked without the choking or the burning, stabbing sensations that left him gasping and gritting his teeth.

He glanced across; yes, Buck was still there, huddled up under the ragged plaid he'd bought from Cumberpatch. Wise purchase.

He lay back down on his side, hauling the canvas up to shield his face while still allowing him to breathe. He'd admit to a feeling of relief at seeing Buck; he'd half-expected the man to decamp and head straight back to Castle Leoch after hearing the truth about his own family. Though, in justice to Buck, he wasn't a sneak. If he'd made up his mind to do that, he'd likely say so—after punching Roger in the nose for not telling him sooner.

As it was, he'd been there, staring into the ashes of the fire when Roger came back. He hadn't looked up, and Roger hadn't said anything to him but had sat down and taken out needle and thread to mend a rip in the seam of his coat.

After a bit, though, Buck had stirred himself.

"Why wait to tell me now?" he'd asked quietly. His voice held no particular note of accusation. "Why not tell me while we were still near Leoch and Cranesmuir?"

"I hadn't made up my mind to tell ye at all," Roger had said bluntly. "It was just thinking about—well, about what we're doing and what might happen. I thought of a sudden that maybe ye *should* know. And . . ." He hesitated for a moment. "I didn't plan it, but it's maybe better so. Ye'll have time to think, maybe, whether ye want to find your parents before we go back."

Buck had merely grunted in reply to that and said no more. But it wasn't Buck's response that was occupying Roger's mind at the moment.

It hadn't hurt when he'd cleared his throat while talking to Buck, though he hadn't noticed consciously at the time.

McEwan—was it what he'd done, his touch? Roger wished he'd been able to see whether McEwan's hand shed blue light when he'd touched Roger's damaged throat.

And what about that light? He thought that Claire had mentioned something like it once—oh, yes, describing how Master Raymond had healed her, following the miscarriage she'd had in Paris. Seeing her bones glow blue inside her body was how she'd put it, he thought.

Now, that was a staggering thought—was it a familial trait, common to time travelers? He yawned hugely and swallowed once more, experimentally. No pain.

He couldn't keep track of his thoughts any longer. Felt sleep spreading through his body like good whisky, warming him. And let go, finally, wondering what he might say to his father. If . . .

97

A MAN TO DO A MAN'S JOB

Boston, MA
December 8, 1980

G AIL ABERNATHY provided a quick but solid supper of spaghetti with meatballs, salad, garlic bread, and—after a quick, penetrating look at Bree—a bottle of wine, despite Brianna's protests.

"You're spending the night here," Gail said, in a tone brooking no opposition, and pointed at the bottle. "And you're drinking that. I don't know what you've been doing to yourself, girl, and you don't need to tell me—but you need to stop doing it."

"I wish I could." But her heart had risen the moment she walked through the familiar door, and her sense of agitation did subside—though it was far from disappearing. The wine helped, though.

The Abernathys helped more. Just the sense of being with friends, of not being alone with the kids and the fear and uncertainty. She went from wanting to cry to wanting to laugh and back again in the space of seconds, and felt that if Gail and Joe had not been there, she might have had no choice but to go into the bathroom, turn on the shower, and scream into a folded bath towel—her only safety valve in the last few days.

But now there was at least someone to talk to. She didn't know whether Joe could offer anything beyond a sympathetic ear, but at the moment that was worth more to her than anything.

Conversation over dinner was light and kid-oriented, Gail asking Mandy whether she liked Barbies and whether her Barbie had a car, and Joe talking soccer versus baseball—Jem was a hard-core Red Sox fan, being allowed to stay up to ungodly hours to listen to rare radio broadcasts with his mother. Brianna contributed nothing more than the occasional smile and felt the tension slowly leave her neck and shoulders.

It came back, though with less force, when dinner was over and Mandy—half-asleep with her arm in her plate—was carried off to bed by Gail, humming "Jesu, Joy of Man's Desiring" in a voice like a cello. Bree rose to pick up the dirty plates, but Joe waved her back, rising from his chair.

"Leave them, darlin'. Come talk to me in the den. Bring the rest of the wine," he added, then smiled at Jem. "Jem, whyn't you go up and ask Gail can you watch TV in the bedroom?"

Jem had a smudge of spaghetti sauce at the corner of his mouth, and his hair was sticking up on one side in porcupine spikes. He was a little pale from the journey, but the food had restored him and his eyes were bright, alert.

"No, sir," he said respectfully, and pushed back his own chair. "I'll stay with my mam."

"You don't need to do that, honey," she said. "Uncle Joe and I have grown-up things we need to talk about. You—"

"I'm staying."

She gave him a hard look, but recognized instantly, with a combination of horror and fascination, a Fraser male with his mind made up.

His lower lip was trembling, just a little. He shut his mouth hard to stop it and looked soberly from her to Joe, then back.

"Dad's not here," he said, and swallowed. "And neither is Grandda. I'm . . . I'm staying."

She couldn't speak. Joe nodded, though, as soberly as Jem, took a can of Coke from the refrigerator, and led the way to the den. She followed them, clutching the wine bottle and two glasses.

"Bree, darlin'?" Joe turned back for a moment. "Get another bottle from the cupboard over the stove. This is gonna take some talking."

It did. Jemmy was on his second Coke—the question of his going to bed, let alone to sleep, was clearly academic—and the second bottle of wine was one-third down before she'd finished describing the situation—all the situations—and what she thought of doing about them.

"Okay," Joe said, quite casually. "I don't believe I'm saying this, but you need to decide whether to go through some rocks in North Carolina or in Scotland and end up in the eighteenth century either way, is that it?"

"That's . . . most of it." She took a swallow of wine; it seemed to steady her. "But that's the first thing, yes. See, I know where Mama and Da are—were—at the end of 1778, and that's the year we'd go back to, if everything works the way it seems to have worked before. They'll either be back on Fraser's Ridge or on their way there."

Jem's face lightened a little at that, but he didn't say anything. She met his eyes directly.

"I was going to take you and Mandy through the stones on Ocracoke—where we came through before, you remember? On the island?"

"Vroom," he said very softly, and broke into a sudden grin, reliving his first exposure to automobiles.

"Yes," she said, smiling back despite herself. "Then we could go to the Ridge, and I was going to leave you with Grannie and Grandda while I went to Scotland to find Daddy."

Jem's smile faded, and his red brows drew together.

"Pardon my pointing out the obvious," Joe said. "But wasn't there a war going on in 1778?"

"There was," she said tersely. "And, yes, it might be a little bit difficult to get a ship from North Carolina to Scotland, but believe you me, I could do it."

"Oh, I do," he assured her. "It would be easier—and safer, I reckon—than going through in Scotland and searching for Roger with Jem and Mandy to look after at the same time, but—"

"I don't need looking after!"

"Maybe not," Joe told him, "but you got about six years, sixty pounds, and another two feet to grow before you can look after your mama. 'Til you get big enough that nobody can just pick you up and carry you off, she's got to worry about you."

Jem looked as if he wanted to argue the point, but he was at the age where logic did sometimes prevail, and happily this was one of those times. He made a small "mmphm" sound in his throat, which startled Bree, and sat back on the ottoman, still frowning.

"But you can't go to where Grannie and Grandda are," he pointed out. " 'Cuz Dad's not where—I mean when—you thought. He's not in the same time they are."

"Bingo," she said briefly, and, reaching into the pocket of her sweater, carefully withdrew the plastic bag protecting Roger's letter. She handed it to Joe. "Read that."

He whipped his reading glasses out of his own pocket and, with them perched on his nose, read the letter carefully, looked up at her, wide-eyed, then bent his head and read it again. After which he sat quite still for several minutes, staring into space, the letter open on his knee.

At last, he heaved a sigh, folded the letter carefully, and handed it back to her.

"So now it's space *and* time," he said. "You ever watch *Doctor Who* on PBS?"

"All the time," she said dryly, "on the BBC. And don't think I wouldn't sell my soul for a TARDIS."

Jem made the little Scottish noise again, and Brianna looked sideways at him.

"Are you doing that on purpose?"

He looked up at her, surprised. "Doing what?"

"Never mind. When you *are* fifteen, I'm locking you in the cellar."

"What? Why?" he demanded indignantly.

"Because that's when your father and grandfather started getting into real trouble, and evidently you're going to be just like them."

"Oh." He seemed pleased to hear this, and subsided.

"Well, putting aside the possibility of getting hold of a working TARDIS . . ." Joe leaned forward, topping up both glasses of wine. "It's possible to travel farther than you thought, because Roger and this Buck guy just did it. So you think you could do it, too?"

"I've got to," she said simply. "He won't try to come back without Jem, so I have to go find him."

"Do you know *how* he did it? You told me it took gemstones to do it. Did he have, like, a special kind of gem?"

"No." She frowned, remembering the effort of using the kitchen shears to snip apart the old brooch with its scatter of chip-like diamonds. "They each had a few tiny little diamonds—but Roger went through before with a single biggish diamond. He said it was like the other times we know about; it exploded or vaporized or something—just a smear of soot in his pocket."

"Mmm." Joe took a sip of wine and held it meditatively in his mouth for a moment before swallowing. "Hypothesis one, then: number is more important than size—i.e., you can go farther if you have more stones in your pocket."

She stared at him for a moment, somewhat taken aback.

"I hadn't thought of that," she said slowly. "The first time he tried it, though . . . he had his mother's locket; that had garnets on it. Definitely garnets, plural. But he didn't get through—he was thrown back, on fire." She shuddered briefly, the sudden vision of Mandy flung on the ground, burning . . . She gulped wine and coughed. "So—so we don't know whether he might have gone farther if he *had* gone through."

"It's just a thought," Joe said mildly, watching her. "Now . . . Roger's mentioning Jeremiah here, and it sounds like he means there's somebody besides Jemmy who's got that name. Do you know what he means?"

"I do." A skitter of something between fear and excitement ran down her back with icy little feet, and she took another swallow of wine and a deep breath before telling him about Jerry MacKenzie. The circumstances of his disappearance—and what her mother had told Roger.

"*She* thought he was very likely an accidental traveler. One who—who couldn't get back." She took another quick sip.

"That's my other grandda?" Jemmy asked. His face flushed a little at the thought and he sat forward, hands clutched between his thighs. "If we go where Dad is, will we get to meet him, too?"

"I can't even think about that," she told him honestly, though the suggestion made her insides curl up. Among the million alarming contingencies of the current situation, the possibility of meeting her deceased father-in-law face-to-face was about 999,999th on the list of Things to Be Worried About—but apparently it *was* on the list.

"But what did Roger mean about seeking Jeremiah?" Joe asked, clinging stubbornly to the point.

"We think that's how you . . . steer," Brianna said. "Focusing your thoughts on a particular person who's in the time you want to go to. We don't know that for sure, though," she added, and stifled a small belch. "Each time we—or Mama—did it, it was always two hundred and two years. And it was when Mama went back the first time—though come to think of it," she added, frowning, "she thought it might have been because Black Jack Randall—Daddy's ancestor—was there. He was the first person she met when she came through the stones. She said he looked a lot like Daddy."

"Uh-huh." Joe poured another half glass and stared at it for a moment, as though hypnotized by the soft reddish light glowing in its bowl. "But." He stopped, marshaling his thoughts. "But other people did go farther. This Geillis your mother mentioned, and Buck? Did he—never mind. Roger *and* Buck *did* do it this time, for sure. So it's possible; we just don't know how."

"I was forgetting Geillis," Bree said slowly. She'd seen the woman only once, and very briefly. A tall, slender figure, fair hair flying in the wind of a murderous fire, her shadow thrown onto one of the standing stones, enormous, elongated.

"Now that I think, though . . . I don't believe she had gemstones when she went back. She thought it took . . . er . . . sacrifice." She glanced at Jem, then looked at Joe, lowering her brows with a meaningful look that said, *"Don't ask."* "And fire. And she never came back the other way, though she planned to, with stones." And suddenly a penny that she hadn't known was there dropped. "She told Mama about using stones—not the other way around. So somebody . . . somebody *else* told her."

Joe digested that one for a moment, but then shook his head, dismissing the distraction.

"Huh. Okay, Hypothesis two: focusing your thoughts on a particular person helps you go to where they are. That make sense to you, Jem?" he asked, turning to Jemmy, who nodded.

"Sure. If it's somebody you know."

"Okay. Then—" Joe stopped abruptly, looking at Jem. "If it's somebody you *know?*"

The icy centipede came rippling up Bree's backbone and into her hair, making her scalp contract.

"Jem." Her voice sounded odd to her own ears, husky and half breathless. "Mandy says she can hear you—in her head. Can you . . . hear *her?*" She swallowed, hard, and her voice came clearer. "Can you hear Daddy that way?"

The small red brows drew together in a puzzled frown.

"Sure. Can't you?"

⸻

THE DEEP LINE between Uncle Joe's eyebrows hadn't gone away since the night before, Jem saw. He still looked friendly; he nodded at Jem and pushed a cup of hot chocolate across the counter to him, but his eyes kept going back to Mam, and every time they did, the line got deeper.

Mam was buttering Mandy's toast. Jem thought she wasn't as worried as she had been, and felt a little better himself. He'd slept all night, for the first time in a long time, and he thought maybe Mam had, too. No matter how tired he was, he usually woke up every couple of hours, listening out for noises, and then listening harder to be sure Mandy and Mam were still breathing. He had nightmares where they weren't.

"So, Jem," Uncle Joe said. He put down his coffee cup and patted his lips with a paper napkin left over from Halloween; it was black with orange jack-o'-lanterns and white ghosts on it. "Um . . . how far can you . . . er . . . you know, when your sister's not with you?"

"How far?" Jem said uncertainly, and looked at Mam. It hadn't ever occurred to him to wonder.

"If you went in the living room right now," Uncle Joe said, nodding at the door. "Could you tell she was in here, even if you didn't know she was in here?"

"Yeah. I mean, yes, sir. I think so." He stuck his finger in the hot chocolate: still too hot to drink. "When I was in the tunnel, in the train—I knew she was . . . somewhere. It's not like science fiction or anything, I mean," he added, trying to explain. "Not like X-rays or phasers or like that. I just . . . ." He struggled for an explanation and finally jerked his head at Mam, who was staring at him with a serious kind of look that bothered him a little. "I mean, if you closed your eyes, you'd still know Mam was here, wouldn't you? It's like that."

Mam and Uncle Joe looked at each other.

"Want toast?" Mandy thrust her half-gnawed piece of buttered toast at him. He took it and had a bite; it was good, squidgy white bread, not the home-baked brown kind Mam made, with gritty bits in it.

"If he could hear her—sense her—from the tunnel while she was at home, he can do it for a good long way," Mam said. "But I don't know for sure that she *was* at home then—I was driving all over with her, looking for Jem. And Mandy could sense him while we were in the car that night. But—" Now *her* eyebrows went together. He didn't like seeing a line there. "She was telling me she was getting colder, when we drove toward Inverness, but I don't know if she meant she couldn't hear him at all, or . . ."

"I don't think I can feel her when I'm at school," Jem said, anxious to be helpful. "But I'm not sure, 'cause I don't think about her at school."

"How far's the school from your place?" Uncle Joe asked. "You want a Pop-Tart, princess?"

"Yes!" Mandy's buttery round face lighted up, but Jem glanced at Mam. Mam looked as if she wanted to kick Uncle Joe under the counter for a second, but then she glanced down at Mandy and her face went all soft.

"All right," she said, and Jem felt a fluttery, excited sort of feeling in his middle. Mam was telling Uncle Joe how far the school was, but Jem wasn't paying attention. They were going to do it. They were really going to do it!

Because the only reason Mam would let Mandy eat Pop-Tarts without a fuss was because she figured she'd never get to eat another one.

"Can I have one, too, Uncle Joe?" he asked. "I like the blueberry ones."

98

THE WALL

HADRIAN'S WALL looked very much as Roger recalled it from a long-ago school trip. A huge thing, standing nearly fifteen feet high and eight feet wide, double stone walls filled with rubble in between, winding off into the distance.

The people were not that much different, either—at least in terms of speech and livelihood. They raised cattle and goats, and the Northumberland dialect had apparently not developed much since Geoffrey Chaucer's time.

Roger and Buck's Highland accents elicited slit-eyed looks of suspicious in-comprehension, and they were for the most part reduced to basic gestures and sign language in order to obtain food and—occasionally—shelter.

With a bit of trial and error, Roger did work out an approximate Middle English for *"Hast come here a stranger?"* From the looks of the place—and the looks he and Buck were getting—he would have said the contingency was remote, and so it proved. Three days of walking, and they were still plainly the strangest men anyone near the wall had ever seen.

"Surely a man dressed in RAF uniform would look even more peculiar than we do?" he said to Buck.

"He would," Buck replied logically, "if he was still wearing it."

Roger grunted in chagrin. He hadn't thought of the possibility that Jerry might have discarded his uniform on purpose—or been deprived of it by whomever came across him first.

It was on the fourth day—the wall itself had rather surprisingly changed, being no longer built of stone and rubble but of stacked turves—that they met a man wearing Jerry MacKenzie's flight jacket.

The man was standing at the edge of a half-plowed field, staring morosely into the distance, apparently with nothing on his mind save his hair. Roger froze, hand on Buck's arm, compelling him to look.

"Jesus," Buck whispered, grabbing Roger's hand. "I didn't believe it. That's it! Isn't it?" he asked, turning to Roger, brows raised. "I mean—the way ye described it . . ."

"Yes. It is." Roger felt his throat tighten with excitement—and fear. But there was only the one thing to be done, regardless, and, dropping Buck's hand, he forged through the dead grass and scattered rock toward the farmer, if that's what he was.

The man heard them coming and turned casually—then stiffened, seeing them, and looked wildly round for help.

"Eevis!" he shouted, or so Roger thought. Looking over his shoulder, Roger saw the stone walls of a house, evidently built into the wall.

"Put up your hands," Roger said to Buck, throwing up his own, palm out, to show his lack of threat. They advanced slowly, hands up, and the farmer stood his ground, though watching them as though they might explode if they got too close.

Roger smiled at the man and elbowed Buck in the ribs to make him do likewise.

"Gud morn," he said clearly and carefully. "Hast cum a stranger here?" He pointed to his own coat—and then to the flight jacket. His heart was thump-ing hard; he wanted to knock the man over and strip it off his back, but that wouldn't do.

"Naow!" said the man quickly, backing away, holding on to the edges of the jacket. "Begone!"

"We mean ye no harm, daftie," Buck said, in as conciliating a tone as he could manage. He patted the air in a soothing manner. "Kenst du dee mann . . . ?"

"What the bloody hell is *that*?" Roger asked, out of the side of his mouth. "Ancient Norse?"

"I don't know, but I heard an Orkneyman say it once. It means—"

"I can tell what it means. Does this look like Orkney to you?"

"No. But if you can tell what it means, maybe he can, too, aye?"

"Naow!" the man repeated, and bellowed, "EEVIS!" again. He began to back away from them.

"Wait!" said Roger. "Look." He fumbled quickly in his pocket and withdrew the little oilcloth packet holding his father's identity disks. He pulled them out, dangling them in the chilly breeze. "See? Where is the man who wore these?"

The farmer's eyes bulged, and he turned and ran clumsily, his clogs hindering him through the clods of the field, shouting, "Eevis! Hellup!" and several other, less comprehensible things.

"Do we want to wait for Eevis to turn up?" Buck said, shifting uneasily. "He may not be friendly."

"Yes, we do," Roger said firmly. The blood was high in his chest and face, and he flexed his hands nervously. Close. They were so close—and yet . . . his spirits went from exhilaration to plunging fear and back within seconds. It hadn't escaped him that there was a strong possibility that Jerry MacKenzie had been killed for that jacket—a possibility that seemed much more likely in view of their interlocutor's precipitate flight.

The man had disappeared into a windbreak of small trees, beyond which some sheds were visible. Perhaps Eevis was a stockman or dairyman?

Then the barking started.

Buck turned to look at Roger.

"Eevis, ye think?"

"Jesus Christ!"

A huge, broad-headed, barrel-chested brown dog with a broad, toothy jaw to match came galloping out of the trees and made for them, its proprietor bringing up the rear with a spade.

They ran for it, circling the house with Eevis on their heels, baying for blood. The broad green bank of the wall loomed up in front of Roger and he leapt for it, jamming the toes of his boots into the turf and scrabbling with fingers, knees, elbows—and likely his teeth, too. He hurled himself over the top and bounced down the far side, landing with a tooth-rattling thud. He was fighting to draw breath when Buck landed on top of him.

"Shit," his ancestor said briefly, rolling off him. "Come on!" He jerked Roger to his feet and they ran, hearing the farmer shouting curses at them from the top of the wall.

They found refuge in the lee of a crag a few hundred yards beyond the wall and collapsed there, gasping.

"The Emp . . . Emperor Had . . . rian kent what the blood . . . y hell he . . . was about," Roger managed, at last.

Buck nodded, wiping sweat from his face. "No . . . very hospitable," he wheezed. He shook his head and gulped air. "What . . . now?"

Roger patted the air, indicating the need for oxygen before he could formulate ideas, and they sat quiet for a bit, breathing. Roger tried to be logical about it, though spikes of adrenaline kept interfering with his thought processes.

One: Jerry MacKenzie had been here. That was all but certain; it was beyond the bounds of probability that there should be *two* displaced travelers wearing RAF flight jackets.

Two: he wasn't here now. Could that be safely deduced? No, Roger concluded reluctantly, it couldn't. He *might* have traded the jacket to Eevis's owner for food or something, in which case he'd likely moved on. But if that were the case, why had the farmer not simply said so, rather than setting the dog on them?

And if he'd stolen the jacket . . . either Jerry was dead and buried somewhere nearby—that thought made Roger's stomach clench and the hairs prickle on his jaw—or he'd been assaulted and stripped but perhaps had escaped.

All right. If Jerry was here, he was dead. And if so, the only way of finding out was to subdue the dog and then beat the information out of Eevis's owner. He didn't feel quite up to it at the moment.

"He's not here," Roger said hoarsely. His breathing was still hard, but regular now.

Buck gave him a quick look, but then nodded. There was a long streak of muddy green down his cheek, smeared moss from the wall that echoed the green of his eyes.

"Aye. What next, then?"

The sweat was cooling on Roger's neck; he wiped it absently with the end of the scarf that had somehow made it over the wall with him.

"I've got an idea. Given the reaction of our friend there"—he nodded in the direction of the farmstead, invisible beyond the green mass of the wall—"I'm thinking that asking for a stranger might be not the wisest thing. But what about the stones?"

Buck blinked at him in incomprehension.

"Stones?"

"Aye. Standing stones. Jerry did travel, we ken that much. What're the odds he came through a circle? And if so . . . they're likely none so far away. And folk wouldn't be threatened, I think, by two dafties asking after stones. If we find the place he likely came through, then we can start to cast out from there and ask at the places nearest to the stones. Cautiously."

Buck tapped his fingers on his knee, considering, then nodded.

"A standing stone isna like to bite the arses out of our breeks. All right, then; let's go."

99

RADAR

J EM FELT NERVOUS. Mam and Uncle Joe were both trying to act as if everything was okay, but even Mandy could tell something was up; she was squirming around in the backseat of Uncle Joe's Cadillac like she had ants in her pants, pulling up her buttoned sweater over her head so her black curls fluffed out of the neckhole like something boiling over.

"Sit *still*," he muttered to her, but he didn't expect her to, and she didn't. Uncle Joe was driving, and Mam had a map open in her lap.

"What are you doing, Mandy?" Mam said absently. She was making marks on the map with a pencil.

Mandy unbuckled her seat belt and popped up on her knees. She'd pulled her arms out of her sweater so they flopped around, and now just her face was poking out of the neckhole.

"I'm an ottopus!" she said, and shook herself so the sweater's arms danced. Jem laughed, in spite of himself. So did Mam, but she waved Mandy back down.

"Octopus," she said. "And put your seat belt back on right now. *Octo* means eight in Latin," she added. "Octopuses have eight legs. Or arms, maybe."

"You've only got four," Jem said to Mandy. "Does that make her a tetra-pus, Mam?"

"Maybe." But Mam had gone back to her map. "The Common, do you think?" she said to Uncle Joe. "It's a little more than a quarter mile across the longest axis. And we could go down into the Public Garden, if . . ."

"Yeah, good idea. I'll let you and Jem off on Park Street, then drive along Beacon to the end of the Common and back around."

It was cold and cloudy, with just a few flakes of snow in the air. He remembered Boston Common and was kind of glad to see it again, even with the trees leafless and the grass brown and dead. There were still people there; there always were, and their winter hats and scarves looked happy, all different colors.

The car stopped on Park Street, across from the tourist trolleys that stopped every twenty minutes. Dad had taken them all on one once—one of the orange ones, with the open sides. It had been summer then.

"Do you have your mittens, sweetheart?" Mam was already out on the sidewalk, peering through the window. "You stay with Uncle Joe, Mandy— just for a few minutes."

Jem got out and stood with Mam on the sidewalk, putting on his mittens while they watched the gray Caddy pull away.

"Close your eyes, Jem," Mam said quietly, and took his hand, squeezing it. "Tell me if you can feel Mandy in your head."

"Sure. I mean, yes. She's there." He hadn't thought of Mandy as a little red light before the business in the tunnel with the train, but now he did. It kind of made it easier to concentrate on her.

"That's good. You can open your eyes if you want to," Mam said. "But keep thinking about Mandy. Tell me if she gets too far away for you to feel."

He could feel Mandy all the way, until the Caddy pulled up next to them again—though she had got a little fainter, then stronger again.

They did it again, with Uncle Joe and Mandy going all the way down to Arlington Street, on the far side of the Public Garden. He could still do it and was getting kind of cold and bored, standing there on the street.

"She can hear him fine," Uncle Joe reported, rolling down his window. "How 'bout you, sport? You hear your sister okay?"

"Yeah," he said patiently. "I mean—I can tell where she is, kind of. She doesn't talk in my head or anything like that." He was glad she didn't. He wouldn't want Mandy chattering away in his head all the time—and he didn't want her listening to his thoughts, either. He frowned at her; he hadn't actu- ally thought of *that* before.

"You can't hear what I'm thinking, can you?" he demanded, shoving his face in the open window. Mandy was riding up front now and looked up at him, surprised. She'd been sucking her thumb, he saw; it was all wet.

"No," she said, kind of uncertainly. He could see she was sort of scared by this. So was he, but he figured he wouldn't let her—or Mam—know that.

"That's good," he said, and patted her on the head. She hated being pat- ted on the head and swiped at him with a ferocious snarl. He stepped back out of reach and grinned at her.

"If we have to do it again," he said to his mother, "maybe Mandy can stay with you, and I'll go with Uncle Joe?"

Mam glanced uncertainly at him, then at Mandy, but seemed to get what he was really saying and nodded, opening the door for Mandy to bounce out, relieved.

Uncle Joe hummed softly to himself as they turned around, went right, and headed down past the big theater and the Freemasons' building. Jem could see Uncle Joe's knuckles showing through his skin, though, where he was clutching the wheel.

"You nervous, sport?" Uncle Joe said, as they passed the Frog Pond. It was drained for the winter; it looked sort of sad.

"Uh-huh." Jem swallowed. "Are you?"

Uncle Joe glanced at him, kind of startled, then smiled as he turned back to keep his eyes on the road.

"Yeah," he said softly. "But I think it's gonna be okay. You'll take good care of your mom and Mandy, and you'll find your dad. You'll be together again."

"Yeah," Jem said, and swallowed again.

They drove in silence for a little bit, and the snow made little scratchy noises on the windshield, like salt being shaken on the glass.

"Mam and Mandy are gonna be pretty cold," Jem ventured.

"Yeah, this'll be our last try today," Uncle Joe assured him. "Still got her? Mandy?"

He hadn't been paying attention; he'd been thinking about the stone circles. And the thing in the tunnel. And Daddy. His stomach hurt.

"No," he said blankly. "No! I can't feel her!" The idea suddenly panicked him and he stiffened in his seat, pushing back with his feet. "Drive back!"

"Right away, pal," Uncle Joe said, and made a U-turn right in the middle of the street. "Gloucester Street. Can you remember that name? We need to tell your mom, so she can work out the distance."

"Uh-huh," Jem said, but he wasn't really listening to Uncle Joe. He was listening hard for Mandy. He'd never thought about it at all before this, never paid any attention to whether he could sense her or not. But now it was important, and he balled up his fists and shoved one into his middle, under his ribs, where the hurt was.

Then there she was, just as though she'd always been there, like one of his toenails or something, and he let his breath out in a gasp that made Uncle Joe look sharply at him.

"You got her again?"

Jem nodded, feeling inexpressible relief. Uncle Joe sighed and his big shoulders relaxed, too.

"Good," he said. "Don't let go."

BRIANNA PICKED UP Esmeralda the rag doll from the floor of the Abernathys' guest room and tucked her carefully in next to Mandy. *Four miles.* They'd spent the morning driving round Boston in circles, and now they knew roughly how far the kids' mutual radar went. Jem could sense Mandy at a little over a mile, but she could sense him at nearly four. Jem could sense Brianna, too, but only vaguely and only for a short distance; Mandy could sense her mother almost as far as she could detect Jem.

She should write that down in the guide, she thought, but she'd spent the afternoon in frenzied arrangements, and right now the effort of finding a pencil felt like searching for the source of the Nile or climbing Kilimanjaro. *Tomorrow.*

The thought of tomorrow jolted her out of her exhausted torpor with a zap of adrenaline. Tomorrow, it would start.

They'd talked, after the kids had gone to bed. She and Joe, with Gail listening in the corner, the whites of her eyes showing now and then, but saying not a word.

"It has to be Scotland," she'd explained. "It's December; ships can't sail until the springtime. If we crossed in North Carolina, we couldn't travel from the colonies before April and wouldn't get to Scotland before the summer. And putting aside the fact that I know what ocean travel in the eighteenth century is like and I wouldn't do that with children unless the alternative was being shot . . . I can't wait that long."

She'd taken a gulp of wine and swallowed, but the knot in her throat didn't go down, any more than it had with the last half-dozen swallows. *Anything could happen to him in six months. Anything.* "I—have to find him."

The Abernathys glanced at each other, and Gail's hand touched Joe gently on the knee.

"Of course you do," she said. "You sure about Scotland, though? What about the people that tried to take Jem from you? Won't they be waiting, if you go back?"

Bree laughed—shakily, but a laugh.

"Another reason to go right away," she said. "In the eighteenth century, I can stop looking over my shoulder."

"You haven't seen anybody—" Joe started, frowning, but she shook her head.

"Not in California. And not here. But I keep watching." She'd taken a few other precautions, too, things she'd recalled from her father's brief—and discreet—memoir of his World War II experiences, but no need to go into those.

"And you have some idea how to keep the kids safe in Scotland?" Gail was perched uneasily on the edge of her seat, as though wanting to spring up and go check on the kids. Brianna knew the feeling.

She sighed and wiped a straggle of hair out of her eye.

"There are two people—well, three—there that I think I can trust."

"You think," Joe echoed, sounding skeptical.

"The only people I *know* I can trust are right here," she said simply, and lifted her wineglass to them. Joe looked away and cleared his throat. Then he glanced at Gail, who nodded at him.

"We'll go with you," he said firmly, turning back to Bree. "Gail can mind the kids, and I can make sure nobody bothers you 'til you're set to go."

She bit her lip to quell the rising tears.

"No," she said, then cleared her own throat hard, to kill the quaver in her voice—caused as much by the vision of the two Drs. Abernathy strolling the streets of Inverness as by gratitude. It wasn't that there were *no* black people in the Highlands of Scotland, but they were sufficiently infrequent as to cause notice.

"No," she repeated, and took a deep breath. "We'll go to Edinburgh to start; I can get the things we need there, without attracting attention. We won't go up to the Highlands until everything is ready—and I'll only get in touch with my friends there at the last minute. There won't be time for anyone else to realize we're there, before we—before we go . . . through."

That one word, "through," hit her like a blow in the chest, freighted as it was with memory of the howling void that lay between now and then. Between herself and the kids—and Roger.

The Abernathys hadn't given up easily—or altogether; she was sure there would be another attempt at breakfast—but she had faith in her own stubbornness and, pleading exhaustion, had escaped from their kind worries in order to be alone with her own.

She *was* exhausted. But the bed she'd share with Mandy didn't draw her. She needed just to be alone for a bit, to decompress before sleep would come. She could hear going-to-bed noises on the floor below; taking off her shoes, she padded silently down to the first floor, where a light had been left on in the kitchen and another at the end of the hallway by the den, where Jem had been put to bed on the big couch.

She turned to go and check on him, but her attention was diverted by a familiar metallic *chunk!* The kitchen had a pocket door, slid half across. She stepped up to it and glanced through the opening, to discover Jem standing on a chair next to the counter, reaching to pull a Pop-Tart out of the toaster.

He looked up, wide-eyed at the sound of her step, held the hot pastry for a second too long, and dropped it as it burned his fingers.

"Ifrinn!"

"Don't say that," she told him, coming to retrieve the fallen tart. "We're about to go where people would understand it. Here—do you want some milk with that?"

He hesitated for an instant, surprised, then hopped down like a towhee, both feet together, and landed with a light thud on the tiled floor. "I'll get it. You want some, too?" Suddenly, nothing on earth sounded better than a hot blueberry Pop-Tart with melting white icing and a glass of cold milk. She nodded and broke the hot tart in two, putting each half on a paper towel.

"Couldn't sleep?" she finally said, after they'd eaten their snack in companionable silence. He shook his head, red hair ruffled up in porcupine spikes.

"Want me to read you a story?" She didn't know what made her say that; he was much too old to be read to, though he was always somewhere nearby when she read to Mandy. He gave her a jaundiced look, but then, surprisingly, nodded and scampered up to the third floor, coming back with the new copy of *Animal Nursery Tales* in hand.

He didn't want to lie down right away but sat very close to her on the sofa while she read, her arm round his shoulders and his weight growing warm and heavy against her side as his breathing slowed.

"My dad used to read to me if I woke up and couldn't go back to sleep," she said softly, turning the last page. "Grandpa Frank, I mean. It was a lot like this; everything quiet." And themselves cozy and bonelessly content, alone together in a puddle of warm yellow light, with the night far away.

She felt Jem's sleepy interest rise.

"Was he like Grandda? Grandpa Frank?" She'd told the kids little things about Frank Randall, not wanting him to be forgotten, but she knew he'd never be much more than a faint ghost beside the vivid warmth of their other grandfather—the grandfather they might have back. She felt a sudden small tearing in her heart, a vivid second of understanding for her mother.

Oh, Mama . . .

"He was different," she said softly, her mouth brushing his bright hair. "He was a soldier, though—they had that in common. And he was a writer, a scholar—like Daddy. All of them were—are—alike, though: they'd all take care of people. It's what a good man does."

"Oh." She could feel him falling asleep, struggling to keep a hold on consciousness, the dreams beginning to walk through his waking thoughts. She eased him down into the nest of blankets and covered him, smoothing the cowlick on the crest of his head.

"Could we see him?" Jem said suddenly, his voice drowsy and soft.

"Daddy? Yes, we'll see him," she promised, making her own voice solid with confidence.

"No, *your* daddy . . ." he said, his eyes half open, glazed with sleep. "If we go through the stones, could we see Grandpa Frank?"

Her mouth dropped open, but she still hadn't found an answer when she heard him start to snore.

100

BE THOSE THY BEASTS?

WHILE IT WAS undeniably true that standing stones didn't bite, Roger thought, that didn't mean they weren't dangerous.

It had taken them only a day and a half to find the stone circle. He'd made a quick sketch of standing stones on the back of his hand with a bit of charcoal, to assist communication, and it had worked surprisingly well. While the scattered people they'd found had regarded them with immense curiosity—and not a few private glances accompanied by whirling motions of the forefinger beside the head—no one had found the visitors more than odd, and everyone had known where the stones were.

They'd come across a tiny village, in fact—consisting of a church, a public house, a smithy, and several houses—where the last household they'd approached had even sent one of their younger sons along to guide Buck and Roger to their goal.

And there they were now: a scatter of stumpy, lichened, wind-scored pillars beside a shallow lake filled with reeds. Ageless, harmless, part of the landscape—and the sight of them filled Roger with a fear that shivered as coldly over his skin as though he stood there naked to the wind.

"Can ye hear them?" Buck muttered under his breath, his own eyes fixed on the stones.

"No," Roger muttered back. "Can you?"

"I hope not." But Buck shuddered suddenly, as though something had walked across his grave.

"Be those thy be-asts?" the boy asked, grinning at Roger. He pointed at the stones, explaining—Roger thought—the local legend that the stones were in fact faery cattle, frozen in place when their drover had too much drink betaken and fell into the lake.

"Sooth," the boy assured them solemnly, making a cross over his heart. "Mester Hacffurthe found es whip!"

"When?" Buck asked sharply. "And where liveth Mester Hacffurthe?"

A week ago, maybe twa, said the boy, waving a hand to indicate that the date was not important. And he would take them to Mester Hacffurthe, if they liked to see the thing.

Despite his name, Mester Hacffurthe proved to be a slight, light-haired young man, the village cobbler. He spoke the same impenetrable Northumbrian dialect, but with some effort and the helpful intervention of the boy—whose name, he said, was Ridley—their desire was made clear, and Hacffurthe obligingly fetched the faery whip out from under his counter, laying it gingerly before them.

"Oh, Lord," Roger said at sight of it—and, with a raised brow at Hacffurthe to ask permission, touched the strip carefully. A machine-woven, tight-warped strip some three inches wide and two feet long, its taut surface gleaming even in the dim light of the cobbler's shop. Part of the harness of an RAF flier. They had the right stones, then.

Careful questioning of Mr. Hacffurthe, though, elicited nothing else helpful. He had found the faery lash lying in the shallows of the lake, washing to and fro among the reeds, but had seen nothing else of note.

Roger noticed, though, that Ridley twitched slightly when Mr. Hacffurthe said this. And after they had left the cobbler's house, he paused at the edge of the village, hand in his pocket.

"I thank 'ee, Master Ridley," he said, and pulled out a broad tuppenny piece that made the boy's face light up. Roger put it into Ridley's hand, but, when the boy would have turned to go, laid his own hand on the lad's arm.

"One thing more, Master Ridley," he said, and, with a glance at Buck, drew out the identity disks.

Ridley jerked in Roger's grasp, his round face going pale. Buck made a small sound of satisfaction and took Ridley by his other arm.

"Tell us about the man," Buck suggested pleasantly. "And I might not break thy neck."

Roger shot Buck a glance of annoyance, but the threat was effective. Ridley gulped as though he'd swallowed a mushroom whole, but then began to talk. Between Ridley's dialect and his distress, the tale took some time to piece together, but at last Roger was fairly sure they had the gist of it.

"Let him go," he said, letting go of Ridley himself. He groped in his pocket and came out with another copper penny, which he offered to the boy. Ridley's face flexed between fear and outrage, but after a moment's hesitation, he snatched the penny and made off, glancing over his shoulder as he ran.

"He'll tell his family," Buck observed. "We'd best hurry."

"We had. But not on that account—it's getting dark." The sun was very low, a brilliant band of yellow light showing at the foot of a cold ochre sky. "Come on. We need to take the direction while we can."

So far as Roger had been able to follow Ridley's story, the strangely dressed man (some said he was a faerie, some thought him a northerner, though there was confusion as to whether this meant a Scot, a Norseman, or something else) had had the ill luck to show up at a farm two or three miles from the stones, where he had been set upon by the inhabitants, these being an antisocial clan called Wad.

The Wads had taken everything of apparent value off the man, beaten him, and tossed him into a ravine—one of the Wads had boasted of it to a drover passing through, who had mentioned the stranger in the village.

The village had of course been interested—but not sufficiently so as to go looking for the man. When Hacffurthe the cobbler had found the peculiar strip of cloth, though, rumors had started to fly thick and fast. Excitement had reached a higher pitch this very afternoon, when one of Mester Quarton's cowmen had come into the village to have a boil lanced by Granny Racket and revealed that a stranger with incomprehensible speech had tried to steal a pie from Missus Quarton's sill and was even now held captive whilst Mester Quarton thought what best to do with him.

"What *might* he do?" Roger had asked. Ridley had pushed out his lips portentously and shaken his head.

"Might kill 'un," he said. "Might take 'un's hand off. Mester Quarton don't hold with thievin'."

And that—aside from a vague direction regarding the location of the Quarton farm—was that.

"This side of the wall, two miles west and a little south, below a ridge and along the stream," Roger said grimly, lengthening his stride. "If we can find the stream before full dark . . ."

"Aye." Buck fell in beside him as they turned toward where they'd left the horses. "Suppose Quarton keeps a dog?"

"Everybody here keeps a dog."

"Oh, God."

101

JUST ONE CHANCE

THERE WAS NO MOON. Undeniably a good thing, but it had its drawbacks. The farmhouse and its outbuildings lay in a pocket of darkness so profound that they mightn't have known it was there, had they not seen it before the light was quite gone. They'd waited, though, for full dark and the dousing of the dim candlelight inside the house, and then an extra half hour or so to ensure that the inhabitants—and their dogs—were well asleep.

Roger was carrying the dark lantern, but with the slide still closed; Buck ran into something lying on the ground, let out a startled cry, and fell head-long over it. The something proved to be a large sleeping goose, which let out a startled *whonk!* somewhat louder than Buck's cry, and promptly set about him with beak and thrashing wings. There was a sharp, inquiring bark in the distance.

"Hush!" Roger hissed, coming to his ancestor's aid. "Ye'll wake the dead, let alone them in the house." He dropped his cloak over the goose, which shut up and began waddling around in confusion, a mobile heap of dark cloth. Roger clapped a hand to his mouth, but couldn't help snorting through his nose.

"Aye, right," Buck whispered, getting to his feet. "If ye think I'm getting your cloak back for ye, think again."

"He'll get out of it soon enough," Roger whispered back. "He's no need of it. Meanwhile, where the devil d'ye think they've got him?"

"Someplace that's got a door ye can bolt." Buck rubbed his palms to-gether, brushing off the dirt. "They'd no keep him in the house, though, would they? It's no that big."

It wasn't. You could have fitted about sixteen farmhouses that size into Lallybroch, Roger thought, and felt a sudden sharp pang, thinking of Lally-broch as it was when he had—he would—own it.

Buck was right, though: there couldn't be more than two rooms and a loft, maybe, for the kids. And given that the neighbors thought Jerry—if it was Jerry—was a foreigner at best, a thief and/or supernatural being at worst, it wasn't likely that the Quartons would be keeping him in the house.

"Did ye see a barn, before the light went?" Buck whispered, changing to Gaelic. He had risen onto his toes, as though that might help him see above the tide of darkness, and was peering into the murk. Dark-adapted as Roger's eyes now were, he could at least make out the squat shapes of the small farm buildings. Corncrib, goat shed, chicken coop, the tousled shape of a hayrick . . .

"No," Roger replied in the same tongue. The goose had extricated itself and gone off making disgruntled small honks; Roger bent and retrieved his cloak. "Small place; they likely haven't more than an ox or a mule for the plowing, if that. I smell stock, though . . . manure, ken?"

"Kine," Buck said, heading abruptly off toward a square-built stone struc-ture. "The cow byre. That'll have a bar to the door."

It did. And the bar was in its brackets.

"I don't hear any kine inside," Buck whispered, drawing close. "And the smell's old."

It was near-on winter. Maybe they'd had to slaughter the cow—or cows; maybe they'd driven them to market. But, cow or no, there was *some-thing* inside; he heard a shuffling noise and what might have been a muffled curse.

"Aye, well, there's something inside." Roger raised the dark lantern, grop-ing for the slide. "Get the bar, will you?"

But before Buck could reach for the bar, a shout of "Hoy!" came from inside, and something fell heavily against the door. "Help! Help me! Help!"

The voice spoke English, and Buck changed back at once. "Will ye for God's sake hush your noise?" he said to the man inside, annoyed. "Ye want to have them all down on us? Here, then, bring the light closer," he said to Roger, and drew the bar with a small grunt of effort.

The door swung open as Buck set down the bar, and light shot out of the lantern's open slide. A slightly built young man with flyaway fair hair—*the same color as Buck's,* Roger thought—blinked at them, dazzled by the light, then closed his eyes against it.

Roger and Buck glanced at each other for an instant, then, with one accord, stepped into the byre.

He is, Roger thought. *It's him. I know it's him. God, he's so young! Barely more than a boy.* Oddly, he felt no burst of dizzying excitement. It was a feeling of calm certainty, as though the world had suddenly righted itself and everything had fallen into place. He reached out and touched the man gently on the shoulder.

"What's your name, mate?" he said softly, in English.

"MacKenzie, J. W.," the young man said, shoulders straightening as he drew himself up, sharp chin jutting. "Lieutenant, Royal Air Force. Service Number—" He broke off, staring at Roger, who belatedly realized that, calmness or no, he was grinning from ear to ear. "What's funny?" Jerry MacKenzie demanded, belligerent.

"Nothing," Roger assured him. "Er . . . glad—glad to see you, that's all." His throat was tight, and he had to cough. "Have ye been here long?"

"No, just a few hours. Ye wouldn't have any food on ye, I don't suppose?" He looked hopefully from one man to the other.

"We do," Buck said, "but this isna the time to stop for a bite, aye?" He glanced over his shoulder. "Let's be off."

"Aye. Aye, we should." But Roger spoke automatically, unable to stop looking at J. W. MacKenzie, RAF, aged twenty-two.

"Who *are* you?" Jerry asked, staring back. "Where d'ye come from? God knows ye're not from here!"

Roger exchanged a quick look with Buck. They hadn't planned what to say; Roger hadn't been willing to jinx the enterprise by thinking that they'd really find Jerry MacKenzie, and as for Buck—

"Inverness," Buck said abruptly. He sounded gruff.

Jerry's eyes flicked back and forth between them, and he caught Roger's sleeve.

"Ye know what I mean!" he said, and gulped air, bracing himself. *"When?"*

Roger touched Jerry's hand, cold and dirty, the fingers long like his own. The question caught at his throat and thickened his voice too much to speak.

"A lang way from you," Buck said quietly, and for the first time, Roger caught a note of desolation in his voice. "From now. Lost."

That struck him to the heart. He'd truly forgotten their situation for a little, driven by the urgency of finding this man. But Buck's answer made Jerry's face, already drawn with hunger and strain, go white under the dirt.

"Jesus," Jerry whispered. "Where are we now? And—and when?"

Buck stiffened. Not at Jerry's question, but at a noise from outside. Roger didn't know what had made it, but it wasn't the wind. Buck made a low, urgent noise in his throat, shifting.

"I think it's part of Northumbria now," Roger said. "Look, there's no time. We have to go, before someone hears—"

"Aye, right. Let's go, then." Jerry had a filthy silk scarf round his neck; he tugged the ends straight and shoved them into his shirt.

The air outside was wonderful after the smells of the cow byre, fresh with new-turned earth and dying heather. They made their way as quickly as they could through the yard, skirting the farmhouse. Jerry was lame, he saw, limping badly, and Roger took his arm to help. A shrill yap came from the darkness, some distance away—then another bark, in a deeper tone.

Roger hastily licked a finger and held it up to gauge the direction of the breeze. A dog barked again, and another echoed it.

"This way," he whispered to his companions, tugging Jerry's arm. He led them away from the house as fast as possible, trying to keep his bearings, and they found themselves stumbling through a plowed field, dirt clods crumbling under their boots.

Buck stumbled and swore under his breath. They lurched from furrow to ridge, half-legged and clumsy, Roger clinging to Jerry's arm to keep him upright; one of Jerry's legs seemed gammy and wouldn't take his weight. *He's been wounded. I saw the medal. . . .*

Then the dogs began to bark, voices suddenly clear—and much closer.

"Jesus." Roger stopped for an instant, breathing hard. Where the bloody hell was the wood they'd hidden in? He'd swear they'd been heading for it, but—the beam from the lantern swung crazily, showing meaningless patches of field. He shut the slide; they'd be better off without it.

"This way!" Buck lurched away and Roger and Jerry followed perforce, hearts thumping. Christ, it sounded like a half-dozen dogs at least had been let loose, all barking. And was that a voice, calling to the dogs? Yes, it bloody was. He couldn't understand a word, but the meaning was as clear as ice water.

They ran, stumbling and panting. Roger couldn't tell where they were; he was following Buck. He dropped the lantern at one point; it fell over with a clank and he heard the oil inside gurgle out of its reservoir. With a soft *whoosh*, it flowered into brilliant flame.

"Shit!" They ran. It didn't matter where, what direction. Just away from the burning beacon and the irate voices—more than one now.

Suddenly they were into a scrim of trees—the low, wind-crabbed grove they'd lurked in earlier. But the dogs were on their track, barking eagerly, and they didn't linger but fought their way through the brush and out again, up a steep hill turfed with heather. Roger's foot sank through the spongy growth into a puddle, soaking him to the ankle, and he nearly lost his balance. Jerry set his feet and yanked Roger upright, then lost his own balance when his knee gave way; they clung together, wobbling precariously for an instant, then Roger lurched forward again and they were out of it.

He thought his lungs would burst, but they kept going—not running any longer; you couldn't run up a hill like this—slogging, planting one foot after another, after another . . . Roger began to see bursts of light at the edges of his vision; he tripped, staggered, and fell, and was hauled to his feet by Jerry.

They were all three half sopping and smeared head to foot with mud and heather scratchings when they lurched at last to the crest of the hill and stopped for a moment, swaying and gasping for air.

"Where . . . are we going?" Jerry wheezed, using the end of his scarf to wipe his face.

Roger shook his head, still short of breath—but then caught the faint gleam of water.

"We're taking you . . . back. To the stones by the lake. Where . . . you came through. Come on!"

They pelted down the far side of the hill, headlong, almost falling, now exhilarated by the speed and the thought of a goal.

"How . . . did you find me?" Jerry gasped, when at last they hit bottom and stopped for breath.

"Found your tags," Buck said, almost brusque. "Followed their trail back."

Roger put a hand to his pocket, about to offer them back—but didn't. It had struck him, like a stone to the middle of his chest, that, having found Jerry MacKenzie against substantial odds, he was about to part from him, likely forever. And that was only if things went *well*. . . .

His father. *Dad?* He couldn't think of this young man, white-faced and lame, nearly twenty years his junior, as his father—not the father he'd imagined all his life.

"Come on." Buck took Jerry's arm now, nearly holding him up, and they began to forge their way across the dark fields, losing their way and finding it again, guided by the light of Orion overhead.

Orion, Lepus. Canis major. He found a measure of comfort in the stars, blazing in the cold black sky. Those didn't change; they'd shine forever—or as close as made no difference—on him and on this man, no matter where each one might end up.

End up. The cold air burned in his lungs. *Bree* . . .

And then he could see them: squatty pillars, no more than blotches on the night, visible only because they showed dark and immobile against the sheet of moving water stirred by the wind.

"Right," he said hoarsely, and, swallowing, wiped his face on his sleeve. "This is where we leave you."

"Ye do?" Jerry panted. "But—but you—"

"When ye came . . . through. Did ye have anything on you? A gemstone, any jewelry?"

"Aye," Jerry said, bewildered. "I had a raw sapphire in my pocket. But it's gone. It's like it—"

"Like it burnt up," Buck finished for him, grim-voiced. "Aye. Well, so?" This last was clearly addressed to Roger, who hesitated. *Bree* . . . No more than an instant, though—he stuck a hand into the leather pouch at his waist, pulled out the tiny oilcloth package, fumbled it open, and pressed the garnet pendant into Jerry's hand. It was faintly warm from his body, and Jerry's cold hand closed over it in reflex.

"Take this; it's a good one. When ye go through," Roger said, and leaned toward him, trying to impress him with the importance of his instructions, "think about your wife, about Marjorie. Think hard; see her in your mind's eye, and walk straight through. Whatever the hell ye do, though, don't think about your son. Just your wife."

"What?" Jerry was gobsmacked. "How the bloody hell do you know my wife's name? And where've ye heard about my son?"

"It doesn't matter," Roger said, and turned his head to look back over his shoulder.

"Damn," said Buck softly. "They're still coming. There's a light."

There was: a single light, bobbing evenly over the ground, as it would if someone carried it. But look as he might, Roger could see no one behind it, and a violent shiver ran over him.

"*Thaibhse,*" said Buck, under his breath. Roger knew that word well enough—spirit, it meant. And usually an ill-disposed one. A haunt.

"Aye, maybe." He was beginning to catch his breath. "And maybe not." He turned again to Jerry. "Either way, ye need to go, man, and now. Remember, think of your wife."

Jerry swallowed, his hand closing tight around the stone.

"Aye. Aye . . . right. Thanks, then," he added awkwardly.

Roger couldn't speak, could give him nothing more than the breath of a smile. Then Buck was beside him, plucking urgently at his sleeve and gesturing at the bobbing light, and they set off, awkward and lumbering after the brief cooldown.

Bree . . . He swallowed, fists clenched. He'd got a stone once, he could do it again. . . . But the greater part of his mind was still with the man they had just left by the lake. He looked over his shoulder and saw Jerry beginning to walk, limping badly but resolute, thin shoulders squared under his pale khaki shirt and the end of his scarf fluttering in the rising wind.

Then it all rose up in him. Seized by an urgency greater than any he'd ever known, he turned and ran. Ran heedless of footing, of dark, of Buck's startled cry behind him.

Jerry heard his footsteps on the grass and whirled round, startled himself. Roger grabbed him by both hands, squeezed them hard enough to make Jerry gasp, and said fiercely, "I love you!"

That was all there was time for—and all he could possibly say. He let go and turned away fast, his boots making a *shoof-shoof* noise in the dry lake grass. He glanced up the hill, but the light had vanished. Likely it had been someone from the farmhouse, satisfied now that the intruders were gone.

Buck was waiting, shrouded in his cloak and holding Roger's; he must have dropped it coming down the hill. Buck shook it out and folded it round Roger's shoulders; Roger's fingers shook, trying to fasten the brooch.

"Why did ye tell him a daft thing like that?" Buck asked, doing it for him. Buck's head was bent, not looking at him.

Roger swallowed hard, and his voice came clear but painful, the words like ice shards in his throat.

"Because he isn't going to make it back. It's the only chance I'll ever have. Come on."

102

POSTPARTUM

T**HE NIGHT SHIVERED.** The *whole* night. The ground and the lake, the sky, the dark, the stars, and every particle of his own body. He was scattered, instantly everywhere and part of everything. And part of *them*. There was one moment of an exaltation too great for fear and then he vanished, his last thought no more than a faint, *I am* . . . voiced more in hope than declaration.

Roger came back to a blurred knowledge of himself, flat on his back under a clear black sky whose brilliant stars seemed pinpoints now, desperately far away. He missed them, missed being part of the night. Missed, with a brief rending sense of desolation, the two men who'd shared his soul for that blazing moment.

The sound of Buck throwing up returned him to a sense of his body. He was lying in cold, wet grass, half soaked, smelling of mud and old manure, chilled to the bone, and bruised in a number of uncomfortable places.

Buck said something horrible in Gaelic and retched again. He was on his hands and knees a few feet away, a blot on the darkness.

"You all right?" Roger croaked, rolling onto his side. He'd remembered, suddenly, the trouble with Buck's heart when they'd made their passage at Craigh na Dun. "If your heart's giving you bother again—"

"If it was, damn-all ye could do about it, is there?" Buck said. He hawked a glob of something nasty into the grass and sat down heavily, wiping his sleeve across his mouth. "Christ, I hate that! Didna ken we'd feel it, this far away."

"Mmphm." Roger sat up slowly. He wondered whether Buck had felt the same thing he had, but it didn't seem the moment for metaphysical discussion. "He's gone, then."

"Want me to go and make sure of it?" Buck said disagreeably. "God, my head!"

Roger rose to his feet, staggering a little, and went and got Buck under one arm, levering him to his feet.

"Come on," he said. "Let's go find the horses. We'll get away a bit, make a wee camp, get some food into you."

"I'm not hungry."

"*I* bloody am." In fact, he was ravenous. Buck swayed but appeared able to stand on his own. Roger released him and turned briefly to look back at the distant lake and the standing stones. For an instant, he recaptured the sense of being part of them, and then it was gone; the gleaming water and the stones were no more than part of the craggy landscape.

There was no way of knowing what time it was, but the night was still pitch-dark by the time they'd retrieved the horses, made their way to a sheltered spot under a cliff face, found water, made fire, and toasted some bannocks to eat with their dried salt herring.

They didn't talk, both exhausted. Roger pushed away the obvious *"So now what?"* and let his thoughts come randomly as they would; time enough for plans tomorrow.

After a bit, Buck got up abruptly and went off into the dark. He stayed gone for some time, during which time Roger sat gazing into the fire, replaying every moment he'd spent with Jerry MacKenzie in his mind, trying to fix it all. He wished passionately that it had been daylight, that he'd been able to see more of his father's face than the brief glimpses he'd had in the beam of the dark lantern.

Whatever his regrets, though, and the cold knowledge that Jerry wouldn't make it back—or not back to where he'd started from, at least (God, what if he ended up lost in yet another strange time? Was that possible?)—there was the one small, warm thing. He'd said it. And wherever his father had gone, he'd carry that with him.

He wrapped himself in his cloak, lay down by the embers of the fire, and carried it with him into sleep.

WHEN ROGER WOKE in the morning, thickheaded but feeling reasonably okay, Buck had already built up the fire and was frying bacon. The smell of it got Roger into a sitting position, rubbing the last of the sleep from his eyes.

Buck blotted a slice of thick bacon out of the pan with a bannock and handed it to him. He seemed to have recovered from the aftereffects of Jerry's leaving; he was disheveled and unshaven, but clear-eyed, and gave Roger an assessing look.

"Are ye in one piece?" It wasn't asked as a rhetorical question, and Roger nodded, taking the food. He started to say something in reply, but his throat was constricted, and nothing much came out. He cleared his throat hard, but Buck shook his head, indicating that no effort need be made on his part.

"I'm thinking we'll head north again," Buck said, without preamble. "Ye'll want to keep looking for your lad, I suppose—and I want to go to Cranesmuir."

So did Roger, though likely for other reasons. He eyed Buck closely, but his ancestor avoided his eye.

"Geillis Duncan?"

"Wouldn't you?" Buck's tone was belligerent.

"I just did," Roger said dryly. "Aye, of course ye do." This didn't come as a surprise. He chewed his makeshift butty slowly, wondering just how much to tell Buck about Geillis. "Your mother," he began, and cleared his throat again.

When Roger had finished, Buck sat in silence for some time, blinking at the last slice of bacon, drying in the pan.

"Jesus," he said, but not in tones of shock. More a deep interest, Roger thought, with some unease. Buck glanced up at Roger, speculation in his moss-green eyes. "And what d'ye ken about my father, then?"

"More than I can tell ye in a few minutes, and we should be on our way." Roger got up, brushing crumbs off his knees. "I don't want to try explaining our presence to any of those hairy buggers. My Old English isn't what it used to be."

"'Sumer is icumen in,'" Buck said, with a glance at the leafless, wind-blasted saplings precariously rooted in the cliff's crevices. "'Lhude sing cuccu.' Aye, let's go."

103

SOLSTICE

December 19, 1980
Edinburgh, Scotland

A PRACTICAL GUIDE FOR TIME TRAVELERS—PART II

It's almost time. The winter solstice is day after tomorrow. I keep imagining that I can feel the earth shifting slowly in the dark, tectonic plates moving under my feet and . . . things . . . invisibly lining up. The moon is waxing, nearly a quarter full. Have no idea whether that might be important.

In the morning, we'll take the train to Inverness. I've called Fiona; she'll meet us at the station, and we'll eat and change at her house—then she'll drive us to Craigh na Dun . . . and leave us there. Keep wondering if I should ask her to stay—or at least to come back in an hour, in case one or more of us should still be there, on fire or unconscious. Or dead.

After dithering for an hour, I called Lionel Menzies, too, and asked him to keep an eye on Rob Cameron. Inverness is a small town; there's always the chance that someone will see us coming off the train, or at Fiona's. And word spreads fast. If anything's going to happen, I want warning.

I have these brief lucid moments when everything seems okay and I'm filled with hope, almost trembling with anticipation. Most of the time, I keep thinking I'm insane, and then I'm really shaking.

104

THE SUCCUBUS OF CRANESMUIR

Cranesmuir, Scotland

ROGER AND BUCK stood at the far side of the tiny square in the middle of Cranesmuir, looking up at the fiscal's house. Roger cast a bleak look at the plinth in the middle of the square, with its wooden pillory. At least there were holes for only one miscreant; no crime waves in Cranesmuir.

"The attic, ye said?" Buck was staring intently at the windows of the top story. It was a substantial house, with leaded windows, and even the attic had some, though smaller than the ones in the lower stories. "I can see plants hanging from the ceiling, I think."

"That's what Claire said, aye. That she keeps her . . . her"—the word "lair" came to mind, but he discarded this in favor of—"her surgery up there. Where she makes up her potions and charms." He inspected his cuffs, which were still damp after a hasty sponge bath at the village horse trough to remove the worst stains of travel, and checked to see that his hair ribbon was in order.

The door opened and a man came out—a merchant, maybe, or a lawyer, well dressed, with a warm coat against the mizzle. Buck shifted to one side, peering to get a look before the door closed behind him.

"There's a servant at the door," he reported. "I'll knock, then, and ask if I can see—Mrs. Duncan, is that her name?"

"For the moment, aye," Roger said. He sympathized entirely with Buck's need to see his mother. And in all truth, he was curious to meet the woman himself; she was his five-times great-grandmother—*and* one of the few time travelers he knew about. But he'd also heard enough about her that his feelings were of excitement mixed with considerable unease.

He coughed, fist to his mouth. "D'ye want me to come up with you? If she's to home, I mean."

Buck opened his mouth to reply, then closed it, considered a moment, then nodded.

"Aye, I do," he said quietly. He shot Roger a sidelong look, though, with a gleam of humor in it. "Ye can help keep the conversation going."

"Happy to help," Roger said. "We're agreed, though: ye dinna mean to tell her who ye are. Or what."

Buck nodded again, though his eyes were now fixed on the door, and Roger thought he wasn't attending.

"Aye," he said. "Come on, then," and strode across the square, head up and shoulders squared.

"Mrs. Duncan? Well, I dinna ken, gentlemen," the maid said. "She's to hame the day, but Dr. McEwan's with her just noo."

Roger's heart jumped.

"Is she ill?" Buck asked sharply, and the maid blinked, surprised.

"Och, no. They're takin' tea in the parlor. Would ye like to step in oot the rain and I'll go and see what she says?" She stepped back to let them in, and Roger took advantage of this to touch her arm.

"Dr. McEwan's a friend of ours. Would ye maybe be giving him our names? Roger and William MacKenzie—at his service."

They discreetly shook as much water as possible off their hats and coats, but within a few moments the maid was back, smiling.

"Come up, gentlemen, Mrs. Duncan says, and welcome! Just up the stair there. I'll just be fetching ye a bit o' tea."

The parlor was one floor above, a small room, rather crowded, but warm and colorful. Neither of the men had eyes for the furnishings, though.

"Mr. MacKenzie," Dr. McEwan said, looking surprised but cordial. "And Mr. MacKenzie." He shook hands with them and turned to the woman who had risen from her seat beside the fire. "My dear, allow me to make you acquainted with an erstwhile patient of mine and his kinsman. Gentlemen, Mrs. Duncan."

Roger felt Buck stiffen slightly, and no wonder. He hoped he wasn't staring himself.

Geillis Duncan was maybe not a classic beauty, but that didn't matter. She was certainly good-looking, with creamy-blond hair put up under a lace cap, and—of course—the eyes. Eyes that made him want to close his own and poke Buck in the back to make him do the same, because surely she or McEwan would notice. . . .

McEwan had noticed something, all right, but it wasn't the eyes. He was eyeing Buck with a small frown of displeasure, as Buck took a long stride forward, seized the woman's hand, and boldly kissed it.

"Mrs. Duncan," he said, straightening up and smiling right into those clear green eyes. "Your most humble and obedient servant, ma'am."

She smiled back, one blond brow raised, with an amused look that met Buck's implied challenge—and raised it. Even from where he was standing, Roger felt the snap of attraction between them, sharp as a spark of static electricity. So had McEwan.

"How is your health, Mr. MacKenzie?" McEwan said pointedly to Buck. He pulled a chair into place. "Do sit down and let me examine you."

Buck either didn't hear or pretended not to. He was still holding Geillis Duncan's hand, and she wasn't pulling it away.

"'Twas kind of you to receive us, ma'am," he said. "And certainly we don't mean to disturb your tea. We'd heard of your skill as a healer and meant to call in what you might say is a professional way."

"Professional," she repeated, and Roger was surprised at her voice. It was light, almost girlish. Then she smiled again and the illusion of girlishness vanished. She drew her hand away now, but with a languid air of reluctance, her eyes still fixed on Buck with obvious interest. "Your profession, or mine?"

"Ah, I'm naught but a humble solicitor, ma'am," Buck said, with a gravity so patently mock that Roger wanted to punch him. Then he added, turning to Roger, "and my kinsman here is a scholar and musician. But as ye see, he's suffered a sad accident to his throat, and—"

Now Roger truly wanted to punch him. "I—" he began, but with the cruel whim of fate, his throat chose that moment to constrict, and his protest ended in a gurgle like a rusty pipe.

"We'd heard of ye, mistress, as I said," Buck went on, putting a sympathetic hand on Roger's shoulder and squeezing hard. "And as I say, we wondered . . ."

"Let me see," she said, and came to stand in front of Roger, her face suddenly a few inches from his. Behind her, McEwan was growing red in the face.

"I've seen this man," he told her. "It's a permanent injury, though I was able to offer some small relief. But—"

"Permanent, indeed." She'd undone his neckcloth in seconds and spread his shirt open, her fingers warm and light on his scar. She shifted her gaze and looked directly into his eyes. "But a lucky one, I'd say. You didn't die."

"No," he said, his voice hoarse but at least serviceable again. "I didn't." God, she was unsettling. Claire had described her vividly—but Claire was a woman. She was still touching him, and while her touch was not in any way improper, it was damned intimate.

Buck was growing restive; he didn't like her touching Roger any more than McEwan did. He cleared his throat.

"I wonder, mistress—might ye have any simples, medicines, perhaps? Not only for my kinsman here, but . . . well . . ." He coughed in a way meant to indicate that he harbored more-delicate ailments that he didn't wish to mention before others.

The woman smelled of sex. Very recent sex. It rose from her like incense.

She stayed in front of Roger for a moment, still looking intently into his face, but then smiled and took her hand away, leaving his throat feeling suddenly cool and exposed.

"Of course," she said, switching smile and attention to Buck. "Come up to my wee attic, sir. I'm sure I've something there that will cure what ails ye."

Roger felt gooseflesh ripple across his chest and shoulders, in spite of the good fire on the hearth. Buck and McEwan had both twitched slightly, and she bloody well knew it, though her face was entirely composed. Roger fixed a glare on Buck, willing his ancestor to look at him. Buck didn't but moved to take Geillis's arm, pulling her hand through his elbow. A slow, hot flush burned up the back of his neck.

McEwan made a very small noise in his throat.

Then Buck and Geillis were gone, the sound of their footsteps and animated voices dying away as they climbed the stairs to the attic, leaving Roger and McEwan both silent, each for his own reasons.

ROGER THOUGHT that the good doctor might be about to suffer an apoplexy, if that was the correct medical term for "blow a gasket." Whatever his own feelings about the abrupt departure of Buck and Geillis—and those were vivid—they paled beside the hue of Hector McEwan's face.

The doctor was panting slightly, his complexion puce. Plainly he wanted to follow the errant pair but just as clearly was constrained by the fact that he had no idea what he might conceivably do when he caught up with them.

"It's not what you think," Roger said, commending his soul to God and *hoping* that it wasn't.

McEwan swung round to glare at him. "The devil it's not," he snapped. "You don't know her."

"Plainly not as well as you do, no," Roger said pointedly, and raised one brow.

McEwan said something blasphemous in reply, took up the poker, and stabbed viciously at the smoking bricks of peat in the hearth. He half-turned toward the door, the poker still in his hand, and the look on his face was such that Roger leapt to his feet and grabbed him by the arm.

"Stop, man," he said, keeping his voice pitched as low and evenly as he could, in hopes of soothing McEwan. "Ye'll do yourself no good. Sit down, now. I'll tell ye why it—why he—why the man's interested in her."

"For the same reason every dog in the village is *interested* in a bitch in heat," McEwan said venomously. But he let Roger take the poker from his hand, and while he wouldn't sit down, he did at least take several deep breaths that restored a semblance of calm.

"Aye, tell me, then—for all the good it will do," he said.

It wasn't a situation that allowed for diplomacy or euphemism.

"She's his mother, and he knows it," Roger said bluntly.

Whatever McEwan had been expecting, that wasn't it, and for an instant, Roger was gratified to see the man's face go absolutely blank with shock. Only for an instant, though. It was likely going to be a tricky bit of pastoral counseling, at best.

"Ye know what he is," Roger said, taking the doctor by the arm again and pulling him toward a brocaded wing chair. "Or, rather, what we are. *Cognosco te?*"

"I—" McEwan's voice died, though he opened and closed his mouth a few times, helplessly looking for words.

"Aye, I know," Roger said soothingly. "It's difficult. But ye do know, don't ye?"

"I—yes." McEwan sat down abruptly. He breathed for a moment, blinked once or twice, and looked up at Roger.

"His mother. His *mother?*"

"I have it on good authority," Roger assured him. A thought struck him, though.

"Ah . . . ye did know about her, didn't ye? That she's . . . one of us?"

McEwan nodded. "She's never admitted it. Just—just laughed at me when I told her where I'd come from. And I didn't know for a long time. Not until I—" His lips clamped abruptly into a tight line.

"I'm guessing ye didn't have occasion to heal her of anything," Roger said carefully. "Does she . . . er . . . has it got anything to do with blue light, by chance?"

He was trying hard to avoid the mental picture of Geillis and Dr. McEwan, naked and sweating, both bathed in a faint blue glow. The woman *was* his several-times great-grandmother, whatever else you liked to say about her.

McEwan gave him a bleak look and shook his head.

"Not . . . exactly. She's a very fine herbalist and not bad at diagnosis, but she can't—do that." He twiddled his fingers briefly in illustration, and Roger felt a faint memory of the warmth when McEwan had touched his throat.

The doctor sighed and rubbed a hand over his face.

"No point in evasion, I suppose. I got her with child. And I could—'see' is not quite the right word, but I can't think of a better one. I could see the moment when my . . . seed . . . reached her ovum. The . . . er . . . the fetus. It glowed inside her womb; I could sense it when I touched her."

A certain heat rose in Roger's face. "Forgive me for asking, but—how do you know that happened because she's . . . what she is? Might it not be the case with a normal woman?"

McEwan smiled—very bleakly—at the word "normal," and shook his head.

"I had two children by a woman in Edinburgh, in—in my own time," he said quietly, and looked down at his feet. "That . . . was one of the reasons I didn't try to return."

Roger made a sound in his damaged throat that was meant to be regretful and compassionate, but whether his feelings or his larynx had got the better of him, it emerged as a rather stern "Hrmph!" and McEwan's color began to rise again.

"I know," he said wretchedly. "I don't seek to—to excuse it."

Just as well, Roger thought. *I'd like to see ye try, you—you—* But recriminations would do no one any good just now, and he stifled whatever else he might have said on the subject, instead returning to Geillis.

"Ye said ye got her"—jerking his chin upward, to where the sounds of footsteps and bumpings were audible overhead—"with child. Where *is* the child?"

McEwan drew a long, trembling breath. "I said . . . she is a very fine herbalist . . . ?"

"Jesus, Lord," Roger said. "Did ye know she meant to do it?"

McEwan swallowed audibly, but kept silent.

"My God," Roger said. "My *God*. I know it's not my place to judge you—but if it was, man, you'd burn in hell."

And with that, he went downstairs and out into the streets of Cranesmuir, leaving the lot of them to their own devices.

⁂

HE'D MADE SIXTEEN circuits of the village square—it was a small square—before getting a precarious hold on his sense of outrage. He stood in front of the Duncans' front door, fists clenched, taking deep, deliberate breaths.

He had to go back. You didn't walk away from people who were drowning, even if they'd jumped into a quagmire on purpose. And he didn't want to think what might happen if McEwan, left to himself, should be overcome by anguish or fury and rush in on the pair in the attic. He *really* didn't want to think what Buck—or, God forbid, Geillis—might do in that case, and the thought galvanized him.

He didn't trouble knocking. Arthur Duncan was the procurator fiscal; his door was always open. The wee maid poked her head out of an inner door at the sound of his footsteps, but when she saw who he was, she drew it in again, doubtless thinking he'd just stepped out for something.

He nearly sprinted up the stair, a guilty conscience now furnishing him with visions of Hector McEwan hanging from the small chandelier in the parlor, helpless feet kicking in the air.

When he burst in, though, he found McEwan slumped forward in the wing chair, face buried in his hands. He didn't look up at Roger's entrance and wouldn't raise his head even when Roger shook him gently by the shoulder.

"Come on, man," he said gruffly, then cleared his throat. "Ye're still a doctor, aren't ye? Ye're needed."

That made the man look up, startled. His face was mottled with emotion—anger, shame, desolation, lust. Could lust be an emotion? Roger wondered briefly, but dismissed the consideration as academic at the moment. McEwan straightened his shoulders and rubbed both hands hard over his face, as though trying to erase the feelings so plainly displayed there.

"Who needs me?" he said, and rose to his feet with a decent attempt at composure.

"I do," Roger said, and cleared his throat again, with a noise like falling gravel. It felt like gravel, too; strong emotion choked him, literally. "Come outside, aye? I need air, and so do you."

McEwan cast one last look up at the ceiling, where the noises had now ceased, then firmed his lips, nodded, and, taking up his hat from the table, came along.

Roger led the way out of the square and past the last house, then up a cow path, dodging heaps of manure, until they reached a drystane wall that they could sit upon. He sat down himself and gestured to McEwan, who sat obediently. The walk had lent the doctor some semblance of calm, and he turned at once to Roger and spread open his collar—this still flapping loose. Roger felt the ghost of Geillis Duncan's touch on his throat and shivered, but it was cold out, and McEwan took no notice.

The doctor wrapped his fingers loosely around the scar and seemed to listen for a moment, head to one side. Then he pulled his hand back a little and felt delicately up higher with two probing fingers, then lower, a small frown of concentration on his face.

And Roger felt it. The same odd sensation of light warmth. He'd been holding his breath under the doctor's touch, but at this realization he exhaled suddenly—and freely.

"Jesus," he said, and put his own hand to his throat. The word had come freely, too.

"It's better?" McEwan was looking at him intently, his earlier upset subsumed in professional concern.

"It . . . is." The scar was still bumpy under his fingers, but something had changed. He cleared his throat experimentally. A little pain, a little blockage—but noticeably better. He lowered his hand and stared at McEwan. "Thank you. What the bloody hell did you do?"

The tension that had been twanging through McEwan since Roger and Buck had entered the Duncans' house finally eased, just as the tightness in Roger's throat had.

"I don't know that I can tell you with any great precision," he said apologetically. "It's just that I know what a sound larynx should feel like, and I can tell what yours feels like, and . . ." He shrugged a little, helpless. "I put my fingers there and . . . envision the way it *should* feel."

He touched Roger's throat gently again, exploring. "I can tell that it's very slightly better now. But there *is* a good deal of damage. I can't say whether it would ever be completely healed—in all truth, I doubt it. But if I were to repeat the treatment—it seems to need some time between treatments, no doubt for the tissue to heal, just as an external wound would. So far as I can tell, the optimum time between treatments of a serious injury is about a month; Geillis—" And here his face twitched violently; he had forgotten. He mastered himself with an effort, though, and went on, "Geillis thinks that the process may be affected by the phase of the moon, but she is . . ."

"A witch," Roger finished for him.

The look of unhappiness had returned to McEwan's face, and he lowered his head to hide it.

"Perhaps," he said softly. "Surely she is . . . an unusual woman."

"And a good thing for the human race that there aren't more like her," Roger said, but then checked himself. If he could pray for Jack Randall's immortal soul, he couldn't do less for his own great-grandmother, homicidal maniac or not. But the immediate problem was to try to extract the hapless soul before him from her clutches before she could destroy Hector McEwan utterly.

"Dr. McEwan . . . Hector," he said softly, and laid a hand on the doctor's arm. "You need to go right away from this place, and from her. She won't merely bring you great unhappiness or imperil your soul—she may well kill you."

A look of surprise momentarily displaced the unhappiness in McEwan's eyes. He looked aside, pursed his mouth, and glanced back at Roger, sidelong, as though afraid to look at him too directly.

"Surely you exaggerate," he said, but the words had no force. McEwan's own Adam's apple bobbed visibly as he swallowed.

Roger drew a deep, unconstricted breath and felt the cold, damp air fresh in his chest.

"No," he said gently. "I don't. Think about it, aye? And pray, if ye can. There *is* mercy, aye? And forgiveness."

McEwan sighed, too, but not with any sense of freedom in it. He cast his eyes down, fixed them on the muddy lane and the rain-dancing puddles in the low spots.

"I cannot," he said, his voice low and hopeless. "I've . . . tried. I can't."

Roger's hand was still on McEwan's arm. He squeezed, hard, and said, "Then I'll pray for ye. And for her," he added, hoping no reluctance showed in his voice.

"Thank you, sir," the doctor said. "I value that extremely." But his eyes had lifted and turned, as though he had no power over them, toward Cranesmuir and its smoking chimneys, and Roger knew there was no hope.

HE WALKED BACK to Cranesmuir and waited in the square 'til the door of the Duncans' house opened and Buck emerged. The man looked mildly surprised—but not displeased—to see Roger, and nodded at him but didn't speak. They walked together to an ordinary, where they got a room and went upstairs to refresh themselves before supper. The ordinary didn't run to a bath, but hot water, soap, razor, and towels went some way to restore them to a decent state of cleanliness.

Buck hadn't spoken a word more than necessary, but he had an odd expression—half pleased and half ashamed—and kept darting sidelong glances at Roger, as though unsure whether to say something but rather wanting to.

Roger poured a cup of water from the ewer, drank half of it, and set the cup down with an air of resignation.

"Tell me you didn't," he said finally. "Please."

Buck shot him a quick glance, looking both shocked at the words and slightly amused.

"No," he said, after a pause long enough to knot Roger's belly. "No, I didn't. I'm no saying I couldn't have, though," he added. "She . . . wasn't unwilling."

Roger would have said he didn't want to know, but he wasn't quite able to deceive himself.

"Ye tried?"

Buck nodded, then picked up the cup of water and dashed the remnants into his own face, shaking them off with a *whoof* of breath.

"I kissed her," he said. "Put my hand on her breast."

Roger had seen the upper slopes of those breasts as they swelled above her deep-green woolen bodice, round and white as snowdrops—but a lot bigger. By a considerable force of will, he kept himself from asking, *"And what happened then?"*

He didn't have to, though; Buck was obviously reliving the experience and wanted nothing more than to talk about it.

"She put her hand on mine, but she didn't pull my hand away. Not at first. She went on kissing me—" He broke off and looked at Roger, one brow raised. "Have ye kissed many women?"

"I haven't kept count," Roger said, with a slight edge. "Have you?"

"Four besides her," Buck said contemplatively. He shook his head. "That was different."

"I'd expect it would be. Kissing your mother, I mean—"

"Not *that* kind of different." Buck touched his lips with two fingers, lightly as a girl might. "The other kind. Or maybe I dinna mean that, quite. I kissed a whore once, and it wasna like that at all." He patted his lips absently for a moment, then realized what he was doing and drew his hand away, looking momentarily embarrassed. "Ever gone wi' a whore?"

"I have not," Roger said, trying not to sound censorious, but not managing all that well.

Buck shrugged, dismissing it.

"Well, so. She kept my hand on her breast while she took her time about kissin' me. But then . . ." He paused, blushing, and Roger drew himself up. Buck, blushing?

"What, then?" he asked, unable to refrain.

"Well, she drew it down, ken, over her body, very slow, and still kissin' me, and—well, I must have heard her skirts rustle, mustn't I? But I wasna paying attention, because when she took my hand and put it on her . . . erm . . . lady part, I thought I'd pass out from the shock."

"Her—was she—it, I mean—naked?"

"Bare as an egg, and just as bald, too," Buck assured him. "Have ye ever heard of such a thing?"

"I have, aye."

Buck stared at him, green eyes wide.

"Ye mean your wife—"

"I bloody don't," Roger snapped. "Don't ye dare speak of Brianna, *an amaidan,* or I'll gie you your head in your hands to play with."

"You and who else?" Buck said automatically, but waved a hand to calm Roger. "Why did ye not tell me my mother was a whore?"

"I wouldn't tell ye something like that, even if I knew it for a fact, and I didn't," Roger said.

Buck looked at him for a moment in silence, eyes direct. "Ye'll never make a decent minister," he said at last, "if ye can't be honest."

The words were said objectively, without heat—and stung the more on that account, being true. Roger breathed in hard through his nose and out again.

"All right," he said. And told Buck everything he knew, or thought he knew, concerning Gillian Edgars, alias Geillis Duncan.

"Jesus God," Buck said, blinking.

"Aye," Roger said shortly. Buck's description of his encounter with his mother had given Roger a vividly disturbing image of Brianna, and he hadn't been able to dismiss it. He hungered for her, and as a result was acutely aware of Buck's lingering images of Geillis; he saw the man's hand absently cup itself, fingers drawing slowly in, as though he were guddling—Christ, he could smell her on Buck's flesh, pungent and taunting.

"So now ye've met her," Roger said abruptly, looking away. "And now ye ken what she is. Is that enough, do ye think?" He was careful to make the question no more than a question, and Buck nodded, but not in answer, more as though he were having an internal conversation—with himself or with Geillis, Roger didn't know.

"My father," Buck said thoughtfully, without actually answering. "From what he said when we met him at the MacLarens' croft, I thought he maybe didna ken her yet. But he was interested, ye could tell that." He looked suddenly at Roger, a thought having struck him.

"D'ye think it was meeting us that made him—will make him," he corrected, with a grimace, "go and find her?" He glanced down, then back up at Roger. "Would I not exist if we hadn't come to find your wee lad, I mean?"

Roger felt the usual sense of startled creepiness at realizations of this sort, something like having cold fingers suddenly laid against the small of his back.

"Maybe so," he said. "But I doubt ye'll ever know that. Not for sure."

He was glad enough to leave the subject of Geillis Duncan, though Buck's other parent was probably no less dangerous.

"D'ye think ye need to speak with Dougal MacKenzie?" Roger asked carefully. He didn't want to go anywhere near Castle Leoch or the MacKenzies, but Buck had a right to do it if he wanted, and Roger himself had an obligation—two of them, as kin and as priest—to help him if he did. And however such a conversation might work out, he doubted very much that it would be as disconcerting as the meeting with Geillis.

As for dangerous, though . . .

"I don't know," Buck said softly, as though talking to himself. "I dinna ken what I'd say to the man—to either of them."

That alarmed Roger, who sat up straight.

"Ye don't mean ye'd go back to her? To—your mother?"

Buck's mouth curled up on one side.

"Well, we really didna say much to each other," he pointed out.

"Neither did I," Roger said shortly, "to my father."

Buck made an indeterminate noise in his throat, and they fell silent, listening to the growing drum of rain on the slates of the roof. The tiny fire dwindled under the rain coming down the chimney and went out, leaving no more than the faint smell of warmth, and after a bit Roger wrapped himself in his cloak and curled up on one side of the bed, waiting for his body to warm enough for sleep to come.

The air through the cracked window was sharp with cold and the tingling smell of wet bracken and pine bark. No place smelled like the Highlands, and Roger found his heart eased by its harsh perfume. He was nearly asleep when Buck's voice came softly to him through the dark.

"I'm glad ye got to say it, though."

105

NO A VERY GOOD PERSON

ROGER HAD INSISTED on camping outside the town, thinking it better to get Buck as far away from Geillis Duncan as was feasible. For once, it wasn't raining, and they'd managed to gather enough in the way of pine twigs for a decent wood fire; pine would usually burn even if damp, because of the resin.

"I'm no a very good person." The words were quiet and took a moment to register. Roger looked up to see Buck slumped on his rock, a long stick in his hand, poking at the fire in a desultory fashion. Roger rubbed a hand along his jaw. He felt tired, discouraged, and in no mood for more pastoral counseling.

"I've met worse," he said, after a pause. It sounded unconvincing.

Buck looked at him from under the fringe of blond hair. "I wasna looking for contradiction or consolation," he said dryly. "It was a statement of fact. Call it a preface, if ye like."

"All right." Roger stretched, yawning, then settled himself. "A preface to what? An apology?" He saw the question on his ancestor's face and, irritated, touched his throat. "For this."

"Ah, that." Buck rocked back a little and pursed his lips, eyes fixed on the scar.

"Aye, *that*!" Roger snapped, irritation flaring suddenly into anger. "Do you have any notion what it was ye took from me, you bastard?"

"Maybe a bit." Buck resumed poking at the fire, waiting 'til the end of his stick caught, then stubbing it out again in the dirt. He fell silent, then, and for a bit there was no sound but the rattle of wind through the dry bracken. *A ghost walking by,* Roger thought, watching the brown fronds within the circle of firelight stir and then fall still.

"I don't say it as excuse, mind," Buck said at last, eyes still fixed on the fire. "But there's the matter of intent. I didna mean to get ye hanged."

Roger made a low, vicious noise in response to this. It hurt. He was damned tired of it hurting to speak, or sing, or even grunt.

"Bugger off," he said abruptly, standing up. "Just—bugger off. I don't want to look at you."

Buck gave him a long look, as though debating whether to say something, but then shrugged, got up, and disappeared. He was back within five minutes, though, and sat down with the air of someone who had something to say. *Fine,* Roger thought. *Get on with it.*

"Did it not occur to the two of ye, whilst reading those letters, that there's another way for the past to speak to the future?"

"Well, of course," Roger said, impatient. He stabbed his dirk into one of the turnips to test it; still hard as a rock. "We thought of all sorts of things—diaries left under stones, newspaper notices"—he grimaced at that one—"and a number of less-useful notions. But most of those options were either too unsure or too risky; that's why we arranged to use the banks. But . . ."

He trailed off. Buck was looking smugly superior.

"And I suppose you've thought of something better?" Roger said.

"Why, man, it's right under your nose." With a smirk, Buck bent to test his own turnip and, evidently finding the results acceptable, lifted it out of the ashes on the point of his dirk.

"If ye think I'm going to *ask* you—"

"Beyond that—" Buck said, blowing on the hot turnip between phrases, "beyond that—it's the only way for the future to speak to the past."

He gave Roger a straight, hard look, and Roger felt as though he'd been stabbed with a screwdriver.

"What—you?" he blurted. "You mean you—"

Buck nodded, eyes casually on his smoking turnip.

"Can't be you, can it?" He looked up suddenly, green eyes catching the firelight. "You won't go. Ye wouldn't trust me to keep looking."

"I—" The words caught in Roger's throat, but he was well aware that they showed in his face.

Buck's own face twisted in a lopsided smile. "I would keep looking," he said. "But I see how ye'd not believe me."

"It's not that," Roger said, clearing his throat. "It's only—I *can't* leave while Jem might be here. Not when I don't know for sure that I could come back if I left and he . . . wasn't at the other end." He made a helpless gesture. "Go, and know I was maybe abandoning him forever?"

Buck nodded, looking down. Roger saw the other man's throat move, too, and was struck by a pang of realization.

"Your Jem," Roger said softly. "You do know where he is, at least. When, I mean." The question was clear: if Buck was willing to risk the stones again, why would he not do it in search of his own family, rather than to carry a message to Bree?

"Ye're all mine, aren't ye?" Buck said gruffly. "My blood. My . . . sons."

Despite everything, Roger was moved by that. A little. He coughed, and it didn't hurt.

"Even so," he said. He gave Buck a direct look. "Why? Ye ken it might do for you; it might have done this last time, if McEwan hadn't been there."

"Mmphm." Buck poked his turnip again and put it back into the fire. "Aye. Well, I meant it; I'm no a very good person. No such a waste, I mean, if I didna make it." His lips twisted a little as he glanced up at Roger. "Ye've maybe got a bit more to offer the world."

"I'm flattered," Roger said dryly. "I imagine the world can get on well enough without me, if it came to that."

"Aye, maybe. But maybe your family can't."

There was a long silence while Roger digested that, broken only by the pop of a burning twig and the distant hooting of courting owls.

"What about your own family?" he asked at last, quietly. "Ye seem to think your wife would be happier without ye. Why? What did ye do to her?"

Buck made a short, unhappy noise that might have been meant for a wry laugh.

"Fell in love wi' her." He took a deep breath, looking down into the fire. "Wanted her."

He'd met Morag Gunn just after he'd begun reading law with a solicitor in Inverness. The lawyer had been called to go out to a farm near Essich, to draw up a will for an old man, and had taken his junior along to see the way of it.

"It took three days, for the auld man was that ill, he couldna attend more than a few minutes at a time. So we stayed wi' the family, and I'd go out to help wi' the pigs and the chickens when I wasna needed inside." He shrugged. "I was young and no bad-looking, and I had the trick of makin' women like me. And she did like me—but she was in love wi' Donald McAllister, a young farmer from Daviot."

But Buck had been unable to forget the lass, and whenever he had a day free from the law, would ride out to visit. He came for Hogmanay, and there was *a cèilidh*, and . . .

"And wee Donald had a dram—or two or three or four—too many and was found in a stall wi' his hand down Mary Finlay's bodice. God, the stramash there was!" A rueful smile flickered over Buck's face. "Mary's twa brothers gave Donald laldy and laid him out like a mackerel, and all the lasses were screamin' and the lads shoutin' like it was Judgment Day. And poor wee Morag was off behind the cow byre, greetin' her heart out."

"You, um, comforted her," Roger suggested, not trying to keep the skeptical note out of his voice. Buck shot him a sharp glance, then shrugged.

"Thought it might be my only chance," he said simply. "Aye. I did. She was the worse for drink herself, and that upset. . . . I didna force her." His lips pressed together. "But I didna take no for an answer, either, and after a bit, she gave up sayin' it."

"Aye. And when she woke up next morning and realized . . . ?"

Buck cocked a brow.

"She didna say anything to anyone then. It was two months later when she realized . . ." Buck had arrived at Mr. Ferguson's rooms one day in March to find Morag Gunn's father and three brothers waiting for him, and as soon as the banns could be read, he was a married man.

"So." Buck took a breath and rubbed a hand over his face. "We . . . got on. I was mad in love wi' her, and she kent that and tried to be kind to me. But I knew well enough it was Donald she'd wanted and still did. He was still there, ken, and she'd see him now and then at *cèilidhean* or the cattle sales."

It was knowing that that had made Buck take the opportunity to sail for North Carolina with his wife and small child.

"Thought she'd forget," he said, a little bleakly. "Or at least I wouldna have to see the look in her eyes when she saw him."

But things had gone badly for the MacKenzies in the New World; Buck had failed to establish a practice as a solicitor, they had little money and no land, and they had no one in the way of kinfolk to turn to for help.

"So we came back," Buck said. He rolled the turnip out of the fire and stabbed it with his stick; the black crust broke and oozed white. He stared at the vegetable for a moment, then stamped on it, mashing it into the ashes.

"And Donald was still there, of course. Was he married?"

Buck shook his head, then knuckled the hair out of his eyes.

"It was no good," he said softly. "It was true, what I told ye about how I came to pass through the stones. But once I'd come to myself and discovered how things were—I kent Morag would be best served if I never came back. Either she'd give me up for dead after a time and marry Donald, or, at the worst, her father would have her back, wi' the bairns. They'd live well—her da had inherited the farm, when his auld one died."

Roger's throat felt tight but it didn't matter. He reached out and squeezed Buck's shoulder, hard. Buck gave a small snort, but didn't pull away.

After a bit, though, he heaved a sigh and straightened up, turning to Roger.

"So ye see," he said. "If I go back and tell your wife what's to do—and, with luck, come back to tell you—it's maybe the one good thing I could do. For my family—for yours."

It took some time for Roger to get his voice sufficiently under control as to speak.

"Aye," he said. "Well. Sleep on it. I mean to go up to Lallybroch. Ye'll maybe go and see Dougal MacKenzie at Leoch. If ye think ye still . . . mean it, after . . . there's time enough to decide then."

106

A BROTHER OF THE LODGE

Craigh na Dun, the Scottish Highlands
December 21, 1980

ESMERALDA'S HAIR was much too red. *Somebody will notice. They'll ask questions. You idiot, why are you even thinking about it? They'd notice a Barbie in a polka-dot bikini a heck of a lot faster.* . . . Brianna shut her eyes for an instant to blot out the sight of Mandy's rag dolly with her scarlet fright wig, brilliant with a dye much brighter than anything achievable in the eighteenth century. She tripped on a stone, said, "S-word!" under her breath, and, her eyes having flown open, took a firmer hold of Mandy's free hand, the other being employed to clutch Esmeralda.

She knew bloody well why she was worrying about the doll's hair. If she didn't think of something inconsequential, she was going to turn right around and run down the rocky slope like a panicked hare, dragging Jem and Mandy through the dead gorse.

We're going to do it. We have to. We'll die, we'll all die in there, in the black . . . Oh, God, oh, God . . .

"Mam?" Jemmy looked up at her, small brow furrowed. She made a good attempt—she thought—at a reassuring smile, but it must have looked less than convincing, judging from his alarmed expression.

"It's okay," she said, abandoning the smile and putting what little conviction she could muster into her voice. "It's okay, Jem."

"Uh-huh." He still looked worried, but he turned his face uphill, and his expression smoothed out, intentness replacing concern. "I can hear them," he said softly. "Can ye hear them, Mama?"

That "Mama" made her hand tighten, and he winced, though she didn't think he really noticed. He was listening. She came to a stop, and they all listened. She could hear the rush of the wind and a slight patter as brief rain swept through the brown heather. Mandy was humming to Esmeralda. But Jem's face was turned upward, serious but not frightened. She could just see the pointed top of one of the stones, barely visible above the crest of the hill.

"I can't, honey," she said, letting out just a bit of the huge breath she'd been holding. "Not yet." *What if I can't hear them at all? What if I've lost it? Holy Mary, Mother of God, pray for us . . .* "Let's . . . get a little closer."

She'd been frozen inside for the last twenty-four hours. She hadn't been able to eat or sleep but had kept going, shoving everything aside, tamping it down—refusing to actually believe they were going to do it, yet making the necessary preparations in a state of eerie calmness.

The leather bag hanging from her shoulder clanked a little, reassuring in its solid reality. Weight might be heavy to carry—but it would hold her steady against the pull of wind and water, secure against the earth. Jem had let go of her hand, and she reached compulsively through the slit in her skirt to feel the three hard little lumps in the pocket tied round her waist.

She'd been afraid to try synthetic stones, for fear they wouldn't work—or might explode violently, like the big opal Jemmy had burst into pieces in North Carolina.

Suddenly she was swept by a longing for Fraser's Ridge—and her parents—so intense that tears welled in her eyes. She blinked hard and wiped her eyes on her sleeve, pretending that the wind had made them water. It didn't matter; neither of the kids was noticing. Now both of them were staring upward—and she finally realized, with a small, flat thump of dread, that she could hear the stones; they were humming, and Mandy was humming with them.

She glanced behind her involuntarily, checking to be sure that they hadn't been followed—but they had. Lionel Menzies was coming up the path behind them, climbing fast.

"F-word!" she said aloud, and Jem whirled to see what was going on.

"Mr. Menzies!" he said, and his face broke into a smile of relief. "Mr. Menzies!"

Bree gestured firmly to Jem to stay where he was and took a couple of steps down the steep path toward Menzies, little rocks sliding under her shoes and bouncing downhill toward him.

"Don't be afraid," he said, coming up breathlessly and stopping just below her. "I—I had to come, be sure you were safe. That you—that you—get away." He nodded upward, looking beyond her. She didn't turn to look; she could feel the stones now, humming gently—for the moment—in her bones.

"We're okay," she said, her voice surprisingly steady. "Really. Er . . . thank you," she added, belatedly polite.

His face was pale and a little strained, but quirked into a small smile at that.

"My pleasure," he said, with equal politeness. But he didn't move to turn and go away. She breathed for a moment, realizing that the frozen core had thawed. She was alive again, completely, and thoroughly on the alert.

"Is there some reason why we might *not* be safe?" she asked, watching his eyes behind the glasses. He grimaced slightly and glanced over his shoulder.

"Shit," she said. "Who? Rob Cameron?" She spoke sharply and heard the creak of gravel under Jem's shoes as he turned sharply, hearing the name.

"Him and his friends, yes." He nodded uphill. "You, um, really should go. Now, I mean."

Brianna said something really bad in Gaelic, and Jemmy gave a nervous giggle. She glared at Menzies.

"And just what were you planning to do if Rob and his band of jerks all turned up after us?"

"What I just did do," he said simply. "Warn you. I'd bloody go if I were you. Your, um, daughter . . . ?"

She whirled round to see Mandy, Esmeralda in the crook of one arm, stumping laboriously up the path.

"Jem!" She took one giant step, seized him by the hand, and they bolted up the hill after Mandy, leaving Lionel Menzies on the path below.

They caught Mandy up right at the edge of the circle, and Bree tried to grab Mandy's hand but missed. She could hear Lionel Menzies coming up behind them. "Mandy!" She grabbed the little girl and stood, panting, surrounded by stones. The hum was higher-pitched and making her teeth itch; she gnashed them once or twice, trying to rid herself of the feeling, and saw Menzies blink. *Good.*

Then she heard the sound of a car's engine below and saw Menzies's face change to a look of acute alarm.

"Go!" he said. "Please!"

She fumbled under her skirt, hands shaking, and finally got hold of all three stones. They were the same kind, small emeralds, though of slightly different cut. She'd chosen them because they reminded her of Roger's eyes. Thought of him steadied her.

"Jem," she said, and put a stone in his hand. "And, Mandy—here's yours. Put them in your pockets, and—"

But Mandy, little fist clutching her emerald, had turned toward the biggest of the standing stones. Her mouth drooped open for a moment, and then suddenly her face brightened as though someone had lit a candle inside her.

"Daddy!" she shrieked, and, yanking her hand out of Brianna's, raced directly toward the cleft stone—and into it.

"Jesus!" Brianna barely heard Menzies's shocked exclamation. She ran toward the stone, tripped over Esmeralda, and fell full length in the grass, knocking out her wind.

"Mama!" Jem paused for a moment beside her, glancing wildly back and forth between her and the stone where his little sister had just vanished.

"I'm . . . okay," she managed, and with that assurance, Jem charged across the clearing, calling back, "I'll get her, Mam!"

She gulped air and tried to shriek after him, but made only a wheezing croak. The sound of feet made her glance fearfully round, but it was only Lionel, who'd run to the edge of the circle, peering down the hillside. In the distance, she could hear car doors slamming. *Doors. More than one . . .*

She staggered to her feet; she'd fallen on the bag and bruised her ribs, but that didn't matter. She limped toward the cleft stone, pausing only to scoop up Esmeralda by reflex. *God, God, God . . .* was the only thought in her head, an agony of unworded prayer.

And suddenly the prayer was answered. Both of them stood in front of her, swaying and white-faced. Mandy threw up; Jem sat down hard on his bottom and slumped there, wavering.

"Oh, God . . ." She ran to them, grabbed them hard against her in spite of the nastiness. Jem clung to her a moment, but then pushed himself away.

"Mam," he said, and his voice was breathless with joy. "Mam, he's *there.* We could feel him. We can find him—we gotta go, Mam!"

"You do." It was Lionel back, breathless and scared, tugging at Brianna's cloak, trying to straighten it for her. "They're coming—three of them."

"Yes, I—" But then realization struck her, and she turned to the children in panic. "Jem, Mandy . . . your stones—where are they?"

"Burned up," Mandy said solemnly, and spat into the grass. "Puh-toody! Yuck." She wiped her mouth.

"What do you mean—"

"Yeah, they are, Mam. See?" Jem turned out the pocket of his breeches, showing her the burnt spot and the smear of carbon black around it, smelling strongly of scorched wool.

Frantic, she fumbled at Mandy's clothes, finding the same scorch mark on the side of her skirt, where the vaporized stone had burned through from her pocket.

"Did it burn you, honey?" she asked, running a hand down Mandy's sturdy little thigh.

"Not much," Mandy reassured her.

"Brianna! For God's sake—I can't—"

"*I* can't!" she shouted, rounding on him, fists clenched. "The kids' stones are *gone!* They can't—they can't go through without them!" She didn't know for sure that this was true, but the thought of letting them try to go into that . . . *that* . . . without the protection of a stone shriveled her stomach, and she nearly wept with fright and exasperation.

"Stones," he repeated, looking blank. "Jewels, do you mean? Gemstones?" "Yes!"

He stood for an instant with his mouth open, then fell to his knees, yanking at his left hand, and the next instant was whacking his right hand feverishly against a rock that lay half sunk in the grass.

Bree stared at him helplessly for a moment, then ran to the edge of the circle, ducked round a stone, and stood flat against it in the shadow, looking out. By peering sideways, she could just see human forms, halfway up the hill and moving fast.

On the other side of the stone, Menzies gave a grunt of pain or frustration and smacked something hard against the rock, with a small cracking noise.

"Brianna!" he called, urgent, and she rushed back, afraid the children were trying to go through—but it was all right; they were standing in front of Lionel Menzies, who was stooping over Mandy, holding one of her hands.

"Curl up your fist, wee lassie," he said, almost gently. "Aye, that's it. And, Jem—here, put out your hand." Brianna was close enough now to see that it was a small glittering thing he put in Jem's palm—and that Mandy's fist was curled around a large ring, rather battered, with a Masonic emblem carved into its onyx—and the twin of Jem's small diamond winking beside it, an empty socket on the other side.

"Lionel," she said, and he reached out and touched her cheek.

"Go now," he said. "I can't leave until ye go. Once you're gone, though, I'll run for it."

She nodded jerkily, once, then stooped and took the children's hands. "Jem—put that in your other pocket, okay?" She gulped air and turned toward the big cleft stone. The racket of it hammered at her blood and she could feel it pulling, trying to take her apart.

"Mandy," she said, and could barely hear her own voice. "Let's find Daddy. Don't let go."

It was only as the screaming began that she realized she'd not said "Thank you," and then she thought no more.

107

THE BURYING GROUND

S HE LOVED LALLYBROCH in winter. The gorse and broom and heather didn't seem to die so much as simply to fade back into the landscape, the purple heather fading to a soft brown shadow of itself and the broom to a cluster of dry sticks, their long flat pods rattling softly in the wind. Today the air was cold and still, and the soft gray smoke from the chimneys rose straight up to touch the lowering sky.

"Home, we're home!" Mandy said, hopping up and down. "Goody, goody, goody! Can I have a Coke?"

"It isn't home, goofy," Jem said. Only the pink tip of his nose and a flicker of eyelash was visible in the gap between his woolly hat and the muffler round his neck. His breath wisped white. "It's—*then*. They don't have Cokes now. Besides," he added logically, "it's too cold to drink Coke. Your tummy would freeze."

"Huh?"

"Never mind, honey," Brianna said, and tightened her grasp on Mandy's hand. They were standing at the crest of the hill behind the house, near the remains of the Iron Age fort. It had been a laborious haul up the hill, but she'd been reluctant to approach the house from the front, where they would have been visible for a good quarter mile, coming across open ground.

"Can you feel Daddy anywhere nearby?" she asked the children. She'd automatically looked for Roger's old orange Morris in the drive as they'd crested the hill—and felt a ridiculous plunge of spirits at seeing neither car nor graveled drive. Jem shook his head; Mandy didn't answer, distracted by a faint bleating from below.

"Iss sheep!" she said, delighted. "Let's go see da sheep!"

"It's not sheep," Jem said, rather crossly. "It's goats. They're in the broch. Can we go down now, Mam? My nose is about to fall off."

She was still hesitant, watching the house. Every muscle was straining, pulling toward it. *Home.* But it wasn't her home, not now. *Roger.* "*The strong, sweet, supple quality he has . . .*"

Of course, she knew that he likely wasn't here; he and Buck would be searching somewhere for Jerry MacKenzie. *And what if they found him?* she thought, with a little thump of something between excitement and fear.

The fear was what was stopping her racing down the hill to hammer on the door and meet whatever of her family happened to be home today. She'd spent the last few days on the road, and the hours on the final walk from where the carter had dropped them, trying to decide—and her mind was still as divided as ever.

"Come on," she said to the kids. She couldn't keep them standing out here in the cold while she made up her mind. "Let's visit the goats first."

The smell of goats struck her the moment she opened the door—pungent, warm, and familiar. Warm, above all; all three humans sighed in relief and pleasure as the animal heat rolled over them, and they smiled at the eager rush and outcry of *mehhs* that greeted their presence.

From the noise that echoed off the stone walls, there might have been fifty goats inside the broch—though Brianna counted only half a dozen nannies, flop-eared and dainty, four or five half-grown, round-bellied kids, and a single robust billy goat who lowered his horns and glowered at them, suspicious and yellow-eyed. All of them shared a rough pen that fenced off half the ground floor of the broch. She glanced up—but instead of the exposed rafters high above that she half-expected to see, there was the intact underside of another floor above.

The kids—her kids, that is, and she smiled at the thought—were already sticking wisps of hay through the fence and playing with the young goats, who were standing on their back legs to peer at the visitors.

"Jemmy, Mandy!" she called. "Take off your hats and mufflers and mittens and put them over by the door, so the goats don't chew on them!" She left Jem to distentangle Mandy from her fuzzy muffler and went up the stair to see what was on the second floor.

Pale winter light from the windows striped the haunches of burlap bags that filled most of the floor space. She breathed in and coughed a little; flour dust was floating in the air, but she smelled the sweetness of dried corn—maize, they called it—and the deeper, nutty smell of ripe barley, as well, and when she nudged her foot against a particularly lumpy sack, she heard the shift and clack of hazelnuts. Lallybroch wouldn't starve this winter.

Curious, she went up one more flight and on the top floor found a good number of small wooden casks arrayed against the wall. It was much colder up here, but the heady aroma of good whisky filled the air with the illusion of warmth. She stood breathing it in for a moment, wanting very badly to be drunk on the fumes, to obliviate her mind, be able not to bloody *think*, if only for a few minutes.

But that was the last thing she could do. In minutes, she'd have to act.

She stepped back onto the narrow stair that wound up between the inner and outer walls of the broch and looked out toward the house, with vivid memories of the last time she had been here, crouched on the stair in the dark with a shotgun in her hands, watching the light of strangers in her house.

There were strangers here now, too, although her own blood. What if . . . She swallowed. If Roger had found Jerry MacKenzie, his father would be only in his early twenties—much younger than Roger himself. And if her own da was here now—

"He can't be," she whispered to herself, and wasn't sure if that was reassurance or regret. She'd met him for the first time in North Carolina, pissing against a tree. He'd been in his forties, she twenty-two.

You couldn't enter your own lifeline, couldn't exist in the same time twice. They thought they knew that for sure. But what if you entered someone else's life twice, at different times?

That was what was turning her blood to ice and making her curled fists tremble. *What happened?* Did one or the other of your appearances change things, perhaps cancel out the other? Would it not happen that way, would she *not* meet Jamie Fraser in North Carolina if she met him now?

But she had to find Roger. No matter what else happened. And Lallybroch was the only place she knew for sure he'd been. She took a deep, deep breath and closed her eyes.

Please, she prayed. *Please help me. Thy will be done, but please show me what to do . . .*

"Mam!" Jemmy came running up the stair, his footsteps loud in the confined stone corridor. "Mam!" He popped into sight, blue eyes round and hair standing half on end with excitement. "Mam, come down! A man's coming!"

"What does he look like?" she asked, urgent, grabbing him by the sleeve. "What color is his hair?"

He blinked, surprised.

"Black, I think. He's at the bottom of the hill—I couldn't see his face."

Roger.

"All right. I'm coming." She felt half choked but no longer frozen. It was happening now, whatever it was, and energy fizzed through her veins.

Even as she hurtled down the stairs behind Jemmy, rationality told her that it wasn't Roger—distance or not, Jemmy would know his father. But she had to see.

"Stay *here*," she said to the children, with so much command in her voice that they blinked but didn't argue. She threw open the door, saw the man coming up the path, and stepped out to meet him, closing the door firmly behind her.

From the first glance, she saw that it wasn't Roger, but the disappointment was subsumed at once in relief that it wasn't Jamie. And intense curiosity, because it must surely be . . .

She'd run down the path, to get well away from the broch, just in case, and was picking her way through the stones of the family burying ground, eyes on the man coming up the steep, rocky path.

A tall, solid-looking man, his dark hair graying a little but still thick, glossy, and loose on his shoulders. His eyes were on the rough ground, watching his footing. And then he came to his destination and made his way across the hill, to one of the stones in the burying ground. He knelt by it and laid down something he'd been carrying in his hand.

She shifted her weight, uncertain whether to call out or wait 'til he'd finished his business with the dead. But the small stones under her feet shifted, too, rolling down with a *click-clack-click* that made him look up and, seeing her, rise abruptly to his feet, black brows raised.

Black hair, black brows. *Brian Dubh.* Black Brian.

I met Brian Fraser (you would like him, and he, you) . . .

Wide, startled hazel eyes met hers, and for a second that was all she saw. His beautiful deep-set eyes, and the expression of stunned horror in them.

"Brian," she said. "I—"

"A Dhia!" He went whiter than the harled plaster of the house below. "Ellen!"

Astonishment deprived her of speech for an instant—long enough to hear light footsteps scrambling down the hill behind her.

"Mam!" Jem called, breathless.

Brian's glance turned up, behind her, and his mouth fell open at sight of Jem. Then a look of radiant joy suffused his face.

"Willie!" he said. *"A bhalaich! Mo bhalaich!"* He looked back at Brianna and stretched out a trembling hand to her. *"Mo ghràidh . . . mo chridhe . . ."*

"Brian," she said softly, her heart in her voice, filled with pity and love, unable to do anything but respond to the need of the soul that showed so clearly in his lovely eyes. And with her speaking of his name for the second time, he stopped dead, swaying for a moment, and then the eyes rolled up in his head and he fell.

SHE WAS KNEELING in the crunchy dead heather beside Brian Fraser before she'd even thought to move. There was a slight blue tinge to his lips, but he was breathing, and she drew a deep cold breath of relief herself, seeing his chest rise slowly under the worn linen shirt.

Not for the first time, she wished fervently that her mother was there, but turned his head to one side and laid two fingers on the pulse she could see at the side of his neck. Her fingers were cold, and his flesh was startlingly warm. He didn't rouse or stir at her touch, though, and she began to fear that he hadn't just fainted.

He'd died—would die—of a stroke. If there was some weakness in his brain . . . oh, God. Had she just killed him prematurely?

"Don't die!" she said to him aloud. "For God's sake, don't die *here*!"

She glanced hastily toward the house below, but no one was coming. Looking down again, she saw what it was he'd held: a small bouquet of evergreen twigs, tied with red thread. Yew—she recognized the oddly tubular red berries—and holly.

And then she saw the stone. She knew it well, had sat on the ground beside it often, contemplating Lallybroch and those who lay sleeping on its hillside.

Ellen Caitriona Sileas MacKenzie Fraser
Beloved wife and mother
Born 1691, Died in childbed 1729

And below, in smaller letters:

Robert Brian Gordon MacKenzie Fraser
Infant son
Died at birth 1729

And:

William Simon Murtagh MacKenzie Fraser
Beloved son
Born 1716, Died of the smallpox 1727

"Mam!" Jem skidded down the last few feet, almost falling beside her. "Mam, Mam—Mandy says—who is he?" He stared from Brian's pallid face to her own and back again.

"His name's Brian Fraser. He's your great-grandfather." Her hands were trembling, but to her surprise she felt suddenly calm at the speaking of the words, as though she had stepped into the center of a puzzle and found herself to be the missing piece. "What about Mandy?"

"Did I scare him?" Jem squatted down, looking worried. "He looked at me just before he fell down. Is he—dead?"

"Don't worry, I think he's just had a shock. He thought we were . . . somebody else." She touched Brian's cheekbone, feeling the soft prickle of his beard stubble, and smoothed the tumbled hair behind his ear. His mouth twitched a little as she did so, the ghost of a half smile, and her heart jumped. Thank God, he was coming round. "What did Mandy say?"

"Oh!" Jem stood up, fast, eyes wide. "She says she hears Dad!"

108

REALITY IS THAT WHICH, WHEN YOU STOP BELIEVING IN IT, DOESN'T GO AWAY

ROGER TURNED HIS horse's head toward Lallybroch, knowing nowhere else to go. He'd taken leave of Brian Fraser six weeks before and had been sad at what he'd thought was a permanent parting. His heart was eased a little now at the thought of seeing Brian again. Also at the certainty of a sympathetic ear, even though there was little he could openly discuss with him.

He'd have to tell Brian, of course, that he hadn't found Jem. That thought was a thorn in his heart, and one felt at every beat. For the last weeks, he had been able to put the brutal ache of Jemmy's absence aside for a little, hoping that somehow, finding Jerry might also lead to finding Jem. But it hadn't.

What the devil it *did* mean was a complete mystery. Had he found the only Jeremiah there was to be found here? If he had . . . where *was* Jem?

He wanted to tell Brian that he'd found the man to whom the identity disks belonged—Brian would ask. But how to do so without divulging either Jerry's identity, Roger's relationship with him—or explaining what had happened to him? He sighed, reining his horse around a large puddle in the road. Maybe better to say simply that he'd failed, hadn't found J. W. MacKenzie—though it troubled him to lie outright to such an openhearted man.

And he couldn't discuss Buck, either. Beyond thought of Jem, Buck was the matter lying heaviest on his mind at the moment.

"Ye'll never make a decent minister, if ye can't be honest." He'd tried to be. The honest truths of the situation from his own selfish point of view were

that he'd miss Buck's company badly, that he was deeply jealous of the possibility that Buck *might* make it to Brianna, and—not least, he assured himself—that he was terrified that Buck *wouldn't* make it through the stones again. He'd die in the void, or maybe be lost once more, alone in some random time.

The truth for Buck was that while it could be argued (and with no little force) that Buck should remove himself forthwith and permanently from the vicinity of Geillis Duncan, going through the stones was maybe the least desirable means of ensuring such an outcome.

To accept Buck's gallant gesture was a temptation, though. If he *could* make it, tell Bree where Roger was . . . Roger didn't think Buck could come back, though. The effects of travel were cumulative, and Hector McEwan likely wouldn't be standing by next time.

But if Buck was willing to risk the crossing, in spite of the very real danger to his own life, surely it was Roger's obligation to try to persuade him to return to his own wife, rather than to Roger's?

He brushed the back of his hand against his lips, feeling in memory the softness of Morag's brown hair on his cheek when he'd bent to kiss her forehead on the banks of the Alamance. The gentle trust in her eyes—and the fact that she'd bloody saved his own life very shortly thereafter. His fingers rested for an instant on his throat, and he realized, with the flicker of surprise that attends recognition of things already long known, that whatever the bitterness of his regrets about his voice, he'd never for an instant wished that she *hadn't* saved him.

When Stephen Bonnet would have thrown Morag's son overboard, Roger had saved the child from drowning, and that at some risk to his own life. But he didn't think she'd done what she'd done at Alamance in payment of that debt. She'd done it because she didn't want him to die.

Well. He didn't want Buck to die.

Did Morag *want* Buck back? Buck thought not, but he might be wrong. Roger was fairly sure that the man still loved Morag and that his abnegation was due as much to Buck's own sense of personal failure as to what he thought Morag's desires might be.

"Even if that's true," he said aloud, "where do I get off trying to manage people's lives?"

He shook his head and rode on through a light mist that wove shreds of fog through the wet black spikiness of the gorse. It wasn't raining, that was one thing, though the sky bore a burden of cloud that brought it down to shroud the tops of the nearby mountains.

He'd never asked his adoptive father anything about the art of being a priest; it was the last thing he'd ever thought of being. But he'd grown up in the Reverend's house and had seen parishioners come every day to the comfortably shabby study in search of help or advice. He remembered his father (and now felt a new oddness in the word, layered as it was with the freshness of Jerry MacKenzie's physical presence), remembered him sitting down with a sigh to drink tea in the kitchen with Mrs. Graham, shaking his head in response to her questioning look and saying, *"Sometimes there's nothing you can give some of them but a friendly ear and a prayer to be going on with."*

He came to a dead stop in the road, closed his eyes, and tried to find a moment's peace in the chaos of his thoughts. And ended, as every priest since Aaron's time doubtless had, by throwing up his hands and demanding, "What do You *want* of me? What the hell should I *do* about these people?"

He opened his eyes when he said that, but instead of finding an angel with an illuminated scroll standing before him, he was confronted by the beady yellow eyes of a fat seagull sitting in the road a few feet from his horse and not discomposed in the slightest by the presence of a creature a hundred times its size. The bird gave him an old-fashioned sort of look, then spread its wings and flapped off with a piercing *screek!* This echoed from the hillside above, where a few more gulls wheeled slowly, barely visible against the paper-white sky.

The presence of the gull broke his sense of isolation, at least. He rode on in a calmer frame of mind, resolved only not to think about things until he had to.

He thought he was close to Lallybroch; with luck, would reach it well before dark. His belly rumbled at the prospect of tea, and he felt happier. Whatever he could and couldn't tell Brian Fraser, just seeing Brian and his daughter Jenny again would be a comfort.

The gulls cried high overhead, still wheeling, and he looked up. Sure enough: he could just make out the low ruins of the Iron Age hill fort up there, the ruins he'd rebuilt—would rebuild? What if he never got back to— *Jesus, don't even think about it, man, it'll drive you crazier than you are already.*

He nudged the horse and it reluctantly accelerated a bit. It accelerated a lot faster in the next moment, when a crashing noise came from the hillside just above.

"Whoa! Whoa, you eedjit! Whoa, I said!" These adjurations, along with a heave of the reins to bring the horse's head around, had an effect, and they ended facing back the way they'd come, to see a young boy standing, panting, in the middle of the road, his red hair all on end, nearly brown in the muted light.

"Daddy," he said, and his face lit as though touched by a sudden sun. "Daddy!"

ROGER HADN'T ANY memory of leaving his horse or running down the road. Or of anything else. He was sitting in the mud and the mist in a patch of wet bracken with his son hugged tight to his chest, and nothing else mattered in the world.

"Dad," Jem kept saying, gasping with sobs, "Daddy, Daddy . . ."

"I'm here," he whispered into Jem's hair, the tears running down his own face. "I'm here, I'm here. Don't be afraid."

Jem took a shuddering breath, managed to say, "I'm *not* afraid," and cried some more.

At last, a sense of time crept back, along with the sensation of water soaking through the seat of his breeches. He breathed and shuddered a bit himself, smoothed Jem's hair, and kissed his head.

"You smell like a goat," he said, swallowed, brushed at his eyes with the back of a hand, and laughed. "Where the *hell* have you been?"

"In the broch with Mandy," Jem said, as though this was the most natural statement in the world. He gave Roger a faintly accusing look. "Where have *you* been?"

"Mandy?" Roger said blankly. "What do you mean Mandy?"

"My sister," Jem said, with the patience children occasionally show for the denseness of their parents. "*You* know."

"Well . . . where *is* Mandy, then?" In Roger's state of surreal confusion, Mandy might just as well have popped up beside Jem like a mushroom.

Jem's face went momentarily blank with confusion, and he glanced round as though expecting Mandy to materialize out of the moss and heather at any moment.

"I don't know," he said, sounding mildly puzzled. "She ran away to find you, and then Mam fell down and broke something and—"

Roger had let go of Jem but grabbed him again at this, startling the breath out of the boy.

"Your mother's here, *too?*"

"Well, sure," Jem said, sounding mildly annoyed. "I mean—not *here* here. She's up there, in the old fort. She tripped on a rock when we were running to catch Mandy."

"Jesus, Lord," Roger said fervently, taking a stride in the direction of the fort, then halting abruptly. "Wait: you said she broke something—she's hurt?"

Jem shrugged. He was beginning to look worried again, but not very worried. Dad was here; everything would be okay.

"I don't think it's bad," he assured his father. "She couldn't walk, though, so she told me to run and catch Mandy. But I found you first."

"Okay. She's awake, though, she's talking?" He had Jem by the shoulders, as much to keep him from disappearing—he half-feared he was hallucinating—as to compel an answer.

"Uh-huh." Jem was looking vaguely about, a slight frown on his face. "Mandy's here *someplace.* . . ." Wriggling free, he turned round slowly, face creased in intent concentration.

"Mandy!" Roger shouted up the hill. He cupped his hands around his mouth and yelled again. "BREE!" He scanned the fort and the hillside anxiously for Bree's head popping up above the ruins or any sign of agitation among the vegetation that might be occasioned by a scrambling three-year-old. No head showed, but a breeze had come up and the whole hill seemed alive.

"Mandy ran away down this hill?" he asked, and, at Jem's nod, he glanced behind him. The land flattened out into moor on the other side of the road, and there wasn't a glimpse of anything that might be Mandy on it. Unless she'd fallen down and was lying in a hollow . . .

"You stay *right here*," he said to Jem, squeezing his shoulder hard. "I'm going to go up the hill and look. I'll bring your mother down." He bounded up the gravel trace that was the nearest thing there was to a path, calling out Mandy's name at intervals, torn between overwhelming joy and terrifying panic, lest it not be real, lest he actually had cracked and was simply imagining that Jem was there—he turned at every third step to check that he *was* there, still standing on the road.

Bree. The thought that she was up there, just above him . . . "Mandy!" he shouted again, his voice cracking. But it cracked from emotion, and he realized in a startled instant that he'd been shouting at full volume for minutes now—and it hadn't hurt.

"God bless you, Hector," he said fervently under his breath, and went on, beginning now to zigzag back and forth across the hill, beating through the sticks of dry broom and birch saplings, kicking at gorse and dead ferns in case Mandy should have fallen, maybe knocked herself out on a rock.

He heard the seagulls shriek above, thin and piercing, and looked up, hoping to see Brianna peering over the wall of the fort. She wasn't, but something called again—thin and piercing, but not a gull.

"Daddeeeee . . ."

He whirled, almost losing his footing, and saw Jem running down the road—and coming round the bend of that road, Buck's horse with Buck atop him, and a wildly squirming bundle with black curly hair cradled precariously in Buck's arm.

He couldn't speak at all by the time he reached them.

"Think ye might have lost something," Buck said gruffly, and handed Mandy carefully down to him. She was a heavy, lively weight in his arms—and smelled of goats.

"Daddy!" she exclaimed, beaming at him as though he'd just come in from work. "Mwah! Mwah!" She kissed him noisily and snuggled into his chest, her hair tickling his chin.

"Where *were* you?" Jem was saying accusingly.

"Where was *you*?" Mandy countered, and stuck her tongue out at him. "Bleah."

Roger was crying again, couldn't stop. Mandy had burrs and foxtails stuck in her hair and in the fabric of her jacket, and he thought she might have wet herself somewhere in the recent past. Buck twitched the reins, as though about to turn and go, and Roger reached out a hand and grabbed his stirrup.

"Stay," he croaked. "Tell me it's real."

Buck made an incoherent noise, and, looking up through his tears, Roger could see that Buck was making an inadequate attempt at hiding his own emotion.

"Aye," Buck said, sounding almost as choked as Roger. He looped his reins and, sliding off into the road, took Jem very gently into his own arms. "Aye, it's real."

109

FROTTAGE

D R. McEWAN WAS a single man and owned a single bed. The bed was presently accommodating four people, and even if two of those people were not full-sized, the general atmosphere was that of the London Tube in rush hour. Heat, random flesh in all directions, and a distinct shortage of oxygen.

Brianna squirmed, trying to find room to breathe. She was lying on her side, back pressed to the wall, with Mandy squashed into a heavily breathing mass between her parents. Roger balanced precariously on the bed's outer edge with Jem draped bonelessly over him, Jem's legs occasionally twitching spasmodically, prodding Bree in the shins. And Esmeralda was taking up most of the single pillow, red yarn hair getting up everyone's nose.

"Do you know the word 'frottage'?" Bree whispered to Roger. He wasn't asleep; if he had been, he'd have been on the floor by now.

"I do. Why, do ye want to try it now?" He reached carefully across Jem and stroked her bare arm lightly. The fine hairs rose on her forearm; she could see them do it, lifting silently in the dull glow from the hearth.

"I want to do less of it with a three-year-old. Mandy's zonked. Is Jem asleep enough to move?"

"We'll find out. I'm going to suffocate if he's not." Roger edged out from under his son, who emitted a loud "mmmm," but then smacked his lips and subsided. Roger patted him softly, bent to check that he was solidly asleep, and straightened up. "Okay, then."

They'd appeared at McEwan's door well after dark, Brianna supported between Roger and Buck, the children at their heels. The doctor, while clearly surprised at this nocturnal invasion of MacKenzies, had taken it calmly, sitting Bree down in his surgery with her foot in a pan of cold water and then going to call his landlady to find a bit of supper for the children.

"A sprain, and not too bad," he'd assured Brianna, drying her foot with a linen towel and expertly palpating her swollen ankle. He passed a thumb up the problematic tendon and noted her wince. "It will just take time to heal—but I think I can ease the pain a bit . . . if you like?" He glanced toward Roger, brow raised, and Brianna breathed in through her nose.

"It's not *his* ankle," she said, mildly annoyed. "And *I'd* certainly appreciate anything you can do."

Roger nodded, to her further annoyance, and McEwan took her foot onto his knee. Seeing her grip the edges of the stool to keep her balance, Roger knelt behind her and wrapped his arms around her.

"Lean on me," he said quietly in her ear. "Just breathe. See what happens."

She shot him a puzzled look, but he merely brushed her ear with his lips and nodded toward McEwan.

The doctor's head was bent over the foot, which he held lightly in both hands, his thumbs on her instep. He moved them slowly in circles, then pressed firmly. A sharp pain shot up her ankle, but died abruptly before she could gasp.

The doctor's hands were noticeably warm on her chilled flesh, and she wondered at that, since they'd been immersed in the same cold water as her foot. One hand now cupped her heel, and thumb and forefinger massaged the puffy flesh lightly, repeatedly, then a little harder. The sensation hovered unsettlingly somewhere between pain and pleasure.

McEwan looked up suddenly and smiled at her.

"It will take a little time," he murmured. "Relax, if you can."

In fact, she could. For the first time in twenty-four hours, she wasn't hungry. For the first time in days, she was beginning to thaw out completely—and for the first time in months, she wasn't afraid. She let out her breath and eased her head back on Roger's shoulder. He made a low humming noise in his throat and took a firmer hold, settling himself.

She could hear Mandy telling Jem a disjointed story about Esmeralda's adventures, in the back room where the landlady had taken them to eat their soup and bread. Sure that they were safe, she gave herself up to the elemental bliss of her husband's arms and the smell of his skin.

> *But the expression of a well-made man appears not only in his face;*
> *It is in his limbs and joints also, it is curiously in the joints of his hips and wrists . . .*

"Bree," Roger whispered to her some moments later. "Bree—look."

She opened her eyes and saw at first the curve of his wrist where it rested on her bosom, the hard elegance of bone and the curve of muscled forearm. But then her focus widened and she started a little. Her toes were glowing with a faint blue light barely visible in the crevices between them. She blinked hard and looked again, to be sure she was really seeing it, but the sound Roger made in his throat assured her that she was—and that he saw it, too.

Dr. McEwan had felt her startlement; he looked up and smiled again, this time joyful. His eyes flicked up toward Roger, then back to her.

"You, too?" he said. "I thought so." He held her foot still for a long moment, until she thought she felt the pulse in his fingers echo in the spaces between the small bones, and then he wrapped a bandage neatly around her ankle and lowered her foot gently to the floor. "Better now?"

"Yes," she said, and found her voice a little husky. "Thank you."

She'd wanted to ask him questions, but he rose and put on his coat.

"Ye'll oblige me greatly by staying here the night," he said firmly, still smiling at her. "I'll find a bed with a friend." And raising his hat to Roger, he bowed and went out, leaving them to put the children to bed.

Not surprisingly, Mandy had put up a fuss at sleeping in a strange bed in a strange room, complaining that Esmeralda thought the surgery smelled funny and was scared of the big wardrobe because there might be kelpies in it.

"Kelpies only live in water, silly," Jem had said, but he also looked a little apprehensively at the enormous dark armoire with its cracked door. So they'd all lain down on the narrow bed together, parents comforted as much as children by sheer physical proximity.

Brianna felt the soft warmth and the haze of exhalation blanketing her bodily exhaustion, a pull on her senses beckoning her toward the well of sleep. But not nearly such a strong pull as her sense of Roger.

> *It is in his walk, the carriage of his neck, the flex of his waist*
> *and knees; dress does not hide him . . .*

She lay for a moment, hand on Mandy's back, feeling the slow beating of the child's heart, watching as Roger scooped Jem into his arms and turned to lay him down on one of the extra quilts McEwan's landlady had brought up with the soup.

> *The strong, sweet, supple quality he has, strikes through the*
> *cotton and flannel . . .*

He was dressed in nothing but shirt and breeks and now paused to shed the homespun breeks, casually scratching his arse in relief, the long linen shirt momentarily rucked up to show the lean curve of a buttock. Then he came to pick up Mandy, smiling over her stertorously breathing body at Bree.

"Leave the bed to the kids, you think? We could make up a pallet with the cloaks—if they've dried out a bit—and quilts in the surgery." He gathered Mandy up like an armful of laundry, and Bree was able to sit up and scoot across the bed, feeling a wonderful movement of air through her perspiration-dampened shift and a brush of soft fabric across her breasts that made her nipples rise.

She turned back the bedding; he moved the children back to the bed, and she covered them and kissed their dreaming faces, kissing Esmeralda for good measure before tucking her into Mandy's arm. Roger turned toward the closed door to the surgery and looked back at Bree over his shoulder, smiling. She could see the shadow of his body through the linen shirt, against the glow of the hearth.

> *To see him pass conveys as much as the best poem,*
> *perhaps more . . .*
> *You linger to see his back, and the back of his neck and*
> *shoulder-side.*

"Wilt bed with me, lass?" he said softly, and put out a hand to her.

"Oh, yes," she said, and came to him.

THE SURGERY WAS cold, after the humid heat of the bedroom, and they came to each other at once, warm limbs and warm lips seeking. The fire in this room had gone out, and they didn't trouble to rebuild it.

Roger had kissed her the moment he saw her on the ground in the fort, grabbing her and lifting her into an embrace that crushed her ribs and nearly bruised her lips. She'd had no objections whatever. But now his mouth was soft and tender and the scruff of his beard light on her skin.

"Fast?" he murmured against her mouth. "Slow?"

"Horizontal," she murmured back, clutching his bottom. "Speed irrelevant." She was standing on one leg, the bad foot elegantly—she hoped—extended behind her. Dr. McEwan's ministrations had eased the throbbing quite a bit, but she still couldn't put weight on it for more than the briefest second.

He laughed—quietly, with a guilty look toward the bedroom door—and, bending suddenly, scooped her up and staggered across the room to the coat rack, where she snagged the hanging cloaks and tossed them onto the floor by the table, that being the cleanest open space visible. He squatted, back creaking audibly and manfully suppressing a groan as he lowered her gently onto the heap.

"Be careful!" she whispered, and not jokingly. "You could put your back out, and then what?"

"Then ye'd get to be on top," he whispered back, and ran a hand up her thigh, her shift rippling up with it. "But I haven't, so ye don't." Then he pulled up his shirt, spread her legs, and came to her with an incoherent noise of deep satisfaction.

"I hope ye meant it about the speed being irrelevant," he said in her ear, a few minutes later.

"Oh. Yes," she said vaguely, and wrapped her arms round his body. "You . . . just . . . stay put." When she could, she let him go, cradling his head and kissing the smooth warm flesh at the side of his neck. She felt the rope scar and gently drew the tip of her tongue along it, making gooseflesh erupt all over his back and shoulders.

"Are you asleep?" he inquired some moments later, suspicious.

She opened one eye halfway. He'd gone back into the bedroom for quilts and was kneeling beside her, spreading one over her. It smelled faintly musty, with a tang of mice, but she didn't care.

"No," she said, and rolled onto her back, feeling wonderful, despite the hard floor, her sprained ankle, and the dawning realization that Dr. McEwan must do operations and amputations on the table. There was a dark stain on the underside, above her head. "Just . . . limp." She stretched out a slow hand to Roger, urging him under the quilt with her. "You?"

"I'm not asleep," he assured her, sliding down close beside her. "And if ye think I'm going to say 'limp,' think again."

She laughed—quietly, with a glance at the door—rolled over, and rested her forehead against his chest.

"I thought I might never see you again," she whispered.

"Aye," he said softly, and his hand stroked her long hair and her back. "Me, too." They were silent for a long moment, each listening to the other's breath—his came easier than it had, she thought, without the small catches— and then he finally said, "Tell me."

She did, baldly and with as little emotion as she could manage. She thought he might be emotional enough for both of them.

He couldn't shout or curse, because of the sleeping children. She could feel the rage in him; he was shaking with it, his fists clenched like solid knobs of bone.

"I'll kill him," he said, in a voice barely pitched above silence, and his eyes met hers, savage and so dark that they seemed black in the dim light.

"It's okay," she said softly, and, sitting up, took both his hands in hers, lifting one and then the other to her lips. "It's okay. We're all right, all of us. And we're here."

He looked away and took a deep breath, then looked back, his hands tightening on hers.

"Here," he repeated, his voice bleak, still hoarse with fury. "In 1739. If I'd—"

"You had to," she said firmly, squeezing back hard. Besides," she added, a little diffidently, "I sort of thought we wouldn't stay. Unless you've taken a great liking to some of the denizens?"

Expressions flickered across his face, from anger to rue to reluctant acceptance . . . and an even more reluctant humor, as he got a grip of himself. He cleared his throat.

"Aye, well," he said dryly. "There's Hector McEwan, to be sure. But there are a good many other people, too—Geillis Duncan, for one."

A small jolt went through her at the name.

"Geillis Duncan? Well . . . yes, I suppose she *would* be here at this point, wouldn't she? Did you—did you meet her?"

A truly extraordinary expression went over Roger's face at that question.

"I did," he said, avoiding her questioning glance. He turned and waved a hand at the surgery window that looked out onto the square. "She lives just across the way."

"Really?" Brianna got to her feet, clutching a quilt to her bosom, forgot about her bad foot, and stumbled. Roger leapt up and caught her by the arm.

"You *don't* want to meet her," he said, with emphasis. "Sit down, aye? Ye're going to fall."

Brianna eyed him, but allowed him to ease her back down to their nest and to pull a quilt up over her shoulders. It *was* bloody cold in the surgery, now that the warmth of their efforts had faded.

"All right," she said, and shook her hair down to cover her ears and neck. "Tell me why I don't want to meet Geillis Duncan."

To her surprise, he flushed deeply, visible even in the shadows of the surgery. Roger had neither the skin nor the temperament to blush easily, but when he *did* describe—briefly, but vividly—what had happened (or possibly *not* happened) with Buck, Dr. McEwan, and Geillis, she understood it.

"Holy moly," she said, with a glance over her shoulder at the window. "Er . . . when Dr. McEwan said he'd find a bed with a friend . . . ?"

Buck had gone off, saying that he'd take a bed at the ordinary at the foot of the High Street and would see them in the morning. Presumably he'd meant it, but . . .

"She *is* married," Roger said tersely. "Presumably her husband would notice were she inviting strange men to spend the night."

"Oh, I don't know so much," she said, half-teasing. "She's an herbalist, remember? Mama does a good sleeping potion; I imagine Geillis could, too."

The color washed up Roger's face again, and she knew, as clearly as if he'd said so, that he was envisioning Geillis Duncan doing something disgraceful with one or another of her lovers whilst lying beside her snoring husband.

"God," he said.

"You, um, do remember what's going to *happen* to her poor husband, don't you?" Bree said delicately. The color vanished instantly from Roger's face, and she knew he hadn't.

"That's one of the reasons we can't stay here," she said, gently but firmly. "There are too many things we know. And we *don't* know what trying to interfere might do, but it's a good bet that it's dangerous."

"Yes, but—" he began, but broke off at the look on her face. "Lallybroch. Is that why ye wouldna go there?" For he'd tried to take her down the hill to the house when he'd rescued her from the fort. She'd insisted that they must go to the village for help instead, even though it meant an awkward and painful three-hour ride.

She nodded and felt a small lump come into her throat. It stayed there as she told him about meeting Brian in the burying ground.

"It's not *just* that I'm afraid what meeting them might do to . . . later," she said, and the lump dissolved into tears. "It's . . . oh, Roger, the look on his face when he saw me and thought I was Ellen!

"I—he—he's going to die in a year or two. That beautiful, sweet man . . . and there isn't any-anything we can do to stop it." She gulped and swiped at her eyes. "He—he thinks he's seen his wife and his son, that they're w-waiting for him. And the—oh, God, the *joy* on his face. I couldn't take that away from him, I just couldn't."

He took her in his arms and rubbed her back gently as she sobbed.

"No, of course ye couldn't," he whispered to her. "Dinna fash, Bree. Ye did right."

She sniffed and groped among the cloaks for something to blow her nose on, settling at last for a stained cloth from Dr. McEwan's table. It smelled of some pungent medicine, thank God, not blood.

"But there's Da, too," she said, taking a deep, tremulous breath. "What will happen to him . . . the scars on his back . . . I—can't stand to think about that and us doing nothing, but we—"

"We can't," Roger agreed quietly. "We daren't. God only knows what I may have done already, finding Jerry and sending him—wherever I *did* send him." Taking the cloth, he dipped it in the water bucket and wiped her face, the cold of it soothing on her hot cheeks, though it made her shiver.

"Come lie down," he said, putting an arm round her shoulders. "Ye need rest, *mo chridhe*. It's been a terrible day."

"No," she murmured, easing down and laying her head in the curve of his shoulder, feeling the strength and warmth of his body. "It's been a wonderful day. I have you back."

110

THE SOUNDS THAT
MAKE UP SILENCE

ROGER FELT HER begin to relax, and quite suddenly she let go her stubborn hold on consciousness and fell asleep like someone breathing ether. He held her and listened to the tiny sounds that made up silence: the distant hiss of the peat fire in the bedroom, a cold wind rattling at the window, the rustling and breathing of the sleeping kids, the slow beating of Brianna's valiant heart.

Thank you, he said silently to God.

He had expected to fall asleep himself at once; tiredness covered him like a lead blanket. But the day was still with him, and he lay for some time looking up into the dark.

He was at peace, too tired to think coherently of anything. All the possibilities drifted round him in a slow, distant swirl, too far away to be troublesome. Where they might go . . . and how. What Buck might have said to Dougal MacKenzie. What Bree had brought in her bag, heavy as lead. Whether there would be porridge for breakfast—Mandy liked porridge.

The thought of Mandy made him ease out of the quilts to check on the children. To reassure himself that they were really there.

They were, and he stood by the bed for a long time, watching their faces in wordless gratitude, breathing the warm childish smell of them—still tinged with a slight tang of goat.

At last he turned, shivering, to make his way back to his warm wife and the beckoning bliss of sleep. But as he reentered the surgery, he glanced through the window into the night outside.

Cranesmuir slept, and mist lay in her streets, the cobbles beneath gleaming with wet in the half-light of a drowning moon. On the far side of the square, though, a light showed in the attic window of Arthur Duncan's house.

And in the shadow of the square below, a small movement betrayed the presence of a man. Waiting.

Roger closed his eyes, cold rising from his bare feet up his body, seeing in his mind the sudden vision of a green-eyed woman, lazy in the arms of a fair-haired lover . . . and a look of surprise and then of horror on her face as the man vanished from her side. And an invisible blue glow rose in her womb.

With his eyes tight shut, he put a hand on the icy windowpane, and said a prayer to be going on with.

PART SEVEN

Before I Go Hence

111

A DISTANT MASSACRE

September 5, 1778

I FOLDED THE CLOTH into a tidy square and used the tongs to dip it in the steaming cauldron, then stood waving it gently to and fro until the compress should cool enough for me to wring it out and use it. Joanie sighed, fidgeting on her stool.

"Don't rub your eye," I said automatically, seeing her curled fist steal toward the large pink sty on her right eyelid. "Don't fret; it won't take long."

"Yes, it does take long," she said crossly. "It takes *forever*!"

"Dinna be giving your grannie sauce," Marsali told her, pausing in her stride on the way from kitchen to printshop, a cheese roll for Fergus in her hand. "Hauld your wheesht and be grateful."

Joanie groaned and writhed, and stuck her tongue out after her departing mother, but whipped it back into her mouth again and looked rather shame-faced when she caught sight of my raised brow.

"I know," I said, with some sympathy. Holding a warm compress on a sty for ten minutes did feel like forever. Particularly if you'd been doing it six times a day for the last two days. "Maybe you can think of something to pass the time. You could recite me the multiplication tables while I grind valerian root."

"Oh, *Grannie*!" she said, exasperated, and I laughed.

"Here you go," I said, handing her the warm poultice. "Do you know any good songs?"

She exhaled moodily, small nostrils flaring.

"I wish Grandda was here," she said. "*He* could tell me a story." The note of comparative accusation was clear in her voice.

"Spell 'hordeolum' for me and I'll tell you the one about the water horse's wife," I suggested. That made her unaffected eye fly open with interest.

"What's a hordeolum?"

"That's the scientific name for a sty."

"Oh." She seemed unimpressed by this, but her forehead creased a little in concentration, and I could see her lips move as she sounded out the syllables. Both Joanie and Félicité were good spellers; they'd been playing with discarded lead type since they were toddlers and loved stumping each other with new words.

That was a thought; maybe I could get her to spell unusual words for me during the compress treatments. The sty was a big, nasty one; her entire eyelid had been red and swollen in the beginning, the eye no more than a gleaming, resentful slit. Now the sty itself had shrunk to the size of a pea, and at least three-quarters of the eye was visible.

"H," she said, watching me to see if that was right, and I nodded. "O, R, D . . ." I nodded again, and saw her lips move silently. "Hor-de-o-lum," I repeated helpfully, and she nodded, more confident. "E, O, L, U, M!"

"Excellent!" I said, beaming at her. "How about . . ." I cast about for another good one, long but strictly phonetic. "Hepatitis?"

"What's that?"

"Viral infection of the liver. Do you know where your liver is?" I was looking through my medicine chest, but appeared to be out of aloe salve. I should ride over to Bartram's Garden tomorrow, I thought, weather permitting. I was out of almost everything, in the wake of the battle. The usual small twinge came in my side at thought of it, but I pushed it firmly away. It would fade, and so would the thoughts.

Marsali appeared suddenly in the kitchen door, as Joanie was carefully spelling "acanthocytosis," and I looked up from my grinding. She was holding a letter in her hand and looked worried.

"Is it the Indian they call Joseph Brant that Young Ian kens?" she asked.

"I expect he knows quite a few of them," I replied, setting down my pestle. "But I've heard him mention Joseph Brant, yes. The man's Mohawk name starts with a 'T,' I think, but that's as much as I feel sure of. Why?" I felt a slight uneasiness at the name. Ian's Mohawk wife, Emily, had been living in a settlement in New York founded by Brant; Ian had mentioned it, very briefly, when he'd gone up there to visit her last year.

He hadn't said what the purpose of his visit was, and neither Jamie nor I had asked, but I assumed it to have had something to do with his fear that he couldn't sire children, as all his babies with Emily had either been stillborn or miscarried. He'd asked me about the matter, and I'd told him what I could, offering what reassurance I could that he might be able to have children with another woman.

I offered up a quick prayer for Rachel's chances, then returned abruptly to what Marsali was saying.

"They did *what?*"

"This gentleman"—she tapped the letter—"says that Brant and his men fell upon a wee place called Andrustown. No but seven families living there." Her lips pressed tight, and she glanced at Joanie, who was listening with her ears flapping. "They plundered and burnt the place, he says, and massa—er . . . did awa wi' a number of the folk who lived there."

"What's that word, Mam?" Joanie asked brightly. "The one that means 'did awa' with?"

" 'Massacred,' " I told her, saving her mother the embarrassment. "It means indiscriminate and brutal slaughter. Here." I handed her the fresh compress, which she applied without protest, frowning in thought.

"Is that different than just killin' someone?"

"Well," I said judiciously, "it depends. You might kill someone by accident, for instance, and that wouldn't be a massacre, though it would certainly be lamentable. You might kill someone who was trying to kill *you,* and that would be self-defense."

"Rachel says ye oughtn't do that," Joanie observed, but merely for the sake of thoroughness. "What about if ye're with an army and have to kill the soldiers on the other side?"

Marsali made a low Scottish noise of disapproval but answered tersely.

"If a man's gone to the army, then killin' is his job," she said. "He does it—mostly—" she added fairly, with a raised brow to me, "to protect his ain family and property. So that's more like self-defense, aye?"

Joanie glanced from her mother to me, still frowning.

"I ken what 'bru-tal' is," she said. "That's bein' mean when ye havena got to. But what's 'in-dis-crim-in-ate'?" She sounded it out carefully, as though about to spell it.

"Without choosing," I said, lifting one shoulder in a shrug. "It means you do something without taking much notice who you do it to and probably without much reason to do it to that particular person."

"Did Cousin Ian's Indian friend have nay reason for burning yon place and killing the folk, then?"

Marsali and I exchanged a glance.

"We dinna ken that," Marsali said. "But it's no a good thing, whatever he meant by it. Now, ye're done. Go along and find Félicité and start in fillin' up the washtub." She took the compress from Joanie and shooed her out.

She stood watching until Joanie had gone out through the back door, then turned to me and handed me the letter.

It was from a Mr. Johansen, apparently one of Fergus's regular correspondents, and the contents were as Marsali had said, though adding a few gruesome details that she hadn't mentioned in Joanie's hearing. It was fairly factual, with only the barest of eighteenth-century ornaments, and the more hair-raising—literally, I thought; some of the Andrustown residents had been scalped, by report—for that.

Marsali nodded as I looked up from the letter.

"Aye," she said. "Fergus wants to publish the account, but I'm nay so sure he ought to. Because of Young Ian, ken?"

"What's because of Young Ian?" said a Scottish voice from the printshop doorway, and Jenny came through, a marketing basket over one arm. Her eyes went to the letter in my hand, and her sharp dark brows rose.

"Has he told ye much about her?" Marsali asked, having explained the letter. "The Indian lass he wed?"

Jenny shook her head and began taking things out of her basket.

"Nay a word, save for his telling Jamie to say he wouldna forget us." A shadow crossed her face at the memory, and I wondered for a moment how it must have been for her and Ian, receiving Jamie's account of the circumstances in which Ian had become a Mohawk. I knew the agony with which he'd written that letter, and doubted that the reading of it had been done with less.

She laid down an apple and beckoned to me for the letter. Having read it through in silence, she looked at me. "D'ye think he's got feelings for her still?"

"I think he does," I answered reluctantly. "But nothing like his feelings for Rachel, surely." I did recall him, though, standing with me in the twilight on the demilune battery at Fort Ticonderoga, when he'd told me about his children—and Emily, his wife.

"He feels guilty about her, does he?" Jenny asked, shrewdly watching my face. I gave her a look, but nodded. She compressed her lips, but then handed the letter back to Marsali.

"Well, we dinna ken whether his wife has anything to do wi' this Brant or his doings, and it's no her that's been massacred. I'd say let Fergus print it, but"—and she glanced at me—"show the letter to Jamie and have him talk to wee Ian about it. He'll listen." Her expression lightened a little then, and a slight smile emerged. "He's got a good wife now, and I think Rachel will keep him to home."

MAIL WAS DELIVERED to the printshop at all hours of the day— and, not infrequently, the night—and by all manner of messengers. Philadel-phia gloried in the best postal system in the colonies, this having been established by Benjamin Franklin only three years before; post riders rode regularly between New York and Philadelphia and over thirty other routes through the colonies.

Given the nature of Fergus's business and the nature of the times, though, almost as much mail arrived by older routes: passed along by travelers, mer-chants, Indians, and soldiers, and shoved under the door in the night watches. Or handed to a member of the family in the street. It was exchanges of that sort during the British occupation of the city that had compelled me to marry John Grey in order to avoid arrest for sedition and spying.

John's own letter, though, arrived sedately in the pouch of a postal rider, properly stamped, and sealed with a blob of yellow wax imprinted with his signet in the shape of a smiling half-moon.

To Mrs. James Fraser, Fraser's Printshop, Philadelphia
From Lord John Grey, Wilbury House, New York

My dear,

I am with my brother and his regiment in New York, and am like to remain here for some time. That being so, I thought I would mention that the Lease of my house on Chestnut Street will run until the End of the Year, and as the Thought of it being left empty to be vandalized or left to ruin distresses me, I conceived the Notion of offering it to you once again.

Not, I hasten to add (lest your intransigent Husband be reading this), as a Domicile but rather as Premises for a Surgery. Acquainted as I am with your peculiar Habit of attracting Persons suffering from Dis-ease, Deformity, or hideous Injury, and being also well acquainted with the Number of Persons presently inhabiting the younger Mr. Fraser's printing Establishment, I believe you may find your medical Adventures more easily accommodated in Chestnut Street than between a Printing Press and a towering Stack of sixpenny Bibles bound in buckram.

As I do not expect you to spend your valuable Time in domestic Labor, I have arranged for Mrs. Figg and a Servant of her choice to remain in my employment for so long as you require them, being paid through my Bank. You will greatly oblige me, my dear, by accepting this Proposition, as it will put my mind at ease regarding the Property. And the Thought of you at work, earnestly administering a Clyster to General Arnold, will greatly enliven the Tedium of my present Condition.

> *Your most obedient Servant,*
> *John*

"What are ye smiling at, Mother Claire?" Marsali inquired, observing me with the letter in hand. She smiled, teasing. "Has someone sent ye a *billet-doux*?"

"Oh, something of the sort," I said, folding it up. "You wouldn't know where Jamie is just now, would you?"

She closed one eye to assist thought, keeping the other on Henri-Christian, who was industriously blacking his father's best boots—and a good deal of himself in the process.

"He said he was going wi' Young Ian to see a man about a horse," she said, "and then to the docks."

"The docks?" I said in surprise. "Did he say why?"

She shook her head. "I could maybe guess, though. That'll do, Henri! *A Dhia*, the state of you! Go find one o' your sisters and tell her to wash your hands for ye, aye?"

Henri looked at his hands, as though astonished to find them completely black.

"*Oui, Maman,*" he said, and, cheerfully wiping them on his breeches, scampered out into the kitchen, bellowing, "Félicité! Come wash me!" at the top of his lungs.

"Why?" I asked, moving closer and lowering my voice slightly—for obviously she'd got rid of Henri-Christian on the little pitchers–big ears principle.

"He's been talking wi' Fergus about going with ye, when ye go back to North Carolina," she said. "If I had to guess, I'd say he's gone to find out what it might cost to move everything"—she made a sweeping gesture, encompassing everything from printing press to loft—"by ship."

"Hmm," I said, as noncommittally as possible, though my heart had leapt—at both the thought of imminent departure for the Ridge and the thought that Fergus and Marsali might come with us. "Do you . . . want to?" I asked cautiously, seeing the line between her brows. She was still a lovely woman, fair and fine-boned, but she was too thin, and the lines of strain sharpened her features.

She shook her head, but in indecision rather than negation.

"I really dinna ken," she admitted. "It's a good bit easier now, wi' the British gone—but they're no so far away, are they? They could come back, and then what?" She glanced uneasily over her shoulder, though the print-shop was empty for the moment. Fergus had had to leave home and live furtively on the outskirts of the city, during the last months of the British occupation.

I opened my mouth to tell her that I doubted this. Hal Grey had told me, under the influence of ganja, that the new British strategy was to sever the southern colonies from the North and suppress the rebellion there, thus starving the North into submission. But I closed it without speaking. Best not to mention that until I found out whether Jamie had told Fergus.

Why didn't I bloody *know* what was going to happen? I asked myself in frustration—and not for the first time. Why hadn't I thought to brush up on American history when I had the chance?

Well, because I hadn't expected to end up in America, was the answer. Just went to show, I supposed. Pointless to spend too much time in planning, anyway, given the propensity of life to make sudden left-hand turns without warning.

"It would be wonderful, if you were to come," I said, as mildly as possible, adding craftily, "so nice to have the children nearby."

Marsali snorted, giving me a sideways glance.

"Aye," she said dryly. "Never think I dinna appreciate the value of a grannie. And when ye leave, Grannie Janet will go, too."

"Do you think so?" I hadn't thought of that. "But Jenny loves you and your children—Fergus is as much a son to her as any of the boys she bore."

"Well, that's maybe true," she admitted, with a brief smile that showed me the radiant fifteen-year-old who had married Fergus on a Caribbean beach twelve years before. "But Young Ian's her youngest, ken? And she's had too little of him. Now he's wed, she'll want to be nearby, to help wi' his bairns when they come. And ye ken Rachel will go where Ian does—and Ian will go where Da does."

That was a shrewd assessment, I thought, and gave her a brief nod of agreement and respect.

She sighed deeply and, sitting down in her nursing chair, took up the top-most item in the brimming mending basket, the threaded needle still sticking up from the garment where she'd last put it down. I had no desire to abandon the conversation and, pulling out a stool, sat down beside her and plucked one of Germain's stockings out of the basket. The workbasket, with its housewife, thread balls, and darning egg, was set beside the mending, and I deftly threaded my own needle, feeling pleased that I could still do that without putting on my spectacles.

"What about Fergus?" I asked bluntly. Because plainly Fergus was the crux of the matter, where Marsali was concerned.

"Aye, that's the rub," she said frankly. "I'd go, and happy, but ye ken how it was for him when we stayed on the Ridge."

I did, and grimaced slightly, stretching the heel of the stocking over the darning egg.

"It's been dangerous in the city, this last year," she said, and swallowed at the memory. "Couldna tell ye how many times the soldiers came to arrest him; they broke up the shop, more than once, when they couldna find him.

And the Loyalists would come and paint slogans on the front wall sometimes. But the danger didna trouble him—so long as it didna threaten me and the bairns."

"And sometimes even if it does," I muttered. "And I don't mean just Fergus. Bloody men."

Marsali sniffed with amusement.

"Aye. But the thing is—he *is* a man, no? He's got to feel he's worth something. He needs to be able to care for us, and that's a thing he can do—and do well—here. I canna see how he'd make a decent living in the mountains."

"True," I admitted reluctantly. It was a hot day, and stifling in the kitchen, with the cauldron simmering over the hearth. Flies or no flies—and there were an ungodly number of flies in Philadelphia—I got up to open the back door. It wasn't noticeably cooler outside, though at least the fire under the big washtub hadn't yet been lit; the girls were still filling it, trudging to and fro from the well with their buckets.

Henri-Christian was nowhere in sight, but had presumably been scrubbed; a filthy black cloth lay crumpled on the doorstep. I stooped to pick it up and saw a folded bit of paper lying on the ground beside the step. It had no direction on it but looked purposeful, so I picked it up and took it back inside.

"Still," Marsali said, barely waiting for me to sit down. "I'm thinkin' that even if we canna go to the Ridge, it might be as well if we were to go. There must be places in the South that could use a printer, even if they're none sae big as Philadelphia."

"Well, there's Charleston," I said doubtfully, "and Savannah. They're just as hot and ghastly in the summer as Philadelphia is, but the winters are milder, I suppose."

She shot me a brief look over the shift she was mending, then set it down on her lap, as though having come to a decision.

"It's no the weather that troubles me," she said quietly. And, bending, she groped under the pile of shirts and stockings, emerging with a handful of grubby notes and frayed letters. Handling these gingerly, as though they carried some disease, she placed them on my knee.

"Any printer in these days gets such things poked under his door," she said, watching my face as I read through the first few. "Especially if ye take a stand. We didn't, for as long as we could, but after a time, ye just canna stand in the middle o' the road any longer."

This was said with a simplicity and acceptance that brought tears to my eyes. The more so with the content of the anonymous notes—for they were all unsigned and in a variety of hands, though some were plainly written by the same person—making it quite clear what the price of standing on the Rebel side might be.

"It was worse, maybe," she said, taking them back and stacking them tidily, "when the British were here. I thought it might stop when they left, but it didn't."

"I don't imagine all the Loyalists left with them," I said, taking a deep breath in order to control myself. I felt as though I'd been punched in the stomach.

"Only the richer ones," Marsali said cynically. "The ones who thought they'd be dragged from their homes or beaten and robbed, without the army to protect them. But it doesna mean the poorer ones dinna have the same opinions."

"Why do you keep these?" I asked, handing them back with two fingers, as though holding them with tongs. "I think I'd throw them into the fire at once."

"I did, at first," she said, tucking the handful of nastiness carefully back into the bottom of the basket. "But I found I couldna forget what they'd said, and the words would come back to me at night and stop me sleeping." She straightened, shrugged, and took up her needle again.

"I told Fergus, and he said the thing to do was to keep them and read them through several times a day, one after the other. Read them tae each other." A brief, rueful smile touched her mouth. "So we did, after the bairns were asleep—we'd sit by the fire and take turns reading them. And he'd make fun o' them, criticizing the grammar and the lack o' poetry, comparing them one to another, and we'd rank them from best to worst . . . and then we'd put them away and go to sleep in each other's arms."

Her hand rested gently on the mound of mending, as though it were Fergus's shoulder, and I smiled.

"Well," I said, and, clearing my throat, produced the note I'd picked up on the step. "I have no idea whether this is another one for your collection— but I found it on the back step just now."

She took it with a raised brow and looked it over, turning it to and fro.

"It's cleaner than most," she observed. "A decent rag paper, too. It's maybe just a . . ." Her voice died away as she opened it and began to read. I could see that the writing inside was brief; within seconds, the blood drained from her face.

"Marsali." I reached toward her, and she thrust the note into my hand and rose swiftly.

Ladybird, ladybird, the note read, *fly away home. Your house is on fire and your children are gone.*

"Henri-Christian!" Marsali's voice was strong and urgent. "Girls! Where's your wee brother?"

112

DAYLIGHT HAUNTING

I FOUND HENRI-CHRISTIAN in the first place I looked: down the street, playing with the two smallest Phillips girls. The Phillipses had ten children, and even Henri-Christian could blend into their household without causing much notice.

Some parents kept their children from coming anywhere near Henri-Christian—whether from fear that dwarfishness was catching, I supposed, or from the popular superstition that his appearance was the result of his mother having fornicated with the devil. I'd heard that one now and then, though everyone in the neighborhood knew better than to say it anywhere in the hearing of Jamie, Fergus, Ian, or Germain.

The Phillipses were Jewish, though, and apparently felt some kinship with a person whose differences set him apart. Henri-Christian was always welcome at their house. Their maid-of-all-work merely nodded when I asked whether one of the older children would walk home with him later, then went back to her washing; it was laundry day all over Philadelphia, and the humid atmosphere was aggravated by a score of steaming washtubs in the neighborhood, all fuming with the reek of washing soda.

I went back quickly to the printshop to tell Marsali where Henri-Christian was and, having relieved her fears, put on my wide-brimmed hat and announced my intent of going to buy some fish for supper. Marsali and Jenny, armed respectively with a laundry fork and a large paddle for clothes-stirring, gave me marked looks—both of them knew exactly how much I disliked doing laundry—but neither said anything.

I had of course been excused from housework while recuperating and, in all truth, was still not up to the labor of hoicking hot, sodden clothes about. I could have managed hanging out the washing, perhaps, but soothed my conscience on grounds that: 1) fish made an easy supper on laundry day, 2) I needed to walk regularly, in order to regain my strength, and 3) I wanted to talk to Jamie, alone.

The anonymous letter had upset me nearly as much as it had Marsali. It wasn't like the other threats she had shown me: those were all specifically political, and while some were aimed at Marsali (for she had run the newspaper alone while Fergus was in hiding), they were of the run-of-the-mill "Rebel bitch" variety. I'd heard such epithets—along with "Tory whore!" and their German and Yiddish equivalents—commonly in the rougher parts of Philadelphia.

This was different. It had the whiff of a refined and intelligent malice, and

I suddenly felt the presence of Jack Randall at my shoulder, so strongly that I came to an abrupt halt and spun round.

The street was busy, but there was no one behind me. No glimpse of a red coat anywhere, though there were Continental officers here and there, in blue and buff.

"Bugger off, Captain," I said, under my breath. Not quite far enough under: I got a wide-eyed look from a round little woman selling pretzels from a tray round her neck. She glanced over her shoulder to see to whom I was speaking, then turned back to me with a look of concern.

"You are all right, madam?" she said in a heavy German accent.

"Yes," I said, embarrassed. "Yes, quite all right. Thank you."

"Take this," she said kindly, handing me a pretzel. "I think you are hungry." And waving away my fumbling attempt at payment, she went off down the street, wide hips rolling, waving a stick of pretzels stacked like quoits and shouting, *"Brezeln! Heiße Brezeln!"*

Feeling suddenly dizzy, I leaned against the front of a building, closed my eyes, and bit into the pretzel. It was chewy, fresh, and rimed with salt, and I discovered that the woman had been right. I *was* hungry. Starved, in fact.

The pretzel hit my stomach and then my bloodstream, imparting an instant sense of stability and well-being, and the momentary panic I'd felt evaporated so quickly that I could almost believe it hadn't happened. Almost.

It *hadn't* happened in some time. I swallowed the last bit of pretzel and, after checking my pulse—strong and steady—set off again toward the river.

I walked slowly; it was midday, and any great exertion would leave me drenched with sweat and very likely light-headed again. I ought to have brought my walking stick but had recklessly decided to do without it. I hated feeling infirm.

I hated feeling . . . *that,* even more. The sudden sense of threat, irrational fear . . . violation. Flashback, the military called it—would call it—in my time. It hadn't happened to me since Saratoga, though, and I'd almost forgotten about it. Almost.

Completely explainable, of course: I'd been shot, come close to dying, was still physically weak. The last time, I'd been in the dark in the forest near a battlefield, alone, lost, and surrounded by violent men. No wonder it had happened then; the situation was much too close to what it had been when I'd been abducted and assaulted—

"Raped," I said out loud, firmly, to the extreme startlement of a pair of gentlemen passing by. I paid no attention to them. No point in trying to avoid either the word or the memory. It was over; I was safe.

Before that . . . the first time I'd been overtaken by that sense of threat, it was at River Run, in the course of a party. But a party where the sense of imminent violence was palpable. On that occasion, Jamie had been nearby, thank God. He'd seen that I was spooked—literally, he assumed—and had given me a handful of salt with which to lay the ghost that haunted me.

The Highlands always had a practical answer, whether the difficulty was keeping a fire smoored for the night, having your cow run dry, or being haunted.

I touched the corner of my mouth with my tongue, found a stray salt crystal from the pretzel, and nearly laughed. I looked over my shoulder for the woman who'd given me succor, but she'd vanished.

"Just as an angel should, I suppose," I murmured. "Thank you."

There was probably a charm for it in the *Gàidhlig,* I reflected. There were dozens, probably hundreds. I knew only a few, mostly those concerned with health (they gave my Gaelic-speaking patients reassurance), but picked the one that seemed most suitable to the situation and strode firmly along, my feet solid on the cobbles, chanting:

> *"I trample on thee, thou seizure,*
> *As tramples whale on brine,*
> *Thou seizure of back, thou seizure of body,*
> *Thou foul wasting of chest."*

And then I saw Jamie, coming up from the docks, laughing at something Fergus was saying, and the world dropped back into place around me.

JAMIE TOOK ONE look at me, took my arm, and steered me into a small coffeehouse around the corner on Locust Street. At this hour of the day, it was all but deserted, and I attracted relatively little attention. Women did drink coffee—when any was to be had—but they mostly drank it at home, in company with friends or at small parties and salons. And while there were grander coffeehouses in London and Edinburgh that women might now and then frequent, the Philadelphia coffeehouses tended to be male preserves of business, gossip, and politics.

"What have ye been doing, Sassenach?" Jamie inquired mildly, taking the tray of coffee cups and almond biscuits from the server. "Ye look—" He squinted at me, evidently searching for a term that would be accurate without causing me to pour scalding coffee on him.

"Somewhat indisposed," Fergus said, taking up the sugar tongs. "Here, milady." Without asking, he dropped three large lumps of brown sugar into my cup. "They say that drinking hot beverages will cool you," he added helpfully.

"Well, it does make you sweat more," I said, taking up my spoon. "But if the sweat doesn't evaporate, it certainly won't make you cooler." I estimated the ambient humidity at roughly a thousand percent, but tipped a little of my sweetened coffee into the saucer and blew on it nonetheless. "As to what I've been doing, I was on my way to buy fish for supper. And what have *you* gentlemen been doing?"

Sitting down had made me feel a good bit steadier, and being flanked by Jamie and Fergus made the odd sense of threat I'd experienced in the street fade a bit. But thought of the anonymous letter on the step raised the hairs on the back of my neck, despite the heat.

Jamie and Fergus glanced at each other, and Fergus raised one shoulder.

"Reckoning our assets," Jamie said. "And visiting warehouses and shipping captains."

"Really?" The thought made my heart lift immediately. These sounded like the first concrete steps toward going home. "Have we got any assets to speak of?" Most of our available cash had gone to pay for horses, uniforms, weapons, food for Jamie's men, and other war-related expenses. Theoretically, Congress would reimburse these expenses, but given everything General Arnold had told me about Congress, I rather thought we oughtn't to hold our collective breath in anticipation.

"A bit," Jamie said, smiling at me. He knew very well what I was thinking. "I've found a buyer for the gelding; four pounds."

"That seems a good price," I said uncertainly. "But . . . wouldn't we need the horse, for travel?"

Before he could answer, the door opened and Germain came in, a bundle of broadsheets under one arm and a scowl on his face. The latter disappeared like the morning dew as he spotted us, though, and he came to hug me.

"*Grand-mère!* What are you doing in here? *Maman* said you went to buy fish."

"Oh," I said, suddenly guilty at thought of the laundry. "Yes. I am—er, I mean, I was just on my way. . . . Would you like a bite, Germain?" I offered him the plate of almond biscuits, and his eyes lighted up.

"*One,*" said Fergus firmly. Germain rolled his eyes at me but took a single biscuit, lifting it with two fingers in exaggerated delicacy.

"*Papa,*" he said, consuming the biscuit in two swift bites, "I think perhaps you should go home."

Both of Fergus's strongly marked black brows rose.

"Why?"

"Because," Germain said, licking sugar from the corner of his mouth and eyeing the remaining biscuits, "Grannie Janet told Mr. Sorrel that if he didn't leave off pestering *Maman,* she would stab him with the laundry fork. She might do it, too," he added thoughtfully, dabbing a finger on the plate for crumbs.

Fergus growled. It quite startled me, as I hadn't heard anything like that from him since he'd been a feral eight-year-old pickpocket in Paris.

"Who's Mr. Sorrel?" Jamie asked, in a deceptively mild tone of voice.

"A tavern owner who passes by the shop on his way to and from his work and stops to buy a newspaper—and to ogle my wife," Fergus said tersely. He pushed back his bench, and rose. "Excuse me, milady," he said, bowing to me.

"Had I best come with ye?" Jamie asked, also pushing back from the table. Fergus shook his head, though, and put on his cocked hat.

"No. The man is a coward. One sight of me, and he will be gone." His very white teeth showed in a sudden smile. "If your sister has not disposed of him already."

He went out, leaving the biscuits at the mercy of Germain, who scooped them tidily into his pocket before going to the counter to deposit the new broadsheets, take away the much-read and coffee-spotted ones from yesterday, and collect his money from the proprietress.

"Whilst you were reckoning assets, did Fergus tell you how well he's doing with the printing business?" I asked, pitching my voice low enough as not to reach Germain.

"He did." Jamie passed a coffee cup under his nose and grimaced slightly. The beverage was nominally coffee—a few genuine beans had likely been included in the brew—but contained a high proportion of chicory and a few other ingredients. I picked a small fragment of charred acorn out of my saucer and added more sugar.

The printshop was in fact very profitable; the more so now, as Fergus's chief competitor, a Loyalist, had left town with the departure of the British army.

"There are a good many expenses, though," Jamie explained. "And some of those have increased since the army left." Paper and ink were more difficult to obtain, with the army no longer protecting transport in and out of the city. And the increased danger of the public roads meant that fewer orders of printed books were shipped and, when they were, must either be insured or risk loss.

"And then there's insurance on his premises, which is expensive," Jamie added. He pinched his nose slightly, then drank his coffee in three large gulps. "Marsali doesna like paying that," he said, gasping a little, "but Fergus kent what happened to my place in Edinburgh. And he told me a few things that Marsali doesna ken, too."

"Such as?" I cast a wary eye at Germain, but he was engaged in what was plainly a saucy conversation with a serving girl at the counter. The girl was two or three years older than Germain but clearly amused by him.

"Oh, the odd threat from folk who dinna like something he's printed or who have their noses put out o' joint because he willna print something of theirs. Bit of sabotage, sometimes: his broadsheets stolen from coffeehouses and taverns and scattered in the street—though he said that's got better since Mr. Dunphy left town."

"Dunphy being the Loyalist printer?"

"Aye. Germain!" he called across the shop. "Have ye other places to visit today? Because if so, ye'd best get to them before your news goes stale."

That made the few customers laugh, and Germain's ears went somewhat pink. He gave his grandfather a measured look, but was wise enough not to say anything, and with a few last words to the counter girl, went out, slipping the small cake she'd given him into his pocket with a casual air.

"You don't suppose he's been picking pockets, do you?" I asked, observing the skill with which this maneuver was accomplished. Fergus had taught Germain a good many of his own techniques in that regard, not wanting the skills to be lost.

"God knows, but all the better if he leaves Philadelphia. He willna find so much scope for that particular talent in the mountains." Jamie craned his neck to see out the window, watching Germain go down the street, then sat back, shaking his head.

"The main thing Fergus hasna told Marsali, though, is about yon French popinjay Wainwright."

"What, the fashionable Percival?" I asked, mildly amused. "Is he still around?"

"Aye, he is. Persistent wee sodomite," he observed dispassionately. "He wrote out a detailed account of what he claims is the story of Fergus's parents, wi' the conclusion that Fergus is the heir to some great estate in France. Fergus says if it had been a romantic novel, it would have been criticized as too implausible and nay publisher would touch it." He grinned at the thought, but then sobered. "Still. Fergus says he hasna the slightest intent o' having anything to do with the matter, as even if it were true, he doesna mean to be a pawn for someone else's interests—and if it's not true, still less."

"Hmm." I had taken to simply eating the sugar lumps by now, rather than mixing them into the problematical coffee, and crunched one between my back teeth. "Why is he keeping that from Marsali, though? She knows about Wainwright's earlier approaches, doesn't she?"

Jamie drummed his hand on the table in thought, and I watched in fascination; he had been accustomed for a great while to drumming the two stiff fingers of his right hand when thinking—the middle and ring finger, which had been badly broken, crudely reset, and frequently re-broken, owing to the clumsy way it stuck out. But I had finally amputated the ruined ring finger after he'd had half of it sliced off by a cavalry saber during the first battle of Saratoga. He still drummed his hand, though, as if the finger were still there, though now only the middle finger struck the tabletop.

"She does," he said slowly. "But Fergus said that there began to be that odd wee bit of . . . something . . . in Wainwright's importunities. No *quite* a threat—but just things like an observation that, of course, since Fergus is the heir to the Beauchamp estate—if he is, in fact—then Germain would inherit the title and land after him."

I frowned.

"I can see that being offered as an inducement—but why is it a threat?"

He gave me a level look over the coffee debris.

"If Germain would inherit this estate—Wainwright's principals dinna really need Fergus, now, do they?"

"Jesus H. . . . Really?" I said. "You—or, rather, Fergus thinks Wainwright and company might *kill* him and then use Germain to get hold of this property or whatever it is they have in mind?"

Jamie gave the ghost of a shrug.

"Fergus hasna lived as long as he has without having a sense of when someone means him harm. And if he thinks there's summat amiss wi' this Wainwright, I'm inclined to believe him. Besides," he added fairly, "if it makes him more willing to leave Philadelphia and come south with us, I'm no going to persuade him he's wrong."

"Well, there's that." I looked dubiously at the dregs of my coffee and decided against it. "Speaking of Germain, though—or, rather, the children in general—that's actually why I was looking for you." And, in a few words, I described the ladybird note and its effect on Marsali.

Jamie's thick auburn brows drew together, and his face took on a look that his enemies would have recognized. I had last seen it in the light of dawn on a North Carolina mountainside, when he had escorted me through woods and meadows, from one cold body to the next, to show me that the men who had hurt me were dead, to reassure me that they could not touch me.

"That was what made me . . . er . . . indisposed in the street," I said, rather apologetically. "It just seemed so . . . evil. But a sort of *delicate* evil, if you know what I mean. It—rather gave me a turn." The dead had their own means of making you remember them, but I felt nothing at the memory of his vengeance beyond a remote sense of relief and an even remoter sense of awe at the supernatural beauty of carnage in such a setting.

"I do know," he said softly, and tapped his missing finger on the table. "And I should like to see that note."

"Why?"

"To see whether the handwriting looks like that in Percy Wainwright's letter, Sassenach," he said, pushing back from the table and handing me my hat. "Are ye ready?"

113

THANKS FOR ALL THE FISH

I HAD BOUGHT A striped bass nearly as long as my arm, along with a mess of crayfish and a gunnysack of oysters from the estuary, and the kitchen smelled delightfully of fresh bread and fish stew. This was a good thing, as stew can always be stretched, and Ian and Rachel, with Rollo in tow, had drifted into the printshop just before supper, so visibly in the throes of wedded bliss that it made one smile—and occasionally blush—to look at them.

Jenny did smile, and I saw her thin shoulders relax a little, seeing Ian's radiant face. I gave the stew a quick stir and came over to stand behind her as she sat by the fire, laying my hands on those shoulders and kneading them gently. I knew bloody well what a day's laundry felt like in the muscles.

She heaved a long, blissful sigh and bent her head to allow me to get my thumbs on her neck.

"D'ye think our wee Quaker lass is wi' child yet?" she murmured to me. Rachel was across the room, chatting with the younger children and very easy with them—though her eyes kept turning to Ian, who was looking at something Fergus had taken out of a drawer in the sideboard.

"They've been married barely a month," I whispered back, though I looked carefully at Rachel.

"It doesna take *that* long," Jenny said. "And plainly the lad kens his job. Look at her." Her shoulders quivered slightly with a suppressed laugh.

"A fine thing for a mother to be thinking about her son," I said under my breath, though I could neither keep the amusement out of my own voice nor say she was wrong. Rachel glowed in the magic light of mingled dusk and hearth fire, and her eyes rested on the lines of Ian's back, even as she admired Félicité's new rag doll.

"He takes after his father," Jenny said, and made a little "hmph" in her throat—still amused, but with a faint tinge of . . . longing? My own eyes went to Jamie, who had come to join Fergus and Ian by the sideboard. Still here, thank God. Tall and graceful, the soft light making shadows in the folds of his shirt as he moved, a fugitive gleam from the long straight bridge of his nose, the auburn wave of his hair. Still mine. Thank God.

"Come cut the bread, Joanie!" Marsali called. "Henri-Christian, stop playin' with that dog and fetch the butter, aye? And, Félicité, put your heid outside and call Germain." The distant sound of boys' voices came from the street, shouts punctuated by the occasional thud of a ball against the front wall of the shop. "And tell those wee heathens I said if they break a windowpane, their fathers will hear about it!"

A brief outbreak of domestic chaos ended with all the adults seated on the benches at table and the children in their own huddle by the hearth with their wooden bowls and spoons. Despite the heat of the evening, the fragrant steam of onions, milk, seafood, and fresh bread enveloped the table in a brief enchantment of anticipation.

The men sat down last, their murmured talk stopping well short of the table, and I gave Jamie a brief, questioning look. He touched my shoulder as he sat down beside me, saying, "Aye, later," under his breath, and nodded at the hearth. *Pas devant les enfants*, then.

Fergus cleared his throat. A small sound, but the children instantly stopped talking. He smiled at them, and their heads bowed over earnestly clasped hands.

"Bless us, O Lord," he said in French, "and these thy gifts, which we are about to receive from thy bounty, through Christ our Lord."

"Amen," everyone murmured, and talk washed over the room like the tide coming in.

"Are ye bound back to the army soon, Ian?" Marsali asked, tucking a damp lock of blond hair back into her cap.

"Aye," he replied, "but not Washington's army. No yet, anyway."

Jamie leaned across me to raise a brow at him.

"Ye've turned your coat, then?" he said. "Or just decided the British pay better?" There was a wry edge to this; he'd not seen a penny of pay and told me frankly that he didn't expect to. Congress wasn't swift about paying anyone, and a temporary general who'd resigned his commission was likely at the bottom of their list.

Ian closed his eyes in momentary bliss, chewing an oyster, then swallowed and opened them, wiping a dribble of milk from his chin.

"No," he said equably, "I'm takin' Dottie up to New York to see her da and Lord John."

That stopped all adult conversation dead, though the children continued to chatter by the hearth. I saw Jenny dart her eyes at Rachel, who looked composed, though considerably less blissful than she had before. She'd known about it, though; there was no surprise on her face.

"Why's that, then?" Jamie asked, in a tone of mild curiosity. "She's not decided Denzell doesna suit her, I hope? For I doubt he's taken to beating her."

That made Rachel laugh—briefly, but out loud, and the company relaxed a bit.

"No," she said. "I believe Dottie to be pleased in her marriage; I know my brother is." The smile lingered in her eyes, though her face grew serious as she glanced at Ian, then turned to Jamie.

"Her eldest brother has died. He was a prisoner of war, held in New Jersey. Her brother Henry received news yesterday confirming his death, but Henry cannot bear the strain of so long a journey yet, especially with the roads so dangerous, and Dottie feels she must go to her father."

Jenny gave her a sharp look, which sharpened a bit further as she turned it on Ian.

"The roads bein' so dangerous," she repeated, with a mild tone that matched Jamie's and fooled no one. Ian grinned at her and took a fresh chunk of bread, which he dunked in his stew.

"Dinna fash, Mam," he said. "There's a wee band o' folk I ken, traveling north. They're agreeable to going by New York. We'll be gey safe wi' them."

"What *sort* of folk?" Jenny asked suspiciously. "Quakers?"

"Mohawk," he said, the grin widening. "Come out wi' me and Rachel after supper, Mam. They'd be that pleased to meet ye."

I could honestly say that, in all the time I'd known her, I'd never before seen Jenny Murray gobsmacked. I could feel Jamie vibrating with suppressed hilarity next to me, and had to look down into my bowl for a moment to regain my own composure.

Jenny was made of stern stuff, though. She took a long moment, took a longer breath, pushed Rollo's nose out of her lap, and then said calmly, "Aye. I'd like that. Pass me the salt, Fergus, aye?"

In spite of the general amusement, I hadn't forgotten what Rachel had said about Dottie's brother Benjamin, and I felt a twist of surprisingly acute pain, as though someone had knotted a length of barbed wire round my heart. *Do you ever make bargains with God?* If Hal had offered such a bargain, evidently God had declined it. *Oh, God, Hal . . . I'm sorry.*

"I'm so sorry to hear about Dottie's brother," I said, leaning forward to talk to Rachel. "Do you know what happened?"

She shook her head briefly, and the firelight, now behind her, cast shadow on her face from the curtain of dark hair.

"Henry had had a letter from their brother Adam. He'd had the news from someone on General Clinton's staff, I think he said. All it said was that whoever had written the letter wished to express their regrets as to the death of Captain Benjamin Grey, a British prisoner of war who had been held at Middlebrook Encampment in New Jersey, and would General Clinton's office please relay this sad news to the captain's family. They'd thought it possible that he was dead—but this seems to put the matter beyond all doubt, alas."

"Middlebrook Encampment is what they call the place in the Watchung

Mountains where Washington took his troops after Bound Brook," Fergus remarked with interest. "But the army left there in June of last year. Why would Captain Grey be there, I wonder?"

"Does an army travel wi' its captives?" Jamie asked, raising one shoulder in a shrug. "Save if they're taken when the army's on the move, I mean."

Fergus nodded, conceding the point, but seemed still to be pondering something. Marsali stepped in before he could speak, though, gesturing at Ian with her spoon.

"Speakin' o' why—why are your friends going north?" she asked. "Hasn't anything to do wi' the massacre at Andrustown, has it?"

Jenny turned toward her son, intent. A closed look came over Ian's face, though he answered calmly enough.

"It does, aye. Where did ye hear o' that?"

Marsali and Fergus shrugged in unison, making me smile involuntarily, in spite of my distress over Hal's son.

"The way in which we hear most of the news we print," Fergus amplified. "A letter from someone who heard of the matter."

"And what do your friends have in mind to do about the matter?" Jenny asked.

"More to the point," Jamie said, twisting to address Ian, "what do *you* have in mind to do about it?"

I was watching Rachel, on the other side of the table, rather than Ian, but I saw a look too faint to be called anxiety cross her brow, relaxing in the next instant when Ian replied flatly, "Nothing." Perhaps feeling this too blunt, he coughed and took a gulp of beer.

"I dinna ken anyone who was there, and as I havena any intent to turn my coat and fight for the British wi' Thayendanegea . . . Nay," he finished, setting down his cup. "I'll go as far as New York to see Dottie safe and then come back to wherever Washington might be." He smiled at Rachel, his face shifting abruptly from its usual appealing half-homely expression to a startling attractiveness. "I need my scout's pay, after all; I've a wife to support."

"Ye must come and stay wi' us, then," Marsali said to Rachel. "While Ian's gone, I mean."

I hadn't time to wonder exactly where she planned to put Rachel—Marsali was ingenious and would doubtless find a place—before Rachel shook her head. She wasn't wearing a cap but wore her straight dark hair loose on her shoulders; I could hear the whisper of it against her dress as she moved.

"I shall go with Ian to fetch Dottie. Rollo and I will stay in camp with my brother until Ian returns. I can be useful there." Her long fingers curled and flexed in illustration, and she smiled at me. "Thee knows the joy of useful occupation, Claire, I expect."

Jenny made a nondescript noise in her throat, and Marsali snorted briefly, though without rancor.

"Indeed I do," I said, my eyes on the slice of bread I was buttering. "And which would you rather find useful occupation in, Rachel—boiling laundry, or lancing the boils on Mr. Pinckney's arse?"

She laughed, and the arrival of Henri-Christian with an empty bowl in his hands saved her replying. He set it on the table and yawned sleepily, swaying on his feet.

"Aye, it's late, wee man," his mother said to him, and, picking him up, cradled him in her arms. "Lay your head, *a bhalaich*. Papa will take ye up presently."

More beer was fetched, the little girls collected the empty bowls and put them in the bucket to soak, Germain vanished outside into the gathering dusk for the last few minutes of play with his friends, Rollo curled up to sleep by the fire, and talk became general.

Jamie's hand rested warmly on my thigh, and I leaned against him, laying my head briefly on his shoulder. He looked down at me and smiled, squeezing my leg. I was looking forward to the Spartan comfort of our pallet in the loft, the cooling freedom of shift and nakedness, and the sharing of whispers in the dark—but for the moment was more than content to be where I was.

Rachel was talking across Marsali to Fergus, Marsali humming quietly to Henri-Christian, whose round dark head lolled on her bosom, his eyes almost closed. I looked carefully at Rachel, but it was much too soon to see any signs of pregnancy, even if— And then I stopped, startled, as my eye caught something else.

I'd seen Marsali through her pregnancy with Henri-Christian. And I was seeing a bloom on her cheeks now that wasn't from the warmth of the room: a slight fullness of the eyelids, and a subtle softening and rounding of face and body that I might have recognized earlier, had I been looking for it. Did Fergus know, I wondered? And glanced quickly at the head of the table, to see him looking at Marsali and Henri-Christian, his dark eyes soft with love.

Jamie shifted a little beside me, turning to say something to Ian, on my other side. I turned, too, and saw that Ian's eyes were also fixed on Marsali and Henri-Christian, with a look of wistfulness that smote me to the heart.

I felt his longing, and my own—for Brianna. Roger, and Jem, and Mandy. Safe, I hoped—but not here, and I swallowed a lump in my throat.

"You'd die for them, happily," Hal had said, in the long night watch when I'd kept him breathing. *"Your family. But at the same time you think,* Christ, I *can't* die! What might happen to them if I weren't here?*"* He'd given me a wry and rueful smile. *"And you know bloody well that you mostly can't help them anyway; they've got to do it—or not—themselves."*

That was true. But it didn't stop you caring.

IT WAS HOT and close in the loft, with the comfortable lingering scents of supper crammed in under the rafters, the more argumentative pungencies of ink, paper, buckram, and leather that had built up all day, and the faintly pervasive scent of mule straw underlying everything. I gasped at the impact as I stepped off the ladder and went at once to open the loading door that looked out onto the cobbled alley behind the shop.

A blast of Philadelphia rushed in, fluttering the stacks of paper: smoke from a dozen nearby chimneys, an acrid stink from the manure pile behind the livery stable down the street, and the intoxicatingly resinous scent of leaves and bark and brush and flowers that was William Penn's legacy. *Leave one acre of trees for every five acres cleared,* he'd advised in his charter, and if Philadelphia had not quite met that ideal, it was still a particularly verdant city.

"God bless you, William," I said, beginning to shed my outer clothes as fast as possible. The evening air might be warm and humid, but it *was* moving, and I couldn't wait to let it move over my skin.

"That's a kind thought, Sassenach," Jamie said, stepping off the ladder into the loft. "Why, though? Is the lad in your mind for some reason?"

"Wh—oh, William," I said, realizing. "I hadn't actually meant your son, but naturally . . ." I fumbled to organize an explanation but gave it up, seeing that he wasn't really attending. "Were you thinking of him?"

"I was, aye," he admitted, coming to help with my laces. "Being wi' the weans and the bairns, and all sae comfortable together . . ." His voice died away and he drew me gently to him, bent his head to mine, and let it rest there with a sigh that stirred the hair near my face.

"You wish he could be part of it," I said softly, reaching up to touch his cheek. "Be part of the family."

"If wishes were horses, then beggars would ride," he said, and let go, with a wry smile visible in the glow from the kitchen below. "And if turnips were swords, I'd hae one by my side."

I laughed, but my eye went to the stack of Bibles where he was accustomed to leave his sword. His dirk was there, his pistols, shot bag, and a scatter of oddments from his sporran, but no sword. I squinted to be sure I was seeing a-right, but I was.

"I sold it," he said matter-of-factly, seeing the direction of my glance. "It's one good thing to be said of war: ye can get a good price for a decent weapon."

I wanted to protest, but didn't. He wore weapons with a lifelong ease, to the point that his knives and guns seemed a part of him, and I didn't like to see him diminished by the loss of any. But without an army commission, he likely wouldn't *need* a sword immediately, and we did certainly need money.

"You can buy another when we reach Wilmington," I said practically, returning his favor by unbuttoning his breeks. They slid off his lean hips and fell, puddling round his feet. "It would be lovely for William to know the truth about Bree and her family sometime. Will you tell him?"

"In the event that he ever comes within speakin' distance of me without trying to kill me?" One corner of his mouth curled ruefully. "Aye, maybe. But I maybe wouldn't tell him *all* the truth."

"Well, perhaps not all at once, no," I agreed. A warm breeze from the window stirred his hair and the tails of his shirt. I fingered the creased linen, warm and damp from his body. "Why don't you take that off?"

He looked me over carefully; I was standing now in nothing but my shift and stockings. A slow smile spread into his eyes.

"Fair's fair," he said. "Take yours off, as well, then."

CLAIRE WAS LOVELY, standing white and naked as a French statue against the deep twilight from the open window, her curly hair a storm cloud round her shoulders. Jamie wanted to stand and look at her, but he wanted a lot more to have his cock inside her.

There were still voices down in the kitchen, though, and he went and pulled the ladder up. Wouldn't do to have Germain or one of the girls scamper up to say good night.

There was a hoot of laughter from Ian and Fergus below, probably at sight of the ladder disappearing, and he grinned to himself, laying it aside. They had their own wives, and if they were foolish enough to sit drinking beer instead of enjoying their beds, it was none of his affair.

Claire was already on their pallet when he turned from the edge of the loft, a pale shadow under the gloom of the ink casks. He eased himself in naked beside her, touched her curving hip; she touched his cock. "I want you," she whispered, and suddenly everything changed.

It was their common magic, but magic nonetheless, the smell of onions and brine on her hands, the taste of butter and beer on her tongue, a tickle of hair on his shoulder, and a sudden rush when she ran a finger down the crack of his arse, which drew him straight up hard between her willing legs.

She made a sound that made him put a hand over her mouth, and he felt her laugh, hot breath against his palm, so he took his hand away and stopped her noises with his mouth, lying full on her for a moment, not moving, trying to wait, not able to wait for the feel of her squirming under him, slick and slippery, rubbing her nipples on his, urging him . . . and then she quivered and made a small noise of surrender that freed him to do as he would, and he did.

JAMIE HEAVED a deep sigh of utter relaxation.

"I have been wanting to do that all day, Sassenach. *Moran taing, a nighean.*"

"So have— Is that a *bat?*" It was: a flittering scrap of detached darkness, ricocheting from one side of the loft to the other. I grabbed Jamie's arm with one hand and pulled a corner of the sheet over my head with the other. It wasn't that I minded bats, as such; a bat whizzing to and fro three feet over my head in the dark, though . . .

"Dinna fash, Sassenach," he said, sounding amused. "It'll go out again directly."

"I'm not so sure of that," I said, slapping something ticklish on my neck. "There are probably any number of insects in here for it to hunt." Clouds of gnats and mosquitoes were inclined to roam in through the open loading window when evening fell, and it was always a Hobson's choice: keep the window closed and die of suffocation, or open it and be chivvied all night by crawling feet and the irritating *sneeeee!* of mosquitoes whining in our ears.

"Ye ought to be pleased about the bat, then," Jamie told me, rolling onto his side and using another bit of sheet to blot a sheen of sweat from his chest. "How many bugs did ye tell me they eat?"

"Well . . . lots," I said. "Don't ask me how I remember this, but according to Brianna's encyclopedia, the average little brown bat can eat up to a thousand mosquitoes in an hour."

"Well, there ye are, then," he said. "I dinna think there can be more than two or three hundred mosquitoes in here just now—it shouldna take him more than a quarter hour to deal wi' those."

It was a definite point, but I was not quite convinced of the virtues of entertaining a resident bat. I did emerge from my makeshift shelter, though, peering upward. "What if more bats come in?"

"Then they'll clear the place in five minutes." He sighed briefly. "D'ye want me to catch him, throw him out, and close the door, Sassenach?"

"No," I said, envisioning Jamie pirouetting around the loft in the dark, either being bitten by a startled bat if he did succeed in catching it or plunging over the edge of the loft in the effort to do so. "No, that's all right. Tell me what you didn't want to say earlier—that will take my mind off it."

"What I—oh, aye." He rolled onto his back, hands clasped on his stomach. "It's only I've been talking wi' Fergus and Ian about coming with us when we leave for the Ridge. Didna want to mention it at table, though. Ian and Fergus should talk it over wi' Rachel and Marsali by themselves first—and I didna want the bairns to hear. They'd go mad with excitement, and Marsali would run me through the heart wi' a meat skewer for stirring them up just before bed."

"She might," I said, amused. "Oh—speaking of Marsali . . . I rather think she's pregnant."

"Is she, now?" He turned his head to me, deeply interested. "Are ye sure?"

"No," I admitted. "I can't be sure without asking her nosy questions and examining her. But I think there's a good chance of it. If so . . . that might affect whether they go with us, mightn't it?"

The prospect of going home was suddenly real, in a way that it hadn't been even a moment before. I could almost feel the breath of the mountains on my bare skin, and gooseflesh rippled fleetingly over my ribs at the thought, in spite of the heat.

"Mmm," Jamie said, though absently. "I suppose it might. D'ye think—if she is wi' child, might the new one be like Henri-Christian?"

"Probably not," I said, though professional caution made me add, "I can't be positive that his type of dwarfism isn't a hereditary condition, because Fergus doesn't know anything about his family. But I think Henri-Christian's is probably a mutation—something that happens just once, a sort of accident."

Jamie gave a small snort.

"Miracles only happen once, too, Sassenach," he said. "That's why all bairns are different."

"I wouldn't argue with that," I said mildly. "But we'll need to be traveling quite soon, won't we? Even if Marsali is pregnant, she won't be more than three or four months along." A small sense of unease crept into my mind. It was early September; snow might begin to close the mountain passes as early as October, though if it was a warm year . . .

"How long will it take, do you think? To get back to the Ridge?"

"Too long to make it before the snow, Sassenach," he said gently, running a hand down my back. "Even if I manage the money and find a ship to take us down to North Carolina—and I'd rather do that—"

"You would?" I blurted, astonished. "*You?* Take a ship? I thought you'd sworn you'd never set foot on one again unless it was the ship taking your coffin back to Scotland."

"Mmphm. Aye, well. If it was only me, then, aye, I'd rather walk to North Carolina barefoot over hot coals. But it's not. It's you, and—"

"*Me?*" I sat up straight, angry. "What do you mean by that? Ahhh!" I clutched my hair and dived into his lap, for the bat had zoomed within inches of my head; I actually *heard* its faint squeaking and the leathery flap of wings.

Jamie laughed, but with a faint edge to it. As I sat up again, he ran a hand down my right side and rested two fingers over the fresh scar there.

"I mean that, Sassenach," he said, and pressed. Very gently, and I kept myself from flinching at the touch—but the scar was still red and tender.

"I'm fine," I said, as firmly as possible.

"I've been shot, Sassenach," he said, very dryly. "More than once. I ken what it feels like—and how long it takes to get your full strength back. Ye nearly fell over in the street today, and—"

"I hadn't eaten anything; I was hungry, and—"

"I'm no taking ye overland," he said, in a tone that brooked no argument. "And it's not only you—though it's mostly you," he added, in a softer tone, smoothing the hair off my face. "But there are the wee bairns, as well, and now Marsali, if she's wi' child . . . It's a hard journey, lass, and dangerous, forbye. Did ye not say the duke told ye the British mean to take the South now?"

"Hmph," I said, but allowed him to pull me down next to him. "Yes, he did. But I've no idea what that might actually *mean,* in terms of where they are or what they're doing. The only battles I'd actually heard of, beyond Lexington and Concord and Bunker Hill, are Saratoga and Yorktown—that's where it ends, Yorktown," I added. "Obviously a few things must happen in between, though."

"Obviously," he said. "Aye. Well, I'll buy another sword when we get to North Carolina and I've money again."

He did in fact have considerable assets—in North Carolina. But there was no way of retrieving any of the gold hidden in the Spaniard's Cave there—even if he had trusted anyone to do so, no one knew where the cave was, save him and Jemmy—and the aging whisky (almost as valuable as the gold, if brought to the coast for sale) was in the same place.

"I suppose the price of a good sword isn't quite enough for ship's passage for nine people—no, eleven, if Ian and Rachel come, too—is it?"

"No," he said thoughtfully. "I said to Fergus that he might consider selling his press. He doesna own the premises, ken—but the press is his." He made a small gesture, encompassing the building around us. "There's my Bonnie in Wilmington, after all."

"Your—oh, your press. Of course." I hid a smile in his biceps. He invariably spoke of . . . well, her . . . with a certain possessive affection. Come to think, I wasn't sure I'd ever heard him talk about *me* that way. . . .

"Aye. Fergus has his mind set that he'll go on bein' a printer, and I think that's wise. Germain's not yet big enough to plow—and poor wee Henri-Christian never will be."

I suppressed my speculations as to just what Germain's reaction might be if forcibly removed from the environs of a thriving city and plunked down behind a plow. He might remember the Ridge fondly, but that didn't mean he wanted to be a farmer.

"What about Richard Bell?" Bell was the Loyalist who had been forcibly deported from his North Carolina home and sent, penniless and friendless, to England, ending up eventually in Edinburgh, where he had found employment as a printer—and where Jamie had encountered him and made the bargain whereby Richard would bring Bonnie to North Carolina and look after her in return for his passage home.

"I dinna ken," Jamie said reflectively. "I wrote to him, to say we were coming to Wilmington and that we must make some arrangement . . . but I've had no reply." This didn't necessarily mean anything; letters frequently were lost or late. Jamie shrugged a little and shifted, stretching as he resettled himself. "Aye, well; let that bide. We'll see when we see. How's our wee friend?"

"Our—oh." I looked up, scanning the low ceiling, but saw no trace of the bat. I didn't hear any whining mosquitoes, either. "Well done, bat," I said appreciatively.

Jamie laughed, low in his throat.

"Remember sittin' on the stoop and watching the bats come out in the summer evenings on the Ridge?"

"I do," I said softly, and turned on my side to embrace him lightly, hand on the curly hairs of his chest. I did remember. The Ridge. The cabin Jamie and Ian had built for shelter when we first came there, and the white piglet we'd bought, who had become the fearsome white sow, terror of the entire neighborhood. Our friends, Jamie's tenants, Lizzie and the Beardsley twins . . . My heart squeezed at some of the memories.

Malva Christie. Poor doomed child. And the Bugs—Jamie's trusted factor and his wife—who had proven a good deal less than trustworthy. And the Big House, our house, gone up in flames, and our life there with it.

"I'll need to build the new house first thing," he said thoughtfully. He laid his own hand on mine and squeezed it. "And I'll make ye a new garden. Ye can have half the money I got for my sword, to buy seeds."

114

BELIEF IS A WISE WAGER

H AL GAVE A MILD snort. "I don't like your going alone," he said.

"I don't like it, either," John said matter-of-factly, corking his hip flask. "But the only person who could effectively go with me is you, and you can't, because of the regiment, so . . . God, I miss Tom Byrd," he said impulsively.

"Your erstwhile valet?" Hal smiled, despite the worry of the situation. "How long has it been since you've seen him? Ten years at least, surely?"

"At least that." Thought of Tom still gave him a slight pang. Tom had left his employment—with deep regret on both sides—in order to marry, and had become a successful publican in Southwark, his wife having inherited a thriving public house from her father. Grey couldn't begrudge him his happiness, but he still sorely missed Byrd, with his sharp eyes, quick mind, and anxious care for Grey's person as well as his clothes.

He glanced down at himself; his current valet managed to keep him decent—a task that he himself admitted to be Sisyphean—but lacked both imagination and conversation.

"You should take Marks, regardless," Hal said, having evidently followed his train of thought without difficulty. "Someone's got to keep you in order." He gave John's uniform a critical look.

"I *can* dress myself, you know," John said mildly. "As for the uniform—" He glanced down and shrugged. "Bit of a brush-off, clean shirt, spare stockings . . . it's not as though I mean to be calling on General Washington."

"We can only hope." Hal's lips pressed together. He'd already expressed his reservations—if anything so violently explicit could be described in such terms—regarding Grey's intent to travel as himself, in uniform.

"I've had quite enough of being arrested as a spy, thank you," John replied. "Beyond the risk of being hanged out-of-hand, the Americans' sense of hospitality . . . though come to think, I'd meant to ask: do you know a Watson Smith? Used to be a captain in the Twenty-second, I think."

Hal frowned in concentration, but his brow cleared almost immediately.

"I do," he said. "A very good officer; did well at Crefeld and Zorndorf." He cocked his head to one side, brows raised. "Why?"

"He's turned his coat; he's now a colonel in the Continental army. I was his involuntary guest for a short time. Nice fellow," Grey added fairly. "Got me drunk on applejack."

"Doubtless with the intent of extracting intelligence from you?" Hal's expression made it clear that he doubted there had been much in that line for Smith to extract.

"No," Grey said thoughtfully. "I don't think so. We just got drunk together. Nice fellow," he repeated. "I was going to express the hope that I wouldn't meet him again—shouldn't like to have to kill him, I mean—but I suppose it isn't beyond belief that I might run into him somewhere." The thought gave him a small, pleasant clench low down in the belly that rather surprised him.

"Anyway," he added, "I'm going in uniform, even if grubby uniform. It won't necessarily keep me from arrest, imprisonment, starvation, and torture, but it *will* save me from being hanged."

"Torture?" Hal gave him a look.

"I had in mind waking up after the applejack," John told him. "And the singing. Have you any idea how many verses the Americans have for 'Yankee Doodle'?"

Hal grunted in response to this and took out a leather folder, from which he extracted a thin sheaf of documents.

"Here are your *bona fides,*" he said, handing them over. "They *may* help—assuming firstly that you're captured or detained, rather than shot on sight, and secondly that your captors take the time to read them."

Grey didn't trouble to reply to this, being occupied in thumbing through the documents. A copy of his warrant of commission; a note from Hal as Colonel of the Regiment, detaching Lieutenant Colonel John Grey temporarily from service and desiring him to undertake the task of locating and assisting one Mrs. Benjamin Grey (née Amaranthus Cowden), widow of Captain Benjamin Grey, late of the Thirty-fourth Foot; a "To Whom It May Concern" letter from Clinton, formally recognizing Grey's mission and requesting that every courtesy and assistance be provided him in consequence thereof; several bills of exchange drawn on Coutts' bank in New York ("Just in case," Hal told him. "In case of what?" "In case you get knocked over and relieved of your gold, halfwit." "Oh."); and . . . Benedict Arnold's note, granting the Duke of Pardloe and his brother, Lord John Grey, permission to abide temporarily in Philadelphia for the purpose of searching for the duke's nephew.

"Really?" Grey said, raising his brows at this last. "Under what circumstances do you think this might be helpful?"

Hal shrugged and straightened his waistcoat. "The fact that you and I are known to General Arnold is worth something. The note doesn't give his opinion of us, after all."

Grey gave the note a critical eye, but, in fact, Arnold had refrained from personalities and had not codified his threats regarding rails and tar and feathers.

"All right." He closed the folder and put it down, laying his hat on it to ensure against walking off without it. "That's that, then. What's for supper?"

JOHN GREY WAS enjoying a confused but pleasant dream involving spring rain, his dachshund Roscoe, Colonel Watson Smith, and a great deal of mud, when he gradually became aware that the raindrops on his face were real.

He opened his eyes, blinking, to discover his niece, Dottie, holding his pitcher in one hand and sprinkling water from her fingertips onto his face.

"Good morning, Uncle John," she said cheerily. "Rise and shine!"

"The last person injudicious enough to say that to me in the morning came to a most unpleasant end," he said, struggling upright and rubbing the sleeve of his nightshirt across his face.

"Really? What happened to him? Or was it a him?" She dimpled at him and set down the pitcher, wiping her wet fingers on her skirt.

"What an improper question," he said, eyeing her.

"Well, I am a married woman now, you know," she said, sitting down with an air of extreme self-possession. "I am allowed to know that men and women occasionally share a bed, even outwith the bonds of matrimony."

"Outwith? Where did you pick up that barbarous construction? Have you been speaking to Scotchmen?"

"Constantly," she said. "But what happened to the unfortunate person who tried to roust you from your slumbers?"

"Oh, him." He rubbed a hand over his head, still surprised at feeling the hair so short, though it had at least grown enough to fall over and lie somewhat flat, rather than sticking straight up like a shaving brush. "He was scalped by red Indians."

She blinked.

"Well, that will teach him, to be sure," she murmured.

Grey swung his legs out of bed and gave her a pointed look.

"I don't care how married you are, Dottie, you are *not* allowed to help me dress. What the devil are you doing here, anyway?"

"I'm going with you to find B-Ben's widow," she said, and all of a sudden her bright façade collapsed like papier-mâché in the rain. Tears welled up in her eyes, and she clamped a hand hard over her mouth to prevent them falling.

"Oh," Grey said. "Oh, my dear . . ." And pausing only to fling on his banyan—even in emergency, there were limits—he knelt beside her and gathered her into his arms.

"It's all right," he said softly to her, rubbing her back. "Ben may not be dead, after all. We think he's not—your father and I." *We certainly hope he's not,* he thought, but opted for the most positive view of the situation.

"You don't?" She choked, sniffed, and sat up a bit, looking up at him with drowned-cornflower eyes.

"Certainly not," he said firmly, and dug in the pocket of his banyan for a handkerchief.

"But why not?" She accepted the proffered linen—somewhat crumpled but not indecently so—and dabbed at her face. "How could he not be?"

Grey sighed, caught between Scylla and Charybdis, as usual when enmeshed in one of Hal's situations.

"Does your father know you're here?" he asked, as a delaying tactic.

"Don't—I mean, no," she said, clearing her throat and sitting up straighter. "I went to his quarters, but he was out, so I came on here to find you."

"How is it that you're sure Ben's died?" Grey stood up and, tying the belt of his banyan, began looking about for his slippers. He knew that Hal hadn't yet written to Minnie about Ben—wouldn't do so unless forced by dreadful certainty—and even if he had, there was no way in which word could have come back to Dottie so soon. And Hal would not have told his daughter the news until he was sure, no more than he would have told his wife.

"Henry told me," she said. She poured a little water onto the handkerchief and commenced repairs to her complexion. "I went to visit him and Mercy, and he'd just had a letter from Adam, telling him . . . you're *sure* he isn't dead?" she asked anxiously, lowering the handkerchief to gaze at him. "Adam's letter said he'd heard it from someone on General Clinton's staff, telling him for sure that Ben had died at a military camp in New Jersey—Middlebrook, I think he said it was called."

"No, we're not sure," he admitted. "But we have reasonable grounds for doubt, and until those have been completely explored, we will proceed on the assumption that he's not. I do have to find his wife, though," he added. "And child."

Dottie's eyes flew wide.

"A *child*? Ben has a baby?"

"Well, the woman who claims to be his wife has a son, or so she says—and she did say that Ben is the father of her offspring." Seeing that there was little alternative, he apprised her of the letter from Amaranthus Cowden that Hal had received in Philadelphia, and its contents.

"Now, as Ben didn't happen to mention this woman to Hal, one of the duties I'm to carry out for your father is the determination as to whether she's telling the truth. And if she is, then of course I will bring her back with me, and the family will take care of her and the child."

"What if she's *not* telling the truth?" Dottie's distress was rapidly being subsumed by a combination of hope and curiosity.

"God knows," Grey said frankly. "Would you like to go and ask Marks to see about breakfast for us, Dottie? I may be out of bed, but I'm in no way equipped to conduct hypothetical conversations before I've had a cup of tea."

"Oh. Yes, of course." She rose, though slowly, plainly still thinking about the revelations, and went toward the door, but paused on the threshold and looked back at him.

"I *am* coming with you," she said firmly. "We can talk about it on the way."

HAL WALKED IN as the kippers and mixed grill were being laid out. He halted for a split second as he saw Dottie, but then came on, more slowly, eyeing her.

"Good morning, Papa," she said briskly, rising and coming to kiss his cheek. "Sit down and have a kipper."

He did sit down, still eyeing her, then switched his gaze to John.

"I had nothing to do with it," Grey assured his brother. "She arrived— how did you get here, Dottie?"

"On a horse," she replied patiently, taking a slice of toast.

"And where is your husband?" Hal asked mildly. "Does he know where you are?"

"Denzell is where his duty takes him," she said, rather tersely. "With the Continental army. Mine takes me here. And of course he knows."

"And he had no objection to your traveling alone from Pennsylvania to New York, over roads infested by—"

"I wasn't alone." She took a delicate bite of her toast, chewed, and swallowed. "Ian and some of his Mohawk friends brought me. The Mohawks were traveling to someplace north of here."

"Ian—is that by chance Ian Murray?" Grey asked, but then answered himself. "I suppose it must be; how many Mohawks can there be named Ian? I take it that he survived his wound, then; I'm pleased to hear it. How did you come to—"

"Dorothea," said Hal, in measured tones, staring at Dottie. "Why are you here?"

Dottie returned his stare, her jaw visibly clenched.

"B-because of Ben," she said, unable to keep her voice entirely steady. "Are you— Papa, are you *sure* he's not dead?"

Hal took an audible breath and nodded.

"I'm sure," he said in his best command voice. But John could see his knuckles whiten as he clutched a teaspoon, and felt the knot in his own stomach tighten in response.

Dottie clearly had her own doubts, judging from her glance at her father, but she obligingly nodded. Being Dottie, of course, she didn't stop there.

"How?" she said. "How do you know? Adam and Henry both think . . . the worst."

Hal's mouth opened a fraction of an inch, but nothing came out.

John thought that Hal ought really to have been prepared for this, but, after all, his brother *had* been having a difficult time. And, in all justice, it was hard to be prepared for something like Dottie.

"I suppose you'd better tell her," John said. "If you don't, she'll likely write to Minnie."

Hal shot him a glance full of venom, fully aware that this helpful suggestion had been made with the intent of forcing him to divulge his reasoning to Dottie—but there wasn't much of a choice, and he did so with as much grace as he could.

"But this Captain Richardson *hadn't* done anything to Willie?" Dottie said, frowning a little. "I thought—"

"Not on this occasion," John said briefly, "but given his earlier behavior over the Dismal Swamp and Quebec, we're somewhat suspicious."

"And the man apparently *has* deserted," Hal pointed out.

"You don't know that. He might have been killed by someone and his body concealed," Dottie pointed out logically.

"He was seen leaving the camp," John said patiently. "Alone. And given what we know and surmise about him, I think we have grounds to consider the possibility that he might be an American agent." He was himself fairly well convinced of it, viewing all his experience of Richardson now with the clarity of hindsight. He'd been an intelligencer himself for some years, and every instinct he possessed was presently shouting *Stinking fish!* with regard to Ezekiel Richardson.

"I blame myself extremely," he said apologetically to Hal. "I should have been on to him much sooner. But I was . . . distracted at the time." Distracted. Blown sideways and more than half obliterated by the news of Jamie Fraser's death. Even the memory of it was enough to close his stomach. He put down the forkful of kipper, untasted.

"All right," Dottie said slowly. Her own breakfast was congealing on her plate. So was Hal's. "So you don't believe Ben is dead, because this Richardson told you he *was*—and you think Richardson is a wrong 'un. But that's . . . all?" She looked intently at her father, her young chin trembling slightly, begging reassurance.

Hal closed his eyes for an instant, opened them, and looked at her directly.

"Dorothea," he said softly. "I have to believe that Ben is alive. Because if he isn't, then your mother will die of heartbreak—and I will die with her."

There was a moment of long silence, during which Grey heard the passage of carts in the street and the muffled voices of his valet and a bootblack in the corridor. Dottie made no sound at all, but he felt he could hear, too, the tears that rolled slowly down her cheeks.

115

THE RAVELED SLEEVE OF CARE

September 15, 1778
Philadelphia

I WOKE ABRUPTLY IN the dark, disoriented and alarmed. For a moment, I had no idea where I was or what was happening—only that something was seriously wrong.

I sat up, blinking furiously in an attempt to focus my eyes. Patted round in confusion and found myself naked, legs tangled in a sheet and wisps of straw prickling . . . oh. Loft. Printshop.

Jamie.

That was what was wrong. He lay next to me, but not still. He was on his side, turned away from me, body contorted, knees drawn up, and his arms crossed tight over his chest, head bowed. Shivering violently, though moonlight showed me the gleam of cold sweat on his shoulders. And making the terrible small whimpering noises that betokened the worst of his dreams.

I knew better than to try to wake him suddenly. Not in a small space with a lot of clutter and a steep drop ten feet away.

My own heart was pounding, and I knew his was. I eased myself carefully down beside him, facing his back. I needed to touch him, to bring him slowly to himself—or to enough of himself that he could recover alone. This wasn't the sort of nightmare eased by talking. Or, sometimes, even by waking.

"God, no," he said, in a heartbroken whisper. "God, *no!*"

I mustn't grab or shake him. I clenched my teeth and ran my hand lightly from the slope of his shoulder down to his elbow, and his skin shivered like a horse ridding itself of flies. That was all right, then. I did it again, paused, and again. He took a deep, horrible gasp, choked with fear . . . but the violent shivering eased a little.

"Jamie," I whispered, and, with extreme caution, touched his back very lightly. If he was dreaming about Jack Randall, this might—

"No!" he exclaimed, in a loud, fierce voice, and his legs straightened, every muscle in his body tight against his skin. "Damn you to *hell!*"

I took a deep breath and relaxed, just a bit. Anger was a thousand times better than fear or pain. Anger would leave him, as soon as he woke completely. The other things tended to linger.

"Hush," I said, a little louder but still softly. Germain often slept by the hearth, not wanting to share a bed with his younger siblings. "Hush, Jamie. I'm here." And with some trepidation, I put my arm round him, lightly, and laid my cheek against his back. His skin was hot; he smelled pungently of our lovemaking and even more strongly of fear and rage.

He stiffened, caught his breath—but I felt his awareness come back: instantly, the way it did when he woke to some alarm, ready to leap out of bed, reaching for a weapon. I tightened my hold and pressed my body against his. He didn't move, but I felt the thud of his heart, beating hard and fast.

"Can you hear me?" I asked. "Are you all right?"

After a moment, he drew a deep breath and let it out in a long, quivering sigh.

"Aye," he whispered, and his hand reached back to grasp my thigh, so tightly that I jerked but managed not to squeal. We rested quietly together for a time, until I felt his heart begin to slow and his skin cool, and then I kissed his back and traced the scars that would never fade from his body, over and over with gentle fingers, until they faded from his mind and he slept in my arms.

THE PIGEONS ON the roof of the boardinghouse made a purling noise, like the sea coming in on a pebbled shore, rolling tiny rounded rocks in the surf. Rachel was making a similar noise, snoring very faintly. Ian found it charming and could have lain watching her and listening to her all night—save that she was lying on his left arm, which had gone numb, and he needed urgently to piss.

As gently as possible, he edged out from under her soft weight, but she was a light sleeper and woke at once, yawning and stretching like a young catamount in the candlelight. She was naked, arms and face the color of just-toasted bread, her body white and her privates under their dark-brown bush a wonderful dusky color that wasn't either rose or violet or brown, but reminded him of orchids in the forests of Jamaica.

She stretched her arms above her head, and the movement lifted her startlingly white round breasts and made her nipples slowly rise. He began to slowly rise, too, and hastily turned away, before it became impossible to do what he'd meant to.

"Go back to sleep, lass," he said. "I just—er . . ." He gestured toward the chamber pot under the bed.

She made a pleasant sleepy noise and rolled onto her side, watching him.

"Does thee mind my looking at thee?" she asked, in a soft voice husked by sleep and earlier muffled shrieks.

He glanced at her in astonishment.

"Why would ye want to?" The notion seemed mildly perverse, but in a distinctly arousing fashion. He wanted to turn his back so he *could* piss, but if she wanted to watch him . . .

"It seems an intimacy of the body," she said, looking at him through half-closed eyes. "A trusting, perhaps. That thee consider thy body to be mine, as I consider mine to be thine."

"Do ye?" That idea surprised him, but he didn't object. At all.

"Thee has seen the most hidden parts of me," she pointed out, and, spreading her legs, drew her fingers delicately between them in illustration. "And tasted them, as well. What *did* it taste like?" she asked curiously.

"Fresh-caught trout," he replied, smiling at her. "Rachel—if ye want to watch me piss, ye can. But ye canna do it if ye talk to me like that while I'm trying, aye?"

"Oh." She made a small snort of amusement and rolled over, turning her back and her very round bottom to him. "Go ahead, then."

He sighed, examining his prospects.

"It will take a minute, aye?" Before she could think of anything else outrageous to say to him, he went on, in hopes of distracting her. "Uncle Jamie and Auntie Claire think of leaving Philadelphia soon. To go back to North Carolina, ken? What would ye think of going with them?"

"What?" He heard the rustle of the corn-husk mattress as she turned over quickly. "Where is thee thinking of going, that thee would not take me with thee?"

"Och, I didna mean that, lass," he assured her, with a quick glance over his shoulder. She was propped on her elbows, looking at him accusingly. "I meant we'd both go. To Fraser's Ridge—Uncle Jamie's settlement."

"Oh." That surprised her into silence. He could hear her thinking about it, and smiled to himself.

"Thee does not feel an obligation to the Continental army?" she asked after a moment, cautiously. "To the cause of freedom?"

"I dinna think those are necessarily the same thing, lass," he said, and closed his eyes in relief as everything relaxed at last. He shook himself and put away the pot, giving himself time to form a coherent sentence.

"The Duke of Pardloe told Auntie Claire that after Saratoga the British made a new plan. They mean to try to separate the southern colonies from the northern ones, blockade the South, and try to starve the North into submission."

"Oh." She moved to give him room to lie down beside her, then snuggled into him, her free hand cupping his balls. "Then thee means there will not be fighting in the North, so thee will not be needed as a scout here—but thee might, in the South?"

"Aye, or I might find another use for myself."

"Outside the army, thee means?" She was trying hard to keep hopefulness out of her voice; he could tell from the very sincere way she looked up at him, and he smiled at her, putting his own hand over hers. He was much in favor of bodily intimacy, but would rather not be squeezed like an orange should Rachel be overcome by enthusiasm.

"Perhaps," he said. "I own some land, ken, on the Ridge. Uncle Jamie gave it to me, some years back. 'Twould be hard work, mind, clearing fields and planting and plowing, but farming is mostly peaceful. Bar things like bears and wild pigs and fire and hailstorms, I mean."

"Oh, Ian." Her face had gone soft, and so had her hand, now resting peacefully in his. "I should love to farm with thee."

"Ye'd miss your brother," he reminded her. "And Dottie. Maybe Fergus and Marsali and the weans, too—I dinna think they'd come settle on the Ridge, though Uncle Jamie thinks they'd maybe travel south with us but settle near the coast. Fergus would need a decent-sized city, if he's to make much living as a printer."

A shadow crossed her face at that, but she shook her head.

"I will miss Denzell and Dottie—but I should in any case, for they will go where the army goes. But I will be very happy if thee does not," she added softly, and lifted her face to kiss him.

RACHEL WOKE instantly. She hadn't been soundly asleep, her body still a-hum from lovemaking, and still so attuned to Ian's that when he gasped and stiffened beside her, she sprang at once into awareness and had her hands on his shoulders, meaning to shake him gently out of his dream.

The next moment, she was on the floor in a tangle of bedding, her husband on top of her and his very large hands vised round her throat. She flopped and wriggled, pushed at him in futile panic—and then, as her breath vanished and brilliant red stars flashed in the darkness of her vision, she got hold of herself and brought her knee up as hard as she could.

It was a lucky blow, though it missed its mark; she hit Ian hard in the thigh, and he woke with a start and let go. She struggled out from under him, gasping and wheezing, and crawled as fast as she could to the corner, where she sat quivering with her arms wrapped round her knees, chest heaving and her heart thumping in her ears.

Ian was breathing heavily through his nose, pausing every so often to grunt or to say something brief—and probably very expressive, if she'd had the wit to understand it—in either Gaelic or Mohawk. After a few minutes, though, he got slowly into a sitting position and leaned back against the bedstead.

"Rachel?" he said warily, after a moment's silence. He sounded rational, and her tight-clasped arms loosened a little.

"Here," she said, tentative. "Is thee . . . all right, Ian?"

"Oh, aye," he said mildly. "Who taught ye to do that to a man?"

"Denny," she said, beginning to breathe easier. "He said that discouraging a man from committing the sin of rape wasn't violence."

There was a moment of silence from the vicinity of the bed.

"Oh," said Ian. "I might have a wee chat wi' Denny, one of these days. A philosophical discussion on the meaning of words, like."

"I'm sure he would enjoy it," Rachel said. She was still unnerved by what had happened, but crawled over and sat beside Ian on the floor. The sheet was lying in a pale puddle nearby, and she shook it out and draped it over her nakedness. She offered half of it to Ian, but he shook his head and leaned back a little, groaning as he stretched out his leg.

"Um. Would thee like me to . . . rub it?" she asked tentatively.

He made a small huffing noise that she interpreted as amusement. "Not just now, aye?"

They sat together, shoulders barely touching, for a bit. Her mouth was dry, and it took some time to work up enough spit to speak.

"I thought thee was going to kill me," she said, trying hard to keep her voice from quivering.

"I thought I was, too," Ian said quietly. He groped for her hand in the dark and held it, hard. "Sorry, lass."

"Thee was dreaming," she ventured. "Does—does thee want to tell me about it?"

"God, no," he said, and sighed. He let go her hand and bent his head, folding his arms atop his knees.

She kept quiet, not knowing what to say, and prayed.

"It was the Abenaki," he said eventually, his voice muffled. "The one I killed. In the British camp."

The words were simple and bald, and struck her in the pit of the stomach. She knew; he'd told her when he came back wounded. But to hear it again here, in the dark, with her back scraped from the floor and her throat bruised from his hands . . . She felt as though the deed itself had just happened in front of her, the reverberation of it shocking as a scream in her ear.

She swallowed and, turning to him, put a hand on his shoulder lightly, feeling with her thumb for the fresh, ragged scar where Denzell had cut to remove the arrow.

"Thee strangled the man?" she asked, very quietly.

"No." He breathed deep and sat up slowly. "I choked him, and I cut his throat, just a wee bit, and then I bashed his head in wi' a tomahawk."

He turned to her then and passed a hand lightly over her hair, smoothing it.

"I didna have to," he said. "Not right that moment, I mean. He didna attack me—though he'd tried to kill me before."

"Oh," she said, and tried to swallow, but her mouth had dried afresh. He sighed and bent so that his forehead rested on hers. She felt the warmth of his nearness, the warmth of his breath, smelling of beer and the juniper berries he chewed to clean his teeth. His eyes were open but so shadowed that she couldn't see into them.

"Is thee afraid of me, Rachel?" he whispered.

"I am," she whispered back, and closed her hand on his wounded shoulder, lightly but hard enough for him to feel the hurt of it. "And I am afraid for thee, as well. But there are things I fear much more than death—and to be without thee is what I fear most."

RACHEL REMADE the bed by candlelight and left the candle burning for a bit, saying that she wanted to read, to settle her mind. Ian had nodded, kissed her, and curled up like a dog beside her—the bedstead was too short for him. She glanced at the corner where Rollo slept; *he* was stretched out straight as a knife, head between his paws.

Ian put a hand on her leg and sank into sleep. She could see him doing it, his face going slack and peaceful, the muscles of his shoulders easing. It was why she'd kept the candle lit, so she might watch him sleep for a little and let the sight of him bring her peace, as well.

She'd put on her shift, feeling obscurely exposed, and though it was hot enough to lie above the sheet, she'd pulled it over her legs, too, wanting to be able to feel Ian when she moved in her sleep. She moved a leg toward him now, slowly, and felt the touch of his knee against her calf. His long lashes cast shadows on his cheeks in the candlelight, just above the looping line of his tattoos.

"Thee is my wolf," she'd said to him. *"And if thee hunts at night, thee will come home."*

"And sleep at thy feet," he'd replied.

She sighed, but felt better, and opened her Bible, to read a psalm before blowing out the candle, only to discover that she had absently picked up *Pamela: Or Virtue Rewarded,* from the bedside table. She gave a small snort of amusement and, all sense of distress now driven from her mind, closed the book, put out the candle, and snuggled down beside her sleeping wolf.

Sometime much later, in the empty hours before dawn, she opened her eyes. Not asleep, but certainly not awake, she had a sense of perfect consciousness without thought. And a distinct and vivid sense that she was not alone.

Ian was beside her; his breath touched her face, but she felt quite apart from him. It was only when it happened again that she realized what had wakened her: a tiny, sharp pain in her belly. Like the pain that sometimes came when she started her monthly, but smaller, less an ache than a . . . stab. A stab of awareness.

She blinked and put her hands over her stomach. The rafters were just barely visible overhead, shadowed with the distant coming of the light.

The pain had stopped, but the sense of . . . company? Of presence, rather. That hadn't gone away. It seemed very odd and completely natural—and of course it was, she thought. Natural as the beating of her own heart and the breath in her lungs.

She had a faint impulse to wake Ian, but that passed almost at once. She wanted to keep this for now, be alone with the knowledge—but not alone, she corrected herself, and sank peacefully back to sleep, hands still crossed over her lively womb.

IAN USUALLY WOKE before her, but she always felt him stir and would rise to the edge of wakefulness to enjoy his sleepy warm smell, the small male sounds he made, and the feel of his legs brushing hers as he swung them out of bed and sat up. He'd sit there on the edge for a moment, rubbing his hands through his hair and getting his bearings on the day, and if she cracked her eyes open, she could see his long, lovely back just in front of her, columnar muscles tanned by the sun and sloping gently down to his neat, tight buttocks, white as milk in contrast.

Sometimes he would emit a small, popping fart and look guiltily over his shoulder. She'd shut her eyes instantly and pretend to be still asleep, thinking that she must be completely besotted to find this adorable—but she did.

This morning, though, he sat up, rubbed a hand through his hair, and stiffened. She opened her eyes all the way, instantly alarmed by something in his posture.

"Ian?" she whispered, but he didn't attend.

"*A Dhia,*" he said, very softly. "Ah, no, *a charaid* . . . "

She knew at once. Should have known from the instant she woke. Because Rollo woke when Ian did, stretching and yawning with a groaning creak of jaw muscles and a lazy thump of tail against the wall, before coming to poke a cold nose into his master's hand.

This morning there was only stillness, and the curled form of what used to be Rollo.

Ian rose and went to him swiftly, knelt on the floor beside the body of his dog, and laid a gentle hand on the big furry head. He didn't say anything, or weep, but she heard the sound he made when he breathed, as of something tearing in his chest.

She got out of bed and came to Ian, kneeling beside him, arm about his waist, and *she* was weeping, quite without meaning to.

"*Mo chù,*" Ian said, running his hand lightly over the soft, thick fur. "*Mo chuilean."* There was a catch in his voice when he said, *"Beannachd leat, a charaid."* *Goodbye, old friend.*

Then he sat back on his heels, took a deep breath, and clasped Rachel's hand very hard. "He waited, I think. Until he kent ye were here for me." He swallowed audibly, and his voice was steady when he spoke again.

"I'll need to bury him. I ken a place, but it's some way. I'll be back by midafternoon, though."

"I'll come with thee." Her nose was running. She reached for the towel by the ewer and blew her nose on one end.

"Ye needn't, *mo ghràidh,*" he said gently, and passed a hand over her hair to smooth it. "It's a long way."

She drew breath and stood up.

"Then we'd best get started." She touched her husband on the shoulder, as lightly as he'd touched Rollo's fur. "I married him, as well as thee."

116

A-HUNTING WE WILL GO

September 15, 1778
First Watchung Mountain

THERE WAS A NEAT mound of droppings by the path, dark and glistening as coffee beans and much the same size. William was leading his mare, owing to her stoutness and the steep nature of the trail, so took the opportunity to stop for a moment and let her breathe. This she did, with an explosive snort and a shake of her mane.

He squatted and scooped up a few of the pellets, sniffing. Very fresh, though not warm, and with the faint oaky tang that meant the deer had been browsing on green acorns. Glancing to his left, he saw the broken brush that marked the animal's passage, and his hand twitched, wanting to wrap itself round his rifle. He could leave the mare tethered . . .

"What about it, owd lass?" he asked the mare, in the accents of the Lake District, where he'd grown up. "Would 'ee carry a carcass, if I shot 'un?"

The mare was maybe fourteen, old enough to be steady; in fact, it would be hard to imagine a steadier mount. She was more like riding a sofa than a horse, with her broad back and sides curved like a hogshead of beer. But he hadn't thought to ask, when he bought her, whether she was used to hunting. Steadiness of gait and a mild temper didn't necessarily mean she'd be fine if he heaved a deer across her back, leaking blood. Still . . .

He lifted his face to the breeze. Perfect. It was straight across the mountainside, toward him, and he imagined he could actually smell the—

Something moved in the wood, snapping twigs, and he heard the unmistakable rustling: the sound of a large herbivorous creature, wrenching mouthfuls of leaves off a tree.

Before he could think twice, he'd got to his feet, slipped the rifle from its sheath as silently as he could, and shucked his boots. Soft-footed as a ferret, he slid into the brush . . .

And, five minutes later, grasped the thrashing stubby antlers of a yearling buck with one hand as he slit the deer's throat with the other, the sound of his shot still echoing off the rocky escarpment above him.

It had happened so fast, it scarcely seemed real, despite the warm-cold feel of the blood soaking into his stockings and the thick smell of it. There was a tick hanging just under the deer's glazing eye, round as a tiny muscat grape. Would it let go at once, he wondered? Or would there be enough blood left for it to go on feeding for some time?

The deer shuddered violently, shoving its antlers hard into his chest, bunched its legs convulsively as though about to make one final leap, and died.

He held it for a few moments, the shredded velvet still on the antlers like rough suede under his sweating palm, the weight of the coarse-haired shoulders growing heavy on his knee.

"Thank you," he whispered, and let go. He remembered that it had been Mac the groom who'd told him that you always thanked a creature that gave you its life—and that it had been James Fraser, some years later, who had killed a huge wapiti in front of him and spoken what he said was a "gralloch prayer" in Gaelic before butchering the beast. But with the deer's blood on his skin and the breeze moving in the wood around him, for once he didn't push those memories away.

He went to check the mare, who was fortunately close to where he'd left her, having merely moved a few yards in order to crop weeds, and who looked at him with tranquil eyes, yellow wildflowers dangling from the corners of her mouth, as though gunshots and the smell of blood were commonplace in her life. Perhaps they were, he thought, and slapped her shoulder companionably.

Here's for you, Ben, he thought a few minutes later, slitting the belly skin. His cousin, nearly six years older than himself, had taken him hunting now and then in the forest near Earlingden, with Viscount Almerding, a friend of Ben's whose preserve it was.

He'd tried not to think of his cousin too much as he'd made his preparations. The greater part of him truly believed that Ben was dead. Gaol fever, according to what Richardson had told his uncle. Not an unusual thing to happen to a prisoner, by any means. And while he was convinced—reluctantly, for it made him burn with shame to have been such a flat as to have been gulled by the man—that Richardson was probably a villain, that didn't necessarily mean that every word from the man's mouth was a lie. Granted, he'd found no other trace of Ben in several weeks of searching.

But there was the small part of his heart that wouldn't give up. And a larger part that would do anything he could to ease the grief of his uncle and father, whatever the truth might prove to be.

"And if you bloody come down to it, what the hell *else* is there for me to do?" he muttered, reaching into the steaming heat of the body and groping for the heart.

At least he'd be welcome when he walked into Middlebrook Encampment, as they called it. A man bearing fresh meat was always welcome.

A half hour later, he'd gutted the carcass and wrapped his canvas bed sack around it to keep off flies. The horse flared her nostrils and snorted in disgust at the smell, but made no great objection when he wrestled it onto her back.

It was late in the afternoon, but this late in the summer it would stay light for some time. Better, he thought, to make his first approach at suppertime. Chances were good that he'd be invited to sit down with someone, and conversation was much easier over food and drink.

He'd gone up to the rocky summit in order to survey the terrain and had to admit that Washington and his engineers had chosen well. From the top of First Watchung Mountain, which he was standing on, the plains before New Brunswick lay clear below. The Continentals could easily keep a beady eye on the British army from their aerie and swoop down to interfere with their movements—and had.

The armies were gone now, though: both of them. The British to New York, Washington's troops to . . . well, wherever they might be at the moment. They weren't *here*, and that was all to the good. But there were people, still, who lived near the encampment.

Ben had been—*was,* he corrected himself fiercely—an officer; an infantry captain, like himself. And captured officers were often billeted upon local householders, under parole. That was the place to begin his inquiries.

"Come on, then, lass," he said to the mare, untying the reins from the sapling he'd wrapped them round. "Let's go and make ourselves welcome."

117

INTO THE BRIAR PATCH

September 16, 1778
Philadelphia

WE'D JUST FINISHED supper and I was wiping Henri-Christian's face with the hem of my apron, when a knock came at the alley door. Jenny, sitting next to me with Félicité on her lap, gave me a quick glance, brows raised. Was this cause for alarm?

I hadn't time to shrug or shake my head; all conversation had ceased on the instant, the children's chatter quelled as though someone had dropped a candle snuffer over them. It was first dark and the door was bolted. Fergus and Jamie exchanged looks and, without a word, both of them rose.

Jamie stood to one side, hand on his dirk—I hadn't realized until this moment that he wore it all the time now, even at table. I heard the shuffle of feet in the alley. There was more than one man out there, and the hair stirred on my nape. Jamie stood relaxed but watchful, weight on his back foot, ready as Fergus lifted the bar.

"Bonsoir," Fergus said calmly, with an interrogative lift at the end of the phrase. A face hovered pale in the dark, not close enough to recognize.

"Bonsoir, Monsieur Fraser." I blinked in surprise; I knew the voice, but had never heard Benedict Arnold speak French. But of course he could, I thought, recovering. He'd led more than one campaign in Quebec. It was a soldier's French he spoke: rough but serviceable.

"Madame Fraser est ici, monsieur?" he said. *"Votre mère?"*

Fergus glanced reflexively over his shoulder at Jenny, astonished. I coughed and eased Henri-Christian off my lap, smoothing his rumpled hair.

"I rather think the governor means me," I said. The governor turned aside and murmured something to his aide, who nodded and retired into the shadows.

"Mrs. Fraser," Arnold said, sounding relieved. Fergus stood aside, and the governor came in, bowing to Marsali and Jenny, nodding to Jamie, before fixing his attention on me. "Yes, I do mean you, ma'am. I beg pardon for my untimely intrusion, sir," he added, turning to Fergus. "I wasn't sure where Mrs. Fraser was residing and was obliged to make inquiries."

I saw Jamie's mouth tighten briefly at this galling reference to our homelessness, but he bowed courteously.

"And I daresay the matter is urgent, sir, since ye come to make your inquiries in person?"

"It is, rather." The governor turned to me. "I come to beg a favor of you, ma'am, on behalf of a friend." He looked a little better than he had the last time I'd seen him; he'd gained a bit of weight and his color was better, but the lines and smudges of strain and fatigue were still plain in his face. The eyes, though, were as alert as ever.

"This would be a sick friend?" I asked, already glancing toward the ladder that led to the loft where we slept—and where the box holding my modest pharmacopeia was kept when I wasn't holding regular surgery hours.

"A matter of injury, ma'am, rather than illness," Arnold said, and his mouth tightened involuntarily. "Severe injury."

"Oh? Well, then, I'd better—"

Jamie stopped me, a hand on my arm and his eyes on Arnold.

"A moment, Sassenach," he said quietly. "Before I let ye go, I want to know the nature of the injury and the name of the injured man. And I also want to ken why the governor comes to ye under cover of night and hides his intent from his own aide."

The color rose in Arnold's cheeks, but he nodded.

"Fair enough, Mr. Fraser. Do you know a man called Shippen?"

Jamie looked blank and shook his head, but Fergus chimed in.

"I do," he said, looking thoughtfully at Arnold. "He is a wealthy man, and a well-known Loyalist—one of those who chose not to leave the city when the British army withdrew."

"I know one of the Shippen girls," I said, with a vague memory of General Howe's lavish leaving party in May—God, could that possibly be only three months past? "I don't think I've met the father, though. Is he the injured party?"

"No, but he is the friend on whose behalf I ask your help, ma'am." Arnold drew a deep, unhappy breath. "Mr. Shippen's young cousin, a man named Tench Bledsoe, was set upon last night by the Sons of Liberty. They tarred and feathered him, ma'am, and left him on the docks in front of Mr. Shippen's warehouse. He rolled off the dock into the river and by a mercy didn't drown, but crept up the bank and lay in the muddy shallows until a slave hunting crabs found him and ran for help."

"Help," Jamie repeated carefully.

Arnold met his eye and nodded. "Just so, Mr. Fraser," he said bleakly. "The Shippens live within two streets of Dr. Benjamin Rush, but under the circumstances . . ."

The circumstances being that Benjamin Rush was a very visible and outspoken Rebel, active in the Sons of Liberty, and would certainly be familiar with everyone in Philadelphia who held similar sentiments—very likely including the men who had attacked Tench Bledsoe.

"Sit down, Sassenach," Jamie said, gesturing to my stool. I didn't, and he gave me a brief, dark look.

"I dinna mean to stop ye going," he said, a distinct edge in his voice. "I ken well enough that ye will. I just mean to make sure ye come back. Aye?"

"Er . . . yes," I said, and coughed. "I'll just—go and get my things together, then." I sidled through the clump of staring children to the ladder and went up as quickly as I could, hearing Jamie's stern inquisition of Governor Arnold begin behind me.

Severe burns—and the attendant difficulties of hardened tar—and very likely fever and infection already started, after a night lying in river mud. This was going to be messy—and possibly worse. There was no telling how badly the young man had been burned; if we were lucky, it might be only splashes of tar that had reached his skin. If we weren't lucky . . .

I set my jaw and began packing. Linen bandages, a scalpel and small paring knife for debridement . . . leeches? Perhaps; there would certainly be bruising involved—no one submitted meekly to being tarred and feathered. I tied a hasty bandage around the leech jar to keep the lid from coming off in transit. Definitely a jar of honey . . . I held it up to the flicker of light from below: half full, a clouded gold that caught the light through brown glass like candle glow. Fergus kept a tin of turpentine in the shed for cleaning type; I should borrow that, as well.

I didn't worry overmuch about the political delicacies that had made Arnold come to me so surreptitiously. Jamie would take what precautions were possible, I knew. Philadelphia lay in Rebel hands, but it was by no means a safe place—for anyone.

Not for the first time—or the last, I was sure—I was glad that at least my own path lay clear before me. The door below opened and closed with a thump; the governor was gone.

I LOOKED AT the rather grubby sedan chair, inhaled the scent of several dozen previous users, and took a firmer grip on my cane.

"I can walk," I said. "It's not that far."

"Ye're not walking," Jamie replied equably.

"Surely you don't intend to stop me?"

"Aye, I do," he said, still mildly. "I canna stop ye going—and I wouldna try—but I can, by God, make sure ye dinna fall on your face in the street on your way. Get in, Sassenach. Go slow," he added to the chairmen, as he opened the door of the sedan and gestured to me. "I'm coming, and I dinna want to gallop so soon after supper."

There being no reasonable alternative, I gathered the remnants of my dignity and got in. And with my basket of supplies settled at my feet and the window slid open as far as it would go—the memories of my last claustrophobic ride in a sedan chair were as vivid as the smell of this one—we set off at a stately jog through the quiet nighttime streets of Philadelphia.

The curfew had been eased of late, owing to protests from tavern owners—and, likely, their patrons—but the overall sense of the city was still edgy, and there were no respectable women on the street, no gangs of rowdy apprentices, or any of the slaves who worked for their masters but lived on their own. I saw one whore, standing by the mouth of an alley; she whistled at Jamie and called out an invitation, but halfheartedly.

"Her pimp'll be a-hiding . . . in the alley with a cosh . . . lay you three to one," the chairman behind me remarked, his remarks punctuated by his breathing. "Ain't as safe . . . as when the army was here."

"Think not?" His partner grunted, then found breath to reply. "Army was here . . . when that officer got his . . . throat cut in a whorehouse. Reckon 's why that . . . drab's out here in her shift." He gulped air and went on. "How you mean . . . to settle the bet, then? Go with her yourself?"

"May be as this gentleman'd do us the service," the other said with a brief, gasping laugh.

"It may be that he won't," I said, sticking my head out the window. "But I'll go and look, if you like."

Jamie and the forward man laughed, the other grunted, and we jolted gently round the corner and down the street to where the Shippen house stood, gracious in its own grounds, on a small rise near the edge of town. There was a lighted lantern by the gate, another by the door. I wondered whether that meant we were expected; I hadn't thought to ask Governor Arnold if he had sent word ahead of us. If he hadn't, the next few minutes might be interesting.

"Any notion how long we might be, Sassenach?" Jamie inquired, taking out his purse to pay the chairmen.

"If he's already dead, it won't take long," I replied, shaking my skirts into order. "If he's not, it could well take all night."

"Aye. Wait a bit, then," Jamie told the chairmen, who were staring at me, mouths agape. "If I havena come out in ten minutes, ye're free to go."

Such was his force of personality, they didn't observe that they were quite free to go at once if they wanted, and merely nodded meekly as he took my arm and escorted me up the steps.

We were expected; the door swung wide as Jamie's boots scuffed the scrubbed stone of the stoop, and a young woman peered out, alarm and interest showing in equal measure on her face. Evidently Mr. Bledsoe wasn't dead, then.

"Mrs. Fraser?" She blinked slightly, looking at me sideways. "Er . . . I mean . . . it *is* Mrs. Fraser? Governor Arnold said—"

"It is Mrs. Fraser," Jamie said, a slight edge in his voice. "And I assure ye, young woman, I'm in a position to know."

"This would be *Mr.* Fraser," I informed the young lady, who was looking up at him, clearly bewildered. "I was probably Lady John Grey last time you saw me," I added, trying for a nonchalant matter-of-factness. "But, yes, I'm Claire Fraser. Er . . . still. I mean—again. I understand that your cousin . . . ?"

"Oh, yes! Please—come this way." She stepped back, gesturing toward the rear of the house, and I saw that she was accompanied by a servant, a middle-aged black man, who bowed when I met his gaze and then led the way through a long hallway to the back stair and thence upward.

On the way, our hostess introduced herself belatedly as Margaret Shippen and apologized prettily for the absence of her parents. Her father—she said—was called away on business.

I hadn't been formally introduced to Peggy Shippen before, but I had seen her and knew a bit about her; she'd been one of the organizing lights of the Mischianza, and while her father had prevented her actually attending the ball, all her friends had talked about her at length—and I'd glimpsed her, lavishly dressed, once or twice at other functions I'd attended with John.

Called away on business, was it? I caught Jamie's eye when she'd said that, and he'd raised one shoulder in the briefest of shrugs. More than likely, Edward Shippen wanted to avoid any public linkage with his nephew's misfortune—and, so far as possible, keep talk about the incident to a minimum. It wasn't a safe time or place to make a point of Loyalist leanings in the family.

Miss Shippen led us to a small bedroom on the third floor, where a blackened, man-shaped object lay on the bed. The smell of tar was thick in the air, along with a distinct smell of blood and a sort of constant low moaning noise. This must be Tench Bledsoe—and wherever had he got a name like that? I wondered, gingerly approaching him. So far as I knew, a tench was a rather undistinguished-looking sort of carp.

"Mr. Bledsoe?" I said quietly, setting down my basket on a small table. There was a candlestick on the table, and by the light of the single flame, I could make out his face—or half of it. The other half was obscured by tar, as was a good bit of his head and neck. The clean half was that of a somewhat plain young man with a large, beaky nose, his features contorted in agony, but not at all fish-looking.

"Yes," he gasped, and pressed his lips tight together, as though even the escape of a single word jeopardized the tenuous grip he had on himself.

"I'm Mrs. Fraser," I said, and laid a hand on his shoulder. A fine shudder was running through him like current through a wire. "I've come to help."

He heard me and nodded jerkily. They'd given him brandy; I could smell it under the aromatic reek of pine tar, and a half-full decanter stood on the table.

"Have you any laudanum in the house?" I asked, turning to Peggy. It wouldn't help that much in the long run, but a large dose might get us through the worst of the preliminaries.

She was quite young—no more than eighteen, I thought—but alert and self-possessed, as well as very pretty. She nodded and disappeared, with a murmured word to the servant. *Of course,* I thought, seeing her skirts whisk out of sight. *She couldn't send him for it.* The laudanum would be with the other household simples, in a closet under lock and key.

"What can I do, Sassenach?" Jamie said softly, as though afraid to break the injured man's concentration on his pain.

"Help me undress him." Whoever had attacked him hadn't stripped him; that was lucky. And most of the tar probably hadn't been boiling hot when it was applied; I smelled burnt hair, but not the sickening stench of cooked flesh. Pine tar wasn't like the asphalt road tar of later centuries; it was a byproduct of turpentine distillation, and might be soft enough to be daubed without needing to be boiled first.

What *wasn't* fortunate was his leg, as I saw at once when Jamie peeled back the sheet covering him. That was where the smell of blood had come from; it spread in a soggy smear on the bedclothes, black in the candlelight, but copper and scarlet to the nose.

"Jesus H. Roosevelt Christ," I said under my breath. Tench's face was dead white and streaked with sweat and tears, his eyes closed, but he grimaced, hearing that.

Jamie set his jaw and drew his case knife, which was sharp enough to shave the hairs on a man's arm. Sharp enough to slice through shredded stocking and damp breeches, spreading the stiffened fabric aside to show me the damage.

"Who did that to ye, man?" he asked Tench, gripping him by the wrist as the injured man reached a tentative hand downward, seeking the extent of the damage.

"No one," Tench whispered, and coughed. "I—I jumped off the dock when he set my head afire, and landed on one foot in the mud. It stuck well in, and when I fell over . . ."

It was a very nasty compound fracture. Both bones of the lower leg had snapped clean through, and the shattered ends were poking through the skin in different directions. I was surprised that he had survived the shock of it, together with the trauma of the attack—to say nothing of a night and part of a day spent lying in the filthy river shallows afterward. The macerated flesh was swollen, raw, red, and ugly, the wounds deeply infected. I breathed in gently, half-expecting the reek of gangrene, but no. Not yet.

"He set your head afire?" Jamie was saying incredulously. He leaned forward, touching the darkened mass on the left side of the young man's head. "Who?"

"Don't know." Tench's hand floated up, touched Jamie's, but Tench didn't try to pull it away. It rested on Jamie's, as though his touch would tell Tench what he needed to know but couldn't bear to find out for himself.

"Think he . . . Way he spoke. Maybe England, maybe Ireland. He . . . poured pitch over my head and sprinkled feathers on. Others would have left me then, I think. But all of a sudden, he turned back and seized a torch . . ." He coughed, wincing against the spasm, and ended breathlessly, " . . . like he . . . hated me." He sounded astonished.

Jamie was carefully breaking off small chunks of singed hair and matted clumps of mud and tar, revealing the blistered skin underneath.

"It's none sae bad, man," he said, encouraging. "Your ear's still there, no but a wee bit black and crusty round the edges."

That actually made Tench laugh—no more than a breathy gasp—though this was extinguished abruptly when I touched his leg.

"I'll need more light," I said, turning to the servant. "And a lot of bandages." He nodded, avoiding looking at the man on the bed, and left.

We worked for some minutes, murmuring occasional encouragement to Tench. At one point, Jamie pulled the chamber pot out from under the bed, excused himself with a brief word, and took it into the hall; I heard him retching. He came back a few moments later, pale and smelling of vomit, and resumed the delicate work of uncovering what might remain of Tench's face.

"Can ye open this eye, man?" he asked, gently touching the left side. I peered up from my station over his leg, to see that the lid was evidently whole but badly blistered and swollen, the lashes singed off.

"No." Tench's voice had changed, and I moved abruptly up to his head.

He sounded almost sleepy, his voice unconcerned. I laid the back of my hand against his cheek; it was cool and clammy. I said something very bad out loud, and his working eye sprang open, staring up at me.

"Oh, there you are," I said, much relieved. "I thought you were going into shock."

"If he hasna been shocked by what's already happened to him, I shouldna think anything would do it, Sassenach," Jamie said, but bent closer to look. "I think he's only worn out from the pain, aye? Sometimes ye canna be bothered to put up with it anymore, but ye're no ready to die, so ye just drift away for a bit."

Tench sighed deeply and gave a small, jerky nod.

"If you could . . . stop for a little while?" he whispered. "Please."

"Aye," Jamie said softly, and, patting his chest, drew the stained sheet up over him. "Rest a bit, *mo charaid*."

I wasn't at all sure that he wasn't trying to die, but there was a limit to what I could do to prevent him, if that were the case. And there was a much more serious limit to what I could do if he *didn't* die.

On the other hand, I had a vivid understanding of exactly what Jamie meant by "drifting away" and of the symptoms of severe blood loss. There was no telling how much blood Tench *had* lost, lying in the river. The fracture had by some miracle not ruptured either of the main tibial arteries—if it had, he'd have been dead long since—but it had certainly made hash of a number of smaller vessels.

On the other hand . . . the Delaware was a fairly cold river, even in summer. The chill of the water might well have constricted the smaller blood vessels, as well as slowed his metabolism and even perhaps minimized the damage due to burns, both by extinguishing the fire and by cooling the burnt skin. I'd whipped a pro forma tourniquet bandage round the leg above the knee but hadn't tightened it; blood loss at the moment was no more than a slow oozing.

And, in fact, the burns *were* minimal. His shirt had been torn open, but the tar on his chest, hands, and clothes hadn't been hot enough to blister his skin—and while there was certainly visible damage to one side of his face and head, I didn't *think* more than a few square inches of scalp had third-degree burns; the rest was redness and blistering. Painful, of course, but not life-threatening. Whoever had attacked him had likely not meant to kill him—but they stood a good chance of doing so, anyway.

"Pitch-capping, they call it," Jamie said, low-voiced. We had moved away to the window, but he nodded back toward the bed. "I havena seen it before, but I've heard of it." He shook his head, lips tight, then picked up the ewer and offered it to me. "D'ye want water, Sassenach?"

"No—oh, wait. Yes, I do, thank you." The window was firmly closed, in accordance with the custom of the times, and the small room was sweltering. I took the pitcher and nodded to the window. "Can you get that open, do you think?"

He turned to wrestle with the window; it was stuck fast in its frame, the wood swollen with humidity and disuse.

"What about the leg?" he said, back turned to me. "Ye'll have to take it off, no?"

I lowered the pitcher—the water was flat and tasted of earth—and sighed.

"Yes," I said. I'd been fighting that conclusion almost from the moment I'd seen Tench's leg, but hearing Jamie's matter-of-factness made it easier to accept.

"I doubt I could save it in a modern hospital, with blood transfusions and anesthetic—and, *God,* I wish I had ether right now!" I bit my lip, looking at the bed, and watching closely to see whether Tench's chest was still rising and falling. A tiny, treacherous part of me rather hoped it wasn't—but it was.

Feet on the stairs, and both Peggy and the manservant were with us again, armed respectively with a stable lantern and an enormous candelabra, Peggy with a square glass bottle clasped to her chest. Both turned anxious faces toward the bed, then toward me, standing apart by the window. Was he dead?

"No," I said, shaking my head, and saw the same half-regretful relief flit across their faces that I had just experienced. I wasn't without sympathy; no matter what their feelings for the injured man, having him on the premises was a danger to the Shippens.

I came forward and explained in a low voice what had to be done, watching Peggy go the color of a bad oyster in the flickering light. She swayed a little, but swallowed hard and drew herself up.

"Here?" she said. "I don't suppose you could take him to . . . Well, no, I suppose not." She took a deep breath. "All right. What can we do to help?"

The manservant coughed behind her in a meaningful manner, and she stiffened.

"My father would say the same," she informed him coldly.

"Just so, miss," he said, with a deference that wasn't all that deferential. "But he might like to have the chance to say it himself, don't you think?"

She shot him an angry glance, but before she could say anything, there was a grinding screech of wood as the window gave way to Jamie's will, and everyone's eye jerked to him.

"I dinna mean to interrupt," he said mildly, turning round. "But I do believe the governor has come to call."

JAMIE PUSHED PAST Miss Shippen and her servant before either could react. He ran lightly down the back stair and came through the house, startling a kitchen maid. Clearly the governor wasn't going to be admitted by the kitchen door.

He reached the front door just as a firm knock sounded, and pulled it open.

"Miss Margaret!" Arnold pushed past Jamie as though he wasn't there—no small feat—and seized Peggy Shippen's hands in his. "I thought I must come—your cousin? How does he do?"

"He is alive." Peggy swallowed, her face the color of the beeswax candle she was holding. "Mrs. Fraser is—she says—" She swallowed again, and Jamie swallowed with her, out of sympathy, knowing all too well what she was thinking of. Tench Bledsoe's shattered leg bones, red and slimy as an ineptly butchered pig's. The back of his throat was still bitter with the taste of vomit.

"I thank you *so* much for sending Mrs. Fraser to us, sir—I couldn't think what on earth we were to do. My father's in Maryland and my mother with her sister in New Jersey. My brothers . . ." She trailed off, looking distraught.

"No, no, my dear—may I call you so? It is my most fervent concern, to help you—your family, to . . . protect you." He hadn't let go her hands, Jamie noted, and she wasn't pulling them away.

Jamie glanced covertly from Arnold to Peggy Shippen, then turned away a little, drawing back. It wasn't hard for them to ignore him; they were focused on each other.

That made matters plain—or at least plainer. Arnold wanted the girl, and wanted her so nakedly that Jamie was slightly ashamed for the man. You couldn't help lust, but surely a man should have enough control to hide it. *And no just for the sake of decency, either,* he thought, seeing a certain look of cautious calculation come into Peggy's face. It was, he thought, the look of a fisherman who has just seen a fat trout swim right under the lure.

He cleared his throat in a pointed manner, and both of them jerked as though he'd run a drawing pin into them.

"My wife says it will be necessary to amputate the injured leg," he said. "Quickly. She requires a few things—instruments and the like."

"I need both the large saw and the small lunar one, the set of tenaculae—the long things that look like fishing hooks—and quite a lot of sutures . . ."

He was trying to keep the list in his head, though it made him ill to envision most of the items, thinking of the use they were about to be put to. Beneath the sense of revulsion and pity, though, was wariness—the same wariness he saw at the back of Benedict Arnold's eyes.

"Does she," Arnold said, not quite a question. His eyes flicked back to Peggy Shippen, who bit her lip in a becoming manner.

"Can ye maybe send your coachman to the printshop?" Jamie asked. "I can go with him and fetch back what's needed."

"Yes," Arnold said slowly, but in an abstracted way, the way he did when he was thinking rapidly. "Or . . . no. Let us rather remove Mr. Bledsoe—and Mrs. Fraser, to be sure—to the printshop in my coach. Mrs. Fraser will have access there to everything she requires, and the assistance and support of her family."

"What?" Jamie exclaimed, but Peggy Shippen was already hanging on to Arnold's arm, her face transformed by relief. Jamie seized Arnold by the arm to compel his attention, and the governor's eyes narrowed.

Jamie's intent had been to demand rhetorically whether Arnold was mad, but the split second's delay was enough to change this to a more politic "There's nay room at the shop for such a venture, sir. We live atop one another, and folk come in and out all day. This willna be a simple matter; the man will need to be nursed for some time."

Peggy Shippen made a small moan of anxiety, and it dawned upon Jamie that Tench Bledsoe was a hot potato, as much—or more—for Arnold as for the Shippens. The last thing Arnold could want, as military governor of the city, was public scandal and disorder, the remaining Loyalists in Philadelphia threatened and frightened, the Sons of Liberty seen as secret vigilantes, a law unto themselves.

Arnold must very much want the incident kept quiet. At the same time, he wanted to be the noble knight, riding to the aid of the very young and enchanting Miss Shippen by caring for her cousin while removing the potential danger he posed to her household.

By bringing it to mine, Jamie thought, his wariness beginning to turn to anger.

"Sir," he said formally. "There is no possibility of preventing the matter from being known, should ye bring yon man into my son's shop. And clearly ye ken the danger of that."

The truth of this was evident, and Arnold paused, wrinkling his brow. But Jamie had fought with the man and kent him well enough; Jamie saw that, having made up his mind to relieve Miss Peggy's concern, Arnold meant to do it, come hell or high water.

Evidently Claire was right in what she'd told him about testosterone, and he'd already known that Arnold was a ram, in terms both of balls and hardheadedness.

"Ah, I have it!" Arnold exclaimed triumphantly, and Jamie saw—with grudging admiration—the general emergent. This admiration disappeared with Arnold's next sentence.

"Lord John Grey," he said. "We could transport Mr. Bledsoe to his lordship's house."

"No!" Jamie said by reflex.

"Yes," Arnold said, but in self-congratulation rather than contradiction; he was paying no attention. "Yes, the ideal solution! His lordship and his brother are much in my debt," he explained to Peggy, with a feigned modesty that made Jamie want to hit him. "And as his lordship and Mrs. Fraser—" At this point, he caught sight of Jamie's face and arrested his speech just in time to prevent exactly such a happenstance. He coughed. "The ideal solution," he repeated. "Will you go and tell Mrs. Fraser what we intend, sir?"

"We?" Jamie said. "I intend nothing of the—"

"What the *bloody* hell is going on down here?" Claire's voice came from the stairway behind him, and he swung round to see her leaning on the banister, a-flicker like a ghost in the light from the tin sconce above her. There was blood smudging her apron, blotches black on the pale cloth.

"Nothing, *a nighean,*" he said, fixing Arnold with a firm eye. "Only discussing where Mr. Bledsoe should be."

"I don't care where he *should* be," she snapped, coming down into the foyer, skirts rustling with agitation. "Where he *will* be is dead, if I can't take care of his leg quickly." Then she noticed the glaring going on betwixt him and Arnold and moved up beside Jamie, looking hard at the governor herself.

"General Arnold," she said, "if you have the slightest concern for Miss Shippen's cousin's life, you'll oblige me by taking my husband promptly to fetch the instruments I need. Hurry!"

Arnold blinked, and Jamie would have smiled had he not been worrit for the lass—she was fierce, but she looked pale, and her fists were clenched in the cloth of her apron. It might have been to keep her from slapping the governor, but he rather thought it was to hide the fact that her hands were trembling—and he realized with a shock that she was afraid.

Not afraid of the circumstance or any future danger—afraid that she couldn't do what she knew she must.

His heart smote him at the thought. He took Arnold firmly by the upper arm, compelling him toward the stair.

"Aye," he said abruptly to Claire. "We'll take the man to Lord John's house, and whilst ye fettle him for the job there, I'll fetch what ye need from the shop. The general will help me to move him."

Arnold's stiff resistance ceased abruptly as he took Jamie's meaning.

"Yes," he said. "Yes, I—" A long moan from above interrupted him, and Claire's face tightened.

"There isn't time," she said, quite calmly. "Miss Shippen—Peggy. Fetch me the largest knife you have in the kitchen, and do it now. Have your servants bring more hot water and cloth for bandages. A strong sewing needle and black thread." Her eyes sought Jamie's, and he let go of the governor at once and went to her.

"Ye're all right, lass?" he said quietly, taking her elbow.

"I am," she said, and squeezed his hand briefly. "This is very bad, though. I don't—I'm sorry, I'll need you to help hold him."

"I'll be fine," he said. "Dinna be worrit. Only do what ye need to do. I promise I willna vomit on him while ye're taking off his leg."

He hadn't actually meant that to be funny, and was surprised—but pleased—when she laughed. Not much of a laugh, but the tension in her arm relaxed, and her fingers were steady on his.

He could tell the minute they entered the room. He didn't know what it was had changed, but clearly Claire had heard the beating of the wings of Death from the floor below; he could sense them now. Bledsoe was still conscious, but barely so; a slice of white showed as one eyelid lifted at their entrance.

"We're here, man," Jamie whispered, sinking to his knees and grasping Bledsoe's hand. It was cold to the touch and clammy with sweat. "Dinna fash, we're here. It'll be done soon."

There was a strong smell of laudanum in the air, together with the stink of tar and blood and burnt hair. Claire was on the other side of the bed, holding Bledsoe's wrist, her eyes flickering from his slack face to the mangled leg.

"Sepsis," she said, quietly but in a normal voice. "Do you see the red line there?" She gestured at the wounded leg, and Jamie saw it clearly: a streak of an ugly dark-red color that he thought hadn't been there before—or perhaps it had, and he'd not noticed. The sight of it made the fine hairs ripple on his shoulders, and he shifted uneasily.

"Blood poisoning," Claire said. "Bacteria—germs—in the blood. It moves very fast, and if it should get into the body proper . . . there's nothing I can do."

He looked up sharp, hearing a tiny tremor in her voice.

"But before that, ye might? There's a chance?" He tried to sound encouraging, though the thought of the alternative made the gooseflesh that much worse.

"Yes. But it isn't a good one." She swallowed. "The shock of the amputation may well kill him on the spot. And if it doesn't, there's still a great chance of infection."

He stood up then and came round the bed to her, taking her gently but solidly by the shoulders. Her bones were close to the surface, and he thought her feelings were, too.

"If he's got a chance, we must give it to him, Sassenach."

"Yes," she murmured, and he felt the shiver go all through her, though the air was hot and close. "God help me."

"He will," Jamie whispered, folding his arms briefly round her. "So will I."

I WAS STANDING in the wrong place. The fact that I understood what was happening to me didn't help at all.

A trained surgeon is also a potential killer, and an important bit of the training lies in accepting the fact. Your intent is entirely benign—or at least you hope so—but you are laying violent hands on someone, and you must be ruthless in order to do it effectively. And sometimes the person under your hands will die, and knowing that . . . you do it anyway.

I had had them bring more candles, though the air in the room was already suffocating. The miasma of humidity and slowly evaporating sweat made the light of the candelabra fill the chamber with a gentle, romantic glow; just the thing for a dinner party filled with wine, flirtations, and dancing.

The wine could wait, and any surgeon dances with death routinely. The problem was that I'd forgotten the steps and was flirting with panic.

I bent to check Tench's heart rate and respiration. He was breathing shallowly but fast. Lack of oxygen, severe blood loss . . . and I felt my own chest tighten, heaving for air, and stood up, giddy, heart hammering.

"Sassenach." I turned, hand on the bedpost, to see Jamie watching me, eyebrows drawn together. "Are ye all right?"

"Yes," I said, but my voice sounded queer even to my own ears. I shook my head hard, trying to clear it. Jamie came close to me and put his hand on mine, where it rested on the bedpost. It was big and steady, and it helped.

"Ye willna help him, lass, if ye faint in the midst of it," he said, low-voiced.

"I'm not going to faint," I said, made a bit testy by anxiety. "I just—I—I'm fine."

His hand fell away, and after a long, searching look into my face, he nodded soberly and stepped back.

I wasn't going to faint. Or at least I hoped not. But I was trapped there in that close, hot room, smelling blood and tar and the scent of myrrh in the laudanum, feeling Tench's agony. And I could *not* do that. I couldn't, I mustn't.

Peggy hurried in, a maidservant behind her, several large knives clutched to her bosom.

"Will one of these do?" She laid them in a clinking heap at the foot of the bed, then stood back, gazing anxiously at her cousin's pale, slack face.

"I'm sure one will." I stirred the heap gingerly, extracting a couple of possibilities: a carving knife that looked sharp, and a big, heavy knife of the sort used for chopping vegetables. And, with a vivid recollection of what it felt like to sever tendons, I picked up a paring knife with a freshly sharpened, silvered edge.

"Do you butcher your own meat? If you have something like a bone saw . . ."

The servant went as pale as a black man reasonably can, and went out, presumably to acquire one.

"Boiling water?" I asked, brows raised.

"Chrissy is bringing it," Peggy assured me. She licked her lips, uneasy. "Do you—mmm." She broke off, narrowly avoiding saying what she so plainly thought: *"Do you know what you're doing?"*

I did. That was the trouble. I knew much too much about what I was doing—from both sides.

"Everything will be fine," I assured her, with a decent appearance of calm and confidence. "I see we have needles and thread. Would you take the biggest needle—a carpet needle, perhaps—and thread it for me, please? And then a couple of smaller ones, just in case." Just in case I had time and opportunity to actually capture and ligate blood vessels. It was much more likely that the only choice I would have was cautery—a brutal searing of the fresh stump to stanch the bleeding, for Tench didn't have enough blood left to be able to spare any of it.

I needed to be alone in my head, in a calm, clear place. The place from which I could see everything, sense the body under my hand in all its particularities—but not *be* that body.

I was about to disjoint Tench Bledsoe's leg like a chicken's. Throw away his bones and flesh. Sear the stump. And I felt his fear in the pit of my stomach.

Benedict Arnold had come in with an armload of firewood and a silver table knife in one hand—my cautery iron, if there wasn't time to stitch. He set them down on the hearth, and the butler began to poke up the fire.

I closed my eyes for an instant, trying not to breathe through my nose, shutting out the candle glow. Denny Hunter had operated on me by candlelight; I remembered watching through a haze of eyelashes, unable to open my eyes more than a crack, as each of the six big candles was lit, the flames rising up pure and hot—and smelling the small iron heating in the brazier beside them.

A hand touched my waist, and, gulping air, I leaned blindly into Jamie.

"What's wrong, *a nighean?*" he whispered to me.

"Laudanum," I said, almost at random. "You don't—you don't lose consciousness altogether. It makes the pain go away—not stop, just seem not connected to you—but it's *there*. And you . . . you know what's happening to you." I swallowed, forcing down bile.

I felt it. The hard probe jabbing its way into my side, startling. The remarkable sense of cold intrusion, mingled with incongruous faint warm echoes of internal movement, the forceful jabs of a child in the womb.

"You know what's happening," I repeated, opening my eyes. I found his, looking down at me with gentleness.

"I ken that, aye?" he whispered, and cupped my cheek with his four-fingered hand. "Come and tell me what ye need me to do, *mo ghràidh*."

THE MOMENTARY PANIC was subsiding; I forced it aside, knowing that even to think about it was to slide headfirst back into it. I laid a hand on Tench's injured leg, willing myself to feel it, find the truth of it.

The truth was all too obvious. The lower leg was a complete wreck, mechanically, and so compromised by septicemia that there was no chance of saving it. I was searching desperately for a way to save the knee; having a knee made a tremendous difference in the ability to walk, to manage. But I couldn't do it.

He was far gone from injury, blood loss, and shock; he was a stubborn man, but I could feel his life flickering in his flesh, dying away in the midst of infection, disruption, and pain. I could *not* ask his body to withstand the longer, painstaking surgery that would be necessary to amputate below the knee—even if I felt sure that such an amputation would be sufficient to forestall the advancing septicemia, and I didn't.

"I'm going to take his leg off above the knee," I said to Jamie. I thought I spoke calmly, but my voice sounded odd. "I need you to hold the leg for me and move it as I tell you. Governor"—I turned to Arnold, who stood with a reassuring arm about Peggy's Shippen's waist—"come and hold him down." Laudanum alone wasn't going to be enough.

To his credit, Arnold came instantly and laid a hand against Tench's slack cheek for a moment in reassurance before taking firm hold of his shoulders. His own face was calm, and I remembered the stories I'd heard of his campaigns into Canada: frostbite, injury, starvation . . . No, not a squeamish man, and I felt a small sense of reassurance from the presence of my two helpers.

No, three: Peggy Shippen came up beside me, pale to the lips and with her throat bobbing every few seconds as she swallowed—but jaw set with determination.

"Tell me what to do," she whispered, and clamped her mouth shut hard as she caught sight of the mangled leg.

"Try not to vomit, but if you must, turn away from the bed," I said. "Otherwise—stand there and hand me things as I ask."

There was no further time for thought or preparation. I tightened the tourniquet, grasped the sharpest knife, nodded to my helpers, and began.

A deep incision, fast, around and across the top of the leg, cutting hard down to expose the bone. An army surgeon could lop off a leg in less than two minutes. So could I, but it would be better if I could manage to cut flaps to cover the stump, could seal the major vessels. . . .

"Big needle," I said to Peggy, holding out my hand. Lacking a tenaculum to seize the large blood vessels that snapped back into the flesh when severed, I had to probe for them with the point of the needle and drag them out, anchor them into the raw, exposed flesh, and then ligate them as fast as I could, whipping thread round them with one of the smaller needles and tying it off. Better than cautery, if there was time . . .

Sweat was running into my eyes; I had to dash it away with my bared forearm; my hands were bloody to the wrist.

"Saw," I said, and no one moved. Had I spoken aloud? *"Saw,"* I said, much louder, and Jamie's head twisted toward the implements on the table. Leaning heavily on Tench's leg with one hand, he stretched to grab the saw from the table with the other.

Where was Peggy? On the floor. I saw the bloom of her skirt from the corner of my eye and felt vaguely through the floorboards the steps of a servant coming to haul her out of the way.

I groped for another suture, blind, and the jar of brandy in which I'd stowed them tipped, spilling on the sheet and adding its sweet stickiness to the atmosphere. I heard Jamie gag, but he didn't move; his fingers squeezed the thigh hard above the tourniquet. Tench would have bruises there, I thought idly. If he lived long enough for his capillaries to bleed. . . .

The saw had been made to disjoint hogs. Sturdy, not sharp, and not well kept—half the teeth were bent, and it jumped and skittered in my hand, grating over the bone. I clenched my teeth and pushed, my hand slipping on the handle, greased with blood and sweat.

Jamie made a deep, desperate noise and moved suddenly, taking the saw from my hand and nudging me aside. He gripped Tench's knee and bore down on the saw, driving it into the bone by main force. Three, four, five dragging strokes, and the bone, three-quarters sawn through, made a cracking noise that jolted me into action.

"Stop," I said, and he did, white-faced and pouring sweat. "Lift his leg. Carefully." He did, and I made the cut from below, long, deep strokes of the knife deepening the incision at an angle to make the flap, joining the cut with the upper incision. The sheet was wet and dark with blood—but not too much. Either the tourniquet was holding, or the man had so little blood left to lose . . .

"Saw again," I said urgently, discarding the knife. "Hold steady! Both pieces." There was no more than a thin section of bone remaining; the spongy bone of the marrow showed, blood flowering slowly from the cut surface. I put no pressure on the saw; the last thing I wanted was to crack the bone in some awkward way. It wasn't working, though, and I looked back toward the line of tools, desperate to find something else.

"Rasp," Jamie said, his voice rough with strain. He nodded toward the table. "There."

I seized the rasp, a rat-tailed thing, drenched it with brandy, and, turning it sideways, filed through the last bit of bone, which parted gently. With a ragged edge, but intact, not shattered.

"Is he breathing?" I asked. I was having trouble breathing myself, and couldn't sense the patient's vital signs—save to notice his heart was beating, because blood was pulsing slightly out of the smaller vessels—but Arnold nodded, his head bowed, intent on Tench's face.

"He'll do," he said, his voice firm and loud, and I knew he was speaking as much to Tench as to me. Now I could feel the stir in the upper leg, a violent reflexive urge to move, and Jamie leaned hard on it. My fingers brushed the discarded lower leg, the flesh horribly flaccid and rubbery, and I snatched them back, wiping them convulsively on my apron.

I swiped the bloody apron then across my face and pushed back loosened bits of hair with the back of my hand. It was shaking; they both were.

What the bloody hell are you shaking now *for?* I thought irritably. But I was, and it took much longer than it should have to cauterize the last few small bleeders—adding the ghastly smell of roasting flesh to everything else in the room; I thought even General Arnold might throw up—stitch the flaps, bandage the wound, and, at last, loosen the tourniquet.

"All right," I said, and straightened up. "Now . . ." But if I said anything else, I didn't hear it. The room revolved slowly round me and dissolved into a flicker of black and white spots, and then everything went black.

118

THE SECOND LAW OF
THERMODYNAMICS

TENCH LIVED.

"I should have known you would," I said to him. "If you were determined enough to survive all night in the river, plainly a mere amputation wouldn't slow you down."

He hadn't enough strength to laugh—the journey by litter to Chestnut Street had left him white-faced and gasping—but he did twitch his mouth enough to qualify his expression as a smile.

"Oh . . . I'll live," he managed. "Wouldn't . . . give 'em . . . the satis . . . faction . . . of dying." Worn out by this, he closed his eyes, chest heaving. I wiped his face gently with my handkerchief, patted his shoulder, and left him to rest.

I had had the litter bearers take him upstairs, to what had been my bedroom, and I closed the door behind me now with a queerly mixed feeling of triumph and depression.

I had spent the morning with Mrs. Figg and the housemaid, Doreen, packing away what remained of Lord John's furnishings—for many had already been shipped to New York—and rearranging the house to serve as a temporary surgery. Even if we were to leave for North Carolina soon—and the sooner the better—I did have to have someplace to put Tench where he could be looked after in conditions approaching comfort and hygiene. And the patients I had been seeing at the printshop could certainly be taken care of more conveniently here.

At the same time . . . being here again brought back echoes of the numb despair I had lived with all those weeks of believing Jamie dead. I thought the bustle of work and the clean sweep of furnishings would perhaps obviate that distant sense of drowning, but at the moment it was an uneasy swirl around my ankles.

Mental oppression was not the only debilitating condition connected with the new situation. Leaving Number 17 to return to the Shippen house, I had been followed in the street by a gang of young men. Mostly boys, but some big fellows of sixteen or seventeen, big enough to make me uneasy with their glances.

Still more uneasy when they began to draw up close to me, taking a quick step to whisper, "King's whore!" in my ear before falling back, or to try to tread on the hem of my skirt, sniggering.

I thought I had seen one or two of them in the mob when I'd brought Hal here. Perhaps they'd followed me then and, finding that I was married to Lord John, assumed I was a turncoat, a traitor to the Rebel cause. Or possibly, I thought, stiffening my spine, they were just troublemaking pipsqueaks.

I whirled round to face them, gripping my parasol. It wasn't much of a weapon, but no physical weapon would have been of use against so many. Even a twelve-year-old boy was likely stronger than I was at the moment.

"What do you want?" I demanded, using the memory of my matron's voice, whipcrack and steel—or at least I hoped I could still do that.

Some of the little warts blinked and took a step back, but one of the bigger ones took a step toward me, grinning. It took all my control not to recoil.

"I don't know, hinnie," he said, looking me up and down with a lazy insolence. "What does a Loyalist *lady* have that we *might* want?"

"A swift poke in the eye is all I can offer you," I informed him crisply, with a meaningful pointing of my parasol. "Apparently I'm walking too slowly and blocking your progress, gentlemen. Do go on ahead of me." Holding his eye with a menacing stare, I stepped into the street and gestured with my parasol, indicating that they should pass on.

That made some of them giggle, but the big fellow flushed a nasty pink that made his adolescent pimples fluoresce. I stepped back farther into the street, in an imitation of politeness, but actually in hopes of attracting some attention.

I was lucky: a rag-and-bone cart was coming down the road, the horse's hooves clopping on the cobbles, and I moved still farther, blocking the way. The carter, aroused from semi-somnolence, half-stood, peering out from under his hat.

"What the devil are you idle buggers a-doing in the road? Get your fat arses out my way!" He raised his whip in a menacing fashion, and the boys, who had started to advance on me, quickly retreated.

The carter stood up all the way, took off his hat, and bowed to me.

"Good day, your ladyship; I hopes I sees you well. Can I offer you a ride, mayhap?" He was speaking in jest; I didn't think he actually knew I had recently *been* a ladyship. He was certainly surprised when I swept up my skirts and mounted his cart, though.

"Home, James," I said, furling my parasol, "and don't spare the horses."

The recollection made me smile a little, but the smile faded at the thought that the louts who had accosted me certainly lived somewhere nearby. I mightn't be as lucky a second time. And at that thought, a wave of cold terror washed over me and I felt a band of soreness across my middle, the chafing and bruising from hours spent tied facedown across a horse's back, being carried helpless to—

"Stop that!" I said sharply to myself. "Stop it at once. I won't have it." They were teenaged boys. I wasn't afraid of . . . But the first man to rape me had been about sixteen; he'd been apologetic about it. I stepped into a narrow alley between two buildings and threw up.

I'd managed to function. I got back to the Shippens' house and collected my things, then returned to the printshop to eat lunch and pack up the rest of my herbs and medicines; Fergus and Germain would bring them to Chestnut Street on their afternoon delivery round.

No one had molested me on the way back to Chestnut Street. I could have asked Jenny to come with me, but pride prevented me. I would *not* let simpleminded fear stop me doing what needed to be done.

But how long can you keep doing it? And what's the point?

"There's always a point," I muttered. "It's someone's life. That's a point."

A life that could be snatched away, thrown away, frittered on a battlefield . . . How many men had died that way? And it didn't stop, it didn't get better. . . . This was an *early* war, for God's sake. An endless chain of wars lay between my lives: the Revolution here, the Great War at the other end—and constant slaughter in between.

The summer was dying; the air was beginning to have a hint of freshness in the mornings, but in midafternoon it still hung thick and heavy. Too heavy to draw a full breath.

I stood for a moment outside Number 17, feeling unequal to going in and dealing with things. After a moment, I turned down the path that led round the side of the house, out to the tiny garden at the back, and sat down on the bench there, among the roses, feeling most unwell.

I DON'T KNOW how long I had been sitting there, head in my hands, listening to the loud buzzing of bees. But I heard footsteps coming down the path and managed to lift my head.

"Are ye all right, Sassenach?" It was Jamie, the large box of medicines and bandages in his arms. And from the look of alarm on his face, it was reasonably obvious that I didn't look all right. I couldn't muster the energy to try to look all right.

"I just—thought I'd sit down," I said, flapping a hand helplessly.

"I'm glad ye did." He set down the box on the yellowing grass and came to crouch in front of me, examining my face. "What happened?"

"Nothing," I said, and without warning began to cry. Or, rather, to leak. There was nothing of the sobbing, convulsive, racking nature of weeping; tears were just streaking down my cheeks without my approval.

Jamie nudged me over a little and sat down beside me, wrapping his arms around me. He was wearing his old kilt, and the smell of the dusty wool fabric, worn thin with age, made me utterly dissolve.

He tightened his grip and, sighing, pressed his cheek to my head and said small, tender things in Gaelic. And in a little time, the effort to understand them gave me a tenuous grip on myself. I drew a deep breath and he released me, though he kept an arm around me for support.

"Mo nighean donn," he said softly, and smoothed hair out of my face. "Have ye got a hankie?"

That made me laugh. Or rather emit a sort of strangled giggle, but still . . .

"Yes. At least, I think so." I groped in my bosom and withdrew a sturdy square of much-laundered linen, on which I blew my nose several times and then wiped my eyes, trying to think what on earth to offer as an explanation for my disordered state—of mind, as well as body. There wasn't any good way to begin, so I just began.

"Do you ever—well, no. I know you do."

"Likely," he said, smiling a little. "What do I do?"

"See the . . . the void. The abyss." Speaking the words reopened the rent in my soul, and the cold wind came through. A shudder ran through me, in spite of the warmth of the air and Jamie's body. "I mean—it's always there, always yawning at your feet, but most people manage to ignore it, not think about it. I've mostly been able to. You have to, to do medicine." I wiped my nose on my sleeve, having dropped my handkerchief. Jamie pulled a crumpled hankie out of his sleeve and handed it to me.

"Ye dinna mean only death?" he asked. "Because I've seen that often enough. It hasna really scairt me since I was ten or so, though." He glanced down at me and smiled. "And I doubt ye're afraid of it, either. I've seen ye face it down a thousand times and more."

"Facing something down doesn't mean you aren't afraid of it," I said dryly. "Usually quite the opposite. And I *know* you know that."

He made a small sound of agreement in his throat and hugged me gently. I would normally have found this comforting, and the fact that I didn't merely added to my sense of despair.

"It's—it's just . . . *nothing.* And so much endless nothing . . . It's as though nothing you do, nothing you are, can possibly matter, it's all just swallowed up . . ." I closed my eyes, but the darkness behind my eyelids frightened me and I opened them again. "I—" I raised a hand, then let it fall.

"I can't explain," I said, defeated. "It wasn't there—or I wasn't looking at it—after I was shot. It wasn't nearly dying that made me look in, see it yawning there. But being so . . . so bloody *frail*! Being so stinking *afraid.*" I clenched my fists, seeing the knobby bones of my knuckles, the blue veins that stood out on the backs of my hands and curved down my wrists.

"Not death," I said at last, sniffing. "Futility. Uselessness. Bloody entropy. Death *matters*, at least sometimes."

"I ken that," Jamie said softly, and took my hands in his; they were big, and battered, scarred and maimed. "It's why a warrior doesna fear death so much. He has the hope—sometimes the certainty—that his death will matter."

"What happens to me between now and then doesna matter to anyone."

Those words swam out of nowhere and struck me in the pit of the stomach, so hard that I could barely breathe. He'd said that to me, from the bottom of despair, in the dungeon of Wentworth Prison, a lifetime ago. He'd bargained for my life then, with what he had—not his life, already forfeit, but his soul.

"It matters to me!" I'd said to him—and, against all odds, had ransomed that soul and brought him back.

And then it had come again, stark and dire necessity, and he'd laid down his life without hesitation for his men and for the child I carried. And that time I had been the one who sacrificed my soul. And it had mattered, for both of us.

It still mattered. And the shell of fear cracked like an egg and everything inside me poured out like blood and water mingled and I sobbed on his chest until there were no more tears and no more breath. I leaned against him, limp as a dishcloth, and watched the crescent moon begin to rise in the east.

"What did you say?" I said, rousing myself after a long while. I felt groggy and disoriented, but at peace.

"I asked, what's entropy?"

"Oh," I said, momentarily disconcerted. When had the concept of entropy been invented? Not yet, obviously. "It's, um . . . a lack of order, a lack of predictability, an inability for a system to do work."

"A system of what?"

"Well, there you have me," I admitted, sitting up and wiping my nose. "Just an ideal sort of system, with heat energy. The Second Law of Thermodynamics basically says that in an isolated system—one that's not getting energy from somewhere outside, I mean—entropy will always increase. I think it's just a scientific way of saying that everything is going to pot, all of the time."

He laughed, and despite my shattered state of mind, I did, too.

"Aye, well, far be it from me to argue wi' the Second Law of Thermodynamics," he said. "I think it's likely right. When did ye last eat, Sassenach?"

"I don't know," I said. "I'm not hungry." I didn't want to do anything but sit still beside him.

"D'ye see the sky?" he said, a little later. It was a pure deep violet at the horizon, fading into a blue-black immensity overhead, and the early stars burned like distant lamps.

"Hard to miss," I said.

"Aye." He sat with his head tilted back, looking up, and I admired the clean line of his long, straight nose, his soft wide mouth and long throat, as though seeing them for the first time.

"Is it not a void there?" he said quietly, still looking up. "And yet we're no afraid to look."

"There are lights," I said. "It makes a difference." My voice was hoarse, and I swallowed. "Though I suppose even the stars are burning out, according to the Second Law."

"Mmphm. Well, I suppose men can make all the laws they like," he said, "but God made hope. The stars willna burn out." He turned and, cupping my chin, kissed me gently. "And nor will we."

The noises of the city were muted now, though even darkness didn't stifle it entirely. I heard distant voices and the sound of a fiddle: a party, perhaps, from one of the houses down the street. And the bell of St. George's struck the hour with a small, flat *bong*! Nine o'clock. And all's well.

"I'd better go and see to my patient," I said.

119

"ALAS, POOR YORICK!"

September 17, 1778
Middlebrook Encampment, New Jersey

TWO NIGHTS LATER, William stood at the edge of a dark wood, watching a lopsided rising moon shed its light over Middlebrook Encampment. His heart was thumping in his ears and he was breathing fast, his hands clenched around the handle of the spade he'd just stolen.

He'd been correct in his assessment of his welcome. He'd roughened his accent and, posing as a young immigrant from England interested in joining Washington's troops, he'd been invited to join the Hamilton family for supper and given a bed for the night. The next day, he'd walked up to Middlebrook Encampment with the eldest Hamilton son, a man about his own age, where he'd been introduced to a Captain Ronson, one of the few officers still there.

One thing had led to another, and, by degrees, he had steered the conversation to the battle at Brandywine Creek and thence to British prisoners of war . . . and eventually he'd been taken to the small burying ground that lay before him now.

He'd been cautious about Ben, mentioning his name only casually among several others—family acquaintances, he'd said, that he'd heard had been at the battle. Some of the men he talked to hadn't recognized the name at all; two or three said, oh, yes, the English viscount, prisoner, billeted with a family called Tobermory, very civil fellow, shame that he'd died. . . .

And one man, a Lieutenant Corey, had said the same thing but his eyes had flickered slightly when he said it. William was wise enough to abandon the subject at once—but brought up Captain Benjamin Grey with someone else, much later and out of hearing of Corey.

"Is he buried nearby?" he'd asked, with a decent assumption of casual concern. "I know his family. I should like to be able to write to them, tell them I'd visited, you know. . . ."

It had taken some effort; the burying ground was well outside the encampment, up on a little wooded knoll, and while some of the graves were neatly ranked, others had been dug hastily, and many were unmarked. His companion was not busy, though, and of a helpful complexion; he went and unearthed the adjutant's ledger in which the dead were listed and, with some poking about, eventually led William to a flattened mound with a piece of lath stuck into it, on which GREY had been scratched with a nail.

"Lucky you came before another winter got at it," his companion had remarked, pulling the lath out and examining it critically. He shook his head, reached into his pocket, and, fetching out a lead pencil, reinforced the name with strong, scrubbing strokes before pushing it back into the earth. "Maybe that will last a bit, in case the family should want to set up a stone."

"That's . . . very good of you," William had said, his throat tight. "I'll tell his family of your kindness." But he couldn't weep for a man he theoretically hadn't known and so swallowed his emotions and turned away, finding something commonplace to talk about as they made their way downhill.

He *had* wept in private, later, leaning against the comforting bulk of the mare, whom he'd named Miranda. She wasn't sprightly, but she was a good horse, and merely whuffed a little and shifted her weight to give him support.

He'd been stubbornly insisting to himself that there must be some mistake. Ben *couldn't* be dead. This belief had been sustained by Uncle Hal's complete refusal to believe the news. And it was plausible; whatever Ezekiel Richardson was up to, he meant no good to the Greys.

But here was Ben's grave, silent and muddy, speckled with the first yellowing leaves of September. And all around him lay the decaying bodies of other men, some prisoners, some Continental regulars, some militia . . . equal, and equally alone in death.

He'd eaten dinner that night with the Hamiltons again, replying automatically to their conversation but concerned with his own misery—and the thought of the much greater misery to come when he had to return to New York and tell his father and Uncle Hal. . . .

William had taken leave of the Hamiltons next morning, consigning the remains of the deer to them, and was followed down the narrow road by their good wishes and hopes that they would see him again with General Washington, when the troops came back to Middlebrook to winter. He'd made it several miles down the mountain, dragging his spirit behind him, when he stopped to take a piss.

He'd been hunting once with Ben, and they'd stopped like this; Ben had told him a particularly scabrous joke, and he'd laughed so much that he couldn't piss and Ben had pissed on his shoes, which made them both laugh harder, and . . .

"God damn it," he said aloud, and, buttoning his flies, stamped back to Miranda and swung up into the saddle. "I'm sorry, owd lass," he said, reining her head around to face uphill. "We're going back."

And here he was, wavering between the conviction that this was madness and the stark fact that there wasn't anything else he could do besides go back to New York, and he wouldn't do that until and unless he had no other choice. At least he might be able to salvage a lock of Ben's hair for Aunt Minnie. . . .

That thought made him want to throw up, but he touched the knife at his waist, took a firmer hold of the spade, and made his way gingerly in among the graves.

The moonlight was bright enough to find footing but not to read most of the markers. He had to kneel and run his thumb over several before feeling the letters G-R-E-Y.

"Right," he said out loud. His voice sounded small and choked, and he cleared his throat and spat—to the side, not on the grave. "Right," he said again, more forcefully, and, standing, took up the spade and drove it into the earth.

He'd started close to what he thought should be the head, but dug in from the side—the thought of driving his spade down into Ben's face made his flesh creep. The dirt was soft, damp with recent rain, but it was heavy work, and despite the coolness of the mountain night, he was soaked with sweat before he'd dug a quarter of an hour. If Ben had died of camp fever, as they said—and come to think, was that sensible? He hadn't been held in the stockade with the enlisted men. As an officer, he'd been billeted with the Tobermorys. How had he come to catch camp fever? But still, if he had, then others would have died at the same time; it was a badly infectious sort of plague, he knew that much.

But if *that* were true, then a number of other men would have been buried at the same time, and buried hastily, to prevent contagion from the bodies. (Oh, *there* was a good thought: he might be opening a grave full of teeming pestilence. . . .) Anyway, if that were the case, the graves would be shallow ones.

This one was. His spade struck something harder than dirt, and he stopped abruptly, muscles quivering. He swallowed and resumed shoveling, more cautiously.

The body had been wrapped in a shroud of coarse burlap. He couldn't see, but a ginger probing with his fingers told him as much. Squatting, he dug with his hands, unearthing what he hoped was the head. His stomach was clenched tight and he was breathing through his mouth. The stink was less than he'd expected, but still definitely there.

Oh, God. Ben . . . He'd been nursing the hope that the grave was empty.

Patting and probing, he made out the rounded shape and took a deep breath, feeling for the edge of the shroud. Had it been stitched? No, the edge was loose.

He'd thought of bringing a torch but had dismissed the idea, not wanting to risk detection. On the whole, he was glad he hadn't. He wiped dirt from his hands onto his breeches and peeled the burlap gently back, grimacing as it stuck to the skin beneath. It came loose with a grisly, rasping sound, and he nearly dropped it and ran. But he steeled himself and touched the dead man's face.

It wasn't as awful as he'd thought it might be; the body seemed largely still intact. *How long will a man lie i' the earth ere he rot?* What had the gravedigger said in reply—nine years? Well, then . . . He'd seen *Hamlet* with Ben and Adam, in London. . . .

William fought back an insane urge to laugh and felt gently over the dead features. The nose was broad and stubby, not Ben's sharp beak—but no doubt the process of decay . . . He slid his fingers over the temple, thinking to see if a presentable lock of hair might—and stopped dead, not breathing.

The corpse was missing an ear. Bloody hell, it was missing *both* ears. He felt again, both sides, unable to believe it. But it was true—and the ears had been missing for some time; even with the nasty slack feel of the decaying flesh, the ridges of scar tissue were distinct. A thief.

William sat back on his heels and tilted up his head, letting out a huge breath. He felt dizzy, and the stars made little pinwheels in his vision.

"Jesus," he breathed, flooded with relief, gratitude, and creeping horror. "Oh, Jesus, thank you! And, oh, Christ," he added, looking down at the invisible stranger in Ben's grave, "*now* what?"

120

A CRACKLING OF THORNS

September 18, 1778
Philadelphia

I WAS HAVING A pleasantly incoherent dream involving autumn leaves and fireflies. The fireflies were red, rather than green, and were floating down through the trees like live sparks, and where they brushed against the yellow leaves, the edges browned and curled as the leaves caught fire. Smoke curled upward through the trees, lazy against an evening sky, pungent as tobacco, and I was walking underneath, smoking a cigarette with Frank . . .

I woke muzzily, thinking how nice it was to see Frank again, followed abruptly by *Dreams don't smell, do they?* along with *I don't smoke,* and then—

"Jesus! We're on fire!" I sat up, panicked and wriggling to get out of the sheets. Smoke was already thick in the loft, drifting layers above my head, and Jamie was coughing, grabbing my arm and dragging me free before I could locate all my limbs.

"Quick," he said, hoarse as a crow. "Dinna wait to dress, come down!"

I didn't dress, but did seize my shift and pulled it over my head as I crawled toward the edge of the loft. Jamie had the ladder over the edge as I reached it and was already started down, shouting in a loud, cracked voice.

I could hear the fire. It rattled and crackled, and the ashy smell of burning paper and the stink of singed buckram was thick in the air.

"In the shop," I gasped, catching up with Jamie in the kitchen. "It's in the shop. The Bibles are burning—the typefoundry . . ."

"Get the weans." He ran across the kitchen, shirttails flying, and slammed shut the door that led into the printshop, from which smoke was fuming in clouds. I ran the other way, into the room that served Fergus and Marsali as living and sleeping quarters, with a smaller loft above, where the children and Jenny slept.

That door was shut, thank God. The smoke hadn't yet reached them. I flung it open, shouting, "Fire! Fire! Get up, get up!" and ran for the ladder to the loft, hearing Fergus swear behind me in French and Marsali's confused "What? *WHAT?*"

My hands were sweating and slipped on the smooth wooden rails of the ladder.

"Jenny! Germain!" I bellowed—or tried to. Smoke was drifting here, too, high up under the roof, and I was coughing, my eyes and nose running.

"Jo-hoan!"

There was one small bedstead, two little humps under the bedclothes. I ran to the bed, flinging back the covers. Joan and Félicité were curled together, Félicité's nightdress rucked up to show her little bottom. I grabbed her by the shoulder, shaking her and trying to speak calmly.

"Girls, girls! You have to get up. Right now. Do you hear me, Joan? Wake up!"

Joan's eyelids were fluttering, and she was coughing, turning her head to and fro to escape the smoke, eyes stubbornly closed. Félicité normally slept like the dead, and tonight was no exception; her head wobbled like her rag doll's when I shook her.

"What? What is it?" Jenny was struggling out of the quilts on her pallet in the corner.

"We're on fire!" I shouted. "Hurry—help me!"

I heard a cracking noise from the kitchen and a scream from Marsali. I didn't know what had happened, but in desperation I grabbed Félicité bodily out of bed, still shouting at Joan to wake up, for God's sake!

I felt the vibration of the ladder against the loft and Jamie was there, snatching Joan up out of the bed.

"The lads, where are the lads?" he asked urgently. In the frantic need to wake the girls, I'd forgotten Germain and Henri-Christian. I looked round in an urgent daze; there was a thin mattress on the floor, flattened and dented by bodies, but no sign of the boys.

"Germain! Joan! Henri-Christian!" Marsali's face popped up over the edge of the loft, pale with fear. "Félicité!" In an instant, she was with me, taking Félicité from me. The little girl was coughing and whining, starting to cry.

"It's all right, *a nighean*, it's all right; you're safe, aye?" Marsali was patting her back, coughing herself as the smoke thickened. "Where are the boys?"

Jamie had shoved Jenny onto the ladder and was following her down, Joan draped over his shoulder, small pink feet kicking urgently.

"I'll find them!" I said, pushing Marsali toward the ladder. "Take Félicité down!"

Something in the shop exploded with a loud *whoosh*—probably a barrel of ink, made with varnish and lampblack. Marsali gasped, clutched Félicité hard, and scuttled for the ladder. I began rootling madly through the bits of furniture and boxes and bags in the loft, calling the boys' names between fits of coughing.

The smoke was much worse now; I could barely see. I was kicking my way through blankets, a chamber pot—unfortunately full—and other things, but there was no sign of Henri-Christian or Germain. Even if they'd been overcome by the smoke, surely—

"Sassenach!" Jamie was suddenly there by my elbow. "Come down, come down! The fire's in the wall; the loft will come down any minute!"

"But—"

He didn't wait for argument, but picked me up bodily and swung me down onto the ladder. I missed my footing and slid the last few feet, knees buckling as I hit the floor. The wall in front of me was alight, plaster shattered and the fire moving, glowing along the edges of the laths. Jamie landed beside me with a thud that shook the floor, seized my arm, and we ran for the kitchen.

I heard a rending crack and then a crash that seemed to happen in slow motion, as the supports to the children's loft gave way and the timbers came down.

"Germain," I gasped. "Henri—"

"Not here," Jamie said, and shook with coughing. "Out, we must get out." The air in the kitchen was a little clearer, but not by much. It was hot enough to sear the hairs inside my nose. Eyes streaming, we made our way across the room to the back door, now standing open, and more or less fell through into the alleyway behind.

Marsali and Jenny were crouched in the privy yard of the house on the other side of the alley, both girls now awake and clinging to them, shrieking.

"Where's Fergus?" Jamie shouted, pushing me toward Marsali. She pointed toward the burning building, screaming something that I couldn't hear over the rumble of the fire. Then there was a second's respite in the noise, and a long, panicked bray split the night air.

"Clarence!" Jamie spun on his heel and ran for the tiny stable, little more than a shed next to the main building. I ran after him, thinking that perhaps the boys had taken refuge there. My bare feet slid on the cobbles, stubbing my toes, but I scarcely noticed, my heart pounding in my ears with fear, lungs laboring to find fresh air.

"Germain!" I heard the shout, faint above the fire, and turned to see a shadow moving just beyond the open door into the kitchen. Smoke was pouring from the door in a thick white column, glowing from the fire beyond. I took a deep gulp of air and dived into the smoke, flailing my arms in a vain effort to dispel enough to see.

One of my flailing arms struck something solid, though, and Fergus collapsed into me, so far overcome with heat and smoke that he couldn't stand. I grabbed him under the arms and dragged him toward the door with that sort of strength that comes from the absolute determination not to die.

We fell out into the alley, and there were shouts from what proved to be neighbors rushing to help. Hands gripped me and pulled me away. I could hear Fergus, gasping and sobbing, struggling against the helpful hands, desperately croaking his sons' names.

Through streaming eyes, I saw the stable roof alight and Jamie leading Clarence out, the torn-off sleeve of his shirt wrapped round the mule's eyes.

And then I heard a shriek that rose above all the noise, fire, neighbors, Clarence's bray. Marsali stood up straight, eyes and mouth round with horror, looking up.

The loading door that led to the kitchen loft was open, smoke and sparks fuming out, and in the midst of it was Germain, dragging Henri-Christian by the hand.

He shouted something, but no one could hear above the racket. There was a muffled *boom* from the loft as another cask went, and the fire blazed up suddenly as the stacks of paper caught, silhouetting the boys in the doorway.

"Jump! Jump!" Jamie was shouting, and everyone else in the alley was shouting it, too, people shoving one another in the effort to get underneath, to help. Germain looked wildly to and fro; Henri-Christian was panicked, struggling to go back into the loft. The rope used to raise and lower loads to a waiting wagon was there, almost within reach. Germain saw it and let go of Henri-Christian for an instant to reach for it, hanging on to the edge of the doorframe.

He got it, and a gasp went through the crowd. His fair hair was standing on end in the wind from the fire, surrounding his head like flames, and for an instant I thought it *was* on fire.

Henri-Christian, dizzy from the smoke, had fallen against the doorframe and was clinging to it. He was too frightened to move; I could see him shaking his head as Germain pulled at him.

"Throw him, Germain! Throw your brother!" Fergus was shouting as loudly as he could, his voice cracking with the strain, and several other voices joined in. "Throw him!"

I saw Germain's jaw set hard, and he yanked Henri-Christian loose, picked him up, and clutched him with one arm, wrapping the rope around the other.

"No!" Jamie bellowed, seeing it. "Germain, *don't*!" But Germain bent his head over his brother's, and I thought I saw his lips move, saying, *"Hold on tight!"* And then he stepped out into the air, both hands clinging to the rope, Henri-Christian's stocky legs wrapped round his ribs.

It happened instantly and yet so slowly. Henri-Christian's short legs lost their grip. Germain's grab failed, for the little boy was already falling, arms outstretched, in a half somersault through the smoky air.

He fell straight through the sea of upraised hands, and the sound as his head struck the cobbles was the sound of the end of the world.

121

WALKING ON COALS

September 19, 1778
Philadelphia

EVEN WHEN THE world ends, things bloody go on *happening*. You just don't know what to do about them.

Everything smelled of smoke and burning. The air, my hair, Jamie's skin, the ill-fitting gown someone had given me . . . Even food tasted of ashes. But, then, it would, wouldn't it? I reflected. It didn't matter; I couldn't eat more than the mouthful or two required for politeness.

No one had slept. The printshop had burned to the ground in the small hours; there was nothing to be done but to beat off flying embers and stamp out sparks in an effort to preserve the nearby houses. By a mercy, it hadn't been a windy night.

The neighbors had given us shelter, clothes, food, and abundant sympathy. None of it seemed real, and I hoped in a vague sort of way that this state of things would continue, even though I knew it couldn't.

What did seem real, though, was the small collection of vivid images that had been literally seared on my mind during the night. Henri-Christian's bare feet, dirty-soled and large in comparison with his legs, sticking out from under his mother's skirt as she cradled him, rocking to and fro, wrapped in a grief too dense for any sound to escape it. Germain, letting go the rope in a frantic attempt to fly after his brother, dropping like a rock into Fergus's arms. Fergus clutching Germain so hard against him that it must have bruised them both, his hook gleaming against Germain's soot-streaked back.

The boys had been sleeping on the roof. There was a small trapdoor in the ceiling of the bedroom loft, which no one had remembered in the panic of the fire.

When Germain began finally to talk, sometime toward dawn, he said they had gone out to be cool and to look at the stars. They had fallen asleep and not waked until the slates they lay on began to feel hot—and by then smoke was rolling up through the cracks of the trapdoor. They'd run across the roof to the other side, where a similar trapdoor let them into the printing loft. Half the loft had fallen away and the rest was on fire, but they'd made it through the smoke and rubble to the loading door.

"Why?" he'd cried, passed from one set of arms to another, ignoring all futile words of would-be comfort. "Why didn't I hold on to him?! He was too little; he couldn't hold on."

Only his mother hadn't embraced him. She held Henri-Christian and wouldn't let go until daylight came and sheer exhaustion loosened her grasp. Fergus and Jamie had eased the small, chunky body from her grip and taken him away to be washed and made decent for the long business of being dead. Then Marsali had come to find her eldest son and touched him gently in his deadened sleep, sorrowing.

The Reverend Figg had once more come to our aid, a small neat figure in his black suit and high white stock, offering his church in which to hold the wake.

I was sitting in the church now, in midafternoon, alone, on a bench with my back against a wall, smelling smoke and trembling intermittently with echoes of flame and loss.

Marsali was asleep in a neighbor's bed. I had tucked her in, her daughters curled up on either side of her, Félicité sucking her thumb, round black eyes watchful as those of her rag doll, fortuitously saved from the flames. So few things had survived. I remembered the constant pang of loss after the Big House had burned, reaching for something and realizing that it wasn't there.

Jenny, worn to the gray-white color of weathered bone, had gone to lie down at the Figgs' house, her rosary in her hands, the wooden beads sliding smoothly through her fingers as she walked, her lips moving silently; I doubted that she would stop praying, even in her sleep.

People came and went, bringing things. Tables, extra benches, platters of food. Late-summer flowers, roses and jasmine and early blue asters, and for the first time, tears ran down my cheeks at this scented remembrance of the wedding held here so little time before. I pressed a stranger's handkerchief to my face, though, not wanting anyone to see and feel that they must try to comfort me.

The bench beside me creaked and gave, and I peeped over the edge of my handkerchief to see Jamie beside me, wearing a worn suit that plainly belonged to a chairman—it had a band round the coat sleeve reading "82"—and with his face washed but the whorls of his ears still grimed with soot. He took my hand and held it tight, and I saw the blisters on his fingers, some fresh, some burst and shredded from the efforts to save what could be saved from the fire.

He looked to the front of the church, toward what couldn't be saved, then sighed and looked down to our clasped hands.

"All right, lass?" His voice was hoarse, his throat raw and soot-choked as my own.

"Yes," I said. "Have you had anything to eat?" I already knew he hadn't slept.

He shook his head and leaned back against the wall, closing his eyes, and I felt the relaxation of his body into momentary exhaustion. There were things still to be done, but just for a moment . . . I wanted to dress his hands, but there was nothing to dress them with. I lifted the hand he held and kissed his knuckles.

"What do ye think it's like when ye die?" he asked suddenly, opening his eyes and looking down at me. His eyes were red as an emery bag.

"I can't say I've really thought about it," I replied, taken aback. "Why?"

He rubbed two fingers slowly between his brows; I thought from the look of him that his head must ache.

"I only wondered if it's like this." He made a brief gesture, encompassing the half-empty room, the well-wishers coming and going in whispers, the mourners sitting, blank-faced and sagging like bags of rubbish, stirring—with a visible effort—only when spoken to. "If ye dinna ken what to do, and ye dinna much want to do anything. Or is it like going to sleep and wakin' up in a new, fresh place and wanting to go out at once and see what it's like?"

"According to Father O'Neill, innocents are just in the presence of God immediately. No limbo, no purgatory. Assuming they were properly baptized," I added. Henri-Christian had indeed been baptized, and as he was not yet seven, the Church held that he lacked sufficient sense of reason to commit sins. Ergo . . .

"I've known people in their fifties who had less sense than Henri-Christian," I said, wiping my nose for the thousandth time. My nostrils were as raw as my eyelids.

"Aye, but they've more capacity for causing harm wi' their foolishness." A faint smile touched his mouth. "I thought I was dead on Culloden field; did I ever tell ye that?"

"I don't think you did. Under the circumstances, I suppose it would have been a reasonable assumption, though—were you knocked out?"

He nodded, eyes fixed on the floorboards.

"Aye. If I'd been able to look about, I should have known better, but my eyes were sealed shut wi' the blood. It was all red and dim, so I supposed I was in purgatory and would just have to wait 'til someone came round to chastise me. After a bit, I supposed boredom was meant to be part of the punishment." He glanced at the tiny coffin on its bench at the front of the room. Germain sat by it, one hand on its lid. He hadn't moved at all in the last half hour.

"I've never seen Henri-Christian bored," I said quietly, after a moment. "Not once."

"No," Jamie said softly, and took my hand. "I dinna suppose he ever will be."

Gaelic wakes have their own rhythm. Fergus and Marsali came in quietly an hour or so later and sat together at first, holding hands near the coffin, but as more people came, the men gradually surrounded Fergus, absorbing him, much as a gang of phagocytes surround a microbe, carrying it along with them, and after a time, as happens normally in such situations, half the men were at one side of the room, talking quietly, and the others outside, unable to bear close quarters and exigent emotion but wanting to lend their presence and sympathy.

The women clustered, first near Marsali, hugging and weeping, then gathering in small clumps with their friends, drifting back to the tables to rearrange things or put out more bread or cakes. Josiah Prentice came with his fiddle, but left it in its case for the time being. Tobacco smoke from the pipes of the men outside drifted through the church in soft blue clouds. It tickled uneasily at the back of my nose, too reminiscent of the fire for comfort.

Jamie left me with a brief squeeze of the hand and went to speak to Ian. I saw them both look at Germain; Ian nodded and moved quietly to his nephew, putting both hands on his shoulders. Rachel hovered nearby, dark eyes watchful.

The bench beside me creaked, and Jenny sat down. Wordless, she put her arm about my shoulder, and equally wordless, I bent my head to hers and we wept for a bit—not only for Henri-Christian but for the babies we each had lost, my stillborn Faith, her infant Caitlin. And for Marsali, now joining us in this sorrowful kinship.

The night drew in, beer and ale were poured, some stronger drink was brought out, and the somber mood of the gathering lifted a little. Still, it was the wake of a child and a life cut short; there couldn't be the sense of shared memory and laughter that there might be for a man who had lived a full life and whose friends had come to share in his death.

Josiah Prentice played his fiddle, but quietly, mixing laments with peaceful tunes and the occasional hymn; there wouldn't be much singing tonight. I wished suddenly and fiercely that Roger were here. He would perhaps have known what to say, in a situation where there was nothing one could say. And even with his ruined voice, he would have known a song to sing, a prayer to offer.

Father O'Neill from St. George's Church had come, tactfully overlooking the unorthodox Quaker marriage of a month before, and stood talking near the door with Fergus and a few other men.

"Poor wee child," Jenny said, her voice roughened by tears but steady now. She was holding my hand, and I hers, and she was looking not at the coffin but at Fergus. "His bairns mean everything to him—and especially our wee man." Her lips trembled, but she pressed them together and straightened her back.

"D'ye think Marsali's breedin'?" she said, very softly, looking at Marsali, with Joan and Félicité clinging to her skirts, Joan's head in her lap. Her mother's hand rested on her hair, gently smoothing it.

"I do," I said, as softly.

She nodded, and her hand twitched, half hidden in the folds of her skirt, making the horns against evil.

More people had come. The Congress was meeting in Philadelphia, and several delegates who did business with Fergus had come. Jonas Phillips and Samuel Adams were both there, chatting by the refreshments table. In a different frame of mind, I might have marveled at being in the same room with two signers of the Declaration of Independence, but, after all, they were only men—though I took it kindly that they'd come.

I looked for Germain every few minutes; now he was standing by the tables with Ian, drinking something from a cup. I blinked and looked again.

"Jesus H— I mean, good Lord. Ian's giving Germain cherry bounce!"

Jenny glanced at Germain's bright red lips, and a quiver of amusement ran through her.

"Canna think of anything better for the lad just now, can you?"

"Well . . . no." I stood up, shaking out my skirts. "D'you want some?"

"I do," she said, and got up with alacrity. "And maybe a wee bite, too. It'll be a long night; we'll need a bit to sustain us, aye?"

It felt better to be up and moving. The fog of grief still numbed sensation, and I didn't look forward to its passing, but at the same time . . . I realized that I *was* hungry now.

The feeling in the room shifted gradually, from the first impact of shock and sorrow, to comforting support for the family, and now to more-general talk. Which was, I realized uneasily, beginning to focus on speculation as to what—or who—had caused the fire.

In the shock and grief of the event, none of us had spoken of it, but even through that numbing fog, the insidious question had hovered like a bat overhead: Why? How? And . . . who?

If anyone. Fire was a common plague in a time when every household had open hearths, and a printshop, with its type forge and its stock of inflammables, was still more vulnerable to simple accident. An open window, a stray breeze, loose papers blowing . . . a spitting ember from a badly smoored fire catching hold . . .

And yet.

The memory of the anonymous letter floated queasily on the surface of my mind. *Your house is on fire and your children are gone . . .*

And the young men who had followed me from Chestnut Street, their stealthy plucking and whispered taunts. God, could I have brought their enmity to Fergus's door?

Jamie had come to stand by me again, steady and solid as a rock, and handed me a fresh cup of cherry bounce. It was like drinking very strong cough syrup, but it was undeniably bracing. Up to the point where you fell down insensible, at least. I saw that Germain had slid slowly down the wall; Rachel knelt next to him and eased him to the ground, then folded her shawl and put it under his head.

The cherry bounce was taking the place of the fog; I thought drunkenness was probably an improvement, on the whole.

"Mrs. Fraser?" A strange voice on my left drew my attention from bemused contemplation of the dark-red depths of my cup. A young man in shabby clothes was standing at my elbow, a small package in his hand.

"She is," Jamie said, giving the young man a searching look. "Are ye needing a physician? Because—"

"Oh, no, sir," the young man assured him, obsequious. "I was told to give this into Mrs. Fraser's hand, that's all." He handed it to me and, with a short bow, turned and left.

Puzzled, and slow with fatigue, grief, and cherry bounce, I fumbled with the string, then gave up and handed the package to Jamie, who reached for his knife, failed to find it—for it had, of course, perished in the fire—and, with a flicker of annoyance, simply broke the string. The wrapping fell open to reveal a small leather purse and a note, folded but unsealed.

I blinked and squinted for a moment, then dipped a hand into my pocket. By a miracle, my spectacles had been downstairs, left behind in the kitchen when I took them off while chopping onions, and Jamie had retrieved them in his hurried foray into the burning house. The stylish handwriting sprang into reassuring clarity.

Mrs. Fraser,

> *I cannot think my Presence would be welcome and I would not intrude on private Grief. I ask nothing, neither Acknowledgment nor Obligation. I do ask that you would allow me to help in the only way that I can and that you will not reveal the Source of this Assistance to the younger Mr. Fraser. I trust your Discretion, as to the Elder.*

It was signed simply, *P. Wainwright (Beauchamp).*

I raised my brows at Jamie and passed him the note. He read it, lips pressed tight together, but glanced at Marsali and the girls, now clustered with Jenny, talking to Mrs. Phillips, all of them crying quietly. Then across the room, to Fergus, flanked by Ian and Rachel. He grimaced very briefly, but his features set in resignation. There was a family to provide for; he couldn't, for the moment, afford pride.

"Well, it probably wasn't him, then," I said, with a sigh, and tucked the little purse into the pocket under my skirt. Numbed as I was, I still felt a vague sense of relief at that. Whatever he might be, might have done, or might intend, I still rather liked the erstwhile Monsieur Beauchamp.

I had no time to consider Percy further, though, for at this point there was a stir among the people near the door, and, looking to see what had caused it, I saw George Sorrel come in.

It was apparent at a glance that the tavern owner had been availing himself of his own wares—possibly as a means of getting up his courage, for he stood swaying slightly, fists clenched at his sides, looking slowly round the room, belligerently meeting the stares that greeted him.

Jamie said something very unsuitable in a house of God under his breath in Gaelic, and started toward the door. Before he could reach it, though, Fergus had turned to see the cause of the stir and had spotted Sorrel.

Fergus was no more sober than Sorrel but was much more upset. He stiffened for an instant, but then pulled himself free of the grasping hands of his supporters and headed for Sorrel without a word, red-eyed as a hunting ferret and just as dangerous.

He hit Sorrel with his fist as the man was opening his mouth. Unsteady as they were, both of them staggered from the impact, and men rushed in to separate them. Jamie reached Sorrel and, grabbing his arm, jerked him out of the scrum.

"I suggest that ye leave, sir," he said, politely, under the circumstances, and turned the man firmly toward the door.

"Don't," Fergus said. He was breathing like a train, sweat pouring down his chalk-white face. "Don't go. Stay—and tell me why. Why have you come here? How dare you come here?" This last was uttered in a cracked shout that made Sorrel blink and take a step backward. He shook his head doggedly, though, and drew himself up.

"I came to—to offer Mrs. Fraser con-condol—to say I was sorry about her son," he said sullenly. "And you ain't a-going to stop me, either, you farting French son of a bitch!"

"You offer my wife nothing," Fergus said, shaking with fury. "Nothing, do you hear? Who is to say you did not set the fire yourself? To kill me, to seize upon my wife? *Salaud!*"

I would have bet money that Sorrel didn't know what a *salaud* was, but it didn't matter; he went the color of beetroot and lunged at Fergus. He didn't reach him, as Jamie managed to grab his collar, but there was a sound of rending cloth and Sorrel jerked to a stop, staggering.

There was a rumble through the room, men and women gathering in a thundercloud of disapproval. I could see Jamie drawing himself up and in, settling himself to haul Sorrel out before someone besides Fergus took a swing at him. A certain shuffling readiness suggested that a number of men had it in mind.

And then Rachel walked between the two men. She was very pale, though a red spot burned in each cheek, and her hands were clenched in the fabric of her skirt.

"Does thee indeed come to offer comfort, friend?" she said to Sorrel, in a voice that shook only a little. "For if that is so, thee ought to offer it to all of those who are met here for the sake of the child. Particularly to his father."

She turned toward Fergus, reaching to put a careful hand on his sleeve.

"Thee will not see thy wife distressed further, I know," she said quietly. "Will thee not go to her now? For while she is grateful for the presence of so many kind folk, it is only thee she wants."

Fergus's face worked, anguish and fury warring with confusion. Seeing him unable to decide what to do or how to do it, Rachel moved closer and took his arm, tucking her hand into the curve of his elbow, and compelled him to turn and to walk with her, the crowd parting in front of them. I saw the curve of Marsali's blond head as she raised it slowly, her face changing as she watched Fergus come.

Jamie took a deep breath and released Sorrel.

"Well?" he said quietly. "Stay or go. As ye will."

Sorrel was still panting a little but had himself in hand now. He nodded jerkily, drew himself up, and straightened his torn coat. Then he walked through the silent crowd, head up, to give his sympathies to the bereaved.

122

HALLOWED GROUND

I N SPITE OF THE neighbors' generosity, there was very little to pack. Nor was there any reason to linger in Philadelphia. Our life there was ended.

There was—there always is—considerable speculation as to the cause of the fire. But after the outburst at the wake, a sense of flat finality had settled over all of us. The neighbors would continue to talk, but among the family there was an unspoken agreement that it made little difference whether the fire had been pure accident or someone's ill design. Nothing would bring Henri-Christian back. Nothing else mattered.

Jamie had taken Fergus to make the arrangements for our travel: not because he needed assistance but as a way of keeping Fergus moving, lest he simply sit down by Henri-Christian's small coffin and never rise again.

Things were both easier and harder for Marsali. She had children to care for, children who needed her badly.

Rachel and I packed what there was to pack, bought food for the journey, and dealt with the final details of leaving. I packed the bits and bobs of my surgery and, with mutual tears and embraces, gave the keys of Number 17 Chestnut Street to Mrs. Figg.

And in the early afternoon of the day following the wake, we borrowed a small cart, hitched up Clarence, and followed Henri-Christian to his grave.

There hadn't been any discussion as to the burial. After the wake, Ian had simply stood up and said, "I know where he must rest."

It was a long way, perhaps two hours' walk outside the city. The heat had broken at last, though, and the air moved gently over us, with the first cool touch of autumn. There was no ceremony to our procession; no Gaelic laments for a life cut short, no professional wailing. Only a small family, walking together for the last time.

We left the road at Ian's signal. Jamie unhitched Clarence and hobbled him to graze, then he and Fergus lifted the coffin and followed Ian into the whisper of the trees, along a small and hidden path made by the hooves of deer, and so upward to a small clearing in the forest.

There were two large cairns there, knee-high. And a smaller one, at the edge of the clearing, under the branches of a red cedar. A flat stone lay against it, the word ROLLO scratched into it.

Fergus and Jamie set down the little coffin, gently. Joanie and Félicité had stopped crying during the long walk, but seeing it there, so small and forlorn, facing the thought of walking away . . . they began to weep silently, clinging hard to each other, and at the sight of them, grief rose in me like a fountain.

Germain was holding hard to his mother's hand, mute and jaw-set, tearless. Not seeking support, giving it, though the agony showed clear in his eyes as they rested on his brother's coffin.

Ian touched Marsali's arm gently.

"This place is hallowed by my sweat and my tears, cousin," he said softly. "Let us hallow it also by our blood and let our wee lad rest here safe in his family. If he canna go with us, we will abide with him."

He took the *sgian dubh* from his stocking and drew it across his wrist, lightly, then held his arm above Henri-Christian's coffin, letting a few drops fall on the wood. I could hear the sound of it, like the beginning of rain.

Marsali drew a shattered breath, stood straight, and took the knife from his hand.

PART EIGHT

Search and Rescue

123

QUOD SCRIPSI, SCRIPSI

*From Mrs. Abigail Bell, Savannah, the Royal Colony of Georgia
To Mr. James Fraser, Philadelphia, Colony of Pennsylvania*

Dear Mr. Fraser,

*I write in response to yours of the 17th inst., apprising my Husband of
your return to America, which was forwarded to him by a Friend in
Wilmington.*

*As you will see from the Direction of this Letter, we have removed
from Wilmington to Savannah, the political Climate of North Carolina
having become increasingly dangerous to Loyalists, particularly to my
Husband, given his History and Profession.*

*I wish to assure you that your Press has been preserved in excellent
condition but is not presently in use. My husband contracted a serious
Ague soon after our arrival here, and it became evident that his Illness
was of the periodic, or relapsing, Kind. He does somewhat better these
days but is unable to sustain the difficult Labor of the printing Trade.
(I will add, should you think of establishing a Business here, that while
the Politics of the Place are a great deal more congenial to those of the
Loyalist Persuasion than those of the northern Colonies, a Printer is
exposed to much Unpleasantness, whatever his personal Beliefs.)*

*Your Press is presently stored in the Barn of a Farmer named
Simpson, who lives a short Distance outside the City. I have seen it and
assured myself that the Instrument is Clean, Dry (it is packed in Straw),
and sheltered from the Weather. Please apprise me of your Desires, should
you wish me to sell the Press and forward the Money to you, or should you
wish to come and fetch it.*

*We are most appreciative of your Help and Kindness, and the Girls
pray for you and your Family every Day.*

*Yours most Sincerely,
Abigail Bell*

William Ransom, to His Grace Harold, Duke of Pardloe
September 24, 1778

Dear Uncle Hal,
You will be gratified to know that your paternal Instinct was correct.
I am very pleased to tell you that Ben probably isn't dead.
On the other hand, I haven't the slightest Idea where the devil he is or
why he's there.
I was shown a Grave at Middlebrook Encampment in New Jersey,
purported to be Ben's, but the Body therein is not Ben. (It's probably
better if you don't know how that bit of information was ascertained.)
Clearly someone in the Continental army must know something of
his whereabouts, but most of Washington's troops who were at the
Encampment when he was captured have gone. There is one Man
who might possibly yield some Information, but beyond that, the only
possible Connection would seem to be the Captain with whom we
are acquainted.
I propose therefore to hunt the Gentleman in question and extract
what Information he may possess when I find him.

Your most obedient nephew,
William

Lord John Grey, to Harold, Duke of Pardloe
Charleston, South Carolina
September 28, 1778

Dear Hal,

We arrived in Charleston by ship two days ago, having encountered a
Storm off the Chesapeake that blew us out to Sea, delaying us for several
days. I'm sure you will not be surprised in the least to learn that Dottie is
a much better Sailor than I am.
She also shows Promise as an inquiry Agent. First thing this morning,
she discovered the Whereabouts of Amaranthus Cowden by the simple Ex-
pedient of stopping a well-dressed Lady on the Street, admiring her Gown,
and then asking for the names of the better Dressmakers in the City, on
the Assumption (as she later explained to me) that Ben would not have
married either a plain Woman or one with no Interest in Fashion.
The third Shop we visited did indeed boast that Miss Cowden (she was
calling herself Mrs. Grey, they said, but they knew her Maiden Name, as
she was residing with an Aunt named Cowden) was a Customer, and
they were able to describe her to me as a slight young Woman of middle
Height, with an excellent Complexion, large brown Eyes, and abundant
Hair of a dark-blond Hue. They could not, however, give me her
Address, as the Lady had recently decamped to winter with Friends in
Savannah. (The Aunt has annoyingly died, I find.)

Interestingly, she styles herself as a Widow, so apparently she was informed—and by whom? I should like to know—of Ben's presumed Death, sometime after the Date of her Letter to you, as otherwise she would certainly have mentioned it.

I also find it interesting that she should be able to afford the Services of Madame Eulalie—and these to no little Extent; I succeeded in inducing Madame to show me her recent Bills—when her Letter to you professed her to be in financial Difficulties owing to Ben's Capture.

If Ben is indeed dead and both the Death and the Marriage proved, then presumably she would inherit some Property—or at least the Child would. But she can't possibly have taken such Legal Steps in the Time between her Letter to you and the Present; it could easily take that long merely to send a Letter to London—assuming that she had any Idea to whom it should be sent. And assuming also that whoever received it would not immediately have informed you.

Oh—she does possess an Infant, a Boy, and the Child is hers; Madame made her two Gowns and a set of Stays to accommodate the Pregnancy. Naturally, there's no telling whether Benjamin is the child's Father. She clearly has at least met Ben—or possibly Adam; she could have got "Wattiswade" from anyone in the Family—but that's not Proof of either Marriage or Paternity.

All in all, an interesting Woman, your putative Daughter-in-law. Plainly our Path lies now toward Savannah, though this may require somewhat more investigative Effort, as we don't know the Name of the Friends with whom she's taken Refuge, and if she is indeed poverty-stricken, she won't be buying new Gowns.

I hope to convince Dottie that she need not accompany me. She's most determined, but I can see that she pines for her Quaker Physician. And if our Quest should be greatly prolonged . . . I will not allow her to be placed in Danger, I assure you.

Your most affectionate Brother,
John

General Sir Henry Clinton, Commander in Chief for North America, to Colonel His Grace Duke of Pardloe, 46th Foot

Sir,

You are hereby ordered and directed to assemble and re-fit your Troops in whatever manner you deem necessary, and then to make Junction with Lieutenant Colonel Archibald Campbell, to march upon the City of Savannah in the colony of Georgia, and take possession of it in His Majesty's name.

H. Clinton

HAROLD, DUKE OF Pardloe, felt his chest tightening and rang for his orderly.

"Coffee, please," he said to the man. "Brewed very strong, and quickly. And bring the brandy while you're at it."

124

BROUGHT TO YOU BY
THE LETTERS Q, E, AND D

IT WAS, OF COURSE, unthinkable that we should sell Clarence. "Do you think he weighs as much as a printing press?" I asked, looking at him dubiously. His tiny stable next to the shop had survived the fire, and while he wrinkled his nose and sneezed when the wind raised a whiff of ash from the charred remains of the printshop, he didn't seem much affected.

"Substantially more, I think." Jamie scratched his forehead and ran a hand up the length of one long ear. "D'ye think mules suffer from seasickness?"

"Can they vomit?" I tried to recall whether I'd ever seen a horse or mule regurgitate—as opposed to dropping slobbery mouthfuls of whatever they were eating—but couldn't call an instance to mind.

"I couldna say if they *can*," Jamie said, picking up a stiff brush and beating clouds of dust from Clarence's broad gray back, "but they don't, no."

"Then how would you know if a mule was seasick?" Jamie himself got violently seasick, and I did wonder how he was going to manage if we did go by ship; the acupuncture needles I used to quell his nausea had perished in the fire—with so much else.

Jamie gave me a jaundiced look over Clarence's back.

"Can ye no tell if I'm seasick, even when I'm not puking?"

"Well, yes," I said mildly, "but you aren't covered with hair, and you can talk. You turn green and pour with sweat and lie about, groaning and begging to be shot."

"Aye. Well, bar the turning green, a mule can tell ye verra well if he's feeling peely-wally. And he can certainly make ye want to shoot him."

He ran a hand down Clarence's leg to pick up the mule's left front hoof. Clarence picked it up and set it down again very solidly, exactly where Jamie's own foot had been an instant before. His ears twitched.

"On the other hand," Jamie said to him, "I could make ye walk all the way to Savannah, pullin' a cart behind ye. Think about that, aye?" He came out of the stall and closed the gate, shaking it to be sure it was securely latched.

"Mr. Fraser!" A shout from the end of the alley drew his attention. It was Jonas Phillips, presumably on his way home to a midday dinner from the assembly room, where the Continental Congress was still locked in struggle. Jamie waved back and, with a nod to me, walked down the alley. While I waited for him, I turned my attention to the jumble of items occupying the other half of the stable.

What little room there was besides Clarence's stall was filled with the things the neighbors had managed to salvage from the remains of the printshop. All of it had the sour reek of ash about it, but a few of the items might be salvaged or sold, I supposed.

Mrs. Bell's letter had caused a certain reevaluation of our immediate prospects. Fergus's press had definitely perished in the flames; the derelict carcass was still there, the metal parts twisted in a way suggesting uncomfortably that the thing had died in agony. Fergus hadn't wept; after Henri-Christian, I didn't think anything could ever make him weep again. But he did avert his eyes whenever he came near the ruins.

On the one hand, the loss of the press was terrible—but, on the other, it did save us the problem of hauling it to . . .

Well, that was another problem. Where were we going?

Jamie had assured me that we were going home—back to the Ridge. But it was late September, and even if we found the money to pay the passage for so many people—and Clarence—and were fortunate enough not to be sunk or captured by an English cutter . . . we would part company with Fergus and Marsali in Wilmington, then go up the Cape Fear River into the North Carolina backcountry, leaving Marsali, Fergus, and the children to go on alone to Savannah. I knew that Jamie didn't want to do that. In all honesty, neither did I.

The little family was surviving, but there was no doubt that Henri-Christian's death and the fire had left them all badly wounded. Especially Germain.

You could see it in his face, even in the way he walked, no longer jaunty and bright-eyed, eager for adventure. He walked with his shoulders hunched, as though expecting a blow to come out of nowhere. And while sometimes he would forget for a few moments and revert to his normal swagger and talk, you could see it when the blow of memory did come out of nowhere to send him reeling.

Ian and Rachel had taken it upon themselves to be sure that he didn't slink away by himself; one or the other was always calling on him to come and help carry the marketing or go out to the forest to look for the proper wood for an ax handle or a new bow. That helped.

If Fergus went to Savannah to retrieve Bonnie, Jamie's original press, Marsali would be hampered and preoccupied by advancing pregnancy and the difficulties both of travel with a family and then of establishing a new home, Fergus needing to devote himself to setting up the new business and dealing with whatever the local politics might be. Germain could so easily slip through the cracks in his family and be lost.

I wondered whether Jenny would go with them—or with Ian and Rachel. Marsali could certainly use her help, but I remembered what Marsali had said, and thought she was right: *"Ian's her youngest. . . . And she's had too little of him."* She had; Ian had essentially been lost to her at the age of fourteen, and she hadn't seen him again until he was a grown man—and a Mohawk. I'd seen her now and then, gazing at him as he talked and ate, with a small inward glow on her face.

I poked gingerly through the pile of remnants. Marsali's cauldron had survived unscathed, though covered with soot. A few pewter plates, one half melted—the wooden ones had all burned—and a stack of Bibles, rescued from the front room by some pious soul. A line of washing had been hung out across the alley; what clothes were on it had all survived, though a couple of Fergus's shirts and Joanie's pinafore had been badly singed. I supposed boiling with lye soap might get the stink of fire out of the clothes, but I doubted that any of the family would wear them again.

Clarence, having finished his hay, was methodically rubbing his forehead against the top rail of his gate, making it rattle and thump.

"Itchy, are you?" I scratched him, then poked my head out of the stable. Jamie was still in conversation with Mr. Phillips at the mouth of the alley, though, and I went back to my explorations.

Under a pile of smoke-stained playscripts I found Marsali's small chiming clock, somehow miraculously intact. It had stopped, of course, but emitted one small, sweet silver *bing!* when I picked it up, making me smile.

Perhaps that was a good omen for the journey. And, after all, even if Jamie and I—and Rachel and Ian—were to set out at once for Fraser's Ridge, there was no chance of reaching the mountains of North Carolina before snow had closed the passes for the winter. It would be March, at the earliest, before we could turn inland.

I sighed, clock in hand, envisioning the Ridge in springtime. It would be a good time to arrive, the weather good for planting and building. I could wait.

I heard Jamie's steps come down the cobbled alley and stop. Stepping to the open front of the stable, I saw that he'd paused at the place where Henri-Christian had died. He stood unmoving for a moment, then crossed himself and turned.

The solemnity left his face as he saw me, and he held up a small leather bag, smiling.

"Look, Sassenach!"

"What is it?"

"One of the Phillips boys found it, scavenging about, and brought it to his father. Hold out your hands."

Puzzled, I did so, and he tilted the bag, decanting a small cascade of surprisingly heavy dark-gray chunks of lead—the type for a complete set of . . . I picked one out and squinted at it. "Caslon English Roman?"

"Better than that, Sassenach," he said, and, plucking the letter "Q" from the pile in my hand, he dug his thumbnail into the soft metal, revealing a faint yellow gleam. "Marsali's hoard."

"My God, it is! I'd forgotten all about it." At the height of the British occupation, when Fergus had been obliged to leave home to avoid arrest, sleeping in a different place each night, Marsali had cast a set of type in gold, carefully rubbing each slug with grease, soot, and ink, and had carried the pouch under her apron, in case she and the children should be likewise forced to flee.

"So did Marsali, I expect." His smile faded a bit, thinking of the causes of Marsali's distraction. "She'd buried it under the bricks of the hearth—I suppose when the army left. Sam Phillips found it when they were pulling down the chimney." He nodded toward the charred spot where the printshop had stood. The chimney had been damaged by the wall falling in, so a number of men had taken it down, neatly stacking the bricks, most of which were intact despite the fire and could be sold.

I poured the type carefully back into the pouch and glanced over my shoulder at Clarence.

"I suppose a goldsmith could make me a set of really *big* acupuncture needles. Just in case."

125

SQUID OF THE EVENING,
BEAUTIFUL SQUID

Charleston, Royal Colony of South Carolina

LORD JOHN AND HIS niece, Dorothea, ate that night at a small ordinary near the shore, whose air was redolent with the luscious scents of baked fish, eels in wine sauce, and small whole squid, fried crisply in cornmeal. John inhaled deeply with pleasure, handed Dottie to a stool, and sat down himself, enjoying the moment of gustatory indecision.

"It's that moment when you can convincingly imagine the delightful prospect of eating everything the establishment has to offer," he told Dottie. "Momentarily untroubled by the knowledge that one's stomach has a limited capacity and thus one must, alas, choose in the end."

Dottie looked a little dubious, but, thus urged, she took a deep sniff of the atmosphere, to which the scent of fresh-baked bread had just been added as the serving maid came in with a great loaf and a dish of butter with a four-leafed clover—this being the name of the establishment—stamped into its oleaginous surface.

"Oh, that smells wonderful!" she said, her face lighting. "Might I have some, please? And a glass of cider?"

He was pleased to see her nibble hungrily at the bread and take a deep breath of the cider—which was aromatic enough to challenge even the squid, his own reluctantly final choice, though this was accompanied by a dozen fresh-shucked oysters to fill whatever crevices might remain. Dottie had chosen the baked hake, though she had only picked at it so far.

"I came down to the harbor this afternoon while you were resting," he said, tearing off a wodge of bread to counteract the grated horseradish mixed with the oysters' brine. "I asked about and found two or three small boats whose owners are not averse to a quick journey to Savannah."

"How quick?" she asked warily.

"It's little more than a hundred miles by water," he said, shrugging in what he hoped was a casual manner. "Perhaps two days, with a good wind and fair weather."

"Mmm." Dottie cast a skeptical glance at the ordinary's shuttered window. The shutters trembled to a blast of rain and wind. "It's October, Uncle John. The weather is seldom predictable."

"How do you know? Madam—might I have some vinegar for the squid?" The proprietor's wife nodded, bustling off, and he repeated, "How do you know?"

"Our landlady's son is a fisherman. So was her husband. He died in a gale—last October," she finished sweetly, and popped the last bite of bread into her mouth.

"Such squeamish prudence is unlike you, Dottie," he remarked, accepting the vinegar bottle from the proprietress and sousing his crisp squidlings. "Oh, God," he said, chewing. "Ambrosia. Here—have one." He speared one with his fork and passed it across to her.

"Yes. Well . . ." She regarded the squid-laden fork with a distinct lack of enthusiasm. "How long would it take to travel overland?"

"Perhaps four or five days. Again, with good weather."

She sighed, lifted the squid to her mouth, hesitated, and then, with the air of a Roman gladiator facing an oncoming crocodile in the arena, put it into her mouth and chewed. She went white.

"Dottie!" He leapt up, knocking his stool over, and managed to catch her as she wilted toward the floor.

"Gah," she said faintly, and, lunging out of his arms, bolted for the door, retching. He followed and was in time to hold her head as she lost the bread, cider, and the half-chewed squid.

"I'm so sorry," she said a few moments later, as he emerged from the ordinary with a mug and a damp cloth. She was leaning against the most sheltered wall of the building, wrapped in his cloak, and was the color of spoiled suet pudding. "How disgusting of me."

"Think nothing of it," he said amiably. "I've done just the same for all three of your brothers, on occasion—though I somehow doubt from the same cause. How long have you known you were with child?"

"I became certain of it about five minutes ago," she said, swallowing audibly and shuddering. "Dear Lord, I will never eat squid again."

"Had you ever eaten squid before?"

"No. I never want to *see* another squid. Bother, my mouth tastes of sick."

John, who was indeed experienced in such matters, handed her the mug of beer.

"Rinse your mouth with that," he said. "Then drink the rest. It will settle your stomach."

She looked dubious at this but did as he said, and emerged from the cup still pale but much improved.

"Better? Good. I don't suppose you want to go back inside? No, of course not. Let me pay, and I'll take you home." Inside, he asked the landlady to make up a parcel of their abandoned supper—he didn't mind eating cold fried squid, but he did want to eat; he was starving—and held this carefully to windward as they walked back to their lodgings.

"You didn't know?" he asked curiously. "I've often wondered about that. Some women have told me they knew at once, and yet I've heard of others who somehow remained oblivious to their condition until the moment of birth was upon them, incredible as that seems."

Dottie laughed; the cold wind had brought some of the color back to her cheeks, and he was relieved to see her spirits recovered.

"Do lots of women discuss their intimacies with you, Uncle John? That seems somewhat unusual."

"I seem to attract unusual women," he said, rather ruefully. "I also seem to have the sort of face that people feel compelled to tell things to. In another age, perhaps I should have been a confessor, if that's the word. But returning to the point"—he took her elbow to guide her round a large pile of horse droppings—"now that you *do* know . . . what shall we do about it?"

"I don't think anything actually needs to be *done* for about eight months," she said, and he gave her a look.

"You know what I mean," he said. "I doubt you wish to establish residence in Charleston until after your child arrives. Do you wish to return to Philadelphia—or New Jersey, or whatever godforsaken place Denzell happens to be at the moment—or shall I make arrangements to proceed to Savannah and remain there for some time? Or—" Another thought struck him, and he altered the look to one of seriousness.

"Do you want to go home, Dottie? To England, I mean. To your mother?"

Her face went blank with surprise, which gave way to a look of longing that broke his heart. She looked away, blinking back tears, but her voice was steady when she turned back to him.

"No," she said, and swallowed. "I want to be with Denzell. All other considerations aside," she added, managing a smile, "he knows how to deliver a baby. His cousin William is *accoucheur* to the Queen, and Denny studied with him for a time."

"Well, that *will* be helpful," Grey agreed, rather dryly. He had himself delivered a child once—completely against his will—and still had nightmares about it.

It was just as well that Dottie didn't want to return to England, though. He'd suggested the notion on impulse but now realized that it might be more dangerous than any of the other alternatives. Since France had entered the war, all English shipping would be at risk.

"I'm thinking that we ought to go to Savannah, though," Dottie was saying. "We're so close, I mean—and if Ben's wife *is* there . . . she might need our help, mightn't she?"

"Yes," he agreed reluctantly. There was a familial obligation. And, after all, unless he *did* take up residence in Charleston for the next eight months, there seemed no alternative to Dottie's traveling, in whichever direction. Still . . . the thought of her giving birth *here*, him responsible for finding midwives and nurses . . . and then she *and* the child would need to be transported . . .

"No," he said, more definitely. "Amaranthus—assuming she does exist—will have to muddle on by herself a little longer. I'm taking you back to New York."

126

THE OGLETHORPE PLAN

Late November

SAVANNAH, UNLIKE MOST American cities, had been carefully planned by its founder, a man named Oglethorpe. I knew this because Mrs. Landrum, the woman from whom we rented our room, had explained to me that the city was laid out according to "the Oglethorpe plan"—this spoken in portentous tones, for Mrs. Landrum was a relative of the aforesaid Oglethorpe and intensely proud of the city and its civic perfection.

The plan called for six wards—a ward being composed of four civic blocks—for business, and four "tything" blocks for houses, these arrayed around an open square. There were ten houses to a block, and the men of a tything trained together for militia duty.

"Though that's not so important now as it used to be," Mrs. Landrum explained to me. "The Indians are still a bother in the backcountry, but it's years since they troubled to come into the city."

I rather thought Indians were the least of it, but as Mrs. Landrum didn't seem concerned about the war with the British, I didn't bring it up. It was apparent from her references that as not only her family but everyone she knew were Loyalists, plainly this was the proper state of things, and pesky nuisances like this "rebellion, as they're pleased to call it!" would soon be put down and we could get tea at a decent price again.

From my point of view, the most interesting thing about Mr. Oglethorpe's plan—in the course of conversation, it was revealed to me that he'd founded not only Savannah but the whole Province of Georgia—was that each house of a tything was provided with a one-mile tract of farmland outside the city and a five-acre kitchen garden closer in.

"Really," I said, my fingers beginning to itch at the thought of dirt. "Er . . . what do you plant?"

The upshot of this conversation—and many like it—was that I made an arrangement to help with the keeping of the kitchen garden in return for a share of "sass" (as Mrs. Landrum puzzlingly referred to green stuff like kale and turnips), beans, and dried corn, as well as a small plot where I could cultivate medicinal herbs. A secondary consequence of this amiable acquaintance was that Rachel and Ian, whose room was below ours, began referring to their unborn child as Oglethorpe, though this was politely shortened to "Oggy" whenever Mrs. Landrum was in hearing.

And the third and most important effect of Mrs. Landrum's friendship was that I found myself once more a doctor.

We had been in Savannah for a few weeks when Mrs. Landrum came up to our room one afternoon and inquired as to whether I might know anything regarding cures for the toothache, she knowing that I had a way with herbs?

"Oh, I might," I replied, with a surreptitious glance at my medical bag, which had been gathering dust under the bed since our arrival. "Whose tooth is it?"

The tooth had belonged to a gentleman named Murphy from Ellis Ward, the one we lived in. I say "had belonged" because I had the badly broken and infected bicuspid out of Mr. Murphy's head before he could have said Jack Robinson, though he was in such pain that he could barely recall his own name, let alone Jack's.

Mr. Murphy was extremely grateful for his deliverance. Mr. Murphy was also the owner of a very small vacant shop on the other side of Ellis Square. It was the work of a few moments to acquire a small shingle with TEETH EXTRACTED on it. And within twenty-four hours of hanging out my shingle, I was proudly depositing my earnings on the kitchen table—which was also my herbal-preparations counter and Jamie's desk, as it occupied the center of our single room.

"Well done, Sassenach!" Jamie picked up a small jar of honey, taken in payment for a nastily impacted wisdom tooth. He loved honey. I'd also acquired two large speckled turkey eggs (one of them filled the entire palm of my hand), a loaf of reasonably fresh sourdough bread, six pennies, and a small silver Spanish coin.

"I think ye could support the family all on your own, *a nighean,*" he said, dipping a finger in the honey and licking it before I could stop him. "Ian and Fergus and I can all retire and become gentlemen of leisure."

"Good. You can start by making supper," I said, stretching my back. Stays did keep you upright through a long day's work, but I was looking forward to taking them off, eating supper, and lying down, in quick succession.

"Of course, Sassenach." With a small flourish, he drew the knife from his belt, cut a slice off the loaf, drizzled honey on it, and gave it to me. "There ye are."

I raised an eyebrow at him but bit into it. Sweetness flooded my mouth and my bloodstream simultaneously, and I tasted sunlight and flowers. I moaned.

"What did ye say, Sassenach?" He was busily buttering another slice.

"I said, 'Well done,'" I said, and picked up the pot of honey. "We'll make a cook of you yet."

THE BASIC ISSUES of housing and food taken care of, plainly the next order of business was to retrieve Bonnie. Jamie had located the Bell family, and three weeks after our arrival in Savannah, he and Fergus had scraped together enough money to hire a cart and an extra mule from the livery stable where Clarence boarded. We met Richard Bell in the morning, and he came with us to the farm of one Zachary Simpson, the farmer with whom Bonnie boarded.

Mr. Simpson cleared away the last of the hay and pulled away the canvas with the air of a magician producing a rabbit from a hat. From the reaction of three-quarters of his spectators, you'd think he *had:* Jamie and Fergus both gasped audibly, and Richard Bell emitted a hum of satisfaction. I bit my lip and tried not to laugh, but I doubted they'd have noticed if I'd rolled on the floor in paroxysms of mirth.

"*Nom de Dieu,*" Fergus said, stretching out a reverent hand. "She's *beautiful.*"

"Best I've ever seen," Mr. Bell agreed, clearly torn between regard and regret.

"Aye." Jamie was pink with pleasure, trying visibly to retain a modest constraint. "Aye. She's bonnie, no?"

I supposed "she" was—if one was a connoisseur of printing presses, which I wasn't. Still, I confessed some fondness for Bonnie; we'd met before, in Edinburgh. Jamie had been oiling some part of her mechanism when I'd returned to find him after twenty years, and she had been witness to our reunion.

And she had withstood the rigors of disassembly, sea travel, reassembly, and months of being immured in a barn with commendable fortitude. A pale winter sun shone through a crack in the barn's wall, making her wood glow with somber pride, and her metal was—so far as I could see—quite free from rust.

"Well done," I said, giving her a small pat. Mr. Simpson was modestly accepting the applause of the crowd for his feat of preserving Bonnie from harm, and I could see that they'd be some time in getting her onto the cart we'd brought, so I made my way back to the farmhouse. I'd noticed a number of chickens scratching in the yard and had some hopes of acquiring fresh eggs.

Marsali's hoard—and Jenny's novena to St. Bride, Queen of the Sea, plus a modest assist from my acupuncture needles (Clarence luckily proved a good sailor)—had got us safely to Savannah, but the requirements of housing ten people and renting premises suitable for a small printing business had exhausted both the Caslon English Roman gold and the insurance money paid to Fergus for the fire's destruction.

With the need for income somewhat acute, Ian and Jamie had found employment at one of the warehouses on the river. A wise choice, as it turned out: in addition to their pay and the odd damaged cask of salt fish or biscuit, being on the docks all day allowed them first—and cheapest—choice from the fishermen coming in with their catch. We therefore hadn't been starving nor yet threatened with scurvy—the climate was mild enough that plenty of green things grew, even in late November—but I was getting tired of rice and fish and winter kale. A nice dish of scrambled eggs, now . . . possibly with fresh butter . . .

I'd come equipped for trading, with several packets of pins and a bag of salt, and Mrs. Simpson and I amicably concluded a bargain for a basket of eggs and a small tub of butter before the men had got Bonnie out of the barn and were sat on the back stoop, comfortably drinking beer.

"What remarkable chickens those are," I said, stifling a small belch. The beer, of Mrs. Simpson's own production, was tasty but strong. The chickens in question were more than remarkable: they appeared to have no legs but to be trundling round the yard on their bottom sides, pecking at their corn with cheerful imperturbability.

"Oh, aye," said Mrs. Simpson, nodding with pride. "My mother brought those—well, their great-great-grandmothers—with her from Scotland, thirty years a-gone. 'Creepies,' she always called them—but they've got a true name. Scots Dumpy, it is, or so a gentleman from Glasgow told me."

"How very appropriate," I said, taking another sip of beer and peering at the chickens. They did after all *have* legs; just very short ones.

"I breed them for sale," Mrs. Simpson added helpfully. "If might should be ye should find yourself in want of a good hen or two."

"I can't think of anything I'd like better," I said wistfully. The rice paddies and palmettos of Savannah seemed infinitely far away from the clean sharp air of Fraser's Ridge . . . but we were in the South, at least. And come March and good traveling weather, Marsali and Fergus should be safely established, and we could turn our faces toward North Carolina. "Perhaps in a few months . . ." I added *Scots Dumpy chickens* to the mental list I was accumulating and returned to the beer.

The men had got the printing press onto the cart, suitably swathed in canvas and repacked with straw for the journey into town, and now came into the house to resume their own well-earned refreshment.

We sat companionably round Mrs. Simpson's scrubbed kitchen table, drinking beer and eating salted radishes. Jamie and Fergus were glowing with excitement and satisfaction; the looks on their faces warmed me more than the beer. Poor Richard Bell was trying his best to be generous and share their delight, but it was plain that he was low in both body and spirit.

I had met him only a few days before, and that briefly, so had not yet cultivated an acquaintance sufficient as to allow me to make him undress and let me palpate his liver, but I was morally certain that the "relapsing ague" Mrs. Bell had written of was malaria. I couldn't say so with complete certainty without looking at his blood cells under a microscope—and God knew when I might ever have one again—but I'd seen enough people suffering from "the quartan ague" or "the tertian fever" as to have little doubt.

Luckily, I had a small supply of Jesuit bark among the selection of herbs and medicines I'd brought with me. It wouldn't cure him, but I could, with luck, limit the more-severe attacks and relieve some of the symptoms. Thinking of this reminded me suddenly of Lizzie Wemyss. Coming to America as Brianna's bond servant, she also had contracted malaria from the coastal mosquitoes. I'd managed to control the disease in her fairly well, but how had she fared in my absence?

"I'm sorry, what did you say?" My attention was jerked back to the conversation, but I added *LOTS of Jesuit bark* to my mental list before replying.

127

PLUMBING

LIKE PLUMBING, MEDICINE is a profession where you learn early on not to put your fingers in your mouth. I smelled my next patient coming and was reaching for the jar of soft soap and the bottle of raw alcohol before she came through the door. And the instant I saw her, I knew what the problem was.

There were two women, in fact: one was a tall, rather commanding-looking woman, well dressed and wearing a hat rather than the usual bonnet. The other was a small, slight girl who might have been any age between twelve and twenty. She was what they called a mulatto, half black and half white, with *café au lait* skin and snub features. I set her lower age limit at twelve only because she had apparent breasts bubbling over the top of her stays. She was dressed neatly but plainly in blue gingham, and she stank like an open sewer.

The tall woman paused, looking me over consideringly.

"You are a female physician?" she asked, in a tone just short of accusation.

"I am Dr. Fraser, yes," I replied equably. "And you are . . . ?"

She flushed at that and looked disconcerted. Also very dubious. But after an awkward pause, she made up her mind and gave a sharp nod. "I am Sarah Bradshaw. Mrs. Phillip Bradshaw."

"I'm pleased to meet you. And your . . . companion?" I nodded at the young woman, who stood with her shoulders hunched and her head bent, staring at the ground. I could hear a soft dripping noise, and she shifted as though trying to press her legs together, wincing as she did so.

"This is Sophronia. One of my husband's slaves." Mrs. Bradshaw's lips compressed and drew in tight; from the lines surrounding her mouth, she did it routinely. "She—that is—I thought perhaps—" Her rather plain face flamed crimson; she couldn't bring herself to describe the trouble.

"I know what it is," I said, saving her the difficulty. I came round the table and took Sophronia by the hand; hers was small and very callused, but her fingernails were clean. A house slave, then. "What happened to the baby?" I asked her gently.

A small, frightened intake of breath, and she glanced sideways at Mrs. Bradshaw, who gave her another sharp nod, lips still pursed.

"It died in me," the girl said, so softly I could scarcely hear her, even though she was no more than an arm's length from me. "Dey cut it out in pieces." That had likely saved the girl's life, but it surely hadn't helped her condition.

Despite the smell, I took a deep breath, trying to keep my emotions under control.

"I'll need to examine Sophronia, Mrs. Bradshaw. If you have any errands, perhaps you'd like to go and take care of them . . . ?"

She unzipped her lips sufficiently as to make a small, frustrated noise. Quite obviously, she would like nothing better than to leave the girl and never come back. But just as obviously, she was afraid of what the slave might tell me if left alone with me.

"Was the child your husband's?" I asked baldly. I didn't have time to beat around the bush; the poor girl was dripping urine and fecal matter on the floor and appeared ready to die of shame.

I doubted that Mrs. Bradshaw meant to die of that condition, but she plainly felt it almost as acutely as did Sophronia. She went white with shock, then her face flamed anew. She turned on her heel and stamped out, slamming the door behind her.

"I'll take that as a 'yes,' then," I said to the door, and turned to the girl, smiling in reassurance. "Here, sweetheart. Let's have a look at the trouble, shall we?"

Vesicovaginal fistula *and* rectovaginal fistula. I'd known that from the first moment; I just didn't know how bad they might be or how far up the vaginal canal they'd occurred. A fistula is a passage between two things that ought never to be joined and is, generally speaking, a bad thing.

It wasn't a common condition in civilized countries in the twentieth century but more common than one might think. I'd seen it several times in Boston, at a clinic where I gave time once a week to provide medical care to the city's poor. Young girls, much too young to be considering the opposite sex in any serious way, becoming pregnant before their bodies had ripened enough. Prostitutes, some of them. Others just girls who had been in the wrong place at the wrong time. Like this one.

A full-term baby that couldn't be forced out through the birth canal, and days of nonproductive labor, the child's head a battering ram against the tissues of the pelvis, the bladder, the vagina, and the bowel. Until at last the tissues thinned and split, leaving a ragged hole between bladder and vagina, or between vagina and rectum, allowing the body's waste to drip out unhindered through the vagina.

Not a matter of life or death, but revolting, uncontrollable, and bloody uncomfortable, too. Sophronia's inner thighs were swollen, a bright, patchy red, the skin macerated by the constant wetness, the irritating fecal slime. Like a permanent diaper rash, I thought, suppressing a deeply visceral urge to find Mr. Bradshaw and make a few fistulas in him with a blunt probe.

I talked to her while I made my examinations, soothingly, and after a little she began to answer me, though still in whispers. She was thirteen. Yes, Mr. Bradshaw had took her to his bed. She hadn't minded. He said his wife was mean to him, and she was—all the slaves knew it. Mr. Bradshaw had been nice to her, gentle-like, and when she fell pregnant, he'd taken her from the laundry and put her to kitchen work, where she'd have good food and wouldn't have to break her back with the heavy linens.

"He was sad," she said softly, looking up at the ceiling while I wiped away the filthy trickle between her legs. "When the baby died. He cried."

"Did he," I said, in what I hoped was a neutral voice. I folded a clean towel and pressed it between her legs, throwing the wet one she'd been wearing into my bucket of vinegar and water. "When did the baby die—how long ago, I mean?"

She frowned, the expression barely rippling the pure young skin of her forehead. Could she count? I wondered.

"Be some time before the sausage-makin'," she said uncertainly.

"In the fall, then?"

"Yessum."

And it was mid-December now. I poured water over my dirty hand and dribbled a bit of soap into my palm. I really must try to get a nailbrush, I thought.

Mrs. Bradshaw had come back but hadn't come in; I'd pulled the curtains over the front window, but her shadowed outline was plain on the cloth, the jaunty feathers in her hat stuck up like a silhouette cowlick.

I tapped my foot thoughtfully, then shook myself into order and went to open the door.

"I *might* be able to help," I said without preamble, startling the woman.

"How?" She blinked at me, and, taken unawares, her face was open, troubled but without the pinched look she'd worn earlier.

"Come inside," I said. "It's cold out here in the wind," and guided her in, a hand on her back. She was very thin; I could feel the knobs of her spine, even through her coat and stays.

Sophronia was sitting on the table, hands folded in her lap; when her mistress came in, she bent her head, looking at the floor again.

I explained the nature of the difficulty, so well as I could—neither of them had any grasp of internal anatomy at all; it was simply a matter of holes to them. Still, I managed to get the general point across.

"You know that a wound can be stitched, to hold the skin together while it heals?" I said patiently. "Well, this is much the same kind of thing, but made much harder by the wounds being inside and the tissues being very thin and slippery. It would be very difficult to mend—I'm not *sure* I can do it—but it is at least possible to try."

It was—just. In the late nineteenth century, a physician named J. Marion Sims had more or less invented the entire practice of gynecological surgery, in order to address exactly this condition. It had taken him years to develop the techniques, and I knew them—had done the procedure more than once. The catch was that you really needed good, solid anesthesia in order to have a chance of success. Laudanum or whisky might answer for cruder, swifter operations, but for painstakingly delicate surgery like this, the patient had to be completely unconscious and immobile. I would have to have ether.

I had no idea how I was going to make ether, living in a small rented house with a number of people whom I really didn't want to risk blowing to bits. And the thought of what flammable ether could do—had done—made me break out in a cold sweat. But seeing the faint hope rise in both their faces, I made up my mind to do it.

I gave Sophronia a small jar of beeswax ointment for the skin of her thighs and told them to come back in a week; I would know then whether it was possible. I saw them out, and as they went away down the street, Mrs. Bradshaw reached out unconsciously and touched Sophronia's shoulder in a brief caress of reassurance.

I took a deep breath and resolved that I *would* find a way. Turning to go inside, I glanced the other way down the street and saw a tall young man whose lean ranginess struck me with a sense of instant recognition. I blinked once, and imagination promptly clothed him in scarlet.

"William!" I called, and, picking up my skirts, ran after him.

HE DIDN'T HEAR me at first, and I had time for doubt—but not much; the set of head and shoulders, that long, decisive stride . . . He was thinner than Jamie, and his hair was a dark chestnut, not red, but he had his father's bones. And his eyes: hearing me at last, he turned, and those dark-blue cat eyes widened in surprise.

"Mother Cl—" He cut the word off, his face hardening, but I reached out and took his big hand between my own (rather hoping that I had got all of the slime off).

"William," I said, panting just a bit, but smiling up at him. "You can call me what you like, but I'm no less—and no more—to you than I ever was."

His severe look softened a little at that, and he ducked his head awkwardly.

"I think I must call you Mrs. Fraser, mustn't I?" He detached his hand, though gently. "How do you come to be here?"

"I might ask the same of you—and perhaps with more reason. Where's your uniform?"

"I've resigned my commission," he said, a little stiffly. "Under the circumstances, there seemed little point to my remaining in the army. And I have business that requires somewhat more independence of movement than I should have as one of Sir Henry's aides."

"Will you come and have something hot to drink with me? You can tell me about your business." I'd rushed out without my cloak, and a chilly breeze was fingering me with more intimacy than I liked.

"I—" He caught himself, frowning, then looked at me thoughtfully and rubbed a finger down the long, straight bridge of his nose, just as Jamie did when making up his mind. And just as Jamie did, he dropped his hand and nodded briefly as though to himself.

"All right," he said, rather gruffly. "In fact, my business may be of some . . . importance to you."

Another five minutes saw us in an ordinary off Ellis Square, drinking hot cider, rich with cinnamon and nutmeg. Savannah wasn't—thank God—Philadelphia, in terms of nasty winter weather, but the day was cold and windy, and the pewter cup was delightfully warm in my hands.

"What *does* bring you here, then, Willie? Or should I call you William now?"

"William, please," he said dryly. "It's the only name I feel is rightfully mine, for the moment. I should like to preserve what small dignity I have."

"Mmm," I said noncommittally. "William it is, then."

"As for my business . . ." He sighed briefly and rubbed a knuckle between his brows. He then explained about his cousin Ben, Ben's wife and child, then Denys Randall, and finally—Captain Ezekiel Richardson. *That* name made me sit up straight.

He noticed my reaction and nodded, grimacing.

"That's what I meant when I said my business might have some relevance to you. Pa—Lord John said that it was Richardson's threatening to arrest you as a spy that caused him to, er, marry you." He flushed a little.

"It was," I said, trying not to recall the occasion. In fact, I recalled only snatches of those empty, glaring days when I'd believed Jamie to be dead. One of those snatches, though, was a vivid recollection of standing in the parlor of Number 17, holding a bouquet of white roses, with John beside me and a military chaplain with a book before us—and, standing on John's other side, grave and handsome, William in his captain's uniform and shining gorget, looking so like Jamie that I felt for a dizzying instant that Jamie's ghost had come to watch. Unable to decide whether to faint or to run out of the room shrieking, I'd simply stood frozen, until John had nudged me gently, whispering in my ear, and I'd blurted out, "I do," and collapsed on the ottoman, flowers spilling from my hands.

Caught up in the memory, I'd missed what William was saying and shook my head, trying to focus.

"I've been searching for him for the last three months," he said, putting down his cup and wiping his mouth with the back of his hand. "He's an elusive scoundrel. And I don't know that he's in Savannah at all, for that matter. But the last hint I had of him was in Charleston, and he left there three weeks ago, heading south.

"Now, for all I know, the fellow's bound for Florida or has already taken ship for England. On the other hand . . . Amaranthus is here, or at least I believe so. Richardson seems to take an inordinate interest in the Grey family and its connections, so perhaps . . . Do you know Denys Randall yourself, by the way?"

He was looking at me intently over his cup, and I realized, with a faint sense of amusement mingled with outrage, that he had thrown the name at me suddenly in hopes of surprising any guilty knowledge I might have.

Why, you little scallywag, I thought, amusement getting the upper hand. *You need a bit more practice before you can pull off that sort of thing, my lad.*

I did in fact know something about Denys Randall that William almost certainly didn't know—and that Denys Randall himself might not know—but it wasn't information that would shed any light on the whereabouts and motives of Ezekiel Richardson.

"I've never met him," I said, quite truthfully, and held up my cup toward the serving maid for more cider. "I used to know his mother, Mary Hawkins; we met in Paris. A lovely, sweet girl, but I've had no contact with her for the last . . . thirty . . . no, thirty-four years. I assume from what you tell me that she married a Mr. Isaacs—you said he was a Jewish merchant?"

"Yes. So Randall said—and I can't see why he'd lie about it."

"Nor can I. But what you do know—you think," I corrected, "is that while Denys Randall and Ezekiel Richardson have heretofore appeared to be working together, now they aren't?"

William shrugged, impatient.

"So far as I know. I haven't seen Randall since he warned me about Richardson, but I haven't seen Richardson, either."

I could sense his rising desire to be up and off; he was drumming his fingers softly on the tabletop, and the table itself shuddered slightly when his leg bumped it.

"Where are you staying, William?" I asked impulsively, before he could go. "In—in case I do see Richardson. Or hear anything of Amaranthus, for that matter. I am a doctor; a lot of people come to see me, and everyone talks to a doctor."

He hesitated, but then gave another shrug, this one infinitesimal. "I've taken a room at Hendry's, on River Street."

He stood, tossed some money on the table, and extended a hand to help me up.

"We're staying at Landrum's, one square over from the City Market," I said on impulse, rising. "If you should—want to call. Or need help. Just in case, I mean."

His face had gone carefully blank, though his eyes were burning like match flames. I felt a chill, knowing from experience the sort of thing that was likely going on behind such a façade.

"I doubt it, Mrs. Fraser," he said politely. And, kissing my hand in brief farewell, he left.

128

GIGGING FROGS

December 22, 1778

JAMIE TOOK A FIRM grip of the back of Germain's shirt and beckoned with his free hand to Ian, who held the torch.

"Look out over the water first, aye?" Jamie whispered, lifting his chin at the black glitter of the submerged marsh. It was broken by clumps of waist-high cordgrass and smaller ones of needlerush, bright green in the torchlight. This was a deep spot, though, with two or three of what the natives of Savannah called "hammocks," though plainly they meant "hummock"—wee islands, with trees like wax myrtle and yaupon holly bushes, though these, too, were of a spiky nature, like everything else in a marsh save the frogs and fish.

Some of the spikier inhabitants of the marsh, though, were mobile and nothing you wanted to meet unexpectedly. Germain peered obediently into the darkness, his gigging spear held tight and high, poised for movement. Jamie could feel him tremble, partly from the chill but mostly, he thought, from excitement.

A sudden movement broke the surface of the water, and Germain lunged forward, plunging his gig into the water with a high-pitched yell.

Fergus and Jamie let out much deeper cries, each grabbing Germain by an arm and hauling him backward over the mud, as the irate cottonmouth he'd nearly speared turned on him, lashing, yawning mouth flaring white.

But the snake luckily had business elsewhere and swam off with a peeved sinuosity. Ian, safely out of range, was laughing.

"Think it's funny, do ye?" said Germain, scowling in order to pretend he wasn't shaking.

"Aye, I do," his uncle assured him. "Be even funnier if ye were eaten by an alligator, though. See there?" He lifted the torch and pointed; ten feet away, there was a ripple in the water, between them and the nearest hammock. Germain frowned uncertainly at it, then turned his head to his grandfather.

"That's an alligator? How d'ye ken that?"

"It is," Jamie said. His own heart was pounding from the sight of the cottonmouth. Snakes unnerved him, but he wasn't scairt of alligators. Cautious, yes. Scairt, no. "See how the ripples come back from the island there?"

"Aye." Germain squinted across the water. "So?"

"Those ripples are coming toward us side on. The one Ian's pointing at? It's coming at a right angle—right toward us."

It was, though slowly.

"Are alligators good to eat?" Fergus asked, watching it thoughtfully. "A good deal more meat on one than on a frog, *n'est-ce pas?*"

"They are, and there is, aye." Ian shifted his weight a little, gauging the distance. "We canna kill one of those wi' spears, though. I should have brought my bow."

"Should we . . . move?" Germain asked doubtfully.

"Nay, see how big it is first," Ian said, fingering the long knife at his belt. He was wearing a breechclout, and his bare legs were long and steady as a heron's, standing mid-calf in the muddy water.

The four of them watched with great concentration as the ripple came on, paused, came on a little more, slowly.

"Are they stunned by light, Ian?" Jamie asked, low-voiced. Frogs were; they had maybe two dozen bullfrogs in their sack, surprised in the water and killed before they kent what hit them.

"I dinna think so," Ian whispered back. "I've not hunted one before, though."

There was a sudden gleam in the water, a scatter of ripples, and the glow of two small burning orbs, a demon's eyes.

"*A Dhia!*" Jamie said, making a convulsive sign against evil. Fergus pulled Germain back farther, making a clumsy sign of the cross with his hook. Even Ian seemed taken back a bit; his hand fell from his knife and he stepped back toward the mud, not taking his eyes off the thing.

"It's a wee one, I think," he said, reaching safety. "See, its eyes are nay bigger than my thumbnail."

"Does that matter, if it's possessed?" Fergus asked, suspicious. "Even if we were to kill it, we might be poisoned."

"Oh, I dinna think so," Jamie said. He could see it now as it hung motionless in the water, stubby clawed feet halfway drawn up. It was perhaps two feet long—the toothy jaw maybe six inches. It could give you a nasty bite, nay more. But it wasn't close enough to reach.

"Ken what a wolf's eyes look like in the dark? Or a possum's?" He'd taken Fergus hunting, of course, when he was young, but seldom at night—and such things as you'd hunt at night in the Highlands were usually running from you, not looking at you.

Ian nodded, not taking his eyes off the small reptile.

"Aye, that's true. Wolves' eyes are usually green or yellow, but I've seen them red like that sometimes, by torchlight."

"I would suppose that a wolf could be possessed by an evil spirit as easily as an alligator could," Fergus said, a little testily. It was clear, though, that he wasn't afraid of the thing, either, now that he'd got a good look; they were all beginning to relax.

"He thinks we're stealing his frogs," Germain said, giggling. He was still holding the spear, and even as he spoke, he spotted something and slammed the three-tined sapling into the water with a whoop.

"I got it, I got it!" he shouted, and splashed into the water, heedless of the alligator. He bent to see that his prey was firmly transfixed, let out another small whoop, and pulled up his spear, displaying a catfish of no mean size, belly showing white in its frantic flapping, blood running in trickles from the holes made by the tines.

"More meat on that than on yon wee lizard there, aye?" Ian took the spear, pulled the fish off, and bashed its head with the hilt of his knife to kill it.

Everyone looked, but the alligator had departed, alarmed by the kerfuffle.

"Aye, that's us fettled, I think." Jamie picked up both bags—one half full of bullfrogs, and the other still squirming slightly from the inclusion of a number of shrimp and crayfish netted from the shallows. He held open the one with the frogs for Ian to toss the fish inside, saying a verse from the Hunting Blessing, for Germain: *"Thou shalt not eat fallen fish nor fallen flesh/ Nor one bird that thy hand shall not bring down/Be thou thankful for the one/ Though nine should be swimming."*

Germain was not paying attention, though; he was standing quite still, fair hair lifting in the breeze, his head turned.

"Look, *Grand-père*," he said, voice urgent. "Look!"

They all looked and saw the ships, far out beyond the marsh but coming in, heading for the small headland to the south. Seven, eight, nine . . . a dozen at least, with red lanterns at their masts, blue ones at the stern. Jamie felt the hair rise on his body and his blood go cold.

"British men-of-war," Fergus said, his voice empty with shock.

"They are," Jamie said. "We'd best get home."

IT WAS ALMOST dawn before I felt Jamie slide into bed behind me, bringing chilled skin and the smell of brine, cold mud, and marsh plants with him. Also . . .

"What's that smell?" I asked drowsily, kissing the arm he'd put round me.

"Frogs, I expect. God, ye're warm, Sassenach." He cuddled closer, pressing his body into mine, and I felt him pull loose the bow of the ribbon that gathered the neck of my shift.

"Good hunting, then?" I obligingly wiggled my bottom into the hollow of his thighs and he sighed in appreciation, his breath warm on my ear, and slipped a cold hand inside my shift. "Ooh."

"Aye. Germain caught a fine big catfish, and we brought back a sack of crawfish and shrimps—the wee gray ones."

"Mmm. We'll have a good supper, then." His temperature was quickly equalizing with mine, and I was drifting pleasantly back down toward sleep—though quite willing to be roused for the right reasons.

"We saw a wee alligator. And a snake—a water moccasin."

"You didn't catch those, I hope." I knew that snakes and alligators were technically edible, but I didn't think we were quite hungry enough to make the challenges of cooking one worthwhile.

"No. Oh—and a dozen British ships full of soldiers turned up, too."

"That's ni— *What?*" I flipped over in his arms, ending face-to-face.

"British soldiers," he repeated gently. "Dinna fash, Sassenach. I expect it will be all right. Fergus and I already hid the press, and we havena got any silver to bury. That's one thing to be said for poverty," he added reflectively, stroking my bottom. "Ye dinna need to fear bein' plundered."

"That—what the bloody hell are they doing *here*?" I rolled over and sat straight up in bed, pulling my shift up round my shoulders.

"Well, ye did say Pardloe told ye they meant to cut off the southern colonies, aye? I imagine they decided to start here."

"Why here? Why not . . . Charleston? Or Norfolk?"

"Well, I couldna say, not being privy to the British councils of war," he said mildly. "But if I was to guess, I'd say it's maybe that there are a good many troops already in Florida, and they'll be marching up to join this new lot. The Loyalists are thick as fleas on a dog all along the coast of the Carolinas; if the army's secured Florida and Georgia, they'd be well placed to advance northward, picking up local support."

"You have it all figured out, I see." I pressed my back against the wall—there was no headboard—and finished retying the ribbon of my shift. I didn't feel equal to meeting an invasion with my bosom uncovered.

"No," he admitted. "But there are only two things to do, Sassenach: stay or flee. It's the dead of winter in the mountains; we canna get through the passes 'til March, and I'd rather not be stravaiging about the countryside with three bairns, two pregnant women, and nay money. And I doubt they'll burn the city, not if they mean it to be a base for invading the rest of the South." He reached up and ran a soothing hand down my shoulder and arm. "It's not as though ye've not lived in an occupied city before."

"Hmm," I said dubiously, but he did have a point. There *were* some advantages to the situation, the chief one being that if an army already held a city, they wouldn't be attacking it: no fighting in the streets. But, then . . . they didn't hold it yet.

"Dinna fash yourself, lass," he said softly, and twined a finger in my ribbon. "Did I not tell ye when we wed, ye'd have the protection of my body?"

"You did," I admitted, and laid a hand over his. It was big, strong, and capable.

"Then come lie wi' me, *mo nighean donn,* and let me prove it," he said, and pulled the ribbon loose.

FROG LEGS OF that size really did look quite like chicken drumsticks. And tasted very like, too, dredged in flour and egg with a little salt and pepper and fried.

"Why is it that the meat of strange animals is so often described as tasting like chicken?" Rachel asked, neatly snaring another leg out from under her husband's reaching hand. "I've heard people say that of everything from catamount to alligator."

"Because it does," Ian answered, raising a brow at her and stabbing his fork into a platter of catfish chunks, similarly coated and fried.

"Well, if you want to be technical about it," I began, to a chorus of mingled groans and laughter. Before I could launch into an explanation of the biochemistry of muscle fiber, though, there was a rap on the door. We had been making so much noise over supper that I hadn't heard footsteps on the stair and was taken by surprise.

Germain popped up to open the door and gazed up in surprise at two Continental officers, in full uniform.

There was a general scraping of chairs as the men stood up, and Jamie stepped out from behind the table. He'd been working in the warehouse all day, after hunting in the marshes half the night, and was not only barefoot but wearing a badly stained, grimy shirt and a faded plaid so worn that it was thin in spots. Still, no one would have doubted that he was the master of the house. When he inclined his head and said, "Gentlemen? Be welcome," both officers took off their hats, bowed, and came in, murmuring, "Your servant, sir."

"General Fraser," the senior officer said, the title not quite a question, as he eyed Jamie's attire. "I am Major General Robert Howe."

I'd never seen Major General Howe before, but I knew his companion, and my hand tightened on the bread knife. He was wearing a colonel's uniform now, and his face was as blandly forgettable as ever, but I wasn't likely to forget Captain Ezekiel Richardson—lately a captain in His Majesty's army, last seen in Clinton's headquarters in Philadelphia.

"Your humble servant, sir," Jamie said, in a tone quite belying the usual compliment. "I am James Fraser but no longer an officer in any army. I have resigned my commission."

"So I understand, sir." Howe's rather bulging eyes scanned the table, flicking past Jenny, Rachel, Marsali, and the little girls before settling on me. He gave a small nod of inward conviction and bowed to me. "Mrs. Fraser? I trust I see you well, ma'am." Obviously, he'd heard the story behind Jamie's dramatic resignation.

"You do, thank you," I said. "Do watch out for the crayfish there, Colonel." For Richardson was standing just in front of the tin tub in which I'd set the crayfish, covered with water and supplied with a few handfuls of cornmeal, with which they'd purge their nasty little entrails over the next twenty-four hours and become safe to eat.

"Your pardon, ma'am," he said politely, moving aside. Unlike Howe, he was chiefly concerned with the men; I saw his eyes touch for an instant on Fergus's hook, dismiss him, then rest on Ian, with an air of satisfaction. What Jamie called a cold grue went down my back. I knew already what they wanted; this was a high-level press gang.

Jamie recognized their purpose, too.

"My wife is well, thanks be to God, General. I expect she would like her husband to remain in that condition, too."

Well, that was fairly blunt. Howe evidently decided there was no point in further civilities and waded in directly.

"Are you aware, sir, that a number of British troops have disembarked just outside the city and doubtless mean to invade and capture it?"

"I am," Jamie said patiently. "I watched their ships come in last night. As for capturing the city, I think they're verra well placed to do just that. And if

I were you, General—and I thank the Lord that I'm not—I should be gatherin' my men this minute and marching out of the city wi' them. Ken the proverb about livin' to fight another day, do ye? I recommend it as a strategy."

"Do I understand you aright, sir?" Richardson put in, his tone edgy. "You decline to join in the defense of your own city?"

"Aye, we do," Ian put in before Jamie could answer. He eyed the visitors in an unfriendly way, and I saw his right hand drop to his side, reaching for Rollo's head, then his fingers curl up tight, missing it. "It's no our city and we're no disposed to die for it."

I was sitting next to Rachel and felt her shoulders lose a little of their tension. Across the table, Marsali's eyes slid sideways, meeting Fergus's, and I saw a moment of silent marital communication and accord. *"If they don't know who we are, don't tell them."*

Howe, a rather thickset man, opened and closed his mouth several times before finding words.

"I am appalled, sir," he managed finally, his face quite red. "Appalled," he repeated, his second chin quivering with outrage—and, I thought, no little desperation. "That a man known for his bravery in battle, his constancy to the cause of freedom, would cravenly submit to the rule of the bloody tyrant!"

"A choice little short of treason," Richardson put in, nodding severely. I raised my eyebrows at this and stared at him, but he sedulously avoided my eye.

Jamie stood looking at them for a moment, rubbing a forefinger down the bridge of his nose.

"Mr. Howe," he said at last, dropping his hand. "How many men have ye in your command?"

"Why . . . nearly a thousand!"

"How nearly?"

"Six hundred," Richardson said, at the same moment that Howe exclaimed, "Nine hundred, sir!"

"Aye," said Jamie, clearly unimpressed. "Those transports carry three thousand men, easily—well armed, with artillery—and they've an entire Highland regiment wi' them, too; I heard their pipes as they came ashore."

Howe's color faded noticeably. Still, he had grit; he kept his dignity.

"Whatever the odds, sir," he said, "it is my duty to fight and to protect the city entrusted to my care."

"I respect your devotion to your duty, General," Jamie said, quite seriously. "And may God be with ye. But I won't."

"We could physically compel you," Richardson pointed out.

"Ye could," Jamie agreed, unruffled. "But to what end? Ye canna make me command men if I refuse to do it, and what good is an unwilling soldier?"

"This is craven cowardice, sir!" Howe said, but it was clear that this was bluster, and poorly acted bluster, at that.

"Dia eadarainn 's an t-olc," Jamie said quietly, and nodded toward the door. *"God between us an evil,"* he said. "Go with God, gentlemen, but leave my house."

"THEE DID WELL, Jamie," Rachel said quietly, after the sound of the soldiers' footsteps had faded from the stairwell. "No Friend could have spoken more wisely."

He glanced at her, mouth quirking.

"Thank ye, lass," he said. "But I think ye ken I wasna speaking from the same reasons a Friend might have."

"Oh, I do," she said, smiling. "But the effect is the same, and Friends are grateful for whatever they can get. Will thee have the last frog leg?"

A small ripple of laughter ran through the adults, and the children, who had been sitting rigid and white-faced during the soldiers' visit, relaxed as though they were balloons that someone had let the air out of and began zooming around the room in relief. Fearing for the tub of crayfish, Jenny and Marsali marshaled them into some sort of order and marched them off home to bed, Marsali pausing to kiss Fergus and adjuring him to be careful walking home alone.

"The British are not in the city yet, *mon chou,*" he said, kissing her back.

"Aye, well—it never hurts to keep in practice," she said tartly. "Come along, ye wee rattans."

The rest of us sat for a time discussing the immediate future and what little might be done. Jamie was right about the advantages of poverty in such a situation—but at the same time . . .

"They'll take whatever food they find," I said. "At least at first." I gave the shelf behind me a quick glance; it was our pantry and held the sum total of the household's stores: a small crock of lard, cloth bags of oatmeal, flour, rice, beans, and parched corn, a braid of onions and a few dried apples, half a wheel of cheese, a little box of salt and a pepper pot, and the remains of a loaf of sugar. Plus our small stock of candles.

"Aye." Jamie nodded, got up, and fetched his purse, which he turned out on the table. "Fourteen shillings, about. Ian? Fergus?" Ian and Rachel's resources amounted to another nine shillings, Fergus's one guinea, two shillings, and a handful of pennies.

"See what ye can get at the tavern tomorrow, lass," he said, pushing a small pile of coins toward Rachel. "I think I can put aside a cask of salt fish from the warehouse. And you, Sassenach—if ye're quick at the market in the morning, ye might manage to get more rice and beans, maybe a flitch of bacon?" Bits of copper and silver winked on the table before me, the King's stolid countenance chiseled in profile.

"There's no good hiding place in our room," Ian observed, looking around. "Nor here. Auntie's wee surgery, d'ye think?"

"Aye, that's what I was thinking. It's a board floor, and the building's got a good foundation. I'll maybe make a wee hidey-hole tomorrow. I shouldna think there's much in your surgery that soldiers would want?" This last was said questioningly to me.

"Only the medicines that are made with alcohol," I said. I took a deep breath. "Speaking of soldiers—I have to tell you something. It may not be important—but then again . . ." And I told them about Ezekiel Richardson.

"Ye're quite sure of it, Sassenach?" Jamie frowned a little, red brows sparking in the candlelight. "Yon man's got a face that might belong to anyone."

"He's not what you'd call memorable, at all," I admitted. "But, yes, I am sure. He has that mole on the side of his chin; I remember that. It's more the way he was looking at me, though. He recognized *me,* I'm positive."

Jamie drew breath and blew it out slowly, considering. Then he put his hands flat on the table and looked at Ian.

"Your auntie met my son, William, in the city the other day—by accident," he said, his voice carefully neutral. "Tell them what he said of Richardson, Sassenach, will ye?"

I did, keeping an eye on the pulse in Ian's throat. So was Rachel; she put a hand quietly on his, which he was clenching in a fist on the table. He glanced at her, smiled briefly, and reluctantly unclenched it, lacing his fingers with hers.

"And what's William doing here, then?" Ian asked, obviously working to keep any hint of hostility out of his voice.

"He was looking for Richardson, in fact, but he's also searching for his cousin's wife, a woman named Amaranthus Grey—or perhaps Cowden," I added. "She might be going by her maiden name. I'd meant to ask if either of you had heard any mention of her."

Both Ian and Rachel shook their heads.

"Thee would remember a name like that," Rachel said. "But thee thinks William doesn't know that Richardson is here?"

"I'm sure he doesn't," I said. "Nor that Richardson has gone over to the Rebels. Apparently."

There was silence for a moment. I could hear the faint clicking of the crayfish in the tub behind me and the slight pop as a fault in the candlewick made the flame bob and dance.

"This man Richardson may simply have changed his allegiance," Rachel suggested. "I know of many who have, over the last two years."

"He might," I said slowly, "but the thing is—John thought he was an intelligencer—a spy or secret agent of some sort. And when someone of that stripe turns his coat . . . you have to ask whether he's turned it once or twice. Or not at all. Don't you?"

Jamie laid a hand on the table, thinking.

"Aye, well," he said at last, and, sitting up straight, stretched himself with a sigh. "If there's aught fishy about the man, we'll ken it soon enough."

"We will?" I asked. He gave me a wry smile.

"Aye, Sassenach. He'll come looking for you. Keep your wee knife close to hand, aye?"

129

INVASION

December 29

W E HEARD THE GUNS soon after dawn. Jamie paused in the act of shaving to listen. It was a distant thunder, irregular, muffled by distance. But I had heard artillery close at hand and felt the sound as an echo in my bones, urging instant flight. Jamie had heard artillery at a much closer range than I and set down his razor, planting his hands flat on the washstand. To keep them from trembling, I thought.

"They're firing cannon from the ships in the river," he said quietly. "And regular artillery from the south. God help Howe and his men." He crossed himself and picked up the razor.

"How far away do you think they are?" I had paused in the act of putting on my stockings and now drew one up, slowly fastening my garter. Jamie shook his head.

"No telling from in here. I'll go out in a bit, though, and then I'll see how the wind lies."

"You're going out?" I asked, uneasy at the prospect. "Surely you're not going to work today." Fadler's warehouse, where he worked as a supervisor and senior clerk, was *on* the river.

"I am not," he said briefly. "But I thought I'd go and fetch the bairns and Marsali and my sister. Fergus will be gone to see what's happening, and I dinna want them left alone without a man." His mouth thinned. "Especially not if the soldiers come into the city."

I nodded, at once unable to speak. The thought of the things that happened—could happen—during an invasion . . . I had, thank God, never lived through such an event but had seen too many newsreels and photographs to be under any illusions as to the possibilities. And there had already been reports of a British company come up from Florida under an officer named Major Prevost, raiding the countryside around Sunbury, running off cattle, and burning barns and farmhouses. Sunbury was not nearly far enough away for comfort.

When Jamie left, I rattled around for a few minutes, undecided what to do first, but then pulled myself together and decided to make a quick visit to my surgery. It would be a good idea to take away my more-valuable instruments—not that any of them had great value; there was no black market in amputation saws (at least not yet . . .)—and such drugs and supplies as might be needed if—

I cut that "if" off sharply and looked around our modest room. I had been keeping only a few staples, like flour and butter, and the more perishable items of food here; anything that could be stored for a while was now hidden under the floor of my surgery. If we were about to have Marsali, Jenny, and the children to stay for an indefinite time, though, I'd best bring back a few more things.

I took my biggest basket and knocked at Rachel's door downstairs. She answered at once, already dressed to go out.

"Ian has gone with Fergus," she said, before I could ask. "He says he will not fight with the militia but that Fergus is his brother and it is his duty to see him safe. I can't complain about that."

"I could," I said frankly. "I'd complain like billy-o if I thought it would do any good. Waste of breath, though. Will you come with me down to the surgery? Jamie's gone to get Jenny and Marsali and the children, so I thought I'd best bring back something for them to eat."

"Let me get my basket."

The streets were full of people—most of them in some process of leaving the city, fetching goods, or drawing carts through the streets, though some were clearly bent on looting. I saw two men break a window and crawl through it into a large house off Ellis Square.

We reached the surgery without incident, though, and found two whores standing outside. They were women I knew, and I introduced them to Rachel, who was much less discomposed by the introduction than they were.

"We're wanting to buy pox cures, missus," said Molly, a sturdy Irish girl. "So many as ye might have to hand and be willin' to part with."

"Are you, um, expecting a—er—rash of the pox? So to speak?" I was unlocking the door as we spoke, calculating whether the current crop of penicillin was likely to be sufficiently potent as to make any difference.

"It don't matter that much whether it works or not, ma'am," said Iris, who was very tall, very thin, and very black. "We'uns plan to sell 'em to the soldiers."

"I see," I said, rather blankly. "Well, then . . ."

I gave them what penicillin I had in liquid form, declining to charge them. I kept the powdered mold and the remnants of Roquefort cheese, though, in case the family might have need of them—and suffered a bolt of vivid fear at the thought of Fergus and Ian, doing God knew what. The artillery had stopped —or the wind had changed—but it started up again as we made our way home, holding our baskets under our cloaks to prevent snatch-and-grab attacks.

Jamie had brought back Marsali and Jenny and the children, all of them carrying what they could in the way of clothes, food, and bedding. There was a long period of total chaos, while things were organized, but at last we sat down to a sort of rough tea, at around three o'clock. Jamie, declining to be involved in the domestic engineering, had exercised his male prerogative of disappearing on vaguely unspecified "business" but, with unerring instinct, reappeared just as the cake was being set out, bearing a large gunnysack full of clams, a barrel of flour, and a modicum of news.

"The fighting's over," he said, looking for someplace to set the clams down.

"I noticed the guns had stopped some time ago. Do you know what's happened?" I took the bag and decanted the clams with a loud clatter into the empty cauldron, then poured a bucket of water over them. They'd keep until supper.

"Exactly what I told General Howe would happen," he said, though not with any sense of pleasure at being right. "Campbell—that's the British Lieutenant Colonel, Archibald Campbell—circled Howe and his men and bagged them up like fish in a net. I dinna ken what he's done wi' them, but I expect there will be troops in the city before nightfall."

The women all looked at one another and relaxed visibly. This was actually good news. What with one thing and another, the British army was quite good at occupying cities. And while the citizenry might justifiably resent the billeting of troops and the requisitioning of supplies, the underlying fact was that there's nothing for keeping public order like having an army living with you.

"Will we be safe, then, with the soldiers here?" Joanie asked. She was bright-eyed with the adventure, like her siblings, and had been following the adult conversation closely.

"Aye, mostly," Jamie said, but his eye met Marsali's, and she grimaced. We probably would be safe enough, though food might be short for a while, until the army quartermasters got things straightened out. Fergus and Bonnie, though, were another matter.

"Luckily, we hadna started up *L'Oignon* yet," she said, answering Jamie's look. "It's only been printing up handbills and broadsheets and the odd religious tract. I think it will be all right," she said bravely, but she reached to touch Félicité's dark head, as though to reassure herself.

We had the clams made into chowder—rather a watery chowder, as we had very little milk, but we thickened it with crumbled biscuit, and there *was* enough butter—and were setting the table for supper when Fergus and Ian came clattering up the stairs, flushed with excitement and full of news.

"It was a black slave who made the difference," Fergus said, cramming a piece of bread into his mouth. "*Mon Dieu,* I'm famished! We haven't eaten all day. This man wandered into the British camp soon after the fighting began and offered to show them a secret path through the swamp. Lieutenant Colonel Campbell sent a regiment of Highlanders—we could hear the pipes; it reminded me of Prestonpans." He grinned at Jamie, and I could see the scrawny ten-year-old French orphan he'd been, riding on a captured cannon. He swallowed and washed the bite down with water, that being all we had at the moment.

"Highlanders," he continued, "and some other infantry, and they followed the slave through the swamp and got well round General Howe's men, who were all clumped together, for of course they didn't know from which direction the fight might come."

Campbell had then sent another infantry company to Howe's left, "to make some demonstrations," Fergus said, waving an airy hand and scattering crumbs. "They turned, of course, to meet this, and then the Highlanders fell on them from the other side, and *voilà!*" He snapped his fingers.

"I doubt Howe feels any gratitude to that slave," Ian put in, scooping his bowl into the cauldron of chowder. "But he ought. He didna lose more than thirty or forty men—and had they stood and fought, they'd likely all have been killed, if they hadn't the sense to surrender. And he didna strike me as a man o' sense," he added thoughtfully.

"How long d'ye think they'll stay, the army?" Jenny was slicing bread and handing out the pieces round the table but paused to wipe a forearm across her brow. It was winter, but with the fire going in the small room and so many people crowded in, the temperature was quickly approaching Turkish-bath levels.

All the men exchanged glances. Then Jamie spoke, reluctantly.

"A long time, *a piuthar*."

130

A SOVEREIGN CURE

I T HAD TO BE done, and it had to be done now. Between Jamie's uneasiness and my own misgivings, I'd put off the question of making ether. But now we were up against it: I simply couldn't do what needed to be done for Sophronia without a dependable general anesthetic.

I'd already decided that I could do the manufacture in the tiny toolshed in Mrs. Landrum's huge kitchen garden. It was outside the city limits, with an acre of open space on every side, this occupied only by winter kale and hibernating carrots. If I blew myself to kingdom come, I wouldn't take anyone else with me.

I doubted that this observation would reassure Jamie to any great extent, though, so I put off mentioning my plans. I'd assemble what I needed and tell him only at the last minute, thus saving him worry. And, after all, if I couldn't obtain the necessary ingredients . . . but I was sure that I could. Savannah was a sizable city, and a shipping port. There were at least three apothecaries in town, as well as several warehouses that imported specialty items from England. *Someone* was bound to have sulfuric acid, otherwise known as oil of vitriol.

The weather was cool but sunny, and seeing a number of red-coated soldiers in the street, I wondered idly whether climatic considerations had had anything to do with the British deciding to switch their theater of operations to the South.

The elder Mr. Jameson—a sprightly gentleman in his seventies—greeted me pleasantly when I entered Jameson's Apothecary. I'd had occasion to make small purchases of herbs from him before, and we got on well. I presented him with my list and browsed among the jars on his shelves while he pottered to and fro in search of my requests. There were three young soldiers on the other side of the shop, gathered in furtive conversation with the younger Mr. Jameson over something he was showing them under his counter. Pox cures, I assumed—or—giving them the benefit of the doubt regarding foresight—possibly condoms.

They concluded their surreptitious purchases and scuttled out, heads down and rather red in the face. The younger Mr. Jameson, who was the grandson of the owner and about the same age as the just-departed soldiers, was also rather pink but greeted me with aplomb, bowing.

"Your servant, Mrs. Fraser! Might I be of assistance?"

"Oh, thank you, Nigel," I said. "Your grandfather has my list. But"—a thought had occurred to me, perhaps jogged by the soldiers—"I wonder whether you might know of a Mrs. Grey. Amaranthus Grey is her name, and I believe her maiden name was . . . oh, what was it? Cowden! Amaranthus Cowden Grey. Have you ever heard that name?"

He wrinkled his very smooth brow in thought.

"What an odd name. Er—meaning no offense, ma'am," he hastily assured me. "I meant . . . rather exotic. Quite unusual."

"Yes, it is. I don't know her," I said, "but a friend of mine said that she lived in Savannah and had urged me to . . . er . . . make her acquaintance."

"Yes, of course." Nigel hmm'd for a bit but shook his head. "No, I'm sorry, ma'am, I don't believe I've ever encountered an Amaranthus Cowden."

"Cowden?" said Mr. Jameson, emerging suddenly from his back room with several bottles in his hands. "Of course we have, boy. Or, rather, not encountered; she's never come in the shop. But we had a request brought by mail, only two or three weeks ago, asking for . . . oh, what was it, my mind is a sieve, Mrs. Fraser, an absolute sieve, I assure you—don't get old, that's my advice—oh, yes. Gould's complexion cream, Villette's gripe water, a box of pastilles to sweeten the breath, and a dozen bars of Savon D'Artagnan French soap. That was it." He beamed at me over his spectacles. "She lives in Saperville," he added, as an afterthought.

"You're a wonder, Granddad," Nigel murmured dutifully, and reached for the bottles his grandfather was holding. "Shall I wrap these, or are we mixing something for the lady?"

"Oh." Mr. Jameson looked down at the bottles in his hands, as though wondering how they'd got there. "Oh, yes! I wanted to ask you, Mrs. Fraser, what it was you had in mind to *do* with oil of vitriol. It's amazingly dangerous, you know."

"Um, yes, I do." I eyed him consideringly; some men would be quite capable of refusing to sell a woman something they thought inappropriate or dangerous, but Mr. Jameson seemed a worldly sort—and he did at least know that I knew the use of medicinal herbs.

"I have it in mind to make ether," I said. The substance was known, I knew—someone or other had discovered it back in the eighth century, or so I was told in medical school—but its use as an anesthetic wouldn't be developed 'til somewhere in the nineteenth century. I wondered idly whether anyone in the intervening eleven hundred years *had* noticed that the stuff put people to sleep, but had inadvertently killed them and thus abandoned further experimentation.

Both Mr. Jamesons looked surprised.

"Ether?" said Nigel, openly puzzled. "Why would you make it yourself?"

"Why would I—what, do you mean that you have the stuff already made up?" I asked, astonished.

Both of them nodded, pleased to be of service.

"Oh, yes," Mr. Jameson said. "We don't always stock it, of course, but with the . . . er . . . army"—he waved a hand, encompassing the recent invasion and occupation—"there are the troop transports, and there will be a great increase of shipping, now that the blockade is not in effect."

"What does the increase of shipping have to do with the sale of ether?" I asked, wondering whether Mr. Jameson might just possibly be right about the effects of advancing age on the brain.

"Why, ma'am," said Nigel. "It's a sovereign cure for the seasickness. Did you not know?"

131

A BORN GAMBLER

I COUNTED MY INSTRUMENTS for the third time and, finding that none of them had escaped since the last count, covered them with a clean linen cloth and patted it lightly in reassurance—whether of the scalpels or myself, I wasn't sure. Silk sutures, gut sutures, needles—the finest embroidery needles obtainable in Savannah. Pledgets, swabs, dressings, rolled bandages. A six-inch willow twig, carefully cleaned of its pith, sanded smooth, and boiled slowly—so as not to crack the wood—to be used as a catheter to stabilize the urethra and bladder and keep urine out of the surgical field. I'd thought of using a larger one for the bowel, but decided that I'd be better using my fingers to manipulate the slippery tissues there—so long as I managed neither to cut nor puncture myself in the process.

Rachel was coming to assist with the surgery, and I'd go through all the instruments and procedures again with her. I'd come down an hour early, though, wanting both to make my final preparations and to spend a little time alone, settling my mind and spirit to the job ahead.

I felt surprisingly calm, considering the complexity and risks of the operation ahead. It could be argued that even if I failed, the poor child couldn't possibly be worse off than she was—but of course she could die as a result of the surgery, from shock, infection, or even accidental hemorrhage. Abdominal surgery was much more serious than trying a transvaginal correction—but given what I had at hand, I thought the chances of achieving a cure were much better that way. And then there was the matter of the curettage that had removed the dead infant; I had no idea what kind of damage that might have inflicted, but if there was any, I might be able to correct it.

I glanced automatically at the shelf where my penicillin factory was working—or at least I hoped it was working, billions of little spores excreting their helpful substance. I hadn't had time in Savannah to establish a good process and test the resultant product; there was, as was so often the case, no guarantee whatever that I *had* usable penicillin in my broth. But I did have a small chunk of very ripe French cheese, acquired at extravagant cost and stirred into a little boiled milk to make a paste; the thick scent of it fought for ascendancy with the pungent smell of ether.

I could hear the early-morning sounds of the city outside, soothing in their ordinariness: the whisk of a broom on pavement, the clop of horse-drawn wagons, a tantalizing smell of hot bread as the baker's boy's quick footsteps passed by. The simple demands of life quickly made routine out of any sort of chaos, and as invasions went, the occupation of Savannah had been reasonably bloodless.

My sense of well-being and calm detachment was interrupted a moment later by the opening of the surgery door.

"May I help—" I began, turning. Then I saw my visitor and altered my remark to a fairly hostile "What do *you* want?"

Captain—no, he was a colonel now; the wages of treason, I supposed—Richardson smiled charmingly at me, then turned and bolted the door. I pulled out a drawer and removed my small amputation saw; it was small enough to handle quickly, and the serrated edge would take his nose off, if my aim was good.

The charming smile broadened into a grin as he saw what I was about, and he bowed. He wasn't wearing a uniform—and no wonder—but was clothed in a decent, rather sober suit, with unpowdered hair tied simply back. No one would have looked at him twice.

"Your most humble servant, ma'am. Have no alarm; I merely wished to make sure we weren't interrupted."

"Yes, that's what I'm alarmed *about*," I said, taking a firm grip on the saw. "Unbolt that bloody door this minute."

He looked at me for a moment, one eye narrowed in calculation, but then uttered a short laugh and, turning, pulled the bolt. Folding his arms, he leaned against the door.

"Better?"

"Much." I let go the saw but didn't move my hand far from it. "I repeat—what do you want?"

"Well, I thought perhaps the time had come to lay my cards upon your table, Mrs. Fraser—and see whether you might want to play a hand or two."

"The only thing I might be inclined to play with you, Colonel, is mumblety-peg," I said, tapping my fingers on the handle of the saw. "But if you want to show me your cards, go right ahead. You want to be quick about it, though—I have an operation to conduct in less than an hour."

"It shouldn't take that long. May I?" Raising his brows, he gestured at one of the stools. I nodded, and he sat down, looking quite relaxed.

"The essence of the matter, ma'am, is that I am a Rebel—and always have been."

"You—what?"

"I am presently a colonel in the Continental army—but when you first knew me, I was working as an American agent in the guise of a captain in His Majesty's army in Philadelphia."

"I don't understand." I grasped *what* he was telling me but couldn't grasp *why* the hell he should be telling me.

"You are a Rebel yourself, are you not?" One sparse brow lifted in inquiry. He really was the most ordinary-looking man, I thought. If he *was* a spy, he was physically well suited for it.

"I am," I said guardedly. "What about it?"

"Then we're on the same side," he said patiently. "When I cozened Lord John Grey into marrying you, I—"

"You *what*?"

"Surely he told you that I had threatened to have you arrested for distributing seditious materials? At which you're very clumsy, I might add," he added dispassionately. "His lordship assured me that he had no personal interest in you whatever and then most obligingly married you the next day. His lordship is a very gallant man—particularly in view of his own preferences."

He cocked his head, smiling in a conspiratorial manner, and a spear of ice shot through my belly.

"Oh, you do know, then," he observed, watching my face. "I thought you would. He's extremely discreet, but I think you a very perceptive woman, particularly in sexual matters."

"Stand up," I said, in my coldest voice, "and leave. Right now."

He didn't, of course, and I cursed my lack of forethought in not keeping a loaded pistol in the surgery. The saw might serve if he attacked me, but I knew better than to try attacking him.

Besides, what would you do with the body, if you killed him? the logical side of my mind inquired. *He wouldn't fit in the cupboard, let alone the hidey-hole.*

"For the third—and last—time," I said. "What do you bloody want?"

"Your help," he said promptly. "I'd originally had it in mind to use you as an agent in place. You could have been very valuable to me, moving in the same social circles as the British high command. But you seemed too unstable—forgive me, ma'am—to approach immediately. I hoped that as your grief over your first husband faded, you would come to a state of resignation in which I might seek your acquaintance and by degrees achieve a state of intimacy in which you could be persuaded to discover small—and, at first, seemingly innocent—bits of information, which you would pass on to me."

"Just what do you mean by 'intimacy'?" I said, folding my arms. Because while the word in current parlance often meant merely friendship, he hadn't used it with that intonation at all.

"You're a very desirable woman, Mrs. Fraser," he said, looking me over in an objectionably appraising way. "And one who knows her desirability. His lordship obviously wasn't obliging you in that regard, so . . ." He lifted a shoulder, smiling in a deprecating fashion. "But as General Fraser has returned from the dead, I imagine you're no longer susceptible to lures of that kind."

I laughed and dropped my arms.

"You flatter yourself, Colonel," I said dryly. "If not me. Look: why not stop trying to fluster me and tell me what you want me to do and why on earth you think I'd do it."

He laughed, too, which lent some sense of individuality to his face.

"Very well. It may be difficult to believe, but this war will not be won on the battlefield."

"Oh, yes?"

"Yes, I assure you, ma'am. It will be won by spying and by politics."

"A very novel approach, I'm sure." I was trying to place his accent; it was English but a rather flat sort of accent. Not London, not the north . . . educated, but not polished. "I assume you weren't soliciting my assistance in the political line."

"No, actually, I am," he said. "If somewhat indirectly."

"I suggest you try the direct approach," I said. "My patient will be arriving very shortly." The sounds outside had changed; apprentices and housemaids were going past in little groups, bound for work or daily marketing. Calls to and fro, the occasional giggle of a flirtation in passing.

Richardson nodded in acceptance.

"Are you aware of the Duke of Pardloe's opinion of this war?"

I was somewhat taken aback by this. Foolishly, it hadn't occurred to me that Hal might have one, outside the requirements of his service. But if ever I had met a man guaranteed to have opinions, it was Harold, Second Duke of Pardloe.

"What with one thing and another, I've never exchanged views with the duke on political matters. Nor with my—nor with his brother, for that matter."

"Ah. Well, ladies often take no interest in things outside their own sphere of interest—though I rather thought you might have a . . . wider appreciation, shall we say?" He looked pointedly from my canvas apron and tray of instruments to the other appointments of my surgery.

"What about his politics?" I asked shortly, disregarding his implications.

"His Grace is a strong voice in the House of Lords," Richardson said, playing with a frayed thread on the edge of his cuff. "And while he was at first very much in favor of the war, his opinions of late have been noticeably more . . . moderate. He wrote a public letter to the first minister in the fall, urging a consideration of reconciliation."

"And?" I hadn't the slightest idea where he was going with this and was growing impatient.

"Reconciliation is not what we want, ma'am," he said, and, pulling the thread free, flicked it aside. "Such efforts will only delay the inevitable and interfere with the commitment of the citizenry that we desperately need. But the fact that His Grace shows this moderation of outlook is useful to me."

"Jolly good," I said. "Get to the point, if you please."

He ignored this and proceeded about his exposition as though he had all the time in the world.

"Were he fiercely committed to one extreme or the other, he would be difficult to . . . influence. While I don't know His Grace well, everything I know *of* him indicates that he values his sense of honor—"

"He does."

"—almost as much as he values his family," Richardson finished. He looked directly at me, and for the first time I felt a flicker of real fear.

"I have for some time been working to acquire influence—whether direct or otherwise—over such members of the duke's family as are within my reach. With, say, a son—a nephew?—perhaps even his brother in my control, it would then be possible to affect His Grace's public position, in whatever way seemed most advantageous to us."

"If you're suggesting what I think you're suggesting, then I suggest you leave my sight this instant," I said, in what I hoped was a tone of calm menace. Though I spoiled whatever effect there might have been by adding, "Besides, I have absolutely no connection with any of Pardloe's family now."

He smiled faintly, with no sense of pleasantry at all.

"His nephew, William, is in the city, ma'am, and you were seen speaking with him nine days ago. Perhaps you are unaware, though, that both Pardloe and his brother are here, as well?"

"Here?" My mouth hung open for an instant and I closed it sharply. "With the army?"

He nodded.

"I gather that in spite of your recent . . . marital rearrangement? . . . you remain on good terms with Lord John Grey."

"Sufficiently good that I would do nothing whatever to deliver him into your bloody hands, if that's what you had in mind."

"Nothing so crude, ma'am," he assured me, with a brief flash of teeth. "I had in mind only the transmission of information—in both directions. I intend no damage at all to the duke or his family; I only wish to—"

Whatever his intentions, they were interrupted by a tentative knock on the door, which then opened to admit Mrs. Bradshaw's head. She looked apprehensively at me and suspiciously at Richardson, who cleared his throat, stood up, and bowed to her.

"Your servant, ma'am," he said. "I was just taking my leave of Mrs. Fraser. Good day to you." He turned and bowed to me, more elaborately. "Your most humble servant, Mrs. Fraser. I look forward to seeing you again. Soon."

"I'll just bet you do," I said, but far enough under my breath that I doubted he heard me.

Mrs. Bradshaw and Sophronia edged into the room, coming close enough to Richardson on his way out that his face wrinkled up in involuntary revulsion at smelling Sophronia, and he cast a startled glance over his shoulder at me—this causing him to collide heavily with Rachel, hurrying in. He waltzed with her for a step or two, finally getting his balance and making his inelegant escape, pursued by my laughter.

This bit of slapstick had partially dispelled the uneasiness he'd brought to my surgery, and I put him firmly out of my mind. Sufficient to the day was the Richardson thereof, and I had work to do. It was with a sense of confidence that I took Sophronia's small hand between my own and smiled at her downcast face.

"Don't be worried, sweetheart," I said. "I'm going to take care of you."

WITH A MODERN hospital and equipment, I would have done the surgery transvaginally. Given my current resources, though, it would have to be abdominal. With Mrs. Bradshaw anxiously perched on a stool out of the way—she wouldn't leave, and I hoped she wouldn't faint—and Rachel carefully counting drops of ether under her breath, I took my best scalpel and cut into Sophronia's fresh-scrubbed belly. The stretch marks left by her pregnancy were fading but still visible on her very young flesh.

I had makeshift stirrups, should I need them, made by nailing blocks of wood to the table at an angle, and I'd put a wadded towel between her thighs, soaked with the antibacterial lotion I'd scrubbed her with, an alcoholic extraction of crushed garlic mixed with a hot-water extract of lemon balm. It smelled pleasantly kitchen-like and did something to kill the sewage smell—as well as germs, I hoped.

The ether, though, was stronger than anything else, and within ten minutes of starting, I began to feel a slight swimming in my head.

"Mrs. Bradshaw," I called over my shoulder. "Will you open the window, please? And the shutters?" I hoped we wouldn't attract any spectators—but the need for fresh air was imperative.

The vesicovaginal fistula was luckily fairly small and in a reasonably easy position to reach. Rachel was holding a retractor for me with one hand, keeping the other on Sophronia's pulse, and administering more ether every few minutes.

"Are you all right, Rachel?" I asked, trimming back the edges of the fistula in order to get a decent field for stitching—the edges were flattened and macerated, and the tissue would shred and pull apart under any sort of pressure. I'd had some hesitation in asking her to help today; I would have asked Jenny, but she was suffering from what was called the catarrh, and sneezing and coughing were the last things I wanted in a surgical assistant.

"I am," she answered, her voice slightly muffled behind her not-quite-sterile-but-at-least-boiled mask. She'd used one of Ian's handkerchiefs for the purpose; it was an incongruously cheerful calico in dark-pink-and-white checks. Ian's taste in clothing was strongly Mohawk.

"Good. Tell me if you feel at all dizzy." I had no idea what I'd do if she *did* feel dizzy—perhaps Mrs. Bradshaw could take over the dropping bottle for a few minutes. . . .

I spared a quick glance over my shoulder. Mrs. Bradshaw sat on her stool, gloved hands clasped tight in her lap and her face pale as a sheet, but she sat firm.

"It's going well so far," I said to her, trying to sound as reassuring as possible through my own chaste white mask. The masks seemed to unnerve her, and she looked away, swallowing.

It really was going well, though. While it was Sophronia's youth that had caused the problem, that also meant that her tissues were healthy, in good shape, and she had considerable animal vitality. If the surgery was successful, if there was little or no subsequent infection, she'd heal very quickly. If.

"Ifs" hover in the air above your head all the time when you're doing surgery, like a cloud of gnats. For the most part, though, they keep a respectful distance, only buzzing dimly in the background.

Done.

"One down, one to go," I murmured, and, dipping a wad of sterilized gauze into my cheese lotion, I daubed some—not without a qualm—over the newly stitched repair. "Onward."

The bowel repair was easier—though more unpleasant. It was quite cold in the surgery—I hadn't lit a fire, not wanting soot in the air—but I was sweating; beads of perspiration ran tickling down the side of my nose and down my neck from my bound-up hair.

I could feel the girl, though, the life of her echoing in my hands, her heartbeat strong and steady—there was a large blood vessel visible on the surface of the uterus, and I could see it pulsing. She'd been lucky in the one thing: the uterus hadn't been perforated, and looked healthy. I couldn't tell whether there was internal scarring, but when I cupped my hand gently over the organ, it felt normal to me. For a moment, I closed my eyes, feeling deeper, and found what I thought I needed. I opened them again, blotted the ooze of blood from the cut tissues, and reached for a fresh needle.

How long? Anesthesia complications were one of the nasty little flying "ifs," and that one flew down and perched on my shoulder. I had no clock or pocket watch but had brought a small sandglass borrowed from our landlady.

"How long has it been, Rachel?"

"Twenty minutes." Her voice was soft, and I looked up, but she was still steady, her eyes fixed on the open belly. She was nearly four months' pregnant, her own belly slightly rounded. "Don't worry," I said to her briefly. "It won't happen to you."

"Surely it *could*?" she said, still more softly.

I shook my head.

"Not if I'm with you when you give birth."

She made a small amused sound and picked up the dropping bottle again.

"Thee will be, I assure thee, Claire."

Rachel was shivering slightly by the time I'd finished; I was wringing wet but feeling the glow of at least temporary victory. The fistulas were repaired, the leakage stopped. I irrigated the surgical field with saline solution and the organs glistened, the beautiful deep colors of the body unmarred by smears of fecal matter.

I paused for a moment to admire the neat compactness of the pelvic organs, all in their places. There was a tiny trickle of pale urine from the catheter, staining the towel with a faint yellow shadow. In a modern hospital, I would have left the catheter in during the healing, but it would be difficult to manage without a drainage bag, and the chances of irritation or infection from the device were likely greater than the possible benefits of leaving it. I eased it free of her body, watching. Within a few seconds, the flow of urine ceased, and I let out a breath I hadn't realized I was holding.

I had taken up a fresh needle threaded with silk, to close the incision, when something occurred to me.

"Rachel—do you want to look? Closely, I mean." Sophronia had had ether within the last couple of minutes and was still deeply under; Rachel checked her color and breathing and then came round the table to stand beside me.

I didn't think she'd be disturbed by the blood or the sight of organs, given the things she'd seen in military camps and battlefields. She wasn't, but she *was* disturbed.

"That—" She swallowed and put a hand to her swelling stomach, very gently. "So beautiful," she whispered. "How the body is made. How such things can be."

"It is," I said, her awe making me lower my own voice.

"To think of her poor infant, though . . . and she no more than a child . . ."

I glanced at Rachel and saw tears standing in her eyes. And I saw the thought cross her face, masked as it was: *It could happen to me.*

"Yes," I said quietly. "Go back to the ether; I'll close the incision now." But as I dipped my hands again in the bowl of alcohol and water, something else occurred to me.

Oh, God, I thought, appalled at the thought. But . . .

"Mrs. Bradshaw," I said. She was sitting with her head bowed, arms wrapped round herself against the chill, perhaps half asleep. When I spoke, though, her head came up sharply.

"Is it over?" she asked. "Does she live?"

"She does," I said. "And, with luck, will continue to do so. But . . ." I hesitated, but I had to ask. And I had to ask this woman.

"Before I sew up the incision . . . I can—do a very minor procedure that will stop Sophronia from becoming pregnant again."

Mrs. Bradshaw blinked.

"You can?"

"Yes. It's a simple thing to do—but, once done, it can't be undone. She'd never be able to have babies." A fresh cloud of "ifs" had formed, buzzing anxiously over my shoulder.

She was thirteen. She was a slave. And had a master who used her. If she were to become pregnant again soon, she might well die during the labor and would almost certainly be seriously damaged. It might never be safe for her to bear a child—but it wasn't safe for any woman, ever. And "never" is a very big word.

Mrs. Bradshaw had drifted slowly toward the table, her eyes twitching toward the exposed, half-draped body, then away, unable either to look or to stay away. I put out a hand, warding her off.

"Don't come closer, please."

"He was sad when the baby died. He cried." I could still hear the sadness in Sophronia's voice; she mourned her child. How could she not? Could I take away the possibility of another—forever—without even asking her what she felt about it?

And yet . . .

If she bore a child, it, too, would be a slave; it might be taken from her and sold. Even if not, it would likely live and die in slavery.

And yet . . .

"If she wasn't able to bear children . . ." Mrs. Bradshaw said slowly. She stopped speaking, and I could see the thoughts crossing her white, pinched face; her lips had all but disappeared, so tightly were they pressed together. I didn't think she was concerned with the fact that Sophronia's value would be diminished if she couldn't reproduce.

Would the fear of damage due to pregnancy stop Mr. Bradshaw from using the girl?

If she were barren, would he feel no hesitation?

"He didn't hesitate because she was twelve," I said, my words cold as pellets of ice. "Would the chance of killing her next time stop him?"

She stared at me in shock, mouth hanging open. She blinked, swallowed, and looked at Sophronia, limp and helpless, body gaping open on the blood-soaked towels, the floor around her thickly spattered with her fluids.

"I think thee cannot," Rachel said quietly. She looked from me to Mrs. Bradshaw, and it wasn't clear to whom she was speaking: perhaps both of us. She was holding Sophronia's hand.

"She felt her child move within her. She loved it." Rachel's voice broke, and she choked a little. Tears welled and rolled down to disappear into her mask. "She wouldn't . . . she . . ." She stopped, gulping a little, and shook her head, unable to go on.

Mrs. Bradshaw put a hand clumsily over her face, as though to stop me seeing her thoughts.

"I can't," she said, and repeated almost angrily, behind the shield of her hand, "I *can't*. It isn't my fault! I tried—I tried to do the right thing!" She wasn't talking to me; I didn't know if it was to Mr. Bradshaw or God.

The "ifs" were all still there, but so was Sophronia, and I couldn't leave her any longer.

"All right," I said quietly. "Go and sit down, Mrs. Bradshaw. I said I'd take care of her, and I will."

My hands were cold, and the body under them was very warm, pulsing with life. I picked up the needle and put in the first suture.

132

WILL-O'-THE-WISP

*S*APERVILLE? WILLIAM WAS beginning to wonder whether Amaranthus Cowden Grey actually existed or whether she was a will-o'-the-wisp created by Ezekiel Richardson. But if so—to what end?

He'd made careful inquiries after receiving Mrs. Fraser's note yesterday; there really was a place called Saperville—a tiny settlement some twenty miles to the southwest of Savannah, in what his interlocutor had told him was "the piney woods," in a tone of voice suggesting that the piney woods were next door to hell, both in terms of remoteness and uncivil conditions. He couldn't conceive what might have made the woman—if she really did exist—go to such a place.

If she *didn't* exist . . . then someone had invented her, and the most likely suspect for such a deception was Ezekiel Richardson. William had been decoyed by Richardson before. The entire experience in the Dismal Swamp still made him grit his teeth in retrospect—the more so when he reflected that, if not for that chain of events, neither he nor Ian Murray would have met Rachel Hunter.

With an effort, he dismissed Rachel from his mind—she wouldn't stay out of his dreams, but he didn't have to think about her while awake—and returned to the elusive Amaranthus.

In purely practical terms, Saperville lay on the other side of Campbell's army, which was still encamped over several acres of ground outside Savannah, while billeting arrangements were made, housing built, and fortifications dug. A large part of the Continental forces that had opposed them had been neatly bagged up and sent north as prisoners, and the chances of the remnants causing trouble for Campbell were minuscule. That didn't mean William could walk straight through the camp without attracting attention. He might not meet with anyone who knew him, but that didn't mean no one would question him. And however innocuous his errand, the last thing he wanted was to have to explain to anyone why he had resigned his commission.

He'd had time, while Campbell was arraying his forces, to take Miranda out of Savannah and board her with a farmer some ten miles to the north. The army foragers might still find her—they certainly would, if the army remained in Savannah for any great time—but for the moment she was safe. All too familiar with military rapacity—he'd seized horses and supplies himself, many times—he wasn't about to take her within sight of the army.

He drummed his fingers on the table, thinking, but reluctantly concluded that he'd best walk to Saperville, making a wide circle around Campbell's men. He wasn't going to find out about bloody Amaranthus sitting here, that was sure.

Resolved, he paid for his meal, wrapped himself in his cloak, and set off. It wasn't raining, that was one good thing.

It was January, though, and the days were still short; the shadows were lengthening by the time he came to the edge of the sea of camp followers that had formed around the army. He made his way past a conclave of red-armed laundresses, their kettles all fuming in the chilly air and the scent of smoke and lye soap hanging over them in a witchy sort of haze.

"Double, double toil and trouble," he chanted under his breath. *"Fire burn and caldron bubble. Fillet of a fenny snake, in the caldron boil and bake. Eye of newt and toe of frog, wool of bat and tongue of dog . . ."* He couldn't recall what came next and abandoned the effort.

Beyond the laundresses, the ground was choppy, the boggy spots interspersed with higher bits of ground, these crowned with stunted trees and low bushes—and quite obviously providing a footing, so to speak, for the whores to ply their own trade.

He gave these a somewhat wider berth and consequently found himself squelching through something that was not quite a bog, but not far off, either. It *was* remarkably beautiful, though, in a chiaroscuro sort of way; the fading light somehow made each barren twig stand out in stark contrast to the air, the swollen buds still sleeping but rounded, balanced on the edge between winter's death and the life of spring. He wished for a moment that he could draw, or paint, or write poetry, but as it was, he could only pause for a few seconds to admire it.

As he did so, though, he felt a permanence form in his heart, a quiet sense that even though he had only these few seconds, he would have them forever, could come back to this place, this time, in his mind.

He was right, though not entirely for the reasons he supposed.

He would have passed right by her, thinking she was a part of the bog, for she was curled over in a tight ball and the hood of her sad-colored cloak covered her head. But she made a tiny sound, a heartbroken whimper that stopped him in his tracks, and he saw her then, crouched in the mud at the foot of a sweet gum.

"Ma'am?" he said tentatively. She hadn't been aware of him; she uncurled suddenly, her white face staring up at him, shocked and tear-streaked. Then she gulped air and leapt to her feet, throwing herself at him.

"Wiyum! Wiyum!" It was Fanny, Jane's sister, alone, daubed with mud, and in a state of complete hysteria. She'd catapulted into his arms; he gripped her firmly, holding her lest she fly to pieces, which she looked very like doing.

"Frances. Frances! It's all right; I'm here. What's happened? Where's Jane?"

At her sister's name, she gave a wail that made his blood go cold and buried her face in his chest. He patted her back and, this failing to help, then shook her a little.

"Frances! Pull yourself together. Sweetheart," he added more gently, see-ing her swimming, red-rimmed eyes and swollen face. She'd been weeping for a long time. "Tell me what's happened, so I can help you."

"You can't," she blubbered, and thumped her forehead hard against his chest, several times. "You can't, you can't, nobody can, you *can't*!"

"Well, we'll see about that." He looked around for someplace to sit her down, but there was nothing more solid than clumps of grass and spindly trees in sight. "Come on, it's getting dark. We need to get out of this place, at least." He set her firmly on her feet, took her arm, and compelled her to start walking, on the theory that one can't be hysterical and walk in a straight line at the same time.

In fact, this seemed to be the case. By the time he'd got her back to the camp followers' area, she was sniffling but no longer wailing, and she was looking where she was going. He bought her a cup of hot soup from a woman with a steaming cauldron and made her drink it, though a remnant thought of the fingers of birth-strangled babes made him forgo one for himself.

He handed back the empty cup and, seeing that Fanny was at least super-ficially calm now, towed her toward the hillock with trees, in search of a seat. She stiffened, though, as they approached, and pulled back with a little mew of fear.

Losing patience, he put a hand under her chin and made her meet his eyes.

"Frances," he said in a level tone. "Tell me what the devil is going on, and do it now. Words of one syllable, if you please."

"Jane," she said, and her eyes began to overflow again. She dashed at them with her cloak-covered forearm, though, and, with a visible effort, managed to tell him.

"It wass a cuwwy."

"A what? Oh, a cully, sorry. At the brothel, you mean. Yes?"

She nodded.

"He wass looking thu the gulls and s-saw J-Jane . . ." She gulped. "He wass a fwend of Captain Hahkness. He wass at da house when he—Captain Hahkness—died. He weckognized huh."

A ball of ice formed in William's entrails at her words.

"The devil he did," he said softly. "What did he do, Fanny?"

The man—a Major Jenkins, she said—had seized Jane by the arm and dragged her off, Fanny running after them. He had taken her all the way into the city, to a house with soldiers standing outside. They wouldn't let Fanny in, so she had stood outside in the street, terrified but determined not to leave, and after a time they had given up trying to drive her away.

The house with soldiers standing outside was very likely Colonel Camp-bell's headquarters, William thought, beginning to feel sick. Presumably Jen-kins had hauled Jane before some senior officer, if not Campbell himself, to denounce her for Harkness's murder.

Would they even bother giving her a trial? He doubted it. The city was under martial law; the army—or, rather, Lieutenant Colonel Campbell—did as it saw fit, and he doubted very much that Campbell would give a whore accused of murdering a soldier the benefit of any doubt.

"Where is she now?" He forced himself to go on sounding calm, though he felt anything but.

Fanny gulped and wiped her nose on her cloak again. At this point, it scarcely mattered, but by instinct he pulled his handkerchief from his sleeve and handed it to her.

"Dey took her to anovver house. On de edge of da city. Dere's a big tree dere, ousside. I tink dey'll hang her, Wiyum."

William was very much afraid they would. He swallowed the saliva that had collected in his mouth and patted Fanny's shoulder.

"I'll go and see what I can find out. Do you have friends here—someone to stay with?" He motioned at the mass of the encampment, where small fires were beginning to glow amidst the oncoming shades of night. She nodded, pressing her lips together to keep them from trembling.

"All right. Go and find them. I'll come in the morning—at first light. Meet me where I found you, all right?"

"Awright," she whispered, and laid a small white hand on his chest, just over his heart. "Sank you, Wiyum."

HIS ONLY CHANCE was to talk to Campbell. Fanny had told him the house where Jenkins had taken Jane was the big gray house north of Reynolds Square; that was the likeliest place to start.

He paused on the street to brush the worst of the dried mud and bits of vegetation off his cloak. He was only too well aware that he looked like exactly what he'd been pretending to be for the last three months: an unemployed laborer. On the other hand—

As he'd resigned his commission, he was no longer under Campbell's authority. And no matter how he personally felt about the matter of his title, it was still his, by law. The Ninth Earl of Ellesmere drew himself up to his full height, squared his shoulders, and went to war.

Manner and speech got him past the sentries at the door. The servant who came to take his cloak stared at him in unmitigated dismay, but was afraid to throw him out, and vanished to find someone who would take the responsibility of dealing with him.

There was a dinner party going on; he could hear the clink of silver and china, the glugging of bottles being poured, and the muted rumble of conversation, punctuated by bursts of polite laughter. His hands were sweating; he wiped them unobtrusively on his breeches.

What the devil was he going to say? He'd tried to formulate some line of reasonable argument on his way, but everything seemed to fall to pieces the moment he thought of it. He'd have to say something, though. . . .

Then he heard a voice, raised in question, that made his heart skip a beat. Uncle Hal! He couldn't be mistaken; his uncle and his father both had light but penetrating voices, clear as cut crystal—and sharp as good Toledo steel when they wanted to be.

"Here, you!" He strode down the hall and grabbed a servitor coming out of the dining room with a platter of crab shells in his hands. "Give me that," he ordered, taking the platter from the man's hands, "go back in there, and tell the Duke of Pardloe his nephew would like a word."

The man goggled at him, mouth open, but didn't move. William repeated his request, adding "Please," but also adding a stare meant to indicate that, in the case of resistance, his next step would be to bash the man over the head with the platter. This worked, and the man turned like an automaton and marched back into the dining room—from which, in very short order, his uncle emerged, polished in dress and manner but clearly excited in countenance.

"William! What the devil are you doing with that?" He took the platter from William and shoved it carelessly under one of the gilt chairs ranged along the wall of the foyer. "What's happened? Have you found Ben?"

Christ, he hadn't thought of that. Naturally, Uncle Hal would assume . . . With a grimace, he shook his head.

"I haven't, Uncle, I'm sorry. I think I do know where his wife is, but—"

Hal's face underwent a couple of lightning shifts, from excitement to disappointment to outward calm.

"Good. Where are you staying? John and I will come and—"

"Papa's here, too?" William blurted, feeling like a fool. If he hadn't been so sensitive about his position and thus avoided anyone from the army, he would have learned that the 46th was part of Campbell's force in short order.

"Naturally," Hal said, with a touch of impatience. "Where else would he be?"

"With Dottie, looking for Ben's wife," William riposted smartly. "Is she here, too?"

"No." His uncle looked displeased, but not altogether displeased. "She discovered that she was with child, so John very properly brought her back to New York—and less properly consigned her to the care of her husband. She's presumably wherever Washington's troops are at the moment, unless that bloody Quaker's had the common sense to—"

"Oh, Pardloe." A stout officer in a lieutenant colonel's uniform and an ornate double-curled wig stood in the doorway, looking mildly surprised. "Thought you'd been taken ill, the way you dashed out." Despite the mild tone, there was an undercurrent in the man's voice that drove a two-penny nail into William's spine. This was Archibald Campbell, and from the visible frostiness with which he and Uncle Hal were viewing each other, Uncle Hal's value as a negotiator might not be what his nephew could hope.

Still, Uncle Hal could—and did—introduce William to Campbell, thus relieving him of the worry of producing adequate *bona fides*.

"Your servant, my lord," Campbell said, eyeing him suspiciously. He glanced over his shoulder, moving out of the way of a pair of servants carrying a massive wine cooler. "I fear that dinner has nearly concluded, but if you'd like, I'll have the servants provide a small supper for you in the office."

"No, sir, I thank you," William said, bowing—though the smell of food made his stomach gurgle. "I took the liberty of coming to speak with you about a . . . um . . . an urgent matter."

"Indeed." Campbell looked displeased and wasn't troubling to hide it. "It can't wait until the morning?"

"I don't know that it can, sir." He'd had a look at the big oak on the edge of town, which he thought must be the one Fanny meant. As Jane's corpse wasn't hanging from it, he assumed she was still being held prisoner in the house nearby. But that was no assurance that they didn't mean to execute her at dawn. The army was rather fond of executing prisoners at dawn; start the day off in the right frame of mind . . .

He got hold of his racing thoughts and bowed again.

"It concerns a young woman, sir, who I understand was arrested earlier today, upon suspicion of—of assault. I—"

"Assault?" Campbell's beetling brows shot up toward the furbelows of his wig. "She stabbed a man twenty-six times, then cut his throat in cold blood. If that's your notion of assault, I should hate to see—"

"Who is this young woman, my lord?" Uncle Hal put in, his tone formal and his face impassive.

"Her name is Jane," William began, and stopped, having no idea what her last name might be. "Uh . . . Jane . . ."

"Pocock, she says," put in Campbell. "She's a whore."

"A—" Hal cut his exclamation off one syllable too late. He narrowed his eyes at William.

"She is . . . under my protection," William said, as firmly as he could.

"Really?" drawled Campbell. He gave Uncle Hal a look of amused contempt, and Uncle Hal went white with suppressed fury—most of which was not suppressed at all in the look he turned on William.

"Yes. Really," said William, aware that this was not brilliant but unable to think of anything better. "I wish to speak on her behalf. Provide her with a solicitor," he added, rather wildly. "I'm sure she isn't guilty of the crime of which she's accused."

Campbell actually laughed, and William felt his ears burning with hot blood. He might have said something imprudent had Lord John not appeared at this juncture, as impeccably uniformed as his brother and looking mildly inquisitive.

"Ah, William," he said, as though he'd quite expected to see his son here. His eyes flicked rapidly from face to face, obviously drawing conclusions about the tenor of the conversation, if not its subject. With scarcely a pause, he stepped forward and embraced William warmly.

"You're here! I'm delighted to see you," he said, smiling up at William. "I have remarkable news! Will you excuse us for a moment, sir?" he said to Campbell, and, not waiting for an answer, gripped William by the elbow, yanked open the front door, towed him out onto the wide veranda, and closed the door firmly behind them.

"All right. Tell me what's going on," Lord John said, low-voiced. "And do it fast.

"Jesus," he said, when William had blurted out an only slightly confused account of the situation. He rubbed a hand slowly over his face, thinking, and repeated, "Jesus."

"Yes," William said, still upset but feeling some comfort at his father's presence. "I'd thought to talk to Campbell, but then when Uncle Hal was here, I hoped . . . but he and Campbell seem to be—"

"Yes, their relationship could best be described as one of cordial hatred," Lord John agreed. "Archibald Campbell is highly unlikely to do Hal any sort of favor, unless it was to escort him personally into the next southbound coach for hell." He blew out his breath and shook his head, as though to clear it of wine fumes.

"I don't know, William, I really don't. The girl—she *is* a whore?"

"Yes."

"Did she do it?"

"Yes."

"Oh, God." He looked helplessly at William for a moment, then squared his shoulders. "All right. I'll do what I can, but I don't promise anything. There's a tavern on the square, called Tudy's. Go there and wait—I rather think your presence will not be helpful in this discussion."

IT SEEMED FOREVER but must have been less than an hour when Lord John appeared at Tudy's. One look at his face told William that he hadn't been successful.

"I'm sorry," he said without preliminary, and sat down opposite William. He'd come out without his hat and brushed at the raindrops caught in his hair. "The girl—"

"Her name is Jane," William interrupted. It seemed important that he insist on that, not let everyone just dismiss her as "the whore."

"Miss Jane Eleanora Pocock," his father agreed, with a brief nod. "Apparently she not only committed the crime but has confessed to it. A signed confession, no less. I read it." He rubbed a hand tiredly over his face. "Her only objection was to the statement that she stabbed Harkness twenty-six times and cut his throat. According to her, she only stabbed him once before cutting his throat. People *will* exaggerate these things."

"That's what she told me." William's throat felt tight. His father darted a glance at him but chose not to say anything in response to this. What he thought was all too clear, though.

"She was trying to save her young sister from being defiled by the man," he said, urgently defensive. "And Harkness was a depraved sod who'd used her—Jane, I mean—abominably! I heard him talk about it. It would have turned your stomach to hear him."

"I daresay," Lord John agreed. "Dangerous clients are one of the hazards of that profession. But was there no recourse available to her other than a carving knife? Most brothels that cater to soldiers have some means of rescuing the whores from . . . excessive importunity. And Miss Pocock, from what Colonel Campbell tells me, is a—er—an—"

"Expensive piece. She is. Was."

William reached out blindly for the mug of beer he'd been ignoring, took a huge gulp, and coughed convulsively. His father watched with some sympathy.

William at last drew breath and sat, staring at his fists, clenched on the table.

"She hated him," he said at last, low-voiced. "And the madam wouldn't have kept her sister from him; he'd paid for her maidenhead."

Lord John sighed and covered one of William's fists with his hand, squeezing.

"Do you love the young woman, William?" he asked, very quietly. The tavern wasn't busy, but there were enough men drinking there that no one was noticing them.

William shook his head, helpless.

"I—tried to protect her. To save her from Harkness. I—I bought her for the night. I didn't stop to think that he'd come back—but of course he would," he finished bitterly. "I likely made things worse for her."

"There wouldn't have been a way of making them better, save marrying the girl or killing Harkness yourself," Lord John said dryly. "And I don't recommend murder as a way of settling difficult situations. It tends to lead to complications—but not nearly as many as marriage." He got up and went to the bar, returning with two steaming cups of hot rum punch.

"Drink that," he said, pushing one in front of William. "You look chilled through."

He was; he'd taken a table in a far corner, nowhere near the fire, and a fine, uncontrollable shiver was running through him, enough to ripple the surface of the punch when he wrapped his hand round the pewter cup. The punch was good, though made with preserved lemon peel, sweet, strong, and hot and made with good brandy as well as rum. He hadn't eaten anything in hours, and it warmed his stomach immediately.

They drank in silence—what was there to say? There was no way of saving Jane, bar some sort of physical assault, and he couldn't ask his father or uncle to join or support him in that sort of desperate caper. He didn't think they'd do it, for one thing. He believed in their considerable affection for him but knew quite well that they'd see it as their duty to prevent him committing folly that could well prove fatal.

"It won't have been entirely in vain, you know," Lord John said quietly. "She did save her sister."

William nodded, unable to speak. The thought of seeing Fanny in the morning, only to tell her—and then what? Must he stand beside her and watch Jane be hanged?

Lord John stood up and, without asking, went back to the bar for another pair of drinks. William looked at the gently steaming cup set before him and then at his father.

"You think you bloody know me, don't you?" he said, but with true affection in his voice.

"Yes, I do think that, William," said his father, in the same tone. "Drink your drink."

William smiled and, rising, clapped his father on the shoulder.

"Maybe you do, at that. I'll see you in the morning, Papa."

133

LAST RESORT

I WAS LYING IN bed beside Jamie, drowsily wondering on what grounds I could induce Mrs. Weisenheimer to collect her urine for me. She suffered from gallstones, for which the most effective herbal treatment I had was bearberry. Fortunately, Mr. Jameson had some of the dried leaf in stock. One had to be careful in using it, though, because it contained arbutin, which hydrolyzed to hydroquinone—a very effective urinary antiseptic, but dangerously toxic. On the other hand . . . it was an effective skin lightener, if applied topically.

I yawned and decided that it wasn't worth the bother of making Jamie come to the surgery and talk to Mrs. Weisenheimer in German about her urine. He'd do it if I asked, but I'd never hear the end of it.

I dismissed the idea and rolled over, cuddling against Jamie, who was peacefully asleep on his back, as usual, but who half-woke at my touch, patted me clumsily, curled round me, and fell soundly asleep again at once. Ninety seconds later, there was a knock at the door.

"*Ifrinn!*" Jamie shot bolt upright, rubbed a hand roughly over his face, and threw back the covers. Groaning, I followed suit less athletically, crawling out of bed and groping blindly for my knitted slippers.

"Let me go. It's probably for me." At this hour of the night, a knock at the door was more likely someone with a medical emergency than one involving salt fish or horses, but given the military occupation of the city, one never knew.

One certainly hadn't anticipated opening the door to find William standing on the other side of it, looking pale and feral.

"Is Mr. Fraser at home?" he said tersely. "I need his help."

FRASER HAD DRESSED at once, taken up a belt with a sheathed dirk and a leather bag upon it, and fastened this round his waist without question. He was wearing Highland dress, William saw, a much-worn, faded plaid. He gathered up a fold of it around his shoulders, nodding toward the door.

"We'd best go down to my wife's surgery," he said softly, nodding toward the thin wall, the laths clearly visible through its plaster. "Ye can tell me there what's to do."

William followed him through the rain-slicked streets, water like cold tears on his cheeks. Inside, he felt parched and dry, cracked leather wrapped around a core of solid terror. Fraser didn't speak on the way but clutched him once by the elbow, pushing him into a narrow space between two buildings, just as an army patrol came round the corner. He pressed hard against the wall, shoulder to shoulder with Fraser, and felt the man's denseness and warmth as a shock.

In the back of his mind was the memory of having been small and lost in the fog on the fells of the Lake District. Cold and terrified, he'd fallen into a rocky hollow and lain there, frozen, hearing ghosts in the mist. And then the overwhelming relief of Mac's finding him, of the enveloping warmth of the groom's arms.

He shoved the memory impatiently aside, but a lingering sense of something that wasn't quite hope remained when the last of the boots trampled out of hearing and Fraser slid from their hiding place, beckoning him to follow.

The small surgery was cold and dark, smelling of herbs and medicines and old blood. There was a sweetish smell, too, strange but familiar, and after a moment's disorientation, he realized that it must be ether; he'd smelled it on Mother Claire and Denzell Hunter when they'd operated on his cousin Henry.

Fraser had locked the door behind them and found a candlestick in the cupboard. He handed this to William, took a tinderbox from the same cupboard, and set the candle alight with a brisk efficiency. The wavering light shone up into his face, and the boldness of his features sprang into view: long straight nose and heavy brows, broad cheekbones and the fine deep modeling of jaw and temple. It was damnably queer to see the resemblance so marked and so close, but at the moment William actually found it an odd comfort.

Fraser set the candlestick on the table and motioned William to one of the two stools, taking the other.

"Tell me, then," he said calmly. "It's safe here; no one will hear. I gather it's a dangerous matter?"

"Life and death," William said, and, with a deep breath, began.

Fraser listened with complete attention, his eyes fixed intently on William's face as he talked. When he had finished, there was a moment of silence. Then Fraser nodded once, as if to himself.

"This young woman," he said. "May I know what she is to you?"

William hesitated, not knowing what to say. What *was* Jane to him? Not a friend, nor yet a lover. And yet . . .

"She—I took her and her sister under my protection," he said. "When they left Philadelphia with the army."

Fraser nodded as though this was a perfectly adequate explanation of the situation.

"D'ye know that your uncle and his regiment are with the occupying army? That he's here, I mean?"

"Yes. I spoke with my—with Lord John and Pardloe. They aren't able to help. I—have resigned my commission," he felt compelled to add. "That hasn't anything to do with why they can't help, only that I'm not subject any longer to military command myself."

"Aye, I saw ye weren't in uniform," he said. He drummed the fingers of his right hand briefly on the tabletop, and William saw with surprise that the ring finger was missing, a thick scar down the back of the hand. Fraser saw him notice.

"Saratoga," he said, with the flicker of something that might have been a smile in other circumstances.

William felt a small shock at the word, things unnoticed at the time suddenly returning to him. Himself kneeling through the night beside Brigadier Simon Fraser's deathbed and a tall man on the other side, a white bandage on his hand, leaning down from the shadows to say something softly in the Scottish tongue to the brigadier, who replied in the same language.

"The brigadier," he said, and stopped abruptly.

"My kinsman," Fraser said. He delicately forbore to add, *"And yours,"* but William made that connection easily. He felt it as a distant echo of grief, a pebble dropped in water, but that could wait.

"Is the young woman's life worth yours?" Fraser asked. "Because I think that consideration is likely what lies behind your—your other kinsmen's"— the corner of his mouth twitched, though William couldn't tell whether with humor or distaste—"failure to help ye."

William felt hot blood rise in his face, anger supplanting desperation.

"They didn't *fail* me. They couldn't help. Are you saying that you will not help me, either, sir? Or can't? Are you afraid of the venture?"

Fraser gave him a quelling look; William registered this but didn't care. He was on his feet, fists clenched.

"Don't bother, then. I'll do it myself."

"If ye thought ye could, ye'd never have come to me, lad," Fraser said evenly.

"Don't you call me 'lad,' you, you—" William choked off the epithet, not out of prudence but out of inability to choose among the several that sprang at once to his mind.

"Sit down," Fraser said, not raising his voice but infusing it with an air of command that made it unthinkable—or at least uncomfortable—to disobey. William glared at him. His chest was heaving and yet he couldn't draw enough breath to speak. He didn't sit down, but he did uncurl his fists and stand still. At last he managed a jerky nod. Fraser drew a long, visible breath and let it out slowly, white in the chill of the dark little room.

"All right, then. Tell me where she is and what ye ken of the physical situation." He glanced at the shuttered window, where oozing damp showed black between the slats as the rain seeped through. "The night's not long enough."

THEY WENT TO the warehouse where Fraser worked, down by the river. Fraser left William outside to keep watch, unlocked a man door at the side, and slid through it with no sound, reappearing a few minutes later dressed in rough breeches and a shirt that didn't fit him, carrying a small burlap bag and two large black kerchiefs. He handed one of these to William and, folding the other diagonally, tied it round his face, covering nose and mouth.

"Is this truly necessary?" William tied on his own kerchief but felt slightly ridiculous, as though dressing up for some bizarre pantomime.

"Ye can go without if ye like," Fraser advised him, taking a knitted wool cap out of the bag, tucking his hair up under it, and then pulling it down over his eyebrows. "I canna risk being recognized."

"If you think the risk too great—" William began, an edge in his voice, but Fraser stopped him, gripping his arm.

"Ye've a claim to my help," he said, voice low and brusque. "For any venture ye deem worthy. But I've a family who have a claim to my protection. I canna leave them to starve if I'm taken."

William had no chance to reply to this; Fraser had locked the door and was already walking off, beckoning impatiently. He did think about it, though, following the Scot through the mist that rose knee-high in the streets. It had stopped raining; that was one thing in their favor.

"For any venture ye deem worthy." Not a word about Jane's being a whore or about her being a confessed murderess. Perhaps it was that Fraser himself was a criminal and felt some sympathy on that account.

Or maybe it's just that he's willing to take my word that I have to do it. And willing to take the devil of a risk to help me.

But such thoughts could do no good now, and he put them out of his mind. They hurried on, soft-footed and faceless, through the empty squares of Savannah, toward the house by the hanging tree.

"I DINNA SUPPOSE ye ken which room is hers?" Jamie murmured to William. They were loitering under the big live oak, concealed not only by its shadows but by the long beards of Spanish moss that hung from its branches and the mist that drifted under them.

"No."

"Wait here." Fraser disappeared in that unnerving catlike way of his. Left to his own devices and further unnerved by the silence, William thought to explore the contents of the bag Fraser had left on the ground. These proved to be several sheets of paper and a stoppered vial of what—un-stoppered—proved to be treacle.

He was still puzzling over that when Fraser was back, as suddenly as he'd disappeared.

"There's no but one guard on the house, at the front," he said, moving close enough to whisper into William's ear. "And all the windows are dark, save one upstairs. There's a single candle burning; it must be hers."

"Why do you think that?" William whispered back, startled.

Fraser hesitated for a moment, but then said, even more quietly, "I once spent a night expecting to be hanged the next morning. I wouldna have spent it in darkness, given the choice. Come on."

It was a two-story house and, while fairly large, simply built. Two rooms on the upper floor at the back, two at the front. The shutters of the upper windows were open, and the glow of a candle flickered in the right-hand room at the back. Fraser insisted on circling the house—at a cautious distance, darting from bush to tree to bush—to be sure of the guard's position. The man, armed with a musket slung across his back, was on the veranda that ran across the front of the house. Judging from his build, he was young, probably younger than William. And by his posture, which was careless in the extreme, he wasn't expecting any trouble.

"I don't suppose they thought a whore would have any friends," William said under his breath, getting a brief Scottish grunt in return. Fraser beckoned and led him round the back of the house.

They passed a window that likely belonged to the kitchen; there were no curtains, and he could see the faint light of a smothered hearth deep inside, just visible through the shutters. There'd be a risk that one or more slaves or servants slept in the kitchen, though—and he was pleased to see that Fraser appeared to be going on that assumption. They moved around the next corner of the house, as quietly as possible.

Fraser pressed his ear to the shutters of a large window but appeared to hear nothing. He fitted the blade of his stout knife between the shutters and, with some difficulty, levered the bolt up out of its brackets. He gestured to William to come and lean hard on the shutter, to keep the bolt from falling suddenly, and with a joint effort composed of dumb-show and frantic gestures—that would likely have seemed comic to anyone not involved in performing it—they succeeded in getting the bloody shutters open without too much racket.

The window behind was curtained—all to the good—but a casement, with a thumb latch that wouldn't yield to Jamie's knife. The big Scot was sweating; he pulled his cap off for a moment to wipe his brow, then put it back on, and, taking the treacle from the bag, he un-stoppered the bottle and poured some of the sticky syrup into his hand. This he smeared over a pane of the casement and, taking a sheet of paper, pasted it onto the glass.

William could make no sense of this proceeding, but Fraser drew back his arm and struck the glass a sharp buffet with his fist. It broke with no more than a small cracking noise, and the shattered pieces were removed easily, stuck to the treacled paper.

"Where did you learn that one?" William whispered, deeply impressed, and heard a small chuckle of satisfaction from behind Fraser's mask.

"My daughter told me about it," he whispered in reply, laying glass and paper on the ground. "She read it in a book."

"That's—" William stopped abruptly, and so did his heart. He'd forgotten. "Your . . . daughter. You mean—I have a sister?"

"Aye," Fraser said briefly. "Ye've met her. Come on." He reached through the hole in the glass, undid the catch, and pulled on the window frame. The window swung open, with an unexpected loud screech of unoiled hinges.

"Shit!" William said, under his breath.

Fraser had said something that William assumed was the equivalent sentiment in Gaelic, but he didn't waste time. He shoved William back against the wall and, with a hissed "Stay there!", faded into the night.

William plastered himself against the wall, heart hammering. He could hear rapid footsteps clattering down the wooden steps from the veranda, then muffled thumps on the damp ground.

"Who's there?" the guard shouted, as he rounded the house. Seeing William, he shouldered his musket and took aim. And Fraser came out of the dark mist like an angry ghost, grabbed the boy by the shoulder, and laid him out with a rock slammed into the back of his skull.

"Hurry," he said, low-voiced, jerking his chin toward the open window as he lowered the guard's limp body to the ground. William wasted no time but heaved himself into the house, squirming across the sill to land almost soundlessly, squatting on the carpet of what must be a parlor, to judge from the dim outlines of the furniture. An unseen clock ticked accusingly, somewhere in the darkness.

Fraser hoisted himself into the open window frame and paused for a moment, listening. But there was no sound in the house save the ticking clock, and he hopped lightly down inside.

"Ye dinna ken whose house this is?" he whispered to William, looking round.

William shook his head. It must be an officer's billet, but he had no idea who the officer might be—probably the major in charge of disciplinary matters. Presumably Campbell had lodged Jane here as an alternative to putting her in the camp's stockade. Thoughtful of him.

His eyes had adapted quickly; there was a dark oblong a few feet away—the door. Fraser saw it, too; his hand rested on William's back for an instant, pushing him toward it.

There was an oval lozenge of glass set into the front door, and enough light came through it to show them the painted canvas floorcloth running down the hall, its diamond pattern black in the colorless light. Near the door, a pool of shadow hid the foot of the staircase, and within seconds they were creeping up the stairs, as quickly and as quietly as two very large men in a hurry could go.

"This way." William was in the lead; he motioned to Fraser as he turned to the left. The blood was beating in his head, and he could scarcely breathe. He wanted to tear off the clinging mask and gulp air, but not yet . . . not yet.

Jane. Had she heard the guard call out? If she was awake, she must have heard them on the stair.

The landing was windowless and very dark, but there was a faint glow of candlelight under Jane's door—he hoped to God it was Jane's door. Running a hand down the doorframe, he felt the knob, and his hand closed round it. It was locked, naturally—but in trying the knob, the heel of his hand brushed the key, still in the lock.

Fraser was behind him; he could hear the man's breathing. Behind the door of the next room, someone was snoring in a reassuringly regular sort of way. So long as the guard stayed out long enough . . .

"Jane," he whispered as loudly as he dared, putting his lips to the crack between the door and its jamb. "Jane! It's me, William. Be quiet!"

He thought he heard a swift intake of breath from the other side of the door, though it might have been only the sound of his own blood racing in his ears. With infinite care, he pulled the door toward him and turned the key.

The candle was standing on a small bureau, its flame flickering wildly in the draft from the open door. There was a strong smell of beer; a broken bottle lay on the floor, brown glass a-glitter in the wavering light. The bed was rumpled, bedclothes hanging half off the mattress . . . Where was Jane? He whirled, expecting to see her cowering in the corner, frightened by his entrance.

He saw her hand first. She was lying on the floor by the bed, beside the broken bottle, her hand flung out, white and half open as though in supplication.

"*A Dhia,*" Fraser whispered behind him, and now he could smell the cut-steel reek of blood, mingled with beer.

He didn't remember falling on his knees or lifting her up in his arms. She was heavy, limp and awkward, all the grace and heat of her gone and her cheek cold to his hand. Only her hair was still Jane, shining in the candlelight, soft against his mouth.

"Here, *a bhalaich.*" A hand touched his shoulder, and he turned without thought.

Fraser had pulled the mask down around his neck, and his face was serious, intent. "We havena much time," he said softly.

They didn't speak. They straightened the bedclothes in silence, put a clean quilt over the worst of the blood, and laid her on it. William wetted his kerchief from the ewer and cleaned the spatters of blood from her face and hands. He hesitated for a moment, then tore the kerchief violently in two and bandaged her torn wrists, then crossed her hands on her breast.

Jamie Fraser was by him then, with a fugitive gleam from the blade of his knife.

"For her sister," he said, and, bending, cut a lock of the shining chestnut hair. He put this into the pocket of the ragged breeches and went quietly out. William heard the brief creak of his footsteps on the stair and understood that he had been left to make his farewell in privacy.

He looked upon her face by candlelight for the first time, and the last. He felt emptied, hollow as a gutted deer. With no notion what to say, he touched one black-bound hand and spoke the truth, in a voice too low for any but the dead to hear.

"I wanted to save you, Jane. Forgive me."

134

LAST RITES

JAMIE CAME HOME just before dawn, white-faced and chilled to the bone. I wasn't asleep. I hadn't slept since he'd left with William, and when I heard his step on the creaking stairs, I scooped hot water from the ever-simmering cauldron into the wooden mug I had ready, half filled with cheap whisky and a spoonful of honey. I'd thought he'd need it, but I hadn't had any idea how much.

"The lassie had cut her wrists wi' a broken bottle," he said, crouching on a stool by the fire, a quilt draped over his shoulders and the warm mug cupped between his big hands. He couldn't stop shivering.

"God rest her soul and forgive her the sin of despair." He closed his eyes and shook his head violently, as though to dispel his memory of what he'd seen in that candlelit room. "Oh, Jesus, my poor lad."

I'd made him go to bed and crawled in to warm him with my body, but I hadn't slept then, either. I didn't feel the need of it. There were things that would need to be done when the day came; I could feel them waiting, a patient throng. William. The dead girl. And Jamie had said something about the girl's young sister. . . . But for the moment, time was still, balanced on the cusp of night. I lay beside Jamie and listened to him breathe. For the moment, that was enough.

BUT THE SUN rose, as it always did.

I was stirring the breakfast porridge when William appeared, bringing with him a mud-smeared young girl who looked like a lightning-blasted tree. William didn't look any better but seemed less likely to fall to bits.

"This is Frances," he said, in a low, hoarse voice, putting a large paw on her shoulder. "These are Mr. and Mrs. Fraser, Fanny." She was so fine-boned that I half-expected her to stagger under the weight of his hand, but she didn't. After a stunned moment, she realized the introduction and gave a jerky nod.

"Sit down, sweetheart," I said, smiling at her. "The porridge is almost ready, and there's toasted bread with honey."

She stared at me, blinking dully. Her eyes were red and swollen, her hair lank under a tattered cap. I thought she was so shocked that she was unable to comprehend anything. William looked as though someone had hit him on the head, stunning him like an ox bound for slaughter. I looked uncertainly at Jamie, not knowing what to do for either of them. He glanced from one to the other, then rose and quietly took the girl into his arms.

"There, *a nighean*," he said quietly, patting her back. His eyes met Willie's and I saw something pass between them—a question asked and answered. Jamie nodded. "I'll care for her," he said.

"Thank you. She . . . Jane," William said with difficulty. "I want to—to bury her. Decently. But I think I can't . . . claim her."

"Aye," Jamie said. "We'll see to it. Go and do whatever ye need to do. Come back when ye can."

William stood a moment longer, red-rimmed eyes fixed on the girl's back, then gave me an abrupt bow and left. At the sound of his departing footsteps, Frances gave a small, despairing howl, like an orphaned puppy. Jamie wrapped her closer in his arms, holding her snug against his chest.

"It will be all right, *a nighean*," he said softly, though his eyes were fixed on the door through which William had gone. "Ye're at home now."

⁂

I DIDN'T REALIZE that Fanny was tongue-tied, until I took her to see Colonel Campbell. She hadn't spoken at all until that point, merely shaking her head yes or no, making small motions of refusal or gratitude.

"You kilt my thither!" she said loudly, when Campbell rose from his desk to greet us. He blinked and sat back down.

"I doubt it," he said, eyeing her warily. She wasn't crying, but her face was blotched and swollen, as if someone had slapped her repeatedly. She stood very straight, though, small fists clenched, and glared at him. He looked at me. I shrugged slightly.

"The'th *dead*," Fanny said. "The wath your prithoner!"

Campbell steepled his hands and cleared his throat.

"May I ask who you are, child? And who your sister is?"

"Her name is Frances Pocock," I put in hastily. "Her sister was Jane Po-cock, who I understand . . . died last night, while in your custody. She would like to claim her sister's body, for burial."

Campbell gave me a bleak look.

"I see that news travels fast. And you are, madam?"

"A friend of the family," I said, as firmly as possible. "My name is Mrs. James Fraser."

His face shifted a little; he'd heard the name. That probably wasn't a good thing.

"Mrs. Fraser," he said slowly. "I've heard of you. You dispense pox cures to the city's whores, do you not?"

"Among . . . other things, yes," I said, rather taken aback by this description of my medical practice. Still, it seemed to offer him a logical connection between Fanny and me, for he glanced from one of us to the other, nodding to himself.

"Well," he said slowly. "I don't know where the—er—the body has been—"

"Don't oo call my thither 'the *body*'!" Fanny shouted. "Her name ith Jane!"

Commanders, as a rule, aren't used to being shouted at, and Campbell appeared to be no exception. His square face flushed and he put his hands flat on the desk, preparing to rise. Before he got the seat of his breeches clear of his chair, though, his aide came in and coughed discreetly.

"I beg pardon, sir; Lieutenant Colonel Lord John Grey wishes to see you."

"Does he, indeed." This didn't seem to be welcome news to Campbell, but it was to me.

"You're clearly busy, sir," I said quickly, seizing Fanny by the arm. "We'll come back later." And without waiting to be dismissed, I more or less dragged her out of the office.

Sure enough, John was standing in the anteroom, in full uniform. His face was calmly pleasant and I saw that he was in diplomatic mode, but his expression altered the instant he saw me.

"What are you doing here?" he blurted. "And"—glancing at Fanny—"who the devil is this?"

"Do you know about Jane?" I said, grabbing him by the sleeve. "What happened to her last night?"

"Yes, I—"

"We want to claim her body, for burial. Can you help?"

He detached my hand, courteously, and brushed his sleeve.

"I can, yes. I'm here upon the same errand. I'll send word—"

"We'll wait for you," I said hastily, seeing the aide frown in my direction. "Outside. Come, Fanny!"

Outside, we found a place to wait on an ornamental bench set in the formal front garden. Even in winter, it was a pleasant spot, with several palmetto trees popping out of the shrubbery like so many Japanese parasols, and even the presence of a number of soldiers coming and going didn't much impair the sense of gracious peace. Fanny, though, was in no mood for peace.

"Who wath *that*?" she demanded, twisting to look back at the house. "What doth he want wif Jane?"

"Ah . . . that's William's father," I said carefully. "Lord John Grey is his name. I imagine William asked him to come."

Fanny blinked for a moment, then turned a remarkably penetrating pair of brown eyes on me, red-rimmed and bloodshot but decidedly intelligent.

"He doethn't *wook* wike Wiyum," she said. "Mither Fwather wooks a wot wike Wiyum."

I looked back at her for a moment.

"Really?" I said. "I hadn't noticed that. Do you mind not talking for a bit, Fanny? I need to think."

———

JOHN CAME OUT about ten minutes later. He paused on the steps, looking around, and I waved. He came down to where we sat and at once bowed very formally to Fanny.

"Your servant, Miss Frances," he said. "I understand from Colonel Campbell that you are the sister of Miss Pocock; please allow me to offer my deepest condolences."

He spoke very simply and honestly, and Fanny's eyes welled up with tears.

"Can I have huh?" she said softly. "Pwease?"

Heedless of his immaculate breeches, he knelt on the ground in front of her and took her hand in his.

"Yes, sweetheart," he said, just as softly. "Of course you can." He patted her hand. "Will you wait here, just for a moment, while I speak with Mrs. Fraser?" He stood and, as an afterthought, pulled a large snowy handkerchief out of his sleeve and handed it to her with another small bow.

"Poor child," he said, taking my hand and tucking it into the curve of his elbow. "Or children—the other girl can't have been more than seventeen." We walked for a few paces, down a small brick walk between empty flower beds, until we were safely out of earshot of both street and house. "I take it that William sought Jamie's help. I thought he might, though I hoped he wouldn't, for both their sakes."

His face was shadowed, and there were blue smudges under his eyes; evidently he'd had a disturbed night, too.

"Where *is* William, do you know?" I asked.

"I don't. He said he had an errand outside the city but would return tonight." He glanced over his shoulder at the house. "I've arranged for . . . Jane . . . to be appropriately tended. She cannot be buried in a churchyard, of course—"

"Of course," I murmured, angry at the thought. He noticed but cleared his throat and went on.

"I know a family with a small private cemetery. I believe I can make arrangement for a quiet burial. Quickly, of course; tomorrow, very early?"

I nodded, getting a grip on myself. It wasn't his fault.

"You've been very good," I said. Worry and the lack of sleep were catching up with me; things seemed oddly non-dimensional, as though trees and people and garden furniture were merely pasted onto a painted backdrop. I shook my head to clear it, though; there were important things to be said.

"I have to tell you something," I said. "I wish I didn't, but there it is. Ezekiel Richardson came to my surgery the other day."

"The devil he did." John had stiffened at the name. "He's not with the army here, surely? I would have—"

"Yes, but not with *your* army." I told him, as briefly as I could, what Richardson now was—or, rather, was revealed to be; God only knew how long he'd been a Rebel spy—and what his intentions were toward Hal and the Grey family in general.

John listened, his face quietly intent, though the corner of his mouth twitched when I described Richardson's plan to influence Hal's political actions.

"Yes, I know," I said dryly, seeing that. "I don't suppose he's ever actually *met* Hal. But the important thing . . ." I hesitated, but he had to know.

"He knows about you," I said. "What you . . . are. I mean that you—"

"What I am," he repeated, expressionless. His eyes had been fastened on my face to this point; now he looked away. "I see." He took a deep breath and let it out slowly.

John was a distinguished soldier and an honorable gentleman, member of an ancient noble family. He was also a homosexual, in a time when that particular attribute was a capital offense. For that knowledge to be in the hands of a man who meant ill to him and his family . . . I wasn't under any illusions about what I'd just done—with three words, I'd shown him that he was standing on a very narrow tightrope over a very deep pit, with Richardson holding the end of the rope.

"I'm sorry, John," I said, very softly. I touched his arm, and he laid his hand briefly over mine, squeezed it gently, and smiled.

"Thank you." He stared at the brick paving under his feet for a moment, then looked up. "Do you know how he came by the—information?" He spoke calmly, but a nerve was jumping just under his injured eye, a tiny twitch. I wanted to put my finger on it, still it. But there was nothing I could do.

"No." I looked back at the distant bench. Fanny was still there, a small, desolate figure, head bent. I turned my gaze back to John; his brow was creased, thinking.

"One last thing. Hal's daughter-in-law, the young woman with the odd name—"

"Amaranthus," he interrupted, and smiled wryly. "Yes, what about her? Don't tell me that Ezekiel Richardson invented her for his own purposes."

"I wouldn't put it past him, but probably not." I told him what I'd learned from Mr. Jameson.

"I told William day before yesterday," I said. "But what with everything"— I waved a hand, encompassing Fanny, Jane, Colonel Campbell, and a few other things—"I doubt he's had time to go to Saperville to look for her. You don't suppose that's the errand he spoke of, do you?" I asked, struck by the thought.

"God knows." He rubbed a hand over his face, then straightened. "I must go. I'll have to tell Hal a few things. Not . . . that, I don't think," he said, seeing my face. "But obviously there are things he needs to know, and know quickly. God bless you, my dear. I'll send word about tomorrow." He took my hand, kissed it very gently, and let go.

I watched him walk away, his back very straight, the scarlet of his coat bright as blood against the grays and faded greens of the winter garden.

⌐

WE BURIED JANE on the morning of a dull, cold day. The sky was sodden with low gray clouds, and a raw wind blew in from the sea. It was a small private burying ground, belonging to a large house that stood outside the city.

All of us came with Fanny: Rachel and Ian, Jenny, Fergus and Marsali— even the girls and Germain. I worried a bit; they couldn't help but feel the echoes of Henri-Christian's death. But death was a fact of life and a common one, and while they stood solemn and pale amongst the adults, they were composed. Fanny was not so much composed as completely numb, I thought; she'd wept all the tears her small body could hold and was white and stiff as a bleached stick.

John came, dressed in his uniform (in case anyone became inquisitive and tried to disturb us, he explained to me in an undertone). The coffin-maker had had only adult coffins to hand; Jane's shrouded body looked so like a chrysalis, I half-expected to hear a dry rattling sound when the men picked it up. Fanny had declined to look upon her sister's face one last time, and I thought that was as well.

There was no priest or minister; she was a suicide, and this was ground hallowed only by respect. When the last of the dirt had been shoveled in, we stood quiet, waiting, the harsh wind flurrying our hair and garments.

Jamie took a deep breath and a step to the head of the grave. He spoke the Gaelic prayer called the Death Dirge, but in English, for the sake of Fanny and Lord John.

> *Thou goest home this night to thy home of winter,*
> *To thy home of autumn, of spring, and of summer;*
> *Thou goest home this night to thy perpetual home,*
> *To thine eternal bed, to thine eternal slumber.*

> *Sleep thou, sleep, and away with thy sorrow,*
> *Sleep thou, sleep, and away with thy sorrow,*
> *Sleep thou, sleep, and away with thy sorrow,*
> *Sleep, thou beloved, in the Rock of the fold.*

> *The shade of death lies upon thy face, beloved,*
> *But the Jesus of grace has His hand round about thee;*
> *In nearness to the Trinity farewell to thy pains,*
> *Christ stands before thee and peace is in His mind.*

Jenny, Ian, Fergus, and Marsali joined in, murmuring the final verse with him.

> *Sleep, O sleep in the calm of all calm,*
> *Sleep, O sleep in the guidance of guidance,*
> *Sleep, O sleep in the love of all loves,*
> *Sleep, O beloved, in the Lord of life,*
> *Sleep, O beloved, in the God of life!*

It wasn't until we turned to go that I saw William. He was standing just outside the wrought-iron fence that enclosed the burying ground, tall and somber in a dark cloak, the wind stirring the dark tail of his hair. He was holding the reins of a very large mare with a back as broad as a barn door. As

I came out of the burying ground, holding Fanny's hand, he came toward us, the horse obligingly following him.

"This is Miranda," he said to Fanny. His face was white and carved with grief, but his voice was steady. "She's yours now. You'll need her." He took Fanny's limp hand, put the reins into it, and closed her fingers over them. Then he looked at me, wisps of hair blowing across his face. "Will you look after her, Mother Claire?"

"Of course we will," I said, my throat tight. "Where are you going, William?"

He smiled then, very faintly.

"It doesn't matter," he said, and walked away.

Fanny was staring up at Miranda in complete incomprehension. I gently took the reins from her, patted the horse's jaw, and turned to find Jamie. He was just inside the fence, talking with Marsali; the others had come out already and were standing in a cold little cluster, Ian and Fergus talking with Lord John, while Jenny shepherded the children—all of whom were staring at Fanny.

Jamie was frowning a little, but at last he nodded and, bending forward, kissed Marsali on the forehead and came out. He raised one eyebrow when he saw Miranda, and I explained.

"Aye, well," he said, with a glance at Fanny. "What's one more?" There was an odd tone to his voice, and I looked at him in inquiry.

"Marsali asked me if we'd take Germain," he said, drawing Fanny in against him in a sheltering hug, as if this were a common thing.

"Really?" I glanced over my shoulder at the rest of the family. "Why?" We had all discussed the matter at some length the night before and concluded that we wouldn't wait until spring to leave Savannah. With the city occupied, there was no chance of Fergus and Marsali resuming publication of their newspaper, and with Colonel Richardson lurking behind the scenes, the place was beginning to seem distinctly dangerous.

We would all travel together to Charleston, get Fergus and Marsali established there, and then the rest of us would go on north to Wilmington, where we would begin to equip ourselves for the trip into the mountains when the snows began to melt in March.

"Ye told them, Sassenach," Jamie said, scratching Miranda's forelock with his free hand. "What the war would be, and how long it would last. Germain's of an age when he'll be out and in the thick o' things. Marsali's worrit that he'll come to harm, loose in a city where the sorts of things happen that *do* happen in wartime. God knows the mountains may be no safer"—he grimaced, obviously recalling a few incidents that had taken place there—"but on the whole, he's likely better off not being in a place where he could be conscripted by the militia or pressed into the British navy."

I looked down the gravel path that led to the house; Germain had drifted away from his mother, grandmother, Rachel, and his sisters and joined Ian and Fergus in conversation with Lord John.

"Aye, he kens he's a man," Jamie said dryly, following the direction of my gaze. "Come along, *a leannan*," he said to Fanny. "It's time we all had breakfast."

135

AMARANTHUS

Saperville
January 15, 1779

SAPERVILLE WAS DIFFICULT to find but, once found, small enough that it was a matter of only three inquiries to discover the residence of a widow named Grey.

"Over there." Hal reined up, nodding toward a house that stood a hundred yards back from the road in the shade of an enormous magnolia tree. He was being casual, but John could see the muscle twitching in his brother's jaw.

"Well . . . I suppose we just go up and knock, then." He turned his own horse's head in at the rutted lane, taking stock of the place as they walked toward it. It was a rather shabby house, the front veranda sagging at one corner where its foundation had given way, and half its few windows boarded over. Still, the place was occupied; the chimney was smoking fitfully, in a way suggesting that it hadn't been recently swept.

The door was opened to them by a slattern. A white woman, but one clothed in a stained wrapper and felt slippers, with wary eyes and a sourly downturned mouth whose corners showed the stains of tobacco chewing.

"Is Mrs. Grey at home?" Hal inquired politely.

"Nobody o' that name here," the woman said, and made to shut the door, this action being prevented by Hal's boot.

"We were directed to this address, madam," Hal said, the politeness diminishing markedly. "Be so good as to inform Mrs. Grey that she has visitors, please."

The woman's eyes narrowed.

"And who in tarnation are you, Mr. Fancy Pants?"

John's estimation of the woman's nerve rose considerably at this, but he thought he ought to intervene before Hal started wheezing.

"This is His Grace the Duke of Pardloe, madam," he said, with maximum politeness. Her face altered at once, though not for the better. Her jaw hardened, but a predatory gleam came into her eye.

"Elle connaît votre nom," he said to Hal. *She knows your name.*

"I know that," his brother snapped. "Madam—"

Whatever he would have said was interrupted by the sudden shrieking of a baby, somewhere upstairs.

"I beg your pardon, madam," Lord John said politely to the slattern, and, seizing her by the elbows, walked her backward into the house, whirled her round, and pushed her into the kitchen. There was a pantry, and he shoved her into this cubbyhole, slammed the door upon her, and, grabbing a bread knife from the table, thrust it through the hasp of the latch as a makeshift bolt.

Hal had meanwhile disappeared upstairs, making enough noise for a company of cavalry. John galloped after him, and by the time he reached the head of the stair, his brother was busily engaged in trying to break down the door of a room from which came the siren shrieks of a baby and the even louder cries of what was probably the baby's mother.

It was a good, solid door; Hal flung himself at it shoulder-first and rebounded as though made of India rubber. Barely pausing, he raised his foot and slammed the flat of his boot sole against the panel, which obligingly splintered but didn't break inward.

Wiping his face on his sleeve, he eyed the door and, catching the flicker of movement through the splintered paneling, called out, "Young woman! We have come to rescue you! Stand well away from the door!

"Pistol, please," he said, turning to John with his hand out.

"I'll do it," John said, resigned. "You haven't any practice with doorknobs."

Whereupon, with an air of assumed casualness, he drew the pistol from his belt, aimed carefully, and shot the doorknob to pieces. The boom of the gun evidently startled the room's inhabitants, for a dead silence fell. He gently pushed the stem of the shattered knob through the door; the remnants of the knob thunked to the floor on the other side, and he pushed the door cautiously open.

Hal, nodding his thanks, stepped forward through the wisps of smoke.

It was a small room, rather grimy, and furnished with no more than a bedstead, dresser, stool, and washstand. The stool was particularly noticeable, as it was being brandished by a wild-eyed young woman, clutching a baby to her breast with her other hand.

An ammoniac reek came from a basket in the corner, piled with dirty clouts; a folded quilt in a pulled-out drawer showed where the baby had been sleeping, and the young woman was less kempt than her mother would have liked to see, her cap askew and her pinny stained. Hal disregarded all matters of circumstance and bowed to her.

"Do I address Miss Amaranthus Cowden?" he said politely. "Or is it Mrs. Grey?"

John gave his brother a disparaging look and turned a cordial smile on the young woman.

"*Viscountess* Grey," he said, and made a leg in courtly style. "Your most humble servant, Lady Grey."

The young woman looked wildly from one man to the other, stool still raised, clearly unable to make head or tail of this invasion, and finally settled on John as the best—if still dubious—source of information.

"Who *are* you?" she asked, pressing her back against the wall. "Hush, darling." For the baby, recovered from shock, had decided to grizzle.

John cleared his throat.

"Well . . . this is Harold, Duke of Pardloe, and I am his brother, Lord John Grey. If our information is correct, I believe we are, respectively, your father-in-law and your uncle by marriage. And, after all," he remarked, turning to Hal, "how many people in the colonies do you think there could possibly *be* named Amaranthus Cowden?"

"She hasn't yet said she *is* Amaranthus Cowden," Hal pointed out. He did, however, smile at the young woman, who reacted as most women did, staring at him with her mouth slightly open.

"May I?" John reached forward and took the stool gently from her unresisting hand, setting it on the floor and gesturing her to take a seat. "What sort of name is Amaranthus, may I ask?"

She swallowed, blinked, and sat down, clutching the baby.

"It's a flower," she said, sounding rather dazed. "My grandfather's a botanist. It could have been worse," she added more sharply, seeing John smile. "It might have been Ampelopsis or Petunia."

"Amaranthus is a very beautiful name, my dear—if I may call you so?" Hal said, with grave courtesy. He wiggled a forefinger at the baby, who had stopped grizzling and was staring at him warily. Hal pulled his officer's gorget off over his head and dangled the shiny object, close enough for the child to grab—which he did.

"It's too large to choke him," Hal assured Amaranthus. "His father—and his father's brothers—all teethed on it. So did I, come to that." He smiled at her again. She was still white-faced but gave him a wary nod in response.

"What is the little fellow's name, my dear?" John asked.

"Trevor," she said, taking a firmer hold on the child, now completely engrossed in trying to get the demilune gorget—half the size of his head—into his mouth. "Trevor Grey." She looked back and forth between the Grey brothers, a frown puckering her brows. Then she lifted her chin and said, enunciating clearly, "Trevor . . . *Wattiswade* . . . Grey. Your Grace."

"So you are Ben's wife." A little of the tension left Hal's shoulders. "Do you know where Ben is, my dear?"

Her face went stiff, and she clutched the baby tighter.

"Benjamin is dead, Your Grace," she said. "But this is his son, and if you don't mind . . . we should quite like to come with you."

UNFINISHED BUSINESS

WILLIAM SHOVED his way through the crowds in the City Market, oblivious to the complaints of those rebounding from his impact.

He knew where he was going and what he meant to do when he got there. It was the only thing left to do before leaving Savannah. After that . . . it didn't matter.

His head throbbed like an inflamed boil. Everything throbbed. His hand— he'd probably broken something, but he didn't care. His heart, pounding and sore inside his chest. He hadn't slept since they'd buried Jane; would likely never sleep again and didn't care.

He remembered where the warehouse was. The place was almost empty; doubtless the soldiers had taken everything the owner hadn't had time to move out of reach. Three men were lounging by the far wall, sitting on the few remaining casks of salt fish and smoking their pipes; the smell of tobacco reached him, a small comfort in the echoing cold fishiness of the building.

"James Fraser?" he said to one of the loungers, and the man pointed with the stem of his pipe toward a small office, a sort of shed attached to the far wall of the warehouse.

The door was open; Fraser was seated at a table covered with papers, writing something by the light that fell through a tiny barred window behind him. He looked up at the sound of William's footsteps and, seeing him, put down his quill and rose slowly to his feet. William came forward, facing him across the table.

"I have come to take my farewell," William said, very formally. His voice was less firm than he liked, and he cleared his throat hard.

"Aye? Where is it that ye mean to go?" Fraser was wearing his plaid, the faded colors muted further by the dimness of the light, but what light there was sparked suddenly from his hair as he moved his head.

"I don't know," William said, gruff. "It doesn't matter." He took a deep breath. "I—wished to thank you. For what you did. Even though—" His throat closed tight; try as he might, he couldn't keep Jane's small white hand out of his thoughts.

Fraser made a slight dismissive motion and said softly, "God rest her, poor wee lass."

"Even so," William said, and cleared his throat again. "But there is one further favor that I wished to ask of you."

Fraser's head came up; he looked surprised but nodded.

"Aye, of course," he said. "If I can."

William turned and pulled the door shut, then turned to face the man again.

"Tell me how I came to be."

The whites of Fraser's eyes flashed in brief astonishment, then disappeared as his eyes narrowed.

"I want to know what happened," William said. "When you lay with my mother. What happened that night? If it *was* night," he added, and then felt foolish for doing so.

Fraser eyed him for a moment.

"Ye want to tell *me* what it was like, the first time ye lay with a woman?"

William felt the blood rush into his head, but before he could speak, the Scot went on.

"Aye, exactly. A decent man doesna speak of such things. Ye dinna tell your friends such things, do ye? No, of course not. So much less would ye tell your . . . father, or a father his . . ."

The hesitation before "father" was brief, but William caught it, no trouble. Fraser's mouth was firm, though, and his eyes direct.

"I wouldna tell ye, no matter who ye were. But being who ye are—"

"Being who I am, I think I have a right to know!"

Fraser looked at him for a moment, expressionless. He closed his eyes for an instant and sighed. Then opened them and drew himself up, straightening his shoulders.

"No, ye haven't. But that's not what ye *want* to know, in any case," he said. "Ye want to know, did I force your mother. I did not. Ye want to know, did I love your mother. I did not."

William let that lie there for a moment, controlling his breathing 'til he was sure his voice would be steady.

"Did she love you?" *It would have been easy to love him.* The thought came to him unbidden—and unwelcome—but with it, his own memories of Mac the groom. Something he shared with his mother.

Fraser's eyes were cast down, watching a trail of tiny ants running along the scuffed floorboards.

"She was verra young," he said softly. "I was twice her age. It was my fault."

There was a brief silence, broken only by their breathing and the distant shouts of men working on the river.

"I've seen the portraits," William said abruptly. "Of my—of the eighth earl. Her husband. Have you?"

Fraser's mouth twisted a little, but he shook his head.

"You know, though—knew. He was fifty years older than she was."

Fraser's maimed hand twitched, fingers tapping lightly against his thigh. Yes, he'd known. How could he *not* have known? He dipped his head, not quite a nod.

"I'm not stupid, you know," William said, louder than he'd intended.

"Didna think ye were," Fraser muttered, but didn't look at him.

"I can count," William went on, through his teeth. "You lay with her just before her wedding. Or was it just after?"

That went home; Fraser's head jerked up and there was a flash of dark-blue anger.

"I wouldna deceive another man in his marriage. Believe that of me, at least."

Oddly enough, he did. And in spite of the anger he still struggled to keep in check, he began to think he perhaps understood how it *might* have been.

"She was reckless." He made it a statement, not a question, and saw Fraser blink. It wasn't a nod, but he thought it was acknowledgment and went on, more confident.

"Everyone says that—everyone who knew her. She was reckless, beautiful, careless . . . she took chances . . ."

"She had courage." It was said softly, the words dropped like pebbles in water, and the ripples spread through the tiny room. Fraser was still looking straight at him. "Did they tell ye that, then? Her family, the folk who kent her?"

"No," William said, and felt the word sharp as a stone in his throat. For just an instant, he'd seen her in those words. He'd *seen* her, and the knowledge of the immensity of his loss struck through his anger like a lightning bolt. He drove his fist into the table, striking it once, twice, hammering it 'til the wood shook and the legs juddered over the floor, papers flying and the inkwell falling over.

He stopped as suddenly as he'd started, and the racket ceased.

"Are you *sorry?*" he said, and made no effort to keep his voice from shaking. "Are you sorry for it, damn you?"

Fraser had turned away; now he turned sharply to face William but didn't speak at once. When he did, his voice was low and firm.

"She died because of it, and I shall sorrow for her death and do penance for my part in it until my own dying day. But—" He compressed his lips for an instant, and then, too fast for William to back away, came round the table and, raising his hand, cupped William's cheek, the touch light and fierce.

"No," he whispered. "No! I am not sorry." Then he whirled on his heel, threw open the door, and was gone, kilt flying.

PART NINE

*"Thig crioch air an t-saoghal ach mairidh
ceol agus gaol."*
*"The world may come to an end, but love
and music will endure."*

137

IN THE WILDERNESS
A LODGING PLACE

I COULDN'T STOP BREATHING. From the moment we left the salt-marsh miasma of Savannah, with its constant fog of rice paddies, mud, and decaying crustaceans, the air had grown clearer, the scents cleaner—well, putting aside the Wilmington mudflats, redolent with their memories of crocodiles and dead pirates—spicier, and more distinct. And as we reached the summit of the final pass, I thought I might explode from simple joy at the scent of the late-spring woods, an intoxicating mix of pine and balsam fir, oaks mingling the spice of fresh green leaves with the must of the winter's fallen acorns, and the nutty sweetness of chestnut mast under a layer of wet dead leaves, so thick that it made the air seem buoyant, bearing me up. I couldn't get enough of it into my lungs.

"If ye keep gasping like that, Sassenach, ye're like to pass out," Jamie said, smiling as he came up beside me. "How's the new knife, then?"

"Wonderful! Look, I found a huge ginseng root, and a birch gall and—"

He stopped this with a kiss, and I dropped the soggy gunnysack full of plants on the path and kissed him back. He'd been eating wild spring onions and watercress plucked dripping from a creek and he smelled of his own male scent, pine sap, and the bloody tang of the two dead rabbits hanging at his belt; it was like kissing the wilderness itself, and it went on for a bit, interrupted only by a discreet cough a few feet away.

We let go of each other at once, and I took an automatic step back behind Jamie even as he stepped in front of me, hand hovering within reach of his dirk. A split second later, he'd taken a huge stride forward and engulfed Mr. Wemyss in an enormous hug.

"Joseph! *A charaid! Ciamar a tha thu?*"

Mr. Wemyss, a small, slight, elderly man, was swept literally off his feet; I could see a shoe dangling loose from the toes of one stockinged foot as he groped for traction. Smiling at this, I glanced round to see if Rachel and Ian had come into sight yet and spotted instead a small, round-faced boy on the path. He was perhaps four or five, with long fair hair, this flying loose around his shoulders.

"Er . . . Rodney?" I asked, making a hasty guess. I hadn't seen him since he was two or so, but I couldn't think who else might be accompanying Mr. Wemyss.

The child nodded, examining me soberly.

"You be the conjure-woman?" he said, in a remarkably deep voice.

"Yes," I said, rather surprised at this address, but still more surprised at how right my acknowledgment of it felt. I realized at that moment that I had been resuming my identity as we walked, that step by step as we climbed the mountain, smelling its scents and harvesting its plenty, I had sloughed off a few layers of the recent past and become again what I had last been in this place. I had come back.

"Yes," I said again. "I am Mrs. Fraser. You may call me Grannie Fraser, if you like."

He nodded thoughtfully, taking this in and mouthing "Grannie Fraser" to himself once or twice, as though to taste it. Then he looked at Jamie, who had set Mr. Wemyss back on his feet and was smiling down at him with a look of joy that turned my heart to wax.

"Izzat Himself?" Rodney whispered, drawing close to me.

"That is Himself," I agreed, nodding gravely.

"Aidan said he was big," Rodney remarked, after another moment's scrutiny.

"Is he big enough, do you think?" I asked, rather surprised by the realization that I didn't want Rodney to be disappointed in this first sight of Himself.

Rodney gave an odd sideways tilt of his head, terribly familiar—it was what his mother, Lizzie, did when making a judgment about something—and said philosophically, "Well, he's lot's bigger 'n me, anyway."

"Everything is relative," I agreed. "And speaking of relatives, how is your mother? And your . . . er . . . father?"

I was wondering whether Lizzie's unorthodox marriage was still in effect. Having fallen accidentally in love with identical-twin brothers, she had—with a guile and cunning unexpected in a demure nineteen-year-old Scottish bond servant—contrived to marry them both. There was no telling whether Rodney's father was Josiah or Keziah Beardsley, but I did wonder—

"Oh, Mammy's breedin' again," Rodney said casually. "She says she's a-going to castrate Daddy or Da or both of 'em, if that's what it takes to put a stop to it."

"Ah . . . well, that *would* be effective," I said, rather taken aback. "How many sisters or brothers have you got?" I'd delivered a sister before we'd left the Ridge, but—

"One sister, one brother." Rodney was clearly growing bored with me and stood on his toes to look down the path behind me. "Is that Mary?"

"What?" Turning, I saw Ian and Rachel navigating a horseshoe bend some way below; they vanished into the trees even as I watched.

"You know, Mary 'n Joseph a-flying into Egypt," he said, and I laughed in sudden understanding. Rachel, very noticeably pregnant, was riding Clarence, with Ian, who hadn't troubled to shave for the last several months and was sporting a beard of quasi-biblical dimensions, walking beside her. Jenny was presumably still out of sight behind them, riding the mare with Franny and leading the pack mule.

"That's Rachel," I said. "And her husband, Ian. Ian is Himself's nephew. You mentioned Aidan—is his family well, too?" Jamie and Mr. Wemyss had started off toward the trailhead, talking sixteen to the dozen about affairs on the Ridge. Rodney took my hand in a gentlemanly way and nodded after them.

"We'd best be going down. I want to tell Mam first, afore *Opa* gets there."

"*Opa* . . . oh, your grandfather?" Joseph Wemyss had married a German lady named Monika, soon after Rodney's birth, and I thought I recalled that "*Opa*" was a German expression for "grandfather."

"*Ja,*" Rodney said, confirming this supposition.

The trail meandered back and forth across the upper slopes of the Ridge, offering me tantalizing glimpses through the trees of the settlement below: scattered cabins among the bright-flowered laurels, the fresh-turned black earth of vegetable gardens—I touched the digging knife at my belt, suddenly dying to have my hands in the dirt, to pull weeds . . .

"Oh, you *are* losing your grip, Beauchamp," I murmured at the thought of ecstatic weed-pulling, but smiled nonetheless.

Rodney was not a chatterbox, but we kept up an amiable conversation as we walked. He said that he and his *opa* had walked up to the head of the pass every day for the last week, to be sure of meeting us.

"Mam and Missus Higgins have a ham saved for ye, for supper," he told me, and licked his lips in anticipation. "And there's honey to have with our corn bread! Daddy found a bee tree last Tuesday sennight and I helped him smoke 'em. And . . ."

I replied, but absentmindedly, and after a bit we both lapsed into a companionable silence. I was bracing myself for the sight of the clearing where the Big House had once stood—and a brief, deep qualm swept through me, remembering fire.

The last time I had seen the house, it was no more than a heap of blackened timbers. Jamie had already chosen a site for a new house and had felled the trees for it, leaving them stacked. Sadness and regret there might be in this return—but there were bright green spikes of anticipation poking through that scorched earth. Jamie had promised me a new garden, a new surgery, a bed long enough to stretch out in—and glass windows.

Just before we came to the spot where the trail ended above the clearing, Jamie and Mr. Wemyss stopped, waiting for Rodney and me to catch up. With a shy smile, Mr. Wemyss kissed my hand and then took Rodney's, saying, "Come along, Roddy, you can be first to tell your mam that Himself and his lady have come back!"

Jamie took my hand and squeezed it hard. He was flushed from the walk, and even more from excitement; the color ran right down into the open neck of his shirt, turning his skin a beautiful rosy bronze.

"I've brought ye home, Sassenach," he said, his voice a little husky. "It willna be the same—and I canna say how things will be now—but I've kept my word."

My throat was so choked that I could barely whisper "Thank you." We stood for a long moment, clasped tight together, summoning up the strength to go around that last corner and look at what had been, and what might be.

Something brushed the hem of my skirt, and I looked down, expecting that a late cone from the big spruce we were standing by had fallen.

A large gray cat looked up at me with big, calm eyes of celadon green and dropped a fat, hairy, very dead wood rat at my feet.

"Oh, *God*!" I said, and burst into tears.

138

FANNY'S FRENULUM

JAMIE HAD SENT word ahead, and preparations had been made for our coming. Jamie and I would stay with Bobby and Amy Higgins; Rachel and Ian with the MacDonalds, a young married couple who lived up the Ridge a way; and Jenny, Fanny, and Germain would bide for the nonce with Widow MacDowall, who had a spare bed.

There was a modest party thrown in our honor the first night—and in the morning we rose and were once more part of Fraser's Ridge. Jamie disappeared into the forest, coming back at nightfall to report that his cache of whisky was safe, and brought a small cask back with him to use as trade goods for what we might need to set up housekeeping, once we had a house to keep again.

As to said house—he'd begun the preparations for building a new house before we had left the Ridge, selecting a good site at the head of the wide cove that opened just below the ridge itself. The site was elevated but the ground there fairly level, and thanks to Bobby Higgins's industry, it had been cleared of trees, timber for the framing of the house laid in stacks, and an amazing quantity of large stones lugged uphill and piled, ready to be used for the foundation.

For Jamie, the first order of business was to see that his house—or the beginnings of it—was as it should be, and the second was to visit every household on the Ridge, hearing and giving news, listening to his tenants, reestablishing himself as the founder and proprietor of Fraser's Ridge.

My first order of business was Fanny's frenulum. I spent a day or two in organizing the various things we had brought with us, in particular my medical equipment, while visiting with the various women who came to call at the Higginses' cabin—our own first cabin, which Jamie and Ian had built when we first came to the Ridge. But once that was done, I summoned my troops and commenced the action.

"YE MAY PUT the poor lass off drinking whisky for good," Jamie observed, casting a worried look at the cup full of amber liquid sitting on the tray next to my embroidery scissors. "Would it not be easier for her to have the ether?"

"In one way, yes," I agreed, sliding the scissors point-first into a second cup, this one filled with clear alcohol. "And if I were going to do a lingual frenectomy, I'd have to. But there *are* dangers to using ether, and I don't mean merely burning down the house. I'm going to do just a frenotomy, at least for now. That *is* a very simple operation; it will literally take five seconds. And, besides, Fanny says she doesn't want to be put to sleep—perhaps she doesn't trust me." I smiled at Fanny as I said this; she was sitting on the oak settle by the hearth, solemnly taking note of my preparations. At this, though, she looked at me abruptly, her big brown eyes surprised.

"Oh, doh," she said. "I twust oo. I zhust wanna thee."

"Don't blame you a bit," I assured her, handing her the cup of whisky. "Here, then, take a good mouthful of that and hold it in your mouth—let it go down under your tongue—for as long as you can."

I had a tiny cautery iron, its handle wrapped in twisted wool, heating on Amy's girdle. I supposed it didn't matter if it tasted like sausages. I had a fine suture needle, threaded with black silk, too, just in case.

The frenulum is a very thin band of elastic tissue that tethers the tongue to the floor of the mouth, and in most people it is exactly as long as it needs to be to allow the tongue to make all the complex motions required for speaking and eating, without letting it stray between the moving teeth, where it could be badly damaged. In some, like Fanny, the frenulum was too long and, by fastening most of the length of the tongue to the floor of her mouth, prevented easy manipulations of that organ. She often had bad breath because, while she cleaned her teeth nightly, she couldn't use her tongue to dislodge bits of food that stuck between cheek and gum or in the hollows of the lower jaw below the tongue.

Fanny gulped audibly, then coughed violently.

"Tha'th . . . *thtrong*!" she said, her eyes watering. She wasn't put off, though, and at my nod took another sip and sat stoically, letting the whisky seep into her buccal tissues. It would in fact numb the frenulum, at least a bit, and at the same time provide disinfection.

I heard Aidan and Germain calling outside; Jenny and Rachel had come down for the operation.

"I think we'd better do this outside," I said to Jamie. "They'll never all fit in here—not with Oglethorpe." For Rachel's belly had made considerable strides in the last few weeks and was of a size to make men shy nervously away from her lest she go off suddenly, like a bomb.

We took the tray of instruments outside and set up our operating site on the bench that stood by the front door. Amy, Aidan, Orrie, and wee Rob clustered together behind Jamie, who was charged with holding the looking glass—both to direct light into Fanny's mouth to assist me and so that Fanny could indeed watch what was going on.

As Oglethorpe precluded Rachel being called into service as a back brace, though, we reshuffled the staff a bit and ended with Jenny holding the look-ing glass and Jamie sitting on the bench, holding Fanny on his knee, his arms wrapped comfortingly around her. Germain stood by, holding a stack of clean cloths, solemn as an altar boy, and Rachel sat beside me, the tray between us, so that she could hand me things.

"All right, sweetheart?" I asked Fanny. She was round-eyed as a sun-stunned owl, and her mouth hung open just a little. She heard me, though, and nodded. I took the cup from her limp hand—it was empty, and I handed it to Rachel, who refilled it briskly.

"Mirror, please, Jenny?" I knelt on the grass before the bench, and with no more than a little trial and error, we had a beam of sunlight trained on Fanny's mouth. I took the embroidery scissors from their bath, wiped them, and, with a pledget of cloth, took hold of Fanny's tongue with my left hand and lifted it.

It didn't take even three seconds. I'd examined her carefully several times, making her move her tongue as far as she could, and knew exactly where I thought the point of attachment should be. Two quick snips and it was done.

Fanny made a surprised little noise and jerked in Jamie's arms, but didn't seem to be in acute pain. The wound was bleeding, though, suddenly and profusely, and I hurriedly pushed her head down, so that the blood could run out of her mouth onto the ground and not choke her.

I had another pledget waiting; I dipped this quickly into the whisky and, seizing Fanny's chin, brought her head up and tucked the pledget under her tongue. *That* made her emit a stifled *"Owy!"* but I cupped her chin and shut her mouth, adjuring her sternly to press down on the pledget with her tongue.

Everyone waited breathlessly while I counted silently to sixty. If the bleed-ing showed no sign of stopping, I'd have to put in a suture, which would be messy, or cauterize the wound, which would certainly be painful.

". . . fifty-nine . . . sixty!" I said aloud, and peering into Fanny's mouth, found the pledget substantially soaked with blood but not overwhelmed by it. I extracted it and put in another, repeating my silent count. This time, the pledget was stained, no more; the bleeding was stopping on its own.

"Hallelujah!" I said, and everyone whooped. Fanny's head bobbed a bit and she smiled, very shyly.

"Here, sweetheart," I said, handing her the half-filled cup. "Finish that, if you can—just sip it slowly and let it go onto the wound if you can; I know it burns a bit."

She did this, rather quickly, and blinked. If it had been possible to stagger sitting down, she would have.

"I'd best put the lassie to bed, aye?" Jamie stood up, gently holding her against his shoulder.

"Yes. I'll come and see to it that her head stays upright—just in case it should bleed again and run down her throat." I turned to thank the assistants and spectators, but Fanny beat me to it.

"Missus . . . Fraser?" she said drowsily. "I—d-t-dth—" The tip of her tongue was sticking out of her mouth, and she looked cross-eyed toward it, astounded. She'd never been able to stick her tongue out before and now wiggled it to and fro, like a very tentative snake testing the air. "T-th—" She stopped, then, contorting her brow in a fearsome expression of concentration, said, "Th-ank y-y-YOU!"

Tears came to my eyes, but I managed to pat her head and say, "You're very welcome, Frances." She smiled at me then, a small, sleepy smile, and the next instant was asleep, her head on Jamie's shoulder and a tiny drooling line of blood trickling from the corner of her mouth onto his shirt.

139

A VISIT TO THE TRADING POST

BEARDSLEY'S TRADING POST was perhaps no great establishment by comparison to the shops of Edinburgh or Paris—but in the backcountry of the Carolinas, it was a rare outpost of civilization. Originally nothing but a run-down house and small barn, the place had expanded over the years, the owners—or rather, her managers—adding additional structures, some attached to the original buildings, other sheds standing free. Tools, hides, live animals, feed corn, tobacco, and hogsheads of everything from salt fish to molasses were to be found in the outbuildings, while comestibles and dry goods were in the main building.

People came to Beardsley's from a hundred miles—literally—in every direction. Cherokee from the Snowbird villages, Moravians from Salem, the multifarious inhabitants of Brownsville, and—of course—the inhabitants of Fraser's Ridge.

The trading post had grown amazingly in the eight years since I had last set foot in the place. I saw campsites in the forest nearby, and a sort of freelance flea market had sprung up alongside the trading post proper—people who brought small things to trade directly with their neighbors.

The manager of the trading post, a lean, pleasant man of middle years named Herman Stoelers, had wisely welcomed this activity, understanding that the more people who came, the greater the variety of what was available, and the more attractive Beardsley's became overall.

And the wealthier became the owner of Beardsley's trading post—an eight-year-old mulatto girl named Alicia. I wondered whether anyone besides Jamie and myself knew the secret of her birth, but if anyone did, they had wisely decided to keep it to themselves.

It was a two-day trek to the trading post, particularly as we had only Clarence, Jamie having taken Miranda and the pack mule—a jenny named

Annabelle—to Salem. But the weather was good, and Jenny and I could walk, accompanied by Germain and Ian, leaving Clarence to carry Rachel and our trade goods. I'd left Fanny with Amy Higgins. She was still shy of talking in front of people; it would take a good deal of practice before she could speak normally.

Even Jenny, sophisticate as she now was after Brest, Philadelphia, and Savannah, was impressed by the trading post.

"I've never seen sae many outlandish-looking people in all my born days," she said, making no effort not to stare as a pair of Cherokee braves in full regalia rode up to the trading post, followed by several women on foot in a mixture of doeskins and European shifts, skirts, breeches, and jackets, these dragging bundles of hides on a travois or carrying huge cloth bundles full of squash, beans, corn, dried fish, or other salables on their heads or backs.

I came to attention, seeing the knobbly bulges of ginseng root protruding from one lady's pack.

"Keep an eye on Germain," I said, shoving him hastily at Jenny, and dived into the throng.

I emerged ten minutes later with a pound of ginseng, having driven a good bargain for a bag of raisins. They were Amy Higgins's raisins, but I would get her the calico cloth she wanted.

Jenny suddenly raised her head, listening.

"Did ye hear a goat just now?"

"I hear several. Do we want a goat?" But she was already making her way toward a distant shed. Evidently we *did* want a goat.

I shoved my ginseng into the canvas bag I'd brought and followed hastily.

"WE DON'T NEED that," a scornful voice said. "Piece o' worthless trash, that is."

Ian looked up from the mirror he was inspecting and squinted at a pair of young men on the other side of the store, engaged in haggling with a clerk over a pistol. They seemed somehow familiar to him, but he was sure he'd never met them. Small and wiry, with yellowish hair cropped short to their narrow skulls and darting eyes, they had the air of stoats: alert and deadly.

Then one of them straightened from the counter and, turning his head, caught sight of Ian. The youth stiffened and poked his brother, who looked up, irritated, and in turn caught sight of Ian.

"What the devil . . . ? Cheese and rice!" the second youth said.

Plainly they knew *him;* they were advancing on him, shoulder to shoulder, eyes gleaming with interest. And seeing them side by side, suddenly he recognized them.

"*A Dhia,*" he said under his breath, and Rachel glanced up.

"Friends of thine?" she said mildly.

"Ye might say so." He stepped out in front of his wife, smiling at the . . . well, he wasn't sure what they *were* just now, but they weren't wee lassies any longer.

He'd thought they were boys when he'd met them: a pair of feral Dutch orphans named—they said—Herman and Vermin, and they *thought* their last name was Kuykendall. In the event, they'd turned out to be in actuality Hermione and Ermintrude. He'd found them a temporary refuge with . . . oh, Christ.

"God, please, no!" he said in Gaelic, causing Rachel to look at him in alarm.

Surely they weren't still with . . . but they were. He saw the back of a very familiar head—and a still more familiar arse—over by the pickle barrel.

He glanced round quickly, but there was no way out. The Kuykendalls were approaching fast. He took a deep breath, commended his soul to God, and turned to his wife.

"Do ye by chance recall once tellin' me that ye didna want to hear about every woman I'd bedded?"

"I do," she said, giving him a deeply quizzical look. "Why?"

"Ah. Well . . ." He breathed deep and got it out just in time. "Ye said ye *did* want me to tell ye if we should ever meet anyone that I . . . er—"

"Ian Murray?" said Mrs. Sylvie, turning round. She came toward him, a look of pleasure on her rather plain, bespectacled face.

"Her," Ian said hastily to Rachel, jerking his thumb in Mrs. Sylvie's direction before turning to the lady.

"Mrs. Sylvie!" he said heartily, seizing her by both hands in case she might try to kiss him, as she had occasionally been wont to do upon their meeting. "I'm that pleased to see ye! And even more pleased to present ye to my . . . er . . . wife." The word emerged in a slight croak, and he cleared his throat hard. "Rachel. Rachel, this is—"

"Friend Sylvie," Rachel said. "Yes, I gathered as much. I'm pleased to know thee, Sylvie." Her cheeks were somewhat flushed, but she spoke demurely, offering a hand in the Friends' manner rather than bowing.

Mrs. Sylvie took in Rachel—and Oglethorpe—at a glance and smiled warmly through her steel-rimmed spectacles, shaking the offered hand.

"My pleasure entirely, I assure you, Mrs. Murray." She gave Ian a sidelong look and a quivering twitch of the mouth that said as clearly as words, *"You? You married a Quaker?"*

"It *is* him! Toldja so!" The Kuykendalls surrounded him—he didn't know how they managed it, there being only two of them, but he *felt* surrounded. Rather to his surprise, one of them seized him by the hand and wrung it fiercely.

"Herman Wurm," he—*he*?—told Ian proudly. "Pleased to meetcha again, sir!"

"Worm?" Rachel murmured, watching them in fascination.

"Aye, Herman, I'm that fettled to see ye doing so . . . er . . . well. And you, too . . ." Ian extended a cautious hand toward what used to be Ermintrude, who responded in a high-pitched but noticeably gruff voice.

"Trask Wurm," the youth said, repeating the vigorous handshake. "It's German."

"'Wurm,' they mean," Mrs. Sylvie put in, pronouncing it *"Vehrm."* She was pink with amusement. "They couldn't ever get the hang of spelling 'Kuykendall,' so we gave it up and settled for something simpler. And as you'd made it *quite* clear that you didn't want them to become prostitutes, we've reached a useful understanding. Herman and Trask provide protection for my . . . establishment." She looked directly at Rachel, who went a shade pinker but smiled.

"Anybody messes with the girls, we'll take care of him right smart," the elder Wurm assured Ian.

"It's not that hard," the other said honestly. "Break just one of them bastards' noses with a hoe handle and the rest of 'em settle right down."

THERE WERE A dozen or so milch goats to choose from in the shed, in varying states of pregnancy. The Higginses had a good billy, though, so I needn't trouble about that. I chose two friendly young unbred nannies, one all brown, the other brown and white, with an odd marking on her side that looked like the rounded fit of two jigsaw-puzzle pieces, one brown and one white.

I pointed out my choices to the young man in charge of the livestock and, as Jenny was still deliberating over her own choice, stepped outside to look over the chickens.

I had some hopes of spotting a Scots Dumpy but found only the usual run of Dominiques and Nankins. Well enough of their kind, but I thought I must wait until Jamie had time to build a chicken coop. And while we could lead the goats home easily enough, I wasn't going to carry chickens for days.

I came out of the chicken yard and looked about, slightly disoriented. That's when I saw him.

At first, I had no idea who he was. None. But the sight of the big, slow-moving man froze me in my tracks and my stomach curled up in instant panic.

No, I thought. *No. He's dead; they're all dead.*

He was a sloppily built man, with sloping shoulders and a protruding stomach that strained his threadbare waistcoat, but big. Big. I felt again the sense of sudden dread, of a big shadow coming out of the night beside me, nudging me, then rolling over me like a thundercloud, crushing me into the dirt and pine needles.

Martha.

A cold swept over me, in spite of the warm sunshine I stood in.

"*Martha,*" he'd said. He'd called me by his dead wife's name and wept into my hair when he'd finished.

Martha. I had to be mistaken. That was my first conscious thought, stubbornly articulated, each word spoken aloud inside my mind, each word set in place like a little pile of stones, the first foundation of a bulwark. *You. Are. Mistaken.*

But I wasn't. My skin knew that. It rippled, a live thing, hairs rising in recoil, in vain defense, for what could skin do to keep such things out?

You. Are. Mistaken!

But I wasn't. My breasts knew that, tingling in outrage, engorged against their will by rough hands that squeezed and pinched.

My thighs knew it, too; the burn and weakness of muscles strained past bearing, the knots where punches and brutal thumbs left bruises that went to the bone, left a soreness that lingered when the bruises faded.

"You are mistaken," I said, whispering but aloud. "Mistaken."

But I wasn't. The deep soft flesh between my legs knew it, slippery with the sudden helpless horror of recollection—and so did I.

I STOOD THERE hyperventilating for several moments before I realized that I was doing it, and stopped with a conscious effort. The man was making his way through the cluster of livestock sheds; he stopped by a pen of hogs and leaned on the fence, watching the gently heaving backs with an air of meditation. Another man employed in the same recreation spoke to him, and he replied. I was too far away to hear what was said, but I caught the timbre of his voice.

"Martha. I know you don't want to, Martha, but you got to. I got to give it to you."

I was not going to be bloody sick. I wasn't. With that decision made, I calmed a little. I hadn't let him or his companions kill my spirit at the time; whyever would I let him harm me now?

He moved away from the pigs, and I followed him. I wasn't sure *why* I was following him but felt a strong compulsion to do so. I wasn't afraid of him; logically, there was no reason to be. At the same time, my unreasoning body still felt the echoes of that night, of his flesh and fingers, and would have liked to run away. I wasn't having that.

I followed him from pigs to chickens, back again to the pigs—he seemed interested in a young black-and-white sow; he pointed her out to the swineherd and seemed to be asking questions, but then shook his head in a dejected fashion and walked away. Too expensive?

I could find out who he is. The thought occurred to me, but I rejected it with a surprising sense of violence. I didn't bloody want to know his name.

And yet . . . I followed him. He went into the main building and bought some tobacco. I realized that I knew he used tobacco; I'd smelled the sour ash of it on his breath. He was talking to the clerk who measured out his purchase, a slow, heavy voice. Whatever he was saying went on too long; the clerk began to look strained, his expression saying all too clearly, *"We're done here; go away. Please go away . . ."* And a full five minutes later, relief was just as clearly marked on the clerk's face as the man turned away to look at barrels full of nails.

I'd known from what he said to me that his wife was dead. From his appearance and the way he was boring everyone he talked to, I thought he hadn't found another. He was plainly poor; that wasn't unusual in the backcountry. But he was also grubby and frayed, unshaven, and unkempt in a way that no man who lives with a woman normally is.

He passed within a yard of me as he went toward the door, his paper twist of tobacco and his bag of nails in one hand, a stick of barley sugar in the other. He was licking this with a large, wet tongue, his face showing a dim, vacant sort of pleasure in the taste. There was a small port-wine stain, a birth-mark, on the side of his jaw. He was crude, I thought. Lumpish. And the word came to me: *feckless.*

Christ, I thought, with a mild disgust, this mingled with an unwilling pity that made me even more disgusted. I had had some vague thought—and realized it only now—of confronting him, of walking up to him and demanding to know whether he knew me. But he had looked right at me as he passed me, without a sign of recognition on his face. Perhaps there was enough difference between what I looked like now—clean and combed, decently dressed—and what I had looked like the last time he had seen me: filthy, wild-haired, half naked, and beaten.

Perhaps he hadn't really seen me at all at the time. It had been full dark when he came to me, tied and struggling for breath, trying to breathe through a broken nose. I hadn't seen him.

Are you sure it's really him? Yes, I bloody was. I was sure when I heard his voice and, even more so, having seen him, felt the rhythm of his bulky, shambling body.

No, I didn't want to speak to him. What would be the point? And what would I say? Demand an apology? More than likely, he wouldn't even remember having done it.

That thought made me snort with a bitter amusement.

"What's funny, *Grand-mère?*" Germain had popped up by my elbow, holding two sticks of barley sugar.

"Just a thought," I said. "Nothing important. Is Grannie Janet ready to go?"

"Aye, she sent me to look for ye. D'ye want one of these?" He generously extended a stick of candy toward me. My stomach flipped, thinking of the man's large pink tongue lapping his treat.

"No, thank you," I said. "Why don't you take it home for Fanny? It would be wonderful exercise for her." Clipping her frenulum hadn't miraculously freed her speech, or even her ability to manipulate food; it just made such things possible, with work. Germain spent hours with her, the two of them sticking out their tongues at each other, wiggling them in all directions and giggling.

"Oh, I got a dozen sticks for Fanny," Germain assured me. "And one each for Aidan, Orrie, and wee Rob, too."

"That's very generous, Germain," I said, slightly surprised. "Er . . . what did you buy them *with?*"

"A beaver skin," he replied, looking pleased with himself. "Mr. Kezzie Beardsley gave it to me for taking his young'uns down to the creek and minding 'em whilst he and Mrs. Beardsley had a lie-down."

"A lie-down," I repeated, my mouth twitching with the urge to laugh. "I see. All right. Let's find Grannie Janet, then."

IT TOOK NO little time to get organized for the journey back to the Ridge. It was a two-day ride; on foot, with goats, it would likely take four.

But we had food and blankets, and the weather was fine. No one was in a hurry—certainly not the goats, who were inclined to pause for a quick mouthful of anything in reach.

The peace of the road and the company of my companions did a great deal to settle my disturbed feelings. Rachel's imitation over supper of Ian's expressions on suddenly meeting Mrs. Sylvie and the Wurms did even more, and I fell asleep by the fire within moments of lying down, and slept without dreaming.

140

WOMAN, WILT THOU LIE WITH ME?

IAN COULDN'T TELL, whether Rachel was amused, appalled, angry, or all three. This discomfited him. He usually *did* know what she thought of things, because she told him; she wasn't the sort of woman— he'd known a few—who expected a man to read her mind and got fashed when he didn't.

She'd kept her own counsel on the matter of Mrs. Sylvie and the Wurms, though. They'd done their wee bit of business, trading two bottles of whisky for salt, sugar, nails, needles, thread, a hoe blade, and a bolt of pink gingham, and he'd bought her a dilled cucumber that was as long as the span of his outstretched fingers. She'd thanked him for this but hadn't said much else on the way home. She was presently licking the vegetable in a meditative sort of way as she rocked along on Clarence.

It fascinated him to watch her do that, and he nearly walked straight off a steep rocky outcrop doing so. She turned round at his exclamation as he scrabbled for footing, though, and smiled at him, so she maybe wasn't that bothered about Sylvie.

"D'ye no mean to eat that?" he inquired, coming up beside her stirrup.

"I do," she said calmly, "but all in good time." She licked the substantial length of the warty green thing with a long, slow swipe of her tongue and then—holding his eyes—sucked deliberately on the end of it. He walked straight into a springy pine branch, which swiped him across the face with its needles.

He swore, rubbing at his watering eyes. She was laughing!

"Ye did that on purpose, Rachel Murray!"

"Is thee accusing me of propelling thee into a tree?" she inquired, arching one brow. "Thee is an experienced Indian scout, or so I was led to believe. Surely one of those should look where he's going."

She had pulled Clarence to a stop—Clarence was always agreeable to stopping, particularly if there was anything edible in sight—and sat there smiling at Ian, cheeky as a monkey.

"Give me that, aye?" She handed him the pickle willingly, wiping her damp hand on her thigh. He took a large bite, his mouth flooded with garlic and dill and vinegar. Then he jammed the cucumber into one of the saddlebags and extended a hand to her. "Come down here."

"Why?" she asked. She was still smiling, but her body had shifted, leaning toward him but making no effort to get off. He understood *that* sort of conversation and reached up, took her by what was left of her waist, and pulled her off in a flurry of skirts. He paused for an instant to swallow the bite of pickle, then kissed her thoroughly, a hand on her bottom. Her hair smelled of pinecones, chicken feathers, and the soft soap Auntie Claire called shampoo, and he could taste the German sausage they'd had for lunch, under the veil of pickling spice.

Her arms were round his neck, her belly pressed against him, and quite suddenly he felt a small hard shove in his own belly. He looked down in astonishment, and Rachel giggled. He hadn't realized that she wasn't wearing stays; her breasts were bound with a simple band under her shift, but her belly was just *there,* round and firm as a pumpkin under her gown.

"He—or she—is wakeful," she said, putting a hand on her bulge, which was moving slightly as tiny limbs poked experimentally here and there inside her. This was always fascinating in its own way, but Ian was still under the influence of her pickle-sucking.

"I'll rock him back to sleep for ye," he whispered in her ear, and, bending, lifted her in his arms. Nearly eight months gone, she was noticeably heavy, but he managed with no more than a slight grunt and, with a care to low-hanging branches and loose stones, carried her off into the forest, leaving Clarence to graze on a succulent clump of muhly grass.

"I RATHER HOPE that it wasn't the meeting with thy former paramour that caused this outbreak of passion," Rachel remarked a short time later, flicking a wandering wood louse off her husband's forearm, which was just by her face. They were lying on their sides on Ian's plaid, naked and cupped together like spoons in a box. It was cool under the trees, but she seemed never to grow cold these days; the child was like a small furnace—doubtless taking after its father, she thought. Ian's skin was usually warm, but for him the heat of passion was no mere metaphor; he blazed when they lay together.

"She's no my paramour," Ian murmured into her hair, and kissed the back of her ear. "It was only a commercial transaction."

She didn't like hearing that and stiffened a little.

"I did tell ye I'd gone wi' whores." Ian's voice was quiet, but she could hear the slight reproach in it. "Would ye rather I had discarded lovers strewn about the countryside?"

She took a breath, relaxed, and stretched her neck to kiss the back of his long, sun-browned hand.

"No, it's true—thee did tell me," she admitted. "And while there is some small part of me that could wish thee came to me virgin, chaste and untouched . . . honesty obliges me to acknowledge some gratitude for the lessons learned from the likes of Mrs. Sylvie." She wanted to ask whether he'd learned the things he'd just been doing to her from Mrs. Sylvie or perhaps from his Indian wife—but she had no wish to bring any thought of Works With Her Hands between them.

His hand lifted and cupped her breast, playing very gently with her nipple, and she squirmed involuntarily—a slow, insinuating squirm that thrust her buttocks back against him. Her nipples were very large these days and so sensitive that they couldn't bear the rubbing of stays. She squirmed again, and he laughed under his breath and rolled her over to face him so he could take her nipple in his mouth.

"Dinna make noises like that," he murmured against her skin. "The others will be comin' along the trail any time now."

"What—will they think when they see Clarence alone?"

"If anyone asks later, we'll say we were gatherin' mushrooms."

THEY MUSTN'T STAY much longer, she knew that. But she longed to stay like this forever—or at least for five minutes more. Ian lay once more behind her, warm and strong. But his hand was now on her stomach, tenderly stroking the rounded mystery of the child within.

He might have thought she was asleep. Perhaps he didn't mind if she heard him. He spoke in the *Gàidhlig*, though, and while she didn't yet know enough of the tongue to make out all he said, she knew it was a prayer. *"A Dhia"* meant "O God." And of course she knew what it was he prayed for.

"It's all right," she said to him softly, when he had stopped, and put her hand over his.

"What is?"

"That thee should think of thy first child—children. I know thee does. And I know how much thee fears for this one," she added, still more softly.

He sighed deeply, his breath, still scented with dill and garlic, warm on her neck.

"Ye turn my heart to water, lass—and should anything happen to you or to wee Oggy, it would punch a hole in me that would let my life run out."

She wanted to tell him that nothing would happen to them, that she wouldn't let it. But that was taking things upon herself that weren't hers to promise.

"Our lives are in God's hand," she said, squeezing his. "And whatever happens, we will be with thee forever."

DRESSED AGAIN, and as seemly as fingers combed through hair could make them, they reached the trail just as Claire and Jenny made their way around the bend, carrying packs and each leading two milch goats, friendly creatures who set up a loud *mehh* of greeting as they spotted the two strangers.

Rachel saw Ian's mother glance sharply at her son, and then her dark-blue gaze lifted at once to Rachel, perched on Clarence's back. She gave Rachel a smile that said, as plain as words, that she knew exactly what they'd been doing and found it funny. Warm blood rose in Rachel's cheeks, but she kept her composure and inclined her head graciously to Jenny—in spite of the fact that Friends did not bow their heads save in worship.

Still blushing, she'd paid no attention to Claire, but after they had gone far enough ahead of the older women and the goats so as not to be overheard, Ian lifted his chin and gestured over his shoulder with it.

"Does aught seem amiss wi' Auntie Claire, d'ye think?"

"I didn't notice. What does thee mean?"

Ian lifted a shoulder, frowning slightly.

"I canna say, quite. She was herself on the way to the trading post and when we first got there, but when she came back from hagglin' for the goats, she looked . . . different." He struggled to find words to explain what he meant.

"No quite what ye'd say someone looks like if they've seen a ghost—not scairt, I mean. But . . . stunned, maybe? Surprised, or maybe shocked. But then when she saw me, she tried to act as though it was all as usual, and I was busy takin' the bundles out and forgot about it."

He turned his head again, looking over his shoulder, but the trail behind was empty. A faint *mehhhh* filtered down through the trees behind them, and he smiled—but his eyes were troubled.

"Ken—Auntie Claire canna hide things verra well. Uncle Jamie always says she's got a glass face, and it's true. Whatever it is she saw back there . . . I think it's with her, still."

141

THE DEEPEST FEELING ALWAYS
SHOWS ITSELF IN SILENCE

IT WAS SOMETIME in the midafternoon of the third day that Jenny cleared her throat in a significant manner. We had paused by a creek where the wild grass grew long and thick and were dabbling our tired feet in the water, watching the hobbled goats disport themselves. One seldom goes to the trouble of hobbling a goat, since they can, if they want to, chew their way free in a matter of seconds. In the present instance, though, there was too much food available for them to want to waste time in eating rope, and the hobbles would keep them within our sight.

"Got something caught in your throat?" I inquired pleasantly. "Luckily there's plenty of water."

She made a Scottish noise indicating polite appreciation of this feeble attempt at wit and, reaching into her pocket, withdrew a very battered silver flask and uncorked it. I could smell the liquor from where I sat—a local forerunner of bourbon, I thought.

"Did you bring that with you from Scotland?" I asked, accepting the flask, which had a crude fleur-de-lis on the side.

"Aye, it was Ian's. He had it from when he and Jamie were soldiering in France; brought it back wi' him when he lost his leg. We'd sit on the wall by his da's house and share a dram, while he was mending; he'd need it, poor lad, after I made him walk up and down the road ten times every day, to learn the use of his peg." She smiled, slanted eyes creasing, but with a wistful turn to her lips.

"I said I wouldna marry him, aye? Unless he could stand up beside me at the altar on two legs and walk me up the aisle after the vows."

I laughed.

"That's not quite the way *he* told it." I took a cautious sip, but the liquid inside was amazingly good, fiery but smooth. "Where did you get this?"

"A man named Gibbs, from Aberdeenshire. Ye wouldna think they ken anything about whisky-making there, but doubtless he learnt it somewhere else. He lives in a place called Hogue Corners; d'ye ken it?"

"No, but it can't be that far away. It's his own make, is it? Jamie would be interested." I took a second mouthful and handed back the flask, holding the whisky in my mouth to savor.

"Aye, I thought so, too. I have a wee bottle for him in my sack." She sipped and nodded approvingly. "Who was the dirty fat lumpkin that scairt ye at Beardsley's?"

I choked on the whisky, swallowed it the wrong way, and nearly coughed my lungs out in consequence. Jenny put down the flask, kirtled up her skirts, and waded into the creek, sousing her hankie in the cold water; she handed it to me, then cupped water in her hand and poured a little into my mouth.

"Lucky there's plenty of water, as ye said," she remarked. "Here, have a bit more." I nodded, eyes streaming, but pulled up my skirts, got down on my knees, and drank for myself, pausing to breathe between mouthfuls, until I stopped wheezing.

"I wasna in any doubt, mind," Jenny said, watching this performance. "But if I had been, I wouldn't be now. Who is he?"

"I don't bloody know," I said crossly, climbing back on my rock. Jenny wasn't one to be daunted by tones of voice, though, and merely raised one gull-wing-shaped brow.

"I don't," I repeated, a little more calmly. "I—had just seen him somewhere else. I have no idea who he is, though."

She was examining me with the interested air of a scientist with a new microorganism trapped under her microscope.

"Aye, aye. And where was it ye saw the fellow before? Because ye certainly kent him this time. Ye were fair gobsmacked."

"If I thought it would make the slightest bit of difference, I'd tell you it's none of your business," I said, giving her a look. "Give me that flask, will you?"

She gave it to me, watching patiently while I took several tiny sips and made up my mind what to say. At last I drew a deep, whisky-scented breath and gave her back the flask.

"Thank you. I don't know whether Jamie told you that about five years ago a gang of bandits who were terrorizing the countryside came through the Ridge. They burnt our malting shed—or tried to—and hurt Marsali. And they—they took me. Hostage."

Jenny handed back the flask, not speaking, but with a look of deep sympathy in her dark-blue eyes.

"Jamie . . . got me back. He brought men with him, and there was a terrible fight. Most of the gang was killed, but—obviously a few got away in the darkness. That—that man was one of them. No, it's all right, I don't need any more." I'd held the flask like a talisman of courage while I told her but now handed it back. She took a long, meditative swallow.

"But ye didna try to find out his name? Folk there kent him, I could see; they'd have told ye."

"I don't want to know!" I spoke loudly enough that one of the goats nearby emitted a startled *meh-eh-eh!* and bounded over a tussock of grass, evidently not discommoded at all by its hobbles.

"I—it doesn't matter," I said, less loudly but no less firmly. "The—ringleaders—are all dead; so are most of the others. This fellow . . . he . . . well, you can tell by looking at him, can't you? What did you call him—'a dirty fat lumpkin'? That's just what he is. He's no danger to us. I just—want to forget about him," I ended, rather lamely.

She nodded, stifled a small belch, looked startled at the sound, and, shaking her head, corked the flask and put it away.

We sat for a bit in silence, listening to the rush of water and the birds in the trees behind us. There was a mockingbird somewhere nearby, running through its lengthy repertoire in a voice like brass.

After ten minutes or so, Jenny stretched, arching her back and sighing.

"Ye'll remember my daughter Maggie?" she asked.

"I do," I said, smiling a little. "I delivered her. Or, rather, I caught her. You did the work."

"So ye did," she said, splashing one foot in the water. "I'd forgotten."

I gave her a sharp look. If she had, it would be the first thing she ever *had* forgotten, at least to my knowledge, and I didn't think she was old enough to have begun forgetting things now.

"She was raped," she said, eyes on the water and her voice very steady. "Not badly—the man didna beat her—but she got wi' child by him."

"How terrible," I said quietly, after a pause. "It—not a government soldier, though, surely?" That had been my first thought—but Maggie would have been no more than a child during the years of the Rising and Cumberland's clearing of the Highlands, when the British army had burned, plundered, and, yes, indeed, raped their way through any number of villages and crofts.

"No, it wasn't," Jenny said thoughtfully. "It was her husband's brother."

"Oh, God!"

"Aye, that's what I said about it, when she told me." She grimaced. "That was the one good thing about it, though; Geordie—that was the brother—had the same color hair and eyes as her husband, Paul, so the bairn could be passed off easy enough."

"And—did she?" I couldn't help asking. "Pass it off?"

Jenny let out a long sigh and nodded, taking her feet out of the water and tucking them up beneath her petticoat.

"She asked me what to do, poor lassie. I prayed about it—God, I prayed!" she said, with sudden violence, then snorted a little. "And I told her not to tell him—tell Paul, I mean. For if she did, what would be the end of it? One of them dead—for a Hieland man canna live wi' a man who's raped his wife nearby, nor should he—and it might be Paul, as like as not. And even if he only beat Geordie and drove him off, everyone would get to know what was behind it, and the poor wee lad—that was Wally, though of course we didna ken that yet, whilst we were talking it over—but the bairn branded as a bastard and the child of rape—what would become of it?"

She leaned down and, scooping up a handful of water, threw it over her face. She put her head back, eyes closed and the water running off her high, sharp cheekbones, and shook her head.

"And the family—Paul and Geordie's? A thing like that would tear them to pieces—and put them at loggerheads wi' us, nay doubt, for they'd be insisting up and down that Maggie was lying, rather than believe such a thing. Fat-heided creatures, the Carmichaels," she said judiciously. "Loyal enough, but stubborn as rocks."

"Thus sayeth a Fraser," I remarked. "The Carmichaels must be something special in that line."

Jenny snorted but didn't reply for a moment or two.

"So," she said at last, turning to look at me, "I said to Maggie that I'd prayed about it, and it seemed to me that if she could bear it for the sake of her man and her bairns, she should say nothing. Try to forgive Geordie if she could, and if she couldn't, keep away from him—but say nothing. And that's what she did."

"What—did Geordie do?" I asked curiously. "Did he—does he know that Wally is his son?"

She shook her head.

"I dinna ken. He left, a month after the bairn was born—emigrated to Canada. No one was surprised at that; everyone kent he was mad in love wi' Maggie and beside himself when she chose Paul. I expect that made it easier."

"Out of sight, out of mind? Yes, I'd suppose so," I said dryly. I thought I shouldn't ask but couldn't help myself. "Did Maggie ever tell Paul—after Geordie left, I mean?"

She shook her head and stood up, a little stiffly, shaking down her skirts.

"I dinna ken for sure, but I dinna think so. For her to tell him, after so long of keeping silent . . . how would he take that? And he'd still hate his brother, even if he couldna kill him right away." Her blue eyes, so like Jamie's, looked at me with rueful amusement. "Ye canna have been marrit to a Hieland man all these years and not ken how deep they can hate. Come on—we'd best gather these creatures before they burst." And she waded off into the grass, shoes in her hand, calling out a *Gàidhlig* charm for gathering livestock:

> *"The Three who are above in the City of glory,*
> *Be shepherding my flock and my kine,*
> *Tending them duly in heat, in storm, and in cold,*
> *With the blessing of power driving them down*
> *From yonder height to the sheiling fold."*

I THOUGHT about it, after everyone had rolled up in their blankets and begun snoring that night. Well . . . I hadn't *stopped* thinking about it since I'd seen the man. But in light of the story that Jenny had told me, my thoughts began to clarify, much as throwing an egg into a pot of coffee will settle the grounds.

The notion of saying nothing was of course the first one to come to my mind and was still my intent. The only difficulty—well, there were two, to be honest. But the first one was that, irritating as it was to be told so repeatedly, I couldn't deny the fact that I had a glass face. If anything was seriously troubling me, the people I lived with immediately began glancing at me sideways, tiptoeing exaggeratedly around me—or, in Jamie's case, demanding bluntly to know what the matter was.

Jenny had done much the same thing, though she hadn't pressed me for details of my experience. Quite plainly, she'd guessed the outlines of it, though, or she wouldn't have chosen to tell me Maggie's story. It occurred to me belatedly to wonder whether Jamie *had* told her anything about Hodgepile's attack and its aftermath.

The underlying difficulty, though, was my own response to meeting the dirty fat lumpkin. I snorted every time I repeated the description to myself, but it actually helped. He was a man, and not a very prepossessing one. Not a monster. Not . . . not bloody *worth* making a fuss about. God knew how he'd come to join Hodgepile's band—I supposed that most criminal gangs were largely composed of feckless idiots, come to that.

And . . . little as I wanted to relive that experience . . . I did. He hadn't come to me with any intent of hurting me, in fact hadn't hurt me (which was not to say that he *hadn't* crushed me with his weight, forced my thighs apart, and stuck his cock into me . . .).

I unclenched my teeth, drew a deep breath, and started over.

He'd come to me out of opportunity—and need.

"Martha," he'd said, sobbing, his tears and snot warm on my neck. *"Martha, I loved you so."*

Could I forgive him on those grounds? Put aside the unpleasantness of what he'd done to me and see him only as the pathetic creature that he was?

If I could—would that stop him living in my mind, a constant burr under the blanket of my thoughts?

I put back my head, looking up at the deep black sky swimming with hot stars. If you knew they were really balls of flaming gas, you could imagine them as van Gogh saw them, without difficulty . . . and looking into that illuminated void, you understood why people have always looked up into the sky when talking to God. You need to feel the immensity of something very much bigger than yourself, and there it is—immeasurably vast, and always near at hand. Covering you.

Help me, I said silently.

I never talked to Jamie about Jack Randall. But I knew from the few things he told me—and the disjointed things he said in the worst of his dreams— that this was how he had chosen to survive. He'd forgiven Jack Randall. Over and over. But he was a stubborn man; he could do it. A thousand times, and still one more.

Help me, I said, and felt tears trickle down my temples, into my hair. *Please. Help me.*

142

THINGS COMING INTO VIEW

IT WORKED. NOT EASILY, and often not for more than a few minutes at a time—but the shock faded and, back at home, with the peace of the mountain and the love of family and friends surrounding me, I felt a welcome sense of balance return. I prayed, and I forgave, and I coped.

This was greatly helped by distraction. Summer is the busiest time in an agricultural community. And when men are working with scythes and hoes and wagons and livestock and guns and knives—they hurt themselves. As for the women and children—burns and household accidents and constipation and diarrhea and teething and . . . pinworms.

"There, you see?" I said in a low voice, holding a lighted candle a few inches from the buttocks of Tammas Wilson, aged two. Tammas, drawing the not unreasonable conclusion that I was about to scorch his bum or ram the candle up his backside, shrieked and kicked, trying to escape. His mother took a firmer grip on him, though, and pried his buttocks apart again, revealing the tiny white wriggles of female pinworms swarming round his less than ideally immaculate small anus.

"Christ between us and evil," Annie Wilson said, letting go with one hand in order to cross herself. Tammas made a determined effort at escape and nearly succeeded in pitching himself headfirst into the fire. I seized him by one foot, though, and hauled him back.

"Those are the females," I explained. "They crawl out at night and lay eggs on the skin. The eggs cause itching, and so, of course, your wee lad scratches. That's what causes the redness and rash. But then he spreads the eggs to things he touches"—and, Tammas being two, he touched everything within reach—"and that's why your whole family is likely infected."

Mrs. Wilson squirmed slightly on her stool, whether because of pinworms or embarrassment, I couldn't tell, and righted Tammas, who promptly wriggled out of her lap and made for the bed containing his two elder sisters, aged four and five. I grabbed him round the waist and lugged him back over to the hearth.

"Bride save us, what shall I do for it?" Annie asked, glancing helplessly from the sleeping girls to Mr. Wilson, who—worn out from his day's work— was curled in the other bed, snoring.

"Well, for the older children and adults, you use this." I took a bottle out of my basket and handed it over, rather gingerly. It wasn't actually explosive, but, knowing its effects, it always gave me that illusion.

"It's a tonic of flowering spurge and wild ipecac root. It's a *very* strong laxative—that means it will give you the blazing shits," I amended, seeing her incomprehension, "but a few doses will get rid of the pinworms, provided you can keep Tammas and the girls from respreading them. And for the smaller children—" I handed over a pot of garlic paste, strong enough to make Annie wrinkle her nose, even though it was corked. "Take a large glob on your finger and smear it round the child's bumhole—and, er, up inside."

"Aye," she said, looking resigned, and took both pot and bottle. It probably wasn't the worst thing she'd ever done as a mother. I gave her instructions regarding the boiling of bedding and strict advice about soap and religious hand-washing, wished her well, and left, feeling a strong urge to scratch my own bottom.

This faded on the walk back to the Higginses' cabin, though, and I slid into the pallet beside Jamie with the peaceful sense of a job well done.

He rolled over drowsily and embraced me, then sniffed.

"What in God's name have ye been doing, Sassenach?"

"You don't want to know," I assured him. "What do I smell like?" If it was just garlic, I wasn't getting up. If it was feces, though . . .

"Garlic," he said, luckily. "Ye smell like a French *gigot d'agneau.*" His stomach rumbled at the thought, and I laughed—quietly.

"I think the best you're likely to get is parritch for your breakfast."

"That's all right," he said comfortably. "There's honey for it."

THE NEXT AFTERNOON, there being no pressing medical calls, I climbed up to the new house site with Jamie. The shield-shaped green leaves and arching stems of the wild strawberries were everywhere, spattering the hillside with tiny, sour-sweet red hearts. I'd brought a small basket with me—I never went anywhere without one in spring or summer—and had it half filled by the time we reached the clearing, with its fine view of the whole cove that lay below the Ridge.

"It seems like a lifetime ago that we came here first," I remarked, sitting down on one of the stacks of half-hewn timbers and pulling off my wide-brimmed hat to let the breeze blow through my hair. "Do you remember when we found the strawberries?" I offered a handful of the fruit to Jamie.

"More like two or three. Lifetimes, I mean. But, aye, I remember." He smiled, sat down beside me, and plucked one of the tiny berries from the palm of my hand. He motioned at the more or less level ground before us, where he'd laid out a rough floor plan with pegs driven into the earth and string outlining the rooms.

"Ye'll want your surgery in the front, aye? The same as it was? That's how I've put it, but it's easy changed, if ye like."

"Yes, I think so. I'll be in there more than anywhere; be nice to be able to look out the window and see what sort of hideous emergency is coming."

I'd spoken in complete seriousness, but he laughed and took a few more strawberries.

"At least if they have to come uphill, it will slow them down a bit." He'd brought up the rough writing desk he'd made and now put it on his knee, opening it to show me his plans, neatly ruled in pencil.

"I'll have my speak-a-word room across the hall from you, like we did before—ye'll see I've made the hallway wider, because of the staircase landing—and I think I'd maybe like a wee parlor there, between the speak-a-word room and the kitchen. But the kitchen . . . d'ye think we should maybe have a separate cookhouse, as well, like John Grey did in Philadelphia?"

I considered that one for a moment, my mouth puckering a bit from the astringent berries. I wasn't surprised that the thought had occurred to him; anyone who'd lived through one house fire, let alone two, would have a very lively awareness of the dangers.

"Oh, I don't think so," I said at last. "They do that as much because of the summer heat as for the danger of fire, and that's not a problem here. We'll have to have hearths in the house, after all. The danger of fire can't be that much greater if we're cooking on one of them."

"Surely that depends who's doin' the cooking," Jamie said, cocking an eyebrow at me.

"If you mean anything personal by that remark, you may retract it," I said coolly. "I may not be the world's best cook, but I've never served you cinders."

"Well, ye *are* the only member o' the family who's ever burnt the house down, Sassenach. Ye've got to admit that much." He was laughing and put up a casual hand to intercept the mock blow I aimed at him. His hand completely enclosed my fist, and he pulled me effortlessly off my perch and onto his knee.

He put an arm round me and his chin on my shoulder, brushing my hair out of his face with his free hand. He was barefoot and wearing only a shirt and his threadbare green-and-brown working plaid, the one he'd bought from a rag dealer in Savannah. It was rucked up over his thigh; I pulled the fold out from under my bottom and smoothed it down over the long muscle of his leg.

"Amy says there's a Scottish weaver in Cross Creek," I said. "When you next go down, maybe you should commission a new plaid—maybe one in your own tartan, if the weaver's up to a Fraser red."

"Aye, well. There're plenty other things to spend money on, Sassenach. I dinna need to be grand to hunt or fish—and I work the fields in my shirt."

"I could go round day in and day out in a gray flannel petticoat with holes in it and it wouldn't make any difference to *my* work—but you wouldn't want me to do that, would you?"

He made a low Scottish noise of amusement and shifted his weight, settling me more firmly.

"I would not. I like to look at ye now and then in a fine gown, lass, wi' your hair put up and your sweet breasts showin'. Besides," he added, "a man's judged by how well he provides for his family. If I let ye go around in rags, folk would think I was either mean or improvident." It was clear from his tone which of these conditions would be the more frightful sin.

"Oh, they would not," I said, mostly teasing for the sake of argument. "Everyone on the Ridge knows perfectly well that you're neither one. Besides, don't you think I like to look at *you* in all your glory?"

"Why, that's verra frivolous of ye, Sassenach; I should never have expected something like that from Dr. C.E.B.R. Fraser." He was laughing again but stopped abruptly as he turned a little.

"Look," he said into my ear, and pointed down the side of the cove. "Just there, on the right, where the creek comes out o' the trees. See her?"

"Oh, *no*!" I said, spotting the smudge of white moving slowly among the green mats of cress and duckweed. "It can't be, surely?" I couldn't make out details at that distance without my glasses, but from the way it moved, the object in question was almost certainly a pig. A big pig. A big *white* pig.

"Well, if it's no the white sow, it's a daughter just like her. But my guess is that it's the auld besom herself. I'd know that proud rump anywhere."

"Well, then." I leaned back against him with a little sigh of satisfaction. "Now I *know* we're home."

"Ye'll sleep under your own roof within a month, *a nighean*," he said, and I could hear the smile in his voice. "Mind, it may not be more than the roof of a lean-to, to start—but it'll be our own. By the winter, though, I'll have the chimneys built, the walls all up, and the roof on; I can be puttin' in the floors and the doors while there's snow on the ground."

I put a hand up to cup his cheek, warm and lightly stubbled. I didn't fool myself that this was paradise or even a refuge from the war—wars tended not to stay in one place but moved around, much in the manner of cyclones and even more destructive where they touched down. But for however long it lasted, this was home, and now was peace.

We sat in silence for a while, watching hawks circle over the open ground below and the machinations of the white sow—if indeed it was she—who had now been joined in her foraging by a number of smaller porcine blobs, doubtless this spring's litter. At the foot of the cove, two men on horseback came into sight from the wagon road, and I felt Jamie's attention sharpen, then relax.

"Hiram Crombie and the new circuit rider," he said. "Hiram said he meant to go down to the crossroads and fetch the man up, so he'd not lose his way."

"You mean so Hiram can make sure he's dour enough for the job," I said, laughing. "You realize they'll have got out of the habit of thinking you're human, don't you?" Hiram Crombie was head man of the little group of settlers that Jamie had acquired six years before. All of them were Presbyterians of a particularly rock-ribbed disposition and inclined to regard Papists as being deeply perverse, if not actually the spawn of Satan.

Jamie made a small noise, but it was one of tolerant dismissal.

"They'll get used to me again," he said. "And I'd pay money to watch Hiram talk to Rachel. Here, Sassenach, my leg's gone asleep." He helped me off his lap and stood up, shaking his kilt into place. Faded or not, it suited him, and my heart rose to see him looking so much as he should: tall and broad-shouldered, head of his household, once more master of his own land.

He looked out over the cove again, sighed deeply, and turned to me.

"Speakin' of hideous emergencies," he said thoughtfully, "ye do want to see them coming. So ye can be fettled against them, aye?" His eyes met mine directly. "Would now be a good time to tell me what's coming, d'ye think?"

"THERE'S NOTHING wrong," I said, for probably the tenth time. I picked at a scab of bark still clinging to the timber I sat on. "It's perfectly all right. Really."

Jamie was standing in front of me, the cove and the clouded sky bright behind him, his face shadowed.

"Sassenach," he said mildly. "I'm a great deal more stubborn than you are, and ye ken that fine. Now, I know something upset ye when ye went to Beardsley's place, and I know ye dinna want to tell me about it. Sometimes I ken ye need to fettle your mind about a matter before ye speak, but you've had time and more to do that—and I see that whatever it is is worse than I thought, or ye'd have said by now."

I hesitated, trying to think of something to tell him that perhaps wasn't quite . . . I looked up at him and decided that, no, I couldn't lie to him—and not only because he'd be able to tell immediately that I *was* lying.

"Do you remember," I said slowly, looking up at him, "on our wedding night? You told me you wouldn't ask me to tell you things that I couldn't. You said that love had room for secrets, but not for lies. I won't lie to you, Jamie—but I really don't want to tell you."

He shifted his weight from one leg to the other and sighed.

"If ye think *that's* going to relieve my mind, Sassenach . . ." he said, and shook his head. "I didna say that, anyway. I do remember the occasion—

vividly"—and he smiled a little at me—"and what I said was that there was nothing between us then but respect—and that I thought respect maybe had room for secrets, but not for lies."

He paused for a moment, then said very gently, "D'ye no think there's more than respect between us now, *mo chridhe*?"

I took a very deep breath. My heart was thumping against my stays, but it was just normal agitation, not panic.

"I do," I said, looking up at him. "Jamie . . . please don't ask me just now. I truly think it's all right; I've been praying about it, and—and—I think it will be all right," I ended, rather lamely. I stood up, though, and took his hands. "I'll tell you when I think I can," I said. "Can you live with that?"

His lips tightened as he thought. He wasn't a man for facile answers. If he couldn't live with it, he'd tell me.

"Is it a matter that I might need to make preparation for?" he asked seriously. "If it might cause a fight of some kind, I mean, I should need to be ready."

"Oh." I let out the breath I'd been holding, somewhat relieved. "No. No, it isn't anything like that. More of a moral question kind of thing."

I could see that he wasn't happy about that; his eyes searched my face, and I saw the troubled look in them, but at last he nodded, slowly.

"I'll live with it, *a nighean*," he said softly, and kissed my forehead. "For now."

143

INTERRUPTUS

THE OTHER MAJOR THINGS requiring a healer's attention in summer were pregnancy and birth. I prayed every day that Marsali had safely delivered her child. Even though it was already June 1, it would likely be months before we had any news, but I had examined her before we parted company—with tears—in Charleston, and all seemed normal.

"Do ye think this one might be . . . like Henri-Christian?" She spoke the name with difficulty and pressed a hand to her swelling belly.

"Probably not," I said, and saw the emotions ripple across her face like wind passing over water. Fear, regret . . . relief.

I crossed myself, with another quick prayer, and walked up the path to the MacDonald cottage, where Rachel and Ian were staying until Ian could build them a place of their own. Rachel was sitting on the bench out front, shelling peas into a basin, the basin sitting comfortably atop her stomach.

"*Madainn mhath!*" she said, smiling in delight when she saw me. "Is thee not impressed with my linguistic facility, Claire? I can say 'Good morning,' 'Good night,' 'How are you?' and 'Bugger off to St. Kilda' now."

"Congratulations," I said, sitting down next to her. "How does that last one go?"

"*Rach a h-Irt,*" she told me. "I gather 'St. Kilda' is actually a figure of speech indicating some extremely remote location, rather than being specified as the actual destination."

"I wouldn't be at all surprised. Do you try to impose the principles of plain speech on *Gàidhlig,* or is that even possible?"

"I have no idea," she said frankly. "Mother Jenny proposes to teach me the Lord's Prayer in *Gàidhlig.* Perhaps I can tell from that, as presumably one addresses the Creator in the same sort of voice that one uses for plain speech."

"Oh." I hadn't thought about that, but it was sensible. "So you call God 'Thee' when speaking to Him?"

"Of course. Who should be a closer Friend?"

It hadn't occurred to me, but presumably that *was* why one used "thou," "thy," et cetera, in prayer; that was originally the familiar form of the singular pronoun "you," even though common English speech had now moved on and lost the distinction, save for the Friends' plain speech.

"How interesting," I said. "And how is Oggy today?"

"Restless," she said, catching the edge of the basin as a vigorous kick made it bounce, scattering peas. "So am I," she added, as I brushed the spilled peas off her petticoat and poured them back into the pan.

"I don't doubt it," I said, smiling. "Pregnancy actually *does* last forever—until suddenly you go into labor."

"I can't wait," she said fervently. "Neither can Ian."

"Any particular reason?"

A slow, glorious blush rose up from the neck of her shift and suffused her to the hairline.

"I wake him six times a night, rising to piss," she said, avoiding my eye. "And Oggy kicks him, nearly as much as he does me."

"And?" I said invitingly.

The blush deepened slightly.

"He says he can't wait to, er, suckle me," she said diffidently. She coughed and then looked up, the blush fading a little.

"Really," she said, now serious, "he's anxious for the child. Thee knows about his children by the Mohawk woman; he said he'd told thee, making up his mind if it was right for him to marry again."

"Ah. Yes, he would be." I laid a hand on her belly, feeling the reassuring pressure of a thrusting foot and the long curve of a tiny back. The baby hadn't dropped, but Oggy was at least head-down. *That* was a great relief.

"It will be all right," I said, and squeezed her hand. "I'm sure of it."

"I'm not afraid for myself at all," she said, smiling and squeezing back. The smile faded a little as she put her hand on her stomach. "But very much afraid for them."

THE WEATHER being fine—and the smallest Higgins teething—we took a pair of quilts and walked up to the house site after supper, to enjoy the long twilight. And a little privacy.

"You don't think we're likely to be interrupted by a bear or some other form of wildlife, do you?" I asked, shimmying out of the rough gown I wore for foraging.

"No. I spoke wi' Jo Beardsley yesterday; he told me the nearest bear is a good league that way—" He nodded toward the far side of the cove. "And they dinna travel far in the summer, while the eating's good where they are. And painters wouldna trouble wi' people while there are easier things to kill. I'll make a bitty fire, though, just on principle."

"How's Lizzie?" I asked, unfolding the quilts as I watched him assemble a small fire with deft efficiency. "Did Jo say?"

Jamie smiled, eyes on what he was doing.

"He did, at some length. The meat of it bein' that she's well enough but summat inclined to bite pieces out o' him and Kezzie to distract her mind. That's why Jo was out hunting; Kezzie stays in when she's frachetty, because he canna hear her so well." The Beardsley twins were identical, and so alike that the only sure way to tell which you were talking to was that Keziah was hard of hearing, as the result of a childhood infection.

"That's good. No malaria, I mean." I'd visited Lizzie soon after our arrival and found her and the brood thriving—but she'd told me that she'd had a few "spells" of fever during the last year, doubtless owing to lack of the Jesuit bark. I'd left her with most of what I'd brought from Savannah. *I should have thought to ask if they had any at the trading post,* I thought—and pushed away the heavy sense of uneasiness that came with the thought of that place, thinking firmly, *I forgive you.*

The fire built, we sat feeding it sticks and watching the last of the sunset go down in flaming banners of golden cloud behind the black pickets of the farthest ridge.

And with the light of the fire dancing on the stacked timbers and the piles of foundation stones, we enjoyed the privacy of our home, rudimentary as said home might be at the moment. We lay peacefully afterward between our quilts—it wasn't cold but, so high up, the heat of the day vanished swiftly from the air—and watched the flickering lights of chimney sparks and lighted windows, in the few houses visible among the trees of the cove. Before the lights were extinguished for the night, we were asleep.

I woke sometime later from an erotic dream, squirming slowly on the lumpy quilt, limbs heavy with desire. This seemed to happen more frequently as I grew older, as though making love with Jamie ignited a fire that didn't quite die but continued to smolder through the night. If I didn't wake enough to do something about it, I'd wake in the morning stupid and foggy with unslaked dreams and unquiet sleep.

Fortunately, I was awake and, while still very pleasantly drowsy, quite capable of doing something about it, the process made much easier by the presence of the large, warm, pungent-smelling male beside me. He shifted a little as I edged onto my back, making a little space between us, but resumed his regular heavy breathing at once, and I edged my hand downward, encountering tumid warmth. It wouldn't take long.

A few minutes later, Jamie shifted again, and my hand stilled between my thighs. Then his hand slid swiftly under the quilt and touched me in the same place, nearly stopping my heart.

"I dinna mean to interrupt ye, Sassenach," he whispered in my ear. "But would ye like a bit of help wi' that?"

"Um," I said rather faintly. "Ah . . . what did you have in mind?"

In answer, the tip of his tongue darted into my ear, and I let out a small shriek. He snorted with amusement and cupped his hand between my legs, dislodging my own fingers, which had gone rather limp. One large finger stroked me delicately, and I arched my back.

"Ooh, ye're well started, then," he murmured. "Ye're slick and briny as an oyster, Sassenach. Ye hadna finished yet, though?"

"No, I—how long were you *listening*?"

"Oh, long enough," he assured me, and, ceasing operations for a moment, took hold of my disengaged hand and folded it firmly round a very enthusiastic bit of his own anatomy. "Mmm?"

"Oh," I said. "Well . . ." My legs had taken stock of the situation much more quickly than my mind had, and so had he. He lowered his head and kissed me in the dark with a soft, eager thoroughness, then pulled his mouth away long enough to ask, "How do elephants make love?"

Fortunately, he didn't wait for an answer, as I hadn't got one. He rolled over me and slid home in the same movement, and the universe shrank suddenly to a single vivid point.

A few minutes later, we lay under the blazing stars, quilt thrown off and hearts thumping slowly back to normal.

"Did you know," I said, "that your heart actually does stop for a moment at the point of climax? That's why your heartbeat is slow for a minute or two after; the sympathetic nervous system has fired all its synapses, leaving the parasympathetic to run your heart, and the parasympathetic decreases heart rate."

"I noticed it stopped," he assured me. "Didna really care why, as long as it started again." He put his arms over his head and stretched luxuriously, enjoying the cool air on his skin. "Actually, I never cared whether it started again, either."

"There's a man for you," I remarked tolerantly. "No forethought."

"Ye dinna need forethought for *that*, Sassenach. What ye were doing when I interrupted ye, I mean. I admit, if there's a woman involved, ye have to think of all sorts of things, but no for that." He paused for a moment.

"Um. Did I not . . . serve ye well enough earlier, Sassenach?" he asked, a little shyly. "I would ha' taken more time, but I couldna wait, and—"

"No, no," I assured him. "It wasn't that—I mean, I just . . . enjoyed it so much I woke up wanting more."

"Oh. Good."

He relaxed with a deep, contented sigh, closing his eyes. There was a waxing moon and I could see him clearly, though the moonlight washed all color from the scene, leaving him a sculpture in black and white. I ran a hand down his chest and lightly over his still-flat belly—hard physical labor had its price, but also its benefits—and cupped his genitals, warm and damp in my hand.

"*Tha ball-ratha sìnte riut,*" he said, putting a big hand over mine.

"A what?" I said. "A lucky . . . leg?"

"Well, limb, really; leg would be overstating it by a good deal. 'There is a lucky limb stretched against you.' It's the first line of a poem by Alasdair mac Mhaighistir Alasdair. 'To an Excellent Penis,' it's called."

"Thought highly of himself, did Alasdair?"

"Well, he doesna *say* it's his—though I admit that's the implication." He squinted a little, eyes still closed, and declaimed:

> "*Tha ball-ratha sìnte riut*
> *A choisinn mìle buaidh*
> *Sàr-bodh iallach acfhainneach*
> *Rinn-gheur sgaiteach cruaidh*
> *Ùilleach feitheach feadanach*
> *Làidir seasmhach buan*
> *Beòdha treòrach togarrach*
> *Nach diùltadh bog no cruaidh.*"

"I daresay," I said. "Do it in English; I believe I've missed a few of the finer points. He can't really have compared his penis to a bagpipe's chanter, can he?"

"Oh, aye, he did," Jamie confirmed, then translated:

> "*There is a lucky limb stretched against you*
> *That has made a thousand conquests:*
> *An excellent penis that is leathery, well-equipped,*
> *Sharp-pointed, piercing, firm,*
> *Lubricated, sinewy, chanter-like,*
> *Strong, durable, long-enduring,*
> *Vigorous, powerful, joyous,*
> *That would not jilt either soft or hard body.*"

"Leathery, is it?" I said, giggling. "I don't wonder, after a thousand conquests. What does he mean, 'well-equipped,' though?"

"I wouldna ken. I suppose I must have seen it once or twice—havin' a piss by the side o' the road, I mean—but if so, I wasna greatly struck by its virtues."

"You *knew* this Alasdair?" I rolled over and propped my head on my arm.

"Oh, aye. So did you, though ye maybe didna ken he wrote poetry, you not having much *Gàidhlig* in those days."

I still didn't have a great deal, though now that we were among *Gàidhlig*-speaking people again, it was coming back.

"Where did we know him? In the Rising?"

He was Prince Tearlach's *Gàidhlig* tutor.

"Aye. He wrote a great many poems and songs about the Stuart cause."

And now that he reminded me, I thought I *did* perhaps recall him: a middle-aged man singing in the firelight, long-haired and clean-shaven, with a deep cleft in his chin. I'd always wondered how he managed to shave so neatly with a cutthroat razor.

"Hmm." I had distinctly mixed feelings about people like Alasdair. On the one hand, without them stirring the pot and exciting irrational romanticism, the Cause might easily have withered and died long before Culloden. On the other . . . because of them, the battlefields—and those who had fallen there— were remembered.

Before I could think too deeply on that subject, though, Jamie interrupted my thoughts by idly brushing his penis to one side.

"The schoolmasters made me learn to write wi' my right hand," he remarked, "but luckily it didna occur to anyone to force me to abuse myself that way, too."

"Why call it that?" I asked, laughing. "Abusing yourself, I mean."

"Well, 'masturbate' sounds a great deal more wicked, aye? And if ye're abusing yourself, it sounds less like ye're havin' a good time."

"Strong, durable, long-enduring," I quoted, stroking the object in question lightly. "Perhaps Alasdair meant something like glove leather?"

"Vigorous and powerful it may be, Sassenach, and certainly joyous—but I tell ye, it's no going to rise to the occasion three times in one night. Not at my age." Detaching my hand, he rolled over, scooping me into a spoon shape before him, and in less than a minute was sound asleep.

When I woke in the morning, he was gone.

144

VISIT TO A HAUNTED GARDEN

I BLOODY *KNEW*. From the moment I woke to birdsong and a cold quilt beside me, I knew. Jamie often rose before dawn, for hunting, fishing, or travel—but he invariably touched me before he left, leaving me with a word or a kiss. We'd lived long enough to know how chancy life could be and how swiftly people could be parted forever. We'd never spoken of it or made a formal custom of it, but we almost never parted without some brief token of affection.

And now he'd gone off in the dark, without a word.

"You bloody, bloody *man!*" I said, and thumped the ground with my fist in frustration.

I made my way down the hill, quilts folded under my arm, fuming. Jenny. He'd gone and talked to Jenny. Of course he had; why hadn't I foreseen that?

He'd agreed not to ask me. He hadn't said he wouldn't ask anyone else. And while Jenny clearly loved me, I'd never been under any illusions as to where her ultimate loyalty lay. She wouldn't have voluntarily given up my secret, but if her brother asked her, point-blank, she would certainly have told him.

The sun was spreading warmth like honey over the morning, but none of it was reaching my cold bones.

He knew. And he'd gone a-hunting.

I DIDN'T NEED to look but looked anyway. Jamie's rifle was gone from its place behind the door.

"He came in early," Amy Higgins told me, spooning out a bowl of parritch for me. "We were all in bed still, but he called out soft, and Bobby got up to unbar the door. I would have fed him, but he said he was well enough and away he went. Hunting, he said."

"Of course," I said. The bowl was warm to my hands, and in spite of what I thought—what I *knew*—was going on, the thick grainy smell of it was enticing. And there was honey, and a little cream kept back from the butter-making; Amy allowed these in deference to Bobby's debauched English tastes, though she stuck to the usual virtuously Scottish salt on parritch herself.

Eating settled me, a little. The blunt fact was that there was absolutely nothing I could do. I didn't know the lumpkin's name or where he lived. Jamie might. If he'd talked to Jenny right away, he could easily have sent word to Beardsley's trading post and asked who was the fat man with the port-wine stain on his face. Even if he didn't yet know and was on his way to find out, I had no means of catching up with him—let alone stopping him.

"A Hieland man canna live wi' a man who's raped his wife nearby, nor should he." That's what Jenny had said to me. In warning, I now realized.

"Gak!" It was wee Rob, toddling round the room, who had seized my skirt in both hands and was giving me a toothy smile—all four teeth of it. "Hungy!"

"Hallo, there," I said, smiling back despite my disquiet. "Hungry, you say?" I extended a small spoonful of honeyed parritch in his direction, and he went for it like a starving piranha. We shared the rest of the bowl in companionable silence—Rob wasn't a chatty child—and I decided that I would work in the garden today. I didn't want to go far afield, as Rachel could go into labor at any moment, from the looks of it. And a short spell of solitude amid the soothing company of the vegetable kingdom might lend me a bit of much-needed calm.

It would also get me out of the cabin, I reflected, as Rob, having licked the bowl, handed it back to me, toddled across the cabin, and, lifting his dress, peed in the hearth.

THERE WOULD BE a new kitchen garden near the new house. It was measured and planned, the earth broken, and poles for the deer fence had begun accumulating. But there was little point in walking that far each day to tend a garden when there was not yet a house to live in. I minded Amy's plot in the meantime, sneaking occasional seedlings and propagules into it between the cabbages and turnips—but today I meant to visit the Old Garden.

That's what the people of the Ridge called it, and they didn't go there. I privately called it Malva's Garden, and did.

It was on a small rise behind where the Big House had stood. With the new house rising already in my mind, I passed the bare spot where the Big House had been, without a qualm. There were more exigent things to be qualm about, I thought, and sniggered.

"You are losing your mind, Beauchamp," I murmured, but felt better.

The deer fence had weathered and broken down in spots, and the deer had naturally accepted the invitation. Most of the bulbs had been pawed up and eaten, and while a few of the softer plants, like lettuce and radishes, had escaped long enough to reseed themselves, the growing plants had been nibbled to scabby white stalks. But a very thorny wild rose brier flourished away in one corner, cucumber vines crawled over the ground, and a massive gourd vine rippled over a collapsed portion of the fence, thick with infant fruits.

A monstrous pokeweed rose from the center of the patch, nearly ten feet high, its thick red stem supporting a wealth of long green leaves and hundreds of purplish-red flower stalks. The nearby trees had grown immensely, shading the plot, and in the diffuse green light the long, nubbly stalks looked like nudibranchs, those colorful sea slugs, gently swaying in currents of air rather than water. I touched it respectfully in passing; it had an odd medicinal smell, well deserved. There were a number of useful things one could do with pokeweed, but eating it wasn't one of them. Which was to say, people *did* eat the leaves on occasion, but the chances of accidental poisoning made it not worth the trouble of preparation unless there was absolutely nothing else to eat.

I couldn't remember the exact spot where she'd died. Where the pokeweed grew? That would be entirely apropos, but maybe too poetic.

Malva Christie. A strange, damaged young woman—but one I'd loved. Who perhaps had loved me, as well as she could. She'd been with child and near her time when her brother—the child's father—had cut her throat, here in the garden.

I'd found her moments later and tried to save the child, performing an emergency cesarean with my gardening knife. He'd been alive when I pulled him from his mother's womb but died at once, the brief flame of his life a passing blue glow in my hands.

Did anyone name him? I wondered suddenly. They'd buried the baby boy with Malva, but I didn't recall anyone mentioning his name.

Adso came stalking through the weeds, eyes intent on a fat robin poking busily for worms in the corner. I kept still, watching, admiring the lithe way in which he sank imperceptibly lower as he came more slowly, creeping on his belly for the last few feet, pausing, moving, pausing again for a long, nerve-racking second, no more than the tip of his tail a-twitch.

And then he moved, too fast for the eye to see, and in a brief and soundless explosion of feathers, it was over.

"Well done, cat," I said, though in fact the sudden violence had startled me a little. He paid no attention but leapt through a low spot in the fence, his prey in his mouth, and disappeared to enjoy his meal.

I stood still for a moment. I wasn't looking for Malva; the Ridge folk said that her ghost haunted the garden, wailing for her child. Just the sort of thing they *would* think, I thought, rather uncharitably. I hoped her spirit had fled and was at peace. But I couldn't help thinking, too, of Rachel, so very different a soul, but a young mother, as well, so near her time, and so nearby.

My old gardening knife was long gone. But Jamie had made me a new one during the winter evenings in Savannah, the handle carved from whalebone, shaped, as the last one had been, to fit my hand. I took it from its sheath in my pocket and nicked my wrist, not stopping to think.

The white scar at the base of my thumb had faded, no more now than a thin line, almost lost in the lines that scored my palm. Still legible, though, if you knew where to look: the letter "J" he had cut into my flesh just before Culloden. Claiming me.

I massaged the flesh near the cut gently, until a full red drop ran down the side of my wrist and fell to the ground at the foot of the pokeweed.

"Blood for blood," I said, the words quiet in themselves but seeming drowned by the rustle of leaves all around. "Rest ye quiet, child—and do no harm."

DO NO HARM. Well, you tried. As doctor, as lover, as mother and wife. I said a silent goodbye to the garden and went up the hill, toward the MacDonalds' cottage.

How would Jamie do it? I wondered, and was surprised to find that I did wonder, and wondered in a purely dispassionate way. He'd taken the rifle. Would he pick the man off at a distance, as if he were a deer at water? A clean shot, the man dead before he knew it.

Or would he feel he must confront the man, tell him why he was about to die—offer him a chance to fight for his life? Or just walk up with the cold face of vengeance, say nothing, and kill the man with his hands?

"Ye canna have been marrit to a Hieland man all these years and not ken how deep they can hate."

I really didn't want to know.

Ian had shot Allan Christie with an arrow, as one would put down a rabid dog, and for precisely similar reasons.

I'd seen Jamie's hate flame bright the night he saved me and said to his men, *"Kill them all."*

How was it now for him? If the man had been found on that night, there would have been no question that he would die. Should it be different now, only because time had passed?

I walked in the sun now but still felt cold, the shadows of Malva's Garden with me. The matter was out of my hands; no longer my business, but Jamie's.

I MET JENNY on the path, coming up briskly, a basket on her arm and her face alight with excitement.

"Already?" I exclaimed.

"Aye, Matthew MacDonald came down a half hour ago to say her water's broken. He's gone to find Ian now."

He had found Ian; we met the two young men in the dooryard of the cabin, Matthew bright red with excitement, Ian white as a sheet under his tan. The door of the cabin was open; I could hear the murmur of women's voices inside.

"Mam," Ian said huskily, seeing Jenny. His shoulders, stiff with terror, relaxed a little.

"Dinna fash yourself, *a bhalaich*," she said comfortably, and smiled sympathetically at him. "Your auntie and I have done this a time or two before. It will be all right."

"Grannie! Grannie!" I turned to find Germain and Fanny, both covered with dirt and with sticks and leaves in their hair, faces bright with excitement. "Is it true? Is Rachel having her baby? Can we watch?"

How did it work? I wondered. News in the mountains seemed to travel through the air.

"Watch, forbye!" Jenny exclaimed, scandalized. "Childbed isna any kind of a place for men. Be off with ye this minute!"

Germain looked torn between disappointment and pleasure at being called a man. Fanny looked hopeful.

"I'm no-t a man," she said.

Jenny and I both looked dubiously at her and then at each other.

"Well, ye're no quite a woman yet, either, are ye?" Jenny said to her. If not, she was close. Tiny breasts were beginning to show when she was in her shift, and her menarche wasn't far off.

"I've s-seen babies bor-n." It was a simple statement of fact, and Jenny nodded slowly.

"Aye. All right, then."

Fanny beamed.

"What do *we* do?" Germain demanded, indignant. "Us men."

I smiled, and Jenny gave a deep chuckle that was older than time. Ian and Matthew looked startled, Germain quite taken aback.

"Your uncle did his part of the business nine months ago, lad, just as ye'll do yours when it's time. Now, you and Matthew take your uncle awa' and get him drunk, aye?"

Germain nodded quite seriously and turned to Ian.

"Do you want Amy's wine, Ian, or shall we use Grandda's good whisky, do ye think?"

Ian's long face twitched, and he glanced at the open cabin door. A deep grunt, not quite a groan, came out and he looked away, paling further. He swallowed and groped in the leather bag he wore at his waist, coming out with what looked like a rolled animal skin of some kind and handing it to me.

"If—" he started, then stopped to gather himself and started again. "When the babe is born, will ye wrap him—or her,"—he added hastily, "in this?"

It was a small skin, soft and flexible, with very thick, fine fur in shades of gray and white. A wolf, I thought, surprised. The hide of an unborn wolf pup.

"Of course, Ian," I said, and squeezed his arm. "Don't worry. It will be all right."

Jenny looked at the small, soft skin and shook her head.

"I doubt, lad, if that will half-cover your bairn. Have ye no seen the size o' your wife lately?"

145

AND YOU KNOW THAT

JAMIE CAME HOME three days later, with a large buck tied to Miranda's saddle. The horse seemed unenthused about this, though tolerant, and she whuffed air through her nostrils and shivered her hide when he dragged the carcass off, letting it fall with a thump.

"Aye, lass, ye've done brawly," he said, clapping her on the shoulder. "Is Ian about, *a nighean*?" He paused to kiss me briefly, glancing up the hill toward the MacDonald cottage. "I could use a bit of help wi' this."

"Oh, he's here," I said, smiling. "I don't know if he'll come skin your deer for you, though. He's got a new son and won't let the baby out of his sight."

Jamie's face, rather tired and worn, broke into a grin.

"A son? The blessing of Bride and Michael be on him! A braw lad?"

"Very," I assured him. "I think he must weigh almost nine pounds."

"Poor lass," he said, with a sympathetic grimace. "And her first, too. Wee Rachel's all right, though?"

"Rather tired and sore, but quite all right," I assured him. "Shall I bring you some beer, while you take care of the horse?"

"A good wife is prized above rubies," he said, smiling. "Come to me, *mo nighean donn*." He reached out a long arm and drew me in, holding me close against him. I put my arms around him and felt the quiver of his muscles, exhausted, and the sheer hard strength still in him, that would hold him up, no matter how tired he might be. We stood quite still for some time, my cheek against his chest and his face against my hair, drawing strength from each other for whatever might come. Being married.

AMID THE GENERAL rejoicing and fuss over the baby—who was still being called Oggy, his parents being spoiled for choice regarding his name—the butchering of the deer, and the subsequent feasting lasting well into the night, it was late morning of the next day before we found ourselves alone again.

"The only thing lacking last night was cherry bounce," I remarked. "I never saw so many people drink so much of so many different things." We were making our way—slowly—up to the house site, carrying several bags of nails, a very expensive small saw, and a plane that Jamie had brought back in addition to the deer.

Jamie made a small amused sound but didn't reply. He paused for a moment to look up at the site, presumably envisioning the outline of the house-to-be.

"D'ye think it should maybe have a third story?" he asked. "The walls would bear it easily enough. Take careful building of the chimneys, though, Keeping them plumb, I mean."

"Do we need that much room?" I asked doubtfully. There had certainly been times in the old house when I'd wished we'd *had* that much room: influxes of visitors, new emigrants, or refugees had often filled the place to the point of explosion—mine. "Providing more space might just encourage guests."

"Ye make it sound like they're white ants, Sassenach."

"Wh—oh, termites. Well, yes, there's a strong superficial resemblance."

Arrived at the clearing, I piled the nails conveniently and went to bathe my face and hands in water from the tiny spring that flowed from the rocks a little way up the hill. By the time I came back, Jamie had stripped off his shirt and was knocking together a pair of rough sawhorses. I hadn't seen him with his shirt off for a long time and paused to enjoy the sight. Beyond the simple pleasure of seeing his body flex and move, whipcord muscles moving easily under his skin, I liked knowing that he felt himself safe here and could ignore his scars.

I sat down on an upturned bucket and watched for a time. The blows of his hammer temporarily silenced the birds, and when he stopped and set the sawhorse on its feet, the air rang empty in my ears.

"I wish you hadn't felt you had to do it," I said quietly.

He didn't reply for a moment but pursed his lips as he squatted and picked up a few stray nails. "When we wed—" he said, not looking at me. "When we wed, I said to ye that I gave ye the protection of my name, my clan—and my body." He stood up then and looked down at me, serious. "Do ye tell me now that ye no longer want that?"

"I—no," I said abruptly. "I just—I wish you hadn't killed him, that's all. I'd—managed to forgive him. It wasn't an easy thing to do, but I did it. Not permanently, but I thought I *could* do it permanently, sooner or later."

His mouth twitched a little.

"And if ye could forgive him, he needn't die, ye're saying? That's like a judge lettin' a murderer go free, because his victim's family forgave him. Or an enemy soldier sent off wi' all his weapons."

"I am not a state at war, and you are not my army!"

He began to speak, then stopped short, searching my face, his eyes intent.

"Am I not?" he said quietly.

I opened my mouth to reply but found I couldn't. The birds had come back, and a gang of house finches chittered at the foot of a big fir that grew at the side of the clearing.

"You are," I said reluctantly, and, standing up, wrapped my arms around him. He was warm from his work, and the scars on his back were fine as threads under my fingers. "I wish you didn't have to be."

"Aye, well," he said, and held me close. After a bit, we walked hand in hand to the biggest pile of barked timber and sat down. I could feel him thinking but was content to wait until he had formed what he wanted to say. It didn't take him long. He turned to me and took my hands, formal as a man about to say his wedding vows.

"Ye lost your parents young, *mo nighean donn*, and wandered about the world, rootless. Ye loved Frank"—his mouth compressed for an instant, but I thought he was unconscious of it—"and of course ye love Brianna and Roger Mac and the weans . . . but, Sassenach—I am the true home of your heart, and I know that."

He lifted my hands to his mouth and kissed my upturned palms, one and then the other, his breath warm and his beard stubble soft on my fingers.

"I have loved others, and I do love many, Sassenach—but you alone hold all my heart, whole in your hands," he said softly. "And you know that."

⁂

WE WORKED through the day then, Jamie fitting stones for the foundation, me digging the new garden and foraging through the woods, bringing back pipsissewa and black cohosh, mint and wild ginger to transplant.

Toward late afternoon we stopped to eat; I'd brought cheese and bread and early apples in my basket and had put two stone bottles of ale in the spring to keep cold. We sat on the grass, leaning back against a stack of timber that was shaded by the big fir, tired, eating in companionable silence.

"Ian says he and Rachel will come up tomorrow to help," Jamie said at last, thriftily eating his apple core. "Are ye going to eat yours, Sassenach?"

"No," I said, handing it over. "Apple seeds have cyanide in them, you know."

"Will it kill me?"

"It hasn't so far."

"Good." He pulled off the stem and ate the core. "Have they settled on a name for the wee lad yet?"

I closed my eyes and leaned back into the shade of the big fir, enjoying its sharp, sun-warmed scent.

"Hmm. The last I heard, Rachel was suggesting Fox—for George Fox, you know; he was the founder of the Society of Friends, but naturally they wouldn't call the baby George, because of the king. Ian said he doesn't think highly of foxes, though, and what about Wolf, instead?"

Jamie made a meditative Scottish noise.

"Aye, that's no bad. At least he's not wanting to call the wean Rollo."

I laughed, opening my eyes.

"Do you really think that's what he has in mind? I know people name their children for deceased relatives, but naming one for your deceased dog . . ."

"Aye, well," Jamie said judiciously. "He was a *good* dog."

"Well, yes, but—" A movement down on the far side of the cove caught my eye. People coming up the wagon road. "Look, who's that?" There were four small moving dots, but at this distance I couldn't make out much more than that without my glasses.

Jamie shaded his eyes, peering.

"No one I ken," he said, sounded mildly interested. "It looks like a family, though—they've a couple of bairns. Maybe new folk, wanting to settle. They havena got much in the way of goods, though."

I squinted; they were closer now, and I could make out the disparity of height. Yes, a man and a woman, both wearing broad-brimmed hats, and a boy and girl.

"Look, the lad's got red hair," Jamie said, smiling and raising his chin to point. "He minds me of Jem."

"So he does." Curious now, I got up and rummaged in my basket, finding the bit of silk in which I kept my spectacles when not wearing them. I put them on and turned, pleased as I always was to see fine details spring suddenly into being. Slightly less pleased to see that what I had thought was a scale of bark on the timber near where I'd been sitting was in fact an enormous centipede, enjoying the shade.

I turned my attention back to the newcomers, though; they'd stopped—the little girl had dropped something. Her dolly—I could see the doll's hair, a splotch of color on the ground, even redder than the little boy's. The man was wearing a pack, and the woman had a large bag over one shoulder. She set it down and bent to pick up the doll, brushing it off and handing it back to her daughter.

The woman turned then to speak to her husband, throwing out an arm to point to something—the Higginses' cabin, I thought. The man put both hands to his mouth and shouted, and the wind carried his words to us, faint but clearly audible, called out in a strong, cracked voice.

"Hello, the house!"

I was on my feet, and Jamie stood and grabbed my hand, hard enough to bruise my fingers.

Movement at the door of the cabin, and a small figure that I recognized as

Amy Higgins appeared. The tall woman pulled off her hat and waved it, her long red hair streaming out like a banner in the wind.

"Hello, the house!" she called, laughing.

Then I was flying down the hill, with Jamie just before me, arms flung wide, the two of us flying together on that same wind.

AUTHOR'S NOTES

Dams and Tunnels

In the 1950s, a great hydroelectric project was started to bring power to the Highlands, and, in the process, many dams with turbines were built. During the construction of these dams, a good many tunnels were built, a number of them long enough to require a small electric train to transport men and equipment from one end to the other. (If you're interested in this project and its history, I recommend a book called *Tunnel Tigers: A First-Hand Account of a Hydro Boy in the Highlands* by Patrick Campbell, though there are several other good sources.)

Now, Loch Errochty does exist, and it does have a dam. I don't know whether it has a tunnel exactly like the one described in the book, but if it did—that's what it would look like; the tunnel and train are taken from multiple descriptions of the hydroelectric constructions in the Highlands. My description of the dam itself, its spillway, and its turbine room are based on those at the Pitlochry Dam.

Banastre Tarleton and the British Legion

There will likely be a certain amount of quibbling about my inclusion of Colonel Banastre Tarleton in the Battle of Monmouth, as the British Legion of which he was a commander (a regiment of mixed cavalry and artillery) was technically not in existence until after General Clinton's return to New York following the battle. However, the British Legion did consist of two separate parts: cavalry, under the command of Banastre Tarleton, and artillery, and these parts were organized separately. The cavalry unit appears to have been in some stage of organization in early June of 1778, prior to the battle, though the artillery unit (reasonably enough, given the problems of equipping and training) was not organized until late July, after the battle, when Sir Henry Clinton had returned to New York.

Now, there is no report that I can find as to the definite whereabouts of Colonel Tarleton during the month of June 1778. While neither he nor his British Legion is listed in the official order of battle, that listing is admitted by every source I could find to be confused and deficient. Owing to the large number of militia units taking part and the irregular nature of the battle (by eighteenth-century standards), various small groups are known to have been there but were not documented, and others were there but under confusing circumstances (e.g., a portion of Daniel Morgan's Rifle Corps was reported as taking part in the battle, but Morgan himself didn't. I don't know whether his absence was the result of illness, accident, or conflict, but apparently he wasn't there, even though he plainly intended to be).

Now, if *I* were General Clinton, in the throes of imminent departure from Philadelphia, and more or less expecting the possibility of attack by Washington's Rebels, *and* I had this nice new cavalry unit forming up in New York—would I not send word to Colonel Tarleton to bring his men on down, to lend a hand in the evacuation and to have a bit of field experience to meld them together as a new unit? I would, and I can't think that General Clinton was less soldierly than I am.

(Besides, there is this interesting thing called novelistic license. I have one. Framed.)

The Battle of Monmouth

The battle lasted from before daylight 'til after dark: the longest battle of the Revolution. It was also by far the messiest battle of the Revolution.

Owing to the circumstances—Washington's troops trying to catch an enemy army fleeing in three widely separated divisions—neither side could choose its ground, and the ground over which they fought was so chopped up and patchworked with farms, creeks, and forests, they couldn't fight in the usual manner, with lines facing each other, nor was it possible to develop effective flanking maneuvers. Thus it wasn't so much a classic eighteenth-century battle as a very long series of pitched fights between small groups, most of whom had No Idea what was going on anywhere else. And it ended up as one of those indecisive battles that no one wins and where no one has any idea for some time afterward what the actual effects of the battle were or would be.

With two hundred–odd years of historical perspective, the general take on the Battle of Monmouth is that it was important not because the Americans won but because they didn't actually lose.

Washington and his troops had spent the preceding winter at Valley Forge, pulling together what men and resources they had and forming those troops into (they hoped) a real army, with the help of Baron von Steuben (who was actually not a baron but thought it sounded better) and other European officers who lent their services either out of idealism (*vide* the Marquis de La Fayette) or from a sense of personal adventure and ambition. (As the Continental army was a trifle lacking in money, they offered instant promotion as an inducement to experienced officers; a mere captain from a British or German regiment could become a colonel—or occasionally, a general—in the Continental army, no questions asked.)

Consequently, Washington was itching to find an opportunity to try out the new army, and General Clinton provided an excellent opportunity. The fact that the new army did acquit itself very well (bar the occasional snafu such as Lee's botched encircling maneuver and mistaken retreat) was a shot in the arm for the Rebel cause and gave both army and partisans new heart to continue the fight.

Still, in terms both of logistics and results, the battle was One Big Mess. While there is a tremendous amount of material on the battle, and a great many eyewitness reports, the fragmented nature of the conflict prevented anyone from ever having a clear idea as to the overall state of things during the battle, and the staggered arrival of so many companies of militia from Pennsylvania and New Jersey meant that some companies were not documented as having been there, even though they were. (Sources note "several unidentified militia companies from New Jersey," for instance. These are, of course, the companies commanded by General Fraser.)

From a historical perspective, the Battle of Monmouth is also interesting because of the participation of so many well-known Revolutionary figures, from George Washington himself to the Marquis de La Fayette, Nathanael Greene, Anthony Wayne, and Baron von Steuben.

Now, when you include real people in a historical novel, you want to balance a realistic and (insofar as is possible) accurate portrayal of them against the fact that the novel is seldom *about* these people. Therefore, while we do see most of them (and what we do see is based on reasonably accurate biographical information[1]), we see them *en passant*, and only in situations affecting the people who are the real focus of the novel.

In regard to the novelistic license mentioned above: a special embossed seal (stamped by the Temporal Authority) allows me to compress time when necessary. True battle aficionados (or those obsessive souls who feel compelled to construct timelines and then fret about them) will note that Jamie and Claire meet with General Washington and several other senior officers at Coryell's Ferry. Some five days later, we find them making preparations on the day of battle, with little or no description of what was happening to them during the interval. That's because, while there was a tremendous amount of moving around, nothing of dramatic note happened on those five days. While I do strive for historical accuracy, I do also know that a) history is often not very accurate, and b) most people who really care about the logistic minutiae of battles are reading Osprey's Men-at-Arms series or the transcript of the court-martial of General Charles Lee, not novels.

Ergo: While all the officers mentioned were with Washington's army, they were not all at dinner on the same night or in the same place. Commanders (and their troops) came to join Washington from several places over the course of the nine days between Clinton's exodus from Philadelphia and Washington's catching him near Monmouth Courthouse (the site of Monmouth Courthouse is now the Monmouth Hall of Records, for the benefit of people who choose to read with a map in hand[2]). The general state of the relations among those officers, though, is as shown during that dinner.

---

1   For example, Nathanael Greene's remarks about Quakers are taken from his own letters, as is his reference to his father's discouraging reading as "tending to separate one from God."

2   With regard to maps and distances, etc., it's worth noting that such things as township boundaries did change between the eighteenth century and the twenty-first. Ergo, Tennent Church is now in Manalapan, New Jersey, whereas originally it was in Freehold Township. The church didn't move; the township did.

Likewise, it seemed unnecessary to depict the mundane events of five days of travel and military conference, just to prove to the meanest intelligence that five days had, in fact, passed. So I didn't.

The Court-Martial of General Charles Lee

Lee's lack of scouting, communications, and (not to put too fine a point on it) leadership led to the massive retreat that nearly scuttled the American attack altogether, this being retrieved by George Washington's personal rallying of the retreating troops. In consequence, General Lee was court-martialed following the battle on charges of disobeying orders, misbehavior before the enemy, and disrespect to the commander in chief; he was convicted and suspended from military command for a year. There would have been a great deal of talk around Philadelphia regarding this—particularly in the household of a printer who published a regular newspaper. However, the Fraser family had other pressing concerns at the time, and so no mention was made of this.

Quaker Plain Speech

The Religious Society of Friends was founded around 1647 by George Fox. As part of the society's belief in the equality of all men before God, they did not use honorific titles (such as "Mr./Mrs.," "General/Colonel/etc.") and used "plain speech" in addressing everyone.

Now, as any of you who have a second language with Latin roots (Spanish, French, etc.) realize, these languages have both a familiar and a formal version of "you." So did English, once upon a time. The "thee" and "thou" forms that most of us recognize as Elizabethan or Biblical are in fact the English familiar forms of "you"—with "you" used as both the plural familiar form ("all y'all") and the formal pronoun (both singular and plural). As English evolved, the familiar forms were dropped, leaving us with the utilitarian "you" to cover all contingencies.

Quakers retained the familiar forms, though, as part of their "plain speech" until the twentieth century. Over the years, though, plain speech also evolved, and while "thee/thy" remained, "thou/thine" largely disappeared, and the verb forms associated with "thee/thy" changed. From about the mid-eighteenth century onward, plain speech used "thee" as the singular form of "you" (the plural form remained "you," even in plain speech), with the same verb forms normally used for third person singular: e.g., "He knows that/ Thee knows that." The older verb endings—"knowest," "doth," etc.—were no longer used.

If you would like to know a whole lot more about the grammatical foundations and usages of Quaker plain speech than most people normally want to, allow me to recommend to you *No Need to be Ashamed of the Plain Language* by Kenneth S. P. Morse

You can find this on the QuakerJane.com website, or Google it (in case that website should no longer be extant).

Scots/Scotch/Scottish

As noted elsewhere (*Lord John and the Brotherhood of the Blade,* see "Author's Notes"), in the eighteenth century (and, indeed, well into the mid-twentieth century), the word "Scotch" and its variants (e.g., "Scotchman") were commonly used (by both English people *and* Scots) to describe an inhabitant of Scotland. The terms "Scottish" and "Scots" were also occasionally used, though less common.

Personally, I don't think political correctness has any place in historical fiction, and therefore those persons in this book who normally would have used "Scotch" do.

Typos and Terminology

Owing to the interesting idiosyncrasies of Scots dialect, some words may appear to be misspelled—but they aren't. For instance, while an English cook may have made her flapjacks on an iron griddle, her Scottish counterpart was frying sausages on a hot girdle. (This occasional transposition of sounds results in such entertaining items as a Scottish dessert known as "creamed crud" ("curd" to the less-imaginative English). It also results in the occasional inattentive reviewer denouncing the occurrence of "typos" in my books. This is not to say that there *aren't* any typos—there always are, no matter how many eyeballs have combed the pages—just that "girdle" isn't one of them.

Besides dialectical idiosyncrasies, there are also the oddities due to obsolete (but entirely accurate) usage. For example, at one point in this book, you will find someone hiding behind a pile of "spiled" barrels. I do *not* mean "spoiled," and it isn't a typo. "Spiled" means that a spile (a small wooden peg or spigot) has been driven into a cask in order to broach it and draw off liquid. So the pile is composed of barrels that have been drained of their contents. (Yes, I could indeed have said "a pile of empty barrels" instead, but what fun would *that* be?)

Bibliography/LibraryThing

Having been an academic for a good long time, I appreciate the virtues of a good bibliography. Having been a reader of novels for a lot longer, I sort of don't think extensive bibliographies belong in them.

Still, one of the side effects of reading historical fiction often is a desire to learn more about events, locations, flora, fauna, etc., described therein. I have a goodish number of references (about 1,500, last time I counted), acquired over the last twenty-odd years of writing historical fiction, and am happy to share the bibliographic information for these.

As it's not convenient to do that individually with a large number of people, I've put my whole reference collection (as of the beginning of 2013, at least) on LibraryThing—this being an online bibliographic site, where people can catalog and share their personal library information. My catalog is public, and you should be able to access all of it using my name as a keyword. (Individual references also include keywords like "medicine," "herbal," "biography," etc.)

ACKNOWLEDGMENTS

It takes me about four years to write one of the Big Books, what with re-search, travel, and the fact that they are . . . er . . . big. During that time, LOTS of people talk to me and kindly offer advice on everything from How to Reseat an Eyeball to what kind of a mess indigo-dyeing really makes, en-tertaining trivia (such as the fact that cows do not like daisies. Who knew?), and logistical support (mostly in terms of remembering when the people in my books were born and how far it is from point A to point B and in which direction—I went to a parochial school that stopped teaching geography in the fifth grade, so this is Not One of My Strong Points, and as for personal chronology, I just don't care whether a given character is nineteen or twenty, but apparently lots of people do, and more power to them).

This being the case, I'm sure I'm leaving out dozens of kindly people who have given me useful information and assistance over the last four years and I apologize for not having written down their names at the time—but I surely do appreciate said information and assistance!

Among those whose names I *did* write down, I'd like to acknowledge . . .

. . . My literary agents, Russell Galen and Danny Baror, without whom my books would not be published as successfully and widely as they are, and I would not have the edifying experience of opening cartons of books written in Lithuanian with my name on the front—to say nothing of the Korean edition of *Outlander* with the pink bubbles on the cover.

. . . Sharon Biggs Waller, for information about the Scots Dumpy and for bringing this charming chicken to my attention.

. . . Marte Brengle, for telling me about the forensic reconstruction of George Washington's face, and Dr. Merih O'Donoghue, for notes on his disastrous dental history.

. . . Dr. Merih O'Donoghue and her ophthalmologist friend, for technical commentary and useful gruesome details concerning Lord John's eye. Also for the teaching model of an eyeball, which adorns my bookshelves and gives interviewers who enter my office the willies.

. . . Carol and Tracey of MyOutlanderPurgatory, for their lovely photos of the battlefield at Paoli, which drew my attention to the Rebel rallying cry "Remember Paoli!" and the discovery of Lord John's unpopular cousin.

. . . Tamara Burke, for bits of homestead and farming lore, most particu-larly for her vivid description of a rooster valiantly defending his hens.

. . . Tamara Burke, Joanna Bourne, and Beth and Matthew Shope, for helpful advice on Quaker marriage customs and absorbing discussions regarding the history and philosophies of the Society of Friends. Any error or license taken with regard to such customs is mine, I hasten to add.

. . . Catherine MacGregor (Gaelic and French, including gruesome lullabies about beheaded lovers), Catherine-Ann MacPhee (Gaelic, phraseology *and* idiom, besides introducing me to the Gaelic poem "To an Excellent Penis" (see below), and Adhamh Ò Broin, Gaelic tutor for the *Outlander* Starz television production, for emergency help with exclamations. Barbara Schnell, for providing the German and occasional Latin bits (If you want to know how to say "Shit!" in Latin, it's *"Stercus!"*).

. . . Michael Newton, for permission to use his delightful translation of "To an Excellent Penis," from his book *The Naughty Little Book of Gaelic* (which I recommend highly, for assorted purposes).

. . . Sandra Harrison, who saved me from Grievous Error by informing me that British police cars do not have flashing red lights, only blue ones.

. . . the 3,247 (approximately) French-speakers and scholars who informed me that I had misspelled *"n'est-ce pas"* in an excerpt of this book posted on Facebook.

. . . James Fenimore Cooper, for lending me Natty Bumppo, whose reminiscences of the proper way to conduct a massacre considerably eased Lord John's journey into captivity.

. . . Sandy Parker (aka the Archivist), for faithful tracking and analysis of the *#DailyLines* (these are tiny snippets of whatever I happen to be working on, posted daily on Facebook and Twitter for the purpose of entertaining people during the long time it takes me to finish a book, as well as a constant helpful flow of articles, photos, and useful nits).

. . . The Cadre of Genealogical Nitpickers—Sandy Parker, Vicki Pack, Mandy Tidwell, and Rita Meistrell, who are responsible for the high degree of accuracy in the beautiful family tree you see on the endpapers of this book.

. . . Karen I. Henry, for bumblebee-herding and for the "Friday Fun Facts" supplied weekly on her blog, *Outlandish Observations.* (The FFF are a collection of fascinating bits of trivia from the books, explored and expanded upon, with pictures.)

. . . Michelle Moore, for Twitter backgrounds, entertaining tea mugs, and a lot of assorted other things that can best be tactfully called "creative design."

. . . Loretta Moore, faithful and timely mistress of my website.

. . . Nikki and Caitlin Rowe, for designing and maintaining my YouTube Channel (which is frankly not something I ever thought I'd need, but a handy thing to have).

. . . Kristin Matherly, who is the fastest website constructor I've ever seen, for her Random Quote Generator, among many other beautiful and helpful *Outlander*-related sites.

. . . Susan Butler, my assistant, Without Whom Nothing Would Ever Be Mailed, a thousand necessary things would not be done, nor would I ever show up for scheduled events.

. . . Janice Millford, Sherpa of the Everest of email and rider of avalanches.

. . . to my friend Ann Hunt, for lovely writing and golden wishes, to say nothing of virtual flowers and raspberry gin.

. . . the title of Chapter 13 ("Morning Air Awash with Angels") is taken from a line of the poem by Richard Purdy Wilbur, "Love Calls Us to the Things of This World."

. . . and the title of Chapter 117, "Into the Briar Patch," is taken from the American folktale "Brer Rabbit and the Tar Baby" (retold by various authors).

. . . whereas the title of Chapter 123, *"Quod Scripsi, Scripsi,"* is courtesy of Pontius Pilate.

. . . Joey McGarvey, Kristin Fassler, Ashley Woodfolk, Lisa Barnes, and a whole passel of other Highly Competent and Energetic People at Random House.

. . . Beatrice Lampe, Andrea Vetterle, Petra Zimmerman, and a similar passel of helpful publishing people at Blanvalet (the German publisher).

. . . As always, great thanks to those practitioners of Eyeball-Numbing Nitpickery whose time and devotion results in a much better book than this would be without them: Catherine MacGregor, Allene Edwards, Karen Henry, Janet McConnaughey, Susan Butler, and especially Barbara Schnell (my invaluable German translator) and Kathleen Lord, copy editor and unsung heroine of the comma and timeline, both of whom always know how far it is from Point A to Point B, even if I would rather not find out.

. . . and my husband, Doug Watkins, who sustains me.

ABOUT THE AUTHOR

Diana Gabaldon is the #1 *New York Times* bestselling author of the wildly popular Outlander novels—*Outlander, Dragonfly in Amber, Voyager, Drums of Autumn, The Fiery Cross, A Breath of Snow and Ashes* (for which she won a Quill Award and the Corine International Book Prize), *An Echo in the Bone,* and *Written in My Own Heart's Blood*—as well as the related Lord John Grey books *Lord John and the Private Matter, Lord John and the Brotherhood of the Blade, Lord John and the Hand of Devils,* and *The Scottish Prisoner;* one work of non-fiction, *The Outlandish Companion;* and the Outlander graphic novel *The Exile.* She lives in Scottsdale, Arizona, with her husband.

www.dianagabaldon.com
Facebook.com/AuthorDianaGabaldon
@Writer_DG

ABOUT THE TYPE

This book was set in Galliard, a typeface designed in 1978 by Matthew Carter (b. 1937) for the Mergenthaler Linotype Company. Galliard is based on the sixteenth-century typefaces of Robert Granjon (1513–89).